Jilly Cooper is a journalist, writer and media superstar. The author of many number-one bestselling novels, including *Riders*, *Rivals*, *Polo*, *The Man Who Made Husbands Jealous*, *Appassionata*, *Score!* and *Pandora*, she lives with her husband, Leo, and five cats in Gloucestershire. She was appointed OBE in the 2004 Queen's Birthday Honours List for her contribution to literature.

www.booksattransworld.co.uk

Also by Jilly Cooper

FICTION
Riders
Rivals
Polo
The Man Who Made Husbands
  Jealous
Appassionata
Score!
Pandora

NON-FICTION
Animals in War
Class
How to Survive Christmas
Hotfoot to Zabriskie Point (with
  Patrick Lichfield)
Intelligent and Loyal
Jolly Marsupial
Jolly Super
Jolly Superlative
Jolly Super Too
Super Cooper
Super Jilly
Super Men and Super Women
The Common Years
Turn Right at the Spotted Dog
Work and Wedlock
Angels Rush In
Araminta's Wedding

CHILDREN'S BOOKS
Little Mabel
Little Mabel's Great Escape
Little Mabel Saves the Day
Little Mabel Wins

ROMANCE
Bella
Emily
Harriet
Imogen
Lisa & Co
Octavia
Prudence

ANTHOLOGIES
The British in Love
Violets and Vinegar

WICKED!

JILLY COOPER

BANTAM PRESS

LONDON · TORONTO · SYDNEY · AUCKLAND · JOHANNESBURG

TRANSWORLD PUBLISHERS
61–63 Uxbridge Road, London W5 5SA
a division of The Random House Group Ltd

RANDOM HOUSE AUSTRALIA (PTY) LTD
20 Alfred Street, Milsons Point, Sydney,
New South Wales 2061, Australia

RANDOM HOUSE NEW ZEALAND LTD
18 Poland Road, Glenfield, Auckland 10, New Zealand

RANDOM HOUSE SOUTH AFRICA (PTY) LTD
Isle of Houghton, Corner of Boundary and Carse O'Gowrie Roads,
Houghton 2198, South Africa

Published 2006 by Bantam Press
a division of Transworld Publishers

A catalogue record for this book is available from the British Library.
ISBN 9780593052990 (cased) (from Jan 07)
ISBN 0593052994 (cased)
ISBN 9780593052983 (tpb) (from Jan 07)
ISBN 0593052986 (tpb)

Typeset in 11/12pt New Baskerville by
Falcon Oast Graphic Art Ltd.

Printed in Great Britain by
Mackays of Chatham plc, Chatham, Kent

1 3 5 7 9 10 8 6 4 2

Papers used by Transworld Publishers are natural, recyclable products
made from wood grown in sustainable forests. The manufacturing
processes conform to the environmental regulations of the
country of origin.

This book is dedicated with love and admiration to two great headmistresses, Virginia Frayer and Katherine Eckersley, and also in loving memory of the Angel School, Islington, and Village High School, Derby

CAST OF CHARACTERS

ADELE

Single mother who teaches geography at Larkminster Comprehensive (otherwise known as Larks).

PARIS ALVASTON

Larks pupil and icon. Founder member of the notorious Wolf Pack.

ANATOLE

Bagley Hall pupil and beguiling son of the Russian Minister of Affaires.

RUFUS ANDERSON

Brilliant and eccentric head of geography at Bagley Hall. Henpecked father of two, liable to leave coursework on trains.

SHEENA ANDERSON

Rufus's concupiscent careerist wife – the main reason Rufus hasn't been given a house at Bagley Hall.

MRS AXFORD

Chief caterer at Bagley Hall.

MISS BASKET

A menopausal misfit who teaches geography at Larks.

BEA FROM THE BEEB

A researcher at the Teaching Awards.

DORA BELVEDON

Bagley Hall new girl. Determined to support her pony and her chocolate Labrador by flogging school scandal to the tabloids.

DICKY BELVEDON	Dora's equally resourceful twin brother who runs his own school shop at Bagley Hall selling booze and fags.
LADY BELVEDON (ANTHEA)	Dicky and Dora's young, very pretty, very spoilt mother. A Violet Elizabeth Bottox, drastically impoverished by widowhood, and determined to hunt for a rich new husband, unobserved by her beady son and daughter.
JUPITER BELVEDON	Dora and Dicky's machiavellian eldest brother, chairman of the governors at Bagley Hall, Tory MP for Larkminster, and tipped to take over the party leadership.
HANNA BELVEDON	Jupiter's lovely and loving wife, a painter.
SOPHY BELVEDON	An English teacher of splendid proportions and great charm. Ian and Patience Cartwright's daughter, and wife of Jupiter Belvedon's younger brother, Alizarin.
DULCIE BELVEDON	Adorable and self-willed daughter of Sophy and Alizarin.
SIR HUGO BETTS	Governor of Larks who sleeps through most meetings.
JAMES BENSON	An extremely smooth private doctor.
THE BISHOP OF LARKMINSTER	A governor of Bagley Hall.
GORDON BLENCHLEY	The unsavoury care manager of Oaktree Court, Paris Alvaston's children's home.
HENGIST BRETT-TAYLOR	Hugely charismatic headmaster of Bagley Hall.
SALLY BRETT-TAYLOR	Hengist's wife, classic beauty and jolly good sort, hugely contributory towards Hengist's success.

ORIANA BRETT-TAYLOR	Hengist and Sally's daughter, a much admired BBC foreign correspondent.
WALLY BRISTOW	Stalwart site manager at Larks.
GENERAL BROADSTAIRS	Lord Lieutenant of Larkshire and governor of Bagley Hall.
'BOFFIN' BROOKS	The cleverest boy at Bagley Hall, a humourless prig.
SIR GORDON BROOKS	Boffin's father, a thrusting captain of industry.
ALEX BRUCE	Deputy head of Bagley Hall, nicknamed Mr Fussy.
POPPET BRUCE	His dreadful wife, who teaches RE. An acronymphomaniac, determined to impose total political correctness on Bagley Hall.
CHARISMA BRUCE	Alex and Poppet's severely gifted daughter.
MARIA CAMBOLA	Larks's splendidly flamboyant head of music.
RUPERT CAMPBELL-BLACK	Former showjumping champion and Tory Minister for Sport. Now leading owner/trainer, and director of Venturer, the local ITV station. Despite being as bloody-minded as he is beautiful, Rupert is still Nirvana for most women.
TAGGIE CAMPBELL-BLACK	His adored wife – an angel.
XAVIER CAMPBELL-BLACK	Bagley Hall pupil and Rupert and Taggie's adopted Colombian son, who has hit moody adolescence head-on.
BIANCA CAMPBELL-BLACK	Xavier's ravishingly pretty, sunny-natured younger sister, also adopted and Colombian.

IAN CARTWRIGHT	Former commanding officer of a tank regiment, now bursar at Bagley Hall.
PATIENCE CARTWRIGHT	Ian's loyal wife – a trooper who teaches riding and runs the stables at Bagley.
MRS CHALFORD	Head of history at Larks. A self-important bossy boots who likes to be referred to as 'Chally'.
TARQUIN COURTNEY	Charismatic captain of rugger at Bagley Hall.
ALISON COX	Sally Brett-Taylor's housekeeper, known as 'Coxie'.
JANNA CURTIS	Larks's very young, Yorkshire-born headmistress.
P.C. CUTHBERT	A zero-tolerant police constable, determined to impose order on Larks.
DANIJELA	Larks pupil from Bosnia.
DANNY	Larks pupil from Ireland.
EMLYN DAVIES	A former Welsh rugby international, known as Attila the Hunk, who teaches history at Bagley Hall and coaches the rugger fifteens to serial victory.
DEBBIE	Ace cook at Larks.
ARTIE DEVERELL	Head of modern languages at Bagley Hall.
ASHTON DOUGLAS	The sinister, lisping Chief Executive Officer of S and C Services, the private company brought in by the Government to supervise education in Larkshire.
ENID	Lachrymose librarian at Larks.
PRIMROSE DUDDON	Earnest, noble-browed, ample-breasted form prefect at Bagley Hall.

VICKY FAIRCHILD	Two-faced but both of them extremely pretty. Cures truancy at Larks overnight when Janna Curtis appoints her as head of drama.
JASON FENTON	Larks's deputy head of drama, known as Goldilocks.
PIERS FLEMING	Wayward head of English at Bagley Hall.
JOHNNIE FOWLER	Good-looking Larks hellraiser; BNP supporter; persistent truant.
LANDO FRANCE-LYNCH	Master of the Bagley Beagles, whose sparse intellect is compensated for by dazzling all-round athletic and equestrian ability.
DAISY FRANCE-LYNCH	His sweet mother, a painter, wife of Ricky France-Lynch, former England polo captain.
FREDDIE	A waiter at La Perdrix d'Or restaurant.
CHIEF INSPECTOR TIMOTHY GABLECROSS	A wise, kind and extremely clever policeman.
MAGS GABLECROSS	The wise, kind wife of the Chief Inspector, part-time modern languages teacher at Larks.
GLORIA	PE teacher at Larks not given to hiding her physical lights under bushels.
THEO GRAHAM	Head of classics at Bagley Hall, an outwardly crusty old bachelor with a heart of gold. Takes out his hearing aid on Speech Day.
GILLIAN GRIMSTON	Head of Searston Abbey, an extremely successful Larkminster grant-maintained school for girls.

LILY HAMILTON	Aunt of Jupiter, Dicky and Dora Belvedon. A merry, very youthful octogenarian and Janna Curtis's next-door neighbour in the village of Wilmington.
DAME HERMIONE HAREFIELD	World famous diva, seriously tiresome, brings out the Crippen in all.
WADE HARGREAVES	An unexpectedly humane Ofsted Inspector.
DENZIL HARPER	Head of PE at Bagley Hall.
UNCLE HARLEY	Jamaican drugs dealer, lives on and off with Feral Jackson's mother.
SIR DAVID 'HATCHET' HAWKLEY	Headmaster of Fleetley, illustrious classical scholar. Later Lord Hawkley.
LADY HAWKLEY (HELEN)	A nervy beauty. Having numbered Rupert Campbell-Black and Roberto Rannaldini among her former husbands, Helen hopes marriage to David Hawkley means calmer waters.
ROD HYDE	An awful autocrat, headmaster of St James's, a highly successful Larkminster grant-maintained school, known as St Jimmy's.
'SKUNK' ILLINGWORTH	Deputy head of science at Larks.
'FERAL' JACKSON	Larks's leading truant, Paris Alvaston's best friend and founder member of the Wolf Pack. Afro-Caribbean, beautiful beyond belief, seriously dyslexic, and a natural athlete.
NANCY JACKSON	Feral's mother, a heroin addict.
JESSAMY	A teaching assistant at Larks.
JESSICA	Hengist Brett-Taylor's stunning second secretary, a typomaniac.

JOAN JOHNSON	Head of science at Bagley Hall, also in charge of Boudicca, the only girls' house. Nicknamed 'No-Joke Joan' because of a total lack of humour.
MRS KAMANI	Long-suffering owner of Larks's nearest newsagent's.
KATA	Larks pupil and wistful asylum-seeker from Kosovo.
AYSHA KHAN	One of Larks's few achievers. Destined for an arranged marriage in Pakistan.
RASCHID KHAN	Aysha's bullying father.
MRS KHAN	Aysha's bullied but surprisingly brave mother.
RUSSELL LAMBERT	Ponderous chairman both of Larks's governors and Larkminster planning committee.
LANCE	An understandably terrified newly qualified Larks history teacher.
AMBER LLOYD-FOXE	Minxy founder member of the 'Bagley Babes', otherwise known as the 'Three Disgraces'.
BILLY LLOYD-FOXE	Amber's father, an ex-Olympic showjumper, now a presenter for the BBC.
JANEY LLOYD-FOXE	His unprincipled journalist wife.
JUNIOR LLOYD-FOXE	Amber's merry, racing-mad twin brother.
LYDIA	Another understandably terrified newly qualified Larks English teacher.
LUBEMIR	Albanian asylum-seeker and safe-breaker, which makes him an extremely useful partner-in-crime to Cosmo Rannaldini.

MR MATES	Larks science master, almost as old as Archimedes.
KITTEN MEADOWS	Larks pupil and sassy, hell-cat girlfriend of Johnnie Fowler.
JOE MEAKIN	Under-master in Alex Bruce's house at Bagley Hall.
ROWAN MERTON	School secretary at Larks.
MRS MILLS	A jolly member of Ofsted.
MISS MISERDEN	Old biddy endlessly complaining about Larks misbehaviour.
TEDDY MURRAY	Randal Stancombe's foreman.
NADINE	Paris Alvaston's social worker.
MARTIN 'MONSTER' NORMAN	Larks pupil. Overweight bully and coward.
'STORMIN'' NORMAN	Larks parent governor and Monster's mother, given to storming into Larks and punching anyone who crosses her ewe lamb.
MISS PAINSWICK	Hengist Brett-Taylor's besotted and ferociously efficient secretary.
CINDY PAYNE	Deceptively cosy New Labour county councillor in charge of education.
KYLIE ROSE PECK	Sweet-natured Larks pupil and member of the Wolf Pack. So eternally up the duff, she'll soon qualify for a free tower block.
CHANTAL PECK	Kylie Rose's mother and also a parent governor at Larks.
CAMERON PECK	Kylie Rose's baby son.
GANYMEDE	Another baby son of Kylie Rose.
COLIN 'COL' PETERS	Editor of the *Larkminster Gazette*. A big, nasty toad in a small pond.
PHIL PIERCE	Head of science at Larks, loved by the children and a great supporter of Janna Curtis.

MIKE PITTS	Larks's deputy head, furious the head's job has been given to Janna Curtis.
COSMO RANNALDINI	Dame Hermione's son and Bagley Hall warlord, with a pop group called the Cosmonaughties and the same lethal sex appeal as his father, the great conductor Roberto Rannaldini.
DESMOND REYNOLDS	Smooth Larkminster estate agent known as 'Des Res'.
ROCKY	Larks pupil and ungentle giant until the Ritalin kicks in.
BIFFO RUDGE	Head of maths at Bagley Hall, ex-rowing Blue, who frequently rides his bike into the River Fleet while coaching the school eight.
ROBBIE RUSHTON	Larks's incurably lazy, left-wing head of geography.
CARA SHARPE	Larks's fearsome head of English and drama.
'SATAN' SIMMONS	Larks bully and best friend of Monster Norman.
SMART	Stalwart Bagley Hall rugger player.
PEARL SMITH	Another Larks hell-cat, member of the Wolf Pack.
MISS SPICER	An unfazed member of Ofsted.
SAM SPINK	Bossy-boots union representative at Larks.
SOLLY THE UNDERTAKER	Governor at Larks.
RANDAL STANCOMBE	Handsome Randal, definitely Mr Dicey rather than Mr Darcy, a wildly successful property developer. One of his private estates of desirable residences, Cavendish Plaza, sits uncomfortably close to Larks.

JADE STANCOMBE	Randal's daughter, sharp-clawed glamourpuss and Bagley Babe.
MISS SWEET	Beleaguered under-matron at Boudicca, reluctantly put in charge of Bagley's sex education.
CRISPIN THOMAS	Incurably greedy deputy director of S and C Services.
TRAFFORD	An unspeakably scrofulous but highly successful artist.
GRANT TYLER	An electronics giant.
MISS UGLOW	Larks RE teacher.
PETE WAINWRIGHT	Genial under-manager at Larkminster Rovers, the local second division football club.
BERTIE WALLACE	Raffish co-owner of Gafellyn Castle in Wales.
RUTH WALTON	A ravishing adventuress, voted on to Bagley Hall's board of governors to ensure full houses at meetings.
MILLY WALTON	The third Bagley Babe, charming and emollient but overshadowed by her gorgeous mother.
THE HON. JACK WATERLANE	Bagley Hall thicko, captain of the Chinless Wanderers.
LORD WATERLANE	Jack's father, who shares his son's fondness for rough trade.
STEWART 'STEW' WILBY	Powerful and visionary headmaster of Redfords, Janna Curtis's former school in the West Riding. Also Janna's former lover.
SPOTTY WILKINS	Bagley Hall pupil.
DAFYDD WILLIAMS	Sometime builder and piss artist.

'GRAFFI' WILLIAMS	Dafydd's son, and captivating, conniving fifth member of the Wolf Pack. Nicknamed 'Graffi' for his skill at spraying luminous paint on buildings.
BRIGADIER CHRISTIAN WOODFORD	A delightful octogenarian, hugely interested in matters military and his beautiful neighbour, Lily Hamilton.
MISS WORMLEY	English mistress at Bagley Hall – poor thing.

THE ANIMALS

CADBURY	Dora Belvedon's chocolate Labrador.
LOOFAH	Dora Belvedon's delinquent pony.
PARTNER	Janna Curtis's ginger and white mongrel.
NORTHCLIFFE	Patience Cartwright's golden retriever.
ELAINE	Hengist Brett-Taylor's white greyhound.
GENERAL	Lily Hamilton's white and black Persian cat.
VERLAINE AND RIMBAUD	Artie Deverell's Jack Russells.
BOGOTÁ	Xavier Campbell-Black's black Labrador.
HINDSIGHT	Theo Graham's marmalade cat.
FAST	One of Rupert Campbell-Black's horses. Aptly named.
PENSCOMBE PETERKIN	Another of Rupert Campbell-Black's star horses.
BELUGA	An extremely kind horse who teaches Paris Alvaston to ride.
PLOVER	Patience Cartwright's grey mare, doted on by Beluga.

1

Larkminster, county town of Larkshire, has long been considered the most precious jewel in the Cotswolds' crown. Throughout the year, its streets are paved with tourists, admiring the glorious pale gold twelfth-century cathedral, the Queen Anne courthouse and the ancient castle, whose battlements descend into the River Fleet as it idles its way round the town.

Larkminster, famous for its splendid beeches and limes and designated England's Town of Trees at the Millennium, was anticipating further fame because its newly elected Conservative MP, Jupiter Belvedon, was hotly tipped to take over the Tory party and oust Tony Blair at the next election.

In his Larkminster constituency, the machiavellian Jupiter was frustrated by a hung Labour and Lib-Dem county council who always voted tactically to keep out the Tories. But in January 2001, to the county council's horror, central government decided to take the running of Larkshire's schools away from the local education authority, who they felt was mismanaging its finances and not adhering sufficiently to the national curriculum. They then handed this task to a private company called S and C Services, the 'S' and the 'C' standing for 'Support' and 'Challenge'.

Larkminster itself boasted a famous public school, Bagley Hall, some five miles outside the town; a choir school attached to the cathedral; two excellent state schools: Searston Abbey and St James's, known as St Jimmy's; and a perfectly frightful sink school, Larkminster Comprehensive, which was situated on the edge of the town's black spot, the notorious Shakespeare Estate.

Like many outwardly serene and elegant West Country towns, Larkminster was greatly exercised by the increase in violent crime, for which it believed the Shakespeare Estate and Larkminster Comprehensive, or 'Larks' as it was known, were entirely responsible.

Randal Stancombe, a Rich List property developer and a hugely influential local player with a manicured finger in every pie, was particularly concerned. Cavendish Plaza, one of his private estates of desirable residences newly built above the flood plain of the River Fleet, was constantly troubled by Larks delinquents mugging, nicking car radios and knocking fairies off Rolls-Royces on their way to school. Randal Stancombe was putting increasing pressure on the police and the county council to clean up the area.

Larkminster Comp had for some years been a candidate for closure. It was at the bottom of the league tables and could only muster five hundred children rattling around in a building large enough for twelve hundred. Taxpayers' money should not be squandered heating empty schools.

Reading the graffiti on the wall, and not liking the prospect of bullying interference from a private company like S and C Services, the then headmaster, Ted Mitchell, had immediately resigned in February 2001. Larks Comp should have been shut down then, but the county council and S and C Services, nervous of the local uproar, the petitions, the poster campaigns, the marches on County Hall and even Westminster and the inevitable loss of seats that occur whenever a school is threatened with closure, dodged the issue.

They should have handed the job to Larks's deputy head, Mike Pitts, a seedy alcoholic who would have killed off the place in a few months. Instead they decided to give Larks a last chance and in April advertised in *The Times Educational Supplement* for a new head. This was why on a hot sunny day in early May, Janna Curtis, head of English at Redfords Comprehensive in West Yorkshire, caught the Intercity from Leeds to Larkminster.

On any journey, Janna overloaded herself with work which she truly intended to do. Aware that Year Eleven would be taking their first English exam in less than three weeks, she should have reread her GCSE revision notes. She should also have checked the English department's activities for the rest of term. Even more important, she should have tackled the pile of information about Larks Comp and the area that she had downloaded from the internet.

But after registering that Larks was underachieving disastrously and those 'right-wing bastards' Randal Stancombe and S and C Services were putting the boot in, she was sidetracked by a

Daily Mail abandoned by a passenger getting off at Birmingham. Despite her horror at its right-wing views, she soon became engrossed in a story about Posh and Becks, followed by Lynda Lee-Potter's much too enthusiastic comments about 'another right-wing bastard': Rupert Campbell-Black.

The train was stiflingly hot. Even if she'd had the money, Janna would never have done anything so revoltingly elitist as travel first class, but she wished air conditioning extended into standard class as well, so she didn't go scarlet before her interview. She was gagging for a large vodka and tonic to steady her nerves, but, on no breakfast, she'd become garrulous. Not that she was going to get the job; they'd think her much too young and inexperienced and she wasn't even sure she wanted it.

Gazing at a cloud of pink and white apple blossom clashing with bilious yellow fields of rape as the train trundled through Worcestershire, Janna reflected that the past three years at Redfords had been the most thrilling of her life. The cheers must have been heard in Westminster the day she and the other staff were told their school had finally struggled out of special measures (the euphemism for a dangerously failing school).

The fight to save Redfords had been unrelenting, but who minded working until midnight, week in, week out, when you were in love with the headmaster, Stew Wilby, who had made you head of English before you were thirty and who frequently put down his magic wand to shag you on the office carpet?

In the end Stew couldn't bring himself to leave his wife, Beth, and had retreated into a marriage far more intact than he had made out. People were beginning to gossip and the warmth of the reference Stew had sent to the governing board at Larks – which he had showed her yesterday: 'I shall be devastated to lose an outstanding teacher, but I cannot stand in Janna Curtis's way' – gave Janna the feeling that he might be relieved to see the back of her.

'Staying with Beth, staying with Beth,' mocked the wheels as the train rattled over the border into the wooded valleys of Larkshire. In her positive moments, all Janna wanted was to escape as far as possible from Stew into a challenge that would give her no time to mourn. Larkminster Comp seemed the answer.

She was met at the station by Phil Pierce, Larks's head of science. Bony-faced, bespectacled, mousy-haired, he wore a creased sand-coloured suit, obviously dragged out of a back drawer in honour of the heat wave and jazzed up by a blue silk tie covered in leaping red frogs.

3

Phil didn't drive Janna to Larks via the Shakespeare Estate to bump over litter-strewn roads and breathe in the stench of bins dustmen were too scared to empty. Instead he took her on the longer scenic route where she could enjoy the River Fleet sparkling, the white cherry blossom in the Town of Trees dancing against ominously rain-filled navy-blue clouds and the lichen blazing like little suns on the ancient buildings.

'How beautiful,' sighed Janna, then bristled with disapproval as she noticed, hanging overhead like birds of prey, a number of huge cranes bearing the name of Randal Stancombe.

'That capitalist monster's doing a lot of work,' she stormed, 'and I didn't realize that fascist bast— I mean fiend was MP here,' as she caught sight of posters of pale, patrician Jupiter Belvedon in the window of the Conservative Club. 'I bet he's in league with S and C Services,' she added furiously. 'Private companies only take over education to make a fat profit.'

'Representatives of S and C Services will certainly be at your interview later,' said Phil Pierce gently, 'so perhaps . . .'

'I'd better button my lip,' sighed Janna, 'and my clothes,' she added, doing up the buttons of the crocus-yellow dress she had bought from Jigsaw after school yesterday.

Looking at the terrace houses painted in neat pastels, their front gardens bright with wallflowers and forget-me-nots, Janna wondered if Larkminster might be too smug, rich and middle class.

As if reading her thoughts, Phil Pierce said: 'This may seem a prosperous county, but there's a very high level of socio-economic deprivation. Eighty per cent of our children are on free school dinners. Many have special educational needs.'

'I hope you receive sufficient funding.'

'Does anyone?' sighed Phil. 'This is Larks.'

Janna was agreeably charmed by the tawny, romantically rambling Victorian building perched on the side of a hill, its turrets and battlements swathed in pink clematis and amethyst wisteria, its parkland crowded with rare trees and with cow parsley and wild garlic advancing in waves on wildly daisied lawns.

Phil kicked off by giving her a quick tour of the school, which was conveniently empty of challenging children because it was polling day at the local elections.

All one needed for outside, reflected Janna, were a pair of secateurs and a mowing machine. The windows could also be mended and unboarded, the graffiti painted over and the chains, taps and locks replaced in the lavatories. The corridors and class-room walls were also badly lacking in posters, paintings and written work by the children. Redfords, her school in Yorkshire, was like walking into a rainbow.

She was disappointed that there were no children around, so no one could watch her taking a lesson. This had always secured her jobs in the past. Instead she was given post to deal with, to show off her management skills, and made a good impression by immediately tackling anything involving media and parents. She was also handed two budgets and quickly identified why one was good, the other bad.

She was aware of being beadily scrutinized by the school secretary, Rowan Merton, who was conventionally pretty: lovely skin, grey eyes, dark brown bob; but who simultaneously radiated smugness and disapproval, like the cat who'd got the cream and found it off.

Still too nervous to eat, Janna refused the quick bite of lunch offered her by Phil Pierce. She was then whisked away to an off-site interview because the governors were equally nervous of the Larks deputy head, Mike Pitts, who, livid he hadn't been offered the job, was likely to grow nasty when sobering up after lunch.

Only as Janna was leaving the Larks building did the heavens open, so she didn't appreciate in how many places rain normally poured in through the roof.

2

Janna was interviewed round the corner, past a row of boarded-up shops, in a pub called the Ghost and Castle, which was of the same tawny, turreted architecture as the school. The landlord was clearly a joker. A skeleton propped up the public bar, which was adorned with etchings of ghosts draped in sheets terrorizing maidens or old men in nightcaps. Rooms off were entitled Spook-Easy and Spirits Bar. The plat du jour chalked up on a blackboard was Ghoulash at £4.50.

Janna giggled and wondered how many Larks pupils were regulars here. At least they could mug up for GCSE in the Macbeth room, whose blood-red walls were decorated with lurid oils of Banquo's ghost, Duncan's murder and a sleepwalking Lady Macbeth. Here Larks's governors, a semi-circle of the Great and the Good, mostly councillors and educationalists, awaited her.

Think before you speak and remember eye contact at all times, Janna told herself as, beaming at everyone, she swivelled round like a searchlight.

The chairman of the governors, Russell Lambert, had tiny eyes, sticking-out ears, a long nose like King Babar and loved the sound of his pompous, very put-on voice. A big elephant in a small watering hole, thought Janna.

Like most good teachers, she of necessity picked up names quickly. As Russell Lambert introduced her, she clocked first Brett Scott, a board member of Larkminster Rovers, who had an appropriately roving eye and looked game for a great night on the tiles, and secondly Crispin Thomas, deputy educational director of S and C Services, who did not.

Crispin, a petulant, pig-faced blond, had a snuffling voice, and

6

from his tan and the spare tyre billowing over the waistband of his off-white suit, had recently returned from a self-indulgent holiday.

Under a painting of the Weird Sisters and infinitely more terrifying, like a crow who'd been made over by Trinny and Susannah, quivered a woman with black, straight hair and a twitching scarlet mouth. Appropriately named Cara Sharpe, she was a teacher governor, supposed to present the concerns of the staff to the governing body.

And I bet she sneaks to both sides, thought Janna.

'Cara is our immensely effective head of English and drama,' said Russell sycophantically.

So she won't welcome any interference on the English front from me, Janna surmised, squaring her little shoulders. At the end of the row, the vice-chairman, Sir Hugo Betts, who resembled a camel on Prozac, fought sleep.

Russell Lambert made no bones about the state of the school: 'Larks is at rock bottom.'

'Then it can only go up,' said Janna cheerfully.

Her audience knew from her impressive CV that she had been a crucial part of the high-flying team that had turned around disastrously failing Redfords. But then she had been led by a charismatic head, Stew Wilby. If she took on Larks, she would be on her own.

She also seemed terrifyingly young. She had lots of dark freckles and wild, rippling dark red hair, a big mouth (which she seldom kept shut), merry onyx-brown eyes and a snub nose. She was not beautiful – her jaw was too square – but she had a face of great sweetness, humour and friendliness. She was small, about five feet one, and after the drenching of rain, her crocus-yellow dress clung enticingly to a very pretty figure. A teardrop of mascara on her cheekbone gave a look of Pierrot.

Phil Pierce, who was very taken, asked her how she would deal with an underachieving teacher.

'I'd immediately involve the head of department,' replied Janna in her soft Yorkshire accent, 'and tactfully find out what's wrong. Is it discipline? Are the children trampling all over him? Is it poor teaching? Academically has he got what it takes, or is he presenting material wrongly? And then, gently, because if he's underachieving he'll have no confidence, try and work it through. After this,' she went on, 'he would either succeed or fail. If the latter, he's not right for teaching, because the education of children is all that matters.'

The semi-circle – except for scowling Cara Sharpe, Rowan

Merton, who was taking the minutes, and Sir Hugo Betts, who was asleep – smiled approvingly.

'What are your weaknesses?' snuffled Crispin Thomas from S and C.

Janna laughed. 'Short legs and an even shorter fuse. But my strengths are that I adore children and I thrive on hard work. Are the parents involved here?'

'Well, we get the odd troublemaker,' said Russell heartily, failing to add that a large proportion of Larks parents were too out of it from drugs to register. 'The children can be challenging.'

'I don't mind challenging children,' said Janna. 'You couldn't find more sad and demoralized kids than the ones at Redfords, but in a few months—'

'Yes, we read about that in the *Guardian*,' interrupted Crispin rudely.

Janna bit her lip; they didn't seem interested in her past.

'I want to give every child and teacher the chance to shine and for them to leave my school with their confidence boosted to enable them to survive and enjoy the world.'

She paused hopefully. A loud snore rent the air followed by an even more thunderous rumble from her own tummy, which woke Sir Hugo with a start.

'What, what, what?' He groped for his flies.

Janna caught Phil Pierce's eye and burst out laughing, so everyone else laughed except Cara and Rowan.

Janna had expected the board to get in touch in a week or so, but Russell Lambert, at a nod from Crispin Thomas, asked her to wait in an ante-room entitled Your Favourite Haunt. Phil Pierce brought her a cup of tea and some egg sandwiches, at which she was still too nervous to do more than nibble. Phil was such a sweet man; she'd love working with him.

Breathing in dark purple lilac, she gazed out of the window at buildings darkened to the colour of toffee by the rain and trees as various in their greenness as kids in any school. Beyond lay the deep blue undulation of the Malvern Hills. Surely she could find fulfilment and happiness here?

She was summoned back by Rowan, looking beadier than ever.

'We've decided not to waste your time asking you to come for a second interview,' announced Russell Lambert.

Janna's face fell.

'It was good of you all to see me,' she muttered. 'I know I look young . . .'

'We'd like to offer you the job,' said Russell.

Janna burst into tears, her mascara mingling with her freckles

8

as she babbled, 'That's wicked! Fantastic! Are you sure? I'm going to be a head, such an honour, I promise to justify your faith, that's really wicked.'

The half-circle smiled indulgently.

'Can I buy you all a drink to celebrate?' stammered Janna, reaching for her briefcase. 'On me, I mean.'

'Should be on us,' said the director of Larkminster Rovers. 'What'll you have, love?'

'Not if she's going to catch the fast train home,' said Russell, looking at his watch, 'and Crispin and I have to talk salaries and technicalities with . . . may I call you Janna?'

Half an hour later on the Ghost and Castle steps, Janna was still thanking them.

'I'd like to walk to the station,' she confessed. 'I want to drink in my new town. Doesn't matter if I get the later train. I'm so excited, I'll float home.'

But as she hadn't yet signed the contract, Russell, not risking Janna anywhere near the Shakespeare Estate, steered her towards his very clean Rover. Despite the stifling heat of the day, he pulled on thick brown leather driving gloves as though he didn't want to leave fingerprints on anything. As he settled in the driving seat, she noticed how his spreading thighs filled his grey flannel trousers.

As they passed the offices of the *Larkminster Gazette*, a billboard announced Randal Stancombe's latest plans for the area.

'That greedy fat cat's got a stranglehold on everything,' spat Janna.

'Wearing my other hat,' reproved Russell, 'as chair of the local planning committee, I can assure you Randal is a very good friend indeed to Larkminster, not least because of the thousands of people he employs.'

Feeling he'd been squashing, he then suggested Janna might like to ring her parents with news of her job.

'Mum passed away at Christmas.' Janna paused. 'She would have been right proud. I wish I could text her in heaven. We came from a very poor family; Mum scrubbed floors to pay for my school uniform, but she loved books and always encouraged us to read. She used to take me to see the Brontës' house in Haworth. I read English because of her.'

'And your father?'

'Dad was a steelworker. He used to take me to Headingly and Old Trafford. Then he left home; he couldn't cope with Mum being ill.' Her voice faltered. She wasn't going to add that her father had been violent and had drunk the family penniless.

She wished she could ring Stew but he'd be taking a staff meeting. Yorkshire was so full of painful memories; she'd be glad to get down south and make a fresh start.

Nothing, however, had prepared her for the anguish of leaving Redfords. Parents and children, who'd thought she'd be with them for ever, seemed equally devastated.

'Why are you living us?' wrote one eleven-year-old. 'I don't want you to live.'

'Are your new children better than us?' wrote another. 'Please change your mind.'

Almost harder to bear was the despair of the older pupils, including some of the roughest, toughest boys, whom she was abandoning in the middle of their GCSE course.

'How will we ever understand *Much Ado* without you? We're going to miss you, miss.'

They all gave her good-luck presents and cards they could ill afford and Janna couldn't look them in the eye and tell them the truth: 'I'm leaving because your headmaster broke my heart and now it's breaking twice.'

Then Stew had done the sweetest thing: he'd had framed a group photograph of the entire school, which every teacher and child had signed. Janna cried every time she looked at it.

Some teachers were very sad she was leaving and wished her well. Others, jealous of her closeness to Stew, expressed their incredulity at her getting the job.

'You'd better cut your hair, you'll never have time to wash that mane every morning. And do buy some sensible clothes.'

'And you'll have to curb that temper and you won't be able to swan into meetings twenty minutes late if you're taking them.'

Waylaid by a sobbing child, Janna would forget about time.

There had also been the hell of seeing Stew interview and appoint her successor: a willowy brunette with large, serious, hazel eyes behind her spectacles – the bloody cow – and everyone getting excited about a Christmas production of *Oliver!* of which Janna would be no part.

Stew had taken her out for a discreet farewell dinner and, because she was moving to the country, given her a little Staffordshire cow as a leaving present.

'I'm so proud of you, Janny. You've probably got eighteen months to try and turn round that school. Don't lose your rag and antagonize people unnecessarily and go easy on the "boogers", "bluddies" and "basstards", they just show off your

10

Yorkshire accent.' Then, pinching her cheek when she looked sulky: 'I don't want anything to wreck your lovely, generous, spontaneous nature.'

'Yeah, yeah. "The only failure is not to have tried",' Janna quoted one of Redfords's mantras back at him.

After a second bottle they had both cried and Stew had quoted: ' "So, we'll go no more a-roving",' but when he got to the bit about the sword outwearing its sheath and the heart wearing out the breast, Janna remembered how they'd worn out the carpet in his office.

I've given him my Bridget Jones years, she thought bitterly. Sometimes she wondered why she loved him so much: his hair was thinning, his body thickening and, apart from the penetrating dark brown eyes, his square face lacked beauty, but whenever he spoke, everyone listened and his powers of persuasion were infinite.

'Little Jannie, I cannot believe you're going to be a head-mistress.' His fingers edged over her breast. 'We can still meet. Can I come home this evening?'

'No,' snapped Janna. 'I'm a head, but no longer a mistress.'

Janna, however, was never cast down for long. At half-term, she had come south and found herself a minute but adorable eighteenth-century house called Jubilee Cottage. Like a child's drawing, it had a path spilling over with catmint and lavender leading up to a gabled porch with 'Jubilate' engraved above the door and mullioned windows on either side. It was the last house in the small village of Wilmington, which had a pub, a shop and a watercress-choked stream dawdling along the edge of the High Street.

Janna could easily afford the mortgage on her splendid new salary. She couldn't believe she'd be earning so much.

Wilmington thankfully was three miles from Larkminster Comp. However much you loved kids, it was a mistake to live over your school. When she grew tired of telling her children they were all stars, she could escape home, wander on her own lawn in bare feet and gaze up at her own stars.

All the same, missing Stew, it was terribly easy to go through a bottle of wine of an evening.

'I shall buy a new car and get a dog,' vowed Janna.

3

From the middle of August, Janna was in and out of her new school familiarizing herself with everything, palling up with Wally Bristow, the site manager, who like most site managers was the fountain of all wisdom.

Wally had short, slicked-back brown hair and wise grey eyes in a round, smiling face as dependable and reassuring as a digestive biscuit. Living but three minutes from Larks, he was always on call except on Thursday evening, when he and a team of bell-ringers rehearsed for Sunday's service in St Mary's Church next door, or on Saturday afternoons when Larkminster Rovers played at home. He was inordinately proud of a good-looking son, Ben, who'd risen to sergeant in the Royal Engineers.

Janna's heart swelled when she saw Wally had repainted the board outside the school in dark blue gloss and written in gold letters: 'LARKMINSTER COMPREHENSIVE SCHOOL. Head Teacher: Janna Curtis'.

'Oh Wally, I've got to make every child feel they're the greatest and discover each one's special talents.'

'Smokin', spittin', swearin', runnin' away, fightin' and urinatin' in phone boxes,' intoned Wally. 'As we can't fill the places, we get all the dropouts that get sacked or rejected by other schools.'

Wally showed her Smokers', a steep, grassy bank down which the children vanished so they could smoke, do drugs, drink and even shag unobserved by the staffroom.

'I don't want to frighten you, Janna,' he went on as they lunched on cans of lager and Marks and Spencer's prawn sandwiches, 'but the kids are running wild. Most of them only come in to trash the place and play football. The rest are off havin' babies or appearin' in court. They're demoralized by the staff,

12

who are either off sick from "stress" ' – Wally gave a snort of dis-belief – 'old dinosaurs hanging on for retirement, or commies who grumble at everything and threaten strike action if you keep them a minute late.'

Wally also warned her of tricky teachers: Mike Pitts, the deputy head, who taught maths, did the timetable and who was always burning joss sticks and scented candles to disguise the drink fumes; and Cara Sharpe, who'd glared at Janna at her interview.

'Everyone hates Cara, but humours her. She wanted Mike as head, and her to get deputy head to look good on her CV. She and Mike are thick as thieves. Don't trust them. Cara's a bitch to the kids.'

'Not any more she won't be. Where are the playing fields?'

'Don't have any: they were sold off by the council. The rest of the land is on too much of a slope and you can't swing a gerbil in the playground.'

The playground was indeed awful: a square of tarmac surrounded by broken rusty railings with no basketball nets and two overhanging sycamores, whose leaves, curling and covered in sinister black spots, provided the only shade.

Everything had deteriorated since Janna's interview in May. A lower-angled sun revealed damp patches and peeling plaster in every classroom. The once lovely garden and parkland were choked with thistles and nettles. Pale phlox and red-hot pokers were broken or bent double by bindweed which seemed to symbolize the red tape threatening to strangle Janna's hopes. An in-tray of forms to be filled in nearly hit the ceiling.

The GCSE results out in late August had dropped to four per cent of the pupils gaining A–C grades in five subjects. Only these gave Larks points in the league tables, and only Cara Sharpe and Phil Pierce, the gentle head of science who'd met Janna at the station, had got most of their children through.

'Phil's a good bloke,' said Wally, 'firm, but very fair. He's always online to answer pupils' homework questions. The kids love him.'

'Why's he still here?' asked Janna gloomily.

'He's very loyal. Trouble with kids here, they leave at sixteen so they don't have to come back and face the music of terrible GCSE results.'

'Where do they go on to?'

'The dole queue or the nick.'

Janna kicked off by tackling her office, which was full of the presence of Mike Pitts, who'd done her job for the spring and

13

summer terms and who clearly hadn't wanted people to follow his movements. The door had a security lock and a heavy dark blind pulled down over the big window hiding a view over the playground to houses, the River Fleet and grey-green woods beyond.

Janna insisted a doubtful Wally remove both lock and blind.

'I want to be accessible to both children and staff.'

Shaking his head, Wally got out his screwdriver.

> 'It really ain't surprising [he sang in a rich baritone],
> That we're rising, rising, rising,
> Soon we'll reach Division One.
> Premier, Wembley, here we come.'

'What's that song?' demanded Janna.

'Larkminster Rovers's battle hymn. We got to the second division last season. Now we've got to stay there.'

> 'Larks is going up the league tables too [sang Janna],
> Soon we'll reach Division One.
> Premier, Wembley, here we come.'

Wally nearly dropped his screwdriver as her sweet soaring voice rattled the window panes.

Having scraped scented candle wax off the furniture and scrubbed the room from top to toe, Janna and Wally painted her office white, hung cherry-red curtains and laid rush matting on the floor.

'I need a settee and a couple of armchairs so people can relax when they come in here.'

'The kids'll trash them, the settee'll be an incitement to rape or teachers grumbling and those white walls won't last a minute,' sighed Wally.

'Then we'll cover them with pictures.'

Up went *Desiderata* and *Hold the Dream* embroidered by Janna's Auntie Glad, followed by big photographs of Wharfedale, Fountains Abbey and Stew's photograph of all the children and teachers at Redfords waving goodbye in front of a square grey school building.

On a side table Janna put Stew's Staffordshire cow and a big bunch of Michaelmas daisies and late roses rescued from Larks's flower beds.

'My goodness, you have been working hard,' mocked Rowan Merton when she looked in a week before term started.

14

As a working wife and mother with photographs of her husband and two little girls all over her office, on the door of which was printed 'Assistant to the Head', Rowan prided herself on juggling. She had wound Mike Pitts round her little finger and clearly didn't fancy extending herself for a woman – particularly one in a denim mini, with a smudged face and her red curls in a ponytail.

'Have you flown in to rescue us?' she mocked. 'Like Red Adair in a skirt?'

'No, I've come to show you how to save yourselves,' retorted Janna tartly, then, remembering Stew's advice about not antagonizing people, added, 'How are Scarlet and Meagan? They must have loved having you to themselves in the holidays.'

Rowan relented fractionally and said they had, then launched into a list of staff requests for broken chairs, desks, leaking windows and computers to be mended.

'And Mrs Sharpe wants a blind. The sun casts such a glare, no one can read the whiteboard in the afternoon.'

Cara Sharpe's own glare, Janna would have thought, would see off any competition.

'And my anglepoise lamp collapses without the aid of two bull-dog clips and the angle being wedged open by the last *Education Year Book*,' went on Rowan. 'If Wally could sort all those things out before term begins?'

'Wally's flat out,' snapped Janna.

Rowan glanced round the office. 'Yes, I can see. Nice settee. We have to watch the budget now S and C hold the purse strings.'

Slowly, Janna familiarized herself with classrooms, halls, gym and labyrinthine adjoining corridors in the main building, which was known as School House. Fifty yards away, the annexe, known as Appletree because it had been built on the site of an old orchard, housed the labs, music, design and technology and food technology departments.

Then she pored over the children's personal files, counting the asylum-seekers, Indians, Pakistanis and Afro-Caribbeans – far fewer than at Redfords. She had also noticed lots of BNPs and swastikas amongst the graffiti: she would have to watch out for racist bullying. She was now frantically trying to memorize the names before term began.

'The ones you have to watch are those going into Year Nine and particularly the Wolf Pack,' said Wally as he carried in a mini-fridge for milk, butter and orange juice, and put jam, marmalade, coffee, tea bags, lots of biscuits, two packs of Mars

15

and Twix bars and a tin of Quality Street in the cupboard. 'These won't last a minute.'

'Oh, shut up,' said Janna, who was gazing down at a photograph of a beautiful black boy with long dark eyelashes and a smile of utter innocence.

Wally glanced over her shoulder. 'He's Wolf Pack. Feral Jackson. Comes into school to play football and start fights. Very druggy background; mother's an addict, off her face all day. Feral went inside at the beginning of the holidays for mugging some women shoppers. His brother Joey was stabbed to death last year. Uncle Harley, his mum's boyfriend, is a mega pusher. That's Feral's best mate, Paris Alvaston.'

Janna looked at the boy's ghostly face, the wonderful bone structure, the watchful pale grey eyes of a merle collie.

'Paris has been in different care homes since he was two,' added Wally. 'Goes AWOL from time to time on trains all over the country searching for his mother. Advertised for a home in the local paper last year, but there were no takers. Shame really.'

'That's terrible.' Janna reached out and switched on the kettle. 'Poor boy.'

'Looks too spooky. Teachers say he's very clever, writes wonderful stories one day, then just puts his name at the top of the paper the next. Everything goes inside. He and Feral are joined at the very narrow hip. Give them a detention and they jump out of the window, climb down the wisteria and run away.

'That's Griffith Williams, known as "Graffi".' Wally pointed to a thickset boy with black curls and wicked sliding dark eyes. 'Graffi was a Welshman, Graffi was a thief . . . But he's a good laugh. Don't stand anywhere near him or he'll graffiti you. That's Pearl Smith: she's got a temper on her, scratch the eyes out of any girl who tries to get off with her boys, particularly Feral. She's trouble. Cuts herself. Got arms like ladders.'

'Well, she's not wearing make-up and having hair that colour in my school,' said Janna firmly as she broke open a packet and dropped tea bags into two mugs. 'That one's pretty.'

'Kylie Rose. Already had one kid at twelve – wanted something to love. Time she spends on her back, she'll have another any minute. Anything to avoid SATs. Those five make up the Wolf Pack.'

'Feral, Paris, Graffi, Pearl and Kylie Rose,' intoned Janna as she poured boiling water over the tea bags and added milk and two sugars for Wally, who carried on with her lesson.

'There are three more you want to watch from Year Nine. One's Rocky; he's autistic. Attention Deficit Disorder they call it

16

these days,' he added scornfully,. 'Nice kid, but violent if he don't get his Ritalin. More serious are "Satan" Simmons – a racist bully, excluded last term for carrying a gun, overturned on appeal because his father's a councillor – and "Monster" Norman. Monster's mixed race' – Wally stirred his tea thoughtfully – 'in that his dad, who keeps walking out, is a quarter black, which Monster denies, which makes him even more of a racist bully. He's also a great snivelling toad, really spiteful, but his mother's a governor, so you can't touch him.'

Janna put her hand over the names: Freddie 'Feral' Jackson, such a beautiful face; Paris Alvaston: no one could forget him either, he looked so hauntingly sad; Griffith 'Graffi' Williams; Pearl; Kylie Rose; 'Satan' Simmons; Rocky; 'Monster' Norman.'

'What's that?' she demanded, noticing a switch inside the well of her desk.

'Your panic button,' said Wally, then, when Janna looked mutinous: 'You don't know what you're up against. Most of our kids come from the Shakespeare Estate. Their parents are crazy people who respect no one. From the beginning of term you're wearing a radio mike, and if there's any trouble, you summon back-up. Someone's always on call on the internal radio link.'

'I'm not bothering with any of that junk. This is going to be a happy school.'

Before the teachers came back, Wally also gave her a sneak preview of the staffroom.

'Why do they need a security lock?' she asked as Wally punched out the code to enter.

'To keep out violent kids and parents.'

'And me too, presumably. God, it's awful! Who'd want to break in here?'

Walls the luminous olive green of a child about to be sick were not enhanced by brown and yellow check curtains. Mock leather chairs in the dingiest browns and beiges huddled dispiritedly round low tables. Staff pigeonholes overflowed, clearly untackled since last term. Three potted plants had baked to death on the window sill. A Hoover, weak from underwork, was slumped against an ancient television set. Health and safety laws and union posters promising significant reductions in workload shared the noticeboard with details of half-price Calvin Klein button-fly boxers and Winnie-the-Pooh character socks. Also pinned up was a letter from Cotchester University announcing that a former pupil Marilyn Finch had attained a second in maths.

17

'For those who remember Marilyn,' Mike Pitts had scribbled across the bottom, 'all our efforts were worthwhile.'

'Only graduate Larks ever had,' volunteered Wally. 'Pittsy taught her.'

'I'm going to have to tackle him on the timetable,' sighed Janna. 'It's covered with drink rings and Year Seven A and Year Eight B are having English with the same teacher in the same classroom at the same time on Tuesday morning – and it gets worse. God, look at that.'

On the breakfast bar, untouched since the end-of-term party, sink and draining board were crowded with dirty wine glasses, moth-filled cups and orange-juice cartons. Scrumpy, beer and vegetable-juice cans littered the floor.

Debbie the cleaner, said Wally disapprovingly, would blitz the place before the first staff meeting tomorrow.

'None of this lot can wash up a cup.'

'We'd better buy them a dishwasher.'

'They'd never load it.'

To the right of the door, imperilling entry, hung a dartboard with two scarlet-feathered darts plunged deep into the bull's eye. Last year's Christmas decorations had been chucked into a far corner between a ping-pong table with one leg supported by a German dictionary and a billiard table with a badly ripped cloth.

'Don't matter,' said Wally philosophically. 'Table's mostly used for late-night nooky.'

'Anyone I know?' asked Janna, who'd moved to examine a big picture frame, which contained cigarette-card-sized photographs of all the staff in order of seniority. Heading these were the Dinosaurs who'd been at Larks for ever. To memorize them, Janna had made an acronym – P.U.B.I.C. – out of the first letters of their names. 'P' for Pitts, 'U' for Uglow (Miss) who taught RE, 'B' for Basket (Miss) who taught geography, 'I' for Illingworth (Mr) who taught science and 'C' for Chalford (Mrs) who taught history.

'That's one I haven't memorized,' mused Janna, 'with the piled-up dark hair and operatic make-up. She must be Miss Cambola, head of music.'

Wally, however, had noticed that into Janna's photograph on the far top left someone had plunged the missing red-feathered dart between the eyes. Hastily Wally whipped it out. Fortunately, Janna had been distracted by the photograph of a good-looking blond man, affectedly cupping his face between long fingers.

'He's not bad.'

'Jason Fenton. Kids call him Goldilocks. Cara Sharpe's toyboy, so hands off. He wanted her job as head of drama and English, and believes in constantly switching schools to jack up his status and his salary. Claims you go stale if you stay more than a year, which upsets the Dinosaurs, who've been here for ever.'

'And him?' Janna pointed to a black-eyed, black-browed, bearded man with dishevelled black hair.

'Robbie Rushton, chief leftie, rabble-rouser and has-bin. Spends his time plotting and telling you what you can't do. Longs for a strike so he can appear on TV again. He and Jason both have the hots for Gloria, deputy head of PE.' Wally pointed to a pouting strawberry blonde. 'Gloria prefers Jason because he's posher and washes more. "Soon we'll reach Division One. Premier, Wembley, here we come,"' sang Wally.

Who the hell had plunged that dart into Janna's photograph, he wondered? She was such a sweet kid. He was determined to protect her.

' "P" for Pitts, "U" for Uglow, "B" for Basket, "I" for Illingworth, "C" for Chalford,' intoned Janna.

4

On 3 September, all the staff came into school for a full day to prepare work and classrooms for the children, whose first day of term was the fourth. New staff were also initiated into school practice: which included what coloured exercise books to use, pupil data files, playground rotas, policy towards parents and bullying, and what was laughingly known as the golden rules of behaviour management.

Janna had decided to break the ice and tradition by scheduling her first staff meeting at five o'clock, rather than first thing. Desperate for it to go well, she had not only memorized names and achievements until her head was bursting, but also ordered in three large quiches and a couple of crates of red and white to jolly things along.

Her day running up to the meeting was frantic: coping with endless requests and demands (mostly, it seemed, not to teach the Wolf Pack), and having a most unpleasant spat with Mike Pitts, who hadn't taken kindly to criticism of his timetable.

'Then do it yourself.'

'No,' countered Janna bravely, 'it's your job to put it right.'

She had fared little better with Sam Spink, the union rep, who had very short hair shaved at the back, a large bottom and an even larger sense of her own importance. Her straining brown leggings stopped at mid-calf leaving a hairy gap above her Winnie-the-Pooh character socks, which seemed to give out signals that she was not all work and no play, and clearly regarded herself as a bit of a card. She proceeded to lecture Janna at great length about not prolonging the school day by a second. Remembering yet again Stew's instruction about not antagonizing colleagues unnecessarily, Janna just managed to keep her temper.

She then had to welcome two newly qualified teachers –
NQTs or Not Quite Togethers, as they were known – pretty,
plump, earnest Lydia who taught English, and pale Lance, teaching history. They were so full of hope and trepidation that Janna
couldn't bear them to be bludgeoned by the weary cynicism of
the other staff and spent longer than she should discussing
Thomas Hardy country and the battlefields, where they had
respectively spent their holidays in order to glean fascinating
information to relay to their classes. Thus she was still talking and
in jeans and a T-shirt when Rowan Merton put her sleek dark bob
round the door:

'Two minutes to kick-off, headmistress.'

'Why didn't you warn me?' screamed Janna.

'You insisted on not being bothered.'

Janna only had time to sling on a denim jacket and slap on
some blusher – God, she looked tired – before belting down the
corridor. Across reception, at her instructions, Wally had strung
a brightly coloured banner saying: 'Welcome back all Larks
teachers and children'.

'So demeaning to refer to the students as children,' grumbled
Sam Spink.

The meeting was held in the non-smoking staffroom. Outside,
a muttering band of lefties, headed by the black-eyed, wild-haired
Robbie Rushton, drew feverishly on last fags. Inside, Debbie the
cleaner had pulled a blinder. The place was gleaming. Janna
made a mental note to buy Debbie a box of chocolates. Gallant
Wally had, in addition, attacked the immediate garden and a
smell of mown grass and newly turned earth drifting in through
the window gave an illusion of spring and fresh starts.

The Dinosaurs had clearly been emailed by a furious Mike
Pitts. Having bagged most of the dingy chairs and chuntering
disapprovingly about 'heads in jeans squandering the budget
on drink', they were getting stuck into the red. Mike Pitts
ostentatiously asked for a mineral water. Skunk Illingworth, who
taught science, stank of BO and wore socks, sandals and shorts,
had just cut himself a huge slice of quiche and filled up a pint
mug with white.

'She's going to have the students out of uniform and calling us
by our Christian names in a trice,' he grumbled.

Heart thumping, Janna glanced round at the sea of faces:
appraising, hostile, suspicious, waiting for someone to make a
move. Thank God, Phil Pierce, who'd befriended her at her
interview, rushed straight over, kissing her on both cheeks and
apologizing profusely for not being in touch.

Like most teachers, he looked fifteen years younger after the summer break. His kind eyes were clear, his hair bleached, his bony face dark tanned. He and his wife had just come back from Kenya, he said. He'd popped in earlier, but Rowan had stressed that Janna was tied up. He hoped she was OK. Then he introduced Miss Cambola of the large bosom, piled-up hair and stage make-up, and Janna scored immediate brownie points by remembering she taught music, was a fine mezzo and sang with the Larkminster Operatic Society.

'You must join us,' said Miss Cambola. 'Wally tells me you have a beautiful voice. We're doing *Don Giovanni* in November and have yet to cast Zerlina.'

'I'm afraid I won't have time,' said Janna wistfully.

'Well anyway, come to supper. Have you met Mags Gablecross? She teaches French part-time.'

'And has a wedding in the offing,' said Janna, shaking hands with a sweet-faced woman in her fifties.

'You are well briefed.' Mags smiled. 'Your predecessor hardly recognized his staff.'

'Oh, thank you,' stammered Janna, 'and your husband's the great detective.'

'He'd like you to say so. He said to call him if you get any hassle.' Margaret popped the Chief Inspector's card into Janna's jacket pocket. 'You must come to supper and meet him.'

Vastly cheered, Janna worked the room, enquiring after new babies, congratulating on engagements and new houses, expressing sorrow over deaths and hearing endless complaints about the new Year Nine and the Wolf Pack.

She was aware of Mike Pitts skulking in a corner not meeting her eyes and Cara Sharpe also avoiding her. In a scarlet dress, which clung to her rapacious, elongated body and matched her drooping vermilion mouth, Cara looked far more attractive than she had at Janna's interview. Her ebony hair seemed softer and curlier, but her face was still as hard as the earth in those poor dead potted plants.

She was also busy upstaging other teachers over their GCSE results. 'How did Mitzi do in geography?' she called across to Miss Basket: one of the Dinosaurs who had buck teeth, a pale, wispy fringe and a twitching face shiny enough to check one's make-up in, and who promptly stepped back into the Christmas decorations with a loud crunch, replying that Mitzi had only got a D.

'You amaze me, she's so easy to teach,' mocked Cara. 'She got A stars in drama, English and English lit. for me.'

Bitch, thought Janna and promptly told a crestfallen Miss Basket, 'You did brilliantly with those asylum-seekers, getting C grades in such a short time.'

Miss Basket blushed with passionate gratitude. Cara looked furious. Then Janna spoilt it by congratulating Basket on a new grandson.

'I never married,' squawked Basket.

Everyone suppressed smiles except Cara Sharpe, who laughed openly before turning glittering eyes on Lydia, the NQT who was the most junior member of her department:

'You've got Year Nine E tomorrow, Lydia, you'll find them a doddle.'

Janna swung round in horror. Year Nine E included the Wolf Pack, Monster and Satan, not to mention autistic, often violent Rocky. They'd eat poor Lydia for the breakfast their parents probably wouldn't provide.

'You must look out for Paris Alvaston,' Janna advised Lydia as Wally topped up their glasses. 'I hear he writes wonderful stories.'

'With respect,' sneered Cara, 'Paris is a no-hoper, like all the Wolf Pack. You have to tell them five times to do anything, they're always late or don't come in at all, and never do their homework. Paris, arrogant little beast, does what he pleases and the others follow suit.'

'Not a doddle then, as you promised Lydia,' flared up Janna, quite forgetting about keeping her trap shut. 'That's a very negative attitude.'

'I'm entirely on Cara's side. The Wolf Pack are beyond control.' A tall man with blond curls and smooth golden-brown skin had joined the group. 'Pearl's a hell-cat and Kylie Rose a nympho. If I'm going to teach them, I want a chastity belt and CCTV in the classroom.'

This must be Jason Fenton, alias Goldilocks. He was certainly pretty, his regular features marred only by rather bulging blue eyes, as though the transformation from frog into Prince Charming had not been absolute.

'We mustn't let past behaviour dictate the future,' Janna said firmly. 'The Wolf Pack are clearly forceful characters.'

'You can't make a difference with that lot,' drawled Jason, 'they're too damaged.'

The room had gone quiet, quivering collectively with expectation.

'If you feel like that,' said Janna furiously, 'you shouldn't be teaching here.'

'I couldn't agree more.' Jason smiled into her eyes. 'I've been

23

trying to see you all day to hand in my notice.' Over the gasps of amazement he added: 'But Rowan Merton wouldn't let me cross your threshold,' and, shoving an envelope into Janna's hand, he turned towards the door.

A striking strawberry blonde in a non-existent skirt and a clinging pink vest glued to her worked-out body, whom Janna recognized as Gloria, the deputy head of PE, gave a wail: 'When are you going, Jase?'

'If one resigns on the first day of term, one can be over the hills and far way by half-term.'

'And *where* are you going?' hissed an incensed, wrong-footed Cara.

'To Bagley Hall as head of drama,' said Jason, filling up his glass on the way out.

'That's an independent,' thundered Sam Spink.

'I know,' murmured Jason. 'Adequate funding, nineteen weeks' holiday, a decent salary and no Wolf Pack: need I say more? Here's to me,' and, draining his glass, he was gone.

Over a thunderous murmur of chat, Janna had to pull herself and the meeting together. Clapping her hands for quiet, assuring everyone she wouldn't keep them long, she then had to express great regret that Larks had had to bid farewell to ten teachers she had never met. There were broad grins when she described a former ICT master as a 'tower of strength', when he'd evidently jumped half the female staff and impregnated two supply teachers, and laughter when she expressed deep regret at the death of some former head, who'd only emigrated with his wife to Tasmania.

'Mike Pitts wouldn't have slipped up like that,' muttered Skunk Illingworth, the science Dinosaur, refilling his pint mug.

'I will get to know you all soon,' apologized Janna. She took a deep breath and looked round. Somehow she must rally them. Then Jason returned. Seeing him grinning superciliously and lounging against the wall, Janna's resolve was stiffened and she kicked off by attacking her staff for their atrocious GCSE results.

'We must start from this moment to improve. If we can get our children to behave, then we can teach them, and they will behave if they're interested.' She smiled at Lydia in the front row.

'They will also behave if this is a happy school and they have fun here as well as learning. We must give them and the school back its pride so they'll stop trashing and graffitiing the place.

'Wally has worked so hard restoring the building over the holidays. Debbie has worked so hard cleaning up in here. Frankly, it was a tip.' Out of the corner of her eye, she saw Wally clutching his head. 'In turn,' she went on, 'I'd like you all to work hard transforming your classrooms. We want examples of good work on the walls and the corridors and colour and excitement everywhere.' Then, beaming at the furious faces: 'And will you all start smiling around the place, particularly at the children, making them feel valued and welcome.'

Only Phil Pierce, Lydia and Lance, Mags Gablecross and Miss Cambola, the busty music mistress, smiled back.

As Janna took a fortifying slug of white, she heard a loud cough to her left and, glancing round, saw Sam Spink tapping the glass of her watch.

'You were saying?' snapped Janna.

Marching over, Sam said in a stage whisper that could be heard in the gods at Covent Garden: 'People have been in school since eight-thirty, nearly nine hours, working flat out to get everything shipshape. Many colleagues need to collect kids from child-minders, others have long journeys home and want to be alert for their students tomorrow. I'm sure you're aware that anything over eight hours is unacceptable. Any minute they'll walk out of their own accord.'

'OK,' muttered Janna, turning to her now utterly captive audience, 'we'll call it a day. I'm afraid it's been a very long one. Thank you all for coming. I look forward to working with you,' then she hissed at Sam Spink, 'and I'll personally string you up by your Winnie-the-Pooh character socks if you ever cheek me in public like that again,' before stalking out.

'Remember always to smile around the school,' Cara Sharpe called after her.

'Never thanked me for taking Year Ten to Anglesey in July,' repeated Skunk as he petulantly emptied bottles, then glasses into his mug.

Phil and Wally were kind and complimentary, but Janna knew she'd blown it.

'This place needs shaking up,' said Phil. 'Would you like to come home for a bite of supper?'

'Oh, I'd love to,' said Janna longingly, 'but I've got so much to do.'

She still hadn't written her speech for assembly and her in-tray, to quote Larkminster Rovers's battle hymn, was 'rising, rising, rising'.

She was also jolted to realize that in the old days, before she'd become part of the high-flying team at Redfords, she'd have probably been out hassling senior management like Sam Spink: was poacher turning keeper?

25

The full moon, like a newly washed plate, followed her home – perhaps she *should* buy the staffroom a dishwasher. Jubilee Cottage was cold, smelt musty and didn't look welcoming because she still hadn't unpacked her stuff or put up any pictures. Most of them, admittedly, were adorning her office at Larks. Poor little cottage, she must give it some TLC along with five hundred disturbed children and at least twenty-eight bolshie staff.

A large vodka and tonic followed by Pot Noodles wasn't a good idea either. She'd promptly thrown up the lot. Then she washed her hair. Nagged to present a more respectable image by her fellow teachers at Redfords, she had had her red curls lopped to the shoulders, then defiantly invested in a pink suit decorated with darker pink roses which should jazz up tomorrow's proceedings.

As heads covered up to ten miles a day policing their schools, she had also bought a pair of dark pink shoes with tiny heels. She laid everything out on a chair. By the time she'd showered and put on a nightie, it was half past twelve.

She fell to her knees. 'Oh please, dear God, help me to save my school.'

If you banged your head on the pillow and recited something last thing, you were supposed to remember it in the morning.

'Feral Jackson, Paris Alvaston, Graffi Williams, Pearl Smith, Kylie Rose Peck . . .' The faces of the Wolf Pack swam before her eyes throughout the night.

Then she overslept and didn't get to school until eight-fifteen.

At the bottom of the drive, in anticipation of a new term, were already gathering lawyers' assistants waiting to hand out leaflets encouraging disgruntled parents to sue the school, pushers lurking with offers of drugs or steroids, and expelled pupils hanging around to duff up pupils they'd been chucked out for terrorizing.

On her desk, Janna found a pile of good-luck cards, but nothing from Stew, not even a phone message. She was also outraged to receive a card on which Tory blue flowers – bluebells, flax and forget-me-nots – were intertwined and exquisitely painted by someone called Hanna Belvedon. Inside was a handwritten note from Jupiter Belvedon, presumably the artist's husband and Larkminster's Conservative MP, welcoming Janna to Larkshire and hoping she'd ring him if she needed help. As if she'd accept help from a rotten Tory.

Out of the window she could see pupils straggling up the drive, smoking, arguing, fighting. Several posters and the welcome-back sign had already been ripped down. There was a crash as a brick flew through a window in reception.

Two minutes before assembly was due to start, Rowan Merton bustled in quivering with excitement:

'You might like to open this before kick-off.'

It was a beautifully wrapped and pink-ribboned bottle of champagne. Darling Stew had remembered. Turning towards the window, so Rowan couldn't look over her shoulder, Janna opened the little white envelope and was almost winded with disappointment as she read: 'Dear Miss Curtis, This is to wish you great luck, I hope you'll lunch with me one day soon. Yours ever, Hengist Brett-Taylor'.

'Who the hell's Hengist Brett-Taylor?'

Rowan was so impressed, she forgot for a moment to be hostile.

'Don't you know? He's head of Bagley Hall.' Then, when Janna looked blank: 'Our local independent school – frightfully posh. He was on *Question Time* last Thursday making mincemeat of poor Estelle Morris. Livens up any programme.'

'Not Ghengist Khan,' whispered Janna in horror, 'that fascist pig?'

'Well, I don't approve of Hengist's politics,' said Rowan shirtily, 'but he's drop-dead gorgeous.'

'He's an arrogant bastard,' who, now Janna remembered, had just poached Jason Fenton, another arrogant bastard. They'd suit each other. She was about to drop the bottle of champagne in the bin, when the bell went, so she put it in the fridge. She might well need it later.

Applying another layer of pale pink lipstick, she defiantly drenched herself in Diorissimo, buttoned up her suit to flaunt her small waist, and jumped at the sound of a wolf whistle.

'You look absolutely gorgeous,' sighed Phil Pierce, who'd come to collect her, 'roses, roses all the way. The kids are going to love you.'

Hearing the overwhelming din of children pouring down the corridor into the main hall, Janna started to shake. The task ahead seemed utterly awesome.

5

Dora, the eleven-year-old sister of Larkminster's Tory MP, Jupiter Belvedon, had heard that the young headmistress starting at Larks, the local sink school, was an absolute cracker. Dora thought this most unlikely. Schoolmistresses in her experience were such old boots that anything without two heads and a squint was described as 'attractive'.

Dora had therefore risen at seven to ride her skewbald pony Loofah along the River Fleet and into Larkminster to check Janna out. Dora also needed to think. She was very exercised because she was starting boarding at a new school, Bagley Hall, in a week's time. Dora's mother, Anthea, kept saying Bagley Hall was like Chewton Glen or the Ritz, but to Dora it was prison – particularly as she'd be separated from Loofah and Cadbury, her chocolate Labrador, who bounded ahead of them putting up duck. Dora was worried about both Loofah and Cadbury. Her sweet father, who'd been dotty about animals, would have looked after them, but alas, he'd died recently and her mother regarded both animals as a tie and a needless expense.

Dora sighed and helped herself to blackberries in the hedgerows. Loofah was much too small for her. He'd need lifts soon to stop her feet scraping the ground. He also bucked, sat down and bit people, but she loved him far too much to sell him. Life was very hard when you had so many animal dependants. Dora edged a KitKat out of her jodhpur pocket to share with the two of them. Her mother, Anthea, was always warning Dora she'd get spots and never attract a boyfriend.

Who wanted soppy boyfriends? thought Dora scornfully.

Dora had thick, flaxen plaits and even thicker curly blonde eye-lashes, which seemed designed to stop the peak of her hard hat

28

falling over her turned-up nose. Her big eyes were the same drained turquoise as the sky on the horizon. Slender, small for her age, she was redeemed from over-prettiness by a determined chin and a mouth frequently pursed in disapproval.

And Dora had much to disapprove of. Her beautiful mother, Anthea, in appearance all dewy-eyed softness, was in reality catting around with loads of boyfriends, including an awful old judge and a rose-grower – both married – and playing the disconsolate, impoverished widow for all she was worth. Fed up with the school run and anxious to enjoy an unbridled sex life, Anthea clearly wanted Dora out of the way, locked up at Bagley Hall.

The sole plus for Dora was that for several years she had been augmenting her income by leaking stories to the press. Her mother's romantic attachments had provided excellent copy.

Bagley Hall should prove even more remunerative. Hengist Brett-Taylor, the head, whom her mother fancied almost as much as Rupert Campbell-Black, was never out of the news. Her twin brother Dicky, who'd been boarding since he was eight and was so pretty he was the toast of the rugby fifteen, had torrid tales of the antics of the pupils.

But alas, her chilly eldest brother, Jupiter, as well as being MP for Larkshire, was chairman of the governors at Bagley Hall and, petrified of sleaze, had already given Dora a stern lecture about keeping her Max Clifford tendencies in check: 'If I hear you've been tipping off the press about anyone at Bagley or in the family, particularly me, there'll be big trouble.'

Jupiter was a beast, reflected Dora, appropriating the family home and all the money when her father died, so Dora, Dicky and their mother Anthea were now crammed into tiny Foxglove Cottage in Bagley village.

Ancient trees stroked the bleached fields with long shadows as Dora reached the outskirts of Larkminster. As she crossed the bridge, the cathedral clock struck eight. Ahead, she could see the beautiful golden houses of the Close, the market and the thriving bustling town. Trotting past St Jimmy's, the highly successful boys' school, entering the Shakespeare Estate, Dora was overtaken by an Interflora van heading nervously towards Larks Comp.

No one drove through the Shakespeare Estate by choice because of the glass and needles all over the roads. Screaming and shouting could be heard issuing from broken, boarded-up windows. Discarded fridges and burnt-out cars littered the gardens. An ashen druggie mumbled in the gutter. A gang of youths, hanging round a motorbike, hurled abuse at Dora as she passed.

Dora didn't care. She called off Cadbury who was taunting a snarling pit bull on a very short lead and looked up enviously at the satellite dishes clustered like black convolvulus on the houses. Her mother was too mean to install Sky in Foxglove Cottage.

Next door to the Shakespeare Estate, as a complete contrast, was a private estate called Cavendish Plaza, which was protected by huge electric gates, security guards and a great abstract in the forecourt, sculpted by Dora's gallery-owning father's most awful artist, Colin Casey Andrews, which was enough to frighten off any burglar, thought Dora sourly.

Cavendish Plaza was one of the brainchildren of developer Randal Stancombe, who was slapping houses, shops and super-markets all over Larkshire and whom her mother also thought was frightfully attractive, but whose hot, devouring, knowing dark eyes made Dora's flesh crawl.

Cavendish Plaza had its own shops and access to the High Street on the other side. Dora, riding on, came to a chip shop with boarded-up windows and a pub called the Ghost and Castle, then stiffened with interest as she saw the notorious Wolf Pack slouching out of the newsagent's, loaded up with goodies. Feral Jackson was breaking the cellophane round a chicken tikka sandwich.

Everyone knew Feral. Although not yet fourteen, he was already five feet nine with snake hips, three-foot-wide shoulders and a middle finger permanently jabbing the air. He'd been up before Dora's mother at the Juvenile Court in the summer for mugging.

'And gave me such a disgustingly undressing look when we remanded him in custody,' her mother had complained.

In the end Feral had been sent for a month to a Young Offenders' Institute, and if he recognized her as her mother's daughter he'd probably knife her as well. Dora shot off down a side road.

Janna's arrival at Larks was, in fact, causing universal excitement.

Rod Hyde, head of St Jimmy's, picked up a magnifying glass to look at a photograph of Janna in the *Larkminster Gazette*. She had nice breasts and an air of confidence that would soon disappear. Pride comes before a fall. Rod Hyde was full of such little homilies. 'Good schools are like good parents,' he was always saying, 'caring and demanding.'

Rod Hyde was very bald but shaved his remaining hair. He had a firm muscular figure, a ginger beard, and believed in exercise and cold baths. St Jimmy's' results had been staggeringly good this year and they were edging nearer Bagley Hall in the league tables.

As a local super head, Rod Hyde was certain his friends, who ran S and C Services, would soon send him into Larks on a rescue mission. He would much enjoy giving Janna Curtis guidance.

Randal Stancombe, property developer, finished working out in his rooftop gymnasium. Before having a shower, he picked up his binoculars and looked down with pride on Cavendish Plaza, his beautiful private estate with its mature trees, still-emerald green lawns and swimming pools, where topless tenants were taking advantage of the Indian summer.

Randal's hands, however, clenched on his binoculars as he turned them towards Larks Comp. He could see all those ruffians straggling in, scrapping, stopping to light fags or worse. Randal's tenants were constantly complaining about stolen cars and streets paved with chewing gum.

Janna Curtis looked pretty tasty in her photograph in the *Gazette*, decided Randal. She might make bold statements about turning the school round, but this Lark had two broken wings. S and C Services were bound to keep her so short of money, she'd soon be desperate for sponsorship. Interesting to see how long she'd take to approach him. Randal loved having power over women.

Randal's daughter Jade, a very attractive young lady, rising fourteen years of age, was starting her third year at Bagley Hall and dating a fellow pupil, Cosmo Rannaldini, the son of Dame Hermione Harefield, the globally famous diva. One forked out school fees mainly for the contacts. Randal would soon ask Dame Hermione to open his hypermall outside Birmingham.

Over at Bagley Hall, Hengist Brett-Taylor, who'd just spent five weeks in Umbria to avoid the middle classes and those with new money, was drafting a speech for the new pupils' parents.

'May I first issue a very warm welcome to all of you here tonight,' he wrote. 'But also point out what will rapidly become clear to you as the years roll by: that the headmaster of Bagley Hall is rather like the figurehead on an old wooden sailing ship. It is vaguely decorative and there is a clear understanding that one really ought to have one if one is to be seen doing the proper thing, but it is of course of absolutely no practical use whatsoever and does nothing.'

Hengist's glow at nearing the top of the country's league tables in both A and GCSE levels was slightly dimmed by having to face

31

several more massive hurdles at the start of term. In addition, he had to address the first staff meeting, the first assembly, the drinks party or 'shout-in' for new staff, not to mention keynote speeches to new pupils and sixth-formers and finally the first sermon in chapel on Sunday week.

The problem was to avoid repeating oneself or descending into platitudes, which was why Francis Bacon's essays, full of invigorating epigrams, was open on his desk. Hengist, who was terrified of boredom, was simultaneously drinking black coffee, listening to Brahms Symphony No. 2 on Radio 3, watching a video of Bagley's first fifteen's recent tour of South Africa and fondly admiring a white greyhound fast asleep on her back on the window seat.

Thank God all the holiday activities – sport and foreign trips – had passed without mishap. 'Toff school goes berserk in convent on rugger tour' could leave a huge clear-up job at the beginning of term.

Hengist gazed out at a sea of green playing fields broken only by the white rugger posts and a little wood, Badger's Retreat, in the distance, to which he kept adding young trees.

The Brahms had finished. Bagley's first fifteen had reached half-time. Picking up the *Larkminster Gazette*, Hengist looked at Janna's picture and shook his head:

'Poor, poor little lamb to the slaughter.'

The Bishop of Larkminster, on his knees in his bedroom in the Bishop's Palace overlooking the River Fleet, was praying without much hope that Janna Curtis, only a child herself, would be able to tame those dreadfully disturbed children who came from such appalling backgrounds. Next moment, he jumped out of skin still pink from his bath as a football parted the magnolia grandiflora and crashed against a pane of his Queen Anne window.

Creaking to his feet and bustling to the window, the Bishop caught a glimpse of white teeth like the crescent moon in a wicked laughing black face as, having retrieved his ball, the invader dropped back into the road. Here his companion, with a can of blue paint, was changing the 'u' in 'Please Shut the Gate' to an 'i'.

'Little buggers,' thundered the Bishop.

The Wolf Pack had no intention of going into school. The grass was too long to play football. So they played in the street. Fists were shaking and windows banged in fury as their ball shed the petals of a yellow rose, then snapped off the head of a tiger

32

lily, before knocking down a row of milk bottles like ninepins.

Feral had finished his chicken sandwich but was still hungry, as he and Paris argued the merits of Arsenal and Liverpool. They once had a fight over whether Thierry Henry was a better player than Michael Owen that had gone on for three days. Feral and Graffi were careful not to mention programmes they had watched last night in front of Paris. Viewing in Paris's children's home was strictly limited. The television was switched off at nine and monitored for sex and violence, which meant no *Big Brother*, *EastEnders*, or *The Bill.*

Pearl Smith, in a vile mood, was kicking a Coke tin. One of the few pupils at Larks who looked good in the hard crimson of the school uniform, she wore a skimpy crop top in that colour instead of the regulation sweatshirt. Her arm throbbed where she'd cut herself last night, after her mother's boyfriend had pushed her across the room for pinching her new baby sister.

Graffi, who'd appropriated another can of paint, was writing 'Stancombe is an asshole' on an outside wall of Cavendish Plaza.

'Very limited vocabulary,' mocked Paris, opening a stolen bar of Crunchie.

'Fuck off, professor,' replied Graffi. 'Teach me some new words then.'

Feral, meanwhile, had opened a nicked *Larkminster Gazette* and was studying Janna's picture.

'Don't look much,' snarled Pearl. 'Crap 'air, crap figure.'

'Oh, I don't know,' said Graffi, to wind her up.

Next moment, Kylie Rose, the fifth member of the Wolf Pack, carrying a pregnancy kit stolen from the High Street, joined them.

'I only got Mum to babysit Cameron by promising I'd go into school,' she told the others, then, peering at the *Gazette*, 'A-a-a-a-h. Janna says she's looking forward to meeting us. Isn't she pretty?'

'Let's go and take the piss,' said Feral, handing the paper to Paris. 'Wally might have mowed the grass.'

Feral could do anything with a football and now, seeing Dora Belvedon approaching, drove it between the conker-brown legs of her pony, Loofah, who reared up. Only Dora's excellent seat kept her in the saddle. Enraged, she rode straight at the Wolf Pack. As he leapt out of the way, Feral slashed at Loofah's reins with a knife, adding in a hoarse deep voice: 'Fuck off, you snotty little slag.'

Next moment Cadbury, the Labrador, came storming to the rescue, barking furiously. Feral, who was terrified of dogs, bolted, followed by the others. Only Paris, who protected and looked after Robin, the old fox terrier who lived at his children's home, stood his ground with hand outstretched, until Cadbury wagged his tail and licked the Crunchie crumbs off his fingers.

He had the palest face Dora had ever seen.

'Don't you dare suck up to my dog,' she yelled.

'Fuck off, you stuck-up bitch,' hissed Paris.

His face stayed with Dora. Apart from the curled lip and gelled, spiky hair, he looked like the ghost on the inn sign of the Ghost and Castle.

6

Assembly at Larks was held in the main hall. On the walls in between doorways leading to classrooms hung bad portraits of former heads: bearded gentlemen in wing collars or wearing cravats with their hair brushed forward. There were also boards listing head boys and more recent heads. How cross Mike Pitts, skulking at the back, must have felt not to have made it up there.

Moth-eaten bottle-green velvet curtains flanked the platform, whose only props included a lectern, a few chairs and, to the right, a grand piano. Behind, having remarkably escaped the school vandals, soared a stained-glass window depicting a languid Archangel Michael with his flaming sword raised to kebab an inoffensive little dragon.

The dragon et moi, thought Janna, unless I catch this mob by the throat. The butterflies in her tummy had grown into blindly crashing pterodactyls as she stood in the wings, trying to concentrate on Phil Pierce's flattering introduction. Although there were only three hundred children after the register had been taken, there seemed an awful lot of them. Above her, chewing gum and surreptitiously chatting into their mobiles, Years Ten and Eleven hung over the balcony rail. In the body of the hall stood Years Eight and Nine, who'd struggled to their feet when prodded by their various form tutors, who ringed them with arms folded like riot police anticipating trouble.

With a thud of relief, Janna thought how attractive the children looked with their bright, curious faces: brown, black, yellow, pink, white, deathly pale, a few tanned, but now tinged with glowing ruby, emerald, violet, sapphire and amber by the light streaming through the stained glass. Both Wally and Phil crossed fingers behind their backs as she bounded up on to the platform, wearing an orange builder's hat.

'Good morning, everyone.' She beamed round at her astonished audience. 'I couldn't decide whether to wear this or a bullet-proof vest, but you all look so friendly, I needn't have worried, so let's kick off with one of your favourite songs.'

Crossing the platform she sat down at the piano and strummed out the introduction to the Larkminster Rovers battle hymn, then, with her sweet, pure voice ringing round the hall, launched into the first verse.

As she reached the second, Miss Cambola, head of music, ran up the platform steps and, in a rich mezzo, splendid bosom heaving, joined in: ' "Europe ain't seen nuffink yet." '

After a stunned silence, everyone else joined in, roaring out the chorus to loud whistling, cheering and stamping of feet.

How at ease she is with the kids, thought Wally as he uncrossed his fingers. And how bonny she looked in her rose suit, with her flaming red curls and her freckles breaking through her make-up.

After a second encore, Janna shut the piano, bowed, then whipped off her hat and held it out to a smiling Phil Pierce, who dropped in a pound coin to roars of laughter.

Janna turned to her audience. 'I'm so pleased to be here.'

'We're not,' shouted a voice from the gallery.

Janna laughed: 'Give me time.'

'She is very pretty,' whispered Kylie Rose, 'and nice.'

'She's ancient,' snarled Pearl.

'I was going through your personal files last night,' continued Janna, 'and discovered some truly excellent work.'

She then praised several children who'd done well in exams and in class.

'I particularly want to commend Aysha Khan's progress in science, and Paris Alvaston's essays, and Graffi Williams's artwork.'

'You can see it on walls all over the town,' shouted a wag.

'I want us to build on these wonderful successes, "rising, rising" like Larkminster Rovers till we get to the top. I'm determined to find what each one of you is good at. Everyone's a star at something. Never be afraid to ask for help or to pop into my office to tell me your problems. I and the other teachers are here to help.'

Seeing Cara Sharpe turn green like the witch in *Snow White* and raising her eyebrows to heaven, Janna took a deep breath:

'I'd like to tell you a story about some begonias, which are kinds of bulbs I planted in pots on the window ledge in my classroom at my last school. I planted seven. They were red, yellow, orange, pink, crimson, cream and white.'

'Oh, get on,' yelled a bruiser Janna recognized as Satan Simmons.

'These bulbs grew very fast on my window ledge,' she went on, 'except one little white one, which didn't put out a single shoot. I was sure it was dead. Days passed and all the others bloomed in wonderful colours, red, yellow, orange, pink, crimson and cream.'

'Cream ain't a colour,' shouted Pearl.

'OK, OK,' went on Janna. 'But as Christmas approached, all the six had finished flowering. I was about to store them for next year and chuck the little white one in the bin, when suddenly it put out leaves and grew and grew until it flowered just at Christmas, when there were no flowers around. And it gave more pleasure than any of the other begonias. So if you're a late developer, don't worry, your time will come.'

Now she'd got their attention, she went on: 'You're all good at something – there are all sorts of exciting new GCSEs. Have you thought of taking one in child development? All you need do is study a little brother or sister.'

'Christ, no,' sneered Pearl, lighting a fag.

Janna's eyes flashed.

'And you're good at smoking, Pearl Smith,' she yelled in sudden outrage. 'You're only thirteen; how dare you ruin your lungs?'

Pearl dropped her cigarette, staggered that Janna knew her name and age.

'I want to see you in my office immediately after assembly,' said Janna ominously. 'You're Pearl's head of year, aren't you, Mrs Sharpe? Please see that she's there.'

Cara Sharpe was hopping. So was Pearl when she reached Janna's office. Her breath was coming in great gasps lifting her little crimson crop top even higher above her groin-level mini.

She seemed to be deliberately breaking every school rule. Her hair drawn back into a cascade of ringlets was dyed more colours than the begonias. Studs gleamed from her belly button, nose and ears, from which, in addition, hung big gold loops. A silver cross nestled in her cleavage. A cat tattoo crawled under a gold ankle bracelet. More alarmingly, scars laddered her arms where she'd cut herself.

Yet with her wide-apart stick legs above killer heels, her sharp nose and chin, her shiny dark eyes, which kept glancing sideways at Janna, and her savage perkiness, she resembled nothing so much as a robin.

'How d'you know my name?'

'Because I care about you,' said Janna gently.

'Don't know me.'

'I want to very, very much.'

Pearl looked sullenly up at the photograph of smiling, waving Redfords pupils. 'Your last school?'

Janna nodded.

'Where is it?'

'Yorkshire.'

'Never been there. Miss Basket, our crap geography teacher, has never been to London.'

Janna suppressed a smile.

'We were the worst school in Yorkshire, right at the bottom,' she said.

'Like us.'

Janna went to the fridge. 'Would you like a Coke?'

'OK. Mrs Sharpe's a bitch.'

'In what way?'

'Blames it on us that she didn't get your job. If our SATs had been better, she would have. She never says anyfing nice when she marks our stuff.'

'How's your new baby sister?' asked Janna.

'Mum wanted to put her in my room – screams all night – and expects me to babysit so she can go out with her toyboy. I said no fucking way. I used to live with my boxer dad, but he's inside for burglary to feed his habit.'

A depressing smell of unflavoured mince was drifting up from the kitchens. I must do something about the food, thought Janna.

'I had a sister who trashed my room,' she said, 'but we get on now. I've heard you're very bright.'

'Paris is the clever one,' said Pearl. 'If he wasn't so cool, he'd get bullied for being a boffin.'

They were interrupted by screams and yells; next minute, Kylie rushed in in high excitement. 'Quickly, miss. Feral and Monster are killing each other in classroom G.'

Not yet wired up, with no thought of summoning back-up or enlisting help from other staff, Janna hurtled down the corridor.

'Christ, she's fast,' gasped Pearl as she and Kylie Rose panted after her.

Half Year Nine E was standing on desks, cheering on the protagonists; occasionally they got so heated, they started punching each other. Graffi was grinning broadly and offering two to one on Feral winning. Paris lounged against the wall pretending to be reading *David Copperfield*, but watching and waiting to jump to Feral's aid.

Young Lydia, suffering a baptism of fire in her first lesson, cringed in a corner, a book called *Dealing with Disruptive Students in the Classroom* sticking out of her pocket.

Janna promptly pummelled and shoved the audience out of the classroom, but they rushed round outside and continued to peer in through the window, applauding and egging on their heroes.

'C'mon, Feral.'

'C'mon, Monster.'

Monster was as huge as a sea lion; Feral, lithe as a panther, prowled round, taunting him, hitting Monster in the eye, which started bleeding, then skipping out of the way as Monster tried to punch him in the stomach. Now they were locked, throwing blows, Feral wincing as he was crushed by Monster's brute strength. Noticing Feral's hand stealing down his jeans, followed by a flash of silver, Janna dived between them.

'Stop it,' she screamed over escalating shrieks and yells. Next moment Feral's knife was thrust in her face, halting within an inch of her nose.

'Pack it in, Feral,' repeated Janna, 'and you too, Monster.'

Chivalry was not in Feral's code, but he admired guts. The rest of the class crept back in through window or door.

'You have a very sexy mouth, Feral,' observed Janna. 'If occasionally you raised it at both corners, and showed your beautiful teeth in a smile rather than an animal snarl, you could look very attractive. And please give me that knife.'

Feral put down his knife and started to laugh, so everyone else did too.

'She's OK,' muttered Pearl.

'I said she was nice,' said Kylie.

'You're wasted on Larks, miss,' observed Graffi, 'you should be refereeing Man U or Arsenal.'

Janna turned to a quivering, ashen Lydia. 'All right, love?'

'F-f-fine.' Then, with hero-worship in her eyes: 'You're the bravest person I've ever met.'

Phil Pierce and Mike Pitts, who were waiting in the passage, were not of the same opinion.

'You stupid fool,' said Phil. 'You could have been killed. Why in hell didn't you call for back-up?'

'I forgot my radio mike,' said Janna, jolted by his rage.

'Well, for God's sake, don't forget it again. This school is not the place for suicide missions.'

Back in her office, Janna was greeted by a smug Rowan.

'I've been trying and trying to page you. Both the Bishop of Larkminster and Mrs Kamani from the corner shop have been on the phone complaining about the Wolf Pack playing football and shoplifting. Evidently Pearl raised her skirt and distracted Mrs Kamani's young son while the boys helped themselves. Next time she's going to press charges.'

It was after six-thirty. People had been banging on Janna's door all day, wanting a piece of her or to give her a piece of their minds. News of her breaking up a fight had whizzed round the building, opinion dividing sharply as to whether she had been incredibly brave or glory-mongering.

Crispin Thomas, ringing from S and C Services, no doubt tipped off by Mike Pitts or Cara, was in the latter camp.

'Feral could have been up on a murder charge and the school brought into disrepute because of your thoughtless irresponsibility,' he snuffled in his asthmatic, pig-like voice. 'And what's this about singing football songs in assembly?'

Janna decided to call it a day and go home.

'Thank you,' she said to Rowan as she took Hengist Brett-Taylor's bottle of champagne out of the fridge, 'you've been a great support.'

Rowan, who knew she hadn't, had the grace to blush.

In reception, Wally was mending windows.

'You did triffic,' he told her. 'Don't listen to the others. Mike Pitts downloaded all his assemblies off the internet. The kids loved you. Just promise to wear that radio mike.'

'It bulks out my skirt at the back,' grumbled Janna.

'Better be wired up than washed up, when you're doing so good,' said Wally.

Maybe, but every poster she'd put up in reception had been ripped down. As she went towards the car park, she discovered someone spraying a large penis in dark browns, purples and pinks on a newly painted wall.

The artist was poised to bolt when Janna called out:

'I don't know how many penises you've seen in your short life, Graffi Williams, but normally the glans is longer. Those testicles, in my experience, are too big, although the wrinkling of the scrotal sac is masterly.'

As Graffi's jaw and his spray can crashed to the ground, Janna went on:

40

'I've got a spare wall in my lounge at my new cottage. I've been wondering how to decorate it. Would you have a moment to pop over at the weekend and give me some ideas for a mural? I'll pay you, but I'd rather you didn't do cocks. There are enough of them crowing in the farm across the fields. Bring Paris, if you like. I'll clear it with the children's home.'

7

After the dark, frenzied intensity of her day, Janna was astonished by the tranquil beauty of the evening. Beyond the hedgerows, slate-blue with sloes and festooned with scarlet skeins of bryony, newly harvested fields rose in platinum-blond sweeps to woods so lush and glossy from endless rain that they appeared to have spent the summer in some expensive greenhouse.

Janna was trying to decide if the orange-gold sheen on the trees was the first fires of autumn or gilding by the setting sun when she plunged like a train into one of Larkshire's dark tunnels: hawthorn, hazel, blackthorn and elder, rising thickly from high banks and impenetrably intertwined overhead by traveller's joy. Down and down she went, until she emerged blinking into the village of Wilmington, passing the duck pond and the village green bordered with pale gold cottages, swerving to avoid a mallard and his wife ambling down the High Street in the direction of the Dog and Duck.

Jubilee Cottage was the last house on the right. As she parked her new pea-green Polo in the street, because the garage was still filled with unpacked boxes, Janna thought she had never been so tired. She'd survived, but the prospect of tomorrow terrified her. Getting out, she caught sight of her neighbour deadheading roses in the mothy dusk, who called out:

'How did you get on? I've been reading about you in the *Gazette*. Come and have a drink, if you're not too tired. I'd have asked you earlier, but I've been away. My name's Lily Hamilton.'

Lily must be well into her seventies, thought Janna, but she was still very beautiful, with gentian-blue eyes, luxuriant grey hair drawn into a bun and a poker-straight back.

'What a lovely garden,' sighed Janna, admiring white

geraniums, phlox and roses luminous in the dusk. 'Mine's a tip.'

'You've been far too busy. I always think one tackles gardens the second year. I'm afraid it's like the Harrods' depository,' she went on, leading Janna into a drawing room crammed with furniture, suggesting departure from a much larger house. Pictures covered every inch of wall. Over the fireplace hung a very explicit nude, with far more rings and studs piercing her voluptuous body than Pearl Smith. Dominating the room was a lovely pale pink and green silk striped sofa, whose arms had been ripped to shreds. The culprit, a vast fluffy black and white cat whom Lily introduced as the General, was stretched out unrepentantly in one corner. In the other lay an even larger stuffed badger. Seeing Janna's frown of disapproval, Lily explained the badger was already stuffed when she acquired him.

'He was in an auction, looking so sad and unloved, I got him for fifteen shillings.'

Wondering if Lily was a bit dotty, Janna waved Hengist's bottle of champagne. 'Why don't we drink this?'

'Tepid champagne is a crime against nature,' observed Lily. 'Let's cool it in the deep freeze and first drink this stuff, which is much less nice.' She filled Janna's glass with white.

Parked between cat and badger, Janna admitted the day had been rough.

'The older staff are so antagonistic, and they're not giving any lead to the younger teachers.'

Then she explained who'd sent her the champagne, which deteriorated into a rant against independent schools and 'fascist bastards' like Hengist Brett-Taylor in particular.

'All those facilities wasted on a few spoilt kids, whose rich parents are too selfish to look after them and just pack them off into the upper-class care of a boarding school.'

'I don't think children in care jet home to Moscow or New York at the weekend,' said Lily. 'Or race up to London. And I promise you, Hengist is a charmer. I'm sure you'd like him if you met him. He doesn't take himself at all seriously, he's awfully good-looking, and he's worked wonders with Bagley. They were a pack of tearaways five years ago. Now they're near the top of the league tables.'

'Perhaps he could give me a few tips,' said Janna sarcastically. 'Although it can't be difficult with all that money and tiny classes and vast playing fields for the kids to let off steam. How d'you know him?'

'My nephew Dicky's a pupil, Dora his twin sister starts this term and Rupert Campbell-Black's children go there as well.'

Which sent Janna into more shivering shock-horror:

'Rupert Campbell-Black's the most arrogant, spoilt, fox-hunting, right-wing bastard.'

'But again, decidedly attractive,' laughed Lily, topping up Janna's glass. 'He does have – even more than Hengist – alarming charm.'

The General heaved himself on to Janna's knee, purring and kneading.

'I must get a cat,' sighed Janna, rubbing him behind his pink ears.

'Do,' said Lily, 'then we can catsit for each other. Why did you take on Larks?'

After a second glass on an empty stomach, Janna found herself telling Lily all about Stew.

'He swore he was going to leave Beth, his wife, and marry me. He just had to see his son graduate, then it was his daughter's wedding, then Beth's hysterectomy, then it was going to be the moment Redfords came out of special measures.

'But the afternoon we found out, he immediately rang up Beth: "Darling, we've done it, put a bottle of bubbly on ice," and booked a table at the Box Tree. They went out to celebrate with the deputy head and his wife. I realized then he'd never leave her.'

'You poor child.' Lily patted her hand. 'For many married people, particularly men, adultery is merely an amusing hobby.'

'He really was a bastard,' mused Janna.

'But a left-wing one this time,' observed Lily.

Janna burst out laughing:

'I was so desperate to get away from the situation, and so longing to be a head, it rather blinded me to Larks's imperfections. Shall we tackle that bottle of bubbly now? And you can tell me why Hengist Brett-Taylor is so attractive and also about Wilmington.'

'Very much "Miss Marple" territory,' said Lily.

'Who's the handsome old gentleman who lives five doors down?'

'That's the Brigadier, Brigadier Christian Woodford. He always salutes my General' – Lily nodded at the cat on Janna's knee – 'when they meet in the street. His wife died recently; nearly bankrupted himself paying her medical bills. She needed twenty-four-hour nursing at home. I don't know if he'll be able to afford to stay.

'He had a terrific war. He's very well read and knows a huge amount about natural history, particularly wild flowers.'

'Like you do,' said Janna, looking at the autumn squills and meadow cranesbill in a vase on top of the bookshelf and the wild-flower books in the shelves. Glancing up at a watercolour of meadowsweet and willowherb, she added, 'I recognize that artist.'

'Hanna Belvedon, married to my nephew Jupiter.' Then at Janna's raised eyebrows, 'Our local MP.'

'Your nephew? But he's another sneering—'

'Right-wing bastard. Here I entirely agree with you,' smiled Lily and then confided that it was Jupiter who had chucked her out of her lovely house in Limesbridge when Raymond, his father and Lily's brother, had died last year. 'He needed the rent money to boost his political campaign.'

'I told you he was a bastard,' said Janna indignantly.

'I shouldn't have sneaked,' sighed Lily, 'but I do think you should have lunch with Hengist. He's got an awfully nice wife and a daughter about your age. You must meet some young people. We're rather a geriatric bunch in Wilmington.'

'I love Wilmington,' protested Janna. 'It's the sweetest village in the world.'

'What fun you've come to live here. Are you desperately tired or shall we have some scrambled eggs?'

Dew soaked Janna's legs. The planets Saturn and, appropriately, Jupiter were rising, glowing green and contained by mist like lights from the angels' electric toothbrushes, as she tottered home after midnight.

What a darling Lily was. After the death of her sweet mother, Janna had plunged into work, and never properly mourned her loss. How wonderful if Lily could become a friend.

Tripping over a boot rack, Janna fell on top of a large bunch of pink and orange lilies wilting in the porch.

'Good luck,' said the card, 'missing you terribly, all love, Stew'.

8

Janna was woken by raging hangover and torrential rain and things went from bad to worse. She found Wally sweeping up more glass from two broken windows. Two door handles had been broken off in the lavatories. The walls in reception had been attacked with a hammer and rain poured in through the roof into the main hall and several classrooms.

Adele, who taught geography and had two children and no husband, rang in sick, so there was no one to take her classes. Another teacher, who hadn't turned up yesterday, wrote saying she'd taken a job in Canada. Ten of the children, believed to be truanting, had evidently gone elsewhere. This hardly put Janna in carnival mood to welcome the new intake of Year Seven: eleven-year-olds fresh from their primary schools.

Leaving Mags Gablecross, who had a free period, to show them round and explain their timetables, Janna took refuge in an empty classroom to fine-tune what she was going to say to their parents. The cleaners had piled the chairs on the tables to show they had swept the floor. Next moment, a tall, handsome hell-raiser from Year Nine, known to be a staunch BNP supporter, staggered in with glazed eyes.

'Good morning, Johnnie Fowler,' called out Janna, proud she'd remembered his name.

Johnnie immediately grabbed a chair and hurled it at her. Just missing her head, it crashed into the whiteboard.

Radio mike forgotten, Janna fled into the corridor, slap into Phil Pierce. She collapsed against his dark blue shirt.

'Help,' she yelped.

For a moment his arms closed around her and she snuggled

into him, heart hammering, breath coming in great gasps, then they both pulled away.

'Johnnie Fowler hurled a chair at me.'

Phil went straight into the classroom, slowly calming Johnnie and sending him back to his own classroom.

'He was coming down from crack.'

'He ought to be excluded or at least suspended,' raged Janna.

'If he goes home, it won't do any good. He'll be out on the street thieving. He mugged an old lady last term. Mother's on her own and can't control him, poor woman.'

Janna felt ashamed. Phil was such a good guy, who had a true empathy with the kids. She was horrified how much she'd enjoyed having his arms round her.

Janna then addressed the new Year Seven parents, who were touched, assuming her frightful shakes were due to nerves at meeting them rather than hangover or Johnnie Fowler.

'Your children will always have a special place in my heart,' she told them, 'because I'm starting at Larks at the same time as they are. We'll go up the school together, and I will learn as much from them as I hope they will from me. I will do everything to make them really enjoy learning. Any problems, please come to me and I hope to welcome you all at parents' meetings.'

She smiled round. The Year Seven parents smiled back. Most of them had been disasters at school and had been phobic about crossing the threshold. Largely from the Shakespeare Estate, they looked like children themselves. If they'd had these kids in their early teens, they need only be in their mid twenties now, which made Janna feel dreadfully old.

As she finished speaking, Mags Gablecross brought in a little girl with huge slanting dark eyes and straight black hair. She was adorable, but sobbing. Mags explained that she came from Paris Alvaston's children's home and had just arrived from Kosovo. Her mother had died in a shootout. Her father was missing, believed killed, in the war. She didn't speak any English and was called Kata.

'Now, which of you is grown-up and kind enough to look after Kata?' Janna asked the children.

Every hand went up.

Afterwards, having just managed to keep down two Alka-Seltzer and feeling incapable of tackling not one, but now two buckling in-trays, Janna informed Rowan Merton she was going to sit in on some classes. Armed with her radio mike, Janna went on to the corridors, fantasizing she was June in *The Bill* or, more likely, a sapper moving from minefield to minefield. She was aware of children roaring past her, swearing, fighting, chatting on their mobiles, drifting in late.

Out of a window, she noticed rabble-rousing Robbie Rushton and Gloria the gymnast creeping in through a side door. They should have been taking geography and PE. No wonder the kids were running wild.

A nice change, however, was Miss Uglow's RE class. 'Ugly', who refused to teach anything but the Bible, was held in equal proportions of terror, respect and love by her pupils.

'Jesus clothed the naked, fed the hungry, and educated the ignorant,' she was telling an enraptured Year Eight, 'which is what I'm doing now.'

Janna smiled and moved on. Rounding the corner, she went slap into Mike Pitts. Obviously tipped off by beady Rowan, he was spluttering to Miss Basket, the menopausal misfit who taught geography.

'As a dedicated professional for twenty-five years, I'm not having some chit of a young woman sitting in on my lessons.' Catching sight of Janna, he turned an even deeper shade of magenta.

Miss Basket melted into the Ladies. Janna followed Mike into his office.

'Could we have a word?'

Mike glanced at the clock. 'I'm teaching in five minutes.'

Clearly a bit of a handsome dandy, judging by past cartoons of him as a cricketer and footballer on the walls, Mike looked dreadful now: his puffy face as bloodshot as his eyes; snowfalls of scurf on the shoulders of his blazer. Joss sticks glowed on his desk. His hands shook as he fussily shoved papers into a blue folder.

Poor man, thought Janna, I usurped him.

'We ought to try and get to know each other,' she stammered. Then, on wild impulse: 'Would you like to come to supper on Sunday?'

'My wife and I prefer to forget school at the weekend.'

Janna flushed. 'Well, perhaps a drink during the week?'

'Quite frankly, I'm too drained. I find if one has fulfilled one's professional commitments, socializing at the end of a working day is not on the agenda. Now, if you'll excuse me.'

Bastard, thought Janna. Feeling the parched earth of a drooping jasmine on the window ledge, she instinctively picked up the green watering can beside it.

'Don't,' yelled Mike, adding hastily, 'I like to look after my own plants. Women overwater.'

That's gin in that watering can, thought Janna, catching a whiff.

Mike glared at her, daring her to confront him.

'We have to work together . . .' Her voice trailed off.

'I must go.'

'I'll come with you,' insisted Janna.

In his classroom, they found a sweet-faced Indian girl in a pale blue sari: a teaching assistant who helped the slower pupils, particularly the foreign ones with poor English, by explaining questions to them and showing them how to write the answers. She was now laying out worksheets and consulting an algebra textbook, and told Janna she had been at Larks for four terms. She loved the job because it was so rewarding seeing understanding dawning on the children's faces and how the slow ones blossomed if you took time to explain things.

'I'd like to start an after-school maths club.'

'Wonderful idea. Come and see me.'

'We must get on,' interrupted Mike, 'the students will be here in a minute.' Tetchily, he handed the Indian girl a page of squares and triangles. 'Can you get me some marker pens and photostat this?'

'She's great,' said Janna as the girl left the room. 'What's her name?'

'I've no idea.'

And Janna flipped. 'This is disgraceful. She's the only black teacher in the school, she's been here a year and you don't know her name.'

'She's only a teaching assistant.'

'Working her butt off for you and the kids. You ought to know everyone in your department and what they're up to, and in the school, you're deputy head, for God's sake.'

'I will not be spoken to like that.'

Both jumped at a knock on the door. It was Rowan Merton, dying to find out what was going on.

'Phone for you, Janna.'

'I'm busy.'

'It's Russell Lambert, our chair of governors. Says its urgent.'

Bitterly regretting her outburst of temper and aware she had made an even more implacable enemy, Janna ran back to her office.

Russell, whom Janna could still only think of as Babar, king of the elephants, head of the Tusk Force, was at his most portentous.

'Good morning, Janna, bad news I'm afraid. Harry Fitzgerald, head of a school in the north of the county, has had a coronary. Ashton Douglas, head of S and C, has just

49

phoned. They want Phil Pierce to take over as head immediately.'

'Can't they take Mike Pitts and his joss sticks?' wailed Janna unguardedly.

'You'll need your deputy head,' reproved Russell. 'You'd be very weak on the maths front if Mike goes.'

'I'll never survive without you,' Janna moaned later to Phil, who had the grace to look sheepish.

'I'm sorry, Janna, I hate to let you down, but I can't resist the chance to be a head.'

He didn't add that Janna had been disturbing his sleep recently: she was so brave but so vulnerable. He loved his wife; safer if he took himself out of harm's way.

'Anyway, Harry Fitzgerald will probably pull through and I'll be back in a few weeks.'

'I'm only cross because Skunk Illingworth will have to be promoted to head of science. He'll be so up himself. When are you going?'

'Tomorrow.'

Crispin Thomas from S and C Services rang later.

'You're providing a bloody sight more challenge than support, swiping my best teacher,' stormed Janna.

Crispin laughed fatly. 'We know, we know. We're going to send Rod Hyde, the super head from St Jimmy's, round to give you a hand next week.'

Outside, rain was still tipping down; the awful playground was filling up with puddles.

'I don't need Rod Hyde. I was hired to run this joint. Our playground needs a makeover for a start,' and Janna hung up because of more screams and yells coming from the direction of the history block.

Running into the classroom, Nine E again, she found tin soldiers and a model battlefield scattered all over the floor. Next moment, a display of shrapnel and shell splinters, the collection of Lance, the newly qualified teacher, went flying. Lance and his teaching assistant were cringing in a corner and the appalling Monster Norman, no doubt feeling he had lost face after his fight with Feral yesterday, had taken centre stage as he menaced a terrified sobbing Asian girl.

'Teacher's pet, teacher's pet,' he hissed. 'Paki swot, Paki swot.'

His victim was Aysha Khan, who'd made such progress after two terms that Janna had singled her out in assembly.

The children, diverted by fights – this was their theatre – had formed a four-deep circle round the participants.

'Black rubbish, black shit,' taunted Monster, then spat in Aysha's face.

'Stop that,' shouted Janna, pushing her way through the crowd, too enraged to be frightened.

Monster, who she noticed had a shadow of moustache on his sweating upper lip, had a lit cigarette in his hand.

'Go home, fucking Paki bitch,' he yelled and was about to burn her arm when Janna dragged his hand away, grabbing the cigarette, stamping on it and turning on him.

'How dare you!'

'Go on,' mocked Monster, 'touch me, hit me, you try it. I'll get you fired, you'll never work again, you sad bitch.'

'You loathsome thug.' Caution had deserted Janna once more. 'Get out of here, you revolting bully.'

'Go on, miss, 'it 'im,' yelled Pearl.

'My mum's a governor.' Monster's evil, sallow, pasty face was disintegrating like goat's cheese in liquid as he gathered saliva in his mouth.

'I don't care. Out, out!'

'Well done, miss,' cheered the children as Monster, already on his mobile to his mother, pummelled his way out of the classroom.

'Are you all right, miss?' asked Kylie Rose. 'Shall I get you a cup of tea?'

In the doorway, Wally was shaking his head again. 'When will you learn, Janna?'

A hovering Jason 'Goldilocks' Fenton was also highly amused.

'Wherever you go, there's a rumpus. So exciting. I might not hand in my notice after all.'

Janna turned on him furiously too. 'Out,' she yelled.

She was picking up toy soldiers and sorting out a mortified Lance – 'I wanted to defend you, but I couldn't somehow. Not sure I'm cut out to be a teacher' – when there was a further rumpus in the corridor.

'Where's Miss Fucking Curtis?' bellowed a voice and Monster Norman's mother, predictably nicknamed 'Stormin'', square, massive and enraged, with a whiskery jaw thrust out, came barging in.

'Why are you always picking on my Martin?'

She raised her fist. Janna got out her mobile.

'If we can't discuss this, Mrs Norman, I'm calling the police. Your Martin was sadistically bullying another pupil.'

Only Wally seizing Mrs Norman's arm stopped her punching Janna in the face.

To Janna's horror, the following day, two governors (Russell Lambert and Cara Sharpe), Crispin Thomas from S and C and Mike Pitts (as deputy head), overturned Monster's exclusion, mostly on Cara's testimony.

'Martin's a sweet, caring boy,' she cooed, 'I've never had any trouble with him.'

'Nor have I,' agreed Mike, who was wearing a purple shirt to match his nose as he helped himself to another extra strong mint.

'He abused Aysha in the most revolting and racist way,' raged Janna. 'He terrorizes half his classmates. We'll never get a happy school with kids like him around.'

'Don't forget you incur a hefty five-thousand-pound fine every time you permanently exclude a pupil,' snuffled fat Crispin, accepting a mint. 'It's not as though you're oversubscribed or rolling in money. You really must be more restrained in your attitude. I'm getting complaints from all over and you've only been here three days. Calling Martin a "loathsome thug" is hardly the way to address challenging behaviour.'

Monster was suspended for three days.

The children were devastated when they heard of Phil Pierce's defection. Their favourite teacher had become just another rat leaving a sinking ship.

9

On Saturday morning, Janna sneaked into Larks to tackle her towering in-tray unobserved by Rowan Merton. Following Stew's maxim that if anything's important, people will write a second time, she chucked ninety-five per cent of her 'bin-tray' into six black dustbin bags. Perhaps Mike Pitts had a 'gin-tray' – he'd locked his office, so she couldn't check his watering can.

Yesterday afternoon, Miss Cambola had flung open the staffroom door and, rattling the teeth of the Dinosaurs and nearly bringing down the whole crumbling building, sang at the top of her voice: 'Thank God it's Friday.'

She had also written on the back of a postcard of Caruso: 'Congratulations! You have survived a whole week and done well, Regards, Maria Cambola', reducing Janna to tears of gratitude.

Having fired off thirty emails, mostly thanking people who'd sent her good-luck cards, Janna made the decision to hold a prospective-parents' evening at the end of the month. This would give her the clout and everyone the incentive to smarten up the school, painting as many classrooms as possible and papering walls and corridors with some decent kids' work, even if she had to write and draw it herself. Full of excitement, she first wrote copy for an ad in the *Larkminster Gazette*, inviting prospective parents to the event, then secondly, a glowing report of Larks's progress and plans for the future. These she delivered to the *Gazette* on the way home.

Earlier in the week, she had rung Mr Blenchley, the care manager of Oaktree Court, Paris's children's home, who sounded bullying and humourless and who had a thick clogged voice like leftover lumpy porridge not going down the plughole.

Little Kata from Kosovo was adjusting to the regime, he said, and it was all right for Paris to come to tea with Graffi:

'But as the lad pleases himself, I doubt he'll show up.'

It was one of those mellow, hazy afternoons only September can produce. Midges jived idly with thistledown. The field at the end of the village was being ploughed up, two men in yellow tractors sailing back and forth over the Venetian-red earth and waving at Janna as she sat in the garden worrying about her first governors' meeting on Monday. There was so much that needed tackling: permission to fire three-quarters of the staff for a start.

A flock of red admirals was guzzling sweetness from the long purple stems of a buddleia bush, but ignoring the honeysuckle next door – like pupils flocking to St Jimmy's and Searston Abbey rather than Larks, she thought sadly. She was just wondering how to galvanize the staff at Monday's morning briefing when the doorbell rang.

To her delight and amazement, it was Graffi, bringing both Paris and Feral. As they swarmed in, laughing and larky as the players in *Hamlet*, Janna suspected they had been enjoying a spliff or two on the way.

'How grand to see you. No Kylie and Pearl?'

'Kylie's minding baby Cameron,' said Graffi, 'giving her mum a day off. Pearl's got a hairdressing job. Don't think she'd have got here on those heels, anyway.'

'Did you walk all the way?' asked Janna, and then thought: How stupid, how else could they have afforded to come?

Taking Graffi by the arm, she led them down the hall into the kitchen, newly painted buttercup yellow and brightened by good-luck cards and framed children's drawings.

'Are you starving? I was planning to give you "high tea", as we call it in Yorkshire, a bit later,' she asked, getting out dark green mugs and a big bottle of Coke.

Opening a jumbo bag of crisps with her teeth, then bending down to pull out a blue bowl into which to decant them, she found all three boys staring at her. Barefoot, wearing tight jeans and a clinging blue-striped matelot jersey, with her wild russet curls escaping from a tartan toggle, she didn't look remotely like a headmistress.

'I don't bother to dress up much at weekends,' she stammered.

'Nice Aga.' Graffi patted its dark blue flanks. 'My mum's ambition's to have one.'

'It was already there when I moved in,' said Janna hastily.

54

She loved the Aga, but felt, like the burglar alarm, it was rather too middle-class.

'Why don't you explore?'

As she put knives, forks and willow-patterned plates on a tray, the boys careered round the house, opening doors and cupboards, picking up and examining ornaments.

'It's fucking tiny,' said Paris, who was accustomed to Oaktree Court, a great house once belonging to the very rich, now ironically inhabited by children who had nothing.

'This bed's fucking large,' agreed Graffi and Feral, who were used to sharing with several brothers and sisters and sometimes a drunken father or fleeing mother, when they discovered Janna's attic bedroom.

Hung with blue gingham curtains, the four-poster only left room for triangular shelves slotted into one corner, a television, fitted cupboards and a dressing table which Janna had to perch on the bottom of the bed to use.

'Fink there's a bloke in her life?' asked Feral.

'Hope not,' said Graffi, breathing in scent bottles.

'Wouldn't mind giving her one,' said Feral.

'Oh, shut up, you're incorrigible,' snapped Paris, who was examining the books, mostly classics, on either side of the bed.

'Whatever that means. This bed's fucking comfortable,' said a bouncing Feral. Then, glancing sideways at Stew's photograph, which, after Monday's flowers, was on show again: 'That must be her father.'

Joyous as otters, they bounded downstairs (emptying the crisp bowl en route) out into the garden, fascinated by reddening apples, French beans hanging from wigwams, potatoes and carrots actually growing in the ground.

'What the hell's that?'

'It's a marrer,' said Graffi. 'My nan used to stuff them.'

Holding it against his groin, Feral indulged in a few pelvic thrusts. 'Looks as though it orta do the stuffing.'

While Paris stopped to stroke Lily's cat the General, who was tightroping along the fence, Graffi and Feral began kicking a football round the lawn. Watching their antics from the kitchen, Janna thought how perfectly they complemented each other. Paris, ghostly pale, seemed lit by moonlight, Feral by the sun. Feral was so arrogant, like George Eliot's cock, who thought the sun had risen to hear him crow. It wasn't just the lift of his jaw, or the swing of his hips, or the lean elongated body that made a red T-shirt, cheap fake leather jacket and black jeans look a million dollars. He'd make a fortune as a model. The long brown eyes curling up at the corner, with thick lashes creating a natural eyeliner, were haughty too; even the huge white smile said, 'I'm superior.'

But, despite this hauteur, like a feral cat he constantly glanced round checking for danger. Made edgy by the alien territory of the countryside, he shot inside when a dozy brown and white cow put her nose over the fence, and ran upstairs to watch football.

Physically, Graffi was a mixture of the two and, with his stocky build, olive skin and wicked dark eyes, needed only a black beret on his unruly dark curls, a smock and an easel to be having *déjeuner sur l'herbe* with naked beauties.

Janna took him into the low-beamed living room, which was painted cream with a pale coral sofa and chairs. Set into one wall was a stone fireplace filled with apple logs. The second wall was mostly a west-facing window overlooking fields and woods. Against the third was an upright piano and floor-to-ceiling shelves for Janna's books, music and CDs. The empty fourth awaited Graffi's genius.

Blown away that Janna trusted him, Graffi borrowed paper and pencil and started sketching. How would she like a view of the cathedral, houses in the Close, softened by lots of trees, a few cows paddling in the river to 'scare Feral away', people walking their dogs on the towpath?

'That sounds champion, as long as you don't graffiti the buildings.'

'Make it look more lived in. Nice place this. My da's a builder, does a lot of work for Randal Stancombe. If you want anything done, he could hide it.' Then, going back to the wall: 'It'll take a few Saturdays.'

'That's fine. You could come Sundays as well.'

'Nah, I'm busy Sundays. Going to look at them cows.' And he wandered off to kick a ball on the lawn with Feral.

Chests of books were lying round, so Paris took them out and put them on to the shelves, his face growing paler as he kept stopping to read. Janna helped him, pointing out favourites: *Rebecca, Middlemarch, Wuthering Heights*, giving him spare copies of Byron, *Le Grand Meaulnes* and *The Catcher in the Rye*.

Paris found the cottage blissfully quiet after Oaktree Court, where someone was always sobbing, screaming and fighting, and wardens or social workers were always asking questions or needling him: 'Get your long nose out of that book. Come on, open up, open up.'

'How long have you loved reading?' asked Janna.

'Since I was about nine. Head teacher of my school in

Nottingham put me in charge of the library, so I could borrow all the books I wanted. I saved up to buy a torch and read under the bedclothes all night. That torch lit up my life.'

Children in care are usually attention-seekers, or, like Paris, internalize everything. Looking at the cool, deadpan face, its only colour the eyes bloodshot from reading, few people realized the raging emotional torrents beneath the layers of ice.

Paris had been two when his mother dumped him on the door of a children's home in Alvaston, outside Derby. He had been clinging on to a glass ball containing the Eiffel Tower in a snow storm – still his most treasured possession. On his royal-blue knitted jumper was pinned a note: 'Please look after my son. His name is Paris.'

No one had ever found his mother. Early adoption was delayed, hoping she'd come forward. Afterwards, there was no one to sign the papers.

Every so often, when the moon was full, longing for his mother overwhelmed him, and he went searching for her on trains round the country. When he was twelve, he had suffered the humiliation of putting his photograph in the local paper advertising for a family. The photograph, taken in the fluorescent light of the children's home, made him look like a death's head. Paris for once had dropped his guard and written the accompanying copy, which Nadine his social worker had rejigged: 'Paris is a healthy twelve-year-old, who has been in care for a number of years. He has a few behaviour problems and needs firm handling,' which, translated, meant trouble with a capital 'T'.

Paris, affecting a total lack of interest, had hung around waiting for the post, expecting Cameron Diaz or Posh and Becks to roll up in a big car and whisk him off to love and luxury. But there had been no takers.

Feral and Graffi had carried him during this humiliation. He, in turn, had carried Feral when his older brother Joey dissed the head of a rival gang, who took him outside and shot him dead. Feral's mother, Nancy, had emerged briefly from a drug-induced stupor to achieve fleeting fame bewailing the loss on television. But as it was only black killing black, the public and police soon forgot and moved on to another tragedy. Nancy turned back to her drugs.

Feral was dyslexic and, ashamed he wrote and read so poorly, truanted persistently. Paris, who was very clever, translated for him and explained questions.

'He's my one-to-one teaching assistant,' boasted Feral.

Out of eighteen homes and eleven schools, Paris's three years at Larks and Oaktree Court had been his longest placement. Terrified of being dragged away to a new care home in another part of the country, he tried not to complain or rock the boat.

'I've got two copies of *The Moonstone*, so here's one for you,' said Janna, 'and here's Lily coming up the path.'

Lily was in high fettle. She had just won a hundred pounds on the three o'clock and been making elderflower wine. Feral and Graffi came scuttling down the stairs for new diversion.

'Boys, this is my friend Lily Hamilton who lives next door, and Lily, these are my friends, Graffi, who's painting me a mural, Paris, who's sorting out my bookshelves, and Feral, who's an ace footballer.'

'Really?' said Lily. 'My nephew Dicky is besotted with Man U; I confess a fondness for Arsenal.'

'That's cool, man,' said Feral approvingly.

'I'm about to watch them on Sky,' said Lily. 'Would you like to come and have a look and test this summer's elderflower wine?'

Needing no more encouragement, Feral and Graffi bounded after her.

10

Paris preferred to stay with the books and Janna. With her sweet face and rippling red hair, she was like those beautiful women in pre-Raphaelite paintings. He tried not to stare. As she handed her books and their hands touched occasionally, she told him about her parents' evening.

'I want the place to look so good, people will really want to send their children to Larks.'

Paris said nothing. Oh God, she thought, he has no parents, I'm a tactless cow. Changing the subject hurriedly, she said she was planning a project on the lark.

'In literature, art, music and real life. I don't know if larks are singing at the moment, but we could take a tape recorder into the fields. I'm going to call the project "Larks Ascending" to symbolize our climb out of special measures.'

' "To hear the lark begin his flight, And singing startle the dull night," ' murmured Paris, handing her a tattered copy of *Anna Karenina*.

' "From his watch-tower in the skies, Till the dappled dawn doth rise," ' carried on Janna, clapping her hands. 'Fantastic, exactly the kind of stuff we need. Will you copy it out for me and perhaps write a poem about a lark yourself?'

Larks were always having to move on because of tractors ploughing and harrowing, and people sowing seed and spraying pesticides and fertilizers, thought Paris bitterly, just like him moving from home to home.

Whoops and yells from next door indicated that Arsenal must have scored.

'Tell me about Graffi,' said Janna as she slotted *Northanger Abbey* between *Emma* and *Persuasion*.

'His dad earns good when he's in work. Nice bloke but the money seems to evaporate in the betting shop or the pub. Graffi's got two elder brothers and a sister; then, after him, his mother had a Downs Syndrome baby, and all the attention goes on her. Graffi gets the shit kicked out of him by the elder kids, but his mother – when she works in the pub evenings and Sundays – expects Graffi, because he's easy-going, to look after his sister. Graffi loves her to bits but he gets jealous and worries she'll be bullied when she goes to primary school next year.'

'Where does he live – on the Shakespeare Estate?'

'Hamlet Street. Feral's Macbeth, Kylie's Dogberry, Pearl's Othello – which figures: she's dead jealous. Monster Norman's Iago, which figures too.'

'Is it really rough?'

'If you want respect, the only way is to act tough and deal drugs,' said Paris. 'Randal Stancombe's sniffing round the place, wants to offer it a leisure centre.'

'So young people have somewhere to go in the evening to keep them off the streets,' volunteered Graffi, returning at half-time.

'I like the streets,' grumbled Feral. 'I don't want no youth club woofter teaching me no ballroom dancing.'

'More walls to draw on,' said Graffi. 'I like that lady next door. She's got terrific pictures on her wall, that nude over the mantelpiece looks straight out of a porn mag. That elderflower wine's not bad neiver; she said it didn't matter as we wasn't driving.'

Out of the corner of her eye, Janna saw Feral pick up a very pretty pink and white paperweight, put it in his pocket, then put it back again.

'What d'you want to be in life, Feral?' she asked.

Feral gave her his huge, charming, dodgy smile.

'Twenty-one, man.'

'I beg your pardon?'

'If you live on the Shakespeare Estate, it's an achievement to stay alive to the weekend,' explained Graffi. 'I've done this drawing of Lily's cat.'

'That's so good.' Janna took it to the light. 'You must give it to Lily. When you get back from the second half, I'll have your tea ready.'

While Paris became immersed in *The Catcher in the Rye*, Janna produced a real Yorkshire tea, with lardy cake, dripping toast, jam roly poly, crumpets and very strong tea out of a big brown pot.

As a returning Feral and Graffi helped her carry it to the table outside, Feral looked up at the kitchen beam. 'What's that long thick black thing called?' he asked.

'Feral Jackson,' quipped Graffi.

'Fuck off, man,' said Feral, who was in a good mood. Arsenal had won resoundingly.

The sinking sun was turning the stubble a soft mushroom pink. Housemartins and swallows gathered on the telegraph wires; rooks were jangling in the beeches; a purple and silver air balloon drifted up the valley, like a bauble escaped from a Christmas tree. As the boys sat down on a rickety old garden bench and devoured everything, helicopters kept chugging overhead.

'Is there an air show on or something?'

'Naaah,' sneered Graffi, 'it's toff kids being taken back to Bagley Hall.'

With only a slight stab of guilt, Janna realized none of her emails had been to thank Hengist Brett-Taylor for his bottle of champagne.

'That dark blue one' – Graffi pointed towards the sky – 'belongs to Rupert Campbell-Black, who my dad hero-worships because Rupert's given him so many winners. And that's Randy Scandal,' he added as Rupert's helicopter was followed five minutes later by one in dark crimson bearing Randal Stancombe's name in gold letters and his logo of a little gold house.

'Randal's got a hot daughter called Jade,' said Feral. 'I wouldn't mind giving her one, wiping the smug smile off her face.'

Paris shivered. Oaktree Court was a grand old building set back from the main road on the way to St Jimmy's and Searston Abbey. Randal Stancombe's henchmen had been spotted in the grounds. Converted, it would make splendid luxury flats in the catchment area of the two schools, and once again Paris's security would be blown.

Seeing the shiver, and how inadequately Paris was dressed in his thin nylon tracksuit and trainers with the soles coming off, Janna suggested they went inside.

'It's nice here,' said Graffi.

'Nadine, your social worker, rang me yesterday,' Janna told Paris.

'Nosy old bitch,' said Paris flatly.

'She spoke well of you,' laughed Janna. 'She said you told the other children fantastic stories at bedtime. Why don't you write them down?'

'Did once. Cara Sharpe said they were crap.'

'That's only her opinion,' said Graffi. 'She's head of drama as well as English but I don't fink she's read a play since she left uni.'

'I told her I wanted to be an actor and she pissed herself.' Paris gave a cackle. 'She said: "With an accent like yours, you've got to be joking."'

For a second, Janna gasped in terror.

'That was extraordinary. That was Cara's laugh and voice exactly.'

'Paris can do anyone,' said Feral.

'Do Mike Pitts,' said Graffi, wiping his hands on his jeans and picking up his pen to draw Janna.

Paris pursed his lips: '"If it weren't for my professional commitment, I'd have left teaching yearsh ago and been earning a million a year running I-Shee-I."'

Janna gave a scream of laughter. Once again the imitation was perfect. Paris had even caught Mike's drunken slur.

Then he did Rowan: '"Ay'm so busy juggling my job, my husband and my two little girls, I forget to have 'me' time."' Paris looked up from under his lashes like Rowan did.

'You're brilliant,' cried Janna, 'you *must* become an actor.'

'"Moost I really? Thut's lovely, in fuct it's chumpion,"' said Paris.

'That's me,' giggled Janna. 'I thought I'd lost my accent a bit down here.'

Paris smiled – and Janna felt truly weak at the knees. He was like some Arctic Prince who'd strayed southwards and might melt any moment in the autumn sunset.

I will do anything to make his life better, she told herself.

They were reserved but not shy, these boys. Although only thirteen or fourteen, they were old before their time, hardened and aged by poverty, loss, lack of security and the contempt of others. But at the same time, they were all hunky: muscular from the fight to survive, and sure of their sexuality.

Overwhelmed with longing for both a lover and a child of her own, Janna was aware that Feral, Graffi and Paris fell halfway between the two. Suddenly she knew she had to send them home.

'We must decide a fee for the mural,' she told Graffi.

'Five grand a day,' Graffi grinned, looking round for the picture he had drawn of her, but Paris had already whipped it.

Janna gave Paris a carrier bag for his books and, for all of them, a big bag of Cox's apples from the tree at the bottom of the garden. But running upstairs for a cardigan, glancing out of her bedroom window, she saw them chucking the apples at each other. Paris, with his long nose still in *The Catcher in the Rye*, stretched out a hand to take a perfect catch as they sauntered up the lane.

Back in the kitchen, the laptop she'd been working on had been opened. Then she gave a gasp of horrified amusement.

To the words: 'Get rid of three-quarters of the teachers, I wish', someone had added, 'Why not start with Cara Sharpe, Mike Pitts, Skunk Illingworth, Chalford (you ain't met her yet), Sam Spink, Robbie Rushton and Hot Flush Basket for a start.' Janna's sentiments exactly.

She ought to work, but she was so pleased to be interrupted by a call from Lily saying she'd enjoyed the wine-tasting as much as Feral and Graffi: 'What delightful boys. Feral's going to help me make sloe gin and Graffi did an excellent drawing of General, caught the angle of his whiskers exactly. If I hadn't fallen out with him, I'd show it to my nephew Jupiter, who's a dealer when he's not being an MP. Feral gave me a spliff.'

'Lily,' said Janna shocked.

'I haven't had one since another nephew, Jonathan, got married. Come and have a drink.'

Janna slept fitfully. Outside her window, Mars blazed golden and angry, a ginger tom cat seeing off a fierce dog. I've got to fight and win, she thought.

11

With Mars in the ascendant, the battle raged on at Larks. On Monday, a physics supply teacher was so unnerved by her first encounter with Year Nine E that she fled down the drive with singed eyebrows and blackened fringe and was never seen again.

'Who was she covering for?' demanded Janna.

Rowan glanced up at the timetable: 'Sam Spink. She's gone to the TUC conference.'

'She never asked me.'

'She cleared it with Mike Pitts last term. There was a memo' – Rowan looked disapprovingly at Janna's dramatically diminished in-tray – 'but it seems to have been chucked away.'

'How long's she gone for?'

'All week. Sam's awfully conscientious. She feels it's crucial to exchange views and keep up with modern legislation.'

'You bet she does, when it involves swilling brandy Alexanders all night in the Metropole.'

Returning from a shouting match in Mike's office, Janna caught Robbie Rushton and Gloria the gymnast sneaking in at midday, claiming that the boat on which they'd been sailing had run aground.

'So will you if you skive any more,' yelled Janna.

A day of hassle left her drained and defensive. Remembering the support the governors at Redfords had given Stew when the going got tough, she looked forward to pouring out her grievances to her own governors, who'd been so friendly at her interview and who were, after all, responsible for Larks's appalling state.

The meeting was held after school in A18, classroom of Robbie

Rushton, who, for once in a hundred years, made a point of working late, so Debbie the cleaner had to sweep and arrange chairs and glasses of water around his martyred presence.

'Robbie's so conscientious,' cooed Cara to arriving governors, as he finally took himself and a huge pile of marking away.

Classroom A18 was one of the worst. Damp patches on the ceiling resembled the map of India and Bangladesh. A rattle of drips was filling up two buckets. Year Eleven, ironically, were studying the story of water: irrigation, the rain cycle, domestic canals and wells. Year Ten, on the other hand, were learning about earthquakes, photographs and diagrams of which also covered the peeling walls. It wasn't long before Janna wished the floorboards would split open and swallow her up.

Mike Pitts wasn't present, but his spies were. Rowan Merton, wafting Anaïs Anaïs, had changed into a clean white shirt and was taking the minutes. Cara, as a teacher governor, having saved Monster Norman from being expelled last week, was thick as thieves and parked next to his mother, Stormin' Norman, also a parent governor.

Bring me my bully-proof vest, muttered Janna.

Kylie Rose's mother, Chantal, another parent governor, held up the whole proceedings by saying: 'Can we discuss this?' at every new item and making eyes at snuffling Crispin Thomas, whom she didn't realize was gay and who looked fatter than ever.

Crispin was accompanied by his boss, Ashton Douglas, S and C Services' Director of Education, an infinitely more formidable adversary who utterly unnerved Janna. His handsome, regular features were somehow blurred like soap left too long in the bath. An air of vulnerability (created by a lisp and soft light brown curls flopping from a middle parting) was belied by the coldest green eyes she had ever seen. Languid as a Beardsley aesthete, Ashton wore a mauve silk shirt, a beautifully cut grey suit and reeked of sweet, cloying scent.

He was now murmuring to Sir Hugo Betts, the camel on Prozac. Sir Hugo was disappointed Janna didn't look nearly as bonny as at her interview, so there would be even less to keep him awake.

Russell Lambert as chairman droned on and on, loving the sound of his own voice and expressing sadness that Brett Scott, the jolly director of Larkminster Rovers, had resigned, not having appreciated the extent of a governor's workload. He had been replaced by a local undertaker, called Solly, who at least can bury us, thought Janna.

She longed to weigh in on the atrocious state of the school, but in a subtle shift of emphasis, she was now held responsible for all Larks's evils. Five other pupils had gone out of county to other schools. Attendance was down by sixty-seven.

'What plans do you have to impwove the situation?' asked Ashton Douglas silkily.

Janna told them about her prospective-parents' evening.

'Hope it's not an *EastEnders* night,' warned Chantal Peck.

Russell then expressed the governors' horror at the disastrous league-table results, with commendable exceptions – they all nodded deferentially at Cara Sharpe. What was Janna intending to do about that?

'I need a massive increase in funding,' said Janna, 'and must smarten up the school. Take this classroom. If you're into virtual reality, we can re-create the monsoon season every time it rains. If we don't mend the roof, we'll need an ark. And moving to Australia' – she tore a peeling strip of paper off the walls – 'we can re-create the eucalyptus.'

No one smiled.

'No, it isn't funny,' agreed Janna. 'We also need hundreds more textbooks; we need to replace four computers. We need an IT technician.

'On the non-teaching side, we need a part-time gardener to sweep up the leaves, which will soon be cascading down from the trees – the only proud thing in this place. Above all we need a decent cook' – both Cara and Rowan Merton were frantically making notes – 'to give the children a really nourishing hot meal in the middle of the day. Dinners here are the only food many of them can rely on, but they're so disgusting, most of the kids won't eat them.'

'Mrs Molly does her best with limited resources,' protested Cara.

'There was a blood-stained plaster in the shepherd's pie on Friday.'

'The shepherd must have cut himself shearing,' murmured Solly the undertaker with a ghostly chuckle.

'And most of all' – Janna plunged in feet first – 'we need some more teachers. Ten of them, including my head of history, Mrs Chalford, whom I've never even met, are off with stress. The only way to attract new talent is to pay them better.'

But no more money was forthcoming.

S and C Services, Ashton Douglas reminded her smoothly, had been brought in by the Government because the local education authority couldn't balance the books. Janna must learn, like everyone else, to economize.

'We must have more money.' Janna banged the table with her little fist. 'You're a private company. You're not in this for love but to make a fat profit, that's why you don't want to give any extra to me. But it's so defeatist to let us self-destruct.'

There was a horrified pause and a flicker of amused malice in Ashton Douglas's cold green eyes.

'Your job, my dear, is to sort out the mess.'

'I've been here a week. If I'm going to sort out this "mess" I need your support. I lost my best teacher last week.' She daren't in front of Cara and Rowan say that Mike Pitts was useless. 'The junior staff are utterly demoralized. The children—'

Clearing his throat, Ashton Douglas cut right across her.

'With wespect, we shouldn't be discussing teaching matters in fwont of Mrs Sharpe. If you need funding, I suggest you look for sponsors in the town: Wandal Stancombe, or Gwant Tyler, our local IT giant. Get the local community on side.'

'Why not mobilize your parents?' suggested Crispin Thomas, smiling at Stormin' Norman and Chantal. 'Last year Searston Abbey and St Jimmy's raised fifteen and twenty thousand pounds respectively.'

'They've got hundreds of middle-class parents who aren't struggling to pay any school fees,' raged Janna. 'Of course they chip in. We don't have middle-class parents at Larks.'

'Ay take exception to that,' bridled Chantal Peck.

'That uncalled-for wemark should be struck from the minutes,' said Ashton. 'If you attwacted more pupils, we could allow you more money. So concentrate on your prospective-parents' meeting. Wod Hyde will also be here to advise you next week.' Then, at Janna's look of outrage: 'You'll find him a bweath of fwesh air.'

'An image that conjures up icy winds blasting in from Siberia,' snapped Janna, 'blowing everything that matters out of the window. I don't want Rod Hyde telling me what to do. I just need more money.

'The children need some treats,' she pleaded. 'They have such bleak lives. We should offer them rewards: a fun day out to look forward to and in recognition of good behaviour.'

'What did you have in mind?' asked Crispin sarcastically.

'The London Eye perhaps, or Tate Modern. A lot of them have never been to the seaside or inside the cathedral or a museum.'

'You'd trust them in a museum?' said Cara incredulously.

'Once they realized we did, they'd start behaving better.'

'Which brings me to behaviour management,' said Russell Lambert. 'We notice you've introduced a new system of mentors.'

'It worked very well at Redfords,' said Janna defensively.

'Means any kid can go to a mentor if they're being bullied or have a problem. I had ten of the more responsible members of Year Eleven photographed last Thursday. Their pictures are now up in the corridors.'

'A needless expense.' Ashton smiled thinly. 'Surely they could have brought photogwaphs from home.'

'It made it more of an honour,' said Janna. 'They look really good.'

There was a knock on the door. It was Kylie Rose, come to collect her mother Chantal and bearing Cameron, a sweet jolly baby who'd inherited his mother's blond, blue-eyed beauty. His charm was lost on Crispin Thomas, however, when his besotted grandmother thrust him into the deputy educational director's arms, particularly when Cameron threw up on Crispin's cream suit.

'Come and see the mentors' photographs,' said Janna hastily, leading everyone off to admire the display, only to find the photographs had already been adorned with moustaches and squints, with the names crossed out and replaced by 'Wanker' and worse.

Janna promptly lost her rag again and shouted at anyone within range. She was just calming down when kind Kylie Rose tugged her sleeve.

'You're easily the best teacher in the school, miss.'

'Am I?' Janna was marginally mollified.

'Easily the best at shouting,' said Kylie Rose.

The governors smirked.

'Phone for you,' called Rowan from Janna's office.

'I'm busy.'

'Says he's an old friend from Redfords.'

Janna shot into the office.

'I tried the cottage,' announced Stew. 'Somehow I knew you'd be still working.'

'Oh Stew.' How lovely to hear the broad, warm, measured Yorkshire accent.

'How are you getting on, love?'

'Horribly. It's hell.' Janna kicked her door shut. 'I hate most of the staff. They gang up. There aren't enough of them. The only nice guy's been hijacked to head up another school. The deputy head's a total lush.'

'What about the kids?'

'Animals, most of them.'

'That's not like you, Janna. What about your PA? She sounded friendly enough on the phone.'

'Worst of the lot. She sneers, sneaks and pumps up my in-tray to demoralize me.' Swinging round, Janna went scarlet; Rowan who must have quietly opened the door was standing outraged in the doorway. 'I've got to go, Stew, ring me later at home.'

But Stew didn't ring back. Why had she moaned so much?

Laugh and the world laughs with you, weep and you weep alone, her mother had always told her. If only she were still alive.

The fall-out was awful. Cara, backed up by Rowan, was straight on to Mike Pitts and the rest of the staff, reporting everything that had been said.

No one would meet Janna's eye the next day. Molly the cook walked out. Even Wally, her dear friend, looked at her reproachfully, until she explained that she wanted to get in some gardening help, to free him for more important tasks.

That same morning, however, Debbie the cleaner, who'd been blown away by the big box of chocolates Janna had given her for blitzing the staffroom, came blushing into the head's office. As she got on so well with Molly's other assistants, how would Janna feel if they took over school dinners on a month's trial?

'Profoundly relieved,' replied Janna. 'Oh, Debbie, thank you, that's the best bit of news I've had for ages. Start today.'

'You deserve some luck,' said Debbie. 'Lots of us think you're 'uman.'

Ironically, Janna was saved by the greatest tragedy. Towards the end of the day, which was 11 September, she was trying to explain Arthur Miller to a sullen group of fifteen-year-olds, who seemed only interested that he'd been married to Marilyn Monroe, when Rowan rushed in to say the World Trade Center had been hit.

Mike Pitts and Cara thought the school should carry on as normal. Janna insisted that this was history and the children must see it.

In no time, Wally had rigged up the big screen attached to a television in the main hall. The excited pupils lugged chairs in from the dining room to watch the terrible events unfold. At first, these were like so many Hollywood films, it was hard for them to understand it was the real thing. But they were soon screaming, sobbing and sometimes cheering. Janna stood to the side of the screen, explaining what was happening.

The Wolf Pack, when they first saw people leaping out of the flaming tower windows, exchanged glances, because they were always escaping that way, but here there was no wisteria to aid their descent, and horror gripped them too.

When it was time to go home, she called for a minute's silence to pray for America and the suffering of its people, thanking God for the courage of the emergency services and hoping as many people as possible had escaped to safety.

Next day at assembly she gave everyone an update on the tragedy and who was responsible, and when fights broke out between the Muslim children and the Hindus and the Christians, she tried to impress on them that ordinary people weren't to blame. She asked the senior classes to write poems about the tragedy. Paris's was marvellous.

As the days passed, a huge mutual interest developed as the children learnt about the courage of the firemen and the brave search-and-rescue dogs. Some of the children said their parents thought Bin Laden was a hero, and more frightful fights ensued.

Cara and Mike Pitts, however, were constantly on the telephone, stirring up trouble. When it was crucial to raise Larks's position in the league tables, why was Janna wasting the entire school's afternoon watching television?

'It's called global citizenship,' protested Janna when Ashton Douglas carpeted her.

'Wod Hyde will be with you tomorrow,' said Ashton nastily. 'He'll sort you out.'

12

Janna had always felt that one of the cruellest humiliations was when heads of very successful establishments known as 'beacon schools' were posted in to sort out failing schools, 'yanking them up by the hair' as the Education Secretary so charmingly put it.

Janna's russet curls were well and truly yanked by the smug and self-regarding Rod Hyde who, as head of St Jimmy's, had been forced to redesign his writing paper to accommodate all the awards and accolades his school had received.

Arriving at Larks, Rod immediately showed how well he got on with Janna's staff, joshing Mike Pitts, Skunk Illingworth and Robbie Rushton, kissing Cara on both hollowed cheeks and warmly quizzing Sam Spink about her week at the TUC conference.

'I'm sure you found it very empowering. You must debrief me over a few jars.'

Janna ground her teeth.

Known as Jesus Christ Superhead, Rod showed off his spare figure and muscular freckled arms by wearing short-sleeved shirts tucked into belted trousers. On colder days, he wore a rust-coloured cardigan to match his ginger beard.

A control freak, Rod received an emotional charge from acting as a 'critical friend', rolling up at Larks, telling Janna what was wrong with her and her school, attacking both her management skills and her teaching.

Janna, on the rare occasions she had time to teach, delivered the national curriculum as if it had been freed from its chains. When, on Rod's first day, Lydia rang in sick at the prospect of teaching *Macbeth* to Year Nine E, Janna took over, refusing to be

71

fazed when Rod parked himself at the back, busily making notes on his clipboard.

It happened to be the day when Rocky, the huge curly-haired autistic boy kept comparatively calm by Ritalin, was in one of his more eccentric moods. Wandering in, he took one look at Rod and shut himself in the store cupboard at the back of the classroom.

'The Macbeths were a glamorous career couple,' Janna was saying, 'like Tony and Cherie Blair or Bill and Hillary Clinton. We tend to think of them as middle-aged and childless, but probably they were young, young enough to have kids who might inherit the throne, which may have been why Macbeth told Lady Macbeth to "bring forth men children only".'

The class then had a spirited discussion on the right age to have children. Kylie Rose said 'twelve'. They then moved on to Macduff being ripped untimely from his mother's womb.

'That's a cop-out, miss,' volunteered Paris.

'I think Shakespeare meant that Macduff's mum had a Caesarean,' explained Janna, 'but you're right, Paris, it is a cop-out.'

How difficult not to be touched when she saw his pale face flood with colour.

'You must also remember Macbeth was a mighty warrior, a fantastic killing machine.'

'Like Russell Crowe in *Gladiator*,' said Pearl.

'Or Arnie in *Terminator*,' said a sepulchral voice from the cupboard.

The class giggled.

'Exactly, Rocky,' called out Janna. 'Macbeth was on a fantastic high having routed the terrorists who were trying to overthrow Duncan, the King of Scotland, who was also his wife's cousin. Mighty Macbeth had been on a killing spree that was hugely applauded. Like scoring a hat trick for Arsenal or Liverpool. The world was at his feet.

'Now tell me, what did Macbeth have in common with Stalin, Hitler and Saddam Hussein?'

'They all had moustaches,' shouted Pearl.

'Like Baldie Hyde,' called out the sepulchral voice from the cupboard.

More giggling as the class stared round at Rod.

'They all deteriorated into tyrants and mass murderers,' said Janna quickly. 'Now, for homework, you've got two choices, one of which may appeal more to the girls, particularly you, Pearl. If you were a costume designer and in charge of make-up, how would you kit out the Weird Sisters?'

'I'd put them in baggy, raggy, gypsy-style costumes,' said Pearl, 'wiv red and purple hair, blackened-out teeth and cruel scarlet mouths.'

'Like Cara Sharpe,' intoned Rocky from his hideout.

'That's enough,' said Janna firmly. 'The other choice is to imagine you're a war correspondent like John Simpson or Kate Adie, and write a script telling the viewers at home about Macbeth's first victory, bringing in the routing of the rebels, the Norwegian support and the butchering of the treacherous Thane of Cawdor, ripping him open or unseaming him "from the navel to the chaps". If you've got time, you could list questions for an interview with Macbeth or Banquo and add Macbeth's possible answers.'

Year Nine E were gratifyingly enraptured and groaned when the bell went. Throughout the lesson, however, Janna had kept seeing Rod Hyde's tongue, green as a wild garlic leaf, as he pointedly yawned. Afterwards he couldn't wait to tick her off.

'You're far too familiar, and if you digress all the time, you'll never get them through their exams.'

'They're not taking GCSEs for nearly three years. I want them to enjoy Shakespeare.'

'And you talk too much,' Rod consulted his clipboard, as they walked back to her office. 'Try to be a listening head rather than a talking one. Don't take this personally,' he added when Janna looked mutinous, 'it's for your own good.

'And you must stop blowing your top. I know we redheads are volatile' – he crinkled his small eyes – 'but you lose dignity every time you raise your voice to students and colleagues. Ashton tells me you displayed unedifying aggression at the governors' meeting. Has it occurred to you that you're the reason so many of your staff are off with stress?'

Janna dug her nails into her palms and counted to ten. Next moment, she and Rod were sent flying by a yelling gang from Year Ten, stampeding like buffaloes towards the playground.

'Don't run,' howled Janna.

'Don't run,' said Rod quietly.

Infuriatingly the gang mumbled, 'Sorry, sir,' and shambled off.

'You must instil discipline here.' Rod shut her office door behind them. 'Coloured hair, beaded necklaces, particularly for boys, rings in the navel or the tongue, and shaved heads must all go.'

Ten days ago, Janna would have agreed with him, but he was irritating her so much, she said she liked children expressing themselves.

'And you should cut down that wisteria, which seems the accepted escape route for most of your hooligans.'

'That wisteria's older than me or even you, and much more beautiful.'

'Dear Janna' – Rod pursed his red lips – 'you're not helping yourself. Caring Cara Sharpe also tells me' – he turned back to his clipboard – 'you've been working here until eleven at night. Terribly unfair to Wally, who has to lock up after you. He does have a life.'

'Wally's never complained,' stammered Janna.

'He's too nice,' said Rod pompously. 'Start thinking of other people. You wouldn't have to work so late if you organized your day better. Now stop sulking and turn on that coffee machine.'

Somehow, Janna managed not to rip him from navel to chaps with her paper knife, but she cried herself to sleep that night. Were the children and staff really acting up and demoralized because she was such a bitch?

For his next visit, Rod called a breakfast meeting at 8.00 a.m.

'You provide the croissants. I'll provide the pearls of wisdom.'

He'd been jogging and dripped with sweat when he arrived. Janna had to watch him getting butter, marmalade and crumbs all over his red beard as he poured scorn on Larks's place in the league tables.

'It'd help if you and Searston Abbey didn't cream off all the best pupils,' snarled Janna. 'Think how disadvantaged our kids are. Most of them have no quiet room at home to do their home-work and no one able to help them. Unemployment's at an all-time high on the Shakespeare Estate, so the kids, as well as helping out with the shopping, have to take evening and week-end jobs to make ends meet. Poor little Graffi fell asleep at his desk this morning.'

'Probably been doing drugs all night,' said Rod dismissively. 'You must get your parents on side. Ours were in school all week-end, installing benches in the playground – that's one reason our results are spectacular. We'll be catching up with Bagley Hall in a year or two and then Hengist B-T will have to look to his laurels. No parent will want to fork out twenty-odd thousand a year only to get thrashed by a maintained school.'

'What's Hengist like?' Janna was annoyed to find herself asking.

'Terminally frivolous and arrogant,' snapped Rod. 'Typical public-school Hooray Henry, far too big for his green wellies.'

As Janna bent down to retrieve a pen, Rod suppressed an urge to pull down her panties and smack her freckled bottom. Sheila, his 'superb wife' of twenty-seven years, an ex-nurse, who called him 'head teacher' in bed, didn't excite him quite enough. One day Janna Curtis would express gratitude for the way he'd imposed discipline on her and her school.

'I shall be spending one to one and a half days a week with you from now on,' he announced.

'How d'you find the time?' asked Janna sulkily.

'I delegate. Ask a busy person.'

On the following day, Rod rolled up in a big black hat, which he left in Janna's office. Later in the morning, passing Year Nine E's history lesson, he found Paris wearing it and doing a dazzling imitation of Rod addressing the troops:

' "As part of our caring and supportive ethos . . ." '

Rod was outraged and snatched back his hat.

'Others make allowances for you, Paris Alvaston, because of your unfortunate circumstances, and you abuse it,' he shouted. 'I shall speak with Mr Blenchley.'

'Mr Blenchley'll make Paris's life hell,' protested Janna.

The Wolf Pack, who also thought Rod's remarks were below the belt, started pelting him with textbooks and pencil boxes and banging their desk lids when he tried to shut them up.

Nor was Rod's impression of Larks improved later in the day, when Graffi caught him whispering to Cara Sharpe just inside the huge stationery cupboard and locked them both in.

Only after an hour did Rowan hear banging and let them out.

Rod had gone maroon with fury. 'How dare you?' he bellowed at Graffi, who was now wearing the hat.

'You and Mrs Sharpe was saying horrible things about Miss,' said Graffi and, jumping out of the window, slithered down the wisteria and ran laughing down the drive.

'This school deserves to be closed down,' exploded Rod.

Janna, meanwhile, was working on her Larks Ascending project for her prospective-parents' evening.

'We need to put everything about larks, how high up they sing, how they nest on the ground, how because of modern farming, they're getting fewer and fewer.'

'Like Larks's pupils,' said Feral.

Janna and Paris raided the dictionary of quotations for poems about larks. Cambola searched for music. Graffi did a wonderful drawing of Rod Hyde as Edward Lear's Old Man with bird droppings on his head and with owls, larks, hens and wrens nesting in his beard. Graffi also helped Janna cover the corridor walls with pictures by the children and torn-out paintings by Old Masters. They tried not to laugh when Mike Pitts wandered in after a lunchtime session at the Ghost and Castle and remarked:

'That Modigliani's not a bad painter. What class is he in?'

Janna knew she ought to sack Mike for drinking, but who would back her up? She ought to sack him for perfidy too. When she came back unexpectedly from a meeting, she found him whispering into her telephone. Seeing her, he flushed even redder and hung up.

Janna had immediately pressed redial, and an answering voice had said, 'Ashton Douglas.'

Janna was so thrown, she revealed who she was and instantly received a bollocking for her treatment of Rod Hyde.

'As part of his caring, supportive ethos, Wod gives of his valuable time and you put up disgusting paintings of him on the wall and treat him with twuculence and disrespect.'

'He's a bloody clipboard junkie who upsets the kids.'

'Your school is spiralling out of control,' said Ashton coldly.

'Ashton to Ashton, dust to dust,' screamed Janna, slamming down the telephone. When it rang again, she was, for once, able to snatch it up before a suspicious Rowan.

'Janna Curtis,' she snapped.

'This is Hengist Brett-Taylor.' The deep lazy voice was laced with laughter. 'I wonder if you'd like to have lunch this week.'

Janna was about to refuse when she saw Monster Norman's mother charging up the corridor, and abandoning her open-door policy, kicked it shut and leant against it.

'Yes, please.'

'How about Wednesday?'

She had a finance meeting at four-thirty, so she could escape early.

'That's OK.'

'I thought we'd go to La Perdrix d'Or in Cathedral Street. Shall I pick you up?'

'No, I'll meet you there.'

'At one o'clock, then. I really look forward to it.'

13

Janna looked forward to lunch with Hengist less and less. She had her prospective-parents' evening the following day and shouldn't be skiving. Nor should she be fraternizing with the enemy with Rowan clocking her every move, particularly when Janna came in in her rose-festooned pink suit, with her newly washed russet curls bouncing around her shoulders.

But, by the time a German teacher and a lab assistant had given in their notice, the boys' lavatories had blocked yet again and Satan Simmons had been carted off to hospital after an encounter with a broken bottle, Janna was ready for a large drink.

Only when she had driven past the Ghost and Castle did she pull in to tart up, not helped by her trembling hands zigzagging her eyeliner, spilling base on her pink satin camisole top and drenching her in so much of Stew's Chanel No 5, big-headed bloody Brett-Taylor would be bound to construe it as a come-on. In an attempt to look school-marmish, she groped furiously for a hairband in the glove compartment, and scraped back as many of her curls as possible. Then she jumped as, in the driving mirror, she caught sight of Rowan, Gloria the gymnast and perfidious Jason Fenton sloping off for an early lunch, no doubt to bitch about her. It was debatable who blushed most when they recognized her car storming off.

Janna grew increasingly flustered because she was late and Cathedral Street long, punctuated with cherry trees and composed of seemingly identical eighteenth-century shopfronts and she'd forgotten the French name of the restaurant – something like Pederast's Door. She was scuttling up and down, when Hengist, who'd been looking out, pulled her in from the street.

'You are absolutely sweet to make it.'

And Janna gasped because he was a good foot taller than she was and undeniably gorgeous-looking, with thick springy dark hair, unflecked by grey, brushed back and curling over the collar. In addition, he had heavy-lidded, amused eyes, the very dark green of rain-soaked cedars, an unlined face still brown from the summer, a nose with several dents in it, a square jaw with a cleft chin and a wonderfully smooth smiling mouth, framing even white teeth, most of them capped after the bashing they had received on the rugger field.

He was conventionally dressed in a longish tweed jacket, dark-yellow cords, an olive-green shirt and an MCC tie, but as his lemon aftershave mingled amorously with Chanel No 5 on the warm windless autumn air, he seemed utterly in the heroic mould. Casting Hector or Horatius who kept the bridge for a Hollywood epic, you would look no further. Beneath the languid amiability, he exuded huge energy, and after the Hydes and Skunks, who'd been her fare for the last month, he seemed like a god.

Janna bristled instinctively:

'I've got a finance meeting; I haven't got long.'

'Then the sooner you have a large drink the better.'

Hengist ordered her (without asking) a glass of champagne and, picking up his glass of red and the biography of Cardinal Mazarin that he'd left on the bar, he led her through a packed restaurant to what was clearly the best table, overlooking the water meadows and the river.

'The view's breathtaking, but you must sit with your back to it, because it's so good for my street cred to be seen with you and it means that all the fat cats lunching here will think: how pretty she is, and pour money into your school.'

'I wish,' sighed Janna.

'I've brought you a present,' said Hengist.

In a blue box tied with crimson ribbon was a long silver spoon.

'I know you feel you're supping or lunching with the devil,' he said, laughing at her. 'I've read all about your views in the *TES* and the *Guardian* – "upper-class care" indeed – but I promise I won't bite except my food, which is excellent here. Thank you, Freddie.' He smiled at the spiky-haired young waiter who'd brought over Janna's champagne and the menu.

'Now get that inside you,' he went on. 'You'll need it to endure the appalling Russell Lambert and the even more appalling Crispin and Ashton. What a coven of fairies you've surrounded yourself with.'

'I don't want to discuss my governors,' said Janna primly and untruthfully.

'I've cracked the governor problem,' confided Hengist. 'We have two meetings a year. One over dinner at Boodle's, my club in London, which they all adore. Then, in early November, they all come down to Bagley for dinner and the night. Sally, my wife, is a fantastic cook. Wonderful smells drift into the boardroom throughout the meeting, so they're desperate to get through it and on to pre-dinner drinks. Then they push off first thing in the morning.

'But my pièce de résistance has been to get the most ravishing mother on to the board, a divorcee called Mrs Walton, so we always get full attendance and all the governors are so busy looking at her boobs, they OK everything.'

Janna tried and failed to look disapproving.

'Sally and I call her the governing body, but she'd be wasted on Ashton or Crispin,' said Hengist idly. 'You'd do better with Brad Pitt.'

'Or Jason Fenton,' snapped Janna.

'Oh dear, I'd forgotten him.'

'Self-satisfied little narcissist. I passed him bunking off with two other teachers today when they thought I'd left for lunch. He'd have been admiring himself in the shop windows if they weren't all boarded up round Larks. I'm over the moon you've taken him off my hands.'

'At least I've done something right.'

Hengist looked so delighted, Janna burst out laughing.

La Perdrix d'Or itself seemed to be celebrating both golden partridge and the guns who killed them. Paintings of partridge or sporting prints of shooting parties in autumn, with birds and yellow leaves cascading out of the sky, adorned the dark-red walls. There were silver partridges and vases of red Michaelmas daisies on the white tablecloths and, like Sally B-T's governors' dinners, the most delicious smells of wine, herbs and garlic were drifting up from the kitchen.

The menu was in French, always Janna's Achilles heel, but Freddie the waiter charmingly translated for her.

'The goat's cheese fritters are out of this world,' said Hengist, 'although they might give you even worse nightmares if you fall asleep during your finance meeting.'

'And the Dover sole's fresh in today,' said Freddie.

'I'll have that,' said Janna with a sigh of relief.

Janna always liked people who looked straight at you, but Hengist unnerved her; those amused appraising eyes never left her face. He was just *so* attractive. Determined not to be a partridge to his twelve bore, she went on the offensive.

'You can't order venison. Poor deer.'

'A poor deer got into the garden last night and demolished the remainder of Sally's roses. He'd have gobbled up your lovely suit in seconds.'

Getting hotter by the minute, Janna was too embarrassed about the make-up on her camisole top to undo her jacket.

'How did you turn Bagley round?'

'Fired a lot of masters. Found several old codgers already dead in the staffroom, which saved me the trouble. We were horribly under-subscribed. Every time the telephone rang, it was someone resigning or removing a pupil. The children were running wild.'

'Sounds familiar.'

'They're still pretty wild,' admitted Hengist. 'You think you've got delinquents at Larks. I've got the offspring of celebrities and high achievers, who are often just as neglected and screwed up. The divorce rate among the parents is frighteningly high.

'My first move was to set off the fire alarm at midnight on my first Saturday of term,' he went on. 'Ten Upper Sixth boys were so drunk, they couldn't get out of bed. In chapel on Monday, I named them all, then fired the lot. The parents, whom I'd alerted, were waiting outside. Then I told the rest of the school, "Your last five days of bad behaviour are up." I think it shocked them. None of the boys kicked out were very bright,' he added. 'One should never fire clever pupils.'

Janna didn't know how to take this patter. Hengist, like jesting Pilate, flitted from subject to subject, never waiting for an answer.

Then he switched tack, unnerving her further by asking her all about herself, her cottage and about Larks. She was too proud to tell him about the antagonism of the staff, but he was so sympathetic, interested and constructively helpful and the cheese fritters were so delicious, particularly washed down by more champagne, Janna was having such a nice time she was ashamed.

'How d'you cope with the workload?' she asked.

'I have a brilliant PA, Miss Painswick, who's a dragon to every-one but me and drives my wife Sally crackers. I appointed a deputy head, Alex Bruce, from the maintained system, who understands red tape and I've no doubt one day will strangle me with it like Laocoön. He *likes* filling in forms. He's a friend of your nemesis, Rod Hyde, same awful class. And I've got a brilliant bursar, Ian Cartwright; he's just back from Africa having extracted two years' unpaid school fees from a Nigerian prince.'

'With so many people looking after you,' asked Janna waspishly, 'what on earth do you find to do?'

'Given the quality of my staff,' murmured Hengist, 'my job

consists largely of keeping out of the way,' and again smiled so sweetly and unrepentantly Janna melted.

'Do you have many women teachers?' she asked as she attacked her sole.

'Alex Bruce's wife, an Olympic-level pest, teaches religious studies, which includes everything except the Bible. Miss Wormly teaches English and we've got a head of science with absolutely no sense of humour, known as "No-Joke Joan". She also runs our only girls' house: Boudicca, a "thankless task". Miss Sweet, the undermatron of Boudicca, takes sex education, poor thing. The girls, who are sexually light years ahead, help her along.'

He's got a divinely deep husky voice, even if I do disapprove of everything he says, thought Janna, unbuttoning her jacket.

'You ought to employ more women,' she said fretfully.

'I'm sure. You don't want a job, do you?'

'I'd rather die than work for an independent school.' Then, feeling she'd been rude: 'This sole is wonderful. How can I stop truancy? It's shocking among the boys.'

'What do they like best?'

'After Hallé Berry, probably football.'

'Start a football club.'

'We haven't got any pitches. Lots of land, nearly ten acres, but we can't afford to have it levelled.'

'I'll introduce you to Randal Stancombe. You're so pretty and he's so rich, he'll give you some money.'

'Do you have a football club at Bagley?'

'No, we're a rugger school.'

'Of course,' said Janna sarcastically. 'I suppose you played rugby for *your* school.'

'Mr Brett-Taylor played rugby for England,' said Freddie. 'Everything all right, sir?'

When he'd gone, Janna asked if there were lots of drugs at Bagley.

'Probably. We only expel on a third offence. Why squander twenty thousand a year? A boy was sacked from Fleetley last week because they found cannabis in his study. He's expected to get straight As and is an Oxbridge cert, so we took him straightaway. His parents are so grateful, they'll probably pay for a new sports pavilion.'

'I can't afford to exclude,' said Janna crossly. 'I get fined five grand every time.'

'Whatever happened to the word "expel"?' sighed Hengist. He quoted softly:

'Shall I come, sweet Love, to thee,
When the evening beams are set?
Shall I not excluded be?'

Stretching out a big suntanned hand, on the little finger of which glinted a big gold signet ring, he gently stroked Janna's cheek.

'Pretty, you are. Don't work yourself into a frazzle over Larks.'

'Don't patronize me.' Blushing furiously, Janna jerked her head away. 'We're just hopelessly underfunded. Bloody rural Larkshire. Can you really introduce me to Randal Stancombe?'

'Of course. Randal wants to build us a vocational wing. When I was young, vocation meant pretty girls becoming nuns and plain ones going off to be missionaries in Africa. Now it means thick boys training to be plumbers and thick girls learning to run travel agencies.'

'I know what "vocation" means,' spat Janna. 'I didn't know you took any thick children.'

'Rupert Campbell-Black's son Xav is destined to get straight Us,' confessed Hengist. 'In compensation, it wildly impresses parents to catch a glimpse of Rupert on Speech Day.'

Janna was getting so flushed with drink, she took off her jacket – sod the spilt make-up. People kept stopping at their table to say hello to Hengist, and praise something he'd written in the *Telegraph* or said on television.

Each time, he introduced Janna, then gave the other person twenty dazzling seconds of charm, before saying they must forgive him, but he and Janna had things to discuss.

'My children aren't thick,' protested Janna when they were alone again. 'They know the players and fixtures of Larkminster Rovers inside out. All I want to do is make a difference to children in a community who don't have the advantages I had. Education is about empowering children to access parts of themselves they haven't accessed,' she concluded sententiously.

Hengist raised an eyebrow. 'Can it really be English language you teach?'

'Oh, shut up,' said Janna so loudly lunchers looked round. 'No, I don't want any dessert. My teachers stop talking when I come into the room: would I had the same effect on the children. Show them any kindness and they spit and swear at you. But now, the wildest of them all, Feral Jackson, comes to tea with me on Saturdays,' she added proudly, 'with Graffi and Paris. Paris is a looked-after kid, I must show you some of his poems, they're brilliant.'

82

Poor little duck, she's adorable when she gets passionate, thought Hengist, only half listening, examining Janna's glowing freckles, the fox-brown eyes, the full trembling mouth, the piled-up Titian hair, which seemed to want to escape as much as she did. Lovely boobs too, quivering in that pink satin thing.

'My children have such terrible lives,' she was saying. 'My old school, Redfords in the West Riding, was an oasis of warmth and friendliness. I want that at Larks.' Tears were now pouring down her cheeks. 'I'm so sorry.' She blew her nose on her napkin.

'I know your old head, Stew Wilby,' said Hengist. 'Met him at conferences. Brilliant man, a visionary but a pragmatist like me.'

He took Janna's hands, stroking, comforting, as if she were a spaniel frightened by gunfire in one of the sporting prints.

'I'll help all I can. S and C Services worry me. I'm not sure they're kosher.'

'Ashton Douglas's vile, and Rod Hyde's a bully,' sniffed Janna.

'Sally likes most people, but she can't bear him,' agreed Hengist. 'Says he's so pompous and stands too close, with terrible coffee breath.'

'How did you find someone as lovely as Sally?' asked Janna wistfully.

'Have you time for another drink?' Hengist waved to Freddie.

'Oh, please. Could I have a gin and orange instead, please?'

Anything, she was appalled to find herself thinking, to extend lunch. Hengist was like the kingfisher or the rainbow, you longed for him to stay longer. Without realizing, she pulled the toggle off her hair.

'Sally, at twenty-one,' began Hengist, bringing her back to earth, 'had so many admirers. She was so pretty – still is – but her father, another head, didn't approve of me. Thought I was a bit of a rugger-bugger and hellraiser, appalled when I didn't get a first. Anyway, Sally turned me down. I was devastated. My own father, however, told me not to be a drip. Said Sally was the best girl I was likely to meet, I must try again.

'So I invited her to the dogs the following night. She wore a pale blue flowing hippy dress. We backed a brindle greyhound called Cheerful Reply. After a drink or two in the bar, we joked that if Cheerful Reply won, Sally would marry me.

'Darling, it was a photo finish between Cheerful Reply and a dog called Bombay Biscuit. So we had several more drinks and a nail-biting quarter of an hour waiting for the result, which was Cheerful Reply ahead by a shiny black nose.

'Euphoric, probably at winning all that money, Sally agreed to marry me. I've never known such happiness: even better than being selected for England.'

'Lucky Sally,' sighed Janna.

'Lucky me. My parents were living in Cambridge at the time,' went on Hengist. 'I took the Green Line bus home, sitting up with the driver, so excited and tanked up, I told him everything and he said:

' "Isn't it amizing how racing dogs influence events?" Wasn't that perfect?' Hengist burst out laughing. 'Sally and I have had greyhounds ever since.'

'What a wonderful story.' Janna shook her head. 'I'd love a dog, but I'm out all day.'

'Take it into school, you're the head, the children would love it. Homesick children at Bagley are always asking if they can take Elaine, our greyhound, for a walk.'

He waved for the bill. As Janna gulped her gin and orange, he paid with American Express, then got a tenner out of his note-case for Freddie.

'Thank you so much,' Janna told the boy. 'Is this a full-time job?'

'No, I'm starting at New College next week.'

'Well done. Where did you go to school?'

'Bagley Hall,' said Freddie.

'One of our nicest boys,' murmured Hengist as he and Janna went out into the sunshine. 'His father walked out, so his mother worked all hours to pay the fees.'

'Why the hell didn't she send him to a comprehensive?'

'Because Freddie was happy with us. A lot of our parents are poor,' said Hengist sharply. 'They just believe in spending money on their children's education rather than cars, holidays and second houses.'

Wow, he can bite, thought Janna.

'Don't forget your spoon.' Handing her the box, Hengist smiled down at her. It was as though the sun had shot out from the blackest cloud. 'Come and see my school,' he said. 'Please.'

'Well, very quickly,' said Janna ungraciously. 'I'll follow you in my car.'

14

I am way over the limit both physically and mentally, thought Janna as, determined to keep up with Hengist, she careered down twisting, narrow, high-walled and high-hedged lanes made slippery by a recent shower of rain.

Bagley Hall, surrounded by exuberant wooded hills, sprawled over a green plain like one of those villages glimpsed from a train where you imagine you might start a thrilling new life.

The school itself was dominated by a big, golden Georgian house, known as the Mansion, which formed one side of a quadrangle. Behind were scattered numerous old and carefully matched modern Cotswold stone buildings, to accommodate 800 pupils and at least 150 staff.

Girls and particularly boys craned to look as Hengist whisked Janna round endless, many of them surprisingly pokey, classrooms. These were compensated for by a library to rival the Bodleian, entire buildings devoted to music or art, a magnificent theatre and a soaring chapel with Burne-Jones windows glowing like captured rainbows.

'Science etc. is over there.' Hengist waved dismissively at an ugly pile through the trees. 'A subject about which I can never get excited; besides, it's the domain of my deputy head, Alex Bruce.'

Outside, he showed her a swimming pool nearly as big as Windermere, running tracks and a golf course. Smooth green pitches stretched eastwards to infinity. To the north, a large bronze of a fierce-looking general on a splendid charger looked out on to an avenue of limes.

'That's General Bagley, our founder, famous for putting down troublemakers after the Black Hole of Calcutta and being effective at the Battle of Plassey.

'Our house is two hundred yards to the west, hidden by the trees,' he added, 'and very pretty. We're very lucky. You'll see it when you come to dinner.' Then, when she raised an eyebrow at his presumption: 'To meet Randal Stancombe. That's Rupert Campbell-Black's adopted son, Xavier, originally from Bogotá.' Hengist lowered his voice as a sullen, overweight black boy surrounded by a lot of chattering white thirteen-year-olds splashed past through the puddles on a cross-country run.

'Xavier's acting up at the moment,' explained Hengist. 'Hard to fade into the background if you belong to such a high-profile white family. Adolescents so detest being conspicuous and Xav's not helped by having a ravishing younger sister, Bianca, of a much lighter colour.'

'Poor lad being saddled with such an uncaring father.' Janna was getting crosser by the minute. 'Having plucked him out of Bogotá, how could Rupert have shunted him off to the vile prison of a boarding school?'

'He wanted to come here,' said Hengist mildly. 'People do, you know, and his stepbrother and -sister both did time.'

When he showed Janna the new sports hall, she really flipped.

'It's a disgrace, kids getting such privileges because they've got wealthy parents. No wonder society's divided. Think how Graffi would thrive in the art department and Paris in the library. Think how Feral would scorch round those running tracks.'

'There's no reason why they shouldn't.'

But Janna was in full flood: 'Why should rich kids have such an easy route in life?' Furious, she snarled up at him, an incensed Jack Russell taking on a lofty Great Dane.

'Janna, Jann-ah,' drawled Hengist, 'by "easy route", I presume you mean being put into "upper-class care". Surely you don't want your precious Larks children subjected to such a "vile prison"? That ain't logic.'

'Stop taking the piss. You know exactly what I mean. I want kids of all classes to go to day schools together, have access to these kinds of facilities and fulfil their potential. All this system does is make your odious stuck-up little toffs despise my kids and make them feel inferior.'

'Dear, dear,' sighed Hengist, stopping to pick up a Mars bar wrapper. 'So it's wicked of me to improve my school because it demoralizes children who don't come here.'

Then he noticed the tears of rage in her eyes and the violet circles beneath them. They had reached a lake fringed with brown-tipped reeds. Falling leaves were joining golden carp in the water. Next moment, a chocolate Labrador surfaced, shaking himself all over Hengist's yellow cords.

On the opposite bank, a blonde head appeared between the fringed branches of a weeping willow and shot back again.

'Dora,' shouted Hengist.

Very reluctantly, a pretty little girl with blonde plaits and binoculars round her neck emerged, followed by an even prettier one, with dark gold skin, laughing brown eyes and glossy black curls.

They were poised to bolt back to school, but Hengist beckoned them over:

'Meet two of my odious stuck-up little toffs, Dora Belvedon and Bianca Campbell-Black, two new girls this term. How are you both getting on?'

'Really well,' said Dora, eyes swivelling towards the chocolate Labrador, who was now chasing a mallard.

Both girls were wearing sea-blue jerseys, white shirts, blue and beige striped ties and beige pleated skirts, which Bianca had hitched to succulent mid-thigh.

'This is Miss Curtis, the new head of Larks,' Hengist introduced Janna. 'Shouldn't you be playing some sort of game?'

'PE, but we both had headaches and needed fresh air.' Frantic to change the subject, Dora turned to Janna, 'How are you getting on at Larks?' she asked politely.

'Very well,' lied Janna. 'Are you Sophy Belvedon's sister-in-law?' Dora brightened. 'I am.'

'Sophy and I taught at a school in Yorkshire,' explained Janna.

'She and my brother Alizarin have got a sweet little baby called Dulcie. All my brothers are breeding,' sighed Dora. 'I'm an aunt four times over; such an expense at Christmas!'

'How's Feral Jackson?' asked Bianca. 'I think he's cool.'

'So does Feral,' said Janna.

'That was an excellent essay you wrote on Prince Rupert, Dora, you obviously liked his dog,' said Hengist. 'And I've been hearing about your dancing, Bianca, I hope you're going to teach me the Argentine tango.'

'It's dead sexy. Women dance really close and rub their legs against men's. Daddy wants to learn it.'

'Is he going to win the St Leger?'

'I hope so.'

'I don't recognize this dog,' Hengist patted Cadbury, who'd bounced up again. 'Whose is it?'

'One of the masters, we don't know all their names yet,' said Dora quickly. 'But we offered to walk him. We'd better get back, he might be worried. Bye, sir. Bye, Miss Curtis. Best of luck at Larks.'

Dog and children scampered off.

'That was a near one,' muttered Bianca. 'We'd better dye Cadbury black. Do you think Mr B-T and Miss Curtis fancy each other? She's very pretty, and he's not bad for a wrinkly.'

Janna, however, was off again. 'How can Rupert Campbell-Black send that adorable scrap to a boarding school?'

'Bianca's a day girl,' said Hengist.

'I thought they all boarded.'

'Not at all. We've got several day pupils, and lots of them go home at weekends, so they can drink and smoke unobserved.' Then he added: 'Come and see my pride and joy.'

The gold hands of the chapel clock already pointed to twenty to four.

I ought to go back. Why am I allowing myself to be swept away by this man? thought Janna as she ran to keep up with his long, effortless stride.

Hengist, who loved trees passionately and was always sloping off in the spring and autumn to rejoice in the changing colours, led her down the pitches to a little wood called Badger's Retreat, which was filled with both newly planted saplings and venerable trees. On the far side, as a complete surprise, the ground dropped sharply down into a broad green ride with beech woods towering on either side and a glorious view of villages, fields and soft blue woods on the horizon.

Janna gasped.

'Lovely, isn't it? Some criminal idiot back in the fifties gave planning permission to build here.' Hengist's voice shook with anger. 'Desirable residences with a view. Every time Bagley runs into trouble, there's talk of selling it off. The moment I got here, I planted more trees to discourage this. Those enormous holes are badger sets. If anyone built houses, the badgers would burrow up through the floors.

'This is what we call the Family Tree,' he added, pointing to a huge sycamore with a single base, out of which three separate trees hoisted a great umbrella of yellowing leaves into the sky. Like three bodies locked in muscular embrace, their trunks gleamed from the recent rain.

'This is the father.' Hengist tapped the biggest trunk, which, from behind, was pressing its chest and pelvis against the mother trunk, with its branches around her and around the child trunk, which was leaning back against its mother. The branches of all three were stretching southwards towards the sun, many of them resting on the ground, as though they were teaching each other to play the piano. The bark, acid green with lichen, was cracked in many places to reveal a rhubarb-pink trunk.

'How beautiful,' breathed Janna, 'like a marvellous sculpture.'

'Like a family, struggling for freedom,' said Hengist, 'yet inextricably entwined and protecting each other. When we first came here, we noticed it, the way families cling together and hide their problems. It was May, and the new leaves were thick and overlapping, like parrots' plumage, concealing trunks and branches.

'We have a daughter, Oriana, who works for the BBC as a foreign correspondent. We did have a son, Mungo, but he died of meningitis.'

Betraying his desolation for only a second, Hengist pulled off a sepia sycamore key.

'I used to tell Oriana she could open any door with one of these and you can too, my darling.' He put the key in Janna's hand, closing her fingers over it.

I must not fancy this man, she told herself.

'Oh look,' said Hengist, 'the Lower Sixth has been here.'

In the long pale grass lay an empty vodka bottle and several fag ends. 'The retakes must have been harder than expected,' he added, picking up a couple of red cartridge cases.

As Janna glanced at her watch and said, 'Help, it's nearly a quarter past four,' Hengist could feel a black cloud of depression engulfing her.

'Thank you for lunch and the spoon,' she stammered as he opened her car door.

'I'd like to help, and I hope it's not just facilities you and I are going to share,' said Hengist, kissing her on the cheek.

'Hum,' said Dora Belvedon, nearly falling out of the biology lab window, 'Mr B-T definitely fancies her.'

15

Hengist Brett-Taylor had been born fifty-one years ago in Herefordshire. His parents were upper-middle-class Liberals and academics: his mother specializing in plants, his father a revered early English history don at Cambridge, hence the choice of Hengist's Christian name. Hengist had been educated at Fleetley and, between 1969 and 1972, read history at Cambridge. Here he got a double Blue for cricket and rugger and later played rugger for England, clinching the Five Nations Cup with a legendary drop goal from just inside his own half. As a result of too much sport and an overactive social life, Hengist, to his parents' horror, only scraped a 2.1.

At a May Ball at Cambridge, Hengist met Sally, a headmaster's daughter, as beautiful as she was straight. Their wedding took place in the chapel at Radley, where Hengist had started teaching history in autumn 1972. A daughter, Oriana, was born in 1973. Hengist had hoped for a son who would play rugger for England and whom he intended to call Orion.

Hengist prospered at Radley and was overjoyed in 1976 when Sally produced a son, Mungo. The birth was so difficult that Sally and Hengist decided two children were enough.

In 1979, Hengist returned to teach history and rugger at his old school, Fleetley, which now rivalled Winchester and Westminster in academic achievement. Fleetley's head, David 'Hatchet' Hawkley, was determined to keep the school single sex, believing that girls distract boys from work.

In 1984, tragedy struck when little Mungo died of meningitis. This nearly derailed Sally and Hengist's marriage, particularly as Sally had just discovered that her husband had been dallying with David Hawkley's ravishing and promiscuous wife, Pippa.

Although Fleetley took only boys, as a huge concession, because Hengist and Sally couldn't bear to be separated from their now only child, David Hawkley had allowed the eleven-year-old Oriana into the Junior School. A contributory factor was that Oriana was far brighter than any of the boys in her class.

Gradually, Sally unfroze and she and Hengist mended their marriage. In 1989, however, Pippa Hawkley had been killed in a riding accident and, going through her desk, a hitherto unsuspecting David Hawkley discovered passionate letters from Hengist, which also contained the odd dismissive crack about David himself. Hengist, therefore, departed from Fleetley under an unpublicized cloud, which not even Oriana gaining straight As in twelve GCSEs could lift.

In 1995, later than if he hadn't screwed up at Fleetley, Hengist had been appointed headmaster of the notorious and wildly out-of-control Bagley Hall. Applying the same foxiness and energy that he displayed on the rugby field, Hengist miraculously turned Bagley round in six years.

Bagley was now snapping at Fleetley and Westminster's heels in the league tables, and lynching every other school at rugger and cricket. Hengist had signed on for another five years until summer 2005 but, easily bored, was looking for new challenges. His ambition was to thrash David Hawkley in the league tables and take over Fleetley when David retired. But he was also toying with the idea of politics. His chairman of governors, steely Jupiter Belvedon, the great white Tory hope, was only too aware that Hengist, as a media star, would add a desperately needed dollop of charisma to the party.

Oriana, meanwhile, had got a first at Oxford and joined the BBC. Although attached to her parents, she couldn't handle the claustrophobia of their love and expectation, and had pushed off abroad as a foreign correspondent. Despite a somewhat contentious relationship, Hengist missed Oriana dreadfully.

One of the reasons Hengist had turned Bagley round was because he was a genius at recruitment. He had so many celebrities among his parents that, in summer, the school helicopter pad wore out more quickly than the wickets.

Interviews with prospective parents took place in Hengist's study, usually in front of a big fire with papers spread all over his desk and everyone relaxing on squashy sofas. Hengist also insisted on the prospective pupil being present and addressing him or her as much as the parents.

To the fathers, who remembered catches flying into his big hands like robins and his dark mane streaming out as he thundered like the Lloyd's Bank horse down the pitch at Twickenham, Hengist was an icon. The mothers just fantasized about sleeping with him. The children said, 'I like that man, I'd like to go to that school.'

As a result Bagley was overbooked until 2010.

Hengist was a great teacher because he was a great communicator. But, because it involved too much hard work, he preferred to leave the GCSE and A level pupils to his heads of department and teach the new boys and girls so he could get to know them. Hengist believed in praising, and always fired off half a dozen postcards a day telling staff or pupils they had done well.

He was a genius at inspiring staff and delegating, but hopelessly bored by admin and red tape, which was why, to relieve himself of this burden, he had appointed Alex Bruce from the maintained sector as his deputy head.

Hengist was aware that the charitable status awarded to the independent schools, which saved them millions of pounds a year, was under threat from the Government unless they could prove they were sharing their facilities with the community and in particular with the local state schools.

Bagley already had a distinguished history of pupils helping in neighbouring hospitals. From the Lower Fifth onwards, each child was allotted a couple of OAPs whose gardens they weeded and errands they ran. But this wasn't quite enough.

What more charming and advantageous diversion, reflected Hengist, to mix philanthropy with pleasure and help out Larks and that adorable crosspatch. And it would so irritate the heads of the other local schools.

16

Larks was revving up for its prospective-parents' evening. All the displays were in place. There was terrific work on the walls, including Pearl's A star essay on dressing the three witches in Macbeth. Year Ten had turned a room into a spaceship. Year Eight were doing agriculture in geography, and although Robbie Rushton had been far too lazy and bolshie to provide any input, his deputy Adele, whom he'd employed to disguise his imperfections, had weighed in and, with the help of the children, created a farm with coloured cut-outs of animals, machinery and a farmhouse kitchen with bread, milk, butter, cheese and a ham on the table.

Graffi, who fancied Adele and had drawn most of the animals and a farmer and his wife, had also created a glorious country scene in reception. This included wild flowers and trees, and larks in their nest, in the young emerald-green wheat or soaring into a red-streaked sky. In the east, he had painted a yawning sun crawling out of bed, and in the west, weary stars wriggling thankfully under the duvet.

Janna had craftily made it seem a great privilege for forty of the better-behaved children to be allowed back into school to welcome and provide tours for visiting parents. Those who'd helped put up displays had been rewarded with Mars bars and letters home requesting their presence.

This had caused sneering from the troublemakers, who'd not been chosen, but who, when a smell of roasting chicken crept out of Debbie's kitchen and Bob Marley began booming over the tannoy at going-home time, felt that they might be missing something – if only the chance to trash.

Feral had been truanting again, but Graffi, Pearl and Kylie had

93

been among the chosen. Alas, Mr Blenchley, angry with Paris for cheeking Rod Hyde, had refused to let him out. Without Paris and Feral, Graffi needed to defend his work more fiercely than ever and, like a little tiger, prowled up and down reception.

The staff had divided into helpers and hinderers. Among the former were Miss Cambola and Mags Gablecross, who had taken children into the fields to try and record trilling larks.

'He's too high, miss,' was the considered opinion, but everyone got muddy and had a laugh.

Wally had painted till he dropped. Countries of the World in lime green now decorated the turquoise corridor walls. Even languid Jason had come to Janna's aid.

'I gather you had lunch with Hengist. How did you find him?'

'With difficulty. I got terribly lost.'

'Charming bloke.'

'If you like arrogant Adonises.'

'Did he mention me?'

'He feels you'll fit in very well.'

Missing the sarcasm, Jason looked delighted.

'Any help needed this evening, I'll be around.'

'If you could provide some evidence of work in progress in the drama department?'

Once Jason decided to lend a hand, Gloria and all the other pretty women on the staff did too.

Lance, although unable to galvanize his class, had himself created a project of life in Tudor England and spent days blackening beams and colouring in doublet and hose.

The hinderers were in a state of mutiny because Janna had ordered them to be on parade. Mike Pitts had left everything to Jessamy, his little Asian teaching assistant. Robbie was sulking because Adele had done so well. Skunk Illingworth carried on reading the *New Scientist*.

Around teatime, Janna caught Cara bitching into her mobile. 'Nobody'll turn up. I'll be away by eight.'

'That is such a defeatist attitude. You've made no effort,' Janna had told her furiously. Shaking with rage, she returned to her office. 'I'm going to kill Cara Sharpe.'

'Kill her tomorrow,' said Debbie, putting a plate of chicken sandwiches, a blackberry yoghurt and a cup of tea on Janna's desk. 'You must keep up your strength.'

'You are champion, the most champion thing that's happened to Larks, your food's utterly transformed the place, and you've added tarragon.' Janna bit gratefully into a sandwich. Then, picking up the *Gazette*. 'Let's look at our ad.'

But, to her horror, there was nothing there: no advertisement nor any part of her glowing report on Larks's future plans.

'I cannot believe it!' The *Gazette* flapped like a captured seagull as she flipped through it a second and third time – nothing. Even more galling, there were big ads and reports on the splendour and overflowing rolls at Searston Abbey, St Jimmy's and the choir school, who were all having parents' evenings this same night.

Colin 'Col' Peters, the *Gazette* editor, was all injured innocence when Janna called him.

'We never received any copy, Miss Curtis.'

'I put it through the letterbox.'

'I'm sorry. We have no record. If we had, we'd have billed you. We're not in the habit of turning away business.'

'I don't believe you. At least send a reporter down here this evening.'

'I'm afraid they're all on other jobs. *Such* a busy night.'

Janna smashed the telephone back on its cradle. What was going on in this town? Keep calm, count to ten, she told herself as she changed into a new dress, the blue of grape hyacinths, which had long, tight sleeves and clung to the bust and waist before flowing into a full skirt. It was demure, but very sexy. Sadly, she felt as sexy as a corpse. Her face, in the mirror, was drained of all colour and confidence.

Smile, Janna, even when you're playing to empty houses.

She hadn't even the heart to chide Gloria who, to wow any fathers, had rolled up in a pink vest and a white groin-length skirt showing off a shocking pink thong.

'Gloria certainly believes in transparency,' observed Mags Gablecross.

As she waited in reception, Janna's mood was not improved by the arrival of Monster Norman and Satan Simmons.

'Who told you to come along?'

'Mrs Sharpe,' sneered Satan.

'I've come to meet my mother,' said Monster.

'If you put a foot out of line . . .' hissed Janna.

'Everything looks splendid,' boomed Miss Uglow, taking up residence in her RE classroom with the latest P. D. James and a bag of bulls' eyes.

'Just remember to be polite to the new parents,' Janna urged the children. 'Show them you're proud of your school, so they'll want to send their kids here.'

The coffee was brewing. Debbie's chicken sandwiches and homemade shortbread were laid out on plates. Fresh rolls awaited the sausages warming in the oven for people who'd come straight from work. The church clock struck seven-thirty.

'Shall we dance?' asked Jason Fenton to Gloria the gymnast, as over the tannoy Bob Marley reassured them that every little thing was going to be all right.

But it wasn't, because no one came. You couldn't even blame the weather. It was a lovely evening, dove grey in the east, rose doré in the west and the first stars competing with Wally's lights up the drive.

'People'll turn up soon. They'll have seen our "Welcome to Larks" sign outside,' Janna reassured the children.

After ten minutes, Graffi abandoned his display in reception and ran down the drive to check. Immediately, Satan and Monster moved in.

' "Due to pesticide and fertilizer, there are few larks about these days," ' read Satan in a silly voice.

'And even fewer prospective parents,' wrote Monster underneath with a marker pen, just as Graffi returned, gloomily shaking his shaggy head.

'No one's coming, miss. Street's empty.'

'They'll probably come on to us from other schools.'

'Here's someone,' cried Kylie Rose in excitement.

But it was only Cara, Mike, Robbie, Sam and Skunk, trooping in from the Ghost and Castle.

'I hope you're not going to insist we hang around if no one turns up,' said Mike.

'Those are for the parents,' protested Pearl as Robbie and Skunk started wolfing chicken sandwiches. 'Tell them off, miss.'

Janna couldn't bear seeing the excitement draining out of the children's faces. Even worse, Rod Hyde kept ringing up.

'We've had two hundred already and they're still flowing in. How are you doing?'

'Oh, go away,' said Janna, fighting back the tears.

'What a waste of money heating the school on such a warm night,' chided Cara.

The boys, also believing in transparency, had started flicking water at the white shirts of the girls, revealing their bras underneath. There was a crash as a window was smashed. Any moment there would be a mass exodus down the wisteria.

Unwilling to take on Graffi, Monster led Satan off to trash Year Eight's farm and, spitting at a cringing Adele, ignoring the screams of the girls, they swept everything off the farmhouse table and hurled a bread board and a papier mâché loaf out of the window. Chucking the farmer and his wife on the floor, they stamped on pigs, sheep and hens, kicked over milk pails and ripped the beautifully constructed tractor to pieces.

'Don't,' yelled Janna, racing up and seizing Monster's arm. Next moment, Graffi erupted into the room, hurling Satan to the ground.

'Fight, fight, fight,' yelled Year Eight, tears drying on their faces as they gathered round.

'Someone's coming,' squealed Kylie Rose.

'It's your mother, Monster,' yelled Graffi, catching him off guard and smashing a fist into Monster's round, pasty face.

Not wanting to have his ears boxed (Stormin' Norman could be as tough on her son as on other people's children), Monster scrambled to his feet, wiping his bloody nose.

Downstairs, Russell Lambert, Ashton Douglas and Crispin Thomas walked into comparative calm. Ashton had gone casual, wearing a beige cashmere V-necked jersey next to his pink-and-white skin, which made his features more formless than ever. Crispin ducked as a cardboard pig flew over the stairwell.

'This is very disappointing,' said Russell as Janna ran downstairs to meet them. 'Sam Spink tells me you've had no one in.'

Crash went another window.

'Turn up the volume,' hissed Janna to Mags Gablecross.

' "Hark, Hark! the Lark",' sang Bryn Terfel, fortissimo, making everyone jump out of their skins.

'Is it a good idea' – Ashton looked disapprovingly at Paris's copied-out poems and Graffi's countryside mural – 'to gwaffiti newly painted walls?'

Explosions from the science lab indicated Year Ten were having fun. As Debbie and her helpers put plates of hot dogs and more chicken sandwiches on the table, Skunk, Robbie and Sam fell on them.

'How caring of Debbie to realize we'd missed supper.'

'Those are for the parents,' repeated Pearl indignantly.

'What happened to the advertisement in the *Gazette*?' asked Ashton.

'They didn't print it, claimed they never got it.'

'It's always wise to check these things,' said Russell heavily, 'shame to squander so much money and time on displays which no one sees.'

I must not cry, Janna told herself.

Five minutes crawled past. Mike Pitts was nose to nose with Ashton Douglas.

'Shall we call it a night?' he was saying. 'Frankly, I've got better things to do.'

'So glad I didn't waste time glamming up my department,'

sneered Cara; then, shooting a venomous glance at Janna: 'Some people accused me of letting Larks down.'

'Ay had to pay someone to mind Cameron,' grumbled Chantal Peck. 'Ay'm going to put in expenses. Told you it would flop on an *EastEnders* night.'

'Please give it another five minutes,' begged Janna.

Noticing the ill-suppressed satisfaction on the faces of Ashton, Crispin and Russell, she told herself numbly: I don't understand why, but they are willing me to fail.

17

Then, suddenly, like the Angel Gabriel emerging from a day in the City, resplendent in a pinstriped suit, dark blue shirt and pretty pink and yellow checked tie, eyes sparking with malice, in sauntered Hengist Brett-Taylor.

'Janna, darling, how are you?'

Striding down reception, he took her hands and, bending down, kissed her on both cheeks.

'It all looks fantastic. My God, you've cheered this place up, and this mural is simply breathtaking. Of course, it's "Larks Ascending" – and the music too,' as, on cue, the tape launched into Vaughan Williams. 'Who's responsible?'

'Well, everyone, but the mastermind's been Graffi Williams here.'

'Brilliant, brilliant.' Hengist grasped Graffi's hands. 'I love the sun and the stars and that beautiful Shelley quote: "The world should listen then, as I am listening now", the prayer of all writers, me included. This is inspiring stuff.' Then he gave a shout of laughter. 'I love the old man with the beard, got that pompous ass Rod Hyde to a T.'

Hengist had been buoyed up by a very successful meeting with two of his high Tory conspirators, who were standing in the doorway and whom he now beckoned over.

'First, this is Jupiter Belvedon, your MP and chairman of my governors at Bagley.'

'Oh, goodness.' Janna found herself shaking hands with a dark, thin-faced, haughty-looking man in his early forties, familiar from posters all round the town, and forgot to bristle because she was so grateful to see anyone. 'Hi,' she gasped, 'welcome to Larks.'

'And Rupert Campbell-Black,' added Hengist.

'Blimey,' whispered Pearl.

'Wicked,' sighed Kylie. 'Oh, wicked!'

'Wicked indeed,' breathed Janna, because Rupert was so beautiful: like moonlight on the Taj Mahal or Monet's *Irises*, or a beech wood in autumn sunshine, which you'd dismissed as clichés because you'd seen them so often in photographs, in the flesh, they – and he – took your breath away.

The antithesis of Ashton Douglas, there was nothing soft in Rupert's face, from the smooth, wide forehead, the long watchful Oxford blue eyes, the hard, high cheekbones, Greek nose, short upper lip and curling but determined mouth. Around Hengist's height, somewhere up in the clouds to Janna, he was broad-shouldered, lean and long-legged.

Only his voice was soft, light and very clipped as he said:

'You don't look like a headmistress. I wouldn't have run away from school at fourteen if they'd looked like you.' Then, glancing down at the battered cardboard collie under his arm: 'Have you lost a dog? This one just flew out of the window.'

Prejudice evaporating, Janna burst out laughing.

'Would you like some shortbread?' asked Gloria.

'Or a chicken sandwich?' said Debbie the cook.

'Or a coffee?' said Rowan.

'Or an 'ot dog?' Chantal Peck rushed forward with a plate.

'I've got one already.' Rupert patted the collie's head.

'I'd adore one, I'm starving,' said Hengist.

'So am I,' said Jupiter.

Rupert shook his sleek blond head. 'I'm OK.'

'You bet you are,' murmured Gloria.

Even Cara Sharpe was looking quite moony.

Jason was feeling very upstaged, particularly as Hengist hadn't recognized him.

'Rupert, as you know, is one of my parents, and a director of Venturer Television,' Hengist told a stunned Janna.

'Has Venturer been in yet?' asked Rupert, who'd noticed Janna was trembling. 'No? I'll give them a ring.'

'Nor have any prospective parents,' said Monster Norman smugly. 'You're the only people who've shown up.'

'D'you have any kiddies, your honourable?' Chantal asked Jupiter.

'One boy.'

'Thinking of sending him to Larks?'

'He doesn't really talk yet.'

'We've got an excellent special-needs department.'

'Even so, he might have difficulty keeping up,' said Jupiter gravely, 'he's only fourteen months.'

'Same as my grandson, Cameron. Frankly, Jupiter, I wouldn't send Cameron anywhere else than Larks.'

Crash went another window. Overhead, it sounded like elephants playing rugby.

'How are you, little one?' Hengist murmured to Janna.

'Hellish. They've trashed the farm we built upstairs; no one's come. I've let the kids down.'

'Leave it to me. You're right about Paris Alvaston. I've just read his poem about a lark; it's miraculous.'

'Hi,' murmured Rupert into his mobile, 'I'm at Larks, get your asses down here.' Then, after a pause: 'Can you rally some parents?' Switching off, he turned to Janna. 'They were on their way to St Jimmy's; they won't be long.'

'I want to see round the school,' said Hengist, who was now talking to the children, praising and discovering who'd done what. 'Are you all going to take me? What's that, England?' He pointed to one of Wally's newly painted acid-green countries.

'No, Africa, dumb-dumb,' giggled Pearl.

'God, these are good.' Grabbing another hot dog, Hengist set off like the Pied Piper, trailing children, all wanting to hold his hand. Reluctantly, Ashton, Russell and Crispin followed him.

Going into classroom B20, he found a scene of total devastation, and Adele trying to comfort the sobbing twelve-year-olds.

There was a pause, then Hengist said, 'This is absolutely brilliant. Look, Ashton, look, Russell, they've re-created a farm in the Balkans.' Putting huge arms round the sobbing little girls, he went on, 'Of course you're sad your farm's been bombed, but you've really captured the pathos of war.'

'Look at the poor farm animals and birds.' Hengist pointed with half a hot dog. 'Animals are always the first casualties of war. Look at that poor lamb with its legs blown off and the cow who's been disembowelled, and everything's been swept off the table.'

Hengist righted the farmer and his wife who'd lost an arm. 'They were just enjoying their tea, poor darlings, when the bomb fell. So sad.'

'Are you responsible?' He turned to a shell-shocked Adele. 'I can only congratulate you; such vision and courage, to destroy something so precious. That tractor's wonderful too. What's your name? Miss Stevens, just the kind of primitive machinery they'd have in Bosnia.'

'Graffi made that,' piped up Janna proudly.

101

'We did it too.' Monster and Satan edged forward. 'We trashed it.'

Janna was poised to annihilate them, but wily old Hengist pumped their hands. 'Well done, a real team effort.'

Robbie was simply furious, longing to push forward to take credit, but Hengist had moved on to Life in Tudor England and, as a fellow historian, was praising a blushing Lance:

'Just the right scarlet for that doublet, a very Elizabethan scarlet.'

Jupiter, meanwhile, was hell-bent on discomfiting Russell, Ashton and Crispin, who were all allied to the hung Labour/Lib Dem county council, who so frustrated his Tory ambition.

'And we'll hang them out to dry at the next election,' he murmured to Rupert as they paused to admire Mrs Gablecross's French café and enquire after her husband, the Chief Inspector, an old friend of them both.

Word had, by this time, got around that Rupert was at Larks and there was a further chance to get on telly, so there was a mass exodus from the other schools with parents and children storming up the drive. A reporter who'd only been at the *Gazette* for a week, tipped off by a Venturer cameraman, also belted over to Larks with his photographer. Hengist immediately introduced them to Janna, then took them by the arm, showing them the Larks Ascending display and the bombed farm.

Satan Simmons and Monster Norman were soon being interviewed.

'We built it up, then trashed it to create a wartime situation,' Monster was saying.

'Like the Chapman brothers or Rachel Whiteread,' said the reporter.

'Yeah, yeah, whatever.'

Photographs were also taken of Rupert, Jupiter and Hengist with Janna. Parents were everywhere, demanding autographs: 'You sending your kids here, Rupert? How's Taggie? Any tips for Cheltenham?'

'We didn't get food at St Jimmy's or Searston Abbey,' said the other parents as they fell on Debbie's hot dogs. 'Lovely atmosphere here. I like these old buildings. More ambience. Hello, Jupiter. He's our MP.'

Jupiter, who reminded Janna of the lean and hungry Cassius, told the *Gazette* that as Shadow Education Minister and Larkminster's MP, he took a great interest in local schools.

'I am delighted Janna Curtis appears to be turning round this one, after only a few weeks. Good to have a young, energetic and

102

charismatic head. You're to be congratulated, Ashton.' He smiled coolly at a seething Ashton Douglas. 'I hope you're providing adequate financial support. Janna tells me she needs textbooks, computers, playing fields and a new roof.'

'We can't have raindrops falling on our head or anyone else's,' said Rupert, looking up from the *Evening Standard.*

Janna got the giggles.

'Ashton, well done,' said Hengist, coming out of a side door, trailing children. 'You must be delighted you chose Janna. I've never seen such a change.'

Ashton looked as though he'd swallowed a wasp.

Venturer Television arrived, filmed the sea of parents and then interviewed Hengist about his interest in Larks.

'Janna and I have been discussing plans to share our facilities,' Hengist told them. 'The council sold off Larks's playing fields, so we'd like to offer them access to ours, and to our libraries, art departments, science labs and running tracks. We're very early in discussions, but it's an exciting project. We'll both learn from each other.'

'We'll teach them fist-foiting, shooting and Formula One driving,' yelled Graffi and was shushed.

'When will this happen?' asked the Venturer presenter.

'I'm off to America and we've got half-term, but very soon after that, I hope. To merit our charitable status, we independent schools must increasingly demonstrate we're of benefit to the community,' Hengist concluded smoothly. 'We've always offered bursaries to bright children; we're merely carrying on a tradition.'

'First I've heard of it.' Russell Lambert was puffing out his cheeks.

'Janna and I' – Hengist smiled in her direction – 'had a working lunch yesterday. She's made a great start, but as one who had problems at the beginning with Bagley, I'd like to offer my support.'

'Rod Hyde's already doing a grand job,' snapped Ashton, 'and I'm not sure how Larks staff will feel about bonding with an independent.'

'We'll have to find out,' said Hengist coolly, 'but three heads are always better than one.'

'Come on, I need a drink.' Rupert was getting bored. 'Can I keep this dog?'

Briefly, Hengist drew Janna aside: 'Pretty dress. At last she rose, and twitched her mantle blue: tomorrow to fresh woods, and pastures new.'

'I don't know what you're playing at,' muttered an utterly confused Janna, 'but thank you for rescuing us.'

'I'll ring you tomorrow.'

'Goodbye, goodbye.' Reluctantly, the children waved Hengist off.

'I'll be in touch,' Jupiter told Janna, then, handing his card to Graffi: 'I'd like to see more of your stuff.'

'That was rather injudicious,' he added a minute later as the black polished shoes of the three men rustled through red and gold leaves towards the car park. 'Do you honestly want Bagley overrun by a lot of yobbos?'

'I want the world to know how good and philanthropic my school is. Caring conservatism must show it has balls,' said Hengist mockingly.

'Are you sure Bagley won't corrupt those innocent Larks hooligans?' asked Rupert. 'Do you really want bricks heaved through your Burne-Jones windows?'

'"We must love one another or die",' replied Hengist sanctimoniously.

'I hope you don't want to get into Janna Curtis's knickers,' warned Jupiter, pressing the remote control to open the doors of his Bentley. 'The Tory party can't afford any more sleaze.'

'I like this dog.' Rupert patted his cardboard collie. 'It can round up the Tory unfaithful.'

Paris lay on top of his bed at Oaktree Court. A girl in the room opposite had been screaming for nearly an hour. Fucking Blenchley, not to let him out, when Janna had been kind enough to pin up his poem beside those of Shakespeare, Milton and Shelley. He murmured longingly:

'Teach me half the gladness
That thy brain must know;
Such harmonious madness
From my lips would flow,
The world should listen then, as I am listening now.'

He would have liked to shag Benita who slept next door, but if ever he left his room, a red light went on in the warden's office.

Shutting his eyes, he dreamt of making love to Janna: 'such harmonious madness'. He must get out of this place.

Waving the *Gazette* next morning, Gillian Grimston, head of Searston Abbey, telephoned Rod Hyde. 'That swine Hengist

Brett-Taylor's never offered us a blade of grass. It's just because Janna Curtis wears tight jumpers and bats her eyelashes.'

'Hengist has always been a ladies' man.'

'I'd hardly call Janna Curtis a lady.'

'It'll all end in tears,' said Rod Hyde grimly, thinking of his stolen hat.

Nor was Randal Stancombe pleased. He didn't fork out £20,000 a year for Jade's school fees only for her to mix with riff-raff.

18

The following evening, Janna recounted the latest events to her new friend Lily Hamilton as they sat at Lily's kitchen table making sloe gin, selecting blue sloes from a pile Lily had picked earlier in the day, pricking each one with a needle before dropping it into a waiting bottle. Lily was progressing much faster because Janna kept pricking her fingers or missing the bottle whenever she got on to the subject of Ashton or Cara or Russell.

'They were foul. If Hengist and his friends hadn't rolled up . . .'

Lily smiled. 'I told you Hengist was nice.'

'I reckon he was more interested in bugging Ashton,' said Janna firmly, but the glow of gratitude still warmed her.

'You're returning your sloes to the pile,' chided Lily.

'Oh help, sorry.'

Just as she was topping up their glasses, Janna's mobile rang.

'Is that Janna?' asked an incredibly plummy voice. 'It's Sally Brett-Taylor. We were wondering if you'd come and dine on October the twenty-sixth. Hengist so enjoyed his lunch with you, and we'll try and rustle up some fun locals for you to meet. As it's a Friday, we won't bother to dress.'

And be running around nude, reflected Janna, then said she'd love to.

'Lovely, eight for eight-thirty, bye-ee.'

'Bye-ee, bye-ee,' muttered Janna as she hung up. 'That was Mrs Brett-Taylor,' she told Lily. 'She sounds very jolly hockey sticks.'

'She's a sweet thing,' said Lily. 'Terribly kind, keeps Hengist on the rails, remembering names, edging him out of parties if he's getting drunk or indiscreet.'

* * *

Janna was further touched on Monday to receive a cheque for three thousand pounds from Venturer Television.

'Hope this might buy a few textbooks,' Rupert had written, 'and your children might enjoy this film.'

It was *Gladiator*, which Janna allowed all the excited children to watch that afternoon as a reward for their good behaviour.

As a result of the prospective-parents' evening, thirty parents put their names down for Larks in autumn 2002 and the editor of the *Gazette* nearly sacked his news editor when a most flattering piece about Larks Comp appeared on the front page. This was accompanied by a smiling picture of Rupert, Hengist, Jupiter and Janna.

Inside were pictures of Graffi, Pearl, Monster and Satan surveying the trashed farm and a large headline: 'Larks Ascending'.

An overjoyed Janna bought twelve copies of the paper and sent photocopies to all the parents. Even more excitingly, the *Gazette* published Paris's poem 'To a Skylark', no longer a blithe spirit, whose trill was a burglar alarm, warning of the pillaging of the countryside.

'Paris Alvaston', wrote Hengist in his diary.

Poor Paris was unmercifully ragged at the children's home.

Sam Spink, meanwhile, called a union meeting to protest against Larks accepting any favours from the private sector. Alex Bruce, deputy head of Bagley, who'd come from the maintained sector, was equally unamused. His friend Rod Hyde had briefed him on the 'challenging behaviour' of Larks's pupils.

'Do we really want these hooligans to invade Bagley? You're always complaining of overwork, Senior Team Leader,' he reproved Hengist. 'Why not let me mentor Janna Curtis? I could slot in a visit to Larks on Fridays.'

'I'm only overworked by things I don't enjoy and Janna Curtis is very pretty,' said Hengist and laughed in Alex's shocked face.

After the parents' evening, Hengist had telephoned Janna as promised.

'I'm deadly serious about Larks and Bagley getting together. But I've got a hellish October. Lectures in Sydney and Rome, a headmasters' conference in Boston, not to mention half-term, so let's aim at early November.'

With that, he had drifted off and, like everyone else, been distracted by the American bombing of Al-Qaeda in Afghanistan, particularly as his daughter Oriana was reporting for the BBC from there.

Larks's pupils, whose spirits had been lifted by Hengist's visit and watching *Gladiator*, fell back into their old ways. Janna seemed to spend her time wrestling with red tape, refereeing fights, putting buckets under leaks and sparring with Rod Hyde, who said:

'Typical Hengist B-T behaviour, swanning in to cash in on the publicity. That's the last you'll see of him.'

It was so humiliating to have nothing to report when the *Gazette* and other papers rang for news of the bonding, and heart-rending when the children kept asking when they'd get a chance to play football on a decent pitch. Janna was too proud to call Hengist, but as the leaves changed colour and tumbled from the trees, she felt enraged he hadn't rung and was determined to look as glamorous as possible at his wife's dinner party.

This was preceded by a day from hell.

In the morning, guilty that she hadn't tapped any local fat cats for sponsorship, Janna had visited Grant Tyler, a Larkminster electronics giant who, with his long, yellow face ending in a pointed chin, looked just like a parsnip.

'And what do I get out of sponsoring Larks?' he had demanded rudely.

'Some of our clever children could do work experience here,' said Janna brightly, 'and might want to work for you as a career.'

Mr Tyler's face had turned from parsnip yellow to the purple of aubergine. 'If you think I'd let your ragamuffins over my threshold—' he had roared, and Janna had walked out leaving him in mid-sentence.

Later in the day she gave Cara Sharpe a final warning for bullying a little Bangladeshi pupil who'd been unable to produce a note explaining her absence because her mother didn't speak or write English.

Janna was also worried about Feral, who'd been truanting persistently. She'd sort him out next week. But tonight she was leaving on time to shower and wash her hair at home and remove the red veins in her eyes with an iced eye pad, before putting on a lovely new off-the-shoulder black dress: all the things she had had time to do before a date with Stew in the old days.

As she came out of Larks, fireworks, anticipating a forthcoming Bonfire Night tomorrow week, were popping all over town. Walking towards the car park, she heard a terrified whine, followed by shouts of laughter. Tiptoeing further into the garden, stumbling down Smokers' Bank, she froze in horror to discover Monster Norman and Satan Simmons in the long, pale grasses above the pond. No doubt carried away by their success in trashing the cardboard animals, they were now trying the real thing and torturing a little dog. They had tied its front legs together; Monster was winding a rope round its muzzle. Satan was swearing as he tied a large rocket to its tail. Monster was also smoking. Having stubbed his cigarette out on the shoulder of the desperately writhing animal, he groped for a lighter and set fire to the rocket's blue paper.

'Stop that,' screamed Janna as both boys leapt out of the flight path.

Seeing her storming down the bank, they bolted, howling with laughter, down the hill over the wall. Next moment, the rocket exploded. Unable to soar into the air, it thrashed around on the ground, shooting out green and bright pink stars, dragging the dog with it.

Whipping off her coat, Janna flung it over the wretched animal, gathering it up, dunking it in the pond. As the sparks finally fizzled out, the dog wriggled. At least it was alive. In the gloom she could see its red and white fur singed on its face, sides and paws. It was a small mongrel with brown ears and a brown patch over one eye. Freeing its muzzle, untying the rocket with frantically trembling hands, Janna carried it up the bank to her car. It was hardly breathing now. Finding Wally and help would waste time. Laying the dog on the back seat, trying not to upset the poor little thing by sobbing, soothing it with: 'Good boy, brave boy, hang on a bit longer, darling,' she hurtled round to the Animal Hospital, off the High Street.

Here a sympathetic vet said it was their first Guy Fawkes casualty, but they were expecting a lot more; that the dog had been very badly burned and would probably lose his tail and an eye.

'It's only just breathing, hasn't got a collar, probably a stray, terribly thin, kinder to put it down.'

The dog, who suddenly seemed to symbolize Larks, gave a whimper.

'Try and save him,' pleaded Janna.

'I'll see what I can do.' The vet looked regretfully at her watch. 'I'm supposed to be at a dinner party.'

'Oh Christ, so am I,' said Janna. 'Can I drop by later?'

'Ring if you'd prefer. You'd better get something on those burns.'

Weeping with rage and horror, Janna plunged into the night. At least she had a proper reason to exclude Monster and Satan, except they'd both deny it. There was plenty of the dog's blood on her, but probably not on them.

Heavens, it was a quarter past eight. She had no time to change or wash her hair. In a lay-by, she ripped off her bloodstained T-shirt, leaving on her old olive-green cardigan and black skirt. Her stockings were laddered to bits. She'd look as poor and scruffy as the toffs would expect a state-school teacher to be, she thought savagely.

She was so distraught, she didn't reach Bagley until nine, where her animosity escalated as various incredibly polite children gave her directions.

'If you like, I'll hop in and guide you,' a little Hooray Henry said finally. 'Should get a good dinner. Mrs B-T's a terrific cook.' Then, noticing the bloodstained T-shirt in the back, he reached nervously for the door handle, until Janna told him about the dog.

'They ought to be shot, or rockets tied to their dicks. That's diabolical. We always give our greyhounds tranquillizers at home when there are fireworks around – at least we did,' he said sadly.

'Here we are,' he announced as the headlamps lit up brilliant red and crimson dogwood and maple and drifts of white cyclamen on either side of the drive.

As they passed arches trailing last year's roses and yew hedges cut into fantastic shapes, including a greyhound, Janna knew she'd come to the right house, which reared up, greyish yellow, shrouded in creeper, with some sash and some narrow casement windows, topped by roofs and turrets on different levels.

'It's a bit of a mishmash,' said her companion. 'Part Elizabethan, part Queen Anne, but very nice.'

A mongrel of a house, thought Janna, but strangely appealing, like the little dog fighting for his life.

'I hope your dog recovers,' said the boy, running round and opening the door for her, 'and you have a good evening.'

'Thank you so much. What's your name?'

'Dicky Belvedon.' As he rang the bell for her, she realized he was Dora's twin.

'How are you getting back?'

'I'll walk. It's not far, and I can have a smoke in peace.'

A plump, middle-aged woman answered the door. Relieved that Hengist's wife wasn't glamorous, Janna was about to apologize for being late, when a truly pretty blonde ran out.

'Hello, Janna, I recognize you from your picture, I'm Sally B-T.'

After her, slipping all over the floorboards, wagging her tail, dark eyes shining, long nose snaking into Janna's hand, came Elaine, the white greyhound. Seeing such a happy, healthy dog, Janna burst into tears.

'You poor darling.' Sally turned, waved to the crowd in the room behind her to have another drink and whisked Janna upstairs. 'What's happened?'

Collapsing on the four-poster in the prettiest blue, lilac and pink bedroom, Janna explained about the dog.

'They're operating now. He was so defenceless and it was Larks children that did it. What can have happened to kids to turn them into such brutes?'

'They don't know any better. But poor little dog, and you've burnt your poor hands. They must be agony. We'll ring the sick bay and get something for them.'

'I'm fine, honestly. I'm so sorry I didn't have time to change.'

There was a knock on the door, and a large glass of gin and orange, followed by Hengist, came round the door.

'Everything OK?'

'No! Poor Janna's had the most awful time.'

Sally, decided Janna – all her antagonism evaporating – was simply sweet. She was terribly Sloaney in her pie-frill collar and tartan blanket skirt, with wonderful rings on her rather wrinkled hands. But she was so friendly and kind.

'Now, please, borrow anything,' she told Janna. 'I'm afraid my make-up's not very exciting. A dash of lipstick and mascara is about my limit, but help yourself. And here's a nice cream shirt, if you're too hot in that cardigan. The bathroom's next door. Don't hurry.'

Having downed half the gin and orange, Janna felt perkier and the urge to spy. The curtains of the huge four-poster were patterned with sky-blue and pink delphiniums. On Sally's bedside table were Joanna Trollope and Penny Vincenzi, on Hengist's, French poetry and a biography of Louis XIV. A big dressing gown in forest-green towelling (to match his eyes) hung on the bathroom door. Janna imagined it wrapped round his hot, wet body. *The Joy of Sex* and *Fanny Hill* were well-thumbed in the shelves. Old maps of Greece and Italy covered the bathroom walls. Water gushed out of a lion's mouth into a big marble basin.

Janna took her hair down, but it looked so lank and straggly she put it up again. Sally's base was too pink, so she merely applied a little cherry-red lipstick to her mouth and blanched cheeks, and took off the shine with a pale blue swansdown powder puff dipped in a cut-glass bowl.

She now needed some perfume. Beautiful was pushing it. She'd smelt it on Sally. Instead, she slapped on a cologne called English Fern and was immediately transported back to La Perdrix d'Or and the wonder of her lunch with Hengist.

Comus, with damp, crinkled pages, was open beside a glass vase of yellow roses. 'What hath night to do with sleep,' read Janna.

You could say that again. She glared at her hollow cheeks and even hollower eyes. Sally's cream shirt falling to her knees like a nightdress made her look even more drained, but anything was better than the dreary cardigan.

Pale but interesting, Janna, she told herself. If that dog pulls through, I'm going to keep him.

19

Hearing the neighing and yelping of the upper middle classes three drinks up, Janna nearly turned and ran. Entering the double doors she found everyone up the other end examining some picture and paused in reluctant admiration because the huge lounge was so warm and welcoming.

Flames leapt merrily in the big stone fireplace. A crimson Persian carpet covered most of the polished floorboards. Battered sofas, armchairs and window seats in fading vermilion, old rose and magenta begged her to curl up on them. Poppies, vines and pomegranates rioting over the scarlet wallpaper battled for space with marvellous pictures. Was that really a Samuel Palmer of moonlit apple blossom? In bookshelves up to the ceiling fat biographies, history, classics, lots of poetry, gardening and art books, all higgledy piggledy and falling out, pleaded to be read. More books jostled with photographs of former pupils on every table, music scores rose from the floor in piles around the grand piano.

Any space left was crammed with family memorabilia: an old-fashioned gramophone with a convolvulus shaped speaking trumpet, a papier mâché HMV dog, busts of Wagner and Louis XIV, a staring female figurehead taken from a nineteenth-century fishing ship, a ravishing marble of Demeter with a sweat band restraining her curls – every object with a story.

This blaze of colour was reflected in a wooden mirror over the fireplace and softened by lamplight falling on great bunches of cream roses.

Never if I pored over *House & Garden* for a million years could I produce a room as beautiful, thought Janna wistfully, then angrily that independent heads must be grossly overpaid to afford places like this.

113

Hengist seemed to have read her mind, because he swung round and bore down on her with another vat of gin and orange.

'You poor darling, poor little dog, bloody bastards, I'd like to ram great lighted rockets up their arses.'

He was wearing a shirt in ultramarine denim, which turned his dark-green eyes a deep Prussian blue. From the breast pocket he produced a tube and a silver sheet of pills.

'The sick bay sent this over for your poor hands. Let me put some on at once.'

'It's only one hand, and it's fine.' Janna snatched the tube, knowing she'd tremble far more if he touched her.

Hengist's suntan had faded; his face was sallow and rumpled rather than golden and godlike. The trips to the States and Sydney must have been punishing, but his spirits were high and his eyes filled with amusement and expectation.

'It's so nice to see you again. I can't wait to open my facilities – such a dreadful word – to your children and particularly you.'

Bloody patronizing Little Lord Bountiful, thought Janna, wincing as she applied the gel, then wiped her hands on her skirt.

'Now swallow these,' ordered Hengist, pushing out two Anadin Ultra. When Janna looked mutinous he added, 'Or I'll hold your nose and stroke your throat.'

Feeding the pills into her mouth, letting his fingers rest on her lips a second too long, he held out the gin and orange for her to wash them down.

'Good girl. Now what are we going to argue about this evening: dyspraxia, ethnic diversity, gifted children?'

'Are my kids ever going to be allowed to play on your pitches?' asked Janna furiously.

'Oh, sweetheart, of course they are.'

'No one believes you.' The hurt and humiliation poured out of her. 'Ashton Douglas, Rod Hyde, Mike Pitts, Crispin Thomas are all sneering at me.'

'Bugger Ashton,' said Hengist, 'although he'd rather enjoy it. I swear the first – no, second week in November. The red carpet awaits. Feral, Graffi, Paris, whoever you like.'

Janna, who'd been staring fixedly at his strong, smooth neck and emerging six o'clock shadow, raised her eyes and found such affection and tenderness on his face, she was quite unable to speak. Thank God, Sally rescued her.

'Janna, come and meet everybody. Be careful, this carpet is a high-heel hazard. You've met Elaine?'

'I have.' Janna ran her hand over the pink silken belly; Elaine, showing herself off to advantage on a russet chaise longue, opened a liquid dark eye and waved a tail in greeting.

The buckets of gin and orange were kicking in and Janna was cheering up, there was so much to look at. The watchful, saturnine Jupiter Belvedon actually pressed both planed cheeks against hers before telling her how much he'd enjoyed visiting her school. He then introduced Hanna, his lovely blonde Norwegian wife, who was as warm and curvy as he was cold and thin, and who must be a colossal asset to him in his constituency.

'Hanna's responsible for those exquisite flower paintings in our bedroom,' explained a hovering Sally.

'They're beautiful,' said Janna. 'My next-door neighbour, Lily Hamilton, has lots of them too.' Then she blushed as she remembered how cruelly Jupiter had turfed Lily out of a lovely house. Fortunately Jupiter, having parked her, had moved off so Janna was able to reassure Hanna that Lily was fine and a wonderful neighbour.

'What's she up to?' asked Hanna.

'Making sloe gin. Keeping us all entertained.'

'I miss her so much,' sighed Hanna.

I am behaving really well at a smart Tory dinner, Janna told herself in amazement. Then, goodness, jungle drums! Sally was introducing her to Randal Stancombe.

Just as black panthers and leopards, sighted in woods and along river banks and terrorizing whole communities, often turn out to be domestic cats with fluffed-out winter fur, Stancombe, despite his fearsome reputation, was in the flesh much less alarming than she'd imagined. He was certainly sexy, with a handsome predator's face, scorching dark eyes that seemed to burn off Janna's clothes, blow-dried glossy black curls and a mahogany suntan, set off to advantage by a linen shirt even whiter than Elaine. Asphyxiated by his musky aftershave and blinded by his jewels, Janna snatched away her burnt hand before it was crushed by his rings.

'Delighted to meet you, Jan, Henge says you're doing a great job at Larks, catch up with you later,' and he turned back to his companion, quite understandably, because she was the most glorious, pampered, expensive-looking beauty with shining chestnut hair, creamy skin, wide hazel eyes and luscious smooth coral lips.

This ravishing adventuress, Hengist whispered in Janna's ear, was *the* Mrs Walton he'd enticed on to the Bagley board as a parent governor, to ensure not only full houses at governors' meetings, but also that the other governors were so distracted by lust that they OKed all the decisions already made by Hengist and Jupiter.

'Very different from *my* parent governors,' giggled Janna, thinking of Chantal Peck and Stormin' Norman. 'When did they meet?'

'About ten minutes ago.'

Feeling his laughing lips against her ear, Janna experienced a surge of happiness. Sally then whisked her off to meet Gillian Grimston, head of Searston Abbey, who had a lot of teeth like a crocodile whose mother had failed to make it wear a brace, and who was asked out a lot because of her ability to offer the Larkshire middle classes an excellent free education, rather than for her charm or good looks. She was patronizing but amiable, and commiserated with Janna on having Rod Hyde on her back.

'He's so conceited and bossy.'

She then banged on about her workload, which had cost her her marriage, and Searston Abbey, which had already raised thousands for Afghanistan war victims, thus giving Janna plenty of opportunity to watch Stancombe freefalling down Mrs Walton's cleavage and only just disguising his irritation when Jupiter joined them.

Determined to crack every aspect of society, Stancombe was not only pressing Hengist to make him a Bagley governor, but having watched Jupiter's rocket-like ascent was anxious to buy into that camp and be a formative influence in Jupiter's break-away Tory party. Jupiter, who liked Stancombe's money better than Stancombe, was playing hard to get.

'The Afghan Fund is part of our caring ethos,' droned on Gillian Grimston, wishing Mrs Walton were one of her mothers.

'I'd rather have an Afghan hound,' giggled Janna. Oh dear, she was getting drunk again.

'Dinner,' announced Sally.

The dining room was equally seductive, with bottle-green jungle-patterned wallpaper, and chairs upholstered in ivy-green velvet round an oak table as dark and polished as treacle toffee.

Light came from red candles flickering amid more white roses and a chandelier overhead like a forest of icicles, which set the regiments of silver and glass glittering.

Ancestors under picture lights looked down from the walls, except for a portrait by Emma Sergeant over the wooden fireplace, which showed the young Hengist, solemn-faced, dark eyes raised to heaven, poised to kick his legendary drop goal at Twickenham. Pausing to admire it, Janna felt Sally's arm through hers.

'I insisted on hanging it there. It was painted some time after the event. Hengist thinks it's awfully showing off, but I so love it.

Hope you didn't get too stuck with Gillian. She's a good old thing and probably a useful ally. Are you OK? Hands not too sore?'

'You are kind,' sighed Janna.

Even kinder, Sally had invited two single men to sit either side of Janna. One was Emlyn Davies, a blond giant with a battered face who taught history and rugger. The other, Piers Fleming, was head of English. Dark and romantic-looking, like Shelley's younger brother, wearing a steel-blue smoking jacket, he confessed he had great difficulty keeping the Bagley girls at bay.

'I'd screw the lot, if I weren't going to be banged up for under-age sex. Some of them are so gorgeous and so precocious, and worst of all' – he nodded across at Stancombe, who was being reluctantly prised away from Mrs Walton – 'is Randal's daughter Jade, and no one can expel her because Daddy's poised to give the school a multi-million pound science block – bloody waste of money.'

They then got on to the more edifying subject of English literature.

Noticing Hengist at the head of the table flanked by lovely Hanna Belvedon and even lovelier Mrs Walton, whose taffeta dress, the stinging emerald of a mallard's head, seemed to caress her body with such love, Janna's spirits drooped. Then Hengist smiled at her and mouthed, 'Everything OK?' And suddenly it was.

Two big glass bowls of glistening black beluga caviar resting on crushed ice were placed on the table, eliciting moans of greed all round. Accompanying them were little brown pancakes, bowls of sour cream, chopped shallot, hard-boiled egg and wedges of lemon.

'Oh, thank you,' said Mrs Walton, as her glass steamed up with the addition of iced vodka. 'Thank goodness I'm staying here and can get legless.'

'Shame with such lovely legs,' Stancombe leered across the table.

How the hell do I eat this lot? wondered Janna.

As if reading her panic, Sally called down the table, 'Do make up Janna's blinis for her, Piers, her hands must be so sore.'

'My favourite food,' confessed Jupiter.

'Where did it come from?' asked Gillian Grimston.

'Moscow,' said Hengist. 'Anatole, one of our pupils and the son of the Russian Minister of Affaires, chucked an empty vodka bottle out of an attic window and nearly concussed the chaplain—'

'And was, I presume, excluded?' Gillian looked shocked.

'Good God, no,' said Hengist, 'Anatole's a lovely boy. Always

117

pays his own school fees in cash – probably laundered – out of a money belt. If only other parents were as prompt.'

'My cheque's in the post,' murmured Mrs Walton.

'Anyway, Anatole's mother was so grateful, she immediately sent us a ton of caviar.'

'Jupiter would kill for caviar,' said Hanna as her husband put two huge spoonfuls on his plate.

And much else, thought Janna. Not Cassius, she decided, he's more Octavius Caesar to Hengist's Mark Antony.

Janna wasn't sure about the caviar. She drowned it in lemon juice and took huge slugs of vodka. Perhaps she should give hers to the emaciated man across the table, who had a tired, bony face and flopping very light red hair, and was already piling a second helping on to his blue glass plate.

'Rufus Anderson, head of geography.' Piers lowered his voice. 'Head in the clouds, more likely, always leaving coursework on trains. Eats hugely at dinner parties because his wife, Sheena, doesn't cook and whizzes up to London to a high-powered Fleet Street job, leaving Rufus to look after the kids. Note his sloping shoulders weighed down by baby slings.'

'Then they should get an au pair,' said Janna sharply. 'Her career is just as important as his.'

'Not at Bagley, it isn't. Wives are expected to be helpmates. Sheena's hopping that Emlyn on your left was offered a job as a housemaster last year and Rufus wasn't. Rufus is miles cleverer than Emlyn or me. Sheena doesn't appreciate she's the only thing in the way of her husband's advancement. That's her down the table hanging like a vampire on Stancombe's every word.'

As Mrs Walton was soft, passive and voluptuous, Sheena Anderson was rapacious and hard. She had sleek black jaw-length hair, a hawklike face only adorned by eyeliner and a lean, restless body. No jewellery softened her short sleeveless black dress.

'I'd love to interview you for the *Guardian*,' she was telling Randal Stancombe.

'They always give me a rough time.'

'Not if I wrote the piece. You could approve copy.'

Like Jack-the-lad-in-a-box, Stancombe kept texting, emailing, doing sums on his palm top, leaping out of his seat to telephone or receive calls, leaving his mountain of caviar untouched.

'We could do it one evening over dinner,' urged Sheena.

But Stancombe was checking his messages. 'Bear with me a minute, Sheen,' and he shot into the hall again. Through the doorway, he could be heard saying, 'Sure, sure, great, great, call you later.' Switching off his mobile, he punched the air. 'Yeah!'

'Good news?' enquired Sally as he slid back into his seat.

'Just secured a plot of land in Colorado, Sal, a ski resort to be exact.'

Janna caught Jupiter's eye and just managed not to laugh.

Gillian Grimston, who'd been subjected to Stancombe's back, was not used to being ignored. 'Where is this resort?' she asked.

'I'm not at liberty to reveal as yet, Gilly.' Stancombe flashed his teeth. 'In fact, bear with me again, Sal and Henge, if I make another call,' and he retreated again.

'That's how he keeps his figure,' said Piers.

Sheena, much to Sally's disapproval, had whipped out and was muttering into a tape recorder.

'How did you get started?' she asked when Stancombe returned.

'As a barrow boy. One of my customer's husbands gave me a job as an office boy in a property company. Kept my ear to the ground. Gave the CEO hot tips until he promoted me to head of the agency division. Two years later I took away all my contacts and started Randal Stancombe Properties. Rest is history. According to the Rich List, in Central London alone we own eight hundred buildings let to blue-chip companies.'

Everyone was listening.

'Despite heavy borrowings at the last count the portfolio must be worth more than two billion.'

Mrs Walton was gazing across the table in wonder. That would sort out the school fees.

'How many million times a million is that?' hissed Janna. 'He should be on the stage.'

'Better on television,' hissed back Piers. 'You could turn him off.'

'To what do you attribute your success?' asked Sheena, who'd left the tape recorder running.

'Hard work, seven days and seven nights a week.'

Stancombe checked his messages again. It was his thin line of moustache, Janna decided, like an upside-down child's drawing of a bird in flight, which gave him a gigolo look.

'Don't you ever play?' purred Mrs Walton.

'According to Freud,' said Janna idly, 'work and love are the only things that matter.'

'And children.' Hanna smiled at Jupiter, thinking how she'd like to paint those white roses.

Stancombe glanced down at his abandoned coal heap of caviar, realizing everyone had finished.

'I've had sufficient. I OD'd on beluga in St Petersburg last week.'

'Christ, what a waste,' exploded Jupiter.

'Did you buy a resortski?' enquired Janna.

Sheena was well named, she decided; she had a sheen of desirability about her but was very opinionated. As conversation became general and moved on to the war, she kept regurgitating whole paragraphs from a piece she had written on American imperialism earlier in the week.

'Hell, isn't she?' muttered Piers.

As he moved on to William Morris on October: 'How can I ever have enough of life and love?' Janna had noticed a sweet little girl gathering up the blue glass plates. Then she realized it was Dora Belvedon, Jupiter's stepsister, who'd emerged from the weeping willow by the lake with Bianca Campbell-Black, the day Hengist had shown her over Bagley.

Now she was bringing sliced roast beef in a rich red wine sauce round on a silver salver.

'Hello, Dora, you'd better tell me what fork to use.'

Dora's mouth lifted at the corner.

'It's very good, I tried some in the kitchen. I hear you met my brother Dicky earlier. I do hope that poor dog recovers.'

Dora loved waiting for Hengist and Sally. If she lurked and kept quiet, guests often forgot she was there, and revealed lots of saleable gossip.

Stancombe for a start was utterly gross, but good copy, and there'd been a lot about Janna Curtis in the press recently. She didn't look pretty tonight with that schoolmarmish hair and shapeless white smock. Mrs Walton, on the other hand, was gorgeous. Stancombe clearly thought so, which might make a story: Dora bustled back to the kitchen, and taking a pad out of her coat pocket wrote 'Randy Randal' and vowed to ring the papers tomorrow.

20

The beef and the creamy swede purée were so utterly delicious, Janna, Sheena and Mrs Walton all simultaneously vowed to take more trouble.

'Thomas Hood's also brilliant on autumn,' Piers was saying.

'You mustn't monopolize Janna,' Sally called down the table.

'He wasn't, we've had a smashing time comparing notes,' protested Janna, who had deliberately concentrated on Piers because the man on her other side was shy-makingly attractive. Outwardly unruffled as a great lion dozing in the afternoon sun, he had a spellbinding voice: deep, lilting and very Welsh, a square, ruddy face, thick blond curly hair, and lazy navy-blue eyes which turned down at the corners.

'Welcome to Larkshire,' said Emlyn Davies as she turned towards him. 'How are you enjoying being a head?'

'Not as much as I'd hoped,' confessed Janna. 'I keep looking back wistfully to the times when my biggest worry was getting a class through GCSE.'

Encouraged by his genuine interest, she was soon telling him all about Larks.

'I made Paris and Feral mentors,' she said finally. 'I thought giving them some responsibility might make them more responsible. You know Feral?'

'Everyone knows Feral.'

'He and Paris are so gorgeous. All the girls are dying to be mentored by them, but Feral's never in school and Paris has his nose in a book and tells them to eff off.'

'Can you buttle, Emlyn?' asked Sally a shade imperiously, 'No one's got a drink at your end.'

'Feral's a dazzling footballer,' continued Janna when Emlyn

121

returned. 'If this bonding between us and Bagley takes off, would you keep an eye on him?'

'I teach rugby.'

'Feral could adjust, he's so fast and can do anything with a ball. If he felt he was achieving, he might come in more often. If Feral stays away, half the school does too and we'll never rise in the league tables.'

Emlyn put a huge hand over hers. 'League tables are shit, so many heads fiddle them. Schools like St Jimmy's and Searston Abbey don't improve: they just reject low achievers. Why should anyone want difficult children if they push you to the bottom?

'When you think of the disadvantages with which your kids from the Shakespeare Estate start, it's as much a miracle to get five per cent of them through as it is for us and St Jimmy's and Gillian to clock up ninety per cent. League tables are about humiliation, delving into laundry baskets and washing dirty linen in public.'

Janna was delighted by the rage in his voice.

'How does an independent teacher understand these things?'

'I taught in comprehensives for nearly nine years.'

'How could you have switched over?' cried Janna in outrage.

'A number of reasons. I like teaching history and the national curriculum's so prohibitive. Nor do I like being bossed around by the Council of Europe. I also like teaching rugby. Bagley was unbeaten last season. Gives you a buzz. I like the salary I get. I adore Hengist and I'm very idle. Here, I get plenty of time to play golf and fool around – "displacement activity" our deputy head Alex Bruce calls it.' He smiled lazily down at her.

'Most Welshmen are small, dark and handsome,' he added, patting his beer gut. 'I'm fair, fat and funny.'

Not handsome, decided Janna, but decidedly attractive.

She hoped he'd ask her out. As if reading her thoughts, he said, 'You must come out with us one evening. We drink at the Rat and Groom. If you're going to be coming to Bagley a lot, someone ought to give you a minibus.'

'I'm not very good at getting sponsorship,' sighed Janna, remembering Mr Tyler who'd looked like a parsnip. 'I get bogged down by administration.' She took a slug of red. 'I'm even wearing my admini skirt.'

Then she noticed the red and white hairs on the black wool, gave a sob, and told Emlyn all about the poor little dog.

'I'm going to call in on the way home. Oh dear.' As she wiped her eyes, smudging Sally's mascara, her elbow slid off the table.

'I'll drive you, I haven't drunk much,' said Emlyn, adding, with a slight edge to his voice, 'Don't want to screw up in front of the boss and his wife.'

'How *kind* of you,' cried Janna, hoping Emlyn might stop her thinking so much of Hengist.

'Can I come too and see this dog?' asked Dora, who was hovering with second helpings. 'Have some more potatoes, Mr Davies, keep up your strength. We had a Labrador called Visitor,' she told Janna, 'who adored fireworks, saw them as coloured shooting. He used to sit barking at them, encouraging them on.'

'Get on, Dora,' ordered Hengist, 'and you move on too, Emlyn, I want to sit next to Janna.'

All the men moved on two places, which meant Randal ended up on Janna's right and, to his delight, on Mrs Walton's left.

Hengist was shocked how wan Janna looked. He didn't tell her about the uproar there had been from Bagley parents reluctant to have Larks tearaways let loose among their darlings.

'How are your hands?'

'Numbed by booze and painkillers. I'm having a lovely time tonight, sorry I snapped at you earlier.'

'It was fear biting.'

'Everything's been getting on top of me.'

Except a good man, thought Hengist. Then he said, 'There's a dinner at the Winter Gardens – tomorrow week – to plan Larkminster's Jubilee celebrations. All the local bigwigs'll be there. Sally can't make it. Come with me; I've got to speak so I can officially announce the twinning of Larks and Bagley.'

'How lovely. Sure I won't lower the tone?'

'Don't be silly. That's a date then. How did you like Emlyn?'

'Wonderful.'

'He is. We didn't lose a match on the South African tour; the boys had a ball but never overstepped the mark. They call him Attila the Hunk. A lot of people raised eyebrows when I tried to make him a housemaster, but the boys adore him and so do the parents. Sadly he refused – said the rugger teams give him enough hassle. You know he played rugger for Wales?'

'Goodness,' said Janna.

'He used to be very chippy, but with success the chips go.'

'Am I chippy?'

'Very, that's why I want to ensure you're wildly successful.' And he smiled with such affection, Janna had to smile back.

'Oh dear, dear,' Piers muttered to Sheena. 'Little Miss Curtis is going to get hurt.'

'What d'you think of Stancombe?' Hengist had lowered his voice.

'Challenging,' said Janna.

'And deeply silly. Parents have to kill to get into one's school; once in, men like Stancombe compete to build science blocks, sports pavilions.'

'And an indoor riding school,' said Dora, putting out pudding plates.

Hengist laughed and patted her arm. 'Dora keeps me young.'

Stancombe had moved on to art. 'I'm a big art person, Ruth. I frequently make large donations to the Tate; they're talking of naming a staircase after me.'

'I'll slide down your banister any time,' murmured Mrs Walton.

'How about making a generous donation to Larkminster Comp?' asked Emlyn idly. 'And give them a minibus.'

'Oh, hush,' said Janna, blushes surging up her freckles.

'What a good idea.' Mrs Walton smiled. 'Then they could name the bus after you.'

'Even a second-hand one,' suggested Hengist. 'If Larks is bonding with Bagley, they'll need transport.'

'I'll think about it.'

'Oh, go on, Randal,' cooed Mrs Walton.

Stancombe was trapped. A muscle was rippling his bronzed cheek, but he was so anxious to impress her.

'Right, you're on, Jan.'

'Oh, thank you,' gasped Janna. 'Thank you so much.'

'Make a note of it, so you don't forget,' insisted Mrs Walton.

'Larks minibus,' wrote Stancombe on his palmtop, then looked across at Mrs Walton, the hunter setting the deer in his sights. 'You owe me,' he mouthed.

'I hope he won't pull out of this science block,' whispered Hengist. 'Alex Bruce insists it'll look good on the prospectus, but oh dear me, builders in hard hats here for over a year and a sea of mud. I'll probably have to take Stancombe's dunderhead son as a quid pro quo, but I'm not having him on my board. And if he wants to get into Boodle's, he'll have to buy the building.'

'Why are you so ungrateful?' asked a shocked Janna.

'At heart, I don't trust him.'

A vibration in Stancombe's trouser pocket signalled an incoming call. Fascinated by Stancombe's mobile, the very latest model, which could actually take pictures and even flashed up on the screen a little photograph of who was calling, Dora shimmied forward to offer Stancombe more wine. Then she nearly dropped the bottle as a disgusting photo of a naked blonde with her legs apart indicated one of Stancombe's girlfriends was on the line. Stancombe hastily killed the call, and started taking photographs of everyone at the table, which gave him the excuse to immortalize Mrs Walton.

All the same, thought Dora, it was a wonderful invention and would hugely help her journalistic investigations to have a little camera inside her mobile. What a good thing too that revolting Stancombe was off his grub. His untouched beef would make a terrific doggie bag for Cadbury, who didn't like caviar.

'My daughter Jade is in a relationship with Cosmo Rannaldini, Dame Hermione Harefield's son,' Stancombe was proudly telling Mrs Walton. 'Dame Hermione was very gracious when Jade went to visit. As Milly and Jade are good friends,' he continued, 'I hope you'll be able to make a long weekend skiing before Christmas.'

'I'm sure we could fit it in.' Mrs Walton's exquisite complexion flushed up so gently, Stancombe could just imagine her generous, sensual mouth round his cock.

'Come home with me tonight,' he whispered.

'I can't really, Sally's offered me a bed.'

'It's awfully kind of you to offer us a minibus,' Janna told him when he finally tore himself away to talk to her. 'I hope you haven't been compromised.'

'No way, I come from a poor family myself, Jan, seven of us in a tiny flat. Your kids deserve a leg-up.'

'I'm particularly grateful for Feral Jackson's sake . . .' began Janna.

Stancombe choked on his drink. He'd been so knocked sideways by Mrs Walton, he'd been manoeuvred, without realizing it, into benefiting his bête noire Feral Jackson, who rampaged through the Shakespeare Estate and nearby Cavendish Plaza terrifying tenants and, only this evening, chucking around lighted fireworks.

Twigging he wasn't exactly flavour of the month, Janna suggested Feral would behave much better if he had a focus in his life.

'It'd better not be my Jade,' snarled Stancombe.

'Rugger channels boys' aggression in an awfully positive way,' said Sally, scenting trouble.

Fortunately Stancombe was distracted by Dora. He liked her shrill little voice, her goucheness, untouched by masculine hand, her antagonism, her tiny breasts pushing through her blue dress, her figure which hadn't yet decided what it was going to do with itself. He wondered if she had any pubic hairs yet. He'd met Anthea, her mother, at Speech Day, a tiny, very pretty lady. Dora was larger than her mother already. That sort of thing made a

125

young girl feel lumpy and elephantine. Dora would benefit from a little attention.

Dora was serving white chocolate mousse with raspberry sauce when she noticed Stancombe's hand burrowing under Mrs Walton's green silk skirt and was so shocked she piled an Everest of mousse on to Mrs Walton's plate.

'Heavens, Dora,' cried Mrs Walton, tipping half of it on to Stancombe's plate, 'are you trying to fatten me up?'

Dora watched appalled as Stancombe removed his hand to spoon up his mousse, then shoved it back up Mrs Walton's skirt.

Marching furiously back to the kitchen, Dora made another note on the pad in her coat pocket, before returning with a brimming finger bowl, which she plonked in front of Stancombe. 'Like one of these?' she hissed.

Emlyn glanced over and roared with laughter. Everyone else was distracted by a querulous knock on the door.

One of Hengist's tricks for keeping people on the jump was to exclude from dinner parties those who felt they should have been invited. A case in point was his deputy head: Alex Bruce, a fussy-looking man with spectacles and a thin, dark beard which ran round his chin into his brushed back hair, edging his peevish face like an oval picture frame. He now came bustling in:

'A word please, Senior Team Leader.'

'It can't be that important.' Hengist patted a chair. 'Have a drink and sit down. You know everyone except Janna Curtis, the marvellous new head at Larks. Janna, this is Alex Bruce, the superpower behind the throne.'

Alex nodded coldly at her, and even more coldly at Mrs Walton, whose presence on the board, making things easy for Hengist and Jupiter, he bitterly resented.

This must be Hengist's cross, thought Janna, the man he feared was going to strangle him in red tape. He certainly looked cross now.

'Joan Johnson's just been on the phone,' Alex told Hengist. 'She caught Amber Lloyd-Foxe and Cosmo Rannaldini snorting cocaine. Dame Hermione was incommunicado when I tried to call, but I took the liberty of suspending Amber Lloyd-Foxe. When I phoned her mother, Jane, she complained it was the middle of the night – it's actually only eleven-thirty – and when I appraised her of the situation, she said: "How lovely, Amber can come to the Seychelles with us." I don't believe Jane Lloyd-Foxe was entirely sober; anyway she refused to drive over and collect Amber.'

Typical, uncaring, public-school parent, thought Janna disapprovingly.

'I'm afraid I hit the roof, Senior Team Leader,' went on Alex.

Cosmo Rannaldini up to no good with Amber Lloyd-Foxe? Randal was also looking furious: was his precious Jade being cheated on?

'Shall we go upstairs?' said Sally, glancing round at the women.

Do they still keep up that ritual? thought Janna, outraged to be dragged away, particularly when she heard Alex recommending exclusion, and Hengist replying in horror that Cosmo was an Oxbridge cert.

21

Upstairs, Sally drew Janna aside on to the blue rose-patterned window seat. 'My dear, it's so nice you're here. Jolly tough assignment, Larks, but I'm sure you'll crack it. You will come to me if I can be of any help?'

Advise me how not to fancy your husband, thought Janna.

'I'm so glad you got on with Emlyn,' went on Sally. 'You must go to the cinema with him and some of the other young masters. I'm awfully fond of naughty little Piers. And you must meet our daughter.' Sally pointed to a photograph in a silver frame on the dressing table.

'Oriana Taylor,' gasped Janna. 'My God! But she's an icon. So brave and so brilliant during September the eleventh and the war in Afghanistan. Hengist never said she was her. I didn't realize. I'd die to meet her, and so would our kids.'

'We must arrange something next time she's home. Oriana is rather left-wing,' confessed Sally. 'Bit of a trial for her father. Having profited from a first-rate education, she now thinks we're horribly elitist.' Sally smiled. 'I expect you do too. She gets into dreadful arguments with Hengist.'

'Does she live in New York full time?' asked Janna.

Sally nodded: 'We had a son; he died.' Oh, the sadness of those flat monosyllables. Sally pointed to a photograph of a beautiful blond boy with Hengist's dark eyes. 'So Hengist misses her dreadfully.'

'I'm so terribly sorry,' mumbled Janna.

'I know you are,' said Sally. 'I'm just nipping downstairs to organize drinks and coffee and pay Dora.'

After that, Janna sat on Sally's four-poster and talked to Mrs Walton, who was really a joy to look at and to smell –

great wafts of scent rising like incense from her body.

'Emlyn's very attractive, isn't he?'

'Extremely, but sadly spoken for.'

'He is?' asked Janna in disappointment.

'He's going to marry Hengist's daughter Oriana.'

'A shrewd career move – lucky Oriana.'

'Lucky indeed. Emlyn's so bats about her he agreed to wait until she'd tried being a foreign correspondent. Alas, she's been so good at it, she seems to have lost any desire to settle down.'

'Oh, poor Emlyn.'

'Sally isn't that displeased by the turn of events; she doesn't think Emlyn's quite good enough,' confided Mrs Walton as she repainted her lips a luscious coral. 'Despite his amiability, he's very left-wing. Hates the Tories, hates the royal family, and hates rich spoilt children. He didn't get a first either, although he's a wonderful teacher. Hengist dotes on him. They have rugger in common, but Sally feels that macho Welsh rugger bugger tradition isn't for Oriana – she needs someone more subtle and better bred. Sally tries not to show it because she's such a gent,' went on Mrs Walton, 'but she also feels Oriana isn't bats enough about Emlyn. I mean, if you had a hunk like that, would you base yourself in New York pursuing all those terrifying assignments?'

Sally wants me to go to the cinema with Emlyn because she knows I fancy Hengist rotten, decided Janna, and if I get off with Emlyn it will free Oriana and get me out of Hengist's hair.

Suddenly, she felt very tired. 'I must go.'

'Let's have lunch,' said Mrs Walton.

'I can't really get away.'

'Well, come to supper then.'

'I'd like that.'

'I'll ring you at Larks.'

At that moment Mrs Walton's mobile rang. It was Stancombe from downstairs.

'I'll call you,' she mouthed at Janna.

How can I ever have enough of love and life, thought Janna as she put on her dreary green cardigan.

Downstairs, she found Jupiter talking to Hengist, who had lucky Elaine stretched out on the sofa beside him with her head in his lap.

Sheena, having dispatched Rufus home to relieve the baby-sitter, was arguing with Piers and waiting to get a lift from Stancombe who was still on his mobile.

Then Janna started to laugh.

'All part of our caring ethos,' Gillian Grimston was droning on to Emlyn, who had fallen asleep in an armchair.

'Caring Ethos,' mused Hengist. 'Sounds like a fifth Musketeer, the priggish older brother of Athos or Porthos. Caring Ethos.' He smiled at Janna, gently setting aside Elaine's head so he could get up. 'Have a drink.'

'I'm off,' she said, 'I'll drive very slowly.'

'You will not, you've had a horrid shock. Emlyn is going to take you,' said Sally firmly.

As they left, Hengist imitated the Family Tree, standing big, strong and dark behind Sally's fairness, his arms wrapped around her: we are an item.

'Will you be home tomorrow afternoon?' he asked Janna. 'I'll drive your car back, and we can discuss where we go from here – put Saturday night in your diary.'

Everything out in the open, so unlike Stew, thought an utterly confused Janna.

'I'd like a word, Sheena,' said Sally as she closed the front door.

Trees brandished their remaining leaves in the wind like tattered orange and yellow banners. Janna tried to quiz Emlyn about Hengist and Sally but, guilty he'd spent half-term and so much money in New York with Oriana rather than with his mother and sick father in Wales, he was uncommunicative.

He didn't say much but he was sweet to make a long detour into Larkminster via the Animal Hospital. The little dog hadn't come round from the anaesthetic, said the nurse, but should pull through. They had saved the eye but probably not the tail. He'd need to spend a few days in hospital.

'And then I'll come and collect him,' said Janna.

I'm going to call him Partner, she decided, then if anyone asks me if I've got a partner, I can say yes.

Most of the Sundays carried lurid accounts of Amber Lloyd-Foxe and Cosmo Rannaldini being suspended for drugs, and everyone blamed the leak on Sheena Anderson.

22

Janna knew that if confronted Monster and Satan would deny torturing Partner. Instead she decided to unnerve them by relating the incident in detail at assembly the following Monday.

'Animals feel pain just as we do. They're more frightened because they have no idea why such evil things are happening.' Her voice broke: 'Partner was such a trusting little dog.'

'Bastards,' spat Pearl.

'Murderers,' sobbed Kylie Rose.

'The bad news is that it was so dark I'm not sure which Larks pupils were involved but the good news is I rang the hospital this morning and despite his horrific burns Partner's getting better all the time. He may still lose his tail but when he comes out of hospital he's moving in with me.'

Cheers from the children.

'I'm going to bring him into school because I know you'll love him and I'm sure he'll recognize the evil bullies who tortured him and we can report them to the police and RSPCA.'

Five minutes after assembly, Rowan gleefully reported that Satan and Monster had been seen belting down Smokers' and over the wall.

'One pair I don't mind truanting,' said Janna.

Feral, on the other hand, was another matter. Each day he missed he slipped further behind. There was no point setting up minibuses, pitches and running tracks if he wasn't there to profit from them.

Paris and Graffi went vague when questioned so Janna dropped a line to Feral's mother asking if she might pop in to discuss her son on the way to Hengist's civic dinner. At least it would give her a chance to check out the dreaded Shakespeare Estate.

Outside she could see shrivelled pale brown leaves tumbling out of the playground sycamores and imagined them falling from Hengist's Family Tree revealing the interlocked incestuous grapplings to the white sky.

She tried not to get excited about Saturday's dinner, for hope would be hope of the wrong thing. At least it would be a change from paperwork and she could finally give her slinky new off-the-shoulder dress an airing. The night before she rubbed lots of scented body lotion into the shoulder that was going to be exposed before falling into a rare and blissful eight-hour sleep.

Waking with optimism, she popped into the hospital to take Partner a bowl of chopped chicken. Still heavily sedated, he greeted her with barks of joy and shrieks of pain as he wagged his poor burnt tail. He really was a sweet little dog, with one ear pointing skywards, a freckled fox's face, a pink nose, sad chestnut-brown eyes, short legs and a rough red and white coat.

'We'll be two short-arsed, mouthy redheads living together,' she told him, 'and exploring the country instead of working all weekend.'

Having measured his neck size and promised she'd fetch him home tomorrow, she spent a fortune in Larkminster's pet shop on a sky-blue collar and lead, a name disk, dog food, pig's ears, a blue ball and a blue quilted basket decorated with moons and suns.

Out in the street, rustling through shoals of red and gold cherry leaves, her happiness evaporated as she caught sight of a *Gazette* poster: 'Is Janna Curtis turning her back on failing Larks?'

Buying a paper, she found a smiling photograph of herself, Hengist and Jupiter at the prospective-parents' day on page three. Accompanying it was a snide story saying she was being wooed by the independent sector and had recently dined with the Brett-Taylors, Jupiter Belvedon, his wife and property tycoon Randal Stancombe. How much longer would she bother with a bog-standard school she had failed to improve?

With a scream of rage, Janna scrunched up the paper, sending three pigeons fluttering up into the rooftops. Why in hell hadn't the piece mentioned Gillian Grimston had been at dinner too?

Larks was always left open on Saturdays for the rare members of staff who might want to catch up or prepare lessons. Fortunately no one seemed to be around when Janna arrived so she would have time to prepare a denial. But as she walked down the corridors, rejoicing in the colour and vitality of the children's work on the walls – Larks was *not* failing – she heard crashes and screams coming from her office and broke into a run.

She was greeted by devastation as a hysterical Pearl, who'd already pulled the books out of the shelves and thrown every file on the carpet with Janna's in-tray scattered on top, was now upending desk drawers.

Her spiky rhubarb-red hair was coaxed upwards like an angry rooster, her coloured make-up was streaked by tears and studs quivered like the Pleiades on her frantically working face.

'Bitch, cunt, slag!' she howled, catching sight of Janna. 'I know you've got the 'ots for Feral, you 'orrible slag, wiv your cosy little tea parties.'

She ripped Janna's date calendar off the wall: pointing a frantically trembling finger at 3 November: '"Feral's mother seven p.m." You never bothered visiting my mum.' She started tearing the calendar to pieces.

'Stop it.' Janna tried to stay calm. 'Steady down. Whatever's brought this on?'

But a screaming Pearl had started on the pictures. Crash went *Hold the Dream* and *Desiderata* over the back of a chair, followed by the big photographs of Fountains Abbey and the Brontës' house at Haworth.

'For God's sake, you'll get glass in your eyes,' pleaded Janna, wondering the best way to grab her.

Crash, sending out another fountain of splintered glass, went Stew's photograph of all the children at Redfords.

Pearl then hurled Janna's Diorissimo against the window smashing both with a sickening crunch, followed by a bottle of ink against the white wall which spilt down over the flower-patterned sofa. Then she picked up Stew's little Staffordshire cow.

'Oh please, no,' gasped Janna.

'You sad bitch!'

Crash went the cow, hitting the fridge and fragmenting into a hundred pieces. Pearl, like a cornered cat now, rather than a furious rooster, was clawing, screaming, spitting. Slowly, slowly Janna talked her down.

'Please tell me what's the matter. I'm not cross, I'm here for you,' until Pearl collapsed sobbing on the ink-stained sofa.

'Thought you liked us, miss, but the paper says you're leaving us for those stuck-up snobs.'

A tidal wave of relief swept over Janna.

'Then they'll have to carry me out in a coffin. I love you at Larks. You're my children and I'm going to take a big photograph of you all and put that on the wall.'

Sally and Hengist, she explained, had kindly invited her to

dinner to meet other teachers and people who might help Larks.

'So we can buy more textbooks and go on more jaunts and invest in some fun, young, new teachers. I'd rather live in a cage full of cobras than teach in an independent school.'

'What about the cow?' sniffed Pearl, picking up a fragment of horn from the carpet. 'Was that precious?'

'Not any more,' said Janna, realizing it was part of a past that had gone away. 'And the only reason I haven't asked you over to the cottage is because of your Saturday job, and I'm not sure how you'd cope with the walk in those heels. The boys are coming tomorrow afternoon instead to meet my new dog. Please come too, and be very gentle with him, boys can be a bit rough. Look at what I bought him at the pet shop.' She opened the carrier bags she'd left in the corridor. 'And let's have a coffee and a chocolate biscuit.'

Later, as, chattering, they made an effort to straighten the room, Pearl noticed the invitation to the civic dinner which Hengist had posted to Janna.

'That's tonight. "Jubilee Dinner". Looks a posh do. I hope we can have a street party. My mum's always going on about how great they was in seventy-seven. Look, to make up for this' – Pearl waved a blue-nailed hand round the devastation – 'I'll make you up for tonight, do your hair, give you a make-over, like. It'd be really cool. Then I could photograph you, put it on the wall like Graffi's pictures and Paris's stories and fucking goody-two-shoes Aysha's chemistry project.' Pearl was suddenly wildly excited. 'I'll find you a dress too.'

'That would be champion,' said Janna. Anything not to shatter this rapprochement. 'Let's meet at five-thirty.'

'Make it earlier,' said Pearl, suddenly authoritive. 'I did the morning stint at the salon. That's where I read the *Gazette*. I need time to do it proper. You go home and have a nice bath. I'll meet you back here at four.'

When Janna dutifully returned, Pearl refused to work her magic in front of a mirror.

'It stresses me to be watched.'

So Janna tugged her desk chair into the middle of the office and got stuck into planning the next human resources meeting, which would cover staffing.

She was sure Ashton Douglas and Crispin would demand redundancies or her budget would never balance. But with any luck the dinosaurs like Mike Pitts, Basket, Skunk, even Cara Sharpe might consider early retirement.

'She's an evil bitch, that Cara.' Pearl peered over Janna's shoulder as she cut her hair.

'If I'm not allowed to look, neither are you,' reproved Janna, 'and not too much off.'

'My mum always says that. I'm going to lift the colour with a few highlights.'

'Not too tarty,' pleaded Janna, 'I'm trying to be an authority figure,' then cautiously enquired about the Shakespeare Estate.

Pearl shrugged. 'Council uses the place as a bin bag to dump all the bad families. Most of the dads are in the nick like mine or on nights and never see their kids.'

Finally, having washed Janna's hair in the Ladies, blow-dried it and made her up from a range of colour that would have been the envy of Titian, Pearl sprayed gold dust on her shoulders. Then, dismissing the black off-the-shoulder number Janna had brought in as too mumsy, she helped Janna into an incredibly short fern-green handkerchief dress which gave her a cleavage worthy of Mrs Walton.

'You look wicked, miss.' Pearl held up Janna's hand mirror, about the only thing unsmashed. 'Now you can look.'

Janna didn't recognize herself. Even under the office strip lighting she looked absolutely gorgeous.

'That can't be me. I look like a film star.'

'Good material to work on,' conceded Pearl.

She had covered Janna's face in light-reflecting moisturizer, then put shimmering highlights on her cheekbones, and narrowed and rounded Janna's squarish chin with blusher, before blending in sparkling powder.

To make the eyes huge and vulnerable she had drawn black along the upper lash line, mingled all the golds, oranges and russets on the lids, then thickened the lashes with three layers of brown mascara.

Most seductive of all, on Janna's big mouth, instead of pale pinky coral, she had used a deep plum red gloss.

'Weeee-ee.' Janna shook her head, swinging rippling cascades of rose red, emerald green and chestnut hair. 'Which flag of the world am I? You're a genius.'

'You look amazing, miss,' said Pearl happily. 'Go out and pull.'

'Where did you find all this incredible make-up?' asked Janna, suspecting it had been knocked off.

'They often pay me in make-up at the salon,' said Pearl airily.

Janna was far too kind to put Pearl down by saying the whole thing was completely OTT and was vastly relieved when Pearl wrapped a long, tasselled flamingo-pink shawl round her shoulders.

'This is lovely and the dress too.'

'My mum's,' said Pearl hastily.

'Won't she mind?'

'Doesn't know – it's my babysitting fee.'

It was only when she was driving to the Winter Gardens, praying none of the big shop owners would recognize their stolen wares on her that Janna remembered she'd promised to pop in on Feral's mother at 12 Macbeth Street. She'd been crazy to pick this weekend. It was like entering a war zone, as coloured stars exploded in dandelion clocks and rockets hissed into the russet Larkminster sky, crashing and banging to a counterpoint of jangling fire engines and screaming police sirens.

How could the people of Afghanistan cope with incessant American bombing – or was she twice as scared because she'd had a baptism of fireworks with Partner a week ago?

The Shakespeare Estate was a concrete hell, hemmed in by a high circular wall, which separated it from the beautiful, prosperous golden town, the serenely winding river and the lush countryside beyond. Cul-de-sacs named after Shakespearean characters ran like spokes in a wheel from this circular wall into a bald piece of land, known as the Romeo Triangle, which had a much graffitied pub, broken seats and a boarded-up newsagent's. Gangs of youths in hoods with sliding walks prowled the streets chucking stones or bangers at Janna's green Polo as she drove past. Rasta and R and B music fortissimo, blaring televisions, couples having violent domestics were interrupted by the screams of prostitutes. Fireworks lit up the crazed emaciated faces of Ixions chained to the wheels of their addictions.

'Never get out of your car and walk,' Pearl had warned.

But there was no space outside number 12, so Janna was forced to park fifty yards away and totter up Macbeth Street on her high heels. All the windows of number 12 were broken or boarded-up. The front garden contained stinking, unemptied dustbins, an old fridge and a burnt-out BMW. No one answered the door, the paint of which was blistered and dented with kicks. Youths, gathering on the pavement, were hurling fireworks into next door's garden. A curtain flickered and Janna caught a glimpse of a terrified old man.

Although number 12 was in darkness, she could hear a ghetto blaster. Perhaps Feral was hiding upstairs. Ducking in terror as a rocket hissed past her head, she ran back down the garden path slap into a very large black man. He had a shaved head and was wearing black leather, a large diamond necklace, ear studs and lots of aftershave, which mercifully blotted out the stench of dustbins.

'What yer doing?' a bass voice with a soft Jamaican accent rumbled menacingly up from his chest.

'Looking for Feral Jackson.'

The big guy gave Janna, as made over by Pearl, the once-over and made an understandable mistake. 'Bit long in the tooth for him.'

'I actually have an appointment with his mother.'

'Pull the other leg – and get off my territory if you don't want your pretty face rearranged.'

Janna winced as he yanked her head upwards and flicked on his lighter. 'On second thoughts I'll forget it if you show me a good time.'

'I beg your pardon?'

'I won't cut you up' – he threatened her eyelashes with his lighter – 'if you give me a fuck.'

Whereupon Janna rose in outrage to her five feet one inch plus four-inch heels. 'How *dare* you. I am Feral's head teacher.'

The big guy looked initially flabbergasted then became very, very cosy and introduced himself as Feral's Uncle Harley.

'And you don't look like an 'ead teacher, little darling.'

'Feral hasn't been in school for three weeks.' Janna tried to steady her trembling legs. 'I'd like to see Mrs Jackson.'

'She's not in; family's gone to the pitchers to see *Shrek.*'

'I just want someone to get him up in the morning and see he does his homework.'

'Look no further,' murmured Uncle Harley.

As he walked her back to her car, approaching gangs of youths retreated like smoke. A prostitute stopped screaming at Janna and slid away like a snake.

'Feral's such a wonderful athlete,' urged Janna. 'A group of Larks children have been invited over to Bagley Hall so he'll get an opportunity to play football on decent pitches and try out their running tracks.'

'He's a lucky young man.' Uncle Harley grew even cosier. 'You got time for a drink?'

'I should be at the Winter Gardens already.'

'Sorry I mistook you.' Uncle Harley took her keys to open the car door, then, adding with massive irony, 'Not safe round here for a nice young lady,' he kissed her hand.

'I hope to see you at one of our parents' evenings.'

'Try and keep me away.'

23

Still shaking with hysterical laughter, Janna reached the Winter Gardens. The dinner was held in a side hall, whose high ceiling was covered with nudging, pinching cherubs reminiscent of the playground at Larks. In one half of the room, tables were laid for dinner and speeches. In the other, because a Lib Dem/Lab hung council had no intention of squandering ratepayers' money, indifferent red or white was being offered to a crowd of bigwigs.

Hengist had not yet arrived, but Pearl's make-over was soon having a dramatic effect. The Mayor, wearing a chain Uncle Harley would have killed for, blamed the Winter Gardens' poor acoustics for the fact he had to bend right over Janna's boobs to hear what she said.

Next minute, parsnip-faced Mr Tyler rushed up with two friends and was just apologizing for his rudeness the week before last when Stancombe appeared by her side, looking sleek and glamorous in a dinner jacket and far more relaxed than he'd been at Sally and Hengist's. 'I can't handle teachers, Jan; so patronizing, do my head in. Don't count you as one; not tonight, particularly. You look very tasty.'

He got out his mobile, took a picture of her and texted it to one of his friends, showing her the message: 'How lucky am I to be invited to functions with ladies like this?' Then, to show off further to Tyler and the Mayor: 'The minibus will be with you by a.m. Wednesday, what colour d'you fancy?'

'The coolest colour, please.' Janna accepted a top-up of white. 'You are kind, it will give our children such street cred.'

'I'm donating a minibus to Larks,' boasted Stancombe to the others, 'so Jan can transport her kids to matches and things.'

'I'll send in the boys to sort out your computers,' countered Tyler.

'I'll pick up the bill for any sports kit,' said one of his friends.

'That would be fantastic,' beamed Janna.

Thank you, Pearl, she thought, sidling away as the Mayor pinched her bottom. She'd never had such an effect on men. Tyler and his mates were clearly irked by the way Stancombe muscled in, but they all deferred to him.

Then Hengist swanned in, instantly stealing Stancombe's thunder: 'Darling, sorry I'm late. Christ, you look amazing.' He kissed her on both shimmering cheeks. 'What have you done?'

'Pearl gave me a make-over.'

'We'll make her head of make-up when we do our joint Larks–Bagley play.' He took a gulp of red and nearly spat it out.

'Christ, that's disgusting.' He waved to a waiter who scuttled over. 'Can you get me a bottle of Sancerre and a large whisky and soda, no ice, and take this arsenic away.' He handed the boy his and Janna's glasses.

'It can't be that bad, Hengist,' grumbled the Mayor.

'It's much worse,' said Hengist, putting an arm round Janna's shoulders. 'Jesus,' he added as the flamingo-pink shawl fell away.

'I'm having a Mrs Walton moment,' giggled Janna.

Hengist couldn't stop laughing.

'I can't work out if you look ten years older or younger than the little teenager you normally resemble. Come and meet everyone important. Oh dear, here come Super Bugger and Sancho Pansy from S and C,' as Ashton and Crispin paused to have their picture taken by the *Gazette*.

Crispin had put on more weight and with his petulant baby face he looked like the bullying older brother of the cherubs rampaging over the ceiling. Ashton's bland pink and white face had been given more definition by a dinner jacket and a black tie but his thinly lashed eyes were as cold green as a frozen fjord. Waiting until Hengist had been distracted by some Tory councillor, he and Crispin cornered Janna.

'You look very Chwistmassy.' Ashton examined her hair. 'Does it wash out?'

'Yes, but I don't.'

'The *Gazette* says you're joining Bagley,' snuffled Crispin.

'When did that rag ever tell the truth? Gillian Grimston was at the same dinner party. Sally invited me to meet some locals, which is more than Mike Pitts, Rod or either of you have ever done.'

'And how's the Bagley bonding going?' asked Ashton.

'Starts next week.'

'Doesn't it threaten your left-wing pwinciples to accept largesse from an independent?'

'Beggars can't be choosers. My children have been let down too often.' Janna's voice rose: 'And it's not as if you're giving us any money.'

Ashton put his head on one side. 'You should weally take a course in anger management.'

'Doesn't she look gorgeous?' It was Hengist back, waving a bottle of Sancerre, topping up Janna's glass. 'Pearl Smith did her hair and make-up. I think we've got another Barbara Daly on our hands. You should let her have a go at you, Ashton, next time you've got an important date,' he added insolently.

'I'm from the *Western Daily Press*, Miss Curtis,' announced a hovering photographer. 'Can I get a picture of your new look? I'll take care of your shawl,' he added whisking it away and arranging her next to a marble vestal virgin with downcast eyes.

'Sacred and profane love,' murmured Hengist. 'I know which I prefer.'

'Can we have you in the photograph too, Mr B-T?' said a second photographer. 'I'm from *Cotswold Life*.'

Ashton and Crispin were hopping. So was Rod Hyde. How dare Janna look so desirable! She deserved a good spanking. Rod had rolled up with Alex Bruce and, like Alex, had rejected the right-wing regalia of a dinner jacket. Gillian Grimston immediately sat down beside them.

'As the leading professional at the Brett-Taylors' dinner party,' she said indignantly, 'why didn't the *Gazette* mention I was there?'

Why wasn't I asked in the first place? thought Alex and Rod darkly and simultaneously.

'Who's that toad-like man with bulging eyes who's just waddled in?' Janna whispered to Hengist.

'Colin "Col" Peters. Editor of the *Gazette*, failed Fleet Street, now enjoying being a big toad in a small pool.'

Janna downed her third glass of wine. 'I'm going to kill him.'

'Not tonight you're not,' said Hengist firmly.

'And the smiley-faced woman in the red trouser suit talking to him looks familiar.'

'That's Cindy Payne, the Labour county councillor in charge of education, hand in glove with Ashton Douglas. Looks like a cosy agony aunt, but she's a snake in sheep's clothing.'

'Snakes eat toads. Col Peters better watch out.'

* * *

140

At dinner Janna found herself sitting next to a CID Chief Inspector with a square, reddish face softened by beautiful long-lashed green eyes, and was enchanted when he turned out to be the husband of her languages teacher, Mags Gablecross.

'Such a lovely woman. If only she worked full time.'

'She says you're working wonders and the kids adore you.'

'I wish the teachers felt the same. They're so terrified of Cara Sharpe.'

'Get her out,' advised Chief Inspector Gablecross. 'She's bad news.'

After a good bitch about Cara, Janna told the Chief Inspector about her encounter with Uncle Harley, which really shocked him.

'Don't ever go near the Shakespeare Estate alone again. Harley's really dangerous and hell-bent on taking the drug trade to new markets all over the West Country.'

Janna drew in her breath. 'Oh dear.'

Across the room she saw Stancombe getting up, making apologies to his table and waving to Janna on the way out.

'See you Wednesday morning, Jan. Give the garage a spring clean.'

'Stancombe's got his eyes on the Shakespeare Estate,' observed the Chief Inspector. 'Always the same procedure. He vows he's going to build cheap houses for first-time buyers – teachers and nurses – then he razes the place to the ground and, like mushrooms, desirable residences spring up.'

He looked down in disgust at his first course of roast vegetables. 'You used to be able to turn down these things with your main course. Now they're everywhere.' He patted his gut.

Janna, who hadn't eaten all day, was tucking in.

'I was worried Stancombe might be after Larks – all those acres of lovely land,' she admitted, 'but I misjudged him, he's just given us a minibus.'

'*Timeo Danaos*,' warned the Chief Inspector.

'Will you come and talk to my kids?' asked Janna.

On Janna's left was a trendy estate agent called Desmond Reynolds, nicknamed 'Des Res', because he found so many middle-class parents desirable residences in the catchment areas of St Jimmy's and Searston Abbey.

He had little chin, talked through clenched teeth and, having discovered she came from West Yorkshire and didn't know the Lane-Foxes or the Horton-Fawkeses, lost interest.

'Five per cent of the properties I sell each year are driven by parents' desire for a better school. Stands to reason,' he went on languidly. 'Pay three hundred thousand for a house in the catchment area of St Jimmy's. In seven years you've not only saved at least a hundred and forty K per child you would have spent on Bagley school fees, but also your house will have trebled in value because you're in the catchment area of such a cracking good school.'

'Why's St Jimmy's so good?' Sulkily, Janna speared a roast potato.

'Because Rod Hyde's a cracking good head.'

'Do your children go there?'

'No, Eton.'

'I suppose people never want to buy houses in the catchment area of Larks?' asked Janna wistfully.

'Never,' said Des Res with a shudder. 'Beats me why Hengist's pairing up with them.'

Glancing round, Hengist caught the desolation on Janna's face and immediately swapped places with Des Res.

Janna took a huge gulp of wine and then a deep breath.

'Stancombe's promised the minibus for Wednesday morning.'

'Come over on Wednesday afternoon then.'

'How do I know your little toffs won't take the piss out of my kids?'

'Send the best-looking. The Wolf Pack are such celebs they'll get badgered for autographs.'

Hengist's flippancy enraged Janna but when she told him about her visit to the Shakespeare Estate he went white.

'Promise, promise never to go there again. Planes may not disappear from the Romeo Triangle but people do.'

'Uncle Harley promised to get Feral back into school.'

'Probably wants him to flog drugs to our "little toffs" when he visits Bagley.'

'Oh God, I hope not.' Then, stammering and angry: 'Desmond Reynolds said he couldn't think why you were wasting your time on Larks.'

'Ah.' Hengist forked up one of her potatoes, 'Because I believe in improving the state system. When I'm old, I want well-educated, positive, happy young adults running this country.' He smiled. 'Or it could be that I fancy you rotten.'

Janna's blush came through Pearl's war paint.

'Stop taking the piss.'

'And because you remind me of Oriana.'

'She's wonderful.'

'And terribly tricky. If only she'd take a nice job with the BBC in Bristol instead of being addicted to trouble spots.'

142

'I'm amazed she can tear herself away from the Shakespeare Estate.'

Hengist laughed. Then, as waitresses stormed on with strawberry pavlova: 'I'd better get back to my seat.'

Against the colourful banners of the Boys' Brigade, the Rotary Club, the Parish Council and the Honorary Corps of Elephants and Buffaloes, the chairman of the county council made a colourless speech laboriously outlining Larkminster's plans for the Jubilee.

He wasn't anticipating a visit from Her Majesty but there were plans for a Jubilee mug and the shops would be decorating their windows. No street parties were planned.

'My children would love a street party,' shouted a now drunk Janna and was shushed.

Noticing Ashton shaking his head and exchanging a pained, what-did-you-expect glance with Crispin and Rod, Hengist thought angrily: They're willing the poor child to screw up. More resolute than ever he rose to his feet.

Miss Painswick had typed out his speech in big print, so he didn't have to wear spectacles; a lock of black hair had fallen over his forehead. As he thanked the waitresses and waiters for all their hard work, they crept back into the dining room to hear him.

'The Queen has been on the throne for nigh on fifty years,' he said warmly, 'never put a foot wrong, and deserves to be celebrated. And, like myself,' he went on slightly mockingly, 'she believes there is no privilege without responsibility.

'We in the independent sector have always recognized there is no justification for our work if pupils grow up to use the benefits of their education only for their own advancement and profit. We at Bagley Hall have a tradition for community work: we go into hospitals, we give concerts in the cathedral, members of the public and other schools use our golf course and our park for cross-country running. We are also clearing ponds around Larkminster and carrying out conservation in the Malvern Hills.'

Then he launched into an attack.

'I appreciate many county councils and education authorities are actively opposed to private education. Larkshire's LEA, in the past, was too busy to answer our letters and ignored our offers of help. S and C Services have shown themselves equally pigheaded. So we approached Janna Curtis direct and to our relief found she puts her children at Larks before her prejudice.

'Larks has been described as a "head's graveyard",' went on

143

Hengist idly. 'One might almost believe S and C and Councillor Cindy Payne are frightened of Janna breaking the mould.'

'Preposterous. Nothing could be further from the truth,' spluttered Ashton.

'Good,' said Hengist smoothly. 'Just to let you know that Larks will be paying their first visit to Bagley on Wednesday.'

'Oh, goodness.' Janna clapped her hands in delight.

Col Peters was writing furiously.

'This has nothing to do with Janna Curtis or helping her students,' hissed Councillor Cindy Payne to Ashton, 'it's Hengist establishing himself as a dove. If Jupiter takes over the Tories, he'll find Hengist a quick seat and give him Education and God help us all.'

Glancing over to the enemy table, Janna noticed Alex Bruce quite unable to hide his jealousy. Hunched like an old monkey throughout Hengist's speech, he had mindlessly wolfed his way through an entire plateful of petits fours. A denied Crispin was almost in tears.

No sooner had Hengist finished, to mixed applause, than the press gathered round him, except for Col Peters, editor of the *Gazette*, who pulled up a chair beside Janna, plonking a bottle of red on the table. Close up he really did look like a toad, his eyes glaucous, fixed and bulging.

'What did you think of that, Miss Curtis?'

'Fantastic.' Janna raised her glass. 'Hengist has been marvellous to us, which is more than you have. Why are you always slagging off Larks? Don't you realize my kids read your rotten paper and are utterly demoralized by your lies?'

A good row was boiling up when Janna was distracted by the peroxide-blonde wife of the chairman of the Rotary Club, who'd drunk even more than she had, and who, passing Councillor Cindy Payne in the gap between the tables, called out: 'Thank God we got Lottie, our grandchild, into Searston Abbey, Cindy, or we'd have had to go private or out of county rather than end up at that dreadful Larks.'

'They'll probably bid for specialist status now they've got Hengist B-T on board,' joked Cindy, who must have been aware of Janna's proximity.

'Crime's Larks's only speciality,' sneered the Rotary chairman's wife. 'They hold their old school reunions in the nick.'

'How dare you slag off my school!' Janna jumped to her feet. 'And you, Councillor Payne, haven't even had the courtesy to visit Larks.'

Seizing Col Peters's bottle, she was tempted to give Councillor

Payne's mousy hair a red rinse, when Hengist grabbed her wrist, increasing pressure so violently she gasped and dropped the bottle, spilling red wine all over Pearl's mother's lovely dress.

'Now look what you've made me do.' She turned, spitting, on him. 'Get off me, you great brute.'

Loosening his grip only a fraction, Hengist dragged her out into the corridor and let her have it:

'When are you going to learn to behave?' he yelled. 'Have you got some sort of death wish? Do you want to wreck everything we're doing to save your school?'

Bursting into tears, Janna fled into the night.

24

Janna woke to find herself on the settee, her breath rising whitely as a reproving sun peered in through the window to dissect her hangover without the aid of anaesthetic. Pearl's mother's green handkerchief dress was her only protection against the bitter cold.

Whimpering and wailing, she pieced together last night's broken dreams. How could she have nearly tipped wine over Cindy Payne, sworn at Col Peters and Hengist, who'd made such a lovely speech about her, then driven home plastered?

As a contrast to such anarchic behaviour, she caught sight of the green and gold serenity of Graffi's mural of Larkshire. He had worked so hard. But now she had stormed out on Hengist, Graffi and his pals would no longer get the chance to run joyously on Bagley's green and pleasant pitches or blossom in art studio, library or concert hall. She had blown it for them and she'd never see Hengist again.

Staggering to her feet, she noticed Pearl's make-up all over the recently upholstered coral settee. Why did she ruin everything? Tottering into the kitchen, wondering if she could keep down a cup of tea, she fell over a padded blue basket and gave a moan of horror as she took in the tins of Pedigree Chum on the window ledge and the blue collar and lead with the newly engraved disk: 'Partner Curtis'. In the fridge was a Tesco's cooked chicken to tempt his appetite.

Glancing at the clock she realized she was due to collect him in three-quarters of an hour. Rescued dogs, particularly ones as traumatized as Partner, needed calm, relaxed owners and she hadn't had the decency to stay sober the night before his arrival. Bloody Larkshire Ladette. And what the hell had she done with Pearl's mother's shawl?

Partner's delighted wagging when he saw Janna was still punctuated by whimpers. His tail, which they'd managed to save and had wrapped in a net gauze dressing, was still very raw and sore.

'Bathe it constantly with cold water,' said the nurse, 'and he'll need antibiotics and painkillers for another fortnight. We ought to keep him in longer, but he's pining in here. He'll do better in a home environment.'

As Janna sank to the floor holding out her arms, Partner crept into them, licking away her tears as they poured from her reddened eyes. 'He needs me as much as I need him,' she whispered.

'Be happy for him,' said the nurse, handing her a box of medicine. 'He's such a brave little dog; we'll all miss him.'

Reluctant to leave at first, Partner perked up in the car, resting his roan nose on Janna's shoulder all the way home. He peed in excitement over the stone kitchen floor before wolfing a huge chicken lunch.

Janna's hangover was hovering like an albatross. She must plan tomorrow's staff meeting. Still cold, she lit a fire. Determined to start as she meant to go on with Partner, she brought his basket into the lounge. Ignoring it, he jumped on to the sofa beside her.

'Not on my new settee,' she said firmly, then caught sight of the streaked make-up and relented.

'Agenda for staff meeting', she read. On top was a note that Mrs Chalford, head of history, who'd been off all term with stress, would be back in school on Monday. Evidently she was a dragon and a bossy boots. The file dropped from Janna's hand.

She was woken by furious barking. Partner, although he was taking refuge under the sofa, was defending his new home against an enchanted Lily.

'What a charming dog. Part corgi, part Norwich terrier, I would say.' Then as Partner, cheered to be attributed with such smart origins, crawled out to lick her hand: 'Oh, your poor little tail. How are you feeling?' she asked Janna.

'Terrible.'

'I've brought you a hair of the dog.' Lily brandished a bottle of last year's sloe gin.

Janna shuddered. 'I'd never keep it down.'

'It's to celebrate Partner's arrival. What are you going to do with him during the day?'

'Take him and his basket to Larks.'

'It's too soon. I'll look after him here until his tail mends.'

'Oh Lily, you're an angel. Are you sure?'

'I expect he'll tree the General to start with, but the old boy needs a bit of exercise.'

'OK, I will have a glass,' said Janna.

As they toasted Partner, Lily said, 'You look terribly tired. What happened last night?'

Janna was about to tell all, when to her horror Partner went into another frenzy of barking and up rolled Graffi, Feral, Paris and this time Pearl. Janna had completely forgotten they were coming.

From Paris's point of view, the afternoons spent at Jubilee Cottage had been the happiest of his life. Afterwards, the memories of gentle football, picking apples and sweeping leaves and twigs for bonfires would be suffused by a golden glow. Best of all had been his hours by the fire with Janna toasting marshmallows and crumpets, the long, leisurely conversations about books, the quiet after the needy, anguished clamour of the children's home. Often, when younger, he had pretended to be his mother and read out loud to himself. Sitting on the floor, not quite letting his head fall on to Janna's little jeaned knees, he had listened to her reading from the *Aeneid*, Aesop's *Fables*, *Paradise Lost* – 'With thee conversing I forget all time' – with no other sound except the swish of Graffi's brushes and the crackle of Lily's apple logs.

Paris had never loved anyone as he loved Janna, but never by the flicker of a pale eyelash would he betray his feelings or embarrass her. He never had any difficulty attracting girls – they lit up like road signs in his headlights as he approached – but it was only an illusion that faded once he'd passed. For, however much they ran after him, inside him was desolation. He must be worthless and unlovable if his mother hadn't wanted to keep him.

Paris didn't have to be back at Oaktree Court until eight o'clock – nine, when he reached fourteen in January – so as the evenings closed in, he would wander the streets of Larkminster: wistful, lonely, pale as the moon, gazing into rooms lit up orange like Halloween pumpkins, bright with books, pictures, leaping fires and mothers, arms round their children's shoulders, as they helped them with their homework.

Bleakly aware that he was incapable of expressing the love that would make him lovable, that he had nothing to offer emotionally, longing for a family would overwhelm him and he would howl at the night sky, reaching for the stars beyond the branches.

What terrified Paris was once Graffi's mural was finished, there would be no excuse for them to roll up at Janna's every weekend, so he kept dreaming up extras for Graffi to include: 'Put Rod Hyde in the stocks.'

As the Wolf Pack rolled up that Sunday, blown in like dry, curling leaves, Paris tried not to feel resentful at having to share Janna with Graffi, Feral and a chattering, first-among-equals Pearl as well as Lily, who was puffing away on the sofa, already stuck into the booze with a fox on her knee, who promptly shot terrified under the sofa.

'Meet Janna's new dog,' said Lily.

'Is it all right if we come today?' asked Graffi.

'Sure,' said Janna weakly.

In agony, Paris noticed her swollen, reddened eyes, ringed by vestiges of Pearl's eyeliner, and loved her more than ever. Had she had bad news? He'd kill anyone who hurt her. Instead he knelt down by the sofa and began to coax out the little dog.

'Come on, good boy.' At least Graffi could string out a few more afternoons adding Partner to the mural.

Janna took a reviving slug of sloe gin. 'You must all speak very quietly,' she begged, 'and avoid any sudden movements. Partner's scared of humans.'

'And I'm scared of dogs,' said Feral, keeping his distance and defiantly bouncing his football.

'It's lovely to see you again,' Janna told him, but noticed in dismay a purple bruise on his cheekbone and that one of his eyes had closed up. She prayed that Uncle Harley hadn't done him over. He was wary of her today, with no sign of that wide, charming, dodgy, insouciant smile.

Later, when conversation moved on to the subject of films, Janna asked if anyone had seen *Shrek*. They all shook their heads, which meant Uncle Harley had lied about Feral's mother taking Feral and the other children to the cinema last night.

While Graffi got down to work, Pearl, her shiny black eyes darting, wanted to hear all about last night. Janna told her, omitting the indecent proposal from Uncle Harley, the row with Col Peters, the attempted wine-drenching of Cindy Payne and the screaming match with Hengist.

'Everyone thought I looked fantastic. Lots of people didn't recognize me. Others who'd previously ignored me were all over me. I felt like a princess.'

'Meet any nice guys?' said Pearl.

Shut up, Paris wanted to scream.

'Think there'll be anything in the paper?'

'Well, they took my picture with Hengist B-T and he told a reporter about your brilliant make-up.'

'Nice guy, Hengist,' observed Graffi, mixing rose madder with burnt sienna to paint in a copper beech. 'Like to see him again.'

'Knowing the *Gazette*,' said Janna quickly, 'they're bound to print the most hideous pictures, but I'll try and get some prints. I'm afraid I spilt wine over your mother's lovely dress and left the shawl behind. I'll get it dry-cleaned.'

'Don't matter,' said Pearl.

'Probably nicked,' murmured a grinning Graffi.

'Shurrup,' snarled Pearl.

Feral was examining the mural. It had come on since his last visit, with a wedding spilling out of the cathedral, dog walkers in the water meadows and otters and fish in the turquoise river.

'It's cool,' he said, then, aggressively bouncing his football, sent Partner under the sofa again.

'Stop it, you're scaring the dog.' There was such ice in Paris's voice and eyes that Feral stopped.

'Why don't you play in the garden?' suggested Janna.

Lily struggled to her feet. 'I'm off to watch Arsenal. You coming, Feral?'

Janna was feeling really ill – perhaps Ashton had spiked her drink. She wasn't up to cooking for this lot and there was nothing in the fridge except Partner's cold chicken.

'How'd you like a Chinese?'

'Wicked,' said Pearl. 'I'll come and help you.'

Paris could have knifed her.

Looking at Pearl's heels, Janna decided to drive.

'Why don't you come with us?' Pearl asked Paris.

'I'll stay with the dog,' said Paris sulkily.

'Oh, would you?' Janna's face lit up. 'He's really taken to you. You're an angel.'

Paris thought he would live after all.

The increasingly bare woods seemed to have been invaded by swarms of yellow and orange butterflies as leaves drifted down. The sun was already sinking.

'Everywhere you look, the colours make you want to be a fashion designer,' observed Pearl as they drove towards Larkminster.

'I met Feral's Uncle Harley last night,' said Janna.

There was a long pause, then Pearl said, 'He's not a real uncle. He's kind of scary, laughing one moment, crazy wiv

150

rage the next. People say he's got Feral's mother hooked on crack' – her voice faltered – 'so he can do what he likes wiv her.'

Listen, listen, listen, Janna urged herself, let Pearl stumble into more indiscretion.

'Don't tell anyone I told you, miss, but Harley's the Shakespeare Estate supplier. Also collects rents for Randal Stancombe. You don't want to be late paying or Uncle Harley cuts you up.' White-knuckled, Pearl's little hands were clenched on her thin thighs.

'He seemed keen for Feral to stop truanting.'

'Only so Feral can push drugs. 'Spect he heard about us bonding wiv Bagley. Means Feral'll have access to rich kids.'

Oh dear. Hengist had said the same thing.

'Uncle Harley gave Feral's brother Joey a gun for his sixteenth birfday, same as a deaf warrant. You didn't hear this from me, miss.'

As they waited outside the Chinese takeaway for their order, which included a double portion of sweet and sour prawns for Feral, Pearl grew more expansive.

'My boxer dad got a prison sentence for burglary, feeding a drug habit. He's convinced Harley shopped him. Last year' – Pearl lowered her voice, shiny robin's eyes darting round for eavesdroppers – 'Feral ran away because Uncle Harley beat him to a pulp. No one went looking for him. Frozen, bleeding to death and half starving, he was forced to crawl home. He's so proud, Feral. Never asks for help, feels he's got nuffink to offer in return. Don't say anyfing, miss. I'm not supposed to know these fings, picked them up, listening.'

'You've been so helpful, Pearl, this'll be our secret.'

'Did they really like my make-up?' asked Pearl.

When they got back to the cottage, Partner only barked once, wagging his tail as Janna went into the sitting room but staying put on the sofa beside Paris.

'Oh look,' shrieked Pearl. 'Sorry, sorry, Partner,' she whispered. 'Graffi's drawn him into the fields wiv you, miss. You've both got the same colour hair.' Then she started to giggle because Graffi had painted in Mike Pitts, Cara, Skunk and Robbie: instantly recognizable as gargoyles.

Janna tried to look reproving. 'I'll never be able to ask any of them for a drink now. Did anyone ring?'

Paris shook his head, noticing how she kept checking her mobile for messages and how she now pounced on the telephone when it rang.

151

Janna felt herself winded by disappointment when, instead of Hengist, it was the shrill voice of Dora Belvedon.

'You probably don't remember me, Miss Curtis. I was waiting at table when you came to dinner with Mr and Mrs Brett-Taylor and we met by the lake. I'm having tea with my Aunt Lily, she says your new dog has arrived. Could I come and see him and bring your shawl back? And I've got a letter for you from Mr Brett-Taylor . . . Miss Curtis?'

But Janna was out of the house in a flash.

Dora had been dying to steam the letter open but wily old Hengist had sealed the blue envelope with green wax, imprinted with his crest of a griffin and a lion.

Dora felt only mildly guilty she had sold the story about 'Bagley beckoning Janna Curtis' to the *Gazette*. Janna would be far happier teaching at Bagley than that horrible Larks.

'I've heard of a new CD that stops dogs being frightened of fireworks, Miss Curtis. You play it every day when they're having their dinner and they get used to the bangs.'

But Janna wasn't listening, she had torn open the envelope and it wasn't just the setting sun reddening her face.

'Darling Janna,' Hengist had written. 'Sorry I bawled you out. I just want to open every door of your advent calendar for you. Very much looking forward to seeing you on Wednesday afternoon. Bring about sixteen to twenty children; they can play football and case the joint and have tea together. I'll ring you this evening. Love, Hengist.'

She was brought back to earth by Dora's gasp of delight. 'Oh, what a sweet dog, he looks like Basil Brush.'

Suddenly Janna's hangover had vanished.

'We're coming over to Bagley next week,' she told Dora. 'Paris and Feral are indoors, and Pearl and Graffi. Do come and meet them.'

Dora sidled away. 'I've come to see Aunt Lily. She misses the family since my horrible brother Jupiter chucked her out of her house. Another time. That is a very cool dog.'

Dora had not forgiven Paris for telling her to fuck off or Feral for kicking his football between her pony Loofah's legs.

Birds were singing agitatedly as the day faded. It was getting cold, so they had tea in the kitchen. It amazed Janna that so much food should vanish so quickly. Feral had cheered up; he'd been at Lily's sloe gin, Arsenal had won convincingly and he was delighted to have an extra helping of prawns. Partner, exhausted by his social afternoon, snored in his blue basket among the moon and stars.

Radiant, able to eat and even keep down a glass of wine, Janna broke the news of the trip on Wednesday.

'Randal Stancombe's been really kind and given us our own minibus to enable us to go to plays and rugby and football matches against other schools, so please stop writing rude things on the walls of Cavendish Plaza.

'And on Wednesday,' she went on, 'a bus load of Larks pupils has been invited over to Bagley on a recce.'

'Wreck will be the operative word,' snapped Paris.

'Send Johnnie Fowler,' taunted Pearl. 'He'll break the place up. I wouldn't want to meet those stuck-up snobs,' she added sulkily.

'How would you all like to go?' said Janna.

'You'd send us?' asked Graffi slowly.

'Yep.' Janna smiled round at their incredulous faces. 'And some pupils from Year Ten, just to look round and have some tea and see what we'd like to do in the future: playing golf, using the running track. The art and the music rooms are to die for; they've even got a rock band.'

'I don't want to go,' said Paris flatly.

'You wait until you see the theatre and the library.'

'Can Kylie come?' asked Pearl.

'I don't see why not.'

'Why us?' muttered Feral. 'We're the school dregs.'

'No you're not,' said Janna crossly. 'I want to show Bagley what attractive, talented pupils Larks has and that, once and for all, our manners are just as good as theirs.'

'Yeah, right,' said Feral, licking sweet and sour sauce off his knife and rolling his huge eyes at Janna, so everyone burst out laughing. From his basket, Partner wagged his gauze-wrapped tail.

'I'd like to go,' said Graffi. 'I'd like to see Hengist again.'

'He really liked your work, Graffi, and your poems,' she added to Paris. 'Please come.'

'OK,' said Paris, 'but what's in it for them?'

'They want to break down conventional social barriers,' said Janna hopefully.

After they'd gone, Lily popped in with some lavender oil. 'Put a few drops on your pillow and you'll fall into a deep sleep. You look much better already.'

Janna was floating on air. She had a bath and sprinkled lavender oil all round her room and on her pillow, then she took Partner out for a last pee and put him in his basket in the kitchen. 'Stay there, love,' she said firmly, then forgot everything because Hengist rang.

'I'm so sorry,' she babbled, 'I just lose it when people attack Larks. I should never have said those awful things to Col Peters.'

'You were suffering from toad rage,' said Hengist.

When she floated upstairs five minutes later, she found Partner out like a light, his ginger head on her lavender-scented pillow. Even his snores didn't keep her awake.

25

Forgetting her own violent antipathy towards private education, Janna was taken aback by the fury produced by the proposed visit to Bagley. The matter was thrashed out at Monday's after-school staff meeting by which time most of the participants had digested as deadly poison the *Gazette* piece with a headline: 'Brett-Taylor confirms Bagley–Larks bonding'.

The copy, which included flip remarks from Hengist about the need to get chewing gum and hooligans off the streets, was accompanied by a glamorous photograph of himself and Janna in front of a vestal virgin. Janna was smiling coyly. Hengist's lazy look of lust was so angled as to be aimed straight down her cleavage.

'Just as though they were playing Valmont and Madame de Merteuil in some amateur dramatics,' spat Cara.

The piece ended with a paragraph about Janna's make-up being created by a Year Nine student, fourteen-year-old Pearl Smith.

' "We like to encourage enterprise in Larks's pupils," joked Miss Curtis.'

Pearl had borrowed a fiver off Wally and rushed out and bought ten copies and a cuttings book.

As staff gathered in explosive mood, down below they could see Janna drifting round the playground chatting, laughing, bidding farewell to the children, adding a last handful of crumbs to the bird table, and praising the new litter prefects who were shoving junk into bin bags.

As she came in Wally, who'd been making garage space for the new minibus, warned her the mood was ugly:

'Don't take any nonsense.'

Already two minutes late, Janna was further delayed by a telephone call.

'It's Harriet from Harriet's Boutique. We were so delighted to see you in today's *Gazette* in one of our gowns.'

'It was a present,' stammered Janna, convinced now that Pearl had nicked the dress. Harriet's was very pricey.

'You looked so lovely,' went on Harriet, 'we wondered if as a great favour, we could blow up the photograph and put it in our window – it would be such a boost to our Christmas display.'

Janna was still laughing as she went into the staffroom. The wind had whipped up her colour and ruffled her hair. She looked absurdly young.

The subject for discussion had been going to be the creation of a Senior Management Team (SMT), or lack of it, because Janna was dragging her heels about appointing a second deputy head to succeed Phil Pierce. If she'd had a flicker of support from any of the heads of department besides Mags Gablecross and Maria Cambola, she might have made more effort.

Now the staff had additional cause for outrage. Rain lashed the windows and relentlessly dripped into three buckets. The only cheery note was a blue vase of scarlet anemones which a grateful parent had given Janna, and which she had plonked in the middle of the staffroom table.

On Janna's right, Skunk Illingworth nearly gassed her with his goaty armpits. On her left, Mike Pitts crunched Polos to hide any drink fumes. Why in hell didn't he kill two birds and drink crème de menthe?

Beyond Mike was Cara Sharpe, who had ripped up the *Gazette* piece. Now, shivering with fury, she was marking essays on the sources of comedy in *A Midsummer Night's Dream* with a red Pentel. Beyond her, Robbie Rushton was spitting blood and applying for a new driving licence. Opposite him presided a returning Mrs Chalford, whom Janna already disliked intensely.

A self-important know-all, she had a smug oblong face and wore a brown trouser suit with a red Paisley scarf coiled round her neck like a python. Insisting on being called 'Chally', she looked as likely to have been suffering from stress as a Sherman tank.

Next to her sat Miss Basket, the menopausal misfit, who had not forgiven Janna for refusing two invitations to supper. She was so red in the face Janna wanted to shove her outside to provide autumn colour.

'Restore work/life balance', 'No one forgets a good teacher', shouted posters on the wall. The younger staff were waiting expectantly for fireworks. Mags Gablecross looked up from the blue and purple striped scarf she was knitting for her future son-in-law and winked at Janna; Jason was reading *The Stage*, Gloria *Hello!*, Cambola the score of *Beatrice and Benedict*. Trevor Harry, head of PE, shook with righteous rage. How dare that shit Brett-Taylor suggest the only exercise Larks pupils got was running away from the police? Old Mr Mates, who taught science, was asleep.

As a heavyweight and official spokesman, Mrs Chalford kicked off. 'I wish to object in the strongest possible terms to learning future plans for our school from the pages of the local rag: future plans which are anathema to the majority of my colleagues who are opposed to any partnership with the private sector. To take only sixteen students is also totally against our caring ethos of equal opportunity for all.'

'The idea has been around since the prospective-parents' meeting,' said Janna reasonably, 'when Mr Brett-Taylor visited Larks.'

'Such bonding is a flagrantly right-wing initiative,' accused Mrs Chalford.

'Not at all, it's a New Labour initiative.'

'I agree with Chally,' butted in Robbie Rushton, who used every steering group or meeting to puncture the atmosphere. 'It is a disgrace that schools charging parents twenty thousand pounds a year should be subsidized for bonding with their impoverished state-school neighbours. Any Labour Government worth its name should be working night and day to abolish the educational apartheid of the independents.'

'Sin-dependents,' murmured Janna.

'As a socialist, I am amazed you're committed to the project,' added Sam Spink.

'Think of the children,' said Janna. 'There is no playing field here where they can let off steam and build up team spirit. Every suggestion box is filled with pleas for more football, more games with other schools. Nor do I want our children to turn into grossly overweight couch potatoes.'

'I object,' said Trevor Harris.

'Later, Trev.' Janna raised her hand. 'As S and C won't help, we have to go elsewhere. If Bagley are prepared to share their facilities with us, we should be gracious enough to accept them for the sake of the children.'

'How are we going to get there?' snapped Mike Pitts.

'Randal Stancombe has given us a minibus,' said Janna. 'It's arriving on Wednesday.'

'That capitalist snake,' hissed Robbie.

'As someone from a desperately deprived background who has clambered out of the poverty trap, I think Randal should be applauded for giving others a chance in life,' snapped Janna.

'Why doesn't he set a good example by sending his children to maintained schools?' said Chally.

'You'll get a chance to ask him on Wednesday; we're having a photo call at Bagley.' Janna took a gulp of water. 'The minibus arrives at midday. We're going over to Bagley in the afternoon. I'd like volunteers to pioneer this first trip.'

The dead silence that followed was only broken by the furious scratch of Cara's pen.

'Hopeless. 1/10', she scrawled across an essay that looked suspiciously like Paris's.

'You amaze me,' she said shrilly. 'After the way you've constantly complained about the cost of supply staff, you're now prepared to impose a further drain on the budget?'

'It'll only be Wednesday afternoons to begin with,' said Janna. 'Later we're going to aim for Saturdays.'

'You cannot expect dedicated, overworked professionals to squander valuable time on something of which they utterly disapprove,' intoned Chally.

'Hear, hear,' agreed most of the room.

'Quite frankly, if I left my post for half a day to commit to this project, which I don't believe in anyway,' said Mike Pitts, 'I'd return to worse problems.'

'I'm sure we'd all like an afternoon off and a chance to see the Burne-Jones windows, but I, for one, thought we were trying to restore work-life balance, not jeopardize it,' pronounced Chally.

'What's in it for Lord Bountiful?' sneered Robbie.

'If you mean Mr Brett-Taylor,' said Janna icily, 'he genuinely wants to help.'

'Rubbish,' hissed Cara. 'He's only interested in his charitable status. Caring conservatism is a classic oxymoron.'

Janna's fingers drummed in counterpoint to the rain dripping into the buckets.

'She's about to lose it,' murmured Jason to Gloria.

'You cannot expect instant decisions without adequate consultation,' reproved Chally.

Mags Gablecross got another ball of mauve wool out of her bag:

'I'd like to go,' she said. 'I'm off on Wednesdays so it won't disrupt the timetable.'

'I'd like to go too,' said Miss Cambola, who was now

orchestrating 'Ding, Dong, Merrily' for the Christmas concert. 'I gather the acoustics for the new music hall are stupendous. I'd like some of our young musicians to join the Bagley orchestra. Cosmo, son of my late countryman, Roberto Rannaldini, is their conductor. His mother, Dame Hermione Harefield, has the most beautiful voice of her generation.'

'Oh, thank you both.' Janna tried to control her shaking. 'We need one more.'

'I'd like to go too,' drawled Jason. He'd score brownie points if he were seen to be giving support to Hengist's pet scheme.

'You've already gone over to Rome,' hissed Cara.

'Thank you, Master Fenton,' sighed Janna.

'I'd like to go as well,' piped up Gloria to Robbie's rage. 'Chance of a lifetime to see their facilities, pick up good practice, must be open-minded, I had an aunt who went to public school.' She smiled adoringly at Jason. 'I'd like to see Bagley.'

'So would I,' sighed Lydia, and was bleached pale by a laser beam of venom from Cara, who then turned on Jason, hissing, 'Who's going to cover for you, Jason?'

'I will,' said Lydia.

She turned even paler when Cara added viciously, 'You know it's Year Nine E.'

'Not quite as challenging as it sounds.' Janna smiled at Lydia. 'The Wolf Pack are coming to Bagley.'

'The Wolf Pack?' Cara's mad escalating laugh made everyone jump. The grey-green roots of her lank black hair gave an impression of poison welling out of her skull. Her red mouth was slack and twitching; her mad malevolent eyes rolled in every direction. Selecting an anemone from the blue vase and ripping off its petals with scarlet talons, she hissed, 'The Wolf Pack? D'you want Larks to be even more of a joke?'

'I've chosen kids who don't normally get recognition and whom I trust,' said Janna simply.

'Just because they've been enjoying cosy weekend tea parties at your cottage. They'll trash the place.'

'Other kids are going: several from Year Ten, plus Aysha, Rocky and Johnnie Fowler.'

'Johnnie Fowler!' said Skunk incredulously.

'Johnnie hasn't been in trouble since he chucked a chair at me on my second day. He's a marvellous cricketer.'

'Who's going to control them?' mocked Cara, selecting another anemone.

'They're very fond of Hengist and have huge respect for Wally who's going to drive the bus.'

159

'Wally as well?' snapped Mike. 'Without a by-your-leave you hijack our site manager. What happens if there's a fire or a fight?'

'Fend for yourself for a change,' snapped back Janna. 'Use the fire extinguisher on both.'

'I wish to register a protest against our students being exposed to snobbish and reactionary peer pressure,' said Robbie pompously.

'Have you got parental permission?' accused Chally.

'I was on the phone first thing this morning,' said Janna triumphantly, 'and didn't get a single refusal. Even Aysha's mother agreed. Parental consent forms have gone home with the kids this evening.'

'How long will you be at Bagley?' demanded Sam Spink, who'd been making copious notes.

'We'll arrive after lunch, at about one-fifteen, and be home about half-five.'

'That could be two and a half extra hours. I'll have to consult the branch secretary. Unfortunately I'm away on Wednesday.'

'What takes you away this time?' said Janna irritably.

'A course on self-assertiveness.'

'Whatever for?' Jason grinned. 'You're far too bossy as it is.'

'How dare you?' spluttered Sam.

Janna decided she was rather going to miss Jason when he moved to Bagley.

Chally looked at her watch. 'It's nearly five o'clock, which leaves no time to discuss the lack of a Senior Management Team. We must have more democratic rule and the opportunity to make informed decisions.'

Her scarf looks set as fast as Hengist's sealing wax, thought Janna. I'm going to see him the day after tomorrow. She fell into a daydream.

'Sorry to railroad you,' she piped up two minutes later as Chally paused for breath, 'but I'm convinced it will boost the children's morale. We're planning a joint play next term.'

Cara gave such a howl of rage, teachers on either side shrank away. 'As head of drama and English I should be consulted on every development.'

'Loosen up, Cara,' drawled Jason, 'it's a great idea.' Then, smiling round the room: 'Means I won't lose touch with you when I move to Bagley.'

'Shall we call it a day?' asked Mike Pitts, who needed a drink.

'Have the rest of Nine E been given the option of going or just your Hell's Angels?' asked Robbie.

Janna gathered up her files. 'That's uncalled for.'

160

'I'm sure Simon Simmons and Martin Norman would love to go,' said Cara ominously.

'They wouldn't,' replied Janna sweetly. 'Both Mrs Norman and Mrs Simmons told me categorically Monster and Satan don't do detentions on Wednesdays, so I hardly think they'd be available to go to Bagley.'

Then she regretted it, instinctively crossing herself as Cara shot her a look of pure loathing. Ripped anemone petals lay like drops of blood on the table. She wants to kill me, thought Janna.

26

Hengist, who, unlike Chally, regarded debate as the enemy of progress and had no desire to discuss anything with his (dreadful word) colleagues, often used chapel to issue orders to subordinates who couldn't answer back.

It was thus on Tuesday morning that he broke the news of the Larks invasion. He softened the blow by asking Primrose Duddon, form prefect of the Lower Fifth, to read a specially selected lesson from St Luke's Gospel.

Primrose Duddon was clever, earnest, noble-browed and already ample-breasted, which ensured normally inattentive schoolboys listened as she read about the Lord throwing a party and, when all his smart friends refused, dispatching his servants into the lanes to invite 'hither the poor, and the maimed, and the halt and the blind'.

'Like some ghastly soup kitchen,' observed Dora Belvedon.

Primrose, reflected Dora, who was sitting in the choir stalls, didn't need the exquisite silver lectern decorated with oak leaves framing the Bagley emblem of a lion sheltering a fawn; she could have rested the Bible on her boobs.

Dora loved chapel. She loved the carved angels in the niches, the flickering lights attached to the dark polished choir stalls, the soaring voices echoing off the wooden vaulted ceiling and the luminous glowing windows, particularly the one opposite, full of birds and animals inhabiting the Tree of Life.

' "For all the saints who from their labours rest," ' sang Dora.

Because she could sight-read and sing in tune, she had been picked for the choir and could thus observe the feuds and blossoming romances of both staff and pupils. Opposite sat her favourite master, Emlyn Davies, far too big and broad-shouldered

162

for his choir stall. Black under the eyes from worry about his darling Oriana who was reporting from Afghanistan, he was surreptitiously selecting the rugby teams for a needle match against Fleetley on Saturday.

Next door were his friends, the elegant, charming head of modern languages, Artie Deverell, who was reading the *Spectator*, and Theo Graham, head of classics, who was bald, wrinkled and sarcastic but revered by his pupils because his lessons were so entertaining.

Next to Theo, looking pained, sat deputy head Alex Bruce, known as Mr Fussy because he was always whingeing about something and who was now pinching the bridge of his nose between finger and thumb. Next to Alex was *his* friend, Biffo Rudge, head of maths, who got so carried away coaching the school eight, he was always riding his bike into the River Fleet. Biffo, a cherry-red-faced bully, with bristling hair like an upside-down nail brush, had a crush on Dora's poor twin brother, Dicky, and (if Dicky were to be believed) dressed up in a black leather dress very late in the evening. Next to Mr Fussy and Biffo was their ally, Joan Johnson, No-Joke Joan, Dora's housemistress, who was hell-bent on making Boudicca, the only girls' house, outstrip the boys' houses academically.

There was no way Joan was going to let Dora rest from her labours like the saints.

In the row in front, romantic-looking Piers Fleming, head of English, was asleep. Not surprising. When Dora had crept out at six o'clock to walk her chocolate Labrador, Cadbury (who was currently living a clandestine existence with the school beagles), she had seen Piers scuttling in, probably from shagging Sheena Anderson in London. Sheena's husband Rufus, head of geography, having dressed and fed himself and his children, and got them to school, was now frantically preparing his first lesson. Piers smelt of Paco Rabanne, reflected Dora, Rufus of baby sick. One could see why Sheena preferred the former.

If she leant back, Dora had an excellent view round the silver lectern of the Lower Fifth – Bagley's equivalent of Year Nine – and the naughtiest form in the school.

Although it contained boffins like Primrose Duddon, and 'Boffin' Brooks, who was both geek and boffin, the Lower Fifth boasted the luscious, long-limbed Bagley Babes. Otherwise known as the Three Disgraces, they included Dora's heroine, Amber Lloyd-Foxe, who had a mane of flaxen hair, exeats on Saturday morning to hunt with the Beaufort and who was now reading love letters from boys at Eton, Harrow and Radley. The second Bagley Babe was Milly Walton: emollient, charming and auburn-haired but overshadowed by her ravishing mother Ruth.

Making up the trio was Jade Stancombe, Randal's 'little princess', who had long, shiny dark hair and was as bitchy as she was beautiful. Jade's street cred had rocketed because of her on-off relationship with Cosmo Rannaldini and because she'd been recently rushed from a party to hospital with alcoholic poisoning to blot out the 'pain of my parents' separation'. Jade had in fact been spoilt rotten all her life, and was miffed because her parents were, for a second, thinking of their impending divorce rather than her.

Everyone was scared of Jade. Milly and Amber loved her for her cast-offs – she seldom wore even cashmere twice – and for trips in the Stancombe jet, though you had to be prepared to endure Randal's groping.

The Bagley Babes indulged in lots of hugging and kissing and, from the humming of vibrators after dark, you'd think bees were swarming. As a new girl, Dora got fed up with making toast and running errands for Jade, and applying fake tan to the small of her very sleek back. She drew the line at shaving Jade's Brazilian.

As well as the Bagley Babes, the Lower Fifths were enlivened by Lando France-Lynch, the Hon. Jack Waterlane and Amber's twin brother, Junior Lloyd-Foxe, who all had Coutts cheque cards and accounts at Ladbrokes and whose sparse intellect was compensated for by their dazzling athletic ability, which had led them to forming their own cricket team: the Chinless Wanderers. With life also revolving round the school stables where they kept their horses and the beagle pack, little time was left for academic pursuit.

And if Babes and Wanderers weren't enough in one form, there was Cosmo Rannaldini, machiavellian master of the universe, and his pop group the Cosmonaughties. Jade Stancombe thought Cosmo was 'sex on cloven hoofs'. Dora thought he was the most horrible boy in the school.

Known as the Bagley Byron, Cosmo had the same lustrous black curls as the poet, but his pale, cruel face was leaner and his dark, soulful eyes less protruding.

'Oh God, our help in ages pissed,' sang Cosmo. Only five foot seven, our little Prince of Darkness had two bodyguards. The first was Anatole, son of the Russian Minister of Affaires, whose vodka bottle chucked out of an attic window was responsible for the glazed expression on the chaplain's face. The second was Lubemir, from Albania, who claimed his family were asylum-seekers, but whose safe-breaking skills and habit of paying school fees with rare works of art suggested rather an affiliation with the Mafia. Pupils tended to seek asylum as Lubemir approached. No one was going to beat up Cosmo with those two around.

Next to the Cosmonaughties sat Xavier Campbell-Black, hunched and miserable. Dora tried to like him because he was the brother of her best friend Bianca, but she'd been horrified recently to see him beating up his horse. Although if you were fat and ugly, and had a heart-rendingly pretty sister after whom every boy in the school lusted, you probably had to take it out on something.

Last hymn over, Dora fell to her knees and really prayed for the safety of Cadbury and Loofah and her dear Bianca, who kept waving and giggling at her from the body of the chapel, and for her brother Dicky, who was always being bullied or jumped on because he was so small and pretty.

Dicky had a much better voice than Dora, but had deliberately sung flat at the compulsory audition, because he'd get even more jumped on if he had to wear chorister's robes.

'Grant me lots of good stories to sell,' prayed Dora.

The twenty pounds from the *Gazette* for the story of Janna dining with the Brett-Taylors wouldn't keep Cadbury in Butcher's Tripe or pay the massive mobile bill from chattering to Bianca. How could she talk to her press contacts without a phone? Life was very hard.

The glazed chaplain was just blessing everyone, when a hitherto absent Hengist swept in, bounding up the steps of the pulpit, as always raising blood pressures and fluttering pulses as he smiled round.

'If I may keep you a moment,' he began in his deep, infinitely thrilling voice. 'You all heard the lesson: "Go out quickly into the streets and lanes of the city, and bring in hither the poor, and the maimed, and the halt, the blind."

'Well, just as the Lord invited the poor to his party, we will be inviting those less fortunate than you to our school tomorrow, when sixteen pupils from Larkminster Comprehensive will spend the afternoon with us.'

A rumble of mirth, interest, disapproval and incredulity swept round the chapel.

'These are children often from tragically impoverished backgrounds, who have only played football on concrete between tower blocks, who often care for handicapped, senile, abusing or drug-addictive parents, who after long days at school have to clean the family home, look after brothers and sisters, iron, cook, shop and hold down evening or weekend jobs to make ends meet.'

Glancing round, moved by his own eloquence, Hengist noticed Cosmo Rannaldini, long lashes sweeping his high cheekbones, playing an imaginary violin, and snapped:

'Save that for the orchestra, Cosmo. Sixteen children from Years Ten and Nine will visit us,' he went on. 'You will recognize them from their crimson sweatshirts and black tracksuits.'

'And yobbo accents,' said Jade Stancombe.

'Takes one to know one,' murmured Amber Lloyd-Foxe.

'A list of both staff and pupils selected to look after our visitors will be found on the noticeboard,' added Hengist. 'I know you and Larks have been sneering at each other for generations, but tomorrow you will have a chance to break down traditional class barriers, and to treat your visitors with the kindness and consideration of which I know you are capable.

'As those selected are too old to kick off with Pass the Parcel, and too young – officially that is' – Hengist raised a thick black eyebrow – 'to break the ice with a large vodka and tonic, we will begin with a team-building exercise in Middle Field, supervised by Mr Anderson and Mr Fleming, which I think you'll enjoy, followed by a tour of the school in general and early supper in the General Bagley Room.

'Tomorrow is only a recce. In future Larks will be spending more time with us and sharing our magnificent facilities. So please look out for anyone looking lost in a crimson sweatshirt and remember our Bagley emblem of the lion protecting the fawn and our motto: "May the strong defend the weak".'

Dora was absolutely livid when she consulted the noticeboard and discovered the Bagley Babes, the Cosmonaughties and the Chinless Wanderers had been chosen to entertain Larks rather than her form. Think of the stories she'd miss.

She was not, however, as furious as Alex Bruce when he saw the list of staff and pupils and realized Hengist had ridden roughshod across his timetable.

Fortunately Miss Painswick, the dragon who guarded Hengist, was off with flu, and Alex was able to storm into Hengist's darkly panelled book-lined office, which was on the first floor of the Mansion and, like the bridge of a ship, enabled Hengist to over-look the playing fields and escape if he saw anyone he didn't like coming up the drive.

Alex's mood was not improved to find Hengist reading *The Times* and listening to some noisy symphony on Radio 3.

'I must protest, S.T.L., on the peremptory way you have imposed your will, hijacking members of staff without any consultation. Who is going to take Piers and Rufus's classes now?'

'Oh, go away, Alex,' said Hengist irritably. 'We must try and learn how the other ninety-five per cent live in this country.'

Alex cracked his knuckles. 'Before you rush into this scheme, S.T.L., we should apply to join the Government Building Bridges programme which for a start would entitle us to some funding.'

'Any initiative from this Government involves far too much red tape.'

'Our parents will be understandably displeased,' continued Alex. 'How can we justify putting up our fees – I got a most offensive letter from Rupert Campbell-Black this very morning – if we reject potential funding?'

Then, as Hengist turned to the crossword:

'I don't expect you realize, grant money could be particularly advantageous to the maintained school involved, funding transport costs and cover for teachers. If you're anticipating any expensive joint productions, you could be depriving your' – Alex was about to say 'precious' but changed it to – ' "friend" Janna Curtis of fifty thousand pounds.'

'Good God.' Hengist put down his pen. 'That's not bad.'

'And there's no reason we ourselves shouldn't apply for a grant retrospectively.'

'Then look into it, you're so good at that sort of thing. Now, if you please.'

But Biffo Rudge, also unchecked by Miss Painswick, had barged in, redder in the face than ever, bellowing, 'Our parents will be up in arms that fees they're struggling to raise are being squandered on the very students from whom they wish their children to be distanced.'

Bringing up the rear, like Boudicca leading her troops into battle, came No-Joke Joan, who had just learnt from the notice-board that the Bagley Babes, none of whom were working hard enough, had been enlisted. Nor did she trust them with Feral Jackson or Paris Alvaston. Couldn't Hengist select three other young women?

'My decision is final,' said Hengist, turning up Brahms's First.

'But S.T.L. . . .' Joan longed to defy Hengist, but her ally Alex Bruce, who'd got her in post at Bagley, was shaking his head.

'Make a note of it – our time will come,' he murmured as a delighted Hengist swooped on an incoming call, then to his horror realized it was Dora's mother, the awful Lady Belvedon whom Painswick would never have let through.

'Quite frankly, Hengist,' she was squawking, 'I don't bankrupt myself as a poor widow in order that Dicky and Dora pick up

167

common accents. The late Sir Raymond would turn in his grave. I also insist the party doesn't include Feral Jackson, who's been up before me and spent several weeks of the summer holidays in a Young Offenders' Institute; a most vindictive fellow.'

Hengist filled in five across and let her run. If he kept saying, 'Yes, yes, yes,' a glowering Biffo, Alex and Joan might go away.

Having ascertained from the noticeboard that the Cosmonaughties, the Chinless Wanderers and the Bagley Babes were all rather surprisingly included in the party to entertain Larks, Cosmo Rannaldini decided to give physics a miss.

Humming Prokofiev's Piano Concerto No. 1, which he was playing and conducting in a concert at the weekend, he sauntered across the quad to the school office to discover Painswick, Hengist's secretary, was off sick. She must be ill to desert Hengist. Instead, Painswick's junior, the ravishing but daffy Jessica, whom Hengist only employed to keep visiting fathers sweet and because her typos made him laugh, was in charge. Jessica was an old friend of Cosmo, having worked as a production secretary on his late father's last film. Jessica wanted to pop down to Bagley village to buy a birthday card for her nan. So Cosmo offered to man the office.

Having checked the weekly bulletins and Hengist's diary, he tapped into Painswick's computer to find out who was coming from Larks, and whistled. Talk about the dregs: not just Johnnie Fowler and his hell-cat girlfriend Kitten Meadows, and Rocky who went berserk if he didn't take his Ritalin – that had possibilities – but all the Wolf Pack.

Feral was four inches taller than Cosmo and had once hit him across Waitrose's drink department. Cosmo did not want his crown as the Byron of Bagley taken away.

He therefore proceeded to email the entire school and most of the parents in histrionic terms, listing the dramatis personae, warning that barbarians were at the gate and that Bagley could anticipate the worst mass rape since the Sabine Women.

'A marauding army of Sharons and Kevs will plunder your cattle and your mobiles. Lock up your Rolexes, iPods and your credit cards; pull up the drawbridge; get the oil boiling on the Aga: we will fight to the death.'

He was just enlarging Janna and Hengist's photo in the *Gazette* to stick on the noticeboard when Dora Belvedon sidled in.

'What do *you* want?'

'To be part of the welcome party when Larks comes over,' said Dora piously. 'It's so important to break down social barriers.'

'Bollocks,' said Cosmo, 'you want to flog the story to the press.'

Unlike his current squeeze Jade Stancombe who considered Dora to be 'a mouthy disrespectful brat', Cosmo rather liked little Miss Belvedon. Her blond plaits were coming untied, her blue-green eyes were suspicious and disapproving and her little nose stuck in the air, but her pursed mouth was sweet. He liked her fearlessness, resourcefulness and jaundiced view of life. She could be trained up as a useful accomplice. And if he won over Dora he could gain outwardly unthreatening access to the desirable Bianca.

'You were waiting at dinner when Janna dined with the B-Ts,' said Cosmo, offering Dora one of Painswick's humbugs.

'So?'

'Must be something going on between Hengist and Janna for him to allow scum like this in here.'

'If you'll stop bullying my brother Dicky . . .'

'Yeah, yeah, whatever. So what gives with Janna and Hengist?'

'She's got a ginormous crush on him. I delivered a sealed love note to her house on Sunday; it was like chucking petrol on a bonfire: whoosh!'

'Is Randal Stancombe after her too?' Cosmo got a fiver out of the inside pocket of his tweed jacket. 'Giving her that minibus?'

'No.' Dora accepted the fiver. 'He was showing off to Mrs Walton. He had his hand up her skirt all dinner – disgusting letch.'

'Lucky Stancombe.'

Dora accepted another fiver, and another after the revelation that Piers Fleming had come in at six that morning.

'Piers likes Sheena Anderson. He put his hands between her bosoms when no one was looking. Thank you.' She shoved yet another fiver into her bra.

'What a decadent world we live in,' sighed Cosmo. 'If we can instigate a punch-up or, better still, a broken jaw tomorrow, it'll make every national. You pick up what you can behind the scenes. Here's my mobile number. I'd better have yours. If you're good, I'll buy you a mobile that takes photographs, then you can photograph the Duddon valley in the shower.'

Sally Brett-Taylor picked up a telephone and rang Larks.

'Janna, my dear, we're so looking forward to seeing you tomorrow. Tell me, what do your chaps really like best to eat?'

Sally was such a brick, reflected Janna, you could chuck her through a window.

169

27

The morning of Larks's visit began for Hengist with a glorious fuck. His favourite breakfast aperitif was going down on his beautiful wife, licking her clitoris, seeing it and the surrounding labia swelling pink, hearing her squeaks and gasps of pleasure, then her breath coming faster until she flooded into his mouth, so slippery with excitement that he could instantly slide his cock inside her.

Sally was like a clearing in the jungle no one but he had ever discovered. No one else knew the joy of making love to her. No one had warmer, softer, sweeter-smelling flesh, or higher, more rounded breasts and bottom, or prettier legs.

Sally's clothes were so straight. No one seeing the silk shirts tucked into the wool skirts which fell just below her knees suspected the luscious underwear: the suspender belts, French knickers and pretty bras in pastel satins; the Reger beneath the Jaeger. Strait is the gate; once through it was all pleasure, which left Hengist purring and utterly relaxed.

Downstairs he switched on the percolator, threw a croissant into the Aga, later smothering it with Oxford marmalade, chatted to Elaine the greyhound and turned on BBC 1 to hear Oriana's latest brief bulletin from Kabul, protesting on the plight of Afghan women. Thank God, she was alive.

Sally knew her husband was excited about Larks's visit. In turn, recognizing the slight widening and worry in Sally's eyes, Hengist murmured that Janna was only an Oriana substitute. 'I like some-one to spar with – chippy, chippy, bang, bang – and she's so desperate to make Larks succeed.'

Sally understood Hengist's craving for novelty. She watched his confident lope, head thrown back, wind lifting his dark hair, shoulders squared. Last leaves were tumbling out of the trees, tossed in every direction, gathering round the bole of a big chestnut, whirling like the tigers circling until they turned into melted butter in *Little Black Sambo*. Sally's heart swelled as she saw Hengist suddenly dance and skip as he rustled through the dry leaves.

She must get on. There was lots to do: organizing smoked salmon and scrambled egg and puds for the Larks pupils; arranging a wrapped bottle of champagne and a light lunch for Randal Stancombe; and masterminding an Old Bagleian reunion dinner this evening.

Swinging out of sight, Hengist ruffled the hair and asked after the parents of two Upper Fourth boys, before grappling briefly with the second fifteen's scrum half and then discussing with him Bagley's chances against Fleetley on Saturday.

'We'll bury them, sir.'

Mist was curling ghostly round the last fires of the beeches as he stopped to joke with gardeners, busy putting the flower beds to rest; ferns hanging limp and dark and a few pinched 'Iceberg' roses being the last inhabitants.

Robins and blackbirds stood round indignantly glaring at a squirrel who, having taken over their bird table, was wolfing all their food. Hengist shooed it off. It was after all the duty of the strong to protect the weak.

It was going to be a beautiful day. The sun was breaking through as he settled into his big office chair, upholstered in burgundy leather, which had once belonged to the Archbishop of Singapore. Radio 3 was playing Brahms's Third Symphony, written when the composer was hopelessly in love, as Hengist leafed through his post. He so adored not being pestered to do things by Miss Painswick.

Then his telephone rang. Jessica wasn't good at fielding calls. This one was from a father, furious that his tone-deaf daughter hadn't been awarded a music scholarship.

No sooner had Hengist put down the telephone than Jessica rushed in to say the *Daily Telegraph* was on the line.

'We wondered what had happened to your copy,' asked John Clare, the hugely respected and influential education editor.

'What copy?'

'On the contribution of competitive sport to the public-school ethos.'

'Christ, when was it due?'

'Yesterday.'

'Jesus, I'm sorry.'

'I can give you till four o'clock.'

'Fuck, fuck, fuck,' yelled Hengist. Painswick would have reminded him. He dialled Emlyn Davies. 'You'll have to kick-start this Larks operation.'

'I've got rugby all afternoon.'

'Not any more you haven't. I'll get shot of this piece as fast as I can.'

'Absolutely fucking typical,' roared Emlyn as he slammed down the telephone.

Next Hengist dialled Alex Bruce.

'I've got to borrow Radcliffe. Someone's got to type this piece.'

'Why can't Jessica?'

'Jessica's not safe. Remember "There's no such word as cunt"?'

Alex Bruce winced. 'High time you learnt to use a computer.'

'You know technology makes me cry.'

'Absolutely typical,' screamed Alex slamming down the telephone and, turning to Mrs Radcliffe, his PA: 'Hengist wants you to type out his article.'

Mrs Radcliffe tried not to look pleased. Hengist was so attractive and so appreciative.

Rufus then rang in and said he wouldn't be able to organize the team-building exercise as one of his children had chicken pox and needed looking after.

'Why can't your wife do it?' snapped Hengist.

'She's in London.'

28

'What is the dress code?' Gloria had asked for the hundredth time.

'Trousers, jumper, warm jacket and flat shoes to run around in,' Janna had replied firmly.

Then, early on Wednesday morning, watched by a bleary-eyed Partner, she had proceeded to wash her hair and scatter rejected clothes all over the bedroom before settling for shiny brown cowboy boots, cowgirl dress in woven pink and blue wool and a dark red jacket with a rich red, fake-fur collar. It looked wacky but sexy and elicited wolf whistles from all the children when she arrived at Larks.

'You said we had to wear trousers,' reproached Gloria, who'd shoehorned herself into her tightest jeans, but added a Sloaney twinset, Alice band and Puffa.

Jason, rolling up in a tweed jacket, grey flannels, a striped shirt and round-necked dark blue jersey, looked as though he'd already crossed over. Mags Gablecross, in a lilac coat and skirt that reminded everyone what a pretty woman she was, was having great difficulty not laughing at Cambola, who looked equipped for a Ruritanian shooting party in a moss-green belted jacket, plus fours and a Tyrolean trilby trimmed with a bright blue jay's feather.

Knowing the other staff were waiting for things to go wrong, Janna had organized everything to the nth degree. Then Chally came bustling smugly into the office. 'Cara's just rung.'

'Yes?' said Janna through gritted teeth.

'The poor dear's sick.'

'Is she ever anything else,' said Janna, instantly regretting it as Chally bridled.

'Let's pretend you never said that. Cara's been signed off with stress for at least a week.'

'She could have rung in earlier,' snapped Janna, thinking of a hundred children with their minds and mouths open and only young Lydia and martyred Basket to cope.

'It was perhaps a mistake for both you and Jason to desert the English department.'

'Cara was perfectly OK last night.'

'Outwardly, perhaps,' reproved Chally. 'Inwardly she was humiliated by your announcing a joint play with Bagley. She feels her authority slipping away – we all do.'

Janna was tempted to throttle Chally with today's bright orange scarf. It was too late to get in a supply teacher.

Instead Wally rigged up a new film of *A Midsummer Night's Dream* in the main hall for the children to watch and then write an essay about.

Janna hugged him. 'Thank God for you.'

Stancombe's minibus was already twenty minutes late. The selected children were getting edgy. No matter that they'd knocked off Bagley's caps for generations. That had been on the streets of Larkminster. Now they faced an away fixture in toff country. Those not chosen to go were jealous and taunting. Fights were breaking out all over the playground.

Matters weren't helped by Kylie Rose turning up in a pretty mauve pansy-patterned wool dress and a little blue velvet jacket, saying she hadn't realized they had to wear uniform.

'And you look wicked, miss,' she added to get the attention off herself.

'She just wants to hook a toff boyfriend,' said Pearl furiously, 'and we're stuck in bloody uniform.'

'That's enough, Pearl,' said Janna. 'And take off those hoop earrings. A dog could jump through them. All right, Aysha?'

Aysha, the cleverest girl in the school, nodded. Despite dark hair hidden by a headscarf, her features were serene and lovely. Inside she fought panic. Her father, in Pakistan on business, was due back any day. Her much more liberal mother had bravely signed today's consent form. If her father found out he would beat both of them.

The boys, wearing massive trainers and tracksuits with the hoods up, were swigging tap water from Evian bottles, unwilling to reveal they couldn't afford spring water.

'Have you taken your Ritalin, Rocky?' asked Janna.

Other boys had discovered that crushed Ritalin snorted gave

174

you a high as good as cocaine and had been offering Rocky ten quid for his daily intake. Rocky liked money to buy chocolate and fizzy drinks, which made him even crazier.

Rocky also had a huge crush on Kylie who led him round like a great curly-polled red bull.

'I want to go on the bus,' he was now grumbling.

'We all do.' Trying to keep her temper, Janna got out her mobile to learn that Stancombe had an important lunch in London, but would arrive at Bagley around three-thirty, officially to hand over the bus, which would be arriving any second.

'It's not coming, it's all a hype,' taunted Monster Norman.

Graffi, Feral and Paris retreated behind a holly bush for a cigarette, which became a second and a third as they all waited.

Then, just when they'd given up, Kylie shouted:

'Here it comes, here it comes, and it's ginormous!'

The bus, the same crimson as Larks's sweatshirts, had black leather upholstery, an upright lavatory like an upended coffin, a television and seated at least twenty-four. On the sides, so no one could mistake its benefactor, was printed in gold letters: 'Larkminster Comprehensive School Bus donated by Randal Stancombe Properties'. On the front the destination said: 'Bagley Hall'.

'Wicked!' yelled the children.

But as they surged forward, struggling to be first up the steps, Satan shouted: 'Yer mother,' to Feral. Next moment Feral had jumped on Satan and Monster on Johnnie Fowler, at the same time aiming a kick at Paris. Graffi leapt to Paris's defence. Everyone was yelling and pitching in, when suddenly the driver climbed down out of the bus. Instantly every child retreated in terror. Then, as he swept off his baseball cap, revealing a dark, shaven head and lighting up the grey day with his diamonds and his white teeth, Janna recognized Feral's Uncle Harley.

'Miss Curtis.' He took her hand. 'As beautiful as ever.'

'What are you doing here?'

'I do a bit of work for Mr Stancombe. Sorry I'm late, the garage was changing the number plates.'

'It's wonderful, thank you so much,' cried Janna as the selected children climbed on in a most orderly fashion.

Janna was about to leap on too, when Rowan came running across the playground: 'Toilets are blocked again, and Mrs Norman's on the warpath.'

A second later, Stormin' Norman came charging across the playground.

'Why isn't my Martin on that bus? Why's he bein' discriminated against, you cheeky cow?' The fist poised to smash into Janna's face stopped in mid-air. 'Mornin', Harley, just discussin' logistics wiv Janna.'

'Fuck off,' ordered Harley, who'd been showing Wally how the bus worked.

Amazingly, Stormin' Norman did.

'You wouldn't like a job here?' asked Janna.

Harley flashed his teeth and advised her to get going. He'd sort everything this end.

'He's dead sexy, your uncle,' said Gloria as Feral tried to get lost against the black leather.

'Quick, miss. Baldie Hyde's just driven up,' shouted Graffi.

Janna needed no further encouragement. Cheered off by other pupils who ran down the drive, banging its sides, the bus pulled away, quite jerkily at first, as Wally became accustomed to the gears.

'I'm going to be sick,' announced Kylie. 'Can we open a window?'

'Nah,' said Pearl. 'It'd fuck my hair.'

As the bus crossed over the River Fleet into the country, pupils charged up and down, trying out the coffin lavatory, fiddling with the windows, standing on the seats to test the luggage rack.

Mags Gablecross, knitting a shawl for a prospective grandchild, handed round a tub of Heroes. Miss Cambola got everyone singing: first 'Swing Low Sweet Chariot', then 'It really ain't surprising That we're rising, rising, rising.'

'Up the fucking social scale,' sang Graffi to howls of laughter.

Outside, the red ploughed fields were covered in flocks of birds having staff meetings.

'Miss, miss, Johnnie Fowler and Kitten Meadows have been in the toilet for five minutes,' cried Kylie.

Janna smiled and walked up and down encouraging everyone.

Paris, ecstatic to be in her company for a whole day, thought she'd never looked more beautiful. The red fur softened her little freckled face. Her perfume made him sneeze and his senses reel, particularly when she sat down and took his hand.

'You'll flip when you see the library. Have you written any more poems?'

'Not a lot.' Actually he was wrestling with one about Janna herself called 'Perihelion'. Such a beautiful word, it meant the point in its orbit when a planet was nearest the sun. He was the planet that craved its moment of perihelion close to his sun: Janna, her flaming hair spread out like the sun's rays.

Love had sabotaged his cool, but he tried to be more

inscrutable than ever, gazing out at old man's beard glittering like cast-aside angels' wings in the hedgerows.

'Here's Bagley, playground of the rich,' said Graffi, catching sight of the big gold house through the thinning trees.

Getting out her powder compact Janna took the shine off her freckled nose and, in the driving mirror, met Wally's wise, kindly eyes, which missed nothing. 'Be careful,' they said.

The bus swung left, through pillars topped with stone lions, up a drive past red and white cows, muddy horses, black-faced sheep, ancient trees in khaki fields; past heroic sculptures; past a sign-post pointing the way to the bursar's office, the science laboratory, the music hall, the sick bay, the headmaster's rooms – Janna gave a shiver. Would there be room for her?

All around, Bagley pupils were walking to classes, girls in sea-blue jerseys, soft beige pleated skirts and slip-on shoes, the boys in tweed jackets and grey flannels. Passing eternal playing fields on the right and the big square Mansion on the left, Wally turned left, then left again up a little drive through a big oak front door into a quadrangle in the centre of which a bronze lion tenderly sheltered a fawn between its paws.

'Bleedin' 'ell,' said Feral, 'it's a fuckin' castle.'

'Bigger than Mr Darcy's house,' conceded Pearl.

'It's Goffic,' breathed Johnnie Fowler, gazing up at the pointed turrets and narrow windows.

'Ah, isn't that lion sweet,' cried Kylie.

As the bus doors buckled, aware of hundreds of eyes looking down at them from offices and classrooms, the Larks children swarmed out into the sunshine, steeling themselves for mockery.

Then, as though one of the heroic sculptures, perhaps Thor, God of Thunder, had come to life, curly-haired, square-jawed, massive-shouldered and battling to curb his fury, Emlyn Davies strode out to meet them.

On Saturday, the five Bagley rugby teams had away matches against Fleetley, the school from which Hengist had departed under a cloud and the one he most wanted to bury.

Emlyn had intended spending the afternoon fine-tuning each team, trying out different moves and combinations of players, before making a final selection. Hengist would be the first to raise hell if Bagley didn't wipe the floor with Fleetley, but had now dragged Emlyn away to oversee his latest self-indulgent distribution of largesse, leaving that pompous woofter Denzil Harper, head of PE, in charge. Sometimes Emlyn loathed Hengist. Everyone had to pick up the fucking pieces.

He had just broken the news that Hengist was irrevocably tied up all afternoon to a stricken Janna and her bitterly disappointed children, when Hengist made him look a complete prat by erupting into the quad, dark hair on end, ink all over his hands.

'*Mea culpa, mea culpa.* I'm so sorry, children. I failed to hand in an essay yesterday and have to stay in all afternoon to write it.' Then, seizing Janna's quivering hands, he kissed her on both flaming cheeks. 'Darling, I'm mortified, how delicious you look. Diorissimo, isn't it?'

Then he turned his spotlight charm on the other teachers – kissing Mags and telling her on what good form her husband Tim had been the other night; praising a piece on Boccherini Miss Cambola had written for last week's *Classical Music*: 'I'd no idea he was such a fascinating character!'; urging Gloria to try out the newest equipment in the gym: 'I'd so value your opinion. What pretty women teach at Larks! And young Jason, hello. I can't remember whether you're in Year Nine or Year Ten,' followed by a shout of laughter, which cracked up the children.

Jason, who'd quickly put his striped shirt collar inside the crew neck of his dark blue jersey because Hengist had, tried to be a good sport.

Then, turning to the children, Hengist explained that with Miss Painswick away and his excitement about their visit, he'd completely forgotten to write his piece for the *Telegraph* about 'the importance of competitive games'. 'You lot, being obsessed with football, know all about that,' he went on, shaking hands with each of them.

'I know Miss Curtis has only chosen special people: Johnnie Fowler, the great cricketer, you must try out the indoor school later. And Aysha, the budding Stephen Hawking, what part of Pakistan d'you come from? I know it well,' followed by a couple of sentences in Urdu.

'And Feral, the ace footballer, whom I am determined to convert to rugger, you're the right build. Lily Hamilton, an old friend, and a fan of yours, Feral, tells me you support Arsenal. And here's Graffi, another old friend, how's the mural of Larkminster going? Janna says it's fantastic. I've just bought a Keith Vaughan for the common room. I'll show it to you later.

'And here's Pearl, who transformed Janna last Saturday, an amazing effort, although you had a lovely subject' – quick smile at Janna – 'will you help us with make-up for our play next term? We're planning to join forces. You must look at our theatre.'

'Yes, please, sir.' Pearl, the cross robin, had suddenly turned into a lovebird.

Yesterday Janna had emailed Hengist photographs of every

child with little biogs, but never expected him to memorize them. She felt overwhelmed with gratitude.

Noting how she was blushing, Paris thought: the smarmy bastard, he's miles too old for her. Then Hengist swung round, his smile so warm and sympathetic.

'And you must be Paris. I love your poems. Janna showed me "The Spire and the Lime Tree". I gather you can also mimic anyone, so you must have a big part in our joint play. You'll find a terrific drama section in the library. Have a look at Wilde, Coward and Tennessee Williams, great writers, great dialogue, great parts for you.'

The boy's looks set him apart, thought Hengist. He has the same sad eyes, pallor, long nose and greyhound grace of Elaine, and I bet he can run away from life just as fast.

And Paris was bowled over like the rest.

Hengist was so good at putting people at their ease: he fired questions and used names to punctuate a sentence, to illustrate how clever he was to remember you out of the thousands of people he met. He had reached Kylie and rocked everyone by asking after little Cameron.

Kylie blossomed like the mauve pansies on her pretty dress. 'He's very well, fank you, sir.'

'Must be hard looking after him and getting your homework done, Kylie, but I gather you're coping brilliantly.'

Janna couldn't fault him. He had screwed up, but as she watched the antagonism and fear melt out of her children, she could only forgive him.

'I'm going to leave you in the large, capable hands of Mr Davies who, until he wrecked his knee, used to play rugger for Wales, which won't impress you, Feral, but will our Welsh Graffi, look you. Everyone wants to be taught history by Mr Davies. His classes are hopelessly over-subscribed. He's easily our most popular master, and has taken the afternoon off to organize your fun and games.'

Emlyn, who'd just been told that Rufus, who'd set up the entire team-building activity, had ratted, refused to be mollified. He was also brick red with hangover and not nearly as attractive in daylight, thought Janna.

Emlyn, in fact, had got wasted last night because he was worried sick about Oriana. God knows what the Taliban might do to one so fearless and beautiful. Then Sally had had the gall to email him first thing. Oriana was safe and sent love. Why the fuck couldn't Oriana call him herself instead of ducking out, like her father, leaving someone else to break the news to the kids.

179

'Mr Davies will take you over to Middle Field to meet our Bagley lot,' Hengist was now saying. 'He's got some rather vigorous game to help you get acquainted. Randal Stancombe is jetting in during the afternoon, so you'll get a chance to thank him for that splendid bus. Then you're free to explore the school; someone will show you round. Don't forget the library, Paris. I'll see you all later. I better get back to my prep.'

'Isn't he awesome?' sighed Kylie Rose.

29

'I'm afraid I won't remember any of your names,' said Emlyn sarcastically as he led them out of the quad, past the lake and the River Fleet in the distance, down to a little white cricket pavilion. Behind this lay Middle Field, which divided Pitch One from the first holes of the golf course and consisted of four acres of rough grass dotted with little copses. Middle Field was also used by the CCF for training exercises. Bagley pupils enjoying peaceful smokes or snoggings were often disturbed by flying balls or invading armies.

On Pitch One, the armies of Larks and Bagley now lined up glaring at one another.

Feral, to appear more menacing, had, like Paris and Graffi, left up the hood of his black tracksuit. Then he clocked the three Bagley Babes, who looked as though they'd been fed on peaches and fillet steak all their lives, who had glossy hair cascading from side partings to below their boobs and gym-honed bodies in cobalt-blue tracksuits and pale ochre T-shirts, which evoked the sea and sand of endless holidays.

Nodding haughtily at Amber, then Milly, then Jade, Feral murmured, 'I am going to have that one, that one and that one.'

'No doubt yelling Sharpeville at the moment of orgasm,' murmured back Paris.

Then Feral reached for the knife in his tracksuit trousers as he recognized sneering, supercilious Cosmo Rannaldini flanked by his two heavies.

'I am Anatole from Russia,' announced the first heavy in a voice as deep as the Caspian Sea, as his narrowed, dark eyes slid over Kylie, Kitten and Pearl.

'And I am Lubemir from Albania,' said the second, whose

black hairline rested on his thick eyebrows like a front on the horizon and whose Slav face was rendered more sinister by dark glasses and even darker stubble.

'And we're Lando France-Lynch, Jack Waterlane and Junior Lloyd-Foxe, from the broom cupboard,' quipped Amber's mousy-haired, merry-faced twin brother.

'Those three are nice,' whispered Kylie, who was also vastly relieved that some of the Bagley contingent were quite plain. There was a boy called Spotty Wilkins who had more spots than face and a geek in granny specs with buck teeth and a huge air of self-importance, who, humming and swaying back and forth, introduced himself as: 'Bernard Brooks from East Horsley, but most people call me "Boffin".'

'Boffin from leafy East Horsley,' murmured Paris, catching Boffin's singsong curate's voice so perfectly, the Bagley Babes started giggling.

'Look at the knockers on that one.' Graffi gazed at Primrose Duddon in wonder. 'Stick out more 'n Boffin's teef.'

'And this is Xavier Campbell-Black,' announced Emlyn because Xav was too shy to introduce himself.

Remembering Rupert from the prospective-parents' evening, all the Larks girls swung round in excitement, which faded as they realized the heavy, hunched, sullen Xavier bore no resemblance to his gilded father.

Next moment the mighty unbeaten first and second fifteens pounded past.

'Sir, Sir,' they shouted to Emlyn, 'we've been dragged out on a fucking cross-country run. We're supposed to be practising ball skills.'

'Buck up, keep moving,' shouted Denzil Harper, head of PE, running effortlessly beside them. A recent Alex Bruce appointment, sporting a snow-white T-shirt and earrings, Denzil had a shaved head and a chunky, muscular body.

I'll kill Hengist and Rufus, vowed Emlyn, if that woofter Denzil injures any of them.

'I want you to split into groups of six,' he told the waiting children, 'mixing both schools as much as possible.'

This meant everyone chose their best friends. Instantly the Wolf Pack drew together, determined to show those fucking Hoorays (Lando France-Lynch indeed) how thick they were.

'Come on, Rocky.' Kind Kylie pulled him into their group.

'We don't want him,' hissed Pearl, 'Rocky couldn't build a team if it sat on his face. Grab Aysha.'

182

As Jade was Cosmo's girlfriend, the Bagley Babes automatically teamed up with the Cosmonaughties. Johnnie Fowler, who wouldn't let sexy Kitten Meadows out of his sight, formed up with four members of Larks Year Ten; the Chinless Wanderers – Lando, Junior and the Hon. Jack – with Bagley mates from the form above. Rejects like Spotty Wilkins and Xavier edged miserably together for comfort.

'A fat lot of mingling that is,' roared Emlyn and proceeded to number members in each group from one to six, and to their outrage ordered the 'ones' to form one group, the 'twos' another, and so on until crimson sweatshirts and sea-blue track-suits were totally mingled.

Outside the cricket pavilion on a trestle table lay a building pack for each group.

'These packs contain simple – depending on your intelligence – instructions on how to build your own hot air balloon,' shouted Emlyn, 'and as you can't fly a balloon without a control tower, here are newspapers for you to create one.'

'This is going to be fun.' Janna smiled anxiously at the mutinous, contemptuous, incredulous faces as Mags Gablecross and Jason rushed round handing out copies of the broadsheets.

'I can't understand papers like this,' grumbled Kitten, un-enthusiastically opening the *Observer*, 'too many long words.'

'To build your balloon,' continued Emlyn, 'you'll also need coloured sheets of tissue paper, cardboard and scissors, which are assembled here on the table. But you win these by passing a number of tests.'

Then, as Janna and Gloria handed out pads of crosswords, puzzles and teasers, Emlyn explained: 'Every time you solve a page of these, you race up to us in the cricket pavilion and if it's correct you'll win yourself either cardboard, scissors or glue, or a sheet of coloured tissue paper. You'll need at least six of those to build your balloon.'

Like the labours of Hercules, thought Paris.

'The other way you can win the stuff you need,' called out Mags, who'd been reading the instructions, 'is by taking part in an orienteering treasure hunt.'

'We're not in the bloody Lower Fourth,' grumbled Cosmo.

'One would not know from your behaviour,' snapped Emlyn. 'You may not have noticed, but amid the autumn colour of Middle Field are hung fifteen orange flags with staplers and directions to the next map reference attached. Here are the maps.' He lobbed them at each team. 'In the frames round them you will find fifteen boxes which each need to be punched with

183

the appropriate map reference. These will entitle you to more tissue paper, glue, etc.'

'Are we going to find treasure?' Amber eyed up Feral.

'Once you've built your balloons,' added Emlyn, 'and you've got an hour and a half, members of the staff will provide hot air.'

'Again,' shouted Junior Lloyd-Foxe to shouts of laughter.

'OK, joke over. Provide hot air to enable them to fly. And there'll be a competition to see whose balloon flies farthest, and for the prettiest and the first finished.'

'And to think I could be curled up in a nice warm classroom learning calculus and being molested by Biffo Rudge.'

'Shut up, Cosmo. Anyone undertaking the treasure hunt must go round in twos in case you get lost.'

'Sounds fun,' Amber smouldered at Feral. 'Shit, I forgot to ring Peregrine.' She groped for her mobile.

'Put that away,' roared Emlyn, 'we're about to start.'

'What is the matter with Attila?' sighed Amber.

Graffi, meanwhile, was immersed in the *Telegraph* racing pages.

Peering over his shoulder, Junior said, 'Singer Songwriter's a good horse.'

'Shining Sixpence's a better one,' said Graffi. 'My dad does work for his trainer. We orta have a bet.'

'I'll ring Ladbrokes,' murmured Junior. 'Hear that, Lando and Jack?' he called out. 'Shining Sixpence in the three o'clock.'

Next moment Lubemir and Anatole were also on their mobiles.

'Shall I put a tenner on each way for you?' Junior asked Graffi.

Aware it would feed the family for a week, Graffi said yes. He'd have to become a rent boy. That Milly Walton was hot.

'Blimey. "He left pubic hair on my mouse",' read Kitten, now engrossed in the *Observer*. 'I didn't know posh papers wrote about this sort of fing. What's "coprophilia"?'

'A kind of cheese, I fink,' said Kylie.

Janna turned on her angrily. 'Concentrate.' Emlyn's increasingly short fuse was getting to her. How on earth had she found him so attractive? With his gut spilling over too-tight chinos, blond hair like an electrocuted haystack, heavy stubbly jaw and angry bloodshot eyes, he looked more like Desperate Dan.

Seeing his beloved Kitten in the same group as evil Cosmo, Johnnie Fowler grabbed Cosmo's collar.

'Don't you lay a finger on my woman.'

'Don't insult my libido,' said Cosmo icily.

'Yer wot?' Johnnie clenched tattooed, ringed fingers.

Nonchalantly, Cosmo sidled off whistling Prokofiev One.

Separated from Anatole and Lubemir, however, he felt vulnerable. He was, in addition, outraged to be teamed with not just Kitten but also Amber, who was making eyes at his arch enemy, Feral, and Lando, who was so thick he made pig shit look like consommé.

Deeply competitive, accustomed to automatic victory, Boffin Brooks was even more outraged to be lumbered with Lubemir, the Hon. Jack, Kylie and the unspeakable neanderthal Rocky, who refused to leave Kylie's side.

'For Christ's sake keep Rocky away from any glue or he'll sniff it,' warned Kylie. 'And the scissors too. If his Ritalin wears off, he'll cut your head off.'

Like a vicar doorstepped by the *News of the World*, Boffin shuddered.

Paris, icier and more remote by the minute to hide his shyness, was in a group which included the even more shy Aysha, monosyllabic Xavier Campbell-Black, Anatole who was reading Pushkin and swigging vodka out of an Evian bottle, and Jade Stancombe.

As Cosmo's friend and his girlfriend respectively, there was no love lost between Anatole and Jade, who made no secret of the fact she had joined the worst group.

' "Woman! when I behold thee flippant, vain, Inconstant, childish, proud, and full of fancies . . ." ' murmured Paris, who'd been reading Keats. Jade was beautiful, but what a bitch.

How he envied Graffi who, oblivious of class difference, was creating his usual party atmosphere, laughing with the ravishing Milly Walton and Junior Lloyd-Foxe, whose father Billy worked for the BBC and brought home riveting gossip about celebs ('Richard and Judy are *so* nice').

Also in their group were Pearl and Spotty Wilkins.

'You could use a concealer on those spots,' Pearl was telling him kindly as they waited for the off.

'You start on those puzzles, Junior,' suggested Graffi, 'and win us some sheets of paper. Pearl's clever, she'll help you.'

'Five, four, three, two, one,' yelled Emlyn, brandishing the starting pistol, then as the chapel clock struck two he pulled the trigger, making members of both schools leap out of their skins, thinking the other had opened fire.

'You have a go at these brainteasers, Feral,' suggested Lando France-Lynch.

'Ain't got a brain to tease, man,' said Feral.

'Nor have I,' agreed Lando.

Amber smiled at Feral. 'Why don't you and I do some orienteering? Hand over the map,' she added to a furious

Cosmo, 'you and Lando can work out the puzzles with Kitten and wind up her jealous boyfriend.'

'Ven two people stand on the same piece of paper in the same house and can't see each other, vere vould they stand?' A perplexed Anatole looked up from another page of puzzles.

'Haven't a clue,' said Jade in a bored voice.

'If they put the sheet of paper under a door, shut it and stood on the paper on either side, they couldn't see each other,' suggested Aysha timidly.

'Brilliant,' chorused Paris, Xav and Anatole.

Admiring her sweet blushing face framed by its black headscarf, Xav wondered what Aysha would look like with her hair unleashed. Not liking attention off her for a second, Jade announced she was going to build the control tower.

'Daddy's got several around the world,' she boasted, picking up the *Sunday Telegraph* business section. 'Oh look, there's a picture of Daddy.'

Ignoring her, Paris was whipping through the crossword even faster than Boffin Brooks.

'Despicable person, five letters beginning with "C"?'

' "Cosmo",' volunteered Lando.

Paris smiled faintly. 'Nice one, but I guess it's "creep". Pleasant facility, seven letters beginning with "A".'

' "Asshole",' drawled Lando.

Aysha blushed. 'Could it be "amenity"?'

'Could indeed, well done, Aysha.' Paris tore off the page, sending her and Xav scurrying off to claim more tissue paper.

The Threes were being held up by Graffi's desire to build a round balloon, rather than one in the recommended cylinder shape.

'It's the wrong way,' protested Junior.

'No it ain't.'

'Bloody is,' said Pearl. 'Graffi's so wilful.'

'Trust me, give me the fucking scissors, and go off and win some more tissue paper in case I screw up,' ordered Graffi.

Tempers and papers were beginning to fray. Under Boffin Brooks's fussy guidance, his team had concocted a scarlet and black cylinder from five sheets of paper, and were now trying to attach round ends to top and bottom.

'You stupid idiot,' screamed Boffin as Rocky's big fist went straight through the tissue paper.

'Don't pick on him, you great bully,' screamed Kylie.

Jade, bored of building her control tower, was putting the boot in.

'You stupid cow,' she cried as Aysha, trying to join their balloon's two emerald and royal blue sides together with trembling hands, also tore the paper.

'Don't talk to her like that,' yelled Xav.

Jade turned on him. 'I can talk to anyone however I like. You know who my boyfriend is.'

'I don't care,' lied Xav defiantly.

'You'll regret this,' hissed Jade.

'Kill each other later,' said Anatole, who was now immersed in the *Sunday Times* business section. 'Ve have balloon to build.'

'You're not being much help.'

A full dress row was quelled by the descent of Mags Gablecross, who chided them for wasting their human resources.

'You've completed the puzzles. Anatole and Jade, go off orienteering; Paris, get on with the balloon and Xav and Aysha, help him after you've finished the control tower.'

Janna and Jason stood at the trestle table handing out tissue paper and cardboard, checking maps to see if each box had been punched correctly.

'You're cheating again, Lubemir, go back and get two to eight punched properly and you too, Rocky, these have all been punched with the same staple. You need fifteen different ones.'

Feral and Amber raced hand in hand through Middle Field, their footsteps muffled by the thick yellow and orange leaf patchwork. They had punched nearly all their map references and collapsed on the roots of a big sycamore to catch their breath.

Amber's tousled mane was falling over eyes, the rich ochre of winter willows. Her breasts heaved beneath her sand-coloured T-shirt.

'Lovely tan,' said Feral.

Amber stroked his cheek. 'Not as lovely as yours.'

Feral laughed, clapping her hand to his face.

'You been away,' teased Amber.

'Inside,' said Feral.

'Poor you, was it hell?'

'Hell, being banged up.'

'What did you do?'

'Mugged a stuck-up bitch; only took her bag and her mobile.'

'My father was always in gaol for hellraising on the

showjumping circuit in the old days. You should compare notes. You're so sexy, Master Feral.'

Feral stretched out a hand and touched a nipple sticking through her bra and T-shirt and very gently ran his finger round and round it, until Amber was trembling with longing to be kissed. He had such white even teeth, such a wonderful smile, such curly black eyelashes.

'It's so important to overcome traditional barriers,' murmured Amber.

Feral found her colouring so exquisite against the yellow hazel, and faded tawny oak, he said, 'You suit autumn.' Putting a hand on her tracksuit trousers, he repeatedly tapped a finger against her clitoris. 'Like that?'

'Amazing.'

Unable to bear the tension, Amber leapt to her feet and stumbled deliberately in a rabbit hole, allowing Feral to catch her. For a second they gazed at each other, burst out laughing, then he kissed her. He smelled so lovely and tasted faintly of peppermint, his tongue flickering as delicately as his fingers had, then growing more and more insistent until her legs would have given way if his arms hadn't held her like steel bands.

'Oh Feral,' gasped Amber, 'talk about lift-off,' then, as his snake hips writhed against hers and his cock seemed about to burst through his trousers: 'I don't think you're entirely in control of your tower.'

'Stop taking the piss, man.'

'Oh, wow,' moaned Amber. As Feral's hand crept inside her T-shirt, her hand in turn slid down his flat belly and thighs and encountered hard steel.

'Ah,' she whispered. 'I see you also dress on the left.'

'I don't take chances.'

Letting her go, Feral whipped out his knife, running his finger down the blade, smiling at her. Amber stood her ground, determined to show no fear. Neither jumped much as they heard Boffin Brooks's strangulated whine.

'Number eight ought to be around here somewhere.'

Reaching up Feral cut through the string which tied stapler and flag to an overhead branch and chucked them into a wild rose bush. Then, putting away his knife, he pulled Amber behind a big oak tree, hand over her mouth to stop her laughing.

'We don't want Boffin catching up wiv us.'

'I've never snogged anyone black before,' murmured Amber, prising off his hand and pulling his head down. 'What have I been missing?'

30

Earlier, in London, Randal Stancombe and Rufus Anderson's wayward wife Sheena lunched on smoked salmon and champagne in one of his many apartments.

'It'll be an excellent photo opportunity,' Sheena reassured him, 'and brilliant for your profile both locally and nationally to help a school that serves an estate with such a high level of deprivation. People will recognize your sincerity about cleaning up the area. If the rest of the press are expected at Bagley at three-thirty I suppose we ought to go,' she added regretfully.

'We could have another drink,' said Stancombe, unbuttoning her dress. Sheena was very tasty and it was one way of finding out if she'd hidden a tape recorder anywhere.

Back at Bagley, the Lower Fourth were studying Tennyson. Poor Miss Wormley, whom the class referred to as Worm Woman, had made the mistake of asking Dora Belvedon for her views on the Lady of Shalott.

'Well, Sir Lancelot with his flowing black curls and his broad brow was pretty cool,' began Dora, 'like a young Mr Brett-Taylor. But next minute he's described as flashing into the crystal mirror. We had a flasher in Limesbridge when we lived there. Our gardener, actually. He was always waving his willy at people, so it must have been a shock for the Lady of Shalott, she'd led such a sheltered life. No wonder she suddenly got her period.'

'Don't be silly, Dora.' Miss Wormley had gone very pink.

'She did too. "The mirror cracked from side to side; 'The curse has come upon me,' cried The Lady of Shalott." They called a period "the curse" in medieval times when my mother was young,

189

so she wasn't going to be much good to Sir Lancelot that day. No wonder he kicked on.'

Apart from Dora's brother Dicky, who had his burning face in his hands, the rest of the Lower Fourth were in ecstasy. They loved it when Dora got into her stride. Dora, however, was frantic to escape.

'I simply must go to the loo, Miss Wormley, I've got a frightful tummy upset. I'll burst all over the floor if I don't.'

And Wormley let her go. Anything to be spared more literary interpretation.

By the time the Lower Fourths had moved on to the next poem, about a snob called Lady Clara Vere de Vere, Dora was falling out of the lavatory window, binoculars trained on Middle Field as the teams shrieked, yelled and raced about.

There was Xavier Campbell-Black actually laughing – that must be a first – with a girl in Eastern clothes. Kylie Rose and the Hon. Jack were having a very heavy snog behind a holly bush. Jack was so dopey, Dora hoped he'd remember to use a condom. Lord Waterlane would go ballistic if he got Kylie pregnant. If only she had a camera, the *Mail* would love that story – talk about Posh and Complications. That dickhead Boffin was grumbling to Mr Davies about something. Dora could just make out Graffi and Milly Walton building a tower together. Janna was looking bleak, probably missing Hengist. And Amber, Dora's heroine, was sauntering out of Middle Field, doing up her bra, straightening her clothes, followed by – yuk! – Feral Jackson. How could Amber fancy him? She wouldn't if she knew he'd kicked a football through Loofah's legs. Dora got out her mobile to ring the press.

Great cheers rent the air as Junior Lloyd-Foxe got a text to say Shining Sixpence had won by five lengths.

'I'm terribly sorry I only got him at ten to one. That's a hundred and thirty quid I owe you,' he told Graffi. 'Thanks for the tip. Bloody good.'

Graffi's balloon would clearly be the most beautiful but not the first completed.

'Come on, Graffi, we must beat that twat Boffin,' pleaded Pearl.

'Rocky and Kylie'll hold him back,' muttered Graffi, gluing on extra strips of violet.

'We must beat that horrible Cosmo.'

'Feral and Lando will hold him back even more.'

'Feral makes up for it by running quick.'

* * *

Cosmo, in fact, was white with rage. He'd always fancied Amber, and she'd pushed off with that snake Feral, leaving him with Lando (who was immersed in week-old racing pages) and only Kitten Meadows to bully, who kept rolling her eyes, clapping her hands over her mouth and giggling.

'Why do you laugh when it's not funny?' he asked evilly.

'Dunno.'

'That's not an answer.'

Kitten flushed, looking round for Johnnie to protect her, but Johnnie, part of Primrose Duddon's team, was gazing longingly at Pitch One. To hit a six on it would be really something.

Having cut out a doughnut-shaped piece of cardboard to re-inforce the bottom disk of violet tissue paper, Graffi shoved his fist through the paper.

'This is where the hot air goes in, Milly.' He lowered his voice. 'You ever come into town?'

'It could be arranged. Here's my mobile number.' Milly wrote it on a fragment of daffodil-yellow tissue paper, shoving it into Graffi's jeans pocket, fingers splaying over his thigh.

'Stop wasting time,' said an envious Spotty Wilkins.

'Your balloon's the prettiest,' said Milly.

Graffi's smile was unwavering. 'No, you're the prettiest.'

To reinforce his team's balloon, Rocky had also been instructed to cut a piece of cardboard shaped like a doughnut and now pretended to eat it. Everyone laughed so Rocky started really to eat it.

'Stop that, you stupid idiot,' screamed Boffin.

'Leave Rocky alone, you great bully,' shouted Kylie. Then, as Rocky went on chewing the cardboard: 'Stop that, you stupid asshole.'

'Now who's being both bullying and offensive,' said a shocked Boffin.

'Rocky's my friend, I'm allowed,' snapped Kylie, adding as an afterthought: 'You're the asshole.'

'Very well said, Kylie,' brayed the Hon. Jack.

Jade Stancombe wasn't happy. Cosmo had ignored her all after-noon. Amber had pulled the divinely wayward Feral. Graffi was so busy gazing at Milly he'd put a fist through his balloon and was frantically patching. The enigmatic Paris, whose beauty was undeniable, was ignoring her. Paris was in fact watching Janna and Emlyn, wondering how that great ape could train his

191

binoculars on a distant rugby game when the loveliest woman in the world stood beside him.

My poor father has spent a fortune on a bus to enable Larks and Bagley to indulge in an orgy, thought Jade furiously, and no one's asked me to join in.

'Why are you staring at me?' she rudely asked Paris, who shrugged and turned back to the balloon to which Lando and Anatole, delighted at their winnings, were proving surprisingly good at adding finishing touches.

Aysha and Xavier were also working well, Aysha deftly gluing the paper Xavier had cut out as they built a beautiful control tower, nearly three feet high with crenellated turrets.

The hour and a half was nearly up. Shrieks of rage, frustration and triumph rent the air.

'I feel like the end of a jumble sale,' said Mags, looking at the empty trestle table from which every scrap of tissue paper had been whipped.

'Finished,' yelled Primrose Duddon, whose team, even with Johnnie on board, had indulged in no dalliance or illicit boozing and had completed their orange and Prussian-blue balloon to loud cheers. As there was no sign of Stancombe, Emlyn presented Primrose with a red rosette.

'Well done,' he told her, then, turning to Janna: 'Should we release the balloons as they come in?'

'More impact if they all go off together,' said Janna, and was nearly sent flying by a furious Boffin.

'Sir, sir, someone's been cheating, cutting free the staplers in the wood so I've been unable to complete our map. Objection! Objection!'

'It's only a game,' said Emlyn, mindful of the gathering press. 'No one's getting any prizes.'

Graffi's round balloon, in diamonds of primrose yellow, shocking pink and violet, was judged to be the most beautiful; Xav and Aysha's control tower the finest; Cosmo's tower the biggest and tallest, which, everyone agreed, figured. Nearly all the participants were chatting and laughing now.

As the balloons were lined up on the edge of the cricket pitch, the chapel weathercock, which had been watching proceedings, swung away as the warm south wind, which would have swept the balloons over the golf course, changed to north-east. Now, with luck, it would carry them over the Mansion.

'Stick 'em up.'

Feral reached instinctively for his knife as Gloria ran out

brandishing two hot-air paint-strippers, followed by Cambola, Jason and Janna bearing hairdriers. Emlyn then handed out cardboard tubes to plug into the cardboard hole in the bottom of each balloon.

'Too phallic for words,' muttered Cosmo as the nozzles of hair-drier and paint-strippers were applied to the lower end of the cardboard tubes.

Emlyn was studying the building pack.

'Are all staff wearing protective gloves and all balloons held firmly by a team member?' he shouted.

'Yes,' went up the cry.

'Well, turn on the heat.'

Scarlet and black, navy and emerald, Prussian blue and orange, shocking pink, violet and yellow, mauve and dark green: the balloons bobbed like tropical fish.

Mauve and dark green, held by Paris as Janna's hairdrier poured hot air inside it, quivered most. Jade put her hand round the cardboard tube, pretending to toss it off, then, encountering an icy look from Paris, blushed and let go.

'Do you like the bus my father gave you?' she demanded.

'It's absolutely wonderful,' cried Janna, 'it'll change our lives. We can't thank him enough.'

'The balloons should take four minutes to fill up,' advised Emlyn.

Kitten stood well back. 'I'm sure the glue's going to catch fire.'

'Out of nuffink, just bits of paper and glue, we've made somefing beautiful,' said Kylie in a choked voice. Like we could be, she thought.

The press had now arrived in force and, with no sign of Stancombe, photographed balloons and happy, excited children.

'Everyone ready?' yelled Emlyn.

'No,' protested Lando France-Lynch.

'He's never been able to get it up,' shouted Junior.

'They'll never fly either,' mocked Cosmo and, as everyone was concentrating on the balloons, whipped Amber's mobile from her pocket.

'Ten, nine, eight, seven, six,' shouted Emlyn. 'Five, four, three, two, one, lift-off.'

Away went the balloons, the tropical fish metamorphosing into a swarm of coloured butterflies, flying over the gold trees into the bright blue autumn sky.

Lubemir and Boffin's black and red balloon caught on the spikes of a sycamore, triggering off a stream of Albanian expletives until a gust of wind freed it to bob after the others.

Sailing south-west over the Mansion, Primrose's orange and Prussian-blue prizewinner stalled on the gold weathercock.

'First time she's bounced on top of a cock,' giggled Amber.

'Let's see how far they go,' said Feral, taking her hand and together they raced through trees and school buildings, followed by a whooping Milly and Graffi, Lubemir and Pearl and, after exchanging shy smiles, by Aysha and Xavier.

'Black shit sticks together,' observed Cosmo. Jade laughed and slid her hand into his.

'Xav has just been very rude to me, I think he needs taking down a peg or two.'

'Or three, or four, or five,' agreed Cosmo. 'It will be arranged.'

'The Montgolfiers always maintained—' began Boffin.

'Oh, shut up, Boffin,' said Primrose.

Janna and Paris stood side by side watching until the last balloon floated out of sight.

'They're a symbol of Larks,' whispered Janna. 'We're going to take off and really fly and so will the partnership with us and Bagley—' Her voice broke.

Turning, Paris saw tears spilling over her lower lashes. Taking the hairdrier from her, he put it on a trestle table, then somehow his hand slid into hers and they smiled at each other.

'God speed,' cried out Janna, as the last emerald and navy balloon bobbed briefly between the tall chimneys, 'such a wonderful omen.'

Paris didn't know when to let go of her hand, so he left it to her.

Interesting, reflected Cosmo, who was standing behind them. Miss Curtis clearly likes toyboys as well as wrinklies.

The rugby fifteens, probably wrecked from all that pounding on hard ground, had gone in, so Emlyn also observed Janna and Paris. She's very near the edge, he decided, and so besotted with Hengist, she's unaware of the havoc she's wreaking on that poor boy.

'That was a great success,' he said loudly.

Janna let go of Paris's hand, and was soon telling the hovering press that 'Larks and Bagley's partnership couldn't have been illustrated taking off in a more romantic and beautiful way.'

31

Stancombe still hadn't turned up, but the Larks and Bagley balloonists, over orange juice and slices of Mrs Axford's cherry cake in the pavilion, were getting on much too well to care. Nor did they notice Cosmo slipping Amber's mobile into the pocket of Feral's tracksuit top, which he'd left hanging on the back of his chair.

Amber and Milly were wildly impressed when they discovered Pearl had done Janna's Winter Garden make-up.

'I mean she's pretty for a wrinkly today, but in that picture with Hengist, she looks like Meg Ryan, and you can see Hengist really, really fancies her,' said Amber.

'Will you make me up one day?' begged Milly.

'Pearl's going to do the make-up for a joint production,' said Amber.

'Then I can quite confidently play Helen of Troy,' giggled Milly.

Pearl was in heaven.

'What d'you want to see this afternoon?' asked Amber.

'The theatre, and Graffi's desperate to see the art department. He's dead talented.'

'Dead lush as well,' sighed Milly.

'Not as lush as Feral,' said Amber.

'Feral's my boyfriend,' said Pearl sharply.

'Ah,' said Amber.

If Feral were taken, which was indeed a body blow, she'd better call Peregrine. She patted her pockets. Where the hell was her mobile?

Johnnie Fowler, who'd been too uptight to have any lunch, had a fourth piece of cherry cake as he discussed safe-breaking and drugs with Lubemir.

'I tried to kill Miss when I were high on crack, so I went cold turkey.'

'Ve vould have allowed you to kill Alex Bruce,' said Lubemir. He turned to Feral: 'Vat vould you like to do this afternoon?'

'Amber Lloyd-Foxe.' Feral shook his head in wonder. 'She's the hottest girl I've seen in years.'

Amber, however, had slid out of the dining room, raided the art department and was racing towards the car park.

Dora, spitting with rage, was leaning out of the science lab window as Stancombe's crimson and gold helicopter finally landed on the grass, to be greeted by a diminished press corps fed up with waiting. As Larks's splendid minibus glided on to the field for the official presentation, no one realized that Amber Lloyd-Foxe had graffitied the back with silver spray paint.

Larks pupils lined up in two rows like ball boys at Wimbledon as Stancombe leapt lithely down on to the grass. Even today, when he'd cultivated an au naturel Richard Branson look – carefully ruffled hair, open-necked check shirt, designer jeans and a shadow of stubble, he didn't get it quite right. The tan was too mahogany and the Dolce & Gabbana label deliberately worn outside his belt.

Striding out to meet him, Alex Bruce explained why Hengist was tied up. Stancombe was incensed.

'You'd have thought . . .'

'I know, I know, I'm afraid our Senior Team Leader is a lawlessness unto himself.'

Next moment, Sheena Anderson had jumped down, and a gust from the helicopter took her black dress over her head to reveal black hold-ups, a neat Brazilian and a wodge of white loo paper shoved between her legs. This was greeted by whoops and wolf whistles. Cosmo whipped out his camera. Dora nearly fell out of the window as a furious Sheena tugged down her skirt.

'Funny place to keep your hanky,' observed Pearl.

'Stan came,' murmured Paris.

Feral laughed. 'You OK, mate?'

'We had a load of press here at three-thirty. They've rather drifted away,' Alex told Stancombe. 'Let's get on with the presentation.'

Rocky, who'd already torn the gold paper off the magnum of champagne, very reluctantly relinquished it so Kylie could present it to Stancombe who, accustomed to the tropical heat of his apartments, was now shivering uncontrollably in the northeast wind.

Janna then came forward to shake his hand.

'It's the most beautiful bus in the world, it's wonderful of you. We are all so grateful.'

A second later Jade, putting on a little girl's voice and crying, 'Daddy, Daddy,' ran across the grass to get in on the act.

'Hi Jadey, how's my little princess?' Stancombe kissed her lingeringly on the mouth.

'Gross,' muttered Milly.

'Can we have a photograph of you and Jade?' asked the *Gazette*.

Meanwhile the helicopter pilot, who'd been kept waiting hours the other end, had charged off to the Gents, whereupon Larks and Bagley pupils swarmed on to the helicopter, examining, pressing buttons, bouncing on the pale beige upholstery, helping themselves to coloured cigarettes.

'Put it back,' said Paris furiously as Feral pocketed a gold ashtray. Sulkily Feral did. A second later, the same ashtray slid into Lubemir's pocket alongside a silver cigarette case. Everyone would blame the yobbos from Larks.

Outside Jade said, 'You know Amber and Milly, don't you, Daddy?'

'Of course.' Stancombe shook their hands. 'And I'd like you to meet Sheena Anderson.' Then, anxious to explain Sheena's presence to Milly: 'Sheen's doing an in-depth profile on me for the *Guardian*.'

'We know Mrs Anderson,' said Milly pointedly.

'How's Flavia?' asked Amber even more pointedly.

'Fine,' snapped Sheena.

'We heard she's got chicken pox even worse than Rebecca. She's got a temperature of a hundred and four,' Milly renewed the attack. 'Mr Anderson was so worried he had to duck out of supervising our balloon-building today.'

'Rufus is such a caring father,' said Jade, who always gave her father's girlfriends a hard time.

Sheena was simply livid.

'How's your mother, Milly?' Stancombe's voice thickened.

'She's really well.'

'Give her my best.'

Why the hell didn't the bitch answer his phone calls?

Bagley and Larks were getting bored. The press were getting restless.

'Why have you given Larkminster Comprehensive such a magnificent bus when you haven't been a huge supporter of the school in the past?' asked the Venturer presenter.

Stancombe, ruffling his hair for the camera, said:

'I feel it's important for disadvantaged youngsters to escape from the poverty trap and, as a consequence, a life of crime.'

As Larks faces fell or set into sullen lines, Janna's eyes met Emlyn's and was comforted to see rage. Stancombe then put an arm round Jade.

'My daughter is a very privileged young lady to be at a school like Bagley. But I've always taught her to treat those less fortunate with kindness.'

'You have, Daddy,' agreed Jade fondly.

'Jade sounds much posher than her dad,' Graffi whispered to Milly. 'Can you learn Posh as well as Spanish, French and German at Bagley?'

'That's what lots of the parents pay for,' said Milly.

Stancombe was kicking himself. By arriving late he had lost crucial coverage. He never should have shagged Sheena – and Larks kids had invaded his chopper. Feral Jackson had just leapt out, pulling at the elastic of a pair of black and red panties as though shooting a catapult at Paris, who was laughing his head off.

Then Stancombe gave a bellow. On the back of the minibus someone had sprayed the words 'Rough Trade Counter' in huge silver letters. The press was going mad photographing it. Alex Bruce was having a coronary.

Lurking in the bushes Amber chucked the can of silver spray paint into the nettles. That would teach young Feral to make a play when he was already in a relationship – and yet, and yet, those kisses had been so magical . . . And what the hell had she done with her mobile?

Fed up with Sheena sticking her tape recorder in everywhere, the press were packing up.

'We'd like the two heads with the pupils,' said a *Daily Telegraph* photographer. 'Any chance we can drag Hengist out?'

'He insisted on not being interrupted.'

'Then we'd better have you in the picture, Mr Bruce.'

Alex was just combing his beard in the minibus wing mirror when Hengist rolled up.

'Randal, you're a brick coming all this way.'

'Randal, you're a brick,' murmured Paris, cracking up Bagley as well as Larks pupils.

As Hengist, Janna, Stancombe and the Larks children, still humiliated and angered by his comments, posed together, a peal of bells floated across the soft autumnal air.

'How lovely,' sighed Janna. 'It must be Wally in the chapel.'

'Thought you only rang bells like that to warn people war had broken out,' quipped Stancombe.

'It already has,' said Paris bleakly.

'OK, chaps.' Hengist waved at the press. 'Got to get back to work. Help yourselves to a cup of tea and a piece of cake inside. Alex'll look after you. Randal, thanks for coming, and I'd like a word with you, Sheena.'

All amiability was wiped off Hengist's face as he drew her aside.

'Glad you're back. Rufus, as you're no doubt aware, is looking after your children, probably contracting chicken pox – or more likely shingles, after the pressure to which you subject him – which means he'll be off for more weeks. Now you're back, you can bloody well take over.'

Sheena flared up immediately. 'The *Guardian* have commissioned this piece. I'm flying straight back to London with Randal to file copy.'

'You can write it from home. Rufus was supposed to supervise operations today. He's paid to look after Bagley's children, not his own.'

Sheena glanced up at Hengist, so handsome, so hard, so contemptuous, and ached with reluctant longing.

'I earn four times as much as my husband,' she said furiously. 'Only way we can make ends meet on his piddling salary since you passed him over as housemaster.'

'Since we passed *you* over as a housemaster's wife. There's nothing wrong with Rufus. If you're capable of earning that kind of money, why the hell don't you get a nanny?'

Quivering with rage, Sheena caught up with Stancombe.

'That bastard B-T's ordered me home to look after the kids.'

'Got a point. Mother's place is with her kids when they're sick.'

'I can't write against that din.'

'You promised I could see copy.'

'I will if there's time; they want it this evening. I'm going to bury the Brett-Taylors if it kills me.'

199

32

Pearl and Graffi were in ecstasy. The drama department were doing *Bugsy Malone* and researching all that thirties kit and make-up. Graffi, having discovered the art department, was going berserk with a spray gun. Miss Cambola had already had a lovely time exploring the music library. Now, wandering round with Kylie, she suddenly heard a pianist pouring forth his soul in a ravishing fountain of sound. Miss Cambola stiffened like a pointer.

'This I must see.' Pushing her way into the music hall, followed by an enraptured Kylie, she found Cosmo at the piano, black curls flying, pale face maniacal as he thundered up and down the keys, producing notes of such crystal beauty, yet somehow managing with his head and occasional free hand to conduct the orchestra as well.

'Stop, stop.' The orchestra slithered to a nervous halt. Cosmo was hurling abuse at them when he heard a footstep and swung round. 'Get out,' he screamed. 'Get fucking out, out, out.'

But Miss Cambola strode on undeterred.

'Maestro,' she cried, sweeping off her Tyrolean hat like a principal boy and seizing Cosmo's pale hand. She kissed it lovingly. 'You can only be the son of Roberto Rannaldini, the greatest conductor of the twentieth century, if not all time.'

Cosmo was mollified. Whatever his contempt for humans, he loved music and was soon gabbling away in Italian. Miss Cambola then introduced Kylie Rose.

'She has an extraordinarily beautiful voice.'

'I must hear it. What instrument do you play, signora?'

'The trumpet,' replied Cambola.

'There's a spare here.'

'The Battle of Waterloo was won on the playing fields of Eton and various other good public schools,' wrote Hengist.

Normally he rattled off journalism. Today he was struggling, especially as Painswick wasn't here to do his research and find out how many acres of playing fields had been sold off in the last twenty years – or hectares. Stupid word. 'Hectors' ought to be sorting out Greeks on the ringing plains of windy Troy.

'Crash, bang, wallop, de dum, de, dah – de, dum, de dah,' anyone would think the Rolling Stones were warming up in the corridor. Hengist glanced irritably up at the timetable. 'Orchestra rehearsal: Cosmo Rannaldini.'

Sixty seconds later, Hengist roared into the music hall—

'For Christ's sake, Cosmo, take that bloody din down.'

Only to find Cambola, Tyrolean hat on the back of her head, jamming away on a trumpet.

Feral, who had a great capacity for kissing the joy as it flies, had just jolted Ex-Regimental Sergeant Major Bilson, who ran the small arms range, by hitting everything in sight. Feral in turn had been fascinated to learn that the sixth-form pupils listed on the walls had sharpened up their shooting here before immediately setting off for two world wars to kill real people and be killed themselves.

Now he was playing golf in the fading light with his new friends Anatole, Lubemir and the Hon. Jack, who seemed a good bloke for a toff and who also supported Arsenal.

'You played before?' Jack asked Feral after a few holes.

'No, man.'

'Christ, well, keep practising, Tiger.'

'My father will sponsor you,' said Anatole. 'We will bury Americans.'

'Golf is excellent game,' said Lubemir. 'You can combine other pleasures, enjoy country air . . .' and, reaching into the bole of an oak tree, he produced what looked like a large stock cube wrapped in cellophane.

'Don't do drugs, man,' said Feral.

'Have a slug of this, then.'

'Nice guy, Emlyn,' observed Feral as neat vodka bit into his throat.

'Tough as sheet,' grumbled Lubemir. 'As punishment he make you run round the pitch in the middle of the night. But you can have a laugh with him. And he takes the teams to the pub when they win matches.'

'Good teacher,' Jack said, who was looking for his ball in the long pale grass. 'Annoying sometimes; always got a reason why the English didn't really win a battle.'

They were passing Badger's Retreat and the Family Tree, its three bodies writhing together in love and resentment. Down below in the valley, lights of farms and cottages were twinkling.

'Very left wing, Emlyn,' Jack went on disapprovingly.

'What's his woman like?' asked Feral.

'Good-looking but even more of a leftie than Emlyn. Wants to abolish public schools, hunting and the House of Lords – what the fuck would my father do all day?'

Feral was teeing up a ball, white as his eyeballs, squinting towards the distant green as he'd watched Tiger do so often on television.

'This is a five,' said Lubemir, passing the spliff to Anatole.

'Oriana is in Afghanistan,' said Anatole approvingly. 'Talking about war, always attacking American imperialism, very good girl.'

'Emlyn must be worried,' said Feral.

'That's why he's so bad-tempered.'

Johnnie Fowler, Kitten and Gloria were having a lovely time working out in the gym with Denzil. Alex Bruce, by contrast, was having a dreadful day. He'd failed to get on television. Hengist had stolen Mrs Radcliffe for another draft. He was furious with Emlyn for sloping off to fine tune the rugby team, leaving that coven of thieves playing golf with Feral Jackson. God knows what they were plotting. Alex had ordered Boffin Brooks, the one dependable boy in the school, not to let Paris Alvaston out of his sight.

Paris was now in the library. He had never seen such rows of temptation, magic carpets waiting to fly him to distant worlds. He had found the plays of Noël Coward and Oscar Wilde. How could anyone be so funny? But Paris couldn't really concentrate; he wanted to write sonnets to Janna. She had held his hand and let him see her cry. If only Boffin would fuck off and stop rabbiting on about IT.

Paris took down a copy of Donne's poems.

> I am two fools, I know,
> For loving, and for saying so
> In whining poetry.

Summed it up really.

Boffin, bored with books, insisted on showing Paris the science lab. Here Dora, forcibly removed from the window by No-Joke Joan, was furiously writing an essay on 'The Journey of the Sperm'.

'The sperms venture inside the womb' – her Biro was nearly ripping the paper – 'trying to swim towards the eggs – yuk – eventually they find them and fertilize them.'

'Do they do the breast stroke or do they crawl?' asked Bianca.

'Dog paddle, I would think. Just imagine all those tiny tadpoles swimming around to produce one. Yuk. Imagine our parents doing that.'

'Being adopted, I don't know who my parents were,' sighed Bianca.

'Must have been beautiful to produce you. My brother Dicky says you're the prettiest girl in the school. Oh, look, here comes that tosser Boffin and Paris Alvaston.'

Dora and Bianca watched Boffin sidle off to chat up No-Joke Joan.

'The old buzzard's looking quite starry-eyed. Boffin's her favourite pupil.'

'He's gorgeous-looking, Paris,' observed Bianca.

Paris's face was as still as a statue, the white streak down the side of his tracksuit trousers emphasizing the lean length of his leg.

'Hengist said we've got to be nice to them,' said Dora, then, edging up to Paris: 'Would you like to take part in an experiment?'

'Depends.'

Dora handed him a piece of stiff white paper and a bottle of blue-black ink. 'Now, drop some ink on the paper.'

So Paris shook out a dark-blue blob, which trembled, then settled.

'Now dip the bit of paper in this flask of water.'

'What for?'

'Trust me. Good. Now watch.'

When the paper was removed from the water the dark blob had metamorphosed into a royal-blue, turquoise and olive-green oval.

'Look,' cried Dora in excitement, 'it's a peacock feather.'

'That's cool,' said Paris, examining it.

'You can all turn from blobs into peacock feathers if you work hard enough,' said a marching-up Joan. 'Now get on with your work, Dora. What are you writing?'

'The Journey of the Sperm.'

'Finding the eggs,' piped up Bianca. 'Dora wanted to know if the eggs were free range.'

'No, the sperm is,' said Paris.

Dora and Bianca got the giggles.

'Don't be sillier than you need be,' snapped Joan.

'I'm going to blow her up soon,' muttered Dora as she handed the peacock feather to Paris.

Paris put it in his pocket, thinking how nice it would be to have a little sister like Dora.

High tea was held in the General Bagley Room, which was used by the debating and literary societies, and for visiting non-crowd-pulling speakers. It was a charming room with flame-red walls, grey silk curtains, framed prize-winning pictures from the art department and a lovely view from the window of the General astride his charger gazing down the Long Walk.

As Hengist still hadn't finished his piece, Sally stood in for him and made the Larks children feel even more special by offering them a great mountain of delectable scrambled egg, dripping with butter and cream and served with smoked salmon and wholemeal toast. Larks, who had never tasted anything so delicious, went back for second and third helpings. A big cheese and onion pie had been set aside for the vegetarians, but everyone tucked into that too and into salads, slices of melon with glacé cherries, fruit salad and chocolate brownies.

'Yum, yum, yum,' said Milly. 'You must come over more often. We don't usually get food like this.'

'Such a happy day,' Mags Gablecross was telling Sally. 'I feel as though I've had a week's holiday. The kids are overwhelmed by such kindness.'

Mags was like a hot-water bottle on a cold night, thought Janna, who was ashamed of feeling so depressed when they were all enjoying themselves. Even Emlyn had shrugged off his ill humour. The teams looked sharper than he'd expected and he was electrified by Feral. If ever there was a natural talent . . . That golf swing was utterly instinctive; he couldn't wait to get him on to the rugby field. Where was he? he wondered.

All around, the children were chattering nineteen to the dozen, arguing about GCSE subjects, football and clothes.

Boffin Brooks, who strongly disapproved of smoked salmon being wasted on such ruffians, noting Aysha and Xav sitting together, contented but not speaking, decided to join them. He was so caring about ethnic minorities.

'Mustn't neglect you two,' he said loudly.

Patronizing bastard, thought Xav, who'd never met anyone as adorable as Aysha. She had the same timidity and sweetness as his mother and he was sure she had the same rippling dark hair beneath her headscarf. He longed to tell her what he couldn't tell his parents: how lonely it was being black in a white family, particularly when, unlike Rupert, he wasn't good at anything.

'There is a myth that independent students don't work hard,' Boffin was saying sententiously. 'In fact I rise at six-thirty and am often still at my computer at eleven at night.'

And I clean the house, cook, wash, iron, shop, go to the mosque, learn from the Koran and do my homework, thought Aysha, and my father still beats me. But Xavier had protected her from Jade. She didn't know how to thank him. He had such a nice face when he wasn't scowling.

'Qualifications are indeed the only things that matter,' went on Boffin.

'No they ain't.' Graffi squeezed Milly's hand. 'Straight As don't teach you how to hang doors or unblock a bog.'

'I agree,' said the Hon. Jack. 'We're learning about agriculture in geography. Bloody waste of time. My father's got a farm. Rufus can't teach me anything new.'

Kylie felt Jack's big hand edging up her thigh. The hand of a lord's son. Her mother would be in raptures.

'I don't like maffs because I don't like our maffs teacher,' said Rocky in his hoarse voice.

'You wouldn't like ours any better,' said Amber. 'He shifts his cock from one leg of his trousers to another, and buries great silent sulphuric farts in his thick tweed trousers. He's called Biffo; ought to be "Whiffo".'

Rocky broke into his hoarse laugh and, unable to stop, lumbered to his feet.

'I'd like to fank everyone at Bagley for having us. Free cheers to Bagley. Hip, hip, hooray; hip, hip, hooray; hip, hip, hooray.'

'You *must* play Bottom next time we do a production of *A Midsummer Night's Dream*,' suggested Cosmo.

'Where's Feral?' said Pearl fretfully.

'You will come out wiv me, won't you?' Graffi murmured to Milly. After his winnings today he could take her to La Perdrix d'Or.

'Course I will. You've got the same lovely accent as Mr Davies. Everyone's got crushes on him, but you've got me over mine.'

33

Hengist felt drained but Christ-like. He had faxed his piece and the *Telegraph* loved it. One shouldn't be so dependent on approval. In the drinks cupboard he found a box of Maltesers given him by some pupil and, realizing he hadn't had any lunch, broke the cellophane and started eating them. His thoughts turned to Janna arriving with her children.

'Round about her "there is a rabble Of the filthy, sturdy, unkillable infants of the very poor",' he quoted idly. ' "They shall inherit the earth." '

Poor child, he'd neglected her shamelessly. He decided to text her: 'Settle your children, then escape and have a drink.'

Shiny-faced, shadowed beneath the eyes, lipstick bitten off, Janna longed to repair her face, but, scared Hengist would have pushed off somewhere else, loathing herself for such abject acquiescence, she was knocking on his big oak door five minutes later.

'How's it gone? I'm so sorry, darling.' Hengist thrust a large glass of gin and orange into her hand.

He'd remembered, but then he'd remembered Kylie had a baby called Cameron. It was so unprofessional to sulk, she must just be cool.

'Your kids have been so nice,' she began. 'The balloons were brilliant, and they've had a really good time since then trying things out. I'm so proud of them,' she added defiantly.

'So you should be.'

His was such a beautiful room: rich dark panelling soaring into the ornate ceiling, William Morris animal tiles round the leaping log fire, red lamps casting a warm glow, lovely photographs on the desk of Sally, Oriana and Elaine, a stuffed bear in a mortar board, overcrowded bookshelves. Noting dilapidated, leather-bound copies of Horace, Aristotle, Saint-Simon and Gibbon, all containing bookmarks, Janna wondered if he'd really read and referred to them all.

Apart from the Keith Vaughan of a thundery twilight, yet to be dispatched to the Common Room, all other available wall space was covered by sepia photographs of past teams, past scholars, past heads, past glories. Such a stultifying emphasis on tradition.

'We've got an old boys' reunion tonight,' said Hengist. 'It's to encourage them to send their sons and daughters here.'

' "This is the Chapel: here, my son, Your father thought the thoughts of youth," ' quoted Janna scornfully.

She ran her hands over a bronze replica of the lion in the quad, dropping his head to lick the little fawn:

'More likely to gobble it up.'

'Debatable,' agreed Hengist.

He looked tired, with great bags under his eyes, but he seemed very happy as he abstractedly went on eating Maltesers.

On a side table Janna suddenly caught sight of a perfectly dreadful figurine of a headless naked woman, with a noose around her long neck and forests of armpit and pubic hair.

'Goodness.'

'Goodness, as Mae West said, has nothing to do with it. Alex Bruce's wife made it for my birthday to remind me not to oppress women.'

'What's she like?'

'Gha-a-a-astly.' Hengist shuddered. 'She carries political correctness ad absurdum and has the relentless cheeriness and verbal diarrhoea of a weather girl. One longs to throw a green baize cloth over her.'

There was a pause. The room was so cosy after the chill winter evening, the flames dancing merrily.

'Dreadful forgetting the *Telegraph* piece, I'm so sorry.' Hengist upended the box of Maltesers.

'Did they like it?'

'John Clare said he did. It probably thumped the right tubs. I ought to write more.'

'I ought to read more,' Janna said fretfully. 'I haven't read a single novel since I came to Larks. I truly hate being a head.'

The guilt she felt about being away from school all afternoon was kicking in. She could no longer bury it beneath her longing to see Hengist again. He's not remotely interested in me, she thought bleakly.

'I don't deserve to be one,' she went on. 'I can't make peace

207

with my staff. They'll never forgive me for having a lovely time today.'

'Don't be silly,' said Hengist gently. 'I like your children very much and I look forward to knowing them and their head-mistress a great deal better.'

'You do?' Janna glanced up, and Hengist was mortified to see her trembling bottom lip and the despair in her big brown eyes.

They were interrupted by an almighty crash, scattering glass everywhere, followed by a second and a further shower of fragments.

Janna screamed; Hengist leapt forward, pulling her against him and out of the way. For a few blissful seconds, his arms closed around her and she felt the softness of dark green cashmere and his heart pounding, and breathed in a faint smell of lemon after-shave and Maltesers.

Then he looked down and she looked up. Both for a second were distracted from the disaster as his beautiful mouth hovered above hers, then reality kicked in.

'Was that some kind of terrorist attack?' she gasped.

Something had smashed the vast bay window overlooking the pitches and to the splintered glass all over the floor were added the shattered remnants of Poppet Bruce's figurine.

'I've found a bit of bush.' Hengist brandished a fragment. 'At least Mrs Bruce's masterpiece is no more. It's an ill window, I suppose.' He grinned in such delight, Janna burst out laughing.

'This is the culprit,' Hengist fished a golf ball out of the fire-place. Striding to the now gaping window, he peered into the dusk, roaring: 'What the hell are you playing at? Christ!' he added as he slowly took in how far the ball must have travelled. Picking up his binoculars, usually used for birdwatching, he caught sight of a distant crimson sweatshirt and a huge, wide grin.

'Your Feral Jackson is the culprit behind the culprit.'

'Oh God.' Janna was appalled. 'We'll pay for it.'

'Feral can pay for it himself when he wins the Masters, if we haven't converted him to rugger by then. God, that was a long way.'

'I'm so sorry, I must take my children home.'

'Feral won't have had supper yet.'

'You've got your old boys' reunion.'

Hengist shrugged. 'We've always got something. Have another drink, it's only five o'clock.' He ran a hand over her hair. 'Sorry you were frightened, but it was a lovely hug.'

34

Over in the General Bagley Room, Graffi and Feral were chatting so much they hadn't noticed Paris's self-absorption.

Feral had come to Bagley determined to trash everything in sight, but he'd had fun; he'd outshot and outdriven everyone else; and he had a new friend called Amber who'd given him her mobile number. Would he have the guts to ring her?

Suddenly the jangling jolly theme tune of showjumping on the BBC rang out.

'That's my mobile,' cried Amber in delight. 'Where is it?'

'Here,' said Cosmo, picking up Feral's black tracksuit top and, before Feral could stop him, whipping a mobile out of the inside pocket. The room went quiet. Cosmo switched it on.

'Hi, is that Peregrine? Hang on a minute. What's your mobile doing in Feral's fleece?' he asked Amber.

'I never touched it.' Feral jumped to his feet, amiability turning to menace, fists clenched, Graffi and Paris beside him.

'I gave it to Feral to look after when we were racing round the wood,' said Amber quickly. 'It was safer with him.'

For a second she and Cosmo glared at each other.

'You said you'd lost it.'

'And now I've found it. Hi, Perry, how are you?'

Graffi pulled a protesting Feral back into his chair.

'I didn't take no mobile.'

'Cool it, man, she gave it to you to look after, she said so.'

'She didn't,' said Feral stonily. 'That was a plant to frame me.'

'What did you go inside for last summer, Feral?' asked Cosmo chattily. 'For nicking a mobile wasn't it?'

Paris stood up and, strolling down the row, pulled Cosmo to his feet. 'Don't even go down that road, you sick bastard,' he said softly. In a trice, Emlyn was beside him.

'It's Janna's day. Don't spoil it for her.'

Paris glowered round, slowly his fist uncurled and dropped to his side. 'You sick bastard,' he repeated.

Boffin, who'd missed this scrap, was still pontificating. 'We do a lot for charity,' he was telling Aysha in his nasal whine. 'We raised twenty thousand pounds for netball courts in Soweto with sponsored runs and cycle rides. Senior students act as mentors to the local primary school. Primrose is very active in this field. We run errands for senior citizens and tend their gardens. We raise a lot for the NSPCC, for cancer patients and other disadvantaged groups.'

Pausing for breath, he smiled smugly round at the Larks contingent. 'And of course today, we've set aside an entire after- noon to entertain you folks.'

'An entire afternoon to entertain you folks,' whined Paris in perfect imitation.

Milly's giggle immediately died. There was a terrible silence.

'Boffin,' said a horrified Amber.

Pearl rose to her feet, hoop earrings flying.

'You lot 'ad us over today,' she yelled. 'If you just did it for bleedin' charity, you can stick it up your ass'ole. In fact you're just a lot of fuckin' ass'oles. Upper class'oles in fact.'

'Upper class-holes,' sighed Cosmo in ecstasy. 'Isn't that perfect. Oh, Pearl of great price.'

Paris, however, had jumped on to the table, padded his way cat- like through the debris of supper and leapt off at Boffin's side, lifting him up by his lapels.

'Take that back,' he hissed.

'Paris,' thundered Emlyn.

'How dare you patronize us.'

Next moment there was a crunch as Paris's knuckles connected with Boffin's buck teeth and hoisted him across the room.

'Stop it.' Emlyn grabbed Paris, clamping his arms behind his back; then, turning on Boffin, who was moaning on the floor, mouth filling up with blood: 'Get up, you deserve everything you got.'

Emlyn proceeded to whistle up Lando and Jack. 'Get him out of here quickly, take him to the sick bay.'

'Wait 'til my father hears about this,' mumbled Boffin, spitting out teeth.

'Save him the cash for a brace,' shouted Lando. 'You should send him a bill, Paris.'

Boffin's remarks had been so cringe-making that everyone cheered as Lando, aided by Jack, Mags and Jason, smuggled him out of a side door.

'Be quiet, everyone,' rapped out Emlyn as Hengist walked in with Janna, who looked as though a smoothing iron had been run over her glowing face.

'I just love being a head,' she was saying. 'It's like being a gardener with slightly too many plants to look after.'

Paris had felt no pain from Boffin's teeth, but he'd rather have roasted in hell than witness the adoring way Janna was smiling up at Hengist.

Out they swarmed into the twilight, rain like the spray from some giant waterfall cooling their hot faces.

Wally, who'd had a wonderful time trying out the bells, hobnobbing with Mrs Axford and talking to RSM Bilson about his son in Iraq, was revving up the bus.

The two schools were bidding each other fond farewells and the Larks pupils were surging on to the minibus when a BMW came hurtling up the drive, screamed to a halt and one of the prettiest women Paris had ever seen leapt out. She was very tall and slim with big anxious eyes and a mass of dark wavy hair. Jeans might have been invented for her.

' "Her eyes as stars of twilight fair; Like twilight's, too, her dusky hair",' he muttered in wonder.

'Christ, look at her,' gasped Feral.

'It's Rupert Campbell-Black's wife, Taggie,' cried an excited Kylie, a great reader of *Hello!*

For a moment, Taggie looked around in anguish, then Bianca came dancing down the steps into her mother's arms.

'I'm sorry, darling,' gasped Taggie. 'The traffic was terrible and I forgot my mobile. I'm so sorry, how are you, how did the dance class go?'

Chucking her stuff in the back, running round to the other side, Bianca waved goodbye to Dora. 'See you tomorrow, I'll text you the moment I get home.'

For a second a shadow flitted across Taggie's face. 'Is Xav around?'

'No,' said Bianca, then irritably: 'He'll be doing prep or watching television. Come on.'

'OK,' sighed Taggie, slotting a seatbelt over the most delectable bosom.

'Oh, that I vas that seatbelt,' sighed Anatole.

'You did give Xav Daddy's and my love?'

'Yes, yes.' For a second, Bianca's sweet face hardened. 'Let's go, we're holding up the bus.'

Neither she nor Taggie saw Xavier lurking under a nearby oriental plane, desperate to catch a glimpse of his mother. He mustn't be a wimp and run to her. Cosmo, alas, had seen him.

'I hear you insulted Jade,' he said softly. 'Getting a bit above yourself, aren't you, black shit? You'll pay for it later.'

A furious Alex caught up with Hengist just as he was leaving his office. 'That window will cost a fortune to replace.'

'I know, but did you see how far the ball travelled? Boy's a natural, and surely we're insured.'

'Not for my wife's gift,' spluttered Alex. 'It's irreplaceable. I know how much care she put into it.' Then an almost coy expression flickered across his face. 'Although if you asked her *very* nicely, she might model you another one.'

'Sweet of her but I'm sure there are worthier recipients than I.'

You bastard, thought Alex.

'A very successful visit, I feel,' said Hengist, whisking off down the stairs.

On the journey back Wally stopped to pick up Graffi's balloon, which was roosting in a hedge like a bird of paradise. The children sang the whole time except when Janna went up to the front and clapped her hands.

'Thank you for behaving so beautifully. I'm right proud of all of you. The Bagley teachers were really complimentary, and thank you for mixing so well with the Bagley kids. Would you like to go back again soon?'

'Yes please,' rose the cry.

Paris didn't sing. He gazed out of the window at the skeletal trees against the russet glow of Larkminster and the cathedral spire, so like one of Rowan Merton's sharpened pencils that he wanted to pick it up and write volumes about his despair.

Imagine running out of school into the arms and soft bosom of a mother as loving as Taggie, who would ask him about his day and sweep him home to tea. Or think of turning right to Wilmington, feeding Partner, cooking supper with Janna and falling asleep in her arms: 'Pillowed upon my fair love's ripening breast'.

Oh God, he wanted a family and a home.

Rocky, after his exertions, had fallen asleep on Kylie's shoulder.

'I really like Jack Waterlane,' she was telling Pearl. 'He was so sweet to Rocky.'

'Same intellectual level,' muttered Graffi.

'Never seen such lovely men as that Emlyn, so macho,' gushed Gloria, 'and that Hengist and that Denzil, who I can assure you is not G.A.Y.'

Feeling there was safety in numbers Wally dropped the children off on the edge of the Shakespeare Estate. Janna shivered at the sight of Oaktree Court, a great Victorian pile with fluorescent lighting and bars on the windows. Paris jumped out, shuffling towards the front door without looking behind or uttering a word of thanks. He couldn't trust himself not to cry.

Humming Prokofiev One, Miss Cambola was joyfully ringing possible dates for a joint concert with Bagley.

'Time for a drink?' Mags asked Janna as they reached Larks.

'Just let me check my messages.'

'Mess' was the operative word. All the displays in reception had been trashed. Rowan had left a note on her desk:

'Did you mean to switch off your mobile? Ring Ashton the moment you get in. Ditto Russell. Ditto Crispin. Ditto Rod Hyde; he left at 6.30. Girl's toilets blocked as well now. Martin Norman rushed to hospital after fight in playground. Three windows broken. Satan on roof chucking down tiles.'

'I'll come and have that drink,' said Janna, just finding time to open a note from Lydia: 'Lovely day; kids very good. We all missed you but heaven without Cara, please burn this.'

Mercifully the Ghost and Castle was empty, except for the skeleton propping up the bar. No disaffected Larks staff in sight. Funny how I lived in the pub when I was at Redfords, thought Janna. Her hair still felt on fire where Hengist had stroked it. Mags insisted on buying the drinks and, between gulps, carrying on knitting the scarf for her future son-in-law.

Mags had the beautiful complexion and sweet unruffled serenity, thought Janna, that a Raphael Madonna might have achieved in middle age if her life had not been torn apart by the tragedy of a son's death.

'Thank you ever so much for coming.'

Mags smiled. 'It was a huge success. You're right to be proud of your children. You've given them so much confidence. Both sides were amazed how much they liked each other.'

Mags prayed the saga of Boffin's teeth wouldn't reach the press. She wondered if she should tell Janna about it, then Janna put everything out of her mind by asking her if she'd like to be deputy head.

'You'd be so good, Mags. The kids love and trust you, and so do the staff. Your lessons are so popular and you don't grind axes all day.'

Looking at Janna's little face, at the pallor beneath the dark freckles and the eyes that never seemed far from tears these days, Mags was deeply touched.

'That's the sweetest compliment I've ever been paid. If you're part-time, people regard you as a dilettante. But truly two and a half days a week are enough for me, so I can be there for Tim when he's on a big case and comes home wiped out, and for the children and soon, fingers crossed, the grandchildren who will all want a part of me and expect me to drop everything. And we've got Diane's wedding coming up. I'm better all round if I don't spread myself too thin.

'I'll support you all the way,' she went on, 'and the others aren't that antagonistic. Sam Spink is a troublemaking cow, but you get that in any school. Forget the Dinosaurs. The rest of the staff like you very much, they're just terrified and poisoned by Cara. You must get rid of her.'

'Hengist and your nice husband said the same thing.'

'Cara made a play for Hengist once, asked him to dance. He rejected her with a finesse only he's capable of.'

'Really?' Janna longed to know more, but didn't want to appear too keen. 'I think Cara's mad. Did you see her ripping apart those anemones? Do you think there's a conspiracy against me?'

Mags looked up, startled.

'The *Gazette* won't leave me alone. There was a piece yesterday about the staff leaving in droves. Russell and S and C deliberately thwart my every move. They seem to be willing me to fail.'

'I'll have a word with Tim,' said Mags thoughtfully. 'You know I disagree passionately with private education, but I have to say both teachers and pupils were terrific today.'

Over at Bagley, Cosmo, Lubemir and Anatole were enjoying their game: shoving Xavier's dark head down the lavatory, holding him under as they pulled the chain.

'Might wash you white, black shit. Black shit should go down the bog,' taunted Cosmo, giving Xav a vicious kick in the ribs.

'Don't bruise him,' reproved Anatole.

'Bruises don't show up on black shit.'

'He is not getting whiter.' Lubemir yanked Xav out by the hair to examine his face. 'Try some bleach.' He emptied half a bottle of Domestos into the water before ramming Xav's head back again.

Xav squeezed shut his eyes so the bleach couldn't burn them

214

but, forced to open his mouth to breathe, gulped and choked as bleach went down his throat.

Cosmo meanwhile, having wolfed down some muesli and a crushed bloc of lavatory freshener, retched and, yanking aside Xav's head, threw up into the lavatory bowl before shoving Xav back again.

'In you go, black bastard.'

Xav thought he'd choke with revulsion and his lungs would explode with pain. Death would be better than this.

Please God, let me die.

Mags had left her Renault outside the Ghost and Castle. As Janna wandered back to Larks's car park, she found the words: 'Go back to Yorkshire you dirty bitch', scrawled in scarlet lipstick across her windscreen.

I mustn't panic, she told herself. It couldn't be Cara, she was off sick. Heart thumping, terrified her brakes had been tampered with, or a mad murderer might rise up in the back to strangle her, she drove very slowly back to Wilmington.

As she leapt out of her car, Partner hurtled out of Lily's house, then stopped at her feet, whimpering and crying.

'I'm so sorry to leave you so long, love,' she said, gathering him up, bitterly ashamed that he was trembling as violently as she was.

Lily admitted that the little dog had missed her dreadfully.

'He's fine with me for a bit, then he seems to panic you're not coming back.'

'I'll take him into Larks tomorrow,' said Janna. 'I guess I need a guard dog.'

35

Janna was so tired, neither terror of Cara nor dreams of Hengist kept her awake. It seemed only a second later that her alarm clock was battering her brain. Six o'clock already. Tugging a pillow over her head for five more minutes, she was roused at a quarter to seven by Partner tugging off her duvet with his teeth.

Thanking him profusely, showering, dressing, wolfing a piece of toast and marmalade, she took her cup of coffee, torch and dog out for a quick run across the fields, soaking her trousers with dew, tripping over molehills, splashing through streams.

'In winter I get up at night And dress by yellow candle-light.'

Partner charged ahead, barking joyfully, chasing rabbits, but as they returned to the cottage, his tummy dragged along the ground, his pointed ear and the remaining plumes on his tail drooped lower and lower at the prospect of Janna abandoning him.

'It's all right, darling, you're coming too.'

Hope springing eternal, Partner gazed up, ginger head on one side, onyx eyes shining, then went berserk, squeaking and jumping four feet off the ground. As she put his basket and a bag of biscuits in the car, he rushed off to collect his lead, then leapt into his basket in the back.

There was an apricot glow in the east. As they passed the signpost for Bagley, she wondered if Hengist ever thought of her. She kept remembering his powerful body thrust against hers. She must find herself a boyfriend.

'I've got you,' she called back to Partner, who swished his tail, then as she crossed the bridge into Larkminster, her mobile beeped. Glancing at the screen, she read: 'Yr toff Bagley friends won't save you, you rancid old tart' and nearly ran into one of the Victorian lamp-posts. She must go to the police.

Shaking uncontrollably, moaning with terror, she sought refuge in the boarded-up newsagent's next to the Ghost and Castle. As she picked up the papers, she was fractionally cheered when the owner, Mrs Kamani, who was always grumbling about the children shoplifting, suddenly announced how delightful they'd been on television last night.

Having installed Partner with a Bonio in his basket under her desk, Janna distracted herself from the foul text message by checking on yesterday's press coverage. It was pretty good except for the *Gazette*, which angled its report on caring Stancombe giving Larks a £25,000 minibus and taking time out from his impossibly busy schedule to fly down to Bagley.

As the purpose of his generosity had been to rescue Larks pupils from the poverty of their ambitions and a life of crime, Stancombe had felt it sadly ironic that after these same pupils had stormed the helicopter during the opening ceremony, several gold ashtrays, a silver cigarette case and a bottle of champagne had gone missing.

'Rubbish,' howled Janna. 'The helicopter was also swarming with Bagley pupils.'

The piece was illustrated by a glamorous picture of Stancombe and Jade, of Larks and Bagley children looking bored, and of Janna, as usual, smiling coyly up at Hengist.

When was Col Peters going to ease up?

Thank God the television coverage would be seen by millions more people than read the *Gazette*.

Most of our parents can't read anyway, Janna was shocked to find herself thinking. The rest of the press had followed Venturer's lead, photographing Kylie in her flowered dress: 'We thought Bagley would be stuck-up snobs, but they were really nice people.'

The *Guardian* had clearly dropped Sheena's piece on Stancombe, who'd be livid. They had however included a charming photo of the black children: Xav, Aysha and Feral, sending Aysha's proud but panic-stricken mother out to buy every copy in case her husband saw it on his return from Pakistan.

Only that most scurrilous of tabloids the *Scorpion* excelled itself by showing Cosmo's somewhat fuzzy pictures of the geography master's wife flashing her Brazilian as she descended from Stancombe's chopper and of 'Rough Trade Counter' on the back of the bus, which had a caption: 'This is what snooty Bagley really thought of Larks'. However, this hadn't stopped 'Toff Love', the caption on a picture of Kylie Rose, 'a 13-year-old single parent', breaking down social barriers with the Hon. Jack Waterlane behind a holly bush.

'Jack's lush,' enthused Kylie Rose . . .

Janna couldn't stop laughing. What would Hengist say? She was brought back to earth by a call from Crispin Thomas furiously cataloguing her iniquities. How could Janna have deserted her post? One would have thought Nelson had gone ashore to frolic with Lady Hamilton during the Battle of Trafalgar.

'If you grant a handful of kids absurd privileges, the rest will act up.'

Janna left the telephone on her desk, made a cup of coffee, and when she picked it up again, Crispin was still snuffling.

'If Rod Hyde hadn't held the fort yesterday . . .'

Oh God, another text message was coming through. Janna steeled herself, but it was from Hengist.

'Hurrah for Toff Love. Ignore *Gazette*, coverage great and should take Sheena down a few square pegs. A bientot. H B-T.'

Trying to keep the silly grin off her face, Janna found Crispin still yakking: 'I'm surprised you have nothing to say to justify such a lapse. It will be top of the agenda at the governors' meeting next week.'

As Wally came in whistling Prokofiev One, Janna handed him a bottle of whisky.

'What's this for? I had a great time. The wife loved seeing us on TV and taped the programme. That Emlyn Davies is a smashing bloke. And that's a nice little dog. Is this Partner? Looks like a cross between a fox and a woodlouse. Come on, boy.'

Partner cowered in his basket.

Then Rowan raced in weighed down by Tesco carrier bags.

'How did it go? Lovely piece on Venturer; the kids looked so happy and you looked so pretty, and you were great, Wally. Oh! This must be Partner, isn't he adorable? Look at his sweet face. He must be part cairn, part Norfolk. Look at his poor bare tail, but I'm sure it'll grow back. Goodness he's sweet.'

Thus encouraged, Partner edged forward.

'We had a lovely day at Bagley Hall,' announced Janna at assembly. 'Later, we'll tell you about it and the wonderful things planned for the future. But first, I want to introduce a new member of Larks. I hope you'll be very kind to him; it's so hard starting late in the term.

'Many of you have been asking what happened to the little dog who nearly died when some cruel boys tied a rocket to his tail.

The answer is he recovered, he's living with me in Wilmington and he's so clever, when I overslept this morning, he pulled the duvet off my bed to wake me up. But he gets frightened on his own during the day and howls, thinking he's been abandoned again. So he's going to come to school every day to be our mascot, bringing us luck. His name is Partner,' she added as Rowan carried him proudly up on to the stage and handed him over.

'I want you all to say "Howdy, Partner", like the cowboys.'

'Howdy, Partner,' roared the delighted children.

Partner quivered at such a big crowd, particularly when Janna carried him down the steps so Year Seven in the front row could stroke him. Then suddenly he caught sight of Paris, who had hugged him and so gently bathed his sore tail and, leaping down, he jumped into Paris's arms.

'Now we really know how much time Paris Alvaston spends at our Senior Team Leader's cottage,' muttered Red Robbie, who was furious that Gloria had had such a lovely time in a capitalist playground yesterday.

'That remark should be withdrawn,' cried an outraged Cambola. She strode up to the piano. 'Now we will sing "All Things Bright and Beautiful", with special emphasis on the Lord God loving all creatures great and small.'

Cambola started playing. The children started singing, but had great difficulty carrying on when Partner put back his ginger head, like the fox in Aesop's fable, and howled until Miss Cambola rose from the piano and conducted him with her pencil, so he howled even louder and the singing broke up because everyone was laughing so much.

As a dog who could end assembly five minutes early, Partner's fame was assured.

36

Cara had only been off sick five minutes before a flood of Larks teachers, realizing how wonderful school was without her venomous demoralizing presence and unable to face the prospect of her return, handed in their notice. These included Adele, Robbie Rushton's deputy, who would now have no means of supporting two little children; Jessamy, Mike Pitts's teaching assistant; Gloria, the gymnast; Lydia and Lance, the newly qualified teachers; and, most surprisingly, Miss Basket, who, because no one else would employ her, everyone thought would ensure her pension by clinging on by her bitten fingernails to the end of time.

Lydia summed up the exodus:

'I love Larks and you, Janna, but I can't handle Cara any more. I feel sick with terror every morning. She's supposed to watch my teaching and encourage me, but I haven't had a page of notes since I've been here. And she punishes me by inciting her favourites to act up. Kitten Meadows stood with her hands on her hips and said, "You're just jealous because I'm hotter than you," then spat in my face. When I complained, Cara just laughed and said, "If you can't handle sassy girls!"

'We're supposed to go to the deputy head if we've got a problem with her, but as he's shagging her anyway, he'd just grass me up, then she'd murder me.

'I'm scared of her, Janna. Please let me leave at Christmas.'

'I'll see what I can do, but please reconsider.' Janna felt bitterly ashamed that she hadn't protected poor Lydia, who'd been so plump and pretty when she'd joined the school, and was now a thin, pale, trembling wraith.

She must tackle Cara, but how?

It was the same at governors' meetings. Although Cara, as a teacher governor, left the room when staff, salary or financial matters were discussed, Stormin' Norman, like Mike Pitts, would report back any snide remarks and Cara would put in the stiletto.

Janna herself grew increasingly fearful as the obscene telephone calls continued. One night her tyres were let down; on another a circle of barbed wire rested against her windscreen.

Some people are terrified of snakes, others of spiders. Janna was terrified of madness. As an imaginative child often left alone at night when her mother went out cleaning, she'd lived in fear that the inhabitants of a nearby lunatic asylum would escape across the fields and come screaming and scrabbling at her bedroom window. Later, dotty Miss Havisham and Mr Rochester's first wife, imprisoned upstairs with her crazy mirthless laugh, had haunted Janna's nightmares. For years, she wouldn't touch apples in case they'd been poisoned by the evil queen in *Snow White*. Most frightening of all was the wicked witch in *The Wizard of Oz*, who, in her sudden appearances and wanton capacity for disruption, reminded her most of Cara.

Thank God for brave little Partner, curled up on her bed or at her feet. Janna longed to put on Dorothy's shiny red shoes, gather him up like Toto and escape down the Yellow Brick Road – but first she must stand up to the governors . . .

Cara in fact limped in a week later, flanked by Satan, Monster and sassy Kitten Meadows, and in time for the after-school governors' meeting. This was held in Cara's classroom, whose walls were covered with masks of everyone from Tony Blair to Maria Callas, gazing sightlessly down from the black walls. Blood-stained rubber knives, instead of scarlet anemones, stood in a blue vase on the table.

Cara looked so deathly pale and red-eyed, and her rasping voice was so pathetically muted, Janna wondered why she had ever been scared of her.

'That's green base and red eyeshadow,' muttered a passing Pearl scornfully.

Fear is the parent of cruelty, but also of sycophancy. Thus staff and pupils were so terrified that Cara, through her KGB system, would learn they had been slagging her off that she returned to a heroine's welcome of cards, flowers and bottles of wine.

There was also a full house at the governors' meeting.

Sir Hugo Betts had had a good lunch and was fighting sleep. Sol the undertaker had just had the satisfaction of burying a very rich local businessman. Cara was flanked by a solicitous Stormin'

Norman and by Crispin, who was wearing dark glasses to hide a stye and flustering Miss Basket who, in the absence of Rowan at the dentist, was taking the minutes on her laptop and kept begging people to 'slow down please'. Basket was also terrified that Cara might have bugged Janna's office and found out why she was leaving.

Ashton Douglas was flipping distastefully through a pile of cuttings on the Bagley jaunt. Sir Hugo Betts put on a second pair of spectacles to admire Sheena's Brazilian. Russell Lambert, his mouth sinking at the corners like the mask of tragedy on the wall, exuded disapproval, particularly at Partner curled up on Janna's knee.

Ashton kicked off, deploring Janna's involvement in the trip to Bagley, 'against the advice and pwinciples of your colleagues and your Labour/Lib Dem county council, who you know are violently opposed to integwation. The result was an unprecedented outbweak of destruction and a lamentable pwess.'

'It was not lamentable, except for the *Gazette*,' protested Janna. 'I've had so many nice emails. It's been so good for the kids' morale.'

Support then came from an unexpected source.

'My Kylie had the most wonderful day of her life,' enthused Chantal Peck.

'We noticed,' said Stormin' Norman sourly.

'Sally Brett-Taylor was most gracious to Kylie Rose, encouraging her to persevere with her singing, because it's a flexible career for a single mother. Cosmo, Dame Hermione Harefield's son, also said Kylie's voice is remarkable. The day was a 'uge success.'

'Because your slag of a daughter got orf with an 'Ooray.' Stormin' Norman was brandishing her short umbrella like a baseball bat.

Chantal, however, decided to rise above this insult.

'Jack is a charmer,' she said icily. 'He's already texted Kylie Rose seventeen times.'

'I'm sure he'd love you as a muvver-in-law,' snarled Stormin'.

'Ladies, ladies,' said Russell smoothly. 'Cara wishes to make a point.'

'I don't feel,' quavered Cara, 'that whoever planned this ill-judged trip appreciated the fragile egos of our students. Anarchy broke out because those left behind felt undervalued.'

' 'Ear, 'ear,' growled Stormin'.

'We have great plans for the future,' said Janna quickly, 'for a joint concert and a joint play next term. The theatre at Bagley is big enough for all our parents and children, so no one will feel excluded.'

'Except the Larks head of drama and English,' said Cara pathetically.

'Please slow down,' wailed Miss Basket.

'We can't spend an entire meeting discussing Bagley Hall and Larks,' said Ashton.

'I would like to register,' boomed Russell Lambert, 'that I found all the publicity so distasteful, I'm contemplating stepping down.'

Janna murmured:

> 'He, stepping down
> By zigzag paths, and juts of pointed rock,
> Came on the shining levels of the lake . . .'

Her thoughts were wandering. Odd that King Arthur and St Joseph, two of the most famous cuckolds in the world, were also regarded as the most noble of men.

'Janna,' said Ashton sharply.

'Sorry, I was miles away,' mumbled Janna, which didn't help.

'We have decided to form a sub-committee to discuss the Larks–Bagley partnership,' went on Ashton.

'Why not a Government enquiry?' quipped Sol the undertaker, winking at Janna.

'Let us move on to the high level of truancy,' went on Russell . . .

'It's down ten per cent,' protested Janna.

'That's not enough.'

'Anyone like one of my choccy biccies?' said Cara, getting a packet out of her bag. 'So many presents and I got forty-two get-well cards.'

'No one's used to you ever taking time off,' gushed Miss Basket, blushing even redder as she met Janna's eye.

'Could we instead move on to wedundancy?' said Ashton.

As teacher governors were excluded from discussions about staff or financial matters, Russell asked Basket and Cara to leave.

'I can speak for all of us in saying how pleased we are you're back, Cara.'

'Hear, hear,' cried Miss Basket.

'Thank you,' whispered Cara.

Crispin leapt up to open the door for them, adding:

'Cara's a lovely woman, such a dedicated teacher.'

'I hope she hasn't come back too soon,' said Russell. 'She looks very pulled down.'

'Wedundancies,' said Ashton. 'I'll make notes now Miss Basket's gone. We've examined your budget situation, Janna. Your only hope is to instigate at least eight wedundancies.'

Janna, who was drawing a picture of Crispin as a pig in a trilby, replied that it was sorted.

Ashton looked up, startled.

'Nine people handed in their notice this week.'

'Whatever for?' said Russell.

Janna took a deep breath. She might as well be hung for a Sharpe as a lamb.

'They're all terrified of Cara.'

'Nonsense,' said Ashton.

'This is disgraceful,' exploded Russell. 'Look at all the cards and flowers greeting her return.'

'Those people were sucking up to her, as his minions fawn over Saddam Hussein. Cara shamelessly favours certain children over others.' Janna looked straight at Stormin' Norman. 'That's why they sent her cards.'

'These are very serious accusations,' said Ashton.

'And very serious transgressions. I have already given Cara three formal warnings for intimidating children, and made a note of numerous others. I also assumed that teacher governors left the room during human resources discussions, so that the rest of the board could talk off the record in the strictest confidence.'

'Of course,' said Russell heartily. 'Within these four walls.'

'I'd therefore like to reiterate that Cara Sharpe is poisoning our school.'

There was a squawk of a tape running out.

'Ha,' said Janna. 'So this meeting is being recorded.'

Pouncing on Stormin's bag, she whipped out a recorder and played it back.

'"Cara Sharpe is poisoning our school",' said the tape.

'I must have left it on by mistake,' puffed Stormin', for once discomforted.

'I'm sure,' said Janna. 'Just for the record, I'm keeping this.' Removing the tape, she dropped it into her bag. Then she turned furiously on Ashton and Russell. 'I don't understand you. Because of my ailing budget you demand redundancies. But when nine teachers hand in their notices, which will cost you nothing compared with the vast amount you'll have to fork out if you have to make people redundant, you don't seem remotely pleased. This saves money, which I thought was your top priority.'

'I agree,' said Sol. 'Janna's achieved what you wanted, cheaply and painlessly, so stop whingeing.'

'Hear, hear,' said Sir Hugo, waking up.

The meeting broke up in uproar.

Only after she had escaped did Janna start shivering. How long would it take Cara to get her revenge?

When she finally got home several hours later, the outside light came on to illuminate a front door daubed with red paint: 'Get out of Larkshire, cradle-snatching bitch'.

Far more dreadful, Partner was frantically sniffing at something on the step. It was a little black cat with its throat cut, its poor body still warm. The nutters were out to get her.

Running into the house, she rang Mags Gablecross and left a terrified, pleading message.

37

After a night with her four-poster shoved against the bedroom door, Janna was passionately relieved first thing to get a call from Chief Inspector Gablecross. He and Mags had been away meeting fellow in-laws and only just checked their messages. Could he pop in around eleven-thirty after break, when hopefully most staff and children would be in lessons?

Janna liked the Chief Inspector as much as when she first met him. The world immediately seemed a better and safer place. Face to face across her desk, rather than side by side at the Winter Gardens dinner, she noticed the shrewdness of his curly lashed green eyes. His rugby player's body, running not unpleasantly to fat, and his slow, soft, gentle voice, evoking the drinking of cider in pubs on the edge of fields of buttercups, reminded her a lot of Emlyn Davies.

And after Janna had reiterated how much she liked and admired Mags, and Gablecross had said how much he liked Partner, who was now chewing on a dried pig's ear, and didn't Janna think he was part dachshund, part corgi, Janna shut the door and told him everything from the daubed windscreen to the murdered cat.

'Cara should be having a rest period,' Janna said finally, 'but she's taking Nine E, which includes the Wolf Pack, because Lydia stayed at home. She's really conscientious but she couldn't hack it now Cara's back.'

Janna was badly frightened, observed Gablecross, but fighting like a little terrier. He admired her guts.

'Could you show me round the school?'

The Chief Inspector had an even more dramatic effect on the children than Uncle Harley. The din in the corridors subsided as though a radio had been turned off. Pupils slid into classrooms. Guilty parties shot into the toilets. Satan Simmons leapt out of a window he'd just broken and set off bleeding like a pig down the drive.

Year Nine E were reading *The Mayor of Casterbridge*, which Paris thought was a fabulous book. Was it possible that his own father had sold him and his mother at a fair, and his mother, unable to support him, had left him on the children's home steps? He was touched Henshaw the Mayor loved Elizabeth-Jane just as much when he discovered she wasn't his natural daughter. Perhaps some father could one day love him. He also liked Hardy's pessimism. He'd have made a good *EastEnders* scriptwriter.

Paris, on the other hand, was churning inside. Lydia, who normally took this class, had thoughtlessly asked the pupils to write an essay about their family tree and bring in photos of their parents and themselves as babies.

Most of the children on the Shakespeare Estate hadn't seen their fathers for years, if ever. Cara was joyfully poised to skin Lydia alive for such gross insensitivity, but meanwhile she intended to have fun and with a cackle picked up Rocky's photograph.

'What a hideous baby you were.'

As Rocky's face fell like a chastised Rottweiler, the class tittered out of fear, rather than agreement.

'You were an even uglier baby, Feral,' went on Cara, 'and goodness me, where did your mother meet your father, Pearl?'

'In the dole queue,' said Pearl sulkily.

' 'Spect it's the only time they did meet,' taunted Satan. In the front row with Kitten Meadows, who'd had a row with Johnnie Fowler, he was egging Cara on. 'Pearl's father's inside.'

'And when my dad comes out, he'll get you if you don't stop fucking bugging me,' spat Pearl.

'Don't swear.' Cara turned with such venom, Pearl shrank away.

Cara had reached Paris. Beside him Graffi, stressed that he had a zit bigger than the Millennium Dome, was texting Milly, whom he was meeting for a first date after school. Paris had had a lousy week. He'd borrowed a copy of *Private Lives* from Bagley library without asking and last night, kids in the home had ripped it to pieces. Inside it had been signed 'To Hengist, love Noël'. He'd meant to give it back, but now no one would believe him. He wasn't sleeping because of Janna; he'd been watching her all week and knew she was unhappy. He'd hardly spoken to her since the Bagley trip, but he'd been taking Partner for walks round the school grounds.

Cara was poised for the kill. Kitten and Satan were grinning in anticipation.

'I see you've forgotten to bring in any photographs or produce an essay, Paris.' Then, when Paris didn't answer: 'Have you lost your tongue?'

'I don't have parents to write about,' he muttered.

'He don't know who they are and he hasn't got no photographs of himself as a baby nor a family tree,' protested Graffi furiously.

'How unfortunate,' drawled Cara, then cruelly intoned:

' "Rattle his bones over the stones; He's only a pauper, whom nobody owns!" '

Only a few grasped the significance of the lines. Fear of Cara inhibited even the Wolf Pack.

Cara detested Paris for his beauty, his brains and, most of all, for his adoration of Janna. She had seen his lovelorn looks and had pieced together torn-up notes in the bin. Stalking Janna herself, she'd had to be very careful not to be apprehended by him.

Gablecross and Janna had just slid into the classroom and witnessed Cara's narrow scarlet back quivering like a cobra poised to strike. At the sight of Gablecross, Feral edged towards the window.

'Where are you off to, Feral Jackson? Sit down,' screeched Cara. Then, turning back to Paris, with her mad laugh: 'I'm not surprised your mother didn't want to keep you. If you only had a fraction more charm . . . Still, I'm sure Janna is like a mother to you, or would you rather be her toyboy?'

Cara had lost it, evil seemed to gush out of her. The class edged away. Only Paris stood his ground. Janna was poised to move in, but Gablecross put his hand on her arm.

'Can't you give me an answer?' screamed Cara. 'You insolent lout.'

'Shut up,' yelled Paris. 'Janna's the loveliest woman in the world. You're just a jealous old bitch.'

Next moment, a mobile rang and Graffi snatched it up. His shoulders hunched in ecstasy: 'Milly, lovely!' As Cara swung round to silence him, he thrust out his palm in a lordly fashion: 'Talk to the hand, dearie.'

Paris made the mistake of laughing. Next moment Cara had whacked him so hard that she left a red handprint darkening on his face; then, as he ducked, balling his fists to strike her, she lashed at him again with the back of her hand. Unable to stay neutral a moment longer, Partner wriggled out of Janna's clutches and, yapping furiously, rushed forward to defend his friend.

'You fucking animal,' screamed Cara, snatching up a pair of scissors lying on the table and jabbing first at Partner, then at Paris.

'Put that down,' thundered Gablecross.

A heavy man but as quick on his feet as Feral's idol, Thierry Henry, he was across the room grabbing Cara's arms from behind and slapping on handcuffs.

'Let me go,' she screeched.

'Cara Sharpe, I am arresting you. You do not have to say anything, but . . .'

'Just like *The Bill*,' cried Kylie in ecstasy.

Janna called Russell Lambert.

'You'd better call an emergency governors' meeting. I've got rid of ten teachers now. I've just fired Cara Sharpe.'

'Hey ho, the witch is dead,' sang the children, racing along the corridors and round the playground and for once no one hushed them. By the afternoon, a raving mad Cara down at the police station had, between bouts of wild laughter, confessed to everything from graffitiing Janna's windscreen to leaving the murdered black cat outside Jubilee Cottage. By late afternoon the teachers, realizing Cara had really gone, started sidling into Janna's office, saying that, after a lot of heart-searching, they'd decided not to resign. Even arch red Robbie Rushton announced that he couldn't live with himself deserting a sinking ship.

Refraining from expressing doubt that anyone else could live with him, Janna took him and everyone else back, and then went out and got drunk with them all in the Ghost and Castle. Mike Pitts bought her a huge gin and orange, and confided that he actually approved of the Larks–Bagley partnership and it would be grand if they could get a football team up and running, then admitted he'd played once for Brentford.

Partner had a wonderful evening, picking up the general euphoria, being fed crisps and pork scratchings, sitting on the bar stool being fussed over as everyone discussed his possible parentage.

'He can take over from Cara as a teacher governor,' said Mags. 'Essential not to have a spy or a sneak.'

Partner dusted the bar stool with his increasingly plumey tail.

The only real resistance to Cara's sacking came from Satan and Monster, who, revved up on crack and armed with crowbars the following morning, threatened Janna on her way to assembly. Partner, however, had barked so furiously before flying at Satan's ankles that both Satan and Monster had fled down the drive. Enough people witnessed this display of canine courage to secure Satan's exclusion and Monster's long-term suspension.

With Monster, Satan and Cara out of the way, children terrorized in the past came flooding back into school over the next few weeks, and attendance went up by twenty per cent.

Partner, who had acquired cult status by seeing off the forces of darkness, also proved a huge help in the battle against truancy. Each week, the class with the best attendance was rewarded with the task of looking after Partner for the next week. Partner adored children and, as long as Janna left her door open and he could pop back and check she was there, was quite happy. He was soon heading and pushing footballs around with his nose and delivering praise postcards, an idea Janna had picked up from Hengist, and certificates of merit. With one child holding one end of the skipping rope, and Charlie Topolski, who was in a wheelchair, holding the other, Partner learnt to skip. When he got tired, he would leap on to Charlie's knee, lick his cheek and curl up.

Because he had suffered himself, the little dog seemed to know instinctively how to comfort a lonely child. Bad readers grew in confidence when allowed to read to Partner. When a school photograph was taken, he took pride of place on Janna's knee.

38

Janna decided to postpone crossing the bridge of redundancies which, if it were anything like the bridge over the River Fleet in the rush hour, would take for ever. Right now she needed a head of English and drama.

In the past Janna had not felt confident enough to bring in her own people. Now Larks was so much happier, she felt justified in approaching Vicky Fairchild, an aptly named beauty of twenty-nine, who looked nearer sixteen. Vicky had long, dark hair, which fell in a thick fringe over melting, dark brown eyes and a pearly complexion, which grew more luminous with tiredness. She was incredibly slender, making the much shorter Janna feel like a bull terrier, and as a member of Janna's department at Redfords, had been an admirer and a huge support.

When Janna rang her to offer her head of drama, adding that as Vicky would have to give in her notice, she presumably couldn't start until the summer, Vicky instantly revealed she was leaving Redfords at Christmas.

'It was so horrible there without you, Jannie.' Then, in her sweet, breathy little girl's voice: 'And I haven't been well. Nothing serious.'

Vicky had also decided to leave because she'd planned to join her boyfriend, Matt, in Bermuda, but that hadn't worked out, so she'd simply adore to come to Larks.

'I love the Cotswolds and I've read all about you forming a partnership with Bagley – that's so cool, I bet they've got a glorious theatre, and Hengist B-T is so inspirational. You've done so well, Jannie, you always know how to motivate people.'

'Larks is a very tough school,' confessed Janna.

'So was Redfords to start with. Oh Janna, thank you so, so much, it's such a compliment.'

231

The governors had been rather stuffy about the sacking of Cara – wasn't it rather a coincidence that Chief Inspector Gablecross had been in the building when one of Janna's favourites, Paris Alvaston, started acting up? Shouldn't Janna be advertising Cara's job? But the special interview panel of susceptible males – Sir Hugo, Sol the undertaker, Russell and Mike Pitts as deputy head – soon forgot their doubts when they clapped eyes on Vicky, glowing in a scarlet suit and long black boots as shiny as her hair.

'This is my dream job,' she told them. 'I really feel I can make a difference. A good drama production can unite an entire school, and raise their profile sky high in the area.'

'She was so interested in Larks,' said Russell Lambert, smoothing his pewter-grey hair, which, translated, meant that Vicky, briefed by Janna, knew Russell's name and occupation as head of the local planning committee and that the *Guardian* had once described him as 'Larks's personable chair'.

As part of the interview, Vicky had to be watched teaching a class. Janna craftily threw her to the Wolf Pack and troublemakers of Year Nine E. Thus Paris, Graffi, Feral and Johnnie sat in the front row, their dropped jaws resting on their trainers. Pearl, Kylie and even sassy Kitten Meadows were equally captivated as Vicky talked about the havoc caused by gang warfare and how Juliet had been let down by her parents and Friar Lawrence.

Then she showed them clips from the fights in the Leonardo di Caprio film, and suggested how brilliant it would be if Bagley and Larks did a joint *Romeo and Juliet* with Bagley as the Montagues and Larks as the Capulets.

'Wiv the Hon. Jack and Kylie Rose as Romeo and Juliet and both sets of parents going ballistic,' shouted Graffi to much laughter.

It was a happy, productive class. If Vicky could handle the Wolf Pack, reasoned the interview panel, she would take on anything, and promptly appointed her.

Effusive in her gratitude, Vicky floated off with Russell to meet Des Res, the smooth local estate agent who'd been so dismissive about Larks at the Winter Gardens dinner. Janna prayed Des wouldn't disillusion Vicky, but she rang ecstatically from the train.

'Des has found me a heavenly flat in the Close and we bumped into Ashton Douglas: such a darling. So is Des. What did you do to upset him, Jannie? I said I wouldn't hear a word against you.'

Lucky to have the kind of beauty that opened doors. Janna glanced at her increasingly lined face in her office mirror.

She in turn was lucky to have a friend like Vicky to stick up for her.

'I'm so sad we didn't have more time to gossip,' went on Vicky. 'Everyone at Redfords is desperate to know how you're getting on.'

'How's Stew?' asked Janna, testing the emotional water.

'Sent his love. He's such a letch, pulled me on to his knee at a party the other day, and he had this huge erection. I don't know how Beth puts up with him.'

Janna was surprised at the pain, as though a lovely Chippendale chair of her past had turned out to be a fake.

'I'm so excited about my new flat – and it's dirt cheap,' added Vicky.

Next day, Janna received a note through her letterbox at home from Des Res. He had several clients who'd be very interested in Jubilee Cottage, would she like a free valuation?

'Is this a hint?' wrote back Janna furiously. 'I'll give *you* a free assessment – you're an absolute shit.'

Having posted the letter, she got her hand stuck trying to retrieve it, and had to hang about until the postman came to open the pillar box.

As a result of Vicky's interview, it was decided that Bagley and Larks would stage a production of *Romeo and Juliet* during the spring term.

Christmas is the cruellest time for children in care. Bombarded constantly by images on television or in the high street of loving families and piles of gold-wrapped presents round glittering Christmas trees, aware that they have no parents or parents that can't look after them, the children rampage, rage, roar and weep at their loss. There is no refuge from their unhappiness.

Janna had tentatively suggested Paris should spend Christmas with her and Partner, with Aunt Lily and the Wolf Pack coming in on Christmas Day, but Paris had flatly refused, still mortified by Cara's cruel jibes about his ambition to become Janna's toyboy and terrified that, alone in the house, he might not be able to control his passion.

So Janna went to Yorkshire to stay with Auntie Glad and Paris remained at Oaktree Court, the sound and fury only redeemed by a navy blue sweater sent him by Janna, which he hid under his bed in case the other inmates nicked it, and by steeping himself in the beauty and sadness of *Romeo and Juliet*.

'Heaven is here,' he kept murmuring:

> 'Where Juliet/Janna lives, and every cat and dog
> And little mouse, every unworthy thing,
> Live here in heaven and may look on her;
> But Romeo/Paris may not.'

If he couldn't have Janna, at least let her be proud of him as Romeo.

39

Vicky arrived in January 2002, and cured truancy among boys almost overnight. Fathers suddenly seemed wildly keen to come in and paint classrooms. Rod Hyde, Ashton and Russell continually described Vicky as a breath of fresh air.

Janna was ashamed of feeling a little disconsolate. She knew her children at Larks were what mattered, but it would have been nice to have a man in her life, particularly as Hengist had been away and inattentive and even more particularly when Vicky came rushing into her office on a late, grey January afternoon, crying:

'Hengist Brett-Taylor has just dropped in and mistook me for one of the kids. He said girls at Larks were getting prettier and prettier, and isn't he drop-dead gorgeous?'

'So was Satan in *Paradise Lost*,' snapped Janna. Was she becoming a disagreeable old crone like Cara? 'Where is he?'

'Oh, he's gone. I said you were closeted with Ashton Douglas, so he said, "Rather Janna than me," and he'd ring you. So exciting we're starting casting *Romeo and Juliet* tomorrow.'

'"We?"' Janna tried to keep the indignation out of her voice.

'The drama departments: Jason Fenton and me. Emlyn Davies. And Hengist wants to have input.'

'So do I,' said Janna grimly.

The auditions took place in the General Bagley Room on a bitterly cold morning. Even with the play cut by nearly a half by Bagley's head of English, Piers Fleming, there were excellent parts not just for the two lovers but for Romeo's friends, Mercutio and Benvolio; Juliet's parents, Lord and Lady Capulet; Friar Lawrence; not to mention Juliet's volatile cousin, Tybalt, Prince of Cats; and Juliet's nurse.

Two hundred children had applied to take part but, as Year Ten and upwards would be occupied with GCSE and A level work through the spring term, it was decided to cast mostly from Year Nine, and name the production 'Cloud Nine'.

Determined Larks shouldn't let the side down, Janna, and Vicky to a lesser extent, had been giving Larks's pupils a crash course in the play and equipping them with speeches to learn or read out. Lit up by her subject, Janna inspired not just Paris, but many others to have a go.

Some had other motives. Kylie was anxious to snog the Hon. Jack again. Rocky went everywhere Kylie did. Pearl was desperate to do the make-up.

Feral wanted to see if Amber Lloyd-Foxe was as disturbing as he remembered. Graffi grasped any opportunity to see Milly. Aysha, forbidden by her heavy father, now back in England, to take part in such immoral frivolity, still longed to see Xavier again. Monster Norman, back in school but missing Satan Simmons and with a massive crush on Vicky, came along for the ride.

The judging panel, sitting at an oblong table armed with pens, notebooks and copies of the text, consisted of Emlyn, who'd been asked by Hengist to keep a lid on everything in case 'naughty little Piers', head of English, went off at half cock. Or whole cock, reflected Emlyn, noticing the way Piers was snuggling up to Vicky, who was reeking of Trésor and ravishing in a raspberry-pink polo neck and short, tight black skirt. On Vicky's other side, whispering into her ear in an increasingly posh voice and looking very public school in a tweed jacket and dung-coloured cords, was Jason.

Piers and Jason had obviously bonded and would need some reining in, particularly where the budget was concerned, or they'd have David Linley designing Juliet's balcony and Stella McCartney her dresses. Beyond Piers was Janna; achingly aware she hadn't seen Hengist since the day of the balloon launch. He'd rung occasionally pleading overwork but now, grabbing the seat on her right, seemed unsettlingly enchanted to see her. Hengist was in fact eaten up with jealousy because his great rival and old boss David Hawkley, head of Fleetley, had been given a peerage in the New Year's Honours list, and been described in *The Times* that morning as the greatest headmaster of the twentieth/twenty-first century.

Hengist wanted to howl. Instead he stroked Partner, who was half asleep on Janna's knee, and said how he'd missed her and they must have lunch and catch up.

Pupils, meanwhile, hung around gossiping, waiting for the off.

The Bagley Babes, Amber, Milly and Jade, all with ski tans paid for by Randal Stancombe, were sitting with Graffi, Feral, Paris, Kylie and Rocky. Jack Waterlane, Junior and Lando had parked themselves in the row behind, also inhabited by a sneering Cosmo, and Anatole the Russian, who was drinking neat vodka out of a teacup.

As Dora Belvedon sidled in, Jade demanded:

'What are you doing here?'

'We were having sex education with Miss Sweet,' replied Dora. 'She was showing us how to roll condoms on to courgettes with the help of K-Y Jelly and got so embarrassed when Bianca asked her what fellatio was that she ran away and we got a free period. So Hengist said I could stay if I was extremely quiet.'

She plonked herself down between Cosmo and Anatole.

'You're incapable of being quiet,' spat Jade.

'Fellatio, fellatio, wherefore art thou fellatio,' sighed Cosmo, who wanted to conduct his beloved orchestra throughout the production but also to play the short, spectacular part of Tybalt.

Feral glanced up at a painting of rugby players leaping in the line-out to distract himself from Amber's thighs. Covered by barely six inches of fawn pleated skirt, they were utterly gorgeous.

'Silly using courgettes as willies,' went on Dora. 'We'll all get a shock when we discover the real thing's red, or pinkish, or purple. They're called zucchini in Italy, I believe.'

'Zucc orf,' said Paris, who'd been miles away in Verona.

To capture his Hooray Henry voice he'd been listening to a tape of Prince Charles; now he was trying to capture the nuances of Jack Waterlane and Lando France-Lynch's voices as they idly discussed snow polo.

'Christ, it's cold, throw another new boy on the fire,' grumbled Cosmo.

Outside, in sympathy, flakes of snow were beginning to settle on General Bagley and his charger.

'All right' – Hengist helped himself to Vicky's tin of Quality Street – 'let's get started, try and keep in alphabetical order. Kirsty, you're first.'

Kirsty Abbot, covered in spots and puppy fat, waddled on and delivered Juliet's speech: ' "Gallop apace, you fiery-footed steeds," ' as though she were taking the register at a primary school. Her audience tried not to laugh. Hengist let her run for sixty seconds.

'Thank you, Kirsty.'

'Useless,' scoffed Jade.

'I'd quite like to play Juliet. I learnt the part while I was skiing,' sighed Amber, 'hissing down the white mountains shouting: "Romeo, Romeo! wherefore art thou Romeo?" nearly setting off an avalanche.' She glanced at Feral under her lashes and yanked her skirt an inch higher.

'Paris Alvaston,' shouted Hengist.

I am Giovanni the lad, Paris was psyching himself up. I've gate-crashed the Capulets' ball, which is dripping with upmarket totty, including Rosaline, the beautiful cold bitch who's rejected me and is now wrapped round a rival. Suddenly I catch sight of little Juliet and realize everything I've felt before has been a mockery. When she leaves the party, I follow her, hanging around her garden, trampling on her father's plants.

As he walked to the centre of the room and turned, he could hear the thud of Partner's tail. For a few seconds he stood absolutely still, eyes shut as if in a trance, then, glancing up at the window, said as softly as the falling snow: ' "He jests at scars, that never felt a wound." '

And the room went still.

> 'But, soft! what light through yonder window breaks?
> It is the east, and Juliet is the sun . . .
> See how she leans her cheek upon her hand!
> O! that I were a glove upon that hand,
> That I might touch that cheek.'

His voice was so filled with tenderness and longing, even Partner wagged his tail again. The only accompaniment was the tick of the clock. Paris then switched to the end of the play, when he discovered Juliet apparently dead in the Capulet tomb.

' "Eyes, look your last! Arms, take your last embrace!" '

Glancing at Janna, Hengist saw her face soaked in tears, and took her hand.

'We've got our Romeo,' he whispered.

As a burst of astonished clapping and foot-stamping greeted Paris's return to his seat, Feral turned to him in amazement.

'You was wicked, man.'

Graffi, Jack Waterlane and Lando thumped him on the back.

Cosmo, his sallow face alight with malice, was less impressed.

'Talk about Kev and Juliet,' he drawled. 'No wonder the Capulets were devastated their daughter had fallen for such a yob.'

'Shut up, Cosmo,' snapped Hengist.

Paris was unmoved.

'I can do it Hooray Henry, if you like.' Shoving one clenched fist into the palm of the other, talking through gritted teeth, he strolled back to the centre of the room. ' "But, sawft! what light through yonder window breaks?" ' and sounded so like Prince Charles, everyone howled with laughter.

Wriggling free, Partner scampered towards Paris, who gathered him up, burying his grin in Partner's fur.

'Well done, Paris,' called out Vicky. 'Those one-to-one rehearsals we've been doing have really paid off.'

A hit so early in the proceedings cheered everyone.

'Now we've got to find him a decent Juliet,' said Jason.

Next moment Alex Bruce rolled up, on whom Stancombe had been putting pressure.

'There's a certain young lady, Alex, who'd be devastated if she doesn't land the lead role in this production.'

Stancombe was threatening not to put up the umpteen million pounds to finance the science block. Alex didn't think he could swing his favourite Boffin Brooks to play Romeo, but he was determined Jade should get Juliet.

Walking into the General Bagley Room, he was furious to find Hengist, who'd claimed he was far too busy to show the Archbishop of some African state round the school, stuffing toffees and giggling with Janna Curtis.

Draining his teacup of vodka, Anatole's turn was next.

'He's got to have a decent part too,' murmured Hengist to Janna, 'so we get another jetload of caviar.'

Anatole was in fact very clever and loved Pushkin, Lermontov and Shakespeare as much as vodka and Marlboro Lights.

'I must give it some velly,' he announced and proceeded to make a wonderfully exuberant Mercutio, teasing Tybalt to fight a duel with him: ' "Tybalt, you rat-catcher, vill you valk?" '

Then, after Tybalt's sword had run him through, his audience, willing him to live, could feel his vitality ebbing away as he swore a plague on both Capulet and Montague houses.

Again, Janna fighting back tears, was hugged by an equally overjoyed Hengist.

'Darling, we've got our Mercutio, and vats of caviar. Anatole's father might even bring Mr Putin to the first night.'

Dora, who'd been given a mobile cum camera by Cosmo for Christmas, was taking pictures. Alex Bruce, not a fan of Anatole, had just bustled off when a heavily pregnant woman in a flowered smock, socks and Jesus sandals waddled in.

'Who's that?' hissed Graffi. 'She's about to pop.'

'Very appropriately she's called Poppet Bruce,' giggled Dora. 'That's Mr Fussy's wife. She is *so* pants. She teaches RE and never mentions poor Jesus. She's also nicknamed "Maternity *Won't* Leave" because she keeps having babies. Can you imagine sleeping with Mr Fussy that many times? Then everyone prays she'll never come back, but she always does. She's the worst person I know.'

'Worse than No-Joke Joan?' asked Amber, applying lip gloss.

'There'd be a photo finish,' said Dora darkly.

From his expression as Poppet approached the panel, looking eager, Hengist clearly felt the same about her.

'Hope you don't mind my joining you,' she said. '*R and J* has such strong RE overtones with Friar Lawrence and an under-age marriage, I hope I may make suggestions.'

'You're welcome today,' said Hengist coolly, 'but too many cooks . . . I'd leave it to the production team.'

Poppet's lips tightened as she pressed her bulge against the table, waiting for someone to give her their seat. Terrified she might explode, Jason leapt to his feet.

'Come and sit down, Mrs Bruce.' Vicky patted Jason's chair. 'I'm Vicky Fairchild, Larks's head of drama. Of course we welcome input. We're planning to have Arab/Israeli overtones in the street fighting and put the play in modern dress with perhaps Friar Lawrence as a mullah.'

'Are we?' muttered Janna to Hengist, who muttered back: 'Friar Lawrence of Arabia.'

To Poppet's noisy approval and much clashing of bracelets, Boffin Brooks read two of Friar Lawrence's speeches in the high fluting voice of a curate at choral evensong.

'Excellent, excellent, Boffin, although I wish you'd read for Romeo.'

'Only with a recycled carrier bag over his head,' muttered Cosmo.

'Essential, in the bedroom scene and with the rise of STDs,' Poppet was now saying, 'that Romeo is shown to wear a condom.'

'And has a green courgette as a willy,' said Milly, 'which Friar Lawrence has grown in his garden.'

'Ah, here's Jade,' cried Boffin.

'Oh good,' said Poppet.

Jade Stancombe's legs were longer and her pleated skirt shorter even than Amber's; her cream silk shirt and blue cashmere jersey clung to her lovely rapacious body.

' "What's in a name? that which we call a rose By any other name would smell as sweet," ' began Jade, overacting appallingly.

Everyone tried not to giggle.

'She's dreadful,' whispered Dora.

'"Thou knowest the mask of night is on my face,"' went on Jade.

'And a whole lot of Clarins,' hissed Dora.

'"The more I give to thee, The more I have, for both are infinite,"' concluded Jade, rolling her eyes and clutching her cashmere bosom.

'Bravo, bravo! That was very convincing, Jade,' called out Poppet.

By contrast, Amber, with her hair piled up, her charming lascivious smile and air of insouciance, decided to go for Lady Capulet – 'just for a laugh' – and was brilliant.

'You're booked,' called out Piers. 'Lady C was only twenty-seven.'

Emlyn wondered how long this was going to last. He had a two-hour period on Hitler and the Nazis and rugby practice for the first and second fifteen after that.

Ah, here was Feral. God, the boy was beautiful. There was a chorus of wolf whistles as he prowled in to audition for Tybalt, 'Prince of Cats', the furious playground bully who picks fights with everyone, who has comparatively few lines but huge impact on the play.

Coached by Paris until he was word perfect, not caring if he got the part, Feral kept exploding into violence:

> 'What, drawn, and talk of peace! I hate the word,
> As I hate hell, all Montagues and thee:
> Have at thee, coward!'

He was booed, hissed, then cheered to the stuccoed ceiling as he sauntered back, grinning, to sit beside Amber.

Cosmo, whose heart was set on playing Tybalt, was not amused.

'Why not give Cosmo Capulet?' Piers was muttering across Janna to Hengist. 'He's the biggest shit in the play, which figures, then Jack Waterlane might just manage the Prince, if I cut his lines to nothing.'

'Good idea,' said Hengist. 'Yes, Vicky?' as she perched on the end of the table beside him.

'At the Capulet ball, why don't we get a wonderful little dancer to play Romeo's ex-girlfriend, Rosaline, and do a fantastically sexy dance with Tybalt, if Feral gets the part – he's an incredible dancer. Then, after being wildly jealous, Paris takes one look at Juliet, and Rosaline is forgotten. It makes the coup de foudre so much more dramatic.'

That was my idea, thought Janna indignantly, particularly when

Hengist congratulated Vicky and put forward little Bianca Campbell-Black, who was being tipped as the next Darcey Bussell.

'Let's audition her. At least it would ensure Rupert rolled up on the opening night.'

'Kylie could sing with the band at the ball,' went on Vicky, 'she's got a lovely voice, and Cosmo's Cosmonaughties must be the band.' She smiled winningly at Cosmo, who smouldered back. He must pull Vicky before the opening night.

Pearl, everyone agreed, would be in charge of make-up.

The auditions were nearly over.

Primrose Duddon of the huge boobs, who'd been taking a Grade 7 piano examination, was now making a pitch for the coveted comedy role of Juliet's nurse. Squawking, slapping her thighs, overacting worse than Jade, she reminded Janna of Sam Spink.

'Thank you, Primrose,' said Hengist after a minute.

They were down to the Ws and no one had been outstanding enough to play Juliet. They couldn't have Jade. Then Milly Walton wandered in. Like Amber, she'd only come along for a laugh and a chance to see Graffi. Her auburn curls were scraped back, her ski tan shiny and Graffi had kissed off all her lipstick in a nearby classroom.

' "My bounty is as boundless as the sea," ' she said thoughtfully. ' "My love as deep; the more I give to thee, The more I have, for both are infinite." '

Then she turned to Graffi and smiled and Graffi's shaggy black locks rose up on the back of his neck, and his toes turned over. Even Paris took his nose out of *The Iliad*.

Hengist turned to Janna, running the back of his hand down her cheek. 'That's our Juliet. Ruth, her mother, will be so pleased. She's always worried about overshadowing Milly.'

I can't help it, thought Janna, when he strokes me I have to purr.

Graffi, being Williams, was the last to go. He was still clapping Milly when a terrible thought struck him. If Paris got Romeo and Milly got Juliet, Paris would spend the whole play kissing and shagging her. Paris was much too good-looking. Graffi hated the thought of his woman making out with someone else.

He had been going to pitch for Benvolio but, nipping off into the nearby dining room, he grabbed a white damask napkin from the table laid for the African Archbishop, folded it into a triangle and wrapped it round his forehead, tying two ends behind his head. Then he grabbed a drying-up cloth from the kitchens, tying it round his waist. Leafing through the text, he found the place and bustled in as Juliet's nurse, the most irritating woman in literature, and brought the house down.

'The nurse in drag, why didn't we think of it?' said Hengist.

'We can cut a lot, but he's hilarious,' agreed Piers.

Then, after all the teasing and horseplay, Graffi's grief when he found his beloved Juliet apparently dead – the scene Primrose Duddon had dreadfully overplayed – was truly touching.

Hengist hugged Janna once more.

'Your boy's come good, darling.' Then, rising to his feet: 'Thank you very much, you all did very well. Think we've found some real stars. Go off and have lunch and we'll let you know.'

40

When the cast list was pinned on the noticeboards of both schools two days later, whoops of excitement and not a little jeering at Larks greeted the news that Paris would be playing Romeo; Feral, Tybalt; Graffi, the Nurse; and Kylie Rose both the Chorus and a blues singer at the Capulets' masked ball.

Janna was particularly gratified that Rocky had been cast as the Capulet heavy who bit his thumb (the Shakespearean equivalent of giving a middle finger) to the Montagues and Monster had landed the small, crucial part of the apothecary who sells deadly poison to Romeo, 'and probably will,' quipped Graffi. Monster was chuffed to bits at the prospect of his own chemist's, open on Sundays, with druggies hanging around. Other members of Year Nine would be filling in as members of the Watch, guards, street fighters, paparazzi and guests at the ball.

The casting over at Bagley caused more ructions. Primrose Duddon, much championed by Poppet and No-Joke Joan, was hopping that Graffi, not she, would be playing the Nurse.

'There are only four parts for young women in the play and the most characterful one's gone to a male student.'

Stancombe was outraged that Juliet had been given to Milly rather than Jade – and so was Jade, particularly when bloody Cosmo applauded the decision, claiming that by no stretch of the imagination or shrinking of the vagina could Jade ever pass as a thirteen-year-old virgin.

Jade was, in fact, over Cosmo. Now it was Paris who robbed her of sleep. She detested indifference and loathed her fellow Bagley Babe Milly for landing the part and the chance to snog and more with Paris for the next two months, particularly as she herself had been cast as Lady Montague, Romeo's mother.

'And this play ain't *Oedipus Rex*,' mocked Cosmo.

Nor had Jade realized Lady Montague only had two lines.

After prolonged hysterics through splayed fingers, it was agreed she could swap with Amber and play the much longer and meatier part of Lady Capulet.

'Lady C was a sassy, glamorous woman in her late twenties,' Vicky explained to Jade. 'And as you're married to a rich peer, with a wedding and a funeral in the offing, there's scope for a fantastic wardrobe.'

Amber, who'd been bribed with a Joseph dress she could keep after the play, was only too happy to play Lady Montague instead, particularly since Pearl, now in charge of make-up, was threatening to add arsenic to the face powder of anyone who flirted with Feral.

Cosmo had been outraged only to be offered Capulet, rather than Tybalt, until he discovered subtleties and ironies in the part as Capulet changed from a kind, tolerant father and genial host to an evil bully. He was delighted that the Cosmonaughties would be playing at the Capulets' ball with Kylie as their lead singer. He intended to bill the school £1500 a night and as the group would be providing the music for a sizzling dance routine performed by Feral and Bianca, Cosmo would be able to clock to the second the comings and goings of the divine Bianca.

Xavier, still terrified of Cosmo, and having learnt that Aysha's father had forbidden her to take part, had refused to get involved with the production. Everyone therefore was relieved Bianca was participating, which would at least ensure the presence of her crowd-pulling parents on the opening night.

'I can't wait to meet Rupert Campbell-Black,' gushed Vicky.

As soon as the play was cast Vicky, a genius at delegating – often a euphemism for extreme laziness – called a staff meeting to discuss what help she needed with the play.

The Larks art department was soon coaxed into designing scenery; Gloria into coaching Bianca and Feral in their dance routine; design and technology into producing costumes and props. Cambola was in cahoots with Cosmo over the music. Johnnie Fowler's father Gary, when sober, was an ace electrician and agreed to help with the lighting.

Once Gary Fowler was involved, other fathers felt impelled to follow suit. Most of them DIY experts, they were soon building and painting scenery, and their wives and girlfriends, having clocked Vicky and determined to keep an eye on their other halves, were giving a hand with costumes – over which there was fierce debate.

Anatole, who had sensational legs, wanted doublet and hose. This meant long skirts for the women, deduced Jade, which meant her even more sensational legs would be hidden, so she pushed for modern dress and won.

'Alex Bruce has a finger in every tart,' grumbled Anatole, who in the end was delighted to wear a Red Army mess jacket and tight black trousers with a red stripe down the side. Other boys in the cast wore paramilitary uniform: berets, peaked caps or red and white keffiyehs borrowed from fathers and masters. Chief Inspector Gablecross provided policemen's uniforms for the Watch. This meant more could be spent on female members of the cast.

Janna contented herself with giving lessons to Year Nine on the background of the play, pointing out its topicality; how innocent people were always caught up in the crossfire of war – particularly domestic violence.

' "Poor sacrifices of our enmity," Old Capulet called them, who'd caused a few in his time.'

Determined Larks would be word perfect, she also helped cast members learn their parts.

Rehearsals took place at Bagley every Tuesday and Wednesday after school from 4.00 to 5.30 p.m., and often in the lunch hour but only using the actors that were needed, which involved endless round trips for Wally.

Caught up in Vicky's enthusiasm, none of the teachers seemed to mind covering for her. Basket had a massive crush. Even Sam Spink was looking quite moony and presented Vicky with a pair of Piglet character socks, causing squeals of delight.

'Piglet is my most favourite character.'

Even though the school was a happier place, Janna herself was still ridiculously overstretched. There was always some desperately crying child needing comfort over cigarette burns or cracked ribs. There was always some furious parent: 'My daughter was top in English last term, why isn't she playing Juliet?'

February brought incessant rain, pouring in through the roof on classes and on coursework, and the heating broke down. The classes not involved in the play were also very jealous. Janna tried to compensate by organizing trips to the ballet or ice skating or football, but she understood how they felt and found it hard to not feel jealous herself. Hengist, so adorable on casting day, had not been in touch since.

Vicky, on the other hand, flaunting those vogue words 'Transparency and Accountability', insisted on keeping her boss up to date with events, particularly late one evening, when she dropped in on a very cold, still-working Janna and announced:

'"My boys", as I call Emlyn, Piers and Jason, are working so hard. Hengist is constantly popping in to see if I'm OK and Sally Brett-Taylor is being so supportive. She's insisting on making Juliet's dress. We discussed it over a drink last night. Jade Stancombe's ordered a dress for the Capulet ball from Amanda Wakeley, which costs well into four figures, which made Ian Cartwright, the darling old bursar, frightfully uptight till I calmed him down.

'His wife Patience is a pet; she teaches riding at Bagley. His 'mistress of the horse', Hengist calls her, claiming Patience couldn't be anyone else's mistress because she's so plain, naughty man! But Patience has agreed to teach Paris to ride, so he can clatter up the gangway when he storms back from exile, believing Juliet's dead.'

'Paris is terrified of horses,' interrupted Janna icily. 'There's no way he should be forced to ride.'

Ignoring her, Vicky glanced over her shoulder:

'What are you wrestling with? Oh, figures. You ought to talk to Ian. Ian Cartwright. He'd be able to sort them out for you. He's been ringing round other independent bursars, checking their fees all week. I thought I might ask him and Patience to supper, and Hengist and Sally and Emlyn, of course. Emlyn is such a tower of strength. I hope you'll come too, Jannie. You ought to get out more, you look so tired.'

Stop patronizing me, Janna wanted to scream.

'I've no time for jaunts,' she snapped, turning back to her computer. 'Sorry, I must get on.'

The following week, however, Vicky forgot to book the bus for Year Ten's ice-skating trip. As a result, dreadful fights broke out. Not only were Year Nine having all the fun and the kudos, no one could organize anything for Year Ten.

When Janna summoned Vicky back from Bagley and bawled her out, Vicky sobbed and sobbed, rivalling the overflowing River Fleet, and fled into the dusk.

Arriving home from work around midnight, Janna was splashing up the path, lamenting yet again that rain had stopped stars, when Partner went into a frenzy of barking. Lily's cottage was in darkness. Catching sight of a huddled figure in the porch, Janna gasped with terror – had Cara escaped from prison?

'Who's there?'

She was overwhelmed with a divine smell of spring. It was a still-sobbing Vicky, thrusting out a huge bunch of narcissi.

'I'm so sorry to let you down, Jannie. I wanted you to be

247

proud of me and put Larks on the map. I've been so thoughtless.'

So Janna opened a bottle and they ended up crying on each other's shoulders, and Vicky staying the night. But once again, as Janna made up a bed on the sofa, the goalposts changed.

'I never meant to make you jealous, Jannie. Has Hengist upset you? He can be so dismissive. Piers and Jason were saying only the other day, it's a shame you've had no input.'

Vicky looked so enchanting curled up under Janna's duvet, cuddling Janna's only hot-water bottle.

And I meant to slap you down for neglecting Year Ten and your tutor group, thought an exasperated Janna, and vowed once again to spend more time at Bagley.

But the following day, Ashton Douglas and Crispin Thomas summoned her to their plush S and C Services headquarters, overlooking an angry, grey and still rising River Fleet.

Even though the appointment was for midday, not a cup of coffee nor a drink was on offer. Janna's spirits were lowered by a huge wall chart, showing Larks at the bottom of the league tables of Larkshire schools.

Both men had big desks side by side. Crispin, who had gained another chin over Christmas and whose pink pullover had shrunk in the wash, was fussily arranging papers. Ashton, wafting his cloyingly sweet chloroform scent, his apple blossom complexion flushed up by tropical central heating, had removed his jacket to flaunt his trim waistline.

S and C must be making a fortune, decided Janna, judging by the fuck-off lighting, the leather sofas in beiges and browns and the suede cushions to match suede cubes on which to rest your feet.

The pictures on the walls were even more impressive. The bunch of red tulips was certainly by Matthew Smith and the lookalike photograph of Beckham by Alison Jackson. Also blown up over the fireplace was the artwork for S and C's latest logo of a grown-up's hand on a child's back both propelling forward and comforting: a symbol of support and challenge, except the hand was placed a little too low. Janna shuddered.

Ashton was examining his very clean fingernails, the diamond set in the gold band on his third finger catching the light.

'This is wather embawassing, but we feel you ought to spend less time at Bagley in future.'

Janna's bag tipped over, spilling out biros, lipstick, hairbrush, perfume, Bonios for Partner and diary on to the thick pale beige carpet.

'I've hardly been near the place,' she squeaked, dropping to the floor to claw back her belongings. 'I've been too busy.'

'Maybe.' Ashton sighed with pleasure. 'But I'm afwaid people are talking about you and Hengist.'

Retrieving a tampon from under Crispin's desk, Janna banged her head.

'I know you feel demonized by the *Gazette*,' went on Ashton, 'but you have a good fwiend in Col Peters. These are the pictures he refused to publish, and instead handed over to us.'

Playing the ace, Ashton produced out of his crocodile notecase a photograph of Janna in Hengist's arms, her cheek rammed against his, her eyes closed in ecstasy. She was wearing a dark blue shirt; a painting of leaping rugby players could be seen in the background.

'This is ridiculous,' she protested. 'This was at an audition surrounded by hundreds of teachers and children. Who took it, for heaven's sake?'

'We're not at liberty.'

'Well, I want to know. Hengist and I were knocked out – Paris Alvaston had just auditioned. We'd found our Romeo. You'll see how brilliant he is on the opening night.'

'Rather unbridled enthusiasm,' observed Crispin. God, he was loving this. 'Particularly when you put it beside this,' and pointed to another shot of Hengist's hand stroking Janna's cheek and then two cuttings of her smiling adoringly up at Hengist at the Winter Gardens civic dinner and on the air-balloon day.

'The cumulative effect is unfortunate,' said Ashton sympathetically. 'We understand. It's so easy for lonely unmarried women of a certain age to develop these cwushes. Hengist is very charismatic, but Sally Bwett-Taylor is such a good egg.'

'There is absolutely nothing between Hengist and me,' said Janna furiously, her face feeling as though it had just come out of the microwave. 'Head teachers have common problems and practice to discuss. Hengist has been genuinely kind and constructive.'

'In future I'd go to Wod Hyde,' urged Ashton. 'He is after all your official mentor. You don't want tittle-tattle to sabotage the excellent work Larks's teachers are doing at Bagley. Vicky Fairchild is first class. Give her her head.'

'I am her Head,' spat Janna.

'No need to be facetious. Just leave Hengist alone.'

Blinded by tears, Janna fumbled her way out to the car park. Ironically, Hengist seemed to feel the same as S and C; he hadn't been in touch for weeks.

Partner, leaping on his hind legs, grinning and scrabbling in ecstasy, body shaken by frenziedly wagging tail, stopped her chucking herself into the swift-flowing river.

You're the only male in my life from now on, she vowed grimly. Vicky can get on with it.

41

Paris was missing Janna desperately. He had to be back in the children's home by eight and was thus denied any of the jolly after-rehearsal get-togethers. He'd invested so much in the play because he thought Janna would be there all the time. He longed to talk to her about his part. Vicky never listened and wanted to impose her own views. Graffi was so busy painting scenery, designing posters, camping it up as the Nurse and snogging Milly, he had abandoned Janna's mural which was nearly finished anyway, so the tea parties at Jubilee Cottage had been scrapped.

The Bagley Babes all fancied Paris like mad, but miffed he was always reading and wouldn't respond, they took the piss out of him instead. Milly was convinced he'd been put off by her costume, which was white muslin, high-waisted, sleeveless, with a buttercup-yellow sash like a little girl's party dress.

'It's so drippy. It's only because Sally Brett-Taylor's made it and Vicky's so far up her,' stormed Milly.

Sally in turn was charmed by Vicky, disloyally thinking how nice it would be to have a daughter with whom you could discuss girly things and who didn't always disagree. She had invited Vicky to supper with Emlyn the night Ireland thrashed Wales, and Emlyn, unable ever to envisage his country's rugby revival, arrived utterly legless. Hengist had had to drive him home before the crème brûlée and let him into his flat. Sally only just stopped herself unbuttoning to Vicky that Emlyn wasn't really the ideal son-in-law. Emlyn also seemed the only male in Bagley not besotted with Vicky. The bursar was making a complete idiot of himself hanging round the rehearsal rooms.

But, as February gave way to March, most of the cast were

251

shaping up splendidly. Feral as Tybalt was an unexpected, if reluctant, star.

' "Why, uncle, 'tis a shame", such a crap line,' he grumbled to Paris.

'Think of Uncle Harley.'

'Everything he does is a shame,' shuddered Feral, then, launching back into his part: '"To strike him dead, I hold it not a sin." '

He was gratified one of the highlights of the evening was going to be his dance with Bianca Campbell-Black at the Capulets' ball.

Normally football was Feral's passion. At every opportunity, down on the grass went the fleece, down twelve feet away went the school bag. Instantly a ball would be kicked between them. But, having agreed *Dirty Dancing* was their favourite film, Bianca and Feral practised their sexy Argentine tango routine, with Bianca rubbing her legs up Feral's, with increasing excitement.

After one particularly successful rehearsal, during which the room seemed to fill up with lustful schoolboys who should have been in lessons and an accompanying Cosmo broke two strings of his guitar, Feral sloped off for a quick game of football while Bianca returned to the changing rooms.

No one was about for her to chatter to – a great deprivation for Bianca. She was just wriggling out of her sweaty leotard when she felt herself grabbed from behind.

'You shouldn't dance so sexily,' said a smoky, bitchy voice as hands crept over her little breasts.

It was Cosmo, who was very strong. Next moment, he'd yanked her against him, clamping her between his legs and bending over her shoulder, forced his lips down on hers.

'Lemme go.' A revolted Bianca, despite writhing like an eel, was unable from this angle to knee him in the groin, even when he plunged his tongue deep down her throat. Retching, gagging, she struggled harder.

Then she heard a crash as a bench was knocked over and Cosmo was dragged off and punched in the face, sending him toppling backwards into a rail of dresses. Feral then opened the window and, gathering Cosmo up, hurled him out on to Sally Brett-Taylor's precious bed of spotted hellebores.

'Keep your filthy hands off her,' he howled. Tugging the window shut, he turned to Bianca, who was struggling to replace her leotard. Seizing Jade Stancombe's big soft dark blue towel, Feral wrapped it round her frantically shuddering body.

'You OK, little darlin'?'

'Yes. No.' Fighting back the tears, Bianca rubbed the back of her hand across her bruised mouth again and again. Cosmo's tongue had been so disgustingly hard, wet and bobbly underneath, her mouth felt raped.

Feral put an arm round her, then, flourishing an imaginary sword with the other: ' "To strike him dead, I hold it not a sin." '

' "Why, uncle, 'tis a shame",' mumbled Bianca.

'It is too.' Feral felt so sorry for her. 'Let's go and find your teddy bear.'

He tried to joke and Bianca had giggled through her tears, but he wanted to kill Cosmo. Bianca was only twelve, but holding her had released some highly unavuncular feelings in Feral.

He so wished Janna was here to advise him and steady the ship.

Vicky seemed to read his mind. As they were waiting in the drizzle for the minibus back to Larks, she could be heard grumbling to Cambola: 'I can't understand why Janna opted out of this production. When she was at Redfords, she never missed a rehearsal. I suppose she was there longer and felt closer to the pupils.'

Seeing the hurt in the children's faces, Cambola snapped that Janna was frantically busy.

'She was never too busy at Redfords,' said Vicky smugly.

Pearl, meanwhile, was taking her responsibility for make-up very seriously and had managed to persuade Paris to let her dye his pale eyelashes and apply dark brown eyeliner before he and Milly were photographed by Cosmo for Graffi's posters.

Cosmo would never forgive Feral, but he was enough of a perfectionist to want to get the best out of Paris and Milly. The results had an unearthly beauty, and posters of the star-crossed lovers were soon plastered all over Larkminster. Tickets designed by Graffi, with a dagger plunged into a bleeding heart, were also selling well.

Paris, as a result, was being teased rotten both at Larks and Oaktree Court, particularly when the inmates got hold of a poster, gave it golden ringlets and a scarlet rosebud mouth and scrawled 'Homo and Juliet, good on you, Woofter' underneath.

'You haven't arrived until you've been graffitied,' Graffi told him airily.

At the beginning of March, three weeks before the opening night, Year Nine and Bagley Lower Fifth had to decide what GCSE subjects they wanted to take in 2004. Ninety per cent opted to take drama with Vicky, almost as many as those who wanted to take history with Emlyn Davies. After such a vote of confidence,

Vicky felt entitled to put pressure on Paris to gallop up the gangway to the stage and when he baulked, to suggest they use a stand-in.

'Cosmo, Lando, Junior, Jack Waterlane, all great riders, could put on your jacket and breeches, thunder up the gangway in the half-light, chuck their reins to Dora, jump across the orchestra on to the stage and exit right into Capulet's tomb. Next scene, which is the interior of Capulet's tomb, you barge in having re-appropriated your clothes.'

'That would work,' mused Jason.

If Emlyn were here, Vicky wouldn't have dared, thought Paris, who was at breaking point.

'I'm not having a stand-in and I'm not doing this fucking play,' he snarled and walked out.

Dora caught up with him halfway down the drive and took his hand. 'Just come and meet Mrs Cartwright – the bursar's wife – she's lovely. They live in the Old Coach House, through the woods.'

The faded leaves on the path matched the brown ploughed fields; other fields were the same pale fawn as the sheep that had been grazing them. The woodland floor was turned emerald by wild garlic leaves.

Dora led a grey-faced, frantically trembling Paris into the yard, where hunters and polo ponies with clipped manes stared out over the bottle-green half-doors. A smell of leather and dung made him want to throw up.

'This is Mrs Cartwright,' said Dora. 'She's a brilliant horsewoman.'

Paris looked unenthusiastically at the big-boned, large-nosed maroon-complexioned woman in the clashing scarlet Puffa.

'Hello Paris,' brayed Patience Cartwright, holding out a rough mottled hand that had never seen a manicure. 'I hear you're a wonderful Romeo.'

Not only did she look like a horse, she sounded like one.

'I don't ride,' he said icily.

'This is Beluga,' said Dora. 'He's extremely kind and loves people, unlike Loofah, my pony' – she stroked the brown and white nose of a small skewbald leaning meanly out of the next box – 'who doesn't.'

'The thing to do is to get on Beluga's back in the middle of the field for a few moments,' advised Patience, 'so if you fall orf it's nice and sawft.'

Paris quarter-smiled. At least he could bone up on his Hooray accent.

'Here's a carrot to sawften him up,' giggled Dora.

The saddle was very slippery and the ground below seemed miles down in Australia, but Beluga had a thick black mane to cling on to. Beluga was also lazy and devoted to Plover, Patience's mare, and therefore quite happy plodding round the fields on a lead rein.

After days of downpour it was a wonderfully gentle, sunny day. Woodpeckers laughed inanely in trees already glowing russet, amethyst and warm brown with swelling buds; the singing birds exhorted him not to be frightened. Very gradually Paris unfroze; sweat dried on his pinched face.

'You're doing really well,' encouraged Patience. 'If ever you want him to stop, just pull very gently on the reins.'

A cock pheasant waddled across their path, showing off ginger, scarlet and bright green plumage and a neat white collar.

'The shooting season's over. Such a relief for him,' said Patience.

'Just like Boffin Brooks as Friar Lawrence,' observed Paris. 'Same silly beaky face and fussy walk.'

Patience brayed with laughter.

'Boffin's a little beast.' She lowered her voice furtively as though a passing rabbit might grass her up. 'He drives my husband Ian mad suggesting to Alex Bruce ways the school could economize. He'd have the stables turned into an IT suite, whatever that might be.'

'Can we go a bit faster?' asked Paris.

'Of course, if you're sure.'

Paris nodded, taking a firmer grip on Beluga's mane.

Patience bypassed the trot, which was bumpy, going straight into a much smoother canter up a green ride flanked with hazels. Paris gave a gasp of terror, but by the time they'd reached the gate on the crest of the hill, he'd settled into the rhythm.

'Can we canter back to the stables?' he asked twenty minutes later.

And they did.

Paris slid off, trembling violently, hanging on to Beluga as his legs collapsed like plasticene. 'Thanks, horse.'

'Awfully well done,' said Patience. 'You're really good with animals. Dora was saying how Elaine Brett-Taylor loves you.'

'Well done,' said Dora, who'd been up in the hayloft watching through binoculars. 'Looks as though you've ridden for ever.'

'Different ball game clattering up the gangway surrounded by a yelling audience,' grumbled Paris.

'We've got three weeks,' said Patience soothingly. 'Come and have a cup of tea.'

She led him into a messy kitchen, with bridles hanging from a clothes horse, plates and mugs still in the sink and ironing, reminding him of Janna's in-tray, rising to the ceiling.

'Christ!' Paris had caught sight of a photograph of a stunningly beautiful girl on the dresser.

'That's my sister, Emerald,' announced Dora, 'and to muddle you completely, she's Mrs Cartwright's daughter.'

How on earth could a dog like Patience give birth to something so exquisite, wondered Paris, then blushed when Patience read his mind and laughed.

'They always say the fairest flowers grow on the foulest dung heaps, but actually we adopted Emerald and when she sought out her natural mother, she turned out to be Dora's mother, Anthea.'

'The old tart,' chuntered Dora, 'having sex before marriage.'

'Dora,' reproved Patience, seeing Paris grinning.

'We adopted both Emerald and Sophy, who's a schoolmistress,' explained Patience, 'and longs to move to the country. She's a great friend of your headmistress, Janna Curtis. I keep hoping to see her at rehearsals so I can introduce myself and ask Janna to supper.'

Glancing out of the window towards Bagley, appreciating the extent and complexity of its spread of buildings, Paris felt himself flushing as he always did when Janna's name was mentioned.

'I must go,' said Dora wistfully. 'Joan's taking prep. Where's Northcliffe?'

'Our golden retriever,' Patience explained to Paris. 'Gone to work with Ian.'

'Cadbury's still living with the beagles,' sighed Dora. 'I wish he could live here.'

'Not sure if Northcliffe would like that, he's awfully territorial. I'll ask Ian.' Patience had taken off her red Puffa to reveal a purple knitted jersey on inside out.

After Dora had gone, she made very strong tea and toast and then surreptitiously scraped mould off some pear jelly entitled 'Poppet Bruce 2000', before discovering to her relief some chocolate spread and a coconut cake stuffed with glacé cherries.

'Were they very young when you adopted them?' asked Paris.

'*Very*, we were so lucky, and they've both got heavenly babas of their own now. It's so crucial for adopted people to have their first blood relation.'

Euphoric that he'd conquered his phobia of horses, Paris, over a second cup of tea and third slice of cake, found himself most uncharacteristically unbuttoning to Patience about his fruitlessly advertising for a family.

'There was no takers. Guess I looked too likely to knife them in their beds.'

'That's horrible.' Patience looked as though she was going to cry. 'Anyone would feel privileged and overjoyed to have you for a son. Everyone thinks so highly of you at Bagley. Your Romeo is the talk of the staffroom.'

Paris shrugged.

'I do hope' – Patience blushed an even darker maroon – 'you'll drop in and see us, like Dora does, even if you don't want to go on riding.'

Seeing Paris's eyes straying to a bookshelf crammed with poetry, much more thumbed than the cookery books, she explained: 'My husband loves poetry. Matthew Arnold's his favourite. I'm awfully badly read, but Arnold wrote a lovely poem called 'Sohrab and Rustum', which has a sweet horse in it called Ruksh who sheds real tears' – Patience's voice trembled – 'when his master unknowingly slays his own son in battle. You must read it.'

'Horses cry when their masters die in the *Iliad*,' said Paris, reaching out his hand for more coconut cake, then pausing.

'Please have it,' begged Patience. 'We used to say whoever had the last piece got a handsome husband and a thousand a year, which wouldn't go very far these days.'

'I could use it,' said Paris.

'I do hope you'll have another go on Beluga. I think you're a natural.'

42

Gradually as March splashed into its third week and Bagley was lit up by daffodils, the excitement began to bite. Wally borrowed a lorry to transport props and scenery made by Larks parents, which included a four-poster painted with flowers for Juliet and a wrought-iron balcony: 'More suited to a Weybridge hacienda,' said Hengist, 'but perfect for sixteenth-century Verona.'

The dress rehearsal in front of pupils from both schools was scheduled for Wednesday evening; the big night for governors, parents and friends would take place on Thursday.

Larks participants spent Wednesday afternoon over at Bagley taking part in a dry run to fine-tune performances, scene shifts and lighting. Glimpses of Paris's naked back view would add excitement to the bedroom scenes. Johnnie Fowler, in charge of his dad's lighting, was determined to catch Paris full frontal.

Amber, meanwhile, was shouting at Alex Bruce:

'I'll pay for my own fucking dress, it was only five hundred pounds,' which is the difference between them and us, thought Graffi, who'd never been paid by Junior for Shining Sixpence's winnings.

All the cast were jittery and Vicky didn't help by ringing in with a migraine. 'So sorry, I've overdone things. I'll try and stagger in later.'

Emlyn took a deep breath and counted to ten.

'Right, let's get started. We all know this is a play about conflict rather than love.'

'Why can't Miss come in instead of Vicky?' sighed Kylie.

The day continued full of spats.

Jade Stancombe, insisting on wearing four-inch heels, fell

down the stairs. A waiter carrying full glasses of coloured water bumped into a bodyguard, soaking the stage, which resulted in Feral and Bianca nearly doing the splits in their tango. Juliet's bed collapsed during her night of passion with Romeo. Everyone burst out laughing when Feral's moustache fell off during a fight.

The instant Juliet's bed had been repaired and her wedding night resumed, Poppet Bruce marched in brandishing a packet of rainbow-coloured Durex.

'R and J are having underage sex; Paris must be publicly seen to be wearing a condom.'

'Surely that's wardrobe's department?' grinned Jason.

'The audience won't see him in the dark,' snarled Emlyn. 'Get out, Poppet.'

'That is not how you should address your deputy team leader's wife,' spluttered Poppet, then, as Emlyn rose to his mighty height, flounced out slamming the door.

'Romeo, Romeo,' sighed Milly, 'wherefore fart thou, Romeo,' producing more giggles.

'Shut up, Milly,' howled Emlyn.

Paris gritted his teeth. His ride up the aisle and his last impassioned speech were still to come.

' "The day is hot, the Capulets abroad . . ." ' Junior Lloyd-Foxe, who had the part of Benvolio, delivered his best and most ominous line.

Next moment, Feral and Cosmo were on the floor, howling, punching, clawing like tomcats.

'Take your hands off her, you sick bastard.'

'Don't give yourself airs, you fucking golliwog.'

'Don't black Cosmo's eyes,' begged Jason as Feral lunged and missed.

'Pack it in,' yelled Emlyn and, when they didn't, he emptied a dusty fire bucket over them. This, as they retreated, spluttering and swearing, did nothing to aid Paris's concentration.

Somehow he managed to gallop Beluga up to the orchestra pit and keep control when Cosmo, to spook the horse, deliberately launched the brass into a deafening tantivy. Chucking his reins to Dora, Paris managed to leap off without touching the floor, run up the plank laid across the pit and dive into Juliet's tomb to a round of applause.

'I don't need no fucking stand-in,' he hissed at Cosmo.

Now Juliet lay before him in her coffin and the half-light. He had just launched into his impassioned soliloquy about the colour still in her lovely face, when he realized Milly, bet by

Amber, had slipped on a red Comic Relief nose, and raised a hand to hit her.

'Don't,' thundered Emlyn, so Paris swore at him, spat on the floor and stalked off the set.

'You stupid bitch,' yelled Emlyn. 'How dare you wind him up like that?'

'It was only a joke to loosen him up,' wailed Milly. 'It's not me he's kissing, it's Juliet. I'm fed up with pandering to him."Paris, Paris, don't upset Paris." What about my needs?'

Graffi, in his Nurse's costume, rushed on to the stage and flung his arms round Milly. 'There, there, lovely, it's OK. Don't bully her,' he shouted at Emlyn.

Milly was touched but rather wished her knight in shining armour wasn't wearing drag and a grey granny wig.

'But soft what brick through yonder window breaks,' intoned Amber.

Although he was consistently bottom in maths, Jack Waterlane had worked out that between appearances on stage, he and Kylie had at least an hour unaccounted for. He had therefore whipped her into the biology lab and hung his red jacket on a skeleton, then they both froze as Poppet Bruce, exuding bossy bustle in her eco-monitor role, rushed by flicking off the lab lights and seemingly giving them her blessing.

'Gosh, we've just had underage sex,' sighed Jack as he lay in Kylie's arms. 'My father had to have sex before polo matches – relaxed him – 'spect I'll win an Oscar now. I love you, Kylie Rose.'

'I love you, Jack,' said Kylie.

It was an hour to the dress rehearsal. No one could find Paris. He hadn't even been to make-up. Everyone was panicking.

'Sometimes he disappears on trains for days,' said Feral, then, turning on Amber and Milly: 'Why'd you wind him up, you stupid cows?'

Patience Cartwright found Paris in Beluga's box, throwing up into an empty water bucket, wiping his face with hay from the rack. At first he wouldn't speak and carried on retching, but when Patience brought him a glass of water, he told her about the red nose, mumbling that he found it so hard without Janna.

'She got me into Shakespeare. Explained things. But she hasn't been to rehearsals for weeks, 'spect she's too busy.'

He slumped against Beluga, his face grey and defeated.

'She probably doesn't want to cramp Vicky's style.'

'Vicky's a stupid bitch.'

Patience felt ashamed at her elation; Ian was besotted with Vicky.

'You've got to be terrified to be any good,' she reassured Paris. 'I once competed at the Horse of the Year Show, and I was so worried about letting Bentley, my horse, down, I spent three hours in the lav. They had to drag me out and then we won our class. I crept into the rehearsal room the other day: you're miles the best in the cast. I'm sure Milly was trying to relax you.'

'I can't kiss her tasting of puke.'

'I always keep spare toothbrushes and toothpaste in case a pupil needs it, and Ian confiscated some peppermint chewing gum yesterday, you can have that.'

'You weren't just saying I was OK?'

He looked so forlorn and despairing, Patience longed to hug him. 'You'll be sensational.'

As soon as he'd gone, Patience called Emlyn. 'Paris is on his way back. I don't mean to interfere, but he needs Janna, he's so alone.'

The dress rehearsal was a great success. When the cheers and clapping finally died down, the cast yelled for Mr Davies: 'Attila! Attila! Attila!' They stamped their feet until, loose-limbed and bleary-eyed, Emlyn shambled on to the stage, where Graffi presented him with a big bottle of red, 'from Larks as a mark of our gratitude'.

'Mr Davies builds us up,' shouted Rocky. 'He puts the boot in, but he's always looking for fings to praise.'

'Why, thank you, Rocky.' Emlyn was touched. 'What about Miss Fairchild and Mr Fenton?'

'We've got fings for them tomorrow, but you do all the work,' said Pearl.

Emlyn was so tired, he would have loved to unwind over a few beers with his friend Artie Deverell, the head of modern languages. Instead he threw the bottle of red into his dirty Renault Estate and drove over to Larks where, although it was after eleven, lights were still blazing.

Inside he thought what a good job Janna was doing. The building might be falling down, but newly painted walls and noticeboards were covered in praise postcards, brightly coloured work and crammed with pictures of the children and their activities: a new baby brother yesterday, a birthday today. Along the corridor, *Romeo and Juliet* posters proudly flaunted yellow 'sold-out' stickers.

Janna was in her office, squealing with frustration as she tried

261

to put back a cupboard, which, as a result of the damp, had fallen off the wall. Her fathers weren't as diligent about do-it-yourself when Vicky wasn't around.

Nor was putting back screws without a screwdriver very easy. 'Bugger, bugger, bugger,' yelled Janna, as a 50p piece slipped out of the groove. The handle of her tweezers had been no more successful.

Then she shrieked as a dark figure filled the doorway. Partner woke up, went berserk, then, recognizing Emlyn's soft Welsh accent, dragged his blue rug across the floor in welcome.

'Fucking cupboard.' Janna gave it a kick. 'How did it go?'

'Wonderfully. They all did so well. Your kids presented this to me.' He dumped the bottle of red on Janna's desk. 'Why don't you open it?'

Rootling round in Wally's toolbox, Emlyn then located four big screws and a box of matches. Putting matches in the holes to make them smaller, he banged in the screws with a hammer.

'That is so cool,' cried an amazed Janna as the cupboard stayed put.

'Can't beat a good screw.' Emlyn took the corkscrew from her.

Noticing the bags under his bloodshot eyes, she said apologetically, 'You must be shattered.'

'No more than you,' said Emlyn, noticing the bags under her bloodshot eyes.

'Why the hell do we teach?' asked Janna, getting two glasses out of a second cupboard.

Emlyn was reading the letter on her laptop.

'Dear Mrs Todd, I thought you'd be pleased that Charlie wrote a wonderful essay on Oliver Cromwell this morning.'

The wine was unbelievably disgusting. If they hadn't needed a drink so badly, Emlyn would have chucked it down the bog.

'I don't think Larks children have much pocket money,' said Janna defensively.

'It was a sweet thought.' Emlyn collapsed on the sofa which still bore Pearl's ink stain. Partner jumped on to his knee.

'Now tell me how it really went.'

When he'd finished, Emlyn said, 'You should have been there.'

'I'm coming tomorrow.'

'Not good enough. I'm told you were always in the thick of things at Redfords. Why have you backed off?'

'I'm frantic,' said Janna defensively.

'Everyone's frantic.'

'Everyone adores Vicky.' Janna tried not to sound bitter. 'I put people's backs up.'

'Vicky lacks your vision,' said Emlyn flatly, 'and she doesn't understand the play. Jason's been terrific, but it's you the kids love. They're dying to show you how far they've come, that they're carrying out your ideas – which Vicky claims are hers.'

'How was Paris?' A defiant, shame-faced Janna wanted to change the subject.

'All to pieces; nearly lost it. Amber, Milly and Jade are fed up they're getting no reaction from him. Why did you stop coming?'

Getting up, he looked at the school photograph. Hands shoved into his pockets, he showed off a surprisingly taut, high, beautiful bottom. He had terrific shoulders too and the bulldog face had charm if you liked bulldogs. Janna longed to throw herself into his arms and tell him how Ashton and Crispin had warned her off. Instead she said, 'I've got a school to save.'

Emlyn could see how reduced in bounce she was and longed to comfort her. In the old days he'd have taken her home for a joyful romp in bed. But there was the cool, white body of Oriana to consider. 'I have been faithful to thee, Cynara! in my fashion.'

Janna anyway was too vulnerable and too nice for half measures.

'Let's go and have supper,' he said instead. 'I know somewhere still open.'

'I've got far too much to do,' snapped Janna, 'but thanks all the same.'

'We all miss you,' said Emlyn as he went out. 'Particularly Paris.'

Returning to Jubilee Cottage, Janna and Partner wandered into the garden. The rain, at last, had stopped and the stars for the first time in days were scattered across the sky like a sweep of white daffodils.

'Give me my Romeo,' she cried out:

> 'And, when he shall die,
> Take him and cut him out in little stars,
> And he will make the face of heaven so fine
> That all the world will be in love with night.'

Oh Hengist! Oh Emlyn! She was so lonely for love and a pair of arms round her.

Even though it was nearly midnight, she rang first Mr Blenchley and then Nadine, Paris's social worker.

'I've got a few spare tickets. It'd mean so much to Paris if you came along.'

43

Paris was gratified next day to get lots of cards, including one from Aunt Lily and another from Nadine, delivered to school by hand: 'So looking forward to seeing you tonight.' Normally she wasn't remotely interested in his academic progress, only his social welfare. There was even a card from the children in the home: 'Sorry we took the piss.'

Patience sent him a silver horseshoe and some chewing gum. Dora had bought him a fluffy black cat, which, entitled 'Dora's pussy', became the subject of much ribaldry. Cadbury sent him a good-lick card.

After last night's success, the cast were cheerful and over-excited.

'You've got to calm down,' Emlyn kept telling them.

It was a glorious evening, with the setting sun flaming the flooded playing fields below a vermilion and Cambridge-blue sky, which was considered a good omen, as the Montagues' uniform was flame red and the Capulets' pale blue.

All afternoon Pearl worked her magic on the cast, particularly Jade, who couldn't stop admiring herself in the mirror. Amber was less sanguine.

'Pearl's still convinced Feral's got the hots for me,' she whispered to Milly, 'but frankly he can't take his big eyes off Bianca C-B. So humiliating to be cuckolded by someone from the Lower Fourth.'

' "There's no trust, No faith, no honesty in men," ' sighed Milly.

Amber was not cast down. Both Eton and Radley boyfriends had sent her huge bunches of flowers and their undying love.

'I'd still like a night with Feral,' she confessed. 'Do you think Paris is gay?'

'That could explain it,' said Milly in delight. 'All the time he's fantasizing I'm Feral, not me. I still fancy him rotten.'

'One can't not,' agreed Amber.

'He stares and stares but it's to observe, not to lust. If Sally Bloody-Taylor hadn't forced me into such a prissy dress with that gross sash, I might have scored.'

Paris was shivering uncontrollably. Thank God he wore a flimsy white shirt in the first act, so the circles of sweat wouldn't show. Already he could hear strains of Tchaikovsky as the orchestra warmed up.

Emlyn was everywhere, calmly encouraging, dealing with last minute crises. 'No, the Prince can't wear gel, Jack, go and wash it out.'

As Mr Khan had shot off to Pakistan on business, Aysha had bravely applied to be a stage hand. Hearing the news from Bianca, Xavier Campbell-Black had applied as well. They had only been working with the cast for a week. Occasionally Xav's hand touched Aysha's as they shifted balconies, beds and coffins around. There were twenty scenes to be set up. They were both very nervous. Aysha looked more beautiful than ever in a shalwar kameez of midnight-blue silk.

Xav had avoided Cosmo and his minions since they tried to drown him in the bog. Now as he and Aysha made sure that Paris's plank was in place, stacked in a corner of the pit ready to form a bridge across the orchestra, Cosmo shouted nastily:

'Good thing you and Miss Khan are black, so the audience needn't see you when you're shifting scenes.'

Next moment, Feral had grabbed Cosmo's dark curls, holding a knife to his throat. 'Take that back,' he hissed.

'I'll have that.' Emlyn grabbed the knife. He also confiscated Anatole's vodka. 'You can get drunk after you're killed off.'

' "Why, uncle, 'tis a shame",' grumbled Anatole.

Jade had got forty-eight red roses from her father, and a huge bunch of pink lilies that she'd sent herself and made a lot of fuss wondering who they came from. Stancombe also sent yellow orchids to Milly. Milly's mother was not as biddable as Stancombe would have liked. He had wanted to arrive with her in the helicopter this evening, but perversely she insisted that, as a governor, she should make her own way.

'When's Hengist going to make me a governor?' grumbled Stancombe.

265

'When a vacancy occurs. No one resigns because meetings are such fun,' said Mrs Walton.

Mags Gablecross and Sally B-T were working flat out on final alterations to costumes.

'Where's Vicky?' demanded Monster fretfully.

'Gone to the hairdresser's,' said Mags dryly. 'She felt the need to pamper herself before her big night.'

'I bought her these flowers,' protested Monster.

'How very thoughtful of you,' said Sally, recognizing five of her rare irises and the only spotted hellebores not squashed earlier by Cosmo. 'I'll put them in water for Vicky.'

Mrs Kamani, thrilled to be sent a ticket, had closed her newsagent's especially early and was now sitting in the second row next to Vicky's proud parents.

Janna crept into the dressing room, where everything seemed chaos. So many ravishing girls and boys. Whatever happened to spots and puppy fat? Such smooth flesh to make up, she thought wistfully, no crevasses for it to sink into.

Milly's streaked ponytail was being brushed out by Sally, before being put up with a white rose. Bianca Campbell-Black, watched surreptitiously by every boy in the room, was being zipped into her scarlet spangled dress.

Feral paced up and down, muttering, ' "Have at thee, coward!" ' He must remember to speak up.

'Who's coming tonight, apart from my mum?' asked Kylie as Pearl toned down her flushed post-orgasmic face.

'Press, parents, friends of the school.'

'Din't know we had any friends,' said Graffi.

' "Why Uncle, 'tis a shame",' muttered Feral.

'I'm going to throw up again,' said Paris.

'No you're not.' Hengist swept in resplendent in a beautifully cut pinstripe suit, sky-blue shirt and dark blue spotted tie. 'The audience are arriving. I want you all down in the General Bagley Room. Take the back stairs so no one sees you.'

On the way they passed props tables groaning with policemen's helmets, Sally's old scent bottles filled with coloured water for Monster's chemist shop, pots of rosemary, camomile and foxglove for Friar Lawrence's garden, phials of fake blood, retractable knives and pistols, which Emlyn constantly checked for the real thing.

Self-conscious yet astounded how newly beautiful Pearl had

made so many of them, the cast took up their positions in rising tiers on three sides of a square. Amber and Jade had become glamorous society hostesses, Milly an innocent vast-eyed angel, towards whom even Paris felt a flicker of lust.

'I look almost as good as Mummy,' sighed Milly.

Graffi, aged up with wrinkles, parsnip-yellow bags under the eyes, a shaggy grey wig and a Norland Nurse's uniform, with a fob watch on his starched bosom, looked nearly fifty and decidedly unattractive. Milly loved him but she wished once again he looked as sexy as Feral who, with his lithe beautiful body encased in black, his amazing tawny eyes elongated to his temples and with a suggestion of ebony whisker, looked indeed the Prince of Cats. Paris had refused blusher or lipstick, but Pearl, with bronzing gel, had warmed his deathly pallor to the olive glow of an Old Master and defined his pale unblinking eyes with eyeliner and mascara. He looked drop dead gorgeous with his officer's peaked cap shoved on to the back of his head.

'I must not fancy Paris,' pleaded Milly.

Standing facing his young audience, Hengist smiled.

'You all look fantastic.' Then, sternly: 'But remember your job tonight is to entertain. Invite the audience on stage with you, invite them to become part of this amazing story. It's all about eye contact, even if you're a bad guy or one of the crowd – look out at the audience.

'Up until now, no one's given more than seventy-five per cent. Tonight I want one hundred and fifty per cent. It's already a great show. I want it to be a brilliant show. I want you to change what the audience feels about you. Your parents are out there, longing to be proud of you.'

Not for Paris, thought Janna in anguish.

'Stand up,' ordered Hengist.

As the children struggled to their feet, the girls swaying on their high heels, his voice became almost messianic:

'Shut your eyes. You are young, you are beautiful, you're energetic, you have ability and gifts. You have time to entertain.'

'Yeah, man.' Rocky punched the air with his fist.

Kylie suppressed a nervous giggle. Aysha was horrified to feel her hand creeping into Xav's, and nearly fainted when he squeezed it back.

'Make the audience want to be what you are,' Hengist's voice dropped seductively: 'Make them adore you. Your job is to break their hearts.'

Against the force of Hengist's personality, Feral wrenched open his eyes and caught Bianca gazing at him; then she smiled

267

shyly. Feral was jolted, he must get a grip on himself. Quickly he looked away. Cosmo, intercepting this exchange, was determined to negate it.

'Good luck, God bless you all,' ended Hengist to a round of applause. Hovering at the back, glancing at the rapt, inspired faces of the children, Janna was reminded once again why he was head of one of the best schools in the country. He could have sent entire armies over the top.

And he looked so divine. The strong features, the ebony eyebrows, the high colour, the slicked-down hair already leaping upwards, the vitality tamed by the dark-grey establishment suit. An arrogant public-school shit, and yet, and yet . . .

'My only love sprung from my only hate', she thought helplessly, stepping out from behind a tier of seats, then leaping back as Pearl shouted, 'Miss, Miss,' and all the children took up the cry.

But Janna had fled, racing down the corridor, losing herself in the crowd gathering in the foyer outside the theatre. All round the walls were Cosmo's blown-up photographs of the cast. Janna swelled with pride. Paris, Feral and Kylie looked so beautiful.

Even more beautiful to the Larks parents was a splendid array of free drink. Two coachloads had been ferried over from the Shakespeare Estate by the heroic Wally and were fast losing their shyness. There was Pearl's mother and her very young lover, who didn't look capable of beating Pearl or anyone else up, and Chantal Peck in gold lurex and a high state of excitement, telling everyone she was a parent governor. Stormin' Norman, in a black trouser suit, had been spoiling for a fight, but her aggression evaporated when she saw the blow-up of Monster as the apothecary. The small stocky man with black curls and naughty laughing eyes, drinking red wine out of a pint mug, must be Dafydd Williams, Graffi's dad.

Out of loyalty to Vicky, but not bothering to change out of very casual clothes, Skunk Illingworth, Sam Spink, Robbie Rushton and Chally had overcome their loathing of private education enough to get stuck into Hengist's drink.

Bagley parents, however, were in the ascendancy.

'Darling darling, kiss kiss, yock yock, ha, ha ha, skiing, the Seychelles, the Caribbean, Egypt, Aspen, Florida, Klosters. Are you going to the Argentine Open? Must come over to kitchen sups,' to show they'd got a dining room. Listening to the confident yelling and exchange of proper names, Janna had forgotten how much she detested the upper middle classes.

It was still light outside; through the open windows, birds were competing with the orchestra. Chantal and Stormin' Norman were pointing out celebs.

'Look, there's Rupert Campbell-Black, ain't he beautiful?'

'Best owner-trainer in the country,' agreed Dafydd, 'and there's Billy Lloyd-Foxe,' as Amber's father, clutching two large whiskies, pushed his way through the throng.

'Never miss him on *Question of Sport*,' said Stormin'. ''Ello Billy, don't drink it all at once.'

Billy grinned back at them: 'I hate running out.'

Dafydd was over the moon and in turn helped himself to two mugs of red.

'And there's Jupiter Belvedon, our Member,' squeaked Chantal. 'Evening, Jupe.'

Jupiter nodded coolly as he joined the group round Rupert Campbell-Black.

'Pity I didn't bring my autograph book,' sighed Chantal.

Such was Janna's paranoia, having been warned off by Ashton and Crispin and imagining everyone would be dubbing her a whore, that she was amazed so many parents hailed her.

'She's so nice, she's our head.'

Maybe all those home visits were paying off.

Randal Stancombe, hovering hopefully round the Campbell-Black clique, kissed Janna on both cheeks. Mrs Walton, ravishing as ever in a Lindka Cierach cream velvet suit, to which she had pinned a big pink rose, Calèche rising like morning mist from her ravine of a cleavage, rushed up and insisted she and Janna have lunch soon.

'I am so thrilled Milly's playing Juliet,' she whispered. 'Randal's livid that poisonous Jade didn't get it. Have you met Taggie Campbell-Black? She can't sleep for worrying Xav's going to move the wrong chair, or Bianca forget her dance steps.'

Janna smiled up at Taggie, who, slender as a young birch, with a dark cloud of hair, kind, silver-grey eyes and soft pink lips, seemed infinitely sweeter and more beautiful than Mrs Walton.

'I gather Bianca's champion,' she said. 'She's doing her dance with one of my most adorable pupils.'

'Is that Feral? Bianca chatters about him all day. Rupert's getting very jealous. But we're so pleased Xav's got involved. Darling, you've met Janna,' Taggie called out to Rupert who, detesting school events, was cringing behind a pillar talking into two mobiles.

Peering out nervously, he waved at Janna.

'I've still got that sheepdog that fell on my head when I visited your school – much better behaved than my dogs.'

Absurdly flattered to be remembered, Janna was thanking him once again for sending *Gladiator* and the huge cheque, when she lost her audience as Rupert muttered, 'Oh God,' and shot behind his pillar again, as a large woman, outcleavaging Ruth Walton and with the wide innocent eyes of a doll, appeared in the doorway awaiting adulation.

'There's Dime Kiri,' shouted Stormin' Norman, who was well away. ''Ello Dime Kiri.'

'That ain't Dime Kiri,' chided Chantal as the large woman expanded like a bullfrog, 'that's Dime Hermy-own, stupid. 'Ello, Dime Hermy-own.'

'It's Dame Hermione, Cosmo's mother, silly old bat. Hengist can't stand her,' said Ruth Walton with rare venom as Randal shot forward to kiss Dame Hermione's hand, determined to harpoon this great whale to open his hypermarket.

'Can I take your photograph, Miss Curtis?' said a shrill voice. It was Dora, ostensibly covering the play for the Bagley school mag. 'Oh bugger, here comes my mother, she's crazy about Rupert.'

'Christ!' Rupert had now disappeared round the other side of the pillar to avoid Lady Belvedon, a very slim pretty blonde, crying: 'Rupert, Rupert.'

'Did I hear Rupert's name?' cried Dame Hermione roguishly and, leaving Stancombe in mid-supermarket pitch, rushed off in pursuit.

Advanced on from right and left, Rupert bolted for the bar.

'Poor Rupert, he's so naughty,' laughed Taggie, then, lowering her voice: 'He can't stand Dame Hermione or Anthea Belvedon, but they're like cats and always crawl over people who are allergic to them.'

'Oh look, he's now been clobbered by Poppet Bruce,' giggled Dora. 'I expect she'll invite him to her workshop on behaviour management.'

Strains of Prokoviev's *Romeo and Juliet* were rising above the din of chat as the five-minute bell went.

'God, I loathe school plays,' grumbled Amber and Junior's mother, Janey, a blonde Fleet Street journalist who'd seen better days. 'This one's going to be even direr, since Bagley bonded with that grotty comprehensive . . .'

Ruth Walton laughed.

'This is the grotty comp's headmistress, Janna Curtis.'

'Oh dear,' said Janey, filling up Janna's glass from her brimming half-pint mug, 'I'm so sorry. You're much too pretty and young for a head. I'm covering this for the *Mail*. I'll say you're charismatic and deeply capable.' Then, as Uncle Harley sauntered in looking sleek and dangerous: 'Who's that utterly ravishing man covered in diamonds?'

'Some African prince,' said Janna slyly.

At least someone's come for Feral, she thought as she waved at Harley. She was also delighted Nadine and Mr Blenchley from Oaktree Court had showed up.

'Christ.' Rupert had joined them again. 'Hermione, Lady Belvedon and that ghastly Poppet: I thought the three witches came in *Macbeth*.'

There was an explosion of flashes as Hengist swept in with Anatole's father the Russian Minister and his glamorous wife, who was wearing a floor-length fur.

'It must have accounted for a hundred bears,' said Dora furiously, 'I'm going to blow her up.'

'I feel one has a duty to support these functions,' Lady Belvedon was telling Stancombe, then squawked as the long pink tongue of Elaine, the greyhound, relieved her of the vol-au-vent she was clutching.

The sixty-second bell was ringing imperiously. As everyone surged into the theatre, Taggie turned shyly to Janna.

'Good luck. I'm so sick with nerves for Bianca, I can't imagine what it would be like to worry about a whole school. You've done so well, Xav and Bianca have really taken to your Larks children.'

If only all posh people were like you, thought Janna, noticing Graffi's dad tucking a bottle of red wine inside his jacket.

'Thank you for helping our Graffi with his muriel,' said his wife.

'You must come and see it,' said Janna happily, then any joy was drained out of her as she saw the Tusk Force: Russell, Crispin, Rod Hyde and Ashton Douglas, in a dark purple smoking jacket, with an uncharacteristically adoring expression on his bland, pink face.

'Dame Hermione.' He seized both her hands. 'You were the most wonderful Elisabetta I ever saw. Pawis nineteen eighty-five.'

'You're very kind.' Hermione bowed gracefully. 'Perhaps you could rustle me up another glass of bubbly?'

'Indeed.' Ashton belted off.

'You're looking very iconic this evening, Dame Hermione,' snuffled fat Crispin.

'Where's Vicky?' asked Russell.

'Backstage.' Rod Hyde's voice thickened. 'The good general is always with his troops.'

Catapulted forward by the crowd, Janna couldn't avoid them.

'Good evening, gentlemen,' she said coolly.

They nodded back equally coolly.

'Good of you to turn up.'

'We felt we must support Vicky,' said Ashton.

Janna glanced at her ticket. 'I must find my seat.'

Next moment, a big warm hand grabbed hers. 'Gotcha,' said a familiar deep husky voice. 'Come and watch with me.'

'I'm sitting with Tim and Mags Gablecross,' shrieked Janna, aware of Ashton and Co's delighted disapproval and wriggling like a stray cat to escape.

'The Gablecrosses won't mind,' said Hengist. 'We started this together, I want to share it with you,' and he dragged her off to sit in the middle of the tenth row, making everyone move up.

'Sally's backstage, doing last-minute repairs,' he told Janna. 'Half our girls are so besotted with your Feral, the other half with your Paris. They've all had to have their costumes taken in.'

Oh God, thought Janna in panic as a flurry of 'Excuse me, sorry, excuse me' indicated that the Tusk Force had taken the seats directly behind her.

I haven't seen Hengist since I last saw you, Janna wanted to scream at them, but then she thought defiantly: I don't care, I don't care. Maybe it's three glasses of wine on an empty stomach, but I still really adore him.

Giving her a slug of Courvoisier from a silver hipflask, Hengist introduced her to two masters on her right.

These were Artie Deverell, the handsome, languid, gentle head of modern languages, whom Mags Gablecross, who taught the same subject, had fallen in love with on balloon day, and Theo Graham, the bald and very wrinkled head of classics, revered for his translation of Euripides.

'I've got Jack Waterlane, Junior, Lando and Lubemir in my house,' whispered Artie. 'Theo's got Cosmo and Anatole, so we both have our crosses.'

The Russian Minister and his wife were seated on Hengist's left. Next moment, everyone jumped out of their skins as Dame Hermione started singing along to Prokofiev.

'Lurex tremendous,' murmured Hengist as Chantal Peck swept up to the front.

44

It was a wonderful theatre, stark and forbidding, with black brick walls forty feet high and black leather seats. Saxophones and clarinets glittered like jewels in the pit; pearly drum skins gleamed in the half-light.

The only prop in front of the crimson curtains was a big cardboard television with the screen cut out. As Prokofiev's menacing 'March of the Capulets' faded away, Kylie Rose appeared inside the now lit-up screen as a presenter.

' "Two households, both alaike in dignity..." ' She held up cards saying Bagley and Larks:

> 'In fair Verona, where we lay our scene.
> From forth the fatal loins of these two foes
> A pair of star-crossed lovers take their laife.'

'Christ,' muttered Rupert, 'she's been here half a term and she talks like Anthea Belvedon.'

Chantal was in ecstasy: Kylie looked so dignified.

Back creaked the crimson curtains to a howl of police sirens and a burst of clapping. Against Graffi's fantastic backdrop of mosques, tumbling twin towers, tower blocks and army barracks strangled by barbed wire was a street in Verona with an ice-cream van, AC Milan posters, a large bullet-pocked Shakespeare Estate sign, and a signpost saying 'Bagley 5 miles, City Centre ½ mile'. There was the Ghost and Castle and Mrs Kamani's newsagent's with a broken window.

Oh God, thought Janna, but, rising out of her seat, she could see Mrs Kamani laughing. Revelling in the roars of applause, Janna forgot her nerves. This was no school production; it was slick, yet bursting with exuberance and passion. Larks's confidence had grown so much, they were as assured as their Bagley counterparts.

Here was Rocky lumbering out of the Ghost and Castle and turning on the Montagues.

' "No, sir, I do not bite my fumb at you, sir, but I bite my fumb, sir. When I have fought the men, I will be civil with the maids, and cut off their heads." '

' "The heads of the maids?" ' demanded Junior.

' "Ay, the heads of the maids or their maidenheads." ' Rocky leered round; the audience laughed.

Then Feral erupted on to the stage to huge cheers and boos.

' "What, drawn, and talk of peace! I hate the word," ' he spat, his fury scattering the Montagues, then paused.

Although the cast knew he'd dried, the audience thought it was terrific timing.

' "I hate the word," ' repeated Feral, recovering, ' "As I hate hell, all Montagues, and thee. Have at thee, coward!" ' And guns were flashing and blanks ringing out.

'That's Bianca's boyfriend,' whispered Taggie. 'Isn't he gorgeous?'

'Very black,' muttered back Rupert.

Paris stood apart in the wings, psyching himself up, mindlessly chewing gum. I am Romeo; I am in Verona; I am empowered; I am lovesick for a woman who hardly knows I exist. *Plus ça change*, he thought bitterly, I am about to crash a ball and fall in love for the first and last time in my life.

'Good luck, Paris.' Vicky's clap on the back nearly shot him on to the stage. 'Remember to speak up.'

Roars of applause greeted each new set, particularly the Capulets' ballroom with long-legged beauties in masks and paparazzi hiding, like Rupert, behind every pillar.

'That's my Jade in cerise,' said Stancombe loudly to Dame Hermione.

'That's my Cosmo playing Lord Capulet in a navy military jacket,' said Hermione even more loudly.

'Shut up,' said Janna.

'Don't wepwove Dame Hermione,' hissed a horrified Ashton.

Cosmo, having played the genial host, whipped off his jacket and joined the Cosmonaughties and Kylie Rose in a number he'd composed called 'Cocks and Rubbers', the words of which were fortunately obscured by the din of the band. Looking at Cosmo's pale dangerous face, ebony curls flopping maniacally as he lashed his guitar, Janna thought: That is one whole lot of gorgeous trouble.

Then the stage cleared for Feral and Bianca's tango. Never taking their eyes off each other, talking through their bodies as they danced, their red-hot passion branded the floorboards. Rupert, woken by his wife just in time to watch them, led the bravoes and thunderous applause. This resulted in two encores, which broke the mood for Paris's big entrance.

'Oh poor boy,' muttered Janna in anguish as the applause petered out.

'He'll be OK,' whispered Hengist.

And Janna moved her body against his so the comforting hand he'd laid on top of hers couldn't be seen from behind by Ashton and Crispin. Any minute, she imagined Crispin's fourth chin resting on her shoulder so he could peep over.

Despite a balloon bursting and Rocky now dressed as a waiter nudging him in the back, saying hoarsely: 'Nibbles anyone?' Paris remained motionless, waiting until he'd got everyone's attention, gazing in wonder at the young girl in white muslin standing with the shy dignity of the daughter of the house at the foot of the stairs.

Pausing for five seconds on that first '"Oh!"' then, glancing up at the flambeaux flickering round the room, he murmured: '"She doth teach the torches to burn bright!"'

'Christ,' murmured Theo and Artie.

I must have that boy at Bagley, thought Hengist.

Offered another swig of Courvoisier from his flask, Janna shook her head, refusing to be distracted for a second. As Paris ended his speech, vowing he'd never seen true beauty till this night, you could have heard a pin and also the jaw of Dora Belvedon drop.

At the moment Paris fell in love with his Juliet, Dora felt herself blasted by similar lightning, as if she was seeing Paris for the first time, and he had become as beautiful, remote and beyond her reach as a stained-glass saint in the chapel.

He was even more heartbreaking in the balcony scene. Cosmo had given her five rolls of film to capture misbehaviour to flog to the nationals. Dora used them all on Paris. Even when Anatole and Feral were being killed off, she could only think of him. The wound made by Cupid's arrow was like the one in Mercutio's side.

'"Not so deep as a well, nor so wide as a church door, but 'tis enough, 'twill serve."'

Dora moaned in terror. She had lost control of her life.

In the dark beside Hengist, Janna had never been prouder or happier, breathing in lemon aftershave, rejoicing as his shout of laughter and the thunderclap of his big hands set off the rest of the audience.

In the interval, reality reasserted itself. Janna resisted going backstage, terrified of intruding. She'd lost so much confidence. She'd just found Tim and Mags and a large glass of wine, when Vicky emerged to hearty cheering from the Tusk Force.

She looked enchanting in jeans and an old petrol-blue jersey, her hair in a ponytail, make-up lightly but carefully applied. Janna was ashamed to find herself wondering if Vicky had got Pearl to add the smudge on her cheek and the violet shadows beneath her eyes.

'So sorry I'm not dressed, everyone,' she cried, 'it's hard to rush round backstage in high heels and glad rags. Is it all right? I'm so close to it!'

The Tusk Force, except for Crispin who had a mouth full of cocktail sausages, assured her it was simply wonderful.

Janna steeled herself to invade the ring of admirers. 'Brilliant, Vicky, congratulations.'

'Your productions were so wonderful at Redfords' – Vicky hugged Janna – 'I so wanted not to let you down.'

'No danger of that,' said Ashton, 'Pawis Alvaston is headed for stardom, I would say.'

'I must rush and have a word with Mummy and Daddy in the auditorium.'

'I hope you'll bring them to the party later,' said a passing Hengist, 'they must be very proud.'

Even with Feral and Anatole killed off, the second half was full of incident. Boffin Brooks had surreptitiously put back the lines cut out of his long speeches as the Friar, and the audience started slow handclapping.

Johnnie Fowler-Upper, as he was now known, had a heavenly time in the bedroom scene, lighting up Juliet's Barbie dolls and Justin Timberlake posters, the Hon. Jack and Kylie snogging illicitly in another corner of the stage, Milly's boobs twice, Paris nude three times, the beauty of his slender wide-shouldered body causing several masters and Ashton to drop their binoculars.

'Very tasteful and dignified,' cried Chantal, seizing Hermione's opera glasses. 'May word, what a botty.'

Hoots of laughter greeted Monster's chemist shop offering Durex at £10 and Viagra at 50p. The mood was brought back on course by Cosmo, no longer the brutal father, but deranged with grief over his daughter. ' "Death lies on her, like an untimely frost Upon the sweetest flower of all the field." '

Then, not on stage until the next act, Cosmo belted off to conduct the orchestra as they broke into galloping music. Suddenly the audience was startled by a clatter of hooves, the doors flew open and Paris thundered up the gangway. Unfazed by the screams and cheers, Beluga reached the pit and slithered to a halt, but as Paris chucked his reins to a starry-eyed, blushing Dora, he realized someone – no doubt Cosmo – had removed his plank.

Should he jump off and race round backstage, which would wreck the momentum, or risk falling into the pit? He chose the latter and scrambled on to Beluga's slippery saddle.

'Careful,' cried Dora in anguish as he took a massive leap, crashing on to the ill-lit stage, struggling to his feet before disappearing into the Capulets' mausoleum.

'Oh, my brave lad,' gasped Janna.

Even when Paris launched into the 'Eyes, look your last! Arms, take your last embrace!' speech and someone yelled: 'She's not dead yet, you berk,' he held the mood.

Tears were pouring down Janna's face and even Rupert was blowing his nose on Taggie's paper handkerchief as Paris drank purple flavoured water out of Sally's scent bottle, which had once contained Beautiful, and collapsed on Milly, gasping:

' "Thus with a kiss, I die",' and did.

'Well done,' whispered Milly, 'you've made it.'

45

The cast were called back again and again – all beaming – except Paris, who looked drained and utterly shell-shocked, but who got the biggest cheer of the night every time he took a bow.

My boy, thought Janna in ecstasy, and her heart nearly burst as Feral and Bianca bounded on hand in hand and slid into a ten-second tango routine, with Feral arching Bianca back until her black ringlets touched the floor, to stampings and cries of, 'More, more.'

Emlyn ensured that there was thunderous applause for every participant from Pearl for her make-up, Graffi for his sets, and Johnnie Fowler for his lighting:

'You should work in a strip club, Johnnie.'

The stagehands filed on until everyone had clapped their hands raw. But at the first pause, Ashton and Rod Hyde called out: 'Director!'

Whereupon the cast all put on their red noses and Primrose Duddon made a glowing breathy speech, handing out bottles to Emlyn, Jason, Sally Brett-Taylor, Mags and Cambola to thank them for all their hard work. Wally was also praised for being a tower of strength and ferrying everyone about in the wonderful Randal Stancombe bus. Wally was then presented with the definitive book on bell-ringing.

'But most importantly' – even Primrose had a crush on Vicky – 'I'd like to thank our wonderful director, Vicky Fairchild.'

Everyone stamped and yelled as Vicky ran on, accepted a vast bunch of pink roses and launched into an orgy of gratitude, for the wonderful chance she'd been given, for the children and teachers at Bagley and Larks, 'and particularly' – dimple, dimple – 'Hengist and Sally for making us so welcome and for all my dear

278

friends at Larks for covering for me. I know I've played hookey a lot but I was so anxious to make a difference.

'And I'd like to thank dear Ashton and Crispin, at Support and Challenge, and dear Russell and all the governors, for being so supportive, and my parents who've come all the way from Harrogate.'

Audience and cast were getting restless. Cosmo, if he hadn't been trapped on stage, would have started up the orchestra.

'Oh come on, Vicky,' muttered Janna.

'Hush.' Hengist patted her arm. 'Let the little poppet enjoy her moment of glory.'

'If you'll just bear with me,' twinkled Vicky.

'Anytime you like, darlin',' yelled Graffi's father, who after the interval had smuggled in an entire bottle of champagne.

Vicky giggled enchantingly.

But Rocky had had enough. Shambling in front of Vicky, he raised a huge red hand. 'And I'd like to fank Miss Curtis, Janna, for believing in us, and making us feel we could do fings and for turning our school round,' he shouted.

This was greeted with cheers, Tarzan howls and fists punched in the air by both Larks and Bagley.

'Get that nutter off the stage,' howled Ashton.

'I was just coming to Janna,' said Vicky tartly.

With all the cuts, the play had lasted only ninety minutes, but it felt like midnight as Janna fought her way backstage to embrace and congratulate a euphoric cast in various states of undress.

'I am right proud. I never believed in a million years you could do so brilliantly.'

In his purple-stained shirt, a burning-hot Paris trembled as she hugged him, but couldn't speak or smile. His head was still in Juliet's tomb, but he was gratified that Nadine and Mr Blenchley, both of whom he loathed, rolled up to congratulate him at the same time as Patience, who in her raucous voice told them how bravely he'd overcome his terror of horses and even more brilliantly circumnavigated the missing plank.

'Plank's been relocated on his shoulder,' murmured Cosmo who, nevertheless, was feeling vulnerable. Judging by the way Feral and Graffi, still in his nurse's uniform, kept scowling in his direction, they were planning revenge.

Cosmo had lost his guards. However much he snapped his fingers, Anatole and Lubemir were ignoring him. Back in the General Bagley Room, where a splendid party was under way, they were happily getting drunk with the opposition.

279

' "Tybalt, you rat-catcher, vill you valk," ' said Anatole for the hundredth time.

Feral grinned, making a feint with a bread knife.

'We can't stop them drinking after such a magnificent performance,' Sally Brett-Taylor was telling Janna as big bowls of lasagne and sticks of bread were placed on a side table. 'But let's at least give them plenty of blotting paper.'

'An Italian dish – appropriate for *Romeo and Juliet*,' Boffin was saying pompously. 'Although at the Capulets' ball they would probably have eaten boar.'

'Unlike us who have to listen to one,' said Anatole, sprinkling Parmesan over Boffin's hair.

Paris, having survived his ride up the aisle, would have liked to retreat to Beluga's stable, thank the kind horse and relive with him every moment of the play. As it was, when he slunk into the party, everyone wanted a piece of him. With such a bone structure, what did it matter if he was monosyllabic?

'Cosmo will invite you back to River House for the weekend,' gushed Dame Hermione.

Cosmo, flipping through the film in Dora's camera, was enraged to find only pictures of Paris.

'They'll be worth a fortune when he gets an Oscar,' protested Dora.

'We need cash now,' snarled Cosmo.

Cosmo was right, thought Dora in panic. How could she support Cadbury or Loofah if she didn't sell stories? What had become of her? She normally had three helpings of lasagne; now she couldn't eat a thing. She couldn't take her eyes off Paris. He was as beautiful as the wild cherry blossom floodlit outside the window. She longed to tell him how wonderful he'd been, but the words stuck in her throat. The hurt was dreadful.

A record player was pounding out music from *Grease*. Amber and Pearl, sharing a surreptitious spliff and a bottle of white, were drowning their sorrows.

'We've lucked out there,' observed Amber as Feral and Bianca, unspeaking, making love with their eyes, danced on and on.

'She's only twelve,' snapped Pearl.

' "Younger than she are happy mothers made",' quipped Amber.

Aysha had gone home. A dazed, deliriously happy Xav gazed out of the window, breathing in the scent of Sally's narcissi, as sweet and delicate as Aysha, who had held his hand.

Janna moved from actor to parent to teacher to technician, praising and thanking. Not realizing Cosmo had been instrumental in Paris not walking the plank, she thanked him too.

She had a lovely chat with Theo Graham and Artie Deverell. Theo seemed keen on teaching Paris Latin and Greek, and quoted Keats about feeling 'like some watcher of the skies When a new planet swims into his ken'.

Artie seemed equally keen to teach Paris modern languages. 'That boy is separate,' he said. 'You can't watch anyone else when he's on stage.'

'Or off it,' sighed Theo.

Kylie unplugged herself for a second from Jack Waterlane's embrace to ask Janna, 'People aren't just saying Larks did good, miss, because we didn't fight or trash anyfing?'

'You weren't good,' said Janna, then, as Kylie's face fell: 'You were utterly sensational.'

'Better'n Redfords?'

'A million times,' said Janna truthfully.

She was pleased when Emlyn, who'd been clearing up the stage, hove into sight clutching a large whisky and asking if she'd had anything to eat.

'Yes,' lied Janna. 'You were the real star. That play was only brilliant because you held everything together.'

'Not for much longer. The Wolf Pack are spoiling for a punch-up.'

'We'd better get them home,' said Janna. 'I'll alert Wally.'

On the way, she was accosted by Stormin' Norman, very drunk and singing Vicky's praises. 'Vicks realized Martin was visually and aurally impaired, put him in the front row and his school work's gone from strengf to strengf.'

Next Janna passed Vicky, surrounded by more admirers than Paris.

'If I had had my way,' she was telling Randal Stancombe, 'your Jade would have been Juliet.' Meeting Janna's eyes, she blushed. 'Well, Jannie, are you proud of us?'

To conceal her galloping disillusionment, Janna was shocked by her own effusiveness. 'It was all great. You did so well.'

'Send us Victoria, Sweetie and Gloria, Long to reign over us,' sang a drunken Lando and Junior.

'It was priceless,' said Vicky, dimpling again. 'Anatole insisted on introducing me to his father, who asked me what I taught. Quick as a flash, dear Anatole said: "She teaches the torches to burn bright, Dad." Wasn't that darling? I must tell Hengist.'

'Hengist has gone,' said Alex Bruce sourly. 'Pushed off to dinner at Head House with the Russian Minister, Rupert and

281

Jupiter. He wouldn't waste time bothering with riff-raff like us.'

Vicky's lips tightened. Janna felt wiped out with tiredness and wondered if it would be letting the side down to go home, but first she must find Wally.

In her search, she bumped into Jason, congratulated him warmly and asked how he was getting on.

'Bloody tiring. I like the work, but you're on call twenty-four hours a day. You can't bunk off at three-thirty like we did at Larks. Thank God it's the end of term.'

'Thank you for working so hard on the play.'

Jason glanced back at Vicky still holding court.

'Come back, Cara,' he said acidly, 'all is forgiven.'

Janna gave a gasp. 'Then I'm not imagining things?'

'You are not. Nothing sucks like success. You turned Larks round. You made the kids understand the play. I know how much Emlyn, Piers and I put in, and how lazy little Vicky has claimed credit for everything. She thanks too much; such women are dangerous . . . And she's after Emlyn.'

'Oh dear.' Janna loathed that. 'He's much too nice.'

'But lonely without Oriana. You two should have dinner.'

Outside, Janna met Patience and thanked her for befriending Paris.

'We love him.' Patience lowered her donkey bray as Nadine and Mr Blenchley went down the steps: 'I just wish we could get him out of that horrible children's home.'

'Oh, so do I.'

'He's such a gentle soul.'

As they spoke, the fist of the gentle soul powered into Little Cosmo's jaw, sending him flying across an empty dining room. Scrambling to his feet in terror, Cosmo managed to leap out of a nearby window, landing this time on Sally's beloved white narcissi and budding crown imperials, followed by a yelling Paris, Feral and Graffi, only slightly impeded by his nurse's costume.

They were all beating the hell out of Cosmo and the crown imperials when Emlyn and the guards of the Russian Minister rolled up, yanking them off by their shirts.

'Lemme go, you fuckers,' howled Paris, escaping back into the fray. 'Lemme get at you, you fucker. How dare you move that plank?'

'How dare you grope my woman?' yelled Feral, also wriggling free.

'Lemme get at him,' bawled Graffi, fob watch and white cap flying.

'Let's all get at him,' shouted the Chinless Wanderers, leaping out of the window and pitching in.

'Stop it,' bellowed Emlyn, hauling Graffi off by the starched white collar of his costume, then, launching into Welsh: 'Back off. Your da's drunk, I need your help to carry him on to the coach before he throws up.'

Swearing and spitting, Graffi backed off.

It was a very warm night. No one could explain why Cosmo was discovered in the flower bed next morning with bruising and mild concussion, but otherwise unhurt, which was more than could be said for Sally's beloved narcissi, trillium grandiflora and crown imperials. Thanks to Emlyn and the Minister's guards, none of this reached the press, which, as a result, was excellent.

Venturer had filmed the whole production, five minutes of which was aired, including Paris's gallop up the gangway and the tango of Feral and Bianca, whose father was, after all, a Venturer director.

46

Mrs Kamani was so pleased to be invited and featured in *Romeo and Juliet*, she gave every Larks child an Easter egg. Janna organized a treasure hunt around the grounds, but she continually had to replace eggs, because they kept being tracked down and gobbled up by Partner.

Everyone had a wonderful time, as did Hengist and Sally, who spent Easter with Anatole's family in Russia.

'We had a treasure hunt for Fabergé eggs,' laughed Sally. 'Hengist and I found one each. Simply heavenly.'

All of which was too much for poor Alex Bruce, still festering over Hengist's lack of concern over Poppet's smashed figurine and being excluded from Hengist's private party after *Romeo and Juliet*, particularly when he discovered that feline smoothie Artie Deverell had been invited.

Then Emlyn Davies, who never showed any respect, announced that as he'd been working all hours on the play, he intended to take two days off to play golf and go racing.

It was high time, decided Alex, to impose some discipline. Staff therefore returned for the summer to find glass panels fitted into their classroom doors so Alex could monitor their lessons.

Theo Graham, head of classics, led the mutiny, promptly hanging his old tweed coat over the panel.

Alex then emailed all staff saying he would be monitoring random classes. Again, Theo led the resistance.

'I've been teaching for nearly forty years; no one's sitting in on my lessons.'

'Well, at least submit a plan for each lesson,' persisted Alex. 'This is required practice in the maintained sector.'

'I don't care, my lesson plans are in here.' Theo tapped his bald head. 'I don't need to write them down.'

Alex was furious and later in April, when Hengist went to America (ostensibly to attend a conference of heads; actually to join Jupiter in talking up their New Reform Party, as it was now officially known, to American senators), Alex decided to introduce daily staff meetings before chapel to discuss targets. This caused uproar.

On the first day only Alex's supporters – Joan Johnson and Biffo Rudge, head of maths – arrived on time: Biffo, because he wanted to seize the most comfortable big brown velvet armchair; Joan, big, meaty, dominating, because she believed in targets. Both she and Biffo rolled up armed with clipboards.

Miss Sweet, sex educator and undermatron of Boudicca, also arrived on time because she was terrified of Joan, as did little Miss Wormley, who was feeling sick at the mid-morning prospect of initiating Amber, Cosmo *et alii* into the erotic subtleties of 'The Love Song of J. Alfred Prufrock'.

The view from the staffroom was already causing controversy. It looked north-west over the shoulder of General Bagley and his charger down the long lime walk, which was just opening into palest acid-green leaf, to the golf course and woods beyond. It was a view which had restored the sanity of many a staff member since the mid nineteenth century, but which was now under threat because Alex Bruce was applying for planning permission to build on this site a new Science Emporium, financed by Randal Stancombe.

Hengist, who would have gone berserk if Alex had threatened a twig on his beloved Badger's Retreat, was comparatively indifferent to the positioning of the new Science Emporium – it had to go somewhere, preferably as far as possible from his office, which faced east, or from Head House, which was tucked away on the other bosky side of the campus, facing south.

And if push came to shove, General Bagley could always be relocated to the lawn below Hengist's office, where more people could admire him. He'd enjoy watching rugger and cricket far more than rats being dissected, and he'd be facing the East and India, where his great career had been carved out.

Alex and Poppet thought General Bagley, who'd won glory at the Battle of Plassey and wreaking vengeance after the Black Hole of Calcutta, was a dreadful old Empire-builder and wanted to get rid of his sculpture altogether.

From eight thirty-five, on the morning of Alex's first meeting, other staff drifted in, grumbling about having no time to walk their dogs, ostentatiously carrying on marking work and preparing lessons. Theo Graham, having scowled at Biffo for pinching the only chair which eased his bad back, perched on the window seat, reading a handful of Paris's poems sent him by Janna. They were very good, particularly one about a dandelion clock, glittering silver then puffed away to decide men's fates. Will she accept my proposal, will I get this job, will I get into Cambridge, is this cancer malignant, it is, it isn't, it is, it isn't. Thank God. My life will go on, but not the dandelion stalk, all its silken feathers flown, given no life in water after such a momentous forecast, chucked down to die on the dusty road.

'Have a look at this.' Theo handed the poem to Artie Deverell who'd just wandered in in a dark blue silk dressing gown, carrying a cup of black coffee, and who, putting the poem in his pocket, stretched out on the staffroom sofa and went back to sleep.

The room was almost full up, so Alex proceeded to involve the staff in a brainstorming session.

'Where d'you think you'll be in five years' time, Theo?'

'In a coffin, with any luck,' growled Theo.

'Don't be fatuous,' snapped Alex.

A disturbance was then created by Emlyn strolling in, still in pyjamas, eating a bowl of cornflakes and reading the *Sun*.

'We're trying to discuss targets and aims, Emlyn,' Alex told him icily. 'Tell us, if you please, the most important ingredient in your teaching plan.'

'A bullet-proof vest,' said Emlyn. 'Crucial for anyone who teaches Cosmo and Anatole.'

'And what is your goal when teaching the Lower Fifths?'

'To get out alive,' grunted Emlyn, not looking up from page three.

'Try to be serious.' Alex was fast losing patience. 'What is the most satisfying part of your lesson?'

'A large gin and tonic afterwards,' snapped back Emlyn.

'And the worst thing about Bagley Hall?' asked Alex through gritted teeth.

'Answering bloody stupid questions like this.'

'And the best?'

'Playing golf and getting wasted with Artie.' Emlyn blew a kiss to the sleeping Mr Deverell.

Alex was beside himself, particularly as Mrs Axford, the school cook, chose that moment to march in:

'Here's your sausage sandwich, Emlyn.'

Emlyn smiled sweetly up at her. 'Thanks so much, lovely.'

'Now we all know why you are so fat, Emlyn,' exploded Alex.

'No we don't,' said Emlyn amiably. 'It's because every time your wife takes me to bed she gives me a biscuit.'

The meeting broke up in disarray and howls of laughter.

The next day, Hengist flew back from America and enraged Alex Bruce by cancelling the meetings, adding they were the stupidest idea he'd ever heard and that good housemasters should be looking after their houses at that hour.

Hengist then embarked on the poaching of Paris Alvaston and the possibility of offering him a free place at Bagley in the Michaelmas term. In this he was much encouraged by the governors, who'd been entranced by *Romeo and Juliet*, and by the number of masters pixillated by Paris's white beauty, in particular Theo Graham and Artie Deverell, who were also impressed by Paris's poems.

Hengist, whose motives were invariably mixed, also wanted to take on a boy who would outshine Alex's favourite, Boffin Brooks, and scupper No-Joke Joan's smug prediction that her girls would soon be outstripping his boys. David Hawkley had also been the subject of a flattering *Sunday Times* profile, and since the death of Mungo from meningitis and with Oriana constantly abroad, Hengist's longing for a son had increased.

Towards the end of the month, therefore, a secret afternoon meeting was held in the tranquillity of Head House to discuss the logistics of Paris's transfer.

Sitting round the highly polished dining-room table, admiring the bottle-green jungle wallpaper and Emma Sergeant's painting of Hengist's legendary drop goal, were Ian Cartwright, the bursar, Crispin Thomas, representing S and C, Nadine, Paris's social worker, Mr Blenchley, who managed Oaktree Court, Janna, who was spitting with Hengist for trying to poach her star pupil, and Hengist himself, who'd been playing tennis and was wearing a dark blue fleece, white shorts and trainers and showing off irritatingly good, already brown, legs.

It was a warm, muggy afternoon; a robin sang in a bronze poplar tree; the cuckoo called from a nearby ash grove; young cow parsley leaves and the emerald-green plumage of the wild garlic spilt in jubilation over shaven green lawns. Beyond, in the park, acid-green domes of young trees rose against a navy-blue cloud, from which fell fringes of rain.

Sally had provided a sumptuous tea of cucumber and tomato sandwiches, a chocolate cake, warm from the oven and thickly spread with butter icing, and Earl Grey in a glittering Georgian silver teapot.

'Who's going to be mother?' snuffled Crispin.

'Who better than you?' mocked Hengist.

Nadine hastily grabbed the teapot. 'I will.'

The next question was who was going to be mother and father to Paris. Having poured out and piled up her plate, Nadine, who was wearing a black trouser suit which couldn't disguise thighs fatter than duffel bags and who, with her short curly fringe, glassy, expressionless eyes and long face, looked like a badly stuffed sheep, proceeded to consult her notes.

She reported that since *Romeo and Juliet*, Paris had had a rough time at Oaktree Court.

'He's too strong to be beaten up, but the inmates have ganged up and trashed his room, torn up his homework, shoved his books, many of them from Bagley library, down the toilet, stolen his school bag and thrown his denim jacket, which you gave him for his birthday, Janna' – Janna blushed as Crispin raised an eyebrow – 'into the boiler.

'As a result, Paris's behaviour has been very challenging. Last week he nearly strangled a boy who ran off with a snow fountain of the Eiffel Tower, the only gift left him by his birth mother.'

'If he moved to Bagley,' continued Nadine in her sing-song voice, helping herself to another tomato sandwich, 'conflict at Oaktree Court would escalate and he would be subject to peer pressure on two fronts. We therefore feel that if he were to go to Bagley, he should leave the care home and be fostered. Over to you, Gordon.'

In his shiny grey suit, with his brutal pasty face, nicotine-stained hands and dirty nails, Mr Blenchley looked both seedy and sinister. He had reached an age when his black and silver stubble merely gave the impression he had forgotten to shave. Hengist, Janna and Ian Cartwright shuddered collectively.

Mr Blenchley then said in his thick, clogged voice that he'd be extremely sorry to lose Paris.

'The lad's been with us for nearly four years; reckon we can congratulate ourselves. Before that he had over twenty placements. In some ways a difficult boy, inscrutable, but very able, needs challenging.'

Mr Blenchley was in fact desperate to get shot of Paris. In the past, the lad had been too terrified of being parted from his friends at Larks, the only family he knew, to blow any whistles. But at five foot nine, whippy and well muscled, Paris could no longer be intimidated into accepting that doors stealthily sliding over nylon carpets and creaking floorboards in the dead of night were the work of ghosts – or that predatory fingers creeping inside pyjama trousers and under little nightdresses were figments of the imagination.

'It costs fourteen hundred pounds a week to keep you at Oaktree Court, you ungrateful little shit,' he had shouted at Paris that very morning.

To which Paris had shouted back, 'Give me the fucking money then.'

'What we feel Paris needs,' chipped in Nadine, 'is a sympathetic foster family, a middle-aged couple whose kids perhaps have grown up. It will be challenging, coming from an institution, however admirable, and a maintained school like Larks, then mixing with the protected, privileged students at Bagley. Paris gets ten pounds a month clothes allowance.'

'Jade Stancombe gets about a thousand,' sighed Hengist.

Janna gazed out into the park at the young green trees in their little wooden playpens. Even trees that soared twenty-five feet still retained their wooden cages. Paris would have no such protection.

'Children of Paris's age seldom find a home,' said Crispin, who'd been too busy filling his face to contribute to the debate, 'because potential adopters think they're too damaged.'

'Paris isn't damaged,' cried Janna in outrage. 'He's a sweet boy, so kind to the little ones and intensely loyal to his friends.' Then, as hateful Crispin smirked again, she went on: 'It would be like trapping a skylark to send him to Bagley, away from Feral and Graffi. What he needs is love and some kind of permanence.'

'I agree,' said Nadine. 'Ideally Paris Alvaston needs a forever family to facilitate the adjustment.'

Hengist had put his chocolate butter icing on the side of his plate. Was he watching his figure or keeping the best bit till last? He kept glancing across the table trying to make Janna laugh each time Nadine murdered the English language, but she refused to meet his eye. She was unable to forgive him for not consulting her before offering Paris a place or for looking so revoltingly sexy in those shorts that she wanted him to drag her upstairs and shag her insensible.

And yet, and yet, however much she loathed the idea of private education, she had to recognize Bagley would give Paris a step up the ladder that Larks never could. But if Oaktree Court had given him such hell for getting posh, surely Bagley would roast him for being a yob?

If only she could foster him herself and provide him with a haven at weekends, half-term and during the holidays. Then she'd have someone to love and to cherish; they'd have such fun together.

But I'm too busy, she thought despairingly.

The spring holidays might never have been. The dark circles were back under her bloodshot eyes. She had 400 kids, 399 if Paris went to Bagley, and a school to save.

'You haven't had any cake.' Ian Cartwright, silly old blimp, was about to slide the last piece on to her plate. 'It's awfully good.'

Janna shook her head. She didn't want anything from Bagley. As the meeting roved on over pros and cons, she fought sleep, finally nodding off only to wake with a start, crying, 'Bagley won't hurt Paris, will they?' making the others stare at her in amazement.

Fortunately, at that moment, Sally Brett-Taylor wandered in, rivalling the spring's freshness in a pale-green cashmere jumper, asking if the teapot needed more hot water and discreetly giving Hengist an escape route by reminding him his next appointment was waiting. Everyone gathered up their papers.

'To sum up,' snuffled Crispin, licking chocolate icing off his fingers, 'unless we can find a foster family for Paris, you wouldn't recommend a move to Bagley.'

'That's right,' said Nadine. 'I think the contrast would be too extreme.'

'Beautiful garden, Mrs Brett-Taylor,' said Mr Blenchley, gazing out on Sally's riot of tulips, irises and fritillaries. 'Do you have a sprinkler system?'

'I prefer to water plants myself.' Sally smiled. 'That way you get to know them individually.'

Like my children, thought Janna. Why did everything at the moment make her cry?

47

Hengist returned from Rutminster Cathedral, where the school choir had been singing at Evensong, around nine. On the bus home he had sat next to Dora Belvedon, who, having somehow discovered the meeting had taken place, was desperate for Paris to come to Bagley.

'Just think, he'll mention you and Bagley one day in his acceptance speech at the Oscars.'

Hengist was greeted by a squirming, pirouetting Elaine, who left white hairs all over the trousers of his dark suit, the jacket of which Hengist hung on the banisters before removing his tie and pouring himself a large whisky.

He found Sally at the drawing-room piano playing the beautiful second movement of Schubert's D Major Sonata, which was slower and easier than the first. Only holding up her cheek to be kissed, she didn't stop. Hengist slumped on the sofa with Elaine to listen, watching the lamplight falling on his wife's pale hair, on Mungo's photograph and on a big bunch of white tulips, which shed petals each time she played more vigorously.

Swearing under her breath at the occasional wrong note in the difficult cross rhythms and vowing to set aside time to practise in the future, Sally reached the end.

'How would you feel about adopting Paris Alvaston?' asked Hengist.

Sally looked down at her hands, closed the music and shut the piano with a snap.

'Or, for a start, fostering him?'

'Not fair to him,' said Sally, with unexpected harshness. 'He'll be conspicuous enough coming from Larks; imagine being the head's son.'

'Easier than if he was our actual child. No one could blame him for my cringe-making idiosyncrasies. Nor would he be upset by other children slagging us off.'

Rising and crossing the room, he massaged Sally's rigid shoulders for a moment, then slid his hands down inside her pale-green jersey, which had been washed in Lux so many times.

'We don't have the time,' said Sally angrily. 'You want Fleetley, the Ministry of Education; you want to write. You have eight hundred children and an army of staff. You're always away and poor Elaine doesn't get enough walks.'

Elaine thumped her bony tail in agreement.

'Paris deserves better,' she went on. 'He needs time, individual attention and a live-in father.' And I don't see enough of you, she nearly added.

As his hands crept downwards, she willed her nipples not to respond. He had such a hold over her.

'It'd only be the holidays, half-terms and weekends,' protested Hengist. 'Give Oriana a bit of competition – a sibling to rival. She might come home more often.'

'Why did she stay away so much in the first place?' At heart, Sally felt she had failed as a mother to the absentee Oriana. Why should she fare any better with Paris?

'The voice of reason,' said Hengist irritably. 'He's such a lovely boy and such a potential star. I could bask in his reflected glory in my dotage.'

As his hands slid over her breasts, he felt the nipples hardening, and Sally felt liquid ripples between her legs.

'I was thinking of you,' whispered Hengist. 'You can always make time. Those geeks today had never eaten anything like your chocolate cake.'

'Janna and Ian Cartwright aren't geeks,' protested Sally, 'although she was looking awfully peaky, poor child.'

'Paris would be company. Mungo—' he began.

'Don't,' gasped Sally. The pain was still unbearable.

'Sorry. I just can't bear the thought of the poor boy being abandoned to that grotesque Blenchley, who I'm sure's a paedophile. His nails looked as though they were steeped in dried blood. Did you know that twenty-five per cent of the homeless are care leavers who've been cast out on the world?'

'Stop it.' Sally clapped her hands to her ears. 'I'll think about it.'

'Elaine loves Paris.' Hengist's hand slipped under the waistband of her skirt, over her flat stomach, to lose itself in warm flesh. 'I'm going to ring Mrs Axford and tell her to wait dinner half an hour.'

Despite his brusque, bossy exterior, Ian Cartwright liked children and, as a fine cricketer and rugby player, had always wanted a son. Since his adopted daughters Emerald and Sophy had married and had their own children, the house had seemed very empty.

Arriving home from the meeting, he could smell shepherd's pie, made from the remains of the cold meat from Sunday's shoulder of lamb. If one carved narrow slices, there was always plenty over. He found Patience crimson in the face, reading *Horse & Hound* as she spread mashed potato over the lamb.

'Good day?' she asked.

'Interesting.' Ian poured them both a glass from the bottle of red with which she was jazzing up the mince. 'Hengist wants to offer a free place to Paris Alvaston.'

'That's wonderful.' Patience tested the broccoli with a fork. 'How brilliant of Hengist.'

'Paris is having a bloody time at the children's home. They're looking for a family to foster him.'

'Oh, poor boy. If only we weren't so old.'

'We may not be. They want an older couple, who, if it worked, might consider adopting him to bridge the gap when he'd normally leave care and be chucked out on the streets.'

Out of the window, Ian could see Northcliffe, the golden retriever who had a tendency to go walkabout round the campus, cantering back across the fields, pausing to pick up a twig as a peace offering.

'Social services won't let him come to Bagley unless they can find someone. "Family find" is the awful expression.'

'Oh, Ian.' Patience sat down. 'Are you sure? We've only just got ourselves sorted.'

'You mean clawed our way back from financial ruin,' said Ian with a mirthless laugh. 'I won't be so stupid again.'

'I'd love to give it a try,' mused Patience. 'Dora simply adores him, so does Northcliffe. But I'm sure he'd find us too square. I don't know anything about Liverpool or pop music or Larkminster Rovers or computers.'

'Why don't we ask him?' said Ian.

They were brought back to earth by the smell of burnt broccoli.

First thing, Ian rang Nadine, who dropped in later in the day and was most enthusiastic.

'Paris loves coming to you. Your daughters and their kids visit often, so he'd have an extended family. You've been cleared by the Criminal Records Bureau; you've experienced the ups and downs of adoption. It could take several months, however, because you'd have to go on a course and undergo some counselling and some extensive interviews, I'm afraid.'

'We've been there. Last time they kept asking about our sex lives,' brayed Patience. 'We're a bit past that now.'

Ian frowned. 'I'm sure Nadine doesn't want to hear about that.'

'Paris's behaviour will probably be very challenging,' said Nadine. 'Looked-after kids invariably test their carers to the limit, just to prove they really care.'

'Just like rescued dogs,' said Patience happily. 'I must start reading the football reports.'

'I can't bear to think of poor Paris trapped in that children's home with that repellent man,' announced Sally the following evening. 'I'm sure we could make time.'

'Too late,' said Hengist, almost accusingly. 'Fools have rushed in. Ian and Patience have offered. They've got to undergo loads of ghastly trials, like the labours of Hercules. But Nadine is taking Paris to "meet with" them shortly. "None but the brave deserves the fair",' he added bitterly and Sally felt reproached.

News of the poaching of Paris flashed round the staffroom.

'Just like a feminist version of the Trojan Wars,' sighed Artie Deverell. 'Lucky, lucky Cartwrights, but bags I be Helen of Troy.'

Dora was in ecstasy:

'I'll come and help you dirty up your house,' she told Patience. 'Social workers don't like prospective foster homes to be too pristine.'

48

The first meeting with the Cartwrights was excruciatingly embarrassing. Paris had only had mugs of tea in the kitchen before, but this time Patience had put on a skirt and make-up and heels she had great difficulty walking in, and had plunged into a drawing-room rat race of best china, silver, bread and butter and strawberry jam and 'Would you like milk, sugar, lemon or another slice of walnut cake?' all to be balanced on one's knees or the cat-shredded arm of a chair.

The drawing room, like Lily Hamilton's, seemed overcrowded with dark furniture, suggesting departure from a much larger house. Every shelf and table was crowded with ornaments or yellowing silver or blossom from the pink cherry outside rammed into vases.

Paris wished Ian and Nadine would bugger off and he could sort things out with Patience. Hitherto he'd only seen Ian flitting round Bagley being bossy about overspending and drooling over Vicky Fairchild. He seemed very old and straight, smelt like Mike Pitts of peppermint and stiff whiskies and kept barking, 'Mind out,' as Northcliffe's plumy tail endangered a precious teacup. He was like Captain Mainwaring in *Dad's Army*; Paris couldn't imagine him wearing jeans or taking him to McDonald's.

'I'm afraid it's bought,' confessed Patience when Nadine congratulated her on her walnut cake. 'I'm not much of a cook.'

Anything would be better than Oaktree Court, thought Paris, where, as if Nigella and Jamie Oliver had never existed, Auntie Sylvia boiled mince, diced carrots and onion in water until they were cooked and turned cod the grey of the ancient pair of knickers, almost divorced from its elastic, which a wagging, singing Northcliffe had just laid at Nadine's big feet.

'Oh Northie,' giggled Patience, grabbing the pants and shoving them under a cushion.

'The most important thing is to hold back and listen,' Nadine had urged Patience, who, however, came from a generation and class who regarded it as a crime not to keep conversation going, however inane, and proceeded to do so.

How the hell was he going to put up with a lifetime of this, wondered Paris. If only he could turn on the television and watch Chelsea play Liverpool.

'This is our granddaughter, Dulcie,' said Patience, picking up a photograph of an adorable child with blond curls. 'She's a darling.'

Paris loved children. The best part of the home had always been making up games and stories for the littlest ones and comforting them when they cried. A few years ago, abuse had been rife; now the pendulum had swung. No careworker was ever on for more than forty-eight hours and the majority were so terrified of being accused of abuse, they wouldn't even take on to their lap a child who'd grazed a knee or been torn away from its parents. Desolation ruled. And if you dared complain of past abuse, you'd be bombarded by social workers, counsellors and therapists, prising you open, gouging out your secrets. Easier to trust no one and keep your trap shut.

There was another long pause.

'Our daughters Emerald and Sophy both married painters,' announced Patience, to explain the large, strange pictures rubbing shoulders with the hunting prints and landscapes on the walls.

'You were in the army, Colonel Cartwright,' accused Nadine, pointing to an oil of a lot of screaming women being mown down by a firing squad and their blood watering the young barley. 'Is this your taste?'

'Certainly not. It was painted by my son-in-law. He's actually a war artist, with work in the Tate.'

'You mustn't be so defensive,' chided Nadine.

Ian turned purple.

'Emerald's a sculptor,' said Patience quickly. 'She made me this adorable little maquette of Northcliffe for my birthday. You can almost see his tail wagging.'

'How old were they when you adopted Emerald and Sophy?'

'Just babies.' Patience reached for more photographs.

Those children had clearly inspired love, reflected Paris. Could he do the same? He was terrified they'd discover, beneath his cool, that he was as needy and desperate to escape as those mongrels pathetically scrabbling at the bars in a dog's home.

'We've got to go through some gruelling interviews,' Patience told him. 'We won't know if we're suitable as parents until August, which is a bore, but more importantly you might hate the thought of living with us.' She tried to stop her voice shaking.

Out in the yard a horse neighed, calling out to its stable mate who'd been taken out for a ride.

'Dunno,' muttered Paris, pulling at a piece of cotton on his chair and releasing an avalanche of horsehair. 'Oh shit.'

'Paris, that's not very nice,' reproved Nadine.

Shut up, Paris wanted to scream, because he didn't know what to say, and was even more terrified that if they found out about his red-haze temper, his light fingers, his capacity for demolition, that he occasionally wet the bed, and was racked by fearful, screaming nightmares, they'd chuck him out after a week, a care leaver destined for homelessness.

'We'd so love you to come and live with us,' stammered Patience, missing the cup as she topped up Nadine's tea. 'But first you must get to know us.'

'That's enough,' snapped Ian. 'Let Paris make up his own mind; there's no hurry.'

'You will come and see us next week?' persisted Patience.

'For Christ's sake,' exploded Ian.

Oh God, they'll reject Ian and me because we don't get on, thought Patience in panic.

'Careful not to invade Paris's personal space,' reproved Nadine.

Paris scowled round at her. 'I can go if I like,' he said curtly.

The following Saturday, they asked Paris if he'd like to go to the cinema, but he said he'd prefer to muck about at home, and spent a couple of hours looking at Ian's military collection, which contained pieces of shrapnel, shells and bullets, and even a bit of marble from Hitler's desk.

'Rupert Brooke and I were at the same school,' volunteered Ian and, secretly thrilled by Paris's interest, presented him with a paperback of First World War poems.

Later, as the evenings were drawing out, Patience took him out to watch the Bagley herd being milked and took a picture of him with Ian and Northcliffe.

Paris's next visit was a disaster. Examining the photographs of beautiful Emerald in the drawing room, he knocked off and smashed the maquette she had modelled of Northcliffe. In terror, he shoved the pieces under the sofa, but missed the tail, which had fallen on a rug.

'I'd better go,' he told Patience, edging towards the door.

'You haven't had any tea – I've got Cornish pasties and chips.'

'Don't want anything.'

'I'll drive you back.'

'I want to walk.'

'Oh look, Northcliffe's tail's fallen off again. I must stick it back.' When she found the other pieces under the sofa, her face fell, then she smiled. 'Doesn't matter, I'm sure Emo can make me another one. I'm always breaking things. I smashed a vase this morning.'

Paris flared up:

'Why aren't you mad at me? You must be, you loved that dog.'

'It's only an ornament that's broken – not a promise or a heart.'

'Oh, for Christ's sake.' Paris stormed out and, crying helplessly, ran all the six miles back to Oaktree Court.

Two days later, he received a letter from Patience.

'Please come to tea next Saturday. Longing to see you.'

It wasn't natural to be so forgiving.

Nadine dropped him off, jollying him along, interrogating him all the way, as though she were forcibly opening an oyster with a chisel. He didn't tell her he was only intending to stay five minutes. Working himself into a rage, heart crashing, his breath coming in great gasps, he marched into an empty kitchen, rehearsing his speech: 'Look, it's not going to work. I want to chuck the whole thing: I can't handle Bagley and sod Hengist and Theo Graham and fucking Homer and Virgil.

'Get out the way,' he yelled, aiming a kick as Northcliffe, carrying a feather duster, bounded towards him in delight.

He was about to sweep all Patience's recipe books on to the floor, and then start smashing plates and mugs so they'd definitely never want to see him again, when he caught sight of his own photographs in a silver frame on the dresser: one of him with Northcliffe, another of him as Romeo. Yet another of him, with Dora and Beluga, Romeo's fiery steed, had been put in a big frame beside pictures of Emerald and Sophy.

Paris blushed and blushed, a huge smile spreading over his face, as Patience bustled in:

'Oh, hello, Paris.' Then, catching sight of the photographs, she added humbly: 'We hope you don't think we're jumping the gun.'

Paris kicked the kitchen table and shook his head.

'It's fine.'

'Thank goodness. Plover's sister's about to foal, the vet's on his way, I thought you might like to help.'

'OK.' Paris then screwed up courage to ask how the interviews were going.

'Pretty well,' said Patience, putting on her red Puffa. 'They do ask extraordinary questions. If normal couples went through such hassle, they'd never have children. But it's all worth it,' she added hastily.

After the foal had been born, all covered in blood and gore, the vet and Patience had shared a bottle of white wine with Paris and congratulated him on having such a calming effect on the frightened mare. When Nadine rolled up, Patience hastily dropped the bottle in the bin.

As he was leaving, she shouted he'd left his jacket, and as she picked it up from the kitchen chair, a photograph of her and Ian fluttered out.

'Must have picked it up by mistake,' muttered Paris. 'No, that's a lie, I wanted one until I moved in, like.'

'Keep it,' said an enraptured Patience.

Watching him go off into the hazy blue evening, Patience hugged herself. Until he moved in, like. She ran to the gate to wave him off.

Back at the home, Paris hid the photo between his under-blanket and the mattress, because he didn't seem to be wetting the bed any more and because Patience and Ian were pretty old and ugly, and he couldn't bear the other kids taking the piss or, even worse, tearing up the photo.

As bursars work extremely hard, Paris saw more of Patience than Ian, who was nervous but determined things should work.

'What'm I supposed to call you?' Paris asked him on the next visit.

'You could call me "Colonel Cartwright", but that's a bit formal, and "Uncle" is silly because I'm not. Would it be OK, if we pass the tests, to describe you as "Paris, our foster son", which would be true, then if things go very well, we can drop the foster.'

'That's good,' agreed Paris. 'I'll call you Mr Ian, if that's OK.'

'Good start,' said Ian.

'As we know each other better, you can call me Patience.'

Paris really smiled for the first time.

'Going to need a lot, if you're taking me on.'

'Next week, why don't we go to IKEA and choose some stuff for your room?' Treading on eggshells, trying not to presume, she added hastily: 'If we don't pass the test, you can always use the room when you come and stay.'

49

In the middle of May, when Bagley was looking at its most seductive, with the setting sun warming the golden stone, cow parsley lacing the endless pitches and the trees still in their radiant young, green beauty, Hengist formally offered Paris a place.

On the wall of Hengist's study, Paris was intensely flattered to see, alongside other triumphs, a framed photograph of himself as Romeo. Then Hengist had added he was also offering a boarding place to Feral, so he and Paris needn't be parted, and when Paris accepted, trying to keep the excitement out of his voice and face, Hengist offered him a glass of champagne to celebrate.

'Patience and Ian are a super couple.' Hengist sat down on the dark red Paisley window seat beside a reclining Elaine, and beckoned Paris to join them. 'A super couple, salt of the earth, although one's not, according to Poppet Bruce, supposed to have salt in anything these days. You'll have fun when their daughters come down – Emerald is stunning – and with young Dora hanging around and lots of horses and a charming dog. But if you find it hard to discuss things with them, speak instead to Theo Graham, who's going to be your new housemaster. Beneath the rather crusty exterior Theo's a sweet man.

'But if you ever think of running away from Bagley' – Hengist was lovingly smoothing Elaine's white, velvet ears – 'I want you to promise to pop in on Sally and me first, and we'll give you some sandwiches and a can of Coke for the journey. Give me your hand and your promise,' and his big suntanned hand enveloped Paris's, which was almost as white and slender as Elaine's.

Paris promised. He'd never met anyone as charismatic as Hengist. The thick, dark hair, olive skin, heavy-lidded eyes, beautiful clothes, the element of danger, the desire not exactly to corrupt but to stir up and subvert reminded him so much of Lord Henry Wotton in *The Portrait of Dorian Gray*. The same sweet, seductive scent of lilac, so memorable in the book, was now drifting in through the window, overpowering the clean, healthy, soapy smell of hawthorn.

Paris had been jealous of Hengist in the past, because Janna smelt so lovely and always seemed to be laughing when Hengist was around. Paris still thought and dreamt of her constantly. At the end of term, they would be split up, but at least before that, at the end of June, she would be coming on the geography field trip, when Larks and Bagley would be taking off together for Wales, and he might slay a dragon for her. He was very proud Hengist had chosen him, and with Feral by his side, he could face anything.

Hengist, predictably, was not just enlisting Feral entirely for Paris's benefit. As a dazzling athlete, who'd really profit from decent coaching and pitches, Feral would bring glory to Bagley. Nor could Hengist resist unsettling that pompous ass Biffo Rudge by installing a gloriously priapic black boy in his house.

Alas, the next day, Feral was summoned off the cricket field, having just been bowled after knocking up a useful fifty in twenty minutes, and flabbergasted Hengist by turning down his offer of a place.

'Kind of you, man, but I don't like the thought of being locked up in the evening.'

He didn't add that he was worried his family would fall apart if he wasn't there to hold it together.

' "Why, uncle, 'tis a shame",' said Paris when he heard the news. Although devastated by Feral's refusal, he wasn't prepared to betray regret or try and talk him round.

'As I'm locked up already, I might as well accept a more upmarket gaol.'

Nor was everyone pleased about Paris going to Bagley. Joan Johnson thought free places should have been offered to clever Aysha, or Kylie for her pretty voice, or Pearl for her artistic skills.

And if the masters at Bagley were excited, the staff at Larks were outraged that Paris would be thrown to the wolves of private education.

Emerald and Sophy Belvedon, who liked to dump their own children on Granny Patience whenever they needed a break, also expressed doubts.

'He'll be bringing his rough friends home and breaking the place up. He's already smashed my maquette of Northcliffe,' raged Emerald. 'And I hope Daddy's not going to get any silly ideas like Jupiter about sons inheriting everything.'

Sophy was more worried that teenagers were wildly expensive and that her parents had just got straight financially after Ian going bankrupt in the nineties.

Janna, meanwhile, had not made it up with Hengist. Ringing up to ask her to lunch, he received an earful, but refused to admit he'd pulled a fast one by poaching Paris.

'Darling, from the moment we met at La Perdrix d'Or, you kept telling me how wonderfully clever Paris was, thrusting his poems and essays at me, saying he needed to escape from the poverty trap. I honestly thought that was what you wanted.'

'Oh, go to hell.' Janna slammed down the telephone.

She was having a very tough summer. The GCSEs loomed and unless their results improved, they would again be branded one of the worst schools in the West. Exams also meant the gym would be out of action, so the children couldn't work off any energy. The Wolf Pack were demoralized and acting up because Paris was leaving. Half the staff were moonlighting and exhausted and tetchy, after four or five hours marking GCSE papers every night.

After the good publicity generated by *Romeo and Juliet*, many parents had put Larks as their first choice. Then the wretched council had changed the bus route, which meant buses no longer stopped outside the school gates and parents, worried about kidnapping and sexual abuse, changed their minds.

One step forward, one step back.

But despite not a week passing without a slagging off in the *Gazette*, Janna felt the school was steadily improving. Thanks to frequent visits from Gablecross's constabulary, there was much less fighting in the playground or in the corridors. Teachers were mostly able to teach. Mrs Kamani no longer complained of shoplifting and rowdy behaviour. Even Miss Miserden, the old biddy who lived at the bottom of the drive, stopped grumbling about Feral's football after Graffi rescued her cat Scamp from the top branch of a pear tree. The children had also been on some terrific jaunts to the seaside, to the Blackpool illuminations, to Longleat and the London Eye. A production of *Oliver!* was planned for next term.

Vicky, who would direct it, was not enjoying the summer term as much as her spring one. She couldn't slope off to Bagley all the time and had to face up to the rough and tumble of Larks.

In the last week in May, in the middle of the GCSEs, having gained Mike Pitts's permission and claiming it was 'vital for her professional development', Vicky sloped off for two days at a National Theatre workshop.

In her absence, Janna discovered a shambles of homework unmarked and work unset. Worse still, Vicky was hardly engaging with her tutor group, with the result that one girl was being so badly bullied, she tried to hang herself with a pair of tights during break.

Janna, who had already received a warning from the girl's mother, had ordered Vicky to sort it out. Vicky had clearly done nothing.

Bitter shame that she herself hadn't prevented it fuelled Janna's anger. Vicky was due back on the Wednesday morning before half-term, then rang in to tell Rowan her train had broken down and she wouldn't be back till after lunch.

She had eventually floated in around two-forty-five, Little Miss Demure in a navy blue suit, with her shining clean hair drawn into a neat bun, pale cheeks flushed, wafting Trésor. Immediately, she started wittering on about 'cutting-edge productions' and 'unique opportunities to discover my own creativity'.

Janna let her run, then let rip, epitomizing every cliché about redheads and fiery tempers. Partner shot under the sofa.

'I trusted you, Vicky. How dare you bunk off like this? Year Eight is totally under-rehearsed for their play on Parents' Day. Year Eleven can't quote a single line from *A View from the Bridge* and they've got Eng. lit. tomorrow. You left no lesson plans for this morning.'

'I rang in,' bridled Vicky.

'You should have come back. Lottie Hargreaves, one of your tutor group, tried to hang herself. We've had the police here all morning. I told you to keep an eye on her. You've let me down!'

'And you've let me down,' shouted back Vicky. 'You never warned me this school was completely out of control. A parent slapped my face the other day.'

'Why didn't you report it?'

'I didn't want to sneak.' Vicky burst into tears and fled.

Overnight, Janna cooled down. The fact remained she needed Vicky. Whatever her limitations, she had reduced truancy among the boys, and with so many children taking drama and English GCSEs next year because of her, Janna couldn't really sack her. She'd better call her in first thing, before she caused too much havoc.

She was greeted on the morrow by a furious Rowan.

'You're not going to like this.'

It was a letter from Bagley's personnel department asking for a reference for Vicky who had applied for a job teaching English and drama. Janna flipped and rang Hengist who, as Painswick had gone to the dentist, picked up the telephone. Bruckner's Eight was on fortissimo. Hengist only turned it down fractionally and when Janna started screaming at him, became quite sharp. Education was a free-for-all. Vicky was entitled to work where she wanted. As long as her notice was in by 31 May, which was tomorrow, she could start in the autumn.

'Anyway, I can't see why you're making such a fuss. You seemed pretty anxious to be shot of the poor child yesterday. I also wanted to make things easy for Paris,' he went on, even more infuriatingly, 'who will feel happier if he's acquainted with a member of staff.'

Out of the window, Janna could see a Year Eleven pupil so deep in last-minute revision, she bumped into an oak tree.

' "All my pretty chickens and their dam, At one fell swoop?" ' she said tonelessly. 'How dare you poach my staff and pupils without asking?'

'Because I knew you'd try and stop me,' said Hengist unrepentantly.

'Vicky has ensured three-quarters of Year Ten will be taking drama GCSE next year.'

'That's great. We can hold joint Larks–Bagley classes. Means I'll see more of you.'

After that, Janna's shouting could be heard all over Larks, and Partner took refuge in Rowan's office.

'I'm not going to talk to you until you cool down,' said Hengist and hung up.

'We're well shot of her, she's an applause junkie and a dozy bitch,' said Rowan, rushing in with a box of tissues and a cup of black coffee laced with brandy. 'Give her a good reference to show you're magnanimous. Lord Brett-Taylor can pick up the pieces when she fucks up.'

'Rowan,' said Janna in awe, 'I've never heard you swear before.'

Janna's magnanimity was sorely tested when she and Vicky met.

'I'm tired of sticking up for you, Jannie.'

'Who first approached you?' asked Janna numbly.

'I don't remember, but Hengist, Emlyn and nice Alex Bruce, such a sweetie, all suggested I'd be an asset to Bagley, and frankly' – Vicky smiled helplessly – 'Hengist is so charismatic, I can't resist the chance of working with him. And if I can ease Paris's transition and Hengist believes I can . . .' Then, misinterpreting the anguish on Janna's face: 'But don't worry, I won't let you down over the geography field trip. Emlyn's going and Hengist even said he might drop in. He's arranged for us to stay in some Welsh stately castle. I can't wait.'

Vicky didn't add that she herself had applied for the job, and at her first interview over lunch with Hengist on Wednesday, had presented him with a rare work on rugby football or that yesterday, after Janna had carpeted her, she had driven over to Bagley and sobbed on Alex's narrow shoulder, telling him:

'Larks is out of control: a Year Nine boy tried to rape me' (mild lunge from Monster) 'and I was punched by a parent' (mild lunge from a mother whose husband Vicky had inveigled into Larks to paint cupboards).

'I loved Jannie so much in Yorkshire,' Vicky had continued to sob. 'She was such fun. Now she seems to have lost her creativity. She's so hard now.'

Dora Belvedon, busy weeding up wallflowers under the window, heard everything, which the following day appeared in the *Gazette* as 'Star teacher and pupil to leave Larks'.

Red Robbie, who'd been hoping to get his leg over Vicky on the geography field trip, was so shocked by her defection to an independent, he flatly refused to go.

Janna also received lots of flak.

'Just learnt of your tragic loss,' emailed Rod Hyde, 'you must try and hang on to your good staff.'

'I don't know what we'll do without our little Vicky to bring sunshine into our life,' moaned Basket.

Monster proceeded to trash the drama department.

I'm just jealous of Vicky having constant access to Hengist and Paris, thought Janna in despair. She wished she could pour her heart out to Emlyn, but he'd taken the opportunity of half-term to fly to Afghanistan to see Oriana.

Janna spent most of the break sobbing for her mother. She had to face up to the fact that hard work cannot blot out loneliness for ever.

The only positive thing she did was to telephone her friend Sophy Belvedon. Sophy was Ian and Patience's daughter, married to Alizarin, the brother of Jupiter, Dora and Dicky. Sophy was also an English and drama teacher, with whom Janna had worked in Yorkshire, who now lived in London.

Sophy was her usual cheerful, adorable self.

'It's so lovely to hear from you. Mum says you're making a brilliant job of Larks. It must be so beautiful down there now.'

'How's Dulcie?' asked Janna. 'She must be nearly eighteen months now.'

'She's heaven, but I'm not sure being a full-time mother's quite me. I'm so turning into a cabbage, leaves are sprouting out of my head. I'm sure some German's going to make me into sauerkraut.'

'You don't want a job, do you?'

'God, I'd love one.'

'Head of English and drama in the autumn.'

'Oh yes, yes please.'

'It's a pretty rough school.'

'Couldn't be rougher than London. Someone chucked a brick through our drawing-room window yesterday. We could get an au pair or perhaps Mum could look after Dulcie during the day. Might put her and Dad off their latest mad project of fostering a looked-after kid of fourteen.'

Alex Bruce, while delighted by the annexing of Vicky, bitterly regretted that Hengist's ability to poach clever children and staff was only equalled by his irrational refusal to boot out the stupid children of his friends.

The Chinless Wanderers: Lando, Jack and Junior, although dazzling at games, were predicted to get straight Us in their GCSE exams in two years' time. Xavier Campbell-Black bumped sulkily along the bottom of the class and his sister Bianca, even more intellectually challenged, had recently revealed that she didn't know on which side Hitler fought in the last war.

Alex was anxious to single out any pupils on the Grade C/D borderline and give them early coaching. Anyone below that level would endanger Bagley's place in the league tables and should be asked to leave.

'Bianca will stay,' said Hengist firmly. 'She's destined to be the next Darcey Bussell. Screw the league tables. We must cultivate individual excellence.'

'You said you wanted to beat Fleetley and ward off any challenge from St Jimmy's.'

'Maybe I did. The secret of greatness is to admit one is in the wrong.'

Hengist's inconsistency drove Alex crackers.

'Thank God this school is in a safe pair of hands,' he told Miss Painswick.

'Thank God for a handy pair of safes,' smirked Little Cosmo, as he and Lubemir cracked the combination of the safe in the school office, photostatted the 2002 GCSE and A level papers stored inside and flogged them for five hundred pounds a go to needy candidates.

'We need never work again,' crowed Cosmo, 'and we're doing

our bit for Bagley by ensuring it does really well in the league tables.'

Having insinuated himself as a regular in the school office by plying Miss Painswick with chocolates and Dame Hermione's latest CDs, Cosmo also overheard Alex chuntering over Bianca's lack of intellect.

After his success at photographing the stars of *Romeo and Juliet*, Cosmo had been asked to do the pictures for the school prospectus and achieved an excellent multicultural mix by putting Anatole, Lubemir, Nordic blonde Amber and Bianca on the cover. No one could sack Bianca if she was in the prospectus.

Cosmo also found the proofs of the prospectus on Painswick's computer and added 'binge-drinking, buggery and Bruce-baiting' to the list of pupils' favourite activities. Fortunately this was picked up and deleted by an amused Hengist.

Alex also had to accept the fact that during Wimbledon, which coincided with the last fortnight of term, Hengist would be virtually incommunicado, claiming to be writing a crucial piece for *The Times*, when all you could hear was the thwack of tennis balls and the rattle of applause.

This year, Anatole's father dropped in for 'an important meeting' and to thwack and rattle were added the chink of bottles and roars of laughter as he and Hengist enjoyed the dazzling Miss Kournikova in the first round.

Hengist fiddled, while Alex burnt with resentment.

50

Field trips are very hard work and enmeshed in red tape, so once Red Robbie refused to go as a matter of principle, the rest of Larks's staff were only too glad to use their disapproval of the private sector as an excuse to opt out. Anyway, they were far too busy marking exams and writing reports.

So Janna buried her pride and pleaded with Robbie to change his mind: 'Next term Year Nine will begin their two-year GCSE course. This trip will whet their appetite not just for geography but for history and English. There are wonderful activities planned. They'll learn self-esteem and the ability to relate to people of a different background.'

Robbie had folded his arms and gazed mutinously up at the damp patch in the ceiling, until Janna lost it.

'You're just terrified of being shown up because Rufus Anderson's such a brilliant head of geography.'

This caused a rumpus, with the senior staff blanking Janna and Sam Spink marching in accusing Janna of humiliating Robbie.

'Good,' snapped Janna.

So in the end, Janna only had Vicky who, having sworn she wouldn't let Janna down, couldn't back out, and Gloria who had a crush on Emlyn, and Skunk Illingworth who would do anything for a freebie and who also had a crush on Vicky, and Cambola who was always game for a jaunt. Mags would have come but her new grandchild was about to be born and the ever dependable Wally had his son, Ben, home on leave.

Batting for Bagley were Rufus and a couple of his young geography teachers, No-Joke Joan who also had a crush on Vicky and didn't want to let any of her young women loose unchaperoned with Cosmo and all those dreadful Larks youths around, and, of course, Emlyn.

As Paris was moving to Bagley, it was felt the field trip would be a good way for him to bond with future form-mates. He was already enduring endless flak at Oaktree Court and at Larks for becoming a stuck-up snob, and as social services hadn't yet confirmed Patience and Ian as his foster parents, it was a time of deep uncertainty.

Paris refused again to betray how gutted he was that Feral – and Graffi as well – had refused to join him on the field trip. Graffi's father was off sick and heavily on the booze again; Feral's domestic life was always shadowy; but both boys were needed at home. Both vowed, as a band of brothers, they would always be friends of Paris, but he knew it would never be the same.

Without the other two he also felt less sanguine about protecting himself against Cosmo and his bodyguards. The female remnants of the Wolf Pack were unlikely to provide support. Pearl would probably go off like a firecracker. Kylie had not only persuaded Chantal to look after Cameron while they were away, but, at the prospect of Kylie becoming the future Lady Waterlane, to also bankroll a snazzy new wardrobe. This included a glamorous dress because everyone had been told to bring something 'eveningy' for a mystery destination on the last night of the trip.

Paris, fretting about his lack of wardrobe, was extremely touched when Ian took him aside and gave him sixty pounds, gruffly bidding him not to spend it all at once. Carrying this out to the letter, Paris nicked some T-shirts and trainers and sauntered out of Gap in unpaid-for dark-grey jeans, which he promptly slashed across the knees and thighs to age them up.

On the morning of departure, Janna was drying her hair when Emlyn rang and said he was dreadfully sorry, he couldn't make the trip. Whereupon Janna, mostly from disappointment and because Emlyn was the only person who could control this mob, lost her temper and bawled him out.

As she paused for breath, Emlyn repeated how sorry he was but that his father had died in the night, from lungs wrecked by a life down the mines, and he was on his way home to Wales to look after his mother and organize the funeral.

A mortified Janna was frantically apologizing when Emlyn displayed a flicker of his old self:

'Now the even worse news. Biffo Rudge has been press-ganged into going in my place. He'll be as anxious to chaperone his boys as Joan is. I'm sorry, lovely, I'll buy you dinner when I get back.'

'I'm the one who's sorry,' wailed Janna, 'I know how you loved him.'

The weather was hot and jungly. The journey in three coaches seemed to take forever. Paris read *Le Rouge et Le Noir*, Rocky the *Mirror* with one finger; Cosmo read the score of *Harold in Italy*; Jade and Milly read each other's palms; Boffin read *A Brief History of Time* and, as litter monitor, bawled out everyone for dropping sweet papers. Amber read text messages from admiring boyfriends; Kylie, who felt sick on buses, tried to look at the pictures in *Hello!* and had to stop near St Jimmy's on the outskirts of Larkminster to throw up.

'You don't think she's up the duff again?' Pearl murmured to Paris.

Whereupon Rocky, realizing he'd left behind his Ritalin, leapt into the driver's seat and drove the bus back to Larks to collect it. Everyone was too petrified of a Ritalinless Rocky to stop him. When the outraged bus driver took over on the second journey, it was noticed how many desirable residences Randal Stancombe was building within the catchment area of Rod Hyde's school.

'These are the sorts of houses you can afford if you don't have to fork out for school fees,' observed Cosmo nastily.

Before leaving, both schools had received individual pep talks on the importance of good behaviour and overcoming the traditional animosities which divide private and state schools.

Cosmo, cash rich from flogging exam papers, had listened in amusement. He liked Emlyn, but they would be much freer without him. Biffo couldn't control an ant. Cosmo had packed a first-aid kit of vodka, brandy, cocaine, grass, Alka-Seltzer, a hundred condoms, the morning-after pill and amyl nitrate, and had had a bet with Anatole that he'd pull both Gloria and Vicky by the end of the trip.

He also fancied a threesome with Milly and Amber, was going to bully Xavier to a jelly and unsettle Paris, to whom he intended to give a rough ride next term, particularly as the Bagley Babes had just announced that, in the absence of Feral and Graffi, their target on the trip was to pull Paris.

As the coaches moved into open country, Cosmo proceeded to ring up Dora, ordering her at pain of death not to forget to water his marijuana plants – not that they would need it, as rain was now chucking itself like lover's gravel against the bus window.

Poor little Dora, being ordered around by a pig like Cosmo,

thought an indignant Pearl, who was sitting across the gangway. Pearl was utterly miserable; her little stepbrother was teething and her mother had discovered fifteen pounds missing from her bag, which Pearl had nicked to pay for a long-sleeved olive-green T-shirt from New Look. This had meant her mother's toyboy couldn't go to the pub, whereupon her mother had hit Pearl and screamed that 'she could bleedin' leave home if there was any more trouble'.

The long sleeves had been needed to cover Pearl's arms, which she'd attacked with a razor and which now throbbed unbearably. Cosmo smiled evilly across at her. He was vile but dead sexy, with his night-dark eyes and his satanic pirate's smile.

Down the bus, Biffo Rudge, noisily crunching an apple as sulphuric farts ruffled his long khaki shorts, was sharing a seat with a pile of Lower Fifth reports.

Cosmo proceeded to convulse pupils from both schools by holding up behind Biffo's seat the air freshener from the lavatory. As the bus crossed over into Herefordshire, plunging into thick forest with glimpses of silver rivers gleaming in the valleys below, Biffo fell asleep. Whereupon Cosmo seized the pile of reports, found his own and wrote 'towering genius' and 'undeniably brilliant' all over it. Buoyed up by the mounting mirth of his audience, Cosmo dug out Boffin's report and scribbled 'deeply irritating', 'unimaginative' and 'stupid twat' all over it, before crying, 'You dropped this, sir,' as Biffo woke up.

At the back of the coach, Vicky had palled up very pointedly with Gloria: 'Such a relief to have someone fun and my age on the trip.'

Now they whispered and played silly games: 'In ten seconds – who would you rather go to bed with, Biffo or Skunk?' followed by squeals of laughter.

Occasionally they cast covetous eyes at Rufus, head of geography, but he was too busy calling his wife and mother, who was looking after the children, even to notice them.

As Cambola was in another coach, Janna was forced to sit with Joan who, despite taking up most of the seat, insisted on clamping a beefy thigh against Janna's.

'All my Lower Fifth students have opted for triple science,' she announced, adding that she was off to a conference in Atlanta at the end of term. 'I'm giving a paper on the Place of the Runner Bean in Teaching Genetics,' she boomed. 'The runner bean is the perfect plant to illustrate multiple pregnancies.'

'Why not Kylie Rose?' murmured Amber to Milly. 'Did you know, Joan rejected seventeen possible gardeners provided by the bursar this week because none of them was ugly enough for us not to jump on him?'

Despite a desire to get off with the opposite sex, Janna noticed a look of relief on the Larks girls' faces when, after an interminable drive, they discovered they would be sleeping in one youth hostel near a river on the edge of a wood, while the boys would be housed four miles away in another.

'Thank goodness,' said Primrose Duddon, 'boys always gobble up all the food.'

In fact the food was awful, spag bol full of gristle, vegetables boiled into abdication and great blocks of jam roly-poly.

'Talk about Calorie Towers,' grumbled Amber.

After supper, if you could call it that, the rain stopped so they dried off the benches outside and Joan brought out her guitar and, led by Cambola, they sang round a dispirited camp fire.

'To think I got myself sacked from the Brownies to end up here,' muttered Amber. 'I need a drink.'

'You'll get cocoa at ten o'clock,' said Joan tartly.

At ten-fifteen, she went round with a basket confiscating mobiles. 'You've all got a long day tomorrow.'

So the Bagley Babes unearthed their second mobiles and rang their boyfriends.

'If anyone tries to escape,' boomed Joan as she marched up and down the rows of beds, 'there'll be trouble.'

'I don't know why we came on this jaunt,' moaned Milly. 'Tomorrow we'll start digging a tunnel.'

As the lights were turned off and everyone stretched out on their hard beds, Kylie, who'd thought by now she'd be curled up with the Hon. Jack, started to cry that she was missing Cameron and Chantal.

'I miss my dog and my horse more than my parents or even my boyfriend,' said Amber, which made Kylie cry even louder, so Jade pelted her with pillows.

For the staff, Janna noted nervously that there were a double and three single rooms.

Joan looked warmly at Vicky. 'I'm happy to share.'

'No, no. You deserve the privilege of a room of your own,' Vicky simpered. 'Gloria and I don't at all mind bunking up.'

Janna, who had watched the girls' faces during that dismal dinner, prayed things would improve tomorrow. Hearing sobs, she went into the dormitory and sitting down on Kylie's bed, patted her heaving shoulder.

'Shall I tell you a story?'

'Please, miss.'

' "O, young Lochinvar is come out of the west, Through all the wide Border his steed was the best",' began Janna in her sweet, soft voice, which in the dark sounded like that of a young girl.

She can't be more than early thirties, thought Amber. It was such a good story, she managed to stay awake to the very end.

51

Things did get better.

'The students have bonded so well that the teachers are redundant,' Skunk Illingworth announced the following evening, froth gathering on his moustache like snow on a blackthorn hedge as he downed a pint of real ale.

He, Biffo and Rufus had sloped off to the local pub, leaving the pupils happy to write up their field notes because, thanks to Bagley's head of geography, they had discovered geography could be really interesting. Rufus, red-blond hair flopping, bony freckled face alight, had charged round Herefordshire, a piece of rock in one hand, a hammer in the other, book open in the grass, explaining the mysteries of the natural world to his enraptured listeners.

Earlier in the day, one group, including Paris, Boffin and Kylie, had carried out a tourist survey in a neighbouring forest. Unfortunately, on a dripping Wednesday morning, there was only a handful of tourists, who got fed up being repeatedly asked the same question. Kylie had even disturbed a couple in flagrante in the maturing bracken.

'When I asked Mr and Mrs Brown from Scunthorpe whether they had travelled here by train, coach or bicycle,' she was now writing in her round, careful hand, 'they told me to f— off.'

Everyone had then piled into the coaches and moved on to the next location, the source of the Fleet, which here was an eight-foot-wide brook, but which swelled into a great river as it passed Bagley, curled round Larkminster and Larks, then flowed on into Rutshire, past Cosmo's mother's house, through Lando France-Lynch's father's land, then skirting Xav's father's land in Gloucestershire.

If I could only climb into a boat and row home, thought Xav, who, that morning, had been punched very hard by Lubemir.

'Each group was allocated a section of the river,' wrote Primrose Duddon in a red and mauve striped notebook. 'We had to test our hypothesis on a "meander", which means the river bending several times, and on a "riffle", which is a fast-flowing, straight section. We rolled up a piece of tin foil, then checked how fast it floated down river.'

Pearl had kicked off her shoes and watched the ball of foil. It was snagged by tawny rushes, then floated on through the brown peaty water. Then she had collapsed on the warm wet grass, waiting for a teacher to tell her to get up. She was about to turn on her stopwatch and see how fast another ball of foil was floating down the far bank, when she felt a hand, as warm as the sun, on her bare legs.

'This is a "riffle",' murmured Cosmo as he ran his hand slowly up her bare legs, roving over her bottom, gently exploring in and out of her shorts. 'And this is definitely a "meander".'

He then lay down beside her on the bank, wickedly squinting sideways at her, stroking her rainbow hair, kissing her forehead, burying his tongue in her ear, murmuring endearments in Italian, his night-dark eyes blotting out the sun. As she turned her head towards him, he kissed her, slowly sucking each lip, then dividing them with his tongue.

A roar of rage interrupted Pearl's moment of bliss.

'Cosmo Rannaldini. Stop that at once.' Then the roar diminished as Joan realized Cosmo was only molesting a Larks student. 'But stop it all the same. You're supposed to be testing the velocity of the river, not the speed of your seduction technique.'

Pearl couldn't wait to tell Kylie.

'Cosmo snogged me. He is so brilliant, my knees gave way and I was lying down.'

The Chinless Wanderers, who weren't remotely interested in riffles and who regarded rivers as places in which you caught salmon or retrieved polo balls, were smoking and listening to the test match. Further down the bank Paris read *Le Rouge et Le Noir*, totally engrossed in Julien Sorel's seduction of the beautiful, much older Madame de Renal leading to passionate mutual love – maybe Janna wasn't such an impossibility.

He had bonded least of the Larks contingent. He was sick of Bagley chat about gap years in Argentina and their parents' splitting up. There was also something sickening about the country, he thought, or the evils man imposed on it. Last year, he'd been haunted by the funeral pyres burning innocent sheep and cattle.

This year it was the rabbits lying in the footpath dying from myxomatosis, desperately trying to crawl away as their bulging eyes were pecked out by huge killer gulls. The girls screamed in horror; Paris turned away retching; Jack Waterlane picked up a log and put one rabbit out of its misery, then another, then another, shouting at the gulls before returning to put a comforting arm round a sobbing Kylie.

Jack wasn't quite such a prat as he seemed, decided Paris.

The gulls were a symbol of the way Cosmo pecked away at Xavier and himself, if given a chance.

Before supper that evening, Paris wandered off from the hostel into the wood to read in peace. Hearing raised voices, he was about to sidle to the right, when he clocked Lubemir's very distinctive accent: 'Fetch eet, black sheet.'

Edging forward through the green curtain of a willow, Paris found a clearing in which Cosmo and Lubemir were playing football. To the left, like an enemy ambush, lurked a huge bed of nettles, giving off a rank, bitter smell as the still hot evening sun burnt off the rain. Beside them stood Xav, fat, hunched, terrified, as Cosmo powered the ball into the nettles.

'Pick it up, black shit.'

Desperate to avoid a beating, wincing from the stings, Xav plunged in and picked up the ball, only for Lubemir to boot it back again. 'Fetch eet, you fat creep.'

For a moment defiance flared: 'Why should I?'

'Because your black skin's too rhinoceros-like to feel stings. Pick it up,' demanded Cosmo.

Paris strolled into the clearing. 'Get it your fucking self.'

'Don't speak to me like that, yob,' said Lubemir insolently.

Paris dropped *Le Rouge et Le Noir*. A second later, his right hook had sent Lubemir flying into the nettles.

Bellowing at the pain, Lubemir yelled, 'Get heem,' to Cosmo.

Cosmo, however, who believed guards should guard themselves, was examining his nails.

Turning on Cosmo, Paris grabbed him by his bright blue Ralph Lauren shirt.

'Want to make the same journey?' he hissed, yanking Cosmo towards the nettles. 'I thought not. Well, fucking lay off Xav.'

Picking up *Le Rouge et Le Noir*, he stalked back to the hostel, with Xav panting to keep up.

'Thanks very, very much.'

317

''S OK. Cosmo's a wimp if you face up to him.'
Xav didn't believe him, but he felt a little better.

'Dear Mum,' wrote Kylie, another twenty-four hours later:

> We're having a brilliant time. We've been clay-pigeon shoot-
> ing, rock climbing and we cycled to a museum. We've also
> been to an art gallery, which Graffi would have loved.
> Everyone friendly – Bagley really nice, Jack gorgeous. We
> write up our notes in the evening when the teachers go to
> the pub, so we can get out the booze and the weed. Today
> some kids went riding. Cosmo raced his horse up behind
> Paris's and made it bolt. Paris fell off.

Paris hadn't any parents to write to. He'd started a card of
a red dragon's tongue, symbol of the Welsh language, to
Patience and Ian, then, not knowing how to address them on the
envelope and deciding it was counting chickens, had torn it up.
His head ached after his fall; if only he was with Janna in the
pub.

Janna enjoyed these pub sessions, discussing the children,
comparing state and private school practice.

'We work much harder in the independent sector,' moaned
one of Rufus's young geography teachers. 'At least you lot can
work at home. We're on call twenty-four hours a day and most
weekends.'

'You have loads longer holidays and we've got so many teachers
off with stress,' said Gloria, returning with another bottle. 'The
ones who aren't work ten times as hard.'

'Hengist doesn't believe in stress or "generalized anxiety" as it's
now known.' Rufus shook his head. 'He expects people to come
in every day.'

'Except for himself,' grumbled Biffo.

'You won't be able to run to your union when you join us next
term,' Joan teased an increasingly alarmed Vicky.

'Hengist is a despot,' complained Biffo. 'When Emlyn had to
pull out, he virtually ordered me to take his place.'

'Poor Emlyn, his father's being buried tomorrow.' Janna found
that he was seldom far from her thoughts. She kept wanting to
call and comfort him, but felt it would be intrusive. She had
arranged a wreath and a card of sympathy signed by everyone on
the trip.

'Hengist is driving down to Wales for the funeral – to show
support,' said Joan dismissively.

'And distribute largesse. The great international in a Welsh rugger town,' said Biffo even more dismissively.

'I think it's lovely of Hengist to go,' protested Janna. 'Emlyn adores him. He is Emlyn's future father-in-law and it'll mean a huge amount to the family.'

'Hengist's probably rather relieved Sally won't have to walk down the aisle on the arm of Emlyn's dad,' observed Joan. 'He's a crashing snob.'

'He is not,' said Janna furiously. 'Hengist gets on with people from all backgrounds.'

'Hark at you defending him,' simpered Vicky. 'I thought the two of you had fallen out.'

Paris had spent Ian's sixty pounds on a pair of shorts, a Prussian-blue shirt and a Liverpool baseball cap, which someone had nicked. As a result, on the third day he got too much sun canoeing. On the way back to the hostel, he started feeling horribly sick and sweaty; his head, after yesterday's fall, ached abominably. Stepping down from the bus, his legs buckled and he fainted.

He came round to find himself on the grass under a spreading chestnut tree, with a rolled towel under his head and Janna fussing over him, and thought he'd gone to heaven. As the bus had drawn up nearer Calorie Towers than the boys' hostel, he was moved to Janna's bed and a doctor summoned, who diagnosed sunstroke.

'With a fair skin like yours, you should never go out without a hat. Realistically you should go home.'

But with Janna holding his hand, mopping his forehead with her own pale blue flannel and looking down with such concern, Paris definitely wanted to stay.

'Perhaps it's better if you're not moved.' The doctor turned to Janna. 'As long as you can keep him cool and quiet?'

'He can sleep in my bed,' said Janna. 'I'm so sorry, love.' She squeezed Paris's hand. 'I should have noticed you weren't wearing a hat.'

She had been swimming and was still in a sopping-wet primrose-yellow bikini, through which goose pimples were protruding like bubble wrap.

'Get something warm on,' advised the doctor, looking admiringly at her speckled body, 'you've had a shock. Don't want you getting a chill.'

Peel off that bikini in here, thought Paris longingly and said:

'I can't take your room.'

'You certainly can and I'm not leaving you either.'

Paris, for the first time in his life, knew the bliss of being cosseted. The Bagley Babes nipped down to the greengrocer's and brought him strawberries and raspberries. Vicky rolled up with lemon sorbet, Gloria with a melon. Paris was embarrassed, yet touched they were so worried. Even Lubemir and Anatole sent apologies and the Chinless Wanderers promised to get him a better horse next time. Finally, Xav shuffled in and offered Paris his mobile.

'You might want to ring someone. No one except my mother rings me.'

'I'll ring you.'

Xav grinned. 'You can't if I haven't got a mobile.' Then, staring at the floor and kicking a table: 'Thanks for sticking up for me. I'm really glad you're coming to Bagley next term.'

Shyly, they exchanged a high five.

Having shooed everyone out, Janna gazed out of the window across the river. She could see thirty or so red and white cows standing together, whisking flies off each other's faces. That's what a good school should be, she thought wistfully, everyone protecting each other.

Despite another deluge, it was still terribly hot. Paris was getting drowsy. As she leant over to straighten his pillow, he could feel the smooth firmness, like almost ripe plums, of her breasts. Soaking the blue flannel in iced water, she trickled it over his forehead, shoulders and chest, like a caress.

'Please don't go away, read to me.'

Janna picked up Matthew Arnold, which had fallen out of his shorts pocket. 'To Paris with love from Patience and Ian', she read on the flyleaf and felt happier that they were kind, educated people who would look after him. She read:

> 'But the majestic river floated on,
> Out of the mist and hum of that low land,
> Into the frosty starlight, and there moved,
> Rejoicing, through the hushed Chorasmian waste,
> Under the solitary moon; he flowed
> Right for the polar star . . .'

'I wonder if he was a riffle or a meander,' mumbled Paris.

He could smell Janna's scent on her sheets. On the table were bottles: magic potions to make her even more beautiful. Gradually Janna's soft, young voice merged with the rain-swollen stream pouring into the river outside. He was asleep.

Oh, the length of those blond lashes. Not wanting him to catch cold, Janna pulled the blanket over him and couldn't resist bending over and dropping a kiss on his damp forehead.

'Good night, sweet Arctic Prince.' If only she'd been able to adopt him.

Paris opened his eyes a millimetre, next moment a tentacle hand had closed round her neck.

'Get away with you,' she protested.

Lifting his head, dizzy this time with longing, Paris kissed her. For a second her lips went rigid, then they relaxed and opened and kissed him back. Then she seemed to shake herself, prised away his hand and laid it on his chest.

'You're delirious,' she told him firmly. 'I must check on everyone else and find myself somewhere to sleep.'

'I love you, miss,' called out Paris, as he drifted into sleep.

52

'You've got to be better by tonight,' Jade Stancombe told Paris next morning as she dropped a box of white chocolates on to his bed. 'We're off to our mystery destination.'

She was followed by Cosmo, who'd clocked the burgeoning friendship between Xav and Paris and, wanting to punish Xav further, decided to take Paris away from him. Cosmo therefore rolled up with mangoes, peaches and Paris's baseball cap, which he claimed he'd found down the seat of a bus.

'But that won't keep the sun off back and front though, like this will,' and he plonked a panama on Paris's head.

'I don't want your fucking hat.'

'You will when you see how much it suits you.'

Paris was about to chuck it in the bin when Janna walked in: 'Oh Paris, you look gorgeous.'

'Just like Jude Law,' agreed Cosmo.

So Paris kept it.

Pearl was terribly excited.

'If you make me up for the mystery party this evening,' Jade had told her, 'you can borrow and keep one of my dresses.'

Then, when Pearl said she hadn't brought much make-up, Jade suggested they buy some in Hereford and proceeded to spend £300, also splashing out £550 on an aquamarine and diamond ring.

'I've brought a nice blue wraparound cardigan with me. You can have that too, Pearl, if you do my hair as well.'

It didn't look as though anyone would need cardigans: the weather was getting steadily hotter and muggier; huge white clouds rose like whipped cream on the horizon.

Terrified of being sent home, Paris kept telling everyone how much better he felt.

'You can come,' said Janna, 'if you take it really easy and keep that hat on.'

The panama was almost unbearably becoming. With the brim over his nose, he could have drifted out of *Brideshead* or *The Great Gatsby*.

But I'm Julien Sorel, he told himself. When I'm sixty, Janna'll be eighty, not a huge gap. Anyway, with her hair in a ponytail and freckles joining up on her face, she looked about fourteen.

As the coaches splashed through huge puddles, they seemed to be galloping back in time. Meadowsweet overran the emerald-green meadows, brown rivers struggled through great tangles of water lilies and dense primeval forests swarmed down the hills.

'That's a riffle, that's a meander,' yelled the children.

'God it's hot, are you OK, Paris?' asked the girls repeatedly.

Joan, the eternal chaperone, marched up and down the coach in search of bad behaviour. Boffin, still engrossed in *A Brief History of Time*, hummed a Bach prelude in a reedy tenor.

'Prince Harry's been done for drink driving,' said Amber, drinking Bourbon out of a Coke bottle, 'he's my hero.'

'Pity he's got a girlfriend,' sighed Milly. 'Boffin Brooks tried to snog me this morning. He must have month-old pilchards lodged in his brace. Where d'you think we're going tonight? It's so exciting.'

Jade stretched out long, newly bronzed and waxed legs.

'Good book?' she asked Paris.

'Very,' said Paris, not looking up.

Rufus was telling Kylie about whales.

'They'll be extinct quite soon.'

'That's really sad.' Kylie's big eyes filled with tears. 'Just like the dildo.'

Pearl had been sad too on the trip to Hereford because Cosmo had gone off in another coach with Vicky. Now he was back sitting beside her, reading *Classical Music* magazine, smiling wickedly, caressing the outside curve of her breast with his little finger.

And so, after four nights of rigorously enforced celibacy, the coaches rolled over the border into Wales. Biffo Rudge sat at the front, directing the driver.

'Here we are,' he shouted as they rounded the corner. On the other side of a wide river, hazily reflected in its water like a forgotten child's fortress, stood Castle Gafellyn against the darkening green trees.

As they crossed the river and drove through huge wrought-iron gates, flanked by rampant lions, they saw that the stern grey walls ahead were softened by rambling pink roses and pale blue hydrangeas.

'Castle Gafellyn was a most important military outpost,' read Biffo from Emlyn's notes. 'An early owner burnt it down to stop it falling into the predatory hands of the English.' He pointed to a square green field framed by crumbling stone walls. 'This was the enclosure into which livestock was herded at night to protect it from the wolves.'

'Sounds just like us,' said Pearl, sticking her tongue out at Cosmo.

I'll teach you, he thought.

'This is the sort of property in which the Macbeths might have resided,' announced Boffin, 'repelling other warlords and of course the English.'

The moat circling the castle was as green, still and smooth as mint jelly; all around dark forest encroached like stealthily invading armies. Like Burnham Wood advancing on Dunsinane, thought Paris, glancing at Janna, whose eyes were wide, her hands clasped in excitement like a child at her first pantomime. She deserved some fun; if only he could provide it.

Once inside, the children swarmed about, peering out through narrow, vertical windows, racing up winding stone staircases leading to turrets. Tapestries, swords and armour covered the walls. Meissen and Ming softened every alcove.

The owner, smooth, pewter-grey-haired, butterscotch-tanned, roving-eyed, was a childhood friend of Hengist called Bertie Wallace, who seemed deeply amused by the whole invasion.

'When one's ancestors have been accustomed to invading English hordes, Larks and Bagley seem very small beer,' he observed dryly as the children fell on tomato sandwiches and rainbow cake.

'It would have been fun to dine in the great hall, but it's so hot, I thought you'd prefer the garden room which opens on to the terrace. Hengist used to stay here as a child,' he told the somewhat awestruck teachers. 'His parents were friends of my parents who sold the place to pay death duties. My wife and I bought it back and are planning to turn it into an hotel, but first it's got to be extensively rebuilt and redecorated. Then I read about Larks joining forces with Bagley and thought you might like to stay here as a climax' – he smiled knowingly at Janna – 'to your trip.'

'You are so kind,' stammered Janna. 'What a treat. The kids have behaved very well so far. I hope they don't get carried away.'

'In olden days, castles like this would have had rushes and

meadowsweet all over the floor instead of carpets,' pronounced Boffin.

A flurry of notes and a burst of *Rigoletto* indicated that Cambola had found the piano. Shrieks of joy echoed round the garden as the children discovered a croquet lawn and the swimming pool, a rippling turquoise expanse of water, framed by limes in sweet scented flower, heavy with the murmuring of bees.

'We can go skinny-dipping later,' purred Amber.

'Or fatty-dipping, in Xavier's case,' said Cosmo evilly.

Bertie, soft-voiced and rakish, was decidedly attractive. Janna could imagine him and Hengist getting up to all sorts of tricks and because he was Hengist's friend, she wanted to make a good impression.

'I cannot think of a more wonderful end to our trip. And it will really help them to relate to history and Macbeth. "This castle hath a pleasant seat; the air Nimbly and sweetly recommends itself Unto our gentle senses",' she quoted happily.

' "This guest of summer, The temple-haunting martlet, does approve By his lov'd mansionry that the heaven's breath Smells wooingly here",' quoted back Bertie. 'I used to be an actor. Hengist told me I'd like you.'

Janna squirmed with pleasure.

A smell of mint was drifting from the kitchen.

'We've got smoked salmon, duck and puds. Do you think they'll like that?'

'Adore it, that's absolutely perfect. Thank you, particularly' – she thought of Calorie Towers – 'after the food they've been having.'

'I'm sorry I won't be with you,' said Bertie. 'A friend's having a dinner party five miles away, so after the servants have served up your dinner and it's mostly cold, I hope you'll forgive me if I hijack them to help my friend. They can clear up first thing. You'll probably feel freer on your own.'

'You're awfully trusting.'

Vicky and Gloria, who, seeing Bertie, had raced to their rooms to tart up, now drifted in.

'What a lovely property,' gushed Vicky.

'I could say the same for you two,' quipped Bertie. 'What amazing taste Hengist has in women.'

'We're expecting him later,' said Vicky. 'Oh, tomato sarnies, how yummy. I've just checked on Paris, Janna, he seems OK.'

Calm down, Janna told herself fiercely. What if Hengist was rolling up just to pull Vicky, who would wear something amazing tonight? 'You are old, Father William.'

Janna's room, at the end of a long corridor, was tauntingly romantic. The big four-poster with deep blue curtains embroidered with silver stars needed only a handsome prince. Other delights included a pale yellow Chinese screen, painted with narrow-eyed warriors, a bottle of champagne in ice and a dapple-grey rocking horse with a rose-red saddle. On the wall was a tapestry of Diana the huntress, her chariot drawn by a purposeful stag who looked very like Joan. Joan, putting an arm round Janna's waist this morning, had definitely slid a hand upwards to grab a breast.

Janna and Joan: perhaps that was her destiny. Collapsing on the bed, she noticed even the blanket had a coat of arms, a golden ram with a motto, 'Fidelis et Constans'. 'An Atkinson Blanket, made in England', said the label. Janna Curtis, made in Wales. Hengist was on the way. Would he be faithful and constant to Sally? She liked Sally so much; how hideous it would be if Hengist were to cheat on her with Vicky.

In another part of the castle, Cosmo, who intended to enjoy his evening, was lacing the fruit cup with vodka and brandy. By studying the guidebook, he had located, ten miles away, a renowned observatory with some adjoining historic troglodyte caves. His suggestion that Skunk and Biffo should give them a ring had resulted in both of them, plus Boffin and Rufus's two minions, being invited to supper to view some rare eclipse and visit the troglodyte caves.

Cosmo had also arranged for his mother to invite Joan and Cambola to *Ariadne auf Naxos* in which she was singing in Cardiff, which would occupy them for several hours.

Rufus should have stayed at the castle too, but getting no answer from his wife Sheena on her mobile or at home, where she should have been with the children, he had panicked and decided to miss dinner and slope home for the evening.

Situation excellent, which meant only Janna, Vicky and Gloria left in charge. If Hengist did show up, reflected Cosmo, Janna would be oblivious to everything else, so his plan to seduce Vicky and Gloria looked feasible.

Cosmo emptied another bottle of vodka into the fruit cup.

53

Before dinner everyone met on the terrace. The pupils in particular were amazed how unfamiliar and glamorous they looked in their party dresses. Jade, made up by Pearl, in a clinging white dress slashed to the waist from top and bottom, showing off St Tropez tan applied by Pearl, her hair plaited and threaded with flowers by Pearl, looked over the top but sensational.

Pearl glowed like a pearl, her normally pinched, sharp, pale little face softened and flushed by sun, love and Jade's flowered dress and pale blue wraparound cardigan.

'Designer clothes are certainly worf the price,' she admitted.

'Because I've got designs on you,' said Cosmo, patting her bottom.

Janna had washed and curled her hair, oiled her body and hidden sleepless nights with a lot of eye make-up. In her bronze speckled dress, which moulded her body and merged with her freckles, she looked like the Little Mermaid.

The children thought she looked stunning, but not as stunning as Vicky, who wore flamingo pink and who, perhaps trying to appear sophisticated for Hengist, had piled up and knotted a pink rose into her dark hair.

Everyone was agreeing they were having a fantastic time, when Bertie Wallace wandered in with a call for Joan Johnson.

'She's gone to the opera,' said Janna.

'It's Hengist.'

'I'll take it.' Vicky grabbed the cordless. 'Hengist, this place is a-mazing. Thank you so much. The kids are ecstatic. You stayed here as a child, Bertie told us. Are you coming over? Oh, what a shame. Of course, I understand. Research is all. Tintern Abbey.

My favourite poem: "That time is past, And all its aching joys are now no more, And dizzy raptures."

'OK, I'll give your love to everyone,' and after a pause: 'Mmm, me too.' Catching sight of Janna's anguished face she added, 'Do you want a word with Janna?' who shook her head frantically. 'OK, thanks for ringing, enjoy your evening.' She handed the cordless back to Bertie. 'Hengist isn't coming, what a pity. He's staying near Tintern Abbey doing some research.'

' "Why, uncle, 'tis a shame",' murmured Anatole.

'Bloody isn't,' murmured back Cosmo. 'When the cat goes arty, the mice begin to party.'

'Where's Tintin Abbey?' asked the Hon. Jack. 'I always liked Tintin.'

'Have a drink,' said Cosmo, handing Janna a huge glass of fruit cup.

How even more amusing to seduce Miss Curtis, who didn't dwarf him and who was looking unusually tempting. Now that really would crucify Master Alvaston.

Fucking Hengist! Paris, also watching Janna, was aware of a dimmer switch turning off the glow in her face. If only he could comfort her.

The sun at thirty degrees was reddening the castle walls; a short shower of rain had scattered pink rose petals over the grass. Delphinium and campanula rose in blue and violet spires. A most heavenly smell of roasting duck mingled with the sweet, heady scent of lime blossom and philadelphus. Vicky and Gloria, succumbing to laced fruit cup and Anatole's deep-voiced blandishments, were getting noisy and sillier.

'I'm dreadfully sorry,' whispered Janna, 'I've got an absolutely blinding headache – a migraine actually. They come on suddenly, I can't see out of one eye.'

'I had one on the opening night of *Romeo and Juliet*,' cried Vicky, 'it was all I could do to stagger in. Poor you. Gloria and I'll hold the fort – or rather the castle.'

Everyone was very solicitous.

'Go and lie down, miss, come back when you feel better.'

'Shall I bring you some iced water?'

Janna could see secret relief in many faces. Without her, joy would be truly unconfined. Paris insisted on accompanying her back to her room.

Let me stay, he wanted to beg. I'll lie down beside you and stroke your forehead as you did mine yesterday.

'Too much sun,' mumbled Janna.

'Do you need a doctor?'

'I'm fine. You go and have fun. I'll probably join you again in half an hour.'

'Sure you're OK?'

The intensity in his face alarmed her. She shouldn't have led him on yesterday. She'd only just managed to shut the door on him and bolt it when the tears poured forth. She was overwhelmed with despair at not seeing Hengist and shock that she could no longer conceal the fact she was hopelessly in love with him.

But what the hell was she playing at? Hengist was a married man, no doubt as faithful and constant to sweet Sally as the Atkinson blanket into which she was sobbing. He was also out of her league. She'd tried to cross the class barriers and found, as the Little Mermaid had when she tried to walk on shore, that she was treading on knives.

Then an imperious knock on the door sent her through the roof. It must be Paris back again. She should never have kissed him, but he'd looked so adorable. The knock became a tantivy. Nervously she opened the door a centimetre, but found the shadowy landing was deserted – perhaps it was the Gafellyn ghost.

The banging had become more insistent, coming from the far side of the room. Padding over the flagstones, she found a bottle-green wool curtain and behind it a rounded Norman door, buckling on its hinges. Oh God, was it Joan or raffish Bertie?

Someone was declaiming the Porter's speech in a strong Welsh accent. ' "Knock, knock, knock . . ." '

Janna opened this second door an inch, breathed in lemon aftershave and almost fainted as the door was thrust open, nearly concussing her. In the dim light she slowly made out a faded Prussian-blue shirt, a sunburnt throat, and eyes, slittier with laughter than the Chinese Warriors. It was Hengist. Ducking his head, he powered his way into the room and pulled her into his arms.

'I thought you were staying near Tintern Abbey.'

'I was, but I couldn't bear the thought of all those aching joys being past. I suddenly wanted a dizzy rapture.'

'I thought you fancied Vicky,' sobbed Janna.

She was so small in her bare feet, Hengist had to pull her chin upwards in order to smile down into her reproachful, bewildered, tearful, mascara-stained face.

'Dear God,' he said, 'from the beginning you've been the one I wanted, the object of my desire.' And when he drew her against him, he was like a great, warm, solid wall; where his shirt was

329

unbuttoned, she felt the burning heat of his body and was shaken by the relentless pounding of his heart.

Then his beautiful, wilful mouth swooped down on hers and she no longer doubted his passion as he kissed her on and on, his big hands closing round her small waist, then moving upwards to caress her high bouncy breasts, then moving down to cup her equally bouncy bottom. Finally, gasping for breath, he buried his face in her clean, silky curls.

'You utterly gorgeous child. Christ, I've fought this.' Then, laughing half ruefully: 'This is an awfully big adventure weekend.'

Janna escaped and paced round the room, heart battling with her head.

'How did you get in here?'

'By a secret passage. It comes out on the edge of the woods. Bertie and I were at school together; I used to stay in the holidays. I can get into every room in this castle.'

'And probably did,' snapped Janna, raging with insecurity, frightened her legs wouldn't hold her any more. 'I cannot believe this.'

'You soon will.' Hengist swiftly unzipped her speckled dress, unhooked her bra, then, gathering her up, dropped her on the blue and silver patchwork quilt.

'We can't,' stammered Janna. 'Sally? The party? How did you know I was here?'

'I tried to ring you but your mobile was switched off. Bertie said you'd sloped off with a headache. You have the sweetest body, look at those adorable boobs.'

Lying down beside her, he swept back her hair, kissed her fore-head and little snub nose, then her lips again, then her nipples, slowly, luxuriously, sensuously. The hand creeping lazily between her legs was so sure.

'Down comes the drawbridge,' he murmured, pulling off her knickers.

In turn he smelt so clean and healthy, and his face was so smooth and newly shaven – Janna was so used to beards and grating stubble – his glorious broad-shouldered body so power-ful, his hair so springy yet silky. As he stroked and fingered her, leaving her quivering with longing, he made no attempt to undress himself.

'I really like Sally,' muttered Janna.

'Hush. Sally's my problem.'

As he drew her into a fairy-tale world inside the star-spangled blue curtains, any principle fled. Through the narrow window, she could see Venus, a glittering silver medal pinned on the deepening blue breast of the night.

'You do want this, darling?' Hengist's hand was roving further afield.

'Oh please, yes,' Janna gasped. 'I'm stunned, that's all. I didn't realize it was an option. I haven't slept with anyone since Stew.'

'I should hope not – you were saving yourself for me.'

'I'm out of practice.'

'We must exchange best practice,' murmured Hengist, spitting on his fingers, finding her clitoris, caressing so gently and expertly.

'I'll give you best practice,' cried a fired-up Janna.

Wriggling out of his embrace, she took over, shoving Hengist back on the bed. Removing his loafers, kissing his bare feet, swiftly unbuttoning his shirt, kissing the dark brown tuft of chest hair, she licked his nipples and his belly button as she undid his belt and unzipped and removed his trousers. For a moment his red check boxer shorts were pegged by a splendidly excited cock, then he eased free and was divinely naked beneath her.

Clambering over his body like a squirrel, she kissed, caressed, sucked and licked until he was moaning in delight.

'For a head, Miss Curtis, you give exquisite head. Aaah . . .' Reaching down, he grabbed her waist and, pulling her up the bed, plunged his splendid rock-hard penis up inside her, which she had no problem accepting in full because she was so bubbling over with excitement.

'Aaah,' groaned Hengist again as her muscles gripped and released him, squeezing and coaxing, 'like the Bourbons, you've forgotten nothing. I'm going to be so selfish, darling, I cannot hold out a second longer, you'll have to catch the next bus. Oh, my Christ,' he shouted, 'here comes the drop goal,' and exploded inside her.

For an age it seemed, they lay giggling and in shared ecstasy.

'Hang out our banners on the outward walls; The cry is still, "he comes",' sighed Hengist. 'Oh my darling. That was even better than scoring at Twickenham.'

As he turned to kiss her, she was made happier by the intense happiness on his face.

'Now, I'm going to make you come lots,' he whispered. And he did.

Time stopped – fantastic, mind-blowing sex blotting out everything.

* * *

Under a weeping willow, whose leaves caressed her far more tenderly, Pearl was seduced by Cosmo, a coupling as brutal and perfunctory as Janna's had been ecstatic.

Retreating into the castle to wash, Pearl reflected it was a shame Cosmo had used a condom or she might have fallen pregnant and qualified for a free flat. At least Cosmo had said he loved her. She hoped Jade wouldn't be angry her wraparound cardigan had been torn.

54

After a glorious dinner, the plates had been stacked and everyone had drifted into the garden to dance under the stars, to snog in the bushes and, because it was such a hot, muggy night, to strip off and leap into the pool. Vicky and Gloria were far too drunk and giggly to worry that it was too soon after dinner to swim.

The scent of philadelphus and lime flower grew headier; more moths dived like kamikaze pilots into the lights round the pool; Jack and Kylie had retreated to the shrubbery; Lando and Junior were playing croquet, trying to hit each other's ankles.

Bertie, who'd gone off to see his mistress, had no intention of returning before dawn.

Paris, wearing just shorts, lay on the grass, admiring the stars; Venus was setting. Above him, the constellation Hercules, arms outstretched, mighty thighs apart, wrestled with his labours. Paris was worried about Janna; she'd been gone three hours. He decided to check her room.

He would have liked to clean his teeth, but someone had nicked his toothbrush. Returning to the dining room, he grabbed and bit into a Granny Smith, poured Janna a glass of orange juice loaded with ice, and set out. Normally at this hour, he'd be confined to his room at Oaktree Court, and he luxuriated in the cold dew beneath his feet and the night air warm on his bare shoulders.

Gradually the screams and shouts round the pool receded. In the moat below, the water-lily leaves gleamed like armour; to the right loomed the castle. Janna's lights were turned off; she must be asleep. O, that he were the pillow beneath her head.

Then he froze as a man appeared at her window, naked to the waist with a magnificent chest and heroic head thrown back, smiling triumphantly and stretching his arms in ecstasy. Not Hercules down from the skies – but Hengist. Then he turned and was engulfed once more in the darkness of the room.

Paris slumped against the castle, body drenched in sweat, heart crashing, ice frantically clattering against the glass in his hand. The whore, the slag! How could she? Women complained of headaches when they didn't want sex – and she'd kissed him first yesterday and not gone into a flurry of outrage, but had parted her lips when he'd kissed her back.

Paris gave a howl and hurled the glass against the wall. Bagley and Larks – 'a plague on both your houses'. In a daze, he staggered back into the castle, heading for the bar. Grabbing a bottle of vodka, he filled a half-pint glass, splashed bitter lemon on the top and downed it in one, then downed a second, spluttering:

'The bitch, the slag.'

Picking up a patterned orange Chinese vase cringing in an alcove, he hurled it against a big gilt mirror, splintering them both. A Tang dog flew out of the window. Gathering up a mahogany side table, Paris hurled it at the bar, smashing glasses, bottles, then swept more glasses on to the floor.

'Fucking slag.'

A bamboo plant had taken off, crashing down on to the keys of the piano, as Rocky wandered in, his mad bull's face crimson, his red curls askew, a bottle of Grand Marnier in his hand.

'What yer doing, man?'

'Wrecking this pervy nob's castle.'

'Right,' yelled Rocky, picking up a large flower arrangement and hurling it against a tallboy. Then he ran into the dining room and started on the debris of duck carcasses and bowls of potatoes and raspberries stacked on the sideboard. There was a sickening crunch as a pile of Rockingham plates fell to the floor. Like Duncan's blood, summer pudding was soon dripping down the pale blue Chinese wallpaper.

Outside, the music was too loud and the dancers and swimmers having too much fun to notice. Someone had found a big yellow ball and Lando and Junior were playing water polo.

Telling herself that first sex with a guy was never very good, still sore from Cosmo's cavalier seeing-to, Pearl wandered back to the party, pausing in horror to see her new boyfriend ferociously snogging Vicky Fairchild, his hand unzipping her flamingo-pink dress.

Going over, Pearl tapped him on the shoulder:

'D'you mind?'

'Piss off,' said Cosmo, with such venom that Pearl shrank away, looking desperately round for someone to tell, but everyone was snogging or swimming.

Running down a grassy path, she bumped into a reeling, half-dressed Jade, who asked:

'Where in hell's Paris?'

'Dunno. Cosmo's a fucking bastard.'

Jade stopped, swaying in her tracks, smiling cruelly.

'What have you and Cosmo been a-doing of? He just texted me.' Jade unearthed her mobile from her bra and held it out.

'Mission acc-come-plished pearls a slag', read Pearl and gave a shriek of rage. 'The bastard. He said he loved me, that I was the biggest fing in his life.'

'You might have been five seconds before he shagged you. Cosmo doesn't let grass grow under his feet, only in window boxes.'

Next moment, Pearl heard the distinctive double beat of a message on her own mobile and read: 'Sorry its over cosmo'.

'Wot dyou mean', texted back Pearl.

'Thanks for terrific sex shame youve just become my X', came back the reply.

'Bstrd how am I supposed to handle this', Pearl replied.

'Ask joan for alka seltzer. now fuck off', texted Cosmo.

Leaving the castle ransacked, Paris found everyone skinny-dipping in the pool. He felt like Actaeon spying on Diana and her nymphs.

A naked Vicky, whose hair had come down, was giggling hysterically and pretending to swim away from Cosmo, who'd just returned from texting. Yanking her back by her hair, Cosmo's hands closed over her breasts.

Very drunk, Paris laboriously undid his belt and stepped out of his shorts. The Bagley Babes, frolicking like Rhine Maidens, gasped as he paused, sleek, white and beautiful. Actaeon had become a moon-blanched Endymion. The only flaw was the tattoo of the Eiffel Tower on his shoulder.

'Jesus,' said Amber.

Letting go of Vicky, leaving her dog-paddling frantically in the deep end, Cosmo scrambled out of the pool, grabbed his camera from his jeans and took a roll of film.

Paris, a glass of neat vodka in his hand, stood gazing into the pool in despair and loathing, then wandered off. After two attempts, a naked Jade managed to struggle out of the pool and ran after him.

'Paris, make love to me,' she called out.

'Fuck off.'

'How come you're so mean to me?'

'Because you're a bitch.'

When Jade slapped his face, Paris slapped her back, then, grabbing her arm, pulled her behind the changing rooms into the shrubbery. He shoved her on the grass and fell on top of her, yelling in pain as her hand clamped around his sunburnt neck, pulling him down to kiss her. Her lovely sleek body writhed beneath his. Her eyes were glazed with lust and booze, Pearl's so carefully applied make-up streaked by water. The coupling, like Cosmo and Pearl's, was violent, fierce, messy and meaningless. The moment it was over, Paris pulled out and walked off.

Bumping into his friend, Pearl, who sobbed hysterically that Cosmo had dumped her by text and told the entire party, he could only say: 'You shouldn't go with trash: sorry, I wish I cared.'

Five minutes later, Pearl stumbled over Jade, passed out on the grass, puked-up raspberries and cream gleaming like blood in the moonlight. Jade was so far gone, she didn't even stir when Pearl produced a kitchen knife and sawed off her twelve-inch plait, threaded with flowers. Then Pearl attacked her own wrist, gasping at the pain and joy of release.

Amber, wet from the pool, caught up with Paris.

'What goings on, Mr Alvaston.'

So Paris pulled her into his arms and shut up her patrician babble by kissing her. He didn't care any more.

'I like you,' he told Amber.

'And I like you.'

It was like being serviced by a unicorn, Amber reflected hazily, or a statue half come to life. Paris's face was dead, devoid of any tenderness. At one moment he called her 'Janna', at another his features seemed about to disintegrate in tears, then set like stone again.

'Oh Christ, oh Christ.'

It was not, as you might say, satisfactory. At least he said 'thank you' as he got to his feet and wandered off.

If he found Milly, thought Paris, he could chalk up a Bagley Babe hat-trick, as Feral had always wanted to do. God, he missed Feral; only Feral would have understood his agony. Then he heard the sound of sobbing. It was Xavier, slumped on a bench, head in his hands, an empty bottle of rum beside him.

'Dad'll never be proud of me. I failed to pull Jade and why haven't I got the guts to kill Cosmo?'

'I'm sorry. I can't help you,' said Paris.

55

Joan and Cambola sang tunes from *Ariadne* all the way home, putting down the hood of the convertible Joan had hired so they could admire the stars. Dame Hermione had been wonderfully gracious and invited them back to her hotel for a cold supper of chicken gelé, wild berries, white chocolate sauce and Pouilly-Fumé. When Miss Cambola had pointed out Cosmo's musical genius, Hermione had replied that Cosmo was 'such a kind boy and very, very sensitive'.

'He gets that from you,' suggested Cambola.

'Indeed.' Hermione bowed her head, then, turning her big, brown eyes on an excited Joan: 'High-spirited maybe, but genius must be untamed.'

It had been after midnight when they'd left Cardiff and her presence.

Overhead, Draco the Dragon, not Welsh this time, had been joined by the Swan and the Lyre, on which Joan would have loved to serenade Dame Hermione. Wild honeysuckle and elderflower bashed in the narrow lanes by her car released a sweet yet disturbingly acrid, sexy smell. The night air was a pashmina round their shoulders. The roads were quiet. Joan took Cambola's hand. They agreed that Skunk and Biffo would have been home hours ago and that Janna was a sensible young woman to leave in charge.

'Janna is like Toscanini,' mused Cambola, 'many wrong things, but redeemed by so much passion and vitality.'

As they drove towards the castle, they heard sounds of revelry by night. Striding down to the pool, Joan's first reaction was delight to see such charming young women frolicking naked in the pool. But her delight turned to horror when she realized they

337

were not only her girls, but Vicky and Gloria also stripped off and extremely the worse for wear. Vicky was wrapped round Anatole, and Gloria snogging unashamedly in the shallow end with Hermione's 'very, very sensitive' little son, who, when Joan bellowed with rage for everyone to stop, gave her a V-sign.

Not making a great deal of potential deputy headway, Joan marched inside to be greeted by devastation. Summer pudding had incarnadined the exquisite blue wallpaper, a glazed brown duck carcass had nested in the chandelier. Empty alcoves reproached her. A raspberry pavlova had been rammed, like a custard pie, into the face of a replica of Michelangelo's David.

Bellowing with rage, blowing her whistle, crunching on smashed Meissen, Ming and Venetian glass, Joan stormed upstairs to find doors ajar and the beds of Jade, Milly and Amber empty. Primrose Duddon wasn't in her room either, nor were Kylie, Pearl or Kitten Meadows.

Red and more fiery than any Welsh dragon, Joan hammered on Janna's door.

'Kerist' – Hengist leapt out of bed – 'it's that porter from Macbeth again. How time flies when you're really enjoying yourself.'

'The moon's gone, get on the balcony,' hissed Janna, kicking his Prussian-blue shirt and white trousers under the bed.

Wrapping herself in a towel for a second time that evening, she opened her door an inch and again was nearly concussed as it was thrust open to reveal Joan bellowing like a Herefordshire bull. Hastily, Janna leapt backwards, aware she must reek of Hengist, his fingerprints luminous on her quivering, sated body.

'How could you let this happen? Downstairs has been totally wrecked. Students and teachers are frolicking naked in the pool. None of my students are in their rooms. As duty officer you're totally to blame.'

Retreating further from a fountain of spit, Janna mumbled she'd been struck down by migraine.

'The worst ever. I lay down for half an hour before dinner; I must have dropped off.'

'Well, get dressed at once,' thundered Joan, 'your students aren't in their beds either.'

Turning, Janna caught a glimpse of the rocking horse, hooded like a prisoner by Hengist's underpants and, fighting laughter, slammed the door and locked it. Equally weak with laughter, Hengist slid in from the balcony.

'Oh dear,' he sighed, 'but quite inevitable after segregating them in separate youth hostels all week. I don't expect they've come to much harm. And quite frankly, that was so miraculous, darling, nothing else matters. I suppose I'd better beat it.'

He was buttoning up his shirt and pausing to kiss Janna, when his mobile rang. It was Joan covering her tracks.

'Sorry to wake you, headmaster, just to alert you that anarchy has broken out at Castle Gafellyn. Janna Curtis was left in charge but deserted her post, claiming a headache. Both Vicky and Gloria are drunk and incapable. Half our students are missing.'

'And where were you and Biffo and Rufus whilst all this was happening?' asked Hengist icily. 'You went to the opera in Cardiff?' After a pause: 'Biffo and Skunk and Boffin went to some troglodyte caves? Surely that was taking coals to Newcastle? Well, you should all have bloody well been there.'

Then, after another long pause: 'Bertie's an old friend and very reasonable. I'm sure the bracelet will turn up.' Reaching out for Janna's pubes, he pulled her towards him, sliding his hand between her legs. 'Try to limit the damage. You've got yourself into this mess; don't call the police. I'm at Tintern Abbey and over the limit, or I'd drive straight over.'

Switching off his mobile, he kissed Janna lingeringly.

'I'd better scarper or we'll both be in trouble. Stick to the migraine story. Joan hasn't got a hairy leg to stand on.'

His feet groped around for his loafers.

'Where are you going?'

'Back down the secret passage. It comes out at the edge of Hanging Wood quarter of a mile away; my car's hidden in the trees. I utterly adore you, that was the best fuck I've ever had.'

'I feel drunk,' sighed Janna, 'and I haven't had a drop.'

'I'll call you,' said Hengist and was gone.

Groggily, Janna dressed. She couldn't stop giggling. She was no doubt about to be sacked, but she didn't care.

I love Hengist, Hengist loves me and two heads are definitely better in bed than one.

Joan meanwhile had stepped over a supine Rocky on the landing, located Lando France-Lynch watching polo on Sky and finally tracked down an orgy in Jack Waterlane's bedroom. Here she found Johnnie Fowler, Monster Norman, Jack, Kylie, Kitten, Junior, Amber, Milly, Cosmo and Anatole, who she'd last seen behaving abominably in the pool, and oh horrors, Primrose Duddon, among the writhing bodies.

Inspired by an internationally prize-winning installation entitled 'Shagpile', which showed models of naked men piled on top of and plugged into each other like Lego, the geography trip participants were trying to create a replica of fornicating bodies.

'Vaitress,' shouted Anatole, falling off the pile and waving an empty vodka bottle at Joan, 'can you get us another drink?'

'How dare you?' thundered Joan.

'Come and join our team-building exercise, miss.' Johnnie Fowler took a hand off Amber's left breast and patted the bed.

'Stop it, all of you, what the hell d'you think you're doing?'

'Don't swear, miss,' giggled Kitten from the middle of the pile.

'You told us to overcome traditional animosities and bond with Larks,' panted Junior, 'and what better way of doing it?' He kissed Kitten's shoulder. 'You beautiful thing.'

'Help,' shrieked Kylie, bucking frantically then collapsing on top of Jack, 'I'm overcoming.'

'Have you seen the state of downstairs?' yelled Joan. 'Thousands of pounds' worth of damage has been done.'

'Not by us,' chorused Shagpile II.

Drawing a dick the length of a conger eel out of a glassy-eyed Milly, Cosmo said chattily, 'Could have been Rocky. He was trashing the place as I passed, probably forgot to take his Ritalin.'

Downstairs, amid the debris, Cambola had swept earth from the hurled bamboo plant off the piano keys and, armed with a large brandy, was singing along as she picked out tunes from *Ariadne.*

Paris, having shed his shorts earlier, couldn't find them. Suspecting Cosmo, he nicked a pair marked Anatole Rostov from the Cosmonaughties' bedroom. Anatole wouldn't miss them; he'd brought six other pairs. Wandering into the garden, overwhelmed by vodka, despair and loveless sex, Paris passed Joan having a squawking match with Vicky.

'You will certainly lose your job, young lady.'

'Doesn't matter, I've got another one to go to.'

'Don't be too sure of that.'

Driven out of Jack's bedroom, Shagpile II were indulging in another shrieking stint of skinny-dipping. Reaching the pool, Paris stopped in his tracks to find Janna counting heads. As though nothing had happened, she turned and smiled at him.

'Oh, there you are. Are you OK?'

Paris was about to shout that she was a fucking slag, when he caught sight of a body in the shallow end, deathly pale even in the moonlight, hair streaming, stick legs askew, and realized it was Pearl surrounded by a flickering halo of blood. At first he thought she must have started her period and to save her humiliation looked round for a towel. Then he realized the blood was gushing from her wrists and, leaping into the water, he dragged her to the side. Hoisting her on to the flagstones, he yelled: 'Quick, she's cut herself.'

Janna rushed forward.

'Oh, poor child. Ring for an ambulance.' Crouching down, she put an ear to Pearl's chest. 'She's breathing, but unconscious, and terribly cold.'

Miss Cambola came running into the garden. 'We must make a tourniquet.' Tearing off her orange and black scarf, she wound it round and round Pearl's arm. 'Put your finger on the knot,' she ordered Paris. Then, turning to Janna: 'We must get her straight to hospital for a blood transfusion. If we meet the ambulance coming the other way, at least we save time.'

'I'll drive, I haven't been drinking,' said Janna. 'What the hell happened?' she asked as a suddenly sobered-up Amber, Junior and Paris helped her and Cambola carry Pearl to Joan's convertible.

'Fucking Cosmo. Shagged her, texted everyone to say she was a slag, then dumped her by text,' said Amber.

Jade, back in her bedroom, was calling her father. 'Daddy, Daddy, I'm having a horrible time. Paris Alvaston tried to rape me, he came on so strong and I didn't want to reject him because he's a yob and Xavier Campbell-Black tried to rape me too. I didn't want to be unkind, but he was drunk and went at me like an animal. I had to knee him in the balls. And, oh Daddy, someone's cut off all my hair, I look hideous. Everyone's drunk; all the teachers are shagging and skinny-dipping.'

'Calm down, princess. Who's in charge?'

'Joan but she bunked off with Cambola to hear Cosmo's mum in some opera and Skunk and Biffo went to look at some lousy eclipse and Rufus's gone home, he thinks his wife's bunked off.'

'Who's in charge?'

'Janna, but she bunked off to bed and now she's taken some girl who's slashed her wrists to hospital. We're staying in such a lovely old castle and Rocky's gone berserk and broken the place up. Everything's out of control. My diamond bracelet's been nicked and oh, my hair, Daddy.'

'Did anyone actually rape you, princess?'

'No, but they tried.'

'Go to bed and I'll fly down and collect you first thing.'

Stancombe came off the telephone and turned to Rufus's wife, Sheena, stretched out beside him on black satin sheets.

'Mission accomplished,' he said triumphantly. 'There's no way the blessed Janna and Larks will survive this disaster.'

'The pupils have bonded so well,' mocked Cosmo as, back in their bedroom, he and Lubemir heated up an electric kettle to light their spliffs on the element, 'that the teachers felt redundant and soon will be declared so.'

'I wonder how the Lower Sixth are getting on with their tour of the battlefields,' pondered Lubemir.

'Ought to start by studying the one downstairs,' said Cosmo.

Alex and Poppet Bruce had spent the day walking in Wales. They had booked into a nearby hotel but, seeing lights still on in the castle, decided to drop in to see Biffo, Skunk, Joan and dear little Vicky and enjoy some free drink.

They found Joan in a state of shock. Desperately guarding her position, fulminating to hide her guilt she had been skiving, she whisked them as quickly as possible out into the garden.

'Where are the students?' asked Alex.

'In their beds.'

'What on earth happened?' asked Poppet, who loved trouble.

'A young woman, Pearl Smith, slashed her wrists. Janna Curtis has rushed her to Casualty. I've been trying to ring Pearl's emergency contact number in Larkminster, but the telephone appears to be cut off.'

'Why did she try to end her life?' pressed Poppet.

'Oh, some love affair,' replied Joan. Dame Hermione would never forgive her if she shopped Cosmo. Anxious to get off the subject: 'And Jade Stancombe has behaved in a most reprehensible way. She was observed in flagrante with both Paris Alvaston and Xavier Campbell-Black. She must be excluded.'

Alex Bruce turned pale.

'We can't exclude Jade. We'd jeopardize our Science Emporium. Stancombe's been supportive when we've fired anyone else's kids, but he wouldn't like it if we excluded Jade. We must limit the damage. Don't call the police or the parents or the ambulance.'

'Janna Curtis insisted on taking Pearl to hospital,' said Joan.

'Well, I suppose Pearl is her responsibility.'

At that moment Biffo and Skunk strode in, laughing heartily.

'Alex, Poppet, how good to see you. We've seen the most dramatic eclipse,' said Biffo. Then, lest Alex should think they'd been skiving, he added that they'd taken Boffin, Alex's favourite pupil with them. 'He couldn't believe his eyes. We've packed him off to bed. No doubt he'll debrief you tomorrow, Alex. I could do with a Scotch, couldn't you, Skunk?'

Joan was just debriefing them about the last six hours, heaping blame on Janna, when Bertie Wallace, hot from his mistress, walked in, whereupon Joan heaped blame on Rocky.

'Quite an achievement,' said Bertie, surveying the devastation. 'Rocky should get a job with the council demolishing old buildings. Fortunately for me, this house is in my wife's name. I doubt if she'll be quite so sanguine, but I expect it's insured.'

Janna rang Joan from the hospital. Pearl, thank God, was out of danger. They had given her stitches and a blood transfusion. She was conscious and Janna had spoken to her. Then she asked if she could have a quick word with Paris.

'I know he's worried.'

Even though it was nearly three a.m., Paris was awake, lying on top of his duvet, gazing at the ceiling. He took the telephone into a deserted bedroom.

'I thought you'd like to know Pearl's going to be OK and you probably saved her life.' Then, when Paris didn't answer: 'She's all right, Paris.'

'You're fucking not.'

'I beg your pardon?'

'If you hadn't sloped off to bed with a made-up headache and Hengist Fucking Brett-Taylor, none of this would have happened, you dirty bitch.'

'What are you talking about?'

'I saw Hengist at your window, stripped off and flaunting his six-pack, you fucking slag.'

'Oh Paris,' pleaded Janna in horror, but he had hung up.

56

Bagley pupils who'd been on the field trip were gated until the end of term, which was only a few days away. As Dora Belvedon had not been among the participants, it fell to Sheena Anderson to sell the story of 'Toff School in Mass Orgy', complete with gory details of skinny-dipping, group sex, trashing of our precious heritage and, finally, of a young woman nearly dying from a suicide attempt.

The person who carried the can was Janna. She was the only head on the trip, and the catastrophe had occurred when she was in charge. She had let the maintained sector down. Hengist was very sympathetic to her plight and had bollocked his staff for leaving her exposed, but he was not prepared, 'for both our sakes, darling', to reveal his part in distracting Janna during the evening.

Parents were fortunately mollified by magnificent exam results released in August, in which Bagley, helped no doubt by Cosmo's leaked papers, had drawn away from St Jimmy's and edged towards Fleetley.

Larks did infinitely better than the previous year: up from four per cent to ten per cent of the pupils getting the requisite five A–C grades known as the Magic Five, but they were still near the bottom of the Larkshire league. Any satisfaction was doused by Ashton Douglas's call.

'Vewy disappointing wesults, Janna. We'll need a post-mortem on these and the geography field trip.'

On the credit side, Pearl bounced back quickly – cheered by all the sympathy and by a large bunch of pink roses on Dame Hermione's account, plus a card from her 'very sensitive' little son saying: 'Sorry, I was a rat. Love, Cosmo.'

Remembering how she had smashed Janna's Staffordshire cow,

Pearl organized a whip-round from both Bagley and Larks children who'd been on the field trip and raised enough money to buy an even prettier Herefordshire cow from Larkminster Antiques.

'Miss loves cows.'

'She don't love Chally or Basket or Spink or Joan,' grumbled Graffi, but he designed a beautiful card, saying 'You're a star' in gold and purple sequins and everyone signed it and wrote fond messages inside apologizing that the trip had gone pear-shaped, but insisting they had had the best time ever, and thanking her for all her kindness.

Janna, overwhelmed, stroked the spotted red and white cow, and blushed and wept with joy over the card. Only after she'd read it half a dozen times did she notice Paris's name was missing.

When asked, Pearl had also blushed. 'Paris gets funny.'

I doubt it, thought Janna.

Paris had blanked her for the rest of the term and when she'd given him a lovely edition of Housman's poems as a leaving present, had just put it back on her desk. How would he treat Hengist, she wondered, when he got to Bagley?

Paris had also fallen out with Feral who, resentful the field trip had been a riot, grew crosser when Paris refused to debrief him and Graffi.

'Did you shag Amber and Jade?'

'Fuck off.'

'Did you shag Vicky or Gloria? Did you shag Miss?'

'I don't want to talk about it.'

Feral then queried the wisdom of moving in with Ian and Patience. 'Be careful, man. People only foster in order to abuse. That Ian looks a fascist perv and she's an ugly cow. I suppose you can always phone Childline.'

Paris, fuelled by rage, misery and apprehension, hit Feral across the playground. The fight went to ten rounds and was not made up. Once again, longing for his lost mother overcame Paris. Two days before the end of term, he vanished, taking to the trains to find her. After two days of panic, social services in Larkminster received a call from a stationmaster in Land's End saying Paris was stopping the night with him and his wife, but would be put on the train back to Birmingham tomorrow. Seeing Nadine's stuffed-sheep face on the platform at New Street, however, beside grim bully Blenchley and Crispin snuffling in disapproval, Paris jumped trains and went off to Edinburgh.

'Children dumped by their mothers never stop looking for

them,' said Nadine, which hardly helped a desperately nervous Patience.

So Paris never said goodbye to Larks, even when he was safely returned to Oaktree Court and started packing up his few belongings in the expectation of moving to the Cartwrights. Janna felt wiped out by guilt. She should have levelled with both Patience and Nadine that Paris had only been thrown off course and was likely to act up appallingly because he'd been let down by yet another mother figure.

'I needn't say I was in bed with you,' she begged Hengist, when he visited Jubilee Cottage after the field trip. 'I can just say some lover rolled up.'

'You're in enough trouble as it is,' said Hengist firmly. 'Some bloody counsellor will worm it out of Paris and then we'll be really in the shit. We deserve a little happiness. It's going to be difficult enough to see each other as it is.'

So, just as Paris felt horribly guilty but let Rocky take the rap for trashing Gafellyn Castle, Janna also kept quiet. Hengist had bewitched her, as blindingly dazzling as low winter sun reflected in icy puddles. She found it impossible not to revel in such unfamiliar happiness.

Throughout the long, hot summer, she was amazed and gratified how often he managed to see her. Luckily, hers was the last cottage in the village, with no house opposite, and Lily's wise sapphire-blue eyes were too short-sighted to recognize Hengist when he crept in during darkening evenings, wearing a confiscated baseball cap, shades and shoes wet from the increasingly heavy dews.

He frequently rolled up with one of Elaine's Bonios for Partner, who, instead of barking, whimpered and wriggled his little body with joy.

When Hengist was unable to see her, he rang, having learnt from his pupils to acquire a second pay-as-you-go mobile so Painswick couldn't trace his calls. He wouldn't, however, write to Janna when he was away. 'Too risky. I trust you, darling, but not the press.' Instead he gave her poetry books with pages marked:

> Ah, love, let us be true
> To one another! For the world, which seems
> To lie before us like a land of dreams,
> So various, so beautiful, so new . . .

'I feel dreadfully guilty about Sally,' Janna told him repeatedly, but Hengist always claimed that was his department.

'I'm not going to lie and say Sally doesn't understand me or sleep with me or love me as I love her. But this is so utterly divine . . .' He buried his lips in Janna's freckled shoulder. 'That's why we must be so careful not to get caught.'

Lovers, like Stew in the past, had refused to say they loved her. Hengist said it all the time. The downside – like jesting Pilate – was that he could never stay for more than an hour or two.

They were in bed one early August afternoon when a naked Janna glanced out of the window and shot back as Alex Bruce jogged by, head held high, spectacles misting up, showing off a spare figure and skinny legs.

'D'you think he's spying?'

'No, determined to win the school steeplechase.'

'When's that?'

'Last Sunday in September. It's Biffo's baby, both staff and pupils take part in a six-mile run round Bagley village and the surrounding countryside. Excellent way of giving unfit masters coronaries. Biffo takes it incredibly seriously. Alex is a lousy games player – can't see a ball – so he's desperate to triumph at cross country. Robot the Bruce. I must keep Paris away from his deplorable wife, Poppet, who'd love to counsel our guilty secret out of him. Anyway, I can think of better ways of keeping fit.' He pulled Janna on top of him.

Hengist was as generous with presents as with his affections: Ralph Lauren shirts; a dusty pink cashmere twinset; a topaz brooch and matching earrings; a little Staffordshire dog; a CD of *Beatrice and Benedict*, Berlioz's lovely opera based on *Much Ado*, because Janna reminded him of the mettlesome lippy Beatrice; a watercolour by Emily Patrick; endless books he'd loved that he hoped she'd enjoy.

Janna was also in heaven because the long summer holiday was the first time she'd had a chance to play house, tend her garden, listen to the Proms and explore the countryside with Partner, who grew in confidence every day. Often she picked blackberries so ripe and luscious in the hedgerows you could fill a bowl in ten minutes. But deep in the wood, the same berries were small, hard and green and would never reach fruition – like so many of her children, trapped by poverty. She vowed once again to start homework and breakfast clubs next term and campaign for a football pitch for Feral.

One muggy afternoon in August, she stood and gazed out of her bedroom window at the yellow shaven fields, the darkening olive-green woods and the gaudy butterflies, glutting themselves on the amethyst spears of 'my buddleia', she thought happily.

She had just been to court with Feral, who, refusing to admit how heartbroken he was at Paris's defection, had got hammered and totalled a stolen car. Bitterly ashamed of his dyslexia and that he could hardly read or write, he was panicking how he could avoid utter humiliation next term without Paris to translate, explain and do his homework.

Even with Dora's frightfully disapproving mother Lady Belvedon on the bench, Janna's impassioned plea that it would be disastrous for Feral to miss the start of his GCSE course, and that she could vouch for his character, won over the other magistrates. When Feral got away with a suspended sentence, his relief was palpable. He clammed up, however, whenever Janna asked him about Paris or his family.

Taking off her rose-patterned suit, worn to charm the magistrates, Janna paused to glance in the mirror. Love seemed to have made her body curvier and softer. Last autumn's head-mistress's bob had grown out, thank goodness; her red curls now nearly reached her nipples. If Hengist thought she was beautiful, maybe she was. He was not due till tomorrow, so she could veg out tonight and watch the four hours of *The Bill* that she'd taped.

'Bugger, bugger,' said a voice.

Returning to the window, Janna found her neighbour Lily, who'd been staying with friends in the Dordogne for a fortnight, forcing a mower through a hayfield of lawn.

'Get on, you utterly bloody thing,' Lily yelled as the mower stalled on a particularly shaggy corner, then hit a bone – probably Partner's, thought Janna guiltily – went into a furious clatter and stopped completely.

'Bugger you.' Lily kicked it several times to no effect. 'My bloody corns!' Then, frantically tugging a wire: 'Don't do this to me, I can't afford to get you mended.'

Next moment, Lily had collapsed on to a rickety garden bench and burst into terrible rasping sobs. Janna was appalled. Ramrod-straight, endlessly kind and merry, outwardly invincible, only occasionally grumbling about her arthritis, Lily seemed indomitable. It was like seeing Big Ben crumbling. Lily was such a good listener and had been such a comfort that Janna wanted to race downstairs, fling her arms round her and return some of the comfort, but felt Lily might feel embarrassed.

Partner, with no such reserve, shot downstairs and out into the garden through the gap in the fence. Dummying past an out-raged General, he leapt on to his friend Lily's knee to lick away her tears.

Grabbing a bottle of white from the fridge, Janna followed more reflectively. Feral was flat broke and had nothing to keep him out of mischief. He'd always got on with Lily when the Wolf Pack came over on Saturday afternoons. Janna would get Lily's mower mended, and Feral could mow her lawn.

She found Lily drying her eyes with Partner's ears, her face ravaged by tears. It was sweet of Janna to suggest Feral, but she could honestly manage.

'Oh please, he's so sad about Paris, and he's desperately broke, you'd be doing him a favour.'

'I always liked Feral,' admitted Lily. 'He had such amazing ball control when he played football on my lawn. He never broke a flower.'

'Well, that's settled then. Let's open this bottle.'

'We mustn't forget to watch Christian Woodford's programme at six-thirty,' said Lily.

The Brigadier, who lived a few doors away, had evidently been asked by Rupert Campbell-Black to do a programme on Dunkirk.

'How exciting,' cried Janna. 'I'll just go and ring Feral.'

Lily's heart sank. She couldn't afford to have her mower mended, let alone pay Feral. Ever since she had been kicked out of her lovely riverside house Lily had existed in this damp, rented cottage on a hopelessly dwindling fixed income – with shares yielding one per cent.

Despite her outward insouciance, Lily was in despair. Although she adored her nephews and nieces, particularly Dora, their constant visits exhausted her physically and financially. She was reduced to selling silver and pictures every month to keep herself in drink and the faddy black and white General in chicken. Some days Lily herself existed on 'pussy's pieces', bought for General from the fishmonger and blackberries picked on walks.

There was another space on the drawing-room wall where she'd last week sold a little Sutherland drawing to pay some bills. Now she'd have to find extra cash to pay Feral and give him a good tea.

349

57

Feral looked as though he needed a good tea when he rolled up two days later. He wore a black baseball cap back to front, black loose jeans, a black T-shirt. Was he in mourning for Paris or did he think black suited him? Rangier than ever, he'd shot up three inches. His tawny brown eyes roved round the kitchen, checking in every corner for ways to escape.

It had been raining heavily. A few muddy gashes, a few roses clouted on the ankles, a clematis taken out altogether and a lot of bad language later, the lawn was mowed and the terrace swept. Lily gave Feral a pie made of potatoes, onions and cheese sauce, blackberry crumble and a glass of sloe gin. He had seconds of everything, as they discussed Arsenal and Larkminster Rovers' prospects for the coming season.

'Football makes me look forward to autumn,' said Lily, 'as fox-hunting used to in the old days.'

The Premiership was due to start on Saturday and the joy of Arsenal winning, or despair at them losing, lasted Feral all week, until excitement about the next game kicked in. But it wouldn't be the same without Paris and the endless arguments they'd had about the relative merits of Emile Heskey or Thierry Henry.

'Paris loved Liverpool,' said Lily idly. 'How's he getting on with his new family?'

'Dunno.'

'You must miss him.'

Feral shrugged.

'How's Graffi?'

'His dad's out of work.'

There was a pause.

'You must meet my friend Brigadier Woodford, who lives four

350

houses away. He might need someone to do odd jobs for him. Rupert Campbell-Black had him on television two nights ago; he was excellent, talking about Dunkirk. Did you come across Rupert's children Xav and Bianca when you went to Bagley?'

'Xav's a no-good nigger,' observed Feral. 'She and I did a dance routine in *Romeo and Juliet*.'

He was desperate to ask after Bianca who, since March, had tangoed through his dreams, but couldn't bring himself to. Instead, he volunteered the information that Randal Stancombe was looking for squatters. 'Pays four pounds an hour, puts them in to bring down the price of a house he wants to buy.'

Lily observed the swallows gathering on the telegraph wires. 'Perhaps I should apply.'

'Bit rough for a lady,' grinned Feral, helping himself to another spoonful of crumble.

Stiffly Lily got to her feet. Taking off her huge sapphire engagement ring and putting it on the draining board, she turned on the hot tap and added washing-up liquid.

'Haven't you got a dishwasher?'

'There's only me. Wouldn't want to risk my best china.'

General the cat appeared at the window. He landed with a thud then ferociously attacked a wooden leg of the kitchen table as the telephone rang. It was Dora. Bianca's friend, thought Feral longingly – as if Rupert Campbell-Anti-Black would let me anywhere near his darling daughter. Fucking upper classes.

'Of course,' Lily was saying, 'no, bring Cadbury, that's fine, perhaps not Loofah as Feral's just mown my lawn most excellently. Yes, stay the night, we can watch *Midsomer Murders*.'

Putting the telephone down, Lily turned back to Feral, lines deepening on her no longer smiling face, utterly exhausted. Feral's tea had taken a lot out of her, and there wasn't any cheese pie or crumble left for Dora's supper. Then she glanced at the draining board. Her ring had gone. She was sure she'd left it there. She should never have put temptation in Feral's way. The great sapphire had been bought to match the blue of her eyes, by a husband she'd loved so much. She glanced at his faded photograph, smiling out at her, and wondered what to do. The sapphire had been like a safety net to keep from the door the wolf, but not the Wolf Pack.

Slowly, painfully, she opened the silver clasp of her red leather purse and with trembling, arthritic fingers gave Feral a tenner for mowing. Then, taking a basket, she went into the garden. It had been a wonderful year for plums; glowing ruby-red, they weighed down the trees like weeping willows. How often recently had she dined on bread and plum jam? Slowly she filled up the basket, swearing and sobbing as a sleepy wasp landed on her third finger where the sapphire had been. Back in the house, she found Feral puffing on a spliff and watching the sports news.

She held out the basket. 'Do you like plums?'

'Never had one.'

'Well, don't break those beautiful white teeth on the stones.' Then, as Feral rolled his eyes: 'You might be able to sell them. I'll decant them into a cardboard box.'

'Fanks, man,' said Feral. With his first glimmer of a smile: 'I could sell them to Paris to put in his mouf, now he's gone all posh at Bagley.'

Lily laughed. Rootling around for an old Whiskas x 12 box, shaking out a spider, she filled it with plums. Handing them to Feral, she noticed the sapphire ring back on the draining board. Dizzy with relief, she had to fight back the tears. For a moment, their eyes met. Again Feral half smiled and shrugged. Then he handed Lily the spliff. Taking a giant puff, she practically burst her lungs.

'You need help wiv Dora's bed?' said Feral.

'You are kind. Actually it's already made up, a teenage friend stayed for a dance last week, only in bed an hour, so I'm afraid I made it up again.'

There was a pause.

'Would you like to come back next week? The grass still grows quickly at this time of year.'

'I'll fink about it,' said Feral.

He longed to feel welcome in an adult world. He needed people to talk to, to feel respect.

'Oh, OK,' he said.

As Brigadier Woodford, who was reading the lesson, drove Lily to Evensong in the next village, they spotted Feral. He was slumped by the side of the road with his Whiskas box, holding up a torn-off piece of cardboard, on which he had written 'Plumes for Sal'.

' "Bring me my white plume",' quipped the Brigadier, slowing down. 'First-rate job you made of Lily's lawn. Well done,' he told Feral and although his garden was awash with plums, he bought a pound's worth. 'Can't resist Lily's plums.'

The collection could have a pound, instead of two, he decided as he drove on. He had skipped lunch at the Dog and Duck, so he could afford to ask Lily to have dinner with him on the way home.

'Your Dunkirk programme was such a triumph,' Lily told him.

'They did seem pleased.'

'With all those Second World War anniversaries coming up, I'm sure Rupert'll ask you to do some more.'

The Brigadier, who had been brought up to be self-deprecating, loved having someone to tell things to. Gratifying how many people at Evensong, even the parson, who was a notorious pacifist, made a point of saying how good he'd been.

'Rupert's going to pay me two hundred pounds,' he confided to Lily. 'Quite extraordinary for a ten-minute waffle. That's twelve hundred an hour.'

'Randal Stancombe will evidently pay us four pounds an hour for squatting.'

'Have to get a new hip before I tried any of that,' grinned the Brigadier.

By the time he'd levered himself out of the car on arrival at the Dog and Duck, to open Lily's door, she'd already clambered out. Good thing there was no shortage of single women in later life. If a husband came home these days, he would be far too crocked to leap into the wardrobe or pull on his clothes in a hurry. He'd had such wonderful escapades when he was young: wives of commanding officers or even of a visiting general. He didn't think his wife Betsy had ever found out, but she'd looked sad sometimes. He'd made it up by nursing her to the end, although he'd often been rather irritable. Now he harboured a secret passion for Lily: so beautiful, so plucky. He suspected she was even broker than he was and wished he could help.

Although over eighty, the Brigadier was tall and upright, with a high colour which tanned quickly and thick hair, brushed back in two wings, in the same steel grey as his moustache.

Lily had refused his invitation to dinner at first because Dora was staying, so the Brigadier had invited them both to the Dog and Duck, where Dora admired the 'gorgeous springer spaniel' on the inn sign, and where it was sheltered enough to eat outside and admire an orange moon floating free of the darkening woods.

Dora, as usual, was brimming over with chat as she fed crisps to Cadbury and tucked into roast chicken, chips and peas.

'Only time to grab a sandwich at lunchtime,' she announced in her piercing voice. 'Patience and I have been getting Paris's room ready. He loves Liverpool, so we put posters of Owen, Gerrard and Emile Heskey on the walls and she's bought him a Liverpool shirt and a red Liverpool mug which says 'You're not drinkin' any more' on the bottom, and a lovely bookshelf and a tuck box with a key, so he can keep private things.

'He's so lucky,' went on Dora, dipping a chip in tomato ketchup. 'That room's got a terrific view of the stables and Patience has painted it a lovely warm corn colour. Ian's been so preoccupied letting the school to a bishops' conference, and getting fees out of parents like my mother who won't pay up, that Patience has been able to splurge. Fortunately, her aunt kicked the bucket and left her some money.'

The Brigadier, famished after no lunch, had nearly finished his shepherd's pie; Dora, getting behind, began feeding strips of chicken to Cadbury.

'Anyway,' she continued, 'Patience has also bought him a television, a radio, a laptop, a tape deck, a mobile and loads of uniform. Ian wanted her to buy it secondhand. Patience wasn't having any of it, so it's all new.'

'Eat up, Dora, darling,' chided Lily, 'it'll get cold.'

'I'll eat your chips if you like,' said the Brigadier, filling his and Lily's glasses with an excellent red.

'And he's got a double bed,' added Dora, aware the entire pub was now listening, 'so he can have women in, with a patchwork quilt. Patience put lots of Emerald and Sophy's old children's books in the bookshelf: *Babar* and *The Happy Prince*, which is what Patience wants Paris to be. I think he's more like Little Kay in *The Snow Queen*. We mustn't let his heart turn into a block of ice. Can I turn my fork over to eat my peas? It's quicker.'

The rising moon had grown paler.

'Not too cold?' asked the Brigadier.

'I'm fine. That was gorgeous. Thank you so much.' Dora shoved her knife and fork together. 'I'm truly full up.' She beamed at him. 'Well, I wouldn't mind some chocolate ice cream, if you insist.'

A second later, she was back to the subject of Paris.

'I only hope he's very grateful because Ian and Patience have gone through so much to become foster parents – oodles of medical tests, and they've got to practise safe sex – sounds like a duet' – Dora pretended to play the piano on the table – 'so that Patience doesn't get pregnant. She's a bit ancient for that, I would say.'

A woman at the next table choked on her quiche. Lily's eyes met the Brigadier's and, as they tried not to laugh, she attempted to steer Dora on to safer subjects.

'How many bishops has Ian let the school to?'

'Millions,' giggled Dora. 'The Bishop of Cotchester's sleeping in Cosmo's study. I hope he'll remember to water Cosmo's marijuana plants.'

58

Head boy at Rugby, a rugger blue with a second at Cambridge, commanding officer of a tank regiment, managing director of a highly successful Yorkshire engineering company, Ian Cartwright had had few setbacks in life until ousted by a boardroom coup staged by directors fed up with his brusque, despotic manner.

He then fell on desperately hard times, lost everything through foolish investment, descended into heavy drinking and nervous breakdown, only surviving on the money his staunch wife Patience earned working in a bar. The nightmare had ended two years ago, when Ian had landed the job as bursar of Bagley Hall, a Hengist appointment, which had been an unqualified success: the previous incumbent having cooked the books. Ian, who was utterly straight, industrious and excellent with figures, soon got the reputation of a man who could 'get things done', which was also a euphemism for being at everyone's beck and call.

Having been delivered from the hell of poverty, Ian was passionately grateful to his deliverer and in truth it was partly to impress Hengist that he had been keen to foster Paris.

Ian had also longed for a son with whom to discuss internationals, test matches and nineteenth-century poetry, who would look up to him, replenish his whisky, bring in logs and share manly tasks.

Although apprehensive, he was determined to do right by Paris and kept quoting *Timon of Athens*: ' 'Tis not enough to help the feeble up, But to support him after.'

Alas, Paris, already in explosive mood, arrived at the Cartwrights' at Ian's busiest time. Bills for school fees had been dispatched on the first day of the holidays and should have been paid – in theory – before the children set foot in school for the autumn term.

This had resulted in a flood of furious letters from parents outraged not only by the increased fees but at having to foot the bill for the demolition of Gafellyn Castle – letters which Hengist, having buggered off to Umbria, had left Ian to answer.

The majority of staff had swanned off on long holidays, leaving Ian to oversee the installation of new kitchens and damp courses and replace faulty windows in their houses and classrooms. No-Joke Joan rang every day from Lesbos to find out if Ian's maintenance men had unjammed the Tampax machine in Boudicca and whether he had looked at her suggestions for a second young women's boarding house.

Little Vicky Fairchild, on whom Ian had a crush, had already wheedled herself a charming flat overlooking the playing fields with a new en suite bathroom; whereupon all the young staff followed suit and wanted one too. In addition, it was Ian's duty in the holidays to let the school to bring in revenue. For the fifth year running, the Church of England had held their conference at Bagley, charming chaps who all wanted to play golf and ride Patience's horses, which ran away with them, which added to the pressure.

In the second half, the school had been taken over by a group of Orthodox Jews, charming chaps too, a source of excellent jokes, but who as part of their religion insisted that their quarters should be plunged into darkness at ten o'clock. They had therefore wrenched out and mislaid most of the infrared lights that automatically came on in the passages as night fell.

Any conference involved a lot of tidying up for Ian's ground staff and maintenance men to prepare the school for the new term. Ian didn't mind, he relished hard work and found Hengist, who only raised hell if his expenses were curbed and the pitches were not mown, a dream boss. The job would have been perfect except for the endless bullying interference of Alex Bruce. Hell-bent on modernizing the school, Alex had insisted Ian learn to use a computer so he could do his own letters and figures and dispense with Jenny Winters, his kind, pretty and brilliantly efficient PA.

Ian was subsequently having a nightmare mastering the beastly machine, which seemed to have tripled his workload.

Normally, as bursar, after he had chased up the parents for payments and settled in the school, he and Patience would have taken their annual three-week holiday in the second half of September. This year, with all the expense of kitting out Paris, they couldn't afford to go.

In late August, when the Cartwrights finally got permission to foster, an exhausted, uptight Ian was hardly in the right mood to welcome and make allowances for Paris. Patience as a reaction became over-conciliatory and dithery, filling every silence with chat, until Ian put her down out of nerves.

Paris was equally uptight, at moving to both a new home and a new school. He loved his new room. He loved his bathroom and, after the fight for often cold showers at Oaktree Court, luxuriated for hours reading in scented baths. He loved his laptop, tape deck and mobile, but since he'd fallen out with the Wolf Pack and Janna, he had no one to ring. The bliss of reading and writing in peace and being able to watch *Richard and Judy* or *Top of the Pops* to the end, without someone throwing a punch or snatching the remote, rather palled when you had all day in which to do it.

After the permanent din of the home where inmates shouted and screamed and were shoved in the quiet room, he found the repressed formality of the Cartwrights unnerving. Nadine had urged them to provide a stable environment with clear boundaries. Ian, tetchy and at full stretch, would return in the evening and order Paris around like an errand boy.

There was the disastrous occasion when Ian asked him to dig some potatoes, and Paris by mistake dug up all the precious half-grown artichokes. Or when Paris was ordered to collect the *Sunday Telegraph* from Bagley village and, settling down to read the football reports on a gravestone in Bagley churchyard on the way home, had crumpled and muddled up all the pages.

Ian, in addition, felt it was his duty to improve others. He started off on Paris's appearance. Sleeveless T-shirts were to be discouraged when they showed off a tattoo of the Eiffel Tower. Soon he was nagging Paris to remove his jewellery. As Paris's ear studs, plaited leather bracelet and necklace of wooden beads, threaded on to a bootlace, had all been presents from Feral, Paris had no intention of complying.

Mealtimes together were also a torment as Ian corrected Paris's pronunciation and table manners.

'It's beetroot, not bee-roo, Paris, and bu-er has a double "t" in the middle. Spoons go on the right and forks on the left and try not to hold your knife like a pencil.'

Patience's erratic time-keeping often meant Paris was summoned to lay the table in the middle of *EastEnders* or *Holby City*. Asparagus lost any initial charm when you were reproached for taking a knife and fork to it.

Even worse horrors occurred at breakfast: plunging your silver spoon into a cavern of phlegm because Patience had under-boiled your egg. It was also impossible to make conversation if your table manners and pronunciation were constantly criticized.

'Leave him alone,' pleaded Patience. 'You're making the poor boy self-conscious.'

'I'm only doing it so he doesn't get teased when he goes to Bagley.'

So Paris left his food and fell into silence. Plates brought to his room when Ian was away were found untouched and gathering flies.

For the first few days he sat with them in the evening, listening to the Proms, watching programmes on archaeological digs and wrecks being brought up from the bottom of the sea. One evening they borrowed and watched a tape of Brigadier Woodford's excellent programme on Dunkirk.

'Woodford lives near Lily Hamilton and Janna Curtis. Evidently he's an awfully nice chap,' observed Ian.

Paris felt the inevitable stab of anguish on hearing Janna's name. Patience felt reproachful. Both Hengist and Janna had promised to be around and help ease Paris's first weeks at Bagley but neither had been near the place, not even a telephone call.

Paris missed the Wolf Pack and Janna dreadfully. Patience couldn't stem his loneliness. She felt she was looking after some-one's dog who pines constantly for his master. Trying to make Paris feel at home, she showed him family albums of her daughters Sophy and Emerald from when they were first adopted, through schooldays and eventually marriage and grandchildren.

'My life is recorded in social service files, not family albums,' said Paris bleakly.

'Not any more,' said Patience brightly. 'You'll be in our albums.'

Not if your poxy husband has his way, thought Paris.

The stingy bugger, furious that his wife had spent so much money on mobiles, laptops and new clothes for Paris, insisted Patience sew the name tapes on herself, rather than avail herself of a school service that only charged 50p a tape. Paris watched her pricking her big red fingers, straining her eyes as she threaded needles.

'At least you're not called something long like Orlando France-Lynch, or Xavier Campbell-Black. Bianca and Xavier are adopted,' bumbled on Patience.

'I know.'

'Bianca's such a happy little soul,' sighed Patience. 'Mind you'

– she lowered her voice – 'Sophy was always much happier and easier than Emerald. Maybe it's younger children.'

To make Paris feel at home, Patience had asked Emerald down for the weekend – sadly Emerald's charming, larky husband Jonathan was in Berlin and unable to accompany her. And the baby Raymond, who might have broken the ice, was left in London with the nanny. Paris found Emerald as beadily bitchy as she was beautiful. She clearly hated seeing him ensconced in the spare room with Liverpool posters rather than her own paintings on the walls.

The evening was chilly, and Ian, showing off, had ordered Paris to fetch logs and coal for a fire. Paris, engrossed in *Great Expectations*, had told Ian to 'piss off' and been sent to his room.

A furious Emerald had followed him.

'How dare you cheek Daddy after all he's done for you, you horrible brat.'

'You could be horrid as a teenager,' protested Patience when Emerald returned downstairs.

'He's a yob,' said Emerald. 'He comes from the gutter and he'll go back there.'

Paris much preferred Emerald's plump, jolly sister, Sophy, Janna's friend, who was going to replace Vicky at Larks in the autumn term. But feeling Sophy might be spying or trying to heal the breach between himself and Janna, whose letters he had continued to tear up, he shut himself in his room whenever she dropped in.

Lying in the bath Paris watched a snail, which had climbed all the way up the wall of the house to escape the incessant rain, its trail glittering in the morning sun, its horns hitting the buffers of the gutter.

Like me, he thought, from the gutter to the gutter.

Term approached. Paris grew more edgy and withdrawn as Bagley staff, back from their holidays, also popped in to check if their windows and sinks had been repaired and to register if he had two heads.

'You're a saint, Patience, adopting at your and Ian's age, and looking after the horses as well. You look exhausted. I hope you're getting paid. Of course he does have a free place.'

And Paris, who'd perfected the art of eavesdropping in care, lurking on stairs and doorways (which was the only way he could learn if he or his friends were being moved on), heard everything.

Watching Patience struggling across the yard with buckets and haynets, he longed to help, but didn't know how to offer.

He would never have survived without Dora, back from a turbulent week in Spain with her brother Dicky, her mother and one of her mother's admirers, a High Court judge.

'Although he was paying for all of us, Mummy didn't want to sleep with him so she insisted on sharing with me, which was so pants. He barged in one night plastered, forgetting I was there, so I whacked him with a black plastic bull.'

Dora's round face and her plump little legs and arms had caught the sun and, rather than plaiting it, she had pulled back her long, blond hair into a ponytail. She was still a tomboy, but as she rolled up with Cadbury and took up residence on his bed, Paris reflected that she might one day have possibilities.

When he tried on his school suit for the first time, both Patience and Dora gasped as its dark severity set off to perfection his pale marble features and lean elegant body. Paris liked the slate grey overcoat. With shades on, he'd look like Feral's Uncle Harley.

'You look cool,' admitted Dora. She consulted the list. 'Two pairs of slip-on shoes. Try a pair on.'

'What am I going to slip on – a banana skin?'

'Are they comfortable?' asked Patience anxiously.

'Very. Change to have a pair that doesn't pinch or let in water.'

A din in the yard outside suggested a pupil had arrived early to drop off a horse. Patience disappeared to welcome them. Dora, who was cleaning tack, remained on Paris's bed, rather randomly applying saddle soap to Plover's bridle.

That tweed jacket must be a cast-off of Ian's, thought Paris. Christ, it was from Harrods, still with the label on, and those pale blue shirts were really cool. It was as though he was being kitted out by Wardrobe for a new play, but who knew if it would be a tragedy or a comedy?

'Let's see your duvets,' asked Dora.

'Thomas the Tank Engine and Beatrix Potter with Peter Rabbit cock-sucking a carrot,' grumbled Paris. 'I am going to get so much piss taken out of me.'

He was now skimming through the Bagley Code of Conduct with increasing alarm. There were pages of rules about not downloading porn.

'I wanted to download some stuff for Patience about Northcliffe' – Dora went very pink – 'but when I logged into golden retriever, it was so disgusting: women actually weeing on men. I don't understand the human race.'

Paris grinned and read on.

' "No one can leave the school without permission." How do they stop me?'

360

'Give you a detention, make you do hearty things like digging the garden and not watching television. The second time they cancel your leave-outs.'

'That'd be a relief, if Ian doesn't loosen up. "Once a week", he read, "all scholars must participate in an activity that involves serving others in the community."'

'Cosmo helps out at Larkminster Hospital,' said Dora. 'He's shagging one of the nurses.'

'Servicing others,' murmured Paris.

'Best way is to find a nice old biddy, weed her garden, then you get crumpets and cake for tea and to watch *Neighbours*. Feral's working for my aunt, Lily Hamilton, mowing her lawn. They get on really well. Janna fixed it up.'

'The happy highways where I went And cannot come again', thought Paris, wincing at the pain.

' "No hats to be worn inside",' he went on. 'That's crazy.'

'They're talking about woolly hats and baseball caps and you're not allowed jewellery.'

'I'm not taking mine off. "In cases of bullying, both victim and bully get counselling."' Paris shivered. He'd heard a chilling rumour about the Pitbull Club in which older boys arranged fights between new boys and bet large sums of money on which one would first beat the other to a pulp.

'What the hell am I supposed to do in my free time?' he added in outrage. 'It says here, "Any scholar caught supplying drugs or having sex gets sacked."'

'Not always.' Dora went to Paris's basin to wash silver polish off Plover's bit. 'You're sacked if you're caught having sex with a girl. If it's a boy, you'd only get three hours' gardening.'

'How d'they work that out?'

'Boys don't get pregnant; it's meant to act as a detergent,' Dora went on helpfully.

'God, listen to this: "Swearing, spitting, chewing gum all incur five-pound penalties." This is a police state. What about smoking and drinking?'

'Fiver first time you're caught, then they double up.'

'What do they do with the money?'

'Goes to charity. Alex Bruce was hopping last term when brilliant Hengist sent the entire six and a half thousand to Greyhound Rescue. But as that tosser Boffin Brooks keeps saying' – Dora put her hands together sanctimoniously – 'one only has to behave oneself.'

361

59

Determined to familiarize Paris with everything, Dora gave him a map and a tour of the school.

'Here's the gym, here's the music school, here's the sick bay. Most important, here's the tuck shop.'

Hengist had put him in Theo Graham's house, a two-storey neo-Gothic building covered in Virginia creeper, which was north-east of the Mansion with a view over the golf course.

'Here's your bedroom-cum-study,' went on Dora, leading him down a corridor. 'They're known as cells.'

The room was tiny – Paris could touch the walls with both hands – and contained a single bed, a desk for his books and laptop and a small cupboard and shelves for his clothes. The joint window was to be shared with the boy in the next cell.

'Who is it? Oh, Smart, he's a rugger bugger; hope he doesn't want the window open all the time. Next year you'll go upstairs to a bigger room of your own. I'll bring your Liverpool posters over later.

'This is Cosmo's cell.' She opened a door on the way out.

'Why's he got a room twice as big as anyone else?'

'Because he's Cosmo. Once he moves in his stuff it'll look like something out of the Arabian nights.

'This is Anatole's.' Giggling, Dora showed Paris the next cell. 'He's got a map of the world as his duvet cover and always sits on the United States because he loathes the Americans so much.'

And I've got Thomas the Tank Engine and Peter Rabbit, thought Paris. How could Patience?

'Oh look, there's Mummy's car outside,' said Dora as they wandered back to the stables.

Although Anthea Belvedon was wildly jealous of Dora's

addiction to Paris and the Cartwrights, it freed her for assignations of her own. Today she had had lunch with Randal Stancombe, who was so attractive, and who hadn't a high opinion of Paris, who'd evidently tried to rape Jade on the field trip.

Having rolled up to collect Dora, Anthea was looking distastefully at the mess in Patience's kitchen (riding boots on the table, washing up still in the sink) while enquiring how Paris was getting on.

'Really well,' said Patience, terrified Paris might walk in.

'Emerald found him gauche and awfully tricky,' went on Anthea. 'Dora said you were awfully upset Paris never said a word of thanks about his lovely room. The working classes never know how to express gratitude, of course.'

'I wasn't upset,' squeaked Patience furiously. 'It's his right to have a nice room.'

'But such an expense: Sky, tape decks and computers – Dora says you emptied Dixons.'

'Mummy, I did not,' screamed Dora, who was standing appalled in the doorway.

Paris had bolted upstairs. Giving a sob, he hurled his precious Liverpool mug against the wall. Then he smashed a china dog, ripped the poster of Heskey off the wall and tipped over the bookshelf.

Hearing crashes, Patience lumbered upstairs, hammering on the door against which Paris had shoved a big armchair.

'Paris, listen.'

'Fuck off,' hissed Paris, grabbing his laptop.

'Anthea's a complete bitch; honestly, she's jealous because Dora loves being here and adores you. We don't expect you to say thank you for anything. We give you things because we love having you here.'

Oh God, it was coming out all wrong. But Paris put down his laptop.

'It'll be shepherd's pie and just you and me tonight; we can eat it in front of the telly.'

'So my crap table manners won't show. I don't want any supper.'

The window was open. Paris slid down the Virginia creeper and off across the yard.

It was only after ten-thirty, when Ian returned home, that Patience realized Paris had taken the car and just managed to stop Ian ringing the police.

'We'll lose him.'

'Bloody good riddance.'

When they went out looking for him they found the car undamaged behind a haystack.

Paris staggered in, plastered, at midnight.

'Go to bed at once, we'll discuss this in the morning,' shouted Ian.

Alex Bruce often rose at six to train for the school steeplechase and to spy on other masters, particularly Hengist's cronies, Artie Deverell and Theo Graham, who were both gay; Emlyn, who was engaged to Hengist's daughter Oriana (sort of); and, more recently, the brusque, dismissive Ian Cartwright: all the King's men.

Hearing shouts from the Old Coach House, Alex broke his journey, jogging up the path, letting himself into the kitchen.

'Can I help?'

He found Dora Belvedon taking everything in, Patience by the Aga, looking miserable, and Ian, as boiling over with rage as Paris was icy with fury.

They all turned to Alex: not an attractive sight. A fringe like a false eyelash hung damply on his forehead, his drenched yellow T-shirt clung to his hollow chest, sweat parted the black hairs on his skinny thighs.

'Can I help?' he repeated.

'No,' snapped Ian.

'You OK, Paris Alvaston?'

'Fine, just fuck off.'

'Paris,' thundered Ian.

'If you'd started at Bagley, young man,' began Alex, 'you'd be fined five pounds for that. I will not allow foul language. I shall leave your foster parents to deal with you.'

'Lando France-Lynch owed the swear fund eight hundred and fifty pounds last term,' piped up Dora, taking croissants out of the Aga and throwing them on the kitchen table. 'Would you like one, Mr Bruce? You look as though you need feeding up.'

Paris went up to his room and slammed the door so hard all the china and glass crowded on the shelves below rattled and clinked. Ian shut himself away in the drawing room with his con-founded computer.

Later, tipped off no doubt by Alex, Nadine the social worker popped in. 'Gather you're having a problem with Paris, Patience.'

'I'm afraid my husband's working and Paris has just gone out. Would you like a cup of tea?'

'Thank you. You must open up.'

364

'We're fine, we love Paris.'

'Don't expect him to love you. When you foster a teenager at best you can expect to be a mentor or an authority figure.'

Did Nadine ever wear anything else but that funereal black, wondered Patience as she switched on the kettle. Getting a packet of chocolate biscuits out of the cupboard, she noticed mice had eaten a hole in one end, and hastily decanted the biscuits on to a plate.

'I know you want to rescue a young life and Paris longs for a family,' bleated Nadine. 'But your expectations are unrealistic. At an age when most adolescents are trying to escape from their parents and forge their own identity, you're going against the grain and trying to form ties. It's not easy.'

Then, seeing the tears spilling down Patience's tired red face: 'He's going to need a lot of counselling.'

It was nearly midnight. Paris still hadn't come home.

'Thank God he's boarding and'll be out of our hair by tomorrow,' exploded Ian. 'How dare he tell Alex Bruce to fuck off.'

Patience felt ashamed that momentarily she agreed with her husband. She felt bitterly let down that neither Hengist nor Janna had yet made contact. She turned out the horses and collapsed into bed.

It was a very warm, muggy night. Moths flying in through the window kept torching themselves on Ian's halogen lamp. Ian winced but there was no time to rescue them. It was after eleven and he was still wrestling with his infernal computer to provide Alex tomorrow with a list of parents who still hadn't paid up. As the whisky bottle emptied, he grew more clumsy. Scrumpled-up paper shared the threadbare Persian carpet with a snoring Northcliffe.

Ian glanced up at the photograph of himself in the Combined Services rugger team, strong muscular arms folded, hair and moustache still black and glossy, eyes clear and confident. He hadn't met Patience then. She was a good old girl, but she no longer stirred his loins, and tomorrow there would be no sweet Jenny Winters to sort out every problem and flash delightful pink flesh and thong as she bent over to pull out a file. On Radio 3, Rupert's older son, Marcus Campbell-Black, was playing a Mozart piano concerto so exquisitely it brought tears to Ian's eyes – a piece Mozart had evidently knocked off to pay bills. Would he had such talent.

Ian hadn't slept properly for weeks. How could he hold down the job of bursar if he wasn't on the ball? He was sixty-one, not twenty-six. He hadn't touched the pile of messages. Boudicca's Tampax machine was still jammed. But at least he'd reached the end of the list of the defaulting parents and tapped in Commander Wilkins, Spotty's father, who'd paid last year with a hogshead of brandy.

Lord Waterlane, Jack's father, had in the past filled up the school deep freezes with venison and grouse, which made marvellous shepherd's pie. Anatole paid his own fees with roubles, Lubemir's father with a Pissarro which turned out to be a fake.

Having been destitute himself recently, Ian felt so sorry for the parents who worked all hours, forgoing cars and holidays and luxuries, to scrape the fees together, and for the grandparents who often paid them and who'd been equally strapped by pension scandals and the collapse of the stock market.

But he didn't feel sorry for Cosmo's mother, the great diva Dame Hermione, who, in lieu of a year's fees, had offered to give a recital to the school with Cosmo accompanying her.

'Normally, Ian, I never charge less than a hundred thousand pounds for a gig, so Bagley's getting a real bargain.'

Lando's parents seemed to be always broke too. Daisy, his mother, had offered to paint Sally Brett-Taylor for free last year. Nor did Amber and Junior's parents, both on high salaries, ever seem to have any money.

Anthea Belvedon, the prettiest little thing, played every trick in the book to avoid forking out since she was widowed two years ago. He'd have to summon her next week. He had a special Paisley emerald-green silk handkerchief, faintly flavoured with lavender, to mop up pretty mothers' tears. What a shame Mrs Walton had shacked up with Randal Stancombe, who'd paid Milly's fees this term. Comforting Mrs Walton had been an even more exquisite pleasure than glimpsing Jenny Winters's thong.

Bagley, overall, was in great financial shape. Since the geography field trip, the waiting list had doubled, as eager off-spring pestered their parents to send them to such a fun palace. Hengist, routing the Education Secretary on *Question Time* last week, had brought another flood of applications. The school was booked solid till 2012. If only Hengist were as good at picking staff. How dare Alex Bruce steal Jenny Winters?

Thank God for that. Ian switched off the computer. But as he emptied the last drop of whisky into a mug entitled Master of the House, he noticed an envelope on the floor. Inside was a cheque signed by Boffin Brooks's frightful father Gordon for five thousand pounds. (Two thousand less than normal because of

Boffin's scholarship.) Gordon always paid at the last moment to avoid both a two per cent penalty and losing interest.

Like most first-generation public-school parents, Sir Gordon Brooks clamoured for his kilo of flesh and would have gone berserk and straight to his good friend Alex Bruce if he'd been chased for non-payment, or if Ian had forgotten to put CBE (for services to export) on the receipt. Why didn't someone export Gordon?

Ian mopped his brow with his shirtsleeve in relief. But when he switched on the computer to delete Gordon's name, he couldn't find the file.

Drenched in sweat, heart pounding, blood swept into his brain in a tidal wave, trying to force its way out. Lightning jagged before his eyes. He was going to have a stroke. Nothing. He'd deleted the fucking thing – two whole days' work with his slow typing. He was far too drunk to type it out again.

'I can't go on.' Ian's head crashed into his sweating hands. He'd get fired; they'd be destitute again. Snoring Northcliffe and Patience's horses would have to go.

He jumped, hearing a crash and rattle downstairs, and shoved the empty whisky bottle under the half-completed *Times* crossword. Hearing a step and a thump of a tail, he swung round. Paris trying to creep in had sent a walking stick flying.

'Where the hell have you been?'

The boy looked whiter than ever – a ghost postillion struck by lightning, haunting the Old Coach House.

'For a walk.'

'Too bloody late.'

Seeing despair rather than rage in Ian's bloodshot eyes, however, Paris asked if he were OK.

'No, I'm not, just wiped a bloody file,' mumbled Ian. 'Need it for Alex Bruce first thing.'

He banged his fist on the table. Everything jumped: the mug tipping over, spilling the last of the whisky on his written notes; *Times* crossword page fluttering down to reveal the empty bottle.

'I can't go on.' Picking up the keyboard, Ian was about to smash it.

Paris, rather encouraged by such loss of control, leapt forward. 'Cool it, for fuck's sake. Get up.' He tugged the keyboard from Ian. 'Lemme have a go.'

Sliding into Ian's seat, he went into MS-DOS and typed in the command to bring up the list of files.

'What's the name of the one you lost?'

' "Unpaid fees 2002 autumn".' Ian slumped against the wall. He didn't dare to hope. Oh, please God.

A blond moth fluttered on a suicide mission towards the lamp. Cupping his hands, Paris caught it. He got up and shoved it into the honeysuckle outside, before shutting the window. Returning to Ian's chair, he scrolled down.

'Reports, expulsions, health, recreations, staff performance, that looks in-eresting – or, as you would say, "intr'sting".' His eyes slid towards Ian. ' "Unpaid fees 2002 autumn." Got it.'

Ian gave a gasp of relief:

'Are you sure?'

'Quite,' said Paris, reinstating the file back on the computer in its original format. 'Do you need to change anything?' Then, scrolling down the list: 'There's that bitch Anthea Belvedon, Campbell-Black, Harefield, Lloyd-Foxe, Waterlane, always the rich buggers that don't pay up.'

'You shouldn't be reading that, it's confidential.'

'I have the shortest memory.'

'Can you delete Gordon Brooks, Boffin's father? He's paid.'

As Paris found the name, highlighted it and hit the delete button, his fingers made an even more exquisite sound than Marcus Campbell-Black.

'Let's print it out,' suggested Ian. 'I can add latecomers in biro. Thank God, Paris, you've saved my life, probably my job.'

Slumped on a moth-eaten sofa covered in a tartan rug, Ian looked utterly exhausted, his eyes red hollows, his cheeks and nose a maze of purple veins, the lines round his mouth like cracks in dry paths.

'Would you like a nightcap?' he asked, desperate for one himself.

Paris grinned. How could a face so shuttered and cold one moment be so enchantingly warm, almost loving, the next?

'Thought caps weren't allowed to be worn indoors at Bagley.'

Getting the joke, Ian laughed.

'All those rules must seem a bit alarming. Have to have that jewellery off, I'm afraid. Wear it when you come back here for leave-outs.'

Ian rose unsteadily and wandered to the much depleted drinks cupboard, pouring a brandy and ginger for Paris and the rest of the brandy for himself, taking a great gulp.

'Thank you, Paris, so much.' Then, seeing the boy's eyes straying towards the crossword: 'Finish it if you like. Got stuck on a Tennyson quote. "Heavily hangs the broad . . .", nine letters, "over its grave in' the earth so chilly." '

'Sunflower,' murmured Paris.

'Of course, well done. "Heavily hangs the hollyhock, Heavily hangs the tiger-lily." Beautiful poem.'

Paris smirked. 'Any time, Ian. And if you have trouble with that computer, ring me or text me on my mobile and I'll whiz out of chemistry and sort it.'

'I suppose those wretched mobiles have their uses,' conceded Ian. 'Sorry, the last few weeks have been rough. All a bit nervous. Promise to telephone or pop into my office if there're any problems.'

'Thank you,' said Paris, feeling much happier.

When Ian looked at his computer next morning, Paris had written, with some scarlet nail polish which Emerald had left in the bathroom, on the frame of the computer screen: 'To remind you to save it.'

60

Paris's first weeks at Bagley were hell. At Larks he'd bunked off any lesson he disliked and been free after three-thirty. Now he was flat out from the moment the bell fractured his skull at six-forty-five until lights out at ten, kept endlessly busy racing from chapel to lessons to games to prep and losing his way despite Dora's map. Used to being easily the cleverest pupil at Larks, he found himself woefully behind in most subjects and, with smaller classes, there was nowhere to hide. Nor had he dreamt rugby would be so brutal, but with Anatole and Lubemir in the scrum, he couldn't expect much else.

His rarity appeal had also gone. An arctic fox occasionally peeping out of the frozen tundra loses his mystery when he's caged in the zoo. Stripped of his lucky jewellery, disfigured by a savaging from the school barber and by his first spots ever (from existing on chocolate, rather than Patience's cooking), he had never felt less attractive. Ian's assault on his pronunciation and table manners had made him miserably self-conscious both in class and at mealtimes.

His first evening was a nightmare, with so many pupils rolling up in flash cars or helicopters with their glamorous parents yelling about mooring the yacht off Sardinia, or stalking in Scotland, or villas in Dubai where the jet-skiing had been out of this world.

Paris nearly died of embarrassment when Patience insisted on humping his stuff across the school into Theo's house, putting Thomas the Tank Engine on his duvet and braying 'hello' to all the other pupils.

'Theo's terrified of parents,' she whispered. 'Probably won't appear for hours. Now let's put up your posters.'

'I'm fine,' hissed Paris.

'Just want to settle you in. Where shall I put this fruit cake?'

'I'll sort it,' Paris almost shrieked. 'I'm OK, just go.'

The moment she left, he was frantically stripping off the duvet cover when his next-door neighbour, Smart, who already had a ginger moustache above his broad grin, wandered in, shouting, 'I'm Smart. Thomas the Tank Engine, fantastic, wish I'd thought of that. Where's the Fat Controller?'

So Paris left it on, and put up a poster of Tennyson between Michael Owen and Emile Heskey.

'Coming to supper?' asked Smart.

Paris wasn't hungry, but he needed an ally. In the dining room, the din was hideous, as they all yakked in their Sloaney way about polo in Sotogrande and the sailing lessons Daddy'd organized in Rock, or chatted to new conquests on their mobiles, or flagged up photographs of them. Paris noticed Xav, sitting alone, sullen and miserable, and felt a louse for avoiding his eye. He also realized he'd made enemies on the field trip. He'd never texted Jade or Amber after shagging them – not having a mobile at the time was no excuse. Boffin, twitchy at the prospect of being usurped by a cleverer boy, was reading the *New Scientist*. Cosmo was smiling his evil smile.

'Hengist really must install a runway, it takes such ages by chopper,' said a familiar bitchy voice.

It was Jade Stancombe, flaunting a butterscotch tan and a ravishing new short tortoiseshell-streaked haircut. Nicky Clarke had repaired the ravages of the sawn-off plait with something far more becoming to Jade's thin, predatory face. Mobile glued to her ear, chatting to some new admirer, she swung round, clocked Cosmo, exchanged a long eye-meet and, walking over, bent down and French kissed him for thirty seconds, sending a shiver through the room. Jade and Cosmo were an item again.

'Love your hair, Jade,' chorused everyone sycophantically.

'Brings out the latent homosexual in all of us,' murmured Cosmo. 'You obviously haven't been abused by the school barber, like our friend Paris.'

Everyone turned round and looked at Paris, who, not giving them time to hail or reject him, chucked down his napkin and, food untouched, stalked out.

'Don't go,' called Amber.

Resisting a temptation to bolt back to the Old Coach House, Paris returned to Theo's house where he found some post on his bed.

Seeing Janna's writing on a dove-grey envelope, Paris dropped it in the bin. Beneath was a parcel from Cosmo, containing a copy

371

of *Tom Brown's Schooldays*. Inside Cosmo had written 'À bientôt, Flashman'.

Finally there was a letter from Sally Brett-Taylor. 'Good luck. Come and have tea with us very soon. Hope your years at Bagley are happy and rewarding.'

Like fuck, thought Paris.

' "The years like great black oxen tread the world," ' he declaimed. ' "And I am broken by their passing feet." '

'At this moment, you can't envisage a day let alone a week at Bagley being tolerable,' said a flat, rasping, mocking voice. 'I'm sorry I wasn't here to welcome you. I'm allergic to parents.'

'Lucky I don't have any.'

'Come and have a drink. Who are you next to? Oh, Smart. A misnomer actually. But he's good-hearted and an excellent rugger player.'

Months spent every summer in Greece and Italy poring over relics and ruins with never a drop of suntan oil had browned and creased Theo Graham's bald head and face like a conker soaked in vinegar. He had jug ears, jagged teeth and, like many school-masters, looked older than his sixty years, but his eyes were kind, shrewd and lively.

'This is my lair,' he said, leading Paris into his study, which reeked worse than a public bar of fags and booze, but which was almost entirely lined with literature, history and philosophy in the original Greek and Latin: ancient books with leather binding or faded dilapidated jackets. As well as a huge desk and an upright piano, the room was densely populated with busts of emperors and great thinkers and sculptures of gods, goddesses, heroes, nymphs, centaurs and caryatids, all poised to embark on some splendid orgy after dark. Paris's eyes were on stalks.

'I hear you're interested in learning Latin and Greek,' said Theo, rootling around under the papers on the desk to find a corkscrew. 'Well, you've come from the Old Coach House to an old coach's house,' and he smiled with great affection.

Adding to the chaos, a huge fluffy marmalade cat padded across the room and landed on the desk, sending half the contents flying.

'At least he's unearthed the corkscrew.' Theo pounced on it. 'His name is Hindsight, so we can all benefit from him.'

Having poured a large glass of red for Paris and an even larger whisky for himself, Theo settled a thunderously purring Hindsight on his knee and asked Paris what other subjects he was intending to take for GCSE. When Paris reeled off English, English lit., French, Spanish, history, geography, drama, business studies, science and maths, Theo heaved a sigh of relief.

'Thank God, none of those new subjects like leisure and tourism. How could one prefer a hotel to Homer?'

Paris took a slug of red and thought for a minute, then said, 'If I could have a night in the bridal suite with Bianca Campbell-Black, sir, I might prefer a hotel, but the *Iliad*'s one of the best books I've ever read.'

'Good,' said Theo happily, 'we should get along.'

Hengist had given a lot of thought to the right house for Paris. Biffo would have got drunk and probably pounced on him. The Bruces would have killed him with petty regulations and counselling. Artie Deverell, gentle, handsome, clever, tolerant, charming, adored by pupils and parents (particularly the latter, who invited him to stay in their villas in Tuscany and Provence for weeks on end), would have been ideal. But Deverell's was always hopelessly over-subscribed, which Graham's never was.

Theo, crotchety, very shy, dreadful with parents and liable to take his hearing aid out on Speech Day, had a house with only a dozen boys. One to whom he was utterly devoted was Cosmo, who returned this devotion. Cosmo was clever and made Theo laugh. As one of the few people who could control Cosmo, Theo also believed that with parents like Dame Hermione and the evil, late Roberto Rannaldini, the boy was entitled to be a monster. Theo also took out his hearing aid when Cosmo and the Cosmonaughties were giving tongue.

If Cosmo started bullying Paris, deduced Hengist, Theo would pick up on it.

Theo drove Alex Bruce crackers calling his Chinese pupils 'Chinks', his Russians 'Little Commies' and banging any child if they were being particularly stupid on the head with an atlas of the ancient world.

Unlike Ian Cartwright he had refused to succumb to Alex's bullying and chucked his first laptop in the lake, continuing to tap away with two fingers on an ancient manual typewriter until Cosmo, terrified the only master who understood him would be eased out, taught him to use a computer.

Theo incurred disapproval because he smoked and drank too much.

'Why am I late?' he would ask his classes.

'Because you drank too much last night, sir,' they would chorus.

A typical holiday in the past would have been riding round Umbria on a donkey reading Plato's *Republic*. Now he took gentler vacations, occasionally grumbling about a bad back. In fact only he knew he had an inoperable tumour in his spine, which was why he drank so much: to ease the pain.

Apart from translating the plays of Euripides and now embarking on those of Sophocles, Theo looked after the classical library and school museum and was in charge of the archives, which chronicled the achievements of illustrious former pupils. Alex Bruce was desperate to scrap the museum and the library and replace them with an IT suite.

'Tradition is the enemy of progress,' he was fond of saying.

Alex was driven demented by Theo, but he was powerless to fire him because Theo got even the dimmest child through GCSE and, because of this and his wonderfully entertaining teaching, his lessons were always crowded out.

One of Bagley's favourite pastimes was watching Artie Deverell and Theo argue. For the duration of an entire cricket match they had been observed marching up and down the boundary waving their arms and shouting over whether Catullus had really been wiped out by love when he wrote his poems or merely portraying someone thus afflicted.

David Hawkley, headmaster of Fleetley, another great classical scholar, had dedicated his translation of Catullus to Theo and every Christmas sent him a litre of malt whisky. This irritated Hengist who longed to be admired by David Hawkley.

'Extraordinary, these new GCSEs,' Theo was now complaining to Paris. 'I gather they're thinking of linking RE and PE as one subject. The mind boggles until one remembers all those old jokes about when the high jump was first invented.'

'When was it?'

'When Jesus cleared the temple.'

Paris laughed.

'Or the first cricket match,' went on Theo, 'when Jesus stood up before the eleven and was bold – or bowled. Interesting that they're always described as schoolboy jokes, never schoolgirl.'

'If you'd been on a geography field trip with Joan Johnson, you'd understand,' said Paris.

At the same time that first evening as Paris was, to his amazement, really enjoying having a drink with Theo, Anthea Belvedon was delivering her son Dicky back to Alex Bruce's house. Here she sought out Poppet Bruce: 'Have you a mo?'

'Of course, Anthea. One of the reasons I'm nicknamed "Poppet" is because people are always "popping in" on me.' Poppet gave a soppy smile.

'My late husband nicknamed me "Hopey",' countered Anthea, 'because I always give people hope.'

After a minute on the importance of reminding Dicky to use his foot-rot cream because he'd infected Anthea's High Court judge on holiday, Anthea moved briskly on to Paris and the riches the Cartwrights had heaped on him:

'Would that I could do the same for my Dora and Dicky.'

'But I thought the Cartwrights were broke,' mused Poppet. 'I hope they're not spending Bagley money.'

'So do I.' Anthea sighed gustily. 'Surely a free place does not mean a free-for-all?'

'I'll have a discreet word with Alex.'

'You won't mention my name.'

'We haven't spoken,' said Poppet.

The upshot twenty-four hours later was a fired-up Patience barging into Alex's office brandishing bills and cheque stubs.

'How dare you accuse Ian of cooking the books? It's actionable. He's the most honest man in the world. He's been flat out through the summer holidays and we've given up our three-week holiday in France this year so we can be home to give Paris a proper start. You and your wife can bloody well apologize to him.'

'We do feel you're in danger of spoiling Paris Alvaston,' spluttered a discomfited Alex. 'His behaviour so far has been very challenging . . .'

Ian, in turn, was later apoplectic with Patience.

'How could you have shouted at Alex? I could have given him a perfectly reasonable explanation. Of course it looks odd you squandering so much on Paris. He could easily have worn a second-hand suit. How can I ask for a rise now?'

Dora, who suspected her mother of sneaking, had also spent too much money on Paris. She must sell some more stories.

Flipping through the papers in the library to assess her market on the first Saturday of term, she came across a piece about parents of truants being given gaol sentences.

If she bunked off for a week, would her utterly bloody mother go to prison? Although her awful old High Court judge boyfriend would probably get her off.

Dispirited, and unable to keep away, Dora wandered off to see Paris. A warm west wind was chasing chestnut leaves round the quad; green spiky husks were opening to drop gleaming brown conkers; the shaggy pelt of Virginia creeper flung round the Gothic turrets of Theo Graham's house was turning crimson.

She found Paris pretending to tackle a distressing amount of homework while listening to Liverpool against Everton on Radio Five, and expressing fury that he'd officially been given Xavier as a 'buddy' to show him the ropes. Talk about linking two social misfits.

Lucky Xav, thought Dora wistfully, but out loud said:

'It won't be so bad, you needn't see much of him after the first week and he might invite you to Penscombe. It's gorgeous. Fabulous horses and Rupert and Taggie are really lovely.'

'And Bianca's even lovelier,' said Paris bitchily. 'Only reason to brown-nose her lousy brother is to get a crack at her.'

Dora couldn't speak for the hurt, as though a huge wasp had plunged its sting deep into her heart, flooding poison through her veins. She knew Paris didn't adore her as she adored him, but he'd never mentioned Bianca, so she'd assumed he wasn't interested.

Seeing her stricken face, her blue eyes widening in bewilderment, Paris felt as though he'd kicked a puppy.

'Oh fuck off,' he snapped. 'You're getting on my tits.'

But as Dora stumbled out, tripping over a pile of books, Paris was livid with himself. He liked Xav as well. Why did he have this urge to hurt and destroy people who were kind to him? He longed to explain to Patience, Dora, even Xav how sad and lonely he was and how sadness came out as anger, but the less you gave people the less they had to hurt you with.

Even Liverpool winning in the dying moments couldn't lift his spirits. On the hall table he found a parcel and a card saying: 'Dear Paris, good luck. Sorry this is late. Love Dora'.

Inside was a really cool Black Watch tartan duvet cover and two pillowcases.

Switching on his mobile, he dialled Dora's number.

'The person you are dialling knows you are calling,' said the message, 'and doesn't give a fuck.'

Meanwhile, on her way out, Dora passed Cosmo's king-sized cell. Glancing in, she saw it now accommodated a baby grand and, on the walls, a Picasso Blue Clown, oriental rugs, an antique gilt mirror and portraits of Cosmo's heroes: the Marquis de Sade, Wagner, Byron and his father, the late Roberto Rannaldini. On the king-sized bed covered with fur rugs lay a dark blue cushion embroidered with the words: 'It's hard to be humble and go to Bagley.'

Seated at the piano, Cosmo was playing and singing Mahler Lieder in a deep, hypnotic baritone of exceptional beauty. He was sporting a black overcoat with an astrakhan collar made famous by his late father, and which much became his night-dark eyes and sallow features.

Hearing a sob, he glanced round to find Dora's sweet plump face dissolving in misery.

'Dora, darling.' Pulling her inside, he shut the door and patted the bed.

'It's very cruel to have fur rugs.'

'I am very cruel. Now, whatever's the matter?' Cosmo stroked her blond hair and retied the blue ribbon on one of her plaits.

'I loathe my mother, I'm sure she shopped the Cartwrights to Poppet, implying they'd been using Bagley money kitting out Paris, whereas Patience has paid for everything out of some money her aunt left her.'

'Patience Carthorse,' drawled Cosmo. 'She ought to be pulling beer barrels round London.'

'She's lovely.'

'Not the word I had in mind. You must be blind and deaf.' Cosmo handed Dora a Bacardi and Coke from his fridge and relit his spliff. 'What else is the matter?'

'Paris is in love with Bianca.'

'And the rest.'

'He told me to fuck off. I gave him a new duvet cover today and earlier a video of *Macbeth*.'

'Young Alvaston needs sorting out,' said Cosmo thoughtfully. He had been reading in the *Observer* that Cherie Blair was offering to defend school bullies in court. What an admirable woman. His mission this term was to make Paris Alvaston's life hell and with Xav as his buddy . . . what an opportunity to kick the shit out of both of them.

It was also high time he bedded Vicky Fairchild.

61

Vicky was not enjoying her first term at Bagley. The workload was appalling and there was no Sam Spink to fight her corner. After cajoling the lovely flat and bathroom out of Ian Cartwright, her charm objective wasn't working as well as she'd hoped. So many of the masters were gay or married and tied up with families. Piers, the head of her department, was rumoured to be having an affair with Rufus's wife, Sheena. Vicky and Jason had seen through each other long ago. Emlyn, easily the most attractive, and with a strange relationship with Oriana from which Vicky was sure he could be detached, was polite but cool, which exhausted the best heterosexual bachelors.

Hengist and Sally were kind, but Olympian and remote, like Jupiter and Juno, and hadn't invited her to a single dinner party.

There were enough boys in the school in love with her and girls, madly admiring, to feed her ego, but she wanted a husband or a steady partner to love and cherish.

Vicky found her thoughts straying rather too often to Cosmo Rannaldini, sexy little beast, with whom she had gone much too far on the field trip. Now he sat, staring at her, a wicked smile snaking round his full lips, unnerving her as she tried to initiate him and the rest of Middle Five B into *The Pardoner's Tale*. Anatole and Lubemir, meanwhile, were playing poker. Milly was painting her nails; Amber was writing to one of her numerous boyfriends; the Chinless Wanderers were studying the *Sun*, deciding which horses to back, except for Lando, lazy great beast, who was asleep.

'Can you tell me, Lando, what Chaucer is trying to say here?' she asked sharply.

Lando opened an eye. 'Can you tell me who the fuck Chaucer is?'

The class fell about.

'Don't use horrible language, Lando, that's another fiver for the swear box. And don't be so obtuse.'

Lando stretched out a large polo-stick-calloused hand for the Collins dictionary. 'What does "obtuse" mean?'

Vicky's lips tightened. She found the Middle Fifths very difficult and not nearly admiring enough – particularly Paris, who, as they had both come from Larks, should have supported her. His stroppy behaviour was becoming the talk of the staffroom with Hengist showing a curious reluctance to put the boot in.

Vicky showed no such reluctance when in the Middle Fifths' next English lesson, three days later, she asked them to describe a happy family experience in the holidays, using simile, metaphor, oxymoron and personification.

'Please, Miss Fairchild,' whispered Milly, 'Paris doesn't have a family.'

'Of course he does. He has the bursar and his wife, his new foster family,' said Vicky, so that everyone looked at Paris. 'You could write a most interesting essay on adjusting to your new placement, Paris, and how Bagley compares with Larks.'

' "Why, this is hell, nor am I out of it",' spat Paris.

'My mother,' piped up Amber, 'says placement is the most difficult part of a dinner party. She always forgets to do a seating plan, and is pissed by the time we get into the dining room. Why doesn't one learn important things like that in maths?'

'I hardly think Biffo'd be an expert,' said Milly. 'It's even worse if you're a single woman. If my mother asks Randal to dinner, is it coming on too strong to put him at the head of the table, or will he be miffed he's not on her right?'

'Don't be silly, Milly,' exploded Vicky.

'Silly Milly,' echoed Jade, sticking her tongue out at Milly.

'Write it as a play, Paris,' suggested Vicky, 'then we could all take parts.'

'Or as a poem,' quipped Cosmo. 'Living with the bursar could not be worser.'

'Shut it,' hissed Paris.

'Paris in fact is quite a poet,' went on Cosmo, dramatically whipping out a rainbow-coloured notebook. 'Listen to this epic about a snail,' which he proceeded to declaim in a camp Cockney accent:

' "O Snile, your gli-ering trile, leads from the gu-er up to anuvver gu-er on which to bang your 'orns." '

As Paris gave a howl of rage, uneasy laughter broke out round the room.

Milly put a hand on Paris's arm. 'Ignore him.'

'Here's another little gem,' continued Cosmo, turning the page, knowing instinctively that Vicky didn't like Paris. 'Here's what our new boy thinks of Bagley:

> 'Death is like a boarding school
> From which you never come home
> Where your name is carved on a gravestone
> Rather than sewn inside your clothes.'

'Doesn't scan,' complained Boffin.

'You bastard,' whispered Paris, turning on Cosmo.

'I think it's rather good,' said Primrose Duddon with a shiver.

'I think it's very good,' came a voice from the back of the class.

It was Piers Fleming, head of English, who'd dropped in to listen to Vicky's class. 'May I?' He grabbed the rainbow-covered notebook and read both the snail poem and the death poem again, but in a normal and beautiful voice.

'The second one,' he went on, 'reminds me of Robert Frost describing a disused graveyard:

> 'The verses in it say and say:
> "The ones who living come today
> To read the stones and go away
> Tomorrow dead will come to stay."

'It has the same icy hand on the heart. I'm going to put forward your poems for the school anthology,' he told Paris. 'We publish it every three years. You're probably too modest to submit your own stuff, so thank you, Cosmo, so much, for drawing it to my attention.'

Cosmo was hopping.

As the bell went and the Middle Fifths packed up, Piers very kindly suggested to Vicky she might fare better with one of the less demanding sets. If Piers and Vicky had seen the Middle Fifths at their next lesson, however, they might have changed their opinion, as the entire set listened enraptured to Theo Graham introducing some of their GCSE Latin texts.

'Poets were like rock stars around the first century AD,' he was now telling them as, hip hitched on to the side of a desk, he puffed away on a forbidden cigarette. 'Just as you lot might enliven an evening with a video or a takeaway or by hiring a stripagram for a party, the Romans sent out for a slave to read poetry.

'Some poets like Martial, who was charming and very witty, recited their own poems at dinner parties, but most of them were read by slaves. You didn't make money as a poet in those days, but people could sponsor you. Horace was earlier, of course, but he was such a good poet – we'll be looking at his stuff in a minute – that a rich Etruscan gave him a farm and a huge estate.'

'Just think if he'd liked your poems, Paris,' giggled Amber. Paris grinned and gave her a middle finger.

Lighting one cigarette from another, Theo shuffled down the row and lifted a lock of Amber's blond hair.

'You'd have been in trouble as a slave, miss, because Italians liked blondes, so lots of society ladies dyed their hair blond, and when it fell out, they shaved the heads of the blonde slaves and used the hair as a wig.

'That's probably why Pyrrha in our first poem was considered such a beauty, Horace describes her as braiding her flaxen locks.'

'Paris would have cleaned up as a poet *and* a blond,' said Milly.

Feeling much happier, Paris came out of Theo's class slap into Poppet Bruce, who was always nagging him to drop in on her and Alex and pour out his soul. Now she wanted him to go public.

'Could you address our Talks Society next week? If a talk is too daunting, I could always interview you.' Paris raised a pale eyebrow. 'It would be such a broadening experience for our group to hear your views on your foster placement and being in care.'

The lad was certainly good-looking, decided Poppet, and the same age as their daughter, Charisma. She was very touched when Paris put a hand in his pocket and handed her a tenner.

'How kind, but you don't have to pay to join our little society.'

'No, it's for the two fines I'm about to get,' said Paris icily. 'You just want me to slag off Patience and Ian, to give you and Mr Fussy ammunition against them. So fuck off.' Then he spat at her feet, just falling short of her grubby sandalled toenails.

Poppet didn't miss a beat.

'I know you're hurting, Paris, and don't really mean it.'

'Hurt is a transitive verb,' snapped Paris, 'and I do.'

Despite half the staff competing to make him tell them if anything was wrong, Paris felt it was as weak to admit terror as to display love and dependency. And so he waited for Cosmo. Whether it was a bomb in the tube or on Big Ben, the terrorists would strike sooner or later. He had already found a rubber snake in his bed and still kept hearing rumours about the notorious Pitbull Club.

* * *

It was after midnight on the second Saturday of term. Theo, after downing a bottle of whisky in his room, had passed out, his snores ripping open the night. Smart, in the next-door cell, had long since wanked himself to sleep over a photograph of Jade Stancombe. Paris could hear the Virginia creeper flapping limp hands against the window, floorboards creaking, Tarquin's ravishing strides, doors softly opening and closing. Just like Oaktree Court. Starting to shake, already drenched in sweat, he pulled Thomas the Tank Engine over his head. The chattering of his teeth would wake the dead.

Suddenly the duvet was wrenched off him and a torch brighter than the full moon shoved in his face.

'Get up, pretty boy.'

'Fuck off.'

'Get up,' repeated the voice.

In the dim light, he could make out a hooded figure, then groaned as the torch was rammed into his ribs.

'You're invited to the Pitbull Club. Move it.'

Paris froze, nearly shitting himself, heart crashing.

'Leave me alone,' he croaked, kicking out at another hooded figure that appeared on the right.

'Come on, Gay Paree.' He knew that voice. Next moment its owner had grabbed his hair, tugging him viciously to his feet.

'New boy's initiation. Let's see how brave you are,' mocked another slighter figure hovering behind.

The figure on the left jabbed him with the torch again. Paris moaned, then, reaching behind him, grabbed the knife from under his pillow. Leaping at the first figure, catching him off balance, pulling him against his own body, clamping him with his left hand, he put the knife against his throat.

The torch crashed to the floor.

The muscular, almost square body, left him in no doubt about the identity of the tormentor.

'Get out, unless you want your throat cut, Albanian pig.'

'Put him down,' ordered the larger of the figures on the right, who had a deep voice, and was moving in. Paris caught a waft of brandy.

'Don't come anywhere near me,' he spat, then, running the blade down Lubemir's cheek, split it open, drawing blood. 'I'm not just shaving him. Next time I'll cut deeper.' Kneeing Lubemir in the kidneys, he sent him crashing to the floor.

'Get him,' said the smaller figure on the right – with less conviction as, in the light from the fallen torch, Paris approached with knife poised.

'You don't scare me,' snarled Paris. 'I'll cut up the lot of you, and you'll lose more than your plait this time, Miss Stancombe.'

Jade gave a gasp, and fled, followed by Lubemir and Anatole.

Down in the cellar, the leader of the pack in his astrakhan coat was admiring his reflection as he snorted coke from a framed mirror lying on an ancient desk. His eyes were glittering but no less cruel.

Other figures stood round self-consciously, rather apprehensively, drinking from bottles or smoking.

Millbank, a new boy in blue-striped pyjamas, almost fainting in terror, was loosely tied to a chair. He had bitten his lip through trying not to cry. Despite the heat from the boilers, he shivered uncontrollably.

'Where's Paris?' snapped Cosmo.

'Won't come,' said Anatole.

'How pathetic is that. Three against one.'

'I'm not risking it,' said Lubemir, removing a blood-saturated handkerchief from his slashed cheek. 'He knows who we all are.'

'How?' Cosmo was hoovering up every last speck of cocaine.

'He listen,' said Anatole. 'How you think he's such a good mimic?'

'I'm going back to Boudicca,' bleated Jade. 'It was bloody scary.'

Cosmo grabbed her arm. 'You're not going anywhere.' Then: 'You can bugger off,' he told Millbank. 'You got off lightly, but don't breathe a word' – he jerked his head at Lubemir, who held the cigarette he'd just lit to Millbank's jumping cheek – 'or we'll really sort you out. Understand?'

'Yes,' sobbed Millbank and fled.

Cosmo turned to the others.

'Are you honestly telling me three of you couldn't sort out that etiolated wimp?'

'He pulled a knife on us,' protested Lubemir.

'Oh dear,' sighed Cosmo, 'I do hope he didn't hold it like a pencil.'

62

Alex Bruce was incensed when Hengist gave any pupil who applied permission to go on the Countryside March. Far too many of the applicants had retakes the next day and would be exhausted and probably hungover.

'And is championing blood sports really part of our Bagley ethos?' asked Alex querulously.

'Damn right it is,' snapped Hengist. 'Bagley Beagles have been going for nearly a hundred years and' – he waved a hand in the direction of Badger's Retreat – 'isn't that country worth saving?'

Patience asked Paris if he'd like to join her on the march.

'Rupert Campbell-Black, Ricky France-Lynch and Billy Lloyd-Foxe are all going. Rupert's taking his dogs. It should be a fun day out.'

Paris replied coldly that he didn't approve of blood sports.

'Alex and Poppet don't either,' said Patience with rare edge. 'It's not just blood sports, it's the whole tapestry and livelihood of the countryside, which this Government is hell-bent on destroying, totally undermining the poor farmers. If hunting goes, thousands of people will lose their jobs, and thousands and thousands more horses and hounds will be put down. People who make such a fuss about killing foxes don't give a stuff about the horrors of factory farming or the dreadful transport of live animals.' Realizing she was shouting, Patience stopped in embarrassment.

'Still bloody cruel.' Paris stalked towards the door. 'Is Ian going?'

'No, he's dining with a supplier.'

'I'll dogsit,' said Paris as a peace offering.

Later he kicked himself when Dora told him that Xav and Bianca were also going, adding:

'Bianca's such an applause junkie, she can't resist crowds and photographers.'

Deliverance seemed at hand when Xav asked Paris to join them. Alas, social services stepped in. Paris couldn't join their party because Rupert hadn't been cleared by the Criminal Records Bureau.

'I can't imagine he ever would be,' said Alex nastily.

Boffin Brooks rose at six most mornings ostensibly to conjugate Latin verbs but in reality to spy on his housemates. Early on the Saturday before the Countryside March, he caught Xav in bed smoking a spliff and reading a porn mag. Noting the ecstasy with which Xav was inhaling, like a chief drawing on a peace pipe, Boffin launched into a sermon in his nasal whine:

'People smoke to look cool, Xavier, or because they're forced to by bullies or peer pressure.'

Boffin's spectacles enlarged his bulging eyes. Shaving his meagre ginger stubble, he had deheaded several spots, reducing his face to an erupting volcanic landscape. His full red lips were salivating at the prospect of reading that disgusting porn mag before he handed it over to Alex.

'I might be fractionally more lenient, Xavier, if you told me who sold you the stuff.'

'I'm not grassing up anyone, so piss off.' Inhaling deeply, Xav blew smoke rings at Boffin.

Boffin looked pained.

'It must be in your blood, Xavier. Colombia not only trains and supports the IRA and many other forms of terrorism, but also destroys billions of lives as the drug centre of the world.'

'Nice place for a weekend break.'

'Only place you won't be this weekend is the Countryside March. My only recourse is to report you to Mr Bruce,' at which point Xav launched himself at Boffin.

'You little idiot,' Hengist yelled at Xavier later in the morning. 'I know how you wanted to go on that march. Why on earth did you screw up? Drugs are not allowed and that's the second time Boffin's teeth have been knocked out in a year. How can I do anything but gate you? Your father will be devastated.'

My father couldn't give a stuff, thought Xav despairingly. He'll just regard it as another cock-up on my part.

* * *

My first leave-out and no one to look after me – thank God, thought Paris as Patience and Ian left the house.

He brushed Northcliffe, partly from self-interest to keep the dog's pale gold hair off his clothes; then he lit a fag and, pouring himself a glass of red, collapsed on the sofa in front of the television, where he was shortly joined by Northcliffe, who was not allowed up when Ian was around. Liverpool had won yesterday, so Paris flicked over to mock the Countryside March for a second and stayed to pray.

'There's Dora,' he shouted in excitement, shoving Northcliffe's face towards the screen as, dressed in jodhpurs and a hacking jacket, Dora marched proudly past chattering to Junior and the Hon. Jack, who were blatantly smoking and shouting to pretty girls among the mass of spectators lining the route.

They were followed by Isa Lovell, former champion jockey, now Rupert Campbell-Black's trainer, with his swarthy gypsy face, and by Rupert Campbell-Black himself, still the handsomest man in England, his eyes the colour of blue Smarties, his face expressionless as he ignored the cheers of the crowd. He was accompanied by half a dozen dogs: lurchers, terriers and Labradors, who kept stopping to fight each other and attack dogs in the crowd, until Rupert called them back.

Inside, Rupert was raging and desolate that Xav as part of the clan wasn't beside him. Instead, running to keep up, was Junior and Amber's father, Billy Lloyd-Foxe, laughing helplessly, grey curls astray, wearing a tweed coat with no buttons and an equally buttonless shirt, held together by his tie.

Reporting the march for the BBC, shouting over the tooting of hunting horns, Billy was giving an unashamedly biased commentary. 'This is the countryside fighting back, making its protest seen and heard, with the largest march London has ever seen.'

Even Paris couldn't restrain a cheer for the three couple of the Bagley Beagles, sterns waving like wheat in a high wind, and in their midst, a large grinning chocolate Labrador pausing to gobble up a discarded Cornish pasty.

'Cadbury,' shouted Paris. Even Northcliffe opened an eye.

In charge of the beagles, blowing their hunting horns, flicking their token whips, were Amber and Lando, glamorous in their teal-blue coats, breeches and black boots.

'I shagged that girl last summer,' said Paris, topping up his glass. He wished he could remember more about it.

And *look* at her: an utterly stunning blonde with the same cool face, blue eyes and ferociously determined mouth as Rupert. It must be his daughter Tabitha, the silver medallist, and that must be her husband Wolfgang who produced films, to whom Xav had promised to introduce Paris: 'So he can discover you.'

Close on their heels came a group who'd clearly had an excellent lunch. According to the commentator, they were former members of the England polo team. Except for Lando's father Ricky, who had a closed, carved, ascetic face and very high cheekbones, they all had handsome, flushed, expensive faces. Two of them, identical twins in their thirties, were holding lead reins attached to the wrists of a beautiful girl. Paris gasped. It was Bianca, inspiring as many cheers and wolf whistles as her father.

She had tied a scarlet bandanna round her dark ringlets and wore a flame-red wool shirt and dark blue breeches which clung to her impossibly supple and slender figure. Her lovely even complexion, the colour of strong tea, was faintly touched with colour. But neither twin could restrain her wonderful wildness. You could more easily have trapped a sunbeam as she skipped and danced, her laughing dark eyes making love to every man in the crowd.

Bloody hell. Paris refilled his glass. For, just behind Bianca and the twins, advancing fast, waving a 'Bring back Blair-Baiting' poster, his black curls flowing out from under his flat cap like Sir Lancelot, strode Cosmo.

'Fuck him,' said Paris, then his heart lifted as Patience came into view. 'There's your mistress,' he chided Northcliffe who was burying a Bonio in the camellia by the window.

Patience might resemble a scarecrow, but she looked so sweet and carefree as she laughed and gossiped to the Hon. Jack's father, David Waterlane and – my God – to Sally Brett-Taylor. It was brave of her to stick her neck out. All three of them were walking backwards now to watch and clap a piper who was leading a large contingent from Scotland, marching behind.

He could just imagine them: knights and ladies of the court, straight out of Tennyson, riding through medieval England on their great horses, a bobbing flotilla of white placards lit by the turning plane trees and Patience part of it. How dare Ian put her down so much? And what a tragedy for Xav not to be there.

I loathe what they stand for, he thought despairingly, but I long to be accepted by them. And Bianca was the only person who might get him over Janna, whom he still missed unbearably. He tried not to think of her. He hadn't glanced at the *Gazette* for weeks, nor been in touch with anyone from Larks. His mobile was dying from lack of use.

If only Janna were here with him now, discussing some poem,

casually ruffling his hair. But if Sally was on the march, that satyr Hengist was probably now at Jubilee Cottage shagging her. Jesus, it crucified him. Paris was about to open another bottle when he realized Rupert was addressing the crowds in Whitehall. The clipped, arrogant, carrying voice hardly needed a microphone.

'We will not let a politically correct but morally corrupt Government dictate to us. We will fight to the death for what we believe in: England, freedom and the countryside.'

'What about Wales, Scotland and Northern Ireland?' reproached Sally Brett-Taylor, over the roar of approval.

'And of course the colonies,' grinned Rupert, chucking an empty hipflask to an adoring fan who rushed off to the nearest pub to refill it.

God, he's a cool bastard, thought Paris, and Xav was his only route to Bianca. Picking up the Cartwrights' telephone he rang Xav. 'Patience and Ian are out. Why don't you come over? Got any weed?'

'Some really strong skunk; it'll blow your mind.'

Happily Alex and Poppet had gone out and the deputy house-master, Joe Meakin, who was new to the job and engrossed in the Sunday papers, was in charge.

'Can I nip over to the Old Coach House? Paris Alvaston's on his own and a bit down, adjusting to a new school and all.'

'OK, don't be late,' said Mr Meakin, glad that Xavier had found a friend. The poor boy seemed so isolated.

'I'll sign myself out,' said Xav, and didn't.

Collecting the skunk, he put a pillow in his bed.

63

'Are you sure it's safe?' he asked Paris ten minutes later. 'If I'm busted again I'll get sacked.'

'Quite safe. Ian's out to dinner; Patience is on the march.'

Having finished the red, Paris handed Xav a glass of Ian's whisky and had one himself.

'Your dad made a good speech; I taped it. I understand now why you wanted to go.'

Xav's face sank into sullenness.

'They wouldn't want a black bastard like me around.'

'Don't talk crap, they all cheered Bianca. Have a look,' said Paris winding back the tape. He wanted to watch her again. 'And hurry up with that smoke. Ian's obviously been watering the whisky; it tastes like gnat's piss. Who are those dirty old men holding Bianca's lead reins?'

Xav looked up from the tobacco and the skunk which he was shredding into a king-sized Rizla.

'The Carlisle twins. Good blokes. The two in front are Bas Baddington and Drew Benedict, friends of my dad's who played polo for England. All terrific studs, who like to wind up Dad, who was the biggest stud of all, by chatting up Bianca. He goes ballistic,' Xav added wistfully. 'He hates people chatting up Mum too. Give me a slug of that Courvoisier; you're right about the whisky.' He emptied it into a nearby plant pot.

'You may not be the brain of Britain,' giggled Paris half an hour later, 'but you're a genius at rolling spliffs.'

Xav had obviously had plenty of practice, and he'd been right about the skunk: it blew their minds, putting them in a really mellow and expansive mood.

There wasn't anything on television and Patience and Ian had crap videos, so they put on a Marilyn Manson CD and, ignoring shouts of 'Turn it down' from all over the campus, they danced. Xav, rocking with the abandon that he drained glasses, was soon rolling another spliff.

After that they got the munchies. Paris remembered a shepherd's pie Patience had left in the fridge, which he put in the oven, and the remains of a boeuf bourguignon, which he fed to Northcliffe. He also found a nice bottle of white and a plate of smoked salmon sandwiches under clingfilm, which they wolfed down, dropping the crusts on the carpet.

Oh help! Paris noticed a cigarette burn on one of Emerald's poncy embroidered cushions and two more on the sofa. He'd sort it later. Drugs made him feel he could conquer anything, be the best guy Cameron Diaz had ever slept with, win the poetry prize, score five goals for Liverpool, have Little Cosmo pleading to be his best friend. Then you came down and descended into the abyss when you wanted to hurt and destroy anyone who loved you.

'Why were you in care?' asked Xav.

'My mum dumped me on the doorstep of a children's home in Alvaston and fucked off. They named me after the town. They reckoned I was about two, so they gave me a birthday on January the thirtieth. Makes me the water carrier – or wine carrier.' He filled Xav's glass with Pouilly-Fumé. 'Aquarians are supposed to be aloof and charismatic. I've worked on it ever since. What happened to you?'

Xav drew deeply on his spliff, eyes like black threads, face impassive, a Hiawatha with puppy fat.

'I was born with a squint and a birthmark, which, probably correctly, is the sign of the devil to the Colombian Indians. So they chucked me into the gutter to die. They shoot stray children along with dogs in Bogotá, so the place looks tidy when foreign leaders roll up. I was rescued by a nun who worked in an orphanage.' Xav's voice grew more bitter. 'Bianca was brought in as a baby when I was about twenty months. She came from a good family, strict Catholics, who forced Bianca's mother to give her up. Dad and Mum had placed an order for her and flown over from England; the nuns threw me in as a job lot. I know nothing about my parents. Bianca's posh but I'm a yob: I can tell that when I look in the mirror.'

Emptying the entire glass of wine, Xav choked. Paris bashed him on the back and said:

'You've got the poshest voice I've ever heard. Birthmark's gone, so's the squint.'

Xav glared glassily at Paris. 'Gets worse when I'm pissed.'

'D'you feel Indian or English?'

'Indian mostly. I love booze, drugs and fast horses. But I've got no stop button. Once I start I can't stop.'

'Your father can't mind that with horses.'

'My father is the most embarrassing person I've ever met. He doesn't give a shit. Wherever he goes everyone gazes at him and Mum and Bianca, and sees how like film stars they are. Then they look at me, and think: Why's that ugly black bastard hanging round them?

'They used to spit at Mum when I was young,' continued Xav bitterly. 'They thought she'd been with a black man. They used to finger my hair and ask her if she ever washed it. I wash the fucking stuff every day. Boy, Mum got angry.' For a second, Xav's heavy face lifted. 'She used to yell at people. But no one ever asked Dad questions about me, because they're too scared of him. So he's never realized there was a problem.'

Xav was rolling a third joint, breaking cardboard off a cigarette packet for them to smoke through.

'Least you've got parents,' said Paris.

The bottle of white was empty. The only thing left seemed to be a bottle of medium-dry sherry. He filled up their glasses.

'Let's drink to yobbos.'

'Yobbos,' shouted Xav, draining his glass. 'Put on some more music.'

Putting on Limp Bizkit, turning up the volume, Paris opened the curtains on a sky full of stars and lit-up windows all over the campus.

'Hear that, you fuckers,' he yelled over the din. 'God stands up for bastards.' Then, as the chapel clock chimed eleven o'clock: 'I've got an idea how we can screw up Biffo's steeplechase.'

On balance, Ian felt the evening had been a success. He had lied to Patience. He hadn't been dining with a supplier, but with Poppet and Alex Bruce, whom he'd taken to *Fidelio* in Bristol – on tickets admittedly given him by a supplier.

This had been to melt the distinct *froideur* which had grown between him and Alex since Patience's shouting match. As Alex wielded more power, Ian was increasingly edgy about losing his job. He knew Patience would disapprove of this move almost as much as Alex disapproved of her going on the march, so he had kept her in the dark.

Fidelio had been ravishing, with a Bagley old girl, Flora Seymour, singing Leonora quite magically. But although the opera was about liberation from tyranny, he didn't feel Poppet and Alex were fans of Beethoven – too militaristic perhaps.

'I prefer Eastern music,' admitted Poppet. 'Or early music on period instruments.'

Both Bruces had worn open-toed sandals and Alex, tieless, had displayed fearful short sleeves when he removed his jacket. They had certainly tucked into the smoked chicken, roast beef, avocado and spinach salad and apricot tart Ian had ordered for the interval, and between them downed the bottle of Beaune.

Ian, who couldn't drink because he'd agreed to drive them, couldn't stop thinking of that bottle of Pouilly-Fumé in the fridge at the Old Coach House.

On the way home, Poppet and Alex talked insufferably smugly about their daughter Charisma, who went to Searston Abbey.

'Of course she's G and T,' boasted Poppet, which turned out to be 'gifted and talented', rather than 'gin and tonic', and which made Ian long for a drink even more.

As they crossed the border into Larkshire, it was still mild enough to have the windows open. Conversation moved on to the challenging behaviour of Paris.

'He's very troubled,' said Poppet firmly, 'and I'm afraid Janna Curtis gave him an inflated sense of his own ability.'

Ian didn't rise, saying they were finding Paris much easier and he seemed to be getting on well with Xavier.

'I'm not liking that,' mused Poppet. 'Xav is very troubled too. I blame Rupert. Xav gets a detention for challenging behaviour and instead of dropping everything to sort out his son, Rupert swans off on the Countryside March.'

'I asked Rupert to discuss Xav's special educational needs recently,' added Alex petulantly, 'and he said: "All Xav needs is a kick up the arse. He's a lazy little sod, like I was at school." '

In the dark, Ian suppressed a smile.

'Rupert of course is troubled,' sighed Poppet, 'and a very private person.'

Only because he runs like hell the moment you appear on the horizon, thought Ian.

Swinging the car in between the stone lions at the bottom of the school drive, Ian was surprised at the number of lights still on. Must be pupils revising for tomorrow's retakes. Someone was playing loud music. Through the trees he could see lights in the Old Coach House; perhaps Patience was home.

'I've got a nice bottle of Pouilly-Fumé and some sandwiches in the fridge,' he told the Bruces. 'It's a long time since supper.'

Paris, if up, could open the bottle for them and hand things round.

'Well, if you insist,' said Poppet.

'Christ,' whispered Paris, who'd been looking out of the window, 'Ian's home and he's brought Mr and Mrs Fussy.' Turning off Limp Bizkit, he chucked the remains of the spliff into the waste-paper basket.

Then he noticed more burns: in the 'Mother's Place is in the Wrong' cushion and on Ian's bridge table and on another of Emerald's cushions, shit, shit, shit. Paris turned the cushions over and shoved a pile of *Horse & Hounds* on the bridge table.

'Gather up the empties at once, man,' he begged, but, cross-eyed and giggling on the sofa, Xav was too far gone.

'Oh, for God's sake.' Paris scooped up at least four bottles and shoved them in Patience's little sewing cupboard, producing a chink and crash of glass, which indicated Ian was already secreting bottles there.

Paris was just trying to identify a smell of burning and shoving a swaying Xav out by the back door when they went slap into Ian, Alex and Poppet coming in through the garage.

'Mr and Mrs Fussy,' said a beaming Xav. 'Have you had a good evening?'

Seeing him momentarily handsome, showing excellent teeth and softened features, Alex thought for a moment Xav had turned into the egregious Feral Jackson. Then he caught sight of the shadow of a birthmark in the overhead light.

'Xavier Campbell-Black,' he thundered, 'why aren't you in bed?'

'Chill, man, I've been counselling Paris. I didn't realize it was so late.'

'You were ordered not to leave your house.'

'I got permission.'

'Something's burning,' said Poppet, fascinated to witness such chaos.

Wrenching open the oven, Ian found a blackened shepherd's pie. Opening the fridge, he discovered the bottle of Pouilly-Fumé and the sandwiches missing and, striding into the drawing room, found an utterly depleted drinks cupboard and took in the mess.

'Paris, come in here at once,' he bellowed.

Everyone unfortunately followed him, whereupon the waste-paper basket containing Paris's discarded spliff, not wanting to be left out, burst into flames.

'Fire, fire,' giggled Xav, emptying the last of the sherry over it,

393

which turned the flame blue. 'Just like the Christmas pudding at home,' he added wistfully.

'We'll be forgetting that drink and sandwiches,' said Alex grimly, 'and take you straight home.' He seized Xav by the arm and turned to Paris. 'And I want you in my office before chapel tomorrow to explain yourself.'

Thank God, the burnt shepherd's pie had blotted out the smell of dope.

Giggling hysterically, Xav tripped over a side table, sending flying a 'World's Best Dad' mug and a Staffordshire dog, and fell flat on his face.

'For God's sake,' exploded Ian.

Xav was as unyielding as a bag of concrete as Paris lugged him to his feet. 'Getta grip,' he hissed. 'I'll help him out, sir.' Anything to escape from Ian's fury.

Outside, the peace of the soft September starlight was disturbed by a tantivy of horns and joyful off-key singing.

> 'The dusky night rides down the sky,
> And ushers in the morn;
> The hounds all join in glorious cry,
> The huntsman winds his horn.'

' "And a-hunting we will go, a-hunting we will go, a-hunting we will go," ' joined in Xav. Lunging forward he yelled, 'Taxi, taxi, take me to paradise,' as a lorry, driven by Patience, with Dora, Jack, Lando and Junior, and several beagles falling out of the windows, came roaring up the drive.

' "The dusky night rides down the sky, the huntsman..." ' began Patience. Screeching to a halt outside the Old Coach House and seeing Xav and Paris, she cried, 'Hello, boys, we've all had such a wonderful day.'

The Bruces, however, lurking in the shadows, felt otherwise, particularly when the beagles poured out of the back of the lorry after Joan's Burmese cat before relieving themselves all over the lawns and the flower beds. The calm of the night was disturbed again as Poppet Bruce's open-toed sandals encountered Northcliffe's regurgitated boeuf bourguignon.

Paris fled to bed, trying to blot out the sounds of Patience and Ian arguing furiously downstairs.

Oh hell, there was the main section of the *Sunday Times* on his bed all crumpled up by Northcliffe, which Ian hadn't read yet and would be crosser about than the booze. The paper lay open at a piece listing the advantages of boarding school which included 'the widening of horizons, the development of autonomy, and the relief from tensions commonly built up in a nuclear family around adolescence'.

Paris buried his face in his pillow. 'I've been catapulted into a nuclear family,' he groaned, 'but I'm the bomb.'

64

As a result of the Countryside March, Bagley received excellent coverage. Many papers carried pictures of Amber, Lando and the beagle pack. The front page of the *Western Daily Press* showed Sally and Patience waving placards. Dora was ecstatic over Nigel Dempster's picture of herself and Cadbury. It would be so good for all her press contacts to be able to put a face to her name. There was however a bitchy piece in the *Scorpion* on the shortness of Rupert Campbell-Black's fuse. Was it due to lack of support from his two sons, Marcus, who was gay and allergic to horses, and his adopted son Xavier, who'd been gated by Bagley Hall (fees £22,000 a year) for undisclosed bad behaviour?

The star of the day was definitely Bianca, who, combining her mother's beauty and her father's ability to dazzle, was considered to be carrying the Campbell-Black torch. This did nothing for Xav's self-esteem, but his street cred rocketed when news leaked out via Dora and the *Evening Standard* that instead of marching, he and Paris had been busted for drunken trashing of the bursar's house.

This, according to the Bruces and a reproachful Nadine, would never have happened if Patience hadn't abandoned Paris so early in his foster placement to defend evil blood sports. Poppet promptly emailed the Cartwrights the telephone number of P.U.K.E., 'which stands for Prevention, Understanding, Knowledge, Education, a support group which takes a non-judgemental view of binge drinking'. 'Call them,' urged Poppet.

Patience put the email in the bin.

Paris and Xav were heavily fined and as punishment had to knock in endless posts and blue and brown flags for Sunday's steeplechase. This enabled them to earmark an outwardly impenetrable clump of rhododendrons and laurels about seventy-five yards from the start.

Xav had planned to invite Paris back to Penscombe that Sunday but the whole school was ordered to stay at Bagley to take part in the steeplechase or at least witness Alex Bruce achieve his personal best.

On a grey dank Sunday afternoon, with fog forecast, the Biffo Rudge Trophy for the first member of staff past the post and the Gordon Brooks Cup for the first pupil, donated by Boffin's father, glittered on a trestle table, reflecting the turning gold limes surrounding Mansion Lawn. Silver shields for the next five in both categories were stacked in a cardboard box.

The six-mile course itself was shaped like the frame of a tennis racquet. Contestants left Mansion Lawn, ran under General Bagley Arch, down the east side of the drive, past thick rhododendron clumps, turned left at the lion gates and continued in a big circle round the villages of Bagley, Wilmington and Sedgeley, turning left again at the lion gates, pounding up the west side of the drive under the arch to the tapes in front of the Mansion.

In chapel that morning, Biffo, nailbrush hair bristling even more fiercely, had sternly set out the rules:

'Students in the past have let down the school and themselves, straying into public houses, cafés and shops along the route. But your target is to be the first back here, where Gordon Brooks and I will be holding the tape. Occasionally pupils have taken short cuts, pretending they have completed the course. Wardens everywhere will be monitoring such transgressions. Any cheating or flouting of rules will be severely punished. Above all act on your own initiative. Don't let anything or anyone distract you from your goal.'

Despite this, all the pubs and shops along the route were staying open expecting excellent business. Janna, Lily and Brigadier Woodford had heaved deckchairs and several bottles and Melton Mowbray pork pies on to the Brigadier's flat roof to enjoy the spectacle.

As kick-off time approached, competitors gathered on Mansion lawn, chatting, shivering, running on the spot and jogging round in little circles.

The smart money for pupils was on Kippy Musgrave, a Lower Fifth beauty, already fleeter than a whippet from running away from lustful masters. Denzil Harper, the ultra-fit head of PE who ran marathons for the county, was favourite for the Rudge Cup, a rather stocky hare who had reckoned without Alex Bruce's tortoise, according to Boffin Brooks.

'I don't approve of gambling, sir, but I've put a whole week's pocket money on your being first past the tape.'

Boffin, his spectacles misting up in an orgy of toadyism, sporting long grey shorts which failed to disguise a bottom wider than his shoulders, breath reeking of breakfast kipper, was also determined to be in the first six.

Members of the first fifteen, including the glamorous captain, Tarquin Courtney, had perfected that rugby star walk, sticking out their chests, straightening their legs backward with each stride to make their thighs judder. Big bruisers, they outwardly treated the whole steeplechase as a joke but underneath, like Alex, they were hell-bent on winning.

Alex himself was in a trance. One must go inside oneself. Following Bianca's example, he had tied a red bandanna round his head; he was flexing his thigh muscles backwards as he swayed and hummed. Poppet, jogging on the spot in shorts and a purple vest, displaying Black Forests of armpit hair, was chopping up bananas for Alex and other runners from his house.

'We want Bruce students in the first six.'

Their G and T daughter Charisma was waiting along the route to ply Alex and Boffin with glucose tablets. Anxious to beat as many masters as possible, No-Joke Joan had, like Alex, been jogging round the campus for weeks.

'Have you seen her thighs?' asked Artie Deverell faintly. 'Like barons of beef.'

'Our Joan would be more interested in the baroness,' murmured back Theo, who was increasingly grateful for swigs from Ian Cartwright's hipflask. Patience, beside them, had gone purple with cold; Ian, looking bleak, had still not forgiven Paris, who hadn't been near the Old Coach House since Sunday and whom he couldn't see anywhere. Probably too ashamed to show his face.

'I want ten pounds on Paris Alvaston for a win,' Dora, currently on three mobiles to various newspapers, told Lando who was keeping a book.

'Don't waste your money, he's two hundred to one.'

'I don't care.'

A chorus of wolf whistles greeted Vicky running out in a clinging pale pink fleece and pink pleated skirt, her hair in bunches.

'I am *so* nervous,' she told Poppet.

Alex detranced enough to say: 'Why not run behind me, little Vicky, until you get into your stride?'

She couldn't fail to be inspired by his tall good figure ahead of her.

' "Mark my footsteps, good my page!" ' mocked Cosmo, still in his astrakhan coat.

'Line up everyone,' shouted Biffo as the big hand of the chapel clock edged towards five to three.

In a long race with over three hundred runners, it didn't matter if everyone started at once, but Mansion Lawn was now entirely covered with competitors. The Mansion itself dozed in a shaft of sunlight which had broken through the clouds.

'Where the hell's Hengist?' muttered Biffo to Joan as he fingered the starting pistol. 'Why is he always deliberately insultingly late?'

'He looked over his shoulder For athletes at their games,' murmured Theo, noticing that Cosmo had at last tossed his astrakhan coat to Dora, and, oh dear, was sliding a thieving hand between Vicky's thighs. There was Smart, stubbing out a fag, but where was Paris? Theo hoped he hadn't done a bunk. Hengist, who was keeping a paternal eye on the boy, had suggested Paris would benefit from a few hours' Latin and Greek coaching a week. Theo sighed. The temptation would be irresistible.

Ah, here at last was Hengist, flushed from a good lunch, laughing, joking, but in no hurry and making no apologies.

Biffo longed to turn the pistol on him.

'Get ready, everyone,' he bellowed. 'Two minutes to the off.'

Alex Bruce had been doing a quick interview with Radio Larkshire.

'Forgive me, the race awaits.'

'Of course, deputy headmaster.'

As Alex strode towards the start line, he passed Emlyn, who'd just enjoyed a long lunch at Hengist's.

'Why aren't you taking part?' he demanded.

'With stars like you, Alex?' Then, when Alex looked simply furious: 'Best of luck.'

Fifty yards down the drive, Paris and Xavier waited in their rhododendron hideout. Paris was watching the start through binoculars. 'One minute to three. Mr Fussy's crouching down with one knee bent, and the other stretched out like the Olympics. Now he's bowing his head. God, he's a twat. OK,' he whispered to Xav.

Crash went the starting pistol, which Paris and Xav had bought on the internet from Bristol last week.

Off set the runners, pounding down the drive, past the rhododendron clump, spilling out on to the roughly mown grass on the left, stepping up their speed to be first through the lion gates.

'Stop,' thundered Biffo, brandishing his unfired pistol, 'that was a false start. Stop the race,' he shouted into his walkie-talkie to Mr Meakin who, desperate to redeem himself after letting Xav out last weekend, rushed forward waving his arms: 'Stop, stop.'

But the leading runners and Tarquin Courtney, who thought Meakin was a wimp and had been ordered not to be distracted by anything, waved two fingers at him and pounded on.

A second later, another avalanche of runners including Vicky and Cosmo sent Meakin flying into a hawthorn bush.

'Blessed are the Meakin for they shall inherit the earth,' shouted Cosmo.

Not until a hundred and fifty or so pupils and masters, including Alex Bruce, had flowed out of the gates did Biffo manage to convince the wardens of the false start.

'Just like the National in nineteen ninety-three,' whinnied Jack Waterlane, who'd been planning to run off and see Kylie, 'except the front runners are halfway to Wilmington.'

Alex Bruce walked back to the Mansion, gibbering with rage, froth flying from his lips.

'Get everyone back. The race must be rerun.'

'Too late,' sighed Hengist. 'Unfair disadvantage to those who've run a mile already; they'll be exhausted.'

'I and many others have been training for months to achieve a pitch of fitness.'

'I know, Alex,' said Hengist sympathetically, 'it's too bad. I felt the same when I did my Achilles tendon just before the England–France game. Run it tomorrow.'

'The sixth form are off to CCF camp.'

'Then we'll have another steeplechase next term.'

'The weather is too unreliable.'

'Who fired that pistol?' spluttered an approaching Biffo.

'Better call a stewards' enquiry,' said Emlyn gravely.

Theo and Artie were having great difficulty keeping straight faces.

'Poor Mr Fussy,' said Patience, 'he was so keen to win.'

'What's going on,' whispered Xav from the dark of the bushes.

'Obviously a terrific row,' said Paris, who'd climbed a rhododendron bush to peer out. 'Biffo's gone purple and is waving his hands. Hengist is trying not to laugh. Poppet Bruce is jumping up and down, saying this is what she hates about competitive games. Her husband's more competitive than anyone.' Paris dropped back on the ground.

'It couldn't have gone better,' said Xav in ecstasy.

'Hush, here comes Boffin Brooks on a bike, we'd better stay put.'

Pedalling furiously, Boffin reached the back runners on the outskirts of Wilmington village.

'Stop, stop,' he yelled, riding straight through them. 'The race is being rerun, stop.'

'Fuck off, Boff,' said Junior, 'it's not the Tour de France.'

'Get off that bike, we were told not to cheat,' called out Lando, coming out of the Dog and Duck clutching four gin and tonics.

'Everyone's got to go back and start again,' panted Boffin.

'Oh, shut up,' grumbled Junior, 'you just want Mr Fussy to win. Throw him in the ditch, Anatole.'

'You're not allowed to drink spirits,' squealed Boffin.

'It's vater, you prat,' said Anatole, chucking Boffin and his bike into the stream that ran along the street.

Five minutes later, help was at hand. Joan had jumped into her British racing green MGB, which the girls in her house had nicknamed Van Dyke, and, hooting imperiously, had overtaken the front runners in Wilmington High Street. Just below a cheering Janna, Lily and Brigadier Woodford, she turned Van Dyke sideways to block the road where it narrowed, before going into the country. The red light of her great roaring face turned everyone back.

'The school buses are on their way to transport you back to the start,' she told them.

'If I have a heart attack,' said Cosmo in outrage, 'I shall get Cherie Booth to represent me.'

Back at Mansion Lawn Alex Bruce was still arguing with Hengist.

'This is a Bagley tradition we must not lose, headmaster.'

'You never stop saying tradition is the enemy of progress,' snapped Hengist, who for once felt outmanoeuvred.

'Someone fired that pistol,' said Biffo furiously. 'I am absolutely determined to get to the bottom of—'

'Kippy Musgrave,' shouted a voice in the crowd to howls of mirth.

'Who said that?' roared Biffo.

Hengist bit his lip. Emlyn, Theo and Artie, standing on the Mansion steps, were openly laughing.

Xav and Paris were in heaven.

'We did it, we fucked the steeplechase.'

They were just about to slope off into the woods and chuck the

401

starting pistol, wiped clean of fingerprints, into a bramble bush when, to their horror, runners came sulkily shuffling back.

'It's bloody unfair, I was in the lead.'

'Dotheboys Hall! I'm going to sue the school.'

'If any masters or boys have coronaries, Alex, I'll hold you personally responsible,' said an outraged Hengist, who'd planned to slope off to Jubilee Cottage. Now he'd be presenting cups at midnight.

Pretending he needed to collect a file, he retreated to his office to ring Janna.

'Sorry, darling, I was so longing to see you, but I can't make it.'

'Probably just as well, Lily and Brigadier Woodford are downstairs getting plastered. I do miss you. But it was terribly funny.'

'Wasn't it? Robot the Bruce is not amused. They'll be pounding past your door again in a few minutes.'

The sun had set, peeping out under a line of dark clouds like a light left on in the next room, as the weary winners, six of them bunched together, finally hobbled through the lion gates into the home straight. A hundred yards behind them, out of eyeshot, concealed by a bend in the road, came the second batch.

Just before the latter turned into the gates, a new willowy, white-blond competitor shot out of the rhododendrons, followed by a smaller, plumper, dark companion. Not having exerted themselves all afternoon, they were fresh enough to catch up with the front runners, and the white-blond boy in a glorious burst of speed began to overtake them.

Perched on the window seat in Hengist's study, peering through the gloom, Theo caught sight of Paris and yelled for the others.

'He's leading. God, he's going to do it, come on, Paris.'

The window seat nearly collapsed as Artie, Emlyn, Hengist, Patience, Ian and Elaine joined Theo, yelling their heads off as Paris passed a panting heaving Denzil and flung his breast against the tape. Xav coming in eleventh was just in the medals.

'Exactly like *Chariots of Fire*,' sighed Dora. She got out her calculator. 'I've made two thousand pounds.'

The joy in Ian's face was enough. Patience was crying openly as Paris accepted the Brooks Cup from an outraged and twitching Gordon Brooks.

'What a triumph, well done, Paris,' said Hengist, shaking him by the hand.

Paris was so overwhelmed by the reception he forgot to scowl at his headmaster. Boffin Brooks and Alex, who were in the second batch and just missed medals, were absolutely livid.

'Never saw Paris Alvaston during the race,' panted Alex.

'Neither did I,' said Boffin.

'It was such a muddle, I'm surprised anyone saw anyone, particularly in the dusk,' said Hengist smoothly.

'I paced myself,' Paris, playing up for the cameras, told Venturer Television. 'Long before I came to Bagley, I perfected my technique running away from the police.'

'I'm convinced it was my counselling,' Vicky was telling everyone.

Back at the Old Coach House, Ian was so delighted he opened a bottle of champagne and shared it with Patience, Dora and Paris.

Perhaps they do like me after all, thought Paris.

Later Hengist rang Janna.

'Paris won; I hope you're pleased. He was so elated he forgot he loathed me. I think we're winning, darling.'

65

As Middle Five B shuffled towards history the following morning, Milly Walton rushed up and kissed Paris.

'Well done, terrific news, you deserve it.'

'Well done,' said Primrose Duddon, blushing scarlet.

'Well done,' said Jade, smiling at him for the first time that term.

'What you talking about?'

'Go and check the noticeboard.'

'Well done, Paris,' said Tarquin Courtney, captain of rugby and of athletics, who had passed his driving test and kept a Porsche in the car park. He knows my name, thought Paris in wonder. Then he went cold. Looking up at the noticeboard, he discovered that after his triumph in the steeplechase, he'd been selected for the athletics team against Fleetley on Saturday.

'This is the one Hengist always wants to win,' confided Tarquin. 'There's training this afternoon. We can sort out whether you're best at sprint or middle distance.'

Oh shit, thought Paris, particularly as next moment Ian charged out of the bursar's office and thumped him on the back.

'Well done, old boy. Patience and I thought we'd drive over to Fleetley to cheer you on. We'll take a picnic. If the weather's foul we can always eat it in the car.'

'What the hell am I going to do?' Paris asked Xav five minutes later.

'Aren't they always pushing steroids outside Larks? You could take some and test positive.'

'Don't be fucking stupid.'

Wandering off down the cloisters Paris went slap into Emlyn, to

404

whom he'd spoken very little since the beginning of term. He wasn't in Emlyn's set for history, and Theo, unable to bear the thought of Paris's beautiful straight nose being broken, had so far managed to get him out of rugby. But Paris trusted Emlyn.

'Can I have a word, sir?'

Thirty seconds later he was in the safety of Emlyn's classroom. Stalin's poster smirked down from underneath his thatch of black moustache. I'll be shunted off to the Gulag any minute, thought Paris.

'I screwed up,' he told Emlyn flatly. 'I didn't win the steeple-chase. I lurked in the bushes and slid into the back of the leaders.'

'I thought as much.' Emlyn dropped four Alka-Seltzers into a glass of water. Yesterday's lunch with Hengist had run into dinner.

Emlyn then got a pile of essays on Hitler out of his briefcase and started to mark the one on the top with a yellow pen entitled Afghanistan Airlines.

Bastard, thought Paris, as Emlyn put a thick red tick halfway down the margin.

'Sit down,' snapped Emlyn. 'Theo showed me that essay you wrote on the *Aeneid*. It was very good. Shame he encouraged you to wimp out of rugby. I suppose he sees you hurling discuses or driving chariots. If you come and play for my under-fifteen side, I'll get you out of athletics.'

'How?' asked Paris sulkily.

'As Hengist still runs this school, rugby takes precedence. It'd also please Ian. He'd go berserk if he knew you'd been cheating in the steeplechase and anything's better than the total humili-ation of running next Saturday.'

Emlyn had reached the end of Cosmo's essay, and wrote: 'A+. You obviously identify with the Führer.'

'OK,' said Paris.

'If you play on my team' – Emlyn grimaced as he downed half the glass of Alka-Seltzer – 'you must give one hundred per cent.'

Emlyn might not have been so co-operative if he hadn't yester-day morning received a telephone call from Janna, saying she was worried about Paris and could Emlyn keep an eye on him.

'Keep an eye on him yourself,' Emlyn had told her disapprov-ingly. 'How many times have you seen him this term?'

'I've been frantic,' replied a flustered Janna. 'We've got Ofsted any minute, and S and C are still refusing to give me any more money.'

So Emlyn said he'd see what he could do, adding, 'Let's have

405

dinner and catch up and I'll tell you how to bamboozle Ofsted. I'll call you.'

As a fine former rugger player, Ian was thrilled, particularly when Emlyn gave Paris private coaching in the basics required of an all-rounder before his first game.

Tackling Emlyn, Paris felt like a flea trying to topple a charging rhino. Emlyn also gave him some videos of internationals to watch with Ian, but Paris still thought it was a strange, brutal, muddy game compared with football. And he already had pierced ears, without having them bitten through.

For the first game, Paris rolled up with hair tangled and unkempt, wearing shirt and shorts still muddy from his brief run in the steeplechase. Nor did he give a hundred per cent because he was terrified of getting hurt.

'If you play hard enough, you won't realize you're hurt till afterwards,' Emlyn assured him at half-time, and once the game was finished took him aside.

'Have you got a girlfriend, Paris?'

Paris went scarlet, kicked the grass and shook his head.

'I should think not, if you go round looking that scruffy. Don't think your hair's seen a brush since the beginning of term.'

'Such a fucking awful haircut' – Paris spat on the grass – 'doesn't deserve one.'

The next game, Paris rolled up with his hair brushed, boots polished, clean shorts. The snow-white collar of his sea-blue and brown striped rugby shirt emphasized his deathly pallor. He was in a foul temper and soon into fights, quite prepared to thump and knee in the groin anyone of either side who bumped into him.

Emlyn kept up a stream of reproof: 'Don't hang on to the ball, don't tackle so high, those boots are to kick balls, not heads in. Rugby's not a free-for-all, it's a team game.'

He was about to send Paris off when the boy scooped up the ball, sauntered towards the posts, kicked a perfect drop goal and raised a middle finger at the other players.

That evening Emlyn called Lando and Junior over to his flat for a beer. The two boys loved the big living room, which had a huge comfortable sofa, a massive television with Sky for all the sport, shelves crammed with books on rugby and history, and a view, once the leaves fell, of General Bagley and the Lime Walk.

Pictures included a few watercolours of Wales, photographs of rugby fifteens, portraits of Emlyn's heroes: J. P. R. Williams,

Gareth Edwards and Cliff Morgan; and in a corner a group photo of himself, a giant towering over giants in the Welsh rugby team. The record shelves were dominated by opera and male voice choirs. On his desk were photographs of his late father, mother and sisters, and the exquisite Oriana, who seemed more distant than his father. If he didn't see her soon, his dick would fall off.

'Which one of you would like to take on Paris Alvaston?' he asked the boys.

'How?' asked Lando.

'In a fight.'

Both boys looked startled.

'We've got to break the ice around him somehow.'

'I will,' said Lando. 'I'm pissed off with the stroppy, arrogant little git.'

The following afternoon was cold, grey and dank with a vicious wind. The Colts were playing to the right of Badger's Retreat, separated from other games by a thick row of conifers.

Passing the Family Tree, seeing Oriana's initials on the trunk, Emlyn was overwhelmed with longing. She hadn't written for three weeks. Was she still in Afghanistan? If he flew out at Christmas, would she be too caught up with work to find time for him? His face hardened. It was a day to take no prisoners.

Within minutes of kick-off, Paris was landing punches, spitting and swearing. Groped too vigorously in a tackle, he turned on Spotty Wilkins, throwing him to the ground, fingers round his throat: 'Keep your fucking hands off me.'

Lando and Junior pulled him off.

Emlyn blew his whistle and formed the boys into a circle.

'I see you're spoiling for a fight, Paris.'

'I've had it with those fuckers.'

'Good,' said Emlyn coolly, 'Lando is only too happy to beat the shit out of you now.'

Lando stepped into the ring, long dark eyes for once alert, massive shoulders, scrum cap and gumshield giving him an inhuman look of Frankenstein's monster, body hard as teak, four inches taller and two stone heavier than Paris.

'Come on, wimp, I'm waiting.'

'This is worse than the Pitbull Club,' hissed Paris, turning on Emlyn. 'You'll get the sack for this.'

'I doubt it,' said Junior, trying to balance the ball on his curly head. 'It's your word against ours and there are lots of trees in the way. Go on, bury him, Lando.'

Lando took a step towards an expressionless but inwardly

quaking Paris. Emlyn was also quaking inside that he'd taken such a risk.

'You can either fight Lando,' he said quietly as Paris raised two trembling fists, 'or become one of the squad, and fight for them rather than against them. You're potentially a bloody good player, you've got the build, the eye and the short-term speed. We'd all be on your side.'

Paris glanced round the group; Junior, Jack, Anatole, Lubemir, Lando, Smartie, Spotty and the rest: all impassive, watchful, much stronger and bigger than him. Then he looked at Emlyn, an implacable giant, with the big smile for once wiped off his face. The pause seemed to go on for ever. He heard a whistle from a nearby pitch and the rumble and hoot of a distant train on which he could be off searching for his mother. But she had left him. Ian and Patience were his only hope. He held a shaking hand out towards Lando.

'OK,' he muttered. 'I've behaved like a twat, I'm sorry.'

'Well done.' Emlyn clapped a huge hand on his shoulder. 'That's the hardest thing you'll ever have to do in rugby.'

'The lads gave him a round of applause,' Emlyn told Janna over a bottle of red in the Dog and Duck that evening. 'They also gave him a lot of ball in the second half, and he played a blinder.'

'You took a hell of a gamble,' reproved Janna. 'Poor Paris could have been beaten to a pulp. You should have been fired.'

'I know.'

'How can you justify such bully-boy tactics?'

'I pray a lot.'

Miffed she wasn't more grateful, he asked her what was the matter.

'Bloody *Gazette* ran a libellous piece today saying: "In a county of too many schools, Larks would be a suitable case for closure."'

'They're only flying kites.'

'Not with Ofsted about to finish us off.'

Janna was also shocked by the change in Emlyn. The fat jester had gone; so had the double chin. His cheeks were hollowed and new lines of suffering formed trenches round his normally laughing mouth. No longer ruddy and bloated, he looked like Ulysses the wanderer returning from an endless and scarring war.

He was wearing too-loose chinos held up by a Welsh international rugby tie, a dark blue shirt and a much darned grey sleeveless pullover which Janna guessed had belonged to his father, about whom over more glasses of red he talked with great pain.

'Like John Mortimer in *A Voyage Around my Father* – that should be a set book – I just feel lonely now he's gone, and racked by lost opportunity. Why didn't I tell him I loved him more often? I betrayed him by going to Bagley – he could never understand it; and although Dad and Oriana were in the same camp, they never really got on. He couldn't comprehend anyone who'd been brought up with every advantage being so ungrateful.'

'How's your mum?' asked Janna.

'Crucified, bewildered, stoical. They'd been together forty years.'

Janna let him talk. It was a pleasure to watch him and to listen. Now the spare flesh had gone, he had such a strong fine face and, after a summer back in the valleys, his lovely lilting voice seemed deeper, with the Welsh open vowels more pronounced.

Oriana, it seemed, had provided little comfort when he'd flown out to see her in the summer holidays.

'She doesn't have the same relationship with her father.'

'But Hengist adores her,' said Janna unguardedly.

Fortunately Emlyn was too preoccupied to notice.

'Maybe, but she doesn't admire what he stands for. She can't understand how sad and guilty I feel. She's too taken up with the present, devastated at the plight of the Afghans. She's got a lead to Bin Laden, and plans to infiltrate herself into some Taliban spy ring. She could easily pass for a boy.'

'Oh poor Emlyn.' Janna topped up his glass.

'Sally and Hengist' – she felt her voice thickening – 'must be out of their minds with worry.'

'I'm sure. But they keep themselves busy. Hengist has been at some conference in Geneva all week. He's expected back this evening.'

Janna was just smirking inwardly because she was going to see him tomorrow, when Emlyn added,

'Why have you fallen out with Paris?'

Janna's glass stopped on the way to her mouth. Careful, she told herself, Emlyn doesn't miss things.

'He was dangerously crazy about you. I always suspected he accepted that place at Bagley as the only possible escape route. He's giving Patience and Ian a really hard time. Trashed their place a few Sundays back, and although he seems to get on with Theo, he's been arguing and swearing and spitting at other teachers.'

'He was used to arguing and swearing and spitting at Larks. I bet you played up at school.'

'I was utterly angelic,' said Emlyn piously. 'I spent my entire

409

school career as still as still' – briefly his face broke into a smile – 'outside the headmaster's office.'

Janna laughed, but her mind was racing.

'Everything Paris loved has been taken away from him,' said Emlyn, his huge hands taking Janna's. 'He lost his mother; endless schools and care homes where he made friends; teachers; foster parents: all taken away. Oaktree Court, however much he loathed it, was familiar. His life's been like living in an airport. All the love and understanding you gave him, I guess he misconstrued it. It's hard for teachers. We have to be so careful not to inspire passion in kids who have had no love, and lead them on to yet another rejection.'

Not just in kids, thought Janna, removing her hands, which felt so comfortable in his.

'Let's get legless,' said Emlyn, about to get another bottle.

Janna shook her head: 'I've got Ofsted in a fortnight. Hengist calls it "Orfsted".'

God, what a slip.

Emlyn looked at her speculatively.

'What happened on the geography field trip?'

Suddenly he was much too big for their corner table, his eyes boring into her.

'I went to bed with a migraine.' At his look of scepticism, she insisted, 'I did truly. I was so tired; I nodded off and missed everything. You're always nodding off,' she added defensively.

'We're not talking about me. Paris was evidently good as gold until the last night. But he's so angry now. Did you turn him down?'

'I don't have to answer these questions,' said Janna furiously.

'Course you don't, lovely, but you're so instinctively warm and tactile. Perhaps he misinterpreted the maternal nature of your affections.'

'Now Paris has got a new school, I'm sure he'll settle down and find himself a nice lass.'

A few days later, Dora was lurking in the main hall, hoping to bump into Paris. She knew his timetable backwards. He was so preoccupied with learning rugby with Emlyn, he hardly noticed her. Late for English, because he'd been practising drop goals, he came hurtling through the yellow lime leaves carpeting Mansion Lawn.

'Shut your eyes,' she called out.

'If it's not seeing the new moon through glass, I'm not interested. Last time I wished for an A star for my Simon Armitage essay, effing Vicky only gave me a C plus.'

'Much better than that.' Seizing Paris by the arm, joltingly aware how he'd thickened out and muscled up since term began, Dora dragged him down the cloisters. 'Now you can look.'

The board was painted in dark blue gloss, like the board outside Larks. Here the gold lettering said 'Notices'. At Larks it said: 'Head Teacher: Janna Curtis'. Oh Christ, when would it stop hurting?

'You don't seem very pleased.

'What for? I'm late for English.'

'Here, stupid.' Dora pointed to a list of names.

In Emlyn's square, clear writing, Paris read, 'France-Lynch (Capt), Waterlane, Lloyd-Foxe, Smart, Rostov . . . Alvaston.' *ALVASTON!*

He couldn't speak; he shut his eyes as warmth flowed through him. He hadn't let Ian, Theo or Hengist down. He'd been picked to play for the Colts on Saturday. Even better, it was a needle match against St Jimmy's, who'd always sneered at Larks and hated Bagley even more. As the first, second and third fifteens would also be playing, the residual resentment between maintained and independent would come bubbling to the surface.

'How d'you feel about St Jimmy's being your first fixture?' asked Dora.

'Great!' Paris punched the air. 'Set a yob to catch a yob. I've always wanted to wipe the smirk off Baldie Hyde's face.'

'Ian and Patience will be *au dessus de la lune*,' said Dora, rushing off to ring the papers.

66

Saturday dawned meanly with the sun skulking like a conspirator behind charcoal-grey clouds, which provided the perfect back-drop for the gold leaves tumbling steadily out of the trees. Distant Pitch Four, where the Colts were playing, was hidden by a net curtain of mist. Despite this, a glamorous photograph of Paris as Romeo, sold to the *Express* by Dora, captioned 'Scrumpet' and announcing his rugby debut and desire to bury St Jimmy's, had attracted a sprinkling of press and a largish crowd.

'Only been playing a few weeks,' crowed Ian, who was watching with Patience, Artie Deverell and Theo, who in an old Prince of Wales check coat and a trilby on the back of his bald head looked like a bookie. Artie noticed with a stab of anguish how grey, now his Tuscany tan had faded, his friend looked in the open air. But Theo was in high spirits and getting stuck into Patience's bull-shots. Five other boys from his little house, other than Paris, Anatole and Smart, were playing on various sides and only two from Alex Bruce's. Boffin Brooks, officious little shit, was one of the touch judges in the Colts game.

Then Theo growled: 'Here comes Rod Hyde, hubristic as ever,' as Rod, having travelled in the first coach singing revivalist hymns with his teams, strode about self-importantly, clapping leather-gloved hands on the shoulders of his 'men' – literally. They looked twice as old and hulking as their Bagley counterparts. Rod was wearing a new black leather coat, tightly belted, to show off his manly figure, and a new big black hat under the brim of which his eyes crinkled at the prettier mothers.

'Mr Hyde who never turns back into nice Dr Jekyll,' observed Theo sourly. 'Ah, here's little Vicky Fairchild with a pretty foot in both camps,' as Vicky, seductive in a long purple coat and a black

412

fur hat, paused to kiss first Poppet and Alex and then Rod and Sheila Hyde.

'Isn't it thrilling Paris is playing?'

'I'm sure your counselling has helped,' said Poppet eagerly.

'I do feel I'm easing his passage,' smiled Vicky.

'The ambition of every Bagley master,' murmured Artie Deverell as the Colts ran on to the field.

'Come on, Bagley,' shouted Bianca and Dora.

'Go for it, Paris,' yelled Dora's brother Dicky. 'God, he looks shit scared. So would I be. Those St Jimmy Colts will never see fifteen again. Look at their moustaches and chest hair. They should have been made to produce their passports. Brute Stevens, their captain, is reputed to have a wife and three children,' he added as, locked together, the St Jimmy's scrum sent Bagley reeling backward.

'Hengist's little laboratory rat is going to be carved up,' said Cosmo approvingly as Paris fluffed three passes and holding on to the fourth was brought crashing down by Brute Stevens.

'That was high,' muttered the crowd. The referee took no notice.

Was it coincidence or had Brute Stevens been deliberately ordered to harass Paris, never Rod's favourite pupil? For the second time as Paris leapt for the ball in the line-out, Brute rammed a thumb down the pockets of Paris's shorts, nearly pulling them off. Around the ground, binoculars rose to a score of masters' eyes.

'Come on, St Jimmy's,' yelled the caring and concerned parents – hearties in Barbours or blazers with badges on their breast pockets, their wives in peaked caps or woolly hats, cheeks purpling against the cold, working up a good hate against Bagley. How dare any school have such splendid buildings, such an excess of land, such arrogant pupils and such a cavalier head-master, who hadn't deigned to make an appearance so they could ignore him. Even the white goal posts and the helicopter pad said H for Hengist.

Sally Brett-Taylor, in a dark blue Puffa, navy-blue and gold Hermès scarf tied under the chin, her exquisite complexion unmarred by the elements, had reached Pitch Four, and was being fractionally more gracious to Sheila Hyde than she would be to the wife of the head of a major public school.

'How good of you to come. The chaps so love a crowd. No, Joan's taken the girls' hockey team to Westonbirt; she'll be so sorry to miss you. Hengist'll be out soon. He always feels person-ally responsible for all four matches. Oh, come on, Bagley. Come

413

on, Colts. Emlyn's been working so hard on them. Well out, Paris. Well done, Smartie. Come on, Junior, come on. Oh, bad luck,' as the whistle went.

Hengist, who'd been in his study with Jupiter thrashing out New Reform's law-and-order policy, which could more profitably have been applied to the Bagley Colts, arrived to find Pitch Four in an uproar, St Jimmy's leading 28–7 and Emlyn in a towering rage.

'We've done all the attacking and had ninety per cent of the ball,' he told Hengist, 'but the bloody bent ref from St Jimmy's is disallowing everything. He's given six penalties against us, none against St Jimmy's. If they knew how to kick straight, the score would be double. Boffin Brooks is touch judge, and can't see a fucking thing – or chooses not to.'

Rod Hyde meanwhile was leaping up and down, bellowing on his side: 'Well played, Wayne, well done, Kevin. Oh, good tackle, Brute. Come on, St Jimmy's,' clapping his great leather-gloved hands together like a walrus.

Bagley Colts, fast losing their tempers, were dramatically down to ten men, five – Junior, Lando, Smartie, Anatole and Spotty Wilkins – having been banished to the sin bin. The rest, like uncut stallions at Windsor Horse Show, were circling the ref.

'I was not orfside,' Jack was yelling, 'and that try was good. Can't you bloody well see?'

'Sin bin,' yelled back the ref.

As the roar of the crowd merged with the whirr of a helicopter, Rod was in ecstasy. Who were the yobbos and the bad sports now? Alex Bruce was also trying not to look smug. If that blockhead Emlyn Davies had introduced a few of Bruce's boys into the Colts, things would be very different. The Colts' moods were not improved at half-time as they sucked lemons and emptied water bottles to be told all the other Bagley sides were wiping the floor.

'High tackle,' yelled Ian Cartwright early on in the second half as Brute put a beefy arm round Paris's neck, yanking him to the ground. 'Did you see that, Hengist?'

But no one had seen anything because Mrs Walton, utterly ravishing and smothered in blond furs, had just rolled up with Randal Stancombe to watch the Colts before taking Milly and Jade to Sardinia for the weekend.

I hope she's happy, thought Hengist as, smiling, he strode down the touchline to welcome them. He was wearing a fawn coat, his hair, always curlier in damp weather, falling over the dark brown velvet collar. St Jimmy mothers, turning as he passed, had to agree reluctantly that he looked even better in the flesh.

Randal was in joshing mood. 'With all your resources and expertise, Hengist, surely the Colts should be thrashing St Jimmy's.'

'Randal!' Rod Hyde strode up, pumping Stancombe's hand.

'You're doing too damn well, Rod.'

'We've been bringing on our young players,' said Rod smugly. 'Congratulations on that takeover, must have taken a lot of time and vision.'

'What takeover?' said Hengist, wrenching his eyes away from Mrs Walton.

He ought to know, thought Randal angrily.

'Both takeovers,' he replied lightly, putting an arm round Mrs Walton. 'Ruth's about to move in with me.'

'If you walk through a head hold your storm up high,' sang Dicky, who'd been drinking vodka in the rhododendrons with Xavier.

Revved up by Emlyn at half-time, the Bagley Colts fought back, and no one fought with more guts than Paris, battered by the terrible strength of the opposition. Tries from Lando and Junior, one of them converted by Lubemir, followed by a stylish drop goal from Anatole, brought the score up to 28–22. Victory was at last within Bagley's reach.

The mist was coming down again; the light fading; the other games were over.

'Come on, Paris,' howled his fan club as he scooped up the ball. Escaping from a tangle of red, blue and brown jerseys and muddy shorts, he streaked down the pitch, pale hair flying, cheers in his ears. Seeing Brute Stevens pounding in like a mad bull from the right, he jinked to the left, bounding along the touchline, burying the ball triumphantly over the line at Boffin's feet.

'Disallow that if you dare, you sad bastard,' he panted, then, raising the ball triumphantly, waved it to the crowds to roars of applause.

In the closing seconds of the game, he had put Bagley ahead. Junior's conversion would clinch it. As photographers raced to get their pictures, Northcliffe broke free, bounding towards Paris, picking up a horse chestnut leaf as a prize. Paris could see Patience wiping her eyes, Ian joyfully brandishing his shooting stick, Theo waving his bookie's hat in the air and Dora and Bianca jumping up and down.

Jack and Anatole charged out of the sin bin to ruffle Paris's hair, and clap him on the back. 'Well done, man.'

Hengist sloped off to report the triumph to Janna.

415

But against all this din, the whistle kept on blowing and not for the end of the match. After a long consultation with Boffin, the ref was walking in Paris's direction.

'I'm afraid the pass was forward and your foot was in touch.'

Paris's muddy face contorted in fury.

'Do you actually know the fucking rules of the game?' he yelled. 'It was not forward and I was not in touch.'

'Don't argue with the ref, you posh bastard,' yelled Brute Stevens.

All the Colts were now shouting at the ref. From all round the ground came booing. Emlyn looked on stonily but impotently.

'I have never witnessed such appalling sportsmanship,' exploded Rod Hyde.

'Come on, we've still got two minutes,' pleaded Smartie.

Once again, Bagley stormed St Jimmy's' end. But tiredness and fury made them fumble.

'Come on, Paris,' he heard Bianca Campbell-Black screaming. Then the whistle blew long and plaintive, the train moving out of the station away from him, and it was over.

Rod Hyde had not been so happy since Margaret Thatcher was booted out of Downing Street. The maintained sector were proving themselves both intellectually and physically superior to the independents. He was already writing the piece in his head for *Education Guardian*. He was so proud of his students. 'Well done, well done.

'Bad luck,' he called out jovially to Emlyn. 'Several of our best players were off from injury. If we'd had our full side, you wouldn't have stood a chance.'

'Come and have tea in the common room,' Sally said hastily to Sheila Hyde.

'We were robbed,' a sobbing Dora was telling the *Mail on Sunday*.

Paris walked back, covered from top to toe in red-brown Larkshire mud, Northcliffe beside him.

'Beautiful, isn't he,' murmured Artie to Theo. 'And, God, he's brave.'

'Paris played a very gallant game,' insisted Ian.

'He did,' agreed Biffo grudgingly. 'There's no denying a first-rate public school can straighten out the most wayward lad.'

Through the twilight, he could see Paris stealthily approaching the little group round Rod Hyde and the ref who, relishing their moment of glory, were loath to leave the pitch.

'Read the fucking rule book next time,' hissed Paris and,

smashing his fist into the face of the ref, sent him crashing to the ground.

There was a horrified pause, interrupted by a burst of cheering from the Bagley Colts.

'Hit him again, he's still moving,' yelled Lando as the ambulance hurtled across the pitch.

67

Hengist loved post-mortems after games. He and Emlyn would play back videos, pinpoint achievements, discuss tactics for next week. Emlyn always saw the cause, while others watched the effect. When everyone else was cheering a try, he could tell you fifteen seconds back what moves had created it. After it was over, he could recount the whole game. He believed if you could get boys to use their brains and think, they'd be much better players and enjoy the game so much more. The boys loved Emlyn for his deep commitment, his expertise, his dedication to transmit the skills he had learnt, his extreme seriousness beneath the jokey exterior.

There was no jokiness in his face that evening as he knocked on Hengist's door.

'Oh dear,' said Hengist a minute later. Throwing a log on the fire, he took a couple of cans of beer out of the fridge.

'I hope you don't mind, I told Paris to report to me up here,' said Emlyn.

Paris climbed the stairs. His neck felt dislocated by Brute's tackles; his knees locked together; his heart battered every bruised rib. Slower and slower he climbed, mocked on all sides by framed photographs of glorious former fifteens.

Inside Hengist's study, Elaine, reclining upside down on a dark green sofa, lifted her tail. Flames dancing and crackling in the red-tiled William Morris fireplace were a cheerful contrast to the bleak faces of the two men, huge shoulders against the big bay window, through which Feral had once driven a golf ball. In the distance could be seen the orange glow of Larkminster.

'Shut the door,' snapped Emlyn.

Hengist retreated to his archbishop's chair, picking up a copy of Matthew Arnold's poems, which fell open at 'Rugby Chapel'.

> Coldly, sadly descends
> The autumn evening [read Hengist]. The field
> Strewn with its dank yellow drifts
> Of withered leaves, and the elms,
> Fade into dimness apace,
> Silent . . .

He must get on with his biography of Thomas and Matthew Arnold. Jupiter was so demanding. Hengist wondered if he really wanted to go into politics.

Emlyn, his normally genial face like granite, paced up and down for a moment, and then let loose his thunderbolt. How dare Paris let down his side, his house and his school and behave like a hooligan on the field.

'And you've let the independent system down, behaving like a yob in front of Rod Hyde, who you know will make political capital out of the whole thing.' Emlyn mimicked Rod for a second. '"We could have told you he'd revert to type." '

After another two minutes of the same rant Hengist, who was a kind man, felt Emlyn was being too brutal. To lighten the mood, Elaine got to her feet and started running on the spot on the window seat, ripping the red Paisley upholstery with her long claws.

'I really feel—' murmured Hengist.

'With respect, headmaster, don't interfere,' snarled Emlyn, then turned on Paris again. 'You realize knocking out a ref is a criminal offence. He could suffer brain damage.'

'No brain to damage.'

'Don't be bloody cheeky,' howled Emlyn, 'just get out of my sight.'

'It's not a laughing matter,' said Hengist sternly, flipping over a page, he read:

> Ah, love, let us be true
> To one another! for the world, which seems
> To lie before us like a land of dreams . . .

It was the same poem he had marked in Janna's copy. Poor Paris, he wondered, was he still hopelessly in love with her?

'Get out,' roared Emlyn.

Elaine shot under a sofa as Paris limped towards the door, shoulders hunched, the picture of desolation. He'd been so proud of being in the team; now he'd blown it. He'd let Bianca down too; he'd heard her screaming for him. Just as his desperately trembling hand reached for the polished brass doorknob, Emlyn drained his beer can and called after him.

'I also have to thank you.' Paris froze. 'If you hadn't knocked out that ref, I'd have been forced to do it myself.'

For a second Paris scowled round at him, then he smiled, slowly, infinitely sweetly. 'Brute Stevens accused me of being a "posh bastard", so I must be making some progress,' and he was gone.

'Christ, how can anyone resist that boy,' sighed Hengist.

From then on Paris began to enjoy Bagley. He played regularly for the Colts. More importantly, Theo Graham began giving him four hours' Latin and Greek coaching a week.

As Theo devoted to him that gift of teaching, that insight into another mind, that patience and ability to inspire and ignite, Paris had his first real glimpse of the enchanted world of the classics and became not altogether of this world. He lost things, he drifted in late, he forgot to eat. He was in love.

Theo was battling to finish his translation of the seven existing plays of Sophocles. Knowing Paris to be confused about his identity, he gave him *Oedipus Rex*, one of the plays he had completed, to read.

'Not only the greatest play ever written,' he told Paris at their first session in his crowded study, 'it's also all about adoption and of the dire consequences of not telling a child it's adopted.

'As an abandoned child' – what Paris loved about Theo was that he never pussyfooted around a subject – 'you must wonder if every man you meet is your father, or every woman you're attracted to is your mother.'

'Perhaps that's why I fancy Bianca,' said Paris dryly, 'who's so young she couldn't possibly be my mother.'

Theo himself had reached an age when he no longer expected reciprocated love, just something to look forward to and dream about at night to distract him from the often terrible pain in his back.

The shadows under Paris's eyes were the pale mauve of harebells, his eyes the grey of overcast skies. He had the straight nose and pallor of an Elgin marble, which Theo would never give back to the Greeks.

Theo now had a second goal, not just to live long enough to complete his translation of Sophocles, but also to get Paris into Cambridge.

68

The week before Larks faced Ofsted, as if deliberately to derail Janna, Ashton and Crispin had finally summoned her to S and C headquarters for the intended pep talk.

A lovely Hockney of a kingfisher-blue swimming pool brightened the beiges of the Evil Office, no doubt reminding the pair of the fortnight they'd just enjoyed in Tangier. Both were tanned, although Ashton must have plastered himself in factor 100 to stop his pink and white skin burning. Crispin was fatter than ever, his primrose-yellow shirt straining at the buttons to reveal his waxed chest. A new goatee beard failed to hide an extra chin. The sun had bleached both goatee and his hair a rather startling orange. The room reeked of Ashton's chloroform scent as he launched straight into the attack.

'S and C were bwought in to waise educational standards in Larkshire but we have just had to pay a massive three-hundred-and-ninety-thousand-pound fine out of our annual management fee purely because you and a handful of rural schools failed to reach their targets. Your GCSE figures were among the lowest in Larkshire.'

'Much higher than last year. We rose six per cent.'

'Not enough. You've let us down.'

'Are you aware' – Crispin glanced at his typed notes – 'your governors called an unofficial meeting because the parents were in such despair over the results and the lack of information provided?'

'Only a few parents,' said Janna, thinking of the pile of cards at the end of the summer term. 'How dare the governors hold secret meetings? It's illegal.'

'A measure of their fwustration,' sighed Ashton.

He's getting a real buzz out of this, thought Janna, looking at his hateful soft features and unblinking serpent's eyes. Putting out a delicately manicured hand, Ashton helped himself to a white chocolate from a shiny mauve box. Crispin's piggy lips watered.

'Your projected intake is also disastwous,' went on Ashton.

'The county council sabotaged that by changing the bus routes,' said Janna quickly. 'No parent is going to allow their eleven-year-olds to walk three-quarters of a mile from the school gates – particularly in winter. We were just getting known as a rapidly improving school then crap press ruins it. A lot of parents changed their minds about coming to Larks after the hopelessly biased reports on the geography field trip.'

'Oh my dear, I was coming to that.' Ashton nibbled another chocolate and finding it lime-centred, lobbed it, to Crispin's distress, into the bin. 'That disaster was of your own making. In this vewy office we warned you not to bond with Hengist B-T. Carried away by his glamour, you flew too near the sun. You were the only head in charge that fatal night. If Alex Bwuce hadn't arrived and taken control, you'd all have lost your jobs. You're lucky Wandal Stancombe didn't have Paris and Xavier Campbell-Black up on a wape charge. Jade Stancombe was evidently so traumatized she couldn't bear to go through the experience again in court.'

'Jade's been going through the same experience since she was twelve. She's a slut.'

'Dear, dear, your language! And after all Wandal's done for you. I hope you're making enough use of that minibus.'

Janna decided to go on the attack.

'I'll never improve my school until you give me more money. We must have more teachers. We must have the roof repaired: reception was flooded last week. We must have more books and more computers—'

'Must, must, must,' interrupted Ashton smoothly: 'I'm amazed you can ask when you've just lost us nearly four hundred thousand pounds. I'd concentwate on pulling yourself together as much as possible before Ofsted next week.'

'The new refuge for asylum-seekers hasn't helped either,' protested Janna, getting to her feet. 'They're great kids, but we're getting six and seven a week, most of them with no English. You just settle them in and find them friends, so they don't totally destabilize established classes, then they move on again. Many of them come from war zones and are used to carrying guns.'

'Then they must feel thoroughly at home at Larks,' said

Crispin nastily, 'and at least they're easing your surplus-places situation, so don't knock it.'

'I bet Rod Hyde hasn't been lumbered with them.'

'That's because Wod's school is overflowing, and if you're going to use words like "lumbered" ' – Ashton pretended to look shocked – 'you shouldn't be in teaching. What was Larks's mission statement about cultivating every child's special excellence?'

'Oh eff off,' screamed Janna and stormed out.

'Good luck with Ofsted,' a highly satisfied Ashton called after her.

69

Janna's determination to conquer Ofsted was not helped by the panicking of her entire staff. At breaktime the day before, even an old hand like Skunk Illingworth was grumbling that he'd stayed up until four in the morning typing out the three-term development plan of the entire science department.

'I didn't,' scoffed Red Robbie, who was ringing jobs in the *TES*. 'All inspectors are failed teachers.'

'Takes one to know one,' muttered Wally who seemed to have painted the entire school, even the bird table, a brighter canary yellow.

During the same breaktime, Enid the librarian had fallen asleep on the sofa clutching a cup of coffee, which dripped on to her fawn flares. She had worked the entire weekend rolling back the date stamp, slapping it on every book in sight to indicate extensive borrowing, even bringing in her own rampageous children to rough up unread volumes. If only Paris were still here: he'd never stopped reading.

The pupils, on the other hand, were gleeful at the prospect of seeing their teachers going through the hoop, particularly silly old Basket who was one long panic attack. Dr Boon, the appropriately named local GP, was getting writer's cramp scribbling sick notes and prescriptions for tranquillizers.

'It may seem obvious,' said Janna as she gave the remaining staff a last-minute briefing, 'but I trust by now you've all familiarized yourselves with the files of every child in your class or tutor group. Please emphasize our positive use of the whiteboard and IT, even if most of our computers need updating. Show the inspectors the children's best work. Tell them the good things about our school. Dress attractively but conservatively – no minis or cleavages.' She looked pointedly at Gloria. 'Be friendly; they're not ogres.'

By which time most of the staff had gone into Red Robbie mode, folding their arms and gazing truculently up at the tobacco-stained staffroom ceiling.

'And when you go to the toilet' – Janna addressed their thrust-out chins – 'for God's sake check, before slagging anyone off, that an inspector isn't lurking in the next-door booth. Finally, the inspectors will be based in the interview room, so if any of the more volatile parents roll up, head them off and ask them to come back later.' Janna forced a smile. 'Frankly you're a terrific bunch so just be yourselves and good luck to you all.'

As well as pupils, teachers and parents, the inspectors would be interviewing the governors, who were sharpening their claws, particularly after Janna had ticked them off at the last meeting for caballing behind her back.

'And please don't badmouth the school,' she had added, 'when we're trying so hard to save it.'

'Could have fooled me,' muttered Stormin' Norman, who was marshalling disaffected parents to put in the boot.

'We just hope you'll keep your students under control,' had been Russell's last word. 'It's we who have to carry the can.'

At least Janna's friends hadn't let her down. Mags Gablecross and Year Nine had produced a marvellous Spanish display of sombreros, tambourines and brave bulls tossing terrified matadors.

Cambola was magicking celestial sounds out of the choir and an orchestra which she'd started. ' "If the trumpet gives an un-certain sound",' she exhorted them, ' "how shall he prepare himself to the battle?"

'Every child matters. Our ethos is to cultivate each child's special excellence and bolster their self-esteem so they confront the future with confidence,' intoned Lydia, Lance and Gloria. 'Every child matters, our ethos is to . . .'

'Please let me not let Larks down,' prayed pretty, very plump Sophy Belvedon, Patience and Ian's daughter, who had taken Vicky's place as head of English and drama and who had proved a huge success.

Mike Pitts, meanwhile, was overdosing on Gold Spot, scurf drifting on his shiny blazered shoulders. Skunk Illingworth ponged so dreadfully, Janna engaged in stench warfare and placed on his desk a deodorant, which he merely returned to her desk.

'This must be yours, headmistress.'

I'm a head's mistress, thought Janna wearily, or would be if I ever got a chance to see him.

Determined not to look like a school-marm, she had invested in a lovely ivy-green suit and a pretty frilled shirt in wild rose pink, which she had laid out with new tights last thing, before falling to her knees: 'Oh dear God, look after my school tomorrow.'

After a restless night, she arrived at Larks at half past seven. Partner, sporting a crimson bow, his red winter coat thickening, bounced ahead, happy to find Debbie, whom he loved and who meant titbits, had already put on a slow cooking goat curry, and was now in reception watering a jungle of potted plants forming the background of the Save the Tiger project. In and out of them drifted gaudy parrots, howler monkeys, sly snakes and splendid amber-eyed tigers. Graffi, who had drawn and cut them out of cardboard for Year Seven to colour, was touching up the tigers' stripes with black gloss.

'That looks grand,' sighed Janna. 'Bless you, Graffi.'

To add authenticity to the tiger display, the schizoid central heating had opted for tropical. Graffi had already removed his crimson sweatshirt. Noticing a big purple bruise on his arm, Janna hoped his father wasn't drinking again.

Reception had also been brightened by flags representing the nationalities of every child in the school. Two more had been added after yet another influx of asylum-seekers on Friday.

Beside the main desk like a welcome committee was a second display entitled 'Movers and Shakers', which included life-size cut-outs of Kennedy, Martin Luther King and Margaret Thatcher.

'Here's hassle,' hissed Graffi as Chally bustled in, her dark brown suit topped with a yellow autumn-leaf-patterned scarf, which Janna found herself sycophantically admiring.

'Yes, everyone likes it,' replied Chally smugly. Having sniffed Debbie's goat curry approvingly – 'a caring gesture to our Afro-Caribbean brethren' – she predictably bristled at 'Movers and Shakers'.

'Black women are deplorably under-represented.'

'Not any more they ain't,' grinned Graffi, splashing black gloss over the faces of Margaret Thatcher, Germaine Greer and Florence Nightingale. 'Florence was a lesbian as well, which makes her even more PC. Silly old bitch getting her effnics in a twist,' he murmured as an apoplectic Chally was fortunately distracted by one of Johnnie Fowler's BNP posters and made a fearful fuss about breaking a nail when she ripped it off the wall.

The young teachers, Lance, Lydia and Sophy Belvedon, yawned as they straightened displays, checked spelling, jazzed up lesson plans and prayed the children would be in a good mood.

'It all looks lovely,' repeated Janna.

In her office the sun had shrugged off its polar-bear coat of dirty white cloud and was shining on the new yellow paint. She was touched to receive good-luck cards from all the Bagley children who'd been on the geography field trip except Paris, and from Sally Brett-Taylor, but worried that the central heating was growing increasingly tropical. She longed to take off her jacket but before the inspector arrived at nine she had to take assembly.

' "Every little thing gonna be all right," ' sang Bob Marley over the public-address system.

'We won't bother with a hymn or a talk today,' she told the packed hall, 'but I'd just like you all to put your hands together, shut your eyes and ask God to look after our school.

'On the other hand,' she continued thirty seconds later, 'God will need your help. The inspectors will be with us for several days, so please be nice to them. Try not to shove or shout, or swear, or drop litter, or your gum.' Glancing around at their anxious faces: 'And try to look happy.'

'How can I look happy when I'm trying to remember all these fings,' grumbled Rocky.

'Above all,' urged Janna, 'be yourselves.'

On cue she received a text from Hengist: 'Above all, *don't* be yourself,' she read, 'or you'll duff up any inspector who criticizes your beloved children. Good luck. When am I going to see you? H'.

Laughing, Janna looked up at the children and said, 'As you file out, I'd like all teachers to double-check the appearance of their classes. Do up your shirt buttons, Kitten, and pull down your skirt. Tuck in your shirt, Johnnie; pull up your socks, Martin. Have you all brushed your hair and cleaned your nails? Miss Basket isn't in? OK, I'll check Nine A.'

She was just working her way down the row of black, yellow, brown, pink and freckled hands, all with commendably clean nails, when she felt Partner's tail bashing her legs, heard whoops of laughter and found herself examining a huge hand, whitened by scars from rugby studs, and with big square nails and fingers.

Looking up, she found Emlyn grinning down at her.

'Oh Emlyn, you are daft.'

' 'Lo, Mr Davies, 'lo Mr Davies.' The children swarmed joyfully around him. 'When are we going to Bagley again?'

'When you learn to behave.' Emlyn produced a big bunch of reddy-brown chrysanthemums from behind his back, 'For your

427

office, lovely, and to match your hair. And these are for your inspectors.' From his pockets he produced packets of herbal, peppermint and fruit tea and a jar of decaffeinated coffee. 'If you don't have any, they're sure to want it.'

'You are so dear,' gasped Janna.

'And you look so pretty in your green suit, just smile and wow them. I must go.' As he kissed Janna on the cheek, all the children whooped again.

'Now, you be particularly good, Miss Curtis has worked her heart out for you lot.'

He was so reassuring and made everything seem so normal, Janna longed for him to stay.

'You're blushing, miss,' accused Pearl.

'It's the central heating,' said Janna hastily. 'Now hurry back to your classrooms, they'll be here in a minute.'

Dear Emlyn, thought Janna, then groaned as her head of PE approached in patent-leather thigh boots, leather shorts and a see-through black shirt.

'You told me to cover up,' protested Gloria. 'That Emlyn's right hunky, isn't he?'

Gloria, it seemed, had, out of nerves, gone out clubbing, and hadn't had time to go home and change.

'Well, for God's sake,' said an exasperated Janna, 'nip down to New Look and get a less transparent top.'

'It's nearly nine,' warned Rowan. 'You're a disgrace, Gloria.'

'You'd better take my shirt,' snarled Janna, dragging Gloria into her office. 'I'll just have to keep my jacket on.'

'I'm ever so sorry. Such a pretty blouse, are you sure?'

'No, I'm bloody not. Put it on.'

In fact Janna's wild rose pink shirt straining over Gloria's thrusting thirty-eight-inch boobs looked even more flagrantly provocative than the see-through black.

Bugger, thought Janna buttoning her wool suit, the temperature was rising by the second.

As Wally gave her brown boots a last polish, there was an enraged banging on the door and Chally barged in.

'Oh, there you are, Wally. Everyone is so stressed, the women's toilet smells like a sewage farm. Can you please put more air freshener in there?'

'And in Skunk Illingworth's classroom,' snapped Janna.

'And I don't know' – Chally's lips tightened – 'who put all those Penhaligon's toiletries in there, the inspector will think we're rolling in money.'

'I did.' Janna was fed up with Chally. 'They were a present. Do you want me to put up a sign saying "Gifted Toiletries"?'

'They're here, they're here.'

Rowan rushed in removing her suit jacket to show off a charming cream linen shirt, straightening Janna's papers, shoving her buckling in-tray under the sofa, then, like a teenager's mum before a dance, straightening Partner's bow tie, before he rushed off sending cardboard, black-faced Margaret Thatcher flying in his haste to welcome the visitors.

As Bob Marley was replaced by Schubert's *Marche Militaire*, such a brisk jaunty tune, Janna found herself marching down the corridor. In reception, the inspector was crouched down admiring the largest of Graffi's tigers.

'This is a very fine beast,' he said. Rising to his feet, he took Janna's trembling hand. 'Wade Hargreaves, and, from your photographs, you must be Janna Curtis.'

Janna had expected an ogre but the man smiling down at her was tall, slim, in his late thirties and with the genial friendliness of a yellow Labrador.

'Welcome to Larks,' said Janna in relief.

'Oh Christ,' muttered Mike Pitts, going green and reversing into his office, 'it's Wade Hargreaves. I sacked him when I was head of maths at Rutminster Comp.'

Wade Hargreaves was accompanied by, amongst others, a spinster called Miss Spicer, who had one of Chalford's draped scarves, short spiky hair, a lantern jaw, disapproving coffee-bean brown eyes and who, having demanded a cup of peppermint tea, seemed disappointed when it was provided. Well done, Emlyn.

From then onwards Janna felt the sharp constant pain of a steel toothcomb being plunged into the scalp and tugged through tangled hair as Wade Hargreaves's team went everywhere, talked to everyone and asked for every lesson plan, file and balance sheet to be taken into the interview room. Brandishing clipboards they moved around devouring timetables, schemes of work, attendance figures, the first tentative coursework of Year Ten, and listening to Sam Spink in her Hogwarts' character socks, her massive thighs spilling over her chair like suet as she charted the inadequacies of Larks's workload agreement.

Mike Pitts, unable to face Wade Hargreaves, disappeared home with stress. By contrast Mags Gablecross was everywhere, guiding, supporting, comforting staff who felt they had cocked up.

'I could have done it so much better,' sobbed Lydia. 'I made a tape about Simon Armitage to nudge my memory but Johnnie Fowler got hold of it and played it back to the class and Miss Spicer.'

'I got Ten C too revved up about Billy the Kid,' said Lance dolefully. 'One of the asylum-seekers pulled out a gun and Miss Spicer said I must remember that the Indians not the cowboys were the heroes.'

But there were good moments.

'Until Miss came, I had no grown-ups to talk to,' Pearl told Wade Hargreaves. 'No one respected me. Now school remembers my birthday, I get a card and a Mars bar and a song in assembly. She's going to help me take a make-up course.'

'Miss is there for the mums,' said Kylie. 'She helps them fill in forms for the social and the courts. She listens when their partners leave them or they can't pay their rent. She filled in my brovver's driving licence for him, and she remembered Cameron's birfday. Lots of teachers don't know all our names. Miss even knows all our babies' names.'

'We get letters to take home in Urdu,' said Aysha, 'so Mum and Dad can understand what's going on. Mum came to parents' day for the first time; there was cake and orange juice and she talked to other mums.'

70

Assembly the following morning was a great success. Kylie Rose lifted the hair on the back of everyone's neck singing 'It's a Wonderful World'. Aysha in her headscarf read from the Koran, Graffi from the New Testament – 'Judge not that ye be not judged' – which made Wade and even Miss Spicer smile. Danijela, one of the new asylum-seekers, read a Bosnian prayer, then the choir sang 'How Lovely are Thy Dwellings' so beautifully as the morning sun streamed through the stained-glass St Michael that even Miss Spicer wiped away a tear and Wade grinned across at Janna.

He was a terrific listener, as still as a wildlife cameraman who knows the only way to score is to move quietly. He and Miss Spicer were unfazed when Graffi's father, who'd been in the pub all day, dropped into the interview room for a quiet kip before going home. Or when Pearl's boxer father, just out of gaol, rolled up to get even with one of the pushers outside the school gates and try and catch a glimpse of his wife and her toyboy friend.

Debbie had been thrilled yesterday when the inspectors lunched in the canteen and had second helpings both of goat curry and rhubarb crumble and were constantly requesting more flapjacks for the interview room.

Things were dicey when they caught up with Feral, sulky because he was having a one-to-one lesson with Sophy Belvedon in the individual learning unit, which had once been the changing rooms before the football pitch was sold off.

Sophy, realizing Feral would only attempt to read if he were interested, had blown up both Sunday's football reports on Arsenal and pages from a biography of Sol Campbell.

'You're not thick, Feral,' Sophy was telling him. 'People are

431

stupidly characterized these days as gifted, able or with needs.'

'I've got needs all right. I need a fag and a shag,' said Feral, grabbing Sophy and burying his sleek face in her splendid breasts.

'I don't think my husband Alizarin would like that.' Sophy edged away her legs and hips, leaving her bosom in Feral's strong grip. 'He's six foot four and built like an oak tree.' Then, as Feral reluctantly released her: 'Not that you're not utterly gorgeous.'

'Wiv needs.' Feral batted his long eyelashes. He liked Sophy but he found it humiliating to be taught on his own. It was all Paris's fault for deserting him.

Wade and Miss Spicer asked Feral a little about work and then about the other teachers.

'Miss went to court with me in August; her evidence got me off. She got me a job working for two coffin-dodgers, mowing, chopping logs and fings; later me and Lily got wasted on sloe gin.

'Most of the teachers are shit here,' Feral went on. 'Chalford's shit, so're Robbie and Skunk, Miss Basket's crap too, she ought to be able to control us. Mrs Gablecross is nice, we can talk to her about anyfing. I need a fag.' Feral shook an empty pack in irritation. 'That no-good mother-fucking nigger-basher Monster Norman pinched my last one.'

'You can't call him that,' said Miss Spicer faintly.

'*You* can't call him that,' corrected Feral mockingly, 'but I can, 'cos I'm black and underprivileged. As a representative of an underprivileged effnic minority, I can call him anyfing I like.'

Sophy tried not to laugh, particularly when Miss Spicer rallied and asked Feral if he felt underprivileged.

'People call you "black shit".' Feral tipped back his chair, testing their reaction through narrowed speculative eyes. 'But if you play football well enough, you earn eighty grand a week and in a few seasons go from being "black shit" to God. That's why I'm gonna become a footballer. Put a recommendation in your report' – he tapped Miss Spicer's clipboard – 'that Larks needs a football pitch.'

'Thank you, Feral and Mrs Belvedon,' said Wade.

Checking the dining room at lunchtime on the second day, Janna's heart sank to see Miss Spicer and a jolly blond member of the team called Mrs Mills tucking into toad in the hole and deep in conversation with Rocky. Did he know that Larkshire had one of the highest rates of teenage pregnancies in the country?'

'Sure,' replied Rocky. 'That's 'cos Kylie Rose lives here.'

'I don't think that's quite right,' said Mrs Mills, who was dieting and reluctantly setting aside a piece of gold, utterly delicious, batter. 'Do you find sex education enlightening, Rocky?'

'Sex education is wicked, man.' Rocky bit suggestively on a sausage. 'They never stop banging on about STDs but they tell you lotsa ways to have sex – blow jobs, going down and fings, anal sex – without getting girls up the duff.'

'That's enough, Rocky,' said Janna firmly. 'Go and get yourself some dessert, you know you like jam roly-poly.'

'Sorry about that,' said Janna, 'Rocky gets carried away. Can I get you some sweet?'

Both Miss Spicer and Mrs Mills felt they'd had enough.

'Would you like to hear my poem about a skylark?' asked Rocky, returning.

'That sounds nice,' said Mrs Mills bravely.

'I heard a skylark singing so sweetly in the sky,' began Rocky, seeing relief dawning on the faces of his listeners, 'but when I looked to find him, he dumped right in my eye.'

'I think I'd like to see the D and T department now,' said Mrs Mills.

'I'll take you there,' said Janna and was just expounding on the splendid work being done when they heard screams. Rounding the corner they nearly fell over Pearl, who was lying on top of Kitten Meadows, holding clumps of her hair in order to smash her head on the stone floor.

'Take it back.'

'No,' squealed Kitten.

'Take it fucking back.' Smash.

'No.' Clawing at Pearl's face with long silver nails, Kitten drew blood. 'You always look fucking crap.'

'Fucking don't.' Pearl smashed her fist into Kitten's face, whereupon Kitten hit Pearl on her left breast.

'Ow,' screamed Pearl.

'Please stop,' called out Basket faintly from the safety of her classroom.

As a crowd gathered – 'C'mon, Pearl, c'mon, Kitten' – Wade Hargreaves emerged from a history lesson, so Janna dived in on the right, ducking blows, trying to prise the contestants apart.

A second later, Sophy Belvedon had rushed up and dived in on the left. As Kitten tried to elbow her in the ribs, she said: 'Won't work, I'm much too fat to feel anything.'

'Stop it, both of you,' yelled Janna.

At that moment Wally arrived and with his superior strength dragged off a spitting, wriggling Pearl.

'Take her to my office,' panted Janna. 'You can go to the gym,' she told Kitten, 'and both of you will have detentions tonight and tomorrow.' Then, when they furiously protested, continuing trying to kick out at each other: 'That's final, now get out of my sight.'

Having administered smelling salts to Basket, Janna, aware that a button had been ripped off her suit and her neatly piled-up hair had come down, retreated to the Ladies where she met Sophy coming out, and said, 'Thanks so much for your help.'

'That Basket's a wet hen.'

'Hush.' Janna put her finger to her lips. Seeing an engaged sign on one of the doors she crept into the next-door booth. Climbing on to the seat and peering over the partition she discovered Miss Spicer knitting and reading *Good Housekeeping* and was so startled she fell back into the lavatory bowl with a shriek.

'Checking for spies?' asked Miss Spicer dryly.

'Sort of.'

'One needs a break from inspection.'

'And from being a head,' sighed Janna.

'Hello,' added Miss Spicer as Partner's snout appeared under her door. 'That is a delightful dog, he seems to know instinctively when a child is sad. He was trailing that pretty fair-haired Bosnian girl this morning.'

Shaking her wet boot Janna climbed down.

'That's probably because we made Danijela our bird girl. Every morning she takes out a tin of scraps which contains rich pickings from the kitchen. We couldn't think why the birds were standing indignantly round with their wings on their hips until we discovered' – Janna's voice quivered – 'Danijela was emptying the tin into her school bag for her friends in the refuge.'

'Can't take on everyone's burdens,' said Miss Spicer briskly, but her coffee-bean eyes were kind as she washed her hands vigorously before applying Bluebell hand cream. Then, painting her small mouth bright orange and rearranging the folds of her scarf, she announced she was off to the Appletree annexe to monitor some science lessons.

Miss Spicer had an eventful day. She was observing one of Mr Mates's experiments when the roof of Appletree finally caved in on her and Year Ten E, who emerged unhurt but much aged by grey, dust-filled hair.

'It worked with the other division,' bleated a shaken Mr Mates, who had to be reassured that the collapsing roof had nothing to do with his experiment.

'How lousy are thy dwellings, oh S and C,' sang Cambola,

whose music department next door had also been submerged.

'They'll have to give us a new roof now,' said Mags Gablecross.

Next day Pearl gave Wade Hargreaves even more pressing reasons.

'I spend half an hour straightening my hair every morning, then the rain pours through the roof and it goes all kinky; that's why Kitten Meadows said my hair was crap and that's why I hit her. If we had new roofs this wouldn't happen.

'My dad's a boxer,' she went on, 'so it's in my genes to land punches. Fights isn't Miss's fault. She's great, and so's Mrs Belvedon, the new English teacher.'

'I'm just going to watch Mrs Belvedon giving Year Eight a lesson on *The Tempest*,' said Wade.

'Oh bugger,' grumbled Sophy, retrieving some dropped folders, then, as Year Eight giggled: 'You'll have to move your table, Stefan and Josef, I'm much too fat to get through that gap.'

'You do sound posh, miss.'

'If you think I'm posh you should hear my mother.'

'Paris is living with her?' asked Kata from Kosovo longingly. 'How's he getting on?'

'Fine.' Sophy was amazed by Larks's ongoing obsession with their lost leader. 'Now to Caliban. My husband Alizarin has done a painting of him.' On the whiteboard appeared a picture of a ferocious-looking beast, half wild boar, half gorilla, but with the saddest eyes.

'See his long nails for digging up pig nuts for his master. Caliban is a really sympathetic character,' Sophy went on, 'he's a bit ugly, but he longs to help and be loved and he says beautiful poetic things. Some horrid sailors are shipwrecked on his island and get poor Caliban drunk, so he makes a fool of himself. He adores Miranda, his boss's daughter.'

A picture of a pretty blonde in a ruff and long Elizabethan dress appeared on the whiteboard. 'But she's in love with some-one else, and I'm sure you all know how it hurts when you love someone who doesn't love you.'

Wade Hargreaves couldn't imagine anyone not loving Sophy.

'And I bet lots of you boys when you go to parties feel shy of chatting up girls, so you drink too much and fall over – well, that's Caliban.'

'He's gentle giant like King Kong,' piped up Kata.

'Exactly.'

'And Monster Norman, except he's horrible.'

'No, no.' Sophy looked round nervously. 'Anyway, this is

Alizarin's picture, and now I want you all to produce your own idea of Caliban. You've got paints on each table and plasticene and paper. Try not to paint each other. Anyone who comes up with an interesting idea can have one or two of these.' She waved a tin of Quality Street. 'Now: ready, steady, go.'

Sitting at the back of the class Wade and Miss Spicer made notes on their clipboards and watched Sophy advising, praising, laughing, screaming with joy – 'That is so good!' – and occasionally remonstrating: 'Don't put that blue brush back in the white pot, Jasper.'

The children, particularly the ones who couldn't speak English, were having a ball. As they slapped on paint or modelled in plasticene or clay, a wonderful zoo emerged.

'I can't do his nails,' wailed Kata.

On cue in pattered Partner and obligingly held up a paw so they could see his claws.

'Good boy.' Sophy hugged him and rewarded him with the Quality Street green-wrapped triangle which was all chocolate.

'That is really cool, Anwar,' she cried, pausing beside a Pakistani boy's desk. 'You've made Caliban look happy because he's asleep. That's in the text: he was so hurt by humans, only in dreams did he find happiness, and when he woke he cried to dream again. This is so good. Brilliant colours too. Lay it out on that chair to dry.'

What a lovely young woman, thought Wade wistfully. Shortly afterwards he was so impressed by another painting of Caliban he sat down on Anwar's picture to study it and was left with red, blue, green and purple splodges all over the seat of his elegant beige suit.

The children screamed with laughter.

'Oh, goodness,' wailed Sophy, 'you look more like a mandrill than a nimble marmoset. I'm so sorry. I'll get it dry cleaned or take it home and wash it for you.'

'Don't give it a thought, I might start a fashion.'

Janna, who'd just been forced into giving Monster a detention for cheeking some other member of the inspection team, was vastly cheered when she peered into Sophy's classroom and saw even Miss Spicer laughing.

As the bell rang for break, Year Eight bore Wade off to the playground to show him the bird table.

'That's a robin.'

'No, stupid, it's a bullfinch.'

'This is the pond,' said Kata, leading him out into the garden. 'We're going to clean it to encourage wild lives. Wally's made a ladder so anything drowning can climb out. And he's going to build a duck house and a bridge to the island.'

'Perhaps Miss Curtis will get you some fish.'

How nice he is, thought Janna, watching from the window, but we mustn't be lulled into a false security.

'Would you like a cup of tea?' she asked as he returned from his tour to her office.

She'd just put on the kettle, when Stormin' Norman roared in. 'You know Martin don't do detentions on a Thursday. You're depriving him of his liberty.'

She was about to punch Janna, who was protesting that surely it was Wednesdays, when Wade stepped out from behind the door, where he'd been admiring some stills from *Romeo and Juliet.*

'I wouldn't.'

'And 'oo the fuck are you?' yelled Stormin' Norman. 'Another of 'er fucking fancy men?' But at least her fist stopped in mid-air.

They were interrupted by the arrival of Chally, bright red in the face.

'One of the Croatians has exposed himself to Year Seven. I said, "We don't do things like that here, Roman, put it away," but he laughed in my face so I called back-up.'

'Front-up, more likely,' said Janna, trying not to laugh.

'This is serious, Senior Team Leader.'

They were distracted yet again by a yell and the crash of plasterboard. Pearl's boxer father had rolled up drunk again and discovered Graffi's father, whom he suspected of once pleasuring his wife, fast asleep in the interview room.

'I told you it was in my genes,' said Pearl smugly as the police arrived to remove both her father and Stormin' Norman.

71

On Friday afternoon Wade called a meeting after school to report on his team's findings. Russell, Ashton and Crispin arrived early. As the interview room had been temporarily totalled by Pearl's boxer dad, they were ushered into Janna's office, where they drank tea, guzzled Debbie's chocolate cake and rubbed their hands in anticipation of a serious drubbing for little Miss Curtis.

Crispin, who was perched on the sofa beside Ashton, murmured that Debbie was an excellent cook.

'She'll be looking for a job tomorrow,' murmured back Ashton. 'I'll put in a good word at County Hall. Perhaps she could come and do for me.'

As Mike Pitts was still off with stress, Mags had been asked by Janna to stand in for him. Pacing up and down outside, Mags had never felt so tired. She was so worried for Janna, who never failed to wear her generous heart on her sleeve.

'Any room for a little one?' said Cindy Payne, the Larkshire county councillor in charge of education, parking her red-trouser-suited bottom on the sofa between Crispin and Ashton. Both men would have liked to edge away but were too firmly wedged.

Russell had commandeered a big upright chair. In his hand was another letter of complaint from Miss Miserden about Larks hooligans swearing and kicking balls into her garden.

'Thought you might like to see this, Inspector.'

Wade, sitting at an imported table shifting papers and flanked by Miss Spicer and Mrs Mills, hardly glanced at the letter before handing it back.

'Sorry to keep you.' Janna rushed in followed by Partner. She settled down at her desk, ramming her hands between her thighs to conceal their trembling. So many things had gone wrong; so many bricks dropped; so many children out of control. Mags, sliding into a little red armchair beside her, squeezed her arm.

Through the window they could see the children running home through the pouring rain, their coats over their heads. After the row at the last governors' meeting, Russell's eyes refused to meet Janna's.

'Hope you survived,' he said heartily to the three inspectors.

'Extremely well,' said Wade, then turning to Janna, 'thank you for your hospitality. We have been made most welcome and given every assistance in forming our opinions.'

Then he unleashed both barrels. Larks in a word was being used by S and C and the county council as a pupil referral unit, or rather a dumping ground for all the rubbish kids with behaviour problems that were expelled from other schools.

'After four days, however, my team and I were delighted to see what efforts are being made by the staff to tackle attendance, unauthorized absence and deplorable behaviour. Support for vulnerable pupils is excellent, as is mentoring. Despite standards being constantly eroded by the behaviour of certain parents and a very disruptive band of children, bad behaviour is dealt with swiftly. Special needs are catered for well within very limited resources. Overall adherence to the curriculum has also been observed.'

Slowly, slowly, Janna felt her foot leaving the bottom of the sea as she drifted upwards towards the sunlight.

Wade consulted his notes. 'The teaching of the older staff is less than satisfactory. Their lessons are often dull, their marking unhelpful.' He pinpointed Chally, Mike Pitts, who had once sacked him, Skunk, Basket, Sam Spink and Robbie. Janna bit her lip: all her *bêtes noires*.

'On the other hand, language teaching was excellent.' Wade smiled at Mags. 'So was Miss Cambola's music and Mr Mates's science.' He then praised Janna's appointments: the new deputy head of history and the head of D and T, and in particular Sophy Belvedon. 'Quite excellent, we much enjoyed her English lesson bringing in both art and drama disciplines.

'Despite the appallingly deprived lives of so many of the children, this is a happy school, a haven which makes many of their lives bearable.'

Russell was rotating his signet ring; Cindy's little dark eyes were like those of an angry swan; Crispin, swelling like a balloon about to pop, seized the last piece of chocolate cake. Janna put her burning face in her hands. She must be dreaming.

'Janna Curtis' – Wade smiled at Janna's bowed head – 'is clearly very popular with pupils and parents for whom she appears to act as a Citizens' Advice Bureau, and by all the staff except the reactionary and the work-shy. She has also had considerable success winning over the community.'

He also praised the excellent displays in reception and on the walls and particularly the hard work and cheerful contribution of Wally and Debbie.

'I shall miss her flapjacks. The beautiful grounds are in good order,' he went on, 'although the children need a playing field.'

Everyone jumped as a football smacked the window.

Much of Wade's disapproval was reserved for the state of the buildings – one of which had collapsed on a member of the inspection team – the atrocious damp, erratic central heating and leaking roofs.

'Which leads me back to the appalling poverty of resources,' he said bleakly. 'We get the impression that both S and C Services and the county council, for some reason, have been deliberately withholding money. From the minutes, the governors appear to have been totally unsupportive to Janna Curtis' – Wade glared at Russell – 'ganging up and scapegoating her. In this they have been hugely aided by a local press so unrelentingly damaging that one might imagine conspiracy.'

As Partner gnawed on an old beef bone given him by Debbie, Ashton lost it.

'Get that bloody dog out of here.' He aimed a kick at Partner, who yelped.

Wade raised an eyebrow. 'If Larks fails,' he concluded, 'it will not be Janna Curtis's fault. As I've said, like its name, Larks is a happy place.'

Janna sat stunned, then, leaping to her feet, ran round and shook hands with a smiling Miss Spicer and Mrs Mills. She turned to Wade and, unable to stop herself, flung her arms round his neck and kissed him, leaving pink lipstick marks on both cheeks.

'Oh, thank you all, thank you, thank you,' she cried tearfully.

'Janna kissed me when we met, Jumping from the chair she sat in,' sighed Wade and then beamed. 'I'm sure you want to pass on the good news to your staff,' he told her. 'I'll be sending you a full report.'

'Thanks so much.' Janna bolted, unable to face the rage of the Gang of Four, who retreated to the Evil Office to lick terrible wounds.

'Curtis clearly dropped her knickers,' said Crispin pouring four large brandies.

'I've never been so insulted in my life,' spluttered Cindy Payne. 'Can we sue?'

'I can only resign,' said Russell. 'Scapegoated indeed. That trollop.'

'You stay put,' ordered Ashton. 'We've got work to do.'

Hengist brought round two bottles of Veuve Clicquot, lit Lily of the Valley scented candles and to the accompaniment of *Capriccio* on Radio 3 gave Janna a bath.

Slowly, lingeringly, he ran soap over her breasts and up between her legs, groping and fingering, then slapped her lightly on the bottom. 'Are you going to be good tonight?'

After he'd dried her, they collapsed in front of the sitting-room fire, made all the more cosy by the relentless patter of the rain outside.

'I cannot believe it,' sighed Janna. 'Wade's looks went everywhere and he seemed to like what e'er he looked on.'

'Your Ofsteady boyfriend, clearly a man of discernment,' said Hengist.

'He virtually accused S and C of malpractice. Cindy looked so pained, Crispin misery-ate most of Debbie's chocolate cake and Ashton went totally silent, but his eyes . . .' Janna shuddered. 'Then he kicked Partner. Spicer was so nice in the end and Wade – well!'

'You bewitched him,' said Hengist.

Pushing her back on the fluffy rug, he ran his tongue along the tender undersides of her breasts, but Janna couldn't get into the mood for sex.

'He loved me for the dangers I had passed,' she murmured, echoing Othello. 'And I loved him that he did pity me. This is the only witchcraft I have used. He realized I'd been scapegoated.'

'I wish you wouldn't butcher a perfectly good noun,' sighed Hengist. 'Scapegoated is worse than showcase.'

'It was the scapegoat curry wot did it,' giggled Janna, 'and probably Sally's good-luck card. I feel so guilty.'

'No you don't,' said Hengist, who was bored with Ofsted. He was due at dinner five minutes ago, was getting a reputation for lateness, and wanted sex now. As if in sympathy, the rain was drumming its fingers on the window. Throwing a log on the fire, which put up a shower of orange sparks, he took Janna's ankles and parted them like scissors, then kissed his way up her warm, scented, freckled thighs.

He loved it when she went quiet, but, surprised by her lack of response – by now she should be writhing, gasping and growing damp – he looked up. She'd fallen asleep.

72

The rage and humiliation of Ashton and Crispin knew no bounds. Ashton, despite his soft features, his lisp and his pretty hands, was a thug who bullied Crispin as relentlessly as everyone else.

'I want evidence to get wid of Janna Curtis,' he ordered his deputy the following morning. 'I don't want her or Larks bouncing back.'

Janna's and Larks's euphoria over Ofsted had been sharply terminated the following week by a couple of knifings in the Shakespeare Estate and a horrific sex murder just over the border in nearby Rutminster. Bethany Watson, the sweetest ten-year-old, had been raped, strangled, then chucked under a pile of rotting hay in a cow byre, leaving a devastated and terrified community. Police were conducting house-to-house searches. Hordes of media hung around, scathingly referring to Larks as 'the Shakespeare Estate sink school'.

Larks mothers were increasingly jittery about their children having to walk home on increasingly dark evenings, because the bus stop had been moved. There were sightings of prowlers everywhere.

Chief Inspector Gablecross had been seconded to Rutminster to lead the investigation. Earlier in the term he had instructed one of his junior officers, PC Cuthbert, to keep an eye on Larks and to break up fights in the playground or at going-home time, when tensions grew high.

PC Cuthbert, despite his blond curls and fresh face, was tough, ambitious, zero-tolerant and determined to rid the town of crime. Influenced by Tim Gablecross and his wife Mags, he was unusual among his colleagues in that he liked Larks kids and felt they had a raw deal. His presence had been a definite plus.

Another plus of the term had been Lily's lectures to the newly formed Wildlife Club. Frantic not to let S and C sell off any part of Larks's beautiful land, Janna had been determined to establish them as a wildlife sanctuary and had been much heartened by Wade Hargreaves's approval.

Lily would arrive with a bootful of plum jam doughnuts and ancient binoculars weighed down with Ascot, Kempton and Goodwood labels and bear the Wildlife Club off on rambles round the grounds, identifying coloured leaves falling from the trees and birds that flocked to the bird table.

They had also sighted roe deer, muntjac, squirrels, rabbits, several foxes and, on a very mild afternoon, an adder asleep on a sunlit pile of leaves, which provoked screams of terror from the children and Monster into picking up a branch.

'Don't hurt him,' Lily had cried. 'Adders are a protected species.'

'His parents must've had unprotected sex to produce him,' observed Feral. 'Nasty killing machine.'

'They ought to practise safe sex,' said Kylie, 'then they wouldn't produce any more babies.'

'Unlike you,' said Johnnie Fowler.

The adder had retreated into the blond grasses.

The pond had also become a focus of interest. The children loved swaying across Wally's narrow bridge to the island on which stood a pale blue duck house, surrounded by willows and white poplars garlanded with brambles and wild roses.

Here, to Lily's great excitement, they sighted a greyish-brown creature covered in red warts, which turned out to be a very rare natterjack toad.

'Looks like somefing the witches'd cook wiv in *Macbeth*,' said Pearl.

'They probably did.' Lily bent down to admire the toad's bright green eyes. 'Natterjacks weren't protected in those days. You must take a photograph, Graffi. Thank you,' she added, as Feral hoisted her to her feet.

Partner, who was devoted to Lily, always accompanied them on these jaunts. The Wildlife Club adored them because Lily was easily distracted into telling them stories about her days in the Wrens, the exotic places she'd visited with her late husband the ambassador and about her wild nieces and nephews who were mostly artists.

The children had instantly taken to Lily because of her genuine kindness, sense of fun and her friendship with Feral who, now her lawn no longer needed mowing, was chopping logs, bringing in coal and sharing spliffs and a passion for Arsenal.

Feral would call her on one of his stolen mobiles: ' 'Lo, Lily, how yer doin', man?' and chat for hours about Sol and Thierry's latest exploits. Lily had started a scrapbook of Arsenal cuttings and encouraged Feral to practise and play as much as possible. Both were secretly very proud of this friendship.

It was Sam Spink, discovering Lily was being paid forty pounds in cash per nature ramble out of the school tin, who predictably sneaked to Ashton Douglas that Lily was entering the school when she hadn't been cleared by the Criminal Records Bureau to work with children.

Ashton promptly banned Lily from Larks on the very November day when a contingent from Bagley Hall was coming over to take part in a ramble. With the honour of Larks at stake, Lily had done a huge amount of cooking, and was understandably upset.

'Hardly likely at my age to jump on children in broad daylight.'

'Quite right,' agreed Johnnie Fowler. 'Lily's too old to be a kiddy-fiddler.'

'We want Lily,' chorused the Wildlife Club.

But S and C were adamant.

'When it's a question of children's safety . . .' Ashton told an enraged Janna. 'Can't think how it's gone on so long.'

'Can't be too careful,' said Sam Spink sanctimoniously.

'Sneak,' hissed Janna.

As a result No-Joke Joan stepped in to lead the ramble.

'Gratifying to have a committed professional,' enthused Chally. 'Joan is a formidable biologist.'

Joan, who'd been regaled with horror stories and instructed to spy by Alex Bruce, was curious to have a look at Larks.

Janna would have fought harder for Lily if she hadn't been besieged by parents frantic about the Rutshire prowler. Yesterday morning Chantal had rung in to report that Kylie Rose was too stressed to come in having caught sight of a suspicious bearded character in a flat cap and dark glasses photographing girls in the playground. Later in the day, three of Year Seven complained they'd seen a bearded prowler lurking between the pond and the car park. Two of the asylum-seekers from Year Eight claimed with graphic mime the same prowler had been flashing on Smokers' Bank.

Today, sightings were coming in thick and fast. What was Janna doing to safeguard the kids, demanded Kitten's mother. Chantal

Peck rang to say that, like the little soldier she was, Kylie would be coming in because she didn't want to miss lessons. Or Jack Waterlane due from Bagley, thought Janna sourly.

Stormin' Norman made the next call. Did Janna realize kiddy-fiddlers went both ways and what provision had she made to protect Martin. Janna had just put the phone down when a sobbing Pearl barged in in a bloodstained shirt, having cut herself.

'My mum must be the only mum at Larks so unconcerned about her kid she hasn't phoned in to make a fuss.'

'Oh Pearl,' sighed Janna, getting out her first-aid kit.

It would need more than Dettol and plaster to heal Pearl.

In assembly, Janna tried to calm everyone's fears. 'When you're terrified, you sometimes see people who aren't there.'

'I saw him, miss, I saw his knife,' came cries from all over the hall.

'He's got a beard and a big red willy wiv a purple knob on.'

'That's enough, Kitten. Make sure you go round in groups of three or four, and never walk home alone.'

'No one wants to walk with me any more,' sobbed Pearl.

'Oh, shut up,' snapped Kitten, throwing a hymn book at her.

Pearl was about to leap on Kitten, but, distracted by Janna's news that good-looking PC Cuthbert would be along soon, she belted off to do her face.

It was a damp, cheerless day. Trees wrapped thick grey mist round their shoulders to protect their last leaves; crows cawed morosely; any minute Dracula's carriage would rumble up the drive.

Joan, as if warding off the powers of darkness, rolled up in a calf-length Barbour, lace-up khaki gumboots and a sombrero worn over a headscarf, so only the lower half of her disapproving brick-red face was visible.

'Like a rubber fetishist's daydream,' muttered Wally.

Joan was accompanied by a giggling Amber, Milly and Jade, a sneering Boffin, a very nervous Primrose Duddon, quivering like a nun entering a brothel, the Chinless Wanderers, armed with hipflasks, and the Cosmonaughties, who had all brought wads of greenbacks to purchase drugs from the pushers who only deserted the gates if PC Cuthbert hove in sight.

'Why hasn't Paris come?' wailed Larks.

'He had double Latin,' explained Amber.

'Oh, did he now,' mocked Monster. 'How fritefly posh.'

446

'Watch it.' Feral bounced his football fractionally faster, then, turning to Amber: 'You're looking good.'

'Almost as good as you,' murmured Amber.

'Why, you're hunkier than ever,' said Milly, hugging Graffi.

'Make sure the students keep away from the bushes,' Chally advised Joan.

Aysha, who had been worried Xav would think her ugly because she had circles under her eyes from not being able to sleep for excitement about seeing him, was devastated when he didn't turn up, although she'd probably have been too shy to speak to him.

'I want some of Lily's fruit cake,' grumbled Rocky.

'You've just had lunch, young man,' reproved Joan bossily, then, blowing her whistle, set off into the mist.

Noticing Cosmo was as fatally glamorous as ever in his astrakhan coat, Pearl couldn't resist trying to attract his attention.

'I saw the prowler yesterday. I was having a quick tinkle in the bushes, and looking round saw his long lens pointing up my bum.'

'Good thing it were only his lens,' leered Monster.

'He was horrible with a flat cap and a perv's beard and shades.' Pearl was famous for exaggeration, but as the mist thickened, everyone shivered and her words gave Milly the excuse to edge near Graffi, and Amber to sidle up to Feral, and Jack to put an arm round Kylie's shoulders. After a cold night, leaves were falling in their thousands, descending without a fight to mould and enrich the earth below.

Joan strode ahead, pointing out different species.

'Look at *Hedera helix*, commonly known as ivy, its little yellow flowers a last feast for the insects. Listen to them humming: hummmm,' she went.

'I want a doughnut,' grumbled Monster. 'Lily brings doughnuts 'n' fudge 'n' chocolate cake.'

Joan turned on him disapprovingly, 'If you want to avoid obesity, young man, you should stop eating between meals.'

'That's an affront to my human dignity,' spluttered Monster, reaching for his mobile. 'I'm telling my mum.'

On Wildlife Club days, feeding the birds was always saved until the rambling party reached the bird table.

Aysha opened the tin, tipping out stale cake, pastry crusts, bacon and birdseed, as the others filled up the nets with nuts.

'Christ, I'm starved,' grumbled Feral, whipping a piece of sponge cake. 'I missed lunch, 'spectin' Lily's doughnuts.' He glared at Joan.

As the rambling party retreated, sharing Lily's binoculars, the birds began to fly in.

'That's a fieldfare,' called out Joan. 'Listen to his cry.' She went into a series of jerky, nervous whistles. 'And here's the redwing, tirra lira, tirra lira, whit, whit. Redwings come south from colder climes. At this time chaffinches and lapwings go round in flocks, you can recognize the lapwing, tirra lira, whoop whoop. There's no need to laugh, Feral Jackson, must you mock everything?'

'Cockadoodle do,' murmured Graffi, sliding his hands inside Milly's fleece.

'Robin's still singing his rich little song.' Putting on a special face, Joan went into another frenzy of whistling and trilling, which had everyone holding their own or each other's sides. Jack and Kylie vanished into the bushes.

'I want a doughnut,' moaned Rocky.

'This is the mating call of the Feral Jackson.' Amber gave three wolf whistles.

'Don't be silly, Amber. Robin will fight over his little bit of garden.'

'Like I'd fight over you,' whispered Graffi. 'You are so beautiful,' he added as he drew Milly into a clump of laurels.

As Joan peered into some long grass, Lando offered Pearl a slug of brandy.

'How's Paris?' she asked.

'Better,' drawled Lando, 'although he can still be moody and aggressive.'

'Note the beech leaves shrivelling.' Joan was pointing in all directions. 'And evergreens in their dark dress like winter furniture: yews, bay trees and over there a Lawson cypress.'

'Joan's getting quite carried away,' muttered Amber from behind a blackthorn copse.

'So am I,' said Feral, sliding his long fingers inside her knickers.

'All animals are preparing for winter. Snails retreat into their shells, squirrels into the trees, even this dear little dog' – Joan patted Partner, who was hanging around for Lily's fudge – 'is developing his thick winter coat.'

As they reached the pond, Joan put a big red finger to her lips: 'We might see the reedling. You can identify him by his brown back and grey and black head, and sometimes orange and lavender feathers. Reedlings are often known as bearded tits.'

'Plenty of those at Larks,' quipped Johnnie Fowler.

In front of the island, a blasted tree had collapsed, half in, half out of the water, its reflection like the strong limbs, torso and thrown-back head of a sleeping god. Above it rose poplar saplings and the whiskery grey ghosts of willowherb.

'I can see a bearded tit,' shouted Rocky.

'That's a moorhen,' reproached Joan.

'Not a hen, I know hens.'

'Note the beautiful yellow and crimson leaves of the bramble.'

'I can see a bearded tit.'

Practically garrotting Rocky, Anatole grabbed Lily's binoculars. Through the willowherb, black disks encountered black disks. Despite the lack of wind, the poplar saplings were shivering to the right of the pale blue duck house, as Anatole caught sight of a bearded figure in a flat cap.

'There is bearded tit on island,' he confirmed in his deep voice.

'It's the prowler!' screamed Pearl. 'He was looking up my panties yesterday. No one believed me.'

'Perv, perv, filthy perv!' chorused the remaining children, who were soon joined by the rest of the party spilling out of the undergrowth in various states of undress and intoxification, yelling: 'Nonce, filthy perving nonce.'

As they searched the water's edge for pebbles to hurl at him, Partner rushed forward barking furiously.

'It's the prowler, miss,' repeated Pearl.

Reluctantly, Joan moved her binoculars from the water. 'Could have sworn I saw a natterjack.' Then, focusing on the island: 'Good God, there is a bloke there.' She blew her whistle. 'Calm down, students. If need be I shall make a citizen's arrest.'

Cheered on, she strode forward. But PC Cuthbert, hell-bent on promotion, who'd been hovering behind a vast cedar, was too quick for her. Racing round the pond, swaying precariously across Wally's bridge, he caught the prowler attempting to escape the same way.

The prowler was indeed wearing a flat cap and dark glasses and sporting a bushy grey beard. Hanging from his neck, binoculars and digital camera clashed against each other. Turning, nearly falling into the pond, he regained the island, calling out:

'Good afternoon, officer, I can explain everything. I've been photographing wildlife for a book I'm writing.' He had a snuffling voice that reminded PC Cuthbert of his aunt's pekingese. Probably an asthmatic.

'May I have a look at your camera, sir?'

The prowler then tried to make a run for it, and in other circumstances would have wondered if he'd gone to heaven when this forceful young constable flung him against the duck house to rousing cheers from the bank and slapped him into handcuffs. In the struggle his beard came off to reveal an orange goatee and several chins.

'I can explain everything, officer,' repeated the prowler. 'My name is in fact Crispin Thomas, Deputy Director of S and C Services, responsible for the education of Larkshire's children.'

'Funny way of showing it, sir.'

'I am actually doing undercover research into challenging behaviour and whether the curriculum is being adhered to in Larkshire's schools. Mike Pitts and Janna Curtis can certainly confirm my identity.' His voice rose as PC Cuthbert dragged him across the bridge.

'Janna's away this afternoon,' shouted Graffi, 'and she don't owe you no favours, and if it's past dinnertime, Pittsy wouldn't know you from his Aunty Vera.'

On disembarking, PC Cuthbert removed the camera from around Crispin's neck, dislodging his flat cap and grey wig to reveal startlingly orange hair.

'That's my property,' screamed Crispin, as PC Cuthbert began looking at the camera's screen.

Clicking through, he found many shots of a questionable nature, namely Pearl urinating and displaying a lot of naked bottom; of sweet little Year Seven photographed from a low angle, their skirts flying as they leapt for a ball; of Kitten Meadows giving Johnnie Fowler a blow job; of Jack Waterlane unhooking Kylie's bra; of Monster sniffing glue; of Graffi and Feral hurling tiles off the roof last Friday and Partner trying to shag Miss Miserden's cat.

An everyday story of Larks Comp – but enough to convince PC Cuthbert he had done the right thing. He wasted no time in summoning back-up in the form of a second officer to ride in the back seat of the car with the prowler.

'I am arresting you on suspicion of taking indecent photographs of children,' he told Crispin and proceeded to caution him.

When Crispin screamed that he was a friend of PC Cuthbert's Chief Constable and would get him sacked and, despite his handcuffs, attempted to run away, Partner rushed forward and nipped him sharply on the ankle.

'Ouch,' screamed Crispin.

'Do any of you recognize this gentleman?' demanded PC Cuthbert.

'Never seen the dirty nonce before in our lives,' lied the children. 'Lock him up.'

Puce, spluttering, swearing he'd sue for wrongful arrest, Crispin was borne off to the station. Joan thought he looked vaguely familiar but it was probably only his identikit photo in the paper. He looked a thoroughly depraved individual. How splendid if he were the Rutshire prowler.

After a very unpleasant session both in a police cell and under interrogation, Crispin was released when a furious Ashton rolled up to identify and bail him.

Chief Inspector Gablecross, who'd been working on poor little Bethany's murder all day, was also able to identify him. But Crispin still had the photographs and the false identity to explain. He was not sure the police believed his excuse about an undercover operation. Ashton was incandescent with rage. How could Crispin screw up so monumentally?

Janna was even angrier when she and Cambola got back from a meeting with the cathedral choirmaster and learnt what had happened, particularly when Hengist rang, having heard the news, and treated the whole thing as a huge joke.

'So perfect for a self-confessed wildlife photographer to cut his teeth on Larks Year Ten and Bagley Middle Fifth. Joan is thoroughly over-excited and longing to go to court.'

'Crispin was lurking on the island to give himself ammunition against us,' stormed Janna.

'I know and he could easily have caught you and me. We must be careful. See you later, darling, and don't wear any knickers.'

73

To Larks's disappointment, the *Gazette* failed to report Crispin's arrest and subsequent release; they were too busy leading on a forthcoming review of Larkshire's secondary schools. According to inside information leaked to them, Larkminster Comp was the preferred option for closure.

Janna was on to Col Peters in a trice.

'What inside information?' she yelled.

'We cannot reveal our sources,' said Col primly.

'You bloody well should when they're libellous and vindictive. You're just putting people off sending children to Larks and utterly demoralizing my parents, teachers and children.'

'Your kids can read our newspaper? They *must* be improving.'

'Bastard!' howled Janna.

As a result Larks pupils were mocked in the street by St Jimmy's, Searston Abbey and even the choir school.

'Sink school, stink school, you're closing down, you'll soon be gone.'

After Ofsted's recommendations, Janna had hoped for more funding or at least that Appletree would be rebuilt. Instead, at the end of the month, Ashton and Crispin, in a fit of spite, ordered Appletree to be boarded up and its science, D and T and music departments to be relocated to the main building. This not only devastated the teachers – Mr Mates had had his labs in Appletree for nearly forty years – but also the pupils, who felt less valued than ever.

When Janna complained, Ashton merely replied bitchily that with so many surplus places, Larks pupils couldn't even be filling the main building.

Hostile and bewildered, the children slipped back into their old, bad ways, particularly the Wolf Pack. Pearl was disrupting every class; Kylie was miserable and doing no work beause she'd just lost a baby. Feral and Graffi were truanting and acting up. The only chemistry the latter two did for the rest of the term was to make up a paste with an ammonium triodide base. This they spread thinly over the platform in the school hall the morning Rod Hyde rolled up on a fault-finding mission and insisted on taking assembly. His pacings up and down the platform triggered off such a series of explosions that, fearing a terrorist attack, there was a stampede out of the hall. Rod, punching pupils out of the way, was at the forefront. On learning the truth, he fired off a furious email to a gratified S and C: 'This school is so dreadful, it must be closed down.'

'My Rod and staff don't comfort me,' moaned Janna as she and Hengist lay in her double bed that evening, so sated with sex they could hardly lift glasses of Hengist's Veuve Clicquot to their lips.

'I had to give Graffi and Feral a detention,' she went on, 'but I had great difficulty not laughing. Pity it didn't blow Rod up. Where are you supposed to be?' she asked.

'Dining with some prep-school heads. The things I do to fill up my school.'

Tomorrow he and Sally were taking Randal and Mrs Walton to the ballet in Paris and a party at the British Embassy afterwards. Clinton and Hillary and a host of luminaries were expected.

'I have to ensure Randal meets everyone, he is such a starfucker. He won't shut up until I nail down the poor dear Queen to open his bloody science block.'

'I'm the one who needs a science block. How's he getting on with Mrs Walton?'

'Moved her into a penthouse flat and picking up her bills, so her spirits will be lifted as well as her body.'

'Improving on previous bust,' giggled Janna.

'God, I'm going to miss you,' groaned Hengist as Janna crawled down, trickling champagne over his cock before sucking it off.

Janna was ashamed how her love affaire with Hengist insulated her at least momentarily against the horrors of Larks. Nor, she comforted herself, was any school with such a glowing Ofsted report likely to be closed down.

The morning after Hengist had left for Paris, she was horrified to see Alex Bruce, in a tracksuit, jogging up the drive on a courtesy visit.

'Thought your Year Ten bods might profit from some

chemistry coaching' – Alex vigorously polished his spectacles – 'now they've started their GCSE syllabus.'

But when he insisted Year Ten remove their coats and baseball caps, spit out their chewing gum and sit at their desks rather than on top of them, they started pelting him with rulers, rubbers and pencil boxes. Then Johnnie Fowler picked up a brick and, pretending it was a grenade, lobbed it at Alex.

'Sending him belting down the drive,' Janna told Hengist when he rang that evening.

'Already training for the next steeplechase,' sighed Hengist.

'The children can't stand him.'

Nor could Alex stand them and wrote an even more damning report to S and C than Rod Hyde.

After that they were into the Christmas frenzy of reports, school plays, end-of-term parties, carol concerts and, apart from an official Christmas card, Janna didn't hear from S and C until January.

It was during mocks, whilst she was appreciating the vast amount of work needed to be put in by Year Eleven before May in order to boost Larks's place in the league tables, that a very amicable letter arrived from Ashton.

In it he wished her a very happy New Year and asked if, after school on 4 February, he could visit Larks.

'At last,' Janna told a staff meeting joyfully, 'S and C have responded to our Ofsted and are going to give us some funding.'

Exhorted by Janna, most of the children stopped trashing and vandalizing and pitched in to make the school look as attractive as possible. As a jokey reminder about the leaking roof, Year Eight had created a rainforest in reception. Janna also aimed to nudge Ashton about rebuilding Appletree and the labs.

The fourth of February dawned bitterly cold, with an east wind howling through every ill-fitting window.

'Pity we can't light a fire with all those DfES directives,' grumbled Rowan as she turned on the storage heater, which Emlyn had dropped in to keep Janna warm on long, late evenings. On a low table, she arranged the pansy-patterned tea set that the children had given Janna for Christmas.

Are pansies quite the right message for Ashton and Crispin? wondered Janna.

On her desk was a copy of the latest Review of Secondary Schools, packed with faulty statistics about Larks's results, attendance, surplus places and future intake. When confronted, smiley-faced Cindy Payne from the county council had airily dismissed them as typing errors, but had made no attempt to correct this publicly. Nor had the review made any mention of Larks's successful Ofsted.

'I must discuss it rationally with Ashton,' Janna told herself. 'I must not lose my temper.'

Thank God the children would be out of the building before he rolled up. There had been far too many fights recently. Many of the kids looked up at her window and waved as they set out for home. She mustn't let them down. Partner, knowing teacups led to biscuits, bustled in wagging ingratiatingly.

'You are *not* to bite Crispin,' said Janna sternly.

'They're here,' shouted Rowan. 'Are you sure you don't mind my sloping off? I must get Scarlet to the doctor.'

'I'll be fine.' Janna ran towards reception, proudly thinking what a contrast the riot of colour in every classroom made to the chill, grey, dying day outside. This was a good and thriving school.

Her first shock was that Ashton had brought Cindy Payne. Her second that they totally ignored all the effort that had been made, even the Indians, cowboys and big toothy horses Graffi had designed for Year Ten's American Wild West display, as they marched along the corridor to Janna's office.

'They've been working so hard,' she said lamely, then after a pause: 'Where's Crispin?'

'He's moved on,' said Ashton, discarding his former deputy as casually as he whipped off an exquisite dark blue cashmere overcoat and palest pink scarf, dropping them over a chair. A pink silk bow tie enlivened a waisted pale grey suit and silver-grey shirt. As usual, he'd drenched himself in sweet, suffocating scent as if to ward off the fetid air of Larks.

Cindy today had matched a red nose and woolly flowerpot hat to the inevitable scarlet trouser suit. But the effect was not one of cheer. Her round face had the relentless jollity of a sister in a ward of terminally ill geriatrics, but her little eyes, like Ashton's, were as cold as the day.

'Those storage heaters are very dear to run,' she said disapprovingly.

'They keep me warm at night when the central heating goes off,' snapped Janna. 'Remembering how saunaed you are at S and C, I didn't want you to catch cold.'

Stop bitching, Janna, she told herself.

Cindy's smile became more fixed, then her face really lit up as Debbie arrived with tea, which included egg sandwiches and a newly baked batch of shortbread:

'Hello, Debs! You do spoil us, what a wonderful spread.'

'What a feast,' said Ashton heartily.

'Shall I be mother?' asked Cindy, flopping on to the sofa, narrowly missing Partner who retreated sourly to Janna's knee. 'I still haven't taken off that half-stone I put on over the festive season, but I won't be able to resist Debs's legendary shortbread.'

Ashton, with an equally greedy expression on his face, was gazing at a blow-up of Paris playing Romeo.

'He got into twouble knocking out a wef last term. Old habits die hard, I suppose.'

'He's playing regularly for the Colts,' said Janna sharply.

'Don't be so defensive,' teased Cindy, hiding the pansies on hers and Ashton's plates with sandwiches. 'A sarnie for you, Janna?'

'I'm OK, thanks.'

Picking up his plate, Ashton moved on to last summer's photograph of the whole school (except for Paris, he noticed, who had probably gone off joy-riding on trains by then). But there was Paris's alter ego, Feral Jackson, another beauty, clutching his football. All the children and teachers were laughing with Janna in the middle with that blasted dog on her knee.

'Nice one of Debs,' he said idly. 'Excellent sandwiches. She's one person who won't have any difficulty getting another job.' Then, as Janna looked up, startled: 'There's weally no easy way to say this, but I'm afwaid Larks is scheduled for closure at the end of the summer term.'

Partner squeaked as Janna's stroking hand clenched on his shoulder. She felt as though she'd stepped back off a cliff with a bullet straight between her eyes.

'But you haven't even seen over it,' she whispered. 'We've spent days making it look lovely.'

'We don't need to see over a school to close it down.'

'But why?' stammered Janna.

'Do you really need us to tell you?' Ashton idly added sweetener to his tea and joined Cindy on the sofa. 'The figures speak for themselves.'

'We had a wonderful Ofsted.'

'The most wonderful Ofsted in the world can't change the fact that you have four hundred and fifty, probably four hundred by now, students wattling around in a building meant for twelve hundred. Your wesults are dreadful, truancy and vandalism are sky high.'

'The latest Review of Secondary Schools was rigged.' Janna could hardly speak through her stiff lips. 'All the figures were wrong and you averaged them over four years, so of course no improvement was discernible. You said they were typing errors, but you never publicly corrected them. We were doing fine until you changed the bus routes and leaked that rumour about Larks being targeted for closure back in November. Why didn't you hang a plague sign over the school gates?'

'You'll have a chance to appeal,' said Cindy cosily, helping herself to two pieces of shortbread. 'My word, these are good; Debbie really is a treasure. We always put our decisions for closure up for public consultation.' At Janna's blank look she added, 'We give people a chance to express their views – public meetings, letters of support, etc. – then in May, the council cabinet will meet to examine these views and put forward recommendations to the Larkshire Schools Organization Committee.'

'If any of their five members vote against closure,' said Ashton, also helping himself to shortbread, 'it'll go to adjudication in the autumn.'

'Unlikely, as you've no doubt got the committee sewn up,' accused Janna.

She looked at the trees outside, disappearing into the twilight, like her school. She was shaking so violently that Partner jumped down and, unnoticed, took refuge on Ashton's navy blue coat.

'Ever since I've been here,' she said bleakly, 'I've battled against a disaffected governing body, a totally uncooperative privatized LEA and a county council who won't give me a penny and who are in league with a vindictive local press.'

'You're making dangerous accusations,' said Ashton sharply.

'Ofsted said exactly the same thing. They knew we were capable of improving if we were given the chance. What about my children?' Janna had a sudden vision of every one of them drowning before her eyes. 'You can't close Larks down. How could anyone in S and C understand? You don't give a toss about continuity. You all move on, like Crispin, if things get rough. What about my teachers? They've made such sacrifices and worked so hard.'

'They'll be wing-fenced,' said Ashton. 'So many have left already; if any jobs are advertised in the county, they'll get first option.'

'Doesn't mean they'll get the job, now they've been tarnished with working at Larks.'

'Is it your career you're worried about?' asked Cindy as if she were dictating to a half-wit secretary. 'You're not old, you'll get plenty of job offers.'

Ashton, who'd been examining his nails, stretched out and

457

selected a nail file from Janna's blue mug crammed with pens.

'Do drink up your tea,' urged Cindy.

Picking up the sugar bowl, Janna emptied it into her cup, then, realizing what she'd done, let the bowl slip from her fingers, so it crashed down on to her cup, smashing them both, spilling tea everywhere.

'Years Ten and Eleven gave me this tea set for Christmas,' she said in a strange, high voice. 'Oh, fuck off, Partner,' she screamed as he leapt off Ashton's coat and tried to lick up the tea.

'There, there,' said Cindy, 'I'm sure that bowl can be mended.'

'But my school can't,' yelled Janna, bursting into tears.

'I know it's a shock when a school closes down.' Cindy struggled to her feet. 'Have you got a friend to come and be with you?'

'Don't fucking patronize me. If you think I'm giving up Larks without a fight . . .' Dropping to the floor, Janna grabbed Ashton's scarf to mop up the tea.

'Give me that.' Ashton seized it back. He was even less pleased to see his coat covered in Partner's hairs. 'Twy not to be gwatuitously unpleasant, Janna,' he continued smoothly, 'you're suffering from hurt pride. I can only advise you to go gwacefully.'

Seeing the murderous expression on Janna's face as her hand grabbed the handle of the teapot, Cindy said hastily:

'We can show ourselves out. Don't get too stressed. I can recommend an excellent counsellor.'

'Anything's better than a county councillor, you fat cow,' shrieked Janna, 'they kill schools.'

'Dear, dear, dear,' said Ashton as they hastened out into the drizzle, 'how did that malevolent hysteric ever get a job running a school? Nothing has ever convinced me more of the rightness of our decision.'

'Thank goodness Alex Bruce and Rod Hyde put in such negative reports.' Cindy tugged her red wool hat over her ears. 'I don't anticipate much opposition, do you?'

'I hope not. Hengist Brett-Taylor might act up; he always had a *tendresse* for little Miss Curtis.'

'But he's so tied up in politics. At least Cavendish Plaza and Haut Larkminster will be on our side. Closing down schools causes such a rumpus. We must rush it through as soon as possible.'

After all, one didn't want to lose one's seat on the county council or all that kudos and fat expenses.

They jumped as a window was flung open.

458

'You won't get away with this, you murderers!'

Two minutes later Janna ran out to a deserted car park, crying uncontrollably: 'My teachers, my children.'

A hundred yards beyond the school gate, she had to leap out of her car and throw up, mostly bile, on the pavement outside the Ghost and Castle.

'Drunk at this hour . . .' chuntered a couple disappearing into the saloon bar.

Only then did Janna realize she'd left Partner locked in her office.

'I'm so sorry,' she sobbed as she recovered him.

But as he snuggled across her thighs, attempting to be the seat-belt she had forgotten to fasten, all she could think was: My career is over. In Yorkshire, they'll say I failed, failed, failed.

She was overwhelmed by a stench of burning wax. Like Icarus, she had flown too near the sun.

74

By contrast, Brigadier Woodford had had such a wonderful piece of news, he had splashed out on two bottles of champagne (Lily's favourite drink, which she could no longer afford), two large cartons of potted shrimps, a beef and ale pie, strawberries and an even larger carton of double cream, and taken them over to Lily's to celebrate.

Lily had lit a fire and they were sitting comfortably on Lily's shabby sofa with the vast fluffy black and white General between them, accidentally brushing hands as they both simultaneously stroked him. Lily had rescued some poor crocuses trampled on the verge outside and, in a white vase in the warmth of the room, they had expanded like purple striped umbrellas with little orange handles. The Brigadier felt his heart expanding like the crocuses.

'God I miss champagne, this is such a treat,' said Lily happily. 'Now, what are we celebrating?'

'Rupert's offered me my own programme. It's going to be called *Buffers*. Each week we'll take a war or campaign in history and get four so-called experts or "old buffers", retired generals and admirals, to sit round a table having frightful rows about strategy and blame. I've got to chair it.'

The genuine delight on Lily's face nearly gave the Brigadier the courage to kiss her.

'How clever of Rupert! You're going to be a star, Christian.'

'Rupert wants to start with twelve programmes. We have to do something called a pilot first, which sounds more like the RAF. You'll have to come on it to add some glamour and talk about the Wrens.' He emptied the bottle into their glasses.

'D'you think we can manage a second?'

'Certainly, with a celebration like this.' As Lily leant across General and gave the Brigadier a peck on the cheek, he had a longing to kiss her passionately on the lips, but was worried it might dislodge his bridge. It was such a long time since he'd made a pass.

'If the pilot works, Rupert wants his father Eddie, who was in the Blues, to be one of the regulars. Said it might stop Eddie tapping him for money if he got an income from television. Frightfully amusing chap, Eddie, thought the programme was going to be called *Buggers*.'

'Probably be even more successful,' said Lily dryly.

Christian guffawed; then, because he didn't feel it was boasting with Lily, 'The Tories have asked me to open their Easter Fair. GMTV want me to go up to London to talk about the possibility of war in the Gulf and Larkminster Rovers wrote asking me to go on their board. I don't know much about soccer.'

'Feral and I will teach you,' said Lily. 'When you score a goal you have to slide to the ground and bare your breast by lifting up and shaking the front of your shirt.'

'Much more excitin' if you did,' snorted the Brigadier. As he heaved himself up to fetch another bottle, he noticed how empty the fridge was except for the strawberries and cream, and also that that dear little watercolour of the church at Limesbridge where Lily grew up was missing. He hated Lily having to sell things. What heaven if they could be together like this every night. Lily could have an 'old age serene and bright, And lovely as a Lapland night'.

General the cat opened a disapproving yellow eye but didn't shift as the cork flew across the room to the accompaniment of a hammering on the front door.

'Oh hell,' said Lily, 'let's pretend we're out.'

But there was no escape as Janna barged in, followed by Partner; nor was there any word of apology as she collapsed on to the dark blue velvet chair by the fire, shaking uncontrollably, her reddened eyes wide and staring.

'Oh Lily, oh Lily.'

'You poor child, whatever's the matter? Give her a drink, Christian.'

'They're closing my school down.'

'They can't do that.'

'They can, they can! What's going to happen to my children and my teachers and Wally?'

'That's rotten luck,' said the Brigadier, handing her a glass. 'You must fight it.'

461

'I know, but I don't know how to. I've been fighting since I took over.' Janna gulped down half the champagne and carried on talking.

Lily, of course, insisted she stay to supper, and divided the potted shrimps and the beef and ale pie for two into three, and buttered a lot of brown bread.

Christian tried not to feel irritated when Janna drank most of the remaining champagne but, incapable of eating, fed all her pie to Partner.

'I forgot to get him any food on the way home, and I left him shut in my office, I'm coming apart at the seams, I've got to be strong for the children. Larks is the only security they know.' She started to cry again. Partner, his front paws on her knees, tried to stem her tears with a beef-flavoured tongue.

'We'll all fight,' promised Lily. 'Hengist will kick up a hell of a rumpus, and so will Rupert. And while my nephew Jupiter isn't my favourite person, he's excellent at putting the jackboot in – anything to discredit Cindy Payne and New Labour.'

'I called her a fat cow.' Janna was twisting a thread hanging out of Lily's green velvet chair cover so violently it broke off and a mass of kapok billowed out. 'Oh God, I'm sorry.'

Whatever happened to stiff upper lips, thought the Brigadier as Janna helped herself to the last of the champagne.

'I've let so many people down.' She sobbed. 'People like Sophy Belvedon and the new head of D and T who've got children and massive mortgages because they've specially bought houses in the area. I feel like a captain who's steered his great battleship on to the rocks.'

Lily patted Janna's shoulder. 'No one could have fought harder.'

The Brigadier felt ashamed. It was only because he'd so wanted to be alone with Lily.

'Oh God, I must tell Russell,' exclaimed Janna. 'So many people to tell – the children are going to be the worst. Can I use your phone?'

Her shaking hand kept misdialling Russell's number. She got the vicar and the local greengrocer before she finally reached him.

'I heard, and I'm not surprised,' he said heavily. 'I gather you were extremely offensive to Cindy when she tried to be supportive. Why must you always construe help as criticism?'

'Their help is like snake venom,' shouted Janna and hung up.

'He knew,' she said flatly. 'Ashton and Cindy must have been straight on to him.'

'I smell collusion,' said Lily. 'First, you must appoint Dora as your press officer.'

Next morning Janna had the nightmare of breaking the news to the staff, taking an extended lunch hour, gathering them into the staffroom, feeling utterly sick at the sight of their stunned faces.

'It can't be true,' muttered Lydia.

Basket burst into tears. 'I'll never get another job.'

'We're going to fight it, of course,' said Janna quickly. 'We've got two months to register protest.'

'It wasn't unexpected,' said Mike Pitts. 'When will the axe fall?'

'Ashton said the end of the summer term, but that's only a few months away.' Janna looked bewildered. 'He must mean summer two thousand and four, and that's only if the Schools Organization Committee are all in favour.'

But when she dialled Ashton to check, he assured her if the Schools Organization Committee were unanimous, Larks would close in summer 2003.

'You can't close it so soon. You particularly can't do that to Year Ten,' whispered Janna in horror, remembering how she'd walked out on her GCSE classes at Redfords. 'Year Eleven will be OK. They'll take their exams in May and we'll be able to see them through before we close down.'

Outside she could see the children in the playground. Graffi and Feral were idly kicking a ball around; Pearl and Kylie were reading the same magazine, stamping their feet to keep warm. All of them were perplexed by their extended lunch hour and, aware some storm was brewing, gathering in edgy little groups, glancing constantly up at her window. Are we in more trouble?

'We can't abandon Year Ten,' she told Ashton firmly. 'What about Aysha and Graffi and Kitten and Johnnie and Feral and Monster, they'll never get a job and out of this hell if they don't get any qualifications.'

'Your beloved Wolf Pack,' drawled Ashton.

'And at least fifty others.'

'Hardly the A team.'

'They bloody are!' yelled Janna, turning and catching Chally raising an eyebrow at Mike Pitts.

'They've been totally disrupted by all the rumour and speculation about closure,' she went on furiously, 'and the incessant bitching of other schools. They haven't completed any coursework, and they'll be chucked out at the end of the summer term into an unfamiliar school for the second year of their course. It's not bloody fair.'

'If their last SATs were anything to go by,' snapped Ashton, 'they're not likely to get any gwades anyway. Straight Us, I'd say.'

'They've got to be given a chance.'

'And you'll have a chance to air your views at the public meeting.'

'I'm afraid it's summer 2003,' she told the staff grimly, 'so we've really got a fight on our hands.'

If anything convinced her of the need to fight it was the anguish and terror of the children. Pearl, sobbing that she'd thought they'd have five terms more; an inconsolable grey-faced Danijela: 'I is only happy with you, this is my home.' 'Who will write our CVs and sign our driving licences,' wailed Year Eleven.

The boys reacted with violence, hurling more tiles off the roof, tearing off door handles, kicking over desks, trashing classrooms; soon they wouldn't have a school to close down. The *Gazette* and the television cameras were soon outside the door. The staff, panicking about lost jobs, gathered in corners, whispering and afraid, many of them blaming Janna.

But even the darkest cloud has a silver lining.

'Can I have a word?' demanded Chally later in the day, shutting Janna's door behind her and rearranging a crimson-leafed scarf before announcing she was off to take up a deputy head's post at St Jimmy's.

'Congratulations.' Janna tried not to display her delight. 'I'm really pleased for you. You'll find it inspirational working with Rod Hyde. Is one of his Senior Management Team leaving?'

'Not that I know of. They need an extra pair of capable hands. St Jimmy's is so over-subscribed.'

Probably soon with an influx of the brightest children from Larks, thought Janna in outrage, but at least I won't have to suck up to you any more, you old bat.

'Every Chally shall be exalted,' sang Cambola when Janna pulled her and Mags into her office to tell them.

'Do you think there's any hope she'll be one of those high fliers who whisks all her key people away with her?' asked Mags.

'What bliss if she took Spink, Skunk, Pittsy, Robbie and Basket,' sighed Janna.

Next moment, a red-eyed Rowan put her dark head round the door. 'Hengist Brett-Taylor on the line, Janna.'

'That should cheer up the poor little duck,' whispered Mags as she and Cambola made themselves scarce.

'Darling, darling!' Hengist was ringing from Brussels. 'I only just heard from Jupiter. Lily Hamilton rang him. She must feel really strongly; first time she's spoken to him since he threw her out of her house. God, I'm sorry, are you OK?'

'Fine.' Janna battled not to cry. 'At least Chalford's just announced she's leaving to be deputy head at St Jimmy's.'

'Two wrongs have certainly made a right there.'

'And when I called Russell last night, an hour after I knew, he'd already been told.'

'Sounds like conspiracy,' Hengist echoed Lily, 'what fun we're going to have exposing them. Don't worry, darling.'

'How can I not? What will happen to my children?'

'I'm sure Bagley can accommodate any of your Year Tens in with a shout. I'd love to have Graffi and Feral and Aysha and mouthy Pearl.' Then, when Janna didn't react: 'You could join Bagley and keep an eye on them. You're always saying how you miss teaching, and I could see more of you.' His voice had grown softer, more husky.

'How can you trivialize such a terrible thing, I'd never teach in an independent,' yelled Janna. 'You've already stolen my teachers, my brightest pupil and my heart, you're not taking anything else,' and she slammed down the receiver.

To her dismay, Hengist didn't ring back. Was she misconstruing genuine help as criticism again?

Two days later she got a letter from Sally.

'Hengist has told me. What a dreadful thing to happen. I'm so sorry. We must save Larks. Hengist has got something up his sleeve.'

75

Affection had grown so strongly between Bagley and Larks that when news of the closure hit the press, mostly via Dora, both schools joined forces to create an uproar.

Graffi's poignant design of a lark escaping from a vicious black cat, with the slogan 'Larks will survive', was soon appearing on balloons, stickers, posters, waving placards and, indeed, scrawled on walls all over Larkminster.

Hengist, to Alex Bruce's fury, blithely encouraged his pupils to join the public protests and marches against both the closure of Larks and the imminent war in Iraq, so they seemed hardly ever in school.

'We bonded with Larks in good times, sir, we're not going to desert them in bad times,' Lando told Alex sanctimoniously.

'But you've got double maths.'

'I don't care,' said Lando, and he raced off to join Graffi and Johnnie on the picket line.

Save our school, boom, boom, boom, save our school, boom, boom, boom, it was so much more fun than lessons.

Tarquin Courtney was only too happy ferrying pickets around in his Porsche. Ashton was demented, particularly when someone spray-painted ascending larks all over his pretty Regency house in the Close.

Lily and the Brigadier were also in the thick of things. In March, to the horror of her nephew Jupiter, Lily whacked a Lib Dem councillor over the head with her placard. Luckily the officer poised to arrest her was PC Cuthbert, who promptly let her off.

Together, she and the Brigadier distracted themselves from the horrors of the war and the stock market by going on marches.

466

Save our school, boom, boom, boom. 'Why does my heart go boom, boom, boom,' sang the Brigadier. The pilot of *Buffers* had been such a resounding success, his presence at Larks demos added considerable gravitas.

Emlyn added physical weight. With Attila the Hunk on the picket line, S and C heavies melted away. With war in Iraq seemingly inevitable, Emlyn was worried sick about Oriana in Baghdad, but he hid it well. He made all his history pupils write letters of protest to County Hall praising Larks, saying how much they'd enjoyed *Romeo and Juliet,* the field trip and the nature ramble in which an S and C executive, hell-bent on closing down Larks, was found in disguise spying in the bushes.

Only Boffin Brooks got under the wire, writing and sealing his own letter, claiming Larks was the most dreadful school he'd ever encountered.

Miss Cambola led every protest, playing 'Hark, Hark! the Lark' on her trumpet. Even Cosmo surprised everyone by proposing a concert in the water meadows near the cathedral. His mother, Dame Hermione, was a friend of the Bishop.

'What could be more lovely, my lord, than classical melodies on a warm summer evening?'

When it leaked out that Cosmo was planning to feature himself and the Cosmonaughties, belting out 'Cocks and Rubbers', among their cleaner lyrics, the Bishop's secretary slipped Cosmo a thousand pounds to go away, half of which Cosmo handed over to Larks.

Poor Feral, who never thought beyond tomorrow, which he thought would be spent at Larks, was terrified. Even incessant Arsenal victories didn't cheer him. He laboriously made his own poster: 'Saive are Skool', which the *Gazette* photographed him nailing up outside Larks. The photograph appeared on the front page, with 'sp' signs in the margin and a caption: 'Another reason why Larks should close'.

Stormin' Norman started a Parents' Action Group, but as most of the action consisted of thumping other parents, it soon fizzled out.

Dora was in her element with the press ringing her every day. In addition, she bravely went from house to house collecting signatures and even organizing a car-boot sale, to which she gave many favourite toys and several of her mother's best dresses.

Paris, pretending not to be interested, read every paper and watched every bulletin. If Larks closed, Janna would leave the area and he'd never see her again. She looked so thin, pale and tense in her photographs. He ached to comfort her.

Ashton and Cindy were getting increasingly rattled. If only the Americans could bomb Larks, but with their track record, they'd probably miss and take out Cavendish Plaza and the Close instead.

As a counter measure, S and C deliberately held their first public meeting to debate Larks's fate on the far side of town on a night when Larkminster Rovers were playing at home. As a result hardly any Larks supporters showed up and instead of pleading her case quietly and reasonably, as she'd intended, a riled Janna lost her cool and a lot of support as she heckled the speakers. A dreadfully dismissive report in the *Gazette* followed.

Meanwhile, Wally with a son, Emlyn with a hoped-for future wife and Hengist and Sally with a daughter were increasingly worried that Bush and Blair would raise two fingers to the UN and plunge into war.

'It's all oil. They don't want the Russians and the French to get their hands on it,' said Hengist.

Wandering across the dry cracked pitches to the Family Tree, he fingered Oriana's carved initials on its trunk. Was she going to be taken from him like Mungo? He longed to ring Janna and find solace in her freckled arms, but he was nervous that any transgression might invoke the anger of the gods, so he walked home to Sally.

Before the second public meeting, which was to take place in late March, Hengist met Rupert and Jupiter at Jupiter's flat in Duke Street, St James's, which had a lovely view over the park lit up by white daffodils and young green willows. A pink moon on its side like a rugby ball hung above Big Ben and the Houses of Parliament. Would they suffer the same fate as the Twin Towers if Britain got into bed with the Americans? wondered Hengist.

The charming flat had once belonged to Jupiter's father, Raymond, a highly successful art dealer. Consequently, the walls were covered with wonderful pictures. On a side table was a photograph of Jupiter, his beautiful sweet-natured wife Hanna and their adorable two-and-a-half-year-old son Viridian.

'That should come in useful when we're electioneering,' said Hengist.

Jupiter, who was as pale as Rupert and Hengist were dark brown from skiing, smiled coolly.

'When are we going to war?' asked Hengist.

'Any minute, pushed as much by the unqualified encouragement of IDS as by Blair's ambition.' Jupiter glanced at his watch.

'I've got to be back in the House in an hour. Would you like a drink?'

'I'd like several,' said Hengist. 'Christ, what a day.'

Rupert looked up from the sofa and the racing pages of the *Evening Standard*. 'Oriana's fantastic on the box.'

'Isn't she? I see her face on every bulletin – so frustrating to touch the screen not her.' For a second Hengist betrayed his desolation, then, reverting to his usual flippancy: 'I was so depressed by my own company, I made the mistake of taking Randal Stancombe for a walk down the pitches this afternoon. He showed an unhealthy interest in Badger's Retreat, but failed to notice leaves leaping out of the wild cherry, breathtaking against a navy blue sky, or the sweeps of primroses and violets. Only sees land as a way of making money.'

'I wouldn't argue with that,' said Rupert.

'Can we skip the nature notes and get on with the meeting?' said Jupiter, pouring Hengist a large whisky.

Hengist turned back from the window where he could see cranes like malignant vultures preying on the city, destroying and rebuilding everywhere.

'We've got to save Larks Comp.'

'Whatever for?' Jupiter looked amazed. 'We can't anyway, once a school's targeted for closure, it's doomed. Only point of public meetings is for the county council and S and C to pretend they've listened to people's views. Anyway,' he went on, shooting soda into his own glass, 'do we really want to antagonize Stancombe, who's good for a massive donation, in order to save a small, pretty awful school? We've also got to work with S and C.'

'You have no heart,' drawled Rupert, getting out a pen to do the quick crossword. 'Janna Curtis was rather pretty, I remember.'

'I can afford to antagonize Stancombe even less,' admitted Hengist, 'he's giving me a six-million-pound science block. But you could take him on, Rupert.'

'I don't mind. His daughter's foul to both Xav and Bianca. What's he got against Larks?'

'He wants it and the entire Shakespeare Estate razed to the ground so they don't lower the tone of his absurdly overpriced Cavendish Plaza.'

'It's the Casey Andrews sculpture in the forecourt that should be razed,' Rupert said. 'Who was the brother of Romulus, five letters?'

'Remus,' said Hengist. 'I suspect Randal's after Larks's land. Whoever buys it, S and C and the county council will make a killing. So this meeting's the ideal opportunity to discredit both

Lib Dem and Labour and make them look like heartless, un-principled shits.'

'I like a good fight,' mused Rupert. 'Taggie and I got together when we were rushing round Gloucestershire, pitching for the Venturer franchise.'

'And Janna Curtis has been very shabbily treated,' pleaded Hengist.

Rupert glanced up, white teeth lighting his dark brown face.

'So you did get into her knickers.'

'Certainly not,' snapped Hengist. 'Caesar has to be above suspicion as well as his wife these days.'

76

The gods appeared to be on S and C's side. On the night of the second public meeting, which was held in a WI hall five miles south of Larkminster, the weeks of dry weather ended in a torrential rainstorm, which halted windscreen wipers in their tracks and turned country lanes into raging rivers.

'Larks parents and teachers'll never turn out in this,' gloated Ashton. '*EastEnders* and the war in its twelfth day will keep them safe in front of the TV. It'll be a walkover.'

He was therefore appalled on arrival to discover chairs being frantically unstacked to accommodate the crowd, a foyer reeking of drying macs and anoraks, and steaming umbrellas huddled together like coloured mushrooms at the back of the hall. The bar was already crowded out.

Emlyn and Wally, desperate to be distracted from the war, had all evening been bussing in parents from the Shakespeare Estate, bribing them with beer, wine, Dawn's hot sausage rolls on the way, and the prospect of a lift home, so they could drink themselves insensible. Stormin' Norman and Pearl's boxer dad were already well away.

They were soon joined by friends and fellow tipplers from the protest marches; Lily, the Brigadier, Ian and Patience Cartwright, whose daughter, Sophy, would be out of work if Larks were shut down.

The Brigadier was rather shyly autographing anti-closure leaflets.

'Love your programme, Brig.'

'All that matters is that every student achieves his or her potential,' intoned Cindy Payne as she hung up her soaking wet cape. One had to have nerves of steel to close down a school.

471

Having heard rumours that both Randal Stancombe and Rupert Campbell-Black were expected, Cavendish Plaza wives, with streaked hair, gold jewellery and beauty department make-up, were out in force. They'd all vote for closure, as would their drenched husbands, who'd nervously left their Mercs and Porsches in the car park before scuttling through the downpour, as would a bristling posse from the Close and the older Larkminster houses.

But there was a dangerously large anti-closure contingent from Bagley: including Dora and Dicky, Bianca, Amber and Milly and the Chinless Wanderers, who, changing allegiance on another front, had become thoroughly excited at the prospect of war in Iraq and kept marching about saluting each other.

'Why aren't you in school doing your prep?' asked Cindy disapprovingly.

'Part of our citizenship course is understanding how local government works,' said Amber piously. 'Mr Brett-Taylor was very anxious we should be present.'

Fuck Hengist, thought Alex, who never swore, even mentally, except in extremis and who had just rolled up with Chally and Poppet, plus her latest baby.

Alex was stressed. Over the weekend Poppet had insisted he look after the kids while she lay outside RAF Fairford protesting against the war. Tonight she had insisted on bringing Little Gandhi and would later breastfeed him. Nothing wrong with that, but this simple act of motherhood seemed to engender such misogyny in his Bagley colleagues.

In the foyer and his father's astrakhan coat, Cosmo examined notices about singing workshops and evenings of circle dancing, as he played 'The Lark Ascending' on his violin. Not missing a trick, he watched the Great and not-so-Good: Ashton, Cindy, Russell, Chally and now Alex and Rod and their wives, drinking cheap red or white in an ante-room. Talk about a witch's coven. And what had happened to Ashton's Sancho Pansy, Crispin?

Cosmo had exchanged a soulful eye-meet with Ashton when he arrived. In front of him, on the floor, he had also placed a dark blue butcher-boy's cap to swell the fund to save Larks. He had already raised two hundred pounds, half of which he intended to keep. His mother, despite her millions, was tight with money.

Inside the hall, Cambola was cheering everyone up playing golden oldies on the tinny upright piano.

' "Night And Day",' sang the Brigadier, sweeping Lily into a quickstep.

'Who's chairing this meeting?' she asked.

'Col Peters.'

'That's totally loaded against Larks for a start; you ought to chair it, Christian. Talk of the devil.'

A hiss went round the hall as Col Peters, more toad-like than ever, put his crinkly black hair and bulging eyes round the door, then retreated to the ante-room.

Dora, meanwhile, was in her element talking on three mobiles.

'Great turnout. I'll ring you the moment it's over, Mr Dacre.'

The rain was growing more frantic, scrabbling against the windows, begging to be let in out of the storm. A shudder and hiss went through those present from the Shakespeare Estate as Uncle Harley walked in in a black fur-lined suede jacket and more jewellery than all the Cav Plaza wives put together.

'Useful if there's a power cut,' giggled Amber.

Having clocked who was present, Uncle Harley took up his position against a side wall where he could watch both platform, hall and gallery, which was also nearly full up.

There was an equal hiss from Cav Plaza, remembering too many broken windows and missing car radios, as Feral slid in bouncing his football. He was absolutely soaked, his black curls flattened, raindrops leaping off his black lashes and running down his shining face. He had just exchanged a damp high five with Lily and the Brigadier, when Bianca, who'd specially worn a new crimson ra-ra skirt and a shocking pink fake-fur coat, leapt up and waved. It was a year since they'd danced together in *Romeo and Juliet*.

'Over here, Feral, I've kept a seat for you.'

Feral had no option; nor did he want one. Padding up the aisle, drenching people as he wriggled along the row, he dropped into the chair next to heaven.

'You're frozen,' wailed Bianca and, putting his ball under her seat, she whipped off her pink coat and wrapped it round him and everyone whooped and whistled. 'No, keep it on,' she cried, doing up the buttons.

Feral beamed.

'Suits you. Wolf in sheep's clothing,' shouted Johnnie Fowler.

Feral rolled his eyes, flung back his head and howled three times. Then he turned to Bianca. 'How yer doin'?' And he couldn't say any more, she was so adorable and gazing at him with such joy, her little shoulders hunched in ecstasy.

'When are we going to dance again?'

'Soon,' said Feral, tapping his feet as Cambola broke into a jazzed-up version of 'Hark, Hark! the Lark', because Janna was trying to slink in unobserved, aware she looked rough, ducking to avoid the exploding of flashes. Larks was about to break up for the Easter holidays and there'd been so many loose ends to tie up with children and teachers leaving, she'd had no time to wash her hair, which, lank and out of condition, she'd pulled back off her pale, pinched, face. She was wearing a silk dress the colour of faded bracken and an amber necklace, both of which Hengist had given her.

But he's not coming, she thought, glancing round the hall in despair and shame that she could think of him when her school was falling round her ears.

'No comment, for the moment,' she told the reporters.

'Miss! Miss!' Pearl shot out and, dragging Janna into the Ladies, applied coral lipstick and blusher to her blanched cheeks. 'That fluorescent light really drains you.'

'It's my Jane Eyre look.'

'Triffic turnout,' said Pearl proudly. 'My boxer dad's come; he's getting pissed with Lily and the Brig.'

'Thank you, dear Pearl.' Hitching up her smile two minutes later, Janna braved the hall, moving from parents to teacher to pupil thanking, cheering, encouraging, only accepting a Perrier water so she didn't lose her rag as she had at the last meeting, before taking her seat in the second row, between Mags and Sophy Belvedon.

As the clock struck half past seven Col Peters, reluctant to wait any longer, trooped on to the platform followed by Cindy, Ashton, Russell Lambert, leading Labour and Lib Dem councillors, and the Bishop of Larkminster, whose window Feral's football had cracked. To accommodate them all, the Prussian-blue curtains on either side of the platform had to be drawn back even further.

Col was then prevented from starting by an avalanche of late-comers, starting off with Sally Brett-Taylor, who ran in wafting Jardin des Bagatelles and looking absolutely stunning in a dark blue velvet cloak over a lilac silk dress and with a rakish lilac sequinned butterfly in her gold hair.

'Looking good, Mrs B-T,' yelled Jack Waterlane to howls of laughter.

Sally smiled, then called up to Col Peters:

'So sorry for being late. Hengist'll be here in a moment.'

'Doesn't Sally look smart? Ah good, here comes Randal,' agreed the Cav Plaza wives in excitement.

They had been admired through Randal's telescope when they sunbathed topless in their gardens. Some of them had been

474

summoned to romp in his Jacuzzi. Randal didn't want that dreadful school nearby; he'd fight their corner.

Here's Stancombe, thought the Shakespeare Estate, better not get too pissed or we might deck him.

Both factions waved sycophantically as Stancombe sauntered in flanked by heavies. He was wearing a dark brown leather jacket, black polo shirt and black cords and looked more attractive than usual, Janna decided. The flash jewellery had gone and his hair had been more becomingly cut with ragged gypsy tendrils softening his predatory face. Was this Mrs Walton's influence? Janna blushed as he caught her staring, particularly when he smiled and waved.

'Don't frat with the enemy,' hissed Mags.

'Daddy, Daddy,' shouted Jade, clambering over the seats to sit with him.

'Hi, princess.' Stancombe kissed her on the mouth.

'Yuk,' said Dora.

Col Peters had just tapped the microphone, hammer poised, when another batch of Larks parents, dug out by Emlyn and Wally, poured into the hall and were reluctantly split up into the remaining single seats.

'There's my da, hope he's sober,' prayed Graffi.

'And my mum,' said Pearl, 'hope she doesn't deck my dad, and Chantal with Kylie and Cameron an' Aysha's mum in a headscarf.'

'That's brave,' murmured Janna to Mags, 'with so much anti-Muslim feeling about.'

Hall and gallery were completely packed out; people were standing among the umbrellas at the back.

'Feral's so vain, we're going to have to gaze at his profile all evening,' Amber, who was sitting just behind him, said acidly.

For Feral was gone. He couldn't take his eyes off Bianca. As if it had a mind of its own, his hand slid into hers; he tried to retrieve it in case he was being forward, but she hung on, gripping it with a surprising strength, gently stroking his palm with little, pink-nailed fingers.

I'm dreaming, he thought, sent reeling by the sweetness of her breath, the faint tang of lily of the valley, the huge, laughing eyes with lashes even longer than his, her pink coat caressing his chin.

'I'm out of luck there,' sighed Amber. 'I'll have to revert to my unrequited passion for Attila.'

Boffin was ostentatiously reading a biography of Marie Curie.

Randal was on his mobile. He'd love to have had Ruth on his arm, but he concentrated better without her. One never knew from where trouble was coming. Rising in his seat, he located Dora taking a photograph of the Bishop. Good, she still had her untidy plaits. He couldn't see if her breasts had begun to bud, but his cock stiffened beneath the *Evening Standard*. He must ask her mother out to dinner next time Ruth was in town. Bloody hell, he'd never expected such a turnout.

Nor had Col Peters, who was prepared to wait no longer. He needed a report of the meeting in tomorrow's *Gazette*, which would be picked up by the nationals.

But in the foyer, Cosmo had launched into 'Hello, Dolly!' as Taggie Campbell-Black ran in, wide-eyed, long-legged as a colt. The fuchsia-pink cashmere shawl she'd flung over her black sequinned dress was already drenched.

That's one woman I'd like even better than Bianca, decided Cosmo.

'Thank you,' he purred as Taggie fumbled in her bag for a fiver. He'd frame it. If he landed Bianca, he could have Taggie as well.

Seeing her husband, not his greatest fan, and Hengist approaching, both in dinner jackets, Cosmo slid into a side kitchen. 'To adjust the temperature in the hall,' he read, 'turn the boiler on or off at the control panel.'

Take more than a switch to control this lot.

Rupert and Hengist were followed by Jupiter. Why's he here? wondered Cosmo. He jumped as Hengist tapped him on the shoulder and handed him a tenner. 'Can you get Mr Campbell-Black a very large whisky?'

Everyone was excited by the latest arrivals, particularly by Jupiter: that really put the evening up a rung. Whose side would he be on? He was already proving a very effective MP.

Furiously, Col Peters raised his hammer, but Hengist was lingering in the doorway, talking intently to the press, asking, no doubt, for any news on Iraq. Janna was shocked how tired he looked. But as he wandered into the hall, he seemed to shrug off his concerns and his face broke into a wicked smile.

'So sorry to hold you up, Col, Ashton, Cindy, Russell, my lord Bishop.' Mockingly Hengist nodded to each in turn. 'Evil night. Fleet's about to burst its banks and sweep S and C away. Hope you've brought your lifebelt, Ashton, you're going to need it before the evening's out. Do kick on, Col,' and, turning his broad, dinner-jacketed back, he edged along the row, shaking hands, hailing Bagley and Larks children, blowing kisses to friends, stopping to grin at Janna – 'Lovely dress, darling' – spying Poppet – 'How's little Gandhi, hope you're resting enough?' – then in a stage whisper to Jupiter, who was following him: 'She's had plenty of rest, lying down in the road to stop the B52s leaving.'

'For Christ sake, sit down,' hissed Jupiter, 'why must you deliberately wind people up?'

Bringing up the rear was Rupert, who stopped to congratulate the Brigadier on the pilot of *Buffers*: 'We got bloody good ratings. I'll ring you tomorrow.'

'Col Peters is going to have a coronary,' observed Mags.

'With any luck,' said Janna. 'Isn't it wonderful Hengist and Co. have showed up?'

Christ, that Campbell-Black/Brett-Taylor/Belvedon faction was hell, thought Emlyn. Only way to shut them up was to cut off their heads – preferably with a guillotine. Hengist was insufferable in this apparatchik-baiting mood. Bloody Hoorays, aren't we wonderful, we all know each other.

Actually the most hip Hooray was Rupert, Emlyn decided, not just because of the beauty of his still, cold toff's face or the casual elegance of his lounging body, but his total indifference to the impact he had on everyone in the room as he devoured print-outs, a large whisky in one hand, the other idly caressing his wife's sweet face as they compared notes on the day. Taggie had removed her soaked shawl and was wearing his dinner jacket round her shoulders.

Even if Oriana came home safely from Baghdad, wondered Emlyn wistfully, would she ever look up at him with a quarter of Taggie's tenderness, or in the adoring way their daughter was gazing at young Feral, still wrapped in her pink fur coat.

Brought up to loathe the Tories, it confused Emlyn that, for some ulterior motive, it was Tories who were coming to Janna's aid and New Labour in their sharp suits, quite unrecognizable from his dad's beloved cloth-cap party, who'd palled up with the beige, open-toed-sandalled Lib Dems to grind the faces of the poor.

Oh God, here was Vicky, putting down her flower-festooned umbrella, rushing towards the platform:

'Col, I am so sorry, I couldn't find anywhere to park. Emlyn dear, could you find me a chair? Oh, Poppet's kept a seat for me.' As she ran along the gap between platform and audience, pausing in front of Janna: 'Jannie, I am *so* sorry it's come to this. Hello, Magsy, hello Cambola, you poor dears.' Vicky was beginning to sound just like Sally. 'I'm so guilty I haven't called,' then, lowering her voice only a fraction: 'And so guilty getting out in time. What a blow too, losing darling Chally. I must find her later.'

'Bitch,' exploded Sophy Belvedon, 'thank God she left before I arrived.'

'What an appalling number of beards,' grumbled Rupert, and jumped out of his skin as Poppet Bruce suddenly cried out, 'Rupert, Roopert.' Thrusting up baby Gandhi, she made him wave: 'Hello, Uncle Rupert.' As Rupert cringed behind Ian Cartwright, Poppet went on: 'And there's Auntie Taggie. Hello, Auntie Taggie.'

Taggie, who'd been hopefully looking round for Xav, waved weakly. As if reading her mind, Poppet yelled out, 'Xav's got another detention, so we couldn't let him out. Sorry. Let's have a word later.'

Seeing her mother red-faced and furious, Bianca whispered to Feral, 'Xav's been caught drinking again. He seems to be pissed all the time.'

'I thought he was mates with Paris,' murmured Feral. Somehow with Bianca's hand in his it didn't hurt so much.

'They used to be really close, but Paris is so taken up with his rugby friends and his extra lessons with Theo, he hardly notices Xav exists any more. Why didn't you ring me?' she asked.

'I wanted to. It's complicated.'

If only Paris held my hand like that, thought Dora.

'Don't worry,' Ashton whispered to Col, 'let them mess around for as long as they like, it'll give them less time to air their non-existent grievances.'

77

At last everyone was settled and Col Peters bashed the table so hard, he spilt all the glasses of water.

'Good evening,' he said. He had a thick, oily voice that seemed drenched in chicken fat. 'Good evening, everyone. We're running behind schedule and as some of you' – he glared at Rupert and Hengist – 'clearly have other engagements, we'd better kick on. We have come together to discuss the proposed closure of Larkminster Comprehensive' – loud boos and cheers – 'and we know you've all got lots to say. We want as many people as possible to air their views, so it'll be easier if you don't interrupt.'

'Save our school,' yelled Johnnie Fowler.

'And show some manners,' snapped Col. 'Not the best way to convince people that your school is worth saving, Master Fowler. I shall now hand over to our county councillor in charge of education, Miss Cindy Payne.'

Hearty cheers from Bruces, Hydes, the Close and Cavendish Plaza.

Cindy, anxious to project a cosy, earth-mother image, had for once abandoned her red trouser suit for a flowing dark brown caftan. Above this her round, ruddy, determinedly smiling face, from which rayed out her light brown hair, bobbed like a setting sun on the horizon.

'I have prayed and prayed for guidance on this issue,' she began, 'and must admit that closing a school is a very painful process.'

'Not for them what's going to make a fat profit,' yelled Pearl's boxer dad to roars of applause. Stancombe's heavies squared their shoulders.

'I didn't hear that,' twinkled Cindy. 'Our aim is to give first-class education to each and every secondary student, which I am afraid Larks Comprehensive is not providing.'

'Who says so?' yelled Monster Norman. 'We isn't complaining.'

'Well said, son,' bellowed Stormin'.

'Closing a school is a painful experience,' Cindy ploughed on, her twinkle becoming fixed, 'but we are convinced this is a democratic decision because the vast majority of local parents have made it quite clear they don't want their children to go to Larks in that they have voted with their feet.' Then, as if taking a run at a fence, she added quickly, 'We've had many, many letters supporting closure, but during this formal consultation period, I'm so sorry, we've only received fifty letters of protest.'

'That's because Larks parents and pupils can't write,' yelled Brute Stevens, the rugger bugger from St Jimmy's.

'Hush, that's unkind,' reproved Cindy fondly.

'It's also fucking out of order,' shouted Johnnie Fowler, jumping on Brute and pummelling the hell out of him. As Johnnie was smaller than Pearl's boxer dad, Stancombe's guards were about to move in when Emlyn pre-empted them.

'Pack it in, for God's sake,' he snarled, peeling Johnnie off like a Polaroid.

'Thank you, Mr Davies,' said Cindy archly. 'Only fifty letters of protest,' she repeated, 'which included ten from a Miss Dora Belvedon, who doesn't even live in the area.'

Screams of laughter and bellows of 'Good on yer, Dora' were interspersed with shouts of 'Shame' and 'Cheat'.

An oblivious Dora was muttering into a tape recorder.

Mags Gablecross then leapt to her feet and introduced herself in a quiet, clear voice. Seeing her approaching the platform clutching a bulging box file, the platform recoiled in horror as if she were a suicide bomber.

'I thought people might be interested in the five hundred and fifty letters we received that were against Larks closing down and our petition signed by more than fifteen thousand people. I didn't want to hand these over before the meeting,' she added politely as she gave the box to a boot-faced Col, 'in case the figures were doctored as they were in your Review of Secondary Schools.' She smiled sweetly at Ashton. 'Please note I've taken a photostat of the petition, Mr Douglas.'

'That is a gwatuitously offensive remark,' snapped Ashton.

'We too have had overwhelming support for closure,' chipped in Cindy. 'Take this excellent letter from a Mr Bernard Brooks.' She waved a piece of paper: ' "Having observed both teachers and pupils at Larks Comp over the last eighteen months, I can honestly say it's the worst school I've ever encountered. I recommend closure instantly."'

There was a roar from the gallery as Graffi stopped snogging Milly and dropped into the hall, slithering across the umbrellas.

'That's Boffin Brooks, you snotty bastard.' Racing up the aisle, Graffi reached into the row, seizing Boffin by his Alex Bruce house tie. 'Don't you dare slag off our school.' Egged on by a roar of Larks approval, he was about to ram his fist into Boffin's face when Johnnie Fowler tugged him off.

'Let me do the honours.'

'Don't touch me,' screamed Boffin.

'Put Boffin in a coffin, boom, boom, boom,' yelled Bagley and Larks in delighted unison.

As Johnnie raised his fist, Emlyn once more shot across the room, prising Johnnie and Graffi off by their collars.

'Stop it,' he bellowed, then, lowering his voice: 'You're not helping Larks.'

'Nor's Boffin, dissing us like that.'

Trying to wriggle free, Graffi made another lunge, but Emlyn hung on, tightening his grip.

'Stop it, both of you.'

'You's choking me.'

Fortunately a nasty scrap was averted by Amber Lloyd-Foxe crying out, 'Oh, why don't you manhandle us, Mr Davies, it's so sexist to pick on boys every time.'

'Why are we being discriminated against?' chorused Kitten, Milly and even Primrose from the gallery. 'We all want to be manhandled by Mr Davies.'

The hall rumbled with laughter.

Blushing furiously, Emlyn dragged Johnnie and Graffi outside and shoved their heads under the kitchen tap.

A scented, blond jangle of jewellery had meanwhile risen to her feet.

'That kaind of behaviour says it all, reely.'

'Oh shut up,' said Pearl, glancing up from the dress she was designing.

'I won't shut up,' said the blonde shrilly. 'As a resident of Cavendish Plaza, Larks kids make our lives a misery. They graffiti our walls, key our cars, carpet our pavements with chewing gum, beat up and spit at our kids. Why should we fork out for security guards to protect us? This isn't the inner city.'

'Larks should be closed down,' shouted a Cavendish Plaza husband in broad pinstripe. 'It's a breeding ground for thugs and drugs. If you live in a pleasant private estate, you don't expect a sink school that is almost a pupil referral unit on the doorstep.'

The platform was nodding in delight as an old biddy knitting in the front took up the cudgel.

'I don't have the privilege of security guards,' squawked Miss Miserden, 'I live next to Larks and I never feel safe in my bed.'

'You'd be quite safe in anyone else's bed, darling,' yelled Graffi, who'd somehow found his way back to the gallery, 'no one's going to jump on you.'

This was followed by more cheers and cries of 'Shame' and 'Disgusting, insulting a pensioner'.

'Who's she?' asked Dora, who was furiously making notes.

'She's the one who brings letters of complaint in every day,' said Junior, who'd been doing work experience on the *Gazette*. 'She's called Name and Address Supplied.'

And so the slanging went on, with the closure brigade attacking Larks and its record and Larks supporters defending it.

When a rather flushed Milly Walton shouted from the gallery:

'We at Bagley love meeting young people from a different background and Larks kids are great, we've had so much fun together,' Randal Stancombe made a note to alert Ruth, who didn't at all approve of her daughter's liaison with Graffi.

Sophy Belvedon then made an impassioned plea for the children and particularly Year Ten, who mustn't be abandoned in mid GCSE course.

'Year Ten will be accommodated and taught much better in other schools,' said Ashton, rising to his feet. It was time this meeting was wrapped up. 'My name's Ashton Douglas,' he told the assembled company smoothly, 'S and C Services Diwector of Opewations.'

'Operations performed without the use of anaesthetics,' shouted Hengist. 'No wonder your collaborator is called Payne. As she keeps informing us: "Closing a school is a Payne-full experience."'

As the audience cheered, Ashton's soft, bland features set into a cement of hatred.

'It is also an unnecessary and dishonest operation,' went on Hengist, rising to his feet, his deep, husky, bitchy voice carrying to every corner. Again he seemed to have shaken off his tiredness and worry. 'This discussion is about surplus places. The education department, we have been told, are very worried about the one thousand six hundred surplus places in Larkshire schools, which will evidently double by two thousand and ten.

'Why then,' he asked coolly, 'if our child population is ebbing away, does the housing department predict that two thousand five hundred extra houses will be built – no doubt roughshod over Larkshire's loveliest green belt – in the next three years? Will all these houses be inhabited by childless couples?' He paused for effect. 'Clearly not, and even more interestingly, that one-off contributions from developers will be put towards new and temporary classrooms to accommodate extra pupils.

'Tut, tut, Ashton, Cindy and Russell, have you enlisted the health department to doctor your figures?

He paused again to allow a roar of approval from Larks supporters.

'It seems that S and C and the county council use figures selectively – just as they rigged the Review of Secondary Schools and, when challenged, blamed the falsely poor figures for Larkminster Comprehensive on typing errors. But did anyone have the decency to admit this publicly?'

'No,' roared at least half the hall.

'I don't know what you're talking about,' spluttered Cindy.

'As a Larkminster county councillor, you don't seem to know what *anyone's* talking about,' cracked back Hengist to more cheers. His dark eyes had recaptured all their old sparkle. 'It's absolutely typical of a Lab/Lib Dim council to have no idea what other departments are up to, or to pretend they don't to achieve their ends. This is a corrupt hung council which ought to be hung out to dry because the only thing that matters to them is selling off Larks's ten acres of prime land and putting millions of pounds into their own and S and C Services' pockets.'

'Save our school!' Stamp, stamp, stamp went a thunder of feet on the parquet as Emlyn grinned across at a flabbergasted Janna.

'Can you tell us' – Rupert had taken up the baton, his light, clipped, contemptuous drawl carrying just as easily round the hall – 'why Randal Stancombe is putting up a large building for Rod Hyde to accommodate extra pupils? This building was commissioned in autumn 2002, at exactly the same time as the Review of Secondary Schools, with rigged figures, was sent out and a report, targeting Larks as the proposed choice for closure, leaked to the *Gazette*.'

'I must protest,' spluttered Rod Hyde.

'Feel free,' said Rupert sarcastically, 'but first, tell us why Larks, particularly after such a good Ofsted report, was chosen to be closed down.'

'Because it's the pits,' yelled Brute Stevens.

As Emlyn grabbed Johnnie Fowler's collar, Cindy saw a chance to dive in:

'As I keep saying, because the people of Larkshire preferred to send their children to other local schools or, failing that, go private or out of county, rather than Larks.'

'Rubbish,' snapped Rupert. 'Plenty of schools in Larkshire have empty desks. The difference is that Larks is sitting on twenty-two million pounds' worth of prime land, with Gap and Borders and Waitrose nearby. S and C have had a catastrophic year; shares in all their other companies have fallen. Selling off Larks would put them nicely in the black.'

Randal Stancombe was by now looking even less amused than Queen Victoria's portrait, which hung on the wall at the end of his row.

'How dare you make these slandewous accusations,' squawked Ashton.

'Because they're true. You've targeted not the most failing school but the one that would bring in the most money. Janna Curtis has been dealt a marked card,' said Rupert chillingly. 'Her only crime was to succeed too well against all the odds, so her character and her school had to be repeatedly blackened by reports in your papers, Col, demoralizing pupils and staff and, in particular, changing the minds of parents intending to send their children there.'

'Oh, well done, Rupert. Col the toad will soon explode,' giggled Dora. 'I am a poet and I do not know it.'

'This is disgraceful,' thundered Russell.

'Disgraceful for Janna and Larks,' shouted the Brigadier.

Janna's face was in her hands, she couldn't believe such incredible support.

Feral gazed at Bianca.

'What are they going on about?'

'I've no idea.'

'This is totally out of order.' Col Peters crashed down his hammer. 'I hope Hengist Brett-Taylor can substantiate these accusations.'

'Only too easily.' Most of the platform, despite the heat, lost colour as, out of his inside pocket, Hengist produced a sheet of paper covered in writing and waved it at the audience. 'This is a list of people likely to profit from the sale of Larks. The wages of Cindy, for example, will be considerably enhanced.'

'How dare you?' squawked Cindy Payne.

'Shall I read it out?'

'Mr Fussy doesn't look too happy either,' whispered Amber.

'Perhaps little Gandhi needs changing,' whispered back Dora.

'Save our school!' Stamp, stamp, stamp, thundered Larks supporters.

'Well?' taunted Hengist.

The big hand of the hall clock was pointing directly upwards: nine o'clock. Saved by the hour and just managing to contain his fury, Col Peters gathered up his papers.

'I'm afraid we've run out of time,' he said.

'Cop out, cop out, read the list, read the list,' roared the hall.

'I have a paper to get to bed with a report of this meeting,' Col said firmly, 'and we mustn't keep Sally and Hengist or Mr and Mrs Campbell-Black from their dinner party.'

'Read out the list,' shouted the *Western Daily Press.*

Hengist laughed and shook his head.

'Not yet. Unlike the editor of the *Gazette,* I feel it more honourable to substantiate rumours before spreading them.'

'Where are you off to?' asked the *Stroud News* as Sally and Taggie hurried towards the exit.

'Highgrove,' piped up Bianca proudly. 'Have a lovely time, Mummy.' Turning to Feral, she handed him three pieces of paper. 'Here's my number, put it in both pockets and in the pocket of your jacket, then there's no excuse.'

Danijela meanwhile had risen trembling to her feet.

'Before we go, I am an asylum-seeker from Bosnia, we love going to Miss Curtis's school, it is our home and best of England.'

Janna's eyes filled with tears.

'Exactly,' called out Jupiter who, having let Rupert and Hengist do his dirty work, totally distancing himself all evening, now moved in for the kill. 'If Larks closes, all its children will have to find new schools, the teachers, cleaners and support staff new jobs. What will happen to the Shakespeare Estate without their school? Larkshire's other schools and several greedy individuals will profit. That's how private business works: targets must be met, so you sell off your best asset.' The whole room had gone silent. 'And so a whole community will be destroyed.'

There was a long pause.

'Save our school,' croaked Rocky.

'Janna Curtis has been dealt a marked card,' murmured Dora to the *Independent.*

'Let's have a quick show of hands,' said Cindy hastily.

'Those in favour of closure?' called out Col Peters, glancing round the hall as a lot of Rolexes and braceleted hands were held up and a County Hall minion did some cursory counting. 'And those in favour of retaining Larks?' Then as a forest of hands sprung up: 'I think that gives closure a clear majority. I will

485

convey the feeling of the hall to the appropriate authorities,' he added and fled the hall to deafening boos.

The place was in uproar. Hengist fighting his way towards the door met Emlyn coming back in.

'Any news?'

'Definitely not Oriana,' said Emlyn, 'it was a British soldier in a car crash, poor sod.'

'Thank Christ.' Throwing back his head, Hengist took in a great breath of relief. 'And for you too. But, oh God, the poor man and his family. I must go and reassure Sally. See you in the morning. Thanks for everything.'

Running through the deluge, Janna caught up with Hengist on the edge of the car park.

'Thank you all ever so much,' she stammered, 'you were wonderful. I must have made you so late for dinner. Where did you get all that amazing info?' Then, when Hengist laughed: 'At least let me see that list of names.'

'You can have it.' He handed her the piece of paper. 'It's Dora Belvedon's essay on why fox hunting shouldn't be abolished. She got an A star.'

'There were no names?'

'Not before I began counting the people who turned green this evening. Rather a good bluff, don't you think? I must go, darling. Just coming,' he called to the others, waiting in Rupert's revving up BMW.

Desire made Janna ungracious. 'You know how I disapprove of hunting,' she said furiously.

'Don't look gift hunters in the mouth, you chippy child. I'll come and see you over the weekend.'

78

Seeing a drenched Janna returning to the hall, Emlyn assumed her air of desolation stemmed from the likely loss of her school and suggested they go and have supper.

He swept away Janna's protests that she had so many people to thank.

'I've got to ferry several busloads of parents back to the Shakespeare Estate. I'll meet you in the Dog and Duck at ten. And put something warm on.'

The pub was packed when Janna arrived. Emlyn had already found a corner table and ordered a bottle of red and two and a half steaks for himself, Janna and Partner.

At the next table sat a group of students from the local agricultural college and their pretty, Sloaney girlfriends, who all had long, clean streaked hair, endless jean-clad legs and were equally excited by Emlyn and Partner. 'What a sweet little dog.'

The men hardly gave Janna a second glance. She must make more effort. She hadn't even bothered to comb her hair.

'So exciting, this war,' cried one of the Sloanes as the pub television was turned up for *News at Ten*, 'one needn't bother to get out a video any more.'

'I feel so sorry for those poor Baghdad dogs,' said a second, 'that terrible howl going up just before the bombing started.'

'Pretty amazing,' said her boyfriend, 'the way you can see the B52s leaving Fairford on television and, unlike British Rail, arriving on time in Baghdad.'

'You feel so guilty sitting in a warm pub when all this is going on,' shivered the first Sloane. 'I'm crazy about Rageh Omar.'

'Not nearly as crazy as I am about Oriana Taylor,' said her boyfriend.

Janna glanced at Emlyn, who put a finger to his lips.

According to Breaking News, as it was now known, the Americans were pushing on towards Baghdad and a British soldier had been killed in a car crash. His parents, the sadness already carved into their faces, showed great fortitude.

'He was such a wonderful young man,' said the mother, 'he'd been ten years in the army and knew it would never happen to him because he was invincible.'

There were clips of the soldier's divine baby and lovely blonde wife, now a widow, but so brave.

Janna blew her nose noisily; even the Sloanes were hushed. Then it was Oriana reporting from Baghdad, her face growing thinner, paler, more shadowed by the minute and looking so beautiful – as if the stars and rockets and coloured smoke behind her were purely backdrop to enhance her fragility and the suffering and outrage in the same dark eyes as Hengist's. Predictably her sympathies were entirely with the beleaguered Iraqis.

'She's awfully left wing,' protested a Sloane.

Emlyn never took his eyes off Oriana's face.

'You must be so proud,' whispered Janna.

Their steaks had arrived. Janna cut up Partner's on a side plate and put it on the floor.

'Oh how sweet,' said the Sloanes, smiling at Emlyn.

Janna, who hadn't eaten all day, found she was starving.

Emlyn, for once, poured his heart out, expressing his doubts that Oriana would ever settle down. 'It'd be like caging a song bird.'

' "We think caged birds sing, when indeed they cry," ' quoted Janna. Seeing Emlyn wince, she asked quickly, 'How did you become an item?'

'More an out-of-sightem, these days,' said Emlyn bitterly. 'I used to glimpse her from afar at Oxford. She broke men's hearts like Zuleika and had the added lustre of having a legendary rugby player as a father. Then, some years later, we actually met at a party, the night Tony Blair won his first election. Both euphoric; suddenly there was hope. We got hammered and ended up in bed. I couldn't believe my luck. The first months were miraculous, but in retrospect I always made the running.'

Janna let him bang on but finally, fed up with hearing about Oriana and having nearly finished her steak because Emlyn was doing the talking, she said, 'That meeting was wonderful,' and, having thanked Emlyn profusely for all his hard work, added, 'And Hengist and Rupert really turned things round.'

When Emlyn didn't say anything, she glanced up and to her horror saw only pity in his eyes.

'You don't think I'm going to save Larks?'

'I don't guess so, lovely.'

'But Hengist ripped them to pieces.'

'Hengist is a fox, he kills for the hell of it. Tonight he got what he wanted: publicly discrediting the Lib Dems and Labour.'

'You think he was only making political capital?' Janna's voice was rising.

'No, no, he's fond of Larks and devoted to you. But at the moment, he's out of it. He lost Mungo, and he's overwhelmed with terror he's going to lose Oriana.'

'But he proved S and C are crooks and in bed with the county council.'

'I know, but despite the bribes they'll dole out and the cut they'll take for themselves, they'll still hand over such a hefty whack to Larkshire's schools. By not saving your school, they'll help everyone else's.'

'Torture the one to save the half-million? Why in hell did you waste your time ferrying all those parents over?' Realizing she was shouting she lowered her voice. 'I'm sorry.'

'Because I couldn't live with myself if we hadn't tried every avenue. I'm truly sorry. I just think S and C's minds are made up and all the protests, placards and petitions are piffle in the wind. They're not going to change anything.'

'I can't give up.' Janna thumped the table in real anguish. 'I'll sell my house or get a second mortgage. At least I must save Year Ten.'

'Hush, hush.' Emlyn came round and sat down beside her, engulfing her with a huge arm. 'I may be wrong.'

'Don't humour me. I only need a hundred and twenty thousand to pay for a handful of staff and for a building to teach them in, just for a year. Jubilee Cottage is too tiny. Just to give them a chance of getting some GCSEs.'

'Don't be unrealistic, lovely. Have another drink.'

'To hell with you, you're so bloody defeatist!' All Janna's Yorkshire vowels spilt out so loudly and angrily that Partner shot off to observe battle from the knees of one of the Sloanes, who were all listening, shocked and fascinated, to every word. 'I'm going to save Year Ten.' Janna wriggled out from under Emlyn's arm and, slapping thirty pounds on the table, gathered up Partner and fled into the night.

The rain had stopped. Climbing the sky was a sad orange

489

half-moon. With a headscarf of black cloud lining her face, she looked like an Iraqi.

'Don't bug me either,' shouted Janna, 'I've got my own war to fight.'

Tomorrow she would seek out Randal Stancombe, who had smiled at her this evening, and ask him for help.

She was so shattered, she didn't check her messages until morning. The first of many was from Mags. Feral had been arrested for pulling a gun on Brute Stevens and, when grabbed by a Stancombe heavy, had misfired, taking an eye out of Queen Victoria's portrait.

As Feral was only fifteen he was later bailed by the Brigadier and the case adjourned.

'How could you, Feral?' stormed Janna. 'Everything was going Larks's way.'

'Brute stole my football and he dissed Bianca,' said Feral. 'He called her a posh black bitch. He showed no respect.'

'None of that'll emerge till the case comes up, which'll be too late for Larks.'

Brigadier Woodford wasn't pleased either.

'If you don't pull yourself together, Feral, and stop carrying guns, you'll be in and out of prison for the rest of your life.'

Feral chucked his jacket and jeans into the washing machine at the launderette deliberately blurring all Bianca's numbers.

The *Gazette* predictably ignored any reference to skulduggery and led on Feral being arrested in front of the Bishop and Ashton Douglas, confirming everyone's worst fears of Larks. They also reported a show of hands in favour of closure and drew attention to Larks's normally vocal headmistress, Janna Curtis, having no words to say in her school's defence.

79

It was not until well into the holidays that Janna screwed up courage to ring Randal Stancombe, who couldn't have been more charming.

'Come and have a drink this evening, any time after seven. I'll warn the guy on the gate.'

How did one dress for a man whom one wanted to convince one was worth a loan or, better still, a gift of £120,000? Peanuts to Stancombe, but the rich got rich by watching the pennies. A hundred and twenty thousand might buy another Ferrari, or a diamond necklace for Mrs Walton, both of which could be sold. You couldn't sell Year Ten.

At least she'd got some sleep and soaked her hair in coconut oil for twenty-four hours so it gleamed glossier than the coat of any Crufts red setter.

She wore a brown velvet pencil skirt and a cotton jersey twin set in the same soft apricot pink as the glow which ringed the horizon as she drove towards Cavendish Plaza.

'One, two, three, four, five, once I caught a big fish alive,' sang Janna.

Despite the deluge on the day of the public meeting, drought and late frosts, as if in sympathy with the war, had bleached the fields khaki. Hungry horses had stripped trees blown down in the gales of their dark bark, leaving pale bone below.

On the car radio she learnt that five Americans taken prisoner had been paraded on television and that, after bashing hell out of the Iraqis for nearly three weeks, the Americans were having the temerity to bang on about the Geneva Convention. She was so ashamed it was Labour who'd taken Britain to war. Great unpatriotic cheers had gone up in the staffroom every time the Iraqis were reported as fighting back bravely.

Stancombe, on the other hand, who was rumoured to be, among other things, an arms dealer, would probably be madly pro-war. She must keep her trap shut.

Janna didn't know which was more beautiful: Larkminster, gold in the setting sun, seen through Stancombe's telescope, which was so powerful she could pick out primroses on Smokers' and even the crumbs Wally, to distract himself from the war, was putting on the bird table, or Stancombe's apartment itself, which was a soothing symphony of sands and terracottas with soft suede sofas, fake fur cushions and fluffy rugs. Two walls of the vast lounge were window, the other two were crammed with wonderful pictures: Rothko, Chagall, Tracey Emin, Sam Taylor-Wood, CDs largely classical and admittedly many of them still in their cellophane wrappings and surprisingly interesting books: biographies of Alan Sugar, Bill Gates and Philip Green rubbing shoulders with Louis de Bernières, Sebastian Faulks, Donna Tartt, a first edition of *Lolita* and even some poetry.

Chopin's Second Piano Concerto rippled through speakers as though Marcus Campbell-Black and the BBC Symphony Orchestra were actually in the room.

'Whatever my feelings for his toffee-nosed father, I cannot get enough of Marcus,' announced Stancombe as, like Venus hot from some exciting, foaming jacuzzi, he welcomed her. His hair was damp and curling on his strong, suntanned neck. He was wearing just a dark blue, crew-necked cashmere sweater and white chinos, which clung to his sleek, still damp body. He smelt of toothpaste and Lynx, his favourite aftershave, as he padded round in beautifully pedicured bare feet.

Janna was flattered he'd glammed up for her, even if he was probably going out later.

'What a gorgeous apartment.'

Stancombe smiled. 'I used to think books and CDs ruined the look, but I've mellowed.'

On a glass side table in an art deco frame was a beautiful photograph of Jade, taken by Lichfield.

'How pretty she is,' sighed Janna.

'Takes after her dad,' joked Stancombe, handing Janna a long, slim glass of champagne; then, suddenly serious: 'She's a bit lost actually. Bloody Cosmo Rannaldini's messed her about.'

Ushering Janna on to a pale brown leather sofa, so vast Janna's little feet only just reached the edge, he sat down beside her.

'Hard being first-generation public school. You pick up the posh accent and the clothes, even the education, but not the roots. People laugh at me because I'm flash and vulgar. They laugh at Jade when she doesn't know things or people or pronounces them wrong. It makes her flare up, easily on the defensive.'

'Like me,' sighed Janna. 'If only I could keep my temper and learn some tact.'

Stancombe clinked his glass against hers. 'To the flash and the vulgar, may we inherit the earth. Problem with education, you've only got one chance. I often think Jade would have been happier at a state school. Nice if she could have been taught by you. You'd have understood her.'

Janna had never felt so flattered or warm inside, particularly when he refilled her glass.

'People like Rupert, Hengist and Jupiter take your money, even ask you to their homes,' he went on bitterly, 'but they never really accept you and they laugh at us behind our backs – even Sally.'

'They were wonderful at the meeting,' protested Janna. 'They came out on a vile night to save me.'

'With respect, they saw it as a chance to rattle the other parties.'

'Oh,' wailed Janna, 'Emlyn said the same thing.'

'Emlyn's one of us.'

'You truly don't think I can save Larks?'

Stancombe shook his head.

Wriggling off the edge of the sofa, which was like falling off the edge of the world, overwhelmed with despair, Janna was tempted to walk straight through the big glass window and splatter on Casey Andrews's sculpture in the forecourt miles below.

On a side table was a *Telegraph* colour magazine open at an interview with Stancombe, photographed in this same flat with Mrs Walton.

'Lovely picture,' she said dully.

'Even with Ruth,' she realized Stancombe was saying a minute later, 'I have to watch myself. She gives me a lot of advice. I thought "mangy" was pronounced like "man".'

'Isn't it? She's so beautiful.'

'Works hard enough at it.'

'And succeeds.'

'She'd get an A star in leisure and tourism. She's in Rome with Milly as we speak.'

Janna could see La Perdrix d'Or, where she and Hengist had had their first lunch, and Larks, appearing at a distance innocent and unscathed with the green blur of spring on its trees – as if for a last time.

'I like a woman who works,' said Stancombe joining her, then, glancing sideways: 'Why are you crying?'

'For Larks.' A great shuddering breath racked Janna's small frame. 'If I can't save it, would you help me to save Year Ten? Only about forty of them. Imagine if your Jade had to leave halfway through her GCSE course. Rod Hyde loathes my children; he'd bully them into the ground. Rutminster Comp's a jungle; they'd just give up.

'I only need a hundred and twenty thousand for some teachers and a new building or to rebuild Appletree. Would you lend me it? You can have my house as security.'

'How much did you pay for it?'

'One hundred and seventy-five thousand; three-quarters of that mortgage. I could sell it.' She wiped her eyes with her sleeve.

'How would you pay your staff?'

'That's why I need a hundred and twenty. Please, please help me.'

Stancombe retreated to get the bottle.

Janna put her hand over her glass. 'I'm driving.'

'A very hard bargain. I need time to think. I'll do all I can. I'll lean on Ashton to keep the school open a bit longer.'

Janna was overwhelmed with weariness. 'I think it'd be too difficult to rebuild now. So many teachers and children have left.'

'If I get you the money . . .' Stretching out a hand, Stancombe caressed the back of her neck . . . 'you've got to promise to sleep with me.'

Janna opened her mouth and shut it again, feeling herself growing very hot and wet as if she were fantasizing about something of which she was ashamed.

Stancombe laughed. 'OK, you need time to think, like me.'

'I must go.' As she jumped away, his hand closed on the scruff of her twinset.

'Why must you?'

'I just ought.'

'The first time I saw you, through this telescope on your first day, you were so bonny with your flaming red hair, like a beacon waiting to light up the town. Next time at Hengist and Sally's, you were so upset, because you'd found that little dog blown up, I still thought you were very tasty, but I'd just met Ruth – the road not taken.'

'I love that poem,' said Janna in surprise.

'Now you're patronizing me and my yob culture, too busy scrabbling his way to the top to read poetry. Then I saw you at the public meeting, I thought how tired and diminished you looked and how cheap your clothes were.'

Janna longed to protest that the dress was pure silk and from Hengist.

'And I wanted to take you under my wing and make your life happier and easier.' Stancombe dropped a kiss on the top of her head and let a leisurely hand move down over her bottom, exciting her unbearably.

'I must go, I've got the same little dog in the car,' she stammered. 'Thank you for seeing me.'

'It's good to talk,' said Stancombe, almost spoiling things.

As she ran to the lift in utter confusion, he caught up with her and pressed the button.

'D'you know the sexiest thing in the world?'

'What?'

'Courage – and you've got it in spades. I'd like to help with your school and I'd like you to help me with Jade, she's so unhappy. Ruth's not the ideal prospective stepmother.'

As he drew her towards him, she felt his wonderfully fit body burning through the blue cashmere, his rock-hard cock practically raping her belly button. So much taller, he had to bend his head to kiss her. Janna gasped and resisted, then her mouth melted beneath his mouth as he sucked and his tongue caressed her lips with such tenderness and delicacy. He was so sexy.

'I want you to look bonny and happy again,' he whispered. 'I want to take those dark circles away and put them back for a different reason, "the lineaments of gratified desire".'

Recognizing the quote, Janna thought: This is ridiculous, he's appealing to my intellectual snobbery.

As the lift opened directly into the flat, she leapt into it.

'That was lovely, thanks ever so much.'

All the way down, she expected him to press a button from above and imprison her deep down in the hellish bowels of the building, for treating with the devil of whom Hengist, Mags and Emlyn so disapproved and yet who had just been so disturbingly adorable.

'One, two, three, four, five, once I caught a big fish alive,' sang Janna to Partner all the way home.

80

'One of the privileges of the great', wrote Giraudoux, 'is to witness catastrophes from a terrace', or, in Randal Stancombe's case, from the air. Flying off to the Far East, he never got back in touch, leaving Janna to her fate. Nor, after their Titanic support at the public meeting, did Hengist, Jupiter or Rupert return to fight her corner.

The war in Iraq, therefore, ended much less decisively than Larkminster Comprehensive when in the middle of May, the School's Organization Committee voted unanimously and conclusively to close it down.

This, although expected, came as a devastating death blow. On the steps of County Hall, a stunned Janna defiantly announced that even if the guillotine had fallen, she would still battle on to save her school. Inside, she knew this was impossible. There was no more money in the kitty.

The following morning, however, she was sitting in the kitchen drinking very strong tea and wondering how to stagger mortally wounded through the rest of her life, when she heard Partner barking at his very good friend the postman. Next moment he had rushed in carrying a blue envelope in his mouth, leaping on to Janna's knee to deliver it. The letter inside was on plain blue paper.

'Dear Janna,' she read, 'I'm sorry about your school. I thought you might need this in your battle to save Year Ten. A banker's draft for £120,000 should now be in your account. Best of luck.'

Janna gave a gasp of disbelief; it must be some cruel joke. There was no address, no signature, only a Royal Mail postmark; nothing to identify who'd given it her. But when she rang her bank in Larkminster, the manager, markedly more friendly and deferential, confirmed the money was indeed in her account, but that the donor had insisted on remaining anonymous.

It couldn't be Hengist, thought Janna, nor Rupert, nor Jupiter, unless Emlyn had told them of her desperate concerns about Year Ten. So she rang Stancombe, gibbering her thanks. After several moments of evasion, there was such a long pause that she thought he had hung up, then he said ruefully:

'I wanted it to be a secret.'

'I cannot believe such kindness. I'll pay you back somehow, I promise.'

'No, no, it's a gift. Lovely ladies deserve a leg-up.' Stancombe laughed softly. 'Just remember our bargain.'

And again Janna felt the warm quiver between her legs.

'I'm off to the States with Ruth on Monday,' Stancombe went on. 'I'll be back in June and we'll find you a building to accommodate your tearaways and get some decent funding from Ashton.'

'I won't accept a penny from him.'

'Don't be stupid. You'll need his help. See you in June.'

'He hasn't failed me, he hasn't failed me.' Gathering up Partner, Janna waltzed him round the room. 'You'll have another year with your friends, darling.'

Then she collapsed back on her chair, unable to comprehend such golden benison after the darkness of yesterday, reeling at the prospect of how much battling would still be needed to get the project off the ground. After she'd worked out the figures, she also realized she would need a lot more money to pay salaries, feed the children and heat and light the building, not to mention exam fees.

Janna remembered very little of the remaining summer term. As dogs moult in hot weather, Larks shed teachers and pupils. Many of the latter returned tearfully from their new schools: 'They called us Larks scum, miss, and put chewing gum in our hair.'

Ashton showed no desire to help Janna find a home for Year Ten. Instead, in early June, he offered her a headship turning round a failing Larkshire school.

'It's a challenge, Janna, restore your sense of self-worth.'

Janna refused; she'd no desire to kill off another school. She continued to refuse jobs and endured the humiliation of all the other schools in the area descending like vultures and slapping different coloured stickers on desks, books, computers and laboratory equipment, which they would collect after Larks finally closed down on 12 July. Enid, who'd built up the library

497

over six years, was in perpetual floods. The choir school was the greediest and earmarked the most.

'The nearer the pulpit, the further from God,' observed Cambola sourly.

Janna felt particularly guilty about teachers like Sophy Belvedon, who'd refused to abandon ship and so heroically carried on helping Year Eleven through their GCSEs that Janna was amazed the vultures didn't slap a coloured sticker on them as well.

Jupiter and Rupert returned to the attack and continued to hassle S and C and the county council, not just on the dodgy ethics of 'closing down' Larks, but also accusing them of diverting the education budget to other areas. Who, for example, had paid for Ashton's Hockney?

S and C and the county council denied everything, but they were rattled, particularly when, after Russell Lambert's resignation as chairman of Larks governors, Brigadier Woodford took over as temporary chairman and asked for the minutes of meetings over the past five years.

They were also fed up to the back teeth with Janna ringing every day demanding a building for Year Ten. Who would rid them of this turbulent priestess? Despite falling S and C shares, even if it would mean a year's delay before getting the big money from the sale of Larks, they decided it might be prudent, and in the end cheaper, to allow Janna to remain on site.

'We must snatch the moral high ground from the Tories,' insisted Cindy Payne. 'Let's go and look at Larks.'

There had been a hosepipe ban and all the little saplings planted by Wally in the autumn had died in the drought. Leaves were falling out of the trees, even though it was only June, as Ashton and Cindy arrived. Janna utterly jolted them by taking them first over the main building. Like an elephant left to die in the jungle, all the flesh had fallen off its bones. Apart from the damp and the boarded-up windows, not a ceiling or a roof tile was in place. Doors had been ripped from their hinges, plugs and lavatory chains torn out, every classroom trashed. Wally had lost heart.

'I wouldn't educate a dog in here,' said Ashton faintly. 'How could this have happened?'

'The children did it. They were so hurt and angry you closed their school.'

Through gritted teeth and because the main building was beyond redemption, Ashton and Cindy agreed two weeks later to rebuild the annexe, Appletree. They then revealed to Janna that

Randal had very, very generously offered to do the job at cost. After all, he was donating a science block to Bagley and a so-called vocational studies unit to St Jimmy's. Appletree would be another example of his wonderful philanthropy.

In the first week in July, therefore, S and C and the county council called a press conference.

'In view of the closure of Larks Compwehensive,' Ashton, in a new mauve striped shirt, told his large audience, 'it has been decided not to diswupt Year Ten in the middle of their GCSE course. S and C Services have therefore decided to pwovide a building in which they can be taught and to put funds towards their education for a further year, until June 2004.'

These funds were of course hugely bolstered by the £120,000 Randal had given to Janna – but he wished this donation to remain anonymous. Ashton, however, did go on to say the rebuilding of Appletree would be supervised by Janna Curtis and carried out, on very generous terms, by Randal Stancombe Properties. Janna was to be given an extended contract until the end of August 2004, to close the school down finally.

'Mercy has a human face,' announced the *Gazette*, alongside a soppy picture of Ashton, which everyone graffitied.

Stormin' Norman appeared on television punching the air instead of anyone else and shouting 'Yes' when the news broke.

'Why isn't Janna Curtis more grateful?' grumbled Cindy Payne.

This was because saving Year Ten was small comfort compared with the anguish of saying goodbye to the other years.

'Why didn't you save us as well?' sobbed the little ones.

'Why didn't you march for us on Drowning Street?'

It was like working in a slaughterhouse, or a vivisection clinic, making their last moments as comfortable as possible. Janna tried heroically to remain cheerful, but on the last day, when the media poured in to photograph the death of a school, she lost it and screamed at them all to booger off.

'Why couldn't I have saved them?' she sobbed to Mags and Cambola as her children set off on their last journey down the drive to St Jimmy's or Searston Abbey or pupil referral units or to uncertain futures and no likelihood of a decent job, unless, in Year Eleven's case, they had notched up a few GCSEs.

Janna felt more and more grateful to Stancombe who was planning to extend Appletree to include a dining room, a big hall, a gym and new labs.

'I'd like to rename it Stancombe House,' she told him when he dropped in with a bottle of champagne after the first day of work.

Stancombe shook his head. 'That'll tell everyone who funded it. It was a gift, remember?'

Although they were alone in the roofless, windowless building and could see a new moon scything its way through the soft blue twilight, Stancombe made no attempt to extract payment. At first Janna thought he was sensitively appreciating her mood of utter desolation, then he shyly confided that he and Ruth were off to Italy and that he was thinking very seriously of asking her to marry him.

When Janna hugged him in delight and urged him to go for it, he assured her that Teddy Murray, his foreman, would keep an eye on everything and told her to ring him on his mobile if she needed help.

Janna was heartbroken to lose Lance and Lydia, who both needed to work full time. She was, however, touched by the teachers who wanted to stay on: Mags, Cambola, Mr Mates, even Basket and Skunk, who she prayed would rise to the challenge. They were all taking early retirement, but were allowed to work two and a half days a week which was all that would be needed to cover the new Year Eleven's GCSE syllabus. This suited Mags who had been only doing two and a half days a week anyway.

Among the younger teachers, sweet Sophy Belvedon had opted to stay. Wally and Debbie would both remain full time and, to the delight of the children, the Brigadier and Lily, who'd both been cleared by the Criminal Records Bureau, would respectively teach history and help Mags out with French, Spanish and German.

One of the nicest compliments came from Rowan who, having signed on for an advanced course in the summer holidays, offered to come in and teach IT.

'I know we've had our differences,' she told Janna, 'but I want to see Larks through to the end and, frankly, anything's better than looking after children full time.'

Gloria was staying on to take PE, so apart from maths and food technology, everything was sorted.

Everyone was being so kind; Janna couldn't think why she couldn't stop crying. There was the afternoon at Appletree when she was dickering over what colour to paint the new hall, when Partner shot off into the park. Janna only just had time to hide her swollen eyes behind dark glasses before he proudly led in Cadbury and Dora.

Dora was delivering a card which said: 'Sorry about your school, good luck, Paris', which nearly set Janna off again.

Dora was also in low spirits. She'd had to spend a lot of time recently counselling her brother, Dicky, because his hero David Beckham had moved to Real Madrid. She had continued to put sweets in Paris's locker but he hardly noticed her. He had been so gorgeous as Jack Tanner in the end-of-term play, *Man and Superman*, it had fanned the flames of her hopeless love for him. But life must go on. Dora cleared her throat.

'I feel one must put something back into the community,' she told Janna gravely, 'so I'd like to offer my services teaching media studies at Larks next term.'

Janna started to laugh and found she couldn't stop. Dora got quite huffy until Janna began to cry, whereupon Dora rushed off to the Ghost and Castle and bought her a quadruple vodka and tonic. When she assured the landlord: 'I'm not a binge drinker, it's for Miss Curtis, whose school has closed down,' he quite understood.

81

Bianca Campbell-Black was so dazzled that Feral had defended her with a real gun at the public meeting, she sent him a new violet and Day-Glo yellow football, a diamond cross and ear studs, did no work through the summer term dreaming of him and throughout the holidays bombarded him with cards inviting him home.

Feral longed to accept. Time and again he hitched a lift or 'borrowed' a car to drive over to Penscombe. On his first visit, he mistook the dear little lodge at the bottom of the drive for Bianca's home and thought how cosily he and she could live there. But when he knocked and was told by an ancient retainer that Bianca lived in the big house at the end of an avenue of chestnuts, whose trunk shadows striped the drive like an endless old-school tie, he turned round and went home.

On subsequent visits through the baking summer, he had borrowed Lily's binoculars and paused on the road out of Penscombe village. Here he had gazed longingly across the valley at fields filled with horses and the long lake squirming in the sunshine beneath Rupert's big, golden house, in the hope of catching a glimpse of Bianca, but knowing there was no way of him ever affording her, particularly as he had a court case pending, and if it was held in September he would be sixteen and named in the paper.

Nor had life in the big golden house during the holidays been peaceful. Xavier had got an even worse report than Bianca, indicating that he hadn't a hope of a single GCSE unless he did four or five hours' work every day in the holidays.

Shut away in his bedroom, ostensibly wrestling with *Macbeth* and the Russian Revolution one stifling mid-August afternoon, Xav looked up at the posters of Colombian beauty spots and fine-looking Colombian Indians, which his mother had had specially framed to make him proud of his origins.

Xav was very aware of the blood of his Indian ancestors flowing through his veins, blood tainted by an excess of drink and drugs, both of which he was now illicitly indulging in. Drunk or stoned, he felt capable of anything; the sadness and terror ebbed away. He forgot he was thick, friendless and had grown fat and spotty by stuffing himself with cake and chocolate when he was coming down.

On the wall hung a little wooden Madonna hollowed out inside to smuggle cocaine. These had been on sale in the Bogotá convent from which he and Bianca had been adopted by Rupert and Taggie. Rupert had nicked one as a souvenir and later given it to Xav, little realizing that Xav was putting it to its original use and, because Rupert himself indulged so rarely, that Xav had been regularly helping himself to his father's stash of cocaine.

At first, Xav had assumed people disliked him at Bagley because he was black, but seeing everyone swooning over Bianca when she arrived, he realized it was just him they didn't like. This was reinforced when Feral, who was much blacker than Bianca, had rolled up, so agile, beautiful and larky that girls fell for him in droves, so Xav could no longer blame his colour for his not getting a girlfriend.

Formerly his great passion and bond with Rupert had been horses, but after a horrible hunting fall in the Easter holidays, when he had smashed his elbow, he had lost his nerve and the one way he could always win his father's respect. If he mounted a horse now, he trembled and poured with sweat. After a few abortive attempts to take him out on a lead rein, Rupert had given up and left him at home.

Finally, Xav's beloved, endlessly wagging, black Labrador, Bogotá, was on his rickety last legs. Rupert had never had any problem with adopting black children. Xav and Bianca were his son and daughter and that was that. Chided in the nineties by a social worker that Xav wasn't making enough black friends, Rupert had insolently bought the boy a black Labrador puppy and called it Bogotá, after Xav's birthplace. The puppy had ironically grown up into the best and truest friend Xav had ever had. Now Bogotá, temporarily oblivious of the arthritis that plagued him, lay snoring at Xavier's feet.

Rupert had been frantically busy all summer running the yard, politicking with Jupiter and Hengist and fighting off takeover bids for Venturer, the television company which he ran with his father-in-law, Declan O'Hara. Venturer was still very successful, but like all independent TV stations, was having an increasing battle attracting advertising.

Nor did the bloodstock market ever sleep, as emails poured in from Tokyo, Dubai and Kentucky. Despite his legendary energy, chronic lack of sleep was making Rupert increasingly ratty and preoccupied, otherwise he might have attributed his son's mood swings to more than adolescent angst.

Hearing a terrific bang and the frenzied barking of dogs, Xav raced out on to the landing with Bogotá hobbling after him. Down the stairwell he could see his mother running white-faced out of the kitchen to be confronted by an outraged Bianca:

'Daddy's shot the television because Mr Blair's on it. I'll just have to go and watch Sky with the lads,' and stormed off.

Taggie clutched her head. She was desperately low both about Xav's deteriorating relationship with the entire family and because she was quite incapable of helping either child with its holiday work. Her agonizing was interrupted by the telephone.

'Helloo, helloo.'

Recognizing the strangulated Adam's apple whine of Alex Bruce, which instantly recalled her own disastrous school days, Taggie started to shake.

'Just checking you're on for our fundraiser for the new science block next week.'

Oh God, she'd forgotten.

'What date is it?'

'Twenty-first of August.'

Taggie went cold. That was Xav's birthday; he went berserk if it weren't celebrated in style. Alex Bruce had caught her on the hop when, back in June, he'd issued the invitation, implying that Xavier's behaviour wouldn't be so 'challenging' or his learning difficulties so excessive if the parental back-up were more committed.

Riddled with shame and guilt, Taggie had weakly accepted but failed to tell Rupert, who was allergic to being gazed at by mothers and forced to put one's hand in one's pocket, when one was already bankrupted by bloody fees.

'Helloo, helloo?' Alex was still on the line. Taggie shuddered at the thought of his pursed red lips framed by beard pressed against the receiver.

'We'll be there,' she bleated.

'Randal Stancombe's agreed to host our promises auction. How about your spouse donating a helicopter trip to the Arc, complete with hospitality, or a peep behind the scenes at Venturer Television? Some of our parents might bid quite high for a chance to appear on *Buffers*.'

'You'll have to ask Rupert,' gasped Taggie and rang off.

Rupert, as she predicted, was insane with rage.

'I'll be in France – there's no way I can get there before nine.'

Taggie said she'd go on ahead, which made Rupert even crosser. He loathed his beautiful wife being out on the toot without him: predators were everywhere.

But his rage was nothing to the sullen fury of Xav that they were abandoning him on his birthday.

'I'm so sorry, darling, I muddled the dates.'

'You should have known it was my birthday from the date. Not that it's my real birthday – that's why you don't care.'

'Don't be bloody to Mummy,' protested Bianca, thinking how unattractively white-tongued and covered in zits her brother looked.

'You can fuck off,' spat Xav, then, swinging back to Taggie: 'Can I have a party at home that night?'

Taggie quailed. 'Of course you can, darling.'

What the hell was Rupert going to say? Mrs Bodkin, their ancient housekeeper, was far too doddery to keep order.

'Will you ask Feral?' pleaded Bianca. 'And Paris? If you ask Paris, Feral might easily come. Oh per-lease.'

'I might.' Xav stormed upstairs, slamming his bedroom door.

Talk about an own goal. Pushing aside a rug and raising a floor board, he lifted out a half-empty bottle of vodka and having filled a tooth mug, hid it again.

He had been so endlessly sulky and difficult at Bagley he had no friends to ask. Girls were repelled by him. Sweet Aysha would never be allowed out by her bullying father. The only reason boys might turn up was to have a crack at Bianca or because the mothers delivering the girls wanted to gawp at the house and his father. He could try the children of his parents' friends: Junior, Amber, Lando and Jack Waterlane. Milly, Dicky and Dora might come. As a brown-nosing gesture, he could ask the hateful Cosmo, but they were probably all away.

Why did his father increasingly hate leaving his dogs and horses and not take them on holidays abroad, so they could row in the Caribbean or Mauritius like everyone else's families? Then he wouldn't have to have a party.

Xav took a slug of vodka, then jumped out of his skin as the door opened, but it was only Bogotá, entirely white face smiling, pink tongue hanging down like a tie, black legs going everywhere.

'You can be guest of honour,' said Xav, giving him a piece of KitKat.

He'd better text people with invitations. He was too shy to telephone. If only Paris were still his friend, then everyone would have come.

Over the next week no one accepted.

'No one answers invitations these days,' Bianca consoled him. Not wanting her brother to be humiliated, she wrote to Feral: 'Xav is having a party on Thursday. Please come, he has asked Paris who would love to see you, so would I. Love, Bianca'.

As the party approached, the spats grew worse.

'How many yobs from Larks are coming?' demanded a departing Rupert.

'I'm not sure,' stammered Taggie.

'They'll chuck all your quiches at each other. For Christ's sake, lock up the silver and bolt all the yard doors.'

Taggie had racked her brains what to give Xav. Before his fall, it had been anything horsey, even on occasion a horse, or a drawing by Lionel Edwards or Munnings. Soon, but not yet, it might be a puppy. Xav didn't want clothes until he'd lost weight. Desperate to placate him, she spent far too much on DVD portables and computer games and mobiles which became cameras. As Rupert was abroad on the day of his birthday, Xav felt free to play up and hardly opened anything, which resulted in a blazing row when Bianca accused him of being an ungrateful pig.

'Mummy's spent days making yummy food and mixing this gorgeous drink.' Bianca pointed to the Pimm's cup floating with exotic fruit in the big blue bowl on the terrace table.

'I wanted people to have Snakebite or Black Russians, not piddling fruit salad,' snapped Xav, who'd been smoking and drinking all day to cushion himself against the nightmare ahead.

At least it was a beautiful evening, with air balloons drifting up the valley out of a soft rose glow in the west and flocks of birds returning home from scavenging in the fields. Beyond the stables, turning poplars soared like paintbrushes dipped in gold.

Taggie had tied scarlet and blue balloons saying 'Happy Birthday, Xav' on the gate and the balustrade running along the terrace, on which panted Rupert's pack of dogs, grateful that the cruel heat of the day was subsiding.

Rupert's horses were still inside to protect them from the flies and because he didn't want them galloping about, laming themselves on the rock-hard ground. From the rim of brown rush on the water's edge, the lake could be seen to have dropped a couple of feet. Eminem on the CD player battled with the roar of combines.

People had been invited for eight. At five minutes to, Taggie hurtled downstairs. Insufficiently dried, her dark hair fluffed out like Struwwelpeter. Her big, silver-grey eyes were red and tired. Never had her and Rupert's huge four-poster seemed more inviting.

'You look lovely,' lied Bianca, her hands shaking as she fastened a double row of pearls round her mother's slender neck.

'And you look heavenly,' said Taggie, very aware that her daughter was showing too much flesh in a pale pink crop-top and ice-blue shorts and wearing far too much make-up. Bianca had ironed her black curls straight, so a long lock fell over one eye. Jewelled flip-flops showed off ruby toenails and Taggie recognized her own Arpège on Bianca's hot, excited body and her own rubies in Bianca's ears. Rupert would have gone ballistic.

Xav was smouldering in the doorway to the terrace.

'Have a lovely evening.' Taggie tried to kiss him, but Xav, humiliated that, in her high heels, his mother was about seven inches taller than he, shoved her away. Although longing to bury his face in her lovely, scented bosom and beg her to make the party disappear, he couldn't thaw out.

'Don't expect we'll be late, Daddy'll have had a long day.' Then when Xav mumbled about olds not spoiling the fun: 'Don't worry, we'll creep in.'

The moment his mother had left, Xav chucked a bottle of gin into the Pimm's cup.

82

Over at Bagley, the Mansion, square-walled and square-windowed like a great doll's house, was softened by floodlights. Someone had tied pink balloons to the bay trees on either side of the front door and left an empty champagne bottle in one of the dark blue tubs. From the open ground-floor windows came the yelping roar of suntanned parents being force-fed drink to elicit more generous promises later in the evening.

On the way in Taggie bumped into dear Patience Cartwright, who, when he'd kept a pony at Bagley, had been one of the few people Xav had liked and talked to.

'Summer has been rather wearying,' Patience now confessed in her raucous voice.

Ian had let the school to a football academy, who'd trashed the kitchens on their last night, and a youth orchestra rehearsing for a prom, which had entailed non-stop Stockhausen and Hindemith. 'If only it'd been a nice Haydn symphony.'

'How's Paris getting on?' asked Taggie, wincing at her gaunt reflection in the hall mirror.

'All right.' Patience touched wood, then, lowering her voice: 'Could we have lunch and compare notes sometime?'

'Oh, do let's.'

'Paris has been a bit up and down. We love him,' Patience went on firmly, 'but we're not quite sure how much he loves us.'

'I know the feeling,' sighed Taggie. Crossing her fingers, she asked: 'Is he coming to Xav's party?'

'Oh dear, didn't he answer? I'm so sorry. He's going to Jack Waterlane's. A whole crowd: Amber, Milly, Junior, Lando, Kylie, Pearl and Graffi have hired a minibus and taken sleeping bags. That's why David Waterlane isn't coming tonight. He won't pay fees, let alone for promises, and he wants to keep an eye on the Canalettos.'

Oh God, thought Taggie in horror. That lot were the core of Xav's party.

The next moment Daisy France-Lynch had hugged her. 'I've got a message from Lando. Will you apologize profusely to Xav, but he'd already accepted Jack's party which is only a couple of miles down the road. Cosmo and Jade are going there too.'

Next moment Dora was offering Taggie a trayful of brimming champagne glasses. 'Can you tell Bianca and Xav I'm terribly sorry I had to work. Mummy gives me no pocket money. Anyway, if Feral turns up, Bianca won't have eyes for anyone else. Paris has gone to Jack Waterlane's,' Dora added wistfully.

Taggie grabbed a drink, gulping down half of it. Poor, deserted Xav. She wanted to rush home to Penscombe but she had to wait for Rupert.

Creeping into the General Bagley Room, which had just been repainted in a glowing scarlet called Firestone, appropriately since so many of the mothers had acquired spare tyres cooking three meals a day for their offspring and visiting friends all summer. Most of them hid these bulges beneath floating flower prints or white caftans to show off suntanned breasts and shoulders.

Led by the frightful Anthea Belvedon, one mother after another charged up saying: 'No Rupert?' in aggrieved tones, as though Taggie'd pushed him over a cliff. Fleeing to avoid No-Joke Joan, who was obviously going to lecture her on Bianca's lack of application, Taggie went slap into Poppet Bruce, beaming like a lighthouse and clutching a hideous baby sucking on a pink dummy.

'Just off to give the babe his supper. Do let's exchange views,' cried Poppet and next moment Taggie found herself perched on a sofa in a side room as Poppet plunged a dishcloth-grey boob into goldfish-mouthing Gandhi.

Oh God, she hoped someone had arrived at Xav's party.

As if reading her thoughts, Poppet said, 'We must encourage Xavier in social skills, he's very troubled.'

'He's very shy,' protested Taggie.

'Last term his behaviour was distinctly challenging. I know parents of adopted children often blame themselves for disasters that happen in any normal families, but you and Rupert lead such full lives, I sometimes wonder if anyone is listening to Xavier.'

'I haven't left the house all summer,' squeaked Taggie, 'and it's difficult listening to someone who won't talk.'

Poppet's bright, cheery eyes were boring into her like diamond cutters. 'Are you able to help him with his maths?'

'I can't do them at all,' gasped Taggie. If only she could ram a dummy into Poppet's mouth.

'Then I advise you to have some coaching. We have a good friend, Mike Pitts, who could come to the house three or four times a week.'

'I don't have the time,' stammered Taggie, which was quite the wrong answer, as Poppet frowned and suggested Taggie made time.

'Nor do I feel Rupert is a supportive father.'

'He absolutely adores Xav.'

'Maybe, but the lad must miss his birth parents. The wound never heals.' Smugly Poppet unplugged baby Gandhi and hooked him on to another dishcloth-grey tit. 'I cannot advise you too strongly' – her tone grew more bullying – 'to take Xav to birth-mother groups. He could then witness grieving mothers coming to terms with giving up their babes and might achieve closure. Have you told Xav everything about his background?'

'I couldn't,' yelped Taggie.

'Have you wondered if your longing for your own children makes you reject Xav in some way?'

'No, no.'

Out of the window, Taggie could see General Bagley gleaming in the moonlight and longed to climb on to the back of his charger so he could gallop her home to Penscombe.

Rescue instead appeared as Hengist, resplendent in a dark blue velvet smoking jacket, appeared in the doorway.

'Taggie, darling, I've been looking for you. Your drink's empty, unlike little Gandhi's.' He and Poppet exchanged smiles of radiant insincerity. 'Come and talk to me.' He pulled Taggie to her feet, sliding his arm round her narrow waist and stubbing his thumb on her protruding ribs. 'You're losing too much weight. Has that bloody Milk Marketing Board been hassling you? I fear the geeks when they come baring breasts.'

Taggie didn't laugh. She was adorable but not very bright. Not that Rupert was the Brain of Britain.

As the gong went, Taggie pulled herself together. 'It was so sweet of Sally and you to send Xav a birthday card.'

'Sweet of Sally – she remembers everyone. She's the light of my life, as you are of Rupert's. I'm terribly sorry Alex has dragged you along to this grisly jaunt in the holidays. It was also Alex's grisly idea for parents to sit at their children's housemasters' tables. Afraid you're lumbered with Poppet and Alex again.'

Next moment Janey Lloyd-Foxe had buttonholed Taggie. 'How are you, darling? I can't wait for Amber and Junior to go back. We'll starve if I don't get some work done soon.'

Janey unnerved Taggie. She was married to Rupert's best friend, Billy Lloyd-Foxe, and was a well-known journalist who always seemed to know more and worse about you than you did yourself.

'Billy always complains he never gets any sex in the summer holidays because I'm so exhausted,' Janey went on. 'Amber and Junior's friends have been pouring through the house all summer.'

Which was more than Xav's had. Retreating to the Ladies, Taggie rang home. 'Are you OK?'

'Fine,' said Bianca. Dropping her voice: 'No one's arrived yet. Hang on, there's the doorbell. We're OK, bye.'

As she belted in from the terrace, Bianca passed Xav downing another mug of fruit cup and Mrs Bodkin in the study, sleeping peacefully through *The Two Ronnies*.

Followed by two striped lurchers, three Labradors and a couple of Jack Russells, Bianca opened the front door. There was no one outside, but the dogs carried on barking.

'Who's there? They're noisy but harmless,' shouted Bianca.

Very slowly, blacker than the shadows from which he emerged, long, lean and relaxed in a soft leather jacket, with the peak of his Arsenal baseball cap over one ear, a diamond cross gleaming at the neck of his black shirt, black jeans glued to his long legs, was Feral.

'Oh Feral!' Joy spread over Bianca's face like the glow in the west returning. 'You found us.'

'I did.' Feral couldn't believe how pretty she looked – and older, with her sleek, black hair and pale pink lipstick and dark liner emphasizing her ravishing mouth and eyes. He no longer felt avuncular, just lustful. 'Not sure about those dogs.'

'They're as dopey as anything.' Terrified he might run away, Bianca grabbed Feral's hand and led him into the hall, which was hung with pictures of horses and more dogs, and past rooms filled with beautiful battered furniture and splendid portraits.

'Who's that old git?'

'Our grandfather. He's been married five times.'

'Must like wedding cake. Looks familiar.'

'He's in *Buffers*.'

'So he is, friend of the Brig.' Then, peering into the library: 'Who reads those books?'

'No one. Mummy can't read; Daddy only reads Dick Francis and the racing pages.'

Out on the terrace, they found Xav, eyes crossed and slumped against the balustrade, just sober enough to say 'Hi' to Feral.

'This cup is cool,' said Bianca, 'I've eaten most of the fruit out of it. I'll get you a glass.'

As she went off to find one, Xav, who admired and envied Feral, offered him a line of coke.

Feral shook his head. 'Don't do drugs. Don't drink much.'

'This'll kick-start you.' Xav plunged the ladle into the Pimm's, picked up Bianca's glass and missed it.

Behind them the house reared up watchfully, ordering them to behave. A lawn to the right was almost as big as a football pitch.

'Paris coming?' asked Feral.

'Not yet,' mumbled Xav, 'evening's young.'

Bianca came back with a glass and filled it. Feral took a cautious sip, then a gulp.

'It is cool, man.' He took another gulp, then, putting down the glass, edged a box out of his tight jeans and handed it to Xav. 'Happy birthday.'

'Thanks.' Xav put it on the table.

'Open it,' nagged Bianca, 'Feral brought it all this way.'

It was a bracelet, consisting of two black straps attached, instead of to a watch, to two silver skull and crossbones flanking the word FUCK in diamanté letters.

Xav's face lifted, showing for a second how good-looking he could be. 'That is wicked, man, really wicked.' He was worried he'd got too fat, but it did up easily.

'Thank Feral,' chided Bianca.

'I was about to, you stupid bitch.'

Feral, who'd been admiring the lake in the moonlight, swung round to defend Bianca, but she shook her head and his fists unclenched.

'It's great,' mumbled Xav. 'Can't wait to wave it at Poppet and Alex,' and he wheeled off into the house.

Justin Timberlake, fortissimo and blaring out over the valley, obliterated the need to talk.

'Don't people complain about the noise?' asked Feral, thinking of the fuss Miss Miserden made at Larks.

'Not really, Daddy owns the land,' said Bianca simply. 'What have you been doing all summer?'

'Working here and there, mostly for Lily and the Brig. He's been doing a series of *Buffers*; I've helped him dress – cufflinks and fings.'

'Daddy says it's going to be a huge hit, the network's taking it. Grandpa's booked for the next series. So naughty, he

512

forgets I'm his granddaughter sometimes and pinches my bottom.'

'Not surprised in those shorts.' Feral drained his glass.

'They ought to do a programme about me called *Duffers*,' said Bianca, filling it up.

'And me.' Feral collapsed on a bench. He wanted to kiss Bianca's ruby toenails in those jewelled flip-flops. 'Can your mum really not read?'

'Hardly at all, she's dyslexic. Suits me, she can't read my diary. Dora's mother's always reading hers.'

'What does yours say?'

'Feral didn't come and see me today. Boo hoo.' Bianca was on the bench beside him, edging up like a kitten. She had no wiles, no defence mechanism; he knew she was dying to be in his arms just as he was to be in hers.

'Are you hungry?' asked Bianca.

'Kind of.' It wasn't cool to say he'd been too nervous to eat all day. 'This drink's strong. Perhaps I should.'

'It'd be nice if you could. Mummy's worked so hard. Poor Xav, I don't think anyone else is coming.'

'Bad for him, suits us.'

There is a limit to the inroads three people, two of them dottily in love, can make on supper for twenty. Feral ate some chicken pie and some chocolate roulade and Bianca toyed with a piece of quiche. Xav had another line of cocaine and another glass of Pimm's and passed out on the sofa.

'Shall we go upstairs?' murmured Bianca, taking Feral's hand, 'Daddy and Mummy have gone to some dinner.'

Drunk with love and fruit cup, Feral had to cling on to the crimson cord to pull himself up the splendid oak staircase.

He would never have followed Bianca upstairs, or even turned up, if he hadn't been boosted by the prospect of a trial with the Rovers on Monday. A contributory factor had also been that this week (earlier than expected) his court case had come up. The Brigadier had accompanied him to court and vouched for his good character. Luckily the magistrates were all fans of *Buffers* and had let him off, and because he was still just fifteen, none of this had been reported in the papers.

Inside Bianca's bedroom, someone appeared to have shredded a rainbow, as clothes she'd rejected littered bed, chair and carpet. As she gathered them up, chucking them on a blue and white striped sofa, Feral admired the daffodil-yellow curtains and the pink and violet quilt on the little four-poster. On the powder-blue walls, framed photographs of Colombian beauty spots – sweeps of orchids, giant water lilies, the lake where the legendary El Dorado was hidden – rubbed shoulders with posters of Michael Owen and Justin Timberlake, which he wanted to tear down. When he was striker for Larkminster Rovers, he'd have his own posters.

'This used to be the nicest spare room, but Daddy hates having people to stay so much, he let me have it.'

Feral leapt for the wardrobe in terror as he heard what he imagined as frantic hammering on the door, but it was only the hooves of Rupert's horses being let out into the fields in the cool of the evening.

'It's like a zoo here,' he grumbled, peering out of the window. 'Graffi'd be in heaven with all these horses and pictures.'

'Bring him tomorrow,' begged Bianca.

Feral had had so many girls, taking what he wanted without compunction, but none had touched him like Bianca, nor been as beautiful. Her clear, pale, coffee-coloured complexion was flushed with rose, her slim, supple body quivering to be entwined with his. He longed to bury his lips in her belly button and progress downward, to caress the delectable curve of buttock emerging from her blue shorts, to feel against his thighs the fluttering caress of her sooty eyelashes. Grown-up things.

But this was a child's room. On the shelves Harry Potter and Jacqueline Wilson fought for space with Barbie dolls, rows and rows of lipsticks and coloured nail polish. She was only thirteen – where the hell could it lead?

Above the bookcase hung a glass plate engraved with the words: 'Welcome to Penscombe, Bianca Maud Campbell-Black. May 1990'.

'I don't remember arriving here, I was only three months old, but Xav does and there were flags and balloons all the way up the drive. Mummy and Daddy crossed the world to find us,' Bianca added proudly. 'They were sad they couldn't have children but so pleased to have us. Our mother is the sweetest woman in the world.'

Feral edged towards her. 'Makes two of you.'

Bianca shrugged. 'Daddy's tricky, I used to be jealous of how much he adored Xav, but now they fight all the time.' She crossed the room, peering out at the empty terrace and the stars nearing their full brightness. 'I'm really sorry, it doesn't look as though Paris is coming.'

'Don't matter.' On her return from the window, Feral reached out for her, realizing she was trembling as much as he was.

'Why didn't you ring me? I gave you my number on three pieces of paper.'

'They ran in the washing machine. I tried once and got your Dad and bottled out. I watched your house across the valley for hours like a stalker.'

'Promise?'

'Promise, promise.'

Grabbing her tiny waist, encountering goose flesh, he caressed the edges of her springy, surprisingly full breasts, then he bent his head to kiss her arched-back throat, then her closed eyelids, the tip of her tiny nose, behind each ear, breathing in the deliciously heady Arpège. Finally he kissed her soft, sweet, pink lips, which parted shyly, her darting tongue touching his, flickering then retreating like a dancer, drawing him into heaven.

As her little hands closed on his head, his hair felt so thick, vigorous and right, compared with the floppy silken tresses of other boys she had snogged, that she clung on. Their first, magic kiss seemed to last for ever.

'Oh Bee-unca,' murmured Feral, collapsing back on to the bed, 'I have dreamt of you.'

'Why, uncle, it isn't a shame at all,' giggled Bianca, collapsing beside him. 'Xav's passed out, Mrs Bodkin's asleep and Mummy won't be back for centuries.'

83

Mrs Axford and her fleet of waitresses were clearing away the main course of chicken supreme with tagliatelle and wild mushrooms when Rupert stalked in. He could have murdered a quadruple whisky, but couldn't drink as he had to fly home. A ripple of excitement ran through the hall as mothers readjusted their cleavages and checked their reflections in little gold compacts. The only man in the room not in a dinner jacket (except Alex Bruce, who'd refused to wear one on principle), Rupert in a crumpled off-white suit and cornflower-blue shirt suddenly made everyone else look overdressed.

Hengist leapt to his feet. 'You've made it, well done, you're over here.'

Rupert had already clocked his wife looking utterly dejected between the appalling Alex Bruce and the just as appalling old queen Biffo Rudge. Serve her right for dragging him along to such a ghastly evening.

'OK?' he asked as he kissed her rigid cheek.

'No one's come to Xav's party,' whispered Taggie in anguish, 'they've all gone to Jack Waterlane's.'

'Might teach him to be nicer to people,' snapped Rupert.

Nemesis descended swiftly with a jangle of ethnic bracelets as a voice cried, 'Rupert, Rupert, you're here,' and Poppet Bruce patted the chair beside her. 'You've got Joan Johnson on your left, so we can enjoy an exchange of views about Xavier and Bianca. You know Alex and Biffo, of course, and Boffin's parents Gordon and Susan Brooks, and Anthea Belvedon.'

'Oh, Rupert and I are old friends,' said Anthea, delighted with an opportunity to captivate. She'd always thought Rupert was gorgeous and wasted on Taggie. How infuriating Dora, watching her every move, was waiting at table and had now rushed over and dumped a large piece of venison pâté in front of Rupert.

'Poor thing, you must be starving. Toast's on the way. How's Penscombe Peterkin?' That was Rupert's star horse, much fancied in the St Leger.

'Awesome, but we need rain, he loathes hard going.'

'Then he wouldn't like sitting between Joan and Poppet,' whispered Dora.

Seeing amusement in Rupert's eyes, Anthea said icily, 'You're supposed to be working, Dora. Had a good day's horse racing, lots of winners?' she called across the table.

'None,' said Rupert.

'Are Meridian going to take over Venturer?' asked Gordon Brooks.

'Not if I can help it.'

Out of the corner of his eye, Rupert caught sight of Hengist, Ruth Walton and his friend Billy Lloyd-Foxe at the next table, laughing their heads off at his plight.

'Trapped between Silly and Charybdis,' sighed Hengist, 'poor Rupert.'

As compensation, Rupert had a direct view of Mrs Walton, golden brown and replete in a beautiful Lindka Cierach dress in old rose silk, with a tiny pink cardigan knotted under her glorious boobs. She smiled lazily at Rupert, who smiled back, an exchange instantly registered by Randal Stancombe. At least he was at the head's table and not Rupert, who made no effort and called him Randolph (if he deigned to recognize him).

Gordon Brooks was now discussing some chemical formula with Joan, so Rupert turned to Poppet. 'How's the new baby?'

'Flourishing, flourishing. His siblings are so supportive. They relish developing their parenting skills. Parenting could be a good GCSE for Bianca.'

'Bit premature, she's only thirteen. Might qualify her for a free house, I suppose.'

'Now you're deliberately misunderstanding me.' Poppet laughed merrily. 'And we need to discuss Xav.'

'He's fine.'

'He has very few friends.' Poppet sipped her cranberry juice reflectively. 'If it's any consolation, Charisma, our eldest daughter, was dreadfully bullied for being severely gifted.'

'Not Xav's problem.'

'They accused Charisma of being "posh".'

'Posh? Your daughter?' said Rupert in genuine amazement.

'Because she always gets A stars. Charisma, of course, is a workaholic.'

'Neither of my children's problem,' snapped Rupert. 'Thanks, darling,' as a grinning Dora exchanged his venison plate for a plate of chicken.

'I've given you lots of mushrooms, they're really good.'

Greedily shovelling up butterscotch ice cream, Poppet trundled on: 'Xav yearns for acceptance by his peers.'

'Peers live in the House of Lords,' said Rupert coldly, 'or they did before Blair gelded the place.'

He glanced across at Taggie. Accustomed to being married to the prettiest woman in the room, he noticed her red, swollen eyes and unbecoming, unruly hair and felt outraged that Alex Bruce was wrapped in conversation with Boffin's mother and Biffo had gone off table-hopping, leaving her stranded. A second later, Biffo's seat had been taken by Sally B-T.

'How's Xav's birthday going? Such a super chap.'

'Are you sure we're talking about the same child?' Rupert answered for Taggie. 'Six weeks into the school holidays, he's emerging as the devil incarnate.'

'Rupert,' gasped Taggie in horror.

Rupert crashed his knife and fork together, chicken hardly touched, fingers drumming, and turning to No-Joke Joan for heavy relief, learnt she'd been giving a paper on the evolution of the potato.

'Does Bianca lack social skills?' he asked finally.

'Quite the contrary. She and Dora Belvedon never stop chattering. I shudder to think of their phone bills. I'm afraid there's little likelihood of Bianca getting any GCSEs unless she buckles down.'

'It's a first step of the most evil tyrants,' Alex Bruce was droning on to Boffin's mother, 'destroying the teaching profession. In the seventies, teachers and academics arrested by Idi Amin never re-emerged because he tortured, then murdered them.'

'What a sensible man.' Rupert took a swig out of a nearby Perrier bottle.

As Alex went purple and stormed off, Poppet renewed her attack.

'There's a wonderful government initiative called Dads and Lads, Rupert. Fathers reading with their sons and helping them with their homework. I'm sure you could give your Colombian lad a lift.'

'Dads and Lads?' said Rupert softly.

'If you and Taggie struggle with the homework,' joined in Joan, 'I think Bianca's only salvation is to board.'

'She will not,' said Rupert, so sharply everyone looked round and Randal Stancombe decided to join the table, taking Alex's chair. He made a great show of kissing first Taggie's, then Anthea's hands, before expressing hope that they were all going to make promises he could auction later in the evening.

'What's on offer already?' asked Poppet.

'Lord Waterlane's offered lunch at the House of Lords,' Stancombe consulted his clipboard. 'Ricky France-Lynch has pledged polo lessons; Daisy his wife has offered to do a free pastel of the person of your choice. Billy Lloyd-Foxe' – he raised his voice so Billy and everyone at the next table stopped talking and laughing – 'has promised a tour round Television Centre, lunch in the canteen and tickets to his programme *Sport and Starboard*.'

'Good old Billy!' everyone cheered.

'What have you offered us, Randal?' simpered Anthea.

'Two weeks in a Caribbean villa and a free flight,' said Randal modestly to more cheers. 'Dame Hermione—' he began.

'Christ, is she here?' Rupert was about to dive under the table.

'Dame Hermione is at a gig this evening,' reproved Joan. 'She has pledged tickets for Covent Garden and supper afterwards. We're still looking for more bumper prizes.'

'How about a night at the Ritz with Rupert Campbell-Black?' yelled Billy.

'Yes, Rupert,' asked Poppet archly, 'what are you going to pledge?'

'A day at the Arc in your private box?' suggested Stancombe. 'And a ride back and forth in your chopper?'

'Or on your chopper,' shouted Janey Lloyd-Foxe to shouts of laughter.

'That would be an exciting pledge,' dimpled Anthea.

'For whom?' snapped Rupert.

'Oh, come on, Rupert, that's not going to break the bank,' chided Stancombe.

'Racing's work. I can't concentrate if I have to spend the day being charming.'

'You'll just have to try harder,' teased Poppet.

'Poor Rupert,' murmured Mrs Walton, 'he does look fed up. Is he ever unfaithful to that sweet, stupid wife?'

'Certainly not,' said Billy with rare sharpness, 'and she's not stupid, Penscombe would crumble without her holding it together.'

'Let's go and cheer him up,' whispered Mrs Walton to Hengist.

Leaving Billy, filling up everyone's glasses with a fresh bottle of red and pulling up two chairs beside Rupert, Hengist muttered:

'Are you OK?'

'Not until you find me a red-hot poker to ram up Mrs Bruce's ass.'

'Hush,' giggled Mrs Walton.

'Those emeralds are stunning,' said Rupert, unthawing slightly, 'and they couldn't have a better setting.'

'Randal brought them back for me from Bogotá.'

What was Stancombe doing there? wondered Rupert. Drug centre of the world; Xav's birthplace. Remembering the happiness and excitement when they'd brought him and Bianca home, he vowed to make things better.

Glancing across at Taggie he saw she was shaking with terror. Toothy Susan Brooks, whose favourite subject was Boffin, had got on to GCSEs and whether it would be too taxing for her G and T son to take fourteen.

'How many did you take, Poppet?'

'Ten, but they were O levels.'

'And you, Anthea?'

'Nine.'

'And you, Ruth?'

'Eight.'

'And you, Hengist?'

'About twenty-five. That's enough of that.' Hengist, who'd also noticed Taggie's twitching face, drained his glass and announced it was time for a pee break before the auction.

But Poppet refused to leave it. 'How many GCSEs did you get, Taggie?' she asked loudly.

'None,' whispered Taggie, colour suffusing her grey cheeks.

'Really?' said Anthea in amazement. 'None at all?'

'I didn't get any either,' said Rupert quickly. 'Never took any.'

'How the hell did you get into the Blues?' asked Hengist.

'I took a civil service exam, which was the equivalent, then went before a selection board at Westbury. I was only in for a year or two before going back to showjumping.'

'No O levels between either you or Taggie,' mocked Poppet.

'One wonders if you could achieve a GCSE today?' Alex quizzed Rupert as he returned to the table.

'Course I could. They're so bloody easy. You can take in calculators and history notes and poetry books. I'd walk it.'

'What a wonderful idea.' Poppet clapped her hands with another mad jangle of bracelets. 'You and Xav must take a GCSE together. English literature. You can read the books he's working on and exchange views at mealtimes.'

'Don't be fucking stupid, I haven't got the time,' snarled Rupert.

'You mean you haven't got the bottle,' taunted Stancombe. 'You wouldn't risk it, knowing you'd fail.'

'I bloody wouldn't.' Rupert had risen to his feet, shaking with rage, about to leap across the bottles and glasses and strangle him.

'Kindly don't swear in front of our spouses,' said Alex querulously.

'Oh fuck off.' Rupert turned back to Stancombe. 'I have got the bottle.'

'Prove it,' taunted Stancombe softly. 'I bet you a hundred grand, which I'll pledge to the Bagley Fund, you can't pass Eng. lit.'

'I'll sponsor you for ten thousand, Rupert,' said Gordon Brooks, 'but only if you get a C grade or above.'

'My newspaper would sponsor you for at least fifty thousand, Rupe,' shouted Janey Lloyd-Foxe leaping up and down in excitement, 'as long as we can have the story. Make a fantastic diary: Rupert takes a GCSE.' She was now scribbling on her wrist.

Offers of sponsorship were coming in from eager mothers all over the room.

'I'll give you twenty-three pounds,' said Dora.

'We'll have paid for the new science block in one night,' murmured Theo Graham.

'Then it's a done deal.' Stancombe jumped on to a chair, shouting, 'Rupert Campbell-Black has agreed to take an English lit. GCSE and has already been sponsored to the tune of two hundred and fifty thousand pounds if he gets a C grade or above.'

Rage no longer robbed Rupert of speech.

'I fucking haven't,' he howled. 'I've got a yard and a television station to run and there is no way I'm taking any exam,' and he stalked out of the hall.

Table Ten were very slow in getting coffee, petits fours and their ordered liqueurs, because Dora, their waitress, had retreated to the sixth-form common room.

'Wicked!' she was whispering into her mobile. 'Rupert Campbell-Black is going to take a GCSE. Yes? I swear. At a promises auction at Bagley. Parents have sponsored him to over a quarter of a million already. It happened after a row with horrible Randal Stancombe, who was taunting Taggie and Rupert for not having any O levels. English lit., I think, although according to his daughter Bianca, Rupert only reads Dick Francis and the racing pages.'

There was no way Dora was going to let that old tart Janey Lloyd-Foxe pip her to the post.

84

Taggie raced after Rupert as he strode towards his helicopter.

'I'm so sorry, I'm so sorry. You were so kind to defend me, it was all my fault.'

As he waited for clearance to fly, Rupert rang Lysander, his assistant, who said everything was as quiet as a mouse.

'Most of the horses are out, except Peterkin and the ones racing on Monday. No sound from the house, hardly any lights on and no music for ages. Party must be over, frankly I didn't see anyone arrive.'

Flying into Penscombe, Rupert looked down at the empire he had created without a single O level. There was the ancient blond house with its billowing woods and venerable oaks skirting a fast emptying lake, more than a hundred horses out in the fields, all weather gallops, indoor school, tennis court, swimming pool, animals' graveyard, and the moonlit ribbon of the Frogsmoor stream, like a white parting down the valley. An empire built up by his own hard work. There was no way he was going to take any fucking GCSE.

He was so angry he ignored the fact his wife was crying. On landing, he went straight to the yard. Penscombe Peterkin whickered at his master's approach, hopeful of being let out to join his friends. The son of Rupert's Derby winner, Peppy Koala, Peterkin had been born and brought up at Penscombe, where everyone loved him. When one of Rupert's jockeys used a whip on him in a race for the first time, the little colt was so outraged, he stopped in his tracks and was never whipped again. Since then, he'd never lost a race. A huge amount was already on him for the St Leger. Rupert patted and gave him a handful of pony nuts and wandered back to the house to find chaos and his wife frantically wiping up pools of sick in the hall.

The dogs had obviously raided Taggie's supper. Stalker, Rupert's favourite Jack Russell, was polishing off a chicken pie abandoned on the terrace table, from time to time dropping pieces on to the flagstones for a patiently waiting Bogotá to hoover up.

Mrs Bodkin was still asleep in front of some X-rated film. Xav's presents were still unopened, little beast.

'I told you not to give him a party,' growled Rupert, avoiding another pile of sick, then catching sight of a black leather jacket over the banister.

Feral had had so many girls before, but this was the real one. The problem was keeping Bianca's love in check. She was so anxious to give him everything. He had removed her bra and stroked her sweet, tip-tilted breasts; he had buried his face in her scented shoulders, stroked her hair and kissed her on and on. They were too preoccupied with one another to hear anyone arriving.

Suddenly the door burst open.

'What the fuck d'you think you're doing? Get away from her, you black bastard,' howled Rupert.

Only when Feral reared up, shaking off the duvet, did Rupert realize Bianca was only naked to the waist and Feral still wearing his black jeans. Standing, he was almost as tall as Rupert.

'I ain't no black bastard, man,' he said with quiet dignity. 'Back in the dark ages, my dad was married to my mum.'

Next moment he had leapt on to the blue striped sofa and jumped out of the window, falling on a yew hedge. But as he dropped down on to the lawn, landing awkwardly, a sharp pain gripped the right ankle of his shooting foot. He gave a groan as he limped away, keeping to the shadows.

'Daddy, how could you?' screamed Bianca. 'We were just snogging. How dare you call Feral a black bastard? I made all the running.'

'You shouldn't bloody be in bed with him,' said Rupert, slightly shaken. 'I suppose your brother's passed out?'

But Xav, sobering up and lurking on the landing, had overheard the row.

'Black bastard?' he yelled. 'Black fucking bastard? I'm black and I'm a bastard. Now I know what you really think of me.'

'Oh, for Christ's sake, it's just a figure of speech.'

'How dare you insult Feral?' sobbed Bianca. 'We were only kissing.'

'Go to bed,' shouted Rupert.

But Xav was fired up.

'My birthday was the day I was wrenched from my mother and chucked out on the streets to die. If only I had died. I've always had shit birthdays.'

'Xav,' pleaded Taggie, running up the stairs, 'that's not true.'

Xav turned on her. 'Shut up! I never wanted you as a mother, I hate you, *hate* you. You never loved me either, because I'm fat, ugly and useless.'

He ran sobbing out of the house, slamming the door in poor limping Bogotá's white face, heading out for the yard. Peterkin was delighted to see Xav, who had been the first person on his back and had often slept in his box. Both horse and boy had moped when Xav went away to Bagley. Xav led Peterkin into the yard by his head collar, jumped on to his back and set off across the fields, flat out towards the main road. Moonlight, more silvery light than day, sculpted dark grey trees and pale grey walls.

'Black bastard, black bastard,' yelled Xav in time to Peterkin's galloping hooves. Cocaine and booze had cushioned him against fear. He wasn't frightened of anything, not even his father. I hate him, I hate him, I hate him.

Rupert had poured himself a quadruple whisky and was just telling himself Xav would come home as soon as he sobered up, when the best horse he'd ever owned and trained passed the window, hurtling towards the main road on rock-hard ground. Rushing out to the yard, Rupert leapt on a mare who was racing on Monday. He'd have to head Xav off.

Xav by this time had turned Peterkin round and, rejoicing he'd got his nerve back, was riding quietly home across the fields, when Rupert thundered up and whacked Xav across the face, yelling:

'Get off that horse, you can bloody well walk home.'

As Xav slid to the ground, he felt all his fuses blow. He watched Rupert pull off his tie and slot it through Peterkin's head collar, then began almost conversationally:

'I know all about you.'

As Rupert paused, he went on:

'I know how much you drugged and boozed. I know you beat up your horses and your first wife. I know you bullied Jake Lovell witless on the showjumping circuit. You're an utterly crap role model. I don't belong to you any more, I want a divorce.' Xav's quiet voice had risen to a scream of pain.

'I dug out my secret files in the cellar. I know I was battered and left for dead as a baby because they thought my birthmark was the sign of the devil. Well, now I'm older, your fingermarks on my face are worse than any birthmark. They're the sign of a devil.' He spat at his appalled father's feet. 'The curse of being your son and a Campbell-Black.'

Hearing screams and shouts, fearful it might be Rupert after him, Feral hobbled faster. Glancing back, he saw Rupert's drive stretched out in the moonlight like a bandage to bind up his broken heart or his totally fucked ankle. No trial, no Bianca.

Next morning, Peterkin was as crippled lame as Feral. All the late editions of the papers picked up the *Independent*'s story about Rupert taking a GCSE.

85

For the first time in her life, Bianca Campbell-Black was utterly miserable. She had always been so proud of her parents, but now her father had revealed himself as a foul racist – and after all her coaxing, Feral had shot back into the jungle again. She kept imagining his cat's eyes shining out of the beech wood behind the house.

The Saturday after Xav's party, she and Dora went into Larkminster to see *I Capture the Castle*, a film Dora loved because she identified with the diary-writing heroine and her large eccentric family. Afterwards, she and Bianca went on to a Chinese restaurant where, as they rolled duck, sliced cucumber and dark sweet crimson sauce in pancakes and harpooned sweet and sour prawns, Bianca relayed the events of the last few days and Dora's eyes grew bigger and bigger.

'Your father was horribly hassled before he left Bagley,' she said in mitigation. 'He'd been trapped by Joan, Mrs Fussy and my mother all evening, then he was manoeuvred into that GCSE which he's been forced to agree to take.'

'That was shocking. Someone must have leaked it to the papers that very night.'

'Shocking,' agreed Dora. 'Some people have no principles.' Then, hastily changing the subject – after all, dinner tonight was being paid for by the *Independent*'s cheque: 'Do you think Feral would be caught in bed with me if I paid him? How ballistic would Mummy go? OK, OK, only joking.'

Dora vowed on this occasion not to ring any newspapers, Bianca was so desolate. She'd eaten nothing. Dora had to finish the spring rolls and prawns and bag up Bianca's duck for Cadbury. Unable to bear seeing her happy friend cast down, she suggested they call on Feral.

It was getting dark. The Shakespeare Estate was only 750 yards away, but they might have been plunging thousands of miles into the depths of hell. Rasta music fortissimo, football commentary, shouts and screams poured out of graffitied buildings. Jeering gangs of youths roamed the streets. Tarts screamed abuse. Addicts, like corpses dug up from the grave, hung stinking and unwashed over broken fences.

'If only Cadbury was here to defend us,' quavered Dora as a snarling Dobermann hurled itself against a gate. 'Shall we try another day?'

'We'll be safe when we find him,' pleaded Bianca. 'Here we are. Macbeth Street, number twelve.'

All Feral's windows were boarded up, as though he no longer allowed himself to look out on the world. The garden was full of burnt-out cars, fridges and wheelless bikes. Running up the path, Bianca hammered on the front door, which was answered by a fat man in a filthy vest, clearly off his face with drugs. Leering, swaying, he beckoned them inside, where Uncle Harley, immaculate as ever in black leather, Feral's diamond cross gleaming at his neck, was watching a revolting film in which a man and a woman were clearly enjoying sex with a little girl.

'Not something you'd show the vicar,' mocked the fat man.

Nearly asphyxiated by a stench of sweat, puke and fags, ready to bolt, but hearing the front door bang behind them, Dora bravely announced they'd come to see Feral.

The fat man jerked his head. 'Next door.'

In the kitchen they found glasses and plates piled high in the sink and a woman, presumably Feral's mother, lying moaning on the floor in a drug-induced stupor, surrounded by playing children.

Then Bianca gasped as she caught sight of Feral, stripped to the waist, shiningly beautiful in this midden of squalor, masculinity in no way diminished by the fact he was working his way through a pile of ironing and trying to feed a yelling baby in a high chair.

Bianca was still speechless, but over the lecherous cajoling of the man in the porn film, Dora yelled:

'It's us, Feral.'

Feral looked up in horror. Hissing like a cornered wild cat, he screamed at them to get the fuck out.

'I wanted to say sorry for Daddy,' sobbed Bianca, 'and see if you were all right.' Then, when Feral said nothing: 'I love you.'

'Well, I don't love you. Get out.' As he hobbled towards them, brandishing the iron in their faces like a riot shield, Dora caught sight of a bandage on his ankle.

Next moment, Uncle Harley had lurched into the room and made a grab at Bianca who, catching him off balance, shoved him crashing against the sink, smashing several glasses. Dora meanwhile had clouted the fat man with her bag and unchained the door, enabling them to flee out of hell. Seeing their terrified faces, a prostitute screeched, 'Taught you a lesson, did it? Don't mess with Uncle Harley.'

Dora and Bianca didn't stop until they reached the bridge. Leaning against it, gasping for breath, Dora couldn't stop shaking.

'What an utterly disgusting, revolting place.'

Bianca couldn't stop crying; her only emotion was sympathy for Feral living with those crackheads.

'That's why he's so poor,' she wailed, 'and why he wouldn't go on the geography field trip, or take up that games scholarship at Bagley. There'd be no one to look after those children. What are we going to do? I daren't tell Mummy and Daddy where I've been.'

'I'll just call Dicky and check Cadbury's OK. I expect they're both watching disgusting porn on the internet too. Then let's take a taxi to Janna's.' Dora put an arm round Bianca. 'Don't cry. She'll know what to do.'

Music louder than any on the Shakespeare Estate poured out of Jubilee Cottage. The Brigadier had been sent a crate of red by a fan and he and Lily were teaching Janna and Emlyn the Charleston. They were all hammered.

'I'm terribly sorry, we haven't got enough for the taxi,' were Dora's first words.

After Emlyn had paid it, Bianca gazed into space shuddering whilst Dora, one hand on her hip, the other gesticulating wildly, described their adventures.

'Poor Feral,' she said indignantly. 'Rupert called him a "black bastard" and chucked him out of Penscombe, although he and Bianca were only snogging, or as Mummy calls it "heavy petting". Mind you, there are plenty of pets at Penscombe.'

Meeting the Brigadier's eye, Lily tried not to laugh.

No one was laughing by the time Dora had finished.

'Oh poor, poor Feral,' whispered Janna.

'We must rescue him,' wept Bianca.

'I think we've all drunk too much to do anything tonight,' said Emlyn. 'Janna and I'll go round in the morning and sort it out.'

'Feral's got a soccer trial on Monday. Should cheer him up,' volunteered the Brigadier.

'I don't think so,' sighed Dora, 'he was lame as a cat.'

'That's from escaping out of my bedroom window,' wailed Bianca. 'It's all bloody Daddy's fault.'

'Better stay the night,' Lily told Dora and Bianca to the Brigadier's regret.

'Shall I come with you?' asked the Brigadier next morning, as he tried to keep down a Fernet-Branca.

'Fewer of us the better, less ostentatious,' answered Emlyn as he coiled his long length into Janna's green Polo.

'Something rotten in the state of Larkminster,' he observed as Janna drove past smashed-up playgrounds, shuttered shops, shells of houses, front gardens full of junk instead of flowers, and parked at the end of Macbeth Street. Emlyn edged her inwards so he could walk on the outside of the pavement.

'Although this is the sort of hell-hole where I should walk on both sides of you.'

At first Feral wouldn't open the door.

'If you're from the social,' observed an old biddy scuttling past, 'they've gone.'

Hearing a baby crying, Emlyn continued thumping.

When Feral finally let them in, they found him alone with three young children and the howling baby, whose nappy he'd just changed. From the mop in a bucket of suds, he'd obviously been cleaning up the floor. There was no fridge. Flies were everywhere.

After a lot of coaxing and a cigarette from Emlyn, he admitted that Uncle Harley and his mother had pushed off abroad to punish him. Gradually, eyes cast down, stammering out the sentences, occasionally returning to his former hauteur, he explained how he'd stolen to feed his brothers and sisters and carried a gun to protect them.

'Harley used my mother as a tom, kept her short of money and drugs, to make her reliant and desperate. Anyfing I earn from Lily and the Brig, she takes to feed her habit. Even if I hide it in the toes of my trainers, she finds it. Does my head in. What'll happen to her? She's not beautiful any more; Harley'll kill her.'

As Feral got up to wave away a swarm of flies settling on a plate of beefburgers, Emlyn noticed him hobbling.

'So you're no good for the trial on Monday?'

'Fanks to Mr Rupert Fancy-Black, I've gotta let the Brig down.'

'Does Harley give you a hard time?'

Feral nodded bleakly. 'He went ballistic I wouldn't deal when I got access to all those rich Bagley kids. Nearly buried me when I turned down that boarding place.'

Now the howling baby was sleeping in her arms, Janna wanted to howl herself. Feral had been so proud, so brave, his constant lack of funds the only giveaway. Emlyn was being wonderful too. With one child on each muscular thigh, and the third watching, he was singing nursery rhymes to them.

'They're not going into care!' Feral became almost hysterical. 'They'll never come back.'

'Only for a bit, while we sort ourselves out,' promised Janna. 'Everyone needs a leg-up occasionally. I accepted money from Randal Stancombe to keep Larks going.'

With trepidation she called Nadine who, fired up by a new scheme to unite social services and the education and health departments, turned out to be an absolute star.

The Brigadier, who had just been cleared by the Criminal Records Bureau to teach history at Larks, had grown so fond of Feral, he asked him to stay until things got straight. Janna would be up the road with Lily next door, so Feral wouldn't be lonely, and he could do the odd job round the house. Nadine then arranged for the children and the baby to be taken into temporary care with a good, kind family in the next village, so Feral could pop in and see them whenever he wanted. Feral listlessly agreed to everything because he saw no other way out. He loved Bianca, but like Juliet she was not yet fourteen; Rupert would always show him the door.

'Rupert called me a "black bastard",' he kept telling the Brigadier.

Feral moved in, but like a feral cat, he couldn't bear being trapped and begged the Brigadier not to lock the doors at night. 'I'll be your guard dog, man.'

86

Janna had worked flat out throughout the summer holidays supervising the rebuilding of Appletree, because the moment she stopped being busy, she was wiped out by guilt, sadness and despair. These feelings were reinforced by record temperatures, dire news of global warming and melting icebergs. Would there be a world at all for the children to inherit?

Despite gallant work by the remaining teachers, there had been so much disruption during the summer term that in the end only eight per cent of Larks children achieved the Magic Five. Ashton was on the telephone in seconds.

'Dear, dear, dear,' he gloated, 'how lucky for you we OK'd Appletwee first. If we'd had a sight of these wesults, you'd never have got your building. I do pray you do better with Year Ten.'

The *Times Educational Supplement* had reported that the proportion of U grades was the highest ever.

'Most of them from Larks,' observed Ashton bitchily.

Janna had also observed a faint neglect of late. Throughout July, Hengist had frequently rolled up at Appletree around dusk to admire work in progress, before making love to her in the long, pale, dry grass of Smokers' with the stars emerging as voyeurs overhead.

'Do you know it's illegal to have sex out of doors?' Janna had teased him on his last visit. 'I'm sure Miss Miserden's got a periscope.'

'It's called outreach, because I reach out for you,' said Hengist.

Above them on the right of an apricot-pink harvest moon, Mars, like an angry red-gold lion tossing his mane, dominated the evening sky.

'This year's belonged to Mars,' said Hengist, as he zipped up his trousers, 'that's why you won your battle over Year Ten, but you must watch Ashton. I don't know what he can still do to hurt you, but I don't trust him. Two thousand and four, thank God, will be Venus's year. She'll shine so brightly, I'll fall in love with you all over again.'

As he smiled down, he noticed, like scratches on a scraper board, new lines on her face.

'Darling, you must get a break. Why not come and crash out for a few days in the house we rent in Tuscany? I'll call you.'

But after that visit in late July she had heard nothing for nearly five weeks. She knew he was back because she'd read in the *Independent* about the fundraising evening and Rupert's GCSE, which he'd only finally agreed to take because all the papers claimed he'd never pass. Janna had been tempted to drop him a line and ask him if he'd like a place at Larks. That would solve any woman-teacher recruitment problem.

Throughout the summer, her thoughts had flickered too often to Emlyn. She was so grateful to him for helping sort out Feral that she called him to say the Welsh National Opera were doing *Turandot* at the Bristol Hippodrome. If she got two tickets, would he like to come?

'And I'll buy you dinner afterwards.'

'I can't, lovely; I've got a lot on.'

And Janna felt snubbed.

'When I suggested another night,' she told Lily, 'he said he was going to see his mother. He hasn't flown anywhere to see Oriana this summer. Do you think' – Janna loathed the thought – 'he's got someone else?'

Lily shook her head.

'I'm sure he's still crazy about Oriana and thinks that somehow, if he's faithful, God will reward him.'

'How complicated,' sighed Janna. 'What's she like?'

'Bit chilly and critical. Ambitious like her father, but she lacks Hengist's warmth and *joie de vivre*.'

87

Hengist was full of joy as he changed for dinner at St Matthew's, his old Cambridge college. He and Sally had had such a magic evening last night, listening to Mahler Three at the Proms and watching a rainbow soaring out of the turning trees, which after rain were all glittering gold in the setting sunlight. They had then rushed up to bed and made such warm, passionate love that they had forgotten their mobiles, lying like lovers side by side on the terrace table, both still working perfectly in the morning, despite a further shower of rain – like our marriage, thought Hengist.

He was still battling not to be too triumphalist over Bagley's leap in the league tables; they were only a place below Fleetley. What matter if, to Alex's fury, St Jimmy's were only five places behind Bagley?

Dear Theo had, once again, got everyone through everything. He must put him forward for a Teaching Award, it would so annoy Alex.

The evening at St Matthew's was all Hengist could have wished for: exquisite food and wine and, although he loved women, as a man who had always charmed his own sex, he found there was something so wonderfully uncorseted about an all alpha-male evening. He loved keeping the table in a roar. He adored the wheeling and dealing, the superior gossip, learning of a brilliant undergraduate who, after he came down, might like to spend a year or ten teaching at Bagley, and dropping in turn hints about a brilliant Bagley boy.

'We plucked him out of the state system and a children's home. Theo's been coaching him.'

There was a lot of chuntering about admissions tutors being forced to accept lower grades from poorer students and a great deal of laughter over Rupert Campbell-Black's GCSE.

'You know him well, Hengist.'

'Love him – but he'd rather die than fail.'

'His son is a rare pianist, I never thought the Grieg could reduce me to tears.'

Over the port, people started table-hopping and the Master drew Hengist into a window seat, and in a voice as soft as the bloom on the black grapes asked him if he'd be interested in Fleetley.

'Hatchet Hawkley's retiring in two thousand and five.'

'The end of a great era,' said Hengist lightly.

'May we put your name forward, Hengist?'

Hengist looked at the wise, knowing face:

'I don't know how delighted Hatchet would be. I used to be one of his junior masters . . . Our son Mungo . . .'

Hengist didn't add that his passionate affaire with Hatchet's wife, Pippa, had only been discovered by Hatchet after her death.

'I know you have painful memories,' said the Master.

'Sally more.' Through the dusk Hengist could see the first yellow leaves falling on yellowing lawns.

'Hatchet has always been laid back about recruitment,' urged the Master, 'you could raise it to new heights.'

'I'll think about it very seriously,' said Hengist with that smile that could melt icebergs.

After a college restoration meeting the next morning, followed by a light, excellent lunch and a trip to buy a lovely oil of a grey-hound for Sally, Hengist was in celebratory mood, and picked up his mobile:

'Darling, I'll be with you around eight and don't wear any knickers.'

As he left, he noticed a mower cutting to pieces any fairy rings on the college lawn.

In Hamburg, negotiating the building of a hypermarket, Randal Stancombe rang Ruth Walton between meetings. Their relationship had recently suffered a setback. Lorraine, his estranged wife, had not been amused when reports on Randal, goading Rupert into taking a GCSE, had referred to Ruth as 'the utterly gorgeous new love of his life'. Nor had Milly; outraged at being banned from seeing Graffi, she had promptly accused Randal of groping her. Ruth had staunchly dismissed this as fantasy on Milly's part, but did suggest it might be better if she and Randal cooled it until next week, when Milly was safely back at Bagley.

Randal now rang in the hope that the coast might be clear. Sadly it wasn't.

'We've got to do Milly's trunk. She's put on seven pounds in the holidays, most of it round the bust.'

Like her mother, thought Stancombe. He must keep his hands off Milly.

'And I've got a Bagley's governors' meeting early evening. After that Milly and I are getting a takeaway; she says we never talk these days.' Ruth added more hot water to a jacuzzi as big as the Bagley lake. 'But once term starts, I'm all yours.'

'What a lovely "all",' purred Stancombe.

Ten minutes later, racked with lust, he decided to kill the meeting and fly home for the night. He bought Milly a bottle of Obsession at the hotel shop and he would sweep her and Ruth out to the La Perdrix d'Or. Somehow he must persuade Ruth to marry him. To hell with Lorraine taking him to the cleaners; he could afford it. Ruth made him feel like a god in and out of bed and after all the surgery he'd paid for, he felt he owned most of her anyway.

As he let himself into the Cavendish Plaza flat he allowed her to live in for nothing, he was touched at first to find candles on a table. Ruth, like the good mother she was, was taking her bonding session with Milly very seriously. Two bottles of his Krug, lobster and strawberries in the fridge were pushing it a bit, as was the Château d'Yquem. There was even a rocket and asparagus salad and, most caring of all, home-made mayonnaise.

On the triple bed, on the other hand, was a Janet Reger carrier bag with a suspender belt, tutu and negligee spilling out, too good even for Milly's trunk, and sweet-scented roses and lilies everywhere.

Stancombe flicked on the machine. The deep, lazy, patrician tones were unmistakable.

'Darling, I'll be with you around eight and don't wear any knickers.'

Clearly this governors' meeting was only for two people. Quivering with clumsy rage, Stancombe removed flowers, food, bottles, underwear – all Ruth's seduction kit – from the flat. He wanted to kill them both so badly, he nearly ran his Ferrari into the Casey Andrews sculpture adorning the exit to Cavendish Plaza. The bastard, the bitch, the bitch, the bastard. His brain was a red fuzz. He'd cancel the Stancombe block at Bagley, but it was already a quarter up, which was more than he was. Desperate for a pretty shoulder to cry on, he drove straight round to Janna's.

Janna had been anticipating a quiet evening. She was delighted to see Lily off on a date with the Brigadier, which would include watching a recording of *Buffers*. Emlyn had swept Feral off to see a Welsh rugby sports doctor about his ankle and spend the night with Emlyn's mother in Wales.

The birds in Janna's garden had stopped singing, too exhausted by caring for their young at the end of the summer holidays. She had just opened a tin of Pedigree Chum for Partner when she heard a car outside.

At first, when she saw the bottles of Krug in Randal's hand, she thought he'd come to exact payment in kind for financing the rebuilding of Appletree. When he plonked them on the kitchen table, along with a bottle of Château d'Yquem and a carrier bag spilling over with pink underwear, she asked him if he'd won the lottery.

She was just hastily washing Pedigree Chum off her hands, when he returned with armfuls of flowers and a carrier bag containing two lobsters, strawberries and a bowl of mayonnaise and told her to put them and the Krug in the fridge.

'How lovely,' squeaked Janna. 'Would you like some of your own drink, or shall I put these in water first?'

Then she noticed Stancombe was wearing a suit and tie, as though he'd just come from the office, that he was shuddering and there was a green tinge to his permatan.

'Whatever's the matter?'

Stancombe slumped down at the kitchen table and started to cry.

'Oh, my poor love.' Running round, Janna put her arms round him. 'Is it Jade? What's happened?'

'Ruth,' sobbed Stancombe.

'Oh my God, is she OK?'

'She's OK, the fucking bitch. She's seeing someone else.'

'Are you sure? She always seems mad about you!'

Ashamed of breaking down, Stancombe blew his nose on a piece of kitchen roll and proceeded to pace up and down the tiny kitchen like a tiger penned in a travelling crate.

Janna took down a vase and as the roses were beginning to droop, found a rolling pin to bash the stems.

'God I loved her, the bitch,' said Stancombe despairingly.

'She was just probably being friendly with whoever.'

'Like hell. I decided to surprise her and she had dinner prepared and my flat decked out for your friend Hengist.'

'Ouch!' The rolling pin crushing her fingers and the rose

thorn plunging into her thumb were nothing to the pain. 'Hengist? It can't be. He and Sally . . .'

'Fucking hypocrite. "My darling Sally", indeed.'

'How long's it been going on?' asked Janna numbly.

'Dunno. A bit – he left a message on her machine telling her not to wear any panties.'

Ouch, thought Janna. Why can't men get a new script?

'He's always treated me like shit,' went on Stancombe, getting the Krug out of the fridge. 'No wonder he wouldn't make me a governor – interrupt their little footsy footsy under the boardroom table. It's the lies I hate, pretending Milly needed some quality time with her mother, when she only wants to be shagged by Mr B-T.'

They went outside and Stancombe and (mostly) Janna drank the first bottle of Krug. Janna had the sprinkler on, defying the hosepipe ban, and kept drenching herself as she moved it round the parched lawn, or leapt up to liberate a Japanese anemone or late delphinium bent double by bindweed. Occasionally an apple thudded to the ground.

Partner, sensing her desolation, stayed very close as Stancombe ranted on and on about expensive trips, surgery, designer clothes for both Ruth and Milly and Milly's school fees.

'Ruth'll be begging for a place at Larks. She won't be able to afford Bagley any more.'

In the middle, Janna rushed next door to Lily's to feed the General and found, instead of cat food, she had emptied a tin of pineapple chunks into his bowl. On her return with the second bottle of Krug, Stancombe was still cataloguing grievances.

'And I'm getting those emeralds back. I really loved Ruth.'

And I really, really loved Hengist, thought Janna. In the dark Stancombe couldn't see the tears pouring down her cheeks.

'I'm so sorry,' she muttered. 'Shall we open this?'

'I've got a better idea.' Seizing her hand, Stancombe dragged her upstairs. 'Nice little property, this.'

' "What gat ye to your dinner, Lord Randal, my son?" ' cried Janna wildly. ' "Make my bed soon, For I'm weary wi' hunting and fain wald lie down." '

'Say again?' asked Stancombe.

'Only an old lay – rather like me,' muttered Janna. Was she going mad? Aware what a pathetic figure she must cut, compared with radiant, bosomy Ruth, she dawdled over undressing, tripping as she tried to escape from her knickers. Stancombe, by comparison, was resplendent, far sleeker than Hengist.

'Why should she cheat on me?' He flexed his muscles in the mirror, then added curtly: 'Put on her underwear.'

'It won't fit.'

Janna's much smaller breasts went straight through the cut-outs for nipples of Ruth's pink lace bra. To stay up, the suspender belt had to be tied behind. The black fishnet hold-ups had to be folded over like long socks.

'God. She knew how to please men,' groaned Stancombe. As he lay back on ivory satin sheets bought to please Hengist, his cock was almost a kingpost supporting the beam. Without any foreplay, Janna was dry as the fields outside and screamed as he tried to force his way in.

'Get that fucking dog out,' yelled Stancombe as Partner rushed yapping to the rescue.

Terrified he might mistake Stancombe's cock for a particularly splendid stick, Janna shoved Partner outside and cautiously rejoined Stancombe on the bed, wondering what to do next. Stancombe had no doubts. Waving his penis like a torch, he said:

'Suck it, you bitch, it won't suck itself.'

So Janna went down on him, hands going like pistons, licking, sucking, flickering, to an accompaniment of whining and scratching from an incensed and banished Partner. Thinking of Mrs Walton's leisurely expertise as she despatched Hengist to heaven, Janna gave a despairing sob.

'Keep going, darling.' Stancombe's hand clutched the back of her head. 'Keep going. Aaah.' And he shot into her mouth.

Stancombe was showered and dressed in five minutes. On the way out he said:

'Sorry. I dumped on you in every way.'

Seeing the misery on his face, she said:

'I'm sure she'll come back.'

'No one cheats on Randal Stancombe.' And he was gone.

Janna felt dirty and utterly desolate. Unable to stop crying, she gulped down the second bottle of Krug to take away the taste of Stancombe.

'Forgo your dream, poor fool of love.'

The pain was so excruciating, she couldn't go on.

Ripping some October pages out of her diary, much aided by Chateau d'Yquem, she settled down to write a suicide note. Lily was away; no one would find her until it was too late.

'My heart has been utterly broken by Hengist Brett-Taylor,' she began. 'My life is no longer worth living.'

When she'd finished, she couldn't find the bottle of paracetamol. As she tried to climb upstairs to look for it, she fell in a crumpled heap on the bottom step and passed out.

* * *

Driving back from Wales early next morning, marvelling at the white biblical rays of sunlight falling through the thinning tree ceiling, Emlyn fretted that he'd snubbed Janna over the Welsh National Opera and *Turandot*. He was so fond of her and in such a muddle about Oriana. He'd almost sensed Oriana's relief when he'd announced he wouldn't be flying out to see her this summer, but it had in no way diminished his longing. Lily, the Brigadier and Sally kept encouraging him to take Janna out. But although he wanted her friendship and her body, he knew if Oriana walked through the door, he'd be as hopelessly hooked as ever, so his muddle was unsorted.

The trip to Wales had at least been a success; the Welsh expert on rugby injuries said Feral's ankle needed only rest. Emlyn's mother had spoilt them both rotten. As he'd just dropped Feral off to visit his brothers and sisters in the next village, Emlyn decided to call on Janna.

Partner was ecstatic to see him and promptly led him to his mistress, who had somehow got herself on to the sitting-room sofa. As she was still asleep (and, he noticed, wearing some very saucy underwear beneath her dressing gown), Emlyn wandered off to the kitchen, taking in the empty bottles, the flowers, the fridge door open, the lobsters inside and blood from Janna's rose-pricked fingers everywhere.

'I wish you could talk, boyo,' he told Partner as he fed him and filled up his water bowl.

Then he picked up an envelope on which was scrawled: 'To whom it may concern – no one probably'.

Inside was Janna's suicide note, scrawled on pages from Yom Kippur to Halloween. Whistling as he read it, Emlyn felt amazement, sadness and fury. Bastard Hengist, bastard Stancombe.

Having fixed himself a cup of very sweet black coffee and a plate of lobster and home-made mayonnaise, he proceeded to mark the suicide note: F for grammar – 'two split infinitives and tenses all to pieces'; G for spelling; U for handwriting – 'almost indecipherable towards the end'; C for imagination; E for narrative skill – 'confused and repetitive'; D for vocabulary – 'somewhat repetitive'. Only for melodrama did he award her A star.

Janna came round at midday to find Emlyn polishing off the strawberries.

'How long has Hengist been shagging you?'

'Don't be ridiculous.' Then, slowly registering the suicide note in his hand: 'About a year and a bit.'

'And Stancombe?'

'Oh, not at all, at all.'

Again Emlyn waved the note.

'Well, maybe last night.' Janna frowned, trying to remember. 'Only to stop the pain.'

'Which must be even worse now judging by the booze you've shipped.'

When she reread the suicide note, complete with Emlyn's marking, Janna started to giggle helplessly.

'You shouldn't make horrible jokes when my heart is broken. Why do I get so hurt?'

'Shouldn't sleep with married men.' Emlyn handed her a glass of Alka-Seltzer. 'If they cheat on their wives, they'll cheat on you.'

'According to this, I didn't sleep with Stancombe.' Janna shuddered.

Emlyn had caught the sun yesterday, his face was tawny brown rather than ruddy, but the expression on it was unreadable. Janna longed to collapse sobbing into his arms. She put a cushion over her face. 'I can't go on. I love Hengist so much.'

'Don't be wet,' said Emlyn briskly, 'you've got forty kids to get through GCSEs. Mrs Walton's the one in trouble. Who's going to bankroll her now? Hengist certainly won't leave Sally.'

'You won't tell anyone about Hengist and me?' pleaded Janna. 'Stancombe hasn't a clue' – she shivered – 'but he's out to bury Hengist.'

'Ruthless in both senses of the word,' sighed Emlyn.

Hengist was in fact extremely twitchy. Not since David Hawkley went through the effects of his late wife Pippa had he been caught out. At first he and Ruth thought the flat had been burgled, then they saw a copy of the Hamburg evening paper. Hengist had made himself scarce. Only later, after Randal had come round and had it out with her, did Ruth ring him at home in hysterics. Sally, thankfully, was staying with her mother.

'Randal heard the message about me not wearing knickers' – Hengist went cold – 'and he's keeping the tape as evidence. He didn't beat me up, but he's chucking me out in the morning and he's stopped all my credit cards and taken back the Merc.'

'God, I'm sorry.'

'It's all your fault,' screamed Ruth. 'Where am I going to live and what about the school fees? You'll have to give Milly a bursary.'

As Milly was definitely C/D borderline, Alex wouldn't be at all amused. Oh dear, how rash he'd been.

'Where did Stancombe go when he found out?'

'Straight round to Janna Curtis.' Then, bitchily: 'You're always saying how good she is with difficult children.'

'Christ.' Hengist had gone even colder. 'What did she say?'

'Evidently they talked for hours, and probably ended up in bed. What the hell am I going to do – sue him for palimony?'

Hengist even in extremis couldn't resist a joke.

'You could get a flat in the catchment area of St Jimmy's. Everybody's doing it for A levels, then the universities couldn't discriminate against Milly for being at a public school.'

'Oh, for Christ's sake, be serious. There's no way Milly's going to a state school. My life is ruined.'

So will mine be if the news reaches Sally, thought Hengist.

In the middle of Friday afternoon, more flowers arrived at Jubilee Cottage. For a moment Janna's heart leapt, hoping that they might be Hengist apologizing, but the card said, 'Thank you for listening, Randal Stancombe'.

Stancombe had already decided to make a play for Anthea Belvedon. It would infuriate Ruth, who disliked her intensely, and it would mean access at last to Little Dora.

88

Hengist did not officially announce that he would be leaving Bagley at the end of summer 2005, because neither the job as Jupiter's Minister of Education nor as head of Fleetley had been firmed up. But from the start of the autumn term 2003 he began dropping hints, setting in train a hunt to find his successor, who must be both a giant and a genius at recruitment. The procedure was to appoint someone at the end of the penultimate year of the departing head, which in Hengist's case would be summer 2004. A small sub-committee of governors would be elected to look for a new head.

Alex Bruce, already hell-bent on getting the job, was consequently even more determined to improve his own house's results by chucking out potential failures like Xavier Campbell-Black. Poppet was already meddling in the leadership struggle by trying to get herself elected to the sub-committee and urging it to monitor applicants to maintain a gender balance. She then encouraged Joan Johnson to put herself forward as a suitable candidate, to which Hengist exploded that after his predecessor, Sabine Bottomley, he wasn't having 'another bloody dyke at the helm'.

A shocked Poppet reproached Hengist for homophobia.

She's probably right, reflected Hengist ruefully.

He had never stopped regretting that he had passed up Artie Deverell as deputy head in favour of the robotic Alex. He had done this not just because he'd wanted Alex to take over all the tasks he detested, but because he'd felt that having a self-confessed homosexual in the job might deter parents. He had been quite wrong. The parents adored Artie, who in his sweetness had never once reproached Hengist for such a betrayal.

Now Hengist was paying for it. Alex, the tortoise to his hare, was slowly imposing his stranglehold. Last term Alex had tried to sack Rufus because missing coursework had been discovered by a cleaner under his bed. Now, on the first Friday of term, the school photograph was being taken and Alex in a frenzy of bossiness was making sure everyone was wearing correct uniform, their hair was brushed and their heights similar. A diversion had been created by Dicky Belvedon, one of the smallest boys in the school; in a desperate attempt to make himself look taller, he had coaxed his hair upwards with pineapple gel, which on a warm, windless September afternoon had attracted a swarm of wasps.

It was only after a blushing, mortified Dicky had returned from washing out the gel, and Alex had finally got everyone settled, that Dicky's sister Dora pointed out that all the Upper Fifths taking GCSEs with Mr Graham were missing, including two star pupils: Cosmo and Paris.

The glorious thing about Theo Graham's classes was that he was not only inspiring on his own subject – the ancient world being populated with people he seemed to know intimately – but also easily diverted onto others.

On Wednesday, the Upper Fifth had discussed in what kind of ship Ulysses would have returned to Ithaca. Today, Theo had produced a cutting about Sutton Hoo, where a lot of Anglo-Saxon remains had been unearthed. They'd even dug up an entire eighty-nine-foot-long ship with its warrior captain buried inside it. Another warrior had been found buried with his horse.

'Imagine your father being buried beside Penscombe Peterkin,' mocked Jade.

Not a road Xav wanted to go down. Peterkin had been scratched from the St Leger. He doubted if his father would ever speak to him again.

'Siegfried was carried down the Rhine on a funeral ship,' murmured Cosmo with an evil smile, 'but he was already dead. Black shit no-hopers like Xavier Campbell-Black ought to be buried alive.'

Theo was about to rebuke Cosmo savagely when Alex Bruce burst in, purple with rage:

'You have forgotten the school photograph, Theo, how dare you keep everyone waiting. You were reminded of this yesterday – very black mark indeed.' Then, as the class poured out of the room: 'And why aren't you using the whiteboard?'

Arriving at the last moment as usual, Hengist ran his eyes over the rows. Xavier looked dreadful, covered in spots, narrowed, dark eyes sliding in his squashed flat face. Hengist was off to London this evening, but tomorrow he'd have the poor boy in for a drink.

He also noticed how grey Theo was looking and hoped Alex wasn't bullying him. And there was Dora's twin, Dicky, cringing behind a couple of bruisers from the first fifteen. Pulling Dicky to the front, because his awful mother would raise hell if he weren't in the picture, Hengist took his place in the middle of the front row beside Sally. God, he hoped Stancombe hadn't shopped him to Alex, who would tell Poppet, who would certainly feel it her duty to tell Sally all about Ruth. Hengist felt extremely exposed.

After the utter humiliation of the school photograph, Dicky Belvedon was still curling up with embarrassment on Friday evening. Dicky was so pretty he had even received a Valentine from Tarquin Courtney. At thirteen, his voice was only just beginning to break, he had little pubic hair and it was a nightmare being called Dick and only having a tiny one, particularly with Cosmo Rannaldini poncing around in the showers brandishing a cock a kilometre long.

Dicky had a passion for Bianca Campbell-Black, but appreciated the competition was too stiff. He was confused because he'd had a wet dream about Paris the other night. He also idolized David Beckham and back in February had written a letter to Beckham commiserating with him for being hit by Alex Ferguson's boot. Beckham hadn't replied.

Dicky had been even more devastated than Dora by the death of his father but, unlike Dora, loved his mother. He tried to over-look her deficiencies and prayed for her in chapel:

'Make my mother marry again, but someone very kind and very rich, who likes me and Dora.'

Like Dora, however, Dicky was a pragmatist, and lionhearted. Running his own shop at Bagley, he did a roaring trade in drink and fags. Wearing one of his mother's wigs, he would make sorties into Bagley village, returning in a buckling taxi, which the more louche and lustful house prefects helped him unload.

Anthea, noting so many pupils hailing Dicky on Speech Days, was always boasting that her son got on with all ages. Little did she realize most of them were customers. One of Bagley's punishments for bad behaviour was having to run ten or twenty times the two hundred yards down to the boathouse and back. Dicky hid a stash of booze in the boathouse. It kept both vodka and white wine cool.

Because his housemaster Alex Bruce was devoted to Anthea, he tended to leave Dicky alone. Not so Xavier, whom Alex had asked Boffin to spy on and who, that Friday evening, was in an explosive mood, fuelled by fast-diminishing supplies of drink and drugs. How dare Cosmo call him a no-hoper and black shit in front of the class?

It was only a week into term and Xav had run out of money. He couldn't help himself to Rupert's cellar or his cocaine stash any more. He was heavily overdrawn at the bank and had gone back to school in such a rage that he'd forgotten to ask for a top-up. He already owed Dicky Belvedon a hundred pounds from last term. Dicky was too frightened of Xav to press for it, but when Xav came storming into his dormitory after supper that Friday night and demanded a bottle of vodka, Dicky stalled.

'You owe me a hundred.'

'So fucking what? D'you want to make an issue of it?'

Dicky didn't. There was something so mad, Neanderthal and truculent about Xav. Dicky extracted a half-bottle of gin from under his mattress. 'You can have this, but it's the last you're having till you've paid up.'

'We'll see about that.' Xavier lurched off.

Dicky sighed. He'd promised the gin to Amber for a midnight feast. He'd better sneak down to the boathouse and get some more. Unfortunately Mr Fussy and Poppet were in the garden celebrating yet another ghastly brat on the way with a supper party, to which Boffin, as Charisma's boyfriend, had been invited, so Dicky didn't manage to escape until after eleven.

It was very dark; only a sliver of moon was mirrored in the depths of the lake as Dicky ran past. The boathouse formed a covered link between the lake and the river. Boats, which could be pushed out into either, floated in rows: long ones known as eights in which the school eights competed at Henley; Biffo's dinghy; and little rowing boats in which juniors occasionally paddled round the lake and where, under a tarpaulin, Dicky hid his booze.

It was spooky inside, just the slap of the water against the boats' sides and a snatch of distant song from the Junior Common Room.

As Dicky emerged with a bottle of gin under his pyjama top and tweed jacket, three figures emerged from out of the curtains of a willow tree and grabbed him. 'Come here, you little bastard.'

Dicky's blood froze. It was Cosmo.

Earlier in the evening, as part of a fiendish plan, Cosmo had pretended to make friends with Xavier.

'I've got some crack,' he lied. 'It'll take your mind apart. And some Charlie – we'll have a party to make up for calling you "black shit" earlier. I was only joking.'

Xav, who had already demolished the half-bottle of gin

or he might have been more suspicious, was absurdly flattered.

'Why don't you get some booze from Dicky Belvedon?' suggested Cosmo.

'He refused me any more earlier,' grumbled Xav, 'but we'll see about that.'

'We certainly will. High time Master Belvedon was done over. He's in your house, Xav, you'll have to lure him out.'

Dicky wasn't in his dormitory and Poppet, Alex, Charisma and Boffin were still squawking away singing madrigals, so Xav had crept out of the house again and he, Cosmo and Lubemir, after a line, had walked in the direction of the boathouse. Meeting Dicky creeping back along the edge of the lake, they had relieved him of his bottle.

'We've other plans for you,' said Cosmo softly. 'We're going to stage your funeral and send you down the river, Dicky.'

'No, please,' begged Dicky, frightened witless, gibbering with horror as they tugged off his clothes and tied his hands behind his back. 'You can have all my booze, it's stored in the last boat under the tarpaulin.'

'We'll have it anyway,' said Lubemir, roping together Dicky's frantically kicking feet, before tying two scarves tightly over his mouth and his eyes. 'This is to punish you for cheeking Xav earlier and refusing to give him any more credit.'

Xav was confused. None of this was quite right, but he was so flattered to be in league with Lubemir and Cosmo.

'Come on, Dicky, into the boat,' said Cosmo. 'Great warriors were buried in eighty-nine-foot ships. Wimps like you don't need anything that long.'

As he identified seats, slides and shoe fastenings beneath his naked back and felt the boat rocking in the water, Dicky realized he was in one of the eights and wriggled and bucked in terror.

'Look at his tiny little dick,' mocked Cosmo, giving it a vicious tweak. 'You don't deserve to live with a cock that tiny, Little Dick. You're in the river now; off you go.'

Panic-stricken, totally disorientated, drenched in icy sweat, Dicky felt the eight give and sway as it slid into open water and moved away.

'Bon voyage,' murmured Cosmo, 'or rather, farewell.'

Then there was silence.

Dicky tried to scream through the scarf as the cold wet fingers of a weeping willow stroked his bare body. In a few minutes the boat would reach the whirlpools and the weir. With his hands and feet bound, he couldn't swim. He couldn't breathe. I'm going to die, thought Dicky, I mustn't shit myself.

89

Charisma Bruce had fallen in love with Boffin after he caringly held her long mousy hair out of the way whilst she threw up into a flower bed during a teenage party.

Now, humming madrigals, she and Boffin walked hand in hand round the lake.

' "A maid and her wight Come whispering by",' quoted Boffin sententiously. ' "War's annals will cloud into night Ere their story die." '

Charisma was wearing a new floaty dress. Her long face looked rather lovely in the moonlight. She and Boffin could hear the croak of frogs and compared notes on the dissecting of other frogs and on future A levels.

'I enjoy *Cracker*,' confessed Charisma. 'It's popular television, of course, but, like Mother, I'm a people person, so I'm going to take psychiatry as one subject.'

When Boffin kissed her, she tasted of cider and her mother's prune and fig sorbet. As a black cloud, indistinguishable from the ebony trees, edged over the moon, Boffin turned on his torch and in its beam, caught sight of one of the eights in the middle of the lake. On closer inspection, he found it contained a wriggling, moaning, naked body.

Charisma, who'd obtained all her life-saving medals, flung aside her shawl and plunged into the water in her floaty dress, which Boffin, diving after her, found floated up most excitingly. Together they towed the boat to the shore.

'Why, it's Dick Belvedon,' said Boffin as Charisma untied the black scarves and wrapped her own shawl round Dicky's frozen, shuddering body.

'Poor little boy, who could have done this wicked thing?'

Cosmo and Lubemir, lurking inside the weeping willow, made a successful run for it, but Xav, off his face with drink and drugs, tripped over a log and went flying.

'Stop,' cried Charisma. As Xavier, trying to struggle to his feet, was caught in the light of Boffin's torch, she picked up her mobile. 'Dad, Dad, come down to the lake and alert the sick bay, Xavier Campbell-Black's tried to murder Dicky Belvedon.'

Rupert and Taggie were in Provence. As neither of their children were speaking to them, they had decided to get away for the weekend and had just enjoyed a most delicious dinner, for once not cooked by Taggie, and reeled upstairs drunk and happy.

Only when Rupert undressed his wife did he realize quite how much weight she'd lost over the summer, particularly on her breasts, which had not dropped because she'd never fed the babies she'd so desperately longed for. Instead she and Rupert had derived incredible happiness from adopting Xavier and Bianca, aware that both had lost parents, vowing to do everything in the world to make them feel happy and safe.

'We will again,' Rupert had promised Taggie over dinner. He found it much easier to forgive Xav now because Peterkin was nearly sound.

Rupert had ordered that on no account should they be disturbed, so the manager had to come upstairs and bang on the door.

'Monsieur Campbell-Black, telephone, it's urgent.'

'Fuck off.'

'It might be one of the children,' said Taggie, wriggling out from under him. Rupert reached for the telephone.

'It's Alex Bruce here, I'm afraid I've had to exclude Xavier. He's not only drunk and stoned but, desperate for a fix, he raided Dick Belvedon's store of booze, then tried to murder him.'

'How?'

'Tied him up, stripped him naked and blindfolded him.'

'All by himself?'

'So it would appear, then put him in one of the eights' boats and, telling him it was the river, sent him out on the lake.'

Rupert went cold.

'Probably just a prank. Is Dicky OK?'

'Far from it. He was in the middle of the lake hyperventilating. Luckily Bernard Brooks and our daughter Charisma were out for a midnight stroll and managed to rescue the lad. Trying to escape the scene of his crime, Xavier fell over a log, so drunk he couldn't get up.'

'If he was that drunk, he couldn't have done all that on his own.'

'Our daughter and Bernard saw no one else. Xav's too inebriated to testify; we've locked him in the sick bay and will have to wait for him to sober up.'

'Fifteen-year-olds don't talk. Where the fuck's Hengist?'

'Our Senior Team Leader's away.' Alex nearly added, As usual.

Hengist was incandescent with rage when he got back next morning. Why the hell hadn't Alex tried to sort it out internally? But by this time, Dora, equally furious with Xav for trying to kill her brother, had leaked the entire story to the *Mail on Sunday*.

Alex, who'd longed to kick Xav out for years, was in heaven, particularly over the publicity. At last, he was man of the hour who'd made the tough decision to rout out bullying. His photograph appeared in all the papers alongside G and T Charisma, Dicky's courageous saviour.

The press, who loved any story about Rupert, proceeded to dig up all his past misdemeanours: drinking and drugging and particularly bullying fellow showjumper Jake Lovell on the circuit.

'Chip off the old Campbell-Black', said the headlincs, accompanying a particularly evil photograph of Xavier, with monotonous regularity.

Almost the worst part was being in emotional debt to Anthea Belvedon, who was really milking it.

'Thank God Sir Raymond is no longer alaive. My Dicky is such a plucky little fellow, he'll bounce back. Of course I won't hold it against you, Rupert, but I do feel, at the very least, we should take a holistic approach and get round the table for family counselling. I and Dicky wouldn't want Xavier excluded. If we discover what happened and why, Dicky and Xav can achieve closure.'

Xavier, who was utterly mortified when he realized what he'd done, had written a letter of apology to Dicky, but he never shopped Cosmo or Lubemir.

Dicky was allowed a few days at home. On the Monday after his terrible boat trip, his mother, having tucked him up in bed, indulged in a little daydream. If Dicky had passed away, heaven forbid, she would have set up 'Dicky's Fund' and campaigned to stop bullying in schools. She would have fundraised tirelessly and lectured in schools and to Government ministers.

'Lady Belvedon talks such good sense and always looks so lovely.'

She could just imagine herself getting an OBE from the Queen, or, with a huge blow-up of Dicky at his most blue-eyed, blond and adorable behind her, talking to Dermot and Natasha on breakfast television.

Heaven forbid, she wouldn't want darling Dicky to die. Dora was a different matter. Anthea had opened an envelope addressed to Dora from the *Scorpion* containing a cheque for three thousand pounds the other day. Dora could jolly well pay her own school fees in future. Perhaps Rupert could pay them for a bit – to make up to her for not suing. Rupert was so attractive – pity about Taggie.

Anthea's musings were interrupted by the telephone and by such an exciting, intimate voice.

'Lady Belvedon, sorry about little Dick, is he OK? Nasty piece of work that Xav Campbell-Black, takes after his dad more than you would think.'

It was Stancombe. Anthea thought of his handsome, sensual face, his dark devouring eyes and his billions.

'Wondered if we could go out for a meal this week.'

'I must be there for my Dicky, but he should be back at Bagley by Wednesday. What about Wednesday evening?'

'Perfect. To avoid the tabloids, as you're such a high profile lady, why not come to my place?'

Life was full of surprises. Lady Belvedon gave Stancombe the best blow job he'd ever had.

Things were also looking up for Dicky. He received a signed football shirt and a get-well card from David Beckham, who was a friend of Rupert, and if Dicky and a friend would like to watch a Real Madrid match one Saturday, Rupert's helicopter was also at their disposal. Dicky definitely thought he'd live.

Xav, who'd gone into rehab, wasn't sure.

'Perhaps he'll meet Feral's mother in there,' said Bianca wistfully.

Such bad publicity for Rupert and Bagley was not good for Jupiter's New Reform Party and he had the temerity to tell Rupert so.

'You're chairman of his governors, why don't you tell Hengist to spend more time there?' Rupert had howled back and wandered off to Venturer to watch a recording of *Buffers*.

Here he had found his father, as one of this week's panel, downing large whiskies in the green room.

General Broadstairs, the Lord Lieutenant and a governor of Bagley, was also on the programme, which resulted in lots of apoplexy and cries of: 'I couldn't agree less.'

Fortunately the contestants were too old to storm very fast off the set and the Brigadier kept the whole thing under excellent control.

Afterwards Rupert had a drink in the bar with the Brigadier, who said he was thinking of asking Ian Cartwright on the programme, what did Rupert think?

'Bit young, isn't he?'

'Sound tank man, read a few books.' Then, after a pause: 'Might get him to bring young Paris with him. I might bring young Feral too. Fun for them to see the inside of a studio, still fascinated by it myself. Think the two boys miss each other.'

The Brigadier longed to tackle Rupert about calling Feral a 'black bastard'. Feral was still so miserable about Bianca, but Rupert was after all the Brigadier's boss, paying him a splendid salary, so he turned to the more neutral subject of Ian Cartwright and then realized Rupert hadn't taken in a word.

'Sorry about Xavier. Couldn't have been the only one. Dicky's small but he's a wiry little chap. Strong mentally too, refusing to shop anyone, like your Xav won't. Where's Xav now?'

'In rehab. Terrible that one doesn't see what's going on under one's nose. Christ knows what we do with him once he's dried out.'

Rupert's despondency was as unusual as it was touching.

'Why not send him to Larks?' suggested the Brigadier. 'Janna Curtis is a genius with disturbed children. The classes are going to be tiny, might get some GCSEs.'

'God in heaven,' cried Rupert in horror, 'it'd make him ten times worse.'

'Christian Woodford suggested we send Xav to Larks,' he told Taggie when he got home. 'Of all the bloody silly ideas. "Do you want to finish him off completely?" I said.'

90

Meanwhile, over at Larks, Janna was heroically forcing herself not to betray her heartbreak over Hengist and having a mad scramble to get Appletree ready in time. She was still searching for a maths master when Mike Pitts called and, having asked for a meeting, rolled up clear-skinned, bright-eyed, with no wine and food stains all over his clothes and asked if he could have his old job back.

'I haven't touched a drop for two months. I so much admire what you've done and I'd like to see my students through to the end.'

Janna leapt up and hugged him, realizing how much paunch and flab he'd lost and how his shakes were from nerves rather than booze – and what courage had been needed to approach her.

'Come back immediately. That is the best news in months,' she cried and, glancing at her watch, added, 'It's nearly six, let's have a vast drink to celebrate.' Then, realizing what she'd said, she screamed with horrified laughter. 'Oh God, sorry, at least we can have a cup of tea and a piece of lardy-cake my auntie sent me from Yorkshire.

'I'm desperate for a maths teacher, and I so need your experience,' she went on, pointing to a rough timetable on the wall as she switched on the kettle. 'I hope it'll work. With only forty-odd children, no one need do more than two and a half days a week. So many of your friends are still here: Skunk, Mr Mates, Basket, Cambola, Mags, darling Sophy Belvedon and Gloria. Lily Hamilton, who speaks masses of languages, is helping out Mags. Brigadier Woodford, who's madly in love with Lily and taught at the Staff College, is tackling history. Wally's going to lend a hand in D and T.'

'What about IT?' asked Mike, mouth watering as Janna cut off two big slices of lardy-cake and drenched them in ruby-red plum jam.

'Rowan's very sweetly staying on to teach it and look after me; she also confided that anything was better than staying at home full time looking after Meagan and Scarlet.'

Mike knew the feeling. For a second, like a butterfly on his upper lip, his ebony moustache quivered. What he didn't tell Janna was the utter nightmare of the last months. No one had wanted to employ him, except Poppet for maths coaching which had come to nothing. His wife had never stopped complaining about having him under her feet, as though he were lying permanently on the kitchen floor singing and waving a whisky bottle, which had not been far from the truth until he forced himself on to the wagon. He felt giddy with relief.

'The place looks superb,' he said, looking round. 'I like all these fawns and sand colours – very soothing.'

'We thought we'd give primary colours a miss, make the children feel it was more like a college.' Janna poured out Mike's tea, remembering the two sugars. 'The only exception is the hall which doubles up as a theatre. Graffi's painted the ceiling sky blue, and covered it in stars, suns and angels, who all have faces like Milly Walton.'

Janna winced, thinking of Milly's mother.

'I'm right glad to see you, Mike.'

'You've cut your hair,' said Mike looking at her for the first time. 'It – er – suits you.'

'Chally would say it's much neater,' said Janna acidly. 'It takes minutes rather than hours to wash in the morning.'

In a gesture of defiance and despair after she'd found out about Hengist and Ruth, she'd rushed into Larkminster and had her shaggy red mane cut off. Now it fell from the crown in a straight hard fringe to an inch above her eyebrows and to an inch above the collar at the back – typical middle-aged head teacher hair: hideous, or rather headious. But Hengist had gone. It was her farewell to love.

Sally Brett-Taylor had popped in several times, replacing many of the dead saplings with new ones from the Bagley plantation, creating a herb garden with Wally and planting plenty of bulbs, so 'we'll have lots to cheer us up in the Hilary Term.'

Each time she arrived, Janna felt glad she and Hengist were over but it didn't lessen her helpless longing.

With Mike on board, everything seemed to be falling into place. Wally hated the sand colours: too much like Iraq where his son was still serving, but he'd applied them with his usual expertise. Only the blue board outside the school had been left empty so the children could think up their own name. Thank God, now Janna was her own mistress, she could call the shots and start term when she chose – several days after bloody Bagley.

Thank God too for Debbie, who would love working in such a shiny new modern kitchen and who had already been freezing curries and pies.

But just a few days before term began, Debbie had sidled into Janna's office with a piece of shortbread for Partner, who immediately leapt on to her knee. Then, eyes cast down, she muttered, 'I'm so sorry, but I won't be staying on at Larks after all.'

'Why ever not?'

'I'm going to work for S and C – or more precisely for Ashton Douglas.'

'You can't. He's a monster!'

Debbie's face went dead.

'I take as I find. He's always been very courteous and pleasant. It'll be nice cooking for one gentleman, dinner parties and things.' Her face softened. 'I've loved working for you, Janna, and little Partner.' She stroked his ginger forehead. 'But there's been a lot of sadness and I'm tired. Forty kids and their teachers is a lot with just me, Moll and Marge. Mr Douglas has got such a lovely quiet house in the Close with a nice top floor for me, Wayne and Brad. And he's promised to get them into the choir school, just two minutes away.'

Wow, thought Janna, Ashton has pulled out the stops.

She felt like the final runner in the relay race, who reaches out for the baton and finds it bashing her over the head.

'I can't bear it,' she wailed. 'I don't mean to rubbish Ashton, but he's been no friend to Larks. I'll try and put up your wages.'

'Thanks all the same, but my mind's made up.'

Where do I find Larks's answer to Nigella Lawson in twenty-four hours, thought Janna.

Bloody Debbie to walk out without notice. Even bloodier Ashton. Then she flipped and sent him an email.

'How dare you poach my cook, you conniving shit. Poaching means dropping into boiling water, so don't you dare hurt or bully Debbie, or I'll cut off your goolies. Janna Curtis'.

The bastard, it was the dirtiest trick he could have played. No army could march on unfilled stomachs.

'Who's going to keep back the best bits of chicken for you?' she asked Partner.

It was dark outside; the wind had risen. The trees were doing aerobics, swaying and tossing their branches from side to side. It was too late to start ringing catering agencies. Then she saw lights. Was it Ashton come to fire her? But Partner, having jumped on the sofa to check the window, first wagged his tail then snuffled madly under the door. Definitely not Ashton. Next moment, Emlyn barged in. He was sweating and wearing a dark blue tracksuit.

'Ashton's poached Debbie,' cried Janna.

'I know.' Emlyn waved an email at her. 'You pressed the wrong button.'

'Ashton deserved it, the bastard. He bribed her with a massive salary and places in the choir school for Brad and Wayne, who both sing like crows with laryngitis. Lemme get at that computer.' Plonking herself down, Janna was about to fire off her rocket to the intended target.

'Pack it in,' snapped Emlyn, 'or you'll get sued for libel and suspended before term begins. Debbie'll come back when she realizes what a shit he is. I'm sorry, lovely.' Then he stopped in his tracks. 'Kerist, what have you done to your lovely hair?'

'I know, it's horrible,' said Janna despairingly. 'But as I'm clearly not a sex object any more, I'm putting all my energies into looking like a head.'

Emlyn smiled ruefully. 'You haven't got the big ass and dinner-lady arms to go with it, angel.'

In the past, Janna had been able to soften and hide the effects of her exhaustion behind long hair and a floppy fringe, but the hard new style exposed the dark circles and the added lines, leaving her with the face of a novice monk unsure of his vocation.

Crossing the room, Emlyn took her in his arms, his big hands ruffling the short crop, then coming to rest on an expanse of bare neck, which reminded him agonizingly of Oriana. But the cut that enhanced Oriana's flawless features did nothing for Janna.

'It'll be easier to keep,' she mumbled into his warm, comforting chest. 'Keep men away, I mean. My love life is over.'

'Bollocks. Ask Sally for some Gro-more. It'll be rippling over your shoulders in a month or two. Mind you' – he squinted down at her – 'you'll appeal to a completely different market now, and have Artie, Theo, Biffo and Joan after you – even Ashton might start pressing his pale grey suit.'

'Yuk,' shuddered Janna, but she started laughing.

It was nice holding her in his arms, reflected Emlyn. Reluctantly, he released her.

'I must go, I'm supposed to be in a staff meeting. It all looks great.' He admired the big collage Janna had made from photographs of every member of the new year Eleven and their teachers.

'I'll have to remove Debbie's photo,' sighed Janna. 'Where the hell am I going to find another cook, and how do I know if any of the children will turn up on the first day?'

'Turn it into a party,' said Emlyn.

And so Janna did – dispatching every child an invitation to 'A launching party at Appletree House to welcome Larks Year Eleven. Buffet 12.30 onwards, no uniform to be worn.'

On the following Monday, the staff settled in, rejoicing over the labs, the IT suite, the light airy classrooms, the big windows that didn't rattle, and the roof which didn't leak despite a downpour outside. They particularly liked the new staffroom, with its circle of comfortable chairs, coffee percolator, fridge, bar, dishwasher and a television with Sky. Randal had done them proud.

On the Tuesday from midday onwards, the children began to drift in. Making the most of the warm September sunshine, many of the girls showed off bare shoulders and midriffs, their flares sweeping the floor. Both sexes, however, looked edgy. Were they going to be the centre of too much teacher attention, drawn into an exam factory and sweatshop?

'It's weird,' grumbled Johnnie Fowler, 'there's no one above us and no one beneaf us.'

But gradually their fears vanished as they were welcomed by a hug from Janna and a glass of Buck's Fizz from Mags, and Bob Marley over the loudspeaker. Everything was certainly going to be all right as they raced round Appletree, admiring the whiteboards and the big windowed dining room, designed with a bar like a Wild West saloon. They were soon swinging on ropes in the gym and screaming with excitement over the boys' lavatory, where as you peed into a shiny steel trough, turquoise and indigo water gushed out and swept it away.

They also loved the hall, with the sky-blue ceiling full of angels looking like Milly Walton. Most of all, they loved the sand colours and beiges.

'Wicked, wicked, wicked, miss, it don't look like a school any more,' shouted Pearl. 'Oh look, TV's arrived. Anyone want mike-up?'

Partner was in heaven to see all his friends again. Janna was particularly pleased to see Aysha. The Brigadier's great coup had been to make a special journey to see Mr Khan, who only dealt with men and whose own father had been in a Punjab regiment. Invited on the set of *Buffers*, flattered to have his brains picked on the Punjabs' courage when the Japs invaded Burma, Mr Khan had finally agreed to let Aysha return to Larks. She looked so pretty in her apricot-pink headscarf and was knocked out by the new labs.

'Kylie Rose has put on a lot of weight,' whispered Cambola. 'Hope it's not what I'm thinking.'

'This drink is yummy,' said Kitten Meadows, 'can I have another one?'

'If you mop it up with some food,' said Mags, running in with a huge shepherd's pie from the Ghost and Castle. Lily, who'd offered to help out in the kitchen, had made several plum tarts and blackberry and apple crumbles.

'We'll start hellfy eating tomorrow,' said Rocky, who'd already had two showers in the changing rooms.

'Like your hair, miss, it's cool,' said kind Kylie.

'It's gross,' said Pearl. 'You'd better let me cut it next time.'

Outside, where the ground had been levelled for a small pitch with goalposts, Feral was playing football with Graffi, Johnnie, Monster and a frantically yapping Partner.

After everyone had had lunch, Janna called them into the hall for a group photograph and Pearl went round taking the shine off everyone's noses.

'I saw Chally in Tesco's this morning,' moaned Basket. 'She was so unkind.'

Janna put her hands over her ears. 'I don't want to hear it.'

'She said, "None of those no-hopers could ever get a job, that's why they're hanging on at Larks for another year."'

'Bitch. We'll show her,' said Janna, clapping her hands for silence. 'I'd like to thank Brigadier Woodford so much for providing the champagne. Is everyone's glass filled up?'

As Sophy and Gloria rushed round with bottles, Cambola played the theme tune from 'Band of Brothers' on the piano, then, as the music faded away, Janna smiled round.

' "We few, we happy few, we band of brothers",' she said softly. 'Today is for welcome and celebration. The purpose of the year ahead is to get some grades and have a ball. You're students now. This is a college. You may have noticed that Wally hasn't painted anything on the board outside because we thought you could kick off by naming your school yourselves.'

'What about Curtis College?' shouted Pearl.

'What about Cool School?'

'What about Shakespeare School?'

The suggestions came from all sides.

'What about Larkminster High School?' Aysha said.

'Because larks fly high, and we're aiming for the stars.' Graffi pointed up at the sky-blue ceiling. 'Bloody good.'

Everyone cheered.

'Larks High it shall be,' went on Janna. 'We've also decided to dispense with a few rules. What causes most rows in schools?'

'Uniform and short skirts,' shouted Pearl, 'and jewellery.'

'Smoking,' said Johnnie, throwing his cigarette into a fire bucket, 'and chewing gum.'

'Mobiles,' said Kylie, as hers rang. 'Hi, Jack, ay can't talk to you right now.'

Everyone roared with laughter.

'Right,' said Janna, 'in future you can smoke, but not in the classrooms, and as long as you don't stub your fags out on our lovely new floors. Ditto chewing gum. You can use your mobiles as long as you ask permission and go out of the classroom to take calls. You can also wear what clothes you like and any jewellery, but be sensible: no hoop earrings and tie back your hair in the labs.

'You've all seen how beautiful your new building is. So please cover the walls with examples of good work, not graffiti. And as we're a band of brothers, please don't bring in any guns or knives. PC Cuthbert' – loud cheers from the girls – 'will be popping in and out. You can also call us by our Christian names if you like.'

'We do, Janna,' yelled Johnnie to more cheers.

'The only sad news,' went on Janna, consulting her notes, 'is that Debbie has left us, so I'm putting up a rota of people who'll help clear away after lunch and load the new dishwasher.'

'Terrific,' interrupted Rocky, 'as long as it's only the women,' which caused a howl of protest from the girls.

'We'd also like two of you to take it in turns to sit in reception doing homework and welcoming guests to the school and offering them tea, coffee or hot chocolate from our wonderful new machine. And please remember to fill up Partner's water bowl.'

'She's very good,' murmured Lily to the Brigadier.

'That's all.' Again Janna smiled round at them. 'Don't hurry home, look around and enjoy yourselves. We may have been called "no-hopers" in the past, but we're going to prove everyone wrong.'

Rocky, who'd been gazing into space, suddenly shouted hoarsely, 'God bless Larks High and all who sail in her. Three cheers for Miss Curtis, I mean Janna.'

'Janna,' shouted everyone, draining empty glasses.

'We few, we crappy few,' sang Graffi happily.

'That went really well,' said Mags as she and Basket loaded up the dishwasher. 'Johnnie must be drunk, I've just seen him doing a high five with Monster.'

'I don't mind doing this today,' Janna said as she shared the last bottle of the champagne between their three glasses, 'but I've got to find a cook. The one I interviewed yesterday was a battleaxe who wanted six hundred pounds a week. Taggie Campbell-Black's coming to see me at three-thirty, I wonder what she wants.'

91

Pupils were still hanging around gossiping when Taggie arrived. Kylie Rose, recognizing her from *Hello!* and most of the papers and determined to be the hostess with the mostess, rushed forward to welcome her, offering her hot chocolate.

'I'm sure there are some biscuits in the kitchen, Mrs Campbell-Black, I'll bring them in.' She ushered Taggie along the corridor, passing Monster and Johnnie, who, having suspended peace talks, were having a fight, then Pearl, in a micro skirt, smoking and shouting, 'You can fuck off,' into her mobile.

As Taggie entered Janna's office, she was shaking worse than Mike Pitts. She was also so tall, long-legged, huge-eyed and vulnerable, Janna felt they were taking part in some Aesop fable about a red squirrel and a giraffe. Partner immediately curled up on Taggie's knee to make her feel at home.

'What a sweet dog.' Taggie had a surprisingly deep, gruff voice. 'Reminds me of my little mongrel, Gertrude. I've got a lurcher now, who's adorable, but you can't cuddle them on your knee. They fall off. All dogs are best dogs, but Gertrude was my best, best dog. What a lovely office.'

Taggie was rattling now and when Kylie Rose arrived with hot chocolate and some Bourbon biscuits, the cup Taggie took from her rattled in accompaniment like a woodpecker.

'Can I get you a tea, miss, I mean, Janna?' asked Kylie, dying to find out why such a star had descended to earth.

'I'm fine thanks. Shut the door behind you, Kylie. How can I help you?' Janna smiled at Taggie.

'I'm looking for a school for Xav when he comes out of rehab next month.'

Janna nearly fell off her chair.

'He was just going into Year Eleven, like your children,' stammered Taggie, 'and Christian Woodford says you're a genius with d-d-d-difficult, unhappy children.'

Janna brightened. 'He did?'

'You can hardly have failed to notice how Xav was expelled from Bagley. Such a public humiliation for both him and Rupert, who's hardly bullied anyone since he left school. Poor Xav's been so difficult since he went to Bagley, I feel terrible not realizing he was drinking and drugging.'

'Tell me about this summer.'

Feeling horribly disloyal, Taggie did so.

'Marcus and Tabitha have done so well,' she said finally, 'and Bianca just floats through life. Xav feels so hopeless. I was the same, the really thick one, between a brilliant brother and sister. Alex Bruce always thought Xav was stupid and was waiting for an excuse to sack him.'

'We have to prove him wrong then.'

Taggie glanced up, not daring to hope. 'D'you mean . . . ?'

'I certainly do. We'd love to have Xav. He was so kind to Paris on the geography field trip and he worked terribly hard during *Romeo and Juliet.* Aysha, who got on very well with him, is staying on at Larks, so he'll have a buddy to look after him.'

Taggie's stammering ecstatic gratitude was cut short by the telephone. The call was equally short.

'Bugger, bugger, bugger.' Janna switched off the handset. 'A cook I interviewed yesterday has decided not to take the job after all. Our wonderful Debbie has been poached by Ashton Douglas.'

Taggie's silver eyes widened like rain rings in a pond.

'Not that horrible smoothie at the public meeting?'

'That's the one.'

'What does the job involve?' asked Taggie.

'Well, basically, dinner every day for about forty. The staff and lots of the children will only be working a two- or three-day week and many of them just have baguettes or salads and rush off and play in the grounds. I've got a very good temp for September starting tomorrow, but after that . . .' Janna splayed out her fingers in despair.

'I know someone who might be able to help you,' said Taggie, colour suffusing her pale face. 'Before I married Rupert I used to cook for dinner parties. I could give it a try until you found someone.'

Taggie had been so desperately low about herself both as a wife and mother that the sun really came out when Janna jumped to her feet in delight and pumped Taggie's hand.

'I can't think of anything more wonderful for Larks's street cred. The children will be so chuffed to have two Campbell-Blacks here.'

'You don't think it'll embarrass Xav?'

'Some mothers, yes, but not you. And I think, as he'll have just come out of rehab, we'll have to keep an eye on him.'

Taggie loved the new kitchens, 'much more modern than ours at Penscombe'.

'I'd like to start a breakfast club,' said Janna as she walked Taggie to the front door, 'even if it's only orange juice and a bacon sandwich. So many of our children face a wall of indifference and hostility beyond the school gates. Xav will find himself one of the very lucky ones. Some of them lead such deprived lives. This is one of the worst cases,' she whispered as, on cue, bouncing his violet and yellow football along the corridor, came Feral. He had lost his sheen like a conker forgotten in a coat pocket. Poised for flight, he looked at Taggie warily as if awaiting blows.

'Hello, Feral, I'm so sorry about the other evening,' she stammered.

'Xavier's coming to Larks,' said Janna.

'Wicked,' said Feral and skittered past them into the dusk.

Back at Penscombe, Rupert was in a foul temper. Where in hell was Taggie? There was no sign of dinner. He'd taken advantage of her absence to have a look at one of his GCSE set books, which he'd found in the library next door: a first edition of *Pride and Prejudice* with the pages uncut, which he'd scribbled notes all over. He hadn't been able to make head nor tail of *Macbeth* and even less of the Ted Hughes poem he'd tackled yesterday. Why had he ever let himself be bullied into taking this bloody exam? If by some miracle he passed, he wouldn't give a penny to Alex Bruce's science block after the way he'd treated Xav.

Hearing a car and joyous barking as dogs bounded down the stairs and along from the kitchen, and old Bogotá looked up hopefully through his sightless eyes praying it might be Xavier, Rupert shoved *Pride and Prejudice* under a cushion. As Taggie ran in, eyes shining, colour back in her cheeks for the first time in days, he thought she'd never looked prettier. How enticingly that white T-shirt clung to her. Dinner could wait; he took her hand: 'Let's go to bed.'

'Something wonderful happened,' gasped Taggie, 'I must just tell you.'

* * *

'Are you out of your mind?' asked Rupert two minutes later, in the soft bitchy voice that always made Taggie want to bolt like a hunted hare. 'Xav is totally unstable, and you're throwing him to the wolves: the flower of the Shakespeare Estate who'll force-feed him glue, steroids and crack cocaine; brutes like Feral Jackson who whip out guns at public meetings, nick cars and beat up old ladies.'

Rupert's icy rage could halt global warming, but Taggie stood her ground.

'Christian Woodford's teaching there, and Lily. They love Feral. You liked Janna. You went out of your way to try and save Larks.'

'For other people's children. You're committing Xav to a crap bunch of teachers and geriatrics, only clinging on because they can't find work anywhere else.'

'Most of them are your age.' Taggie was appalled at her own bitchiness. 'They've just led more stressful lives. Xav's going; I've signed a form.'

'Which you couldn't even read,' said Rupert brutally.

'Janna read it to me. I'm going to give it a try.'

'Shouldn't you have involved Xav "in the decision-making process" as Mrs Bruce would say?'

Taggie lost her temper. 'You haven't tried to find him anywhere. Why are you being so bloody negative?'

'I'm going out.' Rupert snatched up his car keys and stormed off, slamming the door.

Returning at two in the morning, he couldn't have insomnia in the spare room, because he'd given it over to Bianca, so he had to go and freeze in a musty deserted bedroom and let in all the dogs to keep him warm.

'I miss him as much as you,' he mumbled as he hoisted poor blind Bogotá up beside him.

Bianca, next day, was angrier than Rupert.

'I can't tell people you're going to be a cook like Mrs Axford. Who's going to take me to school? You'll have to drop me off at eight in the morning if you're going to get Xav to Larks by eight-thirty. I might as well board, I'm not going to be a latchkey kid.'

Running upstairs, Bianca threw herself down on the pink and lilac quilt and sobbed her heart out. She'd never believed anything could hurt so much. Only this afternoon, as one of the grooms was driving her home, she'd mistaken a rain-soaked trunk halfway down the chestnut avenue for Feral and, leaping out of the car, raced towards him.

If her mother went to Larks, Feral would fall in love with her like everyone else did, she thought despairingly.

What enraged Rupert was the ribbing from Jupiter and Hengist.

'Why don't you take your GCSE at Larks, and make it a full house?' suggested Jupiter. 'Estelle Morris is always ticking off ministers for not sending their children to maintained schools. Think of the brownie points if you sent yourself.'

'Did Taggie say how Janna was?' asked Hengist.

'From that picture in the *Gazette*, she's acquired an Eton crop and completely lost her looks,' said Jupiter.

Hengist missed Janna terribly. He felt so sad and so guilty about her, as if he'd plucked a bunch of wild flowers on a walk and found them dead in the porch three days later because he'd forgotten to put them in water.

92

It was arguable who was more terrified, Xav or Taggie, when they arrived at Larks in late September. Xav had just emerged from rehab, utterly mortified he had nearly killed Dicky and written off Rupert's best horse.

Learning his destination, he panicked: 'I can't go to Larks, they'd skin me alive. They'll have read what I did to Dicky. They'll think I'm some pervy Hooray. Have you seen the hulking brutes like Monster Norman and Johnnie Fowler?'

'Give it a try,' pleaded Taggie, 'I so need your help to read recipes and tell me everyone's names.'

'You do?' Xav looked dubious. 'What'll you do if the other guys slag me off?'

'I'll thump them,' said Taggie.

Xav smiled slightly.

'And there's a sweet girl called Aysha looking forward to seeing you.'

Xav's face brightened. 'I thought she'd gone to Searston Abbey.'

'Brigadier Woodford talked her father round.'

Inside, Taggie was quailing. What if Xav hadn't stopped drinking? She had been comforted by her father, Declan, who was passionately opposed to private education, particularly boarding schools. 'Xav'll get to know all the local children,' he told Rupert.

'Hardly, at thirty miles away,' said Rupert sourly.

'We're to roll up after assembly around ten o'clock so it won't be too public,' Taggie reassured Xav. 'And you don't have to bother with uniform, although you've lost so much weight, we'd better go and buy you some jeans.'

'They'll look too new,' grumbled Xav.

There was a row as they were leaving. How could they possibly abandon Bogotá? He'd get so confused.

'He'll have all the other dogs and the stable lads,' begged Taggie.

'But he's used to having you or me.' Xav was nearly hysterical, particularly when Bogotá tried to jump into the car, missed, fell and, tail drooping, unseeing eyes bewildered, was lifted back into the house.

'Poor old boy,' said Rupert, who'd been deliberately keeping his distance, 'abandoned like everyone else.'

More frightened of his father's icy disapproval, Xav shot into the car. God he could use a drink, or a line. How could he possibly slide unobtrusively into Larks with Taggie in tow, looking utterly gorgeous in a pale pink polo shirt and black jeans?

Dora, who had not forgiven Xav, had also been at work and they arrived to find the school gates swarming with press and television cameras.

Xav grabbed the door handle. 'I'm going home.'

'We can't let Janna down.'

A blond woman thrust her tape recorder through the window. 'Why are you sending Xav to Larks?'

'I've heard wonderful things about it,' stammered Taggie.

'Oh, come on,' said a repulsively familiar toad face with olive-green teeth: Col Peters had turned up in person. 'Larks has just been closed down.'

'Janna Curtis has very kindly offered Xav a place. He's into his second year's GSE' – mumbled Taggie, who could never master initials. 'GECS course. Xav knows a lot of the children and the staff.'

'After the way Xav nearly totalled Dicky Belvedon, he won't have any difficulty holding his own,' sneered Col.

'Is Rupert going to take his GCSE at Larks?' asked a man from the BBC.

'Find his own intellectual level if he did,' quipped Col.

'And Rupert knows all about bullying, doesn't he, Taggie?' The crowd of press were making it impossible for Taggie to push through. Out of the corner of her eye, she could see Wally and PC Cuthbert belting down the drive, but Xav was too quick for them. Leaping out of the car, he grabbed Col's lapels.

'You're one to talk when it comes to bullying,' he yelled. 'Leave my mother alone, you great asshole.'

To his amazement, he was then given a round of applause by the rest of the press.

Next moment, PC Cuthbert had moved in:

'That's enough. Morning, Mrs Campbell-Black, morning, Xav.' He directed them to the car park, then on to reception, where a huge banner said: 'Welcome to Larks High, Taggie and Xavier'.

Cambola played 'The Campbell-Blacks are coming, hurrah, hurrah' on her trumpet, and Kylie stepped forward and presented a bunch of orange freesias to Taggie to a chorus of wolf whistles. No one seemed to be at lessons. Janna came out and hugged them both.

'That your sister, Xav?' shouted Johnnie.

'We're doing media studies, Xav,' giggled Kitten, 'and we just sit round reading the tabloids and about you and your farver all day.'

'Thank goodness you're here, Taggie, we're starving,' shouted Graffi. 'And who's going to win the big race this afternoon, Xavier?'

'Probably Hellespont,' muttered Xav, and a score of mobiles were switched on.

The warmth of his and Taggie's reception was due first to their novelty factor in arriving a fortnight after the beginning of term on a beautiful day, and secondly because Janna's no-hopers were having the time of their lives. In small classes of half a dozen, they were really blossoming, and the teachers who'd stayed on, her 'Golden Oldies' (except for Sophy, Gloria and Rowan) as Janna called them, were regaining their skills, their confidence, and at last having time to teach and prepare their lessons.

After initial doubts about the Brigadier – 'He looks old enough to have been in the First World War,' grumbled Johnnie Fowler – both sexes had been utterly captivated by his lessons, playing war games all over the park, moving pepper pots round polished tables.

An additional advantage was an excellent press, except from the *Gazette*, on Xavier's first day, with several references to his challenging Col Peters for cheeking his mother. His street cred rose even higher when Hellespont won by five lengths.

Xav arrived a scarred, angry, screwed-up ex-junkie, terrified he was going to be beaten up for being posh, thick and black. Instead, he found he was brighter and further ahead in most subjects, particularly in Spanish.

Gradually, as the acceptance of the other children won him over, he began, as Janna had predicted, to appreciate the horror of so many of their lives.

It was Taggie who, because people talked to her, learnt that Johnnie Fowler supported the BNP because his mother had been nearly beaten to death by a black lover and that Monster's dad had arrived last weekend after an absence of five years and left again after a blazing drunken row. Feral's mother had also vanished like smoke, but any moment she and Uncle Harley might roll up and ruin everything. Feral was getting on all right with the Brigadier. His brother and sisters were thriving with the foster parents, but kept escaping to the amusement arcades in Larkminster. Feral had bought the two eldest mobiles, so he could keep track of them, but they kept running up bills. All this Taggie explained to Xav.

Rocky, who was madly in love with Taggie, was building a dog kennel for Bogotá in D and T.

Fearful fights still broke out, particularly between the boys who were so in need of a father figure. Christian Woodford was much admired but a bit old, as were Skunk, Pittsy and Mr Mates. Janna thought longingly of Emlyn, who instantly diffused rows whenever he appeared.

For the first time, Xav found himself looking forward to PE with the glamorous Gloria. He could now get into size 32 trousers; his spots had gone; his hawk-like South American-Indian features were emerging, and suddenly he discovered he was attractive to girls. Pearl and Kitten were both giving him the eye, but Xav still only had eyes for Aysha. Sad, beautiful and timid as the deer that sometimes invaded his father's woods, she was working on her first science module, which had to be finished by Christmas.

'Ask her out,' urged Feral.

'Her dad wouldn't let me near her,' sighed Xav.

Feral knew the feeling. Bianca was boarding at Bagley now and it crucified him to think of her at the mercy of Cosmo, Anatole and the predators of the lower and upper sixths.

During Ramadan, on top of all her school work and helping out at home, Aysha was expected to fast from sunrise to sunset. One afternoon she fainted in the corridor. Xav, who found her, was demented. As he loosened her headscarf and her top button, he couldn't resist kissing her pale lips. Aysha had fluttered open her lashes, smiled as if she'd gone to Mecca, then realized this was earth, cried out in terror, staggered to her feet and fled.

Another of Xav's momentous encounters was with Mike Pitts. Returning to Mike's classroom to collect some forgotten maths homework, Xav found Mike about to take a slug of whisky from a bottle. He had had a gruelling afternoon, with Monster and Johnnie refusing to understand quadratic equations. Xav took a deep breath.

'If you're anything like me, sir, you don't really want to drink that.'

Mike had nearly jumped through the roof, but he lowered the bottle.

'Shall I take it, sir?' Xav felt an awful prig as he emptied it out of the window. 'I'm desperate for a drink whenever I get stressed,' he confessed, 'but if I can somehow get over the moment . . .'

'Thank you.' Mike wanted to beg Xav not to tell anyone. 'Shall we make a pact? If you feel like having a drink, you call me.'

'And if you feel like it,' said Xav, 'you call me – any hour of the night,' he added gravely.

He could feel the dampness of Mike's hand as they shook on it. Xav told no one, but was gratified that he and Mike exchanged three or four calls a week.

Xav was almost proudest that Taggie's cooking had encouraged all the children to switch to school dinners and of how Taggie enslaved them with her gentleness and sweetness when she started helping them with their food technology GCSE. Part of the coursework was to provide a menu and food for Larkminster Rovers Football Club. Taggie was determined to put in a good word for Feral.

As the weather grew colder, more and more children started rolling up to her breakfast club to eat bacon and eggs or croissants with apple jelly from the Penscombe orchard. In addition they joined an after-school club where they could do their homework, undisturbed by yelling families.

The children also saw Xav with his arm round Taggie's shoulders as he deciphered memos and recipes for her, and told him how lucky he was.

'Christ, I wish I was adopted,' sighed Graffi. 'Paris's foster muvver looks like a horse. Yours is like a gazelle, she's beautiful.' Graffi had done some lovely drawings of Taggie, which Xav would have shown to his father if Rupert had been in a better mood.

Sally Brett-Taylor, who often popped in to tend the garden, always sought Xav out to see how he was and give him the gossip, to which Janna was unable to stop herself listening.

Oriana was due home at Christmas for a long stint. Hengist was utterly obsessed with the rugby World Cup.

'If there's any possibility of England reaching the final, he's been asked by Venturer to fly out and cover it. So exciting,' confided Sally. 'He's also been terribly busy writing speeches for Jupiter for the Tory Party conference.'

* * *

Once Larks was up and running, Janna was distracted by a constant stream of visitors. Wendy Wallace wrote a lovely piece for the *Times Educational Supplement*. The BBC in Bristol came over to interview the children and told the viewers how well the experiment was working.

Ashton Douglas was not happy with this publicity, particularly if it established a precedent and failing schools all over the country started clamouring for buildings and funding to enable them to keep going for another year for the sake of a few Year Tens.

Meanwhile Rupert was keeping his distance. He'd enjoyed *The Mayor of Casterbridge*, and in his present mood, was very tempted to auction Taggie at Sotheby's. He'd struggled to the end of act one of *Macbeth*. He only thawed fractionally when Taggie brought him a bottle of Jack Daniel's and a foot of Toblerone with her first pay packet. He yawned like Jonah's whale when Xav and Taggie gossiped about Larks.

'Is Janna interviewing cooks? I thought this was a temporary job?'

'She's trying, but she's got so much to do,' mumbled Taggie, who also had so much to do and was as distressed by Rupert's rage as by Bianca's refusal to come home at weekends.

Bianca, who was too proud to tell her parents how much she loathed boarding, was also furious Xav was having such a good time.

'He gets away at four and often doesn't have homework even in the subjects he's taking. I have to work until six o'clock and have two hours' homework after that.' And she stormed into Miss Painswick's office to ring Childline.

In the second week of October, when the gutters were filling up with leaves and conkers crashing down, Cosmo, Anatole and Lubemir, armed with a huge bottle of vodka for Janna, rolled up at Larks, uninvited, to see what sort of cock-up Xavier was making of his life.

In the corridor they bumped into Xav himself, who started to shake. Fortunately, he was flanked by Johnnie, Monster, Feral and Graffi.

Any skirmish was averted by Janna coming out of her office and offering the Cosmonaughties a cup of tea and lardy-cake and expressing profound gratitude for the vodka.

The trio returned to Bagley absolutely furious.

Why couldn't they smoke, use their mobiles in class, not wear uniform, call the teachers by their Christian names and have cosy lessons on sofas?

'It's great at Larks,' Anatole admitted to the rest of a madly curious Upper Fifth. 'Xav is doing really vell and getting A stars.'

'Boffin Black,' mocked Cosmo, 'born in a Bogotá gutter, he's found his own level. How could Mr Fussy have let such a genius slip through his fingers?'

'Oh, cool it, Cosmo,' snapped Lubemir, who was profoundly grateful to Xav for not shopping him over Dicky Belvedon's boat trip. 'Xav looked really good, he's lost so much weight, and Pearl, Feral, Graffi, Kylie and Johnnie – all of them – sent their best to you,' he added.

'That's nice,' said Amber.

'To me?' asked Paris, looking up.

'No, how funny,' drawled Cosmo, 'no one mentioned you at all, not even Janna, who's had the most awful haircut. They've all forgotten you.'

93

Paris was faring patchily at Bagley. Work, particularly in English, Latin and Greek, was miraculous. He had caught up with and overtaken the class. Playing regularly for the third fifteen had given him a rugger bugger swagger and the friendship of Lando, Junior and Jack Waterlane, who all found his help with both homework and coursework invaluable. In turn they protected him from Cosmo and Boffin, who were furious he had so often supplanted them as teacher's pet.

Things were going less happily at home, where Paris kept on drinking Ian's drink, staying out late, and being sullen and uncommunicative when Ian and Patience's friends dropped in.

Ian was already uptight because of a fee-fixing scandal, which had just broken. As a comparatively new bursar, he had received emails and telephone calls from other independent school bursars round the country, and assumed it was standard practice to compare notes on fees. Now two major public schools had turned supergrass and the independents were being accused of forming a cartel and denying parents the chance to seek cheaper options.

Alex Bruce, predictably, had gone into a frenzy of disapproval, demanding total access to Ian's files and accusing him of sharp practice.

As Alizarin Belvedon, Sophy's husband, was working flat out for a major exhibition in New York and London, and Sophy was working at least three days a week at Larks, Patience frequently looked after their three-year-old daughter Dulcie, which, as well as the yard, meant a lot of work. Dulcie, with blonde curls and huge dark blue eyes, was utterly adorable and very self-willed. She adored Paris and, accompanied by

Northcliffe, trailed constantly round the house after him, interrupting his homework.

The afternoon Cosmo returned from Larks and taunted Paris that no one had asked after him, Paris had stormed out of the classroom and Lando had run after him, trying to comfort him.

'Don't rise, man, Cosmo's just winding you up because he's jealous. I'll walk back to the Coach House with you, I need to check Barbary. He was lame yesterday, and on the way you can tell me the plot of *The Mayor of Casterbridge*.'

But as they shuffled through a burning fiery furnace of leaves, Paris snapped, 'Look it up in the *Oxford Companion to English Literature,* you idle sod. I'm pissed off doing your donkey work,' and ran ahead into the gloom.

Reaching the yard, he found Patience giving the horses haynets and Dulcie, in pale blue denim dungarees and a blue and white shirt, trying to sweep up straw with a fork. Both called out to Paris, but he belted upstairs and slammed his bedroom door.

How could Janna not ask after him? How could Graffi, Pearl and Feral forget him?

' "I am – yet what I am, none cares or knows",' he quoted bitterly. ' "My friends forsake me like a memory lost." ' Glancing round the room, he flipped.

Whoosh went the fixtures, cards and photographs on the mantelpiece. Whoosh off the shelf by the window went the china Labrador head bookends containing his poetry books; crash went pots of felt tips, marker pens and biros, and piles of files and videos, as he tipped over his work table and upended chairs.

'Fuck, fuck, fucking Cosmo.'

'Pawis, Pawis,' said a voice, accompanied by banging on the door. 'Pawis, let me in.' It was Dulcie.

'Fuck off,' screamed Paris, hurling a stapler on the floor so its innards spilled out.

Dulcie looked round in delight. 'Whatyerdoin', Pawis?'

'Trashing this room, now sod off.'

The radio hit the wall with a sickening crunch. A vase of winter jasmine, picked and arranged by Patience, crashed to the floor.

'Let's play twashing,' screamed an enchanted Dulcie, picking up a video of *Macbeth.*

'No,' yelled Paris as she chucked it against a skirting board, following it with a bust of Homer, which lost its nose.

'All fall down.'

'Not that either,' howled Paris as she grabbed a leather-bound copy of the Greek *Epigrams* given him by Theo, and dropped it in the winter jasmine water, before smashing Paris's alarm clock on the floor.

'Twashing, twashing,' crowed Dulcie, pulling books out of shelves.

Only when she grabbed the snow fountain containing the Eiffel Tower, given him by his mother, did Paris finally come to his senses. Catching it just in time and returning it to the window sill, he burst out laughing, and gathering up Dulcie, tossed her in the air until she screamed with even more delight. It was thus how Patience found them.

'We'd better tidy things up before Grandpa gets home.'

Ian was less amused and rang Theo to ask him over for a drink and to seek advice about Paris.

Putting down the telephone, before taking up his translation of Sophocles, Theo looked out of his study window on to the playing fields and woods of the school he loved so dearly. Maybe he'd last another year? He was in terrible pain, but he must cling on to finish Sophocles and to set Paris on course. One felt the ecstasy of teaching and opening up such a receptive mind half a dozen times only in a career.

Hearing a thud, Theo noticed Hindsight, his vast ginger tom cat, had landed on a table by the window, endangering a bust of Socrates, and in greedy pursuit of a peacock butterfly clinging to one of the brown curtains. Groaning, Theo crossed the room and cupped the butterfly in his hands, pulling down the window handle with his little finger. He hated chucking butterflies out in winter but today was perhaps mild enough for it to survive. He laid it on a wisteria stem. Next moment it had taken off into the dusk. Perhaps he could do the same for Paris.

Ignoring Hindsight's filthy thwarted look, he pressed three emerald-green Anadin Ultra out of their silver wrapping and washed them down with neat whisky from the bottle.

Later, he limped over to the Old Coach House, admiring a huge fox-fur ring round the moon – a presage of storms to come.

He liked Cartwright, who poured a good mahogany whisky. He was a little inflexible for Paris perhaps, but kinder and more down to earth than some silly, sandalled, muesli-munching liberal. Noticing a yellow brick road of Wisdens along the bookshelf, Theo was touched when Ian shyly produced Theo's own translation of *The Bacchae* and asked him to sign it. They then got on to their favourite topic, bitching about Alex Bruce.

'The archives are definitely for the chop,' grumbled Ian. 'What does it matter to Alex if Bagley old boys won six VCs or that one got the Templar Prize for a biography of Auchinleck?'

'He's got an even more sinister plan for reports,' growled Theo. 'A computer program limited to a choice of a hundred and forty different phrases to describe a pupil and his work. Christ, when one considers the infinite riches of the English language. "Think of the time you'll save," said Alex. "You've only got a handful of pupils anyway, Theo Graham, and they'll drift away as the classics lose their relevance."'

'"He loves no plays, As thou dost, Antony,"' sighed Ian, '"he hears no music."'

'I hear the scratching of new brooms,' shivered Theo, 'scratch, scratch, scratch along floorboard and carpet, sinister as the dry snake scales crawling up the roof in Rikki Tikki Tavi. I'm sure Hengist is going to Fleetley.'

'God, I hope not,' said Ian in horror as he topped up both their glasses. 'We'll all be for the high jump. Hengist is spending too much time away, not even doing anything worthy like fundraising. He must watch his back. D'you think a word with Sally?'

But the door had burst open and in ran Dulcie, wearing a blue dressing gown and mouse slippers.

Ian's angry face softened. 'Come to say goodnight, darling?'

'Let's play twashing,' cried Dulcie, picking up a photograph of her Aunt Emerald and smashing it on the floor, followed by a cranberry red glass bowl, which Ian, once a fine slip, leapt forward and caught.

'That's enough, Dulcie,' he said sharply, as *The Bacchae* flew across the room.

'Twashing,' cried Dulcie, beaming at her grandfather and briskly upending Theo's overflowing ashtray on the carpet, followed by a Staffordshire milkmaid. 'Pawis and I played twashing this afternoon.'

She took a swig of Theo's whisky and spat it out.

'Ugh, poison.'

'Very possibly,' agreed Theo.

After Patience had bustled in and whisked Dulcie off to bed, Ian said, 'Paris's influence, I'm afraid. He's being tricky at the moment.'

'Testing you,' said Theo. 'He's terrified of losing you and the comfort and security you've given him. I'm photostatting a very good poem called "Yearning Difficulties" he wrote this week. Don't let him know I've shown it to you.'

Upstairs, as Patience read *Jemima Puddleduck* to Dulcie, she was aware of Paris stealing down the landing. He loved listening in, particularly when Patience was teaching Dulcie nursery rhymes. He also loved playing with Ian's old train set, showing Dulcie how to work it with infinite patience because he was enjoying himself so much. It broke Patience's heart that he'd missed out on a childhood.

Pretending they were presents from Dulcie, she'd brought him a teddy bear, a duck for his bath and a CD of nursery rhymes. She'd also rooted out Emerald and Sophy's old copies of *The Just So Stories, The Jungle Book* and Hans Andersen.

Dora insisted Paris was like Little Kay in *The Snow Queen.* 'His heart must be melted before it freezes over completely.'

Paris had filled out from rugby, was nearly six foot and so beautiful, Patience couldn't take her eyes off him. She felt so sorry for poor besotted Dora, who put sweets in his locker, and who was having a horrid time at home.

Randal Stancombe was in hot pursuit of her mother, piling on the presents, inviting Anthea on thrilling trips. He was clearly very taken. Anthea was pretty, clear-sighted, excellent at running a home – Ruth had been a slut and very lazy – and wonderful in bed.

Anthea, in her turn, was captivated by Randal's money, but found him difficult to control; and she'd rather wait until he got his K, so she could move seamlessly from Lady Belvedon to Lady Stancombe. She was touched by the way he wanted to win over her children, but she wished he wouldn't try quite so hard with Dora. So did Dora who, when she was at Foxglove Cottage, slept with Dicky's camel-hair dressing gown buttoned up to her neck and Cadbury, who loathed Stancombe, across her legs.

'I'm going to make myself a chastity belt in D and T,' she told Bianca.

Anthea had made a huge fuss about Stancombe's birthday one Sunday in late November, giving him a beautiful glass engraved with his initials and buying a card to which she insisted Dicky and Dora added their names.

'I don't ever wish him to return happily,' stormed Dora.

Randal was charmed by his present. Then, having said the only thing he'd rather drink from the glass was Anthea herself, spoilt it all by murmuring that:

'Of course, the most precious gift a woman can give a man is her daughter.'

Anthea had gone bright red.

'Don't make disgusting jokes. Dora hasn't had her first period yet and she's not remotely interested in boys except for that gormless Paris Alvaston.'

While Anthea was cooking his birthday lunch next door, an unrepentant Randal had stroked Dora's cheek.

'I'll have to put you down for a few years, then you'll mature like the finest wine.'

Revolted, Dora had stormed off to tell Paris and Dicky as they queued in the drizzle to go into chapel that evening.

'Randal Stancombe is desiccating our father's bed.'

'And we've got to spend Christmas with that poisonous Jade,' sighed Dicky.

'Jade had the gall to complain to Joan she was a victim of peer abuse because Amber chose to go to the cinema with Milly rather than her,' said Dora scornfully. 'Joan took Jade's side. That woman's getting such a hold on Bagley. She's finally got permission for her all-female window in the chapel. She's chosen Elizabeth Fry, Florence Nightingale and Marie Curie, I ask you!'

'Who's Elizabeth Fry?' asked Dicky.

'She was a penis reformer,' said Dora.

'I wish she would do something about mine,' said Dicky gloomily.

Worst of all for Dora, Cadbury was in jeopardy again. He'd been banished from the kennels for gobbling up all the beagles' food, and was back in the air-freshened, floral-print femininity of Foxglove Cottage with Anthea. 'Mummy forgot to get him any Butcher's Tripe, so she fed him on cat food. No wonder he farted throughout their romantic candlelit dinner, just like the bombardment in Iraq. Any minute you'd expect Oriana Brett-Taylor to pop up announcing Breaking Wind.'

Paris laughed. He loved Dora in this mood.

'Now Mummy's threatening to have him castrated because he growls at Stancombe. She's longing to give him away,' exploded Dora, 'so I must go home again next weekend and sort it. I feel so guilty deserting Bianca. She's too proud to go home and I won't be around to protect her from Cosmo.'

I'd protect her, thought Dicky wistfully.

'Poor Bianca's jealous because Taggie and that murderous brute Xavier are getting on so well with Feral.' Grabbing hymn and prayer books, Dora handed them to Paris and Dicky. 'Bianca loves Feral so much and he never rings or texts her.'

Not by a flicker of expression did Paris betray how interested he was.

94

Bianca was indeed miserable. Joan continually hassled her to work harder and she desperately missed Rupert and Taggie and the cosseting at Penscombe. In the past, she had flirted with everyone but escaped in the evenings; now there was nobody to shield her from Jade's bitchiness or Cosmo's lust. So many parents were splitting up. If Taggie and Rupert weren't getting on they might be next. Cruellest of all, Feral had never got in touch.

The following Friday, smelling baked cod which she detested, Bianca decided to skip lunch and wander down the pitches. She had been slightly cheered by an excellent dancing lesson and intimations that she might land the part of Cinderella in the Christmas ballet. Most of the trees were bare now, but the beeches still hung on to a few orange leaves, reminding her of the towering wood behind the house at Penscombe. Feeling the familiar crunch of beech husks beneath her feet, overwhelmed by homesickness, Bianca decided to bury her pride and go home tomorrow. Turning two cartwheels, she started practising dance steps.

Paris, who'd been stalking her like a deer-hunter for days, never revealing his presence, had watched her setting out with that dancer's strut, feet in flat pumps turned out. She was the one everyone wanted: how satisfying to snatch the prize – particularly from Cosmo.

As she reached Badger's Retreat, where smaller trees were protected by larger ones, leaves were still falling. Laughing, shrieking, dark hair escaping, Bianca bounded about trying to catch them like some rite of autumn. Swinging round to catch a red, wild cherry leaf, Bianca caught sight of Paris.

Smiling, she showed no fear.

'What are you doing?' he asked.

'Every time you catch a leaf, it gives you a happy day.' Reaching out, grabbing a dark brown ash frond, she thrust it into his breast pocket. 'Seven leaves. That'll give you a happy week.'

Paris just stared with those light, utterly focused eyes, exciting and unnerving her, lean jaw moving as he chewed gum.

'My father fell in love with my mother when he saw her racing around catching happy days for him.' Bianca snatched a falling yellow hazel leaf and shoved it in his side pocket. 'Daddy kept all the leaves, but felt he was too old and wicked for Mummy. He'd had billions of women before her, like you've had' – she peeped up at Paris from under a thicket of black lashes – 'but Mummy persisted and they've been happy for almost eighteen years – at least they would be if she hadn't taken this stupid job and Daddy wasn't taking this stupid GCSE. So stupid of Feral to say I was out of his league.'

She kicked a red spotted toadstool, did a pas de chat and fell into Paris's arms. Glancing down he saw the despair in her eyes.

'I'm not out of your league, am I?'

'Totally' – Paris spat out his chewing gum – 'but I don't care.'

Once he'd kissed her, she was lost. Scrabbling to remove his school tie, tugging at the short end, she nearly throttled him.

'Lemme do it.' Paris yanked off his own, then hers, then unbuttoned her shirt, pulling her down on a dry, crackling bed of yellow sycamore leaves, black-spotted like leopard skin.

Like both Feral and her father, he had laid so many girls – in the open air, in parks at dusk or on banks in the gardens of care homes – but none as delicately desirable as Bianca as she beamed up at him in ecstasy, her face the same soft shiny umber as the ash frond she had given him.

As he peeled off her tights and knickers, he could smell her body, already hot and excited from dancing and even more so from him.

'D'you really want it?'

'Oh yes, definitely yes.'

Her tiny clitoris was hard as a ball bearing; below lay a buttery sticky cavern, measureless to man and terrifyingly narrow.

'I don't want to hurt you.'

'You won't, you won't.' Then as Paris produced a condom, 'We don't need that, my period's due tomorrow.'

'Better be safe.'

'Well, I'm not going to be sorry.' Unzipping his trousers, she released a cock hard and white as ivory.

'Why isn't it green like one of Mrs Sweetie's courgettes?'

Paris gave a gasp of laughter. 'Shut up.'

'Please, please go on,' begged Bianca, writhing against his lovingly stroking hand as it travelled down her belly, up the insides of her thighs, sliding into her pubes, fingering, stoking, slowly bringing her to ecstasy. 'Oh pleeeeese.'

For a second his cock buckled at the entrance, then straightened.

'Ouch, ouch,' cried Bianca, 'oh bloody ouch.'

Blokes were supposed to recite something boring to stop themselves coming. Paris had been learning the Latin verb *vastare*, to lay waste, but he only reached the future perfect third person singular when Bianca's sleekness and tightness overcame him; three more stabs and it was over.

'I am so sorry,' he muttered.

'Thought you didn't do "sorry".'

Paris slowly opened his eyes to find her laughing up at him.

'I was dying to lose it. Goodbye, virginity.'

Paris wriggled free, falling back on the leaves, ashamed of having come so quickly.

'I'll do it properly next time.' A year ago he'd have said 'proper'.

'When did you get that tattoo?' said Bianca, fingering the Eiffel Tower on his shoulder.

'When I was ten. Saved up my pocket money for a year, sneaked out of the home. Once it was done, nothing they could do.'

Bianca leant up on her elbow, pushing the straight blond hair out of those pale unblinking eyes. 'Do I look like a mature woman of experience?'

'You look beautiful.'

But as the light filtering through the remaining leaves fell on her warm brown skin, her thick dark lashes (such a lovely contrast to her white teeth and the whites of her eyes), Paris was suddenly and agonizingly reminded of Feral, whose great love he had just stolen.

Sitting up, Bianca examined herself.

'I don't seem to be bleeding much. Dora reckons she's ridden such a lot she hasn't got a hymen any more.' Bianca giggled, then squeaked, 'Oh my God, Dora!'

'What about her?' Paris dried Bianca with a handful of leaves.

'She loves you so much.'

'Well, I don't love her. I like her when she's outrageous and funny, but when she hangs around like a kicked spaniel, she does my head in. I don't need a dog, I've got Northcliffe . . .'

He could see the athletics team pounding towards the all-weather track.

'Will your dad horsewhip me?'

'He mustn't know.' Bianca looked aghast. 'I don't want anyone to know – not Feral. Although he probably wouldn't give a stuff. I've just slept with the best-looking guy in the school, and I don't want Jade or Amber scratching my eyes out, or Dora ringing the *News of the World*.'

'Or Cosmo challenging me to a duel,' agreed Paris, tugging on his trousers and buckling the leather belt Dora had given him. ' "Twere profanation of our joys To tell the laity our love." '

'What's that?'

'Some poem.'

'You'll have to help me with my homework, now Dora won't – well, may not want to any more.'

Dora, Bianca reflected, had listened and listened when she'd been miserable about Feral and her mother and boarding. Dora had helped her endlessly with homework, acting out poems so Bianca would remember them. Last week it was one called 'Death the Leveller', and Dora had thrown her riding hat and Bianca's baseball cap down the Boudicca's stairs to illustrate:

> Sceptre and crown
> Must tumble down,
> And in the dust be equal made.

'I feel a pig. What an extraordinary tree' – Bianca patted the trunk – 'all writhing together like dancers.'

'Hengist calls it the Family Tree,' said Paris. 'Look, he, Sally and Oriana have carved their initials on the bark, symbolizing a family clinging together against winter and tempest,' he added bitterly. 'Oriana's supposed to be coming home for Christmas, so Emlyn will be happy again.'

'Talking of families,' said Bianca, testing the water, 'I was going to ring Mummy and ask if I could go back to being a day girl.'

'Don't!' snarled Paris, taking her face between his hands, for a second betraying his need for her. 'Just don't.'

'I'm not going to.' Bianca flung her arms round his neck, kissing him, until her heart was beating louder than the pounding footsteps of the athletics team.

'You're my boyfriend now, aren't you, but above all, we mustn't hurt Dora.'

95

Christmas approached. The erection of Stancombe's Science Emporium seemed to be taking for ever. General Bagley and Denmark, their view of the Long Walk impeded, rose out of a sea of mud. Dulcie spent a lot of time with the builders, who brought her a little wheelbarrow so she could help them. Progress, however, was repeatedly held up by the Lower Fourth doing moonies at the builders from the fire escape.

'Rubble, rubble, toil and trouble,' sighed Hengist.

Poppet Bruce, who was pregnant again, said there was no way she would curtsey to the Queen if she opened the emporium.

'I wish Rupert wasn't taking this GCSE,' grumbled Jupiter. 'He's always working and he's getting even more left wing than Mrs Bruce.'

'He's so seriously stuck into *Macbeth*,' warned Hengist, 'he'll knife you in your bed and take over the Tory Party.'

Nothing could dim Hengist's high spirits. The end of term was nigh and so was his darling Oriana, who was due to arrive at Bagley in time for Christmas and stay at least a week.

Janna's end of term had been a great success, with trips to the pantomime and a carol service at the cathedral, where Kylie Rose had sung 'Mary's Boy Child'. On the last day, the food technology candidates helped cook a glorious Christmas lunch, ending up with more carols, mulled wine, mince pies and every boy in the school trying to manoeuvre Taggie under the mistletoe hanging in reception.

Driving home through the twilight, seeing a fuzzy newish moon like a little pilot light, Janna turned on the car radio to find a voice of exceptional beauty singing 'See Amid the Winter Snow' and burst into tears. She'd thrown herself so wholeheartedly into Larks High, she hadn't given herself time to mourn the loss of Larks Comp or of Hengist, or even her sweet mother, whom she always missed most at Christmas. It was probably exhaustion and still not having a man in her life and wild jealousy of Oriana, because Hengist and Emlyn were so excited about her return.

Among her post on the doormat, however, was a letter from Sally. 'Darling Janna, If you're not busy we'd simply love you to join us for Christmas dinner. Oriana's home and we need some bright attractive young to amuse her. Black tie for the chaps so do dress up. So hope you can make it. Love, Sally'.

Hardly pausing to open a tin for Partner, Janna shot next door to find Lily making fudge and salted almonds.

'Sally B-T's asked me to Christmas dinner.'

'Well, that's very nice, you must go.'

'But I was coming to you.'

'Never mind, you can come on Boxing Day. It'll be fascinating for you to meet Oriana.'

Relieved to see Janna, who'd been very near the edge recently, looking ecstatic, no doubt at the prospect of seeing Hengist again, Lily was too kind to say she and Christian had already refused Sally's invitation to Christmas dinner because they didn't want to desert Janna and Feral.

'Sally said dress up.' Janna glanced at herself in Lily's kitchen mirror, hardly able to see her reflection for photographs of General slotted into the frame. At least her fringe covered her eyebrows now, and Rowan had had a whip-round and the staff had bought her a day of pampering at the local health spa. What could she wear to win Hengist back? But she mustn't think like that, it was so kind of Sally to ask her.

'Naughty Dora's given me a Christmas hamper full of pâté, plum cake and some lovely red,' announced Lily. 'Shall we have a glass now? The end-of-term party was fun, wasn't it?'

'Lovely. Amazing how the Golden Oldies have mellowed; Skunk's so loyal to Larks High he even snogged Basket in the store cupboard.'

'The nicest sight was Xav dancing with Aysha,' said Lily, who was rootling around for a corkscrew, 'so happy, both of them. You'll never guess what Christian has got Feral for Christmas: two tickets for an Arsenal match.'

'Lovely,' said Janna, who wasn't listening. 'Do you really think I should go?'

'You will anyway,' said Lily.

Sally had in fact invited Janna because, a week before

583

Christmas, Oriana had rung and dropped the bombshell that she'd be bringing her producer Charlie Delgado with her for Christmas.

Sally couldn't help bring thrilled as she asked Alison Cox, their housekeeper, to make up the bed in the spare room. She'd always known that Emlyn wasn't the answer for Oriana – too chippy and the wrong class; things like that grated in the end. Emlyn also seemed to have been seeing a bit of Janna recently, so with any luck he wouldn't be too upset about Charlie Delgado.

What a shame Christian and Lily couldn't join them. Christian, she knew, was anxious to have Oriana as a guest on *Buffers* and was longing to hear about the war in Iraq. It was a tragedy too that Artie Deverell couldn't make it. Artie and Oriana loved each other, and he had such a wonderfully emollient effect on both her and Emlyn and could discourse on any subject. But Artie and Theo had decided they needed some sun and taken off to Greece together. Nor could Ian and Patience, who had both daughters staying, make it, so in the end it would be a cosy family party: Janna and Emlyn, Charlie and Oriana, herself and Hengist.

Sally went to the present drawer and found Charlie some cufflinks, English Fern aftershave (which was liked even by men who regarded scent as sissy), David Hawkley's lovely translation of Catullus in paperback, and a jokey yellow silk tie decorated with pink elephants from Elaine.

Sally had been feeling tired, what with all the presents and parties to organize and over a thousand cards now slotted into the drawing-room books in a huge patchwork of glitter and colour, but the prospect of Charlie Delgado had given her a second wind. Not that she was a snob, but Oriana Delgado had a nice ring to it. Although, knowing Oriana, she'd keep her maiden name.

Emlyn, who'd been told in a very casual way that Oriana was bringing some workmate, was getting increasingly twitchy and poured his heart out to Artie on the eve of his and Theo's trip.

'I don't know what she feels any more. She's always been a workaholic, but in the old days she always found time for me and we had fun together. Now I see her on TV growing harder and more glittering. She never answers my emails and puts herself out of communication – as though she and her mobile are both switched off. I'm sure she's got someone else.'

'Only Mungo and the desire to compensate for his death. If he'd lived, she could have shown how much in everything she excelled him. What's she like in bed?'

'Like playing Rachmaninov Three on a soundless piano.

Pouring out love and emotion to no effect somehow. I teach lovesick schoolboys; I don't want to act like one.'

'Sorry to desert you, dear boy, but Theo needs to get away – he wants to see Attica.'

'For a last time?'

'Probably. Poor Paris. He loves Theo and Theo's so desperate not to abandon him. When are you going to Wales?'

'Tomorrow and driving back on Christmas Day.'

On Christmas morning it started to snow, just a few flakes drifting down; by five o'clock it had settled, but Hengist couldn't. He was playing Charpentier's *Oratorio de Noël*, which had reached the jolly jiggy tune of the shepherds on their way to the stable. The house looked ravishing, filled with crimson roses, flame-red amaryllis and white candles everywhere. Holly and pine branches were banked in corners. The whole house smelled divinely of jasmine, pine, orange zest, beeswax and the heady sweet scent of Sally's indoor hyacinths, waxy white and pink flowers rising out of their mossy earth. In the hall, the blond head of the fairy on the top of the Christmas tree touched the vaulted ceiling.

Hengist and Sally had opened their presents earlier. They had so many, and they didn't want to embarrass Charlie Delgado who would have so few. So many of the cards had congratulated Hengist on his wonderful reporting of the World Cup. He still had a dark tan and had not come down to earth. He had managed to get a signed photograph of Jonny Wilkinson for Dora.

He had already received ten copies of Martin Johnson's autobiography and five copies of Lynne Truss's book on punctuation and a digital camera, on which he had just photographed Elaine in an emerald-green paper hat watching a squirrel raiding the bird table, whose roof was already covered with snow three inches thick.

Newspapers kept ringing up for his reaction to Saddam's arrest – pity, strangely – and for his New Year's resolution. To get stuck into his biography of Thomas and Matthew Arnold, vowed Hengist.

Sally had given him an 1867 first edition of Matthew's poems, which included 'Dover Beach', 'Rugby Chapel' and 'Thyrsis'. 'Ah, love, let us be true To one another!' read Hengist. 'And we are here as on a darkling plain . . . where ignorant armies clash by night.'

Sally should have been washing her hair but, ever conscientious, was scrabbling round in old address books to reply to a card from a cook who had left ten years ago. Hengist was therefore delighted to welcome Dora, who'd turned up to waitress, and gave her a glass of champagne.

Dora then told him about lunch at Randal's. 'Dicky got drunk, kept mistaking Randal's furry cushions for cats and apologizing to them. Mummy and Randal are now at home, offering most surprisingly to dogsit. Probably because they want a good bonk.'

After taking a frantically over-excited, capering Elaine for a run in the snow and failing to teach her to catch snowballs, Dora retreated to the kitchen to help Mrs Cox. She had great hopes of tonight. Oriana was a huge star since Iraq. Several newspapers were interested in any titbit about her. Dora couldn't believe her luck when Mrs Cox, who had never really warmed to Oriana and who was utterly devoted to Emlyn, let slip in her indignation that Oriana was rolling up with a new man.

Concentrating on washing up saucepans, Dora didn't reveal how fascinated she was, particularly when Sally breezed in, wet hair in a towel, to check the goose was browning and to remind Coxie that the roast potatoes in their goose dripping should go in at seven-thirty.

'That smoked salmon pâté is delicious, Mrs B-T.'

'I'm glad, Dora. There's plenty of food in the fridge if you're hungry,' suggested Sally, noticing that the parsnip purée and the bread sauce, as well as the salmon pâté, were pitted with Dora's finger marks.

To distract her, Dora said she'd dropped in on Patience and Ian on the way. 'Dulcie's so sweet, she asked me if I was going cattle singing.'

'I'd like a grandchild just like Dulcie,' said Sally.

'I'd like a mother just like you or Mrs Cartwright.'

Sally had written people's names on little cards decorated with holly and mistletoe.

'Shall I put them round the table?' offered Dora. 'You'll catch cold if you don't dry your hair.'

'That's kind. Janna on Mr B-T's right, Emlyn on my right,' said Sally.

'Hengist, Sally, Janna, Oriana, Emlyn, Charlie,' read Dora.

In the shadows of Hengist's study, she switched on her mobile. 'Oriana's got a new boyfriend coming called Charlie,' she murmured. 'I'll keep you posted. So pants for Mr Davies.'

Out of the window, the snow was still falling, transforming the laurels into an army of lop-eared white rabbits.

'She's here, she's here!'

The crunch on the gravel was softened by the snow. Oriana wriggled out of the dark green Peugeot, gathering up parcels and pashminas, a bunch of red freesias between her teeth like Carmen.

'Hi, Mum.'

Oriana had never been a cuddly child, arching her back to wriggle out of every embrace. Now she rested first in Sally's, then in Hengist's arms, pressing her smiling red lips to their cheeks. Softened and glowing as never before, she took Hengist's breath away.

'Hi there, Coxie.' She hugged a startled Mrs Cox before handing her a squashy, scarlet-wrapped present.

'Here's yours, Mum and Dad, Charlie'll be here around eight-thirty. The house looks glorious – I'm so used to New York minimalism and neutral colours . . . and that's new, and that too!' She paused in front of a John Nash of weeping ashes, then a William Nicholson of a child and a dog asleep in a haycock. 'Lovely, both of them.' Then, peering into the dining room: 'That green wallpaper's great.'

'Show's how long you've been away,' said Sally.

From a dark corner of the hall, Dora took pictures on her mobile.

'Who's coming tonight?' asked Oriana.

'Just a very small party. You are staying for a bit, aren't you, darling?'

'Well, at least till the New Year, if that's OK. I want to show Charlie the West Country,' said Oriana, running upstairs to her old bedroom.

'Oh, how lovely you haven't changed anything, except for that sweet little blue chair.' Fingering the Christmas roses and snow-drops in a vase on the dressing table, she said, 'You do know how to make things pretty, Mum.'

She must be in love to be so complimentary, thought Sally.

Hengist gasped when Oriana came down a good hour later. Her slenderness was enhanced by a sleeveless dark brown velvet dress, split to the thigh to show off long greyhound legs and very high heels. Her short spiky hair was softened by pearl drop earrings and, for Oriana, a lot of eye make-up, blusher and scarlet lipstick. She reeked of familiar scent.

'You look absolutely gorgeous, darling.'

She must be bats about this Charlie. Where the hell did that put poor Emlyn?

'Can I take a photograph of you and Mr Brett-Taylor?' asked Dora, sliding in with a champagne cocktail on a silver tray.

Before long, Oriana reverted to being as spiky as her hair.

'You've obviously been fundraising,' she told Hengist. 'Place looks more like a country club than ever, I nearly got lost on the way in. What are you teaching at the moment?'

'First year,' said Hengist, unstoppering the whisky decanter. He intended to get gloriously drunk this evening.

'Hardly extending yourself.'

'It's a very good way of acquainting oneself with a new intake, and, quite frankly, teaching is something I do in my spare time these days.'

Then he tried to tell Oriana about Paris and the brilliant poem he'd written about England winning the World Cup, because for once David (Jonny Wilkinson) and Goliath (Martin Johnson) were on the same side. But he soon realized Oriana was interested neither in Paris nor the World Cup: 'It wasn't reported in the States; it was irrelevant on a global scale!' nor in him fulminating about the dumbing down of the GCSE history syllabus, which now included the restoration of historic houses and the producing of television documentaries.

'The aim is to make it more vocational, Jesus! They're even talking of combining history and geography as one subject. It's madness.'

Noting Oriana yawning, probably jet-lagged, Hengist put another log on the fire and switched to Iraq.

'Seeing Saddam's statue pulled down reminded me of Ozymandias, "round the decay Of that colossal wreck". But I felt unaccountably sorry for the poor sod when he was arrested. Looked as though he'd been sleeping rough outside the Savoy. What's going to happen about Iran?'

'Oh, please don't interrogate me, Dad. We've got all next week, I just need to unwind.'

'Sorry.' Hengist patted her rigid shoulder. 'I'm just so proud of you. Wonderful if you could talk to the school about Iraq, you've got such a fan club here.'

But Oriana was rearranging her spikes in the mirror, a muscle rippling her flawless jawline. She's hellishly nervous, thought Hengist, as he put on a CD of carols sung by his old college choir.

96

Sally knew Oriana was home because her bedroom had been ransacked for tights, shampoo, dental floss; Beautiful had been left unstoppered, Hengist's aftershave ditto. Toothpaste lay like patches of snow in the basin, towels all over the floor. The hair-drier, still plugged in, was on the carpet. Favourite pearl drop earrings were missing from her jewel case.

Sally smiled and put on sapphire earrings instead.

'It came upon a midnight clear . . .' floated up the stairs as she pulled on a midnight-blue skirt and a turquoise frilled silk shirt. A dash of lipstick, a touch of mascara. Thank God for a good skin. Sally hoped Charlie Delgado would think her pretty. She imagined him dark-eyed and slightly Latin; perhaps he'd kiss her hand.

A second champagne cocktail hadn't cured Oriana's nerves; she glanced yet again at the clock and tried to ring someone on the remote control, then, cursing, punched out the number on her mobile.

Emlyn was the first to arrive as the grandfather clock in the hall chimed eight. He'd had a gruelling time with his mother, who was missing his father dreadfully and hinting that the only thing that would cheer her up was grandchildren. Nervous about the evening ahead, he'd done little justice to the Christmas lunch she'd spent so much time preparing. She had cried when he left. He longed to sweep her up and bring her to Bagley, but the contrast between their tiny overcrowded terrace house and the Brett-Taylors' splendour, with all the candles, crimson roses, great glittering tree and the fire leaping in the lounge, would have been hideous.

Aware his dinner suit was crumpled and his face red from lurking outside in the cold, he felt horribly bucolic compared with Hengist, whose cream shirt open at the neck showed off his tan and whose dark green smoking jacket, another present from Sally, emphasized his merry dark green eyes.

'Come in, dear boy. Happy Christmas.'

Emlyn's spirits drooped even further as Oriana ducked her head when he tried to kiss her.

'You look fantastic,' he said, addressing her lowered grey and brown streaked eyelids, then handed her a small square parcel. 'Happy Christmas.'

'Thanks, I'll open it later.'

Was she scared it was a ring?

Dora had no such inhibitions as she swept in with more champagne cocktails.

'Hello Mr Davies. Merry Christmas. What's that, a ring? Randal Stancombe gave my mother a lovely brooch, green enamel mistletoe with pearls as the berries. "Either wear it or put it in a safe," he told Mummy. Then, so she'd find out how much it cost, told her to insure it at once. So pants! Do open it.' She edged forward.

'Come on, Dora.' A grinning Hengist dragged her out of the room. 'Give Oriana and Emlyn a moment together.'

After a long pause, during which Emlyn longed to enfold and kiss the life out of her, he asked, 'How was the flight?'

'OK, except I can't get used to being recognized and pestered for autographs everywhere. It's impossible to be an observer when you're constantly observed.'

'Hasn't hurt John Simpson or Kate Adie,' said Emlyn, more sharply than he meant. 'You're a superstar now, and you look like one. Lovely dress.'

The snow had stopped and the clouds parted to reveal Orion in his glittering glory. Janna wished she could pluck him down from the skies as her escort this evening. She hadn't seen Hengist since before Stancombe caught out him and Mrs Walton. How would she feel about her great lost love? She was so nervous, she couldn't understand why her car wouldn't start until she realized she was trying to jam her seatbelt buckle into the ignition keyhole.

Her lovely day at the health spa yesterday had only made her realize, as hands massaged her face and body, how desperately she needed love in her life.

The snow was falling quietly and steadily again, blotting out caution. Hearing a scrunch on the gravel, Oriana raced to the window. It was not Charlie, but a surprisingly pretty redhead running up the steps as an icy wind blew aside a pashmina the colour of faded bracken to reveal a clinging dress in leopardskin print.

'Darling, darling, "a pardlike Spirit, beautiful and swift".' Opening the front door, Hengist drew Janna into a muscular, lemon-scented embrace. Then, when she glanced up, he kissed her on the mouth, holding her steady as she swayed in amazement and wonder. 'So nice to see you again,' he murmured. 'Have you forgiven me?'

Janna's heart leapt in hope. Did he still care for her? Then he swept her into the lounge, grabbed her a drink and introduced her to Oriana, who had Sally's delicate features but Hengist's colouring, and who, because of her courage and left-wing views, had long been a heroine of Janna's, but who was now looking at her with hostility. Particularly when Elaine, who'd hardly budged when Oriana arrived, now jumped down sleepy-eyed from the sofa to nudge and chatter her teeth in welcome.

'So pleased to meet you. I'm such a fan,' said Janna, taking Oriana's damp hand; then, turning to Emlyn: 'How are you, how was Christmas and your mum?' which made Oriana even frostier. Perhaps she'd heard Emlyn and Janna were friends.

'How's Larks?' Hengist laced her champagne with a slug of brandy. 'You've got to fill me in on everything – and how's Xavier getting on?

'Good,' he said when Janna finished telling him. 'I felt we let him down really badly. And how's the divine Taggie? Is Rupert unfreezing at all?'

It was clear Hengist was on automatic pilot, firing questions, not listening to a word, because he was trying to overhear what Emlyn was saying to Oriana. Not a lot, it seemed. Oriana, equally clearly, was trying to find out what Janna was saying to Hengist.

'How's Xav getting on?' repeated Hengist, and Janna was overwhelmed with sadness.

'Since nothing all my love avails, Since all, my life seemed meant for, fails . . .'

Emlyn looked as though he'd been turned to stone, or rather red brick.

Hengist was deploring universal ignorance again.

'Ninety per cent of secondary-school children interviewed couldn't name a single composer, and seventy per cent of them thought Churchill was the dog in those insurance ads, which is quite funny if it weren't so dreadful. Mind you, teachers aren't much better. Forty-seven per cent, according to the *TES*, couldn't name Charles Clarke as the Education Secretary.'

'They're too busy to read newspapers,' protested Janna.

'Or too out of touch to teach children,' mocked Oriana.

'Janna's head of Larks,' said Hengist.

'I thought it was about to close.'

'It did,' said Janna.

'Not entirely,' said Emlyn evenly, 'it's called Larks High now. I'm going to switch to Scotch, if that's OK, Hengist?'

The restless Oriana had just put on *L'Enfance du Christ* when Sally rushed in.

'Sorry, everyone. Mini crisis with the goose. Janna darling, how lovely you look, such a saucy dress. Emlyn dear, how nice. Hengist, look what Dora's given us, it's an American greyhound calendar, with different photographs of greyhounds for every month.'

Armed with her camera and following Sally into the room, Dora said, 'February's has such a look of Elaine, and April's the spitting image of my father's dog, Grenville, who lives with my sister now, and November's just like Maud who— Smile please, Janna and Mr Davies, and er, Miss Brett-Taylor.'

Headlights shone into the room. There was another crunch on gravel.

'Can you answer the door, Dora?' said Hengist to shut her up, but Oriana had already flown from the room, past the banks of holly and pine, past the white candles and the crimson roses, letting in a blast of icy air before falling into Charlie Delgado's arms.

'Oh, thank God you're here.'

'How's it going?'

'Hairy, but I'm safe now.'

'You are. Now I'm here.'

'So good you've already changed. Let's get your stuff out of the car.'

Two minutes later, with shouts of laughter and excitement, they came back into the house. Charlie's arms were now full of presents and, carrying coals of fire to Newcastle, a huge bunch of crimson roses. Oriana dropped Charlie's very smart suitcase in the hall.

'Come and meet everyone.'

Dora emerged from the shadows and shot back in again in a state of profound shock. For Charlie Delgado was around five foot eleven, lean, raven-haired, lynx-eyed, handsome, wearing an exquisitely cut dinner jacket and very, very female.

'My God.' Hengist's hand flew to straighten his tie and smooth his hair.

Next, thought Janna wearily.

'Oh dear,' said Sally gaily, 'I've screwed up the numbers. Give Charlie a drink, darling, and take her up to the spare room.'

'Oh no, Charlie'll be sleeping with me,' announced Oriana.

97

It was as though a suicide bomber had blown the conviviality of the party to smithereens. An evening of excruciating embarrassment followed.

Dora put her head back round the door, eyes on stalks, and belted off to tell Coxie.

Oriana filled up a glass for Charlie, and was just about to take her upstairs when Hengist said, 'Mummy'll take her,' and dragged Oriana into his study, where neither of them noticed Dora's charging mobile.

Like some outer Mongolian warlord, Ghengist Khan no less, Hengist's eyes had narrowed to slits in his furious brown face.

'What the fuck are you playing at?'

All the radiance had drained out of Oriana. Unfazed by snipers or Scud missiles, she now looked white and utterly terrified.

'I didn't know how to tell you.'

'You could have bloody well tried.'

'I'm gay, Dad. I'm sorry I can't marry Emlyn and provide you with the son who'll play for England.'

'Don't be fatuous. Have you told Emlyn?'

'Not yet. I've never really fancied men.' She was trembling violently. 'I've been so unhappy about it.'

'For Christ's sake, it's just a phase. Scores of people are bisexual.'

'Not me. You and Mum wanted me to be a boy so I guess I tried to please you.' When Hengist opened his mouth to protest: 'No, let me finish. I walked into the Palestine Hotel in Baghdad in April; Charlie was at the bar. Another journalist introduced us. Charlie just stared at me, then said in that glorious deep voice of hers, "Why are you so late?" "What d'you mean?" I stammered.

594

"I've been waiting all my life for you," she said. "I knew the moment you walked into the room."'

Oriana collapsed on the red leather fender seat.

'It was the *coup de foudre* for both of us; we've been living together ever since. I wanted to tell you, Dad.'

'You could have found a better time to do it. Poor Emlyn.'

'I know. But don't think it's been fun.' Having reeled on the ropes, Oriana was beginning the fight back. 'Usually when people announce they've met Mr Right, the champagne comes out and everyone starts ringing round the family. We don't get any of that. No engagement in *The Times*, only being brushed under the carpet and an awareness of murdering one's parents' happiness. I can't help my sexual orientation.'

Through the open curtains, the snow was covering the past, stifling feelings.

Hearing voices, Hengist said, 'We better go back and cause as little hurt as possible.'

Oriana scuttled upstairs.

Next door, Emlyn had turned grey, megalithic, anguish carved on his face. Janna tried to comfort him, but it was like offering junior aspirin to an elephant with a spear through its heart.

Sally, having returned from upstairs, looked equally stunned.

'I'm so sorry.' Janna found herself hugging her. 'I'd better go.'

'No, please don't, we need you,' begged Sally, then lowering her voice: 'It isn't so big a thing.'

Next moment Hengist walked in, also pale, but totally in control, and he put an arm round Sally's shoulders.

'More drinks all round, I guess,' and he poured champagne for Sally and Janna and much darker whiskies for himself and Emlyn.

'I'm afraid our daughter's "come out".'

'Poor Emlyn,' gasped Janna.

'Poor Sally,' snapped Hengist.

They were then joined by Charlie and Oriana, with all her lipstick kissed off.

'Mrs Brett-Taylor, you are so kind,' cried Charlie. 'I've just opened my gifts. These cufflinks are so neat, look' – she shot out her silken ivory cuffs – 'and I'm wearing the perfume, it's delightful.' She held out a wrist for Sally to smell. 'And this is so appropriate.' She waved the pink elephant tie. 'From what Oriana tells me about Brett-Taylor hospitality, I'll be seeing pink elephants of my own in a day or two, and finally Catullus is one of my favourite poets, and translated by Lord Hawkley. He came and lectured us at Smith.'

'"Let's live and love, my Lesbia,"' muttered Janna, who was

starting to get drunk and lippy. ' "Heed not the disapproval of censorious old men," ' and received a filthy look from Oriana.

'I've brought you some bottles of fine wine,' went on Charlie.

Dora, snapping away on her telephone camera, was livid when Hengist gave her twenty pounds and told her to buzz off.

'How are you going to manage? Coxie can't wait on her own, she was hoping to put her feet up with a plate of goose and *The Wizard of Oz*.'

'Go on, hop it.'

Dora rushed off across the snow to the Old Coach House.

'Guess what, Oriana's a lesbian; she's turned up with a tall woman called Charlie. They're sharing a bed, imagine them licking each other, it's so pants.'

Ian and Patience, who'd had several drinks after a gruelling day with Paris, had great difficulty not laughing.

'Shall I go and cheer him up?' asked Dora wistfully. 'Oh well, I'd better toboggan home.'

Charlie proceeded to dominate the conversation. She had spent six years teaching English at Smith before going into television on the news side. She had been everywhere and knew everyone. She was also a know-all, decided Janna, although it might have been to impress the Brett-Taylors.

She immediately recognized *L'Enfance du Christ* on the record player but, on picking up the CD cover, said she preferred Sir Colin Davis's version with Janet Baker singing Mary.

The mistletoe hanging in the hall on the way into dinner was an excuse for a little lecture on druids gathering it by moonlight.

'Mistletoe was alleged to cure infertility,' continued Charlie, 'ill humour and offer protection from lightning.' Then, tucking her arm through Oriana's: 'There should have been some hanging in the Palestine Hotel the night we met.

'Omigod.' She clapped her hands as she entered the dining room. 'How glorious.' Yet the scarlet napkins, crimson roses and army of white candles lighting the room and casting a sheen on the frozen snow outside seemed less suited to the mood of the evening than the dark jungle wallpaper.

Glancing at the place cards, Sally wondered if Charlie ought now to be on Hengist's right rather than hers, particularly as Emlyn was on her left, glowering like some huge cliff face across at Charlie, who was unfolding her red napkin like a matador and banging on about the New York apartment.

'Oriana and I have kept things neutral. Then we can vary the look by adding cushions and throws.'

'We've done the same at my school,' piped up Janna. 'Alas the boys do most of the throwing.'

But Charlie had been sidetracked by a lovely Nevinson of Battersea Power Station, opal smoke drifting in the morning sun, which had been recently hung on the wall opposite.

'Although I prefer the gritty realism of Nevinson's war oeuvre. Oriana, like him, is a war artist. The tautness and poetry of your daughter's reportage, Hengist and Sally, will become TV classics.'

'Oh Charlie.' Oriana blew her a kiss.

They're bitches. Poor Emlyn, thought Janna furiously. How could they chatter away as though everything was normal?

Hengist, who never squandered an opportunity to work a room, was quizzing Charlie about the American political scene, which he and Jupiter were busy cracking. Who were the movers and shakers? Charlie dismissed most of the ones he knew as right-wing bigots.

The first course of smoked salmon mousse and poached scallops was delicious but the latter were definitely undercooked, like eating chunks of female flesh.

Emlyn gagged and put his knife and fork together, suddenly overwhelmed with longing for his wise kindly father, who'd so disapproved of any link with the Brett-Taylors. What was he to do? He could hardly challenge Charlie to a duel. And how did you compete for a woman with another woman, who was so self-assured, so smart and who looked so much better in a dinner suit and her own skin than you did yourself? Emlyn drained his glass of Pouilly-Fumé and poured another one.

Charlie was a slow eater, because she talked so much, which was a good thing, because Coxie was so incensed to be abandoned that she refused to do much waiting.

Oriana and Sally helped her in with the goose, parsnip purée, roast potatoes, sprouts and bread sauce. As Hengist began carving, Elaine sidled round the table, dark eyes bright and loving in anticipation of goodies. On learning her name, Charlie launched into Tennyson:

' "Elaine the fair, Elaine the loveable, Elaine, the lily maid of Astolat." '

'Oh, fuck off,' muttered Emlyn.

'Pardon me?' asked Charlie, then demanded what aspect of American history Emlyn was teaching. Learning it was the Wild West, she hoped Emlyn was stressing the victimization of the Native Americans.

'No one more than Emlyn,' snapped Janna.

'Here you are, Emlyn.' A sympathetic Coxie shoved a

huge plate of goose in front of him. 'I've given you the breast.'

And so it went on. Glasses were filled several times as candle-light etched the deepening crisis on each face. On the surface, people contradicted each other, some with passion, some with dogged authority, while everyone watched. Was Charlie revving up to ask Hengist for Oriana's nailbitten hand? wondered Janna. She had been worried about which fork to use. This lot would hardly have noticed if she'd rammed one into Charlie's arm.

The crimson roses were shedding petals on the polished table like drops of blood. Janna shivered, remembering Cara Sharpe and the scarlet anemones.

Oriana, in truth, was irritated Emlyn was behaving so angrily and gauchely. She could see Charlie was wondering how Oriana could have attached herself for so long to such a boor. Emlyn could be so funny and sharp, but every time Charlie threw him a question, he ignored it like a great vegan sea lion rejecting fish. She also wished her father were less right wing, and her mother less like a crystal lustre, tinkle, tinkle, filling in silences with inane chat.

Janna she couldn't read. She'd been convinced she was her father's latest, but from the way Janna was sticking up for Emlyn, Oriana wasn't sure.

The food was sublime. Never were sprouts more crunchy, potatoes more golden crisp and creamily soft inside, or goose more tender without being fatty. Charlie, who hadn't had any lunch, was particularly taken with the parsnip purée and had a second helping.

'It's Taggie Campbell-Black's recipe,' said Sally, who was now gazing into space.

As Charlie proceeded to annihilate the Bush administration, and make disapproving comments on 'not forgetting the starving worldwide' as more food seemed to go back on everyone else's plates than was put on them in the first place, Elaine was having a field day.

Sally, who'd been fingering the cut-glass ridges of her water glass, suddenly filled it up from the gravy boat without realizing it.

'It's my turn to clear away.' Janna leapt to her feet, stacking up the plates and grabbing Sally's glass.

In the kitchen, she found Coxie in tears and attacking the brandy.

'My dinner's ruined and poor Mr Davies.'

'It was a wonderful dinner. Everyone's upset, that's all.' Janna put an arm round Coxie's heaving shoulders as Emlyn walked in with the goose.

When she and Emlyn came back to the kitchen with vegetables and sauce boats, Janna murmured that Charlie and Oriana were fearfully anti-Bush.

'Except each other's,' snarled Emlyn.

Janna screamed with laughter, then stifled it, stammering how desperately sorry she was about everything.

Returning to the dining room with hot plates, Christmas pudding and brandy butter, they caught Oriana and Charlie in a clinch in the hall.

'Christ!' exploded Emlyn. 'Shall we unjoin the ladies?'

Ignoring him, as a further act of solidarity, Charlie and Oriana moved their chairs together, pulling crackers, putting on paper hats and giggling over riddles. Inside Charlie's cracker was a yellow whistle which she kept blowing.

Janna put the Christmas pudding on the sideboard; Hengist defiantly emptied half a bottle of brandy over it. As he set fire to it, blue flame nearly scorched the ceiling. Emlyn felt similar anger flaring up inside him: Oriana should have levelled with him. Even if there was a certain relief that it wasn't him specifically she didn't fancy, just blokes in general, her lack of response had constantly humiliated him, eroding his masculinity. He'd felt so heavy and ham-fisted, like a rhino trying to shag a gazelle.

'D'you remember how you used to put silver 5ps in the Christmas pudding, Mum?' asked Oriana.

'It was bachelor's buttons in my day,' said Hengist, scooping Christmas pudding into silver bowls, which Janna handed round.

'I wonder who'd qualify for that,' said Sally in a high voice.

Seeing she was shivering, Janna took Emlyn's seat next to her, praising the brandy butter, saying what joy her indoor bulbs had brought the children.

'How nice.' Sally attacked her Christmas pudding, then, putting her spoon down, said:

'D'you remember the time you got Elaine a doggy bag from La Perdrix d'Or, pork chops wrapped in silver foil, and forgot and put it under the tree? By the time you opened it on Christmas night, it had gone orf and stank like hell.' Sally started to laugh shrilly on and on. Janna put a hand on her arm.

'It's OK,' she murmured, 'you're doing fine.'

'I haven't had much practice.'

Hengist, who'd been trying to get some sense out of Emlyn about rugger, glanced across at his wife with such concern.

She's the one he loves, thought Janna. Me, Ruth Walton, even Oriana aren't in the frame compared with her.

'Don't know why everyone goes on about Taggie's cooking,' said Hengist, 'my wife's is just as good. Let's all drink to her.'

After they'd drained their glasses, Hengist filled them up again and proposed a toast to absent friends.

'Mum,' said Janna.

'Mungo,' said Oriana bitterly.

'Dad,' muttered Emlyn with a break in his voice.

He was looking so sad, Janna poked him in the ribs with a cracker. Inside was a key ring attached to a perky little black dog with pricked ears.

'How darling,' said Charlie covetously, 'an Aberdeen terrier. My mother has one.'

'We call them Scotties in England,' said Janna tartly, 'and Emlyn's going to have it.' She dropped it into his dinner jacket pocket.

'Where are Artie and Theo?' said Oriana fretfully.

'Gone to Athens,' said Hengist, 'staying in the Grande Bretagne, lucky things. Artie's hiring a car and they're going on day trips to Corinth and Sparta.'

'Such a shame, I so wanted Charlie to meet them.'

'They're both such dear persons,' said Sally.

'Why are male couples "dear persons" and not women?' said Oriana, who was getting punchy. 'Dad's always slagging off Joan Johnson and Sabine Bottomley, but if they're men, it's fine.'

Hengist and Janna escaped with the pudding bowls.

'Save it for the birds,' he cried as Janna started to tip rejected pudding into the bin. 'Christ, what a bloody awful evening. Is that appalling Charlie going to stay behind and drink port with me and Emlyn?'

But as they returned to the dining room, the grandfather clock struck ten-thirty and Charlie, looking at Oriana with sleepy suggestive eyes, announced she was exhausted.

'Thank you so much, Sally and Hengist, for letting me invade your evening and for your wonderful gifts. If it's OK, I'll give you mine tomorrow after I've unpacked. A very merry Christmas.'

Then she kissed Sally, shook hands with Hengist and Janna and told Emlyn it was good to meet him, and turned towards the door.

'I'm coming with you,' Oriana leapt to her feet.

'No, you're not.' Emlyn grabbed her arm. 'We've got to talk.'

'Tomorrow.' Oriana winced at the exerted pressure, then, thinking her arm would snap like a wishbone: 'Oh, OK then.'

They went back into the drawing room, where neither could be bothered to bank up the dying embers.

Out of nerves, Oriana put a Christmas compilation on the CD player, hastily turning down the sound when the first track was 'O Come, All Ye Faithful'.

Emlyn watched as she idly flipped through the white invitation cards on the chimney piece, then wandered to the window, gazing out at the snow, which, growing too heavy, was sliding off branches and had bowed down her mother's beloved ceanothus to breaking point.

Snow might have fallen on the stretch of white neck between Oriana's dark hair and her brown velvet neckline. This can't be happening, thought Emlyn.

'I'm so desperately sorry.' Her voice was so low he had to move closer. 'I hadn't the guts to tell you. I thought you might have guessed. I'll always love you in my head, but not between my legs.'

'Thanks.' Emlyn helped himself to several fingers of Hengist's whisky. 'How long's it been going on?'

'About eight months. War forces people to take chances, but I just knew it was right.'

She ought to be more contrite, thought Emlyn. She has all the self-righteousness of the infatuated.

'Couldn't we be friends?' she begged.

'I doubt it, not when one's shot down by friendly fire.' As a log fell into the grate in a shower of sparks he went on, 'Hengist won't get his rugby Blue grandson now.' Emlyn removed Hengist's pale blue tasselled Cambridge cap from a bust of Brahms.

'He could.' Oriana swung round. 'Can I ask you a favour? It's a compliment really. Charlie and I want a baby.'

Emlyn caught his breath. Fuck, he'd pulled the tassel off the cap.

'Unto us a boy is born,' sang the CD player.

'Not unto us, it ain't,' said Emlyn flatly.

'It could be. I can't think of anyone in the world I'd rather have as father of my child. You're brave, loyal, funny and such a wonderful athlete.'

'And thick,' said Emlyn. 'You'd provide the brains presumably.'

'Oh, Emlyn.' If he could joke, the worst was over.

She reached out and took his hand, irresistible in her hopeful beauty. 'Daddy'd be so pleased too, he's so fond of you. Will you sleep with me while I'm here, Charlie truly won't mind, but if you can't face that, at least be the donor?' Then when he didn't answer: 'You could have access,' she added.

'You fucking bitch,' said Emlyn softly. 'I joined this school because of you, and sold my principles down the River Fleet. You

601

ruthless bloody bitch. Using your rough trade to provide hybrid vigour. No fucking thank you.'

'No need to be obnoxious,' said Oriana huffily, as though he'd refused to give her a lift to the station. 'I could easily have married you and had women on the side, taken the easy route. But Charlie and I thought about this long and hard.'

'Hardly the operative adjectives.' Emlyn's voice grew in fury. 'There is absolutely no way a child of mine is going to be brought up by a couple of lesbians.'

'Pity,' sighed Oriana, 'our gay male friends have been very supportive and are very happy to oblige. They see the bigger picture.'

'Or bugger picture – we are talking about a child.'

'Charlie would actually prefer IVF to make sure of a girl, but she knows I so want to give Dad a grandson.'

'You've had it all planned,' said Emlyn softly. 'I never, never want to see you again,' and, fumbling with the French windows, tripping over the door ledge, he stumbled off into the blizzard.

Hearing doors slamming and shouting, Hengist, who'd just seen Janna, who should not have been driving, into her car, marched into the drawing room.

Towering over Oriana, terrible as an army with banners, he roared, 'Your mother's devastated. I can't think of a crasser way of hurting her. I'm amazed you didn't announce it on television. Heartbreaking News. And what the hell have you said to poor Emlyn?'

When Oriana told him, adding that she hoped it would be some compensation to Emlyn to feel he was involved, Hengist flipped.

'How can you be so fucking insensitive?'

'You wanted a son, a grandson; I'm doing my best.'

'Not one brought up by two dykes.'

Oriana winced. 'Why are you and Emlyn so homophobic?'

'Children need a father.'

'Charlie and I love each other,' said Oriana. 'You've always surrounded yourself with children who you love more than me. You loved Mungo more than me. I'm just trying to give you another Mungo,' she sobbed.

'Don't drag Mungo into it. Get out, GET OUT, I never want to see you or Charlie again.'

Charging upstairs to her bedroom, Oriana discovered the long, lean, olive-skinned nakedness of Charlie, stretched out across the four-poster. Her high breasts and sleek flat belly would never have need of surgery. Arms on the pillow behind her head showed off armpit hair as glossy as her dark brown Brazilian. On the bedside table awaited oil for fingers that went everywhere, releasing Oriana utterly, driving her to heaven.

'Come to bed, my darling,' called out Charlie softly, then, seeing the anguish on Oriana's face, asked anxiously, 'Whatever's the matter?'

'It's a good thing you haven't unpacked yet,' sobbed Oriana, 'there's no room at this inn.'

Out on the pitches, it was as light as day. In contrast to her master's anguish, Elaine skipped and cavorted, white on white, snorting excitedly, tunnelling her nose along the snow. Hengist, who had no treads on his black evening shoes, fell over twice and heaved himself up. Reaching Badger's Retreat, he found a tall big ash had been blown over in yesterday's gale, knocking most of the branches off the east side of the Family Tree, smashing every sapling springing up around it.

Like Charlie, invading our Christmas, destroying us, he thought. A few remaining branches swung loose like broken limbs. Others were bandaged in snow. Hengist gave a howl and flung his arms round the trunk trying to hold the family together.

From now on, his sights would be set on Paris.

By the time he got home, Oriana and Charlie had departed and he was greeted by a tearful Sally, furious with him for chucking Oriana out.

'It was the way she was born, poor child.'

'Bloody wasn't. How could she treat poor Emlyn like that?'

'She loves Charlie, who was sweet when they left. She apologized and hoped she hadn't come on too strong at dinner, but she didn't know how to handle Emlyn and she was so nervous about meeting us.'

'Bollocks,' raged Hengist, 'she's as nervous as a basking shark.'

98

Dora, of course, leaked the entire story to the press, who came roaring down to Bagley, wildly interested in the coming out of Oriana.

'Of course we support Oriana,' Sally told the *Telegraph*, 'Hengist and I are naturally disappointed as we've always longed for grandchildren and feel life is easier if you have a conventional marriage.'

'If your daughter does something reprehensible,' Hengist was quoted as saying, 'you take it on the chin.'

Rupert put down *Lord of the Flies*, which he was rather enjoying, to ring Hengist to commiserate.

'Same thing happened to us with Marcus. Hell of a shock at the time. But he's very happy with his boyfriend and it didn't do his career any harm.'

Bianca was absolutely fed up with Rupert staying at home to read his set books during the holidays, which meant she couldn't slope off and see Paris. Why the hell couldn't he take up blood sports again?

Although most of the staff at Bagley were very sympathetic towards Hengist, Sally and Emlyn, there was a faction, headed by Poppet Bruce, who felt the Brett-Taylors had been a little too smug about Oriana's achievements.

Janna tried to comfort a monosyllabic, devastated Emlyn, who was outwardly stoical, thinking more of Hengist and Sally. Inwardly he identified with the Brett-Taylors' Christmas tree, which had held up the lights, the tinsel, the fairy and the coloured balls, with everyone oohing and aahing. Now the decorations had gone back into their box until next year, but the tree had been chucked out on the terrace on Twelfth

604

Night, destined for the bonfire. That's how he felt Oriana had treated him.

Somehow he had survived the beginning of term, welcoming back boys, taking lessons and rugby practice, drinking only a little more than usual, refusing to talk to the press, who nevertheless quoted him as saying: 'I feel a proper Charlie, although that's probably Oriana's role now.'

On the other hand, history mocks were never marked down more savagely. Even Boffin Brooks only got a D, while one boy ordered to run ten times down to the boathouse on frozen ground was carted off to the sick bay with a broken ankle. Emlyn was again taking no prisoners. He coped until the second week of term when he and Sally were wandering towards the lake discussing the situation.

The snow had nearly thawed. The brightest thing in the landscape was the warm brown keys of the ashes and Elaine in her red tartan coat, bounding ahead. A soft grey mist was coming down. The press, thank God, had retreated.

'I'm so worried about Oriana's career and her relationship with Hengist,' Sally was saying as she tightened her dark blue silk scarf under her chin. 'He so adores her. When you and she were together, you always made room for him, but Charlie seems to be all-consuming. I doubt, even if he came round, she'd let him back in again.

'I like lesbians,' she added firmly, 'Joan's a dear. But I just feel their chances of happiness are limited and it's more difficult to gain social acceptance because the world is so ignorant and the press is so cruel.'

Emlyn gathered up a remaining patch of snow and hurled it into the lake. 'Guys get excited by the idea, but only if it's two lush blondes on a bed and they can watch or join in. They're threatened by the reality.'

He and Sally were so engrossed they didn't notice Poppet Bruce waiting like Horatius as they stepped on to the Japanese bridge which crossed a narrow stretch of the lake. Poppet looked very cheery in a woolly hat, muffler and gumboots all in orange and, because she was pregnant, she had added a blue and orange wool cloak. She was full of her own Christmas.

'We enjoyed goat's cheese quiche for the festive meal and instead of exchanging Christmas gifts, we donated a goat to a family in Africa. I'm very excited by my latest project: swimming for Asian women.' Then, eyes sparkling with malevolent enthusiasm, she went on, 'I'm so pleased to bump into you, Sally, because I so rejoice for you.'

'Whatever for?' Searching for carp in the grey water, Sally braced herself.

'That Oriana's gay. What a thrill for you and Hengist. What a new and fascinating take it will give you on life, with particular resonance for Hengist who's so homophobic. I would urge him to have immediate counselling. As a professional, I'd be happy to oblige.'

Reading their silence as approval, Poppet turned and walked back across the bridge with them. 'What is more, I much look forward to meeting Charlie Delgado. I so admire her oeuvre. Might Oriana be prevailed on to address the Talks Society, not just about the war, but about coming out? She and Charlie could do a fascinating double act.'

They had reached the other side.

Sally, quite unable to speak, was gazing in horror at Poppet. Not so Emlyn, who was so angry, he gathered up his deputy headmaster's wife and threw her into the lake.

'It's not just Asian women who go swimming. If you were a bloke,' he roared, 'I'd smack you round the face, you insensitive bitch. And you're *not* going to rescue her.' He seized Sally's arm.

As he hurried her away, Sally reflected on life's ironies. She had been so delighted when she thought Oriana had a new man, but now, how lovingly and gratefully she'd have accepted Emlyn as a son-in-law. Furiously spitting out pond weed, Poppet swam to the bank.

Emlyn had hardly got back to his flat and poured himself a vast whisky when Alex Bruce, glasses steaming up in righteous indignation, barged in.

'How dare you chuck Poppet in the lake? You could have killed her and our babe.'

'Witches deserve drowning,' yelled Emlyn. 'My only mistake was not to do it sooner. If you come down to the lake, I'll be happy to hold you under.'

Such was Emlyn's fury, Alex backed hastily away, knocking over a chair overloaded with unopened Christmas presents.

'You're only resorting to vulgar abuse, taking it out on your colleagues, because you can't handle rejection. Oriana is clearly seeking closure.'

'Shut up about Oriana!' Emlyn drained his glass of whisky and got to his feet, his massive frame blotting out any light from the window. Next moment, he had grabbed Alex's lapels, dislodging his spectacles. 'You little weasel.'

'You'll get fired for this.'

'Good,' said Emlyn, 'I couldn't work under the same roof as

you and that vindictive cow a moment longer,' and his fist propelled Alex through the air on to a rickety sofa, sending flying piles of rugby shirts and unmarked mocks papers and face-down photographs of Oriana.

Despite a possibly cracked cheekbone and his terror of this vast, fire-breathing Welsh dragon, Alex felt a surge of satisfaction. Emlyn, with his working-class, state-school background, was an ace in the Hengist-Artie-Theo pack, because he saw good in their traditions, whereas Alex only saw evil. Emlyn was also young, left wing and progressive and so loved by parents and pupils alike that Alex feared him as an outside candidate for headmaster. His loss to the old guard would be immeasurable.

'Can I accept this as your resignation?' he spluttered.

'You certainly can, now get out.'

That day Emlyn walked straight to Janna, who took care of him. For twenty-four hours he was delirious, ranting and raving in the pits of drunken despair. It was hard to tell if the bitch he was inveighing against was Poppet, Charlie or Oriana.

Janna, therefore, hid a letter she had been amazed to receive from Oriana, which apologized for being rude.

'I'm protective towards my mother and I mistakenly thought you were after Dad. Will you keep an eye on her and on Emlyn? I really do care for him and I bungled the whole thing. Charlie sends her best. We hope to see you when we're next in England.'

Janna felt oddly comforted.

'What are you going to do?' she asked Emlyn when he finally sobered up.

'I've been screwed by the Brett-Taylors.' Emlyn gazed moodily into a cup of black coffee. 'Until Charlie rolled up, they had no real desire for me to marry Oriana. To that lot, being working class is worse than being lesbian. Fucking upper classes, fucking independent schools.'

He rubbed his stubble reflectively. 'I might go back to the maintained system; I might go and work for the Welsh Rugby Union. I dropped in on them when I was home at Christmas. They said there was always a job going. I'd like to be part of building up a team to bury England at Twickenham. But for the next two terms, I'd like to help you out at Larks, if you'll have me?'

Janna gazed at him, eyes and mouth opening wider and wider. '*Have* you?' She frantically wiped her eyes. 'It's the best news ever. Are you sure? God, we need you. They love the Brig and Pittsy and tolerate Skunk and Mates, but they worship you. The Brigadier's awesome on Nazi Germany, but he's rusty on the Russian Revolution and it'd be wonderful to have someone to referee fights and see off Ashton Douglas and just have you around.'

Hengist, by contrast, was devastated. He'd lost a marvellous master, a soulmate and a favoured heir apparent. He tried to persuade Emlyn to reconsider.

'We could always claim Poppet provoked you. None of your class has completed its coursework. Their parents are going to be livid. You can't let them down. Look at the way Janna stood by her no-hopers. What the hell are you going to do?'

'Go to Larks to help out Janna,' which didn't please Hengist one bit.

'Well, don't break her heart then. And what about our rugger teams?'

'Denzil will have to get up in the afternoon for a change.'

'Where are you going to live?'

'I've got temporary digs in Wilmington High Street, opposite Brigadier Woodford,' which pleased Hengist even less.

The pupils were equally enraged at Emlyn's departure. Posters and graffiti everywhere demanded his return. Alex was shouted down and booed in chapel and he wrongly blamed Theo when someone painted 'Ite domum' on the roof of his house.

Nor did having Boffin caringly applying rump steak to one's black eye compensate for being called 'Alex Bruise'. Alex festered as he corrected the proofs of his *Guide to Red Tape*, which was due out in June.

Poppet, on the other hand, was nauseatingly forgiving. 'Emlyn was hurting,' she told everyone, 'it came out as anger.'

Artie and Theo walked to chapel past the lake, on whose banks, as a result of the gales, twigs, branches and even ivy-mantled trees were strewn like an antler factory. The wind of change blowing out dead wood, thought Theo, with a shiver.

'How's Emlyn?' he asked.

'Resigned,' replied Artie sadly.

'Is that a verb or an adjective?'

'Both.'

'We have lost our Hector,' said Theo mournfully.

Dora leaked the story to the papers, who all came roaring back to Bagley: 'Top rugby school loses star coach'.

99

The despair of Bagley at losing their star coach was only equalled by Larks's joy at inheriting him. By blacking one of the detested Mr Fussy's eyes, Emlyn had achieved cult status and it rocketed morale to have such an attractive man round the place. Even though it was winter, the gap suddenly increased between jeans and crop tops, skirts climbed, Rowan's dark bob was highlighted for the first time, even Miss Basket, sparked up by snogging Skunk at the Christmas party, drenched herself in lavender water.

'Lovely for the boys to have a role model,' said Mags.

'I'm a roly-poly model,' sighed Sophy, who'd put on seven pounds over Christmas and now joined the netball team in the lunch hour.

Weatherwise, Emlyn's first morning was unpromising, with lowering skies and a bitter east wind sending leaves scuttling like mice across the playground. Inside, all was warmth. Graffi had designed a banner for reception showing a red dragon being greeted by a lot of larks. Pupils wandered in and out of a staffroom thick with cigarette smoke when they wanted to talk to a teacher. The purple and cyclamen-pink ball dresses worn by Pittsy and Skunk as Ugly Sisters in the staff pantomime still hung on a rail with everyone's coats. The noticeboard was thick with cuttings about Larks and a mocks timetable with a red line through it. Thought for the week was: 'Chewing gum: we're gumming down.'

Sophy had brought in her daughter, Dulcie, who was playing with Kylie Rose's Cameron and being monitored by several pupils taking GCSE child care.

Miss Cambola rushed up and kissed Emlyn on both cheeks.

'At last, we have a baritone. We aim to sing the German Requiem in the cathedral.'

At break, Taggie Campbell-Black brought in a rainbow cake she was trying out for coursework and gave Emlyn the biggest slice.

After break he gave his first lesson on the Russian Revolution: a great success, particularly when Rocky retreated once more to the cupboard at the back of the room and kept the class in fits of laughter.

Emlyn told them about the first general strike in Moscow when there was no electricity and Tsar Nicholas, in his amber room, had to read and write his letters by candlelight.

'What was he experiencing for a first time?' asked Emlyn.

'People power,' boomed the voice from the cupboard.

'Excellent, Rocky. Well done.'

Knowing their attention span was short, Emlyn moved on to the Monk with the burning eyes who had such a hold on Queen Alexandra.

'Can anyone tell me his name?'

'Omar Sharif,' intoned the cupboard.

Rocky, who liked talking to adults, wandered into the staffroom during the lunch hour.

'Get out before I kill you,' bellowed the Brigadier in mock fury as Rocky helped himself to Lily's last cheroot.

Both Brigadier and Lily, Emlyn noticed, were in fine fettle, the Brigadier arranging his teaching days to coincide with Lily's so he could give her a lift in and out.

In the afternoon, Janna went through the children's mocks papers with the Brigadier and Emlyn, expressing doubts whether any of them would manage a decent grade in history.

'If they'd been marked down as ruthlessly as they're supposed to be, they'd have been in minus figures,' she added dolefully.

'If it's any comfort' – the Brigadier patted her hand – 'Rupert Campbell-Black asked me to mark his English lit. mocks papers for him. I'm afraid I had to fail him too. In an exam, one really cannot say: "Sylvia Plath's the most fucking awful woman I've ever come across," or, "Mrs Bennet's exactly like Anthea Belvedon."'

Emlyn grinned. 'He got that bit right.'

Emlyn was keen to improve Larks's history marks but, filled with underlying rage against the whole arrogant, elitist public-school system, his ambition was to thrash them at the game at which they considered themselves invincible: rugby football. The boys at Larks were already fired up by the World Cup, so Emlyn had no difficulty in forming a rugby team, who grew markedly less enthusiastic when they had to run through the frozen water meadows before sunrise and train after school in the dark evenings. Admittedly, Emlyn jogged with them and shed twenty pounds and his gut. With his soft Welsh lilt becoming a sergeant major's roar, he had no difficulty keeping the roughest, toughest boys in order, particularly when he dropped them from the team if they didn't shape up.

Johnnie Fowler was kicked out for two weeks because he rolled up in a dirty shirt.

'You're meant to be covered in mud at the end of a game, not the beginning.'

'The washing machine's broke.'

'Go to the launderette.'

'Haven't got no money.'

'Wash it by bloody hand then.'

Emlyn's genius was to draw the most out of players, so they achieved way beyond their own and everyone else's dreams. He knew which boys, like Johnnie and Monster, to slap down and which, like Xav and Rocky, to build up. He was an expert at pin-pointing a player's weakness and finding a solution, adapting teaching to the individual. Rugby, above all, taught boys team-work and to keep their temper. As a result, flare-ups and loutish behaviour within the school dramatically decreased.

Emlyn increasingly appreciated the difficulties in getting these children through GCSE. Not that they were thick, but they were flowers planted in stony, dry, infertile soil, buffeted by winds.

'Try and speak French with your family at home,' he heard Lily urging, '*c'est très bon.*'

'Our family don't even speak in English,' said Johnnie. 'They just throw fings at each other.'

But as the weeks went by, the children gradually mastered the basics of volcanoes, earthquakes, heredity, the rise of Hitler, the Cuban missile crisis, the effect of tourism on world debt, the splitting of the atom, the circulation of the blood, the reflexes of the eye, electricity, dissecting sheep's hearts and learnt how to book a ticket in French or to go shopping in Spanish.

They had fun with geography coursework, deciding where to locate a factory.

'In Miss Miserden's front garden,' said Pearl.

'That won't mean a lot to the examiner,' said Basket.

'Well, Baldie Hyde's back garden then.'

In his coursework, Graffi wrote eloquently about how road-works in Shakespeare Lane, which ran into the Shakespeare Estate, inconvenienced people. 'Makes me late for school. Mum can't get to Tesco's. Dad can't get to the pub. Cavendish Plaza

611

can't get to their hairdressers. Randal Stancombe takes a helicopter, so the rich get inconvenienced less than the poor.'

Emlyn found the teaching much tougher than Bagley; it was like having to crank up an old Ford for the shortest journey when one had been driving a Lamborghini, but the rewards were greater, seeing understanding dawning on children's faces. Increasingly too he admired Janna, how she exhausted herself worrying about Wally's son in Iraq, Mags's premature grandchild, Mr Mates's arthritis.

She was outwardly cheerful, but he realized how near cracking up she was when, one late February morning, she wandered wailing into his history class.

'Look, look, Sally Brett-Taylor gave me these hyacinth bulbs back in October, I put them in a black dustbin bag at the back of the stockroom and forgot about them.'

Thus imprisoned in darkness, the white leaves and stems, from which sprouted tiny, colourless, misshapen flowers, had struggled to a hopelessly etiolated twenty-four inches, hanging pathetically down over the edge of their blue china bowl. Their whiskery roots had completely clogged the bulb fibre.

'They were so desperate to reach the light and flower like the children in the Shakespeare Estate,' she sobbed. 'I left them in the dark; I failed to give them water and light.'

Jerking his head towards the door to tell Feral and Co to scarper, Emlyn put the bowl on his desk and took Janna in his arms.

'It's all right, lovely, it's all right.'

'I killed them.'

'You didn't – it's only this year's hyacinths. The bulbs themselves are fine, they'll flower again next year. Look, already the leaves are turning green in the light, like your kids'll blossom because you've given them love and hope.'

To cheer her up, he took her to the new James Bond film that evening and she slept right through it.

The children at Larks had been so furious when horrible Rod Hyde won a Teaching Award in October that when a small ad appeared in the *Gazette* asking for nominations for next autumn's awards, they decided to enter Janna.

'Miss is such a good filler-in of forms, but we can't expect her to fill in her own,' said Kylie. 'Let's ask Emlyn.'

Gradually Janna became calmer and happier. It was so great to have someone to kick ass so she could concentrate on cherishing.

Emlyn was still gutted about Oriana; he missed Artie and Theo and the pupils at Bagley, but he loved the Brigadier and Wally and even grew fond of Skunk, Pittsy and Mr Mates – and they of him, because he treated them as equals, even regarding them as young enough to be roped into refereeing.

Gradually, as the almond scattered its pink blossom, crocuses purpled the emerald-green spring grass and the days grew longer, Xav's remaining fat turned to hard muscle, Monster, Johnnie and Rocky formed an impenetrable back row, Graffi, talking Welsh to Emlyn to annoy the others, and Danny, a Belfast boy, known as 'Danny the Irish', grew fleet as forwards. Feral, to crown it, was a natural, with the wisdom, the speed, the ability to pass, kick and dodge of a potential international. Like a feral cat, his eyes swivelled the whole time, assessing danger, checking where every-one else was on the field and where they were going to be in five seconds' time.

Emlyn longed to keep him for rugby, but he had made a Faustian bargain. If Feral gave him one term and a sporting chance of beating Bagley, he would put Feral on to the football map. At heart, he hoped Feral might become sufficiently enamoured of rugby to convert.

With Stormin' Norman on the sidelines yelling the heroes on, Larks was gradually transformed into a 'lean, mean, killing machine'.

100

Hengist meanwhile, aware that Bagley needed to do more to bond with the community, challenged Larks to a fun charity rugby match on the last Sunday of term.

Randal Stancombe, as Larks's increasingly self-confessed backer, immediately donated a rugby ball in gold plate, on which the name of the winning team would be engraved.

'And when you move on to your next school,' he told Janna, 'you must carry on the fixture,' murmuring that he had great plans for a new school on the water meadows below the Cathedral, 'a city academy, which you would run.'

Janna couldn't fail to be flattered and although Randal gave her the creeps since their hideous sexual encounter back in September, she had to recognize that with the £120,000, the rebuilding of Appletree and the minibus, which could now take half the school to matches or outings, he had provided fantastic support. So she smiled over gritted teeth when he popped in to show off her brave experiment to high-powered friends, hinting she'd never have pulled it off without his six figure leg-up.

Emlyn detested Randal sauntering in as though he owned the place. As if he could possibly build a school on the water meadows, when they were well below the flood plain. Randal was far more likely to flatten the Shakespeare Estate.

Nor did Randal miss an opportunity to drop in on Taggie's classes. Lady Belvedon might be the blow-job queen, but Mrs Campbell-Black was the stuff of dreams and far too sweet to patronize or put him down as Anthea often did.

'How's your hubby's GCSE going?'

'He's working very hard,' sighed Taggie.

Taggie had another admirer, Pete Wainwright, the new Larks

Rovers under-manager, a bluff, tough Lancastrian, with whom she'd been liaising over her class's coursework. As well as lunch in the director's boxes, this included a pre-match meal for the players and snacks for the crowd.

Pete Wainwright was so impressed, he was thinking of adopting Taggie's menus for the club. Taggie, in turn, was determined 'to screw her courage' (a phrase that came from one of Rupert's set books) to ask Pete to give Feral a trial.

Despite Taggie's success at work, things were not easy at home. Rupert, displaying the same competitive streak that took him to the top as a showjumper and an owner-trainer, was hell bent on winning his bet. Having ploughed his mocks, he had given up drink for Lent and incessantly mugged up his set books as hounds checked between coverts or his helicopter flew him to race meetings round Europe.

Xav seemed much happier, although in despair that Aysha, having completed her coursework in record time, had reluctantly gone back to Pakistan to meet her future husband. Xav was also panicking about the proposed match against Bagley. Would they flay him alive?

Taggie was more worried about Bianca who, on the occasions she came home, was moody and detached: the dancing sunbeam permanently hidden behind dark clouds. Over half-term she'd shut herself away in her room. On the Sunday afternoon, Taggie was wearily clearing away lunch and planning her lesson for tomorrow: 'a cake for a celebration: christening, birthday or wedding', when Bianca rushed in in tears.

'Darling! Whatever's the matter?'

'I don't want to go back to Bagley tomorrow.'

'Oh, angel.' Taggie's heart leapt guiltily: how blissful if Bianca had decided to go back to being a day girl. 'Whyever not?'

'Because I want to go back tonight,' sobbed Bianca, 'but bloody Daddy's so busy writing an essay on *Pride and Prejudice* he'll only take me first thing tomorrow morning. He says I'm obsessed with boys, like Lydia Bennet.'

With the lighter evenings, Bianca had made plans on her return to drug Jade Stancombe's cocoa, climb out of her dormitory window and run to Middle Field, straight into Paris's arms. The effort required for the two of them to be alone added frisson to their affaire. They had made love in Plover's loose box, behind the bicycle shed, in the science lab and the boathouse and had somehow escaped discovery.

Bianca adored Paris; she was reduced to jelly when their eyes met in chapel, or their hands clasped in the corridor. But she found him very difficult to talk to. He was wonderful at making love, his touch so sure and tender, but he was undemonstrative; he told her that she was beautiful, but never that he loved her. There was a detachment and cool about him that fascinated while intimidating her. He was so clever: he sent her witty text messages, wrote her poems she didn't understand and he was always reading. Bianca, who never read, liked chatting, dancing and shopping. It was also impossible to escape Dora who, like a dog suspecting its owners are about to go out, clung ever closer.

Paris had been devastated by Emlyn's departure. Rugby, such a release of aggression, had lost much of its charm. He could always talk to Emlyn, who understood the demons and anger lurking beneath the surface.

Hengist, stung by Oriana's accusations that he'd given up teaching, was now taking the Upper Fifth's history set abandoned by Emlyn. This was a revelation to the pupils because he made the subject so vivid and amusing. On one occasion, they acted out the Munich Conference. Boffin, with his supercilious, toothy face, made the perfect Chamberlain, Lubemir was Mussolini, and the nasty German diplomat demanding more and more of Czechoslovakia was naturally Cosmo.

Lessons went in a flash. Paris wanted to tape every word. You could hear the tramp of jackboots, smell the gas of the concentration camps as Hengist built up the nightmare menace of Nazi Germany.

Hengist, desperately missing Oriana, found great solace in teaching Paris. So did Theo, whose back grew increasingly painful as he laboured to finish Sophocles, but was somehow soothed as he and Paris talked long into the night, devouring the great classical writers.

Obsessed with work, Paris had less time for either Bianca or Dora, but he still went back to the Old Coach House on Sundays, shutting himself in his room to read and work and never too busy to admit Dulcie and Northcliffe, who both loved nothing better than to curl up on his bed.

Paris's over-active imagination was invariably triggered off by things he read. When a Sunday tabloid, early in March, claimed that badly abused children often torture animals and abuse smaller children, he grew utterly distraught, banishing a tearful Dulcie, pushing away a bewildered Northcliffe, terrified of harming them, before trashing his room.

Ian, under continuing pressure from Alex Bruce, was fed up with Paris and increasingly muttering about returning him to care. Only last week, when he had merely removed a leaf from the boy's hair, Paris had clenched his fists and nearly thumped him.

This terrified Patience. As Paris was doing *Macbeth* for GCSE coursework, in a desperate attempt to cheer him up and provide him with inspiration, she drove him, on the third Saturday in March, to see a Royal Shakespeare performance. Paris, who'd wanted to slope off and see Bianca, hardly spoke and listened to a tape of *Lord of the Flies* all the way there.

Poor Patience, no intellectual, was desperately tired and, despite the thunderclaps and battle din, fought sleep throughout the play. She was worried Paris minded being seen in public with such an old scarecrow and tried to keep her raucous voice down. When they went to the bar in the interval, lots of people gazed at the white beauty of Paris in his severe dark grey school suit and then at her, pondering the connection. She had ordered half a bottle of white and some smoked salmon sandwiches, cobwebbed in cellophane, and thought what a ghastly middle-class, middle-aged thing to do.

' "Screw your courage", "Is this a dagger"? We always intoned, "Out, damned spot!" when we had spots at school. *Macbeth*'s so full of quotations,' she gabbled, desperate to keep the conversation going.

Paris answered in monosyllables. Patience longed to get tanked up, but she had to drive home. Conscious of Paris's set, white face beside her on the return journey, she was filled with despair. Ian was right. It wasn't working. He clearly loathed living with them. A small voice inside her also said: He might be more grateful.

It was after midnight when they reached home, greeted by a grinning, sleepy-eyed, singing Northcliffe.

'I do hope the play didn't upset you too much,' said Patience. 'It is very harrowing and so sad at the end.'

As Paris went towards the door, she asked if there was anything about it he'd particularly liked.

'The bogs in the theatre were nice,' muttered Paris and shot upstairs.

Patience went out to check the horses, who at least whickered and were pleased to see her, even when she sobbed into Plover's dappled grey shoulder. When she finally came to bed, she found Ian in a martyred heap. 'Of course I haven't slept, I've been worried stiff about you on those roads.'

Next day was Mothering Sunday – a traditional day for children in care to go berserk because they were made so aware of not having a mother around. Remembering last year's hysterical scenes, when Paris had broken up his room yet again, screaming how he missed his mother and that Ian hated him and anyway, Ian and Patience were so old, they'd die soon and he'd be sent to another foster home, Patience steeled herself.

She'd fed the horses and, as it was a mild day, turned them out in their rugs. She was simultaneously frying bacon, grilling sausages and mushrooms and emptying the bins when Paris walked in. Grabbing the black bin bag and taking it to the dustbins outside, he dropped an envelope on the kitchen table.

He's leaving, thought Patience in panic, oh please God no, but, opening the letter with trembling hands, she found a Mother's Day card of shocking pink roses, with the words 'To a Wonderful Mother' on the front.

'Dear Patience,' Paris had written inside. 'Thank you for *Macbeth*. It was so awesome I couldn't speak afterwards. Love, Paris'.

She had to read it three times before the words swam before her eyes, then she broke into noisy sobs.

'I'm sorry.' An appalled Paris, returning, snatched the card from her. 'I didn't mean to—'

'No, no.' With one large, red hand, Patience reached for the kitchen roll, with the other she snatched back her card.

'It's the most wonderful thing that ever happened. It's just unexpected, that's all. I was worried we were old and boring and you didn't like living here.'

Paris shrugged. 'Well, I do.'

'We want you to stay with us more than anything,' muttered Patience. 'We've tried to act cool because we didn't want to frighten you or make you feel claustrophobic.'

Paris said nothing, but his normally ashen face was flooded with colour.

They were brought back to earth by the smell of burning sausages. Next moment Dulcie marched in with the little wheelbarrow given her by the builders working on the Randal Stancombe science block. Today it was full of sand.

'Those men better get their arses into gear,' announced Dulcie, 'or the building won't be fucking ready in time.'

Patience turned to retrieve the sausages and Paris rescued the bacon on the Aga, both trying to hide their laughter, which diffused the situation.

101

The match between Larks and Bagley's third fifteen took place a week later, on an unexpectedly mild evening. Unbeaten all term, Bagley regarded victory as so certain that the entire team had raging hangovers from a tarts and vicars party the night before. For those in need of succour, Cosmo, still in his dog collar, was circulating with a big brown jug frothing with Alka-Seltzer.

'Attila the Hunk can't work miracles,' he said bitchily, 'even if he does have scores to settle.'

'It'll be more than fifty–nil,' said Lando, who hadn't bothered to wash off his tart's eyeliner and scarlet lipstick. 'I've had a bet.'

Over at Larks, Xav was refusing to get on the bus.

'Please don't make me go back to Bagley,' he begged Emlyn. 'They'll lynch me for bullying Dicky.'

'Not if I'm around. You're the only player with big match experience, who knows the capabilities of the Bagley team.'

As a V-sign to Alex Bruce, who'd sacked them both, Emlyn had made Xav captain. It had been worth it to see the terror and delight on Xav's broad, normally impassive face.

Now terror predominated.

'Cosmo and Lubemir are in the team, they'll bury me.'

'Feral's the one they'll try and bury. You've got to be there for him, to stop him losing his rag. He didn't sleep last night.'

'Nor did I,' grumbled Xav.

Feral ricocheted between longing and panic. Pete Wainwright from Larkminster Rovers was coming to the match and, if impressed, might offer Feral a trial. He might also see Bianca again. Agonizing rumours had filtered through that she and Paris were an item. How could he not murder Paris?

Under his cheerful air of imperturbability, Emlyn was churning worse than his team at the prospect of returning to Bagley, 'the land of lost content', where he'd been so happy and hopeful and so hurt and humiliated by Oriana's coming out. Hengist wouldn't miss an opportunity to emphasize the good he was doing for the community, so the press would be out in force – raking things up.

Hengist, who'd combined a governors' meeting over lunch, had laid on a bar and buffet in the pavilion and buses to transport Larks supporters to the game. He had also invited local bigwigs: the Mayor and the Bishop. Ashton and Cindy who, like Randal, loved to pretend they'd been responsible for saving Larks, had also rolled up.

Ashton, eyeing up the Bagley boys, who were certainly pretty, was in fact feeling bleak. The business pages that morning had launched blistering attacks on S and C and other private companies that had specialized in education. Not only were LEAs they'd taken over not meeting their targets, but the buildings they'd imposed on schools had turned out to be shoddy, poky, taking too long to build and not able to withstand the wear and tear of children. S and C badly needed a hit.

Still, it was hard to be bleak on such a lovely evening. Crowds already thronged the touchline and, although the daffodils were nearly over, primroses starred the banks and a pale haze of green leaf softened many trees, while others were pinky roan from buds about to burst. Heavy rain earlier enhanced the jade green of the pitch.

It was even mild enough for Randal Stancombe to descend from his chopper in a new, exquisitely cut off-white suit. Still smarting from being cuckolded by Hengist, he had rolled up with Anthea Belvedon, radiant in Parma violet, with a calf-length mink flung round her shoulders and a huge sapphire ring on her right hand.

'What a ravishing fur,' sighed Vicky Fairchild.

'A gift from Randal,' said Anthea, loudly enough to be heard by Ruth Walton, who'd just arrived, flushed from lunch, in last year's Lindka Cierach. 'I didn't realize it was going to be so warm – hello, Ruth – Randal and I feel for Dicky, Dora and Jade's sake it's so important to show one's face at such functions.'

'And I'm reporting you to animal rights,' hissed Dora, feeding roast beef sandwiches to Cadbury. 'That coat is so pants.'

Alex Bruce was fuming. How dare Hengist schedule a rugby match on the same day as a GCSE science revision workshop, which no one would now attend. Even Boffin had defected and, already miked up with a silver whistle round his scrawny neck, was poised to referee the game. And how dare Hengist invite back Emlyn, who had nearly drowned Poppet?

'Ten Downing Street is deceptively large once you get inside,' Poppet, several months pregnant, was now boasting to Anthea.

Noticing Mrs Walton looking a shade disconsolate, Cosmo thrust a large vodka and tonic into her hand.

'Ever considered a toyboy?' he murmured.

Hengist, not confident of shaven-headed Denzil, who preferred any game to rugger, was himself revving up the rest of the Bagley third fifteen. 'Never take any team coached by Emlyn for granted. He'll have told them to attack and attack and that nothing matters except getting points on the board.'

'It's still going to be three hundred to nil,' grumbled Lando. 'Christ, my head hurts.'

'Here they are, here they are,' went up the shout as Randal's crimson minibus rumbled up the drive.

'Larks wouldn't still exist without Daddy,' boasted Jade. 'He's given them so much financial support.'

'Oh shut up,' muttered Dora.

Bagley, incensed by the loss of Emlyn, watched Larks emerge with mixed feelings.

'There's Graffi, still lush,' sighed Milly.

Graffi, still grinning although black under the eyes, was reeling with relief because he'd completed his ten-hour art exam earlier in the week and was happy with what he had produced.

'My God,' said Amber, cutting off her conversation with the Master of Beagles at Radley, 'is that really Xavier? He must have lost a couple of stone and grown a foot. Looks quite attractive.'

'Very attractive if one remembers his trust fund,' agreed Milly.

'Hi, Xav.'

'Hello there, Xav,' purred Jade.

'Welcome back, Xav,' shouted Amber.

'Booo!' shouted Dora, who'd been at Dicky's hipflask. 'Have you forgotten he tried to kill my brother?'

'Shut up,' hissed a discomfited Dicky, as an equally discomfited Xav belted across the grass to the visitors' changing room.

'And here comes the Larks Lothario,' shouted Amber.

A pair of black-jeaned legs, as long and pliable as liquorice, were finally followed down the bus steps by a Nike scarlet jacket and a haughty black face.

'God he's awesome,' sighed Milly.

Glancing coldly round, reluctant to take a first step on enemy territory, Feral caught sight of Bianca standing on top of a car, in a bright orange poncho, her dark hair lifting in the breeze; he started violently as they gazed and gazed and gazed at each other.

'Move it, for fuck's sake.'

From behind, Johnnie, Monster and Rocky ejected Feral on to the gravel.

Oh God, thought Bianca in panic, I still love him.

Thank God, thought Feral in ecstasy, she still loves me.

In a daze he glanced up to see if she was real, then, smiling, shaking his head, waving his hands, he reeled after Xav.

Paris, who'd witnessed this eye-meet from the home changing room, felt punched in the gut. Then he saw Janna jumping out of Emlyn's muddy Renault. At first he was shocked how tired, pale and old she looked, but when both Larks and Bagley pupils ran forward to welcome her, and her face was illuminated by that tender, joyful smile, he realized how her new, short, curly hair became her, and how protectively Emlyn was towering over her, sheltering her from the mob as it surged around them.

'Mr Davies, Mr Davies, look, it's Mr Davies back.'

Paris wanted to join the throng and beg Janna's forgiveness and friendship. He wanted to bolt back to the Old Coach House and hide. He couldn't play rugby with so many cross-currents.

'Janna, darling.' It was Hengist, hugging her and then shaking hands with Emlyn. 'Marvellous to see you both. Sally sent her apologies, she's had to go and see her mother.'

Like hell, thought Janna. Normally such a trooper, Sally had taken Oriana's coming out very badly, particularly the press delving around and raising the ghost of Mungo. Today, with Emlyn's return, they would be out in force, and she hadn't been able to face it.

'Tell her her bulbs are being miraculous,' said Janna. 'Sheets of daffodils and hyacinths, even fritillaries; they've cheered everyone up so much.'

'I will; she'll be so pleased. Come and have a drink.'

'Janna can,' said Emlyn. 'I'm going to crank up my team.'

Emlyn found his Larks players strangely silent as with clumsily shaking hands they tried to find the necks of their crimson and yellow striped shirts and zip up shorts less white than most of their faces.

'Ouch,' yelled Johnnie Fowler, as he bit the inside of his cheek instead of his chewing gum.

Emlyn smiled round, steadying them, then placed a rugby ball on the floor in front of them.

'This is your best friend, so don't give him away. He has one destiny, over the line or between the posts. Don't let them bait you, don't swear at the ref, don't spit, or bite, kill the ball, or collapse in the scrum. However much you want to, it'll only put points on the board for the other side, not for us. Watch, watch the whole time.'

Larks parents were out in force. Cigarettes slotted into their lower lips, fathers with tattoos, earrings and T-shirts, they looked so young compared with the tiny sprinkling of Bagley parents.

'S'pose you have to grow old before you're rich enough to afford fees here,' observed Graffi's father, Dafydd, who was getting tanked up with Stormin' Norman.

Pearl's boxer dad had a whole quiche in one hand and a pint of red in the other.

Pearl and Kitten, in crop tops showing off grabbable waists, their purple flares sweeping the damp grass, tossed their shining, straightened manes as they paraded up and down, giggling and being eyed up by the Bagley boys.

Randal moved around pressing the flesh, getting himself and his beautiful suit photographed as much as possible, distributing largesse to the inhabitants of the Shakespeare Estate.

'So pleased Larks is doing well; what subject is your youngster taking in GCSE?'

'Sex and violence,' quipped Dafydd cheekily and regretted it when Stancombe's face blackened and he made a note on his pocket computer.

Through the cobweb-festooned window, Xav could see everyone nudging and staring as his parents arrived. Bianca, full of chat, dragged Taggie off to the bar. Rupert, who had no desire to socialize, stayed in the car with a bottle of brandy and *Opening Lines*, the OCR poetry set book, which, after repeated slugs, he was finding increasingly difficult to understand. He'd never met such a bunch of whingers moaning on about their dreadful childhoods. He could relate to Philip Larkin or Simon Armitage stealing from his mother's handbag and punching an irritating wife, but what the fuck was this guy Stevie Smith going on about?

> To carry a child into adult life,
> Is good, I say it is not.
> To carry the child into adult life
> Is to be handicapped.

In his wild youth, Rupert had had a Rolls-Royce with black windows. He could have done with it now, to stop so many ghastly mothers waving and gazing in. Nor could he avoid seeing Taggie being welcomed by all her dreadful new friends: Pittsy and fearful stinking, whiskery Skunk and that ghastly football manager,

Pete Wainwright, who'd clearly got the raging hots for her, not to mention that fat Welshman who seemed to have bewitched Xav.

Rupert knew he was in the wrong. Since he'd decided to take this wretched exam and Taggie had proved such a hit at Larks, he'd been vile to her and ratty with the children.

Christ, she was even allowing the caretaker Wally to peck her on the cheek. Rupert was finding it as hard to climb out of his mega sulk as to break out of Broadmoor. Bloody hell, Stancombe, looking an absolute prat in his white suit, was now kissing Taggie – pity a snow plough couldn't run him over. Rupert was going to win this bet if it killed him. He took another slug.

Knowing they would expect great things, Paris observed that Ian and Patience had formed a merry party with Artie, Theo, the Brigadier and Lily.

'Larks look alarmingly fit,' grumbled Jack Waterlane as Monster, Johnnie and Danny the Irish thundered past chucking a ball to each other.

'Only because they stayed in last night,' said Anatole.

Bagley's shirts, sea blue with white collars, gave them a look of deceptive innocence. The sun, darting in and out of big white clouds, spotlit the Mansion one moment, an acid-green lime in Badger's Retreat another, Mrs Walton's laughing face as a passing Cosmo waved to her the next.

It was Larks's first glimpse of Paris for eighteen months. He had shot up and filled out, his jewellery had gone, his white blond hair, no longer gelled upwards, was longer with a side parting and, like Rupert Brooke's, poetically brushed back from his forehead. He was as dead pan as ever, but he had a new confidence. Nodding to his old classmates, but not stopping to say hello, he turned to Junior Lloyd-Foxe, yelling at him to pass the ball.

'Parse, parse,' mocked Monster.

'Lord, la-di-da,' shouted Johnnie, 'listen to the Prince of Posh "parsing" the "bawl". He's too grand for his old friends now.'

Paris ignored them, but a flush crept up his cheek.

Bagley won the toss, and chose the Mansion end, with the soft west wind behind them.

'Bagley to kick off.'

'OK, boys,' quietly Xav echoed Martin Johnson, 'let's take this game.'

'Very plucky of your lads to take on Bagley,' Poppet was saying patronizingly to Janna.

'Have you ever seen anything so gross as Boffin's bum in those shorts?' hissed Dora as Boffin blew a shrill plaintive note on his whistle.

Lando booted the ball over the heads of the Larks forwards. Next moment Feral moved into its path, caught it and set off for goal, dodging round Anatole and Lubemir, flashing his teeth at them, charging straight for the Hon. Jack, aiming for his right side, luring him on to his right foot, then bolting past on his left.

'Tackle him,' bellowed Lando, but Lubemir, hurling himself at Feral, only caught air as Feral skipped out of the way, streaking over the line, burying the ball under the posts to ecstatic, flabbergasted cheers.

'That gorilla won't kick it ten yards,' drawled Cosmo, as Rocky, having laboriously readjusted the plastic stand, finally managed to balance the ball on top of it.

'Our Farver,' mumbled Rocky and belted it over the bar to even more flabbergasted cheers.

'Very plucky of you to take on Larks,' Janna told Poppet.

'I ain't no gorilla.' Rocky marched up to Cosmo, shoving a huge fist in his terrified face.

'Rocky, no!' howled Xav.

Reluctantly Rocky lowered his fist.

'If you do that again, Rocky,' Boffin's miked voice echoed round the field, 'I shall send you to the sin bin.'

Three minutes later, Rocky leapt miles in the air in the line-out and catching the ball, passed to Xav, who passed to Graffi, who trundled down the field like a little Welsh pony, black hair tossing, slap into the Bagley defence, powering his way through them and crashing face down in the mud over the line, but with the ball staying firm between his palm and the pitch. Again Rocky converted.

'Rocky by name, Rocky by nature,' yelled the increasingly intoxicated crowd of Larks supporters.

'Steady, steady,' pleaded Emlyn, a great golden bear prowling the touchline. 'Oh Christ, well done,' as Xav kicked eighty yards up the field into touch.

Bagley rallied. Lubemir, winning the scrum, passed to Anatole, who passed to Jack, who found himself running into a solid Berlin wall of defence: Monster, Rocky and Johnnie Fowler, who brought him crashing down. Xav took the ball off him and kicked it up field, where it was gathered up by Feral, who with Ferrari acceleration charged up to the Bagley defence, their gumshields glaring, waiting to flatten him, and popped over a glorious left-footed drop goal.

As he sauntered back, festooned with cheering, thumping,

ecstatic Larks players, Miss Cambola, who'd been practising with Kylie Rose and the choir, started to sing 'Swing Low, Sweet Chariot', as, from all sides, crimson Larks banners were waving.

'That's our tune,' snorted Biffo Rudge.

Bagley were now displaying all the symptoms of nerves, losing in the line-out, high tackling, killing the ball, sledging, biting, resorting to every dirty trick. What was also plain to everyone was that Paris was out of it, passing to the wrong people or the other side, kicking in empty spaces, and when Boffin blew the whistle, first on Monster for high tackling, and then on Johnnie for swearing and spitting at Cosmo, Paris missed two easy penalties.

'Lord Posh, Lord Posh,' barracked the Larks crowd.

'Lord, la-di-da, nose in the air,' bellowed Stormin' Norman to the edification of the entire field, 'you're as useless as tits on a bull.'

Pete Wainwright laughed happily because he was gaining intense pleasure watching Feral. You could see the boy thinking, glancing around each time he had the ball, using his brain. The others mostly kicked and hoped. Xavier was playing beautifully too. It was gratifying to see two black boys working so well together, cleaning up in the white heartland of an English public school. Pete was so pleased to see the delighted pride on Xav's sweet mother's face.

'The directors loved your lunch – it was a great success,' he told Taggie.

Johnnie Fowler's mother, Shelley, swayed up to Rupert's car. 'Your Xav's playing like a little king, Lord Black.' Then, when Rupert lowered the window a millimetre: 'My Johnnie's the good-looking one, didn't go into Larks much in the old days, had a lot of days off, but since Emlyn, Taggie and the Brig's taken over, he's hardly missed a day.' Noticing how handsome Rupert was, she added, 'Would you like me to get you a drink?'

'If you're going that way.'

Seeing Rupert looking more friendly, Poppet Bruce rushed over. 'Rupert, Rupert, how's your GCSE Eng. lit. going?'

'Fine,' snapped Rupert.

'Oh! You're reading *Opening Lines*. Charisma's finding it so enriching. Each poem yielding its meaning.'

'Not to me, they don't. I can't make head nor tail of this chap Stevie Smith.'

'Oh, how priceless.' Poppet went off into peals of laughter. 'Smith's a woman, Rupert.'

'Explains why the poem's such crap.'

'Don't be so sexist. You'll never pass your GCSE that way. Why not join our workshop in the Easter holidays?'

Fortunately relief arrived in the form of Shelley Fowler and a large brandy and ginger.

'Get in,' hissed Rupert, winding up the window.

'Johnnie's got that book too,' said Shelley, picking up *Opening Lines*. 'Didn't understand a word till Janna explained it.'

Half-time. The sides gathered in two groups, towelling away sweat, swigging bottled water, pouring it over their heads. Hengist strode on to the pitch.

'What the hell are you playing at?'

'They're as tough as shit,' protested Jack Waterlane. 'I think I've cracked a rib.'

'They really vant to vin,' grumbled Anatole.

'I've fucked my ankle, sir,' lied Cosmo.

'Well, you better go off for the second half.'

Larks were down to fourteen men: Danny the Irish had cramp. Wally was working on his instep.

Emlyn was talking in a low voice to his team, praising them to the now pink and blue flecked sky, isolating individual triumphs.

'But the second half's going to be tougher; you'll be getting tired. If I sub any of you, it's a compliment, means you've played your hearts out. Rocky, you've been awesome, and Monster and Johnnie.' Emlyn's square face glowed. 'I can't tell you how great it's been, good as scoring for Wales.'

Janna, watching Emlyn's joy, felt conflicting emotions. How glorious to see Larks ascending, but she felt so sorry for Paris.

Dora's despair, on the other hand, was total. She could see Hengist giving the team hell. Poor Paris, head hanging, face concealed by a damp curtain of blond hair, must be feeling suicidal, not just about his dud performance, but about Feral and Bianca as well.

'Stop bullying him,' she shouted. 'It's so unfair.'

Cadbury, who'd been stuffing his face all afternoon, wandered off to drink from Middle Field Pond. Following him, Dora decided she must save Paris.

102

As the pep talk ended and the teams changed ends and took up their positions, they were distracted by howls of laughter and wolf whistles as a streaker came running out of Middle Field and raced across the pitch skipping and dancing, arms outstretched. Her high breasts and bottom were too small to wobble. The waist, in between, as yet lacked definition, the racing legs were still a little plump. A pale blonde triangle was just discernible between her thighs. Her face was hidden by a pulled-down baseball cap.

'Who is it? Who is it?' yelled the delighted and cheering crowd. Then, as the streaker did a cartwheel and two handstands, her baseball cap fell off, her blonde plaits tumbled out and a chocolate Labrador bounded on to the pitch after her.

'My God, it's Dora,' said Lando. 'Look, sir, a streaker.'

Hengist swung round and laughed.

'Good heavens, so there is.'

'Gone away,' brayed Jack Waterlane as Siegfried's horn call rang out joyfully on Miss Cambola's trumpet.

Binoculars and little oblong silver cameras were being raised all round the pitch as the cheers escalated. The press raced along the touchline.

'Go for it, Dora,' yelled both teams, momentarily distracted from despair and elation.

'"Like an unbodied joy whose race has just begun",' murmured Theo.

'Lovely little bottom,' sighed Artie.

Northcliffe growled at the sight of a passing Cadbury. Boffin clamped his hands over his eyes in horror. Anthea, who had been upstaging Poppet, turned back to the pitch.

'Oh look, a streaker, how common. We should never have

allowed this bonding with Larks!' Then she gave an almighty squawk: 'My God, it's Dora. Dicky! Randal! Do something!'

Randal, only too happy to show how fit he was, set off in pursuit.

' "The Assyrian came down like the wolf on the fold," ' murmured Ian Cartwright.

Hot on Randal's heels came Joan. 'Dora Belvedon,' she bellowed, 'come here at once.'

'Sit!' howled Cosmo to roars of laughter. 'Stay!'

Evading capture, circling, Dora galloped up to Paris.

'Get your stupid finger out,' she panted, breasts quivering, face red from running, eyes flashing, hair escaping from her plaits. 'You've got to loosen up and win this game. You can't let Feral beat you.'

As she slid to her knees in the mud, pretending to shake an imaginary football shirt at the crowd, Paris started to laugh. Then he heard footsteps and caught a whiff of aftershave; Randal was thundering in from the left, Joan, like the Paddington-Larkminster Intercity, from the right.

'Come here,' yelled Randal.

'Come here,' bellowed Joan.

The crowd were in uproar. Both Hengist and Emlyn tried to contain their laughter as Dora gave her pursuers the slip again.

Scenting danger, detesting Randal, Paris tugged off his sea-blue shirt to more wolf whistles and belted after Dora, grabbing her and forcing the shirt over her head, but having to loosen his grip as he tried to shove both her arms in. Next moment Dora had scuttled off giggling – slap into Randal.

Alas, in the slippery patch near the goalposts, Randal's Guccis had no grip, and he slid past her flat on his back, covering his lovely new suit in mud. The press went berserk.

'This is the way the gentlemen ride,' shouted Amber, 'gallopy, gallopy, gallopy and *down* in the mud.'

'That ain't no gentleman,' said Cosmo, topping up Mrs Walton's glass.

Dora, running away, turned to laugh, and promptly hit the buffers of Primrose Duddon's vast bosom.

'I've got her, JJ.'

Thundering up, Joan flung her duffel coat round a frantically wriggling Dora.

'How dare you bring Boudicca into disrepute?'

'I had to jolt Paris out of his despair.'

'This way, Dora, to me, Dora,' yelled the photographers, as, clapping and punching the air, Dora allowed herself to be frogmarched up to Anthea.

'Take your daughter home, Lady Belvedon.'

'You little slut,' hissed Anthea, and the next minute had slapped Dora viciously across the face, then again with the back of her hand, catching Dora's pink cheek with Randal's huge sapphire, so blood spurted down Joan's duffel coat and Paris's blue rugby shirt underneath.

'Stop that.' Outraged, Janna shot forward. But Cadbury was quicker. Leaping to the defence of his mistress, he threatened Anthea's tiny ankle with his big white teeth, making her scream her head off.

'Get away, you brute.' Randal, racing up, aimed a vicious kick at Cadbury.

'Don't you hurt my dog,' squealed Dora, kicking Randal in the ankle, spurting blood all over the part of his white suit that wasn't coated in mud, before grabbing Cadbury by the collar.

On cue, Partner, who'd been chatting up his old friend Elaine, rushed up to Cadbury, jumping up and down, licking his ears in congratulation.

'My leg,' shrieked Anthea, pretending to faint into Alex Bruce's skinny arms, as a tiny drop of blood seeped through her flesh-coloured hold-ups. 'I must have a tetanus jab.'

'And a tourniquet,' murmured Amber.

Randal was howling abuse at Cadbury and Dora. It took Hengist to restore order.

'Neither you nor Dora are allowed back on to the field with blood injuries,' he told Anthea. 'You all right, Dora, darling?' Whipping out a blue spotted handkerchief, he mopped Dora's cheek. 'Looks nasty. We better get on with the game. I'm sure First Aid'll sort you out, Anthea. The ambulance is over there. Meanwhile we'd better find Paris another shirt and you take Dora to the sick bay, Joan.' Then, when Joan looked mutinous: '*Now.*'

There was no way he was going to abandon Dora to the untender mercies of Randal and Anthea.

'She can't bring that dog,' announced Joan. 'Hand him over to your mother, Dora.'

'I can't.' Tears, near the surface, spilled over, mingling with the blood on Dora's cheeks. 'Randal will put him down. He and Mummy hate Cadbury.'

'I'll take him.' Ian Cartwright took off his tie for a lead but Northcliffe's golden hackles were up, his teeth bared.

'I'll take him,' said Dicky, borrowing Ian's tie.

* * *

630

As the second half began, Paris, in a no. 16 shirt, could hardly bear to see Dora being dragged off, defiantly yelling: 'Come on Bagley,' to deafening applause from both sides. Joan looked absolutely furious.

Amber shook her head. 'How can that woman, who has no heart, teach us about the heart in biology?'

The heat of the day had subsided; the horizon was ringed with rose; through still bare trees a moon to match the yellow stripe in Larks's shirts was rising to aid the floodlighting switched on for the second half.

'What a dreadful waste of electricity,' chuntered Poppet. 'Why couldn't Hengist schedule this match earlier in the day?'

Johnnie and Graffi, who'd played their hearts out, had been subbed, which gave Graffi the chance to chat up Milly, and Johnnie a chance to chat to the media.

'Emlyn's cool,' he was telling the BBC. 'I always got sent off at football because I had scraps. Emlyn's helped me wiv my anger management.'

'He could give Lady Belvedon a few lessons,' said the interviewer.

Primrose and Pearl were discussing their respective revision of the Russian Revolution.

'We've been watching a video of *Doctor Zhivago*,' volunteered Pearl proudly.

'Hengist is taking us to St Petersburg for a long weekend after Easter,' said Primrose.

The roaring and cheering were continuous now. Bagley had come back with a vengeance and two tries from Paris who, feeling he owed it to Dora, was playing like a man possessed. Rupert had abandoned his sulks and Stevie Smith, and was yelling his handsome head off. 'Come on Xav, come on Larks.'

' "You'll Never Walk Alone",' sang Kylie, her sweet voice ringing out to the accompaniment of Cambola's trumpet, and all the Larks parents, children and teachers joined in.

Janna wiped her eyes. It was wonderful seeing Skunk and Pittsy really cheering, and she was so proud of Emlyn.

Probably the only people not concentrating were Cosmo and Mrs Walton.

'I've always wanted you,' murmured Cosmo. 'Will you come back to my cell?'

'I thought you were injured,' teased a once more radiant Ruth.

'I've sprained my ankle, not my cock. You must give me lessons. One cannot be too good in bed.'

631

Five minutes to go. Bagley was playing catch-up. They were six points behind Larks. A try and a conversion would do it. Somehow Larks hung on with heroic tackling and covering work, but gradually their defence was driven back.

Only a minute to go. Janna couldn't bear to look. Please dear God, for Emlyn's and the children's sake.

Paris had the ball and was scorching down the pitch.

'Come on,' yelled Theo, Artie and the Cartwrights. He was through, but with Aston Martin acceleration, Feral stormed in from the right, tackling him five yards from the line, his arms clamping round Paris's hips, bringing him crashing to the ground. The line was a foot away – beyond it, the heavenly city. Wriggling forward, Paris lost control of the ball, which fell forward over the line.

'Let go of me, you fucker,' he howled, trying to struggle forwards in the mud to touch it down. But Feral clung on. A second later, Rocky had pounded up and kicked the ball into the crowd as the whistle went.

Feral and Paris lay on the ground, hearts thumping, both winded, checking they weren't hurt. Then they turned to look at each other, both faces caked in mud, Paris's as brown as Feral's. For a second, panting and exhausted, they scowled.

Then, as if in a dream, their hands stretched out and, as they grinned, their hands met in a grounded high five.

'You was wicked, man,' gasped Paris.

'We've won, we've beaten Bagley.' All restraint gone, screaming her head off, Janna raced on to the pitch, running from exhausted Larks player to player, kissing their dirty faces before falling into an equally ecstatic Emlyn's arms:

'We did it, we did it.'

Tipping her head right back, Janna smiled up into his rugged, ruddy, overjoyed face, feeling his hot sweating body and his heart pounding against hers. They were brought back to earth by the jeering of Johnnie Fowler.

'Cheer up, you fat commie. At least you came second.'

'Take zat back, you smug little vanker,' howled Anatole.

It was only Emlyn's lightning reaction, dropping Janna, swinging round and catching Anatole's arm before his fist smashed into Johnnie's face, that prevented a riot.

'Break it up, you two,' he roared, in addition grabbing Johnnie's shirt collar, 'or I'll bang your thick skulls together. It's only a game.'

'That's not what you told us in the dressing room beforehand,' panted Johnnie, aiming a kick at Anatole. Then seeing Emlyn's face blacken: 'Sir!'

'That's enough, Anatole,' said Hengist, taking him from Emlyn. 'Be more gracious, you were outplayed.'

103

Ashton, Cindy and Randal, having had a good stretch of their legs to take in Badger's Retreat, were now claiming credit for Larks's victory to *The Times*.

'We felt it crucial to give these disadvantaged youngsters a second chance,' Cindy was saying. 'Yes, "Payne" with a "Y".'

'We're keeping a close watch, of course,' purred Ashton. Catching sight of Hengist, he added, 'Bad luck, you must be very disappointed and surprised.'

'Not when you consider Emlyn's been coaching them,' said Hengist lightly. 'After those rather worrying reports in your Sunday paper today' – he smiled at *The Times*'s reporter – 'about S and C's catastrophic involvement in the educational field, they must regard Larks High, particularly after today's triumph, as the jewel in their crown.' Then, nodding at a scowling Ashton and Cindy: 'Do grab a drink before the presentation.'

Captain Xavier went up to shake hands with Randal in his muddy suit and to collect the gold-plated rugby ball to deafening applause from his parents and those from the Shakespeare Estate, who were already legless.

Xav was followed by his players who, in the floodlighting, cast giant shadows in two directions. But Randal, on the podium (provided by himself), cast the biggest, blackest shadow of all.

Feral was Man of the Match.

'Well played,' said Pete Wainwright, handing him his card. 'For once your supporters didn't exaggerate. Football isn't that different to rugby. Give me a bell and I'll fix a date for a trial.'

'That's wicked, man,' muttered Feral.

Maybe, maybe Bianca soon wouldn't be so out of reach after all. 'Give me time, baby.'

Inside, Hengist was seething, but he'd learnt to be magnanimous in defeat.

'Fantastic victory, Emlyn, terrific entertainment for the spectators.'

Emlyn grinned. 'I think Dora should have won Man of the Match rather than Feral.'

'That bitch of a mother,' exploded Janna.

'Hush, darling,' Hengist took Janna's arm. 'Come and have a drink. You'll want to be with your boys, Emlyn.' It was an order. 'Join Janna and me later. You must be so proud,' he told her as they set off towards the pavilion.

The first pale stars were coming out, as if the deepening blue sky wanted to boast it had primroses too.

'So pleased about Feral's trial,' said Hengist. 'If he needs any advice about converting to soccer . . . ?'

How generous and sweet you are, thought Janna.

'Paris played really well in the end,' she said. Then, as they were out of earshot: 'Do you think he's still hung up about us?'

'Not at all, he's working incredibly hard. Well played!' Hengist ruffled a passing Xav's black hair. 'Really good to see you back. Your parents must be ecstatic.'

As they moved on through a copse of young wild cherry trees, he murmured, 'Are *you* still hung up about us, darling?'

Janna started. Hengist turned her to face him, gazing down at her, laughing eyes for once serious. 'I truly didn't mean to hurt you.'

'But you love Sally,' finished Janna. 'I know – and it doesn't hurt any more,' she added, realizing in amazement it was true. 'It's just lovely we can be friends. I do love you.'

'And I, you,' and he dropped a long kiss on her forehead.

Emlyn, still euphoric, accepting congratulations from Artie and Theo, about to round up his team for the plunge bath, reflected that he hadn't thought about Oriana since he arrived. Irked by being dismissed by Hengist, he glanced idly towards the pavilion, then saw Hengist and Janna had not even reached it but were lurking in the wild cherry copse, talking intimately, smiling at each other; now Hengist was stealing a kiss. Emlyn felt his great blaze of euphoria turn to ashes.

Then soft dark hair brushed against his cheek, and a childish little voice said:

'Well done, Emlyn, I couldn't help cheering like mad for my old school.'

It was Vicky, pretty as ever in a turquoise blazer, with a

schoolboy's turquoise and olive-green scarf round her neck, looking as young as any of her pupils.

'I'm having a party at my flat here tonight. Why don't you come? Lots of Bagley people will be there. You can always stop over in the spare room, if you don't want to drive.'

'I've got to take the team home,' said Emlyn, noticing Hengist and Janna were still gazing into each other's eyes. 'But thanks, I might well look in later.'

Paris wandered towards Badger's Retreat in total confusion. He cringed at the memory of the missed penalties. He'd played atrociously, only redeemed by those tries in the second half, when Dora's streak had shaken him out of his despondency. As if he were coming round after an operation, not knowing how much it would hurt, he hadn't worked out how he felt about Feral and Bianca. Like Philip Larkin in their poetry set book, he'd probably been 'too selfish, withdrawn And easily bored' to love Bianca.

Now he was haunted by the thought of Anthea cutting up Dora's round, sweet face. Randal had ruined his suit; Lady Belvedon had ruined her image as a 'lady' – the vicious bitch. Neither would forgive Dora.

After half an hour, when Emlyn hadn't joined the uproarious party spilling out of the pavilion, happily remembering how lovely his arms had felt round her earlier, Janna went in search of him. She found him among the crowd waving off the still stunned Larks fifteen.

'Are you coming back to the Dog and Duck to celebrate?' Janna tucked her arm through his. 'Lily and Christian and Cambola are just leaving.'

'I'll give it a miss tonight,' said Emlyn brusquely. 'Some of the Bagley teachers are having a party; I said I'd join them.' Not meeting Janna's eyes, he didn't see the hurt and disappointment. 'Can you get a lift with the Brig?'

'Of course,' said Janna in a small voice. 'Thank you for all you did for Larks today.'

But Emlyn had stalked off towards the car park.

As Graffi's father and Stormin' Norman were decanted on to the last bus and went home singing ''Ark, 'Ark! the Lark', Hengist reflected that being a host without Sally was very hard work.

How sweet Janna had looked; he'd have loved to whisk her upstairs to bed. All the same, he felt unusually tired – must be the end of term.

Back in his study in the Mansion, he poured himself a large whisky, put on a CD of Fischer-Dieskau singing *Winterreise* and, picking up his note-laden copy of Matthew Arnold's poems, settled down on the sofa with a weary Elaine's head on his lap. Headmasters' dogs get tired too, trailing after them, her gusty sigh seemed to say.

These holidays, vowed Hengist, he was going to write his book rather than politicking. Jupiter was too bloody demanding.

There was a knock on the door. Elaine, a good judge of character, didn't wag. It was Alex.

'A word, headmaster.'

The bloody man would only accept Perrier and sat bolt upright, as though it would be an act of decadence to collapse into the bear hug of one of Hengist's armchairs.

'That was a catastrophe.'

'Losing to Larks, I agree.'

'No, Dora Belvedon's disgusting display. How should we address the problem?'

'Having that bitch of a mother, not to mention the odious Stancombe as a possible stepfather, should be punishment enough.'

Alex looked pained and cracked his knuckles, his Adam's apple wobbling as he swallowed. 'Anthea and Randal are supportive friends.'

'Not to poor Dora, they aren't.'

'She must be excluded for the rest of the term if not permanently.'

'Don't be fatuous, there are only a few days left. It was just high spirits.' Hengist drained his drink. 'At least she shook Paris out of his doldrums and brightened a dire afternoon.'

'Tomorrow's press will be disastrous.'

Hengist's anger boiled over.

'If you hadn't engineered the departure of the best bloody rugger coach Bagley has ever had, we'd have walked it today.'

'Too much emphasis is placed on competitive sports.'

'Bollocks,' roared Hengist. 'It's crucial for strengthening character, fostering qualities of leadership and channelling aggression. Look how Xavier Campbell-Black blossomed. He looks great and played a terrific match. But you had to kick him out without any kind of investigation. We failed him – and we've made an enemy of Rupert. How d'you think it feels having Campbell-Blacks yelling for Larks? Well, you're not getting rid of Dora. Now get out and wreck someone else's evening.'

* * *

Janna gave herself a talking-to as she made herself a cup of tea the following morning.

'You prayed and prayed that Larks wouldn't be humiliated by Bagley, so for heaven's sake be grateful for very large mercies, and don't go slipping in any prayers about Emlyn. I'm lucky to have you,' she told Partner, who wagged his tail in agreement. Emlyn was amiable enough, but had big feet for treading on paws.

Janna left early to buy a big celebratory cake from the baker's and to drape banners across the gate and reception. She felt the fifteen should tour Larkminster in an open-top bus like the World Cup players.

It was an exquisite morning, with only her and the sun in the quiet street, and celandines opening like more little suns on the banks.

She slowed down as the postman approached.

'Saw you on TV last night, Janna. Great result. That Feral played a blinder. *Scorpion*'s got a cartoon of a Red Dragon carrying lots of larks on his back.'

Janna was enchanted. She must get it framed for Emlyn. Why shouldn't he whoop it up with his Bagley mates. His car wasn't outside his digs. He probably never came home.

As she drove down Wilmington High Street, however, she was flagged down by a scarlet windmill – it was Vicky in a red rugger shirt nearly reaching to her knees, about to get into her pale blue Golf. She wore no make-up; her hair was drawn back and falling in a Jane Austen cascade, pretty as always.

'Jannie, how are you? So sorry to miss you yesterday.'

'What are you doing here?' Janna made no attempt to look friendly.

'Emlyn celebrated victory so full-bloodedly last night,' simpered Vicky, 'I had to bring him home. I'm coaching Jack and Lando at eight o'clock – not that they'll be in any fit state, after drowning their sorrows – so I borrowed one of Emlyn's rugby shirts. Rather fetching.'

I'm not hearing this, thought Janna.

'Emlyn is so gorgeous.' Vicky stretched voluptuously. 'Oriana needs her head – or rather the lower parts of her anatomy' – Vicky giggled coarsely – 'examined. You must come to kitchen sups in my little flat in the hols. Shall I ask Ashton to make up a four, or don't you two still get on? Anyway, must fly.'

'Fuck, fuck, fuck,' said Emlyn looking down from his first-floor window. That had not been the way to get over Oriana.

Dora's streak ensured that Larks's victory over Bagley was headlined in most of the papers.

'Welsh dragon turns heat on old school', said *The Times*.

'Full back', was the *Scorpion*'s caption on a charming, naked rear view of Dora, which she agreed was one way of reminding all her press contacts what she looked like.

104

Larks High's pupils were on such a high on the morning after the match, they failed to notice that both Janna and Emlyn were very subdued. Over at Bagley, an equally ecstatic Cosmo was spending a free period stretched out on the fur-covered triple bed in his study. As token coursework, he was making notes on Andrew Marvell's 'To His Coy Mistress', and thinking about Ruth Walton, who wasn't at all coy and might very soon become his mistress. What a coup. Cosmo was so elated, he had no need of his elevenses spliff.

As it was nearly Easter, he was also playing a CD of his father's recording of the Good Friday music from *Parsifal*. Hearing distraught sobbing and finding Dora and a worried Cadbury outside, he pulled them into the room and slammed the door.

'Whatever's the matter?'

'The music,' wailed Dora. 'It was Daddy's favourite. They played it at his funeral. I miss him so much.'

Cosmo let her cry, tempted to comfort her in the only way he knew. She'd looked extremely fetching streaking round the pitch yesterday.

'Daddy would have saved Cadbury. He liked dogs almost more than people. Hengist's Elaine is the great-niece of Daddy's greyhound Maud. Mummy's so furious about me streaking and Cadbury threatening her, she's insisting he's got to be put down, or castrated, or go to the nearest rescue kennels. I can't let him go. He's my only friend except for Mrs Cartwright,' she added, as Cadbury put a large paw on her knee in agreement.

'Bianca was a best friend, but after she took up with Paris, she got too embarrassed to talk to me. And having sworn she couldn't help herself because he was the great love of her life, she's now bats about Feral again and I so don't want to hear how dreadful she feels about breaking Paris's heart.'

'No, I can see that.' Cosmo handed her a handkerchief and a glass of orange juice.

'Thanks,' sniffed Dora. 'I daren't keep Cadbury at Boudicca, because if Joan finds him she'll shunt him straight back to Mummy and the gas chamber. Mummy's terrified I'll be expelled and she and Randal won't be able to have revolting sex all the time. I think Randal's a paedofeel. He groped my non-existent boobs last time I fell off my skateboard.'

'Hum,' said Cosmo.

'I've got a double period of English. Can Cadbury stay here for a couple of hours?' pleaded Dora.

'Sure.' Cosmo looked at his watch. 'I've got maths, but he'll be OK on his own.'

'Can I use this for water?' said Dora, emptying some alabaster eggs out of a Lalique bowl.

'Yeah,' said Cosmo, 'it's insured.'

Left to his own devices, Cadbury whined for a bit, scratched at Cosmo's door, jumped on to the bed, peered out of the window, growled at Theo's cat Hindsight, then started to sniff round the room. Finding an open packet of biscuits, he devoured them, then smelt something much more exciting under the mattress. Pink nostrils flaring, snorting wildly, tail frantically waving, Cadbury began burrowing.

Double English with Miss Wormley droning on about *The Tempest* seemed to go on for hours. Wheedling a Pyrex bowl of shepherd's pie out of Coxie, Dora rushed over to Cosmo's study to find Cadbury sitting on Cosmo's bed, swaying from side to side, yellow eyes glazed, an inane grin on his panting cocoa-brown face.

'Whatever's the matter with you?' wailed Dora.

Concern turned to panic when Cadbury refused the shepherd's pie. Labradors have to be dying not to eat. Hearing a step in the corridor, Dora leapt to close the door and leant against it. Cosmo, however, shoved his way in.

'Cadbury,' gasped Dora. 'He's been poisoned.'

'Don't be silly, there's nothing poisonous in here; he's probably stuffed his face with too many biscuits.' Cosmo picked up the remains of the packet.

'He's never been ill before – look at him,' sobbed Dora as

Cadbury, pink tongue lolling, swaying like a windscreen wiper, beamed up at Cosmo.

'Looks more like the village idiot than ever.'

'He does not. The vet's too far away' – Dora's voice was rising hysterically – 'You must help me get him to the sick bay.'

'I must not,' snapped Cosmo, who was expecting a call from Ruth Walton. 'I'll get thrown out for harbouring an illegal immigrant.'

Dora didn't care. Rushing outside, she found one of the builder's trolleys which had been nicked last night to wheel home a drunken Anatole.

'Help me,' she begged Cosmo.

'I'm bloody well carrying the front end then. Christ, he's heavy. I'll rupture myself,' grumbled Cosmo as they heaved Cadbury on to the trolley. 'You're on your own now.'

Stumbling, swearing, diving into alleyways and behind trees to avoid Poppet Bruce, who as eco-chief was furiously fingerprinting dropped empties, Dora trundled him round the back of the school.

'Please don't die,' she pleaded. 'Don't give up on me. Please God, save Cadbury, don't make Matron shunt him back to Mummy.'

Luck, however, was on Dora's side. Only two pupils were in the waiting room: a boy with athlete's foot and a girl from Boudicca wanting the morning-after pill.

'It's an emergency,' panted Dora. 'Can I go in first?'

Even better, as she dragged Cadbury through the door, a deep, expensive voice exclaimed, 'Why, Dora, darling, how lovely to see you.'

'Dr Benson. It's even nicer to see you.'

James Benson was the raffishly handsome, ultra-charming private GP who for the last thirty years had looked after her family, the Campbell-Blacks and the France-Lynches.

'Whatever are you doing here?'

'A locum. Rather like working in a sweet shop with so many gorgeous girls around, and talking of gorgeous, you've grown really pretty, Dora.' James Benson smoothed his black and silver hair. 'And so like your father, such a sweet man.'

'Thanks so much.' Dora had no time for pleasantries. 'It's Cadbury I'm worried about, I think he's been poisoned or having some kind of fit. I haven't got time to get him to the vet. Please help.'

Cadbury, dopier than ever, collapsed on the rug, pupils vast, beaming inanely and swaying rather more slowly from left to right.

'He's going to die.' Dora burst into noisy sobs. 'I bet it's Mr Fussy or Poppet who's poisoned him.'

James Benson shot his very white cuffs and looked at Cadbury's eyes, his tongue, listened to his heart, then proceeded to laugh a great deal.

'It's not funny,' exploded Dora.

'I think he'll live.' Dr Benson wiped his eyes. 'If I were you, Dora, darling, I'd take him home, turn down the lights and put on a Bob Marley record.'

'I don't know what you mean,' said Dora huffily.

'I don't know where your dog's been, but he's completely stoned.'

Even Cosmo found this amusing. In fact he was in such a good mood after hearing from Mrs Walton, he forgave Cadbury for tunnelling between two mattresses and locating and swallowing a whole eighth of skunk wrapped in cellophane, and agreed that Cadbury could sleep off his excesses on the fur-covered bed.

'He could have a brilliant career as a sniffer dog,' said Dora in excitement. 'According to the *Daily Mail*, dogs get paid five hundred pounds a morning searching for drugs in state schools.'

'He can start by sniffing out all the drugs at Bagley,' said Cosmo evilly, 'and then we can confiscate them.'

Returning for the summer term, Bagley discovered that Poppet Bruce as eco-chief was becoming more and more of a bully, waddling very pregnant round the corridors, charging vast fines for lights left on or doors not closed to preserve heat.

On a late-night patrol on the first Friday of term, Poppet discerned noises coming from the art department. Hammering on the door, she found it locked and, hearing a crash, fumbled for her master key. 'Let me in, let me in.'

Switching on the light, she was confronted by the excesses of the Upper Fifth's coursework, which included a six-foot straw donkey, a robot Christ on a steel cross, and Lando's sin bin: a flame-red tent painted with demons. Hearing a cough, her gaze was drawn to a naked member of the Upper Fifth, who was clutching a palette in an abortive attempt to hide a very large penis.

'Cosmo Rannaldini,' squawked Poppet, 'what are you doing?'

'You're not going to believe this,' mumbled Cosmo, 'but I come here to be near you.'

'How d'you mean?' asked Poppet, thinking how beautifully the lad was constructed.

'Your p-p-p-picture,' stammered Cosmo, pointing a trembling

finger at Boffin's half-finished but already absurdly flattering portrait of Poppet breastfeeding little thirteen-month-old Gandhi.

'What a caring interpretation,' cried a delighted Poppet.

'Indeed. This is seriously embarrassing,' went on Cosmo, 'but I'm so obsessed with you, Mrs Bruce. I come here sometimes to, er, jerk off in front of your portrait. I have such strong sexual urges, which I don't want to impose on my fellow students. It helps me to destress. Please don't be angry with me.' Cosmo hung his dark, curly head, a tear glittering like a diamond on his cheekbone.

Poppet was deeply moved and very understanding. She appreciated the pain of young love. Cosmo mustn't feel guilty about masturbation. He would get over her and find some lovely young woman of his own.

'Never,' swore Cosmo, 'I think of you constantly. At least let me have hope.'

'Alex and I have a very strong partnership.' Poppet perched on a fibreglass wildebeest. 'Not that I haven't had my admirers.'

'I bet you have.'

Cosmo's penis was pushing most excitingly through the hole in the palette. Alex was rather meanly endowed, although Poppet knew size had nothing to do with pleasure. A snort from the direction of the sin bin made them both jump.

'What was that?'

'Probably a rat. Lando keeps leaving half-eaten Cornish pasties around.'

Poppet noticed Cosmo was shivering. 'You mustn't catch cold.'

'Could you bear to leave me to get dressed?' begged Cosmo adoringly. 'And have a moment of quiet reflection on your words of wisdom?'

'Of course, I'll lock up in a quarter of an hour,' said Poppet. 'Good night, Cosmo.'

'Good night, sweet princess,' said Cosmo soulfully, then, ten seconds later, 'All clear,' and a naked Ruth Walton, who'd been stuffing Cosmo's shirt into her mouth to stop her laughter, emerged from the sin bin into his arms.

'Thank you for saving me.'

'We've got ten minutes.'

'No, we haven't, it's not safe – well, perhaps it is,' gasped Ruth as Cosmo pushed her down on Primrose Duddon's ethnic quilt and plunged his cock into her. 'Oh God, what heaven!'

They escaped down the corridor just in time.

'You are the biggest thing in my life,' confessed Cosmo, kissing her in the shadows of the car park.

'And your thing is the biggest I've ever had in my life,' teased Mrs Walton to hide how enamoured she was.

Cosmo was chuffed to bits. He and Ruth couldn't get enough of each other and the pillow talk was as exciting as the sex. He was learning so much about the governing body and the sexual and social habits of Randal Stancombe. The only blot was that Poppet Bruce, unable to keep a secret, revealed Cosmo's passion to Alex, who was casting even blacker looks in Cosmo's direction.

A fortnight later, Poppet had her baby, another girl, Cranberry Germaine, a little Taurus, whom Poppet breastfed in public at every opportunity, particularly in front of Cosmo: 'To domesticate his passion and help him see my breasts in a different light.' She also bombarded him with leaflets from SHAG: the Sexual Health Action Group.

105

Over at Larks, Feral's football trial, a midweek friendly at Larkminster Rovers, approached. Good as his word, Emlyn spent hours helping Feral transfer back to football, increasingly conscious that he was dealing with genius.

When the trial day arrived, Feral in turn felt more positive than ever before. Emlyn had given him such confidence. If he could get a place with the Rovers, who looked like they'd be going up to the first division next season, he'd soon be on serious money, then he'd be in a position to look after his mother, his brothers and sisters and even ask Bianca out. Suddenly he had hope.

It was a perfect day for football, warm but slightly overcast. The Brigadier, Lily, Janna, Emlyn and, to Rupert's intense irritation, Taggie were all going to the ground to cheer him on. As it was midweek, Bianca couldn't get out of school. Feral was relieved. He needed nothing to distract him.

Feral and Xav, who'd come along to give moral support, made their way to the football ground through the Wednesday market. Xav had already handed Feral a good-luck card of a sleek black velvet cat. Inside it said, 'Stay cool, thinking of you, all love, Bianca'.

Feral was nervous but terribly excited. He was wearing the same socks which brought him luck against Bagley and, doing scout steps, running twenty paces, then walking twenty, dreamt of becoming the next Thierry Henry. No footballer's wife would be lovelier than Bianca; she would light up any stand.

Oh please, God of footballers, this is my one chance to break in.

They were early and as they passed the cheese stall, then

breathed in the smell of beefburgers and rotating golden brown chickens, Xav asked Feral if he were hungry. Feral shook his head. He couldn't have kept down a potato crisp as he skipped to left and right practising moves. They stopped to admire some leather jackets. Xav tried on a black one.

'How does it look?'

'Cool,' said Feral absent-mindedly.

'My father, stupid twat, thinks leather coats are common, so I'm going to buy one. My mother always sides with my father. "Why can't you wear that nice denim jacket?" Parents get on my tits.'

Xav, who was very antsy about the GCSEs ahead, tried on a brown jacket, then decided the black one was nicer.

'Blacks look good in black,' agreed Feral.

'I'll have it.' Xav produced a Coutts cheque book, a sheaf of identification and wrote a cheque for £160.

'Parents are never off your back,' he went on irritably as he pocketed the receipt. 'My father never gave a stuff about my working hard until he started this stupid GCSE. My mother's over the moon because Larkminster Rovers are so excited by her coursework ideas. If you land this job, you'll probably live on Steak Taggie for the rest of your life.'

'Shut up, you spoilt bastard,' snapped Feral. 'You don't deserve no respect, man. Every kid in the school wants to be you, living in a palace wiv horses, buying coats wiv what would keep most families for a monf. You've a beautiful sister, your mother's a lovely woman – your dad's a shit, admittedly, but he's always been there for you. You're fucking smuvvered wiv love, and you can't stop dissing them. For Chrissake, stop whingeing.'

A gust of wind blowing blossom out of the trees scattered pink petals over them, as they scowled at each other, fists clenched. Then Feral said:

'Sorry, man. I'm uptight about the trial, didn't sleep last night.'

They did a high five. Feral glanced at Xav's Rolex; there was still time to buy Janna some flowers.

'She's always been there for me.'

Just as he was paying for a bunch of red carnations, he felt a faint scratch on his back. Swinging round, he saw a corpse – almost a skeleton – with a white scabby face, thinning hair, unseeing bloodshot eyes: a nightmare life in death against the technicoloured riot of the flower stall.

She had bruises and cuts all over her arms, was wrapped in stinking rags and trembled uncontrollably in what Feral instantly recognized as an advanced state of heroin withdrawal.

647

'Have you got a pound for a cup of tea?' she mumbled.

'Mum,' whispered Feral in horror.

Xav took Feral firmly by the arm.

'You've got a trial, it's your big chance. You've got to walk away from her.'

'Fifty pence for a cup of tea,' whined Feral's swaying mother.

Xav gave her a fiver and frogmarched Feral towards the football ground. They could see the flags and the stands ahead, but as they reached the High Street, Feral turned and bolted back, disappearing into the crowd. Janna's red carnations fell from his hand and were trampled underfoot.

Xav searched for Feral everywhere, but fruitlessly. By the time he turned up at the match, play had been going on for half an hour and everyone had washed their hands of him.

Pete Wainwright, who'd set the whole thing up, was apoplectic with rage. 'Made me look a complete prat. It's obvious the lad's got no commitment.'

Lily, Janna and Taggie in the stands were devastated; the Brigadier and Emlyn hopping mad with fury. How could Feral have bottled out of the thing he wanted most in the world?

'It isn't as though any of the trial players are a quarter as good as him. He'd have walked it,' exploded the Brigadier.

Rupert who, not trusting Taggie with flash football managers, had at the last moment rolled up as well, said the whole thing was 'absolutely typical'.

Seeing Xav, they all charged down the stands.

'What the hell's happened?'

As Xav finished explaining, Rupert launched into blistering invective. 'It's not worth investing a bloody penny in him.'

'It was his mother, for Christ's sake,' shouted back Xav. 'You wouldn't leave someone like that.'

'I'll come and help you look for him,' said Janna.

'So will I,' said Emlyn.

Having combed the market and the main streets, they tried the Shakespeare Estate. Janna ran up the path past the burnt-out car and the stinking dustbins. A pretty black girl, reeking of sex and booze, her great body shown off by tight orange vest and rucked-up yellow mini, answered the door.

'We're looking for Feral,' begged Janna, then flinched as the girl was joined by a leering Uncle Harley, clearly off his face and zipping up his trousers.

'Nice to see you, Miss Curtis.'

'Have you seen Feral?'

'He's not here. He in trouble again?'

'Feral obviously daren't go home,' Janna told Emlyn as she jumped back into his car.

A distraught Xav didn't get back till late evening. There had been no sign of Feral or his mother, so Emlyn had called the police.

'I'm sorry,' Xav told Rupert defiantly, 'but I admire Feral more than anyone I've ever met.'

Next day the police found Feral hiding out under the railway bridge. His mother beside him, drifting in and out of consciousness, was rushed to hospital. The police had been searching for her anyway on three drug-related offences. The following day, she just avoided a prison sentence by promising to go into rehab and was admitted to a local drying-out clinic.

'I'm jolly well going to pay for six weeks of it,' said Taggie.

'Don't be bloody stupid,' snapped Rupert, particularly when Taggie threatened to sell her diamonds.

Feral, suicidally aware he'd let everyone down, ashamed that he'd been too frightened of her getting arrested to take his mother to hospital, was amazed that the Brigadier allowed him back. Lily was there when, head drooping, a picture of dejection, he walked through the door.

'Come and sit down.' Lily patted the sofa.

Collapsing beside her, Feral broke into the most piteous sobs.

'So sorry, Lily, so sorry, man.'

It broke the Brigadier's heart.

'Poor fellow, poor fellow,' he said, patting Feral's heaving shoulders. 'So pleased you're home. Missed you around the place very much. Tried my hand at cooking corn beef hash for tonight, but have a dry Martini first.'

106

All round Larks, as the summer term began, Wally had nailed up signs saying: 'Get your finger out and your coursework in. All your hard work will be worthless unless you write tidily.'

The teachers stood over the children, reading, redrafting, adding, criticizing handwriting, improving spelling and grammar and finally marking each piece of coursework.

Staff teaching the same subject, like Skunk and Mates, or Janna and Sophy, would then read coursework by each other's pupils, to see if they felt the grades given were fair.

'I do feel this mark's a little too generous for Feral,' sighed Janna.

'A little,' agreed Sophy, 'but marking him up seemed the only way of helping him get a grade.'

There was a drama over the food technology coursework, which included lunch for the hospitality boxes at Larkminster Rovers. The chicken and vegetable jalousie, which consisted of chicken legs wrapped in ham with pepper and tomato sauce, smelt so delicious that Rocky wandered in and scoffed four of the entries. As the external examiner was due in an hour, Taggie felt justified in remaking them herself, just in time.

Other members of staff felt it was like Christmas all over again, as they packed up coursework and despatched it to the examining board. They needed a pantechnicon to accommodate the contribution from design and technology, which included Danijela the Bosnian girl's beautiful blue and green embroidered wedding dress and Rocky's six-foot dog kennel. On the side he had written in pokerwork: 'Dog house I will live in if you do not pass me'.

Other packages included geography projects on traffic-calming and the shaping of industrial development and RE dissertations on death and dying, which seemed a welcome option to the exams ahead, which began on 14 May with Urdu listening.

In Xav's view, Aysha had been listening to a great deal too much Urdu claptrap from her bullying father.

He and Aysha had revised together in the Larks garden, she helping him with science, he her with Spanish and French, occasionally getting electric shocks when their hands touched.

'You must get an A star in Urdu to beat my vile ex-housemaster's wife,' said Xav. 'She and her awful daughter Charisma are taking the subject to show off.'

'How's your dad getting on with English lit.?' asked Aysha. Her little diamond nose stud glinted in the sunlight. Her face and hands were the soft brown of Penscombe Peterkin's glossy coat. As she raised big, brown, almond-shaped eyes to him, Xav's heart shook his body like an overloaded washing machine.

'My dad is very short-fused and not concentrating enough on the yard,' he replied gloomily. 'Hasn't had as many winners as last year. I tried to give him a few tips I'd learnt in business studies, but he told me to get stuffed. Got a good horse called Fast running on the twenty-eighth.'

' "Do not adultery commit; Advantage rarely came of it",' intoned Rupert.

What a ridiculous syllabus! Of all the sins teenagers committed, adultery must be bottom of the list. Half the poems on the other hand seem to be cooing over new babies, the last thing one wanted to encourage in the young. A poem by some woman called Pilkington (who'd only lived thirty-eight years, so God had struck her down) claimed the only way to get on in politics was to tell lies, which didn't dispose Rupert to join Jupiter and Hengist in their proposed coup.

The whole anthology was deeply silly.

Fed up with poetry, Rupert slotted *Pride and Prejudice* into his Walkman. Not a bad book, quite funny, and he completely identified with Darcy: sound fellow, looked after his friends and his tenants, ran his estate well, couldn't be bothered with riff-raff like Mrs Bennet.

Rupert was still spitting because he'd received a letter from Aysha's father, Raschid Khan, who owned a curry house in Larkminster, asking him to stop Xav pestering Aysha. Damned cheek. Both children were black. Xav was clearly desperately in love. Rupert's daughter, Tabitha, had been besotted by a tractor driver called Ashley and got over him, thank God, but he hated to see Xav so unhappy about Aysha's arranged marriage.

As soon as the summer term began, the press, nudged by Dora, had started ringing Bagley for reports on Larks's Golden Boy, only to be told by Hengist that he was confident that not only Paris, but all the school's candidates, would excel in their forthcoming exams. They were all working extremely hard.

This was not strictly true. Boffin and Primrose Duddon had been working steadily all their school careers. Paris had worked hard since he'd been at Bagley. The rest of the year had been cramming knowledge into their heads, aided by caffeine and speed, but only for three weeks. Even the promise of an oil well and his own six-bedroom dacha hadn't motivated Anatole. Even the promise of a Ferrari if he achieved straight As had not halted Cosmo's nightly visits to Mrs Walton, whom he had installed in a cottage on the far side of Bagley village.

Disapproving of all work and no play, Poppet urged her RE students to keep up their voluntary work and 'enrichment activities', which enraged Lubemir, Anatole and Cosmo. How could they enrich themselves by flogging exam papers, when Alex Bruce had once more changed the combination on the school safe? Why should generations of Bagley pupils profit from their enterprise and not they?

Primrose Duddon was overwhelmed how popular she'd suddenly become, enjoying heady weekends staying with the Lloyd-Foxes, helping Amber and Junior with English revision, and at Robinsgrove where, with his dark, sleek head resting on her splendid breasts, she had initiated Lando France-Lynch into the mysteries of the double helix and the circulation of the blood.

Paris's first exam was Latin on the afternoon of 18 May. The night before, Hengist, just off a plane after a big speech in Washington, summoned Paris to his study in the Mansion to check things were all right.

Still in crumpled off-white trousers and a purple shirt, Hengist had hung his jacket and tie over Darwin, the ancient stuffed gorilla, which Alex and Joan had recently sacked from the biology lab on the grounds that he would be too scruffy for Randal's Science Emporium. In an excess of Bruce-baiting, Hengist had rescued Darwin from the skip, placing him beside the stuffed bear and topping him with his own mortar board.

Elaine, enchanted to have her master home, was following Hengist round, nudging him in friendship, sweeping off with her long tail the pile of faxes, emails and letters Hengist couldn't be bothered to look at.

Switching off his telephone, Hengist hung a 'Do Not Disturb' notice on the door, tore the gold paper off a bottle of Moët and prepared to give Paris his full attention.

It was a perfect evening. Cricket games were in their last overs. Cow parsley foamed along the rough meadow between pitches and golf course; buttercups streaked the fields beyond. An over-poweringly sweet scent of lilac drifted in through the big open windows.

'Don't be silly,' Hengist murmured fondly as Elaine jumped then trembled as the champagne cork flew out. 'You've heard enough of those in your time.'

Perched on the dark red Paisley window seat, Paris could just see the lake. Here Artie Deverell lounged in a panama hat and a deckchair, with several bottles of Sancerre cooling in the water among the forget-me-nots, reading his favourite poems in his gentle bell-like voice to his favourite GCSE candidates.

'I bet he's chosen Lamartine's "Lake" or Baudelaire's "Voyage to Cythera".' Hengist handed Paris an excitingly large glass. 'Poetry that no longer appears on any exam syllabus. Great literature, as William Rees-Mogg was saying recently in *The Times*, teaches us to understand human nature. People still sulk like Achilles, get mad with jealousy like Othello, loathe their step-father like Hamlet, have happy marriages like Hector and Andromache.' For a second Hengist's finger caressed Sally's sweet face in the photograph on his desk. 'Literature, Rees-Mogg rightly claims, is the road to the general understanding of the heart and the head. History's the same. If you study William's conquest of England in ten sixty-six, you can appreciate how the Iraqis feel today.'

'Mr Bruce doesn't feel like that.' Paris rose to his feet, gazing at Hengist's books with a longing most boys would reserve for Sienna Miller. 'He's hell-bent on chucking out the classical library and Theo's archives.'

'Not while I'm running this joint. This bloody Government is already destroying public libraries. Wants them to replenish their entire stock in five years, in the name of multiculturism and vibrancy. Jesus! I can accommodate Darwin' – he patted the gorilla on the shoulder – 'not sure there's room in here for the archives.'

'You will protect Theo. He's such a cool teacher,' Paris

stammered and blushed. 'He read us Plato's description of the death of Socrates the other evening, tears pouring down his cheeks the whole time. It was awesome, but I think he's very near the edge.'

'I'll make a note of it,' said Hengist gravely, noting how exhausted Paris looked. His bloodshot eyes glowed like rubies in the intense white face.

'I know how hard you've been working, but this time in a month, you won't remember a single equation or date you've forced into your tired brain.'

'I have to say, sir' – Paris took a gulp of champagne, and moved to sit down on what was left of the sofa by a stretched-out Elaine – 'I was gutted when Mr Davies left, but your classes are wicked, just as interesting as Mr Graham's. I can relate now to Lenin, Khrushchev, the Tsar, even to Hitler and Stalin. You don't make us take sides. Emlyn was always pushing for the underdog, the peasants, the Jews or the communists, but you show us tyrants don't start off wrong, they're often convinced they were doing right. Like in Euripides. I suddenly find I'm right behind Medea. You're like Euripides, sir.'

'Why, thank you, Paris. I've been called a lot of things. Which English set book did you like best?'

'*Macbeth*. Wish I'd been able to take it in the exam, rather than just as coursework.'

'Rupert Campbell-Black has very strong views on *Macbeth*.' Hengist shook his head. 'I so hope he's going to pass. I toned down some of his ideas in which he described Malcolm as a "heartless shit" for being so bracing with Macduff just after his wife and children had been butchered. The Prince of Wales would have handled it far more sympathetically, according to Rupert.'

'That's right,' said Paris.

Down below, he could see Dora scouring the ground with her eyes one moment, looking round for him the next, with Cadbury bounding after her. He'd had a disturbing dream last night: Dora had rescued him from a particularly horrible children's home, and held him safe and kissed him. It had been lovely, but Dora was only a child, sexually light years behind Bianca. He must stamp on any feelings.

'Dora's been great,' he added to Hengist. 'She's helped me to revise, testing me on everything. Pity she's not taking her GCSEs. She knows the textbooks backwards.'

'I'm devoted to Dora,' said Hengist. 'I'll never forget inviting her in for a glass of champagne on her birthday her first term and asking her with what adjective would she best like her friends to describe her. She said, "There." I said, "That's not an adjective." And Dora said, "I'd like my friends to say I was there for them." '

'And she is,' said Paris.

'How are you getting on with Ian and Patience?' he asked.

'OK. Patience took me to *Macbeth*. Brilliant production, except the weird sisters were sleek, young and glamorous, which is garbage: Shakespeare categorically states they had beards and were ugly. And they can't have been in Macbeth's imagination, because Banquo saw them too.'

'Rupert explained it as Macbeth and Banquo being off their faces with drugs,' volunteered Hengist, 'like the entire US Army in Iraq.'

'Magic mushrooms, perhaps,' suggested Paris.

' "The instruments of darkness tell us truths",' murmured Hengist, then, regretfully: 'I must go and change. We're dining with the Lord Lieutenant – such a sweet, boring man, I'll never stay awake. Look, you'll walk these exams. Try and write legibly and read through if you've got time. Examiners are awfully keen on inessentials like punctuation and spelling. Easy to ignore if you're writing at the gallop.'

Paris finished his glass of champagne. If he hadn't been a bit drunk, he would never have tried on Hengist's mortar board. With it tipped over his long nose, and shielding his red eyes, his blond hair floating, he looked so ravishing, Hengist caught his breath.

'Certainly suits you better than Darwin. You must go to my old college, and get the first Matthew Arnold and I, upsetting our fathers so dreadfully, didn't get.'

As Hengist showered, watching the black hairs flowing down in deltas over his strong muscular chest and thighs, he was gripped with excitement. What a transformation in two years! Paris was able to relax, joke, put forward opinions, even exchange compliments. Hengist imagined his first book of poems, dedicated to 'Hengist Brett-Taylor, without whom . . .'

Ian, Patience and Theo, too, must be doing a good job. All the same, the boy would have fared even better with him and Sally. If he took the job at Fleetley, could he take Paris with him? If he went into politics, a beautiful adopted son would be great for his image. Christ, he mustn't think like that. He missed Oriana so much. Even in Washington he hadn't rung her. Not a word had been exchanged. Was Sally speaking to her secretly?

Wrapped in a big red towel, wandering to the window, Hengist saw Paris sprinting down to the lake to join Artie and his friends.

In the Bruces' back garden he could see Boffin, his nose in his revision folder, and Alex smugly rereading a proof of his *Guide to Red Tape*. He must get on with Tom and Matt. Please God, prayed Hengist, make Paris do better than Boffin.

107

'Before the GCSEs, you can expect panic attacks, moodiness, tears and temper tantrums,' Janna sighed to Taggie, 'and that's just the parents.'

The staff weren't behaving much better. Despite the outwardly convivial atmosphere, Pittsy was desperate his maths candidates should do much better than Skunk's scientists. Basket wanted better grades than Sophy and Cambola. Even sweet, calm Mags and jaunty Lily got snappy with Emlyn and the Brigadier over hijacked marker pens. There was so much at stake.

Discounting art and Urdu, which Graffi and Aysha had already taken, exams started in earnest with business studies on the morning of 21 May. The evening before, Janna took refuge among the cow parsley on Smokers', breathing in a heady mingling of wild garlic and balsam, watching the last scarlet streaks of the sunset jazzing up the black silhouette of the cathedral and listening to the exquisite singing of the nightingales in the laurels. Partner, who'd been rabbiting, was drinking out of the pond, avoiding the tadpoles the children had been too busy revising to collect in jam jars.

Like Orpheus visiting the underworld, Janna was still shaking from dropping off good-luck cards to houses in the Shakespeare Estate. If her children scraped just a few GCSEs, they could escape from that hell-hole. Johnnie, Rocky, Monster, Danny the Irish, whose father had just been arrested for punching a particularly irritating female social worker, were all light-fingered and, with no job prospects, would revert to crime and the streets.

Aysha would be beaten within an inch of her life if she didn't get the Magic Five. Kylie was expecting a second child any minute and her voice would need to take off like Charlotte Church's to support them both. Feral had the back-up of the Brigadier and Lily, but although he'd tried hard, she doubted if he'd get any grades except PE. At least Rocky was ensured a good D and T grade with his massive dog kennel.

Graffi worried her the most. Ever since his da Dafydd had been sacked for cheeking Stancombe at the rugby match, he'd been blacked by other firms and drunkenly out of work. Dafydd's mood had not been improved by his dotty mother, known as Cardiff Nan, moving in with them. Graffi, stacking shelves all night in Tesco to make ends meet, was constantly hijacked during the day to mind both his little handicapped sister Caitlin and Cardiff Nan in their enclosed worlds.

Graffi was clever. He'd already got a starred A for art and could easily notch up the Magic Five if he could get some sleep and somewhere quiet to revise. Earlier, she had found him fallen asleep in reception, brush in his hand dripping black gloss on to the floor, in the middle of painting a lucky black cat ringed with gold horseshoes.

The sun and the nightingales had disappeared into the darkness. Going indoors, Janna checked the gym, where in the half-light, like a chessboard, each white square table a metre apart, awaited exam papers. Partner's claws clattered on the floorboards as he sniffed around.

Going into her office, Janna jumped as her mobile rang. Emlyn? she thought ever hopefully, but the number was unfamiliar. The sinister, lisping stammering voice was not.

'Pwepared for tomorrow, Janna? After all our effort, support and financial commitment, I hope you're not going to let us down. Wemember how you hassled us to give your kids a chance to get some gwades? Now it's your turn to deliver; the world is watching, you owe us spectacular wesults.'

'You've got the wrong number, this is not Sadists Anonymous and I'm taping this conversation, so bugger off.'

Janna slammed down the receiver. How dare Ashton wind her up when she needed to be at her most calm and cheerful? She longed to unlock the safe and photocopy every paper. Not that it would help the children unless she wrote the answers for them. By the time Rocky, Feral and Danijela had struggled to the end of the business studies case histories and worked out what questions needed answering, time would be up. Oh God, had she pushed them beyond their capabilities?

If only she could call Emlyn, but since the rugby match their stand-off had continued. But whatever his sadness over Oriana, Emlyn had gallantly thrown himself into the Larks GCSEs, even to the unprecedented step of getting himself to the breakfast club most mornings and conducting question-and-answer sessions until the history candidates were date perfect. Often the Brigadier had joined him, performing a splendid double act.

Over at Bagley, Alex Bruce tiptoed along the landing after lights out. Hearing murmuring coming from the junior dormitory, he drew closer, then smiled as he heard Boffin's voice: 'Please remember in your prayers that over the next four weeks I'll be taking my GCSEs.'

It was nearly midnight at Penscombe, but still stiflingly hot. The shrill neigh of a horse trembled on the night. Earlier, Xav had bravely delivered a good-luck card to Aysha's house and been sent packing.

Now he looked out on a tossing silver sea of cow parsley and ebony woods menacing as an approaching tidal wave on the horizon. Bogotá panted at his feet. *Understanding Business*, black with notes, lay open on his bed.

Xav had never more wanted a drink to take the edge off his nerves and his sadness. He had shouted at his poor mother for asking for the hundredth time if he were all right, and threatened to punch Bianca for pestering him for the millionth time not to forget to pass on Feral's good-luck card, which she'd put in his school bag. There was a knock on the door.

'Bugger off,' hissed Xav.

It was Rupert, bearing a cup of cocoa.

'Thought this might help you sleep. Know what you're going through. I'm shit scared already and I'm doing only one subject; you're doing loads.'

'Thanks.' Xav took the cup. 'Not so much money on me. You've got to wipe that smug smirk off Stancombe's face.'

The cup of cocoa, the first and last Rupert would ever make, was absolutely disgusting. The cocoa was still in powdery lumps, sugar hadn't been added and, by not sieving the milk, Rupert had left a thickening layer of skin on the top. Xav was so touched by his father's concern, he drank the lot, managing not to gag.

'Those marketing ideas aren't bad,' admitted Rupert, 'although I doubt if direct mailing the Shakespeare Estate would find us any new owners.'

To Xav's amazement, the cocoa sent him to sleep.

'"Nessun dorma!"' sang Miss Cambola, but pianissimo so that it wouldn't wake her fellow lodgers.

When she'd taken O levels, far too many years ago, her English had been so poor, she'd failed everything except music. Her set pieces had been Brandenburg Four, the Egmont Overture and the 'Waldstein'; she could still remember every note. The last year had been such a joy; Cambola absolutely dreaded the future. Kylie had such an exquisite voice, but would she ever be able to use it?

Over at Wilmington, the Brigadier couldn't sleep. All his un-relaxed bones were aching. Had he simplified the Great War enough? Would they ever remember the essentials? Feral had received a lot of good-luck cards – even one from his mother in rehab, whom he'd promised to ring after every exam. Business studies this morning, however, had been considered beyond him, so, getting up at five, the Brigadier left him to sleep.

Out in the deserted street, every car had a cat stretched out on the bonnet or underneath, like a union meeting. Lily's cat, General, obviously the shop steward, lay in the middle of the road, and strolled off huffily as the Brigadier started up his car. Noticing ominous pewter-grey clouds over Larkminster, he prayed the forecast rain would hold off. As had been proved in elections, the working classes tended not to come out in bad weather. He and Emlyn would have to jump into Stancombe's minibus and round up the defectors.

The cuckoo was singing in a nearby wood as he reached the next village. In the churchyard, the graves, like swimmers in a marathon, nearly disappeared in a white sea of cow parsley and wild garlic flowers. The yellow roses he'd put on his wife's grave on Ascension Day were shedding their petals. He wondered if she'd rest in peace if she knew he was plucking up courage to propose to Lily.

The church door creaked as he went in, followed by another creak as Lily, kneeling in a front pew, struggled to her feet.

'Don't believe prayers work unless one kneels down,' she confessed. 'Couldn't sleep, just popped down here to wish them luck.'

Without rouge and lipstick, Lily looked pale; pink moisturizer ringed her nostrils; her face was as rumpled as the bed in which she'd tossed and turned. There was a white hair on her upper lip and a big bunch of dark and light purple lilac, with stems bashed, on the pew beside her.

'I so want them and Janna not to be humiliated.'

The Brigadier's heart expanded with love.

108

Over at Larks, from eight o'clock onwards, Partner, sporting a smart crimson bow tie, welcomed everyone with joyful barks. Across one whole wall of reception, defiantly defacing Ashton's property, Graffi's grinning black cat juggled gold horseshoes and lashed a tail at a lark ascending into gold clouds. In black letters, Graffi had also named each candidate and wished them all luck.

The heady smell of Sally and Lily's flowers, however, couldn't disguise a reek of cheap scent, sweat and terror. No one could face Taggie's cornflakes and croissants; they could hardly keep down a cup of tea.

With their hair drawn back and twisted up into knots, their smocks with shoelace straps showing off bare shoulders, and their jeans flopping round their ankles, the girls looked like extras in a BBC Jane Austen ball scene above the waist, and the technicians making the film below it.

But their pale faces, seamed with strain and weariness, came straight out of a Dickens slum scene. Every so often, one of the girls would break into terrified sobs and trigger off the others.

'Got the runs, miss.' 'Toilet's blocked, miss.' 'Stink makes you frow up.' 'Fink I've come on.' 'Miss, I'm goin' 'ome.'

'No, you're not,' said Janna firmly.

After quick prayers in assembly – 'May an angel ride on your shoulders' – Cambola played them out with 'Hark, Hark! the Lark' on the trumpet.

Now at the far end of the gym, Mags Gablecross sat calmly smiling, ticking off candidates as she called out their names in alphabetical order.

Xav being Campbell-Black was one of the first in. Taggie gave him a huge hug.

'Can I have a hug too?' asked Rocky.

Danijela's little teeth were chattering frantically.

'Even my buttyflies have buttyflies.'

Danny the Irish, who'd only come in because she had, held her hand.

'I'm so exhausted I can't remember my candidate number,' moaned Pearl.

'Can I have a hug?' Monster begged Taggie, his lower lip trembling like a little boy's.

Inside the gym, the windows were too high to reveal anything except ever-darkening purple sky.

'At least we can hang ourself on the ropes,' sighed Kylie, whose bulge was so big she could hardly get at her desk.

'That's not a metre between your desks, Danny and Danijela,' called out Mags as she checked everyone had written their names and numbers properly. 'If you want to hold hands, do it after the exam.'

Aysha, a bruise darkening her cheek, cast down her eyes, terrified of looking at an anguished Xav.

As Janna watched the tail-enders forlornly filing to their doom, she wanted to ask if they'd packed their pencil boxes themselves.

'Perhaps we should strip search you for mobiles,' she joked.

'Yes, please,' giggled Kitten, 'but only if Emlyn does it.'

'Kitten Meadows, you've never worn a long skirt in your life, what have you got hidden?' shouted Pearl.

'Shut up, all of you,' yelled Cambola.

Turning, Janna noticed Emlyn leaning against the wall watching her. He had just rounded up and brought in Johnnie Fowler. 'Worse than getting a mustang into a lorry.'

'I feel like Gérard Houllier,' confessed Janna, watching through the door as Mags handed out the papers. 'Once they're on the field you can only pray, we can't even substitute Boffin or Cosmo.'

'Don't expect too much, they've crammed a two-year course into one year, but it's been such a fantastic year. It'll stand them in good stead for ever,' said Emlyn. As his big, warm hand gathered up hers and squeezed it, she let it lie there.

'Everyone here?' demanded Mags, consulting her list. 'No Feral?'

'He's not taking business studies, miss.'

Mags looked round the room. 'Graffi's not here either.'

At that moment, a schoolmaster bringing back the birch, the rain lashed the window panes.

'I'll go and find him,' said Emlyn, letting go of Janna's hand.

Torrential rain scrabbled and clawed at his windscreen; rotting fruit, veg, fag ends and needles flowed into the cul-de-sacs of the Shakespeare Estate. Emlyn found Graffi wandering down Hamlet Street. It was hard to tell if his face was soaked by tears or rain; his black curls hung in rat's tails.

'Cardiff Nan's fucked off.'

'Hop in and leave her.'

'Can't, she's left all her clothes at home.'

'A Welsh undresser.'

'She'll catch her death.'

'I'll find her after I've dropped you at Larks.'

'Can't do the exam now, it's too late. My hands are frozen.' Graffi was shaking uncontrollably. 'I can't write.'

'You can have a go.'

Five minutes later, having swapped his drenched T-shirt for Emlyn's jersey, which reached his knees, Graffi slid into the gym to giggles and cheers from his supporters.

'I've got the shakes, I can't do this.' He picked up the paper and read: 'Greenstreet PLC are planning to build their fifth supermarket on the edge of an ancient and much-loved country town. Question one: How should they set about winning local acceptance and planning permission?'

Familiar territory, Mr Randal Greenstreet, thought Graffi.

'Well, maybe I can.' He picked up his pen.

The silence of the exams was interrupted only by occasional expletives, rain grapeshotting the windows, sweet papers rustling, tummies rumbling, the click of Mags's knitting needles and the pacing of Cambola, the invigilator, up and down the rows, to be replaced after thirty minutes by the clattering of Gloria's high heels.

Gloria, dreaming of PC Cuthbert, didn't notice Kitten's denim skirt falling open to reveal useful business terms and formulas written on her succulent thighs. Distracted by the sight, Monster lost his train of thought. Pearl opened her KitKat, turning it over thoughtfully. On the back, with a compass, she had also scratched terms and formulas.

Sweating when they came in, the bare-shouldered girls were now shivering.

I'm three-quarters through. I can do it, thought Xav joyfully. Looking across, he met Aysha's eyes. He wanted to kiss her purple bruise better.

Even Rocky, vast in his tiny desk, like Bultitude Senior in *Vice Versa*, was writing slowly but steadily.

'Got my period,' announced Pearl. 'Got to go to the toilet.'

Out she went, returning in a spitting rage.

'Who removed *Understanding Business* out of the toilet cistern?'

Over at Bagley, Stancombe's Science Emporium was being built for the Queen's visit in the first week in November and the builders continued to make an unconscionable din: bang, bang, drill, drill, setting the children's teeth on edge, so the GCSE exams were being taken in the newish sports hall.

Well into business studies, Primrose was writing steadily. Paris was thinking, then scribbling frantically, wishing he could instead write a short story about the idealistic young couple in Question Three, who were trying to make their garden centre break even by taking in another director.

Amber was writing to her boyfriend at Harrow. Boffin was filling pages and pages, between smirking and cracking his knuckles. Cosmo had polished off his paper in half an hour and was writing to Mrs Walton. He did hope Milly wouldn't want to come home and veg for a week at half-term.

Plugged into Jade Stancombe's ear, and hidden by a curtain of tortoiseshell hair, was a little mobile, the latest technical device from the Philippines, which as she tapped in the number, gave her the answers to each question as slowly or as fast as she chose. For this relief, she had almost forgiven Daddy for shacking up with Anthea Belvedon, particularly as he'd promised her a thousand pounds for every A grade.

Gloria had been replaced as invigilator by Basket, whose spangled flip-flops, daringly acquired in Skunk's honour, flapped as she padded up and down, doing everyone's heads in.

'Turn down the fucking volume,' snarled Monster.

The rain was easing, the windows framing grey clouds topped with white rather than purple.

Mags put down the shawl she was knitting for Kylie's baby.

'You've got five minutes left.'

Danijela burst into tears, gazing helplessly at her hardly touched pages. Others scribbled final answers or tried to reach into the depths of their memories, as one might rootle in a bag for a taxi fare, and find nothing.

'Put down your pens, please.'

Dazed, like miners coming up into the light, they spilt out into the drizzle. They had an hour and three-quarters to eat and drink something before PE theory that afternoon. Feral, bouncing his football, had just arrived; Partner, barking round his feet, hoped for a game.

'Howdya do?' Feral asked Xav.

'Not bad, once I got going. I've got a card for you.'

Pearl the drama queen was making her usual fuss.

'I've failed, I've failed. Couldn't do any of it. We wasn't taught the syllabus.'

'Yes we was,' said Kitten. 'I thought it were easy.'

Janna rushed round encouraging and consoling.

'First one's always difficult. Sure this afternoon'll be much easier. Just make certain you have a proper dinner.'

It had been hard to settle to anything this morning, all she could think was that Emlyn had held her hand.

PE theory lasted two hours. Feral had got top marks in the practical exam, but he couldn't make head nor tail of this paper. So he slowly deciphered Bianca's card.

It was her parents' last-year's Christmas card, with a picture of Penscombe Peterkin gambolling in the snow with Rupert's Jack Russells.

Inside were printed the words 'Merry Christmas and a Happy New Year' and at the bottom 'Rupert and Taggie Campbell-Black'. There was no way Rupert would ever wish him any happiness, thought Feral wearily.

'Dearest Feral,' Bianca had written. 'This card is the right one because I want to know you next Christmas and the next and the next, for ever. Good luck, I miss you, please ring me. All love.'

With a groan of despair Feral shoved the card in his pocket and gazed at the blank pages of the booklet in which he was supposed to write down his answers. The princess and pauper: how could he ever give Bianca the life she deserved?

When Graffi got home from his night shift at Tesco, the dawn was already breaking and his father roaring drunk and raging mad.

'How dare you let out Cardiff Nan? Day centre brought her back and fucking charged me for the loan of a dressing gown,' and he hit Graffi across the lounge.

109

PE theory was followed by information technology, German listening and religious studies, leading up to the big one, English lit., on the Friday morning before half-term. For Rupert, the Thursday had been punctuated by telephone calls from skittish Bagley mothers, including the fearful Dame Hermione, saying that as they'd pledged large sums of money, they did hope to be rewarded with a party if he got a good grade. The final call at midnight had been from ghastly Stancombe, saying he hoped Rupert was going to honour his promise and roll up at Cotchester College tomorrow.

'There's a lot at stake.'

'The stake should be through your fucking heart,' howled Rupert and hung up.

Randal turned gleefully to Anthea, stretched out naked on his bed beside him. 'Pressure getting to his Highness.'

'Good,' said Anthea. 'Ay hope he gets a U. He's always been far too big for his raiding boots.'

Rupert was so livid, he'd never sleep now. In the old days of showjumping, or when he was Minister for Sport, he could always ease the tension by pulling a groom or a groupie. Now he was mocked by an entire library of books, which he'd never read, and by *Lord of the Flies* reminding him how horribly he was bullying darling Taggie at the moment, by being so sulky and resentful. Thank God term would be over in a few weeks and she'd be back home with him again. But would she be bored? Had Larks whetted her appetite for more company and excitement: for bloody Pete Wainwright or that fat Welshman?

Rupert wished he could have taken the exam at Larks instead of Cotchester College, which would be swarming with press. But when he'd dropped into Jubilee Cottage to ask Janna, she had very sweetly said his presence in the exam room would be far too distracting.

'The girls would all gaze at you, and the invigilators too, enabling all the lads to cheat like mad and no one would notice. You're still the most attractive man in the world,' she added, blushing furiously.

'Huh – doesn't get me anywhere.' Rupert had stalked off into the sitting room and been blown away by Graffi's mural.

'That's so bloody good. Christ! There's Rod Hyde and ghastly Ashton in one of his poncy mauve shirts and that asshole Bishop. What's he called, Graffi? He must come and do one of the hunt before bloody Blair closes it down.'

Rupert's mood didn't improve on the morning of the exam. Taggie and Xav had left for Larks and weren't even there to wave him off. The forecourt of Cotchester College was swarming with press, including a grinning Venturer camera crew.

'To me, Rupert', 'Look this way, Rupe', 'Over here', they shouted, as Rupert deliberately parked his dark blue BMW in the space reserved for the Dean of the College, and, gathering up *Lord of the Flies, Death of a Salesman*, and *Opening Lines*, leapt out like a snarling tiger.

'God, he's lush,' sighed a presenter from Sky.

'What have you learnt from your studies of English lit.?' asked the *Guardian*.

'That the term "mature student" is an oxymoron.'

'Randal Stancombe says you haven't got a hope in hell,' taunted the *Scorpion*.

'Stancombe's an expert on hell,' snarled Rupert. 'Now, get out of my way.'

He was about to pick the *Scorpion* reporter up by his lapels when he was distracted by a vast fluffy black pantomime cat padding up to him, purring loudly and rubbing itself against his thighs.

'What the fuck?' Rupert was about to punch or kick the cat away, when a deep gasping familiar voice spoke.

'I've just come to bring you luck.'

Rupert's scowl widened into a huge smile, his voice cracked: 'Oh Tag, darling, oh Tag,' as he pulled the cat to its feet and into his arms.

'Purrrr, purrrr,' giggled the cat, tickling his face with its whiskers.

Rupert was still laughing as he sat down. Oblivious of his fellow candidates, he got out a blue fountain pen and wrote his name and number. Then, opening the paper, he read the first question on *Lord of the Flies*: 'Describe the importance of Jack in this novel.'

' "This is a good island",' wrote Rupert, with a sigh of relief. ' "We'll have fun." '

Finishing his answer on *Death of a Salesman*, he had half an hour left for poetry and to explain the ways Seamus Heaney and Dannie Abse wrote about the father/son relationship in two poems, which he'd enjoyed and identified with. Heaney was sound on ploughing and he liked the Abse line about his son playing pop music and 'dreaming of some school Juliet I don't know'. He'd never get a chance to meet Aysha if Raschid Khan had his way.

Thank God there wasn't a question on that whining bitch Sylvia Plath.

Having finished the paper, Rupert felt very flat. Cursing himself for things he should have put in, he shook off the press, and drove straight to Larks to collect Xav. Taggie would already have left to collect Bianca from Bagley.

As he hurtled down the back roads, he noticed the cow parsley turning green and going over and the chestnut candles scattering their creamy petals. He'd been too busy to appreciate them and now he'd have to wait until next year. The baton had been taken over by hawthorn, exploding everywhere in white-hot fountains, its soapy bath-day smell competing with the reek of wild garlic, much stronger now the leaves were yellowing and decaying.

Thank God he'd be able to concentrate full time on racing once more. A new dark brown filly called Fast was running in the first race at York. Pulling into the Larks car park, where, judging by the 'Please Be Quiet' sign, Eng. lit. was still going on, he switched on the little television on his dashboard.

Next second, a white van with Star of Lahore Curry House printed on its side drew up, driven presumably by Raschid Khan. Rupert had been about to take a large swig of brandy out of his hipflask, but Khan looked the sort of evil bugger who'd report him to the police.

Fast was dancing round the paddock looking almost too well. The bookies had her at twelve to one. Rupert was about to ring Ladbrokes, when he noticed Mr Khan, despite his air of extreme disapproval, sneaking a look at the television.

'Hi,' said Rupert.

'Good afternoon,' replied Mr Khan stiffly.

'I know who you are,' drawled Rupert. 'You have an exceptionally clever daughter. In my experience, the more you tell teenagers not to see each other, the more they want to.'

Mr Khan was about to close his window, when Rupert added:

'The attachment is as abhorrent to me as it obviously is to you.' Then, when Mr Khan looked astounded: 'Do you honestly think I want Xavier, with all he is likely to inherit, to chuck himself away on a total nobody?'

'A nobody?' Quivering with fury, Mr Khan inflated like a turkey cock.

'By comparison,' said Rupert coldly.

'That's a racist remark.'

'You're the racist,' snapped back Rupert, 'being foul about my son, who's much blacker than your daughter, who I gather is utterly enchanting. My wife Taggie is almost more devoted to her than Xav is.'

'There is nothing more to be said. Aysha is engaged to be married.'

'Right. If you'll forgive me,' said Rupert, punching out Ladbrokes' number, 'I've got a potentially very good horse in this race. If you want to take a chance and have a bet, the odds are excellent.'

There was a long pause. In the dust of the car park, two robins were quarrelling over a feather. Mr Khan, unable to resist a flutter, extracted a tenner from a paperclip full of notes in his breast pocket and handed it over. 'I will have a bet.'

Matters dipped when Fast, no doubt excited to be carrying Rupert's dark blue and emerald green colours for the first time, took off at the start and ran halfway round the course, before her jockey could pull her up. She then lined up with the starters, set off at a cracking pace, and with Mr Khan and Rupert both yelling their heads off, lived up to her name by flying down the straight to win by six lengths.

'You've made a hundred and twenty pounds,' said Rupert jubilantly, 'and I've just bought one fantastic horse.'

When Xav and Aysha wandered wearily out of English lit., deliberately keeping their distance, utterly dejected at the prospect of not seeing each other for ten days, they were flabbergasted to see Rupert and Raschid Khan leaning against Rupert's car, deep in conversation.

'Xav tried to introduce marketing to my yard.'

'Aysha tried to introduce food technology to my restaurant, which I would be honoured if you would visit one evening.'

'How did you get on, Dad?' asked Xav nervously.

'Not bad, might have scraped a G. How about you?'

'Not great, I've never understood that Heaney poem. Is his father senile, or is he haunted by his memory?'

'Senile, if he's anything like me. Have you met Mr Khan? Fast just won by six lengths.' Rupert turned back to Raschid: 'Why don't you, your wife and Aysha come to Epsom one day next week?'

'How could you schmooze up to that terrible guy?' exploded Xav as Rupert drove over the bridge towards Penscombe. 'He blacked Aysha's eye last week.'

'No, he didn't, Aysha's younger sister did that. Aysha wanted to revise and turned off *EastEnders*. Raschid told me,' said Rupert smugly.

Winding down his window, narrowly missing a jogger, Rupert chucked Sylvia Plath into the River Fleet.

110

Half-term wasn't helpful. The candidates felt they deserved a break, but guilty if they eased off and lost momentum, particularly on the Monday after, when faced with two heavyweights: geography and double science. As a result of being in a confined space, everyone had colds or tummy bugs and the heat wave had kicked in. At nine-thirty it was already like an oven in the gym. Sophy was invigilating and unless she walked in the straight line required of sobriety tests, her splendid bulk sent papers flying and candidates into fits of nervous giggles.

They were just about to start geography when Johnnie Fowler was found to be missing. Then Janna ran in saying Johnnie's sister had rung to say at the prospect of two such gruelling exams, Johnnie had gone 'on the booze, then on the rob' and been arrested.

'Go and bail him,' Skunk Littlewood begged Emlyn, 'he's got double science this afternoon. He could get a B.'

Emlyn found Johnnie in a cell, cross-eyed with hangover.

'What happened?'

'I got hammered, mugged an old lady for anuvver round, but I was so drunk I didn't realize it was Graffi's Cardiff Nan, what had escaped. It's not funny,' he grumbled. 'Anyway, I don't want bailing. Can't I stay here and miss science, maffs, French, D and T, English, anuvver bleeding geography and German and history and more science?'

'Come on,' said Emlyn.

Outside, he fed Johnnie black coffee and later chicken soup and dry toast and got him back in time for science.

'Don't,' groaned Johnnie, clutching his head as the other candidates gave him a round of applause.

Monster had had baked beans for lunch; consequently, his farts were worse than Skunk's heat-wave armpits.

'I'm going to faint,' said Johnnie, even more so a minute later when he opened the paper, which was a brute. 'And to fink I could be kipping in some nice cell.'

'Holy shit.' Feral screwed up his paper and walked out, bouncing his football.

'Don't give up,' the Brigadier, who was hovering in the corridor, begged him, 'you've got plenty of time and an extra half-hour for being dyslexic.'

'If I stared at that paper for a hundred years, I couldn't do a word of it, so don't get yer hopes up, Brig, I'm going to play football.'

Pearl unfurled another KitKat weighed down with equations. Within twenty minutes the room was almost empty; only Graffi, Aysha, Xav (because it gave him the chance to gaze at Aysha), Kitten and Pearl were left.

'Bloody hell,' said Graffi, 'I need a fag and a piss.'

'Hush,' said Basket in horror.

'And for you to take off those fucking, squeaking shoes.'

'Nuffink on circulation, nuffink on the heart, nuffink on the solar system, or electricity or radiation,' raged Pearl as they came blinking and utterly dispirited into the sunlight.

'I thought it were easy,' said Kitten and got punched in the face by Pearl.

Over at Bagley earlier, Mr Fussy hung round the sports hall, hurrying in his students, 'Don't be late, don't be late,' hell-bent on smashing Theo's record of getting everyone through.

Milly, practising a yoga relaxation technique Poppet had urged on her, was nearly asleep. Jade made another mental note not to thrust her fingers through her hair and reveal the tiny transmitter in her ear.

Lando was at the back, murmuring, 'Define a quark, define a quark. It's the sound that an upper-class duck makes,' and laughing at his own joke so much, he was furiously hushed by Boffin. From where Lando was sitting, he could admire the splendid swell of Primrose's left breast. Cosmo, having finished his paper, was reading *The Secret History*.

When it came to the two-hour maths exam the following day, Xav was determined not to let Pittsy down. Ex-alkies should stick together.

'If Mrs Rock borrowed £2,000 at ten per cent compound

interest and paid it back together with total interest after two years, what would be her total repayment?' read Xav.

'£2,420', he wrote a minute later.

Over at Bagley, the Philippine gremlin whispered £2,420 in Jade's ear, in answer to the same question. Jack Waterlane, utterly defeated by the same paper, was relieved to receive a text message on his smuggled-in mobile, saying Kylie Rose had gone into labour.

When in doubt, take the easier option. As Jack ran out of the exam hall, Biffo, who was invigilating, leapt down from his chair and chased after him. The best way of stopping Biffo following him, decided Jack, was to take Biffo's car. Although he was only sixteen, Jack had been driving tractors round his father's estate since he was ten and, leaving a furiously windmilling Biffo, set off at ninety miles an hour for the hospital.

Kylie Rose's face when he walked into the maternity ward made everything worthwhile.

'I thought you' – groan – 'was in the middle of a maffs paper,' progressed to, 'Oh' – groan – 'of course I'll marry you.'

Chantal spent the rest of the labour crying with joy.

Lord Waterlane, when he rolled up some hours later, was in a towering rage. On the other hand, Jack's mother, Sharon, who insisted on referring to herself as Lady Shar, had once been a nightclub hostess and a hell of a goer. David had always suffered from *nostalgie de la boue* and found Chantal, who was only thirty, extremely pretty and, after all, Kylie had given birth to a boy.

'We're going to call him Ganymede David,' she told her future father-in-law proudly.

The first English paper, which also contained literature questions, was on 10 June. Dora, knowing this was a crucially important subject to Paris, had finally tracked down five four-leafed clovers and, with Patience's help, had glued them on a card. 'Dear Paris,' she had written inside, 'Good luck in English and all your other exams, you'll do brilliantly. Love, Dora'.

Her timing, admittedly, was lousy. A thoroughly strung-up Paris, flanked by Junior, Lando and Jack, was just going into the exam when Dora had rushed up, thrusting the card into his hand. Paris glanced down.

'What the fuck?'

'Please open it.'

Paris gazed at her in disbelief.

'Just fuck off, can't you see I'm busy? Get out of my life and leave me alone.'

Dora cried great rasping sobs all round the pitches, missing French. Artie Deverell, who'd picked up on the exchange, dispatched Bianca, not the ideal person, who found Dora sitting on a log sobbing into Cadbury's shoulder.

'Good thing Labradors like water,' observed Bianca.

Dora went on crying.

'Paris is heartless, Dor. Even when he was crazy about me, he couldn't show it. It's his upbringing; he doesn't know how to express love, he hasn't had any practice. He's got a slice of ice in his heart.'

'Put not your trust in Arctic Princes,' sobbed Dora.

Jade Stancombe, in the evening, was more brutal. 'You were like an autograph-hunter interrupting Tiger Woods as he teed up at the eighteenth hole. Paris just tore up your card and chucked it in the bin. Stop making a fool of yourself; he's out of your league.'

In the sports hall earlier, Paris dispatched Housman and Hood's rosy view of childhood: 'Lands of Lost Content'. Poets all seemed to have had wondrous childhoods and gloomy, insecure old ages.

I've had a gloomy, insecure childhood, thought Paris; God help me if the rest of my life is even worse. I remember, I remember the children's homes where I wasn't born.

He turned to the next question: 'Describe a place you hate.'

I hate my own heart [wrote Paris] because it is cruel and hard. My best friend, Dora, is honourable and good like Piggy in *Lord of the Flies*. She has helped me revise all my exams: where the world moves and sits in space, Martial's recipe for happiness, drumlins, the Battle of Arginusae and the trials of the Generals. She gave me a beautiful good-luck card decorated with four-leaf clovers, but I tore it up and told her to piss off, because I was uptight. I would like to apologize to Dora on behalf of all my sex. Where women are concerned, we always get things wrong and I most of all. Dora is well named because she is adorable.

I hate my heart because it lets me down; its beat quickens when I hear beautiful music or poetry, but when a friend tries to get close, it freezes over. To twist Catullus: whenever I love, I seem to hate or resent as well. We dissected a pig's heart in biology, but if you dissected my heart, it would pump not blood but poison.

'A place I hate,' wrote Boffin Brooks, 'is the headquarters of the Tory Party.'

The place I hate is my deputy headmaster's drawing room. He calls it a lounge, which is a complete misnomer because no one could lounge in such an uncomfortable place [wrote Lando]. The chairs are ramrod hard; the sofas murder your coccyx. No parents stay more than five minutes because he offers such tiny glasses of indifferent sherry and doesn't want anyone to linger. There are no pictures, no books except the very odd scientific manual. When you enter, you always get a lecture on bad behaviour.

'The place I hate is a vivisectionist's laboratory where the animals' vocal cords are cut on arrival so their screams cannot upset the staff or visitors,' wrote Amber and made herself cry even more cataloguing other iniquities.

Glancing round, Primrose Duddon smiled sympathetically and shoved a box of Kleenex in her direction.

I like Primrose, decided Amber, I like her much better than Milly or Jade. Primrose had helped her with revision beyond the call of duty. Amber resolved to buy her a cashmere jersey as a thank-you present. On the other hand, it would take a lot of cashmere to accommodate Primrose's splendid bosom and might be rather expensive. Better to give her scent instead.

111

The sun had long since set, but it was still so hot that, despite wearing only shorts, a cotton shirt and loafers, Theo had left his study windows wide open. In the past month, he had been soothed by the 'liquid siftings' of the nightingales in the laurels. Tonight they had all departed – like pupils at the end of term. Would he still be alive next year to hear them?

He had been wrestling with a difficult letter in answer to a telephone call telling him one of his favourite old boys, Jamie Pardow, had been killed in Iraq.

'We kncw you were fond of each other,' Jamie's father had said, 'in fact in his very last letter home, he said: "If you see Theo, tell him I'm still not tucking my shirt in."' The father's voice had cracked then and he'd had to ring off.

Such a lovely boy. Theo shook his head. He should be writing reports. He should be working on Sophocles. Instead, he poured another large Scotch to wash down a couple more painkillers. A bottle of morphine, illegally prescribed by James Benson, was hidden behind the books, for when things became unendurable.

Would he could take something to ease the ache in his heart that after the end of term he wouldn't see Paris for eight weeks. In a way it would be a relief. He needed to be alone to calm his fever, to think about the boy. He knew Ian Cartwright, Cosmo and even Dora were jealous of their friendship. He must try not to favour him next term.

On a positive side, he was delighted Paris was on course for A stars in Greek and Latin. Hengist, who had a key to the school safe and, against all the rules, often looked at finished papers, had reported exquisite translations of Homer and Virgil, wise, witty, lyrical comments on Ovid and Horace and Iphigenia's pleading for Orestes and flawless unseens in the language papers. How Socrates would have loved him.

Paris, according to Hengist, had also submitted brilliant papers in other subjects, including a matchless first history paper. 'He writes so entertainingly.'

Paris had science tomorrow morning and a second history paper in the afternoon, covering the Russian Revolution and Nazi Germany, which had both fascinated and haunted him. Then it was all over.

Although it was after eleven, golden Jupiter was the only star visible in a palely luminous blue sky. The trees on the edge of the golf course, olive green in the half light, seemed to have faces, hollow-eyed, too, after a month of exams. The mingled stench of rank elderflower and decaying wild garlic was overwhelming.

As Hindsight padded in, leaping on to the table, Theo grabbed his glass – there was enough whisky spilt over the reports and his translation of Sophocles already – and guided the cat's fluffy orange tail away from the halogen lamp. A mosquito was whining around his bald head looking for a late supper; Theo lit yet another cigarette to deter it.

He smiled briefly as he caught sight of a poster on the wall Paris had had framed for him for his birthday, which showed a woman with a balloon coming out of her mouth saying: 'I'm voting for Martial, he's not clever, he's not honest, but he's hand-some.' Alex had banished it from Theo's classroom as being too sexist.

Theo had seen a lot of Paris in the last ten days. Not entirely, he was realistic enough to recognize, because Paris relished his company. The boy, it appeared, had been so gratuitously cruel to poor little Dora that that dear, kind, soul Patience Cartwright had ticked him off roundly. This had so shocked Paris, he had since shunned the Cartwrights' and spent his evenings working in the library or talking to Theo. Theo suspected and genuinely hoped Paris was much fonder of Dora than he let on. He could do worse. Dora was brave, resourceful and good-hearted.

The evenings together had been an exquisite pleasure. They had listened to music and discussed books and Paris's choice of AS levels: Greek, Latin, theatre studies and English. Paris also brought Theo the latest gossip. How Lando had been caught lis-tening to the Empire test match on his walkman during science, how Anatole had mistaken downers for uppers and slept peace-fully through French, and how Boffin, 'stupid twat', was already immersed in one of next year's set books: *The Handmaid's Tale.*

* * *

Hengist was in Washington, due back this evening, but grounded by a strike. He had nevertheless rung in to wish Paris luck in his final history paper tomorrow.

Theo emptied the bottle into his glass. On his desk lay an advance copy of Alex's *Guide to Red Tape* (or *Tape* as it was now known), which the self-regarding idiot had presented to Theo to illustrate that he, Alex, despite being busier than anyone, was capable, unlike Theo and Hengist, of meeting deadlines.

Theo, instead, turned to Aeschylus, whose *Philoctetes*, covered in drink and coffee rings, he'd been reading earlier. Philoctetes, driven crazy by a snake bite, as he was by his ransacked spine. How admirable was Maurice Bowra's translation:

> Oh Healer death, spurn not to come to me.
> For you alone, of woes incurable, are doctor,
> And a dead man feels no pain.

Theo hoped this were true. Awful to reach the other side and immediately find oneself bound on a wheel of fire, like Ixion.

Back in his cell, Cosmo peeled off his mother's blond wig, which she'd worn for *Norma* and in which he had disguised himself in his walk down to Bagley village to pleasure Ruth Walton.

He had finished *The Secret History*, the best book he had ever read, in which young people had totally waived morality and taken justice into their own hands. He had put on Matthias Goerne, a voice of unearthly beauty, singing Bach cantatas and was flipping through scores for the end-of-term concert. But he was not happy.

He had spent half an hour earlier mending Theo's DVD machine, but Theo's eyes still didn't rest on him with as much tenderness as they rested on Paris. No matter that he was going to get straight A stars and one for shagging from Ruth Walton, Cosmo wanted to be loved best by all the people by whom he wanted to be loved best. Even Hengist had rung from Washington to wish Paris luck.

He never rang me, thought Cosmo bitterly.

Cannoning off the walls on his way to bed around midnight, Theo saw a light on in Paris's room and went in. On the Thomas the Tank Engine duvet lay the boy's dark green history revision folder. In his sleeping hand was clutched the Greek *Epigrams* which Theo had given him for his sixteenth birthday. Theo was touched.

Paris looked so adorable with the lamplight falling on his long blond lashes and silky, flaxen hair. Playing cricket without a cap had brought a sprinkling of freckles and a touch of colour to his pale face. In sleep, the wolf cub relaxed and one could appreciate the beauty and casual grace of his body. Theo removed the Greek *Epigrams.*

Cosmo, skulking on the landing on the lookout for trouble, froze at the sight of Theo's battered copy of Philoctetes and his late-night whisky outside Paris's bedroom.

Suddenly terrible screams ripped the night apart, followed by anguished sobbing, which slowly subsided. Five minutes later, Cosmo, lurking in the shadows, saw Theo, a faint smile on his cadaverous features, coming out of Paris's room and going through the green baize door into his own apartment.

Cosmo retired to his cell and, setting aside the end-of-term concert scores, lit a fag, poured himself a large brandy and reflected. Alex Bruce wasn't his greatest fan, particularly since the Poppet art department incident. Poppet had even asked Cosmo to address the Talks Society on the morality of onanism. It wouldn't hurt to win some brownie points.

After a preliminary rootle round Theo's study, Cosmo let himself out of the front door, dropped his empty brandy bottle in Poppet's bottle bank and knocked on the Bruces' door. Alex, awake, much enjoying a third read of *Tape*, was soon reassuring Cosmo that he had done exactly the right thing.

Telling each other it was for Paris's sake, they let themselves into the house and to Theo's study, which thankfully looked out over an entirely deserted golf course. Judging by the bottles in the waste-paper basket, Theo was unlikely to wake up.

Alex's lips pursed at the overflowing ashtrays and the pile of reports unmarked, except by whisky stains. From Theo's desk drawer, Cosmo unearthed some love poems to Paris in Greek.

'Who was it said Greek letters on a blank page look like bird's footprints in the snow?' asked Cosmo, then when Alex clearly didn't know the answer, added, 'These are pretty explicit, sir, and those letters here, here, here and here, spell Paris, although it could be the Paris who triggered off the Trojan War.'

'I doubt it.' The gleam of triumph in Alex's eyes was obscene, particularly when, from under Theo's desk drawer lining paper, Cosmo pulled ravishing nude photographs of Paris, with the Eiffel Tower tattoo on his right shoulder, as well as a DVD in a plain brown wrapper.

Hearing a crash, they both jumped out of their skins, but it was only Hindsight arriving through the window.

'I'm amazed that cat hasn't died from passive smoking,' said

Alex, shoving him out again. Breathing more heavily than a French bulldog on the job, Alex then fastidiously parked his bottom on Theo's rickety chair and put the DVD into the machine, which came up with a film of ravishing naked youths re-enacting classical myths with men sporting curly hair and ringleted beards.

'That's Narcissus and that must be Ganymede,' volunteered Cosmo.

'Don't look.' Alex clapped a sweating hand over Cosmo's eyes.

'All part of my development,' said Cosmo, tugging the hand away.

The mosquito, earlier deterred by Theo's cigarettes, whined, circled and plunged her teeth into Alex's arm.

'I thought Mr Fussy was going to pounce,' Cosmo told Anatole next morning. 'I couldn't tell if he was more turned on by the porn or the chance to nail Theo. The Martial voting poster on the wall and *Red Tape* chucked in the bin were the *dernière paille*.'

112

Arriving at the police station in the early hours of the morning, Theo was locked in a windowless cell measuring five foot by eight foot and strip-searched. This included a policeman getting out a latex glove and telling him to bend over. He was then moved to another cell, by which time, deprived of whisky, cigarettes and morphine, he was crawling up the walls. Every so often, officers lifted the flap in the door to look at him.

He realized he had entered the twisted world of the morally repulsive when he saw the stony contempt on the faces of the two interrogating officers, one man, one woman, who obviously wanted to find out if he were part of a wider paedophile ring.

'I'm innocent.'

'Those photographs and that DVD weren't innocent, sir.'

'They were planted. Look, I need to make a telephone call, I'm worried about my cat.'

'Cat's least of your worries, sir.'

The policewoman clearly found him distasteful. He'd grabbed a maroon polo neck knitted for him by an aunt, but was still in his shorts, knees continually knocking together. Stinking of booze, fags and sweat, grey stubble thickening, he must cut a repugnant figure. They had removed his shoelaces and his belt, so his shorts kept falling down.

As the night wore on, they kept trying to make him confess.

'I'm innocent, I never laid a finger on the boy.'

'What about those nude photographs?'

'Never saw them before in my life; you won't find any of my fingerprints; must have been taken years ago – Paris has got a completely different haircut.'

'And the images of an obscene nature on the DVD machine?'

'The sixth form gave it to me as a Christmas present. I can't work the damn thing.'

'And the poems?'

'Certainly, I wrote those.' Theo groaned; his back was excruciating. 'Nothing obscene about them. I've been framed.'

'They all say that. You're in denial, Theo. Admit your guilt, you'll feel so much better. Then you can be put on a course for sex offenders.'

'And never teach again.'

'You were carried away, you'd had a bit too much to drink. Do you always entertain young boys alone? D'you sit close to them? D'you always make a habit of going into their rooms at night?'

Sadness overwhelmed Theo. Paris must have shopped him.

'If you confess,' the policewoman was now saying cosily, 'you might easily get off. Crown won't want a lengthy trial; happens a lot.'

The only reason he might confess, thought Theo, as the sky turned from electric blue to the rose pink of sunrise, was to get some more morphine.

In the morning, he came up before the magistrates and was given police bail, on condition that he didn't get in touch with anyone from the school.

'You must not speak to any members of staff,' he was told, 'or discuss the incident with anyone. You're to have no contact with the boy or any of the pupils. You must give an address well away from the school.'

Theo gave them the name of a dilapidated cottage on Windermere, left him by the aunt who'd knitted the maroon polo neck.

The case would now be adjourned for a pre-judicial review, which might take three weeks. Theo would come up in court three weeks after that. If the magistrates decided there was a case, it would be tried in a Crown court, probably not before Christmas.

Outside the court, Theo found Biffo, who had been selected by Alex as a safe bet to pack up his belongings. Biffo had also driven over in Theo's ancient Golf, which was loaded up with books, clothes, bottles of pills. He had also packed Theo's credit cards and cheque books, the seven plays of Sophocles, the manuscript in progress and Theo's notebooks.

'Where's my cat?' demanded Theo.

'I couldn't find him.' Biffo couldn't meet his eyes. 'All the police cars and disturbance must have scared him.'

'You must find him!' Theo was nearly in tears. 'I've had him since he was a kitten.'

'You often left him in the summer holidays.'

Biffo, Theo felt, at last had a legitimate excuse for detesting him.

'You've got to help me, Biffo, I must talk to Paris and Hengist.'

'You can't talk to anyone. Hengist is still away, anyway. You can ring me, here's my number, but only about things unconnected with the case.'

'I'm not resigning, I'm innocent.'

'I can't discuss it.'

Theo gave Biffo the address and telephone number of his cottage in Windermere. 'At least give it to Artie.'

'I can't promise anything. I've filled your car up with petrol.'

'Please try and find Hindsight, I'll pay for someone to come and collect him.'

Theo was still missing when Paris returned from his history exam. Barging into his housemaster's sealed-off study, he found whole shelves of books and Theo's manuscript gone, and Biffo nosing around.

'Is Theo back?'

'Gone away.'

'Where?'

'I'm not at liberty to say.'

'Don't be fucking stupid. I need to phone him. He never said goodbye; what's he supposed to have done?' Paris was nearly hysterical, particularly when Hindsight jumped in through the window and, mewing piteously, started weaving round his legs. 'Theo must have been pushed; he'd never leave without Hindsight. Tell me.'

Biffo backed away as, from a miniature Greek urn on Theo's desk, Paris grabbed a pair of scissors.

'I'll have those,' said Dora, grabbing the scissors as she marched in with a plate of cod from the kitchens and the *Larkminster Gazette*, which she handed to Paris.

'Page three,' she added as she started to cut up the cod for Hindsight.

'Bagley master arrested over sex abuse claim', Paris read the headline, then, with dawning disbelief, the copy: 'Theo Graham, aged 59, a housemaster who frequently took groups of boys on trips to Ancient Greece, was arrested last night for harbouring images of an obscene nature, but was released on police bail this morning.'

Paris turned on Dora. 'You didn't flog this story?'

'Certainly not. Poor Mr Graham's been victimcised.'

'Who's he supposed to have jumped on?'

'Why, you, of course.'

The temperature had dropped; a mean east wind was systematically stripping the petals off Sally's shrub roses. The A Level candidates were still wrestling with law and French papers and police cars were parked outside the Mansion when Hengist finally got back to Bagley.

Marching into Alex's office, he found his deputy head in a high state of almost sexual excitement, forehead white, eyes gleaming more than the gold rims of his spectacles, whole body shivering with self-righteous disapproval, damp patches under the arms of his shirt, whose sleeves were held up by frightful garters.

'What the hell's going on?'

'Very grave news, S.T.L. Theo Graham's been arrested.'

'Whatever for?'

'Sexually abusing Paris Alvaston.'

'Don't be ridiculous, Theo'd never jeopardize a boy's exams like that.'

'His baser nature overcame him,' said Alex heavily.

'Is Paris OK?' demanded Hengist. 'Did he take his history paper?' Then realizing how self-interested that sounded: 'What's he got to say?'

'He became hysterical and leapt at both Biffo and the policeman when asked the simplest question, which pre-supposes . . .'

'Bloody nothing,' roared Hengist.

'Theo entered Paris's room last night. Bloodcurdling screams were followed by desperate sobbing.'

'Probably a nightmare. Too much *Macbeth*, or mugging up Stalin's purges and the death camps, for Christ's sake. The boy's always been highly strung. Who reported this?'

'One of his peers, Cosmo Rannaldini.'

'Whoever believed a word Cosmo says?' said Hengist contemptuously. 'He'll have rung up the *Scorpion* by now.'

'I think not.' Alex put steepled fingers to pursed lips. 'Concerned for a fellow student, Cosmo behaved caringly and approached me late last night. I phoned the police instantly. They arrested Theo in the early hours.'

'For Christ's sake, Alex, why didn't you talk to Theo or ring me?'

'Your mobile was switched off. I consulted with Biffo, Joan and the bursar who, as the foster father, was very concerned.'

'You always wanted Theo out because he resisted your bloody modernizing.'

'We are accountable for our students' safety. In Theo's drawers were found naked photographs of Paris' – let Hengist think the police discovered them – 'poems dedicated to Paris of a homo-erotic nature and an obscene DVD of child pornography.'

Hengist looked out of the window at a blackbird splashing in the bird bath: such an innocent joyful pleasure. He felt a great sadness and said with less certainty, 'Theo's been framed.'

'I'm sorry, S.T.L.' Alex pinched the bridge of his nose. 'I know you were fond of the old boy. I was fond of him too. The whole thing has been most distressing.'

And you want me to feel sorry for you, thought Hengist.

'When did Paris find out?'

'We didn't apprize him this morning. I didn't want to stress him before a science paper.'

'Your subject, natch,' snarled Hengist. He wanted to hurl Alex to his death through the window.

'By lunchtime, Paris was searching for Theo. Rumours were circulating. The story had broken on Radio Larkminster. So Poppet broke the news to Paris, saying Mr Graham was helping the police with their enquiries.'

'Poppet? How did Paris take that?'

'Hard to tell, he never says much.'

'Jesus, if he's screwed up history, deputy heads will roll. I'm telling you, Alex, it's a set-up. Cosmo was clearly jealous of Theo's closeness to Paris.'

'Even if Paris does deny everything,' said Alex smugly, 'the photos and the pornography are enough to suspend him. I emailed the parents first thing. Better they knew before it hit the press. I've already received several back, and many supportive phone calls.' Alex handed Hengist a sheaf of paper. On top was a fax from Randal Stancombe: 'Hope that bloody nonce goes down and gets the thrashing he deserves. He's always sidelined my Jade.'

The second came from Boffin's mother: 'I don't want my Bernard at risk.'

'With an arse that size, he'd hardly be in jeopardy,' said Hengist contemptuously.

'That was uncalled for. I've arranged for Jason Fenton, who knows a little Latin, to take Theo's classes. Fortunately, the classics don't attract many students. Goodness knows who's going to write Theo's reports.'

Alex paused as Miss Painswick, who'd never been berserk about Theo either, rushed in in a state of high excitement.

685

'Oh, you're back, headmaster. Thank God, there are so many messages.' Then, turning to Alex: 'The police want to talk to you, Mr Bruce, and afterwards, the press would like a word.'

Quivering with self-importance, Alex bustled off.

'The *TES* want that piece on the advantages of the baccalaureate by tomorrow,' Painswick added to Hengist.

Finding the general office empty, Hengist unlocked the safe and took the GCSE history papers, which had just been handed in, upstairs to his office and groaned when he saw Paris's booklet. The boy had scrawled his name: Alvaston, Paris; his candidate number; and signed his name at the bottom. The rest was gibberish, the work of a fast unravelling mind. What did they expect with yet another father figure snatched from him?

Hengist was demented; his great scheme fucked. He turned to Boffin's booklet. In his greed to get at the paper, the little beast had forgotten to put his name at the top, only his candidate number which ended with a three which could easily be curved and billowed out into an eight.

Hengist glanced through the questions.

'The main reason for the collapse of the provisional Government in 1917 was the work of Lenin and the Bolsheviks. Discuss.'

That was a doddle.

'Do you agree that the increased Nazi support in the period 1930–32 was due to the personal appeal of Hitler?'

Hengist suddenly had a better plan. Picking up the telephone, he rang Painswick.

'I better get shot of that *TES* piece before anything else blows up, Miss P. Won't take more than an hour. I don't want to be disturbed.'

Alex was relishing his interview.

'Mr Graham was a scholar of the old school, officer. He had that rather Greek thing of cultivating friendships with boys, never girls, and insisted on working one to one with vulnerable youngsters like Paris Alvaston. He liked to flout convention.

'Believing in transparency, officer, I installed glass panels in classroom doors so one could monitor practice. Theo Graham deliberately hung his coat over the panel. He could be very subversive.'

An hour later, Hengist was just deciding how best to handle the Theo debacle when his office door was pushed open and Elaine flew in, throwing herself on him, chattering her teeth in delight, circling and sending all the urgent messages flying. She was followed by Sally, who'd clearly been crying.

'Darling, why didn't you tell me you were back? This is so terrible.' Quickly she kissed Hengist. 'Thank God you're here. Poor Theo could never have done this. We've got to rescue him.'

'I'm just off to nail Alex, come with me.'

In Alex's office, they found Poppet dropping some herbal painkiller made from drops of valerian into a glass of water, which Alex gulped down noisily, his Adam's apple heaving. Hengist couldn't bear to look at him and went to the window, from which he could see pupils, aware of some great crisis, milling about, talking, glancing worriedly up, then looking away.

'What did the police say?'

'They're taking it very seriously.'

'So am I. They've hijacked my best teacher,' snapped Hengist.

'And granted him bail,' said Poppet, who was now massaging her husband's shoulders. Alex closed his eyes.

On a side table, copies of *A Guide to Red Tape* rose to the ceiling.

'I've signed you a copy, S.T.L.'

Then, when Hengist didn't answer, Poppet said accusingly, 'Alex didn't get any sleep last night.'

'Didn't bloody deserve to.'

'Alex has a duty of care for young people,' reproached Poppet.

'Theo's name should never have been released to the media before there was any proof of guilt,' said Sally furiously. 'Why couldn't it have been dealt with internally, Alex?'

'Things are so much better handled in the maintained system,' piped up Poppet. 'Theo could have sought help from the union. We could have called an emergency meeting of the governors. The union rep would have then rolled up with the offending member.'

'If they can persuade the offending member to withdraw,' added Alex – for a second Hengist's eyes met Sally's – 'i.e. resign at once, things can be hushed up.'

'Why should Theo resign?' shouted Sally. 'He's innocent.'

Theo drove north until he found a church that was open, such was his need of sanctuary. How would he cope without James Benson's morphine? But the pain in his heart was far crueller.

Gasping for breath, he collapsed in a front pew, resting for a long time . . . When he looked down, he saw a pool of tears on the stone floor of the church.

687

Over at Larks, insulated against the outside world, the Brigadier and Emlyn heaved sighs of relief to find the history paper had included a question about the number of people killed on the Somme.

'On the other hand,' said Emlyn, 'Rocky's just informed me he was so pleased he remembered to tell the examiner we'd never have won World War I if Hitler hadn't attacked the Russians. How d'you get on?' he asked Feral.

'Bad as usual.' Feral shot outside to join his friends, who, euphoric the last exam was over, were playing football. Partner raced about yapping encouragement, particularly to Feral, who seemed to have wings on his heels. No one could stop him as he found goal again and again.

But what was the use? I'm thick, thick, thick, he told himself as he psyched himself up to ring his mother to let her know he'd screwed up yet again.

Pete Wainwright had just rolled up with a crate of wine to say thank you for the suggestions Taggie and her class had put forward for the Rovers' next season's menus. Bottles were therefore being opened in the staffroom to celebrate the end of the GCSEs when Emlyn walked in looking wintry.

'Afraid I can't stay.'

'Whyever not?' asked the Brigadier, who was mixing a pink gin for Lily.

'I've got to go over to Bagley. Artie's just phoned. Theo was arrested last night for possession of child porn and sexual abuse.'

'Paris?' whispered Janna.

'So it seems.'

'I don't believe it.'

Oh God, she thought, we should never have let him go to Bagley.

113

The last exam at Larks was followed two nights later by the end-of-term prom. Janna and her staff had such a frantic scramble getting everything ready that they had scant time to agonize about Paris and Theo – particularly as they were full of their own regrets that the year of grace was almost over.

Lily spent the day of the prom at home making sausage rolls and mushroom vol-au-vents for the buffet supper and trying not to cry. She was going to miss her Larks friends horribly, particularly seeing so much of the Brigadier. They'd planned a dance routine of Fred Astaire songs as a cabaret. Christian, rather smug he could still fit into them, was going to wear tails, and Lily had been forced to sell a last piece of Georgian silver to pay for a blue silk ball dress and pretty silver shoes in which to perform. Her cottage was achieving fashionable minimalism faster than she would have liked.

Lily was nervous of making an idiot of herself. If she drank enough to give herself courage she'd probably fall over. One of the numbers was 'Stepping Out with My Baby', and how could she pass as a 'baby' when she was over eighty with hair drawn into a dreary bun? If only she could afford to go back to Sadie, her darling Larkminster hairdresser, who'd cut her hair so beautifully.

As she packed bottles of elderberry wine into a cardboard box, she wondered who would feed the birds at Larks or the silver carp gliding, like Concorde, through the pond. She mustn't cry. Weeping at her age so devastated one's face. Sometimes she thought Christian loved her, but she was terrified her bridge might dislodge if he kissed her, leaving a great red toothless gap, and her body undressed was not a pretty sight, and with her too-long grey hair down, she looked like a witch.

Despite being poor, Lily had never stinted on General, who, too fat for the cat door, was mewing to go out. Wiping her eyes with a drying-up cloth, she opened the front door to find Pearl on the doorstep, weighed down by make-up kit.

'You've been so kind to me Lily, I fort I'd give you a make-over.' Then, at Lily's look of alarm: 'You've got such pretty hair, I'd love to cut it, and there's a new blue rinse called Sapphire Siren to bring out your blue eyes.'

'It's very kind. I'm not sure.'

'You'll look great.' Pearl marched into the house, dumping her cases in the kitchen. 'You've got such lovely skin. Christian says you're wearing blue tonight for the cabaret.'

'It's a secret,' squeaked Lily. 'We may not do it, depends how the evening pans out.'

'Everyone's looking forward to it,' said Pearl. As she unpacked her bottles, six tenners from the Brigadier crackled comfortingly in her breast pocket.

'I think I'll cut your hair before I wash it. Have you heard about Paris? Do you think Mr Graham's really been giving him it up the bum?'

'I'm sure not,' said Lily faintly.

'I often wondered whether Paris wasn't a woofter. Never made a pass at me,' said Pearl.

The rest of the staff kept trying to send Janna home early to make herself beautiful. Twenty years wouldn't be enough, she thought wearily; she'd need her jaw wired up in a permanent smile to get her through the evening.

She had been trying to complete the children's year books and certificates of achievement, when Sally had popped in with 'a bit of blotting paper': namely a mountain of smoked salmon wrapped in cling film and 'some nice white wine for you and Emlyn to drink behind the bus shelter'.

Janna thanked her profusely and, thinking for the first time Sally looked her age, begged her to stop for a cup of tea.

'My dear, I'd have loved to – look how well those oriental poppies are doing – but we're all in a bit of a state over Theo and Paris. Paris hurled a brick through Alex's window last night, because no one will give him Theo's address. Emlyn's been wonderful with him, but the poor boy's hysterical, says he'll only talk to the police if he's allowed to talk to Theo first, which the police say is impossible. Nadine and Cindy Payne are putting their oars in; press everywhere.'

The sympathy in Janna's eyes prompted Sally to further revelations. 'Emlyn's also had a bit of a shock, poor boy. Oriana's expecting a baby – I'm not sure who the father is – due in November.' For a second Sally's face crumpled. 'I'm sure I'll love it once it's born, but Hengist doesn't want anything to do with it or Oriana. He's terribly cut up about Theo. Oh Janna, I do hope you don't feel we've failed Paris.'

Janna was reassuring Sally she didn't and was kissing her good-bye when Randal Stancombe came on the line. God, how she now hated his oily, over-intimate, threatening voice.

'Hi, Jan, can I be frank? Feel rather let down; I didn't get an invite for tonight's end-of-term do. Didn't think our friendship was that shallow.'

'Oh, it isn't, it isn't.' Janna curled up in embarrassment. 'It's only small, just staff and children.'

'Don't weaken,' mouthed Rowan from the doorway.

'But do drop in,' mumbled Janna.

'I'm actually taking Jade out for a meal, but we'll look in on the way. You asked any media?'

'No. Doesn't mean the bastards won't turn up.'

'Gosh, you're brave,' said Bianca, 'I should so die of embarrassment if Mummy was tempted on to the dance floor.'

'Unlikely,' said Xav as he tied his black tie. 'Dad's ordered me to shoot anyone who comes near her.'

He was delighted that the waistband of his DJ trousers had had to be taken in six inches and the legs let down.

Downstairs, Rupert helped his wife, ravishing in a scarlet halterneck, load chocolate torte and bowls of strawberries into the car.

'Keep an eye on her,' he said to Xav. 'You both look marvellous.'

He wouldn't have admitted to a soul, that he couldn't wait to get back and finish *Emma*. Mrs Elton was even more like Anthea Belvedon than Mrs Bennet.

'I'll be down in a minute, pour yourself a drink,' Lily shouted down the stairs as Christian Woodford put the elderberry wine, the crumbles and the sausage rolls into the car.

The Brigadier choked on his drink as Lily came down the stairs. Her short silver-blue hair softly caressed her cheekbones, brought out the intense blue of her eyes and matched a dress short enough to reveal the most charming ankles. She had pawned all her jewellery except her sapphire engagement

691

ring and her pearls, which she asked him to do up.

' "My precious Lily! My imperial kitten!" ' sighed the Brigadier, letting his fingers linger on her neck.

With his white tie and tails setting off his golfing tan, his fine square features and his thick silver hair, the Brigadier looked infinitely handsomer than Fred Astaire and Lily told him so.

'Could you also zip up my dress, which is beyond my arthritic fingers?'

'Much rather unhook it,' said the Brigadier, who had this afternoon signed a two-year Venturer contract to make another series of *Buffers*, along with some poetry drama documentaries kicking off with 'Horatius' and 'Morte d'Arthur'.

' "Steppin' Out With My Baby",' sang the Brigadier, smiling at Lily as they reached the outskirts of Larkminster. For a moment, he thought he was back in the last war, as, like submarines gliding stealthily through the blue evening, stretch limos with black windows kept overtaking them. Then out of these limos on to the Appletree forecourt, like a conjuror's coloured handkerchief, spilled the children, the boys in hired tuxedos with red, blue, green and tartan bow ties, the girls in pink or mauve satin trouser suits or ball dresses showing off pearly shoulders and pretty legs, enhanced by jewelled high heels and sparkling ankle bracelets.

With their hair descending in ringleted waterfalls and secured with combs decorated with flowers, their faces glittering with excitement, they could have been re-enacting the Netherfield ball from their set book. Intoxicated by their new beauty, they tore around Appletree, taking photographs, shrieking how wicked each other looked. Judging by the giggling, they'd already been at the booze.

The boys were fingering the Brigadier's tailcoat.

'That retro shawl collar's dead cool, Brig, did you get it from Matalan or the internet?'

'It's my own,' confessed Christian, 'I used to wear it night after night to dances. I like your gym shoes, Graffi.'

'Fort I'd treat myself.' Graffi waved a dark blue and pale blue trainer with a two-inch heel in the air. 'They cost a hundred and ten quid. What d'you think of Beckham's new hair?'

'Not as good as mine,' said Rocky, patting four-inch-high vermilion-gelled spikes. 'And you look even gooder, Lily.'

As the others laughed and agreed, Lily told them they all looked wonderful too.

The hall had been utterly transformed. Mags had blocked out any light from the big windows with full-length black curtains, which she and the other teachers had covered in silver and gold paper stars. On the stage below a huge glittering blue sign saying 'Larkminster High School Prom 2004', a group of suntanned men in black, known as the Butchers (as in 'I'm butcher than you'), were belting out 'American Pie'.

From the ceiling, concealing Graffi's angels, who all looked like Milly Walton, hung hundreds of coloured balloons like an inverted bubble bath. The floor was carpeted with dancers, gyrating under the flickering lights, clapping their hands above their heads. Many of the boys wore luminous rings in blue, emerald or red round foreheads or necks. The air was a dense fog of cigarette smoke.

Chairs for spectators had been grouped along one wall on either side of a trestle table, offering Coca-Cola, lemonade and Fanta. Officially, because Ashton or Cindy might gatecrash, the evening was dry.

I could murder a proper drink, thought Lily.

As if reading her mind, Janna glided out of the dancers. She had at long last had a chance to wear her slinky black velvet dress, off one freckled shoulder and split to the thigh on one side. With the front of her hair coaxed upward in smaller russet spikes than Rocky's, her huge eyes ringed with raw sienna, her big trembling mouth painted scarlet, she looked as young suddenly as any of her pupils.

'You look stunning! Isn't Pearl a genius,' she and Lily shouted to each other over 'American Pie'.

'Keep this for yourself,' added Janna, filling a glass with Sally's white, then handing bottle and glass to Lily.

'What's that?' Lily noticed Janna was drinking straight from a Fanta bottle.

'Teachers' lemonade, taught me by a primary head. No one can tell it's half filled with vodka. Will you crown the Prom King and Queen for us?'

'As long as I don't have to make a speech. Who's won it?'

'Wait and see. But it's a grand result.'

Next moment Pearl had rushed up.

'I want a group photograph of my favourite teachers,' she said bossily. 'That's you, Pittsy, you, Janna, you, Taggie and the Brig and Lily.'

Flattered, the five lined up as Pearl spent ages getting them in the right position. 'You go behind Janna, Taggie, and Lily in front of Pittsy, or we can't see you. Where's Emlyn? I'd like him as well.'

'Oh, get on,' grumbled the Brigadier, 'Lily and Taggie need top-ups.'

Dutifully they all waited as Pearl peered into her viewfinder, then, suddenly saying: 'Oh, I'm bored with this,' she wandered off to photograph someone else.

'Little madam,' exploded the Brigadier as Janna and Lily got the giggles.

'It's the first time I've seen Aysha's hair in four years. She looks absolutely gorgeous,' said Pittsy as Aysha timidly followed Xav on to the floor to join the big circle of dancers.

Aysha had only been allowed to attend the prom if she was chaperoned. As a result, Mrs Khan sat in the darkness watching her daughter, knowing how sad Aysha would be tomorrow. At least tonight, as she swayed in flowing turquoise chiffon before Xav, she could forget her heartache.

'Get Mother Khan some teachers' lemonade,' suggested Wally.

'Where's Emlyn?' asked Janna for the hundredth time.

'He was here shifting furniture until the last moment,' said Cambola, who kept dragging boys on to the floor to dance; they lasted thirty seconds before belting back to their mates.

Outside, the sky was pale grey, the lace mats of elderflower caressing the window panes. Thinking Basket looked rather fetching in her tobacco-brown crimplene, Skunk led her off for a stroll.

They were passed as they went out by Feral wandering in, late because he'd been playing football. Unable to afford a tuxedo, he still looked a million dollars in black jeans and polo neck.

'"Here's mettle more attractive",' cried Cambola, bearing him off to dance to loud cheers.

114

Janna was dancing with the children again, singing along to Katie Melua as she rotated two pink luminous flowers above her head, surrendering herself to the music.

'One forgets how young she is,' Lily murmured to the Brigadier, adding doubtfully, 'You don't think our cabaret's too old for them?'

The Brigadier squeezed her hand.

'To use a mendacious expression of Randal Stancombe's: "Trust me."'

'Talk of the devil,' complained Lily as Randal, resplendent in a dinner jacket, pink carnation in his buttonhole, appeared in the doorway.

I'd like to be his arm candy, thought Kitten, running her hand through her hair and sticking out her breasts. Oh hell, he'd brought a woman. No, it was that bitch Jade.

Graffi, drunk and furious with Stancombe for sacking his father, reeled over and handed him his glass, which Stancombe was about to drink out of, then realized it was empty.

'Get me a Bacardi and Coke,' Graffi ordered him airily, then, at Stancombe's look of fury: 'Oh, I fort you was a waiter.'

'Graffi!' Anticipating punch-ups, Janna ran off the dance floor. 'Hello, Randal, let me get you a drink.'

'Evening, Janna, looks as if you're enjoying yourself.' Stancombe then dragged her into the corridor, pointing to walls on which Graffi had caricatured every child in the school. 'Made a bit of a mess of the property.'

'Nothing a lick of paint won't cure,' answered Janna defensively. 'One day, Graffi's murals'll be worth more than this place put together.'

'Your geese are always swans,' sneered Stancombe.

Suddenly photographers seemed to be everywhere.

'Go away, this is a private party,' Janna told them furiously.

'Just a few piccies,' insisted Stancombe, 'with the kids beside the minibus,' which had suddenly appeared, parked in the forecourt.

'I can't drag them off the dance floor.'

Jade, Kitten and Pearl were insincerely congratulating each other on their dresses. Jade in Versace was miffed they were looking so good. She was used to being the belle of the ball. Feral, Graffi, Johnnie, Danny the Irish, even Xav, all looked gorgeous. Why weren't any of them asking her to dance?

'Come and dance,' Rocky asked her a minute later.

'Thanks, but I'm not stopping. Daddy's about to make a statement to the press,' answered Jade as the music died away.

'As one who has enriched these youngsters' lives,' Stancombe told the reporters, 'I've been haunted by the statistics that it's six times as difficult for kids from poor homes to go to uni.'

'You did it without a degree, Mr Stancombe,' said a blonde from the *Scorpion* admiringly.

'I was lucky,' admitted Stancombe modestly. 'I only hope my not insubstantial financial contribution to Larks High has paid off and the students get some good grades.'

'Oh, shut up,' muttered Janna.

'Can we have a photograph of you dancing with the kids?' asked the *Gazette*.

'You'd better do it,' Janna urged the children, as the band started up again, 'then he'll push off.'

Stancombe, however, had turned back to Janna.

'Terrible news about Theo Graham. I'd castrate all paedophiles.'

'Hengist is convinced he's innocent.'

Stancombe was about to argue, when he noticed Xav, euphoric after another dance with Aysha, bopping off the floor and demanded, 'How did your dad get on in his Eng. lit. exam?'

'Very well,' replied Xav coldly, then as Stancombe's eyebrows shot up. 'My dad does everything well. He's got a horse running on Saturday called Poodle. I'd have a big bet if I were you. It's the only way you'll pay the money you owe the Bagley Fund when the results come out.'

Scenting trouble, it was Xav's mother this time who rushed over.

'Ah, the lovely Taggie – a quick dance?' Randal seized her hand.

'I don't think so.' Xav stepped in front of his mother, scowling up at Stancombe. 'My father asked me to look after Mum – he wouldn't like it one bit if she danced with you.'

Stancombe, who now much regretted leaving his guards behind, said furiously:

'I can only assume you've been drinking.'

'I don't drink,' said Xav.

'I'll get even with you and your arrogant bastard of a father.' Hurrying Jade towards the door, Stancombe went slap into Emlyn.

'I was just saying,' he yelled over the band, 'Theo Graham ought to be castrated and not allowed near vulnerable youngsters.'

'Get out,' growled Emlyn, holding open the door.

Jade suddenly longed to stay. As she watched Xav rushing back to Aysha, she decided he'd become very attractive, not least in the way he'd stood up to her father. She'd love to join the great ring of dancers. She wished she had friends like that. It was all her parents' fault for not sending her to a comprehensive.

'Come on, princess,' shouted Randal.

'You OK?' Janna asked Emlyn, noticing how tired he looked, but his answer was blotted out by a roll of drums. It was time for the awards.

'At least it might mean the music is a bit less loud,' the Brigadier murmured to Lily.

Janna grabbed the mike and announced she was now going to give each pupil his or her year book and certificate of achievement.

'I'd rather have some money,' shouted Rocky to roars of applause, which continued as each child went up and Emlyn took photograph after photograph, because everyone wanted a record of themselves beside Janna.

When it was Johnnie's turn, he grabbed Janna, kissing her on and on to whoops and catcalls until Emlyn tapped him sharply on the shoulder: 'That's enough.'

'Your turn now, Mr Davies,' chorused the children, screaming with laughter as Emlyn handed a blushing Janna his handkerchief to wipe off her smudged lipstick.

Who would have dreamt a year ago, I could have had a ball at a ball without a drop of booze? thought Pittsy.

Janna then thanked all the children for making the year so memorable and rewarding.

'I'd also like to say on behalf of all the weird staff who came to teach you, that we've never had it so good.'

'Hear, hear,' shouted Skunk, squeezing Basket's spare tyres.

'And I'd like to thank all the teachers, wondercooks' – Janna smiled at Taggie – 'terrific dinner ladies, Rowan and, most of all, Wally, who's taken care of us all, and made this evening possible.'

'Don't forget Mistah Davies,' shouted Graffi.

'And of course, Emlyn, thank you all.'

Pittsy then seized the mike and admitted:

'In twenty-nine years of teaching, this is the best year I've ever had because of that woman over there.' He pointed to Janna, to deafening applause. 'She's the best boss I've ever had—' His voice cracked. 'She's been dead good.'

Are they talking about me, wondered Janna in bewilderment, particularly when a big screen to the right of the band lit up and there was Kylie, clutching her new baby and singing: 'To Miss . . .' instead of 'To Sir, With Love'.

'Oh hell,' grumbled Pearl. 'There goes my make-up again,' as Janna's tears swept away a flotsam of mascara and glitter, particularly when Kitten curtsied and presented her with a gold pen engraved 'To a great head'.

'Thank you ever so much and I'll write to you all with this pen.' Janna mopped her eyes with Emlyn's handkerchief. Then, desperate to get the praise on to someone else: 'And now Lily is going to crown the Prom King and Queen, voted by their peers.'

'I first have to read the citations,' said Lily, putting on her spectacles and joining Janna in the middle of the floor.

' "We thought you was very snooty when you joined Larks," ' she read, ' "but we realized you was just shy and now you're a good friend to all of us." Very nice too.' Opening the envelope: 'And our Prom Queen is none other than Aysha Khan.'

Aysha gasped and clapped her hands over her eyes:

'I don't believe it.'

As Xav proudly led her up, Mrs Khan stood up and cheered, then shushed herself in horror. Lily placed a gold cardboard crown, inset with red, blue and green jewels, on Aysha's dark head, and the room erupted.

'She looks absolutely gorgeous,' sighed Pittsy.

'She certainly does,' agreed a grinning Xav as he slid back into the crowd, but not for long, as Lily read out the next citation.

' "We was worried when you came to us, but you mixed in really well, and you was never posh." ' Hands trembling with excitement, Lily ripped open the envelope. 'And the Prom King is Xavier Campbell-Black.'

More deafening roars of applause followed as Lily had difficulty getting the crown over Xav's Afro.

'Thank you so much,' shouted Xav, 'I can't believe this.'

'Nor can we,' yelled Graffi. 'Never had a poof on the frone since James I.'

'Give your queen a kiss,' shouted Pearl, and Xav turned and kissed Aysha on the lips for the first time since Ramadan, and Aysha, after a terrified glance at her tearful, ecstatic mother, who had nearly finished her bottle of teachers' lemonade, kissed Xav back to a thunder of stamped feet.

'Look at Taggie,' whispered Lily as Xav's mother wiped her eyes with her crimson pashmina.

Xav and Aysha reopened the ball, never taking their eyes off each other. A second later, Emlyn led a laughing, protesting Taggie on to the floor.

'It's so refreshing,' beamed Mrs Khan as Janna replaced her Fanta bottle.

Supper followed and the starving hordes fell on tuna and cucumber sandwiches, bridge rolls filled with egg mayonnaise, Lily's sausage rolls and vol-au-vents, Sally's smoked salmon sandwiches, strawberries, blackberry crumbles and chocolate torte.

The girls were back on the floor dancing together, flashing lights picking up glossy tossing curls and gleaming bare shoulders. Janna was among them, swaying like a maenad, waving a glittering blue butterfly in figures of eight.

Why haven't I asked her to dance? wondered Emlyn. What am I afraid of?

Out in the limos, groups were drinking Cava and smoking weed. Others were signing each other's T-shirts, certificates and year books. There was a second roll of drums. 'It's now time for your cabaret,' shouted the lead singer, 'performed by Brigadier Christian Woodford and Mrs Lily Hamilton.'

Clapping and whooping, the dancers retreated to be joined round the edge of the floor by others running in from the cars.

Lily fled to the Ladies, shaking with terror. If only she'd had a little more to drink. Pearl was waiting when she came out of the loo.

'Just let me fix your face.'

Getting out a brush, she added blusher to Lily's blanched cheeks, used another brush to repaint her trembling lips and another to fluff up her hair, before spraying on some rather bold scent.

'You look great, Lily. Let's hide that bra strap, and straighten your dress, off you go. Good luck.'

The children had begun to stamp their feet and slow handclap.

Christian, waiting with a mike in his hand, was looking anxious, but his smile was beautiful, even when Lily muttered, 'You got me into this bloody thing,' as he led her on to the floor.

'Doo di doo, doo di doo di, doo di . . .' sang the Brigadier in a delightful baritone, then, brandishing both mike and a large green umbrella, launched into 'Singing in the Rain', ending up with a little tap dance round Lily, before sweeping her into 'Stepping Out With My Baby'.

For a second, Lily stumbled; the Brigadier held her tightly and they were off. It was such a beautiful tune.

After that Lily was fine. In no time, Christian was singing 'Cheek To Cheek', as with faces pressed together, they glided round the floor.

Lily would never in a thousand years have accused the Brigadier of showing off, but she was not displeased when he too stumbled, and this time it was she who had to hold him up.

The pupils, utterly entranced, bellowed their approval.

'Good on yer, Brig. Wicked, Lily. Come on, Fred and Ginger, give us an encore.'

'I'm out,' said Lily firmly, so the Brigadier, gazing into her eyes, sang 'Our Love Is Here To Stay'.

Seizing Basket's hand, Skunk stole off into the moonlight.

'I love you, Xav,' whispered Aysha.

'Hic,' said Mrs Khan.

How much longer can I go on staying cheerful, wondered Feral as, in the middle of the floor, the Brigadier beamed down at Lily.

'Oh, cut to the chase, Brig,' shouted Graffi, 'you know you love her.'

'I believe I do,' said Christian, kissing Lily on the forehead.

As the band broke into 'YMCA', the hall filled up again. Monster was dancing with Mrs Khan, Rowan with Pittsy, Wally with Janna, Sophy with Graffi, and Rocky with Gloria.

Aware that his wits might be needed if fights broke out, Emlyn, unlike Mrs Khan, had stayed off the drink. Watching the high jinks on the floor, he thought: They're all so pixillated by the transformation of the school and themselves, they've forgotten the dark to come.

Tonight for him had been a cut-off point. Before, despite everything, he'd had the faint hope that Oriana might realize Charlie was a dreadful mistake. Now she was pregnant, it was over.

' "You're The One That I Want", ' sang the bronzed lead singer.

115

It was the last dance; Johnnie hand in hand with Kitten, Pearl with Graffi, Feral with Janna, Danny with Danijela, all formed a great circle. The dope-smokers, who'd got the munchies and been raiding the buffet, came racing on to the floor, sandwiches in their hands, as the balloons came down. Yellow, emerald, blue, pink, scarlet and orange, a technicolour snowstorm cascaded into the flickering lights until the ground was one great technicolour bubble bath.

Then the boys waded in, as if this was what their huge trainers had been awaiting all evening, symbolically stamping on the balloons, bang, bang, bang, followed by the girls leaping in with their stilettos, pop, pop, pop, as though war had broken out.

Instinctively, Janna had dropped Feral and Graffi's hands looking round for the tranquillizers for Partner, then remembered he was safe at home.

'Summer Days' sang the band, as dancing went on over an ocean of shredded rubber. Some of the balloons had been saved. Kitten had six, Danijela had one and burst into tears when Rocky popped it with a cigarette. Feral kept back an orange one, in case Bianca was in the car collecting Xav.

It was stiflingly hot in the smoke-filled hall. Everyone was glad to surge out into the cool of the night.

A glittering full moon, like a halo searching for its lost saint, clearly felt upstaged by the splendid explosion of fireworks which followed. Golden fountains overflowed, surging silver snakes belched forth great flurries of blue sparks, rose-pink Roman candles and hissing orange Chinese dragons were followed by a series of colossal bangs, producing screams from the spectators.

Bounding round, setting alight Catherine wheels, avoiding

701

squibs, launching off rockets, Emlyn was glad he'd stayed sober, particularly when Rocky lurched forward.

'Want to light a rocket, want to light a rocket,' and fell flat on his face, lit cigarette narrowly missing the remaining fireworks in the box.

Heaving him up, Emlyn allowed him to light one, which, with a sound like Velcro being ripped apart, soared gloriously upwards, before tossing its emerald and royal blue stars over the Shakespeare Estate.

At the end, more blazing white-hot stars spelt out the words 'Goodbye Larks High', then faded, bringing everyone back to reality with a bump.

Suddenly Mags was reassuring sobbing pupils: 'This school is a launching pad not a crashing down to earth.'

As Pearl in her pretty periwinkle-blue dress wept on her shoulder, Janna could feel her desperate thinness.

'I'm going to miss you, miss.'

Janna was quickly drenched as child after tearful child came up.

'Thank you, miss, for everything.'

'You're the bravest girl I know.' Mags was comforting an inconsolable Aysha.

Cambola, clinging to her trumpet, was also in floods. She had no family, no husband, no job; her pupils were all.

'Do drop in for a cup of tea whenever you're passing,' she begged as each one came up.

'Never been kissed by so many pretty women,' said Pittsy.

Even Skunk was getting his fair share of hugs and shrieks, as cheeks were tickled by his bristly beard and moustache. The girls far more enjoyed weeping on Emlyn's chest. Kitten was clinging to him, leaving frosted-pink lipstick all over his shirt, when he glanced across at Janna, seeing her tears glittering in the moonlight. Setting Kitten gently aside, he crossed the grass, gathering up Janna's soaked body, and she let herself go.

It was such a haven, amid such desolation, to feel his arms round her; he was so big, solid and warm. She knew he was still carrying a torch for Oriana, but she wished he'd go on hugging her for ever.

Emlyn, meanwhile, thought: My heart is in smithereens over Oriana, but it feels nice with my arms round Janna; I'd like to keep them there.

'Can I give you a lift home?' he murmured into her spiked hair.

Janna's heart leapt. 'Oh yes, please.'

'At last,' said Lily, turning in satisfaction to the Brigadier.

Gradually the limos glided away. Most of the teachers had retreated to the staffroom, where the pink and purple ball dresses still hung from the Christmas pantomime and the cuttings from the rugby match against Bagley: 'Comp thrashes Posh', curled on the noticeboard. Mags had pinned up Monster's definition of a mentor: 'Someone you can talk to, an adult what ain't your parents, but is a friend.'

'Once they realized we weren't on supply, they began to trust us,' said Pittsy.

The telephone rang.

'I've been phoning all evening,' screeched Miss Miserden. 'Never heard such a noise. A rocket landed on my patio. Scamp shot up the pear tree. I'm about to call the police.'

'When we have another party,' said Pittsy sarcastically, 'we'll give you a warning,' but as he replaced the receiver, his face crumpled. 'But there never will be. Best boss I ever had.'

Putting off the evil day, to cheer up her staff, Janna had organized some jaunts for later in the week. The list, also pinned up, included the Barbican and Kensington Palace to see Princess Diana's clothes collection one day, a clay and archery shoot on another, with a buffet at school to include partners on another, then a fun supper just for Larks staff the next.

None of this cheered up Cambola, sobbing in the corner: it was like the end of an opera tour. Tomorrow, we rest.

As Janna waved the band off with profuse thanks, Rupert and Bianca arrived to collect Taggie and Xav, who was clutching his crown.

'He was voted most popular boy in the school,' cried Taggie.

Rupert put a hand on Xav's shoulder. 'That's better than grades, well done.'

'Is it all right if we drop Aysha and Mrs Khan off on the way?' whispered Xav, 'I think someone's spiked her drink.'

Bianca had jumped out of the BMW, big dark eyes searching everywhere for Feral. Reading her mind, Xav said, 'I'm sorry, he's gone home, I tried to keep him.'

Bianca shrugged and huddled into the back. Feral, hidden behind the big swamp cypress, watched the BMW roll down the drive, before fleeing into the night.

Emlyn was desperate to leave, suffering the edginess of not drinking, jangling his car keys attached to a black plastic Scottie with a tartan collar. He found Janna in the IT room gazing abstractedly at a computer screen, where Larks High School, like

703

a house in a twister, rolled hopelessly over and over into a bright blue eternity.

'I saved you this.' Emlyn handed her a red balloon, splaying his fingers over hers. 'Let's go.'

'I'll just say goodbye to the others.'

Outside the staffroom, however, they found Danijela in tears.

'This school is my home.'

Emlyn gritted his teeth as Janna, the eternal hostess, put Basket's beige cardigan round Danijela's thin shoulders. Janna was just making her a cup of tea when Monster wandered in.

'My mum's not answering.'

'Where is she?'

'Moved house if she's got any sense,' quipped Rocky.

'She's asleep. Probably can't hear the doorbell,' whined Monster.

'Pissed,' mouthed Wally from behind his back.

'My bruvvers and sisters are asleep, no one won't let me in,' he whined.

'So you walked back here, poor Martin.' Janna poured boiling water over Danijela's tea bag.

'I got nowhere to go.' Monster looked round pathetically.

There was a long pause. Pittsy looked at his feet, so did Cambola, so even did Mags and Emlyn. Janna counted to ten.

'You better come home with me, Martin. We'll put a note through your mum's door: "I'm in Miss Curtis's house." You'll have to sleep on the sofa.'

Then she caught sight of Emlyn, his face a death mask.

'I'm off. Night, everybody.' He gathered up his car keys and was gone.

Janna caught up with him in reception. Graffi's black good-luck cat grinned down at her unsympathetically.

'Come in for a drink on the way home,' she pleaded. 'We can put Monster to bed.'

'Where?' snapped Emlyn.

'In the lounge. We can talk in the kitchen.'

'Talking wasn't what I had in mind.'

Janna's heart started to thump in excitement, then faltered as Emlyn said, 'And I'm not coming to any of those jaunts next week, I've got interviews.'

'You what?' Janna fought back tears of disappointment. Every trip had been planned with him in mind. 'Who with?' she asked, following him through the front door.

'The Welsh Rugby Union, among others.'

Out in the warmth of Midsummer Night's Eve, the bitter acid

tang of elder and the overwhelming sweetness of the white philadelphus mingled to symbolize the bitter sweetness of the evening.

'You're lovely, Janna; all things to all children,' said Emlyn bleakly, 'but you're not going to change. I'm fed up with women who want to save the world.'

As he strode towards his car, Janna ran after him. 'I'm sorry about Oriana's baby. I know you're upset: please talk to me about it.'

'I don't need any counselling. Poppet Bruce had a go earlier.' And he was in his car, storming down the drive, not even bothering with lights or a seatbelt.

Janna couldn't bawl her heart out because of Monster.

'So much food left,' she said, returning to the staffroom. 'If we put it in the fridge, the children can have it tomorrow.'

'There isn't going to be a tomorrow,' sobbed Rowan.

Cambola, however, switched off her mobile, tears drying on her beaming face.

'Jack and Kylie have just asked me to be godmother to little Ganymede.'

Both the Brigadier and Lily had been drinking, so they left the car at Larks and took a taxi to Elmsley church, where the Brigadier put a balloon on his wife's grave. Then they walked hand in hand down the tree tunnel with shafts of moonlight piercing the leaf ceiling lighting on Lily's pearls and the Brigadier's diamond shirt studs.

Pearl had forced a fish-paste sandwich on Lily, made by her mum, to keep up her strength, so Lily had to do something to sweeten her breath. Pearl's proffered Juicy Fruit chewing gum might have pulled her bridge out. Fortunately, she always kept three boiled sweets in her bag, one for the walk there, one for the walk home and one just in case. The just in case was blackcurrant, which she was sucking furiously.

Despite his outward sangfroid, the Brigadier was more nervous than he had ever been under fire.

Just outside Wilmington, they paused to rest against a five-bar gate. The Brigadier took a deep breath. Lily looked so beautiful with her silvery hair and her face bathed in moonlight.

'Darling Lily, I fell in love with you on the second of October two thousand, the day you moved into Wilmington.'

There was a crunch of boiled sweet as he took her in his arms, kissing her gently then passionately, and both their teeth stayed put.

'Oh, Christian, my Brigadearest,' sighed Lily.

'If I go down on one knee, will you help me up afterwards?'

'Of course.'

'Sweetest Lily, will you do me the great honour of marrying me?'

'Oh yes, yes I will.'

Anxious to kiss his betrothed, Christian held out a hand, Lily gave it a tug, but he was too heavy for her, and next moment had pulled her down on the grass beside him. The only way they could clamber up, some time later, still laughing helplessly, was gate bar by gate bar.

Back at Larks, Graffi and Johnnie, who'd been indulging in a hilarious spot of dogging, observing Basket's plump white bottom bobbing up and down in Skunk's heaving Vauxhall, had returned to the staffroom to mob up Janna.

'Not sure Monster wants to come home with you, miss. Finks you're going to jump on him.'

'There's a perfectly good lock to the lounge door,' snarled Janna. 'Come on, Martin, I can't abandon Partner any longer.'

Having once bound a firework to Partner's tail, Monster showed even more reluctance to spend the night under the same roof.

'He'll get me in the night, miss.'

Janna drove home very slowly, tempted to knock on Emlyn's door, but there was no car outside. She had great difficulty not strangling Monster, particularly when the hulking great beast announced he was starving, then complained the scrambled eggs Janna made him were too sloppy.

Partner growled so much at such ingratitude, Janna let Monster sleep in her bedroom, and heard the key turn in the lock.

Outside, it was getting light, the longest day dawning after the longest saddest night. Except for the jaunts, which were meaningless without Emlyn, Larks was over. She must face up to the fact that she was totally, hopelessly in love with him and had utterly blown it by not being there when he needed her. Having sobbed herself to sleep, her first lie-in for weeks was interrupted by pounding on the door at six o'clock.

'Can you run me into Larkminster, miss? It's my paper round.'

116

'Teachers should never go on holiday for at least a fortnight after the end of the summer term,' Pittsy was always saying. 'One needs two weeks at home unwinding and invariably contracting some bug, then fourteen days abroad in the sun, before a fortnight psyching oneself up for the rigours of the autumn term.'

Janna had no such luxury. She had to work out her contract with S and C until the end of August, leaving Appletree immaculate for the new incumbents, whoever they might be, and supervising the removal of property by neighbouring schools, who were so avaricious, she was tempted to put a 'do not remove' label on Partner's collar.

To depress her further, it rained throughout July and August as estate agents and developers splashed through the school grounds, skips filled with water and rubble, windows were boarded up, machinery dismantled and cork and whiteboards ripped down, until only Janna's office remained operational.

In it, apart from her personal belongings, were a framed photograph of the staff and children of Larks High in happier days and the computer and printer, out of which the GCSE results would thunder.

Still on the wall was the cupboard Emlyn had put up by non-chalantly hammering in the screws. Janna never dreamt she would miss him so dreadfully. Her constant companion as a child had been a vast English sheepdog, whose huge reassuring presence she kept imagining round the house for months after he died. So it was with Emlyn. He had landed his grand job with the Welsh Rugby Union, but, according to the Brigadier, he was hoping to get back to Larks for Results Day on 26 August. The children so longed to see him.

Even after term was ended, they hadn't been able to accept the dream was over and still piled in every day: 'Let's play bingo, miss,' or offering to help her clean the building and littering it with Coke cans and crisp packets.

As Results Day approached, they grew increasingly jittery about not getting enough grades to qualify for sixth-form places in colleges or other schools, or for a good job, or to satisfy their parents, or to not feel a fool in front of their friends.

None of them aspired to the miracle of the Magic Five, which would give Larks a point in the league tables.

In the evenings, Janna had visited every parent on the Shakespeare Estate, trying to explain that further education didn't just mean top-up fees and the loss of a family breadwinner.

She was most worried about Feral, who'd left the sanctuary of the Brigadier's cottage and moved with his mother into a two-bedroom flat so poky there was hardly room for his football. If his mother stayed off drugs until Christmas, her other children might be returned to her. But she was so listless and easily cast down, Feral was terrified she'd lapse, particularly if Uncle Harley rolled up again. He hated leaving her, even to stack shelves with Graffi every night.

As Janna was shredding confidential papers referring to the staff at Larks, she had come across one of Feral's essays which young Lydia had kept. He must have dictated it to Paris.

My dream [he had begun] is to leave home when I'm nineteen and be married by the time I'm twenty to the girl I stay with for the rest of my life and have two children. I'm going to buy a house in a nice area for my children to grow up decently. I will buy a car for my wife. She can go to work or look after the children. I'm going to give her a big posh kitchen worth £1,000 and go on holiday three times a year, twice abroad and once to Skegness.

'Well done, Feral,' Lydia had written, 'work hard and chase your dream.'

It was dated March 2002, just after he had met Bianca. Oh, poor Feral, Janna nearly wept, the desire of the moth for the star.

At least this year the incessant rain had kept alive the saplings Wally had planted last autumn; perhaps they might symbolize the survival of her children.

Against all this, she longed constantly for Emlyn and could have done without Basket popping in, flashing Skunk's diamond and saying, 'I know you'll find a Skunk of your own when you least expect it,' until Janna nearly kicked her teeth in.

Janna shared Wednesday 25 August with Mags and Pittsy, closeted together in her office, sworn to secrecy until the official release time which was eight o'clock on the morning of the twenty-sixth.

The results arrived by email and, as they were downloaded, were logged on to a big wall chart with a list of candidates' names in alphabetical order down the left-hand side, and the subjects starting with history along the top. It was surprising Miss Miserden didn't ring up and complain about the shrieks and yells of excitement as the trio caught sight of and analysed each result.

'We're going to need several king-size boxes of tissues tomorrow,' confessed Mags, 'but, bearing in mind how far behind they were at the beginning of the year, haven't some of our no-hopers done well?'

Pittsy was delighted he'd got more candidates through than Skunk or Basket. Serve them right for being so smug. The Brigadier and Emlyn had done very well in history, Mags and Lily in languages, Janna and Sophy in English.

Over at Bagley, the mood was less rowdy, but just as feverish, as, in scenes resembling Wall Street, department heads reached for their calculators to check if they'd beaten other departments, or set in train computer programmes to work out the crucial percentage of children who'd got the Magic Five. Could they have overtaken Fleetley, St Paul's or Wycombe Abbey, or shaken Rod Hyde off their heels?

Miss Painswick was flapping around so that the moment the official results came in tomorrow and were checked for inconsistencies, they would be faxed or emailed immediately to candidates on yacht, grouse moor, Aegean isle or, in Paris's case, the Old Coach House.

At six o'clock on the morning of 26 August, Janna dressed herself in a clinging new yellow and white striped T-shirt and tight sexy white jeans, in case Emlyn showed up. She then drove to the central post office in Larkminster to pick up the envelopes with coral labels containing official result slips for each candidate.

After yesterday's downpour it was a beautiful day: very hot with a bright blue sky flecked with little cirrus clouds and larger grey cumulus clouds, behind which the sun kept disappearing, as if to illustrate the miseries or splendours of each candidate.

The press awaited Janna at Larks.

'How's Rupert Campbell-Black done?'

'No idea.'

'And his son, Xav, the thick one?'

'I'm not going to tell you.'

She then rushed into her office and spent the next hour with the other staff, shoving the results into envelopes for each child, checking them against yesterday's emails. Aysha had got an A star, not an A, for maths, Kitten an E rather than a D for English lit.

'I nearly wore *my* white jeans,' said Rowan, 'but I thought it was too casual for such an important day. Oh look, here's an email from Emlyn. Oh no! He's had to fly out on some pre-season rugby tour. He sends huge love to us all and good luck. The kids will be gutted.'

Et moi aussi, thought Janna, Oh Emlyn! But she must hide her despair; it was the children's day.

Most schools just pin up the envelopes on the wall for pupils to collect. Janna, however, sat in her office determined to go through every result with every child as they lined up in the corridor, frantically chewing gum, faces dead, pacing up and down.

'I'm going to get all Gs.'

'I'm going to get straight Us.'

Pearl, shaking and sobbing, had to be carried by Mags and Cambola into Janna's office – Pearl the former truant and disaster area. Janna jumped up and hugged her.

'Oh Pearl, this is one of the best results in the school. B in English, C in history, C in home economics, C in maths, C in science. D in business studies. Well done.'

Pearl was turned to stone like Niobe, when, like the fountain, her tears gushed out.

'I don't believe it, miss. I done brilliant.'

'You certainly have.'

'I got the Magic Five,' shrieked Pearl, racing round the playground hugging everyone. Then she rang her mother and then the factory where her boxer dad worked, asking them to broadcast the results over the tannoy, then rushed off to the toilets to redo her face before she faced the press.

Back in Janna's office, there were more yells of excitement and cries of 'Good lad, well done', 'Good girl, you've got a B in RE and a C in geography and a C in home economics', as stunned candidates reeled out of the room. Graffi, despite stacking shelves, had got four Cs and an A star for art and was calling his parents. Danny the Irish had managed a B and two Cs, Kitten was over the moon to get four Cs and a D in English, until she heard Pearl's grades were even better and blamed it on a social life so much more active than Pearl's.

Johnnie, against all the odds, had notched up two Bs and four Cs.

'I worked, like, hard,' he told the press, 'but I'd have screwed up, like, if it hadn't been for Emlyn and the Brigadier getting me here.'

Janna was so good at comforting the sad ones. Danijela was inconsolable. She'd only got an A in D and T for her blue and green wedding dress and a C in food technology.

'But that's brilliant. You spoke no English when you came here, you can always retake the others.'

Janna was also euphoric about Rocky, who'd been special needs level three and on the at-risk register, but had still got a B for his D and T dog kennel, a C for history and a D for business studies.

'He must have learnt more in that cupboard than we thought,' laughed Pittsy.

Kylie had notched up three Ds, a B in child care and an A star in music, which enchanted Cambola. Chantal had arrived with Cambola's little godson, Ganymede, who looked just like Jack Waterlane, and, thoroughly carried away, was now telling the press: 'My Kylie Rose is destined for music college. She done superior to her hubby, the Honourable Jack, who may well stay home and mind Cameron and Ganymede.'

'Jack'd love that,' muttered Graffi. 'He'll be able to drink and watch racing on TV all day.'

Graffi couldn't believe those results. The Magic Five. His father had just rolled up with Cardiff Nan and was looking at him with new respect.

'Good luck,' called out everyone, as, trembling and terrified, Aysha crept into Janna's office.

'I don't want to let down my dad.'

'No fear of that.' Janna clasped her hands. 'You got an A star for science, an A star for Urdu, Bs for history and English, an A star for maths and Cs for French and Spanish. Best result in the school, Aysha. Your parents will be so thrilled.'

Aysha gazed at the results slip for a moment; a storm of relieved weeping followed.

'Do you think Dad will let me see Xav now?'

'I'm sure he will.' Janna plied her with Kleenex. 'Get out,' she screamed as a cameraman shoved a lens in through the window.

Summoned by mobile and text, excited parents were soon storming the playground, bearing flowers in cellophane, cards in coloured envelopes, and accepting paper cups of wine handed out by Wally, who was beaming from ear to ear. He'd helped out all year with D and T and his pupils had done really well.

Pearl's boxer dad, who'd been allowed the rest of the day off, was hugging Pearl's mother. Pearl, thoroughly above herself, was telling the television cameras: 'The world is my lobster. I was planning to go into hairdressing, but getting the Magic Five, I've gotta refink my options.'

A dazed Aysha had already been offered places at four schools, but would she be allowed to take up any of them?

The press were now photographing pupils jumping for joy, tossing their papers in the air, the eternal cliché only before afforded to St Jimmy's and Searston Abbey.

'Where's Emlyn? What can have happened to Feral?' asked everyone. 'Where's Xav?'

117

Over at Penscombe, none of the Campbell-Blacks had slept. The plan was to go into Larks to collect Xav and Taggie's results, making a slight detour on the way to Cotchester College to discover Rupert's English lit. grade. Both Rupert and Xav would have preferred to learn their fate in solitude.

The fact that Rupert had just flown in from the Athens Olympics, where his daughter Tabitha and her horse had been in the medals, had, on the one hand, made him incredibly proud. On the other, he was now even more anxious that Xav would be utterly demoralized if, by contrast, he didn't notch up a single GCSE.

To steady his nerves, Rupert was riding around the estate, followed by his pack of dogs. He admired two yearlings, Macduff and Thane of Fife, known as Fifey, checked fences and noted the casualties of summer: rusty branches hanging like broken limbs from the sycamore, field maples eaten to bits by the squirrels. The dawn redwood, prematurely russet, looked a goner too. Despite the rain, it had been an incredibly fecund year, elders already crimson black with berries, brambles covered in gorging wasps.

The sun was coming through the clouds to highlight a triangle of jade field one moment, and touch the shoulder of a beech tree – Shall we dance? – the next. Since he had read English lit., he appreciated nature and character so much more.

It was bliss having Taggie home again, but they had all found it difficult to settle this summer, worrying about three different sets of results.

This is a good horse, thought Rupert: dark bay, strong, confident, too slow to race, the perfect hunter, but hunting would be banned soon. Democracy was gradually being eroded, but did he really mind enough to go back into politics?

There had been so much rain, the fields had only just been topped. Buzzards screamed overhead searching for carrion; a fox had caught a pigeon, its dark grey and light feathers all over the stubble – not a good omen. Nor was the single magpie rising squawking out of the wood.

'Morning, Mr Magpie, how's your wife? How many A to C grades did your children get? You piebald smartass,' snapped Rupert.

Dear God, he prayed, if Tag gets some children through food technology and Xav just one or two decent grades, he'd gladly give up his English lit. pass. Everyone knew he was a philistine. Helen, his first wife, had told him often enough.

Xav huddled in his room, hugging smelly, old, comforting Bogotá, who was too old to join the pack on the ride.

What if he got no grades at all? Mr Khan and Alex Bruce would gloat and say I told you so. He couldn't bear the humiliation, but he couldn't miss a chance of seeing Aysha one last time. Bianca, equally desperate for a last chance to see Feral, banged on his door.

'We ought to go, it's nearly eleven.'

She was wearing red shorts, red boots and a sleeveless crimson T shirt.

'You look cool,' said Xav.

Taggie was in the kitchen praying and unloading the dishwasher, when the telephone rang. It was Mags.

'My dears, are you coming in? Good, but I thought you might like Xav's results in advance.'

Taggie, a potato masher in one hand and two mugs hanging on the end fingers of the hand holding the telephone, sat down on the window seat, just missing Bianca's kitten.

'Can you read them again?' she gasped a minute later.

'And again?' a minute after that, then a minute later. 'And again.'

Afterwards there was a long pause.

'Are you all right?' asked Mags anxiously. 'I thought you'd like to hear the food technology results as well.'

'Yes, no.' All Margaret could hear was sobbing. 'I'll ring you back.' Taggie slotted back the telephone.

Walking back from the yard, noticing dew-spangled spiders all over the lawn, Rupert caught sight of Taggie running out on to the terrace, the same sun lighting up the tears pouring down her face.

'It's all right, darling.' Rupert raced up the lawn, folding his wife in his arms, struggling to hide his disappointment. 'He was Prom King and he's got friends; that's much more important. He worked really hard too.'

But he so wanted to pass, said a voice inside Rupert, we should have fought harder to keep him at Bagley.

Taggie was still sobbing.

'It's all right.' Rupert gritted his jaw. 'We'll look after him. I could never take exams.'

'No, no,' Taggie gulped and gasped. 'He passed. He got four Cs and a B for Spanish. The Magic Five, and D grades in all his other subjects.'

Rupert shut his eyes. Back went his head as he breathed in deeply and incredulously.

'You did it,' he muttered. 'You had the courage to send him to Larks.'

'Shall we go?' Xav walked out, saw his mother crying and knew all was lost. 'Sorry,' he mumbled.

His parents pulled him into a sodden hug.

'You got it,' said Rupert. 'They've just rung. You got the Magic Five.'

'That is really wicked,' said Xav.

Rupert put a crate of Veuve Clicquot in the car. Taggie was so happy she couldn't stop giggling. Glancing at the back, she noticed Bianca gazing out of the window, her painted scarlet lips moving: 'Please God, give me Feral,' and put a hand back on her daughter's knee.

In Cotchester, the roads were blocked with mothers frantic to collect their children's results from various schools. The forecourt of Cotchester College was swarming with mature students comparing results and with even more press, who raised their cameras and tape recorders as Rupert approached, but warily. In his time, the Golden Beast had broken more than a few photographers' jaws. Today he didn't look in a party mood. Rupert had withdrawn his bargain with God. He'd mind like hell if he failed.

Pushing through the swing doors, he entered the exam room, waving his student card.

'Can I have my GCSE result?'

'Oh, it's you, Mr Campbell-Black,' said the woman at the table reverently. 'We hoped you'd come in.' She coughed loudly.

As secretaries suddenly appeared, peering excitedly through the glass panel behind her, she handed him a sealed envelope, her kind round face full of concern.

'Summer 2004,' read Rupert, 'Campbell-Black, Rupert Edward. English Literature GCSE, Grade B.' He gasped. 'There's no mistake?'

'None. Many congratulations.'

'My God.' Rupert leant over the table and kissed her on both cheeks.

Out in the sunshine he sauntered over to the assembled press.

'How d'yer do, Rupert?'

'B for bloody brilliant.' He brandished the slip of paper. 'And two fingers to Randal Stancombe, who now owes the Bagley Fund a lot of money, and my first wife, Helen, now Lady Hawkley, who always told me I was thick.'

Taggie was so excited she nearly ran over an old man wheeling a tartan bag across a zebra crossing.

Back at Larks, Monster was moaning he'd only got Cs for English and business studies, after working like stink.

'That's terrific, well done,' said Janna, making Monster feel so good that he decided to ring Stormin', who was on nights and asleep at home.

If you can wake her, thought Janna bitterly, you horrible gooseberry, who ruined my last chance with Emlyn.

Only Feral had bombed totally. Not a single grade, nothing above a G – darkness at noon. He was now on his mobile, huddled in misery.

'Didn't do enough revision, I guess, sorry, Brig, sorry, Lily. See you both later.'

As he rang his mother, Graffi and Kylie were hovering to comfort him.

'There's good news and bad news, Mum. First the bad news, I failed all my exams. Yes, all of them. But the really good news to cheer you all up, is everyone else in the school passed somefing.'

Heroically brave, he deserved an A star for courage. Janna bit her lip as she remembered the essay of hope about the girl to whom he stayed married for the rest of his life and took on holiday to Skegness.

Kylie put an arm round his shoulders. 'How was your mum?'

'OK,' lied Feral. 'Not now, perhaps later,' he added to Partner, who was nudging him to play football. Oh God, he prayed, don't let the bad news start Mum off again.

Everyone – children, parents and press – was knocking back the bottles of white and red. Graffi's dad was getting legless with Pearl's boxer dad and mum and Stormin' Norman, who'd just arrived. Even Raschid Khan, sipping apple juice, was looking quite mellow.

'I agree, Raschid,' Dafydd Williams was saying. 'None of my family's ever been to uni, we work in factories or on the building, we don't go on to better things.'

Janna climbed on to Appletree steps and clapped her hands. 'I'd just like to thank and congratulate all the children who worked so hard and made such fantastic progress. These are a terrific set of results. The greatest thing in life is an ability to pick yourself up from the floor and you all did this, and I'd like to thank your parents for all their support.'

A second later Feral had grabbed the microphone from her, clutching his battered violet and yellow football like a hot-water bottle with the other. In his deep hoarse voice, gallant in defeat, he thanked particularly Janna and the teachers.

'For being so brilliant, and giving us the best year of our lives. They've taken a year out to look after us and no one's worked harder than they have.'

What on earth's he going to do now? thought Janna despairingly.

'Oh, look,' cried Chantal, as the press went berserk, photographing a new arrival.

For a horrible moment, Janna thought it might be Stancombe, then she realized it was Pete Wainwright, grinning on the edge of the crowd. Last week, he'd been appointed manager of Larkminster Rovers and was now a god in Larkshire.

Shaking off the press, he came over and shook Janna's hand. 'How did Taggie's class do?'

'Fantastic,' said Janna.

'She coming?'

'I hope so.'

Pete Wainwright glanced across the euphoric, teeming playground at Feral, a picture of desolation slumped against the fence, listlessly tapping his football back and forth to Partner, dark head on Graffi's shoulder as Graffi patted him on the back.

'Ain't the end of the world, man.'

'Certainly isn't,' said Pete Wainwright, joining them. 'Here's something to cheer you up, lad.' He handed Feral a typed envelope.

Feral stared at it stupidly.

'Well, open it and read it,' ordered Pete.

'You ought to know, man, I didn't get no English.'

'I'll read it,' said Graffi. 'Wow!' he said after a quarter of a minute. 'Fuckin' hell, fuckin' wicked!' and went into a series of

Tarzan howls. 'Mr Wainwright's offering you a job, man, as a junior player at Larkminster Rovers, starting next week.'

Feral swung round in bewilderment.

'I ducked out of that trial.'

'I know, and I know why you did. I saw you playing one evening after exams. Emlyn showed me some tapes. You'll have to clean a few boots to start with, spend a bit of time observing on the bench. But you're good and so was that speech you just made. I like generosity in my players.'

Feral tried to read the letter.

'It ain't no wind-up?'

Janna by this time had rushed up, hugging Feral, telling everyone the good news. 'Oh Pete, this is really wicked.'

After that Feral, like Pearl, got thoroughly above himself.

'I'm going to be the next Thierry Henry,' he yelled, punching the air, 'and I'll be so fucking rich, I'll be able to take out that bastard Rupert Campbell-Black – in fact he'll be crawling to have me marrying his daughter.'

'He probably will,' said a dry voice behind him.

It was Rupert, who'd just arrived with Taggie and Xav.

'Feral's got a job,' cried Janna as the press surged forward, 'with Larkminster Rovers. And well done, fantastic results!' She hugged Xav. 'And well done, Taggie.'

'Taggie, Taggie!' The children surged round her: 'I got a B.' 'I got a C.' 'I got an A.' 'I got a C.'

'I can't believe it.' Taggie tried to hug them all.

Meanwhile, Rupert had turned to Feral.

'I've brought you a congratulatory present,' he drawled.

And Bianca erupted out of the car and, stopping, gazed at Feral, who gazed at her in wonder.

Slowly, they moved towards each other. Seizing her hand, chucking his ball to Partner, Feral led her off into the garden.

'I thought your father didn't approve of Feral,' whispered Kylie.

'He's just got a B in English lit.,' whispered back Xav, 'I think he'd even accept Tony Blair as a son-in-law.'

Having congratulated Taggie on her food technology triumph, Janna was now hugging Rupert – such a pleasure as he was so handsome.

'Randal is going to be furious about your B.'

'Good,' said Rupert. 'I should be congratulating you and apologizing for doubting that you and Larks would be the best thing for Xav. He's found himself.'

Across the playground, Xav was surrounded by friends, thumping him on the back.

'I've bought a few bottles, they're in the car,' added Rupert. 'Which one's Graffi? I want a mural in the long gallery.'

Feral, wiping off crimson lipstick and grinning like the Cheshire cat, later talked, somewhat warily, to Rupert, who said,

'Sorry I called you a black bastard.'

'It's OK, man. If I caught my daughter in bed with some no-good nigger, I guess I'd call him the same thing.'

They looked at each other, dislike melting away.

'Thank you for looking after Xav.'

'Thank you for beating Stancombe. He's a bastard, really evil, and I know, man.'

'You do interest me. Why don't you come out to lunch with us?'

'I'd like to, man' – Feral looked longingly at Bianca, who was dancing by herself, as lightly as the thistledown drifting in from the long grass – 'but actually I'm lunching wiv Lily and the Brig. I'm going to be a witness at their wedding,' he added proudly.

'Hmmmm, that sounds a party that'll go on,' said Rupert. 'You'd better come to lunch tomorrow.'

Grinning, very tentatively they exchanged a high five.

Round the back of the building, Rupert tracked down Graffi spraying in large purple letters: 'Graffi Williams for the Tate, Feral Jackson for Wembley, Randal Stancombe for the High Jump.'

'Excellent sentiments.' Rupert handed Graffi a paper cup of champagne. 'But I want something marginally more figurative for Penscombe. Are you anti blood sports?'

'Not if you pay me well enough,' said Graffi.

'Then I'd like you to do the hunt.'

Feral and Bianca were dancing in the hall.

Graffi's board saying 'Larkminster High School Prom 2004' had been thrown in the bin, but the silver moon and stars still curled on the long black curtains.

'And I will take Feral and cut him out in little stars, and he will make the face of heaven so fine,' said Bianca softly.

Feral picked up a fragment of balloon.

'Since Romeo and Juliet, I haven't fort of anyone or anyfing but you. I couldn't ask you to be my girlfriend when I had nothing to offer. Now I have.'

'I'll come and watch you every week.'

'Every goal will have your name on it.'

'You will come to lunch tomorrow, won't you, or it'd break my heart.'

Feral drew her into his arms. Both of them had to hold each other up, as he kissed her.

Later Bianca was approached by a man from the *Daily Express*. 'Your family's done so well today. Your mum's candidates all got through, Rupert got a B and Xav the Magic Five.'

'I've done best.' Bianca did a joyful handstand, peering back and up from between her arms and black waterfall of hair. 'They got Bs and Cs, but I got Feral Jackson.'

118

Over at Bagley, the celebrations were no less euphoric, as faxes and emails spread over the globe to Lando France-Lynch playing polo in Deauville, Lubemir in a casino, Anatole on a yacht and Cosmo on top of Mrs Walton.

'In my case, my angel,' boasted Cosmo, 'GCSE stands for Great Cock Satisfaction Ensured.'

There was as much press interest in Bagley as there had been at Larks, particularly when a jubilant Hengist announced that not only Cosmo Rannaldini and Primrose Duddon, but Paris Alvaston had achieved straight As and A stars, and Bagley appeared to have gone above Fleetley in the league tables.

Paris who, as it was still holidays, was one of the only boys in school, was bewildered by his results and ran straight over to Hengist's study.

'I couldn't have got an A star in history, sir,' he panted, 'I trashed my second paper.'

'You're imagining things,' Hengist said firmly. 'You'd been working too hard and were understandably upset about Theo. You didn't know if it was Christmas or Easter when you took that last paper. I saw it. It was fine.'

'I wrote gibberish,' insisted Paris.

'Strange things have happened this year. A boy at Fleetley evidently got an A star in English lit. and missed an entire P3 module. Your first history paper must have been exceptional. Ian and Patience will be delighted.'

They were. Ian had opened a bank account and put in £25 for each brilliant grade, totalling £250, but Paris wasn't happy.

'I want to ring Theo.'

'You can't, I'm afraid.' Hengist went to the fridge and got out a bottle of white. 'Let's have a drink to celebrate.'

'I want to ring Theo.'

'You can't. How many times do I have to tell you the police have expressively forbidden any contact.' Hengist ran his hand through his hair. 'Imagine how I'd like to ring him, but I don't want to prejudice his case.'

'How can it, if I just thank him and give him my grades?'

'Biffo'll tell him.' Hengist was rootling round for a corkscrew.

'Who?' asked Paris quickly.

'Someone will,' said Hengist quickly. 'Oh look, Rupert and Xav are on the box, turn the sound up.' But Paris had shot out of the room.

Hengist shook his head. He must calm Paris down.

After some lovely film of Penscombe, the lunchtime news cut to Sian Williams in the studio. What a pretty thing she was; Hengist turned up the volume.

Xavier Campbell-Black, she told the viewers, who'd been excluded from Bagley Hall for bullying last September, had just notched up five A–C grades at his new school: Larkminster High. A maintained school had thus succeeded where a prestigious independent had failed.

Xav used to be such a fat slob, thought Hengist, now he was clear-eyed, smiling, good-looking and confident.

'I made so many friends at Larks,' he was now saying, 'I didn't need to bully anyone. I found teachers who believed in me and helped me to understand. It helped that my mother joined the staff as a teaching assistant. Everyone she taught food technology to passed.'

'Did you find the teaching better at Larks?'

'Much,' said Xav, who'd been at the Veuve Clicquot, 'and Alex Bruce, my housemaster at Bagley, was a twat.'

Hengist choked on his drink as the interviewer hastily asked Xav about Rupert's B.

'He's laid back, my dad, but he worked incredibly hard and we're all really proud of him.'

Now it was Rupert's turn. Age cannot wither him, thought Hengist, particularly when he's happy, mouth and long eyes lifting.

'I'm knocked out by my wife Taggie's results,' admitted Rupert, 'and Xav's and my own.'

'Who taught you?'

'Well, Miss Jennings at Cotchester College gave me some very good coaching, but mostly I read and wrestled on my own.

722

Couldn't understand a word of it at first. Lucky to have Xav's headmistress, Janna Curtis, and Bianca's headmaster, Hengist Brett-Taylor, to tell me when my ideas were crap.'

'And by passing you won your bet with Randal Stancombe, for an undisclosed sum.'

'Not at all undisclosed, it was a hundred thousand pounds, which is not going to worry Stancombe. He spends that in a day on aftershave and greasing palms.'

'Bastard,' howled Stancombe, who was watching the same news, 'and he got that treacherous bitch, Janna Curtis, and that shit, Hengist, to help him. No wonder he got a B. They've obviously been cramming him. After all I've done for Hengist. Building the Science Emporium and his taking Ruth off me. My God, I'll bury all three of them.'

Alex Bruce, also watching, was even more outraged. How dare that insolent brat call him a twat, and how could he have got the Magic Five? Janna Curtis must have shown him the papers. Even more distressingly, Lando and Jack had ploughed science, so Alex still hadn't equalled Theo's record of getting everyone through.

Worst of all, his star pupil Boffin Brooks had not achieved straight As. He had just had Sir Gordon Brooks in a towering rage from his villa in Portugal.

'There's no way Bernard could only have got a B in history. It's one of his strongest subjects. That's why I donated five thousand for a history prize, which will now go to some other student.'

'Rest assured, Gordon, I shall approach our Senior Team Leader and appeal. May I have a word with Charisma?' She was staying with the Brookses.

'I can't understand, Dad, I only got a B for Urdu,' whined his G and T daughter.

The last parents and children had drifted away; only Mr Khan lingered.

'You have a brilliant daughter,' pleaded Janna, 'won't you just consider her going on to sixth-form college?'

'She has a husband waiting for her in Pakistan. He has been very patient. He is a good man and will take care of her.'

'But she's so young— Excuse me, that's my mobile.'

It was Hengist. 'Darling, I've just seen the one o'clock news. Well done, Xav, how brilliant and what a smack in the face for stupid Alex for letting him go. How did the others do?'

After Janna had told him, and about Feral's fantastic new job, she asked after Paris.

'Wonderful.' What purring content in Hengist's voice. 'Straight As and A stars for Greek, Latin, both Englishes and history. Absolutely wonderful.'

Janna was ecstatic.

'Ian and Patience must be so thrilled.'

'Relieved, as well. Little Amber did surprisingly well, too.'

'How's Paris in himself?'

'Withdrawn. We had a bit of a set-to just now. He wanted to ring Theo and tell him about the A stars to give him some comfort. But he mustn't get in touch. All the press are hanging round. They all know it's Paris, but he can't be named because the so-called "offence" began when he was fourteen.'

'Oh God, poor Theo. Will he get off?'

'Christ, I hope so. The evidence is pretty damning. Case comes up later in the year, bound to coincide with the Queen's visit. The press'll make a meal out of two old queens. One shouldn't laugh.'

Janna had taken refuge in her office; glasses and discarded envelopes were everywhere.

'Jade only scraped five Cs, which won't please Stancombe,' Hengist was now telling her, 'and, by the way, I've just seen Rupert on the box saying how much we helped him and slagging off Stancombe. It's going to be a long time before dear Randal forgives either of us.'

'I don't care.'

'I do miss you. Let's have a drunken celebration before term starts.'

Dear Hengist, Janna smiled as she switched off her mobile.

Outside the playground was empty; Mr Khan had gone. Tomorrow, she thought wearily, she'd continue the battle to stop the parents chucking it all away. Lily's wedding was at two-thirty; she'd better step on it. Hastily, she toned down her flushed cheeks and shrugged on her white jacket. What did it matter how she looked, if Emlyn wasn't going to be there?

'Next week,' she told Partner as she tied a white silk bow round his neck, 'you and I will look for a job and probably somewhere to live. Today all that matters is those fantastic results.'

But as she splashed Diorissimo on her wrists, Ashton rang.

'I can see why you haven't phoned, Janna, these wesults are dweadfully disappointing.'

'Disappointing?' cried Janna in outrage. 'They're brilliant. You should focus on where those children came from. No one expected them to get any grades at all. You forget there are four pass grades below C. They may not all have got brilliant grades but they got grades. It's a miracle.'

724

'Janna, Janna,' sighed Ashton, 'exonerating yourself as usual. It's going to be tewwibly difficult justifying all the extwa funding you've had from the DfES. We expected far better.'

'My kids really worked, so did my teachers,' yelled Janna. 'What d'you know about work, sitting in your ivory tower surrounded by hundreds of apparatchiks doing fuck all on vast salaries? Don't talk to me about wasting money.'

'No need to be offensive. You've failed, that's all, but there's no point in talking to you in this mood.' Ashton rang off.

Like a slow puncture, Janna's pride and delight ebbed out of her.

'These are the children that God forgot,' she whispered in horror as she gazed up at the happy, optimistic group photograph on the wall. 'I'm not going to change anything for them; I just suffered from hubris, putting them through exams because I wanted to prove to the world that I was a brilliant head.'

119

To ward off her desolation over Emlyn's absence and Ashton's vile remarks, Janna got dreadfully drunk at Lily's wedding and danced most of the night away with a euphoric Feral and Lily's whacky, charming family, who included Dicky and Dora. Lily, in the same blue dress she'd worn to the prom, had no need of Pearl's make-up. Never was a bridegroom prouder than her Brigadearest.

Next morning, groaning with hangover, Janna went over to Larks. She had only three days left to leave the place shipshape. Wally had lent her a van to clear out her belongings. At first, as she drove up the drive, she thought a television crew had rolled up, then she realized the place was swarming with workmen; one of them, in a bulldozer, had just smashed down half a dozen of Wally's saplings. Drawing closer, she recognized Teddy Murray, Stancombe's foreman, who'd supervised the rebuilding of Appletree.

'What the hell are you doing?'

'Taking over,' said Teddy curtly.

'On whose authority?'

'Stancombe's, of course.'

'Stancombe?' said Janna in horror as another bulldozer crushed Sally's oriental poppies. 'What's he got to do with it?'

'Owns the property. Just paid twenty-five million.'

'Don't be ridiculous.'

'See for yourself.' Teddy waved a heavily tattooed hand towards the bottom of the drive and the hayfield of a lawn outside the ruins of the main buildings, where two big crimson signs announced 'Randal Stancombe Properties'.

'What's he planning to do?'

'Search me. Slap luxury houses all over it. Flog it to some supermarket giant. Flatten the Shakespeare Estate and move in some decent customers. All part of his caring "clean up Larkminster" campaign.' Just for a second sarcasm predominated over indifference in Teddy's voice. 'Now, if you'll excuse me, Janna . . .' Revving up he smashed down two willows.

'Stop it,' screamed Janna, but he had wound up his window, so she ran into Appletree, to find all her stuff had been dumped outside her office.

She was on to Stancombe in a flash.

'Have you bought Larks?'

'I have indeed.'

'You never said anything.'

'You never let on you were coaching Rupert Campbell-Black, you treacherous bitch.'

'I didn't help him,' protested Janna. 'Rupert showed me one essay, from which I deleted a few swear words.'

'After all the support I gave you,' howled Randal, 'I don't feel predisposed to help you ever again.'

Janna gave a gasp of horror as, outside the window, she noticed a JCB gouging out the pond. What would be the fate of Concorde, the carp and the natterjack toads?

'Anyway,' went on Stancombe, 'I put up the money for Appletree, so I own it anyway,' and he hung up.

120

Boffin Brooks's sense of grievance was aggravated on his return to Bagley to find both Cosmo and Paris had better grades.

'I couldn't have got a B in history,' he spluttered to Alex. 'I remember every word I wrote, I could only have got an A star.'

Urged by Charisma, Boffin had started wearing blue tinted contact lenses, which gave him a glazed, almost defenceless look – definitely Alex's blue-eyed boy.

'I have already contacted the exam board,' Alex reassured him, 'to request a clerical check that your history marks were added up correctly. If need be, there are good friends I can phone in the exam world, but I don't want to be accused of pulling strings.'

Together they tackled Hengist, who was bogged down writing beginning-of-term speeches and welcoming new pupils and masters. He was not in a co-operative mood, telling Boffin not to be a bad loser and employing a lot of uncharacteristically hearty clichés like 'biting the bullet' and 'taking it on the chin'.

'We were also warned,' he added sourly, 'that only a limited number of candidates in each subject, irrespective of how well they did, were going to be allowed A stars. You were just one of the unlucky ones. The goalposts have been changed by this bloody Government.'

Boffin and Alex winced collectively.

'It's tough,' concluded Hengist, then begged to be excused because the Queen's Private Secretary and the Lord Lieutenant, General Broadstairs, who was also a Bagley governor, were coming to see him about the royal visit. 'You cannot imagine the red tape. You should give them a copy of your book, Alex.'

Alex's smile creaked.

Getting up, Hengist opened the door. 'We've got just

728

under eight weeks. I hope everything's going to be ready in time.'

Retreating down the stairs, Alex swelled with rage; after all the spadework he'd put in on the royal visit, as usual, Hengist swanned in when it suited him.

'I'm going to appeal,' whined Boffin. 'There's no way I got a B. Mr Brett-Taylor never encourages me.'

Alex was equally determined not to let his star pupil down.

'I shall request the return of your answer paper and have the marks checked, then we'll ask for a total remark. It costs around sixty pounds; Bagley can foot the bill.'

'What a beautiful school,' said the Private Secretary as Elaine left white hairs all over his dark suit, 'and what a beautiful dog.'

'Isn't she?' said Hengist happily. 'People think she's snarling, but she's really smiling.'

'We have Labradors, they smile too,' said the Lord Lieutenant, producing a file already as big as the Larkshire telephone book.

'I want Her Majesty to have a really nice time,' said Hengist, pouring Pouilly-Fumé into three glasses. 'I know she's got to open the Science Emporium, but I thought she might like to watch some polo if the weather's fine and meet the school beagles? One of our star pupils, Paris Alvaston, might read out one of his beautiful poems and, of course, Cosmo Rannaldini, another star pupil, will be conducting the school orchestra and his mother, Dame Hermione Harefield, in a welcoming fanfare.'

'That sounds a good start,' said the Lord Lieutenant.

'Recently, we bonded with a comprehensive,' Hengist told the Private Secretary, 'who did very well in their GCSEs. It would be a miracle for them if Her Majesty could hand out the certificates.'

Later, with an entourage of press officers and detectives, they walked a possible course. Approaching the Science Emporium, still a pile of rubble, they passed General Bagley's statue.

'That's a fine beast.' The Private Secretary patted Denmark's gleaming black shoulder.

'Isn't he?' agreed Hengist. 'And his rider, our founder, General Bagley, is, I think, a distant relation of Her Majesty's mother.'

'How interesting.' The Private Secretary made a note. 'Her Majesty might like to refer to that in her speech. We'll need potted biogs, in advance, of all the people she's going to meet.'

No one was more excited about Paris's results than Dora.

'Ha, ha, ha, hee, hee, hee,' she sang to her friend Peter on the *Mail on Sunday* a few days later. 'Boffin Brooks has got a B.'

'Any more news of Theo Graham?'

'None, poor thing, he can't get in touch with us or we with him, until after his court case. Paris has been transferred to Artie Deverell's house. Artie's really nice, but Paris can't forgive him for not being Theo and Paris nearly strangled Cosmo yesterday for suggesting Hengist was stupid to put Paris into the house of yet another shirt-lifter.'

'How's the Queen's visit?'

'Chaos. Mrs Fussy's refusing to curtsey and wants a dust sheet put over General Bagley. No one can decide on the right shade of red carpet. But guess what, I've bought a man's wig and a white coat which I've splattered with paint so I can pose as a workman and listen in on meetings, so expect some good copy.'

'Good girl.'

'Randal Stancombe, my mum's grotesque boyfriend, is flooding the place with workmen to get his Science Emporium up in time. It's even got a space centre, so hopefully once it's finished we can land Poppet and Alex on Mars for good.'

'And your handsome headmaster?'

'Utterly euphoric we've gone above Fleetley in the league tables and off next month to Bournemouth to the Tory Party conference with my brother Jupiter.'

Awaiting Rupert's helicopter to fly him to Bournemouth, Hengist took Elaine for a quick walk down to Badger's Retreat. In one hand, he had a piece of toast and marmalade, in the other, a private and confidential letter from David 'Hatchet' Hawkley, now Lord Hawkley, the head of Fleetley.

Dear Hengist [he read],
This is a difficult letter to write. This week you will be offered the job of headmaster of Fleetley, a school I have loved and cherished for twenty-five years. I have long deliberated over whether you are the right person to succeed me. You are a genius at recruitment and getting the best out of both masters and pupils, you are hugely entertaining, charismatic, with a foot in the old world and the new, and generally filled with the milk of human kindness.
In the past we have fallen out . . .

This was a massive understatement. Hengist righted himself after nearly falling down a rabbit hole. He had feared David Hawkley would block his candidacy, but in his fairness, he had not. The letter ended: 'Look after my school, I trust you.'

Hengist was touched. It was a huge olive branch. Looking

down, he saw Elaine had nicked his toast and marmalade. But would Fleetley remind Sally too much of Mungo and Pippa, David's then wife, and would it turn out to be a grander, more rigid version of Bagley?

Here he could offer Paris the odd glass of champagne and the run of his books; here he could refuse to disband the school beagles and allow Dora to keep her chocolate Labrador. Could he cope with the lack of freedom? Hengist sighed. Jupiter had just offered him Shadow Education, which would be a complete change of career and an adventure.

Sally would make the perfect minister's wife and Hengist had written Jupiter such a cracking conference speech that by next year he might have seized power. Hengist was flying down to make a fringe speech on education, before flying up to St Andrews in time for dinner at the Headmasters' Conference.

He glanced back at David's letter. He couldn't take on both Fleetley and Education. David, who was a great friend of Theo's, had added a PS: 'To sadder matters, how can we rescue Theo? I am convinced of his innocence. We must battle to clear his name and enable him to finish Sophocles. You have the greater clout.'

Hengist had reached Badger's Retreat. A robin sang in a hawthorn bush, its orange breast clashing with the crimson haws. Like a unicorn, Elaine bounded through the trees he had planted and nurtured. The ground was littered with conkers, which always gave Hengist a stab, remembering how he'd collected them for Mungo.

The Family Tree, its keys turning coral, had lost much of its charm since he'd thrown Oriana out, but, still clinging together, the three trunks and many branches had survived the onslaught of the fallen ash. Perhaps he and Oriana might be friends one day.

Bagley was a far more beautiful school than Fleetley, which, although fed by the same River Fleet, was a squat, grey, Georgian pile surrounded by very flat country. Hengist believed he would miss Badger's Retreat most of all.

Heavens! He must hurry. There was Rupert's dark blue helicopter, in which it would be so cool to arrive at the Headmasters' Conference this evening.

He would earn far more money in politics than at Fleetley. The paths of glory lead but to the gravy train, reflected Hengist.

121

Jupiter's speech was a wow, constructive and marvellously bitchy about the Opposition. Then word got around about Hengist's fringe speech and the main hall had emptied, particularly of young MPs, who had crowded in to hear his good tub-thumping stuff about the real England and freedom from the stranglehold of the curriculum and Brussels.

'Let them be our allies but not dictate our way of life.'

So many interviews and congratulations followed, he only just reached St Andrews in time for dinner. The conference was being held in a lovely hotel, the St Andrews Bay, overlooking the golf course, which was being buffeted by an angry, grey North Sea.

Fiddling to get Radio 3 and the television working, emptying a miniature Bell's into a glass, Hengist called Sally.

'I'm in the most enormous suite, I wish you were here to share it. The guest speaker, some lady novelist, will address us in the Robert Burns Room.'

Sally loved Burns and had, when they first met, compared Hengist with John Anderson, my jo of the bonnie brow and the raven locks. Hengist, in turn, had recited 'My love is like a red, red rose', to her at their wedding.

'Jupiter's speech was marvellous,' cried Sally, 'terrific jokes and he seemed so warm and sort of sincere.'

'That must be a first. I'm moving towards accepting his offer, if you can cope with the incessant ripping apart by the press.'

'As long as we're together.'

'That's the only certainty. Can I fuck you the moment I get home?'

'The Bishop's coming to lunch . . .'

'I'll get there early then. I love you so much and a pat for Elaine.'

Hengist always enjoyed the Headmasters' Conference and never more so than tonight, when Bagley had finally gone above Fleetley. Whilst changing for dinner, many of the heads had seen clips of his and Jupiter's speeches, or his helicopter landing, and he was subjected to a lot of rather envious joshing.

'You going into politics, Hengist?'

'As a head, is one ever out of them?'

'Did you write all Rupert's coursework?'

Then, in lowered voices: 'Sorry about poor old Theo Graham.'

Listening to the cheerful roar of 250 like minds, anticipating a very good dinner, Hengist thought what a good bunch of chaps they were. Personable was the word. There were intellectuals, like David Hawkley or Anthony Seldon at Brighton College, who'd written a biography of Blair, or Martin Stephen, who'd just taken over St Paul's, who wrote excellent historical novels. These men had read hugely and could pick up any literary allusion. A new breed, more interested in management and marketing, had hardly read a book.

Except for a sprinkling of headmistresses, the membership was all men. Milling around they could be mistaken for army officers out of uniform, showing half an inch of clean, pink neck between hair and collar, wearing trousers that when they sat down rose to sock level above highly polished shoes.

'The *Guardian* described us as "grey men in grey suits",' grumbled old Freddie Wills of St Barnabas. 'Not true: we're in navy blue, mostly pinstripe.' With cheerfulness breaking in with flamboyant ties, thought Hengist: technicolour checks or swarming with elephants or dolphins.

They had listened all day to seminars.

'Jenni Murray was excellent on gender,' Freddie Wills told Hengist, 'but Andrew Adonis predictably told us "the Labour Party loves us", because they want to bleed us white propping up city academies. Don't seem to realize most of us have a hell of a struggle making ends meet.'

Then, a few feet away, standing in front of a mural of a 1930s' golf match, with players in pancake caps and plus fours showing off well-turned ankles, was David 'Hatchet' Hawkley, appropriately hawklike, immensely distinguished, his shyness so often coming across as brusqueness.

Hengist waved in greeting. 'Thank you for your letter.'

'You got it? Good. Better get into dinner. You're at my table.'

Hengist, already high on a successful Bournemouth and three

large whiskies, found himself seated between the jolly lady novelist guest speaker and David's second wife, Helen.

As her previous husbands had included such unashamed Lotharios as Rupert Campbell-Black and Cosmo's late father, Roberto Rannaldini, it was hardly surprising Lady Hawkley insisted on accompanying handsome David everywhere. A red-head with big, yellow eyes and the nervous breediness of a fallow deer, she was easily the most beautiful woman in the room.

Hengist would far rather have been seated with his chums, fellow junior masters in earlier schools, particularly as, through a vase of yellow carnations, Hatchet Hawkley was watching his every move. Would Helen follow Pippa and fall under Hengist's spell?

In fact, Hengist found Helen earnest and a dreadful intellectual snob. Having clocked him landing in Rupert's helicopter, she immediately tackled him on Rupert's B grade.

'Do we need any more proof that GCSEs are getting easier?'

'Rupert worked very hard,' protested Hengist, who hadn't eaten all day and was buttering his roll, 'and he's discovered he rather likes English lit. There's a copy of *Henry Esmond* in the helicopter and he's mellowed since the old days, when he was Lord of the Unzipped Flies. He's so delighted Taggie did so well and Xav got the Magic Five, he's thinking of turning Penscombe into a second Bloomsbury.'

Oh God. Hengist realized he'd goofed. Helen was clearly so scarred by her marriage to Rupert, she loathed any reference to the success of his second marriage. She had now put her knife and fork together, rather like her legs, leaving her divine russet slab of pâté untouched. Hengist was tempted to ask if he could have it, but this would probably be construed as too intimate a gesture by David, who was still peering at them through the carnations.

Hengist still hadn't decided one hundred per cent between Fleetley or politics.

'We're putting your ravishing Tabitha and her horse on the front of the *Old Bagleian*,' he told Helen, 'although no one could look less like an Old Bag. We're all so proud of her silver!' Then he realized he'd goofed again. He'd forgotten how jealous Helen was of Tabitha, whom he supposed looked too like Rupert.

'You look absolutely stunning,' he murmured. 'Most heads' wives resemble overgrown tomboys, short pepper and salt hair, slim figures: senior, senior prefects. It's not homosexual, just that most heads feel easier with boys. How are you looking forward to David retiring?' he went on. Christ, he hoped they didn't move into a cottage on the Fleetley Estate.

'We've got a house in Umbria,' said Helen, 'and we're looking for somewhere in Dorset. We're both going to write. David's doing Aeschylus and I'm working on a literary memoir.'

Hengist was about to say Helen's inside story of marriage to Rupert and Rannaldini would sell much better than any translation of Aeschylus, but just stopped himself. 'We'd better get another bottle.' He tipped back his chair.

At the next-door table, two of his dearest friends, Tim Hastie-Smith, head of Dean Close, and Pete Johnson, head of Millfield, were discussing Colin Montgomerie's triumph in the Ryder Cup. As waitresses and waiters in grey silk cheongsams rushed in with the main course – large squares of roast lamb and shiny brown parsnips – Hengist turned to the lady novelist, who said she was writing about two schools and asked him to tell her about being a headmaster.

'Big egos and like this' – Hengist plunged his knife into his lamb to reveal its pink interior – 'very square but tender inside.'

'I must remember that,' laughed the lady novelist. 'What else makes a great head?'

'Ability to fill the school and pick first-class staff.'

'Energy and charm?'

'Certainly.' Hengist filled up her glass.

'Intellect?'

Hengist shook his head. 'Huge self-belief is much more important.'

'Have you ever won anything at the Teaching Awards?'

'No, that's a state-school affair, even though Lord Hawkley's one of the judges. They think we have it too easy.' He noticed she was looking down at some speech notes on her lap.

'Don't be scared, we'll be a terrific audience, so used to laughing at parents' weak jokes.'

'I'm going to end by quoting from "Rugby Chapel", about heads as heroic great souls leading and inspiring others on to the city of God.'

' "Ye, like angels, appear, radiant with ardour divine!" ' quoted back Hengist. 'They'll love that.'

The lady novelist was thrilled Hengist was writing a biography of Thomas and Matthew Arnold.

'Will you send me a review copy?'

'How bad was that school, Larks something, you joined up with?' shouted old Freddie Wills across the table.

'Well, they had a geography mistress who'd never been to London,' said Hengist, howling with laughter, so everyone else joined in.

Anyone could charm the birds off the trees, reflected David enviously, with a packet of Swoop, but Hengist could charm the birds away from a loaded bird table on the coldest of winter days, because it was so much more fun to be in his presence.

He, Freddie and the lady novelist, who'd probably end up in bed with him later, were discussing a collective noun for heads.

'You've got a pride of lions, a gaggle of geese,' said Freddie.

'How about a hurrah of heads?' suggested the lady novelist.

'Or a "Hail, fellow, well met" of heads?' volunteered Hengist.

Aware that Hengist was having far more fun with the plump lady novelist with the loud laugh and shiny face, Helen knew she had been crabby. She had always found him disturbingly attractive. With his sallow skin, laughing slit eyes, dark curls rising from his smooth forehead and spilling over the collar of his dinner jacket, he looked like some Renaissance grandee. His height, strength, merriment and overwhelming vitality made one long to be in bed with him.

'How's my ex-stepson, Cosmo?' she asked. 'As obnoxious as ever?'

'Probably,' said Hengist, 'but he's very clever. I'm afraid he makes me laugh.'

With no Sally to drag him home, Hengist had a lovely end to the evening, drinking the minibar dry in his suite and playing bears round the furniture with his friends.

'Are you going into politics, Hengist?'

'No, no, I could never leave teaching.'

122

Next morning, Hengist had a frightful hangover and didn't get away as early as he'd hoped. This was the way to travel though, flying over magenta ploughed fields flecked with gulls, like waves on a wine-dark sea. Down below was St Andrews, with its ancient university and town hall built of big, proud, yellow stone, the colour of the turning trees. What a lovely place for Sally and him to retire to. A seat of learning, where he could at last write his books. Perhaps he didn't want Fleetley *or* politics.

At midday, the helicopter dropped him at Bagley, sending the leaves flying upwards, then whizzed off to take Rupert racing.

Dropping little bottles of shampoo and body lotion on Miss Painswick's desk, although her body was not somewhere he wished to go, Hengist asked if anything interesting had happened.

'Only these.' She handed him two letters marked 'private and confidential', one presumably offering him Shadow Education, the other asking him to take over Fleetley in the Michaelmas Term of 2005. Hengist pocketed them.

'How was the trip? asked Miss Painswick. 'You were awfully good at Bournemouth.'

'And awfully bad at St Andrews. Could you get me a vast Fernet-Branca?'

'Mr Bruce is in your office, by the way, says it's urgent.'

Bounding up the stairs, Hengist was amazed to find Alex sitting in his archbishop's chair, flipping disapprovingly through his mountainous in-tray. Alex's blackcurrant eyes glittered behind his spectacles with the same air of excitement as when Theo was arrested.

Feeling even more in need of a hair of the dog, Hengist edged towards the whisky decanter, then, dropping a St Andrews Bay Hotel bath cap on the big oak table in front of Alex:

'I've brought you a present. I know how you like transparency.'

Alex didn't smile.

'You'd better sit down. Something very serious has occurred.'

Not Sally? Hengist felt a lurch of terror, but Painswick wouldn't have been looking so cheerful.

' "Lay on, Macduff," ' he said lightly.

'I'd like you to explain this.' Alex chucked an exam script down on the table. 'This was handed in as Paris Alvaston's second history paper.'

Hengist picked it up and went cold to his bones. His heart stopped, then began to crash out of control. 'So what?'

'That is not Paris's writing. Only four people knew the combination to the safe: the exam officer, Ian Cartwright – who as Paris's foster father was not a disinterested party – Miss Painswick and yourself.'

'Course it's not Cartwright. I can't imagine Painswick achieving an A star either.'

'We've checked with a graphologist' – although he'd have recognized anywhere that arrogant, flamboyant scrawl seen so often on praise postcards – 'it was your writing, headmaster.'

There was a crash of cut glass on glass as Hengist poured himself a large whisky. For Paris's sake, he mustn't give in without a fight and prepare a defence, which of course was non-existent.

In a flash, he realized he would lose his school, Shadow Education and Fleetley, and Paris would lose his A star. It might have been better if Sally had died. She was so straight and true, the disgrace that would submerge him would kill her anyway.

It was a few moments before he realized Alex was saying, 'I suppose you couldn't bear your little guinea pig to fail.'

Then he backed away as Hengist turned on him, like a raging lion:

'It was your bloody fault. If you hadn't shopped Theo in the middle of GCSEs, Paris would never have screwed up. He was knocked sideways by Theo leaving.'

Hearing a thud, they both jumped.

'We're busy,' called out Alex.

The door flew open and in bounded Elaine, hurling herself on her master with joyful squeaks, then racing round the room knocking over a side table, a waste-paper basket and a vase of scarlet dahlias with her thwacking tail, before jumping on the window seat to indulge in some scrabbling running on the spot.

'Get that beast out of here,' screamed Alex. In no way could he more have asserted his new ascendancy.

Elaine was followed by Sally. Devastated by the Oriana saga, she had been looking tired and drained for some time. Now, with highlighted, newly washed hair softening her sweet face and a pale blue cashmere jersey caressing her breasts, she looked utterly ravishing.

'Darling, when did you get back? How lovely. The Bishop's caught up in traffic, but he'll be here in half an hour.' Time for sex, her eyes smiled. 'And some prospective parents have turned up.' Then, noticing a muscle bounding in Hengist's jaw and Alex's face longer than a tomb stone: 'What on earth's going on?'

'I regret our Senior Team Leader has been caught cheating,' said Alex heavily.

In the distance, Hengist could see spirals of mist, the ghost of his career, curling up from Badger's Retreat. ' "O! the fierce wretchedness that glory brings," ' he said bleakly.

'Hengist wouldn't cheat,' cried Sally in outrage. 'He's the most honourable man.'

Hengist turned back, stroking Elaine, who, wagging her tail gently and joyfully, was gazing up from the ripped window seat.

'I'm afraid it's true.' He tried to meet Sally's eyes. 'Paris found out Theo'd been arrested and made such a cock-up of his paper, I wrote it instead.'

'Oh, Hengist,' Sally clung on to the back of the sofa, 'how could you? Poor Paris could have retaken it! He'll be mortified, the press will crucify him after all the crowing about A stars.'

'Paris Alvaston, in fact, suspected foul play,' intoned Alex. 'Joan Johnson overheard him saying he couldn't possibly have got an A star, as he'd trashed his second history paper.'

Loathing herself, Sally turned to Alex: 'Does this have to get out?'

'My duty is to the other students,' said Alex primly, 'and I must immediately inform the chair of governors.'

There goes politics and Fleetley, thought Hengist. His heart was thumping relentlessly, his knees shuddering together.

'As I'm not prepared to be an accessory to a crime' – Alex cracked his knuckles – 'I have also alerted the police.'

'Oh dear,' sighed Hengist, draining his whisky, 'such a bad effect on recruitment. To have one master arrested looks like misfortune, but two, definitely carelessness.'

'Don't be so bloody flippant,' yelled Sally.

Elaine vanished under the sofa.

'Theo's was a lapse, motivated by lust,' said Alex sanctimoniously. 'This is a far greater crime. Who knows how many papers Hengist tampered with? Our entire year's GCSE marks could be declared null and void. I'm sure Fleetley will appeal.'

A smell of moussaka was drifting from the kitchens. In two neighbouring practice rooms, pupils could be heard hammering out pieces for the Queen's visit.

Alex sat back in Hengist's chair. Perceptibly, he was shrugging on the mantle of power. I hope he gets it better cut than his suits, thought Hengist irrationally.

As Sally slumped on the sofa, he could see the line of her suspender belt through her grey skirt and that she was wearing sheer black stockings and high heels.

'It's a sad way to end your career, Hengist, but I have to think of Bagley,' sighed Alex. Then, seeing a Panda car emerging from the Memorial Arch: 'Here come the police.'

As he opened the door, Miss Painswick nearly fell into the room.

'The new parents will be old parents if they're kept waiting much longer,' she said tartly, 'and the Bishop's arrived.'

Alex smoothed his beard. 'I will entertain his lordship.'

'Mrs Cox has made celeriac purée,' said Sally in a high voice, 'the Bishop liked it so much last time.' Turning to Alex, she stammered, 'Hengist only did it for Paris's sake.'

'No, I didn't, I did it for myself, said Hengist. 'I'd invested so much in Paris, I couldn't bear him to fail.'

'You have brought independent schools and the entire exam system into disrepute,' said Alex, no longer feeling the need to conceal the extent of his loathing. 'You could get five years.'

What a dreadful combination, thought Hengist, Alex and ruin staring one in the face.

After lunch, in a frenzy of righteousness, Alex rang his chair of governors, not only to tell him about the cheating, but that Hengist had been knocking off a member of the governing body.

'Good God, not the Bishop of Larkminster?' said Jupiter in alarm.

'No, and a parent too, I'm talking about Ruth Walton.'

Jupiter said, 'Good God,' a second time. He'd always fancied Mrs Walton. One of his favourite sayings was: 'That man's the true conservative Who lops the moulder'd branch away.' There was no way Hengist was going to get Education now.

Putting down the telephone, Jupiter was about to dial Fleetley, then, remembering Lord Hawkley would be still at the Headmasters' Conference, he called the St Andrews Bay Hotel.

123

Hengist was arrested, taken down to the station for questioning and kept overnight. Dora, dying to find out what was going on, in overalls, wig and the guise of smartening up the general office for the Queen's visit, was so shocked as she assimilated the terrible truth that she managed to paint Miss Painswick's coat, as well as an entire wall, vicarage green.

Sally retreated to Head House, sat on the bed in which she'd been looking forward to Hengist making love to her, and cried. She'd never dumped on others. She'd been too busy listening to other people's problems and, unlike the clubbable Hengist, had always kept her distance. So she was now intensely alone.

What would happen to them? Hengist would never get another job in teaching. Nor would the New Reform Party look at him and – apart from the terrible disgrace – what would they live on? They had always spent a fortune on entertaining, on pictures, books and the garden, but never bothered to buy a house or save any money. When he had gone abroad on school or political business, Hengist had invariably picked up the bill. And how would such a free spirit ever survive in prison?

Randal Stancombe, who loved hospital cases, decided as night fell to call on Sally. The humiliating amount of coverage over Rupert getting his GCSE, abetted by Hengist and Janna, had increased his detestation of all three. He'd zapped Janna by moving the bulldozers in on Larks; now he was overjoyed to learn, from a very over-excited Poppet Bruce, of Hengist's arrest.

'How's Sally?'

'In shock. I took round some organic hot cross buns and offered her counselling, but she insisted on being on her own. I'm sure she's hurting.'

741

Randal had always fancied Sally. What sweet revenge to take her off Hengist. Champagne might be too celebratory a gesture, so he settled for a huge bunch of bronze chrysanths.

He didn't tell Anthea of his plan, even though she'd been delighted by the turn of events. Sally and Hengist had always shown their preference for Anthea's late husband, Sir Raymond, and constantly displayed favouritism towards Dicky and particularly Dora. Anthea didn't feel Sally deserved any sympathy, so Randal decided to make a mission of mercy on his own.

Showering in his penthouse at Cavendish Plaza, he drenched himself and the blue spotted handkerchief with which he had so often wiped away ladies' tears in lavender water rather than Lynx. Lynx would come later. If there were people with Sally, he'd just leave the flowers with a caring message: 'Thinking of you, Randal', which would soften her up for a later pounce.

Nice property, Head House, thought Randal as he pressed the doorbell. How long would Alex let her stay on?

Sally had clearly been crying a great deal; her face was blotchy and swollen, bloodshot veins intensifying the blue of her eyes. Upset by her mistress's tears, Elaine rushed to the door hoping Randal might be Hengist to make her better.

At first Sally didn't recognize Stancombe. With his mahogany tan and huge circular shield of bronze chrysanthemums, he resembled a Zulu warrior.

'I only popped in, Sal, to offer my condolences,' and he was over the threshold.

He could tell she was in a state. She was shuddering uncontrollably, the fire had not been lit, none of the sidelights had been turned on and she had obviously been trying to persuade that bloody dog to eat. An untouched bowl of chicken curled and dried on the carpet.

'You shouldn't be on your own.'

'It's awfully kind, but I'm better that way. Rupert thinks Hengist will be bailed first thing tomorrow, unless he comes up before Anthea Belvedon. Oh, I'm sorry, Randal, it's Rupert's way of joking.'

'I know,' said Randal bleakly, 'only too well.'

Sally started frantically plumping cushions. 'I don't mind for me, but Hengist was so excited about the future. He would never have touched Paris's paper if Paris hadn't been so devastated by Theo's arrest. Hengist wasn't there to reassure him and came back to find Paris had put in a completely dud paper, just signed his name and a few incomprehensible sentences. So Hengist answered the paper for him.'

'No wonder Paris got an A star,' said Randal coldly. 'I don't approve of cheating, Sally.'

'Neither do I, but Hengist has lost everything.' She started to cry. 'Please go.'

'I'm not leaving you like this.'

Randal had changed his hair, Sally noticed mindlessly, it was shorter and gelled upwards like an oiled, black pincushion. Turned upside down, he could be used to spike up the leaves littering the lawns outside. He was now telling her she was a fine woman.

'Look at that dog, Sal, asleep on its back, taking up nine-tenths of the settee, leaving you no space. Hengist is the same, taking up nine-tenths of your life. You've devoted yourself to a taker who wasn't worth it.'

'That's not true.'

'Hengist broke my heart.'

'Your heart?' Sally stopped plumping a silver wedding cushion in which the embroidered initials H and S had been entwined.

'I cared very deeply for Ruth, then discovered she and Hengist were having a relationship.'

'Ruth's a great friend of both of us!'

'Hengist is a persuasive guy. He also had a relationship with Janna Curtis. Sorry to be brutal, Sal, but you're too straight and sincere not to know the truth.'

Sally gazed at him bewildered. 'But Janna's such a dear.'

'Stands to reason.' Randal paced the room turning on radiators. 'If ladies are sweet to you, you'll invite them to your posh dos and they'll have a chance to pop upstairs for a quickie with Hengist.'

'Don't be revolting. How dare you? Hengist is such a super chap and so kind, mothers, pupils, schoolmistresses are always falling in love with him.'

Stancombe produced a trump card. 'Here's a love letter he wrote Ruth and a picture of them in Paris. She left it under the lining paper in my penthouse apartment.'

Sally glanced at a very loving photograph in some nightclub and a letter which began: 'Ah love, let us be true To one another!' in Hengist's writing, and threw it aside. Randal had his blue spotted handkerchief at the ready.

'Get out, you revolting sneak,' yelled Sally.

'I could make you happy' – a squirt of Gold Spot – 'I can't bear to see you so alone,' and Randal had grabbed her, tugging her towards him, burying his full, cruel lips in hers, pressing his muscular body against her.

'You b-b-bastard,' screamed Sally.

'My, you're a foxy lady,' panted Stancombe as under her discreet cashmere jumper, he'd discovered splendid breasts, supported by a pale blue lacy bra. Putting his other hand up her tweed skirt, he encountered stockings and suspenders but no panties; remembering Hengist on the answerphone to Ruth: 'Darling, don't wear any knickers,' he added, 'You know you want it, Sally.' He would have taken her on the sofa if it hadn't been for Elaine.

'I don't,' shouted Sally. 'If you don't get out I'll call the police,' and gathering up Volume One of the *Shorter Oxford Dictionary*, she clipped him round the ears, sending him reeling backwards, splintering an occasional table.

'Why, you vicious cow . . .'

Rushing to her mistress's defence, Elaine nipped Randal on the back of his thigh, then darted off as the doorbell rang.

'GET OUT,' sobbed Sally.

Randal, in his haste, had not shut the front door properly. Next minute Paris, clutching a half-bottle of Ian's brandy, marched in. 'I wanted to see you were OK. Oh, sorry.'

Elaine accompanied Paris, snaking her long nose into his hand, whacking his jeans with her tail.

'Randal was leaving,' gasped Sally, hastily reloading her bra and pulling down her jersey.

'Good,' said Paris, noticing a trickle of blood flowing from Randal's forehead.

'You'll regret it, Mrs Brett-Taylor. I came offering support,' shouted Randal, banging the front door behind him.

Paris went to the kitchen and poured Sally a large brandy, which she choked on but which warmed her.

'What did he want?'

'To gloat. He brought some hideous flowers.'

'Bin them.'

'Not the flowers' fault, must give them the chance of a few more days of life.'

Sally slumped, shivering, on the sofa. Both Ruth and Janna . . . Oh, Hengist. And he'd sworn after Pippa: never again. Wretchedness was sinking in as his laughing, open, reassuring face looked down at her from Daisy France-Lynch's charming little portrait on the right of the fireplace . . . Paris, having topped up her glass, was meanwhile consumed with his own concerns.

'I'm sorry, but no one will tell me the truth. Did Mr Brett-Taylor switch my and Boffin's papers?'

'No, he wrote yours. It was a very wrong thing to do. But he knew how brilliant you were and couldn't bear you not to produce the goods.'

'So Boffin really did only get a B.'

Paris's satisfaction, however, was short-lived.

'According to Dora, who's been hanging around Painswick's office, Hengist will be fired if he doesn't resign, so both Theo and Hengist lost their jobs because of me.'

Paris was deathly white now, trembling in horror.

'It's not your fault.'

'And if Hengist goes, Artie will be next and Ian and Patience will be turfed out.'

'Theo may well get off.'

'But Hengist's career's ruined.'

'No, no, there are thousands of things he can do – write his books . . . Oh, God.' Tears were pouring down Sally's face; shock was taking over as she knelt by the fire, sweeping up non-existent ashes.

'What did Stancombe really want?'

'To badmouth Hengist. Oh, Paris . . .' Sally wiped her eyes with a sooty hand, 'I shouldn't be telling you, but Randal said Hengist had been . . . been . . . having an affaire with Ruth Walton. I didn't want to believe it, but he produced such a happy photo of Hengist and Janna in Paris.' She clutched her head. 'I mean Ruth.'

'Janna?' said Paris unthinkingly. 'That was in Wales.'

'Then it's true.' Picking up the lovely little Staffordshire dog, which had fallen off the occasional table during Randal's descent, Sally promptly dropped it on the fender where it smashed in a dozen pieces. 'Oh no, watch out for Elaine's paws, that was a wedding present.'

'I'm sorry.' Clumsily Paris swept up the pieces. 'I never told anyone. I caught them on the geography field trip. He was at her bedroom window.'

'So that was why you never came and saw us?'

'Sort of. Fuck, I never meant to tell you.' He tipped the fragments into the waste-paper basket.

Sally couldn't stop crying. Paris wasn't embarrassed; people had always been crying in the children's home. He put his arms round her. 'I'll look after you. I'm sure they were one-night stands and one thing is certain: Mr Brett-Taylor adores you. Like Brutus, you are his true and honourable wife, as dear to him as the ruddy drops that visit his sad heart.'

'Oh P-p-p-p-paris.'

He was stroking her hair; Elaine snuggled up on the other end of the sofa, so he stroked her too.

745

'You ought to go,' gulped Sally.

'Have you got a best friend I can ring?'

'Not really, Hengist was my best friend.'

Paris felt so sorry for her. He gave her another top-up of brandy, then kissed her juddering mouth very tentatively.

'Hush, please don't cry.'

Sally struggled like a captured bird, then went still.

Paris was amazed by the voluptuousness of her body. Sliding his hand up her silken black legs, he encountered shaved pubes, or did women her age go bald down there? It felt smooth, then sticky. Her legs were long and slim and there was only a tiny roll of fat round her waist.

Sally gave a moan as his hand slipped between her legs and slowly, caressingly, moved upwards. The other hand unhooked her bra; out tumbled beautiful, high breasts, still darkened by the Tuscany sun.

'I always dress up for Hengist when he's been away,' she muttered.

For thirty years, only Hengist in his heavyweight strength had made love to her. Paris was Narcissus, Adonis, Endymion, a slender Greek youth with a body and a cock as hard and white as marble. He didn't give her time to think, because it was the only way he knew of lessening both their anguish. It was quick and, because of his kindness, extraordinarily cathartic.

Afterwards, as if she were Little Dulcie, he removed the rest of her clothes, dressed her in a white cotton nightgown and put her to bed.

'Got to do my teeth.'

'Do them in the morning, they won't fall out.'

Then he filled up a hot-water bottle and found her a sleeping pill in the bathroom cupboard.

'I don't take them,' protested Sally. 'Hengist tries to cram too much in and has bouts of insomnia.'

'Take one now.'

Sitting on the bed, Paris stroked her face.

'Elaine,' she mumbled.

'I'll take her out and see she gets something to eat.'

'And the poor, hideous flowers.'

'Yeah, yeah. Don't feel guilty in the morning. I reckon Hengist owed us.'

She was woken from heavy sleep by the telephone. It was Oriana.

'Mum, it's just come over the internet. "Toff school head arrested for cheating". Is it true?'

746

Sally shook herself into consciousness.

'I'm afraid so.'

'What happened? How could Dad?'

Clutching the telephone, Sally wandered groggily downstairs. Paris had put Stancombe's chrysanthemums in the mauve bucket with which Mrs Cox cleaned the kitchen floor. There was a bowl of untouched cold roast beef beside Elaine.

'You're beautiful,' Paris had written on the hall mirror in marker pen, 'all the guys fancy you.'

Oriana was still talking: 'Dad threw up his entire career for one GCSE?'

'I guess so,' said Sally, 'and we're getting a divorce.'

'That's not like you, Mum.'

'I can cope with cheating but not being cheated on.'

Echoing her father last Christmas, Oriana told the press that 'when one of your family does something reprehensible, you take it on the chin.'

124

Once Sally demanded a divorce, Hengist seemed to lose any interest in fighting his case. Despite Rupert bringing down an ace barrister to defend him, he refused to offer any excuse. His actions had been unforgivable. He apologized unreservedly for the distress he had caused a great school and particularly his wife and Paris Alvaston. He appeared unmoved when he was subsequently sent down for three months. Life without Sally was such hell anyway, it didn't much matter whether he was locked up or not. He insisted on no visitors.

Bagley was devastated. Hengist had been hugely popular. He had raised the school's profile at the same time as his own, and any liberty he had taken with his globe-trotting he had returned in glamour, vision, kindness and fun.

'"There hath passed away a glory from the earth,"' sighed Cosmo.

Bagley also loved Sally. They knew how tirelessly she had shored up Hengist, how kind she had been, particularly to the non-teaching staff, how many miserably homesick children she'd comforted, how diligently she'd rammed coronation chicken into square plastic boxes and raced up motorways to organize fundraising dinners.

Now the dream was over. She and Hengist had split up and were to be chucked out of their ravishing house because Poppet and Alex, as acting head, wanted to move 'their brood' in before Christmas. Ideally, they would have liked Sally, who'd met Her Majesty on numerous occasions, to be out before the Queen's visit, but were loath publicly to appear uncaring. Then there was the little hurdle of the next governors' meeting when, hopefully, Alex would be confirmed as head with a salary of £150,000 a year.

Poppet kept dropping in on Sally to measure up rooms and windows and offer counselling. 'I'm sure once you leave Bagley, you'll find it easier to achieve closure.'

'Should we organize a leaving present?' she asked Alex. 'After all, Sally is leaving Hengist *and* Bagley. Perhaps a small refrigerator or a Dyson; I expect she and Hengist have only one between them.'

'And who will have custody of Elaine?' sobbed Dora, who would no longer be able to boost her pocket money and pick up stories waiting at Hengist and Sally's dinner parties.

'At least Alex and Poppet won't need Pickfords to move their lack of furniture,' drawled Amber. 'They could probably get it all into Van Dyke. Joan is definitely flavour of the month. Lando's got her at ten to one to get deputy head rather than Biffo.'

Rumour and suspicion were swirling round like autumn mist. Alex was determined to scrap the school beagles before February 2005, when hunting was bound to become illegal, and close the stables, which pandered to an elitist few and was the centre of subversive activity. He had also introduced a tagging system to ensure pupils were always in the right lesson and safe in their houses by eight o'clock.

'There'll be no more shagging in Middle Field,' sighed Milly as they waited to go into chapel, 'and Theo won't be allowed back even if he's proved innocent. Stancombe's builders are pulling down the classical library and the archives as we speak. Look what I've just found in the skip: Theo's translation of *Medea*.'

Paris snatched it. 'I'll have that.'

The press had a field day. Ashton Douglas was interviewed at length about his 'great wegret' that, against his better judgement, he had allowed Paris Alvaston to be plucked from the security of a care home and thrust into the hothouse atmosphere of a rich decadent public school, where he had had to suffer the humiliation of being cheated for when an exam was beyond his capabilities.

Col Peters's hatchet job in the *Larkminster Gazette*. 'The Head that wasn't there', picked up by all the nationals, listed Hengist's away days, leaked by Alex. Alex, photographed very flatteringly, was quoted as saying his goal was to put Bagley back on the rails and engage with the wider community.

In the same *Gazette* there was a profile of Ashton Douglas, entitled 'Schools Saviour', with a picture of him accepting a cheque from Randal Stancombe for £25,000,000 for the sale of Larks High School, which would go towards the education of

Larkshire's children. Randal was quoted as saying he had very exciting plans for the area, including health and sports centres, playgrounds, a row of shops, even a police station for the Shakespeare Estate.

Nudged by Randal, Alex had immediately axed all Hengist's plans for the Queen's visit, liaising with the Lord Lieutenant and the royal household and guaranteeing Randal as much access to Her Majesty on the day as possible.

'Engaging with the community', Alex had also invited a lot of local movers and shakers to meet the Queen, but had pointedly left out Artie, Ian and Patience and, more seriously, Biffo, who was even more upset when he saw the agenda for the next governors' meeting and discovered he was not being put forward for deputy head.

'You promised me this, Alex, when I supported you over the Theo business.'

'That was before I analysed your maths results, which could have been better,' replied Alex coldly. 'You're nearly sixty, Biffo, and not cutting it any more. Of course I want you on side, but suggesting Sally Brett-Taylor be allowed to stay on was not helpful. I'd rather you didn't make suggestions like that.'

Alex speedily assumed the role of head. He'd been running the school for the last two years anyway. Now, like a second wife, he was determined to exorcise every trace of the Brett-Taylors; for a start, ordering the digging up of Sally's glowing, subtly coloured autumn borders and replacing them with regiments of clashing bedding plants.

Alex knew nothing of the art world, but had recently been putting out feelers for the right person to paint him. At some function, Poppet had met an interesting artist called Trafford, who, responsible for some ground-breakingly obscene installations, had been nominated for the Turner. Trafford, who was coming down for a recce next week, also had some challenging ideas, according to Poppet, about a sculpture to replace General Bagley and Denmark. Everyone knew of Arnold of Rugby, why not Bruce of Bagley? mused Alex.

He was gratified how many of the press were ringing him up for quotes, and now that he was appearing on the box a lot, he'd invested in contact lenses, like his icon Jack Straw, and a new wardrobe. Channel 4 was coming down for a programme entitled 'Whither Independents?' – or should it be 'Wither?' Alex had quipped to the researcher. They'd be filming outside, so Alex intended to wear a smart new raincoat in fashionable stone, belted to show off his good figure, which he'd acquired in

750

celebratory mood the day after Hengist had been forced to resign.

The new raincoat was hanging in the general office when Dora, who was highly displeased with all Alex's pointless innovations, wandered in with cups of coffee for herself and Miss Painswick.

'Why is Tabitha Campbell-Black no longer on the front of the *Old Bagleian*?' she demanded. 'She's an icon.'

'Equestrianism is regarded as elitist,' explained Painswick sourly. 'Mr Bruce is replacing her with a picture of the Science Emporium.'

'How pants is that?' Dora was leaning forward to read the list of acceptances for the Queen's visit, which Painswick was typing out, when Alex walked in, causing her to jump and spill coffee all over his raincoat.

'Oh bugger, sorry, Mr Bruce.'

'Don't swear. Sorry isn't enough. You will take that raincoat to the dry-cleaner's, pay for it and return it by tomorrow when I need it. Why are you hanging round here anyway? You should be in . . .' He pressed a button on the tagging computer. '. . . French lit. Why hasn't Mr Deverell reported you?'

'Mr Deverell doesn't need the tagging system because we all love him. No one misses his lessons.' Dora glanced up at the clock. 'I'm only a minute late.' Grabbing the raincoat, she shot out of the office.

Later in the day, Dora returned sulkily to Boudicca. There was no way she was going to fork out for dry-cleaning, so she chucked Alex's mac into Joan's washing machine. Next morning, attaching safety pins and a couple of coloured tags to prove it had been dry-cleaned, Dora hung it back in the general office.

Alas, when Alex flung it on to go into the Long Walk with Channel 4, he was horrified to discover it had shrunk to mid-thigh, and wouldn't remotely button up. Alex was so thrown, he didn't get half his points across and forgot to plug *A Guide to Red Tape*. After the crew had gone, he summoned Dora in a fury.

'Those dry-cleaner's shrunk my raincoat.'

'They couldn't have. Perhaps you've put on weight.'

'Don't be ridiculous. I've weighed eleven stone two since I left Bristol.'

'You should have flung it round your shoulders like a matador.'

'Just shut up. Where's the receipt?'

'I chucked it away.'

'Well, find it then.'

'That Polly Toyboy on the phone for you, Mr Bruce,' called out Painswick.

751

Sidling out of the office, Dora remembered there had been a piece of paper with writing on in the mac pocket, which she'd left on her bedside table.

As Cosmo was as anxious as she was to depose Alex and bring back Hengist's very benevolent despotism, Dora showed Cosmo the piece of paper later in the day. 'It's in Mr Fussy's wincy little writing and it says: ' "BC Green Dolphin, six o'clock, August 27th", plus a mobile number.'

'What's BC?' pondered Cosmo.

'Before Christ – Mr Fussy's so old; and my God, that's Stancombe's number. Engraved on my heart. My mother's always ringing it.'

Next day, while Painswick was at lunch, Dora and Cosmo checked Alex's diary.

'He should have been at an "Against Gender Bias Workshop" in Birmingham at six o'clock on the twenty-seventh.' Cosmo clicked his tongue. 'Our Senior Team Leader has been moonlighting.'

Cosmo was a regular of the Green Dolphin, a trendy country pub, two miles from Bagley. Hanging on the walls beside fishing nets, tridents and leaping dolphins, was a mug engraved with his name.

As Lubemir had immediately cracked Alex's tagging system, Cosmo escaped that evening to the Green Dolphin to chat up his friend Susie the barmaid. Fortunately the place was virtually empty.

'Your usual?' asked Susie, getting down his mug and filling it up with a concoction made up of black vodka, Tia Maria and Coke, entitled Black Russian. He was a one, that Cosmo, with his soulful eyes and flopping curls.

Susie remembered 27 August well, because they were all there: 'Ashton Douglas, Alex Bruce, Rod Hyde, Col Peters (the revolting pig), Russell Lambert (the planning permission king, who allowed Stancombe's horrible expensive houses on the edge of the village here, blocking out the view from my mum and dad's cottage), Des Reynolds, smoothie pants, and his lordship, Randal Stancombe. They had a private room and drank buckets of Bolly, obviously celebrating something.'

'It's called "engaging with the wider community",' said Cosmo, making notes. 'Strange, or not so strange bedfellows: Randal, Alex and Rod perhaps, but what were Russell and Ashton doing there? I bet Stancombe handed out a few suitcases of greenbacks or Caribbean villas as going-home presents.'

As 27 August had been around the time Stancombe got his hands on the Larks land, Cosmo decided he must try and get into Stancombe's office. Difficult when he'd treated Jade in so cavalier a fashion – and when Stancombe had changed the locks after he split up with Ruth Walton. Alex Bruce had also put such a lock on his files recently, so Cosmo decided to try and gain access to those of another member of the party: Ashton Douglas at S and C.

There were advantages to having a famous mother. That very evening, Dame Hermione invited Ashton Douglas to a little supper party the following night in her beautiful house in neighbouring Rutshire. Ashton, an opera buff, was in heaven, kissing Hermione's white hands, almost too excited to eat his lobster pancakes.

Afterwards Dame Hermione sang to the guests, and during 'Where e'er you walk' gazed directly at Ashton.

Later, over a glass of Kummel, she told him:

'My son is obsessed with citizenship, Mr Douglas. He's taking it for AS level. He has such a feeling for his fellow citizens and the work of the Borough. It would be so wonderful' – Hermione opened her big brown eyes – 'if he could do a few days' work experience in your fascinating office to learn about education.'

'We'd be honoured, Dame Hermione,' said Ashton warmly, who had no idea of Cosmo's capacity for evil and thought he looked fetchingly like a Caravaggio catamite as, back home for the weekend, he sat quietly in the window seat engrossed in a book called *Know Your Town Hall*, which was actually a jacket wrapped round *L'Histoire d'O*.

'Bingo,' crowed Cosmo next day to Dora. 'I'll get access to Ashton's offices and find out exactly what's going on.'

Fortunately, most of the Lower Sixth were out on work experience and Alex was too obsessed with the Queen's visit to bother about Cosmo's destination.

'My interesting news is that my Aunt Lily and the Brigadier are planning to fight the development at Larks,' Dora told Cosmo, 'because the builders are endangering natterjack toads and loads of rare wild flowers, which aren't out at the moment, but which the Brigadier, who is a keen bottomist, recognizes by the leaves.'

'Ashton Douglas is also a keen bottomist,' said Cosmo. 'I'd better wear steel underpants. I might even write a musical called *Kiddy Fiddler on the Roof*.'

125

Paris was in despair, overwhelmed by the misfortune he'd brought on Bagley.

'You've created even more havoc than the Paris who started the Trojan Wars,' Boffin told him nastily as they came out of prep the following dank October evening. 'First Theo, then Hengist chucked out; both their careers ruined; Hengist's marriage wrecked. Artie, Biffo and your dear foster parents'll be next for the chop. Alex doesn't like fossils.'

Somehow Paris managed not to throttle Boffin. He'd caused enough trouble already. Bagley had completely lost its charm. Back at the Old Coach House, Ian was not sleeping and his temper grew shorter as Alex delved into every aspect of the school's finances. There was no Hengist or Emlyn for Paris to have fun with any more and every time he popped in to cheer up Sally, he found her unravelling with despair, and felt hideously responsible.

He loathed Dora and Cosmo having secrets and whispering in corners together. He liked the charming and emollient Artie, but didn't have the same bond with him that he had with Theo. Where the hell was Theo and how was his back and how was he getting on with Sophocles? And Paris had worries of his own. He'd be seventeen in January and if Patience and Ian didn't want or could no longer afford to keep him, he'd be out of care and on to the scrap heap, no doubt joining the criminal classes and the homeless, like so many care leavers.

Alone in the dusk, Paris punched the wall of the Mansion several times until his knuckles ran with blood, like Oedipus's beard after he'd pierced his eyeballs again and again with the brooch pins of his hanged wife and mother, Jocasta. A passage

Theo had translated with such terrifying vividness. Paris shuddered. There was still one trail he hadn't followed up.

On his way back to Ian and Patience's for supper, having wrapped his hand in bog paper, he dropped in on Biffo to return a maths textbook. He found the old boy plastered in a thick fog of smoke, farts and drink fumes. The fire had gone out; Biffo was three-quarters down a bottle of red; another bottle lay in the waste-paper basket.

'Are you OK, sir?' Paris relit the fire, then played a sneaky trick. 'We're looking forward to you being deputy head.'

Like an old walrus confronted by an eskimo's harpoon, Biffo glowered at him. 'Not getting it.'

'Everyone thinks it's a done deal.'

'Huh, Alex says I'm not cutting it any more. Results not good enough.'

'You got me through maths, you must be a bloody genius.'

Paris waited for Biffo to nod off, then he grabbed his red leatherbound book filled with the addresses of old boys and other masters. Many entries had a diagonal through them and were marked RIP. There was only a handful of women's names.

He was half an hour late back at the Coach House. His steak pie had dried in the oven; Dulcie, expecting a goodnight kiss, had refused to go to bed. Ian and Patience were in their coats, waiting to go out.

'What's the point of a tagging system if you bloody well ignore it?' yelled Ian. 'Alex has been on, demanding where you are. It's Patience and I who get it in the neck. Have you no consideration? What the hell have you been doing?'

'Looking for my real parents,' shouted Paris, running upstairs and slamming the door.

The following evening, Cosmo rang Dora in triumph. He had had a brilliant first day at S and C.

'I found several references to BC at the Green Dragon and other places. It must be some kind of club. The one on the twenty-seventh of August seems to be definitely celebrating Randal finally buying Larks. They had another get-together the day Hengist was arrested. They've obviously been trying to get their hands on the Larks land for ages. There was an email from Ashton to Rod Hyde way back in November 2002 saying – listen to this: "Despite all our efforts, Janna Curtis is not failing as expected. We must also watch our step, as she is accusing us of rigging figures and results and changing boundaries and bus stops."'

There was a pause.

'Have you heard a word I said, Dora?'

Dora, who'd been holding her breath like a baby, gave an almighty bellow.

'What in hell's the matter?'

'Paris has run away. He left an envelope with twenty-five pounds in to pay Ian back for not getting history. Then he said he was sorry for all the misery he'd caused and not to try and find him. And worst of all, there was no Hengist to give him a can of Coke and some sandwiches for the journey.' Dora bawled even louder.

'What an applause junky. Can't bear to be out of the limelight for a second,' sighed Cosmo, then, in a kinder voice: 'He'll come back when he's cold and hungry.'

Alex immediately alerted the police and the social services and, while blaming the whole experiment on Hengist, was desperate for Paris's return. The last thing he'd wanted was a crisis distracting either the governors when they met next week, or the media when they should be concentrating on the Queen's visit.

The police were very reassuring. Lads often ran away after a family row. At least he'd left a note; he'd probably be home in the morning.

But Paris did not come home. As the days crawled by, Ian and Patience sank into blacker despair. Patience wouldn't leave the house in case he returned. Dora kept bunking off classes and at night, combing the woods with Northcliffe and Cadbury.

'Where's Pawis?' cried Dulcie over and over again.

Ian couldn't concentrate on anything. How could he have shouted at Paris on that last evening? Taking a wireless into the bursar's office, he listened to every bulletin until Alex grew very sharp with him.

'It's only a foster child, after all.'

Pleading for help, Dora rang all her media contacts, who wanted to know if Paris was having woman trouble.

'Are you his girlfriend, Dora?'

'No, but I'd like to be. He's so beautiful, I'm sure he's been kidnapped.'

'We just want him home and safe,' Ian and Patience told the press.

'He might go to Feral or Emlyn,' suggested Dora. 'If he'd known where Theo was, he'd have gone to him.'

'We've checked Theo Graham,' said Chief Inspector Gablecross, 'but there's no sign.'

'And he can't go to Hengist,' sobbed Dora, 'because he's in prison.'

Sally felt desperately guilty. She never should have slept with Paris. They hadn't again, but he'd been so adorable, popping in most days, holding her in his arms and sending her praise postcards. Calling on the Old Coach House, Sally found Patience mucking out the horses, her mobile in the breast pocket of her tweed coat. Her face was utterly devastated by tears, her eyes huge purple craters.

'Oh Sally, we tried so hard not to crowd him; now we realize how desperately we love him. It's all our fault. Paris's last words to us were that he was going to find his real parents. Ian thought he was just trying to hurt us. We should have stayed in, but Poppet was holding some awful parenting workshop, and we felt we should go to gain brownie points.'

Patience collapsed sobbing on a hay bale.

Over at Wilmington, Janna had been equally devastated, not least by Hengist's arrest. Jubilee Cottage was on the market, the 'For Sale' sign creaking desolate in the east wind. As a hair shirt and to pay the mortgage, she was filling in for a head of English on maternity leave in the next county, which meant an hour's drive there and back every day, leaving poor bewildered Partner alone in the house, ripping up carpets, scrabbling at doors and biting the ankles of estate agents, who showed fewer and fewer people over the house.

Patience had called to tell her Paris had bolted.

'He so admired you, Janna. He might easily turn up.'

'Oh God, I probably won't be here, I'm working miles away and such long hours.'

'Poor Paris was devastated about Theo and Hengist. Alex is being such a brute turfing Sally out in November. She's just been here. Paris found out Ian and Artie were under threat too, poor boy. He must have felt all his security crumbling.'

As Janna switched off the telephone, she wondered if she ought to stay home, just in case Paris did turn up.

He loved me once, Atthis, long ago.

In need of comfort and the comfort of comforting, Janna rang Sally and thought she'd got the wrong number when the call was answered by a deep, lilting, utterly unforgettable voice that set her heart crashing.

'Emlyn. I must have misdialled. I wanted Sally.'

'I've just driven down to see her.'

There was an interminable pause.

Oh Christ, she'd craved the sound of that voice for the longest four months of her life, now she couldn't think of anything to say.

'How's the Welsh Rugby Union?'

'Fine.'

There was another long pause.

'Emlyn, I wrote to Sally about Hengist. How is she?'

'Not great.'

He was making no effort. He was still angry with her.

'Sally didn't write back and she's usually so punctilious. Is she OK?' Janna was so frantic to see Emlyn, she added, 'Shall I pop round?'

'I wouldn't. That bastard Randal told her Hengist was having an affaire with Ruth.'

'Oh no!'

'Randal was trying to pull Sally; then he told her about Hengist and you. Paris, caught off guard, confirmed it.'

Janna gave a wail of anguish.

'I can't bear it, poor Sally. Oh my God, I'm sorry. But it was over months ago.'

'Was it?' said Emlyn bleakly.

'Truly, truly, when I found out about him and Ruth, when you marked my stupid suicide note. Oh, please tell Sally she's the only person he's ever loved.'

'I'm sure she'll find it a great comfort,' said Emlyn acidly. 'I've gotta go.'

'Please, please don't.'

But he'd hung up.

Sobbing wildly, Janna drove over to Bagley and parked in the hedgerow at the bottom of the drive.

After an hour, listening to the screech owls and watching the moon rise through the mist, she heard the familiar racket of Emlyn's Renault, careering and bumping down the drive. She prayed he'd turn left towards Wilmington, but she only caught a glimpse of his thick blond hair before, with a screech of tyres, he hurtled right towards Wales.

Patience and Ian sank deeper and deeper into despair. They had never known there were a hundred hours between each tick of the clock, and no sleep in the night, as a day became a week. There was no trace anywhere of Paris.

The police, by the increasing gravity of their demeanour, clearly felt something must have happened to him and suggested Ian and Patience appealed to the public for information at a press conference. This was absolutely packed out – the Arctic Prince being an on-going story.

The Cartwrights tried to be very stiff-upper-lipped, but they looked dreadful, hollow-eyed, trembling, their clothes falling off them and when Patience had to speak, she broke down.

'Honking away like a red-nosed reindeer,' shuddered Cosmo who was watching with Painswick and Jessica on the portable in the general office. 'Not much incentive to return.'

'We love him so much,' brayed Patience, her blotched face collapsing. 'We just want him to come home and know he's safe.'

'For God's sake, pull yourself together, woman,' hissed Ian.

'We were fostering him, but we wanted to adopt him,' struggled on Patience, 'if he'd have liked it, that is, but we never told him, we were so frightened of being pushy. We all miss him, particularly our little granddaughter Dulcie and Northcliffe our dog, who just sit waiting by the front door. Paris is such a super chap.'

'Cringe-making,' drawled Cosmo.

'Oh, shut up,' said Jessica and Painswick, who were both in tears.

After Ian and Patience, Nadine was interviewed and very indiscreetly confessed that she blamed herself: 'The placement was too middle class and Mr and Mrs Cartwright were too elderly to foster a teenage boy.'

126

When Hengist resigned so suddenly, Jupiter Belvedon, as chairman, had telephoned the rest of the governors and suggested they invite David Hawkley to attend the next meeting, to advise them on steadying the ship. This was agreed to be an excellent idea, particularly since Lord Hawkley was leaving Fleetley, and as he'd been touring schools with the Great and the Good looking for a Head of the Year for the Teaching Awards, he would have many fresh ideas.

It was also agreed that as the Queen's visit was so imminent, it would be better to have a holding meeting beforehand to discuss logistics and mull over possible candidates to take over as head, then schedule a second meeting shortly after Her Majesty's visit, when they could have a jolly post-mortem and probably confirm a shortlist for the new head.

The only person deeply displeased by this development was Alex, who wanted the matter sewn up. Gathering allies, he suggested that a previous winner of Head of the Year at the Teaching Awards, Rod Hyde of St Jimmy's, should be invited to join the meeting as an impartial adviser, as well as Joan Johnson, the favoured candidate for deputy head; also that to discuss arrangements for the Queen's visit Randal should be brought in at half-time.

As none of these three would be able to vote for anything, Jupiter and the board agreed.

The governors had all loved Hengist and were very upset by his departure. Meetings in his day had been held in London over an excellent dinner at Boodle's, or at Bagley after a luscious lunch laid on by Sally with plenty to drink. Alex intended to scrap both these procedures. They were expensive, and people couldn't think straight if they were drunk.

Poppet, however, didn't want her hospitality to compare unfavourably with Sally's, and before the meeting, which was held at three o'clock on the fourth Friday in October, laid on a light buffet and soft drinks.

As a result, General Broadstairs, the Lord Lieutenant, who'd been up since five cub hunting and was absolutely starving, helped himself to most of Poppet's quiche, imagining it was a first course, which left cheese and cress sandwiches, plain yoghurts and figs for everyone else.

Jupiter retreated to a corner with David Hawkley:

'Any more thoughts on joining us on Education?'

'I'm sixty-five,' said David firmly, 'much too old for politics and about to retire.'

'Can you resist a chance to play God with the education of this country's children? Greek and Latin in every primary school?'

They were distracted by Poppet, bringing in and insisting on breastfeeding nineteen-month-old Gandhi.

'At least the lucky little sod's got a drink,' grumbled Jupiter as, hungry, resentful and very sober, the governors filed into the boardroom next door.

Here they were further distressed to find a less faded square on the magenta damask walls, between the portraits of General Bagley and Sabine Bottomley. This, at the last meeting, had been inhabited by Jonathan Belvedon's lovely, smiling portrait of Hengist, with his hand on Elaine's head and Sally's photograph on the bookshelf behind him.

'Beautiful picture. Hope it's been given to Sally,' chuntered the Lord Lieutenant.

Alex smiled thinly. Having learnt Jonathan's portraits went for over two hundred thousand pounds on the open market, a discreet sale could buy a lot more IT equipment.

Outside in the park, leaves were drifting downwards in free-fall. Jupiter sat at one end of the long polished table, with David Hawkley on his left and the Bishop on his right. Alex sat at the other end flanked by Joan and Rod Hyde, rigid with disapproval to be among the governing body of an independent school.

Miss Painswick, a box of Kleenex beside her, was taking the minutes and tearfully assuring Ruth Walton there was no news yet of Paris.

The Bishop kicked off with prayers, including one for Paris's safe return, then, when everyone was seated, added: 'I'd like to express the governors' universal regret at the departure of Hengist Brett-Taylor. We've all enjoyed Hengist's friendship and

761

marvellous hospitality and felt privileged to be part of an exciting adventure in turning Bagley into a great school. The lapse that toppled him was regrettable, but understandable.'

'Hear, hear,' said everyone but Alex and Rod and Joan.

The first item on the agenda was the appointment of a new head.

'I'd like to stick my neck out,' said Joan bravely, 'and say that Alex has been virtually running the school for the past three years.'

Jupiter gave her a glare which said, 'You're a new girl so shut up,' and announced that it was essential to look at outside candidates.

'We always have. Several were being considered when it was rumoured that Hengist was taking over Fleetley on Lord Hawkley's retirement' – he smiled at David – 'and I think we should follow these through. Not that I don't think Alex is doing an excellent job.'

'Then appoint him as head,' urged Rod Hyde. 'Schools should not be allowed to drift. A strong hand on the tiller.'

'I suggest we need more time before making a decision,' said the Lord Lieutenant, thinking what a damned attractive woman Ruth Walton was and the more meetings the better.

Ruth, in turn, was thinking that David Hawkley was utterly divine: strong, macho, brilliant and so gravely good-looking. Taking off her suit jacket, she breathed in deeply.

Alex then said he didn't wish to speak ill of the departed, but he did feel Bagley should be run more economically. So much of the land wasn't being utilized; so many bursaries had been offered to foreign pupils, particularly if the mother was, er, good-looking.

'And talking of good-looking women,' butted in the Lord Lieutenant, 'what about Sally Brett-Taylor, to whom we're all devoted? She should be allowed to stay in Head House till she finds somewhere suitable to live.'

'Hear, hear,' said all the governors, except Alex and his allies.

'Surely she could be lent one of the cottages off the campus,' suggested Rod Hyde, 'then Alex and Poppet, whom I see as the ideal couple to run Bagley Hall, could take over Head House immediately. It's hard even for acting heads to be constantly reminded of unfortunate past regimes. It divides loyalties.'

'I agree with Rod,' said Joan. 'Head House is a symbol of authority. The school needs strong management at once, particularly during the Queen's visit.'

Outside the window, Jupiter could see his sister Dora and

Bianca Campbell-Black marching up and down brandishing placards saying: 'Bring back Hengist Brett-Taylor'.

Marching the other way, with a four-foot penis destined for the body parts zone of the Science Emporium balanced on his shoulder like a musket, came a grinning Stancombe workman, reducing Bianca and even a tear-stained Dora to fits of giggles.

'Let's leave this decision until after the Queen's visit,' said Jupiter.

One of the school cooks then came in with tea and biscuits, on which everyone fell.

Stirring Sweetex into his cup, feeling he wasn't making sufficient headway, Alex said, 'Before Randal arrives to brief us, I would like to raise the matter of Theo Graham, whose case is due to come up next month.'

'I hoped the police were dropping the charges,' said David Hawkley quickly.

'The evidence is so overwhelming. It really pains me to do this,' lied Alex, 'but you should look at these.' Walking down the table, he placed copies of the poems and the photographs of Paris in front of Jupiter. 'The DVD of young boys of such a distressingly pornographic nature is still with the police.'

David Hawkley read one poem, then another and another, the hair lifting on the back of his neck. They were exquisite.

'Theo and I were at Cambridge together,' he said coldly. 'He is a man of utter integrity. I cannot believe he would ever touch a boy.'

'His base nature clearly overcame him,' intoned Rod.

'My problem' – Alex had returned to his seat – 'is whether to look for a new head of classics. A Mr Margolis is filling in for Theo, but my inclination would be to phase out the dead languages at Bagley.'

'You what?' thundered David Hawkley.

'Whatever the outcome of the case,' Alex battled on, 'if we let Theo back into school, the no-smoke-without-fire brigade would never let up. Theo's only two or three years off retirement. With a small pay-off, he could enjoy exit with dignity.'

'Theo is one of the greatest classical scholars of his age,' said an outraged David. 'If there's any further chance for your scholars to be taught by him, they should take it.'

'I agree with Alex,' butted in Rod Hyde, taking two more biscuits. 'Mud sticks. Bagley has had such appalling press recently, they must prove they're serious about rooting out corruption.'

'Almost all the boys in Theo's house have been dispersed, anyway,' Joan joined in the attack.

'Not quite all of them,' said a voice, and in walked Paris.

In one hand he was carrying a dark blue carrier bag patterned with gold Roman emperors, in the other a furiously leaping and mewing cat basket.

What a beautiful boy, thought David. Adonis bathed in moonlight. He'd never seen anyone so pale.

Miss Painswick dropped her shorthand notebook and burst into noisy sobs. 'Oh Paris, thank God you're safe.'

'Where the hell have you been?' Alex had gone as magenta as the wallpaper. 'The entire country's looking for you. How dare you vanish like that and then barge in here? Go to my office at once. I'll deal with you later.'

'You'll deal with me now,' said Paris coolly.

'Show some manners to your headmaster,' bellowed Rod Hyde.

'Deputy head,' countered Paris. 'I've come to talk about Theo.'

'This is not the time,' screeched Alex, 'and don't let that cat out.'

But Paris had opened the basket.

'He'll pee everywhere.' Jupiter snatched up his papers in alarm.

'No, he won't, I gave him a run five minutes ago.'

Everyone watched mesmerized as Hindsight landed on the table with a thud. The Bishop proceeded to pour some milk into a saucer and was delighted when Hindsight padded over and drank the lot.

'What a fine cat. Must have been thirsty.'

'Like most of us earlier,' giggled Ruth Walton. 'It's a lovely cat.'

Alex had had enough. Marching down the table, he grabbed Paris's arm. 'Get that cat and yourself out of here, at once.'

'I want to talk about Theo,' persisted Paris, prising off Alex's skinny fingers.

'As one person who has never given an account of that night,' said Jupiter, 'Paris is a crucial witness and should be heard.'

'Hear, hear,' piped up Miss Painswick, receiving a daggers look from Alex.

'This is Theo's cat,' said Paris, running his finger round and round Hindsight's plumey tail. 'He'd be an even better witness.' Then, out of the Roman-emperor-patterned bag, he produced an ivy-green leather folder filled with manuscript paper. 'Which one of you's Lord Hawkley?'

'I am.'

Paris flushed. 'Your translations of Catullus and Ovid are really cool.'

'Thank you.' David's hatchet face softened fractionally.

'Theo asked me to give you this with his love. It's Sophocles,' said Paris. 'Much better than your rotten *Guide to Red Tape*,' he added over his shoulder.

'Sophocles.' David was down the table in a flash, grabbing the folder, opening it, stopping to read bits in wonder, then flipping through to the end. 'My God, he finished it.'

'All seven plays, the night before last,' said Paris. 'I wrote out the final pages for him.'

'You were ordered not to contact Theo Graham.' Alex was spluttering, hysterical, impotent with rage. 'How dare you? This could compromise his trial.'

'Theo's dead,' said Paris flatly, seeing a flare of relief in Alex's eyes. 'He died yesterday in my arms.' Then, turning like a viper on Rod: 'Make something of that, you prurient bastard.'

The Bishop crossed himself. 'Took his own life.'

'Not at all, he had an inoperable tumour on his spine, claimed it came from being stabbed in the back so often.' There was only the slightest quiver in Paris's voice. 'He's been on morphine for weeks. Dr Benson's been looking after him. He drove up to Windermere this morning and signed the death certificate. He gave me a lift here.'

'I'm very sorry,' said a shaken Ruth Walton. 'Milly was devoted to Theo.'

David Hawkley put down Sophocles, a tear running down his cheek.

'How did you know where I was, Paris?'

'I rang Fleetley. They said you were here.'

'Why didn't the police find you at Windermere?' demanded Joan.

'They were evidently sniffing around last week. I only found him on Monday. At least we had three days together. Merciful death came at last,' he said carefully, 'and a dead man knows no pain.'

Hindsight, ready to witness more drama, settled himself, purring loudly, on the Bishop's knee. Paris strolled back to Alex and stood over him. 'You broke Theo's heart,' he said softly. 'He loved Bagley and his archives. They were his life, but he knew once Hengist had resigned, you'd never let him back.'

'You were told not to go near him,' repeated Alex, clearly jolted. 'Where did you get his address?'

'From Biffo's phone book. Poor old bugger was drunk with despair that even though he'd helped you get rid of Theo, you were still going to dump him: "Biffo, you're not cutting it any more." The sudden mimicry of Alex's reedy whine was so exact, the governors shivered.

'At least Biffo had the decency to make sure Hindsight was safely delivered to Theo's door in Windermere in July,' Paris told Alex contemptuously. 'You'd have put him down.'

'That is quite enough on the subject,' boomed Joan.

'I loved Theo,' said Paris softly and defiantly. ' "Forty thousand brothers Could not, with all their quantity of love, Make up my sum." '

Glancing across the table at Alex, Rod nodded knowingly.

'I know about shirt-lifters and bum bandits!' Paris snarled at them. 'Since I was three, I've defended my ass in children's homes and foster homes all round the country.'

God he's wonderful, thought Mrs Walton as Hindsight, finding the Bishop's knees a trifle bony, settled on her bosom to get a better view all round.

'Theo never laid a finger on me.' Paris's voice trembled. 'The only thing he touched was my heart. He opened my mind; he shared things with me. Yes, I loved him, but not in the way you stinking pervs would understand. The night before the second history paper, I had a nightmare. I woke and found a man in my room, and screamed until I realized it was Theo; he was just turning off my bedside light and putting my books away. He calmed me down. I was so knackered cramming for history, in which I was so desperate to please Hengist, I fell back asleep at once.'

'What about the photographs?'

'They must have been taken on the geography field trip. Look at my hair now.' He shook his head so it flopped over his face.

'And the poems?' David handed them to Paris, who took a minute or so to translate the first one.

'I've never seen it before; it's beautiful.' For a moment he seemed about to lose it. 'It's a privilege to have inspired such love.'

No wonder Hengist cheated for him, thought David.

'Last night, after Theo'd died' – Paris had regained control of himself – 'I went outside. It had been grey and windy all day, but suddenly every star in heaven was out: Pegasus and Aldebaran, the Pole Star and the Great Bear, who Theo told me was once Callisto. They'd all come out to welcome a new star to heaven. I felt happy he'd got a lot of fans up there.'

Paris slumped against the wall, his face in his hands. Miss Painswick and the Bishop blew their noses. Everyone jumped at the sound of slow clapping as Cosmo sauntered in.

'Very good, Paris, you should really go on the stage.'

'Get out,' howled Alex.

'This is a private meeting,' said Jupiter icily.

Ignoring them both, Cosmo helped himself to a biscuit and, murmuring, 'Hello Hindsight,' stroked the cat and briefly the splendid bosom of Mrs Walton, who had earlier tipped him off that Theo's future was on the agenda.

'I shopped Theo,' he told the flabbergasted company, 'because I was jealous of Paris. Artie, Hengist, Theo, Sally, the bursar, even Emlyn were always fussing over him. I took and then put the nude photos under the lining paper of Theo's desk. I made out to Alex, who doesn't read Greek, that the poems were much dirtier. Theo asked me to get his DVD machine working, so I shoved in a pornographic DVD for a joke. When I heard screaming coming from Paris's bedroom and Theo came out, it seemed the perfect opportunity.'

'This is disgraceful,' thundered David Hawkley, who, being married to the widow of Cosmo's father, the late Roberto Rannaldini, was aware of Cosmo's capacity for transgression.

'It is,' agreed Cosmo soulfully. 'In fact, I was so ashamed when it all backfired, I confessed to Mr Bruce what I'd done and he simply wouldn't believe me, because he wanted Theo and Hengist out so badly. He's keener on new blood than Dracula. There won't be a master left at Bagley, at this rate.' He smiled lovingly at Mrs Walton.

Alex was quivering with rage:

'How dare you tell such lies!'

The governors were clearly astounded. Even Jupiter looked shocked. And where does that put my deputy headship? wondered Joan.

'You can both get out,' said Jupiter.

At that moment, Miss Painswick's assistant, the comely Jessica, knocked on the door. 'Mr Stancombe's downstairs.'

Aware he'd put in a dud performance, Alex ordered Jessica to show Randal up at once, so they could regain the ascendancy, revealing the mysteries of the Science Emporium.

The governors, however, needed a few more minutes to decide whether Cosmo was telling the truth about Theo.

'Cosmo Rannaldini is a compulsive liar,' spluttered Alex. 'Any of my colleagues will bear this out. Theo is past history. Bagley must move on.'

'I think this whole affair'd better be set aside for reflection until after Her Majesty's visit,' said Jupiter.

Joan, who was watching Paris with difficulty shoving Hindsight back in the cat basket, decided to seize the initiative.

'Where are you going, Paris? Someone must alert the authorities that you're back. Have you any idea how much police

767

time you've wasted? What the dickens d'you think you've been doing?'

'Finding my real parents,' snapped Paris.

On the Mansion steps, he and Cosmo faced each other.

'Plans are afoot to oust Mr Fussy,' said Cosmo. 'I'm doing work experience at S and C this week to get dirt on him.'

Then there was a long pause as a workman passed them in the half-light, buckling under a huge gall bladder.

'Thank you for rescuing Theo's reputation,' said Paris softly, 'and that's for fucking it up in the first place,' and he hit Cosmo down the steps, before gathering up Hindsight and disappearing into the October gloom.

127

Over at the stables, Patience took the thousandth call from an increasingly frantic Dora.

'I'm so sorry, nothing I'm afraid. The police still think something might come out of our television interview. I'll ring you the moment we hear anything, and, darling, it's getting dark, don't go looking in the woods, it's not safe with just Cadbury.'

'Where's Paris?' wailed Dulcie, who was staying the night.

Patience had even greater cause for anguish. If the governors rubber-stamped Alex as head at today's meeting, she and Ian would be out of the Old Coach House by Christmas – so there would be nowhere for Paris to come home to.

A fatalistic Ian had left the office when Painswick went in to take the minutes and, in anticipation of their departure, was mindlessly sorting out drawers in the sitting room. He had discovered one of Paris's notebooks. On the first page the boy had scribbled 'Paris Cartwright' over and over again, then the initials PC, then 'politically correct', then 'Mr Wright', 'Mr Wrong', 'Paris always Wrong'. Then 'Dora Cartwright', then 'Paris Alvaston Cartwright' over and over. Out of the middle pages fluttered a picture of Theo and a piece of paper with a blob, coloured olive green, turquoise, royal blue and shaped like a peacock's feather. Perhaps there had been something between him and Theo.

Overwhelmed with despair and longing, Ian gave a sob. If only he'd been more demonstrative towards the boy. Next moment, the notebook crashed to the floor as Paris walked in, ducking nervously as though expecting blows and recriminations.

Ian just took his hand and shut his eyes for a moment, then he mumbled, 'It's very, very good to see you, Paris.'

'You're out of logs, I'll get some.'

'Would you like a gin and tonic?'

'Yes, please.'

How sweet-faced the boy was, even though he looked as if he'd been sleeping rough, and had lost a hell of a lot of weight.

By the time Paris struggled back with the logs, Patience had been alerted and came galumphing downstairs.

'Oh Paris, how lovely to see you, we've missed you.'

She longed to hug him. Little Dulcie, who came rushing in in her blue pyjamas, had no such reserve and hurled herself into Paris's arms with screams of joy. Paris hugged her back, colour suffusing his shadowed face. A minute later Northcliffe bounded in, singing at the top of his voice, dragging one of Patience's huge bras like a mini Himalayas.

'The mountains have truly come to Mahomet,' observed Ian. 'I'll get some ice.'

Outside, he made a discreet telephone call.

'It's OK, Sally, he's home.' Then, not knowing the permutations: 'Could you let Janna know? And Feral too, if you get a moment.'

If only he could ring Hengist in prison.

After that, they didn't leave Paris for a second, fearful he'd vanish. Paris couldn't stop yawning.

'Your bed's made up,' stammered Patience, 'if you'd like to spend the night.'

'Please,' said Paris. 'There just one problem.' Patience's heart stopped. 'I acquired a cat on my travels; he's outside.'

Patience laughed in relief.

'That's wonderful, we've got far too many mice and Northcliffe loves cats.'

They were just feeding Hindsight a tin of tuna when Dora rang.

'Bloody cow, bloody tagging system, Joan won't let me out. Is he really back?'

'Have a word,' said Patience, going off to fill a hot-water bottle. Paris was already in bed when she knocked on the door, an equally weary Hindsight curled into the back of his legs.

'I'm really sorry,' he said. 'Until I saw you and Ian on TV, I didn't realize.'

Patience sat down on the bed and took his hand.

'Doesn't matter; you're home. Ian is so pleased. He just loves having another chap around the house.' She tucked the hot-water bottle in beside him. 'Sorry there aren't any flowers.'

'That's OK – flowers are for guests. What really pissed me off was Nadine saying we were wrong for each other. You know I said that about running away to find my real mother and father?'

Patience nodded, quite unable to speak.

'Well' – Paris's hand tightened on hers – 'I guess being away taught me, if it's all right with you, that I did find them – that you and Ian *are* my real parents.'

Patience still couldn't speak, but she nodded frantically.

'I don't need to call you Mum and Dad, I'm just grateful I've found people I love, who, however horrible I am, seem to love me, so I can start again.'

'Oh, Paris.'

A tear splashed on to his hand.

Paris's eyelids were drooping.

'You're tired, shall I read to you?'

Paris nodded, but still clung to her hand.

Taking down Hans Andersen's fairy tales, Patience turned to 'The Snow Queen', and began: ' "Attend! We are now at the beginning. When we get to the end of our story, we shall know more than we do now," ' but by the time she'd finished the first paragraph, Paris was asleep.

128

It was time for the high noon of the school year, the National Teaching Awards, in which hundreds of teachers, including all the regional winners and their partners, are invited for a splendid weekend in London. Activities included a grand ball on Saturday night, seminars, and sightseeing. The climax, however, was the televising of the national winners receiving their awards at the Palace Theatre on Sunday afternoon, followed by a riotous party and no teaching the following week, because it was half-term.

The winners in the ten different categories had been originally nominated by two members of their school community. Their schools were then visited by regional judges and later by a team of national judges, amongst whom was Lord Hawkley.

'The Awards are an amazing celebration of teaching,' he told the *Observer*, 'although, of the six hundred people crammed into the Palace Theatre on Sunday, I will be one of the only public-school voices. No member of an independent has ever won an award.'

This year Alex Bruce, because of his clean-out at Bagley and his brilliant (except for Lando and Jack) science results and, of course, his *Guide to Red Tape*, was hoping to be the first. Rod Hyde, who'd formerly won Head of the Year, was hoping to score again.

A thousand years ago, it seemed, when Janna had been teaching English at Redfords, Stew Wilby had talked about putting her forward for an award. Now it would never happen. She no longer had a school to nominate her.

It was half-term Sunday, and she had reached rock bottom. The head of English on maternity leave for whom Janna was covering had brought in her adorable baby last week, and Janna had been overwhelmed with despair that she would never have Emlyn and his babies and the family life for which she so desperately longed.

In a bleak week, Stancombe, after a few hiccups – like the Brigadier pointing out the presence of fritillaries and natterjack toads in the grounds – had obtained a compulsory purchase order on both Larks buildings, to make way for – he'd finally come clean – a supermarket development.

The *Sunday Express* had rung for Janna's comments:

'Why don't you write us a piece about your battle to save Larks?'

'And call it Tesco of the D'Urbervilles,' screamed Janna.

She had been to the gym earlier, pounding out her hatred of Randal and Ashton on the machines. She ought to spend the rest of the day painting the kitchen some enticing pastel shade, as no buyer had yet come forward. Instead, she turned listlessly to the lonely hearts ads in the *TES*.

'Beautiful female,' she read, 'thirty, five foot seven, slim, brown hair, green eyes, enjoys long walks, reading, keeping fit, good wine.'

How bloody conceited to describe oneself as 'beautiful'.

'Eighteen-year-old woman, enjoys power boating, weightlifting, GSOH,' said the next ad, 'seeks female for friendship, possibly more.'

Janna supposed GSOH stood for good sense of humour – that was bloody conceited too.

How would she advertise herself? she wondered.

'Titchy carrot-haired loudmouth, failed head, near alkie, lousy SOH, seeks' – Oh God – 'Emlyn Davies for infinitely more than friendship.'

The Brigadier was revving up for his new series bringing epic poems to life. He and Lily were so dottily in love, Janna didn't want to be a dampener, and it was almost a relief they were in Rome recceing the first programme about Horatius keeping the bridge.

Still fatally drawn to Larks, Janna decided to go for a walk there and see the trees, probably for the last time. At least on a Sunday afternoon the bulldozers would be still.

Leaping out of the car, Partner immediately found a stick three times as big as himself and kept tripping over molehills as he lugged it round. The place looked desolate: great craters filled with rain, huge trees knocked over, bottles rammed into the tennis-court wire, the bird table still on its side in the playground. Catching sight of her, a robin shot forward hopefully.

The door to Appletree was open. As she wandered the corridors, she could hear the ghost voices of children. On the staff room wall, someone had scribbled: 'School's out for summer.' Underneath someone else had written: 'School's out for ever.'

'You will go through a time when everything hurts,' murmured Janna.

Still trying to negotiate his huge stick through the doorways, Partner dropped it and went into a flurry of barking, then scampered on ahead. Following him into the gym, Janna discovered the back view of a blond man in a navy blue jersey, so tall he could gaze out of the high window at the town. His hands were shoved deep into the pockets of his dark grey trousers, showing off a high, tight, beautiful bottom.

Janna lost her temper. 'Stop gloating, you bloody developer,' she shouted, then, as he turned round, she gasped, 'Emlyn!'

'I thought I'd find you here. Hello, boyo.' He stooped to gather up Partner, who, squeaking with delight, frantically licked his square blushing face, giving both humans a moment to collect themselves.

'I've got an invite for two for the Teaching Awards,' Emlyn said ultra-casually. 'Wondered if you'd like to come. We'd be home by ten. Artie, as well as Alex, has been nominated for an award. The first independent teachers ever.'

In panic, Janna grabbed back Partner. 'I can't leave him. He's terribly depressed. I have to abandon him during the day; Lily and the Brigadier are away.'

'They're back,' said Emlyn. 'They said they'd love to dogsit.'

Janna was confused. When they'd last spoken, Emlyn had been so antagonistic.

'I've got too much to do. I've got to paint the kitchen.'

'Paint the town red instead. It's a grand do.'

Then she noticed he was wearing a white frilled evening shirt under his blue jersey.

'This is a set-up.'

'Sure it is.' The warm, wide, unrepentant smile transformed his square, heavy face. 'Pearl's even waiting at home to do your make-up.'

After a lot of persuading, Janna went back and changed into the bronze-speckled Little Mermaid dress she'd worn to the geography field trip party in Wales. Full of chat, Pearl was determined to make Janna look beautiful rather than outlandish and straightened her hair so it fell in a sleek russet cascade to her collar bones.

'Knowing what a blubber you are, I'm not giving you any mascara on your lower lashes. Emlyn says it's a box-of-tissues evening, miss.' Then, as Janna pestered her for news of the children: 'Feral got two goals for the Rovers yesterday; Johnnie and Kitten have split up again; Kylie's up the duff again – no, maybe she ain't.'

The Brigadier and the new Mrs Woodford applauded when Janna came downstairs wrapped in her bracken-brown pashmina.

'What an incredibly pretty girl you are,' said Lily. 'Don't worry about Partner, he can have the extra piece of steak I'd bought in case you felt like having supper with us.'

'Here's a little something for the journey,' said the Brigadier, handing Janna a silver flask of vodka and tonic.

The sky was brilliant blue and the sun set behind them like a huge blood orange. Torrential rain nearly turned them back at Windsor. Emlyn wanted an update on the Larks children and regaled her with Bagley gossip gleaned from Artie. Poor Dora was evidently outraged because her bitch of a mother had had even poor Cadbury castrated. Cosmo, on the other hand, had been delighted to receive a red Ferrari for his GCSE results.

Emlyn's muddy Renault Estate as usual looked as though he lived in it. Books, newspapers, CDs, laptops were piled high and amid the chaos were a half-empty crate of beer, a midnight-blue velvet jacket in cellophane back from the cleaner's, clean shirts, new socks and underpants still in their packaging. The Christmas Scottie, she noticed, still bounced from his car keys – probably as a wistful reminder of Oriana.

Janna was even more confused. Why was Emlyn being so nice when he'd been so angry before? She ached to put a hand on his great chunky thigh or stroke his big strong hand on the wheel. He'd lost more weight, was muscled up and was clearly revelling in the new job.

'The boys are beginning to express themselves and play in their Welsh way, lots of attack and guile, and we've got a brilliant new centre called Gavin Henson.'

He even had cautious hopes of the Six Nations in 2005.

'What will it be like tonight?' asked Janna.

'Lots of on-message celebs handing out awards and attributing their entire success to some inspirational teacher; lots of winners attributing their success to everything from the school gerbil to the site manager; constant emphasis on the team effort rather than the individual, belied when rival heads are discovered throttling each other in the bog.' Emlyn's huge shoulders shook with laughter.

In London, the trees had hung on to their leaves; rain-soaked, shining gold, they softened every building.

'This city now doth like a garment wear the beauty of the afternoon,' sighed Janna, gazing in vodka-aided ecstasy at the gleaming river beneath glittering bridges and the London Eye, a silver halo tossed aside by some falling angel.

Teachers were decanting from buses and milling round outside the theatre as they arrived.

'Janna Curtis,' cried a pretty blonde, 'you did so well for your Year Elevens. Look, it's Janna, you know, from Larks High,' she called out to her friends, who all gathered round to praise Janna.

'You're much prettier than your picture.' 'Is that your partner?' 'Isn't he lush?' 'You put up such a good fight.'

'They've read every word about me,' squeaked Janna. 'So up yours, Ashton.'

As Emlyn, who'd been shrugging himself into the dark blue velvet jacket, shepherded her firmly through the crowd into the Green Room, large glasses of champagne were thrust into their hands.

'Oh look, there's Ted Wragg, he's so funny.' Janna took a huge gulp. 'And there's Lord Hawkley, and that redhead with him is Rupert's ex-wife. Taggie's much prettier,' she added defensively.

'Better have some blotting paper.' Emlyn beckoned a waitress bearing a basket full of chicken and prawns on long-pointed sticks.

'God, they look delicious' – Janna grabbed four – 'and those sticks are perfect for pricking bubbles as a "critical friend" – and talk of the devil, here come Rod and Alex.'

'What's going on in your neck of the woods?' a BBC minion was asking them solicitously.

'The Queen's opening our new Science Emporium on Wednesday week,' Alex was boasting.

'Goodness, it'll be Sir Alex soon,' said the minion admiringly. 'The other Sir Alex better look to his laurels.'

The smug smile was then wiped off Alex's face. 'What are you doing here, Janna Curtis? You can hardly qualify as a past winner or a nominee this evening.'

'Nominees up, Mother Brown,' sang Janna, doing a little dance. 'I came with Emlyn,' she announced happily, then, thrusting out her glass to a passing waitress, 'I'd love another one.'

The BBC minion, who had shiny dark hair streaked with scarlet and caramel, introduced herself as 'Bea from the Beeb' and said, 'Janna Curtis, I so admire your stand in Larkshire. We're so delighted you could make it.'

'Have you had a great weekend?' asked Janna.

'Amazing! Last night's dance was fabulous, and teachers are such lovely people, so modest and self-effacing; they hate being singled out from their colleagues for praise.'

'Alex and Rod are just like that,' enthused Janna.

Emlyn choked on his drink.

'Although one headmaster,' admitted Bea from the Beeb, 'who didn't win last year, was so furious he had a nervous breakdown.'

'There are the warning bells, we'd better go in,' said Rod frostily.

'Is that gorgeous guy your partner?' whispered Bea.

'I wish,' sighed Janna.

Not wanting to let her spirits droop a millimetre, she managed to secrete a three-quarters-full bottle of champagne under her pashmina as she and Emlyn flowed with the laughing, excited tide into the auditorium.

It was a lovely little theatre, with cherry-red velvet seats and cherry-red boxes, like the drawers Janna hadn't pushed in before she left: those spilling over with rejected clothes, these with teachers, or with technicians manning a huge overhead camera like a pterodactyl to capture the Great and the Good in the audience.

'Oh hell,' said Janna, 'Rod Hyde and his admired wife and Alex and Poppet are just across the aisle.'

Poppet, in an extraordinary white broderie anglaise mob cap and a milkmaid's dress, was flushed with success from delivering her first TROT workshop.

'TROT stands for Total Recognition of Transpersons,' she was eagerly telling the Education Secretary. 'So enriching to exchange views with other caring professionals.'

'Silly bitch,' muttered Janna; then, as a female bruiser in the row in front swung round disapprovingly, 'You could use that one in your back row.'

'Hush, or we'll get thrown out,' warned Emlyn. He caught sight of Janna's bottle: 'What have you got there?'

'Petrol,' said Janna.

Emlyn tried and failed to look reproving.

They were in wonderful seats about ten rows from the front. Technicians, checking camera angles and locating possible winners, scuttled around in pairs, one carrying the camera, the other the wires, as though he was holding up the long tail of a mouse.

The beautiful set was hung with panels in Three Wise Men colours: glowing scarlet, amethyst, turquoise, and sapphire blue.

A midnight-blue canopy overhead glittered with little stars. On the red and gold podium awaiting the first winner, was one of the awards. Named a Plato, it was a gold curved oblong with one end fashioned into the profile of a Greek god.

'He's got Rupert Campbell-Black's nose,' observed Janna. 'What a lovely party,' she added to Emlyn. 'There's David Miliband. He looks as though he's still in Year Ten.'

Emlyn had temporarily found room for his long legs in the gangway. 'You will tuck them inside when we begin?' begged a returning Bea admiringly.

Emlyn was so broad-shouldered, Janna also found it impossible not to brush against him as he leant in to avoid technicians racing past. There is not room in this theatre, nor in all the world, to contain my love for him, she thought helplessly as she took another slug of champagne.

A handsome organizer was now telling the audience they were here to celebrate excellence in education. 'To ensure maximum media exposure for the profession we all love, we want you to shout and clap as much as possible.'

'Hurrah,' yelled Janna, clapping like mad.

'I've been used and abused by the BBC,' grumbled an old trout in the row behind. 'I will not clap to order.'

There were so many shining bald heads and spectacles in the stalls reflecting the television lights that no other lighting was needed. Gales of hearty laughter, no doubt to show off their GSOH, greeted every joke from the warm-up man.

'All round the theatre, you'll find teachers seated in areas. There's Northern Ireland to the left in the dress circle and Wales over on the right.' Emlyn raised a hand to two young women teachers. 'And right over there are the Larkshire contingent. Look, they're waving at you.'

Janna waved back. 'Where's Yorkshire?'

'In the gallery.'

'Oh my God, there's Stew,' gasped Janna.

'Who?' Emlyn swung round sharply.

'My old boss.' He's put on weight, she thought.

She was brought back to earth by a roll of drums.

'Pray silence for your head boy of the evening,' said a voice, and on came Eamonn Holmes, who, despite a sombre dark suit and red spotted tie, looked, with his sweet little face and naughty grin, much more like the terror of Year Seven.

'Welcome to the Oscars of the teaching profession,' he said, looking round at the audience. 'Now you'll know what it's like to be in assembly.'

'He can't say that,' gasped a hovering BBC minion, 'it'll diminish them.'

'You're not allowed to make jokes about gowns and mortar-boards, or about Whacko and canes,' whispered Emlyn.

There was another roll of drums, and actor Bill Nighy ambled somewhat nervously on to the stage to present the award to the Primary Teacher of the Year. As a photograph of him as a dear little boy appeared on the screen above the podium, he talked charmingly and deprecatingly about his school days, then announced the winner, who, from the gasp of joyful surprise, turned out to be a charming brunette sitting in the row opposite Emlyn.

As she ran down the aisle and mounted the steps to the platform, Janna cheered and cheered. The clips of her brilliant rapport with the children were so touching that the tears spilling down Janna's cheeks became a cascade when she glanced side-ways and saw the winner's incredibly proud husband also crying his eyes out.

From then onwards, Janna worked her way through her box of tissues and her bottle. All the winners – from Best New Teacher, the Teacher Who Used IT Most Imaginatively, to the Teaching Assistant of the Year – were so brilliant, innovative and imaginative, and the children so sweet, and the celebrities so exciting. Janna loved Sanjeev Bhaskar and had always been a fan of Imogen Stubbs, beautiful, clever, posh, but also a true socialist.

129

Rupert arrived at the Palace Theatre alone and in a foul temper. The last time he could remember being in London on a Sunday, except for the Countryside March, was when he'd taken his ex-wife Helen out on a first date – and look what trouble that had got him into.

He'd only agreed to give away an award because Jupiter had insisted it would be good for his image and that of the New Reform Party to get in with the lefties. Except for Janna and Hengist, who'd both lost their schools, he loathed the teaching profession. They'd been so bloody patronizing about his GCSE and got so uptight if you mentioned their long holidays.

Now, still in his dark blue overcoat so he could make a quick get-away, Rupert stood in the Green Room drinking whisky, watching the whole thing on a monitor and thinking he'd never seen so many ghastly beards in his life, nor so many old boots built like semis in Croydon and with Tim Henman hair. Rupert loathed very short hair on women, even more than beards, particularly when it showed off hulking great necks. Talk about the planet of the napes. Rupert was so fed up, he couldn't be bothered to laugh at his own joke.

He'd been listening to the big match on the car wireless. Feral would shoot himself if Man U broke Arsenal's run of 49 wins. It was a measure of Rupert's increasing fondness for Bianca's boyfriend (whom he'd watched scoring two goals for the Rovers yesterday) that he'd started taking an interest in soccer as well as English literature – any minute he'd be taking up Morris dancing.

There in the audience was that stuffed shirt David Hawkley, married to Helen, stepfather to Tabitha and Marcus. How small the world was. Muttering about gravitas, Jupiter was determined to give Education to David in place of Hengist, who'd been so much more amusing. Rory Bremner had done over Jupiter last night – bloody funny.

'Isn't it a fun evening?' Bea from the Beeb broke into his thoughts with a plate of smoked salmon sandwiches. 'You should have seen all those major civil servants, not known for their frivolity, bopping on the dance floor last night.'

'Letting their lack of hair down,' said Rupert sourly.

He loathed civil servants even more than teachers.

On the other hand, the blonde now accepting a Plato for school and community involvement was very pretty. He could happily have got involved with her. Lovely legs too; perhaps teachers weren't such boots.

Again and again the camera crews ran backwards down the gangway, as though they were filming royalty, and the little stars in the indigo firmament brightened as each winner, the real stars of the evening, mounted the stage.

'When's Artie going to get his award?' asked Janna.

'I'm afraid it's gone to that head of science, two categories back,' whispered Emlyn.

'Artie should have won,' protested Janna noisily, and was shushed. As her big gold programme kept sliding off her knees, rather than bury her head in Emlyn's lap when she retrieved it, she leant down to the left, which gave her the chance to take another slug from her bottle.

Emlyn was half laughing, but she wished he'd loosen up and get into party mode. He still seemed tense and watchful as the lights turned his face glowing ruby, then sapphire, then aquamarine, then Lenten purple, each time more gorgeous. I love him, thought Janna helplessly. I just adore him.

'I know it's going to be Rod Hyde,' she cried in despair, then cheered and cheered, because the winner of the Lifetime Achievement Award wasn't Rod, but a darling old duck from a London primary who let the children run all over her office in the lunch hour.

'Please be quiet,' hissed the horrified Number Eight in the row in front.

Janna would have raised two fingers, if Emlyn hadn't held grimly on to her hands.

'You've got to behave yourself.'

'That's it for the evening,' said Janna, then nearly fell off her chair with excitement as a blow-up of a beautiful sulky little boy appeared on the screen, and a grinning Eamonn Holmes announced one last award to be presented by someone often described as 'the handsomest man in England', an owner/trainer, ex-showjumper and Minister for Sport, who'd called himself 'the most immature mature student' when he recently gained a 'B' in GCSE English literature.

And on stalked Rupert to a frenzy of wolf whistles and catcalls. He still had his overcoat on, but smiled slightly when Eamonn asked him the Arsenal/Man U result.

'Rooney scored in extra time,' replied Rupert. 'It's his birthday. He's a Scorpio like me.

'I was so useless at school,' he went on, in his clipped, flat drawl, 'that I normally don't like schoolmasters or -mistresses one bit, but I have to confess, watching the television in the Green Room, I have seen some fantastic examples of teaching that might have galvanized even myself.

'I'm here to hand out a special new award: the People's Prize, to the teacher whom the most pupils, parents, teachers and members of the public all round the country felt had done the best and most heroic job, and in the winner's case, pulled in five times as many votes as the rest put together.

'This was a head who fought against all odds for their school,' went on Rupert, 'and kept it open under remarkable circumstances, who inspired confidence in children who believed they were worthless, who inspired the staff into believing every teacher can teach and every child achieve, and who never gave up on a child.'

Tears rushing down Janna's cheeks took away the rest of Pearl's make-up. 'What a wonderful person she must be,' she murmured and, turning, seeing tears in Emlyn's eyes, added, 'Don't be sad.'

As she stroked his cheek, he trapped her hand.

The cameras were slowly creeping up the aisle.

'And the winner . . .' As, utterly deadpan, Rupert slowly opened the gold envelope, Alex Bruce, halfway out of his seat and deliriously punching the air, was sent flying by the overhead camera.

'The winner . . .' repeated Rupert with a triumphant smirk, 'is one of the few schoolmistresses I like: Janna Curtis of Larkminster High School.'

An explosion of cheering rocked the theatre, particularly from the South-West and from Yorkshire up in the gallery.

'I don't believe it,' gasped Janna, turning to a tearful, beaming Emlyn.

'Well done, lovely, you did it, just watch these clips.'

Among the television crews who'd been doorstepping Larks for the past year had been one from the BBC. Now they showed clips of Janna racing round hugging all the team when they beat Bagley at rugby; yelling, 'You're worse looters than the Iraqis,' at Searston Abbey staff when they arrived prematurely to remove earmarked books and computers; crawling across the park, waving branches of swamp cypress, bringing Birnam Wood to Dunsinane; and finally of her praising or comforting her children on Results Day.

Glowing testimonials followed from Stormin' Norman and Chantal Peck, who said Janna was just like a 'Citizen's Advaice Bureau,' and the Mayor of Larkminster, who said she was a 'cracker'. Even the Bishop described her as a 'very live wire'.

Then there were clips from children all round the country who'd followed Larks's progress on the news.

'Janna seems so nice, we'd love to go to her school.'

Finally, Dora appeared saying how much they'd all liked her at Bagley.

'I cannot believe this,' muttered Janna as the film came to an end.

'Yes, you can.' Standing up to let her out, Emlyn steadied her, before setting her off on her tottering path.

Utterly shell-shocked and extremely drunk, she staggered up on to the stage, where Rupert caught her, enveloping her for a second inside the blue silk lining of his overcoat.

'Bloody marvellous, darling. Can you manage a few words?'

Turning, Janna reached out for and nearly missed the microphone. Freckles were the only colour in her face. As her speckled Little Mermaid dress, damp with champagne and tears, clung to her, people could see how thin she was.

'It's been a wonderful evening,' she began. 'I've never been so proud of my profession.' Then, pulling her thoughts together: 'I'd like to thank everyone who voted for me, and all the Larks teachers and children who worked so hard, and the parents, and particularly the anonymous donor who gave us a hundred and twenty thousand pounds so we could keep Larks open for another year, although S and C Services and the county council did eff-all to help us,' she added to equal laughter and gasps of disapproval.

'Rather a looshe cannon,' murmured a grinning Rupert, thinking there was something infinitely touching about Janna's little bitten nails clutching the mike.

'And we'd never have done it without the help of the staff and children from Bagley Hall,' she went on defiantly, adding, over a storm of booing, 'particularly without Hengist Brett-Taylor.'

'Hear, hear,' shouted Rupert.

'Cheat!' yelled the audience.

'Hear me out,' yelled back Janna. 'We must stop demonizing the independents as they demonize us. We've got to work together for all children. Hengist gave so many of our pupils a chance. He enabled Paris Alvaston, for example, to learn Latin and Greek. This is a Plato' – she brandished her award – 'but how many of you can quote a single line Plato wrote?'

There was a long pause.

'Plato said democracy leads to despotism, which is happening in this country today, when schools are closed down just because the powers-that-be want to make a fat profit selling off the land.'

The horror and alarm on the faces of the majority of the audience turned to sympathy as Janna burst into tears.

'But what does it matter? How can I be a great head if I lost my school? All I want is my children back.'

Emlyn was on his feet about to vault on to the stage. Rupert and Eamonn were moving forward when a dirty violet and yellow football rolled across the stage towards Janna's feet, followed by Cameron Peck, followed by his mother, carrying Ganymede.

'I'm training as a nursery nurse,' Kylie Rose told the audience, 'and taking singing lessons.'

She was followed by Aysha and Xavier, hand in hand, who were going to the same FE college. Graffi, waving a paintbrush, unrolled a scroll showing a draft of the mural he was painting for the long room at Penscombe. Kitten, looking breathtaking, was modelling and back in love with Johnnie, who was working in a racing car garage. Danijela was altering clothes at Harriet's Boutique. Monster had got a job working as a bouncer in a night-club and, despite Rooney scoring in extra time, a beaming Feral came bouncing on, like Tigger, in Larkminster Rovers orange and black colours, leading a giggling Bianca, who was in turn leading Rocky, who was working on the Penscombe Estate as a chippy, until miraculously, every Larks High pupil was crowding the stage.

Pearl came last strutting around with her royal-blue rooster hair.

'I did Miss's make-up earlier,' she announced, then, turning to Janna: 'Looks as though you could do wiv a touchup, miss. Miss didn't have a clue we was all coming up, or she was getting an award. Mr Davies organized the whole fing. I'm working wiv Trinny and Susannah now, so I get paid for telling people they look gross. And if anyone wants my card . . . ?'

The audience smiled fondly, particularly when Pearl took Janna's hand: 'Larks didn't die, miss. Honest. We just want to say it lives on in us and in all our memories, so thank you for everything you did.'

Great were the cheers and the rejoicing as they were all swept off the stage to make way for Lords Puttnam and Attenborough.

Afterwards it passed in a dream. Dazed and amazed, all Janna wanted to do was get stuck back into the champagne and talk to the children and find out about Graffi's dad and Feral's mum. But once Pearl had redone her face, everyone, particularly the press and the photographers, wanted a piece of her.

Overwhelmingly important at the back of her mind was what was Emlyn's part in it? Had he come over to Larks merely to lure her up to London? Had he persuaded all the children to vote for her because he cared for her or was it the altruism of a colleague wanting justice and recognition for a colleague?

She must ask him. She was just taking another slug of champagne to give herself courage, when Stew, her old head from Redfords, hove into sight and kissed her on both cheeks.

'Well done. I couldn't be more proud. Good, you stuck up for Hengist Brett-Taylor. Nice man, if misguided. I must have trained you jolly well. It's a crime you're doing supply,' he continued, lowering his normally loud commanding voice. 'How'd you like to be deputy head at a city academy I'm taking over in Lancashire?'

'Oh Stew, it's good to see you. You haven't met Emlyn Davies.'

The two men shook hands without enthusiasm.

'You must have been planning this for weeks,' said Stew, then, turning back to Janna: 'Mike Pitts has been telling me that everyone decided Emlyn would be the best person to hijack you, darling.'

Janna was hazily wondering why she loved Rupert calling her 'darling', but bitterly resented it from Stew. He was also too old for that trendy short hair at the front, as though a rat'd been nibbling it all night. Then she looked up at Emlyn, who didn't have a millimetre of meanness or weakness in his big kind face.

'What happened to Artie's award?'

Emlyn looked sheepish. 'I made that bit up.'

She was now seeing him through swirling black clouds.

Next moment Bea from the Beeb was asking, 'Could you bear to have your photograph taken with the rest of the winners?'

'All right, but don't go away,' Janna begged Emlyn. 'I want to ask you something. Oh look, there's David Puttnam, my hero. Oh dear, I don't feel very well.' She suddenly buckled, stumbled and flopped to the ground.

'She's fainted, give her some air,' shouted Stew.

'I think you'll find she's passed out,' said Emlyn. 'I'll take her home.'

Janna's children, quite used to bringing parents back from the pub, hoisted her aloft and carried her out of the theatre.

' "Go, bid the soldiers shoot",' said a grinning Rupert.

'Utterly deplorable,' chuntered the Bruces and Hydes.

'So unnecessary to bring up Hengist. She only won that award because of all the publicity,' grumbled Poppet.

'Shut up, you jealous old bitch,' shouted Aysha to everyone's utter amazement.

Emlyn wrapped Janna in her bracken-brown pashmina and his jacket and drove her back to Larkshire with the winter stars, Castor and Pollux and the big and little Dog Stars, accompanying him all the way home.

Janna was a winter star, he thought wistfully. The darker the night and things had got at Larks, the more brightly and cheerfully she had rallied everyone. She looked about fifteen; occasionally she muttered in her sleep, but as he took her little hand in his, she slept on.

She had been so reluctant to accompany him earlier and so defensive until she got pissed. Was she still keen on that asshole Stew, or on Hengist, whom she'd defended so fiercely this evening?

Using her keys to let himself into her cottage, he put her down in the hall while he switched off the burglar alarm. Next moment Partner hurtled in from next door, but even when he barked joyfully and rushed up and down hurling all his toys in the air, Janna didn't stir.

'I hoped I'd carry you over the threshold a different way,' Emlyn told her as he took off her shoes and put her to bed in her clothes, then, dropping a kiss on her lips and switching off her mobile, he left her Plato in her arms.

130

Janna was woken by *Newsnight* on the landline, congratulating her and asking her to come on the programme that evening. Clutching her head, wincing at white sky glaring through the window, noticing the time, she gave a screech of horror. She'd be fatally late for work.

'Can I call you back?'

But, as she started scrabbling for clean pants and tights, she caught sight of herself still in her bronze speckled party dress and then of the Plato gleaming in the dark folds of the bedspread, and, attempting to piece last night together, she remembered it was half-term.

Having splashed her face with cold water, scraped moss off her tongue and cleaned her teeth, she tottered downstairs. There was no note anywhere. What had been Emlyn's part in all this?

She was simultaneously reassuring Partner she'd feed him in a second and groping for Alka-Seltzer when a hammering on the door made her clutch her head again.

Outside Lily was looking distraught.

'You were wonderful last night, Christian and I were so proud, but, darling, I've done something dreadful.'

'You've never done anything dreadful.'

But Lily, it seemed, had been having a tidy-out, prior to moving into a new house, and had discovered a recorded delivery she'd taken in for Janna two days after the Prom.

'I was so excited to be marrying Christian, I must have shoved it to one side and forgot to give it to you.'

'Couldn't matter less. The only thing that matters at the moment is finding the Alka-Seltzer. It's probably a final reminder from the Gas Board . . .' Janna's voice trailed off. 'Goodness, it's Emlyn's writing.'

'Oh dear, that's even worse, I'm so sorry.' Janna hadn't seen Lily so upset since her mower broke down.

'Truly doesn't matter.'

'Come and have a drink at lunchtime and tell us all about the awards.'

'Sure, thanks.' Ripping open the envelope, Janna wandered back into the kitchen.

> Darling Janna [she read incredulously]
>
> I'm so sorry I was such a complete shit last night. I lost my temper because I wanted you to myself so badly and quite rightly you put the kids or rather Monster first. You probably won't want to but could we start again? You may be still crazy about Hengist and I had so much to work through with Oriana. But suddenly the prospect of not seeing you every day for the rest of my life fills me with such utter despair. I know you're busy winding up Larks, but why don't you come up to Wales next weekend? My mother longs to meet you, and there's a good head's job coming up in a school near here.

Janna couldn't read any more. She was blushing too much and reeled into the garden, collapsing on to the old garden bench surrounded by rotting apples, oblivious of guzzling wasps wooed out of hiding by such a warm windless day.

Emlyn had written this letter on the day after the prom, recording it to make sure it reached her, and she'd never replied. That's why he'd ducked out of Results Day, been so curt on the telephone when she'd rung him at Sally's and so tense and guarded yesterday.

'The prospect of not seeing you every day for the rest of my life fills me with such utter despair . . .' Oh Emlyn.

It broke her heart to think of him, waiting for the post and by the telephone, convincing himself she didn't care.

Then panic gripped her – perhaps he'd moved on, and found some Blodwyn to love. She didn't remember any emotions betrayed yesterday. He hadn't even bothered to leave a note. Looking up for guidance, she found the glaring white sky dalmatianed with liver spots. Midges shifted around like footballers adjusting before a corner.

She had to call Emlyn at once. Racing into the house, she switched on her mobile, which rang instantly, and she swooned with disappointment to hear a light, patrician, rather patronizing voice. It was Oriana, who'd seen the Teaching Awards.

'Well done getting a Plato, and thank you for sticking up for Dad.'

'Did I?' wondered Janna. The whole thing was such a haze.

'It was very brave of you,' continued Oriana, 'I'm so pleased they didn't edit it out.'

'I haven't watched the tape yet.' Janna sat down on a kitchen chair on top of a pair of trainers, feeling defensive.

Perhaps Oriana wanted Emlyn back.

'Was it really OK?'

'Fabulous. Charlie and I both cried.'

'How's the baby?' asked Janna, feeling more cheerful.

'Due in a month, thank God.'

Partner was pointedly shoving his empty bowl round the floor. As Janna reached for a tin of Butcher's Tripe, Oriana asked:

'Have you been to see Dad in prison?'

'He doesn't want any visitors,' sighed Janna.

'You're not still in love with him?'

'Oh goodness no,' stammered Janna.

'You deserved that award,' went on Oriana briskly, 'but frankly Emlyn orchestrated the whole thing. He got cramp writing all the kids' nominations and transcribing the tapes of the parents who couldn't write. Theoretically you shouldn't have won because you don't have a school any more, but Emlyn kept on at them.'

Oriana's awfully upfront, thought Janna, and how does she know so much about what Emlyn's been up to?

'Why did he make such an effort?' she asked sulkily, then felt utterly deflated at Oriana's reply.

'Because he has an innate sense of justice.'

'So did Pontius Pilate,' grumbled Janna.

'I'm now going to break a confidence,' announced Oriana.

Janna, who had been trying to rotate the tin-opener handle with the same hand that was holding her mobile, let go of the tin, which crashed to the floor as Oriana added:

'It's high time you realized it was Emlyn who gave you that hundred and twenty grand to save Larks.'

'Emlyn?' whispered Janna. 'Oh God, he couldn't have! And I spent so many hours banging on to him about Randal, and how Randal couldn't be all villain if he was capable of such generosity. I even speculated whether it could be Hengist or Rupert. Emlyn never said a word. Oh, how heroically kind of him—' Her voice broke. 'I never dreamt. Where did he get the money from?'

'He was saving up to buy himself and me a really nice house,' said Oriana reprovingly.

'This is terrible,' groaned Janna. 'That was why he was always so poor, not able to fly out to see you in Iraq, not flying out to watch England and Wales in the World Cup, refusing to go Dutch to the opera. Oh God, why didn't he tell me?' Her brain was reeling all over the place, as though its steering had packed up on a mountain road.

'And why me?'

'Because he loves you,' said Oriana.

'What did you say?' whispered Janna.

'Because he loves you. Look how he's given and given and given to you, ferrying your children and their parents to public meetings, organizing entire productions of *Romeo and Juliet*, even coming to teach at Larks, which must have been a helluva culture shock. Making sure of your career by getting you a Plato. What have you ever done for him?'

'Listened ad nauseam when he rabbited on and on about you,' snapped Janna. 'And you're one to talk after the revoltingly contemptuous way you treated him. I've never seen anything so horribly cruel and humiliating and in your face as you and Charlie last Christmas.'

To her amazement, Oriana laughed.

'Good – now I'm convinced you love him too. Well, it's payback time, so go and find him.'

'Are you sure he loves me? He didn't say anything last night.'

'You've got to make the first move.'

'Where is he?' gasped Janna.

'Training with the Welsh squad at the Vale Hotel in Glamorgan, just the other side of Cardiff,' rattled off Oriana. 'Exit thirty-four on the M4. Should take you an hour and a quarter. It's known as the Lucky Hotel, because entire teams hole up there before big matches and really bond and thrive – I'm sure you and Emlyn will do the same. And you can jolly well ask Charlie and me to your wedding.'

As she rang off, the purr of the telephone sounded like a great contented cat. Looking down, Janna saw Partner had the tin between his paws. 'Sorry, darling.' In a daze, she emptied the contents into his bowl. Then she wandered round the room, warming her hands on her burning face, trying to take in the enormity of Emlyn's colossal sacrifice. And bloody Randal had let her believe he'd given her the money, and let everyone else think so too. She'd murder him. But what did Randal matter? She must get to Emlyn.

All shaking fingers and thumbs, she tried to dial his mobile, but it was switched off. It was twenty to one now. He might only be training in the morning.

Gathering up Partner and her car keys, she ran out barefooted and still in her party dress to her green Polo. Never had the little car hurtled so fast, rattling poor Partner from side to side in the back. Respite came for him twice. First at the Severn Bridge, rising like huge palest green Aeolian harps over the shining levels of the Bristol Channel and needing a £4.60 toll. Janna, however, had forgotten to bring any money. In his booth, the toll-keeper, who had 'Carpe Diem' tattooed on his brawny arm, was utterly intransigent: no £4.60, no Wales. Fortunately a man in the fast-growing, hooting queue behind a sobbing, pleading Janna had last night seen the Teaching Awards and said it would be a privilege to pay her toll.

Gibbering her thanks, scribbling his address to return the money, Janna scorched on even faster. Partner's second respite came when his mistress was flagged down by a traffic cop as she was passing Cardiff. Fortunately the traffic cop had also seen the Teaching Awards and on learning Janna was trying to reach Emlyn Davies, who was a local hero, put on his blue flashing lights and gave her a police escort. This was a good thing, because she'd reached a state when she was muttering, 'M34, exit four', and would never have reached the Lucky Hotel without help.

But gradually the turning trees grew thicker, thronging the edge of the motorway like rugby crowds cheering her home. And there was the Vale Hotel in its lovely green valley, a beautiful Palladian house with red roses still flowering behind little box hedges and flags hanging limp in the windless air.

And there, even lovelier – she gave a shriek of joy and relief – was Emlyn's Renault, easily the dirtiest, scruffiest, most over-loaded car in the place. Two women in white towelling dressing gowns, on their way to the spa, directed her to the Indoor Training Arena.

Tearing up a little hill to a big green building hidden by trees, Janna barged inside, past a big sepia photograph of Emlyn's hero, Gareth Edwards, through a glass door and found herself in a vast enclosed area, half the size of a rugby pitch and carpeted with artificial grass. It was so like a huge hangar, she half expected Kenneth More to roll up or a Hercules to taxi in after a hard night's work.

Instead, twenty odd members of the Welsh national squad, mostly pale-faced, black-haired, black-eyed and gloriously hunky, were running about practising back moves, set line-outs and tack-ling great red rubber bollards; and there, towering over them, shouting, encouraging, advising but not as sharp or focused as usual, in a grey tracksuit adorned with the three Welsh feathers, was her own golden-haired, ruddy-faced Hercules down from the skies.

'Emlyn,' screamed Janna, 'oh Emlyn.'

'Janna,' gasped Emlyn as, lovely as the Olympic torch approaching its final destination, still in her party dress, bare-armed and barefooted, she hurtled across the bouncy green grass towards him.

Six feet away, she halted, panting for breath, fighting back the tears.

'Oh Emlyn,' she gasped, 'I only got the letter you sent me back in June after the prom this morning. Lily signed for it, but she was so excited about Christian proposing, she shoved it in a drawer.'

Then seeing his face lighten in incredulous hope and bewilderment, she stumbled on:

'It's been the most miserable time of my life for me too. At first I blamed it on losing Larks, but now I realize I said goodbye to that months ago, and it was only you I was missing. I just love you to bits. I don't care where I live as long as it's with you.'

As she edged towards him, they were both oblivious of the flower of Welsh rugby also gathering round, transfixed with interest to see one of their normally roaringly articulate coaches utterly lost for words.

'And what is more' – Janna brushed away the tears – 'Oriana told me about the money. Emlyn, it was all your savings for her and your future and you never let on. I can't even begin to thank you and for all the other things you've done for me.'

'A lot of that money was left me by Dad,' mumbled Emlyn. 'Nothing would have pleased him more than it being spent on Larks. Oriana ought to be shot.'

'So ought Randal,' admitted Janna, but she was not to be deflected.

She was so close now she could feel the heat of his body and, looking up, see the dark underside of his blond curls, his massive torso heaving and his square jaw gritted in an attempt not to break down.

'D'you remember once asking me what I'd most like in the world?' she asked.

'You said a waiting list.'

'Well, I've changed my mind,' sobbed Janna. 'I want a wedding ring, and the chance to spend the rest of my life loving you and paying you back for all the kindness.'

When Emlyn just gazed at her and said nothing, she stammered, 'But only if you haven't changed your mind and still feel those wonderful things you said in your letter.'

It is difficult even in a fast lift to rise from darkest hell to heaven so quickly. Emlyn still couldn't bring the words out. Below him Janna's flaming red hair seemed to fan out as cheerfully as a bonfire on a grey winter day, and her love seemed as true and real as the grass beneath her little feet was artificial.

'If I still feel like that?' asked Emlyn slowly as, softly as a falling leaf, his hand touched her soaked cheek. 'Oh God, lovely, if only you knew.'

Wiping his eyes, pulling her into his arms, enfolding her in a great bear hug, looking down into her adorable face, where every freckle seemed to be declaring its love, he kissed her on and on and on until the ecstatic Welsh rugby squad gave them a standing ovation.

'With breath control like that, Emlyn,' shouted one of the forwards, 'you should be teaching underwater swimming.'

'Aren't you going to introduce the lady?' shouted a back.

The fast lift had clearly reached heaven. With a huge smile and an arm about a dazed but beaming Janna, Emlyn glanced round at the squad. 'I'd like you to welcome the future Mrs Davies to Wales,' he said proudly.

Instantly there was a patter of tiny feet as Partner, having wriggled out of the Polo window and conned his way to the training area, happily took up his position beside them.

131

Two days before the Queen's visit, Dora, utterly outraged that Alex Bruce had banned all dogs from the campus and wearing a 'Ban the Ban' badge on each lapel, accompanied Artie Deverell and his two Jack Russells, Verlaine and Rimbaud, round Bagley village.

Dora loved Artie because in his languor, sensitivity, extreme kindness and slight air of helplessness, he reminded her so much of her late father, Raymond. Artie, in turn, was devoted to Dora. When his feckless, totally unsuitable chef boyfriend had finally walked out two years ago, it had been Dora who'd mounted a relief operation, which resulted in every member of the Upper Fourth bringing round their cod in cheese sauce, cooked in food technology, for his supper that evening.

Today she was in full flood. 'It's so pants of Alex changing everything,' she stormed. 'The eventing and polo teams and the beagles were going to meet the Queen at the gate and act as outriders up to the Mansion. You know how she loves horses and dogs. And Paris was going to recite a beautiful poem he'd written.

'Instead the poor dear's got to listen to an IT lesson, watch Poppet teach RE and then tour that stupid Science Emporium and witness Boffin perform some stupid experiment, splitting the atom or finding a cure for bird flu. Although Mr Fussy's flapping around so much, he'll give us bird flu anyway.'

Passing the charming cottage where Cosmo had installed Mrs Walton, reaching the White Lion, they wistfully breathed in the smell of lamb braising in red wine, parsley and garlic. School food had deteriorated depressingly since Poppet's lentil-loaded, salt-free regime had taken over.

'If we turn left here, down Stream Lane,' Dora told Artie, 'we can sneak the dogs back to your house undercover via Badger's Retreat and the golf course. I've done it often enough with Cadbury.'

It was a mild, windless day; gold leaves clogged the dark waters of the stream. Birds sang sweetly in the rain-soaked air. The path was strewn with tawny willow spears.

' "Yellow, and black and pale, and hectic red," ' quoted Artie, as the Jack Russells bounded ahead, stopping to fight and snuffle down rabbit holes.

'Hengist wanted the Queen to watch a history lesson,' said Dora crossly.

'Might have been tricky,' mused Artie, wondering nervously, as he lit a cigarette, how far Poppet's no smoking ban extended. 'The Upper Fifth are doing the Russian Revolution, the Middle Fifth, the English Civil War.'

'And we're doing the French Revolution,' giggled Dora, chucking a stick for the dogs. 'Might have been a bit tactless, all those kings and queens having their heads chopped off. But she'd have seen some terrific teaching. Hengist's lessons were wonderful. We were making a guillotine and tumbrels when he was arrested. The acting head of history Mr Fussy's roped in promptly put them on the skip. He keeps groping Bianca; we call him the Randy Republican.

'Emlyn was a terrific teacher too,' Dora sighed, as they crossed over a wooden bridge back on to Bagley land. 'Exciting about him and Janna getting married; I hope they ask me to the wedding. And wasn't it lovely her getting that Teaching Award and not Mr Fussy, and all the Larks pupils coming on to the stage. I think Paris was upset not to be part of it, he was very fond of Janna,' Dora added wistfully, 'and he's terribly upset about the bursar being booted out at Christmas. I do wish Hengist would come back.'

Oh, so do I, thought Artie.

Ahead, after a night of downpour, serpents of opal blue mist were writhing out of Badger's Retreat.

Artie let Dora run on. Since Hengist, his real, never-confessed love, had left, Bagley had lost its lustre. Artie had already had numerous approaches from other schools. Even Fleetley was putting out feelers. But he had loved Bagley so much and, like Theo, so longed to end his days here, he couldn't rouse himself to go to interviews.

In his breast pocket was a letter from Hengist.

'Dear Artie, I'm so sorry I let you down. If I'd made you deputy head as you deserved, none of this sorry business would have happened. Please look after Sally and the school if you can. Yours ever.'

Yours never, thought Artie sadly.

'Couldn't you be head?' Dora's shrill voice broke into his reverie.

'I don't think Mr Bruce would like that.'

'Everyone loathes him.'

'That's enough,' said Artie firmly, dodging to avoid a stick which Dora in her rage had thrown straight up in the air.

'My God,' he exploded as they reached Badger's Retreat, 'they've daubed red spots on everything, even Hengist's Family Tree.'

'Mr Fussy must be going to chop them down. He thinks woods are pointless. And he's banished Cadbury so the Queen won't meet him, which will be a great disappointment to her. Instead she'll have to listen to Alex's boring speech. Poor Painswick has to keep on retyping it when she's not ringing the Met. Office to check the weather: "Oh, it's you again, Miss Painswick, it's going to bloody chuck it down."'

'And what's more . . .' Dora retrieved the stick, teasing the Jack Russells, who launched into a frenzy of yapping.

'For God's sake,' hissed Artie in alarm, 'they'll get arrested.'

'And what's more' – Dora chucked the stick – 'I was in the general office and quite by chance caught sight of the agenda for the next governors' meeting, and I promise you General Bagley and Denmark are for the chop. Because the General was an imperialist who kicked ass after the Black Hole of Calcutta, Poppet wants him toppled like Saddam Hussein and replaced, I would think, by some manky statue of Mr Fussy brandishing a test tube and a copy of *Red Tape*.'

Artie was appalled. 'They can't pull down General Bagley. It's a beautiful sculpture.'

'And Denmark's so realistic, I always want to give him an apple.'

'And the General was a most civilized old boy,' protested Artie, 'who took copies of Racine and the *Iliad* to India with him, kept springers, was an excellent watercolourist, then left all his land and his house to found this school.'

'Well, I do know' – Dora glanced furtively round – 'that Mr Fussy, who knows eff all about art, has asked an artist called Trafford to come up with alternative suggestions. I bet he doesn't realize Trafford, who is a best friend of my brother Jonathan, is wildly expensive and often charges twenty thousand for a maquette.'

Despite his horror at the threat to the General, Artie laughed. 'Trafford has certainly made a convert of Poppet,' he said. 'She much admired his latest installation: *Tranny by Gaslight: The Story of a Sex Change.*'

'Working title: *From Willy to Womb.* It's absolutely disgusting,' thundered Dora, 'and cost half a million pounds. And I bet she hasn't seen *Sister Hoodie,* Trafford's video of a teenage girl beating up an old woman.'

'How can Poppet accuse our beloved General of colonialism,' said Artie indignantly, 'when her new best friend Randal Stancombe is busy colonizing Larkshire?'

As they neared Bagley and Artie hid both Jack Russells under his coat, they passed Theo's old house, now the home of the Randy Republican, who'd put a picture of Trotsky in the window.

'I'm determined to plant an oak tree in Theo's memory,' said Artie, 'but Alex is resolutely against it.'

'He's also banned school fireworks tonight for the first time in twenty years,' raged Dora, 'because they leave even more mess than dogs.'

132

Twenty-four hours to go. To the excitement of the female pupils, Bagley swarmed with hunky security men and sniffer dogs checking everywhere for weapons and explosives.

The red carpet couldn't be laid yet because the white gloss on the corridor wainscots was still wet. The sea-blue curtain covering the plaque on the Science Emporium wall, which the Queen would unveil to commemorate her visit, had fallen off when Joan Johnson jerked it back in rehearsal, but was now firmly secured. The splendid lavatory, specially built for the royal visit and nicknamed the 'Roylet', had been equipped with pot pourri and Bluebell, allegedly the Queen's favourite soap and toilet water. The framed print of *The Laughing Cavalier* had been replaced by a more neutral field of poppies and relocated in the dressing room of Dame Hermione Harefield, who, with her demands for vintage champagne, four dozen yellow roses and her own private loo, was causing far more hassle than the dear Queen.

There was good news however. The forecast was fine, if chilly, and Alex's bible the *New Scientist* had accepted, alongside a huge turnout of press and television who didn't realize all the celebs, including the Russian Minister of Affaires and Rupert Campbell-Black, had cancelled out of loyalty to Hengist.

'What story do you want to tell the Queen about the school?' General Broadstairs, the Lord Lieutenant, who was a governor anyway, had asked Alex on their first meeting after Hengist's departure, and Alex had replied that he wished to 'showcase Bagley's scientific and technological achievements in an emporium which would be the envy of scientists the world over'.

What Alex really wanted was to nail the top job and for people to love him more than Hengist. He was furious Janna had won an award and had finally got together with that Welsh gorilla who'd tried to drown Poppet, but he supposed they deserved each other.

Alex didn't find diplomacy easy. He had failed to thwart Poppet's plan to serve vegetable curry for everyone after the Queen had gone. Randal Stancombe too, once he'd learnt Boffin was performing some ground-breaking experiment in front of the Queen, had insisted that his Jade must present the Queen with her bouquet. Alex didn't dare say he'd promised that role to Little Dulcie who, with her wheelbarrow, had laboured harder on the emporium than any of the workforce. He didn't need to appease Patience and Ian, quite the reverse, but he must buy Dulcie a teddy bear. Randal had also insisted that Dora, who, as Jade's potential stepsister, might be jealous, must present Her Majesty with some dog she'd made specially in pottery. Alex hated kow-towing to Randal and Poppet. Once he was head, he'd call the shots.

The Queen had several other engagements on the same day in Larkshire. It was essential none of them overran. She was due to reach Bagley at 11.30 and must, on pain of guillotine, leave by 12.30 to reach a hospital on the outskirts of Larkminster at 12.50.

After endless telephone calls and meetings with local police and members of the royal household protection team and the route being rewalked and the itinerary reworked to the final second, an increasingly uptight Alex insisted on one more, school only, rehearsal after lunch.

Biffo, acutely aware his job was on the line, had been given a stopwatch and put in charge of operations. Searching for a stand-in for the Queen, he promptly roped in Trafford, the louche artist invited down by Alex and Poppet to provide an alternative to General Bagley, whom he found eating a doughnut and reading a porn mag in the staffroom.

'And since you're so good at acting,' Biffo added bossily to Paris, 'you can double up as Lord Lieutenant and headmaster until Alex gets here. Anyone involved in events the Queen is going to witness can take up their positions around the route.'

Dora should have been standing by General Bagley's statue waiting to hand over her pottery dog immediately after Jade had presented the Queen with her bouquet. Reluctant to miss anything, however, Dora had managed to lose herself among a group of Lower Fifths, including Bianca, whom Biffo had grabbed as they came out of the dining room to act as press.

After all, no one is more qualified than me, rationalized Dora.

Trafford, meanwhile, attempting to appear more royal, had topped his shaved head, designer stubble and pig-like features with the large rose-trimmed mauve felt hat Miss Painswick had bought specially for the big day, reducing everyone to fits of giggles. Thus encouraged, Trafford pretended to jump out of a limo outside the Mansion steps, saying in a high voice:

'My husband and I, what a beautiful school, we haven't been here before.'

'Stop being silly, Trafford,' snapped Biffo, consulting his notes. 'Now, as Lord Lieutenant, Paris, you present Jupiter Belvedon as chair of governors and MP for Larkminster to Her Majesty.'

'Who will try and flog her a picture,' quipped Trafford, 'and take eighty per cent.'

'Shuddup,' said Biffo through gritted brown teeth. 'And now Paris presents Alex to Her Majesty and now you, Poppet.'

'And Poppet will give me a nice curtsey,' said Trafford.

'I will *not*,' squawked Poppet, 'I don't bend my knee to anyone.'

'Right,' said Trafford.

'Then, as headmaster, I present Mr Randal Stancombe, who's donated this wonderful building to Bagley for the furtherance of science,' said Paris, getting into the swing of things.

'And then his wife,' prompted Biffo.

'Mrs Hyacinth Bouquet,' muttered Dora.

'Who said that? That's not funny,' roared Biffo.

'Push orf,' announced Paris. 'One says that every five seconds to the press: "Push orf."'

'Then you present Mr Ashton Douglas,' said Biffo.

Everything went comparatively smoothly until they reached the Science Emporium.

'We're now touring these splendid zones.' Trafford was getting more regal by the second. 'My word, Mr Randal Stinkbomb, this is awesome, particularly this.' Trafford peeled a 'Bring back Hengist' sticker off a vast replica of the pancreas. 'How long have you been building this, Mr Stinkbomb? Push orf, press, although not if you're as ravishing as you are,' he added to Bianca.

Paris meanwhile was watching Dora, who was laughing so much she could hardly write in her reporter's notebook. He remembered her showing him how to make that peacock feather: 'Would you like to take part in an experiment?'

'How truly interesting,' trilled Trafford as the royal party entered the Zone of Chemical Investigative Science. 'My husband and I simply dote on chemistry.'

'Wake up, Paris,' snapped Alex, 'as headmaster you should be presenting Boffin.'

'As what?' drawled Paris sarcastically.

'Like this. I'm here, I'll do it,' said Alex, striding up. 'Your Majesty, may I present Bernard Brooks, the son of Sir Gordon and Lady Brooks, one of Bagley's most gifted and talented pupils, who's going to perform a ground-breaking experiment.'

Alex turned lovingly to Boffin who, dressed in white coat and goggles, his sparse light brown hair tied back, an expression on his shiny, spotty face of a priest preparing communion wine, was pestling silver and reddish powders together in a mortar.

'In this invention,' said Boffin pompously, 'I'm combining iron oxide and aluminium in order to weld railway tracks together.'

'You must patent it and sell it to British Rail,' gushed Trafford, pushing Painswick's hat to the back of his head, 'and our royal train will rattle more safely over it.'

'Boffin is so pants,' muttered Dora as Boffin carried on mixing, gazing round to see he had everyone's attention.

'Buck up, Boffin,' said Biffo curtly, 'we're ten seconds behind schedule.'

'Would anyone thus have hurried Archimedes?' reproached Poppet.

'Such procedures must not be rushed,' agreed Alex.

Next moment the Zone of Chemical Investigative Science was rocked by a mighty explosion that showered the floor with glass as the windows blew in and bottles and containers of chemicals flew off the shelves and everyone was blown six feet across the room.

'It's a bomb, it's a bomb.'

'Clear the building,' yelled Biffo as, amid shouting, screaming and sobbing, people fell over themselves to escape.

Paris, however, had only one thought. Grabbing Dora, he pulled her under the nearest table, shielding her with his body. As black smoke engulfed the room to a crescendo of choking and coughing, he became aware of delicious softness.

'Get out of here, everyone out!' bellowed Biffo.

Paris stayed put and, as the smoke cleared, he looked down and saw Dora, blond eyelashes mascaraed with soot, face blackened, but her eyes still duck-egg blue, widening as they gazed up at him. In them and in her sweet, pink, trembling mouth he saw no fear, only love.

Oblivious of the chaos around them, with a feeling of utter rightness and coming home, he dropped his head and kissed her, feeling her breastbone rise as she gasped in wonder, her mouth

801

opening and her tongue creeping out tentatively to meet his. Paris put his hands on either side of her sooty face, stroking back her hair, smiling slowly, joyfully: 'It's happened,' he whispered, 'at last I can love you,' and he kissed her again.

'And I love you.' Dora choked slightly. 'I always have.'

'Paris Alvaston,' thundered Joan, whose red tie had been blown off, 'come out from under that table at once. You're un-accounted for outside. Watch out for broken glass. Who's that with you? Dora Belvedon, I might have guessed. What do you think you're doing?'

'Covering the visit for the school mag,' said Dora faintly.

Scrabbling up, pulling Dora to her feet, Paris brushed soot and glass off her blue jersey and pleated skirt as reverently as if he'd unearthed a hitherto unread play by Euripides. Unaware of every-one sobbing and shouting around them, he looked down at her in wonder:

'You and I were the chemical reaction that triggered off that explosion.'

'We were?' stammered Dora.

'What just happened to us could have blasted a man on to Venus, or broken the light barrier, or proved that God needn't exist because we do. Not even the universe began with a bigger bang, oh, darling Dora,' and he buried his lips in hers a second time.

'Paris!' thundered Joan.

'I cannot understand what happened,' Boffin's voice curled petulantly through the smoke. 'Perhaps too much aluminium?'

'What were you trying to achieve?' asked an ashen protection officer.

'A revolution in railway safety. It'll work next time. Ouch!' Boffin gave a furious squawk as Lando emptied a fire bucket into his face.

'You're an asshole, Boffin.'

'Thank God no one's been hurt.' Joan Johnson was comforting a shaken Poppet, who quavered that everyone was going to need counselling.

'Except those two,' giggled Bianca and everyone turned to see Dora, both feet off the ground in excitement, locked in Paris's arms.

133

The sight of Paris in a clinch with Dora proved the last straw for Stancombe, who'd just rolled up and taken stock of his ransacked emporium.

'You've got less than twenty-four hours to repair this building,' he howled at Teddy Murray. 'You can work all through the night. I want every man in Larkshire on the job.'

Such was his determination that even Graffi's father Dafydd was dragged out of the Ghost and Castle to help. Fortunately the damage was mostly confined to the one chemistry zone, which would need the windows mended, the walls replastered and repainted and all the flasks and containers replaced and refilled.

Boffin inevitably received an earful from Stancombe:

'Of all the fucking stupid, criminal things to do!'

To Boffin's fury, even Alex agreed with the royal household protection team and the local police that even if the building were declared safe in the morning, the Queen would open and tour the emporium and speak to the students but witness absolutely no experiments.

'Dad will not be pleased,' said Boffin ominously.

Despite unearthing splendid skulduggery at S and C Services, Cosmo and the rest of the Lower Sixth, returning from work experience, were gutted to have missed the fun. Cosmo was further irritated to find the ladder outside his room had yet again been removed by the protection officers. How could he ever escape to pleasure Mrs Walton? Replacing it, he leant a Randal Stancombe board across the bottom rung.

Although heavy frost was forecast, the lawn behind the Mansion, on which stood General Bagley and Denmark, was shielded from an icy north wind howling down the Long Walk by

803

the vast, if temporarily damaged, bulk of the Science Emporium. Although the General was oblivious to cold, the pupils lugging four hundred chairs for the not so Great nor Good through the dusk and placing them under a blue striped awning were grateful for the shelter.

'Ha, ha, ha, my mother's twenty-two rows back, next to Rod Hyde,' crowed Dora, examining the seating plan. 'She will go ballistic.'

The pupils dispersed wearily to supper and prep, but Dora lingered and was discovered by Alex Bruce hosing down General Bagley and Denmark and chatting to security men and their dogs.

'So many pigeons have dumped on the poor old boy,' explained Dora, aiming the hose at the General's bristling moustache, 'we must wash it off. After all, he is our founder.'

Not for much longer, thought Alex, then ordered Dora to buck up and get back to Boudicca.

The moment he'd bustled off to urge on the frantic activity in the Zone of Chemical Investigative Science, a lurking Paris emerged from the shadows carrying gin and tonic in two paper cups. Balancing them on Denmark's quarters, he stood back to admire the big horse, gleaming like jet, in the lights from the emporium.

'Looks much better. Sure you're warm enough? I like winter, you can see so many more stars now the leaves have gone.' Running his hand in wonder over her little, cold face: ' "and thou art fairer than the evening's air Clad in the beauty of a thousand stars".'

'Oh Paris,' said Dora, gruff with embarrassment and delight, 'that is so poetic.'

'Marlowe said it first,' Paris admitted; then, in bewilderment: 'I just feel a great Niagara of love has been released from inside me.'

'How heavenly is that?' Dropping the hose, Dora wriggled into his arms. 'How did it happen?' she asked, gasping for breath a minute later. 'I wanted it for so long.'

'I suddenly remembered you giving me the peacock feather. Bad things happened in the past, which made me bad at loving and at letting people get close.'

'Not any more.' Dora hugged him so tightly, he groaned. 'I'm here for you now,' and she kissed him again.

It was only when the abandoned hose started snaking around, soaking their legs, that she looked down and squeaked in excitement, 'I've got a brilliant plan.'

As Graffi's father Dafydd wandered past with a tool kit, she called out that they needed his help. Dafydd was only too happy. The entire workforce, he said, was on the verge of going on strike because Little Dulcie wasn't presenting the bouquet.

Much later, having downed two bottles of red to calm his nerves after the explosion, Biffo Rudge thought he'd seen a ghost, then realized it was Dora Belvedon astride Denmark, training a hose on the General's hat.

'What on earth are you doing?' he bellowed.

'I miss my pony so much' – Dora pretended to cry – 'Mr Bruce kindly allowed me to spruce up Denmark and the General. I'm just washing behind the General's ears.'

'Horse must have Arab blood' – Biffo patted Denmark – 'with those curved ears and wide eyes and that lovely dish face. Bagley was a good fellow too, not your usual military bonehead.'

'Isn't it tragic Mr and Mrs Bruce want to melt him down?' said Dora innocently.

'First I've heard of it,' exploded Biffo. 'Talk about the old order being ripped away.'

'Our founder flounders,' sighed Dora, 'and after he gave us our lovely school. But if he looks nice and clean tomorrow, more people will want to keep him. I've only got a bit more pigeon crap to get off, Mr Rudge, and then I'll race back to Boudicca.'

Fortunately, Alex Bruce was distracted during the evening by a crisis. The protection teams refused to allow in any more chemicals before the Queen's visit, so all the glass vessels being replaced in the Zone of Chemical Investigative Science had to be filled up with coloured water, by which time it was nearly ten o'clock.

'No longer Dirty Denmark,' said Dora, finally handing the hosepipe back to Dafydd. 'Do you want me to roll it up?'

'No, you get home, lovely. We'll be working all night. Shame Hengist's left, he wanted all the Larks kids to collect their GCSE certificates from the Queen, then bloody Bruce killed the idea. Chantal Peck had already bought her hat and been practising her curtsey all round the estate.'

'That's really sad,' said Dora. 'How's Graffi?'

'Triffic. He and Rupert are thick as thieves. Rupert's tickled pink with his muriel and I'm getting some triffic winners.'

Over in his minimalist living room, soon to be abandoned for the vast splendour of Head House, Alex was yet again going through his speech with Vicky Fairchild. The explosion in the emporium had removed his eyebrows so he could no longer raise them quizzically to make a point.

'Just a little more warmth in the words "Your Majesty",' cooed Vicky. 'I know how shy you are, Alex, but let the caring persona shine through.'

Upstairs, Poppet slept soundly. Tomorrow's outfit, a crimson, yellow and green bandanna and a warm wool ketchup-red smock, was already folded on a chair. Little Cranberry Germaine was yelling her head off, but let Alex deal.

Alex plugged Cranberry on to Poppet's left breast and reflected that if tomorrow went well, he'd be voted head by the governors on Friday and could have mistresses like Hengist. He'd always admired Vicky Fairchild.

Sally Brett-Taylor turned over a sodden pillow. Tomorrow, so no one would be embarrassed and because she couldn't bear to look at the butchered school gardens, she'd make herself scarce. She must also pull herself together and find somewhere to live. In the old days, Elaine had slept, often on her back, on the chaise longue at the bottom of the bed. Now she kept vigil in the hall, painful for her bony legs and elbows, always facing the front door, pining, not eating, hoping Hengist would walk in. How do you explain to a dog that Master has gone to kennels?

Sally was pleased to learn from Patience, on the Bagley bush telegraph, that Paris and Dora had finally got it together and yet she was sad. Paris had comforted her during the bleakest time of her life. Like the Marschallin, she must let him go with both hands.

Post-Mrs Walton, Cosmo crept back into Bagley very happy. Work experience had been equally rewarding. He had found the initials BP in Ashton's diary for tomorrow night, after the Queen's visit. Amber, at work experience at the *Gazette,* had found BP on the same date in Col Peters's diary. Dora had found it in Mr Fussy's.

Cosmo had also discovered, when a card arrived in a mauve envelope from the egregious Crispin Thomas, that it was Ashton's birthday tomorrow. Cosmo had therefore arranged for Dame Hermione, when she serenaded the Queen, to slip in a 'Happy Birthday to Ashton'.

Cosmo, who went every which way to gain what he wanted, even promising Ashton a blow job for his birthday, had introduced Lubemir into S and C's offices as a comely bit of rough trade.

Tomorrow, he and Ashton would spend all morning at Bagley, he to conduct his mother and the school orchestra, Ashton to be presented to the Queen. This would leave the office unguarded for Lubemir, who had already unearthed the shadow of an email from Alex to Ashton on 6 October: 'HB-T resigned. BR ours.'

What the hell was BR? Was it a typo for BC or BP? After a lot of thought, Cosmo decided it must be Badger's Retreat, so Stancombe could chop down Hengist's beloved trees, which had since been daubed with red plague spots, and, with Russell fiddling planning permission, slap desirable residences with a view all over the area.

Lubemir had also dug up so much shit on the bringing down of Janna and BC was looking increasingly like Birthday Club and BP like Birthday Party.

Russell had a planning office in County Hall and Milly Walton, working as a clerk in another department, had found a BP in his diary for tomorrow night. A good day's work.

On his way back to his cell, Cosmo called Milly's mother:

'Angel, can you do one thing for me? Suck up to Stancombe tomorrow, pretend it might be on again and see if you can wheedle your keys back. I desperately need to get into his files. I love you.'

Going upstairs Cosmo found Paris in his own cell, wrapped against the cold in a Black Watch tartan duvet, reading John Donne and looking happier than ever before.

' "She is all States, and all Princes, I, Nothing else is",' mocked Cosmo.

Paris flushed slightly. 'Whatever.'

Cosmo then debriefed him on the day's findings. 'Nasty little den of thieves going to that party tomorrow night,' he said finally. 'None of them has written down the address, so we may have to trail one of them.'

'Not in anything as obvious as your Ferrari,' chided Paris, but when Cosmo added that it was Ashton's birthday tomorrow, all the luminous happiness drained out of Paris's face.

'The third of November,' he said bleakly, 'that means he's forty-five tomorrow.'

'How d'you know?'

'Does he have a lisp, can't say his Rs, and have a big watch on the inside of his wrist and stink of asphyxiatingly sweet aftershave like poison gas?'

'That's the one.'

Paris shut his eyes, remembering the blindfolding, so every other sense was heightened, the holding down, the soft caressing hands, the laughter. The terrible pain and indignity going on and on, the grunting and heavy breathing: 'Shut up, you little wat or we'll weally hurt you.' The suffocating scent he could now smell on Cosmo.

As Paris glanced up, Cosmo was shocked by the depths of suffering in his face. He was shaking violently.

'How d'you know him?'

'I was the birthday present at his fortieth birthday party,' Paris said flatly. 'Not a bweeze, being gang waped.'

'My God, where was this?'

'In Oaktree Court, in a back room. I never saw any of them; they blindfolded me and tied my hands. God knows how many of them had me, I lost count. I don't know if Blenchley, the care manager, was one of them. Next day he told me I was imagining things. If I said anything, he'd move me on or have me taken out.'

Cosmo shook his head in bewildered admiration. 'And you never grassed?'

'I was only eleven, I was too ashamed, I felt so dirty. Who would have believed me? I was terrified of losing my friends. Ben Longstaff, who ran away from the home after threatening to grass them up, died in a very suspicious fire.'

If Paris had looked up, he would have found genuine compassion on Cosmo's face. 'I'm truly sorry. Was that why you screamed when Theo came into your room?'

'Yes.'

'Christ, I'm sorry,' repeated Cosmo. 'We'll nail them. Can you handle Ashton being here tomorrow?'

'It's OK.' Paris wandered towards the window. Through the newly bare trees he could see Dora's window in Boudicca. 'I can handle anything now.'

134

Bagley Hall was still in shock and in a growing state of mutiny over Hengist's departure. Both staff and pupils missed his warmth and genuine interest, his great laugh, even his bellows of rage. All they could think was how much he would have enjoyed welcoming the Queen, bounding down the Mansion steps, rubbing his big hands in joy, sweeping her off on a magical mystery tour of the school.

Instead they had to suffer Mr Fussy as powerless as Canute to keep back the great gold tidal wave of leaves unleashed by last night's frost, which now covered pitch, path and, mercifully, most of the hideously clashing flowerbeds. Mr Fussy was doing his nut and blaming every leaf on the bursar and his groundsmen.

Tension had also gripped Boudicca.

'Who's used all the hot water?' screamed Jade Stancombe. 'I'm handing the Queen her bouquet, I ought to have priority.'

Joan in a pinstripe suit was inspecting nails, hair, even breath for alcohol and that everyone was wearing the regulation on-the-knee sea-blue coat and beige skirt, with sufficiently polished shoes.

'And you're all to leave your mobiles behind.'

In the Science Emporium, the brightest pupils, their hair tied back, wearing white coats and goggles, nervously waited at their benches, ignoring the 'Bring back Hengist' stickers attached to the liver, the colon and the interactive whiteboards.

In the RE suite, the Lower Fifth played pass the parcel with a gurgling baby Cranberry and awaited Poppet to give them a lesson on birth as a rite of passage.

Outside, beneath a bright blue sky, crowds lining the route and gathered on the battlements shivered in the icy east wind. Inside the warmth of the Mansion, as the welcome party paced the black and white checked hall floor, Jupiter, Poppet and the Lord Lieutenant's wife, who'd arrived early because she'd driven down from London, were the only people not nervous.

Sweat crystalled Alex's forehead and was beading Ashton Douglas's discreet beige make-up. Stancombe's estranged wife, Lorraine, wheeled in for the occasion to present a united front, had disappeared yet again to powder her rebuilt nose. Stancombe constantly readjusted his gelled black spikes and his new, dark blue suit in the big gilt mirror. Jupiter was being gratifyingly friendly for once, and by chatting up Lorraine had freed Stancombe to rebond with Ruth Walton. Looking particularly sumptuous in an old rose velvet suit, Mrs Walton was clearly delighted to ignite an old flame.

Jupiter wanted Stancombe's billions for New Reform. But would this entail asking him to join the party executive, which might mean losing Rupert and Lord Hawkley, who had both formed an antipathy towards Stancombe? Bugger Hengist for letting them down.

'The Principal is within a quarter of a mile,' the Officer in Command, having received the message on his radio mike, told the welcome party and other relevant security units around the school grounds.

'I cannot think why you're all so nervous, she's only a senior citizen,' said Poppet as Ashton and Lorraine discreetly re-powdered their noses. Even with a respray, Ashton's cloying aftershave was fighting a losing battle with the stench of vegetable curry drifting from the kitchens.

'Wise of the Queen to move on to lunch at Larkminster Hospital,' murmured Jupiter.

'Sally Brett-Taylor always provided the most delicious luncheon and the most beautiful flowers,' grumbled the Lord Lieutenant's wife, not known for her diplomacy. 'Garden's gorn off dreadfully, might be in a municipal park. Sweet thing, Sally. Is she here?'

'Sadly not invited.'

Nor were the bursar, Patience and Little Dulcie, as they forlornly lined the lower drive, waving flags alongside villagers and children from the local primary, only catching the briefest glimpse of the Queen as her car with its cavalcade of cars and motorbike outriders sailed past.

Oblivious of a demo of pupils waving 'Bring back Hengist' placards and Trafford and the Randy Republican on the battlements brandishing red flags and crying, 'Down with the Monarchy', the Queen stepped out of her car. Accompanying her were her personal protection officer, a lady-in-waiting, who had potted biographies of everyone the Queen was going to meet in her handbag, and the Lord Lieutenant in his splendid uniform with its epaulettes, medals and stars.

Anthea Belvedon, twenty-two rows back, swamped by the 399 dignitaries, was absolutely hopping that no one could see how lovely she looked. On a big screen, she could see the crowds ringing Mansion Lawn and Randal bending over Her Majesty like a street lamp and his ghastly common wife being presented as well. There was Ruth Walton, laughing away, when Randal had sworn it was over between them, and Poppet looking ridiculous in that fearful bandanna and ghastly red smock to disguise the fact she hadn't got her figure back. Now she was refusing to bob to the Queen. So rude.

I should be over there, thought Anthea darkly, I'm supposed to be a close friend of Randal and Poppet.

Beside Anthea, Rod Hyde and Gillian Grimston of Searston Abbey were equally unhappy. Why had they been confined to very hard seats under an awning with 398 nonentities and not been introduced to Her Majesty like Ashton and Russell Lambert?

Any deficiencies in Poppet's bob were more than made up for by Dame Hermione's curtsey, more regal than any queen, as she sank to the floor in her Parma violet Chanel suit, a saintly expression in her wide brown eyes.

This distribution of largesse was cut short when her son Cosmo leapt on to the rostrum, sharply tapped the lectern and swept the school orchestra into the National Anthem, involving his mother in an undignified scramble to her feet. All four verses were sung fortissimo, rattling the Mansion windows and dislodging more leaves, followed by 'Here's a Health Unto Your Majesty' and Randal's Largo, as it was now known.

Everyone was heaving a sigh of relief and preparing for the Queen to move on to the RE and IT suites, when Hermione clapped her hands and announced: 'Somebody here, Ashton Douglas, head of education in Larkshire, has a birthday today. I'm sure Your Majesty would like to join me in wishing Ashton many happy returns.'

Ashton looked as though he'd been kissed under the mistletoe. Paris, round the other side of the school, watching him on the same big screen as Anthea Belvedon, fingered his knife.

And Dame Hermione was off: 'Happy birthday to You-hoo!'

Randal, Alex and the Lord Lieutenant were as purple or red as the polyanthus clashing in a nearby flowerbed. Finally Hermione swept off.

'My mother's kind of hard to stop,' sighed Cosmo.

Her Majesty was just moving on when Hermione's dresser, who'd been bunged a tenner, cried out, 'Encore,' and, whisking out of her dressing room, Dame Hermione obliged.

Alex was about to have a coronary. There were still two students taking Duke of Edinburgh Awards to be presented and they now had only half an hour left and had to whiz through the lesson in the IT suite with no time to look at the pupils' work.

'We'll have to switch to plan B and cut the RE lesson,' said the Officer in Command.

Alex turned pale. 'We can't, my wife . . .'

Dora, waiting beside General Bagley's statue to make her presentation and also watching events on the big screen, put down her blue box and wrote in her notebook: 'Her Majesty is running behind in her tight schedule.'

Everyone was commenting on how tiny and pretty the Queen was. How kind her blue eyes; how genuinely warm and radiant her smile; how becoming her amethyst hat trimmed with palest green feathers and how even a colour as harsh as the purple of her coat couldn't diminish her flawless pink and white complexion.

On to the Randal Stancombe Science Emporium, where the royal party toured the different zones and exclaimed in wonder at the giant tree you could walk inside and the huge ear that could be taken apart and the echo chambers, giant fibre-optics and heavenly light displays. On to the Zone of Chemical Investigative Science, which, although miraculously restored with coloured water in all the containers, seemed rather dull after yesterday's excitement.

'The Queen has the ability to make everyone feel special. Even republicans become monarchists in her presence,' wrote Dora.

Not so Poppet Bruce, who, white-faced, tight-lipped, was determined to divert the Queen back in the direction of RE, rites of passage and little Cranberry.

'I am of course known as the Queen of Arts,' Dame Hermione was telling everyone, 'and why isn't my very good friend Rupert Campbell-Black here?'

Even without Rupert, however, the media were agreeing that the Randal Stancombe Science Emporium was a triumph, that Randal would be assured his handle and Alex Bruce the headship of Bagley.

As the Queen finally emerged from this futuristic Nirvana, it was at last the turn of Anthea and the 399 very cold other dignitaries on their hard seats to hear Alex's speech of welcome in front of General Bagley's statue with the Science Emporium towering in the background. Afterwards, Randal would say a few words about his part in the great endeavour. Jade and Dora had taken up their positions beside Denmark's hindquarters.

Paris was crowded together behind the barricade with the rest of the Lower Sixth to watch the ceremony. Gazing across at Dora clutching her blue box, wishing it was his hand rather than the east wind ruffling her pale blonde hair, Paris was overwhelmed with love. The knife was to protect Dora from harm as much as to stab Ashton. He hated to leave her to carry out their great plan, but her official position beside Denmark made it possible.

Having practised a little bob, Dora turned round and smiled at him. Witnessing this exchange, Randal Stancombe, even at his finest hour, felt a skewer dipped in acid plunged in his heart. His great speech, his knighthood, Ruth Walton were as nothing to his lust for Dora Belvedon. He could see the gap of pink flesh between her skirt and her rolled-over brown socks. He was brought back to earth by the Queen's gloved hand patting Denmark:

'What a splendid animal.'

Alex in turn patted the mike, cleared his throat, raised his head self-importantly and began very, very warmly: 'Your Majesty, on behalf of students, teachers, parents, governors and supporters of Bagley Hall, I would like to thank you very much for visiting us today. It is a huge honour and marks an historical moment of our development.'

Nothing's going to stop him taking over now, thought a despairing Artie, gazing down from a staffroom window.

'On this momentous day for Bagley Hall and for science . . .' Alex was getting into his stride.

Goodness, the Queen's good at looking interested, thought Dora. As her eyes flickered towards Paris, he nodded. Imperceptibly, Dora's hand slipped between Denmark's back legs.

At first, people thought the heavens had opened; then, as there was no rattle of rain on the blue striped awning, they decided it must be a burst pipe. There was a gasp of consternation as the splatter continued and a great gush of water was located, splashing on General Bagley's plinth and spilling on to the grass.

Bewilderment, rage, horror, shock and broad grins could be seen on individual faces as it struck home that the torrent of very yellow liquid was pouring out of Denmark's cock.

'Quick, quick, he's staling,' yelled Amber. 'Stand up in your stirrups, General.'

There was a rumble of laughter. For a second, Her Majesty's face twitched. The photographers were going berserk, snapping Denmark and his gushing yellow cascade from all angles.

'The Empire Strikes Back,' murmured Artie in ecstasy.

For once, the Lord Lieutenant, the personal protection officer and the Officer in Command were at a loss.

'Stop it,' howled Randal. 'For Christ's sake, someone stop it.'

'Try one of Sweetie's condoms,' suggested Dora.

Then, to distance herself from blame, she rushed forward, trying to stem the flow with her notebook, but the torrent swept it aside like driftwood. A proffered bucket overflowed in a few seconds, a policeman's helmet met the same fate, as did the end of Miss Painswick's parasol rammed up as a catheter.

'Try a tourniquet,' said Dora.

But no one was around to solve the problem. Alex had not issued any invitations to the bursar's team of maintenance men. Randal was casting furiously about for one of his plumbers, but after twenty-four hours on, and having been ordered to 'bloody well hop it,' they had understandably done so. None of his work-force had been inclined to stay anyway after the snubbing of Little Dulcie.

'What a pity Graffi and Rocky were uninvited,' piped up Dora, 'they'd have stopped it.'

Like Don Giovanni's Commandatore, impervious to the Victoria Falls beneath him, General Bagley gazed fiercely at the Science Emporium: 'Serve you right, Mr Bruce, for trying to melt me down.'

'Can't stop it, sir,' a drenched security man muttered to the Lord Lieutenant. 'Better move on.'

Alex, meanwhile, had lost it, trying with rolling eyes to blurt out his last two crucial paragraphs about a breeding ground for the Hawkings and Einsteins of the future and thanking Randal for his historic contribution, but Denmark peed on.

The pupils and most of the audience were by now quite unable to contain their laughter. Rod Hyde and Gillian Grimston, even Ashton and Russell, were not displeased: Poppet and Alex had got a fraction above themselves recently.

Most of the school just thought: Hengist would have known how to handle it, turning the whole thing into an enormous joke. The gold hands of the school clock had edged round to 12.25. No time for Randal's speech.

'I would like to ask Your Majesty to mark your visit by unveiling a commemorative plaque,' mumbled Alex.

At least the sea-blue curtain didn't come away in Her Majesty's hand and the dark blue Parker pen worked when she signed the visitors' book. Joan, standing like a retired Guards officer in her pinstripe suit, tugged down Jade's skirt to just above her knees before she shimmied forward to present a big bunch of orange lilies and chrysanthemums, which the Queen passed on to her lady-in-waiting. Jade then managed to redress the balance a fraction by explaining it was her father, Randal Stancombe, who had bankrolled and masterminded the Science Emporium.

Then it was Dora's turn. Aware of so many of her media contacts watching, she once again turned and smiled quickly at an impossibly proud Paris, before executing a beautiful curtsey.

The Queen said she remembered Dora's father and how sorry she'd been when he died. Dora in turn said she was very sorry when the Queen had lost one of her corgis in a fight, but that she'd obtained a photograph of Pharos.

'You must miss her, so I've made you a model.'

Peering into the box at Pharos sitting on a royal blue satin bed, for a second the Queen bit her lip and Dora was afraid she was angry. Then she said Dora's version was lovely and very like Pharos and thanked her very much.

She was about to move on, the wind lifting the green feathers in her hat, when something in her kind face made Dora take a deep breath: 'As the most powerful person in the land, could Your Majesty possibly bring back our headmaster Hengist Brett-Taylor? We feel the heart has been torn out of our school since he left and we'd like him back.'

'That's enough,' exploded Alex as the Queen smiled and, handing the blue box to her lady-in-waiting, moved on. Alex was so livid, he forgot to present her with a copy of *A Guide to Red Tape*.

Many pupils and staff positioned on the other side of the Mansion didn't think they'd get a chance to see the Queen close up, but she left from a different side, passing Trafford high up in the battlements, who grabbed Miss Painswick's Union Jack and cheered his head off. On the way down the drive, Her Majesty was near the window and able to wave and smile at Little Dulcie.

135

Meanwhile, like the far-distant Oxus, a steady yellow stream of liquid still flowed out of Denmark's cock.

'Heads will roll,' screamed Alex. 'Who filled up that horse with water and how dare Dora Belvedon ask the Queen to bring back Hengist? It was probably her that filled up the horse, she was hanging round it long enough last night.'

The day couldn't have gone worse. He would now have to cope with Poppet's rage, because the Queen never reached RE. Not to mention Gordon Brooks, apoplectic because he'd driven all the way down from Manchester to find Boffin's experiment had ended up on the cutting-room floor. Stancombe was understandably angriest of all. All the press would concentrate on General Bagley's horse, no doubt already writing tomorrow's headlines about the Royal Wee, and hardly mention his heroic and historic contribution. And he'd just seen that white devil Paris Alvaston kissing Dora yet again.

Alex then had to host vegetable curry for nearly eight hundred, without any drink.

The day couldn't get worse, but it did when Dame Hermione slipped a bill for fifty thousand pounds into his top pocket.

'What is this?'

'My fee, Alex. I've given it to you at half-price for Cosmo's sake and of course there'll be ten per cent off if you pay cash, which I know you can,' she added roguishly.

Alex was jolted. How could she know any such thing?

'There was no question of a fee,' he spluttered.

'Indeed there was. I never give my services for nothing, even if it's a fee for charity. A performance like today's takes so much preparation – like you, I am a true professional.'

816

How dare she? It was Cartwright's fault, he'd obviously agreed a fee with her. Cartwright could get out before Christmas.

The vegetable curry lunch in the great hall without any alcohol was not a prolonged affair, but it gave Ruth Walton time to commiserate with Randal Stancombe.

'The Science Emporium is awesome; posterity will always remember you for it.' Then, lowering her voice: 'I've missed you so much, Randal, why don't you pop round for supper tonight?'

'I'd like that, Ruth,' said Stancombe.

Rod Hyde, meanwhile, was sitting in a window seat with Anthea Belvedon, whom he regarded as a very pretty lady and an excellent JP.

'Why don't you pop round later for a jar?' he asked. 'I could show you over St Jimmy's. I'm sure our school could sort out your Dora. We're thinking of starting a boarding house for challenging students.'

'I'd like that,' said Anthea, who wanted to pay back Randal for bringing Lorraine and flirting with Ruth Walton. She was fascinated to hear about Rod's new villa in the Seychelles and thought he was rather excitingly masterful.

Poppet, determined to regain the ascendancy, insisted after lunch that Trafford unveil his ground-breaking maquette of a sculpture to replace General Bagley. The royal party had gone, but there were plenty of dignitaries and press still around. Trafford, creator of *Shagpile*, *Tranny by Gaslight* and *Sister Hoodie*, was always good copy.

Poppet, requesting quiet with a cymbal clash of bracelets, pointed to the maquette in front of her on the table, but hidden by a tarpaulin. She then introduced Trafford: 'One of our most exciting Young British Artists, who'd like to introduce his concept of a new work of art to replace General Bagley, whose image many of us strongly feel to be outdated.'

A great rumble of disapproval at her words turned to envy as the artist in question was seen to be holding a large glass of whisky.

'General Bagley's like, male, imperialistic, aggressive,' Trafford told his now very hostile audience. 'I wanted to create something like female, tender, loving and of the age.'

Poppet was in ecstasy, nodding in agreement as Trafford drained his whisky and whipped off the tarpaulin to reveal a maquette of two very stocky women going down on each other.

Alex turned green; his wife was made of sterner stuff.

'How apt – an act of reciprocal love,' she cried. 'Do we have a title?'

'It's called *Minge-drinking*,' said Trafford.

Hengist would have given everyone the rest of the day off. Alex, true to his puritan ethic, insisted afternoon lessons went on as usual. Stancombe then joined him in the head's office, where, judging by the shouting, the battle of Randal's Handle was joined. After twenty minutes, Randal stormed out and Alex went on the rampage.

He had never been so humiliated in his life. He was determined to track down the ringleaders responsible for the General Bagley fiasco. Denmark was still peeing merrily and to top it, some joker had leant a sign saying 'Flood Warning' against the General's plinth.

136

At dusk, a very tired Dora ran back to Boudicca to change out of her school suit. Trying to absorb the enormity of the last two days' events and the miracle of Paris loving her, she was suddenly racked with terror.

Up to now she had led a charmed life at Bagley. Hengist had adored her and after he'd gone to prison she'd been protected because her mother was a great friend of Alex and Poppet. But if Anthea had been relegated to row twenty-two under the awning, her mother had clearly lost caste and there would be nothing to stop Alex expelling her for begging the Queen to bring back Hengist.

If, in addition, she were expelled for the General Bagley escapade, Paris as her accomplice might get chucked out too and she'd never see him again, or Patience and Ian, who'd been so lovely, or Cosmo, Bianca or Artie or all her friends.

Paris had just texted her to ask where she was and she'd texted back to say she'd see him at supper. Cosmo, who'd managed to infiltrate himself into the unveiling of Trafford's sculpture, had also texted her that he'd overheard horrible Rod Hyde asking her mother for a drink at St Jimmy's later. Dora shivered as she remembered how well Anthea and Rod seemed to be getting on, on their hard seats. Her mother would love St Jimmy's because it was free. And how dare the old bitch not pop back to Foxglove Cottage to feed and let out Cadbury, then smack him if he made a puddle?

Dora had reached her dormitory and just taken off her suit jacket, when Joan barged in, bellowing:

'You were hanging round General Bagley's statue last night, Dora Belvedon, and you're no doubt behind that disgusting act of sabotage. Well, you're for the high jump. Mr Bruce wants to see you in his office at once.'

'OK, OK.' Dora raced out of Boudicca towards the Mansion, but the moment she was out of sight, she turned right instead of left, belted down the drive and didn't stop running until she reached Foxglove Cottage.

She was just being knocked sideways by an ecstatic Cadbury when her mobile rang. It was Stancombe. He'd tracked down an event horse called Kerfuffle, advertised in *Horse & Hound*, in which Dora had expressed an interest on her last leave-out.

'Lots of people are after him. Want to come and see him this evening?'

Looking at a horse was much better than being expelled and, out of the corner of her eye, Dora noticed Cadbury had chewed up one of Anthea's new silver sandals.

'Yes, please,' she said.

'Where are you?' asked Stancombe.

'At Foxglove Cottage.'

'Where's Mummy?'

'Having a drink with Rod Hyde.'

'Good. Don't tell her anything until we've bought the horse. She'll say I'm spoiling you. I'm tied up as we speak. I'll send a car to fetch you. See you in a bit.'

Dora was not pleased when creepy Uncle Harley rolled up ten minutes later. She'd only taken Cadbury into the garden, fed him and chucked the remains of her mother's sandals in next door's dustbin; she'd had no time to ring Paris to tell him where she was going or change out of school uniform into jodhpurs.

Uncle Harley was not pleased when Dora insisted on bringing Cadbury and sitting in the back with him.

'Who's going to guard your mum's house?'

'Who's going to guard me?' snapped Dora.

Outside, night had fallen like a shroud. No stars or moon pierced the sooty gloom as they left Bagley village and sped out of reach of street lamps, lighted windows or even chinks of light under doors, deep into thickly wooded country where trees writhed under the rising wind's lash, down by-roads carpeted with red and orange leaves, which danced in the headlights like the flames of hell. Even Uncle Harley's jewellery didn't lighten the dark. In horror Dora realized she'd forgotten her mobile.

'Can I borrow your telephone to ring my boyfriend?'

'There's no signal here.'

Dora clutched Cadbury tighter. Kerfuffle had better be good. As Uncle Harley turned through pillars topped by winged monsters, with eagles' heads and lions' bodies, and drove up a long, pitted, bumpy drive, Dora couldn't see any horses beyond the rusty broken railings. As the car rattled over a sheep grid, she thought she must be careful of Cadbury's legs if they had to make a run for it. Ahead towered a house, shaggy with leafless creeper, which fell over the windows like too-long fringes.

'Where are we?' she asked nervously.

'Here,' said Uncle Harley.

Meanwhile, over the border in Rutshire, Mags Gablecross, avid to hear details of the Queen's visit to Bagley, was awaiting her husband the Chief Inspector's return for supper, when the telephone rang. It was Debbie, Larks's former cook, asking if Mags knew of Janna's whereabouts.

'She's in Wales with Emlyn. They're getting married, isn't it lovely?' Then, when Debbie didn't react: 'Are you OK, Debs?'

'Yes – no. I'm worried, Mags. I've handed in my notice here. Janna was right all along about Ashton. He's vile and he never stops watching my boys. I think he's put a two-way mirror in the shower.'

Mags shuddered. 'How horrible.'

'It may sound stupid, but I think something evil's going on. Russell Lambert had a birthday party here at Ashton's place back in August and instead of wanting me to help out, Ashton insisted I looked tired, and packed me and the boys off to the seaside for the weekend.

'Anyway, it's Ashton's birthday today. Stancombe called him first thing about some party this evening. I picked up the phone by mistake and got the impression' – Debbie's voice shook – 'Randal was lining up some little girl "for dessert" – those were his words – then Ashton laughed and said he'd be bringing something much more to his own taste.'

'You don't know where this party's going to be?'

'No idea.' Debbie started to cry. 'I thought I was imagining things but Brad went to his dad for the day, and when I got back from Tesco's this evening, there was no one home. When I phoned Brad's dad, he said he'd dropped Brad off an hour ago and Ashton had insisted on minding Brad until I got back.'

'There was no note?'

'Nothing. Oh Mags, I'm so worried Ashton has kidnapped him.'

'I'll get on to Tim at once,' said Mags.

Over at Bagley, Paris was equally demented. Dora hadn't returned to supper and she wasn't answering her mobile. There was no sign of her at Boudicca when he dropped in and when he raced down to Foxglove Cottage, the place was in darkness.

'Randal's always had the hots for her. I know the bastard's going to serve her up at Ashton's birthday party and dispose of her afterwards. I can't handle it, Cosmo. I love her so much.'

'Randal's safe with Ruth,' said Cosmo soothingly, 'she asked him over to supper.'

'Well, fucking ring and check if he's there.'

'Bit early. I don't want to rouse his suspicions. Oh, OK then.'

Mrs Walton answered immediately: 'Randal? Oh, it's you, Cosmo darling, any chance of you popping over later? I seem to have been stood up by Randal. Cosmo! Cosmo!'

But Cosmo had hung up.

137

Stancombe must have been looking out because the moment the car drew up, the heavy studded oak front door creaked open and he pulled Dora in out of the bitter cold. Inside it was tropical, which had given him the excuse to wear nothing but a very white, mostly unbuttoned shirt, black velvet trousers and a great deal of Lynx – hardly horse-buying kit, reflected Dora. The sort of soppy music her mother liked was belching out of speakers.

There was no furniture in the high vaulted hall, but Stancombe led her into a large drawing room with flames leaping in a big fireplace, walls lined with mirrors and leather sofas, fur cushions and a floor covered in thick, dark shagpile. In one corner, four-legged and big as a Welsh cob, stood a vast television. In another was a table covered in glasses and a trolley groaning with every kind of drink. In the centre of the room stood a strange padded leather table about three feet off the ground. Twigs and rose thorns clawed and scrabbled at the windows, like the buried-alive trying to escape from their coffins. At least the windows had handles in case she wanted to make a quick getaway.

Cadbury's hackles had gone straight up, his pink lip curled, his normally genial yellow eyes were hard and reptilian. He had no use for Stancombe, who in turn was furious Dora had brought a chaperon, but decided not to make a fuss. She looked so adorable in her school tie with her chubby little legs sticking out from underneath her beige pleated skirt and flesh visible in the gaps between the buttons of her white shirt.

Anthea was too mean to buy Dora new uniform until she was absolutely bursting out of it, and would have been appalled if she'd realized how additionally seductive this made her daughter look. Stancombe, who'd just taken the brake off any inhibitions with a vast line of coke, felt himself boiling over with lust.

As Dora plonked herself down on a brown leather sofa, Cadbury wandered off to explore, which suited Stancombe. It would enable him to shut the bloody dog away in another room.

'What would you like to drink?'

'A crème de menthe frappé,' said Dora airily, 'but shouldn't we see Kerfuffle? Another buyer might get there first.'

'He's in the stables, only five minutes from here.' Stancombe waved vaguely in the direction of the window behind her.

'I want to try him out.'

'Of course. They've got an indoor school.' Hell, he'd forgotten how to frappé ice. He was so on fire, he'd melt anything he touched.

'Wasn't the Queen lovely?' said Dora brightly. 'I thought it went so well.'

Stancombe picked up a steel hammer. 'It was a cock-up from start to finish. Whatever one's reservations about Hengist B-T, he'd have known how to run a show like that. Alex couldn't run a piss-up in a brewery.' Bash, bash, bash! The ice was going everywhere.

'It's awfully hot,' said Dora, 'can we open the window?'

'Take off your cardi, then I can admire your sexy figure. You get tastier every time I see you. Said I ought to put you down like a fine wine but I think you're grown-up enough for love now.' As he handed her her drink, his fingers caressed hers.

'I am too,' beamed Dora as he sat beside her. 'I've got a boyfriend. I've wanted him to be my boyfriend for nearly three years, since he played Romeo.' She took a gulp of crème de menthe. 'That's lovely, rather like mouthwash, but I don't want to be drunk in charge of an event horse. I've always fancied older men,' she went on dreamily. Stancombe preened, then scowled as she added, 'Paris is two years older than me.'

If I bang on about Paris, it'll put him off, thought Dora hopefully. He won't dare try anything if he's Mummy's boyfriend.

'Would you like a tour of the house?' murmured Stancombe.

Suddenly aware of his burning thigh pressed against hers, Dora jumped to her feet. 'I'd rather see Kerfuffle – and where's Cadbury? I bet he's found the kitchen.'

She ran out into the hall and, turning left, discovered herself in a room with a vast double bed and walls lined with more mirrors. On the bedside table was a pair of handcuffs, some manacles and an evil-looking black whip with a long lash, which was certainly not intended to be used on Kerfuffle.

Dora froze, increasingly aware she was in the presence of evil.

' "The Good Life",' sang Sacha Distel sforzando. No one would hear screams over that.

Next moment, Stancombe had grabbed her, hands going everywhere, like the sinewy tentacles of a mad, starved octopus. 'Little Dora,' he whispered, crashing his horrible, hot, full lips down on hers, ramming his great, hard, fat tongue between her teeth.

'Don't,' squealed Dora, 'let me go, you disgusting old man, or I'll bite your tongue off. I'll guillotine your willy. I trusted you because you're Mummy's boyfriend. She's a JP and I'm under age. She'll bang you up for this. Stop it. STOP it!' She tried to knee him in the groin as shirt buttons under siege were pinging everywhere.

'You know you want me,' taunted Stancombe, as wildly excited by her antagonism as by her plump, young flesh.

'I bloody don't, I've got a boyfriend.'

'That's where you're wrong.' Stancombe was tearing off her shirt, scrabbling for the hook of her pink gingham bra, about to rip it off in his frustration. 'You need a real man, not that little wimp.'

'I don't, he isn't, I love Paris.' Dora aimed a kick at Stancombe's shins.

'Stop it, you snotty little bitch.' As he pinned her against a mirrored wall, she was impaled by an erection big as a rounder's bat. 'Can't you get it into your fucking head, Paris is gay.'

'Don't be stupid,' panted Dora. 'He wasn't gay with my friend Bianca, or Amber, or your stuck-up daughter. You're just as green with jealousy as that crème de menthe.'

'Paris is a little tart,' hissed Stancombe. 'Look at the way he flashed his ass at Theo and Hengist and Artie and Biffo, all eating out of his hand.'

He was foaming at the mouth, veins like snakes writhing on his forehead. Dora had never seen anyone so angry and would have been scared witless if she hadn't been so furious.

'Come and look at this.' Grabbing her hand, Stancombe dragged her back into the living room where he pushed her down on the leather sofa. Then he took a video from the shelf and rammed it into the television.

Dora took a gulp of crème de menthe. She must get out and where the hell was Cadbury? Next moment, ridiculous, jiggy music flooded the room and despite everything, she burst out laughing at the sight of a lot of fat, naked old men dancing round, whooping and drinking out of champagne bottles. It was like the Elephants in 'Carnival of the Animals', except they had waggling willies instead of trunks.

'Oh yuk, yuk, yuk cubed,' cried Dora as they started groping each other, fondling and slapping each other's bottoms. Then she gave a gasp.

'My God, that fat one's Russell someone, Mummy knows him, he's the planning officer. And there's revolting Ashton Douglas who Dame Hermione sang happy birthday to. He's got his socks on too; expect he's frightened of getting verrucas. God, how gross – and there's Col Peters, vile pig and Rod Hyde' – Dora couldn't help giggling – 'with a wincy little willy.'

But when Stancombe fast-forwarded the tape, Dora shrieked in real anguish to see that Russell Someone was humping away – 'Oh God, no!' – on top of a thin, very young girl, lying on her front on the same leather table that was in the centre of the room, with her face concealed by flopping white-blonde hair. Although her hands were tightly tied together in front and Rod Hyde and Col Peters were laughing and holding her down, she was putting up a hell of a struggle.

'My God, poor little girl,' screamed Dora, 'he's raping her. How can you allow something so terrible? Turn it off, I can't look.'

'Yes, you can,' hissed Stancombe, yanking her head back towards the screen as the camera zoomed in. 'Look at the Eiffel Tower on his shoulder. That's your little rent boy.'

'My turn, my turn,' Ashton was now yelling, prising off Russell and taking over, to whoops of excitement from the others, and shafting away with unparalleled viciousness.

'Just watch,' gloated Stancombe as, in close-up again, the camera captured below the blindfold a long nose, lips curled back in agony, and teeth plunged into the black leather. The exquisite bone structure could only belong to Paris.

'You revolting pervert,' screamed Dora, hammering her fists against Stancombe's chest, 'you were raping him, that's what the Upper Sixth threatened to do to my brother Dicky. How dare you hurt Paris when he was a little boy in a children's home with no parents to protect him? That is the most disgusting, horrible thing I've ever seen.'

Rushing towards the television, Dora pressed the eject button, grabbed the video and, yanking open a window, hurled it out into the bushes.

'You stupid bitch,' howled Stancombe, 'you'll pay for it.'

'How could you film something so sick?' howled back Dora. 'So you could blackmail Ashton and Rod Hyde if they stepped out of line?'

'That's enough, it's your turn now, no one knows you're here.'

But as Stancombe lunged at her, they were both distracted by excited squeaking. Shoving Stancombe off balance with all her might, Dora ran to yet another room, a sort of study with a big desk. Here she found Cadbury, his pink nose deep in a wardrobe, his tail going like a windscreen wiper on speed.

'Drop!' yelled Stancombe, hurtling forward and kicking Cadbury viciously in the ribs.

'Don't hurt him,' screamed Dora, grabbing a steel lamp.

But Cadbury had been living at home with Anthea and shut in the kitchen and kicked in the ribs once too often. Next moment he'd thrown himself at Stancombe, knocking him to the floor, standing over him, growling furiously.

'Bastard dog.' Stancombe tried and failed to grab Cadbury by the balls.

'Ha, ha, ha,' panted Dora, 'serves you right for persuading Mummy to have him castrated. Pity she didn't have you done at the same time.'

When she first peered into the wardrobe, she thought she'd stumbled on a linen cupboard, then slowly realized Cadbury had sniffed out pillows and pillows of white powder.

'Good boy, good, clever Cadbury, keep him there.' Dora rushed next door and seized the handcuffs. Wrenching a terrified Stancombe's hands behind his back, she clicked them shut. Then she bound his ankles very tightly with her Boudicca house tie.

'That's a reef knot – only thing I learnt in the Brownies. You won't get out of that, nor would Joan approve of such disgusting language,' she added, pulling his green silk handkerchief out of his pocket and shoving it in his raging mouth.

'Let's see what else you've got in here.' Returning to the wardrobe, Dora found several briefcases bulging with notes and, at the back, a sleek, black gun, which she laid on the desk.

'You evil man . . .' Then, horror and revulsion taking over from a sense of achievement: 'How dare you do that to my boyfriend?'

Picking up the house telephone she dialled 999.

'I want to speak to Chief Inspector Gablecross, it's very urgent.' Then, after a pause during which Stancombe wriggled like a netted tuna to free himself: 'Hello, Chief Inspector, this is Dora Belvedon, could you come at once? I've just conducted a citizen's arrest on Randal Stancombe. He's in big trouble. He's got a lot of white stuff in his cupboard that doesn't look like baby powder.

'My dog, Cadbury, deserves a medal, he's been so brave. I've tied Stancombe up but he's not in carnival mood, so please hurry. I've no idea where I am, but it's quite grand with pillars at the bottom of the drive topped with monsters . . . now I remember, Mr Brett-Taylor's got one on his crest: they're griffins. The park railings are all broken and could never keep a horse in and it's a very shaggy old house with high ceilings. There's the doorbell, it might be Uncle Harley back, so please hurry.'

As the bell rang more insistently, Cadbury barked, uncertain whether he ought to rush to the door or guard Stancombe, who mumbled furiously through his handkerchief that Dora would now be for the high jump.

The doorbell rang again. Grabbing the gun, holding it behind her back, Dora tugged open the door to find Ashton Douglas, with his arm round a beautiful fair-haired little boy, cooing, 'Come on, Bwad, you'll love this wonderful house. Good evening,' he added with his thin smile. Then, clocking Dora's ripped, undone shirt, paused, unsure what game she might be playing. 'I've got an appointment with Mr Stancombe.'

'He's not here.'

There was a crash from next door.

'It's a man mending the boiler,' squeaked Dora.

Ignoring her, Ashton ushered Brad into the study.

'What the hell?'

Cadbury growled, but with more uncertainty. He needed another line of coke.

'Don't untie him, Mr Douglas,' ordered Dora, whipping out the gun, 'or I'll fill you full of lead. The police are on their way and this gun is loaded.'

'Don't be silly, little girl,' said Ashton, hastily shielding himself with a terrified Brad.

Oh help, thought Dora as the doorbell rang yet again.

'You wouldn't dare fire that gun, put it down.' Ashton, setting Brad aside, was about to untie Stancombe's feet.

'Oh yes I would.' Aiming above Brad, Dora shut her eyes and pulled the trigger. As a bullet shattered the mirror above his head, Ashton dropped Stancombe's ankles. 'And next time you go kiddy-fiddling,' she added furiously, 'take your socks off.'

'What are you talking about?' spluttered Ashton.

'A disgusting film of you gang-raping Paris.'

Ashton's face turned as green as his suddenly panic-stricken eyes. Next moment, Brad made a bolt for it. Catching him with her left hand, Dora drew him close: 'It's OK, you're safe now.'

Someone was leaning on the bell. Backing towards the front door, keeping her eyes on Ashton, Dora put on a deep voice and cried: 'Who's there?'

'Open up,' said a familiar, reedy voice.

'Mr Fussy,' exploded Dora as she opened the door.

Alex was disguised by a false beard, a deerstalker and dark glasses; his open-neck shirt, however, revealed his wobbling Adam's apple.

'Your friends are in there, you disgusting old man.'

Seeing the gun and Nemesis in the form of a Middle Fifth student with her clothes torn off, Alex turned and bolted slap into the arms of PC Cuthbert, who'd been working out with Gloria and who had no difficulty arresting Alex and slapping him into handcuffs.

PC Cuthbert was accompanied by a policewoman, into whose arms Dora thrust a sobbing Brad. Rushing back to Stancombe's telephone, punching out numbers, she was deep in conversation as Paris erupted into the room, fists clenched, eyes blazing, snarling like a snow leopard about to spring.

'Where's Dora, what the fuck's going on?'

Cadbury thumped his tail as Paris took in Stancombe flailing on the ground, Ashton cringing in the corner and Dora with all her buttons ripped off, putting back a receiver. Completely losing it, Paris leapt forward, enfolding her in his arms, clinging to her like a drowning man to driftwood, frantically kissing her over and over again.

'Are you OK? Omigod, what did that bastard do to you? Did he hurt you?'

'I'm fine, honest. I was just ringing Paul Dacre to ask him to hold the front page.'

For a moment Paris gazed down at her in disbelief, exasperation and then love.

'For fuck's sake, I've been through every hell in the world worrying about you. No one knew where you were. I thought I'd never see you again.' Paris's voice broke as, trembling violently, he clutched her tight. 'And don't watch, you bastard,' he added, giving Stancombe a big kick.

'I left my mobile behind, I wanted to ring you but I couldn't,' gasped Dora who, as reality reasserted itself, had started trembling far worse than Paris. 'I had to be brave for Cadbury and because I was so desperate to see you again.'

Tears were trickling down Paris's cheeks.

'I imagined such terrible things happening to you, I can't tell you . . . They're like . . . so terrible.' Having furiously wiped his eyes with his sleeve, still clutching Dora, he turned towards Ashton.

'Many happy weturns, Mr Douglas, wemember me?'

His voice was so filled with contempt and loathing that Dora shivered, Cadbury dropped his ears and Ashton backed terrified into the cupboard.

'We've never met,' he gibbered.

'Yeah, we did. On your fortieth birthday, remember, at a waif-swapping party at Oaktree Court,' spat Paris. 'I don't figure this birthday's going to end quite so well for you.'

For a second his fingers tightened convulsively on Dora's arms, then, as she said shakily, 'It's OK, I'm here for you, I love you,' police poured into the house.

'Break it up, you two,' said Cosmo, tapping them on the shoulder a few minutes later. 'Well done, Cadbury. Christ! Look at that Charlie.' He snorted a pinch from a claws-punctured bag. 'It's very good; I suppose we can't have the odd kilo for rounding up this gang of thieves?'

'How did you ever find me?' asked Dora, still keeping the firmest hold on Paris.

'We followed Mr Fussy,' said Cosmo, nodding at Alex who was remonstrating with PC Cuthbert.

'I can explain everything, officer.'

'And I can tell you, Alex, baby,' called out Cosmo chattily, 'that like Trafford's minge-drinkers, you're going down for a long, long time.'

While Col Peters, Russell Lambert, Des Res and Rod Hyde were being rounded up, all on their way to the party, Dora had a brief private word with Chief Inspector Gablecross.

'There was this hideous video in the machine which could send this lot to the electric chair. Could Paris possibly not see it? I chucked it out of that window into some bushes in the direction of the stables.'

'There aren't any stables,' said Chief Inspector Gablecross grimly. 'You've been very lucky; Stancombe's a very dangerous man. You must have been frightened.'

'I had Cadbury,' said Dora fondly, 'and, frankly, when a true writer gets on to a good story, they feel no fear.'

138

The police proceeded to fillet Stancombe's various properties and unearth every kind of skulduggery, more drugs and arms in other deserted warehouses and evidence that he had massively bribed Ashton, Rod Hyde, Alex Bruce, Russell, Desmond Reynolds and Col Peters with villas in hot countries and huge dollops of cash.

For these rewards, they had been instrumental in stitching up Janna and ousting Hengist from power, so Stancombe could get his hands on both the Larks land and Badger's Retreat, with, eventually, his eyes set on the water meadows and razing the Shakespeare Estate to the ground.

Stancombe and Uncle Harley were also convicted for importing and dealing in millions of pounds' worth of Class A drugs. In addition, Stancombe's inability to resist a chance to blackmail or keep in line the others by filming every birthday party had provided enough evidence to send the entire gang to prison for many years.

As there were at least a dozen other incriminating videos, Chief Inspector Gablecross managed to retrieve the one Dora had chucked in the bushes and never used it in evidence.

'Now Mr Fussy's gone, Hengist can have his job back,' said Dora happily.

Fussygate, however, was the third scandal to rock Bagley and, at the governors' meeting in mid November, it was unanimously decided, at Jupiter's instigation, to appoint Artie Deverell as headmaster.

Hengist wasn't due out till after Christmas and nobody knew if he'd even want to come back. Better to root out all corruption.

Ian and Patience were asked to stay on and Wally and Miss

Cambola invited to join the staff. Artie would also have liked to have invited his friend Emlyn Davies back as deputy head, but Emlyn was finding both his marriage and his job with the Welsh Rugby Union far too exciting.

The photograph of Tabitha Campbell-Black and her horse was restored to the front of the *Old Bagleian* magazine. Aided by Artie, Lord Hawkley set about clearing Theo's name and overseeing the publication of his epic translation of Sophocles. A new classical library, large enough to contain the archives, was also commissioned. Randal Stancombe, it was noted, didn't tender for the job.

Other excitements included Dora and Cadbury getting their faces in all the national press and Cadbury getting his chance to meet the Queen after all, when he won an award for gallantry.

Just after Christmas, Artie Deverell was faced with his first challenge: a letter from Joan Johnson, saying in future she would like to be known as Mr John Johnson.

'She can take over Artie's old house,' observed Cosmo, 'and at least she won't be hassled to address the Talks Society.'

139

Hengist was released from prison in January, to the sorrow of his fellow inmates. He had written their letters, sorted out their financial and emotional problems and, when pressed, regaled them with hilarious anecdotes of the great and famous.

None of them felt he had committed a crime.

'When we took SATs at school, Henge, our 'ead gave us the answers.'

Despite his cheerful exterior, they were aware too of a heart-break no prison doctor could cure.

Whilst inside, Hengist had kept up with the outside world, reading with pride of Jack Waterlane, Lando and Amber scuffling with the police over the hunting ban, with huge pleasure of Janna and Emlyn's marriage, noting without surprise the increasing closeness of Jupiter and David Hawkley, and, with amazement, the rounding-up of the Birthday Party club.

Being in prison, no one could ring him up for quotes.

'We'll sort out the nonces, Henge, if any of 'em end up 'ere,' promised his friends.

Artie Deverell was now at the helm, but in no hurry to desert his exquisite Regency house, so there was no longer any pressure on Sally to leave Head House. But she was so unhappy she wanted to escape as soon as possible. It was just the mental paralysis induced by having to dispose of twenty thousand books, innumerable works of art and beautiful cherished furniture; it was as harrowing as distributing beloved animals if you're forced to close down a zoo.

Since she'd demanded a divorce, Sally hadn't seen or spoken to Hengist. He had refused to allow her or anyone else to visit him in prison. Anxious not to embarrass pupils or staff, he returned to Bagley to pick up some books and clothes on the Sunday before the start of the spring term. Sally therefore said she'd make herself scarce.

Hengist arrived in a blue van lent him by Rupert and, before going into Head House, wandered up the pitches to Badger's Retreat. At least this had been saved from Randal's bulldozers. It was bitterly cold and had been trying to snow, but only with the coming of night was it starting to settle. Flakes swirling against a dark yew reminded him of a bottle-green polka-dotted dress with a full skirt that Sally had worn on their first date.

How he had missed his trees in prison, and his stars, only a few of which at a time could be seen through his cell window, and most of all, his white dog, whom he kept thinking he saw in the snow shadows.

The tall ash that had taken the huge side branch off the Family Tree when it fell the night Charlie visited Bagley and Oriana came out had been sawn into logs. These had been neatly stacked, as had the logs from the branches off the Family Tree. Two men were making a bonfire out of the brushwood. All our life tidied away, thought Hengist. On other trees, where branches had been sawn off, the circular scars had not closed up at the top, like horseshoes nailed to the trunk.

I could do with some luck, reflected Hengist.

Oriana coming out had been such a tiny thing compared to losing Bagley, Fleetley and Education. Although Education would have been a two-edged sword, now he fully appreciated the ruthlessness of Jupiter, who had scuppered any hope of his return to Bagley. It was some comfort that Rupert had resigned from the New Reform Party.

But none of this mattered a jot compared to losing Sally and the desolation of stretching out in bed and finding her no longer by his side and having no one to share and recapture the tragedies and triumphs and laughter of thirty years.

Above, the snow now lining the limbs of the trees was like the body lotion Sally had rubbed into her arms every day, always making herself soft and beautiful for him. He had thrown away a pearl far richer than his tribe.

The three figures of the Family Tree, although battered, were still locked together. This year's riveted olive-green buds were already formed; Hengist picked up one of the curling sepia leaves with its cherry-red stem and put it in his pocket.

'"I have lived long enough,"' he quoted wearily:

'And that which should accompany old age,
As honour, love, obedience, troops of friends,
I must not hope to have.'

Oh, he'd loved his troops of friends, but they were as nothing,
again, compared with losing Sally. He had let her down, taken
her for granted, betrayed her. For the first time in years, in
prison, he'd had time to think.

He passed a young oak tree, planted 'In loving memory of that
great scholar and schoolmaster, Theo Graham'. Hengist wished
him well, free of pain in the Elysian Fields.

That must be Artie's work. The earth, although frozen, was
newly dug. Artie would make a strong, wise and compassionate
head.

Hengist had sent ahead a list of the books he particularly
wanted and, arriving at the house, found them awaiting him in
packing chests in the hall. On the hall table was a huge pile of
post, including an emerald-green carrier bag with an envelope
attached.

Recognizing the spiky handwriting, Hengist opened it:

Dear Mr Brett-Taylor [Paris had written],
 I wanted to thank you for everything. I've just retaken
history, and it was dead easy. I should get an A star, so a
middle finger to Boffin Brooks. I'm staying on now that Mr
Deverell's head and I'm going to work really hard to go to
your old college at Cambridge. I won't have any problem
with top-up fees as Theo left me everything.
 I'm sorry for all the trouble I caused you and Mrs B-T.
Please don't take this wrong, but it meant a lot that you
cared enough to cheat for me.
 Love from Paris
 PS Dora sends her love too.
 PPS These are for the journey.

Opening the carrier bag, Hengist found a can of Coke and
some tomato sandwiches with the crusts cut off, and broke down
and wept for the first time since he'd been arrested. Finally,
deciding he must pull himself together, he opened a second
letter, also recognizing the flashy, green scrawl.

'Dear Hengist,' Cosmo had written, 'I wonder if I could interview you for a programme I'm making for Channel 4 called
Cheating Heads.'

And Hengist laughed until he cried, and this was how Sally

found him as she tiptoed into the hall: once again the radiant, handsome, happy man she'd married. But when he turned, starting violently, she could see the deep lines of grief etching his face and that his thick, dark hair had gone completely grey.

'I didn't know you were going to be here,' he began.

'I wanted to see that everything was ...' stammered Sally, clutching on to the front door handle for support.

Next moment the lights went out and the whole campus was plunged in darkness.

'Oh sugar, I lent the torch to Dora. She and Paris have taken Elaine for a walk.'

Jumping every time they bumped into each other, aching with longing, they found some candles in the kitchen and lit them from the gas cooker. Taking a lit candle into the drawing room to light more candles, Hengist could dimly see the snow outside tumbling down, blanketing everything in whiteness, making the ugliest shapes beautiful. Thinking sadly that he would never have cause to read it again, Hengist spread the pages of the *TES* on the remains of last night's fire. To his amazement, after few seconds, the pages leapt into flame. From the ashes, thought Hengist.

Sally brought down thick jerseys for them both. Hengist noticed her hair had been newly washed – probably not for him – and her faint, familiar scent of red roses made his senses reel as it mingled with the smell of white hyacinths in the peacock-blue bowl on the low centre table. Sally had always staggered her planting of bulbs so they brought joy throughout the dark winter.

Hengist poured them both large Armagnacs and they sat on the carpet in front of the fire, separately pondering on the impossibility of dividing up their possessions or their lives.

Take what you want, they had both written to each other. But as the firelight flickered over the room, Sally noticed the bronze greyhound Hengist had given her to celebrate Cheerful Reply's victory, which had sealed their engagement. Then all the wedding presents, the little Sickert from her father and mother, the green Victorian paperweight from David Hawkley, the Rockingham Dalmatian from Rupert Campbell-Black and his then wife, Helen. How could you cut Sickerts and greyhounds in half? Or that lovely photograph of Oriana on graduation day or of Mungo on his first day at prep school?

On the piano – had Sally been playing it? wondered Hengist – was the music for the entrance of the priests in *The Magic Flute*, which had been played at their wedding. Next to it was a wedding photograph of Sally looking ecstatically happy. After a second glass of Armagnac and with the warmth of the fire bringing colour to her blanched cheeks, she looked just as young and pretty as on their first date.

'I feel guilty about taking so long, when Artie must want to move in,' she said helplessly, 'but I just don't know how to divide things up.'

'I'll cut out my heart and give it to you, it's yours anyway,' said Hengist in a low voice. 'I never wanted to leave, but I'd destroyed our marriage. I'd let you down irrevocably. It was the only option. You were right to tell me to go.'

'What are you going to do?' asked Sally.

'Write, I suppose. There's Tom and Matt to finish and I might have a crack at the novel on the Fronde. I'm sure it would sell more than Alex's apparatchik lit. I got a nice letter from Transworld saying they'd be interested in my memoirs.' Then, with difficulty: 'How's Elaine?'

'She misses you appallingly, she really pined.' Sally's voice trembled. 'In her gentle way, she never complained, but I think she should go with you.'

Then the lights flickered and went on. Both Hengist and Sally scrambled to their feet, gazing at each other, both aged as though blasted by lightning, but frantic to reach out.

'Fuck, fuck, fuck,' howled Hengist as the doorbell rang.

There was a pause, followed by quick steps, then a dark head came round the door. The skin was so smooth, the big eyes so large, clear and purple-shadowed, Hengist thought at first it was a pupil returned early.

'Hello, Mum,' said Oriana, then her face lit up:

'Dad, I didn't know you were here.'

'Just going,' mumbled Hengist.

A wail from the hall made them all jump.

'I've brought Wilfred, if that's all right.'

Going out into the hall, Oriana returned with the most adorable baby, strong, deep-blue-eyed, chubby-faced, with already a down of dark hair. Sally took him in ecstasy.

'What a splendid little chap.' She gazed at him in amazement that something so wholesome and beautifully formed should emerge from such a strange, unpropitious union.

'Look at his sweet hands and his lovely skin, and I love that track suit, it must be American, they make such fun clothes. Oh Oriana, he's heavenly.'

After a minute she handed him on to Hengist.

'I hope you don't mind us giving him Hengist as a second name, Dad,' stammered Oriana.

'Not at all. Very gratifying; he's beautiful,' said Hengist in a choked voice as he gazed in wonder at his grandson.

'We chose a fantastic guy as a donor,' said Oriana, 'a baseball champion, a summa cum laude at Harvard, so Wilfie'll probably end up playing rugger for England after all.'

Profoundly relieved that her parents were taking it so well, Oriana then asked them if they'd like to come to New York for the christening next month.

'Charlie's parents are utterly spooked by the whole me and Charlie scenario,' she went on. 'You two would add a wonderful normality to the whole thing and be brilliant for my street cred.'

'Not me, surely,' said Hengist quickly.

'Hush,' said Oriana, reaching up to kiss his rigid cheek.

'Where is Charlie?' asked Sally.

'In the car.'

'She must be frozen, go and get her.'

'Only if you'll agree to come to the christening and stay on for a week or two. You both need a holiday.'

Sally didn't answer. The grandfather clock continued its jerky tick.

Outside Hengist could just make out Elaine hurtling home through the snow, kicking up a white spray like a downhill racer. But still, for him, the chasm loomed. Still Sally didn't speak; then her hand slipped into his.

'Yes, we will,' she cried joyfully, 'that would be grand, Daddy and I would simply love to be there.'

ACKNOWLEDGEMENTS

During the four years I have been writing *Wicked!*, so many people from both the maintained and independent sectors helped me, that a list of them all would be longer than the book. Most of them were insanely overworked, which made their generosity with their time and ideas all the kinder.

I should add that all were in some way experts in their field, but because *Wicked!* is a work of fiction I only took their advice in so far as it suited my plot. The end product is no reflection on their expertise.

I must start by thanking two inspired heads from the maintained sector: Virginia Frayer and Katherine Eckersley, to whom *Wicked!* is dedicated, because of their devotion to their pupils and the heroic attempts both made to save two wonderful schools, the Angel, Islington, and Village High School, Derby, from closing down.

Both Virginia and Katherine are happily now in other jobs, but at the time they talked to me for hours with great courage and allowed me access to their schools. I was also lucky to receive similar help from another inspiring head, Gill Pyatt of Barnwood Park, Gloucester. This school met a happier fate in 2005, when the Tories snatched control of Gloucestershire and with an hour to spare dramatically reversed an inexplicable decision by the County Council to close it down. To prove the point, Barnwood Park was later in the year declared the fourth most improved school in the country.

I was also made hugely welcome by two other brilliant local heads, Jo Grills of Stroud High and Vivienne Warren of Archway, who let me rove round their schools talking to pupils and witnessing inspirational teaching. Other great heads included

Nigel Griffiths of John Kyrle School, Ross-on-Wye, Paul Eckersley of Selby High, Aydin Onac of Tewkesbury School, Jan Thompson of Cranham C. of E. Primary, Chris Steer of Sir Thomas Keble. I am also grateful for the shared wisdom of an awesome trio of former heads, Anthony Edkins, Jill Clough and Marie Stubbs.

The independent sector was equally helpful and I owe a massive debt of gratitude to two most humane and charming head-masters: Martin Stephen of St Paul's and Tim Hastie-Smith of Dean Close. They were always there when I needed help and gave me wise and witty advice on everything from royal visits to the endless speeches that bedevil a head at the beginning of term. In Tim's case, because Dean Close is indeed geographically close, I was allowed frequent access to his lovely school and enchanting staff and pupils.

I was also uniquely privileged to be able to pick the very con-siderable brains of two charismatic former heads, Dennis Silk of Radley and Ian Beer of Harrow, and to enjoy the beguiling com-pany of Tom Weare of Bryanston, Peter Johnson of Millfield, Angus McPhail of Radley and Jennie Stephen of South Hampstead High School.

An incredibly valuable slant on school life was provided by headmasters' wives, who included Diana Silk, Angela Beer, Joanne Hastie-Smith, Joanna Seldon, by a headmistress's husband John Thompson and masters' wives Dee Brown and Emily Clark.

I would like to thank Hamish Aird, our son's Social Tutor and former Sub-Warden of Radley, for his wisdom over the years. Special gratitude is due to Colin Belford, Deputy Head of Archway, for his advice on everything and for being an absolute charmer, to Tony Marchand, Deputy Head (Academic) at Dean Close, for his help on exam procedure, and to Simon Smith, Deputy Head of Brighton College, who invited me down to his school to witness a most successful partnership scheme between the College and Falmer, a local comprehensive, which was crucial to the plot of *Wicked!* Martin Green from Brighton College, Norma Smith and Rose Styman from Falmer and both sets of pupils were also marvellously eloquent on the subject.

The teaching I witnessed on numerous occasions made me long to be back at school again. From Stroud High, Kathryn Loveridge was inspirational on the *Odes* of Horace, and Andy Webb on *Romeo and Juliet*, as was Guy Burge from the Angel, Islington, on English grammar, Steve and Ray Jones from Village High School on all aspects of GCSE history, Paul Davies from Dean Close on the Russian Revolution, Claire Matthews and John Evans from Archway respectively on *Macbeth* and football, while from

Barnwood Park, Ursula Jeakins excelled in French, Gill Moseley on music and Beverley Atkinson, Head of Science, was particularly brilliant on explosions.

I also had most rewarding input from other wonderful teachers: Veronica Rock, Colin Dodds, Judith Drury, Di Medland, Dominic Hayne, Jose Hellet, Vanessa Macmillan, Anita Bradnum, Suzy Hearn, Sue Dean, who wrote a wonderful pantomime, Jill Barrow, Bob and Fran Peel, Andrew Cleary, Andrew Robinson, Vaughan Clark, Justin Nolan, Ailsa Chapman, Corinne Pierre, Trish Hillier, Carole Roome and Josephine Sutton.

In order to experience the terrors of teaching, I did give a two-hour lesson at Barnwood Park, in which I tried to explain to different groups the mysteries of writing a book and seeing it through to publication. As homework I set a task of designing a book jacket for *Wicked!* The results were fabulous and the children delightful. Nevertheless I needed to sleep for three days afterwards and was, as a result, even more overwhelmed with admiration as to how teachers can go so cheerfully through the same process day in, day out, thirty-nine weeks of the year – partly because they get such fantastic support from the non-teaching staff. On this front I'd like to thank Naomi McMahon, Marian Shergold, Margaret Turner, Clare Walsh, Brenda Dew, Ann Cave, Ali Sim and Jane Harrington for the support they in turn gave me.

I'm also grateful to those unsung heroes, the governors, who put in hours of unpaid work supporting their respective schools, and who were particularly patient in explaining the role they play. They include Peter Nesbitt, David Corbett, Deborah Priestley, Mark Westbrook and Mark Barty-King.

The true heroes of *Wicked!*, however, are the pupils. It is impossible for me to express my appreciation of those who helped me and the enthusiasm with which they entered into the whole adventure. Not a day passed without letters decorated with Pooh and Eeyore or Wallace and Gromit winging their way from Bryanston or Queen Anne's, Caversham, cataloguing the latest high jinks whilst stressing how hard everyone was working!

A stars must go to Tom Barber of Dean Close, for his marvellous run-down on life at a public school, to Carl Pearson, whose beautiful essay *My Dream* is reproduced on page 708, to Mabel McKeown and Anastasia Jennings for such entertaining dispatches from the front and to Karina Clutterbuck, who showed me how to turn an ink blob into a peacock feather.

Other pupils, who regaled me with riotous anecdotes and painstakingly initiated me into the mysteries of mocks and modules, include Henrietta Abel-Smith, Phoebe Adler, Jenny Frings, Alana Nash, Sam Muskett, Georgia Morgan, Georgie Klein, Jessica Seldon, Kit Cooper, Frankie Hildick-Smith, Ned Wyndham, Max Morgan, Teddy Chadd, Theo Hodson, Freddie Miles, Robbie McColl, Sarah Kilmister, James Bowler, Harriet Manners, Georgie Clarkson-Webb, Leo Robson, James Merry, Michael Dhenin, Sam Rogerson, Dean Monahan, Charmaine Moss, Michelle Pickering, Lauren Doble, Harry Flinder, Natalie Torr, Carmelita Winslow, Anthony Scott and many others.

I cannot emphasize too strongly how genuinely bright and good-hearted these children were and would like to stress that although pupils, teachers, parents and supporting cast behave by turns heroically and simply dreadfully in *Wicked!*, no character is based on anyone living. Any coincidence is accidental, unless they are as eminent as Her Majesty the Queen or Lord Puttnam and appear as themselves.

I was lucky enough to be invited on four occasions by Lord Puttnam to one of the happiest events in the school calendar, the National Teaching Awards. Here I enjoyed great teaching, was beautifully looked after by Carolyn Taylor and Sarah Davey and revelled in the company of the Awards' irrepressible anchorman Eamonn Holmes and BBC producer, Kate Shiers. I hope I will be forgiven for inserting an extra category into the 2004 Awards.

A hugely enjoyable event in the independent calendar was the 2004 Headmasters' Conference in St Andrews, where I stayed at the lovely St Andrews Bay Hotel and found myself in the company of Titans. Here I would like to thank Martin Stephen for inviting me and Roger Peel and Chris Addy for their wonderful organization.

A large section of *Wicked!* is taken up with all aspects of GCSE, which I found unbelievably complicated, particularly when I introduced a mature student. I must thank Helen Claridge, Moira Gage, the exam officer of Stroud High, Cathie Shovlin of OCR, Madeleine Fowler and Yvonne Hutchinson-Ruff of Stroud College. They were all heroic in their attempts to explain things. I hope the liberties I've taken aren't too flagrant.

Education has many luminaries supporting it from the outside, so I am equally grateful to Margaret Davies of Capita, who came in like Red Adair in a skirt to galvanize the LEA in Gloucestershire, to Andrew Flack, Director of Education at Derby City Council, to Dr Judy Coultars, Human Centre Technology Group, University of Sussex, to Jonquil Dodd, Senior Research Officer (Performance) Gloucestershire Education; and from Gloucestershire Social Services: Margaret Sheather, Executive

Director, Alan Barton, Complaints Manager and Cathie Shea, Looked-After-Children Manager of Gloucestershire Social Services, Pat Gifford, Education Liaison Officer, Gloucestershire Children and Young People's Services, and to the staff of the former Causeway Care Home, Stroud. All nobly gave me their time.

I also had wonderful advice from Anne Clark, Lib Dem Councillor for Cotswold District Council and from Tory Councillors Jackie Hall and Andrew Gravells of Gloucestershire County Council who were both hugely instrumental in saving Barnwood Park School from closure in the nick of time.

My characters, both human and animal, sometimes fall ill and make miraculous recoveries, so I was lucky to be able to consult Dr Laurence Fielder and Dr Tim Crouch at Frithwood Surgery and John Hunter and his team at Bowbridge Veterinary Surgery. Carole Lee and Judy Zatonski from Greyhound Rescue, West of England and the Celia Cross Trust inspired me on Greyhounds.

I needed an exciting team-building activity in *Wicked!* to unite my two schools when they first meet. Hazel Heron of Roedean suggested I spoke to Ian Davies of Pinnacle Training, who in turn suggested a brilliant competition when groups of pupils compete to be the first to build and fly a hot air balloon.

There is a lot of rugger in *Wicked!* Here I got wonderful assistance from Matthew Evans of BBC Cardiff, David and Justine Pickering, Ralph Bucknell, Phil Butler and in particular from Stephanie Metson, Marketing Manager of the beautiful Vale Hotel, Glamorgan, known as the Lucky Hotel, because subsequently successful teams so often hole up there before big games. Stephanie showed me the vast indoor arena and entertained me royally.

On the sartorial front Robert Hartop of Grooms Formal Hire, Andoversford, initiated me into the latest fashion in men's evening wear, while Mariska Kay and Lindka Cierach advised me on lovely women's clothes. Duncan Armstrong, my bank manager at Coutts, and Stephen Foakes, my former bank manager, were brilliant on money. Dear Stephen Simpson of Hatchards is again to be hugely thanked for tenaciously tracking down any books I needed. Sounds Good of Cheltenham did the same for CDs. I am extremely grateful too to the resourceful and unflappable Phil Bradley of Cornerstones for driving me from school to school.

I am also indebted to Diane Law at Manchester United, Andrew Yeatman at the Met Office, Marc Stevens at the LSO for answering complicated queries and to Mike Zealey of ISIS, Lyn Sweeney and Sarah Hutchens for checking facts.

Gloucestershire police, as always, have been marvellous, answering my endless questions with patience, humour and imagination. I'd particularly like to thank Inspector Chris Hill for his advice on royal visits, Marie Watton, DC Liz Smith and Child Protection Officer DC Ian Bennett.

Last year saw the tragic, untimely death of Gil Martin, horse and lurcher lover and ex-super sleuth of Gloucestershire CID, who for fifteen years had advised me on all matters criminal. Gil was a brilliant, kind, enchanting man, whose loss to his family and legion of friends is immeasurable.

One of my heroes in *Wicked!* spends twelve years in care. On a train to Swindon, I was therefore very lucky to meet Josephine Cook, who told me most movingly about her experiences as a foster child. I am also grateful to Phil Frampton and Paolo Hewitt who each survived heartbreakingly harrowing childhoods in care to produce marvellous memoirs: *The Golly in the Cupboard* and *The Looked After Kid* respectively. Both books were an inspiration and both men, I'm proud to think, have become friends.

I am also beholden to the authors of the following books which provided both enlightenment and factual background: *Ahead of the Class* by Marie Stubbs, *Handsworth Revolution* by David Winkley, *But Headmaster!* by Ian Beer, *Why Schools Fail* by Jill Clough, *Special* by Bella Bathurst and the invaluable *Good Neighbours* by the Independent Schools Council.

Journalists do not automatically expect kindness from their own profession. Few, however, could have been more charming and helpful than Sarah Bayliss, editor of *The Times Educational Supplement*'s *Friday Magazine*, Rachel Johnson, Julie Henry, Amelia Hill, Geraldine Hackett, Quentin Letts, Chris Bunting, Will Woodward, Jo Scriven and Fay Millar of the Brighton *Argus*. I must also thank *The Times Educational Supplement*, who produce enough good stories every week to furnish a hundred novels, for keeping me up with events. Our local press were also an endless support. Ian Mean of *The Citizen*, Anita Syvret of the *Gloucestershire Echo*, Skip Walker, former editor, and Sue Smith, present editor of the *Stroud News & Journal*, so often paved the way for me with local schools.

Gold stars must especially go to *Guardian* writer Jonathan Freedland and Wendy Wallace of *Friday Magazine* whose moving pieces on the imminent closing of the Angel, Islington, and the rejuvenation of Village High School, Derby, sowed the seeds of so much of *Wicked!*

My friends, as usual, deserve straight As. Caterina Krucker, a lecturer in modern languages, was a shining example of the passion and effort that goes into preparing and delivering a great lesson. Edward Thring was magisterial on bursars, Marcus Clapham great on Greece, Pete Hendy on Ofsted and anything scientific, Andrew Parker Bowles on racing and Bill Holland on music. Peter Clarkson, Associate Lecturer on Art History at the Open University, lent me endless books and his marvellous thesis on the concept of chivalry and mediaevalism in Cheltenham public school architecture, and Paul Morrison was illuminating on developers. John and Anne Cooper valiantly tried to untangle the red tape of education law. Jo Xuereb-Brennan was dazzling on acronyms. My brother Timothy Sallitt and his wife Angela were funny as ever on everything. Other friends who came up with great ideas include Shona Williams, Jill Reay, David Fyfe-Jamieson, Derick Davin, Jane Workman, Peregrine Hodson, Marion Carver, Tim Griffiths, Susannah and Bill Franklyn, Sue Lauzier, Jane Farrow, Bill Holland, Liz and Michael Flint, Rosemary Nunneley, William and Caroline Nunneley, Marjorie Dent, Heather Ross, Anna Gibbs-Kennet, Rupert Miles, Roz Murray-Smith, Anna Wing, Janetta Lee, Joyce Ball and Karina Gabner.

I must also apologize to all the people who helped me who I have forgotten to include.

My marvellous publishers Transworld are a constant joy to deal with and I was particularly touched that Gail Rebuck, Larry Finlay and Patrick Janson-Smith kept in touch during the long haul, and never chided me for delivering late.

At the risk of adjectival overkill, I am convinced I have the sweetest, most encouraging editor in Linda Evans, the nicest, most charismatic publicity directors in Nicky Henderson and Patsy Irwin and the kindest, wisest, most cheering-up agent in Vivienne Schuster of Curtis Brown. No author is so blessed. Nor should Laura Gammell, Anneliese Bridges and Stephanie Thwaites who assist them, be forgotten. Nor Richenda Todd, my brilliant copy-editor, and Deborah Adams, who gave splendid help at proof stage.

On the home front, it is hard to describe my gratitude to my PA Pam Dhenin for masterminding the production of such a vast ungainly manuscript. I thank her for her tolerance, huge encouragement and for never complaining about my appallingly indecipherable writing as draft after endless draft was followed by interminable corrections and checking. Great chunks of the manuscript were also typed equally brilliantly and heroically by Annette Xuereb-Brennan, Mandy Williams, Pippa Birch and Zoë Dhenin, who all deserved A stars for pitching in with suggestions, and producing the most beautiful typescript at phenomenal speed. Zoë Dhenin is also to be thanked for checking endless facts and tracking down everything from hotels in Baghdad to Croatian Christian names.

Other A stars should be awarded to my wonderful housekeeper Ann Mills and to dear Moira Hatherall, who restore order out of chaos, prevent the house disappearing under a tidal wave of paper and provide so much comfort and laughter.

Most of all I must thank my sweet family for putting up with force ten sighs and utter neglect for months on end. My husband Leo, our son Felix and his wife Edwina, our daughter Emily and her husband Adam Tarrant, our grandson Jago, and five excellent cats, all provide an essential mix of love, fantastic copy and endless good cheer.

Connecting with Culture

Readings for Writers

Greg Barnhisel

Duquesne University

PEARSON

Boston   Columbus   Indianapolis   New York   San Francisco
Upper Saddle River   Amsterdam   Cape Town   Dubai   London   Madrid
Milan   Munich   Paris   Montreal   Toronto   Delhi   Mexico City
São Paulo   Sydney   Hong Kong   Seoul   Singapore   Taipei   Tokyo

Senior Acquisitions Editor: Lauren A. Finn
Senior Marketing Manager: Sandra McGuire
Senior Supplements Editor: Donna Campion
Production Manager: Denise Phillip
Project Coordination, Text Design, and Electronic Page Makeup: Integra
Cover Design Manager: Wendy Ann Fredericks
Cover Designer: Nancy Sacks
Cover Photo: John Lund/Blend Images/Gettyimages
Senior Manufacturing Buyer: Roy Pickering
Printer/Binder: R.R. Donnelley/Harrisonburg
Cover Printer: R.R. Donnelley/Harrisonburg

Library of Congress Cataloging-in-Publication Data
Barnhisel, Greg
  Connecting with Culture / [edited by] Greg Barnhisel.—1st ed.
    p. cm.
  ISBN-13: 978-0-205-74188-5 (alk. paper)
  ISBN-10: 0-205-74188-6 (alk. paper)
  1. College readers.   2. English language—Rhetoric—Study and teaching
  (Higher) I. Title.
  PE1417.B357 2012
  808'.0427—dc23

                                                          2011029792

10 9 8 7 6 5 4 3 2 1—DOH—14 13 12 11

ISBN 10: 0-205-74188-6
ISBN 13: 978-0-205-74188-5

Contents

Chapter 2   What Does it Mean to "Write Critically?"   30

Chapter 3   What Does it Mean to "Write Persuasively?"   59

Chapter 6   How Do We Work Today, and How Will We Work Tomorrow?   229

Chapter 7   What Makes a Family?   295

Chapter 8   What Spaces Do You Inhabit?   340

Chapter 9   How True Is Scientific "Truth"?   424

Chapter 10   Are We What We Eat?   516

Preface

The first-year writing course—the course for which *Connecting with Culture* is designed—frequently serves as a cornerstone for a college's general-education requirements. The first-year writing course trains students in the critical reading, critical thinking, and writing skills necessary for many of their other classes. But at the same time the first-year writing class is also a place where students make connections between disciplines, between ways of thinking, between ideas. Writing classes put ideas in conversation with each other; the student's job is to make explicit the connections between those ideas, and then to connect those ideas with the student's own. For this reason, the central intellectual exercise this book encourages is *making connections*. Chapters 1–3 of this book stress these key skills, and particularly emphasize the importance of careful, critical reading (a skill which appears to be in decline, as many instructors have observed).

Connecting with Culture's readings chapters (4–10) consist of thematically connected pieces, and the reading questions that follow ask students to identify and respond to those connections. While "connection" in the sense of linking diverse ideas and arguments is the method that this book uses to teach writing, the book is also thematically concerned with another important meaning of "connection": our use of communications technology. To be "connected" is, of course, to be in communication with a network, whether the Internet or a cell phone network or a college intraweb. Many of the pieces in each of the readings chapters focus on the effect of our communications technologies and how the new world that these technologies are forging will affect students' future work lives, family lives, intellectual development, and even physical health.

These readings take a diverse range of positions of this issue of being perpetually connected. Andrew Sullivan describes, in Chapter 4's "Why I Blog," how the practices people have developed for reading material on the Web helped him and many others to create an entirely new genre of writing: the blog. Several authors in several different chapters examine the unexpected consequences of our connected lives on job searching, on our privacy, and on what we eat.

In one of my favorite pieces in the entire book, Zadie Smith reviews the 2010 film *The Social Network*, a fictionalized version of the genesis of Facebook. For Smith, being "connected" virtually seems to substitute for real kinds of connections between people, and she wonders, "is that all there is?" It is not enough for her just to be "connected" through our technologies to other people and places. There's connection—and there's real engagement. In Smith's view, the metaphor of "connection" that we increasingly use to refer to the ways that our technologies allow us to communicate is losing a sense of real personal connection—a Facebook friend and a real friend, Smith suggests, are quite different.

In a larger sense, this text encourages students to "connect" to the larger issues going on in the culture around them. Many commentators—including Ron Alsop in his piece on "The 'Trophy Kids' Go To Work" in Chapter 6 of this book—have suggested that the "millennial generation" is unprecedentedly inward-looking and narcissistic; they connect with the world around them, the argument goes, only as spectators or as seekers of diversion or praise. While it is uncertain that any generation can be so characterized, the readings and written questions in *Connecting with Culture* are intended to draw students into cultural conversations around issues—"connecting" them to these conversations and inviting them to contribute.

FEATURES OF THE TEXT

Instruction in Reading, Writing, and Argument

Connecting with Culture combines three chapters of writing and critical-reading instruction with seven chapters of readings in broad cultural topics. The instructional chapters are predicated on the belief that critical reading suffers because the writing in digital environments privileges brevity, immediacy, and casualness. Chapter 1, "What Does It Mean to 'Read Critically,'" acknowledges the value and importance of this kind of writing but at the same time lays out a way for students to develop, and instructors to teach, a critical-reading process more suited for the longer, more complicated, and more nuanced readings that students will be doing in college. In Chapter 1, for instance, students are asked to differentiate knowing, comprehending, and recalling material they've read, and to use those preliminary stages to then "question the text." Chapters 2 and 3 put those skills into practice in low-stakes writing exercises. While Chapter 2 centers on student writing informed by critical reading of sources, Chapter 3 provides a brief introduction to the classical appeals, to audience analysis, and to identifying audience, forum, occasion, and the appeals in rhetorical analysis.

Included in the first chapter are three graphics intended to call attention to key problems in doing online research. Annotated screenshots explain three of the most popular places where students begin their research work: a Google search, a Wikipedia entry, and the front page of a news-aggregator site. Students need to read their Web resources with the same critical, analytical eye that we are encouraging them to apply to the readings in the book, and these graphics are intended to underscore this imperative.

Readings Arranged Thematically

Each of the seven readings chapters is divided into two "clusters": one a set of four or five readings on a very specific issue from a variety of social and political perspectives, and one a set of three or four readings that give broader takes on the issue. Each cluster, moreover, features multiple *kinds* of writing, from blog posts to journalism to cultural criticism to academic or scholarly writing, and the headnotes and questions following each reading ask students to take the piece's audience and forum into consideration. Each chapter includes several source-based readings accompanied by questions that require students to examine precisely how this author chose, read, incorporated, and documented sources in the article. Some readings in each chapter will be taken from the very contingent and temporary world of online-native writing—blogging or user-generated comment forums—with explicit attention in the headnotes and reading questions to how the temporariness of those arenas generates a particular *kind* of content (as with Sullivan's "Why I Blog"). In fact, one of the readings even includes the comment thread from the original online text, and asks students to think about how a piece of writing changes when the writer can and does interact with readers. The readings chapters also include images such as editorial cartoons, advertisements, photographs, stills from movies and TV shows, screen captures, and so on. Similar questions follow the images, asking students to "read" images using the same rhetorical-analysis tools as they employ in analyzing verbal texts.

Apparatus for Analysis and Writing

Questions after each reading include three types with distinct purposes:

- "Summarizing the Text" questions help students understand central ideas within the text;

- "Establishing the Context" questions examine how the author appeals to his specific audience and takes into consideration forum and occasion;

- "Responding to the Message" questions ask students to create connections either between the reading and another in the book or between the reading and other material from outside the text, including their own experiences.

In addition, questions at the end of each chapter include the below.

- "Questions for Short Projects or Group Presentations" offer opportunities for brief writing in which students connect ideas and readings from the chapter to pieces in other chapters or to material in the larger world;

- "Questions for Formal Essays" can be used for longer and more formal essay prompts. Some are grounded solely in a single text; some ask students to compare multiple articles from the book; some explicitly encourage outside research in the pursuit of a larger topic; and others present opportunities for multimodal writing projects such as a photo essay, a feature story for a magazine, a Web site with hyperlinks, and more.

SUPPLEMENTS

Instructor's Manual

The Instructor's Manual for *Connecting with Culture* has been designed to provide guidance for inexperienced instructors and veterans alike. The IM includes general ideas about how instructors might approach teaching the first three chapters, as well as specific suggestions for in-class activities and formal writing assignments that can supplement the material in the chapters themselves. For the seven readings chapters (4–10), the IM includes answers to the readings questions that follow each selection as well as ideas for teaching the clusters as units unto themselves.

Instructors don't always love to teach books sequentially, from page 1 through to the index. We like to bring our own ideas and direction to our writing courses. For that reason, the IM includes a set of alternate tables of contents and syllabi for instructors who might want to organize their courses along thematic lines, according to the genres of writing included in the book, or in order to foreground modes of argument (definitional, evaluative, proposal, etc.). These sample syllabi and alternate TOCs should help any instructor reconfigure the content of the book to better suit his or her particular approach to teaching the first-year composition class.

mycomplab ▌ The only online application to integrate a writing environment with proven resources for grammar, writing, and research, MyCompLab gives students help at their fingertips as they draft and revise. Instructors have access to a variety of assessment tools including commenting capabilities, diagnostics and study plans, and an e-portfolio. Created after years of extensive research and in partnership with faculty and students across the country, MyCompLab offers a seamless and flexible teaching and learning environment built specifically for writers.

ACKNOWLEDGMENTS

Thanks and gratitude for ideas, inspiration, moral support, and hard work go to Craig Bernier, Jennifer Collins, Michelle Gaffey, Nora McBurney, Mary Parish, Dean Rader, Jonathan Silverman, Jeff Stoyanoff, Dan Watkins, and Mike Wong. The faculty and staff of the first-year writing program and the English department at Duquesne University deserve thanks not just for all the ideas I get from being around you, but for doing such a great job at teaching writing. Of course, this book would not exist without Lauren Finn and the staff at Pearson Longman. Finally, as ever, thanks and love to Alison, Jack, and Beckett for your help and patience.

Thanks also go to all of the colleagues who reviewed the manuscript and who offered keen insights: Jo Ann M. Bamdas, Palm Beach State College; Allison Boldt, Middle Tennessee State University; Tamara Ponzo Brattoli, Joliet Junior College; Patricia Boyd, Arizona State University; Mary A. Cooksey, Indiana University East; Jennifer Diamond, Bucks County Community College; Marilu dos Santos, South Suburban College; Kevin Dyer, North Carolina Central University; Jason D. Fichtel, Joliet Junior College; Africa Fine, Palm Beach State College; Amy Friedman, Temple University; Carole Ganim, Miami University Middletown; Rachael Groner, Temple University; Lisa Grunberger, Temple University; Barbara E. Hamilton, Montclair State University; Kerry A. Hillis, Middle Tennessee State University; Adrianne Hopes, Montclair State University; Brooke Hughes, California State University, Bakersfield; Cecile Kandl, Bucks County Community College; Parmita Kapadia, Northern Kentucky University;

Martin Lastrapes, Chaffey College; Vanessa McLaughlin, Penn State University; Shannon R. Mortimore-Smith, Shippensburg University; Patty Schumacher, Northern Kentucky University; Lisa Shaw, Miami Dade College North; Lori Vail, Green River Community College; Shannon Walters, Temple University; Stacia Watkins, Lipscomb University; Kathryn Wymer, North Carolina Central University; Richard Zumkhawala-Cook, Shippensburg University.

What Does it Mean to "Read Critically?"

In 2004, the National Endowment for the Arts (NEA), a U.S. government agency, released a report entitled "To Read or Not To Read" that concluded that the number of Americans who read literature for pleasure was plunging. Three years later, an Associated Press poll found that 27 percent of Americans hadn't read a book in the previous year. Declaring that the decline of reading was a "national crisis," NEA head and poet Dana Gioia explained in a press conference that

> Reading develops a capacity for focused attention and imaginative growth that enriches both private and public life. The decline in reading among every segment of the adult population reflects a general collapse in advanced literacy. To lose this human capacity—and all the diverse benefits it fosters—impoverishes both cultural and civic life.

But wait. Something about the conclusions that Gioia, and many other commentators, drew seems wrong. The NEA survey documented a drop in the number of Americans who read *literature*. The AP's poll asked people about whether they read a "book." But Gioia's statement says that there was a decline in "reading"—does the evidence actually support his point? Can one "read" things that are not books?

Obviously, one can. We all spend our days "reading" a vast array of texts: magazines, newspapers, text messages, emails, Web pages, Facebook updates, billboards, lecture notes. Because of the explosion

Former National Endowment for the Arts chairman and poet Dana Gioia

of information technology, many of us read *more* than we used to, spending hours surfing the net and reading Web pages. Books, too, are not necessarily books anymore, as anyone with a Kindle or an iPad can attest. And if we expand our definition of *reading* beyond the obvious one of "looking at words," we read even more. If *reading* also means "deciphering meaning in symbols and actions and events," we "read" facial expressions, we "read" advertisements, and we "read" buildings and clothing and cars for what they tell us about the inhabitants and wearers and drivers. By this logic, it's far from true that reading is in decline.

So on this level, Gioia seems to have committed what's called a *logical fallacy*—he's drawn a conclusion from insufficient evidence, made a potentially false generalization. But does this mean that we should discount his point entirely? Gioia says that reading "develops a capacity for focused attention and imaginative growth." This capacity "enriches both private and public life," and its decline, or loss, "impoverishes both cultural and civic life."

While one might not agree with Gioia's implicit assumption that only *literature* does these good things, his argument about what reading does has much more traction. Most of us believe—as Gioia appears to, as well—that we must develop the ability to give "focused attention" to some matters. Many issues that we wrestle with in our society are extremely complex and require focused attention in order to understand them. Without giving focused attention to, for example, the complexities of the American health care system or the dynamics of climate change, our national debate about how to handle these issues will be "impoverished."

Another of Gioia's implicit assumptions is probably pretty valid or widely held: when we read literature, we give it a kind of focused and sustained attention that we don't give to other things we read, such as emails or text messages or billboards or celebrity gossip posted on a website. Literature in particular, and books in general, requires us to focus on the words and concepts and to *extend* our attention—reading a book may take weeks, and we must keep its ideas in our heads and mull them over even during the times we are not actually reading. Thinking deeply and over a long period of time about an idea is a wonderful way to form a mature and rea- soned response to that idea, and reading literature fosters that kind of thinking.

Building on what Gioia said, one of the premises of *Connecting with Culture* is that careful reading is a fundamentally necessary and ethical act in a democracy. Our society is grounded on the premise that all citizens have an equal right to express themselves; the right to vote and the right of free speech guarantee that. And since a democ- racy makes decisions by weighing the various arguments about an issue, it is crucial that we read and understand those arguments—it's our ethical obligation to our fellow citizens, and it's our social obliga- tion to make the best decisions for our society. So even though this NEA report and the AP poll might not be as alarming as Gioia or many others made them out to be, there are important differences between reading books and literature and reading text messages and Web dispatches, and the skills cultivated by reading and really engag- ing with longer pieces are skills crucial to our civic life and personal intellectual development.

Furthermore, both of these studies raise the "why" question. Why is reading on the decline? Some easy ideas proliferate—blaming the Internet always seems to be popular, for instance, and others speculate that there are just so many other ways out there for people to get their entertainment. But the reports don't suggest causes for the phenomenon so much as they conjecture possible results of it (such as the impoverishment of our democracy). Taking in these reports, many readers or audiences might be spurred to wonder about *why* fewer people read literature.

Finally, just because something is happening now doesn't mean that it will necessarily continue to happen in the same way. In fact, in 2009, the NEA released another study (entitled *Reading on the Rise*) concluding that *more* people were reading literature, that a higher percentage of adults were reading literature, and that the demographic group that showed the greatest increase in literary reading—+21 percent—was

18- to 24-year-olds. Knowing this, how does it change our understanding of the 2004 NEA study and the 2007 AP poll?

What I've just done in the preceding paragraphs is engage in what's called **reading critically**. Critical reading is the foundation for much of what you'll do in college, and helping hone your critical-reading skills is a primary aim of this book.

Critical reading begins simply with comprehension: do you understand what the writer is saying? Most of us are able to accomplish reading at that level, unless we are reading material meant for specialists in a particular field—a manual for software coders or an article in a pharmacological journal. But critical reading doesn't stop at mere comprehension.

After basic comprehension, the next step a critical reader takes is to compose—even if only mentally—a rough **summary** of the writer's point. In your writing classes, often your instructors will have you actually write a summary, but the object of a summary is to help you **understand the writer's point and argument so well that you can accurately put it in your own words and work with it**. When you read something difficult that you need to understand and retain, you probably already do this: you complete reading the text and then create a brief summary of it for further use, almost as a "mental note."

After the summary, a critical reading proceeds to **analysis**. Analysis, in turn, consists of dozens of separate operations. Although many are performed just in our minds, the previous responses to Gioia did a few explicitly. For one, I identified **unstated assumptions** in Gioia's comments, and I also questioned the **definition of key terms** such as *reading*. How can a definition be anything but an unquestioned fact? Gioia seemed to be saying that reading was what we did to literature, while the analysis countered that we read all sorts of other texts. In the later chapters of this book, you will be provided with many questions that will help you in the process of analyzing a piece of writing. Analysis also includes identifying what the text is doing— identifying a phenomenon and speculating about the possible results of that phenomenon—and what the text is *not* doing.

Finally, a critical reading forms the basis for an **informed response**. You'll notice that the response to Gioia's words and to the report and poll agreed and disagreed with parts and used their ideas as starting points for other ideas. A critical reading can provide us with the ability not only to respond to the text directly, but also to use that text to develop our own ideas about related topics. Through this, we "enter the conversation" about an idea, even if the original text is one with which we disagree.

In this chapter, we'll look at strategies for active, engaged, critical reading, in order to prepare you to conduct critical readings and written responses to the writings included in this book.

WHAT'S THE USE OF CRITICAL READING?

Why, a critical reader of this chapter might ask, is critical reading so important? Particularly if we are being asked to read material that might be (to put it neutrally) of minimal interest to us, why is it important to expend that extra energy? There are at least two good answers for this.

Although, as the author, I like to think that thousands of readers purchased this book out of a fascination with the topic, I realize that pretty much everyone looking at this page was required to buy and read this book in conjunction with a writing class, probably of the first-year composition variety. I will also conclude that most people who take such courses do so because they're required; that they want to fulfill their requirements because they want to obtain their degree; and that they want a degree because it qualifies them, directly or indirectly, for a career.

Given that, here's my first answer to the "why" question. **Because college isn't about rote memorization and recitation**. Of course, any degree program in any major will include some work that is just memorization. History, organic chemistry, nursing, information sciences, even philosophy and art—all of these programs require students to retain and, at some point, regurgitate lists of facts. However, all of these programs also require students to **apply** that knowledge, to **respond to** that knowledge, to **use that knowledge** in new ways, even to **question where that knowledge came from**. These skills— which can differentiate barely competent employees from innovative professionals—come from critical reading.

The habits you'll develop by critically reading the texts in this book, then, will prepare you for the things you'll have to do in your profession. As a pharmacist, you might not remember what Andrew Sullivan had to say about blogging, and as a lawyer, you may not need to use Stephen Dubner's debunking of the "locavorism" movement. However, your ability to read, understand, summarize, question, respond to, and extrapolate from information *will* be of use in those professions, and any other profession.

Reading, understanding, and retaining information is a necessary first step toward knowledge. Critical reading, though, takes you to where you can assess the value of that information, use it in new ways, and synthesize it with other information.

The second reason that critical reading is a crucial skill has less to do with your education than it does with your future as a participant in a democratic society. In the United States, we make important decisions through a process of civic dialogue. Politicians, corporations, interest groups, and voters express their views on an issue in simple ways (informal meetings) and sophisticated ways (television commercials, websites, speeches). But all of those expressions are examples of **rhetoric**—attempts to persuade you of something.

Rhetoric demands critical reading. Primarily, it's important to be able to pull apart *how* something is attempting to move you to action. Is it playing on your emotions? Does the solution it proposes actually solve the problem? Are the facts it relies upon valid? But we must also critically read rhetoric in order to hear the other participants in our society, and understand what they actually are saying. Critical reading isn't just critical; it's a form of respect for someone else's words and ideas.

THE FIRST STEP IN CRITICAL READING: KNOWING, COMPREHENDING, AND RECALLING

It goes without saying that the first step in critical reading is simply understanding what a text or passage has to say, and being able to repeat that understanding or even to put the information presented in the text into one's own words. Let's take a simple example. Read the following text, and then close the book and say or write down—in your own words—the information it presents.

In poker, a flush beats a straight.

Easy, right? Perhaps not. It's certainly easy to "know" this information and "recall" or repeat it back to a listener in one's own words: "In poker, a flush is superior to a straight."

But in order truly to "comprehend" or understand it, this passage demands quite a bit of specialized knowledge from the reader. First of all, a reader must know that "poker" is a game played with a standard deck of playing cards—"standard" meaning the Anglo-American deck consisting of four suits (diamonds, hearts, clubs, and spades), each with an ace, nine numbered cards, and three "face cards." One must also know that "flush" and "straight" are descriptions of types of "hands"—a way of classifying the cards one holds at a given time. Finally, one must know that a "flush" describes a "hand" with five cards of the same suit, and a "straight" indicates a run of five cards in sequential order.

The point here is that simple knowledge and recall don't necessarily also indicate comprehension. This example might be simple for you, but let's take another couple of examples to demonstrate that "knowing" and "recalling" don't necessarily mean "comprehending":

The EKG shows atrial fibrillation.

Or

Antinomianism was a product of Pauline times.

Both of these examples are more difficult than the first one to put into your own words. That's because each relies on **specialized vocabulary**. You may have already noticed that, in the classes you are taking in college, you are exposed to much more specialized vocabulary than you ever have been. Every discipline, every class has its own words and terms that aren't used anywhere else. More problematic is that these specialized words can't be skipped over: in order to understand the sentence at its most basic level, you need to understand those words.

Comprehension, then, requires that a reader identify any terms he or she doesn't understand and find out what those terms mean in that specific context. Identifying key terms, and knowing what those terms mean in that text, is necessary for critical reading. You are already familiar with several ways of figuring out what a term means. You can ask the instructor. You can see if it's in the textbook's glossary. You can look up the term in a print or online dictionary, or simply perform a Web search for the term (this can be especially valuable, as it should bring up both definitions and uses of the term in context).

It's also often possible to find the definition of the term in the text itself. Frequently, when a writer uses a word that might be unfamiliar to an audience, he or she will make a point to define it immediately:

> Antinomianism, *the belief that Christians were not subject to the laws God laid down for the Jews,* was a product of Pauline times (*the era in which St. Paul lived*).

Whether a writer will define a term immediately or not depends on the **intended audience** for a work. In a scholarly work written for theologians and historians, the writer would not bother to define *antinomianism*—the audience would understand what that word meant. However, in a textbook or in a magazine article, the writer would not assume that the audience understood the term and would be likely to offer a definition.

When moving into specialized territory or scholarly writing, you might notice that some familiar words are used in a different context and might even have a completely different meaning. Take this sentence:

> Candida epiglottitis is an emergent condition.

Certainly, a nonspecialist would need to look up *Candida epiglottitis*, although from the combination of "condition" in the sentence and the suffix *-itis,* it would seem that the term refers to some kind of a medical problem. (It's also likely that such a sentence would exist only in a text that was clearly about health or medicine.) However, what about that other word—*emergent*? Most English speakers know that *emerge* means "to come forth" or "to rise up," but how is this applicable here? Is Candida epiglottitis a condition in which something rises or comes out—perhaps out of the epiglottis? Here, *emergent* is a specialized medical term meaning "demanding prompt action" or "urgent"; *emergent* and *emergency* are closely related. A critical reader would need to ask questions of the text, and of his or her own knowledge, and not assume that a familiar word, used in a different context, has a stable meaning.

Comprehension doesn't just mean that you understand the dictionary or specialist definition of a term. An active, critical reader needs to identify key terms within a text that are "at issue"—terms about whose meanings people might disagree. Sometimes the definition of those terms is actually the point of the text. Take a term such as *feminist*, for instance. What does it mean? Is a feminist someone who hates men and wants women to be given special privileges? Or is a feminist someone who feels that men and women should be treated equally under the law?

The definition of such terms can even be the very subject of the text, because the terms carry powerful connotations. Take *terrorist* for example. Certainly, most people would agree that Osama bin Laden and members of Al Qaeda are terrorists, but what about other groups that engage in antigovernment action? Early American patriots attacked British goods and sabotaged British business in actions such as the Boston Tea Party—were they terrorists? What about John Brown, who attacked the federal garrison at Harper's Ferry, Virginia, in order to instigate a slave rebellion? What about the Biblical character Samson? When a person is called a *terrorist*, he or she becomes subject to certain legal punishments that other people, committing similar actions, avoid. Also, when the term *terrorist* is appended to a person, the American public will treat that person with hostility and fear. So it can be in someone's interest to persuade an audience that a group or person is a terrorist. A critical reader must always keep in mind the power of language to elicit an emotional response from an audience, and be aware of when a writer is using these words to achieve such effects.

Finally, achieving comprehension or even basic knowledge and recall of a text can be difficult when the actual writing is complicated or convoluted. This can be the result of stylistically poor or simply ungrammatical writing, but just as often the complexity of a well-crafted sentence can stand in the way of understanding the sentence, as in the following lead sentence from Henry James's 1909 preface to his 1904 novel *The Golden Bowl*:

> Among many matters thrown into relief by a refreshed acquaintance with "The Golden Bowl" what perhaps most stands out for me is the still marked inveteracy of a certain indirect and oblique view of my presented action; unless indeed I make up my mind to call this mode of treatment, on the contrary, any superficial appearance notwithstanding, the very straightest and closest possible.

This is by no means James's longest or most complicated sentence, even within this preface, but since it is the first sentence of the text, it particularly demands the attention of a critical reader. The best way to decipher a complex sentence is to start by simply breaking it down to its most basic elements: its subject and verb. The essential structure of the James's sentence is "X is Y." On one side of the equation—the X—is the phrase "what perhaps most stands out," or more simply "what stands out." On the other side of the equation is the word *inveteracy*—a word we likely will have to look up. (It means "persistence" or "the state of having been long established.") So, the basic structure of the first part of the sentence is that "what stands out is the persistence."

What stands out in what context? we ask next. That appears to be "Among many matters thrown into relief by a refreshed acquaintance with 'The Golden Bowl.'" So, what stands out among other things that are "thrown into relief"—or brought forth like a relief sculpture—when he "refreshe[s]" his "acquaintance with," or goes back to, his novel *The Golden Bowl*, is the persistence of … what? Here we progress to the last part of the sentence: "a certain indirect and oblique view of my presented action." These terms are all pretty abstract—who is viewing? Does "my presented action" refer to the way he presented action in his own novel *The Golden Bowl*, or does it refer to something else? We have to hold that idea "in abeyance"—keep it in the back of our minds and let him explain it later; since this is the lead to a longer piece, he certainly will.

James's sentence provides another complication in that it includes a semicolon. Contemporary American usage requires that unless it is being used to separate the elements of a list, a semicolon must divide two complete independent sentences. The clause following the semicolon here is introduced by the conjunction "unless," meaning "except," and making the clause after the semicolon a sentence fragment. (Such usage was acceptable at the time James wrote.) So, what is the exception here? "Unless," James says, "I make up my mind to call this mode of treatment." What is "this mode of treatment"? "This" in the phrase indicates that a "mode of treatment" was previously mentioned. It seems that "this mode of treatment" is a reference to James's "indirect and oblique view of my presented action." So, this part of the sentence says, "Unless I choose to call this 'view' or 'mode'"… what? "The very straightest and closest possible."

The sentence is constructed, therefore, on an opposition, and each pole of the opposition occupies one side of the semicolon. Put in simpler terms, the sentence means something like this:

> When I read *The Golden Bowl* again, what stands out is the indirect and oblique view of the action—unless I choose to say that what seems 'indirect and oblique' is actually as straight and close as is possible.

From here, we can simplify this even further:

> The action in *The Golden Bowl* might seem to be described in an indirect and oblique way, but I could also say that it could not be any straighter or more direct.

This is still a pretty tough idea, but it is much easier to understand than it was in James's original words.

Critical reading, therefore, must start at the most basic level of comprehension. What can be different about the kinds of materials that you'll be reading in college is that they'll likely be more specialized, include vocabulary that may be obscure or have unfamiliar meanings, and utilize sentence structure that requires extra time and attention. It's unlikely that the same kinds of basic reading strategies that you use for reading emails or news articles on the net will be sufficient for reading the more challenging and demanding material presented to you in your college classes; therefore, it's important to be ready to expend that extra time and energy on just figuring out what the writer is *saying*. **Critical** reading comes next.

Exercise 1.1: Summarizing

Summarize the following passages in two sentences at most.

1. This Abstract, which I now publish, must necessarily be imperfect. I cannot here give references and authorities for my several statements; and I must trust to the reader reposing some confidence in my accuracy. No doubt errors will have crept in, though I hope I have always been cautious in trusting to good authorities alone. I can here give only the general conclusions at which I have arrived, with a few facts in illustration, but which, I hope, in most cases will suffice. No one can feel more sensible than I do of the necessity of hereafter publishing in detail all the facts, with references, on which my conclusions have been grounded; and I hope in a future work to do this. For I am well aware that scarcely a single point is discussed in this volume on which facts cannot be adduced, often apparently leading to conclusions directly opposite to those at which I have arrived. A fair result can be obtained only by fully stating and balancing the facts and arguments on both sides of each question; and this cannot possibly be here done. (Charles Darwin, "Introduction" to *On the Origin of Species*)

2. Between these sections commercial relations have sprung up, and economic combinations and contests may be traced by the student who looks beneath the surface of our national life to the actual grouping of States in congressional votes on tariff, internal improvement, currency and banking, and all the varied legislation in the field of commerce. American industrial life is the outcome of the combinations and contests of groups of States in sections. And the intellectual, the spiritual life of the nation is the result of

the interplay of the sectional ideals, fundamental assumptions and emotions. (Frederick Jackson Turner, *The Frontier in American History*)

3. A state or region taken over by jihadists will not last long before declining into extreme poverty and backwardness and savagery. There are no exceptions to this rule. We do not need to demonstrate again what happens to countries where vicious fantasists try to govern illiterates with the help of only one book. And who will be blamed for the failure? There will not, let me assure you, be a self-criticism session mounted by the responsible mullahs. Instead, all ills will be blamed on the Crusader-Zionist conspiracy, and young men with deficiency diseases and learning disabilities will be taught how to export their frustrations to happier lands. (Christopher Hitchens, "Handing the Swat Valley to the Taliban was shameful and wrong," Slate.com 9 March 2009. http://www.slate.com/id/2213246/)

4. Read the following article, and write a one-paragraph summary of it. Be sure to identify the author's thesis, and identify places where the author seems to be addressing a specific audience.

"Gangsta Kobe"

Scott Andrews

I love this picture. I saw it being sold as a poster by a vendor at Venice Beach. He also was selling images of Marilyn Monroe with thuggish tats on her body. But it was this picture of Kobe that fascinated me more.

I saw it and laughed before I even understood what I was laughing at. I stared at it, fascinated by it and by my fascination with it. As I tried to understand my reaction to this gunslinging Kobe, I was reminded of reception theory. Yes, even on a sunny day in Venice, with bikini-clad girls rollerblading past, over the din of the construction of yet another medical marijuana dispensary, and lit by the flashes from the digital cameras of a thousand German tourists, I could wax wonk-like about a bootleg poster.

Must I over-analyze everything? Yes. Yes, I must.

In literary studies, reception theory is an attempt to explain the process by which audiences understand texts. Traditional literary studies had concentrated on what an author might have intended to communicate with a text, but reception theory (and reader response theory) concentrates on the reader's interpretation, regardless of how that meaning deviates from the author's intent.

One of the many influences on how a person receives a text is his/her community. People who share a culture, an economic class, or a community are likely to interpret a text in similar ways. And if the maker of a message shares this connection with the audience, it is more likely the audience will generate an interpretation similar to the maker's intended message. The further apart creator and audience are, the less likely they will be in agreement.

As I stared at Gangsta Kobe, I knew I had no way of knowing what its creator meant to convey since I didn't know who had made it. And I knew that what the poster could mean would depend a great deal upon who was looking. Is the poster celebratory? Does it appeal to people who see themselves as gangsters? Are they embracing Kobe as one of their own?

This seems odd when you think he so clearly is NOT one of them. He is a multi-millionaire. He spent much of his childhood in Italy, where his father played pro basketball. He did not grow up in the American inner city. He did not know the mean streets. He is more scampi than Scarface. However, Los Angeles is obsessed with the Lakers. Gangsters are obsessed with the Lakers. The people who identify with gangsters, even though they may go to church every Sunday, are obsessed with the Lakers. And so perhaps they claim him as one of their own, and they dress him up in the images from pop culture paraphernalia they are familiar with—movies, rap and hip-hop videos, CD covers, etc.

Do they imagine Kobe sharing their fantasies of fighting back against a system they may feel oppresses them? Is this poster some kind of Robin in the "Hood fantasy? Do they dream of Kobe following Public Enemy's instructions to "Fight the Power"? Do they hope Kobe will descend from his gated community, arm his merry band of bodyguards, and cause some serious mayhem?

Or is the image mocking? Does it appeal to an audience that sees Kobe as unlike themselves and similar to those lower-income people who identify with gangsters? Does the poster suggest that Kobe, despite his millions and comfortable childhood, is a gun-wielding criminal at heart? Is it a racist poster? It may appear comical, but perhaps beneath the laughter is a quiet fear about the violence that can come from black anger.

Is it the celebration of the wannabe? You know, Seth Green's character from *Can't Hardly Wait.* Jamie Kennedy's character from *Malibu's Most Wanted.* Does this poster hang in the bedrooms of nerdy boys across L.A., boys who wish they could be as cool as Kobe? Boys who mash up being cool and being black with being gangsta? Ultimately, I cannot know what the poster means. And the fascination it holds for me is exactly the fact that I cannot know. I am fascinated not by what its ultimate meaning might be—that is rather UNfascinating—but by its simultaneous and conflicting and irresolvable messages.

QUESTIONING THE TEXT

Making sure you fully understand a text—that you can put that text into your own words and accurately express the author's stance—is only the first step in critical reading, but it is absolutely crucial. Once you understand a writer's point well enough that you can summarize it in your own words, you can move on to the next step: questioning the text.

That's not right, actually. Questioning the text is something that a critical reader does throughout. Think about what you do when you approach a text—literally, a text. When a friend texts you, even before you read that message you bring to your reading some knowledge about the context of the message and how that context affects the message's meaning. You use that knowledge to ask questions about the text and its context—what it says, who is sending the message, when it is being sent, how the message is being sent.

First of all, you likely know the person who is texting you (and if you don't know that person, you may conclude that the text message is actually spam). A message saying "let's hit the American Eagle sale now!" from a friend means something different than that same message from a sender you don't know.

When a message is sent also affects its meaning. That message sent at 10 a.m. on a Saturday means something different than the same message sent at 2 a.m. on a Tuesday. The forum itself—the text message—also affects the meaning of a message. A text is offhanded, casual; you won't expect a serious proposal or statement to be delivered, out of the blue, through a text. (Think of how unacceptable it would be to break up with someone through a text.) These three processes of critical reading (summary, analysis, informed response), you might be surprised to know, are things you already do without even thinking about it.

Although it might seem far-fetched, these are the same processes a critical reader is aware of when approaching a more formal or complicated message. The words themselves, after all, are only part of a message: a message consists of the words plus the context in which it is embedded. Some components of the context include:

1. The sender (writer/speaker) of the message. What is this person's relationship to the issue addressed by the text? To the receiver(s) of the message? For example, an essay on what it means to play basketball well might be interesting and insightful when written by Kenzaburo Takahashi, but if the byline reads "Michael Jordan," any reader who knows who Michael Jordan is will read the essay differently.

2. The forum in which the message appears. A federal subpoena ordering you to "Be at the courthouse on Monday at 10 a.m." means something different than the same sentence in a *Travel & Leisure* magazine article about sightseeing in Oxford, Mississippi. A long essay analyzing the motivations of Pakistani insurgent groups on a blog means something different than that same essay when it appears in a reputable political magazine or is sent to you as part of a politician's campaign mailer. When your friend posts a status update on Facebook saying "I need help," you'll likely understand that to mean something different than if that friend called the same message out in a crowded street.

3. The time when the message appears. "We must take up arms against the Germans" would be a bizarre statement today, but in 1940, that same message had a very different meaning.

4. The intended audience of the message. A statement made in private, to a particular person, can mean something entirely different than that statement made to any other person—or to the general public.

All of this is just to say that the **context** of a message (the sender, forum, time, and intended audience) contributes meaning to the **text** or words. The text and context together are the **message**.

Read the following essay, from the Canadian newsmagazine *Maclean's*, and answer the questions that follow.

Look, Over There. It's a Black Guy!

Kevin Chong

Earlier this year, Axe Deodorant launched a clever advertising campaign in Canada called "Game Killers." In the ads, a game killer is anyone—be it a boorish friend or a caddish adversary—who gets between a man and the object of his affection. In one, a game killer called "British Accent Guy" woos a young woman in front of her fuming boyfriend. "While re-arranging this game killer's face is tempting," a voiceover suggests, "what could you do to those teeth that shoddy dentistry hasn't?" What's interesting about the ad isn't so much the punchline, or its suggestion to "Keep Your Cool" and not sweat these interlopers, but the casting: while British Accent Guy and the girl are white, the hero—the average guy whose game is being threatened—happens to be black.

Similarly, last year, in a Molson's commercial that advises a *realpolitik* approach to meeting women, a black man at a nightclub coaches a friend (not shown): "Remember, you're a quarterback! A quarterback!" And in an Old Navy ad that recently aired in the United States, a young white woman misinterprets a fashionable (but affordable) scarf from her Asian boyfriend as a wedding proposal. The relaxed commingling of ethnicities feels neither revolutionary nor gimmicky. It simply reflects the contemporary world, especially among younger people.

It was not so long ago that TV shows like *Seinfeld* and *Friends* were lambasted for their white-bread visions of New York City, and that minorities popped up only in commercials or programs that explicitly pursued a multicultural aesthetic. These days colour-blind casting is catching on. But it seems to be happening most quickly not in art house movies, but in places many would deem unsophisticated: deodorant and beer ads, sex comedies like *The 40-Year-Old Virgin*, and action films like *2 Fast 2 Furious*.

There's *Harold and Kumar Go to White Castle*, centered around two pot-smoking Asians and their quest to get to a fast-food restaurant. Some of the film's jokes address the stoners' ethnicity, but the biggest laughs revolve around their marijuana-induced munchies. Or take last summer's *The 40-Year-Old Virgin*. One running gag involved the inability of a character, played by Paul Rudd, to get over an ex-girlfriend who had dumped him years earlier. In a small but noticeable bit of colourblind casting, the ex-girlfriend was played by a South Asian actress, Mindy Kaling.

Compare these films to a list of 2006 Oscar nominees for Best Picture: *Brokeback Mountain*, *Capote*, *Goodnight, and Good Luck*, *Munich*, and *Crash*. Of these highbrow mainstream films, only the winner, *Crash*, which is explicitly about race relations, features any non-white actors in major roles. Lowbrow culture is apparently better able, or more willing, to reflect an ethnically mixed world.

The casting seems almost incidental. "With the exception of certain clients—government agencies that have mandates to represent a cross-section of the community," says Nancy Mauro, an advertising copywriter, "I've never had a client suggest specific ethnic casting." That said, savvy marketing is clearly part of the story. In 1997, for instance, long before *Queer Eye for the Straight Guy*, Volkswagen ran an ad in which two men—one black, one white—find an abandoned armchair that they load into their VW Golf. The ad inspired much talk about whether the two characters were a gay couple. "If research shows that a significant percentage of gay men purchase this vehicle, or have the potential to," says Mauro, "a smart marketer will cast the target as the hero of the spot." And when seeking a suitable love interest for Will

Smith in the romantic comedy *Hitch*, producers reportedly chose Eva Mendes because they felt her Cuban-American heritage would appeal equally to black and white audiences.

Within the films, too, race remains a factor. *Harold and Kumar* deals with racists who joke about the Karate Kid and Apu (the convenience-store clerk from *The Simpsons*). And in *The 40-Year-Old Virgin*, the black and South Asian stereo salesmen trade barbs about drive-by shootings and turbans. There's a good dose of self-conscious cultural jokes—a nod, perhaps, that the portrayal wouldn't ring true otherwise. Still, this may be better than completely ignoring race. "The one danger in colour-blind casting is that it can make it seem as if all racial problems have already been solved," says Carmen Van Kerckhove, co-founder of the U.S. blog Mixed Media Watch. A truly colour-blind society wouldn't require rose-coloured glasses.

Maclean's 1 July 2006

Exercise 1.2: Critical Reading Questions

Summarizing the Text

1. What is Chong's thesis?
2. What evidence supports his thesis?

Establishing the Context

3. When did this appear? How might that time be different, in terms of this issue, from today?
4. Chong is a Canadian journalist, and this article appeared in Canada's most important newsmagazine. How is the article specifically Canadian? Are there ways in which the American context surrounding this issue might be different?
5. What is Chong's tone here? Is this a serious or light-hearted article? Does he use humor? How does this affect the tone?

Responding to the Message

6. Chong's article focuses specifically on the representation of members of minority groups in films, television programs, and commercials. Do other kinds of advertising (billboards, print magazines, Internet) either support Chong's thesis or work as a counter-argument? Why?
7. Does Chong have an unspoken assumption about what he wants to see? Is he assuming that we all *want* a "color-blind society"? How does that assumption inform his argument?
8. Are we reaching a point at which race no longer matters when it comes to advertising?

WHAT'S YOUR POINT?

A basic distinction that a critical reader must make is between texts that simply **inform** and those that **make an argument**. You might remember from your grammar-school days differentiating between "fact" and "opinion." The statement that "The earth orbits the sun" is a fact, whereas the statement "Strawberry is the best ice cream flavor" is an opinion.

Sometimes differentiating between fact and opinion, though, isn't so easy. An opinion isn't necessarily just a preference, as in the ice cream example. Sometimes, an opinion comes in the form of a hypothesis, or a synthesis of information. "Slavery caused the Civil War" might be one example. Another scholar, historian, or ordinary person might disagree with this statement. However, most writers who make such arguments are aware that some audiences might disagree and will offer evidence in support of this statement. You'll notice that nobody— at least since the 1700s—has felt the need to offer evidence to persuade people that the earth orbits the sun.

One test you can perform on some texts to determine whether they are arguments is to **falsify the claim** and see whether the statement still makes sense. "The earth does not orbit the sun": that's pretty clearly nonsensical, and easily disproven. But how about "Emissions of carbon dioxide from human activities are causing the earth's climate to heat up"? To the vast majority of scientists studying this phenomenon, this is a clear statement of fact, and the argument that human activities don't contribute to the warming of the planet is also nonsensical. However, a large number of people outside of the scientific community, and a few people within that community, disagree. Some argue that the earth is not warming up. Some who grant that the earth is warming insist that other factors, not carbon dioxide, are the culprits. Others state that the warming is not human caused.

You'll be confronting opinion, in other words, that demands a different kind of response than "No, chocolate is the best." The statement about global warming may be a hypothesis or an opinion, but to refute it, one needs evidence, an understanding of the underlying issues, and sometimes even professional credentials. A critical reader must identify when a writer is making those moves: positing something as a thesis, and then offering evidence to support that thesis. A writer who is doing this is likely expressing an opinion.

As you learned in the previous section, the **context** of a message also affects its meaning—and even whether a message is a statement of fact or an opinion. Take the time in which a text is written. "The earth orbits the sun" would have been a statement of opinion in the 1600s, and Copernicus, Galileo, and others had to offer powerful evidence to hostile and skeptical audiences in support of that statement. But today, it's a statement of fact.

Why is it important to distinguish between fact and opinion? Primarily, it's key to identify when someone is trying to persuade you of something—stating an opinion and offering support for that opinion—so that you are aware that there might be other opinions on that issue. A critical reader needs to identify when someone is attempting to convince or persuade him or her of something, because this should spur our reader to approach the information, well, more critically: to judge whether the claim makes sense, to evaluate the evidence offered in support of that claim, and to identify strategies employed by the writer to "push the buttons" of the reader.

So, when confronted by a piece of writing on an unfamiliar topic, how is a reader without specialized knowledge to know what's an opinion? Context clues can help. Where does this piece of writing appear? A textbook that is specifically meant for use in a classroom, more than likely, strives to be factual. Your instructors' lectures are probably factual rather than argumentative. On the other hand, much of the writing in magazines and online journals advances and supports opinions, even when it appears to be just "informative." Professional journals, even scientific journals, frequently contain opinions—deeply informed, highly sophisticated opinions supported by expertise and research, but opinions nonetheless.

Certain types of statements are likely to be opinions. Claims that one thing **causes** something else—smoking causes cancer, for example—begin as opinions or hypotheses and require support to become factual statements. An **evaluative** claim is almost always an opinion. Evaluative claims boil down to someone saying that something is "good" or "better" or "the best." Many statements of opinion come in the form of **categorical** claims, or arguments that a specific thing fits into a larger category and that, in the process, offer a definition of the category. "Chipotle isn't a fast-food restaurant" might be an example of a categorical claim, as it requires that the writer define what a "fast-food restaurant" is.

Are these statements of fact or arguments?

1. The United States suffers from an obesity epidemic.

This is an argument. Think back to the earlier section about knowing and understanding. Are there any terms here that readers might not understand? Not on first glance, but ask yourself questions. What is *obesity*? Who defines it? At what point does a person become obese? Also, what is an *epidemic*? We all have a general idea of what this word means—a disease that sweeps through a population and infects a significant proportion of that population—but when does something go from simply being "widespread" to being an "epidemic"? In a later chapter, you'll read several takes on this issue, some arguing for the position and others arguing against it on various grounds.

2. The human species is the product of evolution.

This is a sticky one. Most of us are familiar with the theory of evolution—the notion, popularized by Charles Darwin in the nineteenth century, that life forms adapt to their conditions and change over the generations to be better suited for their environment. However, not everyone believes this "theory," and in fact many powerful and influential belief systems strongly deny that evolution occurs. A 2009 Gallup poll showed that only 39 percent of Americans believe in evolution.* Some critical readers point to the fact that even scientists call evolution a "theory," not a "law." However, others refute this, countering that in science, a "theory" indicates an explanation for a natural phenomenon that essentially has the status of a law, and that no credible scientists doubt that evolution happens. Whether this statement is an argument or simply an assertion of fact, therefore, depends upon the audience being addressed.

Exercise 1.3: Fact or Argument?

Evaluate the following statements. Are they facts or arguments—and if they are arguments, where might the disagreement occur?

1. Social-media technologies such as Facebook and Twitter allow people to communicate with large numbers of preselected "friends" or contacts instantaneously.

2. Social-media technologies such as Facebook and Twitter undermine our ability to think carefully and critically, substituting short bursts of rhetoric for reasoned argument.

3. Social-media technologies such as Facebook and Twitter will change the ways that companies communicate with their customers.

4. The requirement for all undergraduates to take theology is an anachronism and should be eliminated.

5. The requirement for all undergraduates to take theology is intended to ensure that our graduates understand the nature of Methodist higher education.

6. The requirement for all undergraduates to take theology stems from our university's Methodist mission.

Exercise 1.4: Thesis Statement or Information?

Read the following passages. Which makes an argument, and which simply presents information?

1. Trains running on a "light-rail" system are smaller and run at a lower speed than do trains on a traditional rail system, but they are larger and go faster than standard trams or streetcars. The proposal presented to the city council calls for funding construction of a single-line light rail that would run from downtown Austin to Buda.

---

* Newport, Frank. "On Darwin's Birthday, Only 4 in 10 Beleive in Evolution." Gallup. 11 Feb. 2009. Web.

2. Austin should build a light-rail system that passes through the southern half of the city. This system would alleviate the traffic problems on I-35 and other major arteries in South Austin, and it would significantly decrease air pollution in the area, improving the quality of life for local residents.

READING AS A BELIEVER AND READING AS A DOUBTER

Peter Elbow, one of the most prominent American teachers of writing, asks students to play a little game with texts they are reading. This game—reading as a believer and reading as a doubter—can serve as an excellent final stage of critical reading.

When we read as a believer, we temporarily adopt all of the writer's values and beliefs; we "side with" the author. Reading in this way encourages us to fully understand the logic of the writer's argument and empathize with the values and beliefs that underlie the text. Having finished reading a text as a believer, then, we reread as a doubter. In this second reading, we exercise our critical skills fully. In the logic of the argument, are there flaws? Does the author rely on a shared definition that not all readers agree upon? Does the author assume that X causes Y, when in fact that relationship is in doubt? Does the argument require that all readers feel a particular way about one of its components?

Read the following article first as a believer then as a doubter, then answer the questions following the text.

Terrorists in the Heartland? Chill

Steve Chapman

The idea of having an al-Qaida presence in Illinois, even locked up behind bars, is a horrifying prospect. That's what we have to confront now that the Obama administration has decided to move some Guantanamo inmates to a prison in Thomson, a small town in the northwest corner of the state. How will we sleep nights with terrorists in our midst?

Probably about like we do right now. From the shrieks of alarm, you'd think no bloodthirsty jihadist had ever occupied a cell in one of our correctional facilities. As it turns out, there are already some 35 domestic and international terrorists privileged to reside in the Land of Lincoln.

Run into any at Wal-Mart lately? Seen one cut in line at Dunkin' Donuts? Me neither.

Just a few weeks ago, a federal judge sentenced Ali al-Marri, a convicted al-Qaida sleeper agent who had undergone terrorist training and met with alleged 9/11 mastermind Khalid Sheikh Mohammed, to eight years behind bars. A former student at Bradley University in Peoria, he is now serving his term at the federal prison in Marion. Yet Illinoisans have somehow stifled their impulse to curl up into the fetal position awaiting certain doom.

A lot of politicians nonetheless insist the risk of relocating detainees to Thomson is intolerable. All seven Republican House members from Illinois vehemently object.

They signed a letter drafted by Rep. Mark Kirk predicting the state would become "ground zero for jihadist terrorist plots, recruitment and radicalization" and insisting that "al-Qaida terrorists should stay where they cannot endanger American citizens."

Being locked up in what will become a supermax prison, however, means they will be in a place where they can no more endanger American citizens than they can party with Paris Hilton. If housing jihadists would provoke attacks here, why hasn't Osama bin Laden carried out massacres in Florence, Colo., whose supermax penitentiary holds several terrorists?

Kirk warns that an inmate who needs more than routine medical care will have to get it at the nearest military hospital, which happens to be in his district—raising all sorts of security risks. Fear not. No inmate has ever left Guantanamo for treatment. The Pentagon says it won't move anyone to Thomson until it ensures the medical unit can "handle all foreseeable detainee health conditions, just as it has done at Guantanamo for the past seven years."

A common theme among Republicans running for senator and governor is that the inmates shouldn't be moved anywhere, because there is no reason to close Guantanamo. Obama's decision, charges Senate candidate Patrick Hughes, is just keeping "a campaign promise to an antiwar, left-wing" faction of his party.

But it's not just Birkenstock-shod peaceniks who support the idea. Former Joint Chiefs of Staff chairman Colin Powell has endorsed it. So has Gen. David Petraeus.

Last year, John McCain vowed to close Gitmo if he became president. There were other presidential candidates who disagreed. You know what? They lost.

The opponents see no risk in keeping Guantanamo open and no gain in getting rid of it. But plenty of military people think the status quo is about as satisfactory as a dead skunk in the living room.

Former Navy General Counsel Alberto Mora told Congress that high-ranking officers "maintain that the first and second identifiable causes of U.S. combat deaths in Iraq—as judged by their effectiveness in recruiting insurgent fighters into combat—are, respectively, the symbols of Abu Ghraib and Guantanamo."

The Bush administration's purpose in putting the captives at the U.S. naval base in Cuba was to keep them beyond the reach of federal courts, so it could do whatever struck the fancy of Dick Cheney and

Donald Rumsfeld. But the Supreme Court has repeatedly asserted that Guantanamo cannot be a lawless zone. The executive branch has to follow the Constitution even there.

Moving the prisoners to American soil would affirm the startling proposition that we consider ourselves bound by the rule of law. It wouldn't make veteran terrorists give up the fight. But it would deprive them of an emblem of torture and abuse that inspires anti-American fury and endangers American lives.

When the detainees arrive here, I predict, Illinoisans will pay attention for about five minutes and then go on calmly with their lives. At least the grownups will.

Chicago Tribune 17 December 2009

Exercise 1.5: Critical Reading Questions

Summarizing the Text

1. What is the **thesis** of this article?

2. What can you conclude about the **context** of the article—where did it appear? Who are its intended readers? What is the issue that Chapman is addressing? What is the climate of opinion about this issue?

3. Having read the article as a **believer**, summarize the argument in two to three sentences. What evidence or sub-points does Chapman use to support his thesis?

Establishing the Context

4. What tone does Chapman adopt here? How does this support the argument he is making?

5. What are the counterarguments to Chapman's claim that he includes? How does he defuse or refute them?

Responding to the Message

6. Having read the article as a **doubter**, list several potential objections one might have to Chapman's article. Is his portrayal of those who don't share his opinion fair? Does he ignore other possible arguments that might go counter to his? What assumptions does he rely upon that not everyone might share?

7. **Respond** to the article. Do you believe that housing convicted terrorists in a prison facility in Illinois is a good idea? Why or why not? What other authority figures or prominent people oppose Chapman's claim, and what are their arguments? Do you think that al Qaeda terrorists can be safely housed in American prisons?

PUTTING IT TOGETHER

Critical reading, then, requires several steps. Although I have set them out here in a sequence, most readers engage in all of these steps simultaneously.

1. **Understanding** the thesis, key terms, and logic of a text.

2. Being able to **summarize** that text, comprehensively, in your own words.

3. Identifying the key elements of the **context** of a text and how the context and text together create the **message**.

4. Reading as a **believer** so as to fully understand and empathize with the writer's message.

5. Reading as a **doubter** so as to identify unstated assumptions, logical flaws, and fuzzy terms used by the writer, and evaluate how they affect the validity and persuasiveness of the message.

6. **Responding** to the message by comparing it with one's own feelings about the subject, values, personal experience, and store of knowledge.

Critically Reading the Web: Search Engine Results

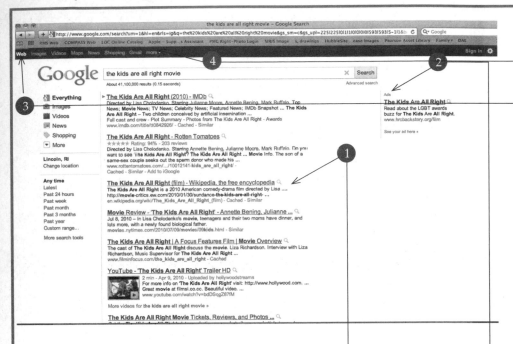

1   Search Ranking

The "algorithm," or formula, by which Google ranks the results of a search is a trade secret—it's Google's most valuable possession. However, certain elements of this algorithm are well-known. Unlike previous search engines, which ranked the relevance of a site according to how often the term being searched for appeared on the page, Google ranks a site's relevance according to *how many other sites link to it.* That is, Google has decided that if a great deal of other web sites think that a site is a good source about something, that's probably true. How might a company or organization game this?

2   Sponsored Results

Appearing on the first screen of a Google search result is incredibly valuable—searchers will go to this site, and if the searcher is looking to buy something, he or she may buy something from the first site encountered. For this reason, web designers want their sites to appear as high up on a list of results as possible. Failing that, a company can just pay Google to appear on the first page—but Google will put those results in a colored box on top of the search results or in a column on the right. (Both are labeled "Ads.")

Web, Images, Videos, etc.

By default, Google searches web sites that offer primarily text. But a searcher can also specify that the search look only at images or videos or maps or news sites or shopping sites. The problem here is that Google doesn't know what's *in* a photo or video unless someone has labeled it—anyone might be able to recognize Lady Gaga, but Google can't. Fortunately, it's very likely that the text near the image or video refers to the image or video—so if Google finds a blog entry in which "Lady Gaga" appears multiple times, it will assume that an image or video there is of Lady Gaga, and so it will appear in the search results.

 ### Google Scholar

Google has become an empire: its stated goal is to index all of the world's information, from photographs to sounds to videos to maps to books. Google Books, a work in progress, seeks to scan (and make available for searching) every book ever printed. Google Scholar is a subdivision of Google's ordinary text search engine that limits its purview to *scholarly* sources. Because of this, its results tend to be more credible.

The World Wide Web is so vast that it requires "search engines"—computer programs that go out and, at the speed of light, search out what you're looking for. But search engines aren't smart: all they can do is what they are programmed to do. Knowing how these programs work can help you use them better. Google, by far the most popular search engine, got that way by doing its job extremely well and extremely quickly. But as it came to dominate web searching (handling about two-thirds of all searches in the U.S. market in 2011), companies and groups who wanted to make sure they were ranked at the top of Google searches have learned how to game the system. You, too, can benefit by learning a little bit about how Google works—it'll help you research smarter and more quickly.

Critically Reading the Web: Wikipedia

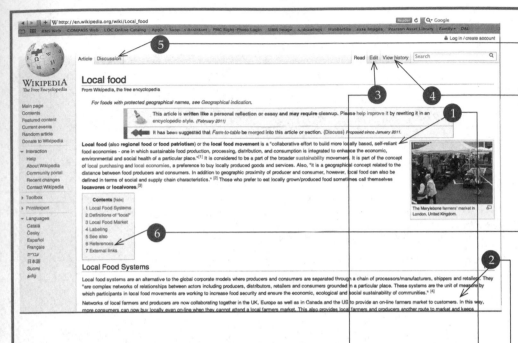

① Article

This is the page to which you are directed when you search for a topic. A Wikipedia entry consists of a general introduction, a table of contents in which each element links to the corresponding section of the entry, and the sections of the entry itself.

② Writers

Who wrote this entry? Where did the text come from? The short answer is "anyone." But you can find out exactly who wrote every part of each entry—that is, if you're willing to settle for usernames and IP addresses (a computer's identification number on the Internet).

③ Edit

This link brings you to a page on which the entry is laid out in simple HTML (hypertext markup language)—the code that tells web pages how to make links and depict text. The "edit" function is what sets Wikipedia apart from any other encyclopedia. Go ahead—try it. Go to "Edit" and make a change. Save the change. Go back to the entry's page. Bingo: you've altered a Wikipedia entry. What does this say about Wikipedia's reliability?

History

The history page records every change made to this page. This is one of Wikipedia's defense mechanisms against sabotage. When a malicious user repeatedly inserts false or irrelevant information in an entry, Wikipedia's volunteer editors disable that user's ability to edit Wikipedia entries. Unfortunately, such malicious users can only be identified by usernames or computer IP addresses—and someone who is determined to evade this system can always create a new identity or use a different computer.

 Discussion

The more popular the topic, the more controversial the entry, the more interesting the discussion. Check it out—here is where Wikipedia editors and writers debate what should go in an entry, how to keep an entry objective and unbiased, and how to maintain Wikipedia's "house style"— the format of an entry.

 References/External Links

These are the sources the entry's writers used. They run the gamut fron random web sites to peer-reviewed scholarly papers. If you are starting your research with Wikipedia, your next step might be to check out some of these references.

Wikipedia is one of the most popular, most visited sites on the internet. Wikipedia is a "user-generated encyclopedia"—but what does that mean? Unlike with a traditional published encyclopedia, whose entries are written by professional writers and experts in the field, Wikipedia's articles are all written by volunteers, users of the site. Wikipedia's genius and greatest drawback is that *anyone* can write or edit or alter essentially any entry. Wikipedia draws upon the "wisdom of crowds," the idea that a large mass of people, working together, will generate the right answer to questions. (See Katherine Mangu-Ward's profile of Wikipedia founder Jimmy Wales in chapter 4 for more background on Wikipedia.)

Generally, Wikipedia isn't considered an acceptable source in an academic paper. It has no credibility among audience. This doesn't mean that no Wikipedia entry is valuable; thousands of them are the clearest and most user-friendly introductions to a subject. But thousands of them are erroneous, deceptive, or incomplete. It's best to use Wikipedia as a place to start your research—to start thinking about a topic.

Critically Reading the Web: News Aggregators

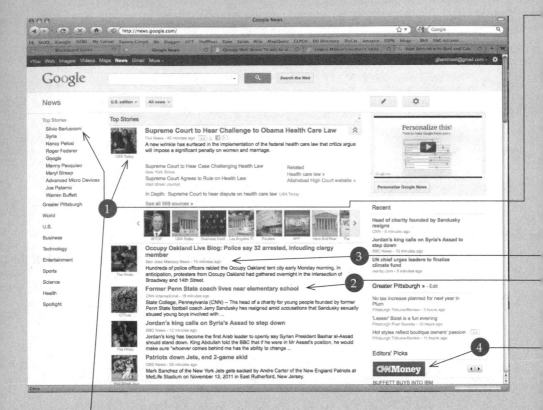

① What's Chosen?

News-aggregator sites want to be your destination—they want you to bookmark them and go there regularly to check out the latest happenings. Failing that, they figure out how to appear at the top of search results. Even if a site features links to "hard" (serious) news, more people will click their way there when it indexes "hot" topics such as celebrity news, sensational crime, or funny stories. Many news sites are also politically slanted, and will link to stories that support their political stance (and ignore stories that work against that position). And while Google News tries to maintain neutrality, other sites aggregate news to advance a political position. The Drudge Report and Newsmax are popular sites with a conservative perspective on current events; the Huffington Post and Raw Story are two prominent sites coming from the political left.

① Why Are the Links Placed Where They Are?

The editor of the news-aggregator site puts links to stories that he/she thinks will be the most popular in the most prominent sites on the page—above the headline, or on the top corners. Aggregator sites with a political slant will tend to put those stories that advance their perspective in those slots—even if those stories might not otherwise be popular. By doing this, they get people talking about those stories.

② Who Writes the Headlines?

The news-aggregator editors do. Many times, the headline on the news-aggregator site is quite different than the headline on the site where the story originally appeared. News-aggregator editors will do this to boost traffic or try to shape readers' understandings of what a story means.

③ How is a News Site Different Than a News Aggregator?

Simple: a news aggregator simply links to news stories written for other sources (newspaper, cable news networks, magazines, and the like). A news site employs its own reporters who write those stories. News sites and news aggregators are rarely related—and their business interests are often opposed.

④ How Does a News Aggregator Make Money?

News aggregators make most of their money from advertising that appears on their front pages, and from selling information they learn about their readers by tracking readers' movements on the web. New sites, by contrast, make a little money when news-aggregator sites link to their stories, but most news sites get their primary revenue from another part of their operations.

News aggregator sites might be killing the newspaper business, or they might be its savior. News aggregators gather ("aggregate") stories on a particular topic that searchers want to find. But who writes these stories? Are they credible and reliable? The stories come from sites that bill themselves as news sites. These might be national news organizations, such as the *New York Times* or Reuters; they might be local television stations or newspapers; or they might be blogs or other sites that look like objective news, but in actuality are slanted or unreliable. When you use research in your paper, it's important to know your sources are good. How can you tell the difference between a "real" news site, and a site that just looks like the news?

What Does it Mean to "Write Critically?"

In the previous chapter, we learned that reading critically involves three components: summary, analysis, and response. Ordinary reading, of course, begins with simple comprehension: passing your eyes over words so that their meanings register in your conscious mind. But often this kind of reading is neither deep nor lasting. You've probably noticed how you can read an entire email or article on the Web and then barely be able to recall what it said three minutes later. In fact, you may have made the mistake of applying this ordinary reading technique to an assignment for school, only to find that a quiz or discussion required you to have read the article much more attentively.

Critical reading requires much greater attention and active participation in the reading process than you may be accustomed to giving. As you are no doubt experiencing in your classes, it's often not enough to casually skim an article or chapter. Most of the time, you'll need to understand the argument and main points that a piece of reading contains, you'll need to retain that understanding, and you may also need to have your own response to that argument and those points prepared. Reading this way is a good habit to develop, and you'll discover that as you get to be a better reader, it won't take as long.

In many ways, the same situation holds when it comes to writing. On one hand, unless you are an uncommonly comfortable and confident writer, it's tough to write on autopilot, the way most of us can skim or read automatically. But on the other hand, even if you struggle with writing, it's likely that with a little effort you have the ability to compose sentences that sound smooth and intelligent and easy to understand. The problem is that this kind of writing often doesn't *say* all that much.

WRITING THAT GOES DOWN EASY ISN'T ALWAYS GOOD WRITING

This kind of writing—writing that has a familiar and comfortable surface but lacks depth—is often what we produce when we try to imitate other writers or the sound of authoritative writing. Imitation is an important part of writing; a good writer is probably able, even unconsciously, to imitate any number of writers or types of writing, from text-message language to the inscrutable abstraction of bureaucratic language to the hopped-up rhetoric of political talk radio.

Imitation, though, is just a tool, not an end in itself. A good writer uses this tool to help get across his or her message to an audience. However, writers who are less confident tend to use imitation for its own sake, hoping just to blend in so that readers don't pay too much attention to them. This happens especially frequently in the kind of writing that you are beginning to do: academic writing.

"IN TODAY'S SOCIETY, ..."

Let's take an example. Students often find that *starting* a paper is the hardest part of writing the paper. A good opening to a paper must grab the reader's attention, lead into the writer's argument, and establish the writer as a voice worth listening to. As a hypothetical, imagine the following assignment prompt:

> In several American cities, "needle exchange" programs—some sponsored by government agencies, some by private groups—allow drug addicts to exchange used hypodermic needles for clean ones, in an effort to stop the transmission of deadly diseases such as HIV/AIDS and hepatitis C. Critics of these programs (which are illegal in some states) charge that they perpetuate drug abuse, while supporters counter that there will always be illicit drug use, and fighting these diseases is of greater benefit to society. What do you think? Does the harm of needle exchange—making drug abuse safer and easier—outweigh the benefits? Use the poster below in your answer.

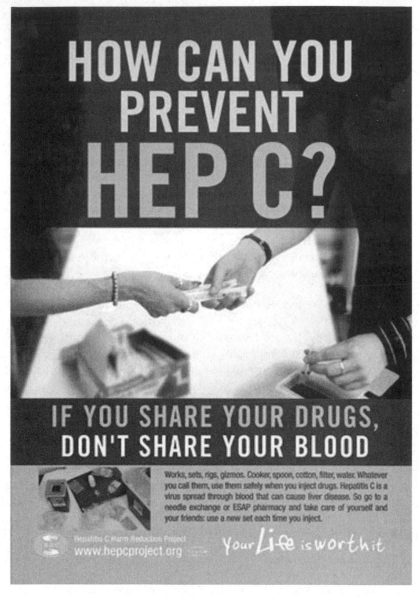

A poster for the "Hep C Project," a harm–reduction group aimed at preventing needle drug addicts from spreading hepatitis C.

What is our hypothetical student going to say? The question asks the student to take a stand on an issue (needle exchange), ground that stand both in a claim about cause and in a comparative assessment of costs and benefits, and use primary-source evidence to support her argument.

Our hypothetical student needs to do several things: decide what she thinks about needle exchange programs on a gut level, then weigh the competing claims of the pro- and anti-needle exchange camps, then construct an argument about whether the harms outweigh the benefits of such programs. So rather than jump right into the tough business of constructing a thesis, our student decides that it's better to start with something familiar in the hope that it will give her some momentum:

> In today's society, drug abuse is a serious problem. This can be seen in the posters for needle-exchange programs, which show that we need to fight the harmful effects of addiction.

You all have seen, and may well have written, openings like that. What's *good* about this opening is that it's familiar and smooth. It feels like a lead-in, and it makes a broad statement that nobody really can argue with. Contrast that sentence with the blunter, choppier opening another student might write:

> Needle exchange is wrong. Drug abuse is a terrible thing and when you give addicts clean needles there's no reason for them to quit using. The posters show this, with their use of distasteful drug slang like "works" and "rigs." We as a society need to do everything we can to eliminate drug addiction.

That sounds a lot less smooth and doesn't have the same familiar flow of the first opening. It jars the ear. However, read both openers again and think about what they *mean*. Opener one, our "In today's society" example, essentially says that "drug abuse is important today" and we can see this from the posters. The other makes the argument that needle-exchange programs only perpetuate drug abuse. Which one is better? Which one makes an argument that answers the question posed by the paper prompt?

Opener two does. When you look at it, opener one actually doesn't make any sense. It posits something that is so universally true as to not be worth saying: today, drug abuse is an important issue. Well, sure, but can you name a time when that wasn't true? Is "today's society" characterized by its drug problems, but earlier societies were not? Furthermore, what characterizes "today's society"? This year? The last twenty years, after the crack "epidemic" of the 1990s? Everything since the 1960s? The century after Prohibition? Finally, if you look even closer, you'll see that the opener doesn't even answer the question: it does not take a stand on whether the drawbacks of needle-exchange programs outweigh their benefits.

What this hypothetical student has done is reach for the familiar, to imitate what sounds like a good model. "In today's society drug abuse is an important issue" sounds authoritative. It's hard to argue with.

It follows the "start broad, then get specific" model we are often taught in high school. It imitates well. What it doesn't do is say anything or answer the question.

ANSWERING THE QUESTION

It may seem obvious, but the first step in critical writing is often just answering the question you've been asked. Certainly in high school you've already had experience answering questions for a *kind* of academic audience. You might have been asked to "compare and contrast" two kinds of societies or "describe" a chemical reaction. In personal essays, you probably explained what you did over a summer vacation or explained why you want to attend a particular university. These kinds of writing came from specific questions that were probably quite simple to understand and answer.

Here is where the difference between academic writing and other forms of writing can become quite clear. Granted, for the writing assignments in your classes, you are also going to be responding to specific questions: "Identify three symptoms of aphasia," for example. But sometimes those questions can be difficult to understand, and sometimes, even if you understand what the question is asking, it's hard to know whether your response actually answers it.

Let's start with the earlier example. "Do the problems caused by needle-exchange programs outweigh the benefits?" it asks. We concluded that "The posters show that drug abuse is a problem today" doesn't actually answer that question. Why?

Let's simplify the question in the prompt: "DOES the harm OUTWEIGH the benefits?" This question wants us to assert whether the harm that comes from a particular program is greater in magnitude than the benefit that program offers. Simply saying that "drug abuse is a problem today" doesn't answer the "OUTWEIGH" part of the question.

What about the other answer?

> Needle exchange is wrong. Drug abuse is a terrible thing and when you give addicts clean needles there's no reason for them to quit using. The posters show this, with their use of distasteful drug slang like "works" and "rigs." We as a society need to do everything we can to eliminate drug addiction.

This certainly isn't a great thesis. It's too blunt, and while it does make clear to the reader what the paper will do, it doesn't really give the reader an idea of *why* needle exchange programs are wrong. The vivid detail the writer seizes upon (the drug slang) isn't, by itself, persuasive. But there is something effective there—the writer tries to leverage the distaste that most readers will have about intravenous drug use as support for the claim. But it's not there yet.

So, to create an effective thesis what we need to do is somehow link the three elements that we are trying to add together to make a thesis (these are the elements that the paper prompt specifies):

1. a stance on needle-exchange programs,

2. an assessment of the good such programs do by limiting the spread of disease,

3. an assessment of the harm such programs do by "promoting" or at least not fighting drug abuse, and

4. a reference to the needle-exchange program posters.

We are trying to argue, in essence, whether X (good) is greater or lesser than Y (harm), and then to use that comparison to either endorse or condemn needle-exchange programs. In addition, the prompt asks us to use the poster images as evidence to support our claim. A thesis paragraph that incorporates all of these elements—that answers the question—might look like this:

> Intravenous drug abuse is a scourge, ruining the lives of addicts and their families. But the damage isn't limited to those closest to the users. Society also suffers when users share dirty needles and pass dread diseases, such as HIV or hepatitis C, between each other and then on beyond the circle of addicts. Needle exchange, where addicts can trade in used, contaminated needles for clean ones, stops the spread of disease. And although the general public might be disgusted by the details of IV drug use when they see posters for needle-exchange programs, and feel that we should focus our efforts on eliminating drug abuse, in the end we need to realize that such programs meet an immediate need, and that their benefit to society as a whole outweighs the fact that they might do little to get addicts to clean up.

Does this pass the test? Let's see: the benefits (disease prevention) of X (needle-exchange programs) outweigh the harms (not doing much to stop drug abuse). This thesis answers the question.

In addition, the thesis implicitly lets the reader know what the rest of the paper will do. The thesis, as written, suggests to the reader that the paper will lay out facts about IV drug use and evidence that needle-exchange programs slow the spread of disease (such evidence is necessary to bolster the key claim that they do in fact slow infection rates). The writer will grant that needle exchange probably does little to stop drug abuse, a tactic that makes the writer seem more reasonable and knowledgeable. Finally, the writer indicates that she will use the posters as evidence that the general public probably finds IV drug use viscerally distasteful, which could lead them to disagree with her.

The tough part in any argument is actually connecting the dots, and this will be the challenge for this writer. How effective is needle exchange at reducing disease transmission rates? How much does it cost? Who pays for it? Is it more effective than just trying to get addicts to quit? How many people does it affect? And, apart from the questions about efficacy, what about the moral issues? Should a society ever do anything to enable a behavior that it otherwise condemns? Isn't drug abuse illegal? Don't needle-exchange programs help people break the law? The immediate benefits of lower disease rates may outweigh the immediate harm of not working to stop drug abuse, but what about the larger problem of ignoring or even promoting lawbreaking?

Responding to more complicated, more nuanced questions than you may have previously been used to is probably the first way college writing will differ from your high school writing experience, and it's important always to make sure that you actually answer the question that you've been asked. If you find yourself unsure about whether or not you are answering the question, you can generally talk to your instructor (in class, after class, during office hours, or through email) to make sure you're doing it. You can also take advantage of services such as your university's Writing Center, if it has one, to help with this.

MAKING SURE YOU HAVE A THESIS

What is a thesis? It's the main point of your paper. It's your argument. It's a summary of everything you are going to say. All of these things are correct. So if we all understand what a thesis is, why is it often so hard to write one?

Sometimes it's simple to tell when you are actually writing a thesis. In response to the needle-exchange example, the writer was asked to weigh the costs and benefits of a program. Obviously, a thesis in response to that question needs to make a statement: X is greater, Y is greater, X is greater in the short term but not in the long term, X is greater in one way but lesser in another, and so forth.

But particularly in your writing classes, you'll be writing papers that demand theses that do something else. Often, you'll be asked to analyze someone else's argument, and construct your own argument in response. In answering these kinds of questions, particularly when they are on difficult or controversial topics, students have trouble differentiating between "summary" and "argument." A "summary," as we learned in Chapter 1, is a shortened version of another piece of writing. An "argument" is a statement of opinion about another piece of writing—about its thesis, use of evidence, appeals to its audience, validity, or other questions.

To stick with our needle-exchange topic, read the following opinion piece from a newspaper and think about how you might answer the question that follows:

> Analyze and respond to the following editorial. What is Martin's thesis? What claims does he make, and what evidence does he use? Finally, do you agree with his argument?

The Conservative Case for Needle Exchange

William Martin

The specter of a ruinous budget shortfall has darkened the mood of the current Texas Legislature. In a climate with a mandate to slash spending, bills that seek new or increased funding—no matter how valid the need—seem doomed from the start.

Paradoxically, one of the earliest bills filed for the 140-day biennial session, a public-health outreach program that would include distribution of sterile syringes to injecting drug users, may benefit from the tight economic environment. While this is a controversial issue, and many people believe that needle exchange programs simply facilitate or condone illegal drug use, there is a powerful conservative argument for why it is nonetheless good public policy.

House Bill 117, authored by Rep. Ruth Jones McClendon, D-San Antonio, seeks no state money. It would simply allow local health authorities or nongovernmental organizations to use either private or public funds to establish disease-control programs that offer blood testing, education about the transmission and prevention of communicable diseases, and exchange of used syringes for new ones. Vitally important, these programs would also help participants gain access to effective treatment for their addiction.

Obviously, injecting illegal drugs—particularly in the corrupted state in which they typically reach the retail market—is risky business. This inherent risk is substantially increased when users share needles contaminated by blood-borne diseases, most notably HIV/AIDS and hepatitis. The actual result is stunning. According to the Centers for Disease Control and Prevention, nearly 30 percent of new cases of HIV/AIDS and 60 percent of hepatitis C can be traced to injecting drug use. Small wonder that politicians at all levels have long sought to deny drug users easy access to needles and to punish them whenever they are found with one.

While understandable at a superficial level, this policy rests on a demonstrably false premise. Addicts deprived of clean needles do not give up their drugs; they inject them with contaminated needles, and they contract deadly diseases. One may regard such outcomes as a matter of just deserts, but even the most punitive of politicians pause in the face of the economic drain these diseases create. The average lifetime cost of treating a person with HIV/AIDS is currently estimated to be $380,000. Lifetime costs of treatment for hepatitis C can exceed $300,000. Texas has the fourth-highest rate of HIV/AIDS in the nation, with an estimated 63,000 Texans currently living with HIV, and at least 300,000 with hepatitis C.

Many people infected with these diseases receive little or no medical treatment, but of those who do, public funds bear a high proportion of the cost. From 2002 to 2007, state Medicaid costs for HIV/AIDS services totaled more than $476 million; the cost of treating hepatitis C reached nearly $160 million. That did not include outlays by private payers, insurance companies, local hospital districts or federal programs like Medicare and Veterans Affairs.

Well-run syringe exchanges can dramatically reduce the spread of these diseases. A Johns Hopkins study of the Baltimore City Needle Exchange found that, after six years in operation, the incidence of HIV in Baltimore decreased by 35 percent overall and 70 percent among the approximately 10,000 participants in the program. Even more striking, epidemiologist Don Des Jarlais, director of research at New York's Beth Israel Medical Center and a leading expert on syringe exchange, reports that the incidence of new HIV infections among injecting drug users in New York City has dropped to less than 1 percent per year. "We appear," he said, "to be very close to eliminating injecting-related transmission in a city with over 100,000 injecting drug users."

At least 10 major studies, conducted by such organizations as the National Academy of Science, the Centers for Disease Control and the American Medical Association, have unanimously concluded that access to clean needles reduces the incidence of blood-borne diseases and neither encourages people to start injecting drugs nor increases drug use by those who are already users. Syringe exchange is an accepted part of public health programs in almost all countries of Western and Eastern Europe, Central Asia, and Australia and New Zealand. Even the hyper-conservative ruling mullahs in Iran have approved of syringe exchange as a way to fight an HIV/AIDS epidemic spread mainly by drug users.

Texas is the only state in the union that still flatly prohibits the purchase or possession of syringes for the purpose of injecting illegal drugs. Some religious and social conservatives have opposed exchange programs, contending that they abet addiction and facilitate sin, but legislators themselves have increasingly accepted the counterintuitive scientific evidence.

Sen. Bob Deuell, a conservative Republican and a practicing doctor, sponsored similar bills in both 2007 and 2009. "At one time," he recalled, "I was opposed, but I looked at the data. When people have disagreed with my vote, I've shown them the data and asked them, 'How could I argue with that?'" A fiscal conservative, Deuell also noted that syringe exchange makes good economic sense: "It costs us a fortune to treat HIV and hepatitis C. It's breaking the budget."

Deuell's support of needle exchange does not rest on science and economics alone. "I look at it from the Christian viewpoint," he said. "What would Jesus do? We need to show compassion and try to help.

[Addicts] are God's children, too. When they need new needles, this puts them in touch with someone who might reach them. The very act of handing them clean needles says, 'Your life has value to me. I want you to know that we care about you. When you want to get off, we're here to help you.' If they're in a back alley, using a dirty needle, there's no chance of that."

This argument resonates on both sides of the aisle in the Capitol congregation. In 2009, it was Republicans on the House Public Health committee who organized a special session to hear pro-syringe testimony from religious leaders and others engaged in faith-based outreach to drug users. That panel challenged the morality of applauding churches that minister to AIDS victims but prohibiting a proven means of preventing the disease itself.

In 2007, Deuell's bill, essentially identical to McClendon's current version, passed the Senate by a 23-8 vote (12 from Republicans) but was blocked in the House by the chair of the Public Health Committee, who refused to allow a committee vote. In 2009, a similar bill sailed through the Senate again with an equally bipartisan 23-6 tally, and the House committee sent the bill forward with a 7-3 vote. Observers expected the full House to pass it easily, but the legislative clock ran down on the 140th day, leaving needle exchange and other worthwhile bills orphaned for lack of a vote. In the current session, the Senate will wait to see what the House does, but with only two new senators taking office, one from each party, continued solid support seems assured.

Some supporters of syringe exchange fear that new Republicans in the House might have a knee-jerk negative response to McClendon's bill, imagining it to be just one more Democrat effort to undermine morality and religion in the Lone Star State. The more optimistic expect that the newcomers will quickly see that syringe exchange has wide bipartisan support (Rep. Susan King, R-Abilene, a registered nurse on the Public Health Committee, has signed on as a co-author, as has Rep. John Zerwas, R-Simonton, another physician), is grounded in sound science, is supported by devout religious colleagues and will actually save the state millions of dollars.

Passing a syringe-exchange bill won't balance the state's budget, but it may be one of few opportunities Texas legislators will have this year to improve public health, show compassion for the afflicted and save money in the bargain.

Texas Tribune, 23 February, 2011.

What might be a good thesis in response to the question?

In his editorial "The Conservative Case for Needle Exchange," William Martin argues that although most conservative people think IV drug abuse is wrong, their own conservative values should push them to support needle-exchange programs, for those programs save the government money.

This statement, although a very accurate summary of Martin's argument, doesn't state *the student's* argument—in fact, it's only a summary. The assignment called for a *response* to Martin.

In this paper I am going to respond to William Martin's argument that conservatives should support needle-exchange programs because they save the government money, and conservatives want the government to spend less money.

Although this thesis brings the student writer into it, and it summarizes Martin's thesis, it doesn't actually let the reader know what the student's response *is*.

In an editorial from the *Texas Tribune*, William Martin argues that needle-exchange programs are effective in slowing the spread of disease and are cost-effective, as well. Because they save the government money, he argues, conservatives should support these programs. Although I grant that such programs do slow the spread of disease, and do trim health-care expenditures, I think it is dangerous to implicitly endorse the tragedy of IV drug abuse. We should spend our money on fighting drug abuse, on educating people about the dangers of addiction and of needles, not on giving addicts clean needles.

This thesis clearly states what the paper will be *arguing*, and it sets forth a basic outline of what the paper will accomplish in the process of making that argument. In just about every paper you'll write in any college class, you'll be making some kind of argument—you'll be looking at evidence, applying that evidence to a question, perhaps adding in your own feelings about the question, and coming up with an argument.

So, a *thesis is a statement of opinion*. It's your opinion, based on evidence, about the question your instructor has posed to you. (An introduction that says "I will look at X," like the second one given earlier, isn't a statement of opinion—it's a statement of the fact that the paper will do the things it says it will do.) A thesis statement must be *arguable*—you must be able to present evidence in support of your thesis and have the possibility of persuading an open-minded audience—and a statement of fact isn't that. "William Martin argues that needle-exchange programs are effective and should be legal" is a statement of fact. "I will respond to William Miller's argument" is a statement of fact. "I agree with some of what Miller says, but I think he's wrong in some places" is a statement of *opinion*.

Differentiating between statements of opinion and statements of fact can be difficult. Certainly you learned "fact vs. opinion" back in elementary school, but the issues in question in college papers can be much more sticky, and something that seems like indisputable fact might not seem like that to experts.

PREFERENCES AND OPINIONS

So, if you can't argue a fact, does that mean that all opinions are arguable and, therefore, possible theses? Well, no. Some statements of opinion are simply statements of *preference* and are unarguable. What differentiates a statement of preference from an argument is that it boils down to the unstated assumption that "I like it." Statements of preference can be as simple as "Chocolate milk is better than strawberry milk" or as seemingly complex as "Mozart is a finer composer than Haydn," but both of those statements boil down to the basic idea that "I like X better."

The borderline between a statement of preference and an arguable statement of opinion can be pretty fuzzy. An entire genre of writing— the review—is essentially an extended statement of preference. Similarly, "Mozart is a finer composer than Haydn" is a statement of preference to most audiences, but among classical-music conductors, it could be an arguable proposition.

What can make a statement of preference an arguable proposition is whether or not the speaker and the audience share criteria for judgment. Let's take the chocolate milk statement as an example. What are your criteria for exalting chocolate milk over all other flavored dairy products? "I like it best." "It tastes best." These criteria aren't necessarily shared between the speaker and the audience.

Classical-music conductors, though, might view the proposition "Mozart is a finer conductor than Haydn" to be an arguable proposition. Among this community of experts, there are certainly commonly held criteria about what makes a "fine" or "the finest" composer—the fact that such conductors would universally hold Mozart in higher esteem than, say, a commercial jingle writer demonstrates this. Presumably, since this group holds these criteria in common, they can compare both Haydn and Mozart to those criteria, and see which one excels. But even here, those criteria might not apply: they are too blunt; they only show that both Mozart and Haydn are fine composers, but they cannot objectively differentiate between degrees once they are describing such highly accomplished exemplars of the profession. Again, this probably becomes an argument of preference or taste.

Exercise 2.1: Fact or Opinion or Preference?

Look at the following thesis statements. Which are facts, which are preferences, and which are opinions and, therefore, possible theses? If it might be a preference *or* argument depending upon the audience, explain what the audience would have to be to make it an argument.

1. Of all of the restaurants on campus, Subway is the best.
2. Of all of the restaurants on campus, Subway offers the healthiest food.
3. Of all of the restaurants on campus, Subway's food is the most appealing to college students.
4. Professors might not like it, but texting in class is here to stay.
5. Students who text in class get worse grades than students who don't.
6. Professors who ban laptops in class are behind the times.
7. Professors who ban laptops in class are worse teachers than those who allow laptops.
8. Organic chemistry is so difficult, the best way to teach it is by using three-dimensional modeling.

FINDING THE THESIS

In a short piece of writing, the thesis frequently comes near the end of the first paragraph. In fact, the five-paragraph-essay model essentially demands that the last sentence of the first paragraph be the thesis. But as you read more, and exercise your critical-reading skills, you'll find that writers put their thesis in all sorts of places. In the "Gangsta Kobe" article from Chapter 1, the thesis comes almost as the last sentence of the article.

Nor is it necessary for a thesis to be stated explicitly. It's hardly uncommon for an article, especially a longer one, to have an **implicit thesis**—one that is never stated in clear one-sentence form. Other articles or essays might have a thesis that is broken into parts—the author must prove one point, and then another related point, and then assert at the end of the article that these two points add up to something unexpected (which becomes the article's thesis). As you read, be sure you account for this.

You can do the same thing. Although your instructor may have a preference, or may even require that you state your thesis explicitly and place it in a particular place in your paper, there are no hard and fast rules about what a thesis must look like, where it must appear, or whether a piece of writing even has to have a thesis statement. What matters is that *what you are arguing is clear to the audience*. The point of a thesis is to boil down a longer piece of writing into a single statement that the reader can keep in mind as he or she considers the argument and the evidence that the writer—you—offers in support of it.

JOINING THE CONVERSATION

Although it's likely that thesis statements are familiar, one thing that differentiates academic writing from writing that students have done earlier is the notion of "joining the conversation" around a particular issue. Basically, what this means is that rather than learning about a topic as something that is fixed and settled (which might have been part of a "report" assignment), students may now be expected to see a particular topic as something on which people, including scholars and experts, have different opinions. Through research, writers learn the facts about the matter, and then they identify what the most important or dominant of the differing opinions and perspectives on the issue are. (This is what is often called an "overview.") For such papers in college classes, students may also be asked to offer their own take on the issue—to connect with, and then join, that conversation.

Obviously, issues of political importance lend themselves well to this kind of work, and they're pretty common in writing classes. Let's take a simple example: in a given writing class, the students are asked to take a stand on "Should capital punishment be abolished?" For many students, this might seem an easy task; they've thought extensively about the morality and practicality of capital punishment before. "No way," the student might say: "If they kill someone, they deserve to die. End of story." Here, the writer has an **opinion** on the issue but hasn't yet joined the conversation.

In order to join the conversation surrounding capital punishment, it's necessary to learn more about the issue, even if your basic stance on it is so firm that it'll never be shaken. What are the most important and influential stands on the issue? Who are the leading spokespeople and writers on the issue? What are the relevant facts about capital punishment? How does capital punishment work? Is it used in every state? Was it ever banned? How many executions happen in an average year? Is the death penalty imposed by a judge or a jury? What crimes trigger the death penalty? Does this differ from state to state?

One can find this information in basic reference works such as encyclopedias, Wikipedia, and books on the criminal-justice system. For more specialized, precise, and reliable information, sources such as the websites of the U.S. Justice Department, the Supreme Court of the United States, or advocacy groups such as Amnesty International are invaluable and bring credibility to one's paper.

Having learned the central facts about the issue, a writer will then move on to surveying the range of opinion. Finding various stances on the issue is as simple as entering "death penalty" or "capital punishment" into a Google search box. However, the work doesn't end there. The first page of results for this Google search isn't an accurate representation of the most influential or important stances on the death penalty (or any other issue).

Searching "capital punishment," I came up with two Wikipedia pages, the home pages for three prominent anti-death-penalty advocacy groups, two personal pro-death-penalty home pages, and two sites that bill themselves as giving an objective "pro-con" overview. Anti-death-penalty arguments dominate this material, giving no indication that a majority of Americans consistently support capital punishment. It's imperative to bring one's critical reading skills—particularly the practice of identifying the credibility of the writer or group that produced the Web page or article—to each of the pages consulted.

That said, this basic Google search will unearth many of the key arguments for and against capital punishment. Digging underneath the binary "yes/no" stances, we find these (and many other) underlying claims:

> Capital punishment serves as a deterrent to murder.
>
> Capital punishment has not been shown to diminish the crime rate.
>
> Killing humans for any reason is always wrong.
>
> The Bible endorses capital punishment when it says "an eye for an eye, a tooth for a tooth."
>
> Members of minority groups are much more likely to be convicted and executed, even when they have committed the same crimes as whites.
>
> Capital punishment reinforces our society's commitment to the sanctity of life.
>
> States should decide for themselves whether to permit capital punishment.
>
> Because their lives are at stake, defendants in capital cases must be provided excellent lawyers.
>
> Capital punishment isn't cost efficient.
>
> By allowing capital punishment, the United States puts itself in the company of nations such as Iran, China, North Korea, and Saudi Arabia.

REFINING YOUR STANCE

Starting with an opinion, we moved on to researching the facts about the issue and now have developed a rudimentary understanding of the history of the death penalty and how it is imposed. Then, we found a range of opinions on the issue—not just yes/no stances, but explanations of why and how. What we have are the raw materials of—the notes for—a good *overview* of the issue.

Frequently, the next step is to express your own stance on the issue. Let's take the hypothetical situation posed earlier: a supporter of the death penalty has been assigned a paper in which he must give an overview of the issue and argue for his position. Now that he understands the issue in much greater detail than he did before, he can write this part of the paper.

Finding the Implicit Assumption

"I support the death penalty," our hypothetical student says. Now, he has to answer the question of "why." Let's have our hypothetical student examine his own beliefs for a minute, in order to discover what the "implicit assumption" is behind this claim.

> Why do I support capital punishment? Capital punishment is the most final and irreversible punishment we can impose. Most of the time, it's imposed only on the most final and irreversible crime—murder. Ending someone else's life is so extreme that it merits a special kind of punishment, something going beyond just confinement in prison. It also helps that this punishment really does fit the crime—kill someone, and you die. Therefore, capital punishment is just (it reflects the extremity of the crime) and simple (there's no negotiating about how long to hold someone in prison, or in what kind of conditions).

The implicit assumption behind the claim "The death penalty is right because it is simple and just" is "those penalties that are simple and just are right," or "we should seek to impose penalties that are simple and that mirror the crime committed." This implicit assumption, or what some rhetoricians call a "warrant," reflects your basic beliefs, and ideally you'll share this assumption with your audience.

This might seem difficult to understand at first, so let's look at a few other examples. "You should get a college degree because over the course of your life, the odds are that you'll earn significantly more money." Standing behind this claim is the idea that "it is a good thing to earn more money, and a person should do what he or she can to make that possible." Alternately, a professor may counsel that "while a degree in philosophy might not seem like it'll lead you right into a profession, I think that you'll find that the skills we teach in philosophy will prepare you for any number of professions; in addition, it will equip you with critical-thinking skills that will enrich your life in ways that you can't imagine right now." Underlying this claim are the assumptions that "having broad training is better than having specialized training, even if specialized training might be more immediately remunerative" and "you should want to enrich your life."

Exercise 2.2: Critical Thinking Exercise

What are the implicit assumptions behind the following claims?

1. Capital punishment is right because it serves as a deterrent to murder.

2. Capital punishment should be abolished because it has not been shown to diminish the crime rate.

3. Capital punishment is immoral because killing humans is always wrong.

4. Capital punishment is moral because the Bible endorses it.

5. Capital punishment is unfair because members of minority groups are much more likely to be convicted and executed, even when they have committed the same crimes as whites.

6. Capital punishment reinforces our society's commitment to the sanctity of life.

7. States should decide for themselves whether to permit capital punishment.

8. Because their lives are at stake, defendants in capital cases must be provided excellent lawyers.

9. Although its advocates argue that it is simple and cheap, capital punishment in the United States costs more per prisoner than simple incarceration would, and thus isn't cost-efficient.

Using the Implicit Assumption

A good writer is aware of his or her implicit assumptions before getting involved in a conversation about an issue. Our hypothetical student's assumption that "those penalties that are simple and just are right" will appeal to some listeners or readers but not to others. Think back to the implicit assumptions behind the claims given earlier: they argue, variously, that a punishment should be fair, should not disproportionately fall upon one group of people (apart from criminals), should serve the purpose of deterring crime, and should use resources effectively. A listener who is most concerned with *fairness*—whether the death penalty is imposed equally upon all people who commit the same crime—is probably not going to be swayed by an argument grounded on the justice and simplicity of capital punishment. Our hypothetical student is talking about the punishment in *theory*, whereas the listener is concerned about how it works out *in practice*.

This isn't to say that the two parties can't talk to each other. When two speakers or writers have incompatible warrants, they may choose to shift the discussion from one about issues to one about warrants. Rather than "The death penalty is right because it's just and simple" versus "the death penalty is wrong because minorities are much more likely to be sentenced to it," the speakers might choose to talk about "What is most important in a legal punishment—that it be simple and clear in theory, or that it be fair and equal in application?" What's important to keep in mind, as you are engaging in the process of writing critically about texts, is to drill deeply into your text to uncover your author's implicit assumptions, and to make sure that you don't take it for granted that everyone shares *your* implicit assumptions.

INCORPORATING DIFFERENT VOICES: SUMMARY, PARAPHRASE, QUOTATION

Throughout this process of engaging with diverse ideas about a topic, we encounter these ideas primarily in language. That is, we *read* or *hear* these ideas, whether they are on a newspaper's website, on a blog, or even in a classroom lecture or discussion. Some of these ideas will be exciting and provocative; others will hold no relevance or interest.

But—and this is one of the key aspects differentiating college writing from other kinds of writing, particularly that done in high school—when a writer responds to those ideas, he or she is now expected to respond *directly* to them, and in a way that permits a reader to go back to the writer's original sources. And in doing so, the writer is expected to be conscientious about *accurately* capturing what those sources say, and not misrepresenting their ideas or words. As this chapter has made clear, college writing is more about weighing competing ideas than it is about transcribing or swallowing them whole, and so writing teachers want students to be able to "put ideas into play" with each other. This requires that writers genuinely understand those ideas.

Almost all writers entering college have worked with secondary sources before. For high school research papers, teachers often require a set number of sources and may even specify that some of those sources must come from books or other printed media. Although students often enjoy engaging in research, the actual process of putting those sources into the paper often becomes a chore—students will select the minimum number of sources and just pick a random quote from the source so that they meet the assignment's requirement. Writing teachers sometimes call this the "crouton" effect—quotes from outside sources just float on top of the student's actual writing but don't really become *part* of the paper and, in fact, stick out (like a crouton on top of a salad).

Such assignments—research papers requiring a specified number of outside sources—are also common in college writing classes. But as students begin engaging with more intellectually challenging subject matter, writing teachers expect more from their students in terms of the use of outside sources. In particular, writing teachers want writers to *select carefully* sources that are relevant to the paper and credible to an academic audience, and they want writers to *digest* those sources—to understand them in full, rather than just finding a quote that seems to fit the purpose of the paper. Good, relevant sources, fully understood and "digested" by the writer, don't stick out like croutons.

When a writer incorporates a secondary source, he or she is really lending space to another writer, another voice. There should be a good reason to do so, since the primary purpose of a paper is to express *the writer's* ideas in *the writer's* voice. Secondary sources provide evidence for a point that the primary writer wants to make; they add credibility to the primary writer's argument; they might offer particularly apt or clever wording. But a writer should always remember that secondary sources are not the point of the paper, but rather a tool to be used in the paper. They should work *for* the writer.

There are three basic means by which writers incorporate others' words and ideas into their own work: summary, paraphrase, and quotation. These three modes of using outside sources are probably already familiar to most beginning college writers. But even though writers at this level still use these three basic tools, two things change when one writes for an academic audience.

First, the ideas and often the words of the secondary sources are likely to be much more complicated than anything that college writers have encountered before. This may not seem relevant at first; after all, it's just as easy to pull a quote out of a difficult journal article as it is to find a quote in a Facebook status update. But it's especially imperative for a writer who uses complicated or difficult secondary sources really to understand those sources and to "translate" them for the reader— explaining clearly what they mean, and showing how they are relevant to the argument at hand. With complicated or difficult materials, even finding the thesis statement or essence of the source's argument can be an achievement and requires genuine intellectual work (and critical reading, as discussed in the previous chapter).

Second, a university is an intellectual community, and as such it holds to particular values and practices. Central to these practices is the commandment that "one does not take credit for work that is not one's own." When a writer uses a secondary source, he or she must accurately explain to the reader what that source is saying but must also make clear to the reader which are the *source's* words and ideas and which are the *writer's*. Writers do this in several ways at once: by using signal words and phrases, by stating explicitly in the text who is responsible for an idea, and by citing and documenting the source and where they accessed it.

Signal Words and Phrases

The first thing to do when using a secondary source is to signal to the reader that the next words or ideas come from another writer. Writers do this with **signal words** or **phrases**:

> This university needs to stop selling apparel made at Indonesian sweatshops. After all, **as Martin Luther King said in his "Letter from Birmingham Jail,"** "injustice anywhere is a threat to justice every-where."

> The current political preoccupation with reducing the federal deficit **seems to disprove former Vice-President Cheney's statement that** "deficits don't matter."

Although Oracle CEO Larry Ellison blithely stated that online privacy is dead, I think that we need to pay closer attention to how companies such as Google and Facebook are using our data.

When Gloria Steinem said that "a woman needs a man like a fish needs a bicycle," she inspired millions of women to be more independent.

Signal words and phrases call the reader's attention to the identity of the speaker who has been invited into the paper, which can be valuable when the writer wants to draw upon that speaker's credibility (or *ethos*, as you'll read about in the following chapter). Signal words and phrases also make it clear that the writer is not trying to claim credit for those words or ideas; this subtly works to bolster the writer's own credibility. Finally, such signal words or phrases, particularly in a piece of writing that is engaged extensively with someone else's words or ideas (as in a review or response paper), help the reader differentiate the writer's ideas from the source's.

Exercise 2.3: Critical Writing

Choose an article from one of the readings chapters. Write sentences that quote from the article that you select. Vary the phrases and words you choose so that you produce:

1. One sentence in which the signal word or phrase comes before the quote
2. One sentence in which the signal word or phrase is inserted in the middle of the quote
3. One sentence in which the signal word or phrase follows the quote
4. One sentence with a signal phrase that fully introduces the author of the quote
5. Three sentences using words besides "said" to introduce the quote

Summary, Paraphrase, Quotation

Once you decide that a source offers you something important that you could not come up with on your own, you'll then need to decide how to use it, and how much of that source is necessary to include in your paper. For instance, do you need to refer to the argument or facts included in a full article, a chapter in a book, or an entire book? Or do you need to explain only a small section of the work? An example might be a portion of a long chapter in which the financial instruments called "credit default swaps" are described—you might not need the entire chapter, but you do need the book's definition of credit default swaps, which is better than one you might be able to generate. Finally, sometimes you might need just a single sentence, phrase, or even word, as in the Steinem and Martin Luther King quotes given earlier.

A *summary* is a significantly shortened and simplified version, written in your own words, of a longer secondary source. In a paper for your Media Studies class, you might be asked to respond to Farhad Manjoo's *True Enough*, a discussion of our current electronic-media environment. (An excerpt from that book appears in Chapter 4.) In order to respond to it, you'll have to summarize it—not just a chunk of it, but the whole thing—and make sure you are accurately identifying its key points. A summary of *True Enough*, incorporated into a writer's own introductory paragraph and set off with signal phrases, might look like this:

> The media environment is changing more quickly than it ever has. The means by which we get the news, the content of the news itself, and even the way we read and understand the news are all undergoing dramatic shifts. **Journalist Farhad Manjoo addresses these issues in his 2008 book *True Enough***. In this work, **Manjoo argues** that the breakdown of the "old media" environment—caused largely by the growth of electronic media such as cell phones and emails and blogs as well as 24-hour news channels—is causing people to consume only news that already agrees with what they believe. Because of this, the whole idea of a "fact" that we all share is disappearing. **Manjoo engages** in case studies of, among others, the "Swift Boat" incident in the 2004 presidential election, the group of conspiracy theorists who believe that the U.S. government was behind the 9/11 attacks, and the community of parents of autistic children to make his case that current communications and media technology allow us to wall ourselves off from ideas or facts that we find inconvenient.

Summary might seem easy—how hard could it be to write three or four sentences?—but it's actually a task that requires that you have fully understood the source text. In order to summarize, you have to identify the key argument of the source text and its most important pieces of evidence, most surprising insights, and the ways in which it anticipates counterarguments. It requires critical reading, in other words.

Exercise 2.4: Summarizing

Choose two of the readings in Chapters 4 to 10 and summarize each one in a single paragraph. Start your first sentence with "In [title], [author] argues that [thesis of the piece]." Then identify the most important points and provide them for your reader.

Writers use paraphrase when it is important not just to get the basics of a longer piece, but to restate a portion of someone else's writing in detail. In a paraphrase, you use *your own words*—this is extremely important—but you try to approximate as closely as possible the meaning of the source passage. Writers often paraphrase when an original author uses technical jargon or a difficult or bureaucratic style; the goals are to get the meaning of the passage across to the reader effectively and to embed the point of the original passage in the writer's own work and style.

Exercise 2.5: Paraphrasing

Choose a passage from one of the articles in cluster one of Chapter 4—the Carr or Willen articles would work well. Paraphrase that passage in your own words, making sure to get all essential details in there (summaries frequently omit details).

Quoting is the use of a secondary source you are probably most familiar with and have used the most. Ironically, though, it should probably be used the *least* of these three options for incorporating secondary sources.

Why is that? Primarily, it's because the reader reads your writing to hear you, and thus when you are allowing someone else to speak—when you are lending another voice some of your valuable real estate — the reader doesn't hear you. For the most part, when you are trying to point out or refute or respond to someone else's ideas and points, it's best to use summary and paraphrase. That way, the reader hears your voice, you can pick and choose what you want to emphasize or downplay in the original source, and you demonstrate to your reader that you have a mastery of the ideas of the original source.

The flip side of this is that student writers tend to rely on quotes when they *don't* fully understand what a source is saying. It's harder work to critically read and be able accurately to summarize or paraphrase a source than it is to pull a seemingly representative quote out. Don't let quoting from a source be a shortcut that you use to bypass fully understanding the source.

Quoting is appropriate, even necessary, when a writer has said something in a particularly memorable fashion. "'I have a dream that my four little children will one day live in a nation where they will not be judged by the color of their skin but by the content of their character,' Martin Luther King Jr. said"; this would be much less impressive paraphrased as "Martin Luther King said that he hoped his children wouldn't be judged on their skin color but on who they were."

Quoting is also important when your writing task is primarily a detailed and sustained explanation of, response to, or refutation of another text. In an analysis of poetry, you'll certainly want to quote exact words and phrases; in a rebuttal to a political speech, you'll pull specific passages and terms and respond directly to them. When the actual words of the text to which you are responding are central to your own writing task, it's more likely that quoting is the best choice.

Crediting Sources

Finally, it should go without saying that whenever you use someone else's ideas or words in any way, you must credit them. A responsible academic writer does this in two parts. First, the writer alerts the reader that a particular idea or set of words comes from someone else. The signal words and phrases discussed earlier are the most common way of achieving this. Second, the writer provides all of the information necessary for the reader to consult the exact source, in the exact form, from which the writer got the words or ideas. This isn't an either/or situation; a writer must do *both* every time he or she uses an outside source.

It's quite important for writers to make sure that they signal to readers that they are taking words or ideas from an outside source. A quote thrown into the middle of a passage of prose—even one with a clear conceptual connection to what you're writing about—without any introduction or identification of who is speaking is disconcerting and undermines the writer's authority:

> Although many of the finest ski areas on the East Coast are in Vermont, the Pocono Mountains of Pennsylvania have several very good, if small, slopes. For those who can't or don't wish to ski, some of these resorts offer inner tubing, as well. "Who needs skis to hurtle down a snowy mountain? At least a half-dozen ski areas in the Pocono Mountains in eastern Pennsylvania offer sledding on an inner tube." The Pennsylvania state tourism board should promote these areas more than it does.

Writing teachers bemoan the crouton effect of the previous passage: the quote is thrown in and doesn't mix well with the rest of the passage. A simple signal phrase smoothes the paragraph out nicely and puts the writer fully in control:

> Although many of the finest ski areas on the East Coast are in Vermont, the Pocono Mountains of Pennsylvania have several very good, if small, slopes. For those who can't or don't wish to ski, some of these resorts offer inner tubing, as well. As the *New York Times* noted in 2009, "who needs skis to hurtle down a snowy mountain? At least a half-dozen ski areas in the Pocono Mountains in eastern Pennsylvania offer sledding on an inner tube." The Pennsylvania state tourism board should promote winter tubing more than it does.

This passage, though, is missing the second component of responsible use of outside sources: documentation. Every writing teacher or school has a preferred citation style (MLA, APA, Chicago, or another), but in any style you use, there'll probably be two elements: a brief citation in the text and a fuller entry in a bibliography or works-cited list that appears at the end of the paper. The two elements are separated, generally, because it would be too obtrusive (especially in a paper that uses numerous sources) to have a full bibliographic entry in the text—this would be annoying to read.

So, with a signal phrase, in-text citation, and works-cited entry in MLA style, our passage would look like this:

> Although many of the finest ski areas on the East Coast are in Vermont, the Pocono Mountains of Pennsylvania have several very good, if small, slopes. For those who can't or don't wish to ski, some of these resorts offer inner tubing, as well. As Dave Caldwell noted in the *New York Times* in 2009, "who needs skis to hurtle down a snowy mountain? At least a half-dozen

ski areas in the Pocono Mountains in eastern Pennsylvania offer sledding on an inner tube" (Caldwell). The Pennsylvania state tourism board should promote winter tubing more than it does.

> Caldwell, Dave. "Winter Weekends: Tubing in the Poconos." *New York Times* 2 January 2009. Web. 16 December 2010.

Citations and bibliographical entries are necessary whether you are quoting, paraphrasing, or summarizing. Check with your instructor and consult your writing handbook or style manual about specific procedures (e.g., footnotes versus in-text citations; where a citation goes when a paragraph is entirely a summary).

So, to sum up:

- The primary purpose of your writing is to express your own ideas and thoughts. Even though secondary sources are often necessary, they should serve your purposes as a writer, not overwhelm your voice.

- When you move from expressing your own ideas and thoughts to summarizing, paraphrasing, or quoting someone else's, you need to alert the reader to this shift through a signal phrase.

- Choose among summary, paraphrase, and quotation based on how long the source is, to what extent your writing project directly engages with the secondary source, and whether the impact or memorability of the original lies in the original wording.

- When using any ideas or words from a secondary source, it's necessary to cite that source.

- Citations serve two purposes: to inform the reader that these words or ideas are not yours and to allow the reader to consult the exact source, in the exact form, that you did.

- A shorthand citation should appear in the text or as a footnote, informing the reader that this idea or these words come from a secondary source.

- This shorthand citation should point to a full bibliography or works-cited entry that appears either at the end of the text or in a footnote.

JOINING DIFFERENT KINDS OF CONVERSATIONS

Browsing through, researching, and using in your own writing the words and ideas produced by other writers are among the most important steps in learning about, and then joining, societal conversations about important issues. Where do such conversations happen? The writing classroom, often, is one place—and it's generally a safe place for students to try out new ideas and ways of arguing.

But in a large, pluralistic, democratic society such as ours, conversations about important issues (such as the death penalty) primarily happen in places or "forums" such as magazines, newspapers (online or print), blogs, cable news programs, listservs, talk radio, social-networking sites such as Facebook, television commercials, and, yes, even personal conversation. These forums provide us space to learn about and express our own feelings on important issues.

Ours isn't an ideal society in this way, of course. Not everyone has an equal voice—the powerful, the wealthy, and the well connected have a much easier time being heard than those who are not so privileged. And as has always been the case, some of the voices would rather persuade by any means possible than fairly examine the evidence; be open about their assumptions, biases, and stakes in the issue; and be truthful with audiences. A savvy critical reader (as you are no doubt becoming) learns to spot biases, identify how the forum can affect a message, and discern when a speaker or writer is attempting to mislead an audience. We learn this by reading, by spending time on Facebook or on blogs, or by talking with others and learning about what's going on under the surface.

Then, you might want to take part in those conversations. You might do so by expressing yourself in a class discussion. You might join in a dorm-room debate. You might start a blog, contribute a comment to a news story on the Web, or write a letter to the editor of the school or local paper. You might call in to a talk show or email a public official.

In doing so, you'll notice that each forum has particular expectations and conventions for contributions to it. Talk radio, for example, often values callers who use inflammatory language and that boil issues down to simple black-and-white alternatives. Talk radio also appreciates contributions that are extremely concise and snappy.

Comments on blogs, on the other hand, often use a great deal of slang; are casual; and rely on in-jokes and specialized lingo, such as "noob" or "pwn" (terms derived from video-game culture that respectively refer to an inexperienced person and to the act of utterly dominating or humiliating an opponent). Contributions to online forums often include hyperlinks to other, related content.

In class, by contrast, even when you are discussing a controversial or emotional issue, it's likely that your professor *doesn't* want some of the things that work well on talk radio or blogs—insults, inflammatory language, oversimplification. Contributions to this forum should be carefully stated, should focus on the issue rather than on attacking other speakers, and should put the issue in the context of the class's main focus.

Exercise 2.6: Assumptions and Conventions

Find, read, and contribute to five different forums—social-networking site, letter to campus newspaper or publication, comment forum on a news story, comment forum on an entertainment-oriented site such as YouTube, and political blog. Describe the different conventions of each forum.

THE ACADEMIC CONVERSATION

Conversations that take place in academia—the world of research and teaching, the world you inhabit now—have their own conventions. Some, such as how to make contributions in a class, you are learning about and probably beginning to master. Others, in particular the conversations that take place between scholars, you may have started listening in on, especially if you are taking upper-division classes.

In what are called the "knowledge professions" (academia, for example), scholars and experts study subjects and issues and questions and express their views on the matters at hand in formal ways: through peer-reviewed books and journal articles, through attending conferences and listening to one another's research findings, through applying for grants and evaluating grant applications, and even through direct contact. (The Internet itself, in fact, began as a way for scientists to share data and communicate with one another.)

The conventions of the academic conversation may seem strange or even pointless. Why all of the footnotes? Why the insistence on documenting every statement? Why the impenetrable vocabulary? How can a nonexpert tell a statement of fact from a statement of opinion? These matters can be baffling for students, who are not only expected to read and decipher such material, but also to start to write in the same way— to cite all facts, to provide a "literature review" of relevant scholarship, and to adopt the stylistic conventions (such as the use of the passive voice) of a particular discipline.

A common objection to these specialized and even alienating means of communication is that they lack "common sense" and intelligibility. Particularly when the subject under discussion is something of immediate public importance, it seems suspicious when writers are using language and concepts that the "layperson" (another word for nonspecialist) cannot understand.

TAKING THE ACADEMIC CONVERSATION OUT OF THE ACADEMY: A CASE STUDY

In recent years, the debate about whether or not human activity is changing the climate of the earth in catastrophic ways has been the arena for a controversy between specialists and non-specialists. Lay readers cannot, for the most part, understand the language or ramifications of the scientific articles that present the primary evidence for climate change, and other writing that attempts to "translate" this science for a wider audience (such as Al Gore's film *An Inconvenient Truth*) is attacked, with some justification, for oversimplifying a complex process.

In 2009, a set of emails between climate-change researchers surfaced, emails that seemed to suggest that a few of these scientists had been "fudging their data" or altering results in a way that would strengthen the case that the earth is warming. Climate-change skeptics argued that these emails proved that the science behind global warming is tainted, and thus that the earth is not heating up due to human activity. Climate scientists responded that although these pieces of data and these specific studies might have been faulty, they were only one piece in a much larger edifice of research undergirding the theory that human activity was warming the earth.

Although this is fundamentally a conflict about science and public policy, in another sense the climate-change controversy is an enormous test case about *critical writing*. The scientists, accustomed to speaking only among themselves, attempted to convey their conclusions to a mass audience and expected that the science would speak for itself. However, when these scientists entered the larger societal conversation about what, if anything, we should do about this purported "global warming," they discovered that other voices (from oil companies to libertarian citizens to dissenting scientists) skeptical about climate change and the proposed solution to this supposed problem were more effective at communicating their message to an audience of non-specialists.

These skeptical voices pointed out that human-caused climate change was still only a "theory," and that some scientists still doubted the conclusion that this climate change was either human caused or catastrophic. They also crafted effective, if at times cynical, messages that drew upon people's misunderstanding of science and mistrust of politicians. As a result, the American public's belief that humans are causing catastrophic climate change has *diminished* in recent years, even as the science behind this conclusion has strengthened.

In the end, the scientists had to learn that, if you want to have an impact on society at large, *how you communicate* is just as important as *what you are saying*. Faced with growing public skepticism, a large group of some of the most prominent scientists in the United States published the following extraordinary letter to *Science* magazine (the leading publication of the American scientific establishment, and one of the most important places in which the scientific conversation is conducted) in an attempt to regain control of the conversation.

Please read the letter and answer the questions that follow. In the next chapter, we will continue to examine this letter for its *persuasive* or *rhetorical* strategies. For the purposes of this chapter, focus simply on how it makes its argument and what that argument is.

Climate Change and the Integrity of Science

From 255 members of the National Academy of Sciences:

We are deeply disturbed by the recent escalation of political assaults on scientists in general and on climate scientists in particular. All citizens should understand some basic scientific facts. There is always some uncertainty associated with scientific conclusions; science never absolutely proves anything. When someone says that society should wait until scientists are absolutely certain before taking any action, it is the same as saying society should never take action. For a problem as potentially catastrophic as climate change, taking no action poses a dangerous risk for our planet.

Scientific conclusions derive from an understanding of basic laws supported by laboratory experiments, observations of nature, and mathematical and computer modeling. Like all human beings, scientists make mistakes, but the scientific process is designed to find and correct them. This process is inherently adversarial—scientists build reputations and gain recognition not only for supporting conventional wisdom, but even more so for demonstrating that the scientific consensus is wrong and that there is a better explanation. That's what Galileo, Pasteur, Darwin, and Einstein did. But when some conclusions have been thoroughly and deeply tested, questioned, and examined, they gain the status of "well-established theories" and are often spoken of as "facts."

For instance, there is compelling scientific evidence that our planet is about 4.5bn years old (the theory of the origin of Earth), that our universe was born from a single event about 14bn years ago (the Big Bang theory), and that today's organisms evolved from ones living in the past (the theory of evolution). Even as these are overwhelmingly accepted by the scientific community, fame still awaits anyone who could show these theories to be wrong. Climate change now falls into this category: there is compelling, comprehensive, and consistent objective evidence that humans are changing the climate in ways that threaten our societies and the ecosystems on which we depend.

Many recent assaults on climate science and, more disturbingly, on climate scientists by climate change deniers, are typically driven by special interests or dogma, not by an honest effort to provide an alternative theory that credibly satisfies the evidence. The Intergovernmental Panel on Climate Change (IPCC) and other scientific assessments of climate change, which involve thousands of scientists producing massive and comprehensive reports, have, quite expectedly and normally, made some mistakes. When errors are pointed out, they are corrected.

But there is nothing remotely identified in the recent events that changes the fundamental conclusions about climate change:

(i) The planet is warming due to increased concentrations of heat-trapping gases in our atmosphere. A snowy winter in Washington does not alter this fact.

(ii) Most of the increase in the concentration of these gases over the last century is due to human activities, especially the burning of fossil fuels and deforestation.

(iii) Natural causes always play a role in changing Earth's climate, but are now being overwhelmed by human-induced changes.

(iv) Warming the planet will cause many other climatic patterns to change at speeds unprecedented in modern times, including increasing rates of sea-level rise and alterations in the hydrologic cycle. Rising concentrations of carbon dioxide are making the oceans more acidic.

(v) The combination of these complex climate changes threatens coastal communities and cities, our food and water supplies, marine and freshwater ecosystems, forests, high mountain environments, and far more.

Much more can be, and has been, said by the world's scientific societies, national academies, and individuals, but these conclusions should be enough to indicate why scientists are concerned about what future generations will face from business-as-usual practices. We urge our policymakers and the public to move forward immediately to address the causes of climate change, including the unrestrained burning of fossil fuels.

We also call for an end to McCarthy-like threats of criminal prosecution against our colleagues based on innuendo and guilt by association, the harassment of scientists by politicians seeking distractions to avoid taking action, and the outright lies being spread about them. Society has two choices: we can ignore the science and hide our heads in the sand and hope we are lucky, or we can act in the public interest to reduce the threat of global climate change quickly and substantively. The good news is that smart and effective actions are possible. But delay must not be an option.

Science, 7 May 2010.

Exercise 2.7: Critical Reading Questions

1. Who is the intended audience of this letter? What are the textual clues that make that clear?

2. What is the thesis of the letter?

3. How does the letter identify and respond to (or "rebut") those who disagree with its argument?

4. The letter lists five points (i–v) that it poses as indisputable facts. Do you agree that these are statements of facts, or do you believe that they are statements of opinion? If you believe that they are opinions, what evidence would it take to make them facts?

5. Does the letter use specialized vocabulary or require specialized knowledge? If you feel it does, identify places in which it does so.

3
What Does it Mean to "Write Persuasively?"

*R*hetoric. You've probably heard the term before. It's likely that if you've heard the term, it was being used dismissively. "That's all just typical party rhetoric," a television commentator might say. "There's a lot of rhetoric out there about this issue," says a politician, "but I'm here to tell you the truth." *Rhetoric* and *truth*, in fact, are often seen to be opposites. But what is rhetoric? What does it have to do with "truth"? And what does it have to do with the writing you do in college?

Rhetoric, in contemporary English, has come to mean "the use of language to persuade." When we speak of rhetoric, we generally are talking about the kind of language that is intended to get an audience to think or do something—to convince or persuade them of something. Language that is strictly informational (for example, "the sun rises in the east") isn't considered rhetoric. But if this is the *denotation* (or the dictionary definition) of rhetoric, the *connotation*—the added meanings a word carries by the way it's frequently used—is that of empty or bombastic or needlessly biased speech. To call something *rhetoric* is to say that you shouldn't take it as fact, and that you should watch out for the tricks it might use on you.

THE TOOLS OF PERSUASION

Before talking about rhetoric, we should probably just review the basics of communication. All acts of communication require three elements: a sender of a message, a message, and a receiver. (The three are often diagrammed as a "communications triangle.") This is true whether the message is intended to persuade or to inform. In addition, all acts of communication take place in a "situation"—a time and a place—and through a "medium" of communication—direct one-to-one speech, a telephone, a printed magazine, the radio, a police officer's bullhorn, a blog's comment section.

In crafting an effective message, a *rhetor* (someone who is using rhetoric) must think about how each of these elements might affect the act as a whole. Shouting "Fire!" in a crowded theater is a different kind of communications act than an executioner shouting "Fire!" to a firing squad, or a basketball coach urging a hot shooter to "Fire!" away, or a beleaguered scoutmaster pointing to the "Fire!" he just successfully kindled after an hour of frustrated effort. The message is the same in all of these, but the *meaning* is different because of the differences in speaker, audience, and situation. In expressing your happiness at making the dean's list, you'll express it differently to your best friend, to your rival who *didn't* make the list, to the professor who spent extra time with you to get you up to speed, and to your parents.

Persuasive speech relies particularly heavily on how rhetors account for audience, medium, message, and situation. Let's look at a hypothetical example of persuasive speech and see how those affect it. Imagine a student—perhaps someone like yourself. This student has an important paper due in her writing class on Friday: the problem is that she also has an accounting exam, a double shift at her off-campus job, and a weekend trip planned. It's a perfect storm of obligations that are almost certainly going to prevent her from being able to give this paper the attention it deserves. Her job: persuade her professor to give her a one-week extension on the paper. In this situation, we have the following elements:

- SENDER: student
- MESSAGE: allow me an extension on this paper
- AUDIENCE: professor
- PLACE: professor's office
- TIME: during office hours
- MEDIUM: speech

How do these elements affect the message? First of all, *audience*. The audience is the professor. The prof has made a rule that our hypothetical student is asking her to bend, so clearly she has a stake in upholding it—the prof instituted this rule (the deadline) for a reason and is trying to achieve something through this rule. However, the professor's ultimate objective is to help the student learn to write. Our student might presume that the underlying principle behind the deadline is the professor's convenience and thus might try to craft the message to appeal to the professor's desire for convenience: "I know you want all the papers at once, so that you can grade them all at the same time, but I will have my paper to you only a week later—this shouldn't inconvenience you greatly." It's unlikely this will sway the professor, who—even if she *did* institute the rule for her convenience, might not want to acknowledge that. It might be smarter, and more effective, for the student to appeal to the professor's desire to help the student learn to write. What might that request sound like?

The other elements also affect how our student will craft the message. Making this request in the relative privacy of the professor's office might be more effective than asking for an extension in class; the prof might fear that granting an extension to one person in front of the class will spur other students to ask for an extension. The time—office hours—is important, as well, only in the sense that it is the *appropriate* time to make a request of a professor. Running up to the prof at lunch, or trying to catch her in the halls between classes, is likely to be ineffective. The medium—speech—is also relevant, as our student will be in the physical presence of the prof.

Exercise 3.1: Using the Concept

Think of several times in the past day or so when you have attempted to persuade or convince an audience of something. Then draw up a description of this attempted act of persuasion, listing the six elements (sender, message, audience, place, time, and medium) and how you took the last three into consideration in crafting that message. Try to choose situations in which the medium differed: a spoken message, a message by telephone, a text message, a Facebook post, and so on.

ETHOS: WHY SHOULD YOU LISTEN TO ME?

On top of the basic elements of communication described earlier are what have come to be known as "rhetorical appeals." Rhetorical appeals—known as *ethos*, *pathos*, and *logos*—are the choices that a rhetor makes in designing his or her message to be persuasive to the particular audience in this particular situation and through this particular medium.

In our hypothetical communicative act, the student is the speaker; there's nothing she can do about this (she can't hire an attorney, for example). However, an effective rhetor takes care in crafting the *way* he or she comes across. Our student could slouch in to the professor's office and demand an extension because her life is so busy right now. She could try to garner sympathy from the professor; she might even carp a little bit. Or she could use a respectful and serious posture and tone of voice and say, "I realize that this might inconvenience you, and that my overpacked schedule this week isn't your problem, but is there any way I could have an extension on this paper? Given my other commitments, I just can't give this paper the time and energy it deserves, and I'd like to do a good job on it, because it's important to me."

The choice between the two is a choice of *ethos*. In the first, the student is thinking that emotion (pity) might sway the prof. "I have so much to do, and your assignment is just another thing!" this *ethos* appeal says. It could work: the prof might have a reputation for pitying overscheduled students or for being a softie on deadlines. But this first appeal is fundamentally about the *speaker*—give me this (an extension) because of things that I have done and that I need to do.

The other *ethos* choice might be called "the responsible grown-up." The student identifies the values held by the audience—the desire for the student to learn to write better, the need for the student to put in concentrated time and energy on the writing process in order to achieve that—and appeals to those values in the *audience*. In the first example, the speaker's *ethos* is as a fundamentally self-concerned person; in the second, the speaker creates an *ethos* of being attentive to other people's needs and values. The argument ("give me an extension") is the same; the *message itself* differs because the *ethos* differs.

Ethos is, then, the speaker's answer to the question "Why should you believe me? Why should you listen to me?" *Ethos* describes the speaker's credibility or authority to speak on a particular topic. Experts in a field, high officials, well-respected people, those who have achieved something important in a particular area will all have a great deal of *ethos* when making an argument about that field of expertise or accomplishment.

One size rarely fits all when it comes to *ethos*. Generally, a speaker will want to seem knowledgeable about a topic, unless the audience is suspicious of sophistication or acquaintance with a particular subject. In fact, a speaker might use the lack of knowledge or education as part of an *ethos* appeal: "Now, I may not be a fancy big-city lawyer, and I may not have gone to Harvard, but I do know a few things..." An effective rhetor may change his or her *ethos* appeal for the same message depending upon the audience and the situation. Speaking to an audience of enthusiastic supporters at a fund-raiser for a Democratic Senate candidate, President Obama will come across very

Martin Luther King speaking

differently than he will in the State of the Union address, even though the message—"support my programs"—is identical.

A writer's passion about a topic conveys *ethos*, as well. Making an argument about an explosive topic, a writer may want to come across as the voice of reason or, on the other hand, might want to seem even more passionate than the audience itself—it all depends on the audience, the nature of the issue, and the occasion.

Marshalling other authorities on a topic is part of *ethos*. When Martin Luther King compared himself to St. Paul in his famous "Letter from Birmingham Jail," he sought to point out to his audience (clergy) how similar his situation was to that of a man whom the Christian priests and ministers venerate. (This can lead to overreaching, as when cult leaders compare themselves to Jesus Christ or Moses.) Conservative politicians often cite Ronald Reagan in their appeals, as conservative audiences tend to greatly admire Reagan, and liberal politicians frequently allude to Franklin Roosevelt, a favorite of liberal audiences. *All* sides tend to claim that they are in the tradition of such American heroes as Abraham Lincoln or Thomas Jefferson, as they know that almost all Americans have positive feelings about these presidents.

Exercise 3.2: Critical Reading Question

Look back at the "Climate Change and the Integrity of Science" letter at the end of the previous chapter. In one paragraph, identify *all* of

the ways in which this letter uses *ethos*. Then, having listed all of
these, synthesize them: what do they all have in common? How are
all of these *ethos* appeals linked? Can you come up with a summary
statement about the *ethos* appeal of this letter as a whole?

ETHOS IN YOUR OWN WRITING

In writing for your classes, you can make yourself more persuasive by
effectively using *ethos*. In this rhetorical situation—a student learning
about an issue or a subject, and making an argument about that subject
to an instructor who, presumably, knows more about the topic—it's of
paramount importance to come across as also *knowledgeable*. Whether
or not a student has carefully and critically read a piece of writing
comes across very clearly when a student summarizes that piece—and
a student who hasn't fully understood a piece of writing to which he
or she is responding immediately loses credibility.

The outside sources a writer brings in are central components of a
writer's *ethos*. As Chapter 2 pointed out, by incorporating a secondary
source, the writer gives his or her seal of approval to that source,
saying, "I'm going to let someone else say this for me, because he or
she can say it better than I can or is more knowledgeable." So, when a
writer gives someone else's voice a prominent place in his or her own
writing, and that source turns out to be unreliable, the writer's own
ethos takes a major hit. Many of your classes will require that all of
your sources be peer-reviewed, scholarly research from journals and
books; in those classes, using non-scholarly sources will immediately
undermine your *ethos*.

It's particularly important to be vigilant about what you are
quoting and citing off the Web, because many advertisers, interest
groups, and other biased or unreliable voices have spent a great deal of
time and money making sure that their sites come up on the first page
of search results. Because of this, it's important to go beyond the first
few hits on a search engine and to seek out credible, impartial sources
on a topic. Search engines such as Google do some of that work for
you, for Google ranks results based on how many other sites link to a
site (a lot of sites linking somewhere suggests that a site is credible to a
large number of people). However, just because a site is *popular* doesn't
mean that it's *credible for use in an academic paper*.

Ethos goes beyond the argument and what sources the writer
includes. Student writers want their instructors to think they have
worked hard on and thought deeply about their papers; a tightly edited,
neatly printed, and carefully proofread paper conveys this to the audience. Sloppy language and presentation suggest to instructors—fairly or
not—that students have been careless with their research and argument.

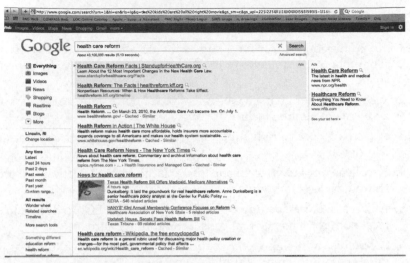

Screenshot of a Google search for "health care reform." Note that the first two results are "sponsored links"—advertisements.

Finally, the very voice a writer chooses is part of *ethos*. Is the writer too casual about a complicated topic? That might indicate that the writer doesn't fully understand the subject. Does jargon make the writing impenetrable? The writer might not have fully digested the original sources.

And what about using the first person ("I") in a college paper? Except in personal essays, high school teachers tend to forbid the first person in essays. But in college, and in particular in your college writing classes, it might be perfectly okay to use the first person (check with your instructor).

As always, though, think about *ethos*. A writer using the first person wants the readers to think explicitly about him- or herself. Sometimes that's effective, as in a paper in which the writer's strong feelings bolster the argument, or when anecdotal evidence from the writer's own life might be valuable. An argument about standardized testing in secondary schools would be strengthened by the personal presence, through the first person, of a writer who has just emerged from four years of standardized testing. But in other rhetorical situations, student writers will probably want to minimize their own presence in the writing, such as in an essay about health care policy largely drawing upon the facts and opinions of expert secondary sources.

Exercise 3.3: Critical Reading Questions

Suggest an effective *ethos* appeal (describe how the speaker/writer will want to come across, and suggest some particular points or language or authorities he or she might want to employ or cite) for the following rhetorical situations.

1. An admissions officer for a large state university giving a presentation about the university to a group of seniors at an elite prep school

2. A social worker giving a job-skills workshop to young offenders at a juvenile detention facility

3. A lacrosse coach motivating her team to forget about last week's bad defeat

4. A college professor trying to get a large lecture section to stop texting in class

5. An organizer persuading a group of corporate CEOs to donate to a local nonprofit agency that runs a community garden

6. A scientist applying to the National Institutes of Health for a $1 million grant to fund a study on hepatitis

7. A college sophomore interviewing for a prestigious summer internship at a law firm

8. An affluent suburban teenager trying to gain entry into an underground urban hip-hop club

PATHOS: MOVING THE AUDIENCE

If *ethos* refers to the ways that the speaker or writer claims authority to speak or write on a topic, *pathos* is the Greek term for how the speaker or writer seeks to move the audience emotionally. In both cases, though, the appeal is always contingent upon the rhetorical situation: the nature of the message (the argument), the audience, and the occasion.

You've been using *pathos* appeals all your life without even thinking about it. When you were eight years old, your sniffling mantra of "please please please??" was a *pathos* appeal: you were attempting to move your parents through pity and through their desire to make their child happy. But there is nothing essentially juvenile about *pathos* appeals, as some of the most famous pieces of rhetoric of the twentieth century demonstrate. "We have nothing to fear but fear itself," Franklin Roosevelt reassured panicked Americans as they faced the economic collapse of the Great Depression, attempting to counter their fright with his calm strength. "We shall fight with growing confidence and growing strength in the air; we shall defend our Island, whatever the cost may be," Winston Churchill told a demoralized Great Britain in 1940, appealing to and attempting to bolster Britons' patriotism and determination to resist Nazi Germany.

Pathos is powerful because it tends to be easier to move people to action through touching their emotions than through appealing just to their intellect. Effective writers judiciously employ *pathos* appeals. *Pathos* can be a dangerous tool, though, because of how emotion can overwhelm logic and fact. Demagogues tend to use heavily emotional arguments to move people to do unwise or cruel things, and powerful emotion often moves us to prefer simple solutions to problems rather than more complicated (and effective) ones. In times of crisis, as well, we are more susceptible to emotional appeals than we would be otherwise, and rhetors (from commentators to the president) often try to take advantage of that.

In his 2009 State of the Union address, President Obama used the example of Ty'sheoma Bethea, a young girl who wrote him to call attention to the sorry state of her school, to make the argument that we should provide more funding for education. The president could have cited endless statistics about the superior outcomes produced by better schools or quoted teachers and education scholars on the subject, but the emotional punch of hearing Ty'Sheoma's own words—and the powerful image of Ty'Sheoma, a young girl from a small South Carolina middle school, sitting next to Michelle Obama in a place of honor—carried the argument home in a way that a more fact- or logic- or *ethos*-based appeal could not have.

First Lady Michelle Obama and Ty'Sheoma Bethea at the State of the Union Address, 24 Feb. 2009.

Exercise 3.4: Critical Reading Questions

Describe the *pathos* appeals of each of the following short passages.

1. And today, as you leave the loving bosom of South Salem High School and make your way into the cold world, keep with you the memories. French Club, that party junior year, Senior Skip Day, Homecoming, just hanging with your friends in front of your locker during lunch. Remember where you came from, and remember that South will always be a part of you.

2. Look, we were defeated last week. But we fought hard and we showed heart. And this week, we are going to fight harder. We are going to defend that ball. We are going to run right over their backs and into the end zone. And we are going to smash them back onto their half of the field when they get the ball. We are going to win this game.

3. Mom, I really need a car. Everyone on my floor has a car, and so on Friday nights everyone goes out, except for me. I'm stuck here in the dorm with the losers. I don't have any friends, and I don't eat anything except the stuff they serve at Commons. I miss your cooking. I miss my friends. If I had a car, this year would be so much better.

4. Zoning this tract for commercial development is a terrible idea. Because of its proximity to the highway, it's pretty certain that we're going to end up with a massive strip mall, with just more fast-food, more stores that you can find anywhere else in the world. Just more sprawl and sameness and cars and asphalt and dirty air and endless traffic.

Pathos appeals are common in political discourse, particularly in such forums as talk radio, debate shows, speeches, and campaign advertisements. "If we elect X, we will be in danger from the terrorists" plays upon our fear of terrorism and our desire to protect our nation and our families from danger. "Y is way out of the mainstream" stokes our sense of us and them—we want to be part of the "mainstream," and thus if Y is "out of the mainstream" she must have strange, disturbing ideas.

Conservative activists have been particularly effective at using emotionally charged naming: in the 1990s, the term *family values* was popularized to describe people who held to a traditional model of a married, two-parent family, particularly one in which the father was the primary breadwinner. The intended effect of this was to suggest that those who supported or lived in other kinds of families (same-sex parents, single parents, blended families) were "anti-family." The estate tax—the tax on large estates passed on to descendants at the death of the owner—was rebranded the "death tax," with the intention of making us feel that paying a tax for dying was ludicrous. In debates about the budget, those who seek to increase taxes on high earners call those taxpayers "the rich" or "the wealthy," whereas those who oppose such tax increases refer to them as "job creators." The first word choice seeks to make us resent "the wealthy"; the second intends to make us feel that those people's wealth benefits us.

What we call *loaded language* (terms such as *family values* or *death tax*) is a powerful and often subtle way to convey an emotional appeal. Loaded language refers to the use of terms with powerful emotional connotations rather than terms with more neutral resonance. "Estate tax" becomes "death tax." "Anti-abortion" becomes "pro-life." "Conservative" becomes "right-wing extremist." In analyzing rhetoric, it is important to pay attention to how a writer uses loaded terms to move his or her audience emotionally, and to identify the particular words and terms the writer uses to accomplish this.

Exercise 3.5: Critical Reading Questions

Identify the loaded terms in the following passages. What emotions and associations are they intended to create or stoke or reinforce in their audiences?

1. Conservatives and lying. It's just like Hitler—repeat a lie enough times, and it becomes the truth.
2. Melissa Sczymczyk is a family woman, a mother of two boys and two girls, and a loving wife. She also wants to be your voice in the state capital.
3. WE MUST DEFEND THIS HOUSE! UnderForce gear prepares real athletes for the battlefield. Don't go into combat without UnderForce.
4. Whether it's a quiet evening at home, curled up with a good book under a wool blanket, or a get-together with good friends and good conversation, Warmth of the East Teas are the perfect companions.
5. My professor is the worst. She's so unfair—she grades on the harshest curve and has the strictest attendance policy of any professor at this college.
6. Professor Severin is known throughout the university for her challenging classes and her high expectations of her students. She's rigorous but if you pass, you'll know a lot more than you did when you enrolled.

PATHOS IN YOUR OWN WRITING

In many college writing situations, a heavy reliance on *pathos* isn't necessary and can even be detrimental. As we said before, "the academy" (the world of higher education) values knowledge for its own sake above almost anything else, and thus the kinds of writing one does in college—even when they are persuasive—tend to be about developing or demonstrating knowledge. Audiences that are looking for knowledge and objectivity, in turn, may be put off by writing that attempts to move them emotionally—"you're trying to make me *feel* rather than *think*," they might respond. So it's important to think carefully about when and how to employ emotion as a persuasive strategy within an academic context.

An emotional appeal, however, can be effective with an academic audience when it is one tool (preferably a secondary one) among many. For example, let's say that in a health care ethics class, the assignment is to write a rebuttal to a ban on stem-cell research. A purely logical argument might hinge on the benefit of this technology to society: lifting the ban on research using stem cells derived from human embryos—which must be destroyed in the process—could possibly result in large numbers of people with currently incurable conditions being able to receive life-saving therapies.

Largely a logical argument, this thesis overlooks many people's profound ethical objection to the destruction of a human embryo and thus seems like a heartless calculation: the potential for improved health of mature humans is worth more than the embryos. This writer might be well advised to add an element of emotion here, to diminish the cold calculation of the original thesis. Personalizing the argument might work: a story about the terrible suffering of a family member with ALS (Lou Gehrig's disease) who might be helped by a stem-cell-derived therapy, for example, might affect the audience emotionally and diminish the sense that the writer is simply weighing existing lives against those of developing embryos.

Anecdotes can effectively carry *pathos* to an audience. As speech makers have always known, a small personal anecdote that illustrates the larger point the speaker is trying to make can be much more effective than a mass of irrefutable statistics and logical argument. We tend to understand things through stories; we "relate" to them and bring to bear both our cognitive and our emotional intelligence.

Exercise 3.6: Using the Concept

Describe your college three times using loaded language.

1. In a two- to three-sentence passage, use loaded terms that would appeal to a student who is seeking out a college with extremely rigorous academics.

2. In another passage, describe your school to a college finder–type site and emphasize the college's social side (or lack of one).

3. And in a third, describe the school to the parents of a prospective student who are looking to send their child to a school that will carefully look after this child, both academically and personally.

LOGOS: THE LOGIC OF AN ARGUMENT

Returning to our communications triangle, we have covered the sender of the message (*ethos*, or how a speaker/writer makes him- or herself credible to an audience) and the receiver of the message (*pathos*, or how a speaker/writer moves an audience emotionally). The Greek term for the rhetorical appeal that centers on the message itself is *logos*, which is, not coincidentally, also the Greek word for "word." *Logos* refers to the actual content, in particular the logic, of the message itself.

What does this mean? The most basic question *logos* answers is "does the message make sense?" It might seem like it should go without saying, but a thesis and its corresponding evidence and underlying assumptions have to match. For example, let's take as a hypothetical a municipal question: whether or not to put a stoplight at the corner of Greene and Parsons Streets. A speaker in favor addresses the council with the following argument:

> The city should put a stoplight at the corner of Greene and Parsons because the intersection is dangerous for pedestrians. This intersection has been the site of several car versus pedestrian accidents in the past few years, and a stoplight would protect pedestrians.

Although seemingly a simple argument, several logical premises are embedded here, and for the argument to make sense, all of these premises must be demonstrably true—or at least acceptable to the audience. Among these are:

1. It is true that there have been car vs. pedestrian accidents at this intersection.

2. It is true that we as a city wish to minimize car vs. pedestrian accidents.

3. The number of car vs. pedestrian accidents at this intersection is greater than we as a city think is acceptable.

4. Stoplights reduce or eliminate car vs. pedestrian accidents.

5. Among all possible ways to reduce car vs. pedestrian accidents, a stoplight is the best.

Simple, right? Not so much. Certainly, this seems like an ironclad argument at first glance. But apply our critical thinking to this and we can find weaknesses. First of all, there will always be car vs. pedestrian accidents. It is also likely that a stoplight would reduce these accidents (as the pedestrians would have a walk/don't walk sign, and cross traffic a red light), but a stoplight doesn't *eliminate* such collisions— it would be easy to find examples of car vs. pedestrian accidents in intersections with stoplights. So a stoplight will probably diminish the problem, but it will not eliminate it.

Second, we must be sure that our solution is actually the best solution—that it doesn't solve one problem while causing several others. If we all agree that we want to achieve these goals, can we achieve them differently, in ways that might be preferable? First of all, a stoplight cannot eliminate the problem; at best, it can reduce it. This is certainly a good thing. But might a stoplight have other negative effects that might outweigh the benefits of reducing such collisions? A stoplight will impede the flow of traffic, and Greene St. might be a major artery that the city wants flowing freely. Can pedestrians cross Greene St. a few blocks up, where there is already a stoplight? Walkers can be hit even at a controlled intersection; might a pedestrian overpass be an even better way to reduce or eliminate deaths? Or is the cost too great?

Logos, then, is the appeal of being logical—of the facts being factual, and relating to each other in the way that the speaker claims. The *logos* of an argument, like all other parts of it, might differ for different audiences. The argument that reducing taxes will increase overall tax revenue can rely on relatively fuzzy evidence when made to an audience of non-specialists: "With lower taxes, there will be more investment, which will lead to more jobs, which will lead to more people paying taxes—and greater revenue for the government." The logical chain here seems to make sense. But an audience of economists is going to need a lot more than that—the logic and the actual evidence are going to need to be much more specific and credible to persuade that audience.

Exercise 3.7: Analyzing an Essay

Read the following essay by a first-year writing student named Mike Wong, in which Wong responds to the argument made by the journalist Maggie Jackson in her 2008 book *Distracted* that our increasing reliance on technology, and the cognitive and behavioral habits this engenders, is causing us to lose our ability to give anything focus or full attention. (A different section of *Distracted* appears in Chapter 4.) Please keep in mind that Wong's essay has not been line edited; he makes some errors in usage, grammar, and citation/documentation. Mark all such errors that you find, and answer the questions that follow the essay.

Rebuttal to Maggie Jackson's *Distracted*

Mike Wong

In Maggie Jackson's *Distracted*, she argues that traditional "intensive" (Jackson 161) reading, an activity where a reader absorbs knowledge contained in the text through careful consideration of its content, and which leads towards deeper thoughts, deeper understanding, and the ability to probe beneath the surface of texts and ideas, is suffering due to modern trends caused by technologies such as the Internet and Google which lead users to "skim the surface of information" (Jackson 159). As evidence for her claim, Ms. Jackson cites studies from the National Assessment of Adult Literacy (NAAL) and provides some anecdotal evidence from students at the New Jersey Institute of Technology (NJIT). However anecdotes are not satisfactory evidence to support a claim, and her use of the NAAL study to prove that technology is causing a decline in our ability to find deeper meaning in what we read is incorrect because that study was not an experiment and thus can prove no causation. Furthermore the same study by the same organization shows the opposite of her claim: that reading comprehension is on the rise. In fact, counter to her beliefs, many argue that the internet is not just a mess of unedited and fragmented information which readers simply skim but rather is the pinnacle of modern technology, allowing readers to access unprecedented levels of scholarly text, academic articles, journalistic reports, and philosophical discourses from all over the world from vast digitized collections of these works.

In Jackson's argument to prove that modern technology like the Internet has led towards a degradation of our ability to think deeply about what we read, she starts with a valid point about the importance of reading; however, as her argument develops we see that her sources become shakier and her reasoning less guided by facts. She begins with the idea that the simple act of reading "transforms mere marks on a page into meaning" (Jackson 182) but that reading also does much more than that: "Reading gives us a deeply meaningful framework for living" (Jackson 159). We can intuitively see her point, namely that reading helps people understand new ideas, see new connections, and understand the world on a more fundamental level; however, when she says that we are losing this ability to extract deeper meaning from what we read because we are becoming "extensive readers" (Jackson 161); she fails to back up such a bold claim with solid evidence. Instead she implies that the sheer vastness of the internet simply forces us to skim over such insurmountable quantities of information. Jackson says that the Web shapes us into "extensive readers" (Jackson 161); people who "dance on the surface of a thousand texts, skimming over billions of words…across the mesmerizing Web" (Jackson 161). She asserts that because there is such a plethora of available text online, "we risk losing our means and ability to go beneath the surface and think deeply. This is the second collective loss after trust that we nurture in a time of distraction" (Jackson 155). Then to make it all the more disheartening she stresses that when we do actually intend on reading something on the Web, popular search engines like Google provide us with results where expert sources are put on par with opinionated blogs and irrelevant information. So overall she feels that technology like the Internet causes readers to shift from being able to delve beneath the surface of one text and understand its meaning to skimming across the surface of the many texts that are now available online, and that the tools we have created are so easy to use that they allow us to forgo critical thinking in information gathering and provide good and bad results, which she believes will hurt our ability to think critically overall.

To support her claim that the Web's nearly unlimited access to information paradoxically hurts our ability to read at a higher level, Jackson relies on the 2003 NAAL survey results by Mark Kutner *et al.* in *Literacy in Everyday Life; Results from the 2003 National Assessment of Adult Literacy.* From his conclusions she points to such alarming quotes as "only 30 percent of college graduates can understand a simple document such as a food label" (Jackson 155). To explain such surprising data, Jackson blames our "steady diet of Web info" (Jackson 155). However when looking at the survey one finds that even the authors of the NAAL document state that "The purpose of this report is to examine the relationship between literacy and various self-reported background factors. This report is purely descriptive" (Kutner 9). Thus we can see that no causal relationships can be derived from their survey because it is not an experiment and so Jackson cannot draw the conclusion that the rise of the Web is causing our decline in reading abilities instead of some other lurking or confounding variable. Furthermore, we see that in the actual document they are only examining topics like "how parents and guardians with different literacy levels interacted with the children living in their homes around issues related to literacy" (Kutner 9) and not how the Web has affected reading abilities. Besides all this, the study actually shows that reading levels have improved in several areas. For instance, the NAAL assesses three types of reading—

> *Prose literacy.* The knowledge and skills needed to perform prose tasks (i.e., to search for, comprehend, and use information from continuous texts). Prose examples include editorials, news stories...*Document literacy.* The knowledge and skills needed to perform document tasks.... Document examples include job applications, payroll forms, maps...and food labels... *Quantitative literacy.* The knowledge and skills required to perform quantitative tasks (i.e., to identify and perform computations, either alone or sequentially, using numbers embedded in printed materials). Examples include balancing a checkbook. (Kutner 5)

—and they show quantitatively, in the very same study that Jackson used to say we are facing a reading dark age, that the average score was intermediate in the prose and document category and average scores had increased in the quantitative category since 1993 when the last study was done: "On the document scale, the percentage of adults with *Intermediate* literacy increased. The percentage of adults with *Below Basic* quantitative literacy declined between 1992 and 2003, and the percentage of adults with *Intermediate* quantitative literacy increased" (Kutner 13). Additionally, as the graph on page 15 shows, average scores for every group in the three categories tested, prose, document, and quantitative skills increased by a statistically significant amount for 5 of the 6 different races/ethnicities studied (Kutner 15). Also, another one of Jackson's sources, the National Endowment for the Arts, reports that instead of a decline in the reading abilities of today's youth, we actually see an increase in their literacy skills: "*Reading on the Rise*, the National Endowment for the Arts' new report," issued in 2008 "documents a significant turning point in recent American cultural history. For the first time in over a quarter-century, our survey shows that literary reading has risen among adult Americans...There has been a decisive and unambiguous increase among virtually every group measured in this comprehensive national survey" (Gioia 3) and also that "the youngest group (ages 18-24) has undergone a particularly inspiring transformation" (Gioia 4) referring to the 21 percent increase in literacy from 2002 to 2008 in that age group. These results regarding literacy rates alone do little to refute Jackson's point, but when we combine these statistics with the results of the NAAL survey we start to get a truer picture of reading levels in this country. Not only are people reading more, as literacy rates in "virtually every group" (Gioia 3) increase, but also the ability to "search for, comprehend, and use information from continuous texts" (Kutner) is on the rise. So we aren't just reading more, we understand more as well. Thus, while we cannot prove that the internet promotes the reading prowess of our population, we can at least show, using her own sources, that Jackson's claims that the internet, with its unlimited access to documents, damages our ability to read and understand what it is that we are reading are at best unsubstantiated and at worst pure falsehood. Overall then, based on information from her own sources, I would claim that reading in this country is not in a period of decline, rather we see an increase in our ability to extract meaning from what we are reading, whether it be prose, document, or any other form of literature.

Besides her claim that the internet has so much information that we are being forced to skim its "infinite texts" (Jackson 173) and thus forfeit our ability to "delve beneath the surface" (Jackson 173), she also claims that the tools we have developed to help us search the internet are leading us to poor quality information that we tend to just eat up. This adds to her overall message that we're suffering from declining reading abilities by underscoring the potential danger that not only is there a lot on the Web but what see is largely unreliable. To support this claim she looks to anecdotal evidence from students at NJIT: "All I did was type around and Googled" (Jackson 166). Additionally she cites her experiences sitting in on a class where she observes such things as "most of the other students paid no attention" (Jackson 162) in order to help paint a gloomy picture of our futures, however in terms of information to prove her point such vignettes of a classroom offer nothing but an emotional appeal that leads her readers into thinking if students aren't paying attention in class they must not be smart enough to sift through information on a Google results page.

I in no way find this argument about the deleterious effect of search sites convincing. Her point that sites like Google strip away our critical-thinking powers and feed us poor results is alarmist, whereas I argue that the internet has a striking potential to positively impact the world. If we truly live in time where literacy rates and literary skills are increasing, as statistics suggest, then the internet will certainly be a powerful tool to take us new levels of access and understanding. If we go by the old adage that knowledge is power, then each and every one of us with an internet connection has an unprecedented level of power. At its core the Internet is a way to obtain information from anywhere. It is a place for us to flex our rising literary acumen on texts from all over the world. The existence of millions of opinionated blog and rants disguised as facts on the internet is only one side of the story. Simply because the internet makes it easier to find unreliable information does not mean it causes our thinking skills to atrophy, because the other side of the coin is that the internet provides unprecedented access to credible sources as well. The internet is a tool for us to use; we are not used by it as Jackson almost seems to be implying. We are in no way limited to only blogs or unedited information, rather through the internet we can look to scholarly websites like those from universities, places like Jstor.com that store journals online, and Google's own feature that will search only published scholarly text. Furthermore, Google, a favorite target for Jackson, is now in the processes of digitizing academic, philosophical, and primary source documents from the great research libraries in the country in the Hathi Trust project. Universities like Yale, Princeton, Penn State, and others have all offered up their collections and as of July 2010, "6,630,296 total volumes or 2,320,603,600 pages" (Hathi Trust) of these documents have been digitized. Surely now we can see that while her point that some popular search engines like Google "place irrelevant or mediocre sites on par with expert ones" (Jackson 163), we are not limited to using only those searches or sources, and this is the real power of the Web, it is un-limiting. With it we have the freedom to turn to vast collections of well researched work now available online. That is the point of the internet: it is not restrictive, it is liberating, we can with simply our fingers look to find any trust worthy information we want. Therefore instead of saying that our tools direct us towards mediocre information I would assert that through the Internet we have the power to find and access vast collections of scholarly work from all over the world like never before.

Overall, Ms. Jackson's argument that the enormity of the Internet is causing us to skip over information instead of understanding what we read is unfounded. Similarly her claim that the methods we use to find things on the internet further limit our ability to find information worth understanding is gloomy stretch of the truth. In reality, studies show that not simply our literacy rates but more importantly our ability to think about what we read, understand its meaning, and extract information from what we read are improving. Furthermore we can see that the internet is not just full of poor quality information but rather there are massive amounts of credible information available and it can all even be accessed easily through popular search sites like Google. In fact, considering what studies show about our increasing literacy rates combined with our growing power to understand the information contained in what we read and the power of the internet to provide us with relevant credible information I would think that we are not on the cusp of a cultural dark age but rather at the leading edge of a bright future.

Critical Reading Questions

1. Where does Wong challenge the *logic* of the text he is rebutting?
2. What is the counterclaim that Wong makes?
3. On what logical claim does Wong ground his counterargument?

Is There an Information Overload?

CHAPTER INTRODUCTION

In a series of television commercials for Microsoft's Web search engine "Bing," people in various settings—a restaurant, a grocery store, a middle-class home—go glassy-eyed when answering simple questions, and can only respond only with a tidbit of information or a question related to the last word in the question. None of the information actually answers any of the questions, or is related to any of the other information. The phenomenon is contagious, and soon every person in the room is spouting random facts or statements.

This silly scene represents our "search overload," according to Microsoft. So much information is available to us on the Internet that we can never find the most relevant answer when using a search engine; ironically, the plethora of information available to us ends up distracting us from what we are really trying to do and *not* answering our questions. (The solution to this problem, the commercial insists, is of course Bing.)

Silly and entertaining, the commercial does make concrete an anxiety many feel today: that the Internet has made so much more information available that we are no longer able to find what we want. Information overwhelms us—"getting information off the Internet," the personal-computing pioneer Mitchell Kapor famously said, "is like taking a drink from a fire hydrant." This is particularly true for

Getting information off the Internet is like taking a drink from a fire hydrant.

Mitchell Kapor

those not of the "Web generation," those who grew up in a different information environment. But even the most savvy, most connected young people occasionally feel intimidated by the mass of information out there—or at least by the stickier question of *what* information is valid and relevant.

The phenomenon of more information actually hindering decision making is called *information overload.* Information overload isn't anything new—sociologists, psychologists, and others have been studying it since the 1960s. But technology has accelerated it remarkably in recent years—in particular, wireless communication technology (cell phones), computer software, and the Internet. Now, formerly disconnected repositories of information are connected and available to anyone with an Internet connection. Dictionaries, medical compendia, the voting records of American members of Congress, scores of 1915 baseball games, the entire contents of major libraries— any of us can access any of it in seconds. We are all the richer for it, certainly.

But we have all been in situations in which the massive amount of information available has been an *obstacle* to making a decision. How many of us have been feeling poorly, Googled our symptoms, and ended up certain that we were suffering from a dread disease? Without all of this information at our fingertips, we might never have heard of "necrotizing fasciitis," much less feared that it was eating our own arms. In so many arenas—choosing a college, finding a restaurant for lunch, evaluating whether there is such a thing as "clean coal technology," locating the name of a celebrity's baby—the fire hydrant of information can be too much and can make judgment harder.

Moreover, we are also still in the infancy of the "information age." How will this connectedness and this access to information change us, theorists and critics and politicians and educators wonder. How will it change our societies? Our personal relationships? Education? Jobs? It is far too soon to tell.

We are seeing, though, early indications of what might happen. Popular uprisings in nations such as Iran, Tunisia, and Egypt have been driven and facilitated by modern communications: text messaging, satellite television news channels, and social-networking sites. This might be good, a chance for democracy to flourish ... unless it's bad and brings to power a repressive or aggressive regime that knows how to use technology effectively. The net can be a powerful tool to spread the truth or to spread lies. And as Farhad Manjoo points out in this chapter, those who intend to spread lies increasingly rely on information overload to get their ideas past our B.S. detectors. With so many opinions out there, everything begins to seem equally valid.

On the personal level, information is changing our lives in ways that affect all of us daily. Email, cell phones, social-networking sites, and other forms of inexpensive and convenient electronic communication allow us to stay in much closer touch with friends and family than would have been possible before—but is it better to have a lot of casual friends or a few intense friendships? Cyberstalking, "sexting," embarrassing photos or videos posted on the net: all of these are new phenomena, and society has not yet learned how to handle them. In many ways, the experiences of the "net generation" are teaching the rest of us how to handle this new world.

This chapter provides several diverse responses to the question "what is the information age doing to us?" Nicholas Carr, Maggie Jackson, and Farhad Manjoo all suggest that information overload and dependence on technology are atrophying our intellectual capabilities. When we "outsource" our brain work to machines and computer algorithms, they suggest, we lose the ability to make critical decisions about important issues. Jackson even warns that we may lose our ability to give full attention to anything, and thus end up in a "new dark age."

Although many commentators—including many in this book—assume that "the digital generation" has a preternaturally deft command of all technology, Siva Vaidhyanathan counters that there is a wide gulf between knowing a little about a new tech tool (which most young people do) and knowing how to take advantage of our gadgets and software. Notwithstanding their unshakable self-confidence, he argues, most of his students don't actually know as much as they think they do about the tools that shape their lives.

An indispensible tool for students (and professors) is the community-authored Web encyclopedia Wikipedia. In her fascinating profile of Wikipedia founder Jimmy Wales, Katherine Mangu-Ward explains the genesis of one of the most popular sites on the Web and argues that Wikipedia's success is concrete proof of the validity of libertarian, laissez-faire ideas about economics and governance.

Two writers take on the question of how we receive and convey information. The eminent political writer Andrew Sullivan explains, in "Why I Blog," the appeal of the blog form, with all of its immediacy, emotionalism, and potential inaccuracy. And Matthew Willen reflects on the "cultural climate of plagiarism"—the sense held by many members of the digital generation that anything on the Web is free and available for anyone's use, as well as the erosion of academic integrity among today's college students.

Finally, Ta-Nehisi Coates and Zadie Smith discuss diametrically opposed ways in which being "connected" online has changed their personal lives. Coates, a self-described "30-year-old gamer," describes the appeal of online gaming, and the pleasure he takes in the casual online interactions inherent in such games. Smith, echoing E. M. Forster, concludes that being connected isn't all it's cracked up to be, and that she prefers her connections to be "real," not digital.

CLUSTER ONE: WHAT IS THE NET DOING TO US?

Is Google Making Us Stupid?

Nicholas Carr

The writer Nicholas Carr ignited a firestorm of controversy when he published "Is Google Making Us Stupid?" in the Atlantic Monthly *in 2008. Carr, who writes on the intersection of technology, information, and business, suggested that the ways we access, use, and have become dependent upon information from the Internet is adversely affecting the very ways we think—our cognition.*

"Dave, stop. Stop, will you? Stop, Dave. Will you stop, Dave?" So the supercomputer HAL pleads with the implacable astronaut Dave Bowman in a famous and weirdly poignant scene toward the end of Stanley Kubrick's *2001: A Space Odyssey.* Bowman, having nearly been sent to a deep-space death by the malfunctioning machine, is calmly, coldly disconnecting the memory circuits that control its artificial "brain. "Dave, my mind is going," HAL says, forlornly. "I can feel it. I can feel it."

I can feel it, too. Over the past few years I've had an uncomfortable sense that someone, or something, has been tinkering with my brain, remapping the neural circuitry, reprogramming the memory. My mind isn't going—so far as I can tell—but it's changing. I'm not thinking the way I used to think. I can feel it most strongly when I'm reading. Immersing myself in a book or a lengthy article used to be easy. My mind would get caught up in the narrative or the turns of the argument, and I'd spend hours strolling through long stretches of prose. That's rarely the case anymore. Now my concentration often starts to drift after two or three pages. I get fidgety, lose the thread, begin looking for something else to do. I feel as if I'm always dragging my wayward brain back to the text. The deep reading that used to come naturally has become a struggle.

I think I know what's going on. For more than a decade now, I've been spending a lot of time online, searching and surfing and sometimes adding to the great databases of the Internet. The Web has been a godsend to me as a writer. Research that once required days in the stacks or periodical rooms of libraries can now be done in minutes. A few Google searches, some quick clicks on hyperlinks, and I've got the telltale fact or pithy quote I was after. Even when I'm not working, I'm as likely as not to be foraging in the Web's info-thickets, reading and writing e-mails, scanning headlines and blog posts, watching videos and listening to podcasts, or just tripping from link to link to link. (Unlike footnotes, to which they're sometimes likened, hyperlinks don't merely point to related works; they propel you toward them.)

For me, as for others, the Net is becoming a universal medium, the conduit for most of the information that flows through my eyes and ears and into my mind. The advantages of having immediate access to such an incredibly rich store of information are many, and they've been widely described and duly applauded. "The perfect recall of silicon memory," *Wired*'s Clive Thompson has written, "can be an enormous boon to thinking." But that boon comes at a price. As the media theorist Marshall McLuhan pointed out in the 1960s, media are not just passive channels of information. They supply the stuff of thought, but they also shape the process of thought. And what the Net seems to be doing is chipping away my capacity for concentration and contemplation. My mind now expects to take in information the way the Net distributes it: in a swiftly moving stream of particles. Once I was a scuba diver in the sea of words. Now I zip along the surface like a guy on a Jet Ski.

I'm not the only one. When I mention my troubles with reading to friends and acquaintances—literary types, most of them—many say they're having similar experiences. The more they use the Web, the more they have to fight to stay focused on long pieces of writing. Some of the bloggers I follow have also begun mentioning the phenomenon. Scott Karp, who writes a blog about online media, recently confessed that he has stopped reading books altogether. "I was a lit major in college, and used to be [a] voracious book reader," he wrote.

"What happened?" He speculates on the answer: "What if I do all my reading on the web not so much because the way I read has changed, i.e. I'm just seeking convenience, but because the way I THINK has changed?"

Bruce Friedman, who blogs regularly about the use of computers in medicine, also has described how the Internet has altered his mental habits. "I now have almost totally lost the ability to read and absorb a longish article on the web or in print," he wrote earlier this year. A pathologist who has long been on the faculty of the University of Michigan Medical School, Friedman elaborated on his comment in a telephone conversation with me. His thinking, he said, has taken on a "staccato" quality, reflecting the way he quickly scans short passages of text from many sources online. "I can't read *War and Peace* anymore," he admitted. "I've lost the ability to do that. Even a blog post of more than three or four paragraphs is too much to absorb. I skim it."

Anecdotes alone don't prove much. And we still await the long-term neurological and psychological experiments that will provide a definitive picture of how Internet use affects cognition. But a recently published study of online research habits, conducted by scholars from University College London, suggests that we may well be in the midst of a sea change in the way we read and think. As part of the five-year research program, the scholars examined computer logs documenting the behavior of visitors to two popular research sites, one operated by the British Library and one by a U.K. educational consortium, that provide access to journal articles, e-books, and other sources of written information. They found that people using the sites exhibited "a form of skimming activity," hopping from one source to another and rarely returning to any source they'd already visited. They typically read no more than one or two pages of an article or book before they would "bounce" out to another site. Sometimes they'd save a long article, but there's no evidence that they ever went back and actually read it. The authors of the study report:

> It is clear that users are not reading online in the traditional sense; indeed there are signs that new forms of "reading" are emerging as users "power browse" horizontally through titles, contents pages and abstracts going for quick wins. It almost seems that they go online to avoid reading in the traditional sense.

Thanks to the ubiquity of text on the Internet, not to mention the popularity of text-messaging on cell phones, we may well be reading more today than we did in the 1970s or 1980s, when television was our medium of choice. But it's a different kind of reading, and behind it lies a different kind of thinking—perhaps even a new sense of the self. "We are not only *what* we read," says Maryanne Wolf, a developmental psychologist at Tufts University and the author of *Proust and the Squid: The Story and Science of the Reading Brain.* "We are *how* we read." Wolf worries that the style of reading promoted by the Net, a style that puts "efficiency" and "immediacy" above all else, may be weakening our capacity for the kind of deep reading that emerged when an earlier technology, the printing press, made long and complex works of prose commonplace. When we read online, she says, we tend to become "mere decoders of information." Our ability to interpret text, to make the rich mental connections that form when we read deeply and without distraction, remains largely disengaged.

Reading, explains Wolf, is not an instinctive skill for human beings. It's not etched into our genes the way speech is. We have to teach our minds how to translate the symbolic characters we see into the language we understand. And the media or other technologies we use in learning and practicing the craft of reading play an important part in shaping the neural circuits inside our brains. Experiments demonstrate that readers of ideograms, such as the Chinese, develop a mental circuitry for reading that is very different from the circuitry found in those of us whose written language employs an alphabet. The variations extend across many regions of the brain, including those that govern such essential cognitive functions as memory and the interpretation of visual and auditory stimuli. We can expect as well that the circuits woven by our use of the Net will be different from those woven by our reading of books and other printed works.

Sometime in 1882, Friedrich Nietzsche bought a typewriter—a Malling-Hansen Writing Ball, to be precise. His vision was failing, and keeping his eyes focused on a page had become exhausting and painful, often bringing on crushing headaches. He had been forced to curtail his writing, and he feared that he would soon have to give it up. The typewriter rescued him, at least for a time. Once he had mastered touch-typing, he was able to write with his eyes closed, using only the tips of his fingers. Words could once again flow from his mind to the page.

But the machine had a subtler effect on his work. One of Nietzsche's friends, a composer, noticed a change in the style of his writing. His already terse prose had become even tighter, more telegraphic. "Perhaps you will through this instrument even take to a new idiom," the friend wrote in a letter, noting that, in his own work, his "'thoughts' in music and language often depend on the quality of pen and paper."

"You are right," Nietzsche replied, "our writing equipment takes part in the forming of our thoughts." Under the sway of the machine, writes the German media scholar Friedrich A. Kittler, Nietzsche's prose "changed from arguments to aphorisms, from thoughts to puns, from rhetoric to telegram style."

The human brain is almost infinitely malleable. People used to think that our mental meshwork, the dense connections formed among the 100 billion or so neurons inside our skulls, was largely fixed by the time we reached adulthood. But brain researchers have discovered that that's not the case. James Olds, a professor of neuroscience who directs the Krasnow Institute for Advanced Study at George Mason University, says that even the adult mind "is very plastic." Nerve cells routinely break old connections and form new ones. "The brain," according to Olds, "has the ability to reprogram itself on the fly, altering the way it functions."

As we use what the sociologist Daniel Bell has called our "intellectual technologies"—the tools that extend our mental rather than our physical capacities—we inevitably begin to take on the qualities of those technologies. The mechanical clock, which came into common use in the 14th century, provides a compelling example. In *Technics and Civilization*, the historian and cultural critic Lewis Mumford described how the clock "disassociated time from human events and helped create the belief in an independent world of mathematically measurable sequences." The "abstract framework of divided time" became "the point of reference for both action and thought."

The clock's methodical ticking helped bring into being the scientific mind and the scientific man. But it also took something away. As the late MIT computer scientist Joseph Weizenbaum observed in his 1976 book, *Computer Power and Human Reason: From Judgment to Calculation*, the conception of the world that emerged from the widespread use of timekeeping instruments "remains an impoverished version of the older one, for it rests on a rejection of those direct experiences that formed the basis for, and indeed constituted, the old reality." In deciding when to eat, to work, to sleep, to rise, we stopped listening to our senses and started obeying the clock.

The process of adapting to new intellectual technologies is reflected in the changing metaphors we use to explain ourselves to ourselves. When the mechanical clock arrived, people began thinking of their brains as operating "like clockwork." Today, in the age of software, we have come to think of them as operating "like computers." But the changes, neuroscience tells us, go much deeper than metaphor. Thanks to our brain's plasticity, the adaptation occurs also at a biological level.

The Internet promises to have particularly far-reaching effects on cognition. In a paper published in 1936, the British mathematician Alan Turing proved that a digital computer, which at the time existed only as a theoretical machine, could be programmed to perform the function of any other information-processing device. And that's what we're seeing today. The Internet, an immeasurably powerful computing system, is subsuming most of our other intellectual technologies. It's becoming our map and our clock, our printing press and our typewriter, our calculator and our telephone, and our radio and TV.

When the Net absorbs a medium, that medium is re-created in the Net's image. It injects the medium's content with hyperlinks, blinking ads, and other digital gewgaws, and it surrounds the content with the content of all the other media it has absorbed. A new e-mail message, for instance, may announce its arrival as we're glancing over the latest headlines at a newspaper's site. The result is to scatter our attention and diffuse our concentration.

The Net's influence doesn't end at the edges of a computer screen, either. As people's minds become attuned to the crazy quilt of Internet media, traditional media have to adapt to the audience's new expectations. Television programs add text crawls and pop-up ads, and magazines and newspapers shorten their articles, introduce capsule summaries, and crowd their pages with easy-to-browse info-snippets. When, in March of this year, *The New York Times* decided to devote the second and third pages of every edition to article abstracts, its design director, Tom Bodkin, explained that the "shortcuts" would give harried readers a quick "taste" of the day's news, sparing them the "less efficient" method of actually turning the pages and reading the articles. Old media have little choice but to play by the new-media rules.

Never has a communications system played so many roles in our lives—or exerted such broad influence over our thoughts—as the Internet does today. Yet, for all that's been written about the Net, there's been little consideration of how, exactly, it's reprogramming us. The Net's intellectual ethic remains obscure.

About the same time that Nietzsche started using his typewriter, an earnest young man named Frederick Winslow Taylor carried a stopwatch into the Midvale Steel plant in Philadelphia and began a historic series of experiments aimed at improving the efficiency of the plant's machinists. With the approval of Midvale's owners, he recruited a group of factory hands, set them to work on various metalworking machines, and recorded and timed their every movement as well as the operations of the machines. By breaking down every job into a sequence of small, discrete steps and then testing different ways of performing each one, Taylor created a set of precise instructions—an "algorithm," we might say today—for how each worker should work. Midvale's employees grumbled about the strict new regime, claiming that it turned them into little more than automatons, but the factory's productivity soared.

More than a hundred years after the invention of the steam engine, the Industrial Revolution had at last found its philosophy and its philosopher. Taylor's tight industrial choreography—his "system," as he liked to call it—was embraced by manufacturers throughout the country and, in time, around the world. Seeking maximum speed, maximum efficiency, and maximum output, factory owners used time-and-motion studies to organize their work and configure the jobs of their workers. The goal, as Taylor defined it in his celebrated 1911 treatise, *The Principles of Scientific Management*, was to identify and adopt, for every job, the "one best method" of work and thereby to effect "the gradual substitution of science for rule of thumb throughout the mechanic arts." Once his system was applied to all acts of manual labor, Taylor assured his followers, it would bring about a restructuring not only of industry but of society, creating a utopia of perfect efficiency. "In the past the man has been first," he declared; "in the future the system must be first."

Taylor's system is still very much with us; it remains the ethic of industrial manufacturing. And now, thanks to the growing power that computer engineers and software coders wield over our intellectual lives, Taylor's ethic is beginning to govern the realm of the mind as well. The Internet is a machine designed for the efficient and automated collection, transmission, and manipulation of information, and its legions of programmers are intent on finding the "one best method"—the perfect algorithm—to carry out every mental movement of what we've come to describe as "knowledge work."

Google's headquarters, in Mountain View, California—the Googleplex—is the Internet's high church, and the religion practiced inside its walls is Taylorism. Google, says its chief executive, Eric Schmidt, is "a company that's founded around the science of measurement," and it is striving to "systematize everything" it does. Drawing on the terabytes of behavioral data it collects through its search engine and other sites, it carries out thousands of experiments a day, according to the *Harvard Business Review*, and it uses the results to refine the algorithms that increasingly control how people find information and extract meaning from it. What Taylor did for the work of the hand, Google is doing for the work of the mind.

The company has declared that its mission is "to organize the world's information and make it universally accessible and useful." It seeks to develop "the perfect search engine," which it defines as something that "understands exactly what you mean and gives you back exactly what you want." In Google's view, information is a kind of commodity, a utilitarian resource that can be mined and processed with industrial efficiency. The more pieces of information we can "access" and the faster we can extract their gist, the more productive we become as thinkers.

Where does it end? Sergey Brin and Larry Page, the gifted young men who founded Google while pursuing doctoral degrees in computer science at Stanford, speak frequently of their desire to turn their search engine into an artificial intelligence, a HAL-like machine that might be connected directly to our brains. "The ultimate search engine is something as smart as people—or smarter," Page said in a speech a few years back. "For us, working on search is a way to work on artificial intelligence." In a 2004 interview with *Newsweek*, Brin said, "Certainly if you had all the world's information directly attached to your brain, or an artificial brain that was smarter than your brain, you'd be better off." Last year, Page told a convention of scientists that Google is "really trying to build artificial intelligence and to do it on a large scale."

Such an ambition is a natural one, even an admirable one, for a pair of math whizzes with vast quantities of cash at their disposal and a small army of computer scientists in their employ. A fundamentally scientific enterprise, Google is motivated by a desire to use technology, in Eric Schmidt's words, "to solve problems that have never been solved before," and artificial intelligence is the hardest problem out there. Why wouldn't Brin and Page want to be the ones to crack it?

Still, their easy assumption that we'd all "be better off" if our brains were supplemented, or even replaced, by an artificial intelligence is unsettling. It suggests a belief that intelligence is the output of a mechanical process, a series of discrete steps that can be isolated, measured, and optimized. In Google's world, the world we enter when we go online, there's little place for the fuzziness of contemplation. Ambiguity is not an opening for insight but a bug to be fixed. The human brain is just an outdated computer that needs a faster processor and a bigger hard drive.

The idea that our minds should operate as high-speed data-processing machines is not only built into the workings of the Internet, it is the network's reigning business model as well. The faster we surf across the Web—the more links we click and pages we view—the more opportunities Google and other companies gain to collect information about us and to feed us advertisements. Most of the proprietors of the commercial Internet have a financial stake in collecting the crumbs of data we leave behind as we flit from link to link—the more crumbs, the better. The last thing these companies want is to encourage leisurely reading or slow, concentrated thought. It's in their economic interest to drive us to distraction.

Maybe I'm just a worrywart. Just as there's a tendency to glorify technological progress, there's a countertendency to expect the worst of every new tool or machine. In Plato's *Phaedrus*, Socrates bemoaned the development of writing. He feared that, as people came to rely on the written word as a substitute for the knowledge they used to carry inside their heads, they would, in the words of one of the dialogue's characters, "cease to exercise their memory and become forgetful." And because they would be able to "receive a quantity of information without proper instruction," they would "be thought very knowledgeable when they are for the most part quite ignorant." They would be "filled with the conceit of wisdom instead of real wisdom." Socrates wasn't wrong—the new technology did often have the effects he feared—but he was shortsighted. He couldn't foresee the many ways that writing and reading would serve to spread information, spur fresh ideas, and expand human knowledge (if not wisdom).

The arrival of Gutenberg's printing press, in the 15th century, set off another round of teeth gnashing. The Italian humanist Hieronimo Squarciafico worried that the easy availability of books would lead to intellectual laziness, making men "less studious" and weakening their minds. Others argued that cheaply printed books and broadsheets would undermine religious authority, demean the work of scholars and scribes, and spread sedition and debauchery. As New York University professor Clay Shirky notes, "Most of the arguments made against the printing press were correct, even prescient." But, again, the doomsayers were unable to imagine the myriad blessings that the printed word would deliver.

So, yes, you should be skeptical of my skepticism. Perhaps those who dismiss critics of the Internet as Luddites or nostalgists will be proved correct, and from our hyperactive, data-stoked minds will spring a golden age of intellectual discovery and universal wisdom. Then again, the Net isn't the alphabet, and although it may replace the printing press, it produces something altogether different. The kind of deep reading that a sequence of printed pages promotes is valuable not just for the knowledge we acquire from the author's words but for the intellectual vibrations those words set off within our own minds. In the quiet spaces opened up by the sustained, undistracted reading of a book, or by any other act of contemplation, for that matter, we make our own associations, draw our own inferences and analogies, foster our own ideas. Deep reading, as Maryanne Wolf argues, is indistinguishable from deep thinking.

If we lose those quiet spaces, or fill them up with "content," we will sacrifice something important not only in our selves but in our culture. In a recent essay, the playwright Richard Foreman eloquently described what's at stake:

> I come from a tradition of Western culture, in which the ideal (my ideal) was the complex, dense and "cathedral-like" structure of the highly educated and articulate personality—a man or woman who carried inside themselves a personally constructed and unique version of the entire heritage of the West. [But now] I see within us all (myself included) the replacement of complex inner density with a new kind of self—evolving under the pressure of information overload and the technology of the "instantly available."

As we are drained of our "inner repertory of dense cultural inheritance," Foreman concluded, we risk turning into "'pancake people'—spread wide and thin as we connect with that vast network of information accessed by the mere touch of a button."

I'm haunted by that scene in *2001*. What makes it so poignant, and so weird, is the computer's emotional response to the disassembly of its mind: its despair as one circuit after another goes dark, its childlike pleading with the astronaut— "I can feel it. I can feel it. I'm afraid"—and its final reversion to what can only be called a state of innocence. HAL's outpouring of feeling contrasts with the emotionlessness that characterizes the human figures in the film, who go about their business with an almost robotic efficiency. Their thoughts and actions feel scripted, as if they're following the steps of an algorithm. In the world of *2001*, people have become so machinelike that the most human character turns out to be a machine. That's the essence of Kubrick's dark prophecy: as we come to rely on computers to mediate our understanding of the world, it is our own intelligence that flattens into artificial intelligence.

This article available online at: http://www.theatlantic.com/magazine/archive/2008/07/is-google-making-us-stupid/6868/

Critical Reading Questions

Summarizing the Text

1. Carr's argument boils down to a warning about our increasing reliance on information from the Internet, and on Google in particular, as a way of organizing that information. What does he fear might be the effect?

2. How is Frederick Winslow Taylor's approach to management coming to govern our minds, in Carr's formulation?

Establishing the Context

3. The *Atlantic Monthly* is a long-established American magazine that has historically published some of the best American writing, including short stories and long-form journalism. How does it affect the meaning of this text that it appears in a forum so devoted to everything Carr's view of the Internet is *not*?

4. Carr historicizes his argument, suggesting that this current development might end up being like other cognitive revolutions brought about by technology. Those revolutions had unforeseen effects on the human brain, he shows. But he seems to ignore ways in which the Internet, and Google's organizing of it, could have other effects. What might those be?

Responding to the Message

5. It seems that as the technology to record information becomes more widespread and easier to use, humans' ability to remember diminishes accordingly. Anthropologists studying preliterate societies have noted their impressive memories in comparison with those of literate societies, and Carr seems to be arguing that the Internet and current technology might be a leap

of the same order as the creation of the printing press. What do you think? Is it harmful to "outsource" much of our thinking to an Internet application such as Google?

6. How has the presence of electronically delivered and catalogued information changed your life? What place does print—everything from books to billboards to newspapers—have in your daily experience of information?

"Truthiness" Everywhere

Farhad Manjoo

Manjoo, the technology columnist for the online magazine Slate.com, posed a provocative question in his 2006 book True Enough *from which this excerpt is taken: just how true does something have to be, or seem, in order to be generally accepted as truth? We may be moving into an age, Manjoo suggests, when something just needs to be "true enough" for a critical mass of people to accept it.*

Late in the holiday shopping season of 2005, the technology columnist Robin Raskin began to worry about a hidden danger posed by a popular gadget that many American parents were then contemplating buying for their kids: pornography was popping up on the iPod. Apple had just released a version of the ubiquitous white-plastic-and-steel music player that was also capable of displaying video clips, and although the company marketed the device as a way for people to watch television shows, innovators online envisioned many less seemly possibilities. "There's scores of 'iPorn' everywhere," Raskin warned in one of several television appearances at the time. The iPod had become "a pedophile's playground," she said, and Apple was doing little to stem the smut.

Raskin's anti-iPod admonition grew out of what she calls an abiding interest in "digital kids." Children today use technology in ways that absolutely bewilders older people, and Raskin, a mother of three who has been writing about computers for more than two decades, has made it her mission to steer parents away from trouble. In the 1990s, she edited *Family PC* magazine, where her regular column, which was titled "Internet Mom," took as its refrain the dangers of the Web, instant messaging software, and other technologies that were spidering into American homes. *Family PC* folded in the tough advertising market that followed the September 11, 2001, terrorist attacks, but Raskin, who hoped to launch another lifestyle magazine one day, continued to go on TV to review certain gadgets. When she saw that the iPod might pose a menace to children, the Internet Mom was determined to sound the alarm.

That unseen dangers lurk in everyday objects is a cliché of local news—"Have you just eaten something that's going to kill you? Details at 11—and Raskin's iPorn pitch piqued news directors everywhere. Raskin, a pert middle-aged woman with short brown hair and a deep, authoritative voice, also makes good TV. You might picture her as the Martha Stewart of consumer technology—direct but not rude, friendly but not perky.

And so it was that one morning in December 2005, Raskin found herself on Pittsburgh's Fox affiliate, WPGH Channel 53, calling the iPod one of the "scariest" gifts of the season. iPod-porn, she said, was a scourge that parents needed to fight. On KGUN, an ABC station in Tucson, Raskin got similarly worked up, saying that iPorn "is free, it's on Apple's iTunes—it's not like they're hiding it anywhere." The ABC station in Columbus, Ohio, featured Raskin's warnings as part of a report by Kent Justice, a consumer correspondent who produces a regular segment called "On Your Side." Justice told viewers, "If you didn't know it, now prepare for it: hundreds of Web sites are selling iPorn."

A total of nine stations aired the Internet Mom's warning about the iPod. Most also featured an additional message from Raskin—and it's here that this story finds its legs. It's here that we begin to skip past the truth, past the conventional definition of factual, unbiased news and into a newer, murkier category of information.

Along with her warning concerning iPorn, Raskin used her time on TV to put forward recommendations for what she'd determined were a few "safe" holiday tech products. She touted a modern version of the old Coleco video game system—"$19.99 as a stocking stuffer!" she exclaimed in one interview—as well as an update of Pac-Man and a popular Japanese game called We Love Katamari. But these weren't unbiased reviews. Raskin was pushing the products because three companies—Panasonic, Namco, and Techno Source—had hired her to sell their wares during news appearances.

Raskin says that rather than acting as a "journalist," her true role on television during these segments was that of a "spokeswoman." Indeed, she'd approached the news stations with the iPorn story only as a way to hook them into running her demonstrations of sponsored products. "It was a great, grabbing headline," she says of the pornography angle. The TV stations were aware of Raskin's benefactors; she had disclosed the arrangement to them, and her solicitations had come through DS Simon, a public relations firm that commonly sends out marketing requests to local news outlets. Everyone on TV knew the game. Only the people at home were in the dark....

On October 17, 2005, on the premiere of his late-night show, the comedian Stephen Colbert coined the term "truthiness," and it was good. For Colbert, who plays a blowhard TV pundit à la the

Fox network's Bill O'Reilly, "truthiness" conveyed a neat précis of a strained worldview: Stephen Colbert believed America to be split between two camps whose philosophies could never reconcile—those who *"think* with their *head"* and those who *"know* with their *heart."* Colbert himself was a proud *knower*, and "truthiness," he explained, was the quality of a thing *feeling* true without any evidence suggesting it actually was. The archetypal example was George W. Bush's decision to invade Iraq. "If you *think* about it, maybe there are a few missing pieces to the rationale for war," Colbert conceded. "But doesn't taking Saddam out *feel* like the right thing, right here in the gut?"

Colbert planted "truthiness" in a fertile field, in soil full of it, you might say. At the time, combatants in Washington were battling over a vacancy on the Supreme Court, a situation bound to erupt in plumes of hot air. But the term really took off a month and a half after Colbert's debut, and it was popular culture rather than national politics that presented the key exhibit in building the case that the world had gone truthy.

The news concerned the author James Frey, whose memoir *A Million Little Pieces*, which told of Frey's harrowing trip through addiction, criminality, and a hard recovery, had just won the publishing industry's most lucrative prize—Oprah Winfrey had picked it for her televised book club. But early in 2006, the muckraking Web site the Smoking Gun, which began to look into Frey's story in order to find a mug shot of the writer to post online (the memoir told of several stints in jail), reported that it had found serious flaws in his tale. There was no evidence that Frey had lived through much of what he'd written. *A Million Little Pieces* was stacked on the nonfiction shelves, but Frey had invented large swaths of it.

Then came the moment of truthiness: Winfrey defended Frey. Even if his details couldn't stand up to scrutiny, she told CNN, the "underlying message of redemption in James Frey's memoir still resonates with me, and I know it resonates with millions of other people who have read this book." It wasn't that Winfrey didn't believe the Smoking Gun's findings. Rather, she didn't think they mattered. The revelations were "much ado about nothing," she said, suggesting that what had really happened to Frey was less important than what one *believed* had happened to Frey. *A Million Little Pieces* felt real, and that was enough.

It's true that Oprah Winfrey later stepped back from the lie. After the *New York Times* columnist Frank Rich, a hardworking beat cop against the official sanctioning of lies, criticized her blasé attitude toward the truth, she invited Frey and his publisher to her show and sternly dressed them down. Winfrey also told her audience, "I made a mistake, and I left the impression that the truth does not matter." She added, "To everyone who has challenged me on this issue of truth, you are absolutely right."

Yet there was something in the air. There had been for some time. Oprah's jaunt into the dark side only proved that no one was safe from the fakery flooding the culture.

If there was a central font of fallacy, it was the war in Iraq, which, like the war in Vietnam, split wide the gulf between reality and perception, between what people wanted to be true and what was true. None of what had been said about Iraq—about its links to terrorism, about the deadly weapons it harbored, about the mission there having already been accomplished, and democracy having already taken root—none of it fit with reports describing the reality in Iraq.

But the White House's efforts to script the truth reached, as well, beyond the war. Early in 2005, for instance, *USA Today* reported that the Department of Education had covertly hired Armstrong Williams, a conservative commentator, to promote the Bush education plan, called No Child Left Behind, on TV and on the radio. Williams, who is black, was contracted to sell the plan to black audiences and to other minority journalists. He did so enthusiastically, even persuading the comedian Steve Harvey to invite Secretary of Education Rod Paige twice to Harvey's morning radio show. Williams maintains that he genuinely supported the White House's education policies. But he didn't tell his audience that he'd been paid $240,000 for his efforts.

It soon emerged that Williams wasn't the only pundit on the dole. The *Washington Post* and *Salon* found that the Department of Health and Human Services employed two other commentators, Maggie Gallagher and Michael McManus, as consultants on another federal social project, the president's proposal for strengthening American marriages. While working for the government, each had praised the Bush marriage plan in their columns, but neither had revealed their conflicts of interest. Late in 2005, the *Los Angeles Times* reported that the Pentagon had hired the Lincoln Group, an upstart Washington PR firm, to run an elaborate pro-American propaganda operation in Iraq. At the same time that Bush officials were praising the independence and vibrancy of Iraq's newly liberated press, the Lincoln Group was translating stories produced by U.S. officials into Arabic and then bribing Iraqi journalists or hiring Arabs to pose as journalists in order to disseminate the phony news through the Iraqi media.

Thus by the time Colbert took to the airwaves, by the time James Frey landed in trouble, the rift between the actual and the artificial had already become a topic of wide discussion. For many on the left, it was Bush himself who stood as the clear cause of it. A born-again Christian who credits unquestioning faith with saving him from delinquency, Bush is notoriously, even proudly uncurious about the world. Online, many bloggers highlighted this detachment by branding themselves members of "the reality-based community." This was a reference to an infamous and revealing interview that an unnamed Bush aide had once given to the journalist Ron Suskind. According to the aide, opponents of Bush were part of "what we call the reality-based community"—a label not meant to be complimentary, because to the aide, "discernible reality" was a stock of faltering value. The United States was "an empire now, and when we act, we create our own reality," the official told Suskind. "And while you're studying that reality—judiciously, as you will—we'll act again, creating other new realities, which you can study too, and that's how things will sort out."

How could this happen? How did we land in a place where a political official feels comfortable publicly dismissing "discernible reality"?

Investigating the rise of carelessness toward "reality" is, of course, the headlong purpose of this book. But I've been driving at a theory more pervasive than the peculiar psychology of one president, the transgressions of a single dominant political machine, or the aims of certain powerful players. The truth about truthiness, I've argued, is cognitive: when we strung up the planet in fiber-optic cable, when we dissolved the mainstream media into prickly niches, and when each of us began to create and transmit our own pictures and sounds, we eased the path through which propaganda infects the culture.

Video news releases and satellite media tours suggest the ultimate cultural expression of these forces: they show us what might become of the world—or, indeed, what has become of the world—in an age of easy lying. Today, marketers, political operatives, and others who want to convince you of the virtue of some thing or idea—whether it is a Swiffer duster, a Nokia headset, a presidential candidate, a certain education policy, or the "truth" about global warming—can go about the business of persuasion covertly, without divulging their motives or even *the fact that they're engaged in persuasion*. Propagandists have become experts at mining the vulnerabilities of the many-media world (for instance, the dubious ethics of bottom line–watching local news operations). They've adopted a range of methods to exploit the current conditions—some are as benign as the covert placement of products in films and TV shows, but others are more questionable, such as planting VNRs on the news, or buying up pundits, or spreading their messages anonymously and "virally" through blogs, videos, and photos on the Web.

Technically, what these operatives aim to do is capture one or many of the forces I've discussed so far: *selective exposure*, in which we indulge information that pleases us and cocoon ourselves among others who think as we do; *selective perception*, in which we interpret documentary proof according to our long-held beliefs; *peripheral processing*, which produces a swarm of phony experts; and the *hostile media phenomenon*, which pushes the news away from objectivity and toward the sort of drivel one sees on cable.

In practice, what propagandists are doing is simpler to describe: they've mastered a new way to lie....

There is an interesting story about how we got to this point. It begins, as so many tales of deception do, in the tobacco industry—specifically in the early 1990s, within the assaulted confines of the second-largest cigarette company in the United States, R. J. Reynolds, better known as RJR, the makers of Winston, Salem, and Camel. These were difficult times for cigarette manufacturers. As Americans began to learn about the pervasive risks of tobacco, dangers the industry had long understood and suppressed, calls for regulating cigarettes attracted wide public support. Local, state, and even national politicians proposed a web of restrictions: raising cigarette sales taxes, banning smoking in public places, recognizing tobacco as a dangerous drug.

The industry had long maintained a legendary lobbying and public affairs apparatus, and it had succeeded, miraculously, for decades, in pushing back most antismoking efforts. But now the party was burning out. Americans were turning against cigarettes. The opposition was visceral, a matter of life and death. How could any marketing campaign reverse this reality?

For executives at RJR, the answer, initially, was to go after the base. Like long-shot politicians everywhere, RJR hoped to rouse a sleeping mass of like-minded combatants—a "smokers' rights" army, in this case—that could face down the coming advance. About a fifth of Americans smoked cigarettes, and occasionally some would contact RJR with tales of dispossession. Smokers' employers hassled them when they lit up at work, their towns contemplated doubling and tripling the cost of their habit, they were being kicked out of restaurants and bowling alleys and the layabout places they'd considered havens. In the mid-1980s, RJR, following the lead of its rival Philip Morris, launched a monthly magazine catering to America's smokers. *Choice*, it was called, and that's how its pages painted the issue: smoking was a fundamental freedom, and it was under attack.

Choice depicted the world as a place of woe for smokers. It urged them to act. Smokers needed to stand up, write letters, call their legislators, circulate petitions, and fight for what was theirs. To reinforce the message, RJR also began to organize "smokers' rights" chapters across the country, arranging for citizens to come together to discuss how to battle the growing legions of antismokers. "Field coordinators" working for the company rented local meeting spots and recruited smokers, and they instructed the groups according to a slick PR manual the firm had produced. The manual offered tips on the mechanics of activism and policy making—how to recruit others to the fight, how to get noticed by politicians and the media—and it urged smokers to think about their struggle in epic terms. Tobacco was "more deeply rooted in our nation's heritage than any other commodity," the manual declared, and those protecting its legacy were acting in the tradition of the American revolutionaries, the women who'd fought for suffrage, and those who'd campaigned for civil rights. "Successful movements like these are not just in the history books," RJR told smokers. "One of them is happening here and now, and you're part of it!"

You can think of RJR's fostering of smokers' rights as an attempt at the direct route of marketing. In organizing smokers, RJR was selling its message as plainly as Dick Cavett once sold Lawry's Seasoned Salt. The company didn't hide its own interests. Throughout the 1980s and early 1990s, in fact, RJR ran a number of advertisements in which it boasted of its courage to speak out for what it believed. "We know some of you may question what we say because we're a cigarette company," it said in one ad. "But we also know that by keeping silent, we've contributed to this climate of doubt and distrust."

The spots often pleaded with nonsmokers to consider the feelings of smokers. "We feel singled out. We're doing something perfectly legal, yet we're often segregated, discriminated against, even legislated against." The solution to the impasse, the company said, was painfully obvious: "common courtesy." If smokers and nonsmokers would only be civil to each other—the smoker asks whether others wouldn't mind if he lit up, the nonsmoker doesn't try to get cigarettes banned from every public place—tobacco would cease to be a contentious public issue. At the bottom of each of these spots, one image was given prominence: the firm's logo, "R.J. Reynolds Tobacco Company," stenciled out in a stylish serif font.

But smokers' rights never caught on. The problem was the smokers themselves. They had, as it turned out, little sympathy for their pushers. According to the industry's own research, many hated their addiction and wanted to quit. A large number even supported restrictions on smoking. RJR struggled to fill the smokers' rights meetings. The few die-hards who joined seemed to do so only for the free cigarettes and lighters the company handed out; they hardly looked like the Martin Luther King Jrs. of smoking.

Worse, RJR's direct appeals engendered tremendous opposition. Every time the company ran an ad, it got more feedback from critics than from supporters. Dozens of people would cut out the newspaper spots, scribble responses to each of the company's points, and mail back their thoughts. An advertisement would declare, "We're not criminals," and a critic would write back, "You are breaking one of the Ten Commandments—Thou shall not kill." There's a famous industry story, first reported by *Mother Jones* magazine, that describes one RJR field coordinator's encounter with a woman who came to a smokers' rights meeting holding a shoe box. When the company man introduced himself, the woman said, "I want you to know my mother got an invitation to this meeting." Holding out the box, she added, "She died of lung cancer. I brought my mother to your meeting."

In the summer of 1994, after the Food and Drug Administration and the Occupational Safety and Health Administration announced that they were looking into regulating tobacco, RJR signaled a shift in its strategy. The firm published a newspaper ad that differed in a subtle but telling way from its previous campaigns.

In this ad, the company's name was scaled down to small type; the protagonist here was not RJR, the money-loving industrial giant, but instead it was *you*—the typical American citizen. Indeed, right up at the top of the page was a big photograph of one such specimen. He was a middle-aged man in jeans and a work shirt, cuffs rolled up, a wide smile on his face. His baseball cap sported the word "Minnesota." You could tell by the way he leaned against his pickup truck that he was a man's man, no time to talk. And this fellow, let's call him Heartland Man, came to us with a plain-spoken complaint: "I'm one of America's 45 million smokers. I'm not a moaner or a whiner. But I'm getting fed up. I'd like to get the government off my back." He went on to make an expansive case. The move to restrict cigarettes, he warned, would harm everyone, not just smokers. Because once the government banned cigarettes, it'll "go for liquor and fast food and buttermilk and who knows what else. There's a line of dominoes a mile long."

A few months after the ad was published, Mongoven, Biscoe, and Duchin (MBD), a Washington PR firm that worked for RJR, proposed that the company sponsor an entire campaign inspired by the grievances of the Heartland Man. The effort would have little to do with new tobacco regulations or, really, with smoking or the rights of smokers; instead, the new campaign would take aim at a larger, more universal scourge, one whose dimensions every American, whatever his politics or preferred vice, could be expected to appreciate: the government was getting too damn powerful, too damn nagging, too damn invasive.

MBD asked hundreds of organizations that ordinarily didn't take a stand either way on smoking to join the effort. Soon, the campaign, which MBD called the Get Government Off Our Back project— referred to by insiders as GGOOB; "guh-goob," if you wanted to say it out loud—had attracted an impressive array of member groups. The U.S. Chamber of Commerce signed on, as did the Traditional Values Coalition, the National Rifle Association, Small Business of America, the Seniors Coalition, and the Home School Legal Defense Association, among many others. Perhaps GGOOB's most important member group was Americans for Tax Reform, whose founder, the influential conservative operative Grover Norquist—a man known for fighting taxes and government programs with the restraint that General Sherman brought on his march to Savannah—enthusiastically pressed GGOOB's case with reporters and Washington policy makers.

But one name was left out of the lengthy list of stars joining the new project. RJR, which sponsored GGOOB and had provided substantial donations to many of the groups that agreed to join, took no credit for the campaign. Nor did any other lobby with obvious ties to the tobacco industry. Indeed, to look at GGOOB's papers and press releases, you'd never guess a cigarette connection. In one position paper released by the group, a frequently-asked-questions section posed, "How did Get Government Off Our Back get started?" The true answer was that RJR's public relations company founded it. Instead, the document said that GGOOB was created at the "grassroots," by "loose networks of business groups, civic groups and other organizations" who'd come together more or less spontaneously. Why was GGOOB necessary now? The paper didn't say it was because RJR wanted to beat back new regulations on its business. Rather, GGOOB was necessary because if nobody acted soon, "the American system could be in danger of collapsing under the weight of big government." There was that line of dominoes a mile long.

GGOOB, plainly, was a front group. As Dorie Apollonio and Lisa Bero, two researchers at the University of California, San Francisco, who first uncovered the project's connections, explain, in starting up GGOOB, RJR found a way to push its own agenda in a "politically palatable" manner. It's true that many of the groups involved in GGOOB were deeply conservative; most fit the mold of Americans for Tax Reform, ardent antitax campaigners and small-government advocates who were not particularly representative of the country at large. Still, their motives represented a vastly more powerful organizing force than the narrow, unpopular aims of RJR.

Remember that RJR wasn't getting anywhere with the direct appeal. When the company tried to sell its ideas straight—when it took out ads asking for some consideration, when it sketched out the possibility of some middle ground on the issue of smoking— people dismissed it. Polls showed antitobacco fervor rising around the country. Even smokers wouldn't join its side. Now, by taking its propaganda underground—by turning the battle into one about big government rather than big tobacco and, crucially, by hiding its own association with the plan—RJR could ride toward its goals upon a cresting wave of antiregulatory activism. And that's exactly how the plan played out.

In its first major action, GGOOB declared March 1995 national "Regulatory Revolt Month" and celebrated the invented holiday with rallies in several states, some of which drew hundreds of supporters. The rallies were extensively covered in the local media, but the press did not report—because the press did not know—that these were tobacco-funded affairs. GGOOB also asked state lawmakers to pledge to oppose new government rules. Impressed by the project's apparent popularity, dozens of legislators, mainly Republicans, signed the promise. They, too, weren't told that they were joining a cigarette company's cause; presumably, many would have reconsidered had they been aware who was behind the GGOOB curtain.

In Washington, Republicans who'd recently taken over both houses of Congress pushed GGOOB's call to put a freeze on all new federal health and environmental regulations. Their bill didn't pass, but men like Norquist enforced a tough line against federal rules, and by the end of 1995, it was clear that GGOOB had succeeded in its effort to derail the harshest proposed restrictions on cigarettes. The FDA prohibited tobacco advertisements aimed at teenagers, but it did not impose any of the strict rules—including an outright ban on cigarettes—that the industry had long feared. A rule by the Labor Department to restrict smoking in the workplace, meanwhile, went nowhere. GGOOB succeeded. But the real victor, of course, was RJR.

A skeptic might point out that GGOOB merely won a battle but that tobacco still lost the war. In the years since RJR's tricky PR effort, after all, many of the restrictions it once fought have come to pass. Today the vast majority of Americans aren't allowed to smoke at work, and in many places it's illegal, not to mention uncouth, to wield a cigarette in public. The culture, more important, has shifted, so that the very thought of smoking as a "heartland" habit feels like a notion from the distant past. Yet it is precisely the tobacco industry's general failures that prove the importance—and the lasting appeal, to propagandists— of a deceptive PR plan like GGOOB.

By the 1990s, probably nothing could have saved cigarette companies from the fate they've suffered since; if you kill four hundred thousand people every year, and if the public comes to realize you're killing four hundred thousand people every year, no sort of PR campaign will win you permanent favor. But that's just what's so remarkable about GGOOB—the project helped to hold back a few big losses for the industry at a time of clear and growing antipathy toward cigarettes, and it worked only because, in the public mind, GGOOB had nothing to do with cigarettes. GGOOB showed that you can engineer a marketing win even if your position was ridiculous (a ban on cigarettes might lead to a prohibition on buttermilk!), even if your product was killing people, even if your own customers, people who were neurochemically addicted to what you sold, were on the fence about what you did. All you had to do was fight your battle from another front. All you had to do was don a disguise. You just had to lie.

The annals of tobacco burn bright with scams like GGOOB; at the risk of comically understating the case, it's fair to say that this was far from the only time a cigarette company came upon the utility of hiding the truth from the public.* But there was still something noteworthy about GGOOB, something seminal in its design and constituency that can be traced, over the years, to the bog of truthiness we find ourselves navigating now, more than a decade afterward.

If you look through the many PR pros and consultants working with RJR of the early 1990s, you find a clutch of players who turn up, with surprising frequency, at the sites of several of the major scuffles over truth we've witnessed since the millennium. Among these RJR all-stars are three men who merit special mention: Thomas Synhorst, who worked for years as an aide to Republican senators Charles Grassley and Bob Dole, was a part-time field coordinator for RJR and was responsible for conducting the company's smokers' rights operations in the Midwest. Douglas Goodyear was an executive at Walt Klein and Associates, a public relations and marketing company in Denver that worked closely with RJR on many projects, including GGOOB. And Timothy Hyde was RJR's in-house public affairs chief, involved in virtually all of its campaigns, including GGOOB.

In 1997, these three men got together to create a lobbying and public relations firm of their own. They called the partnership the DCI Group. If the name sounds forgettably generic, that's in keeping with DCI's ethos. On behalf of some of the largest companies in the world, DCI pulls strings in the shadows, fostering positive outcomes by creating the appearance of a groundswell of public support. Its entire business is creating projects like GGOOB.

Tales of DCI's sneaky coalition-creation efforts are legion. In the late 1990s, when the federal government was trying to break up Microsoft over antitrust charges, the software company hired DCI— among several other lobbying firms—to cook up ways to enhance its standing in the capital. DCI appears to have helped the company found at least one pro-Microsoft industry group, Americans for Technology Leadership, whose president, an amiable fellow named Jonathan

---

*To name one other remarkable example: The health policy researchers Elisa Ong and Stanton Glantz, also at UCSF, found that around the same time that RKR was working on GGOOB, Philip Morris, the world's largest cigarette maker, directed its public relations firm to create a front group focused on the grand-sounding idea of "sound science." Philip Morris's PR firm sent letters to thousands of scientists asking them to join the new group, the Advancement for Sound Science Coalition, which called on the government to be cautious when using science in determining how to regulate businesses. Many of the people who signed on didn't know they were working for a cigarette company; Philip Morris documents show that the firm made sure to treat the scientists in a way that made them "feel" that they (the scientists) were dictating the front group's strategies. Steven Milloy, the Philip Morris employee who directed the effort, has since gone on to find much success in the business of sound science. He now runs a Web site call JunkScience.com and is a frequent commentator on Fox News, where he regularly dismisses findings—on global warming, secondhand smoke, and other health and environmental threats—that threaten industry. Journalists Chris Mooney and Pual Thacker, among others, have reported that Milloy regularly receives money from cigarette and oil companies.

Zuck, was frequently quoted in the press as offering sensible-sounding reasons why Microsoft should be left alone.

I say that DCI's role in the creation of ATL is only *apparent* because the story has never been definitively unraveled, and one rarely knows for sure what has happened in cases involving DCI. When ATL officials lobbied members of Congress, state officials, and reporters on behalf of Microsoft, they purported to be completely independent from the company and from DCI. But ATL's executive director was also an employee of DCI, and Microsoft and several groups funded by Microsoft were listed as its founding members. ATL's murky role so agitated Oracle, one of Microsoft's main rivals, that it hired a private investigation firm to look into the group. But Oracle's P.I.s couldn't get very close to the truth, either: the gumshoes were discovered when they tried to pay the janitors at ATL's Washington office for bags of trash belonging to the advocacy group.

In 2003, Nicholas Confessore, a writer for *Washington Monthly* magazine, discovered that DCI had branched out into an even more creative propaganda venture, one that Confessore labeled "journa-lobbying." At the time, a magazine named *Tech Central Station* was gaining some notice on the Web, especially among conservative bloggers, who appreciated its wonky but engaging discussions of controversies in science, technology, and economics. *TCS*, which the journalist James Glassman founded at the height of the Internet boom, often espoused the pseudo-libertarian point of view that has long attracted certain geekier sects online. *TCS*'s writers, for instance, did not look favorably on regulations to curb greenhouse gases or the government's move to break up Microsoft or federal efforts to control drug prices. Though the magazine's style wasn't for everyone, even critics of *TCS* didn't doubt its writers' authenticity. Glassman had previously worked at the *New Republic* and the *Atlantic Monthly*, and he'd edited the Capitol Hill newspaper *Roll Call*. He was a real journalist.

Except maybe not anymore. As Confessore discovered, *Tech Central Station*, unbeknownst to its readers, was covertly published by the DCI Group, and DCI and *TCS* shared owners, employees, and office space. Moreover, many of the DCI Group's corporate clients were also "sponsors" of *TCS*, and *TCS*'s editorial positions, seen in this light, made a lot more sense. Among the benefactors were ExxonMobil, Microsoft, and PhRMA, the trade group that represents the pharmaceutical industry.

Glassman denied that the DCI connection affected his site's content.[*] He may have genuinely believed that, just as the scientists working for cigarette company front groups believed they'd independently arrived at the positions that favored their bosses. But that *TCS*'s punditry closely orbited the positions of its sponsors was evident on a host of issues, even beyond global warming, telecom policy, prescription drugs, and Microsoft.

---

[*]Late in 2006, DCI sold the site to its editor, Nick Schultz, and Glassman left the company to found a magazine called *The American. Tech Central Station* is now called *TCS Daily*.

In the spring of 2006, the writers Charles Wilson and Eric Schlosser published *Chew on This,* a version of Schlosser's earlier book *Fast Food Nation,* this one meant to educate schoolchildren on the dangers of eating junk food. In response to the book and to the coming *Fast Food Nation* movie, McDonald's, according to internal documents obtained by the *Wall Street Journal,* launched a vigorous campaign to "discredit the message and the messenger"—the messenger here being Schlosser.

McDonald's was one of DCI's sponsors, and soon its strategy came to life on Glassman's *TCS* in a feature called "Fast Talk Nation." The *TCS* site attacked *Chew on This* and included a form letter for parents to print out and send to schools where Schlosser and Wilson were speaking. The letter alleged that Schlosser favored legalizing marijuana—this was a reference to *Reefer Madness,* Schlosser's book examining the cost of the black market in drugs—and that he wasn't fit to lecture to kids. In an afterward to *Chew on This,* the authors wrote that "headmasters and principals received e-mails, letters, and phone calls urging them to cancel our visits."

No schools did. And when the press found the McDonald's/ DCI/*TCS* connection, "Fast Talk Nation" was taken down. Still, you can see in this example the efficacy of the secret attack, of stealth PR. What DCI built, in *TCS,* was a system to "launder" ideas, as Confessore called the practice. By filtering the positions of corporations through creative and highly readable pundits, DCI could apply a sheen of respectability, of legitimacy, to naked business agendas. McDonald's, by itself, could not criticize Schlosser; it couldn't risk its image, for one, and people would have dismissed what it said anyway, just as they'd ignored what tobacco companies had said about cigarettes. Why would you believe anything *McDonald's* told you about junk food and kids?

But when the idea is separated from the company, when doubts about Schlosser are raised by all sorts of groups that sound well-meaning, and when blogs and discussion forums you're reading keep alerting you to the *TCS* page on Schlosser's sketchy past, well, then, don't you have to wonder? You don't know that McDonald's is part of this campaign. You don't even know there *is* a campaign. So if you're a parent, maybe you pause before picking up *Chew on This.* Or maybe you write a letter to a school. Many did, getting roped in to a machine built by DCI, *TCS,* and McDonald's, without even knowing it.

I can't provide you with anything near an exhaustive catalog of DCI's machinations; to do so would turn this book into a directory of mendacity, and, more to the point, it'd be impossible. Much of what the firm does we do not know. That's the essence of DCI: we hear about its actions only when it slips up in some way, or when canny reporters start nosing around in areas usually left unexplored.

It seems safe to say that DCI created front groups for Microsoft. But what about the fake groups we haven't uncovered? Lobbying firms have become skilled at the tactic, known as "astroturfing,"* and it's unclear how many phony coalitions representing other clients have littered the discourse and altered public policy over the last couple of decades.

Similarly, stories of DCI's political push-polling operations occasionally find a way into the papers. In these schemes, operators call up voters and pretend they're pollsters conducting a survey, but instead of soliciting information, they attack an opponent. DCI seems to have carried out some of the infamous push-polls against John McCain that Bush operatives designed during the 2000 Republican primary in South Carolina. In one poll, operators called McCain "a liar, a cheat, and a fraud." But nobody has ever proved DCI's involvement, and it's likely that nobody ever will. It seems plausible that DCI has conducted other push-polls in other elections. But we don't know of them.

Meanwhile, there's evidence that DCI is slinking further into the digital shadows. Around the time that the film *An Inconvenient Truth* was released in theaters, a short animated video criticizing the Al Gore global warming documentary began to make the rounds on online video-sharing sites. The cartoon was something like a spoof of Gore's famous touring slideshow on climate change, with the former vice president lecturing a bunch of bored penguins on the dangers of carbon emissions—although really the spot was so unfocused and underproduced that it was difficult to know what it was getting at. There seemed to be nothing more sophisticated to it than the joke that Al Gore is wooden and boring (which is not to downplay its rhetorical potential; the joke that Gore is boring has certainly attained a cloying permanence, if late-night TV is a guide).

The video was posted on You Tube by someone going by the handle "toutsmith." He identified himself as a twenty-nine-year-old in California, apparently an ordinary You Tuber, and there was no reason to suspect that he wasn't; anyone of more nefarious connections would probably have offered a more substantive response to Gore's polemic.

But there was something—something very small—that set the penguin video apart from the millions of other amateur political productions vying for attention on the Web. As a *Wall Street Journal* reporter discovered, someone had bought up ads on Google pointing to the penguin movie. Why would a homebrew political agitator take out ads? Because, of course, this wasn't home brew. The *Journal* reporter had a brief e-mail discussion with "toutsmith," and he examined the fellow's messages to see how they'd been routed through the Internet. It turned out that toutsmith's e-mail was coming from a computer belonging to—wait for it—the DCI Group. To this day, though,

---

*The term was coined in 1986 by that font of political quippery, the late Texas senator Lloyd Bentsen.

that's about all we know of the plan. DCI has refused to comment on its role in criticizing the Gore movie (the firm refuses to comment on all of its work). Was the penguin video part of some larger campaign? Are there other DCI-sponsored videos online criticizing Gore? Or are some blogs or MySpace profiles, or video games possibly supported by the firm? And if there were, would we ever know it? How would we ever find out?

The point is not that the DCI Group doesn't tell the truth. What is important is the design and the nature of its lies, and how difficult they are, now, to dig up. Only recently have investigators begun to unearth the awesome reach of the tobacco industry's propaganda operation during the 1980s and 1990s, and the successes have mainly come about because millions of cigarette documents are now public and searchable, a result of government lawsuits against manufacturers. But the players who touted tobacco are now free agents, and they're working in a system that is vastly more sympathetic to their game.

In fact, all we know about any of this is fragmentary. There is a story about how these things work, but we can only guess it. In a suite in Redmond or San Antonio or Dallas or Detroit or Mountain View or Washington, a CEO or a candidate muses on the necessity of confronting a certain public danger.[*] Here the message gleams; it's simple and direct, maybe as plain as, *We need to get the government off our backs*, or *This movie will be trouble.*

Later, down in Government Affairs, company men versed in minutiae turn musing into strategy, as they outline aims and aspirations, identifying necessary goals: guaranteeing that there are three commissioners supporting the company in the FCC's examination of unbundling obligations of incumbent local exchange carriers, for example, or holding up the effort in Congress on corporate average fuel economy standards. From there, the thing is shipped to a shop like DCI, where the work begins. Eager old hands mold strategy into a full-bore campaign, the effort getting dirty now, coalitions rising out of the swamp. Americans for Economic Progress, People Against Environmental Radicalism, the Committee for Common Sense—each of them is given a staff of experts and prognosticators, souls who clamor for news attention and earnestly press their reps on behalf of the many they say they represent.

There are mailings and newspaper ads, experts are corralled, and, depending on the scope, there might be a phone bank operation, online videos, video news releases, a letter-writing campaign, or manufactured rallies in several cities. The message is sent, too, to the journalistic operation down the hall and to others known to be friendly, and here

---

[*]Google, whose motto is "Don't be evil," is among the firms recently known to have hired the DCI Group.

writers and anchors take to the project with aplomb, making the sponsors' case so elegantly, so convincingly, that people don't even think to ask about connections.

There must be a few lies along the way, certainly. Americans for Economic Progress is really one American, a man in a cubicle in an office on K Street. Coincidentally, it's the same cubicle that houses the Committee for Common Sense. The experts are on the take, and aren't quite experts besides. The videos picture events that are not replicable in reality. The phone bankers are phony. The journalists, well, they've got problems; they'll say anything, those guys.

But these things can be excused, they're not going to matter because all along the way, the connections have been severed: as the message slips away from the company or the candidate, the sponsor recedes from responsibility, and by the time the bloggers get to it, the lie has spread blamelessly throughout. Real people are invested in the message now, actually fighting on its behalf. This is the key, really, to the enterprise. By now, so many have participated so enthusiastically that the message has become a thing of the culture. And when that happens—if you've set up a whole reality that says something false is true, and if so many people have bought into that reality and are even defending it—one has to ask, Is it really even a lie anymore?

Critical Reading Questions

Summarizing the Text

1. How does Manjoo use Stephen Colbert's term *truthiness*? What does that term mean?

2. Understanding this article requires that the reader keep in mind many acronyms. What are DCI, VNRs, ATL, TCS, GGOOB, and RJR? How does Manjoo use each of these entities to build his argument?

Establishing the Context

3. Written in 2006, at a time when many people had grown extremely skeptical of the Bush administration and had come to believe that the war in Iraq had been dishonestly sold to the nation, this book takes for granted a degree of cynicism in the public. Has public cynicism about the information we receive from the government grown or diminished or remained steady since then? What evidence do you have for your answer?

4. Skepticism about the truthfulness of official bodies—such as the government—is one of the strategies used by the public relations (PR) industry to make "truthy" claims, Manjoo argues. What is one example—either from

Manjoo or from your own experience—of a claim that gained traction partly because of a hostility to what the government or another powerful entity was saying about the issue?

Responding to the Message

5. Some things that Manjoo might consider "truthy"—such as the widespread objections to the teaching of the theory of evolution and the proposed "intelligent design" hypothesis—others believe are in no way similar to the corporate-friendly PR of such projects at GGOOB. Where do you stand on this issue?

6. In many ways, *where* a story gets told contributes as much to its credibility as what the story is, and how likely it seems. Can you think of an example of a story that began as a rumor or an Internet gossip item that gained credibility as it moved into what some call the "mainstream media"?

7. How do you evaluate the credibility of information you find on the Internet or on the television news?

Reflections on the Cultural Climate of Plagiarism

Matthew S. Willen

Reports of an "epidemic" of plagiarism have cited statistics purporting to show that anywhere from 40 percent to 90 percent of students cheat by cut-and-pasting from the Internet at some point in their college careers. Why do students plagiarize? In this article, Matthew Willen (Associate Professor of English and director of the first-year writing program at Elizabethtown College in Pennsylvania) offers some answers to that question. This article appeared in Liberal Education, *the magazine of the American Association of Colleges and Universities.*

If frequency of e-mail distribution is any indication, college professors and administrators indeed took notice of last fall's article in the *New York Times*, "A Campus Fad That's Being Copied: Internet Plagiarism" (Rimer 2003), on Rutgers Professor Donald L. McCabe's recent study of cheating in college and universities. I received four copies of the article: two from faculty colleagues on my campus, one from a campus administrator and another from a colleague at a university where I formerly worked. As a writing teacher, I receive many articles and announcements about cheating from colleagues, though never four of the same piece. The figures cited in the *Times* article are worthy of attention—38 percent of surveyed college students admitted to "cut and paste" plagiarism from the Internet during the year surveyed, while a slightly higher number (40 percent) that probably overlaps with the first group acknowledged plagiarizing from written sources.

These numbers demonstrate that cheating is a problem on college campuses and that the Internet is probably not making matters better, but plagiarism is certainly not a new phenomenon. Educators have attended and continue to attend to plagiarism in positive ways that help students better recognize, understand, and avoid it: we educate students on how to properly work with sources; teach them about standards of academic integrity; help them to understand academic culture; and explain the ramifications, both intellectual and ethical, of cheating. Some schools have developed pledges and honor codes to help cultivate an ethos of integrity on campus. As an extra measure, many instructors address the problem by designing projects which make plagiarizing difficult.

Yet incidents of plagiarism persist, and, as these numbers suggest, they are probably on the rise. This persistence, in spite of efforts to teach students what plagiarism is, why it is unethical, and how to avoid it, makes clear that the circumstances which lead a student to choose to plagiarize are considerably more complicated than the omnipresence of the Internet or simply not knowing any better. In fact, the high percentage of students who willingly admitted to "cut and paste" plagiarism for McCabe's survey is evidence enough that they do know what they are doing.

As director of a freshman writing program, I frequently deal with incidents of and issues related to plagiarism. I never cease to be surprised by the fact that many students who plagiarize are bright, well-intentioned students who, in fact, do know better. Most are students who possess moral convictions and ethical standards that would prevent them from stealing food, money, or clothing. Yet when it comes to the theft of another person's words or ideas, these same students appear to be guided by a different "moral compass." So writes David Callahan, in *The Cheating Culture* (2004, 14), as he examines the pervasiveness of cheating in American society that allows individuals to transgress those very convictions and standards that otherwise apply. Obviously, there is some sort of disconnect here, and if we are going to effectively address the problem of plagiarism on college campuses, we must understand the conditions that underlie this disconnect.

Cultural conditions

What are the circumstances that compel students to choose to go against their own moral and ethical standards and to plagiarize? This is no doubt a perplexing question, and I make no pretense of addressing it in all of its complexity here. McCabe's comments cited in the Times article, though, suggest one way that we might begin to think about it. He explains that "undergraduates say they need to cheat because of the intense competition to get into graduate school, and land the top jobs." The need that students express should not be taken lightly. Surprisingly, McCabe indicates that this need is not an effect of the expectations or requirements for courses being unreasonable; nor are the pressures created by workloads, deadlines and poor time management the primary issues. Instead, this need reflects an anxiety about the future, an anxiety reinforced by their experiencing higher education as professional preparation that is a highly competitive, high stakes endeavor.

It is not difficult to imagine some of the reasons for students' experiencing higher education this way. From a young age, both parents and the schools inculcate by a narrative that presents the conventional path to success—to living a good life—as paved with good grades, good SAT scores, and acceptance into a good college. All of these, it is assumed, lead ultimately to a good job. Historically, there has been some truth to this narrative, but when confronted with current economic uncertainties, it seems rather inadequate. Graduates now find themselves in intense competition for opportunities for the success myth that are more limited than they were at other times in the past.

The success narrative comes to college with students where it unintentionally continues to be supported in ways that we tend not to recognize. We continue to present the "top graduate school" and the "good job" (expressions which could stand to be unpacked) as the hallmarks of educational achievement, and we celebrate and distinguish those individuals who excel by these norms by providing them with honors and other forms of recognition.

We certainly want to acknowledge the achievements of our best and brightest students, but doing so in these ways suggests to all students that individual accomplishments evidenced by good grades are what is really important; top grades do provide the competitive edge. The effect of this critique can be especially problematic in a cultural climate that has become increasingly obsessed with competition and the accumulation of material wealth. In *The Cheating Culture* (2004), Callahan attributes this obsession to the rise of the market as the "dominant cultural force" in the latter part of the twentieth century, with the consequent effect of performance and profitability becoming the keys to success.

In this climate what counts most are numbers and results, and those who get results, those who make the grade, *regardless of how they go about doing it,* reap the benefits. As Callahan suggests, the fact that opportunities for graduates are becoming more limited; that the middle class in American society is shrinking; that the rewards for coming out on top seem astronomical (think for instance of CEO salaries), it is not surprising that, when faced with a choice between preserving one's integrity or doing what is unethical but may ensure some measure of success or security, many students will choose the latter.

Again, these are complex issues that demand greater attention than I have the space to give them here. My intention, though, is to consider that the conditions that lead students to choose to plagiarize might be located in a broad cultural climate that privileges an unhealthy competitiveness and the results that it garners as the means to the limited opportunities and material wealth by which success is measured. By thinking of the conditions that make plagiarism an option, we may begin to consider additional, and perhaps less obvious, measures for contending with its persistence.

Value of learning

We might, for instance, pay more attention to the way that we present writing to our students by showing them that we value the process of writing—which includes invention, drafting, collaboration, revising, and editing—and not simply the final product as what is essential to their learning. For students who see the objective of a college education as the attainment of top grades to provide the edge over others competing for the same limited opportunities, such an education can easily become less about learning and more about results. In this paradigm, writing tends to be viewed as a commodity whose value is measured exclusively in terms of the grade for which it is exchanged. It fails to acknowledge the essential functions that the activities involved with producing the document play in the learning process. We need to stress that writing doesn't simply document what they know on a topic; its processes enable comprehension of the topic. From a pedagogical perspective, the real crime of plagiarism is less that it is dishonest than that it precludes learning.

A logical place to begin the work of recasting the value of writing is in the freshman composition courses required for most college students. This effort would require that the instructors shift attention from creating projects that make plagiarism impossible, to designing those that reveal the ways writing contributes to learning; it requires providing opportunities to reflect on this dimension of writing that remains misunderstood by many students. Moreover, it necessarily needs to be consistently followed in other classes. To this end we might do a better job explaining why and how we require different types of writing in the assignments that we create for all of our courses, instead of simply listing how many points or what percentage of the final grade a paper is worth. Listing points or percentages to the exclusion of an explanation of how a project contributes to learning explicitly casts the text as commodity, its value only in the final product. Moreover, these efforts need to be extended by evaluation methods that take into account the process of production as well as the quality of the product.

Campus ethos

It seems important as well to continue finding ways to cultivate a campus ethos of integrity. Instituting honors codes and pledges of integrity have been effective towards this end. An earlier study by McCabe and his associates (2001), for instance, demonstrates that schools that had some form of code or pledge of integrity experienced significantly lower incidents of cheating than those without.

In addition to these efforts, it may be useful to reflect on the ways that our institutional and pedagogical practices continue to reinforce and reward aggressive competitiveness and an individualistic me-first climate, to the exclusion of recognizing those who have contributed to the integrity of a campus or local community. Now more than ever, it is important to develop ways to acknowledge those sorts of contributions.

Changing campus values may grow from and make possible conversations on campus about the nature of success and what it might mean to live well. This kind of conversation could help students to better see their education not simply as an obligatory credentialing experience but as an opportunity to investigate and define the values that inform the life decisions they make and will be called upon to make beyond the campus.

Consequences of decisions

Finally, many of us are probably in need of dealing with incidents of plagiarism and enforcing policies concerning cheating more strictly. From my experience working with faculty members in both supervisory and consulting roles, I see that many are willing to treat a case of plagiarism as a learning experience, as an instance of a student misunderstanding the rules, and to provide the student with the opportunity to redo an assignment. Having done this myself, I understand that the impulse stems from a commitment to student success and to helping students learn. It is one thing, however, to make this sort of allowance in a freshman-level course when students are learning about matters of academic integrity; it is quite another thing to make this allowance for students beyond the freshman year.

If we are to assume that the standards of and methods for maintaining academic integrity are something that all students learn in their first year at college, then we undermine our own ethical and educational standards if we do not expect students to apply that knowledge in subsequent courses. How we deal with incidents of dishonesty is open to some discussion. Failing or dismissing a student or placing him or her on academic probation—the traditional stated consequence for cheating—may not be the most effective methods for dealing with the problem. If cheating is both an ethical transgression and evidence of a failure to learn, it harms the academic community as much as it does the individual. We may do well to name just how plagiarism compromises the integrity of a community, and to develop disciplinary methods that compel a student who cheats to contribute to building community in some constructive way.

Overall, these are difficult steps that don't necessarily target plagiarism directly. Perhaps they are most difficult because they ask us to examine the ways in which our basic and unquestioned pedagogical and institutional practices may be complicit in creating a climate of values that unwittingly supports plagiarism. At this juncture, however, it is important that we begin attending to some of the larger, difficult cultural issues that may be contributing to this problem. In my view, one of the most important things that a liberal education can provide students is the ability to see how the choices they make are situated in cultural contexts and to consider critically the far-reaching effects (rather than simply the individual effects) of choosing one course of action as opposed to another. These suggestions are intended to point in that direction.

Works Cited

Callahan, D. 2004. *The cheating culture: Why more Americans are doing wrong to get ahead*. Orlando, FL: Harcourt Inc.

McCabe, D. L., L. K. Treviño, and K. D. Butterfield. 2001. Cheating in academic institutions: A decade of research. *Ethics and Behavior* 11: 219-32.

Rimer, S. 2003. A campus fad that's being copied: Internet plagiarism. *New York Times*, September 3.

Critical Reading Questions

Summarizing the Text

1. What are some of the circumstances that spur students to plagiarize, according to Willen?

2. How can colleges and universities best prevent students from plagiarizing, in Willen's view?

Establishing the Context

3. Although it may seem like the Internet and cut-and-paste technology have existed forever, in the context of American universities they are new phenomena. How does Willen attempt to give some historical context to his argument?
4. Who is Willen's audience for this article? (One clue: look at where it appeared.) How might this article be argued differently had it been aimed at another audience—students, parents, people uninvolved in higher education?

Responding to the Message

5. Is Willen just letting students off the hook by, essentially, blaming society for the prevalence of plagiarism?
6. Without naming names, of course, discuss any instances of Internet plagiarism that you have committed or seen while at college. Do you think that a different campus "ethos of integrity" might have prevented those incidents? Do you think the prospect of stricter punishment, such as expulsion, would do the trick?

Generational Myth

Siva Vaidhyanathan

Siva Vaidhyanathan has written extensively on information technology, publishing, and society, and in recent years he has become an important voice in the debate about the ultimate ramifications of Google's ambitious undertakings. His latest book is The Googlization of Everything (And Why We Should Worry). *This essay appeared in the* Chronicle of Higher Education, *a weekly newsmagazine aimed at professors and administrators in universities and colleges.*

Consider all the pundits, professors, and pop critics who have wrung their hands over the inadequacies of the so-called digital generation of young people filling our colleges and jobs. Then consider those commentators who celebrate the creative brilliance of digitally adept youth. To them all, I want to ask: Whom are you talking about? There is no such thing as a "digital generation."

In the introduction to his book *Print Is Dead: Books in Our Digital Age* (Macmillan) last year, Jeff Gomez posits that young Americans constitute a distinct generation that shares a sensibility: resistance to the charms of printed and bound books. Gomez, who has been a sales-and-marketing director for a number of global publishers, has written a trade book whose title and thesis demand that we ignore it. Alas, I could not.

"The needs of an entire generation of 'Digital Natives'—kids who have grown up with the Internet, and are accustomed to the entire world being only a mouse click away— are going unanswered by traditional print media like books, magazines, and newspapers," Gomez writes. "For this generation—which Googles rather than going to the library—print seems expensive, a bore, and a waste of time."

When I read that, I shuddered. I shook my head. I rolled my eyes. And I sighed. I have been hearing some version of the "kids today" or "this generation believes" argument for more than a dozen years of studying and teaching about digital culture and technology. As a professor, I am in the constant company of 18- to 23-year-olds. I have taught at both public and private universities, and I have to report that the levels of comfort with, understanding of, and dexterity with digital technology vary greatly within every class. Yet it has not changed in the aggregate in more than 10 years.

Every class has a handful of people with amazing skills and a large number who can't deal with computers at all. A few lack mobile phones. Many can't afford any gizmos and resent assignments that demand digital work. Many use Facebook and MySpace because they are easy and fun, not because they are powerful (which, of course, they are not). And almost none know how to program or even code text with Hypertext Markup Language (HTML). Only a handful come to college with a sense of how the Internet fundamentally differs from the other major media platforms in daily life.

College students in America are not as "digital" as we might wish to pretend. And even at elite universities, many are not rich enough. All this mystical talk about a generational shift and all the claims that kids won't read books are just not true. Our students read books when books work for them (and when I tell them to). And they all (I mean all) tell me that they prefer the technology of the bound book to the PDF or Web page. What kids, like the rest of us, don't like is the price of books.

Of course they use Google, but not very well—just like my 75-year-old father. And they fill the campus libraries at all hours, just as Americans of all ages are using libraries in record numbers. (According to the American Library Association, visits to public libraries in the United States increased 61 percent from 1994 to 2004).

What do we miss when we pay attention only to the perceived digital prejudices of American college students? Most high-school graduates in the United States do not end up graduating from four-year universities with bachelor's degrees. According to the National Center for Education Statistics, in 2007 only some 28 percent of adults 25 and older had completed bachelor's degrees or higher. Is it just college-educated Americans who are eligible for generational status?

Talk of a "digital generation" or people who are "born digital" willfully ignores the vast range of skills, knowledge, and experience of many segments of society. It ignores the needs and perspectives of those young people who are not socially or financially privileged. It presumes a level playing field and equal access to time, knowledge, skills, and technologies. The ethnic, national, gender, and class biases of any sort of generation talk are troubling. And they could not be more obvious than when discussing assumptions about digital media.

As Henry Jenkins, a media-studies professor at the Massachusetts Institute of Technology, wrote on his blog last year, "Talking about youth as digital natives implies that there is a world which these young people all share and a body of knowledge they have all mastered, rather than seeing the online world as unfamiliar and uncertain for all of us." Such discussions, he said, also risk ignoring the different ways young people use digital tools, from listening to compact discs to blogging to posting clever videos on YouTube to buying stuff on eBay.

In reaction to Jenkins's post, Leslie Johnston, now at the Library of Congress, wrote on her blog, "I have worked with faculty in their 60s who saw something in being digital decades ago and have worked in that realm for years. I have worked with colleagues—librarians and faculty—in my own age group (I'm 44) who hate all technology with a passion and others who embrace it in all ways. I have worked with students at three different research universities who could not care less about being digital."

On my blog, Sivocracy, Elizabeth Losh, writing director of the humanities core course at the University of California at Irvine and author of the forthcoming *Virtualpolitik: An Electronic History of Government Media-Making in Time of War, Scandal, Disaster, Miscommunication, and Mistakes* (MIT Press, 2009), kept the online conversation going: "Unlike many in today's supposed 'digital generation,' we learned real programming skills—with punch cards in the beginning—from the time we were in elementary school. What passes for 'media literacy' now is often nothing more than teaching kids to make prepackaged PowerPoint presentations." Losh also pointed out that the supposed existence of a digital generation has had an impact on education, as distance-learning corporations with bells-and-whistles technology get public attention while traditional classroom teaching is ignored.

Once we assume that all young people love certain forms of interaction and hate others, we forge policies and design systems and devices that match those presumptions. By doing so, we either pander to some marketing cliché or force an otherwise diverse group of potential users into a one-size-fits-all system that might not meet their needs. Then, lo and behold, young people rush to adapt to those changes that we assumed all along that they wanted. More precisely, we take actions like rushing to digitize entire state-university library systems with an emphasis on speed and size rather than on quality and utility.

Ask any five people when Generation X started and ended. You will get five different answers. The borders of membership could not be more arbitrary. Talking as if all people born between 1964 and (pick a year after 1974) share some discernible, unifying traits or experiences is about as useful as saying that all Capricorns are the same. Such talk is not based on any sociological or demographic definition of a generation; it's based on whatever topic is in question.

Invoking "generations" demands an exclusive focus on people of wealth and means, because they get to express their preferences (for music, clothes, technology, etc.) in ways that are easy to count. It tends to exclude immigrants and non-English-speaking Americans, not to mention those who live beyond the borders of the United States. And it excludes anyone on the margins of mainstream consumer or cultural behavior.

The baby boom was a real demographic event. But what baby boomers share is Medicare—or at least they will soon. That's pretty much the end of the list. America, even in the 1950s and 1960s, was too diverse a place for uniform assumptions to hold true. It's even more diverse now.

Historical phenomena such as the Vietnam War matter to entire populations in complicated ways. Vietnam affected almost everyone in America who was 18 to 25 at the time. But it affected everyone differently. Let's not pretend that the war was not traumatic to those older than 25. Those who served did not share the zeitgeist with those who resisted. Women and men experienced it differently. The poor tended to serve. The rich did not. Remember how many people assumed in 1972 that there was some great generational mood or attitude that would pull voters to George McGovern in the first election in which 18- to 20-year-olds could vote? Why don't we ask President McGovern how that turned out?

By focusing on wealthy, white, educated people, as journalists and pop-trend analysts tend to do, we miss out on the whole truth. Generation X and the Greatest Generation are just the stuff of book titles. And they are not even good books.

The strongest argument against the idea of generations was raised first by the 18th-century philosopher David Hume. People are constantly being born and dying, Hume noted. So political sensibilities (to cite one phenomenon often assigned to generations) tend not to be cleanly associated with a single cohort. They change gradually. That's why human history has so few revolutions. And when there are revolutions, they tend not to separate generations.

I realize that by puncturing the myth of generations, I am pitting myself against one of the giants of 20th-century social theory,

Karl Mannheim. In his 1927 essay, "The Problem of Generations," Mannheim answered Hume by positing that generations are not demographically determined, but historically. Big events forge common identities. And proximity to an experience matters more than birth year. In other words, a Mannheimian generation might exist among all people who breathed in the ash and dust of the Twin Towers in New York City in 2001. But it might exclude people of the same age who merely watched the event on television from a comfortable couch in Madison, Wis.

Nor, Mannheim wrote, is a generation like an association, in which one claims membership or allegiance. Generation is a fluid and messy social category, not unlike class, he argued. As with class, members don't always know they are members. Members of generations, like classes, share "a common location in the social and historical process," he wrote, that predisposes them to certain modes of thought and action. A generation is one element of a fuller theory of cultural cohesion, mutation, and transmission.

Mannheim was arguing for an eclectic model of social analysis, one that does not rely too heavily on positivist principles of precision and accountability. He also wanted to use the concept of generation to delineate a set of human traits that biology alone could not explain. Finally, he wanted to establish that one's intellectual position in society is influenced by much more than class position, as orthodox Marxism of the day insisted. Thus generations were important explanatory mechanisms in his "sociology of knowledge."

By trying to do all that work, Mannheim's generations quickly crumbled. Generations seemed only to exist within nations, not across them; continuity existed between and among age cohorts; diversity of thought existed among members of a generation. Even if Mannheim's generations might have existed as a stable social category, they no longer do. Germany, Hungary, and England in the 1920s were hardly as diverse and globalized as those countries are now.

None of this means that nothing changes. Nor that we should not study youth, even privileged subcultures of youth, and their particular needs and problems. History is not static. Demography matters. But today's young people—including college students—are just more complicated than an analysis of imaginary generations can ever reveal. There are far better ways to study and write about them and their interactions with digital technologies than our current punditry offers.

A short list of the best of those who are studying and writing about the effects of digital media on youth must include Eszter Hargittai, a sociologist and associate professor of communications studies at Northwestern University, who has received a major grant from the John D. and Catherine T. MacArthur Foundation to study digital communication and youth. In a recent paper in Information, Communication

& Society, "The Participation Divide: Content Creation and Sharing in the Digital Age," Hargittai and Gina Walejko conclude that the habit of creating digital content and sharing it across digital platforms correlates with a person's identity traits. When asked in an interview in the May 2 issue of *The Chronicle* which demographic groups are less Web-savvy than others, Hargittai responded that women, students of Hispanic origin, African-American students, and students whose parents have lower levels of education tend to have less mastery of the inner workings of digital technology than other groups do.

Hargittai explained why we tend to overestimate the digital skills of young people: "I think the assumption is that if [digital technology] was available from a young age for them, then they can use it better. Also, the people who tend to comment about technology use tend to be either academics or journalists or techies, and these three groups tend to understand some of these new developments better than the average person. Ask your average 18-year-old: Does he know what RSS means? And he won't."

A 2007-8 fellow at the Berkman Center for Internet and Society, at Harvard University, and a doctoral candidate at the University of California at Berkeley, danah boyd, has done a series of in-depth qualitative studies of young people's use of digital communication. In her paper "Why Youth (Heart) Social Network Sites: The Role of Networked Publics in Teenage Social Life," published in a volume edited by David Buckingham, *Youth, Identity, and Digital Media* (MIT Press, 2008), she has observed how digital spaces give young people a sense of autonomy and control that, for example, planned access and limited loitering spaces at shopping malls do not. She has also sparked an online conversation, however, by noting how the migration of some young people from MySpace to Facebook reflects a strong class component.

As Susan Herring urges in an insightful article, "Questioning the Generational Divide," also in the Buckingham volume, we should move our gaze from dazzling technologies and two-dimensional exotic beings—so-called "digital natives"—to young people themselves.

Even in her unfortunately titled yet sharp book, *Generation Digital: Politics, Commerce, and Childhood in the Age of the Internet* (MIT Press, 2007), the American University communications professor Kathryn C. Montgomery has criticized the news media for characterizing "all young people in monolithic and simplistic terms, defining them almost exclusively on the basis of technology."

But Montgomery is not alone in selling a book about a generation while undermining belief in its existence. The most prominent scholarly project aimed at making sense of the effects of digitization on young people remains invested in the notion that they "constitute a distinct tribe": Digital Natives, conducted at the Berkman Center by its former executive director, John Palfrey. In August, Palfrey and Urs Gasser gave us *Born Digital: Understanding the First Generation of Digital Natives* (Basic Books), which argues that kids today are fundamentally different from the rest of us because their default modes of interaction involve mixing and mashing digital files and exposing (and rewriting) themselves through online profiles and avatars. That assumption bolsters the policy positions that the investigators already embraced: that the law should allow young people to remix and share bits of culture, while helping them respect and manage privacy. The policy goals are laudable. And the research is interesting. But Palfrey and Gasser did not need to render young people exotic to make their points. The concept of "born digital" flattens out the needs and experiences of young people into a uniform wish list of policies that conveniently matches the agenda of digital enthusiasts and entrepreneurs of all ages. Indeed, it is interesting that Palfrey and Gasser deny that their subjects constitute a "generation," conceding in their introduction that they are describing only the challenges of privileged young people.

Most alarming, Mark Bauerlein, a professor of English at Emory University, has recently written a jeremiad against young people and their digital habits, *The Dumbest Generation: How the Digital Age Stupefies Young Americans and Jeopardizes Our Future* (Jeremy P. Tarcher/ Penguin, 2008). Well, if there is one way to ensure that young people do not read more books than necessary, it is to call them dumb in the title of a book. The book is strongly argued, but the voices of those who concern the author are curiously absent.

There is much to admire in the book. Bauerlein assembles impressive evidence that American youth are terribly served by our current educational system. He deflates the grand folly of strategies like putting computers in the classroom and assuming that students will learn skills by sitting in front of them. But in blaming the digital movement for the problems of education, and government in general, he is off the mark.

Yes, young people may favor social-networking sites to the exclusion of political, news, or in-depth intellectual or cultural-commentary sites. But if the form is different, the malady is old. After all, Neil Postman, the late New York University professor who originated the anti-media jeremiad with *Amusing Ourselves to Death* (Viking, 1985), blamed television for restructuring our thought patterns and retarding our ability to think complex thoughts.

If the concept of a generation is unenlightening at best and harmful at worst, why do we persist in describing cultural, historical, and social change as generational? Sociologists have subsumed Mannheim's generational declarations within sophisticated theories of the "sociology of knowledge" and the "collective memory" of inherited culture. And professional historians rarely employ generations as historically determinative categories. Still, sociologist-sounding consultants like Neil Howe and the late William Strauss have built nice careers publishing shallow primers—like their books on millennials—on how to market goods and services to cartoon versions of various generations. They have pretty much owned the generations field to the point where real scholars will even cite their definitions of when baby boomers and Generation X begin and end. Howe and Strauss go to show you that you'll never go broke in America marketing to marketers. Or marketing to those who claim membership in particular generations. Journalists like Tom Brokaw invoke generations to forge rickety generalizations about people who were young in the 1940s and 1960s. Americans love thinking in generations because they keep us from examining uncomfortable ethnic, gender, and class distinctions too closely. Generations seem to explain everything.

But there is more to it. People fervently declare and defend generational identity. They clearly get something out it. Perhaps it's the same satisfaction that one gets out of other tribal identities, what Émile Durkheim called the "collective effervescence" of performed rituals. Feeling part of the "Woodstock generation" must generate some sort of warmth, comfort, or false nostalgia for those who caught the 1970 documentary film but missed the bus to the festival back in 1969.

We should drop our simplistic attachments to generations so we can generate an accurate and subtle account of the needs of young people—and all people, for that matter. A more responsible assessment would divorce itself from a pro- or anti-technology agenda and look at multiple causes for problems we note: state malfeasance or benign neglect of education, rampant consumerism in our culture, moral panics that lead us to scapegoat technology, and, yes, technology itself. Such work would reflect the fact that technologies do not emerge in a vacuum. They are subject to market forces, political ideologies, and policy incentives. More important, such work would not use young people as fodder for attacking wider social problems.

Too often we reach for easy, totalizing explanations for cultural phenomena, constructing cartoons of digital youth that have a tone of "gee whiz" or "shame, shame" to describe these new and odd creatures. The Who may have started this whole mess by recording an anthem steeped in the collective effervescence of "My Generation." But the Who also assured us that "The Kids Are Alright."

Critical Reading Questions

Summarizing the Text

1. It is a commonplace assumption, and has become a stereotype, that the younger generation is much more savvy and capable when it comes to all

forms of technology than are their elders. Nonsense, says Vaidhyanathan: there is no such thing as a digital generation. Explain how he supports this argument.

2. The question of how to define a *generation* is central to this argument. How does Vaidhyanathan complicate the (often media-created) notion of a generation?

Establishing the Context

3. The *Chronicle of Higher Education* is the primary magazine for college and university faculty and administrators. What is Vaidhyanathan's main aim here: is it to offer practical tips to college professors on how to reach their students? Is he attempting to refute a commonly held belief about students? What does this article have to say to students themselves?

4. How does Vaidhyanathan situate himself within a cultural discussion? What kinds of sources is he citing and responding to? Few of them are specifically about twenty-first-century technology and students—why? What does this tell you about the aims of his argument?

Responding to the Message

5. Do you see yourself as belonging to a generation that has some kind of common experience, such as the "Woodstock generation" of the 1960s or the "Lost Generation" of the 1920s? What is the nature of your generation's identity?

6. In this article, Vaidhyanathan implicitly argues that students don't know as much as they think they do about how to access and use information with technology. Is he right? Why or why not?

Generation Why?

Zadie Smith

Zadie Smith's 2000 debut novel White Teeth *marked the emergence of a major new voice in English fiction. She followed* White Teeth *with* The Autograph Man *(2002) and* On Beauty *(2005). Since September 2010, she has been a professor in New York University's creative-writing program. This essay, a review of the 2010 film* The Social Network, *appeared in the* New York Review of Books.

How long is a generation these days? I must be in Mark Zuckerberg's generation—there are only nine years between us—but somehow it doesn't feel that way. This despite the fact that I can say (like everyone else on Harvard's campus in the fall of 2003) that "I was there" at Facebook's inception, and remember Facemash and the fuss it caused; also that tiny, exquisite movie star trailed by fan-boys through the snow wherever she went, and the awful snow itself, turning your toes gray, destroying your spirit, bringing a bloodless end to a squirrel on my block: frozen, inanimate, perfect—like the Blaschka glass flowers. Doubtless years from now I will misremember my closeness to Zuckerberg, in the same spirit that everyone in '60s Liverpool met John Lennon.

At the time, though, I felt distant from Zuckerberg and all the kids at Harvard. I still feel distant from them now, ever more so, as I increasingly opt out (by choice, by default) of the things they have embraced. We have different ideas about things. Specifically we have different ideas about what a person is, or should be. I often worry that my idea of personhood is nostalgic, irrational, inaccurate. Perhaps Generation Facebook have built their virtual mansions in good faith, in order to house the People 2.0 they genuinely are, and if I feel uncomfortable within them it is because I am stuck at Person 1.0. Then again, the more time I spend with the tail end of Generation Facebook (in the shape of my students) the more convinced I become that some of the software currently shaping their generation is unworthy of them. They are more interesting than it is. They deserve better.

In *The Social Network* Generation Facebook gets a movie almost worthy of them, and this fact, being so unexpected, makes the film feel more delightful than it probably, objectively, is. From the opening scene it's clear that this is a movie about 2.0 people made by 1.0 people (Aaron Sorkin and David Fincher, forty-nine and forty-eight respectively). It's a *talkie*, for goodness' sake, with as many words per minute as *His Girl Friday*. A boy, Mark, and his girl, Erica, sit at a little table in a Harvard bar, zinging each other, in that relentless Sorkin style made famous by *The West Wing* (though at no point does either party say "Walk with me"—for this we should be grateful).

But something is not right with this young man: his eye contact is patchy; he doesn't seem to understand common turns of phrase or ambiguities of language; he is literal to the point of offense, pedantic to the point of aggression. ("Final clubs," says Mark, correcting Erica, as they discuss those exclusive Harvard entities, "*Not* Finals clubs.") He doesn't understand what's happening as she tries to break up with him. ("Wait, wait, this is real?") Nor does he understand *why*. He doesn't get that what he may consider a statement of fact might yet have, for this other person, some personal, painful import:

> ERICA: I have to go study.
>
> MARK: You don't have to study.
>
> ERICA: *How do you know I don't have to study?!*
>
> MARK: *Because you go to B. U.!*

Simply put, he is a computer nerd, a social "autistic": a type as recognizable to Fincher's audience as the cynical newshound was to

Howard Hawks's. To create this Zuckerberg, Sorkin barely need brush his pen against the page. We came to the cinema expecting to meet this guy and it's a pleasure to watch Sorkin color in what we had already confidently sketched in our minds. For sometimes the culture surmises an individual personality, collectively. Or thinks it does. Don't we all know why nerds do what they do? To get money, which leads to popularity, which leads to girls. Sorkin, confident of his foundation myth, spins an exhilarating tale of double rejection—spurned by Erica and the Porcellian, the Finaliest of the Final Clubs, Zuckerberg begins his spite-fueled rise to the top. Cue a lot of betrayal. A lot of scenes of lawyers' offices and miserable, character-damning depositions. ("Your best friend is suing you!") Sorkin has swapped the military types of *A Few Good Men* for a different kind of all-male community in a different uniform: GAP hoodies, North Face sweats.

At my screening, blocks from NYU, the audience thrilled with intimate identification. But if the hipsters and nerds are hoping for Fincher's usual pyrotechnics they will be disappointed: in a lawyer's office there's not a lot for Fincher to *do*. He has to content himself with excellent and rapid cutting between Harvard and the later court cases, and after that, the discreet pleasures of another, less-remarked-upon Fincher skill: great casting. It'll be a long time before a cinema geek comes along to push Jesse Eisenberg, the actor who plays Zuckerberg, off the top of our nerd typologies. The passive-aggressive, flat-line voice. The shifty boredom when anyone, other than himself, is speaking. The barely suppressed smirk. Eisenberg even chooses the correct nerd walk: not the sideways corridor shuffle (the *Don't Hit Me!*), but the puffed chest vertical march (the *I'm not 5'8", I'm 5'9"!*).

With rucksack, naturally. An extended four-minute shot has him doing exactly this all the way through the Harvard campus, before he lands finally where he belongs, the only place he's truly comfortable, in front of his laptop, with his blog:

> Erica Albright's a bitch. You think that's because her family changed their name from Albrecht or do you think it's because all B.U. girls are bitches?

Oh, yeah. We know this guy. Overprogrammed, furious, lonely. Around him Fincher arranges a convincing bunch of 1.0 humans, by turns betrayed and humiliated by him, and as the movie progresses they line up to sue him. If it's a three-act movie it's because Zuckerberg screws over more people than a two-act movie can comfortably hold: the Winklevoss twins and Divya Navendra (from whom Zuckerberg allegedly stole the Facebook concept), and then his best friend, Eduardo Saverin (the CFO he edged out of the company), and finally Sean Parker, the boy king of Napster, the music-sharing program, although he, to be fair, pretty much screws himself.

It's in Eduardo—in the actor Andrew Garfield's animate, beautiful face—that all these betrayals seem to converge, and become personal, painful. The arbitration scenes—that should be dull, being so terribly static—get their power from the eerie opposition between Eisenberg's unmoving countenance (his eyebrows hardly ever move; the real Zuckerberg's eyebrows *never* move) and Garfield's imploring disbelief, almost the way Spencer Tracy got all worked up opposite Frederic March's rigidity in another courtroom epic, *Inherit the Wind*.

Still, Fincher allows himself one sequence of (literal) showboating. Halfway through the film, he inserts a ravishing but quite unnecessary scene of the pretty Winklevoss twins (for a story of nerds, all the men are surprisingly comely) at the Henley Regatta. These two blond titans row like champs. (One actor, Armie Hammer, has been digitally doubled. I'm so utterly 1.0 that I spent an hour of the movie trying to detect any difference between the twins.) Their arms move suspiciously fast, faster than real human arms, their muscles seem outlined by a fine pen, the water splashes up in individual droplets as if painted by Caravaggio, and the music! Trent Reznor, of Nine Inch Nails, commits exquisite brutality upon Edward Grieg's already pretty brutal "In the Hall of the Mountain King." All synths and white noise. It's music video stuff—the art form in which my not-quite generation truly excels—and it demonstrates the knack for hyperreality that made Fincher's *Fight Club* so compelling while rendering the real world, for so many of his fans, always something of a disappointment. Anyway, the twins lose the regatta, too, by a nose, which allows Fincher to justify the scene by thematic reiteration: sometimes very close is simply not close enough. Or as Mark pleasantly puts it across a conference table: "If you guys were the inventors of Facebook you'd have invented Facebook."

All that's left for Zuckerberg is to meet the devil at the crossroads: naturally he's an Internet music entrepreneur. It's a Generation Facebook instinct to expect (hope?) that a pop star will fall on his face in the cinema, but Justin Timberlake, as Sean Parker, neatly steps over that expectation: whether or not you think he's a shmuck, he sure plays a great shmuck. Manicured eyebrows, sweaty forehead, and that coked-up, wafer-thin self-confidence, always threatening to collapse into paranoia. Timberlake shimmies into view in the third act to offer the audience, and Zuckerberg, the very same thing, essentially, that he's been offering us for the past decade in his videos: a vision of the good life.

This vision is also wafer-thin, and Fincher satirizes it mercilessly. Again, we know its basic outline: a velvet rope, a cocktail waitress who treats you like a king, the best of everything on tap, a special booth of your own, fussy tiny expensive food ("Could you bring out some things? The lacquered pork with that ginger confit? I don't know, tuna tartar, some lobster claws, the foie gras and the shrimp dumplings, that'll get us started"), appletinis, a Victoria's Secret model date, wild house parties, fancy cars, slick suits, cocaine, and a "sky's the limit" objective: "A million dollars isn't cool. You know what's cool?... A *billion* dollars." Over cocktails in a glamorous nightclub, Parker dazzles Zuckerberg with tales of the life that awaits him on the other side of a billion. Fincher keeps the thumping Euro house music turned up to exactly the level it would be in real life: the actors have to practically scream to be heard above it. Like many a nerd before him, Zuckerberg is too hyped on the idea that he's in heaven to notice he's in hell.

Generation Facebook's obsession with this type of "celebrity lifestyle" is more than familiar. It's pitiful, it pains us, and we recognize it. But would Zuckerberg recognize it, the real Zuckerberg? Are these really *his* motivations, *his* obsessions? No—and the movie knows it. Several times the script tries to square the real Zuckerberg's apparent indifference to money with the plot arc of *The Social Network*—and never quite succeeds. In a scene in which Mark argues with a lawyer, Sorkin attempts a sleight of hand, swapping an interest in money for an interest in power:

> Ma'am, I know you've done your homework and so you know that money isn't a big part of my life, but at the moment I could buy Harvard University, take the Phoenix Club and turn it into my ping pong room.

But that doesn't explain why the teenage Zuckerberg gave away his free app for an MP3 player (similar to the very popular Pandora, as it recognized your taste in music), rather than selling it to Microsoft. What power was he hoping to accrue to himself in high school, at seventeen? Girls, was it? Except the girl motivation is patently phony—with a brief interruption Zuckerberg has been dating the same Chinese-American, now a medical student, since 2003, a fact the movie omits entirely. At the end of the film, when all the suing has come to an end ("Pay them. In the scheme of things it's a parking ticket"), we're offered a Zuckerberg slumped before his laptop, still obsessed with the long-lost Erica, sending a "Friend request" to her on Facebook, and then refreshing the page, over and over, in expectation of her reply.... Fincher's contemporary window-dressing is so convincing that it wasn't until this very last scene that I realized the obvious progenitor of this wildly enjoyable, wildly inaccurate biopic. Hollywood still believes that behind every mogul there's an *idée fixe*: Rosebud—meet Erica.

If it's not for money and it's not for girls—what is it for? With Zuckerberg we have a real American mystery. Maybe it's not mysterious and he's just playing the long game, holding out: not a billion dollars but a hundred billion dollars. Or is it possible *he just loves programming*? No doubt the filmmakers considered this option, but you

can see their dilemma: how to convey the pleasure of programming—
if such a pleasure exists—in a way that is both cinematic and comprehensible? Movies are notoriously bad at showing the pleasures and
rigors of art-making, even when the medium is familiar.

Programming is a whole new kind of problem. Fincher makes a
brave stab at showing the intensity of programming in action ("He's
wired in," people say to other people to stop them disturbing a third
person who sits before a laptop wearing noise-reducing earphones) and
there's a "vodka-shots-and-programming" party in Zuckerberg's dorm
room that gives us some clue of the pleasures. But even if we spent half
the film looking at those busy screens (and we do get glimpses), most
of us would be none the wiser. Watching this movie, even though you
know Sorkin wants your disapproval, you can't help feel a little swell
of pride in this 2.0 generation. They've spent a decade being berated
for not making the right sorts of paintings or novels or music or politics. Turns out the brightest 2.0 kids have been doing something else
extraordinary. They've been making a world.

World makers, social network makers, ask one question first: How
can I do it? Zuckerberg solved that one in about three weeks. The other
question, the ethical question, he came to later: Why? Why Facebook?
Why this format? Why do it like that? Why not do it another way?
The striking thing about the real Zuckerberg, in video and in print, is
the relative banality of his ideas concerning the "Why" of Facebook.
He uses the word "connect" as believers use the word "Jesus," as if it
were sacred in and of itself: "So the idea is really that, um, the site helps
everyone connect with people and share information with the people
they want to stay connected with...." Connection is the goal. The quality of that connection, the quality of the information that passes through
it, the quality of the relationship that connection permits—none of this
is important. That a lot of social networking software explicitly encourages people to make weak, superficial connections with each other
(as Malcolm Gladwell has recently argued[1]), and that this might not be
an entirely positive thing, seem to never have occurred to him.

He is, to say the least, dispassionate about the philosophical questions concerning privacy—and sociality itself—raised by his inge-
nious program. Watching him interviewed I found myself waiting for
the verbal wit, the controlled and articulate sarcasm of that famous
Zuckerberg kid—then remembered that was only Sorkin. The real
Zuckerberg is much more like his website, on each page of which,
once upon a time (2004), he emblazoned the legend: *A Mark Zuckerberg
Production.* Controlled but dull, bright and clean but uniformly plain,
nonideological, affectless.

---

[1]See "Small Change: Why the Revolution Will Not Be Tweeted," *The New Yorker*, October
4, 2010.

In Zuckerberg's *New Yorker* profile it is revealed that his own Facebook page lists, among his interests, Minimalism, revolutions, and "eliminating desire."[2] We also learn of his affection for the culture and writings of ancient Greece. Perhaps this is the disjunct between real Zuckerberg and fake Zuckerberg: the movie places him in the Roman world of betrayal and excess, but the real Zuckerberg may belong in the Greek, perhaps with the Stoics ("eliminating desire"?). There's a clue in the two Zuckerbergs' relative physiognomies: real Zuckerberg (especially in profile) is Greek sculpture, noble, featureless, a little like the Doryphorus (only facially, mind—his torso is definitely not seven times his head). Fake Mark looks Roman, with all the precise facial detail filled in. Zuckerberg, with his steady relationship and his rented house and his refusal to get angry on television even when people are being very rude to him (he sweats instead), has something of the teen-age Stoic about him. And of course if you've eliminated desire you've got nothing to hide, right?

It's *that* kind of kid we're dealing with, the kind who would never screw a groupie in a bar toilet—as happens in the movie—or leave his doctor girlfriend for a Victoria's Secret model. It's this type of kid who would think that giving people *less* privacy was a good idea. What's striking about Zuckerberg's vision of an open Internet is the very blandness it requires to function, as Facebook members discovered when the site changed their privacy settings, allowing more things to become more public, with the (unintended?) consequence that your Aunt Dora could suddenly find out you joined the group Queer Nation last Tuesday. Gay kids became un-gay, partiers took down their party photos, political firebrands put out their fires. In real life we can be all these people on our own terms, in our own way, with whom we choose. For a revealing moment Facebook forgot that. Or else got bored of waiting for us to change in the ways it's betting we will. On the question of privacy, Zuckerberg informed the world: "That social norm is just something that has evolved over time." On this occasion, the world protested, loudly, and so Facebook has responded with "Groups," a site revamp that will allow people to divide their friends into "cliques," some who see more of our profile and some who see less.

How "Groups" will work alongside "Facebook Connect" remains to be seen. Facebook Connect is the "next iteration of Facebook Platform," in which users are "allowed" to "'connect' their Facebook identity, friends and privacy to any site." In this new, open Internet, we will take our real identities with us as we travel through the Internet. This concept seems to have some immediate Stoical advantages: no

---

[2]See Jose Antonio Vargas, "The Face of Facebook: Mark Zuckerberg Opens Up," *The New Yorker*, September 20, 2010.

more faceless bile, no more inflammatory trolling: if your name and social network track you around the virtual world beyond Facebook, you'll have to restrain yourself and so will everyone else. On the other hand, you'll also take your likes and dislikes with you, your tastes, your preferences, all connected to your name, through which people will try to sell you things.

Maybe it will be like an intensified version of the Internet I already live in, where ads for dental services stalk me from pillar to post and I am continually urged to buy my own books. Or maybe the whole Internet will simply become like Facebook: falsely jolly, fake-friendly, self-promoting, slickly disingenuous. For all these reasons I quit Facebook about two months after I'd joined it. As with all seriously addictive things, giving up proved to be immeasurably harder than starting. I kept changing my mind: Facebook remains the greatest distraction from work I've ever had, and I loved it for that. I think a lot of people love it for that. Some work-avoidance techniques are onerous in themselves and don't make time move especially quickly: smoking, eating, calling people up on the phone. With Facebook hours, afternoons, entire days went by without my noticing.

When I finally decided to put a stop to it, once and for all, I was left with the question bothering everybody: Are you ever truly removed, once and for all? In an interview on *The Today Show*, Matt Lauer asked Zuckerberg the same question, but because Matt Lauer doesn't listen to people when they talk, he accepted the following answer and moved on to the next question: "Yeah, so what'll happen is that none of that information will be shared with anyone going forward."

You want to be optimistic about your own generation. You want to keep pace with them and not to fear what you don't understand. To put it another way, if you feel discomfort at the world they're making, you want to have a good reason for it. Master programmer and virtual reality pioneer Jaron Lanier (b. 1960) is not of my generation, but he knows and understands us well, and has written a short and frightening book, *You Are Not a Gadget*, which chimes with my own discomfort, while coming from a position of real knowledge and insight, both practical and philosophical. Lanier is interested in the ways in which people "reduce themselves" in order to make a computer's description of them appear more accurate. "Information systems," he writes, "need to have information in order to run, but information *underrepresents reality*" (my italics). In Lanier's view, there is no perfect computer analogue for what we call a "person." In life, we all profess to know this, but when we get online it becomes easy to forget. In Facebook, as it is with other online social networks, life is turned into a database, and this is a degradation, Lanier argues, which is based on [a] philosophical mistake…the belief that computers can presently represent human thought or human relationships. These are things computers cannot currently do.

We know the consequences of this instinctively; we feel them. We know that having two thousand Facebook friends is not what it looks like. We know that we are using the software to behave in a certain, superficial way toward others. We know what we are doing "in" the software. But do we know, are we alert to, what the software is doing to us? Is it possible that what is communicated between people online "eventually becomes their truth"? What Lanier, a software expert, reveals to me, a software idiot, is what must be obvious (to software experts): software is not neutral. Different software embeds different philosophies, and these philosophies, as they become ubiquitous, become invisible.

Lanier asks us to consider, for example, the humble file, or rather, to consider a world without "files." (The first iteration of the Macintosh, which never shipped, didn't have files.) I confess this thought experiment stumped me about as much as if I'd been asked to consider persisting in a world without "time." And then consider further that these designs, so often taken up in a slap-dash, last-minute fashion, become "locked in," and, because they are software, used by millions, too often become impossible to adapt, or change. MIDI, an inflexible, early-1980s digital music protocol for connecting different musical components, such as a keyboard and a computer, takes no account of, say, the fluid line of a soprano's coloratura; it is still the basis of most of the tinny music we hear every day—in our phones, in the charts, in elevators—simply because it became, in software terms, too big to fail, too big to change.

Lanier wants us to be attentive to the software into which we are "locked in." Is it really fulfilling our needs? Or are we reducing the needs we feel in order to convince ourselves that the software isn't limited? As Lanier argues:

> Different media designs stimulate different potentials in human nature. We shouldn't seek to make the pack mentality as efficient as possible. We should instead seek to inspire the phenomenon of individual intelligence.

But the pack mentality is precisely what Open Graph, a Facebook innovation of 2008, is designed to encourage. Open Graph allows you to see everything your friends are reading, watching, eating, so that you might read and watch and eat as they do. In his *New Yorker* profile, Zuckerberg made his personal "philosophy" clear:

> Most of the information that we care about is things that are in our heads, right? And that's not out there to be indexed, right?… It's like hardwired into us in a deeper way: you really want to know what's going on with the people around you.

Is that really the best we can do online? In the film, Sean Parker, during one of his coke-fueled "Sean-athon monologues," delivers what is intended as a generation-defining line: "We lived on farms, then we lived in cities and now we're gonna live on the internet." To this idea Lanier, one of the Internet's original visionaries, can have no profound objection. But his skeptical interrogation of the "Nerd reductionism" of Web 2.0 prompts us to ask a question: What kind of life?[3] Surely not this one, where 500 million connected people all decide to watch the reality-TV show *Bride Wars* because their friends are? "You have to be somebody," Lanier writes, "before you can share yourself." But to Zuckerberg sharing your choices with everybody (and doing what they do) *is* being somebody.

Personally I don't think Final Clubs were ever the point; I don't think exclusivity was ever the point; nor even money. E Pluribus Unum—that's the point. Here's my guess: he wants to be like everybody else. He wants to be liked. Those 1.0 people who couldn't understand Zuckerberg's apparently ham-fisted PR move of giving the school system of Newark $100 million on the very day the movie came out—they just don't get it. For our self-conscious generation (and in this, I and Zuckerberg, and everyone raised on TV in the Eighties and Nineties, share a single soul), *not being liked* is as bad as it gets.

Intolerable to be thought of badly for a minute, even for a moment. He didn't need to just get out "in front" of the story. He had to get right on top of it and try to stop it breathing. Two weeks later, he went to a screening. Why? Because everybody liked the movie.

When a human being becomes a set of data on a website like Facebook, he or she is reduced. Everything shrinks. Individual character. Friendships. Language. Sensibility. In a way it's a transcendent experience: we lose our bodies, our messy feelings, our desires, our fears. It reminds me that those of us who turn in disgust from what we consider an overinflated liberal-bourgeois sense of self should be careful what we wish for: our denuded networked selves don't look more free, they just look more owned.

With Facebook, Zuckerberg seems to be trying to create something like a Noosphere, an Internet with one mind, a uniform environment in which it genuinely doesn't matter who you are, as long as you make "choices" (which means, finally, purchases). If the aim is to be liked by more and more people, whatever is unusual about a person gets flattened out. One nation under a format. To ourselves, we are special people, documented in wonderful photos, and it also happens that we

---

[3]Lanier: "Individual web pages as they first appeared in the early 1990s had the flavor of personhood. MySpace preserved some of that flavor, though a process of regularized formatting had begun. Facebook went further, organizing people into multiple-choice identities, while Wikipedia seeks to erase point of view entirely."

sometimes buy things. This latter fact is an incidental matter, to us. However, the advertising money that will rain down on Facebook—if and when Zuckerberg succeeds in encouraging 500 million people to take their Facebook identities onto the Internet at large—this money thinks of us the other way around. To the advertisers, we are our capacity to buy, attached to a few personal, irrelevant photos.

Is it possible that we have begun to think of ourselves that way? It seemed significant to me that on the way to the movie theater, while doing a small mental calculation (how old I was when at Harvard; how old I am now), I had a Person 1.0 panic attack. Soon I will be forty, then fifty, then soon after dead; I broke out in a Zuckerberg sweat, my heart went crazy, I had to stop and lean against a trashcan. Can you have that feeling, on Facebook? I've noticed—and been ashamed of noticing—that when a teenager is murdered, at least in Britain, her Facebook wall will often fill with messages that seem to not quite comprehend the gravity of what has occurred. You know the type of thing: *Sorry babes! Missin' you!!! Hopin' u iz with the Angles. I remember the jokes we used to have LOL! PEACE XXXXX*

When I read something like that, I have a little argument with myself: "It's only poor education. They feel the same way as anyone would, they just don't have the language to express it." But another part of me has a darker, more frightening thought. Do they genuinely believe, because the girl's wall is still up, that she is still, in some sense, alive? What's the difference, after all, if all your contact was virtual?[4]

Software may reduce humans, but there are degrees. Fiction reduces humans, too, but bad fiction does it more than good fiction, and we have the option to read good fiction. Jaron Lanier's point is that Web 2.0 "lock-in" happens soon; is happening; has to some degree already happened. And what has been "locked in"? It feels important to remind ourselves, at this point, that Facebook, our new beloved interface with reality, was designed by a Harvard sophomore with a Harvard sophomore's preoccupations. What is your relationship status? (Choose one. There can be only one answer. People need to know.) Do you have a "life"? (Prove it. Post pictures.) Do you like the right sort of things? (Make a list. Things to like will include: movies, music, books and television, but not architecture, ideas, or plants.)

But here I fear I am becoming nostalgic. I am dreaming of a Web that caters to a kind of person who no longer exists. A private

---

[4]Perhaps the reason why there has not been more resistance to social networking among older people is because 1.0 people do not use Web 2.0 software in the way 2.0 people do. An analogous situation can be found in the way the two generations use cell phones. For me, text messaging is simply a new medium for an old form of communication: I write to my friends in heavily punctuated, fully expressive, standard English sentences—and they write back to me in the same way. Text-speak is unknown between us. Our relationship with the English language predates our relationships with our phones.

person, a person who is a mystery, to the world and—which is more important—to herself. Person as mystery: this idea of personhood is certainly changing, perhaps has already changed. Because I find I agree with Zuckerberg: selves evolve.

Of course, Zuckerberg insists selves simply do this by themselves and the technology he and others have created has no influence upon the process. That is for techies and philosophers to debate (ideally techie-philosophers, like Jaron Lanier). Whichever direction the change is coming from, though, it's absolutely clear to me that the students I teach now are not like the student I once was or even the students I taught seven short years ago at Harvard. Right now I am teaching my students a book called *The Bathroom* by the Belgian experimentalist Jean-Philippe Toussaint—at least I used to *think* he was an experimentalist. It's a book about a man who decides to pass most of his time in his bathroom, yet to my students this novel feels perfectly realistic; an accurate portrait of their own denuded selfhood, or, to put it neutrally, a close analogue of the undeniable boredom of urban twenty-first-century existence.

In the most famous scene, the unnamed protagonist, in one of the few moments of "action," throws a dart into his girlfriend's forehead. Later, in the hospital they reunite with a kiss and no explanation. "It's just between them," said one student, and looked happy. To a reader of my generation, Toussaint's characters seemed, at first glance, to have no interiority—in fact theirs is not an absence but a refusal, and an ethical one. *What's inside of me is none of your business.* To my students, *The Bathroom* is a true romance.

Toussaint was writing in 1985, in France. In France philosophy seems to come before technology; here in the Anglo-American world we race ahead with technology and hope the ideas will look after themselves. Finally, it's the *idea* of Facebook that disappoints. If it were a genuinely interesting interface, built for these genuinely different 2.0 kids to live in, well, that would be something. It's not that. It's the wild west of the Internet tamed to fit the suburban fantasies of a suburban soul. Lanier:

> These designs came together very recently, and there's a haphazard, accidental quality to them. Resist the easy grooves they guide you into. If you love a medium made of software, there's a danger that you will become entrapped in someone else's recent careless thoughts. Struggle against that!

Shouldn't we struggle against Facebook? Everything in it is reduced to the size of its founder. Blue, because it turns out Zuckerberg is red-green color-blind. "Blue is the richest color for me—I can see all of blue." Poking, because that's what shy boys do to girls they are scared to talk to. Preoccupied with personal trivia, because Mark Zuckerberg thinks the exchange of personal trivia is what "friendship" *is*. A Mark Zuckerberg Production indeed! We were going to live online. It was going to be extraordinary. Yet what kind of living is this? Step back from your Facebook Wall for a moment: Doesn't it, suddenly, look a little ridiculous? *Your* life in *this* format?

The last defense of every Facebook addict is: *but it helps me keep in contact with people who are far away!* Well, e-mail and Skype do that, too, and they have the added advantage of not forcing you to interface with the mind of Mark Zuckerberg—but, well, you know. We all know. If we *really* wanted to write to these faraway people, or see them, we would. What we actually want to do is the bare minimum, just like any nineteen-year-old college boy who'd rather be doing something else, or nothing.

At my screening, when a character in the film mentioned the early blog platform LiveJournal (still popular in Russia), the audience laughed. I can't imagine life without files but I can just about imagine a time when Facebook will seem as comically obsolete as LiveJournal. In this sense, *The Social Network* is not a cruel portrait of any particular real-world person called "Mark Zuckerberg." It's a cruel portrait of us: 500 million sentient people entrapped in the recent careless thoughts of a Harvard sophomore.

Critical Reading Questions

Summarizing the Text

1. Smith draws a distinction between "Generation 2.0" and "Generation 1.0." What are the characteristics of each? Why does she consider herself a member of Generation 1.0?

2. Who is Jaron Lanier, what is his argument, and how does Smith use his argument in her article?

Establishing the Context

3. Smith's article is, at least nominally, a review of *The Social Network,* and a traditional movie review is intended to help people decide whether to see the film. How much of the article actually evaluates the film?

4. Smith argues that the movie gets some important elements of the real Zuckerberg's life wrong. Does this undermine the movie as a whole? What does Smith conclude about the message of the movie from the changes that Sorkin and Fincher made to Zuckerberg's story?

Responding to the Message

5. Smith implicitly argues that Zuckerberg's fascination with connection is directly opposed to other people's desire for privacy. Are these two terms necessarily in conflict? Research how your online information is collected and used by such sites as Facebook, Google, Amazon, iTunes—where do you fall in the connectedness–privacy spectrum?

6. Is Smith giving too much importance to one person, one website? Is the information age reducing us to being mere data points and consumer preferences? Respond to Smith's worried argument about where we, as individuals in a larger society, are going.

Still from *The Social Network*

This still from the 2010 film The Social Network *shows Jesse Eisenberg, portraying Facebook founder Mark Zuckerberg, walking in for a meeting with a potential investor. Another Internet pioneer (Sean Parker of Napster, played by the singer/actor Justin Timberlake) advised him to show no respect to the people seeking to invest in his company, as a psychological tactic to intimidate them.*

1. "Read" this photo—its composition, the contrast between Zuckerberg's clothes and the office building, and Eisenberg's bearing and expression. If you had no idea what *The Social Network* was about, what message would this image convey?

2. How does Eisenberg's dress and expression convey his character's attitude toward the world? Compare this image of Eisenberg as Zuckerberg to Zadie Smith's description of his portrayal of the Facebook founder.

CLUSTER TWO: HOW DO WE RELATE TO OUR TECHNOLOGY?

Wikipedia and Beyond: Jimmy Wales' Sprawling Vision

Katherine Mangu-Ward

In this article, which appeared in the libertarian magazine Reason, *Katherine Mangu-Ward argues that the success of Wikipedia provides evidence in support of the theories of economist Friedrich Hayek and against those who would push for more centralization (of markets, governments, or control of information). As you read, pay attention the ways in which Mangu-Ward uses a profile of a person to make a larger argument about politics and society.*

Jimmy Wales, the founder of Wikipedia, lives in a house fit for a grandmother. The progenitor and public face of one of the 10 most popular websites in the world beds down in a one-story bungalow on a cul-de-sac near St. Petersburg, Florida. The neighborhood, with its scrubby vegetation and plastic lawn furniture, screams "Bingo Night." Inside the house, the décor is minimal, and the stucco and cool tile floors make the place echo. A few potted plants bravely attempt domesticity. Out front sits a cherry red Hyundai.

I arrive at Wales' house on a gray, humid day in December. It's 11 a.m., and after wrapping up some emails on his white Mac iBook, Wales proposes lunch. We hit the mean streets of Gulf Coast Florida in the Hyundai, in search of "this really great Indian place that's part of a motel," and wind up cruising for hours—stopping at Starbucks, hitting the mall, and generally duplicating the average day of millions of suburban teenagers. Wal-Marts and Olive Gardens slip past as Wales, often taciturn and abrupt in public statements, lets loose a flood of words about his past, his politics, the future of the Internet, and why he's optimistic about pretty much everything.

Despite his modest digs, Wales is an Internet rock star. He was included on Time's list of the 100 most influential people of 2006. Pages from Wikipedia dominate Google search results, making the operation, which dubs itself "the free encyclopedia that anyone can edit," a primary source of information for millions of people. (Do a Google search for "monkeys," "Azerbaijan," "mass spectrometry," or "Jesus," and the first hit will be from Wikipedia.) Although he insists he isn't a "rich guy" and doesn't have "rich guy hobbies," when pressed Wales admits to hobnobbing with other geek elites, such as Amazon founder Jeff Bezos, and hanging out on Virgin CEO Richard Branson's private island. (The only available estimate of Wales' net worth comes from a now-removed section of his own Wikipedia entry, pinning his fortune at less than $1 million.) Scruffy in a gray mock turtleneck and a closely cropped beard, the 40-year-old Wales plays it low key. But he is well aware that he is a strangely powerful man: He has utterly changed the way people extract information from the chaos of the World Wide Web, and he is the master of a huge, robust online community of writers, editors, and users. Asked about the secret to Wikipedia's success, Wales says simply, "We make the Internet not suck."

On other occasions, Wales has offered a more erudite account of the site's origins and purpose. In 1945, in his famous essay "The Use of Knowledge in Society," the libertarian economist F.A. Hayek argued that market mechanisms serve "to share and synchronize local and personal knowledge, allowing society's members to achieve diverse, complicated ends through a principle of spontaneous self-organization." (These are the words not of the Nobel Prize winner himself but of Wikipedia's entry on him.) "Hayek's work on price theory is central to my own thinking about how to manage the Wikipedia project," Wales wrote on the blog of the Internet law guru Lawrence Lessig. "One can't understand my ideas about Wikipedia without understanding Hayek." Long before socialism crumbled, Hayek saw the perils of centralization. When information is dispersed (as it always is), decisions are best left to those with the most local knowledge. This insight, which undergirds contemporary libertarianism, earned Hayek plaudits from fellow libertarian economist and Nobel Prize winner Milton Friedman as the "most important social thinker of the 20th century." The question: Will traditional reference works like *Encyclopedia Britannica*, that great centralizer of knowledge, fall before Wikipedia the way the Soviet Union fell before the West?

When Wales founded the site in 2001, his plan was simple yet seemingly insane: "Imagine a world in which every single person on the planet is given free access to the sum of all human knowledge. That's what we're doing." In case that plan didn't sound nutty enough on its own, he went on to let every Tom, Dick, and Friedrich write and edit articles for that mystical encyclopedia. "Now it's obvious that it works," says Wales, "but then most people couldn't get it." And not everyone gets it yet. Wales has his share of enemies, detractors, and doubters. But he also has a growing fan club. Wikipedia, which is run by Wales' nonprofit Wikimedia Foundation, is now almost fully supported by small donations (in addition to a few grants and gifts of servers and hosting), and many of its savviest users consider it the search of first resort, bypassing Google entirely.

Wikipedia was born as an experiment in aggregating information. But the reason it works isn't that the world was clamoring for a new kind of encyclopedia. It took off because of the robust, self-policing community it created. Despite its critics, it is transforming our everyday lives; as with Amazon, Google, and eBay, it is almost impossible to remember how much more circumscribed our world was before it existed.

Hayek's arguments inspired Wales to take on traditional encyclopedias, and now they're inspiring Wales' next big project: Wikia, a for-profit venture that hopes to expand the idea beyond encyclopedias into all kinds of Internet-based communities and collaborative projects. If Wikia succeeds, it will open up this spontaneously ordered, self-governing world to millions more people. Encyclopedias aren't the only places to gather knowledge, and by making tools available to create other kinds of collaborative communities, Wales is fleshing out and bringing to life Hayek's insights about the power of decentralized knowledge gathering, the surprising strength of communities bound only by reputation, and the fluidity of self-governance.

Jimbo

Wales was born in Huntsville, Alabama, in 1966, the son of a grocery store manager. He was educated at a tiny private school run by his mother, Doris, and grandmother, Erma. His education, which he has described as "a one-room schoolhouse or Abe Lincoln type of thing," was fairly unstructured: He "spent many, many hours just poring over the *World Book* encyclopedia." Wales received his B.A. in finance from Auburn University, a hotbed of free market economists, and got his master's degree in finance from the University of Alabama. He did coursework and taught at Indiana University, but he failed to complete a Ph.D. dissertation—largely, he says, because he "got bored."

Wales moved to Chicago and became a futures and options trader. After six years of betting on interest rates and currency fluctuations, he made enough money to pay the mortgage for the rest of his life. In 1998 he moved to San Diego and started a Web portal, Bomis, which featured, among other things, a "guy-oriented search engine" and pictures of scantily clad women. The *en déshabillé* ladies have since caused trouble for Wales, who regularly fields questions about his former life as a "porn king." In a typically blunt move, Wales often responds to criticism of his Bomis days by sending reporters links to Yahoo's midget porn category page. If he was a porn king, he suggests, so is the head of the biggest Web portal in the world.

Bomis didn't make it big—it was no Yahoo—but in March 2000 the site hosted Nupedia, Wales' first attempt to build a free online encyclopedia. Wales hired Larry Sanger, at the time a doctoral candidate in philosophy at Ohio State, to edit encyclopedia articles submitted voluntarily by scholars, and to manage a multistage peer review process. After a slow start, Wales and Sanger decided to try something more radical. In 2001 they bracketed the Nupedia project and started a new venture built on the same foundations. The twist: It would be an open-source encyclopedia. Any user could exercise editorial control, and no one person or group would have ultimate authority.

Sanger resigned from the project in 2002 and since then has been in an ongoing low-grade war with Wales over who founded Wikipedia. Everyone agrees that Sanger came up with the name while Wales wrote the checks and provided the underlying open-source philosophy. But who thought of powering the site with a wiki?

Wikis are simple software that allow anyone to create or edit a webpage. The first wikis were developed by Ward Cunningham, a programmer who created the WikiWikiWeb, a collaborative software guide, in 1995. ("Wiki wiki" means "quick" in Hawaiian.) Gradually adopted by a variety of companies to facilitate internal collaboration (IBM and Google, for instance, use wikis for project management and document version control), wikis were spreading under the radar until Wikipedia started using the software.

Wales characterizes the dispute with Sanger as a fight over the "project's radically open nature" and the question of "whether there was a role for an editor in chief" in the new project. Sanger says he wanted to implement the "common-sense" rules that "experts and specialists should be given some particular respect when writing in their areas of expertise." (Sanger has since launched a competitor to Wikipedia called Citizendium, with stricter rules about editors' credentials.) They also differed over whether advertising should be permitted on the site. Not only does Wikipedia allow anyone to write or edit any article, but the site contains no ads. Yet it allows others to use its content to make money: The site Answers.com, for example, is composed almost entirely of Wikipedia content reposted with ads.

When Nupedia finally shut down for good in 2003, only 24 articles had completed its onerous scholarly review process. In contrast, Wikipedia was flourishing, with 20,000 articles by the end of its first year. It now has 6 million articles, 1.7 million of which are in English. It has become a verb ("What exactly is a quark?" "I don't know. Did you Wikipedia it?"), a sure sign of Internet success.

The Troublemaker

An obvious question troubled, and continues to trouble, many: How could an "encyclopedia that anyone can edit" possibly be reliable? Can truth be reached by a consensus of amateurs? Can a community of volunteers aggregate and assimilate knowledge the way a market assimilates price information? Can it do so with consistent accuracy? If markets fail sometimes, shouldn't the same be true of market-based systems?

Wikipedia does fail sometimes. The most famous controversy over its accuracy boiled over when John Seigenthaler Sr., a former assistant to Attorney General Robert F. Kennedy, wrote about his own Wikipedia entry in a November 2005 *USA Today* op-ed. The entry on Seigenthaler included a claim that he had been involved in both Kennedy assassinations. "We live in a universe of new media," wrote Seigenthaler, "with phenomenal opportunities for worldwide communications and research—but populated by volunteer vandals with poison-pen intellects."

The false claim had been added to the entry as a prank in May 2005. When Seigenthaler contacted Wikipedia about the error in October, Wales personally took the unusual step of removing the false allegations from the editing history on the page, wiping out the publicly accessible records of the error. After the *USA Today* story ran, dozens of the site's contributors (who call themselves "Wikipedians") visited the page, vastly improving the short blurb that had been put in place after the prank entry was removed. As in a market, when a failure was detected, people rushed in to take advantage of the gap and, in doing so, made things better than they were before. Print outlets couldn't hope to compete with Wikipedians' speed in correcting, expanding, and footnoting the new Seigenthaler entry. At best, a traditional encyclopedia would have pasted a correction into a little-consulted annual, mailed out to some users many months after the fact. And even then, it would have been little more than a correction blurb, not a dramatic rethinking and rewriting of the whole entry.

But well-intentioned Wikipedians weren't the only ones attracted to Seigenthaler's Wikipedia entry. Since the article appeared, Seigenthaler says, he has been a constant target for vandals—people whose only goal is to deface an entry. He has been struck by the "vulgarity and meanspiritedness of the attacks," which included replacing his picture with photos of Hitler, Himmler, and "an unattractive cross dresser in a big red wig and a short skirt," Seigenthaler tells me. "I don't care what the hell they put up. When you're 80 years old, there's not much they can say that hasn't been said before. But my, they've been creative over the last months."

Seigenthaler's primary concern these days is about the history page that accompanies each Wikipedia article. Even though various allegations against Seigenthaler have been removed promptly from the main encyclopedia entry, a record of each change and reversion is stored on the site. Many of the comments, says Seigenthaler, are things he would not want his 9-year-old grandson to see.

Seigenthaler says he never intended to sue (surprisingly, the site has never been sued), but he worries that Wales will eventually find himself in legal trouble unless he takes more action to control what appears on the site: "I said to Jimmy Wales, 'You're going to offend enough members of Congress that you're going to get more regulation.' I don't want more regulation of the media, but once the Congress starts regulating they never stop." Coverage of the scandal was largely anti-Wikipedia, focusing on the system's lack of ethical editorial oversight. Sample headline: "There's No Wikipedia Entry for 'Moral Responsibility.'"

Wikipedia's flexibility allows anyone who stumbles on an error to correct it quickly. But that's not enough for some detractors. "There is little evidence to suggest that simply having a lot of people freely editing encyclopedia articles produces more balanced coverage," the editor-in-chief of *Encyclopedia Britannica* said last year in an online debate hosted by *The Wall Street Journal.* "On the contrary, it opens the gates to propaganda and seesaw fights between writers." Another *Britannica* editor dissed Wikipedia by comparing it to a toilet seat (you don't know who used it last). A host of academics charge Wikipedia with having too casual a relationship with authority and objectivity. Michael Gorman, former president of the American Library Association, told the *San Francisco Chronicle* in 2006, "The problem with an online encyclopedia created by anybody is that you have no idea whether you are reading an established person in the field or someone with an ax to grind." Last summer at Wikimania 2006, a gathering of Wikipedians and various hangers-on at the Harvard Law School's Berkman Center for Internet & Society, university professors expressed concern that their students were treating Wikipedia as an authoritative source. In January the history faculty at Vermont's Middlebury College voted to ban the use of Wikipedia in bibliographies. Wales has issued statements telling kids to use Wikipedia as a starting point, but not to include it in their bibliographies as a final source. Good Wikipedia articles have links to authoritative sources, he explains; students should take advantage of them.

Referring to the Seigenthaler controversy during his opening remarks at Wikimania 2006, Wales got one of the biggest laughs of the weekend when he said: "Apparently there was an error in Wikipedia. Who knew?" Wales and the hundreds of Wikipedians could afford a giggle or two because the entry had long since been corrected. This wasn't a traumatic incident to Wikipedians because they admit error hundreds of times a day. There is no pretense of infallibility at Wikipedia, an attitude that sets it apart from traditional reference works, or even *The New York Times;* when an error is found it doesn't undermine the project. Readers who know better than the people who made the error just fix it and move on.

Wikipedia's other major scandal hasn't been quite as easy for Wales to laugh off, because he was the culprit. In 2005 he was caught with his hand on the edit button, taking advantage of Wikipedia's open editing policy to remove Larry Sanger from the encyclopedia's official history of itself. There has been an ongoing controversy about Wales' attempts to edit his own Wikipedia entry, which is permitted but considered extremely bad form. After a round of negative publicity when the edits were discovered, Wales stopped editing his own profile. But in the site's discussion pages, using the handle "Jimbo Wales," he can be found trying to persuade others to make changes on this and other topics. If he wanted to, Wales could make these and other changes by fiat, then lock out other editors. But he doesn't. If the individuals that people Wales' experiment in free association choose to ignore his pleas, as they occasionally do, he takes a deep breath and lets it happen.

Wales isn't the only one who has tried to use Wikipedia to rewrite history. In January 2006, all edits originating with the House of Representatives were briefly blocked after staffers for Rep. Martin Meehan (D-Mass.) were caught systematically replacing unflattering facts in his entry with campaign material; among other things, they removed a reference to his broken promise not to serve more than four terms. In the fall of 2006, officials from the National Institute on Drug Abuse dramatically edited their own entry to remove criticism of the agency. In both cases, the editors got more than they bargained for: Not only was the original material quickly restored, but a section describing the editing scandal was tacked on to each entry.

Then there are edits that are less ideological but still troublesome. Wales has adopted Hayek's view that change is handled more smoothly by an interlocking network of diverse individuals than by a central planning authority. One test of the rapid response to change in Wikipedia is how the site deals with vandalism. Fairly often, says Wales, someone comes along and replaces an entry on, say, George W. Bush with a "giant picture of a penis." Such vandalism tends to be corrected in less than five minutes, and a 2002 study by IBM found that even subtler vandalism rarely lasts more than a few hours. This, Wales argues, is only possible because responsibility for the content of Wikipedia is so widely distributed. Even hundreds of professional editors would struggle to keep six million articles clean day in and day out, but Wikipedia manages it fairly easily by relying on its thousands of volunteer contributors.

The delicate compromise wording of the entry about abortion is an example of how collaborative editing can succeed. One passage reads: "Most often those in favor of legal prohibition of abortion describe themselves as pro-life while those against legal restrictions on abortion describe themselves as pro-choice." Imagine the fighting that went into producing these simple words. But the article, as it stands, is not disputed. Discussants have found a middle ground. "It's fabulous," says Wales, citing another example, "that our article about Taiwan was written by Mainlanders and Taiwanese who don't agree." That said, other entries—such as the page on the Iraq War—host ongoing battles that have not reached equilibrium.

Skeptics of Wikipedia's model emphasize that the writers have no authority; there is no way to verify credentials on the site. But Wikipedia seems to be doing OK without letters after its name. In 2005 the journal *Nature* compared the accuracy of scientific articles in Wikipedia with that of *Encyclopedia Britannica.* Articles were sent to panels of experts in the appropriate field for review. Reviewers found an average of four errors in Wikipedia entries, only slightly higher than *Britannica*'s average of three errors per entry.

The Federalist

One way to understand what makes Wikipedia unique is its reaction to the threat of blackout by the Chinese government. When government censors in China blocked the Chinese-language Wikipedia page and demanded that the content be heavily censored before it was unblocked, the site's Chinese contributors chose to lie low and wait. Wales agreed to let them handle it. Eventually the site was unblocked, although its status is always precarious.

Wikipedia's decision not to censor its content selectively in order to meet the demands of the Chinese government was easy, since it would be almost impossible to do anyway. The "encyclopedia that anyone can edit" would have to employ a full-time staff just to remove objectionable content, which could be added back moments later by anyone, anywhere. The diffuse responsibility for the content of Wikipedia protects it from censorship.

By leaving such a big decision to the community of Chinese Wikipedia users, Wales made good on his boast that he's "a big supporter of federalism," not just in politics but in the governance of Wikipedia. Wales tries to let communities of users make their own decisions in every possible case. "It's not healthy for us if there are certain decisions that are simply removed from the democratic realm and are just 'the Supreme Court says so,'" he argues. "I would even say this about abortion, although I'm a big pro-choice guy. It's not clear to me that it's such a great thing to have removed it completely from politics."

Politically, Wales cops to various libertarian positions but prefers to call his views "center-right." By that he means that he sees himself as part of a silent majority of socially liberal, fiscally conservative people who value liberty—"people who vote Republican but who worry about right-wingers." The Libertarian Party, he says, is full of "lunatics." But even as he outlines all the reasons why he prefers to stay close to the American political mainstream, Wales delicately parses the various libertarian positions on intellectual property and other points of dispute without breaking a sweat. He swears to have actually read Ludwig von Mises's 10-pound tome *Human Action* (which he ultimately found "bombastic and wrong in many ways"). And of course, he credits Hayek with the central insight that made Wikipedia possible.

Wales' political philosophy isn't confined to books. Pulling onto yet another seemingly identical Florida highway during our day-long road trip, Wales blows past the Knight Shooting Sports Indoor Range, lamenting that he hasn't made it to the range in a long time. "When I lived in San Diego," he says, "the range was on my way home from work." Wales used to be preoccupied with gun rights, or the lack thereof. "In California," he says, "the gun laws irritated me so much that I cared, but then I moved to Florida and I stopped caring because everything is fine here."

Wales, whose wife Christine teaches their 5-year-old daughter Kira at home, says he is disappointed by the "factory nature" of American education: "There's something significantly broken about the whole concept of school." A longtime opponent of mandatory public school attendance, Wales says that part of the allure of Florida, where his Wikimedia Foundation is based, is its relatively laissez-faire attitude toward homeschoolers. This makes it easier for Wales and his wife to let Kira (a tiny genius in her father's eyes) follow her own interests and travel with her parents when Wales gives one of his many speeches abroad.

Kira has recently become interested in Ancient Egypt, and a few books on the subject lie on the kitchen counter of their sparse house. When she was younger, Kira was transfixed by digital clocks, staring at one minute after minute, trying to guess which number would be next. "She just needed time to do that," says Wales. "Once she figured it out, she stopped. Christine and I were a little worried, but we let her do her thing, and it turned out fine."

Likewise, Wales says he prefers the users of his encyclopedia to make their own decisions about governance and follow their own peculiar interests wherever possible; things usually turn out fine. "Simply having rules does not change the things that people want to do," he says. "You have to change incentives."

One of the most powerful forces on Wikipedia is reputation. Users rarely identify themselves by their real names, but regular users maintain consistent identities. When a particularly obnoxious edit or egregious error is found, it's easy to check all of the other changes made by the same user; you just click on his name. Users who catch others at misdeeds are praised, and frequent abusers are abused. Because it's so easy to get caught in one stupid mistake or prank, every user has an incentive to do the best he can with each entry. The evolution of a praise/shame economy within Wikipedia has been far more effective at keeping most users in line than the addition of formal rules to deal with specific conflicts.

"It's always better not to have a rule," Wales says. "But sometimes you have to say, 'Don't be a dick.'" On the English Wikipedia, there is a rule that you can't undo someone else's changes more than three times. It is formalized, a part of the system. But Wikipedias in other languages have a more casual approach to the same problem. Wales himself sometimes talks to troublemakers. "I try to talk jerks into adopting a three-revert rule as a principle for themselves," he says.

Wikipedias in different languages have developed their own policies about practically everything. Only one point is "not negotiable": the maintenance of a "neutral point of view" in Wikipedia encyclopedia entries. Wikipedia has been uniquely successful in maintaining the neutrality ethos, says Wales, because "text is so flexible and fluid that you can find amongst reasonable people with different perspectives something that is functional." ("Most people assume the fights are going to be the left vs. the right," Wales has said, "but it always is the reasonable versus the jerks.")

The jerks range from the Chinese government to the giant penis guy. But mostly they're regular contributors who get upset about some hobbyhorse and have to be talked down or even shamed by their communities.

Although he professes to hate phrases like "swarm intelligence" and "the wisdom of crowds," Wales' phenomenal success springs largely from his willingness to trust large aggregations of human beings to produce good outcomes though decentralized, market-like mechanisms. He is suspicious of a priori planning and centralization, and he places a high value on freedom and independence for individuals. He is also suspicious of mob rule. Most Wikipedia entries, Wales notes, are actually written by two or three people, or reflect decisions made by small groups in the discussion forums on the site. Wales calls himself an "anti-credentialist" but adds that doesn't mean he's anti-elitist. He likes elites, he says; they just have to duke it out with the rest of us on Wikipedia and his other projects.

"Jimmy Wales is a very open person," says his friend Irene McGee, the host of the radio show *No One's Listening* and a former *Real World* cast member. "He has very genuine intentions and faith in people. He'll come to San Francisco and come to little Meetups that don't have anything to do with anything, just to find out what's going on. He'll go to meet the kid in this town who writes articles and then meet with people who run countries. He can meet somebody really fancy and he could meet somebody who nobody would recognize and tell the story as if it's the same."

The Individualist Communitarian

Rock star status can be fleeting, of course. Whether Jimmy Wales will still be meeting fancy people who run countries five years from now may depend on the success of his new venture, Wikia. Wikipedia is here to stay, but the public has an annoying habit of demanding that its heroes achieve ever more heroic feats. Wikia is an attempt to take the open-source, community-based model to profitability and broader public acceptance.

Consider, for instance, the astonishing growth and readership at the Wikia site devoted to Muppets. At a little over one year old, the Muppet Wiki has 13,700 articles. Every single one is about Muppets. Interested in an in-depth look at the use of gorilla suits in the Muppet movies? No problem. Just type in "gorilla suits" and enjoy a well-illustrated article that documents, among other things, the names of actors who have worn an ape outfit for Jim Henson. There is a timeline of all things Muppet-related. An entry on China details Big Bird's reception in the People's Republic. The site is astonishingly comprehensive and, perhaps more impressive, comprehensible to a Muppet novice.

This ever-expanding encyclopedia of Muppetry is just a tiny part of Wikia. It is an arguably trivial but hugely telling example of the power of open publishing systems to enable professionals and amateurs to work together to aggregate vast amounts of data and conversation on topics and areas ranging from the serious to the sublime. Founded in November 2004, Wikia communities use the same editing and writing structure as Wikipedia. The site provides free bandwidth, storage, blogging software, and other tools to anyone who wants to start an online community or collaborative project. If you don't care for Kermit the Frog, you can try the Your Subculture Soundtrack, an "interconnecting database of the music scene" with more than 5,600 articles. Many of them are just enormous lists of discographies, lyrics, or guitar tabs. The topics of other Wikis range from *Star Wars* to polyamory to transhumanism. Wikia also includes collaborative online projects such as the Search Wiki, an effort to create an open-source competitor to Google where a Wikipedia-style universe of users rates websites and sorts the search results instead of relying solely on an algorithm.

In December, Wikia announced that its first corporate partner, Amazon, had committed $10 million to further development of the project. Amazon's money added to the $4 million kicked in by angel investors earlier in the year. Amazon and Wikia have not integrated their services, but Wales has not ruled out the possibility of cooperation at a later date, spurring not entirely tongue-in-cheek rumors of a joint Wikipedia-Amazon takeover of the Web. The site plans to make money by showing a few well-targeted, well-placed ads to massive numbers of community members and users.

Amazon founder Jeff Bezos (a supporter of Reason Foundation, the nonprofit that publishes this magazine) has spoken enviously of Wikipedia's collaborative model, expressed his regret that Amazon's user reviews aren't more like wikis, and credited Wikipedia with having "cracked the code for user-generated content." Bezos "really drove this deal personally," Wales says, adding that he was in the enviable position of vetting potential investors.

Wales is reluctant to get into more precise detail about what exactly Wikia will do, or what the communities or collaborative projects will produce, since that will be up to the users. This reticence turns out to be, in part, philosophical. Wikia is radically devoted to the idea that if you provide free, flexible tools, people will build interesting things. It's the same concept that drives Wikipedia, but expanded to nonencyclopedic functions. Like the rest of the cohort sometimes dubbed "Web 2.0"—YouTube, MySpace, Blogger, and other services that emphasize collaboration and user-generated content—Wales is relying on users to make his sites interesting. It isn't always easy to explain this to investors. "Before Wikipedia, the idea of an encyclopedia on a wiki seemed completely insane," says Wales. "It's obvious that it works now, but at the time no one was sure. Now we're going through the same moment with Wikia."

Perhaps because of the indeterminate nature of the final product, Wales has opted for the '90s approach of "build the site now, make money later." Industry analyst Peter Cohan thinks Wikia isn't likely to fall into the same trap as the busted Internet companies of the dot-com era. "Wikia is getting two and a half million page views a day," he says, "and it's growing steadily. There are people who are willing to pay for those eyeballs." (It has been growing at about the same rate as Wikipedia did at this stage of its development.) Still, says Cohan, there will be some hurdles for Wales, who is known only for his non-profit work. "When you bring money into the picture it might change the incentives for people to participate in this thing," he says. "When people know that there is no money involved, then ego gets involved and it's a matter of pride."

Wales is banking on strong communities to give Wikia the staying power that flash-in-the-pan Internet sensations or more loosely knit social networking sites lack. Wales is plugged into social networking sites (and has more than a few online friends/fans), but he says he finds the exhibitionism and technical precocity of MySpace somewhat creepy.

It might sound strange, but Wales' interest in community dovetails nicely with his interest in individualism. No one is born into the Muppet Wiki community. Everyone who is there chooses to be there, and everyone who participates has a chance to shape its rules and content. People naturally form communities with their own delicate etiquette and expectations, and they jealously guard their own protocols. Each one is different, making Wikia communities fertile ground where thousands of experimental social arrangements can be tried—some with millions of members and some with just two or three. Like the "framework for utopia" described in the libertarian philosopher Robert Nozick's *Anarchy, State, and Utopia*, Wikia maximizes the chance that people can work together to get exactly what they want, while still being part of a meaningful community by maximizing freedom and opportunities for voluntary cooperation.

Wikia boosters contend that many existing online communities would benefit from the kind of curb appeal a wiki offers. The firm hopes to co-opt, buy, or duplicate them. Wikia CEO Gil Penchina, formerly of eBay, is a frequent-flyer-miles enthusiast, for example. But most of the sites now haunted by airfare obsessives deal in nitty-gritty details and are useless to the outsider hoping to figure out the best way to get a free ticket by gaming various frequent-flyer plans, or by finding fares listed erroneously as $3.75 instead of $375. "This makes it hard to monetize that content," says Wales. "People just come and look around and don't find what they want and leave." Incorporating those same geeks into a wiki community could make their considerable knowledge available to outsiders and make the page more welcoming to advertisers. If lots of outsiders looking for a good price on a specific product can use the site, advertisers will compete (and pay) to grab their attention.

For now, Wikia makes money solely from Google ads running on its community pages. Wales says this is because they're "lazy" and because Google ads are a good way to generate a little revenue while they "build communities." Since its 2004 launch, Wikia has spent exactly $5.74 on advertising—a small fee for Google analytics to track stats on the site. "That makes our ad budget about 25 cents per month," Wales grins. It's early yet to expect a big push to generate revenue, but this charming laziness could be troublesome if it persists much longer.

Wikia now has 40 employees, including a handful of Polish programmers—a huge staff compared with the three people it takes to run Wikipedia. With 500,000 articles on 2,000 topics produced by 60,000 registered users in 45 languages, the network of websites is growing fast. The biggest wikis are dedicated to *Star Trek* and *Star Wars*. Wales is partial to the wiki devoted to the TV show *Lost*. He also admires the Campaign Wiki, which among other projects has neutral voter guides for elections.

Even as Wikia relies on Google ads for its only revenue at the moment, Wales recently has started to talk publicly about building a search engine using open-source tools, a project Wales casually calls "The Google Killer." Wales hopes the transparency and flexibility of an open-source model will discourage the gaming of the system that plagues Google. A search for "hotels in Tampa" on Google, a search I tried before my trip into town to interview Wales, yields nothing useful, just a jumble of defunct ratings sites and some ads that aren't tailored to my needs. By using a community of volunteers who will rerank results and tweak algorithms, Wales hopes to get useful results in categories that are particularly subject to gaming.

The Pathological Optimist

Later that December afternoon, after an excellent Indian lunch in a Florida strip mall, Wales proposes that we hop back into the Hyundai for a stop at the "fancy mall" in the Tampa area. En route to the Apple store, he surveys the bright lights and luxury goods for sale and announces that he is generally pretty pleased with how things are going in the world. In fact, he calls himself a "pathological optimist." On issue after issue, he pronounces some version of "things aren't that bad" or "things are getting better": People are more connected than they used to be (thanks, in part, to Internet communities), the wide availability of ethnic food has made the American diet more inter- esting, bookstore mega-chains are increasing the diversity of media available in America, entertainment is increasing in quality, gun rights are expanding, and so on. Tempted to get involved with free speech activists, Wales, a self-declared "First Amendment extremist," says he drew back because real repression doesn't seem likely. "There's a lot of hysteria around this," he says—concerns about censorship that aren't supported by the facts.

Wales is optimistic about the Internet too. "There's a certain kind of dire anti-market person," he says, "who assumes that no matter what happens, it's all driving toward one monopoly—the ominous view that all of these companies are going to consolidate into the Matrix." His own view is that radical decentralization will win out, to good effect: "If everybody has a gigabit [broadband Internet connec- tion] to their home as their basic $40-a-month connection, anybody can write Wikipedia."

Wales' optimism isn't without perspective. After reading Tom Standage's book about the impact of the telegraph, *The Victorian Internet*, he was "struck by how much of the semi-utopian rhetoric that comes out of people like me sounds just like what people like them said back then."

Among Wikipedians, there is constant squabbling about how to characterize Wales' role in the project. He is often called a "benevo- lent dictator," or a "God-King," or sometimes a "tyrant." While the 200,000 mere mortals who have contributed articles and edits to the site are circumscribed by rules and elaborate community-enforced norms, Wales has amorphous and wide-ranging powers to block users, delete pages, and lock entries outside of the usual processes. But if Wales is a god, he is like the gods of ancient times (though his is a flat, suburban Olympus), periodically making his presence and preferences known through interventions large and small, but primarily leaving the world he created to chug along according to rules of its own devising.

After spending a day cruising the greater Tampa Bay area, I find myself back at the Wales homestead, sitting with the family as they watch a video of Wales' daughter delivering a presentation on Germany for a first-grade enrichment class. Wales is learning German, in part because the German Wikipedia is the second largest after English, in part because "I'm a geek." Daughter Kira stands in front of a board, wearing a dirndl and reciting facts about Germany. Asked where she did her research, she cops to using Wikipedia for part of the project. Wales smiles sheepishly; the Wikipedia revolution has penetrated even his own small bungalow.

People who don't "get" Wikipedia, or who get it and recoil in horror, tend to be from an older generation literally and figuratively: the Seigenthalers and *Britannica* editors of the world. People who get it are younger and hipper: the Irene McGees and Jeff Bezoses. But the people who really matter are the Kiras, who will never remember a time without Wikipedia (or perhaps Wikia), the people for whom open-source, self-governed, spontaneously ordered online community projects don't seem insane, scary, or even particularly remarkable. If Wales has his way—and if Wikipedia is any indication, he will—such projects will just be another reason the Internet doesn't suck.

Critical Reading Questions

Summarizing the Text

1. What is the argument here? What is Mangu-Ward's thesis about Wikipedia?
2. What did Friedrich Hayek argue about how markets allocate goods? How can an encyclopedia be relevant to an argument about economics?

Establishing the Context

3. *Reason* magazine is aligned with the libertarian philosophy, which opposes governmental intervention in most social arenas and tends to support deregulation of markets of all kinds and private ownership of most sectors of society. How does Mangu-Ward relate Wikipedia to libertarian ideas?
4. In what ways has Jimmy Wales adopted "federalism" in his administration of Wikipedia? How did this affect the community of Wikipedians in China? Given what you know about China's political and social environment, how does this position Wikipedia in relation to the interests of the Chinese government?

Responding to the Text

5. Do you use Wikipedia? What do you use it for? Did this article and its explanation of how entries are written change your opinion of the value of the site?

6. Mangu-Ward puts two terms in opposition: *federalism* and *centralization*. Although she uses them specifically to describe Wikipedia's governance, in what other arenas might this opposition be useful?

A New Dark Age?

Maggie Jackson

Author of the Boston Globe's *"Balancing Acts" column, journalist Maggie Jackson writes on issues relating to the balance of work and life. In her 2008 book* Distracted, *from which this excerpt is taken, Jackson argues that "the way we live is eroding our capacity for deep, sustained, perceptive attention"—or, to put it in the terms of this book, our willingness or ability to engage in critical reading.*

I am alone inside a glass booth, enveloped in a swirling storm of dialogue snippets, data shards, and clashing storylines. This is a play, for an audience of one. Within the booth is a tiny cybercafe, with a table, two chairs, a fake daisy in a vase, and a Mac computer. Sit down, press a button, and the play begins—disembodied, prerecorded, unshared. Over a soundtrack of clinking dishes and laughing customers, I hear two hushed voices, talking as if from another table. A man and a woman are meeting secretly, worried that their spouses are having a cyber-affair. The Mac comes to life and unfurls an instant message chat: the virtual whispers of the cyber-lovers. I listen and read, as the two couples simultaneously, online and offline, debate whether cyber-love is real, whether harm has been done. "We haven't cheated, if that's what you're thinking," says one. "Then why do I feel guilty?" his virtual lover retorts. The parallel scripts wash over me, clashing and overlapping, competing for my gaze and for my ear.

I listen twice and then try the next booth, and the next. There are six in all, a half dozen playlets, each no more than twelve minutes long, told by and through computers. These are the Technology Plays—six faceless, mechanized dramas of passion, mistrust, and dehumanization, unfolding at the touch of a button.[1] This smorgasbord of experimental theater is on display in the soaring atrium of a college library in upstate New York. Just before the plays are dismantled, I have driven three hours to see them. Here on this dreary campus on a raw November day, I am looking for clues to understanding our own increasingly multilayered, mutable, and virtual world. Are these six mini-plays absurd slices of science fiction or reflections of our own lives of snippets and sound bites? Are they meaningless theatrical peep shows or dramatizations of the real shadows creeping over our lives?

Enter Booth 2, Richard Dresser's *Greetings from the Home Office*. Now I am sitting at an office desk, cast as the new hire in a corporate office that's roiled by a possible accounting scandal. A telephone rings. A frantic woman colleague is calling to say that the boss is covering up his misdoings. The smooth-talking boss telephones next to say that the whistleblower should be ignored; she is his bitter ex-lover. "I'm saying this for your own good," the boss purrs. Rapid-fire calls are punctuated by the interjections of a meddling secretary on an intercom. Ultimately, I'm forced to decide whom to trust, based on incomplete information and faceless relations. It's the age-old game of office politics done blindfolded, execution-style. In another play, *Chip*, a seemingly banal ATM transaction goes wrong when the machine rejects the identity chip allegedly implanted in my finger. The machine and a bank representative on the telephone shout contradictory commands as I hear machine-gun-firing security guards close in. The experience is at once comic and frightening. When the machine orders me not to turn around, I can't help but give a terrified peek over my shoulder. The Technology Plays are equal parts video game, amusement park ride, and high-tech storytelling. Oh-so briefly, you are sent hurtling into fantastical worlds where you are asked to fix what you can't see, decide what you don't understand, relate to those you cannot fully trust. The narratives are fragmented. The experience is disorienting. This is not how we live. Or is it?

I close the door of the last booth and walk back to my car. I've talked to no one all afternoon except a faceless woman whom I called on my cell phone about a technological glitch. (A man wordlessly comes to fix it.) The next day is Thanksgiving. The campus is silent and nearly deserted, with only a few backpack-toting students milling about. In twenty-four hours, most will be gathering with family, as will I. But going forward, I can't shake the lingering unease left by these fragments of plays. They manage to distill in brief much of how we live: tossed and turned by info-floods, pummeled by clashing streams of rapid-fire imagery, floating in limitless cyber-worlds, all while trust and privacy and face-to-face moments slip from our grasp. Twelve-minute plays for a one-minute world. Push the button and the next morsel of "real life" unfolds. Guess again, a soupçon of information will suffice. Do you dare peek over your shoulder? Can you clearly see the way ahead?

We can tap into 50 million Web sites, 1.8 million books in print, 75 million blogs, and other snowstorms of information,[2] but we increasingly seek knowledge in Google searches and Yahoo! headlines that we gulp on the run while juggling other tasks. We can contact millions of people across the globe, yet we increasingly connect with even our most intimate friends and family via instant messaging, virtual visits, and fleeting meetings that are rescheduled a half dozen times, then punctuated when they do occur by pings and beeps and multitasking. Amid the glittering promise of our new technologies and the wondrous potential of our scientific gains, we are nurturing a culture of social diffusion, intellectual fragmentation, sensory detachment. In this new world, something is amiss. And that something is attention.

The premise of this book is simple. The way we live is eroding our capacity for deep, sustained, perceptive attention—the building block of intimacy, wisdom, and cultural progress. Moreover, this disintegration may come at great cost to ourselves and to society. Put most simply, attention defines us and is the bedrock of society. Attention "is the taking possession by the mind, in clear and vivid form, of one out of what seem several simultaneously possible objects or trains of thought," wrote psychologist and philosopher William James in 1890. "It implies withdrawal from some things in order to deal effectively with others, and is a condition which has a real opposite in the confused, dazed, scatter-brained state which in French is called *distraction*, and *Zerstreutheit* in German."[3] James came tantalizingly close to understanding at least one aspect of this mysterious phenomenon whose inner workings eluded philosophers, artists, historians, and scientists for centuries. But today, we know much more about attention, and all that we are learning only serves to underscore its irrefutable importance in life. Attention is an organ system, akin to our respiratory or circulation systems, according to cognitive neuroscientist Michael Posner. Attention, as James astutely understood, is the brain's conductor, leading the orchestration of our minds. And its various networks are key not only to higher forms of thinking but to our morality and even our very happiness.

Yet increasingly, we are shaped by distraction. James described a clear and vivid possessing of the mind, an ordering, and a withdrawal. We easily recognize that these states of mind are becoming less and less a given in our lives. The seduction of alternative virtual universes, the addictive allure of multitasking people and things, our near-religious allegiance to a constant state of motion: these are markers of a land of distraction, in which our old conceptions of space, time, and place have been shattered. This is why we are less and less able to see, hear, and comprehend what's relevant and permanent, why so many of us feel that we can barely keep our heads above water, and our days are marked by perpetual loose ends. What's more, the waning of our powers of attention is occurring at such a rate and in so many areas of life, that the erosion is reaching critical mass. We are on the verge of losing our capacity as a society for deep, sustained focus. In short, we are slipping toward a new dark age.

A dark age? Certainly, the notion seems so far removed from our techno-miraculous era that the mere mention of the subject appears irresponsibly alarmist. Amid our material riches, abundant information, and creative leaps, how can we be headed toward a time of decline? How can I speak of cultural slippages when we are able to decipher the genome, map the ocean floor, and plumb the depths of the brain to begin understanding something as abstract and intangible as attention? But take a closer look. The parallels between dark ages past and our times are clear and multiplying, and the erosion of attention is the key to understanding why we are on the cusp of a time of widespread cultural and social losses.

Consider first that a dark age is not a one-dimensional time of unending disintegration. Rather, it is a distinct turning point in history, a period of flux that often produces great technological and other gains yet ultimately results in a declining civilization and a desertlike spell of collective forgetting. The medieval era was a fertile time technologically, marked by the invention of eyeglasses, glazed windows, fireplaces, windmills, and stirrups, along with the compass, mechanical clock, and rudder.[4] Yet by the sixth century, all of continental Europe's great libraries not only had disappeared but the *memory* of them was lost to an emerging feudal society, notes Thomas Cahill.[5] After the fall of the mighty Mycenaean Empire in the tenth century BC, the Greeks improved upon the great rowing ships of the time and upon military tactics such as the phalanx. For the first time, the olive was cultivated as a food. Yet overall living standards slipped dramatically, and advances in carving, building, the arts, and farming slipped away as Greece entered a five-hundred-year-long dark age. Beads of amber came to be made of bone. Painted murals and elaborately carved gems gave way to clay modeling. The dead were buried in the crumbling ruins of beautiful buildings. Even writing declined in the time between the waning of the script called "Linear B," and the adoption of an alphabet.[6] A dark age can dazzle if you fail to see the whole. But inexorably, such a time leads to "a culture's dead end."

Chillingly, many of these shifts parallel the current trajectory of our civilization. I'm not arguing that we'll soon be living in wooden huts and burying our dead in ruined landmarks, yet we, too, are in the midst of a time of innovations, flux, and impending decline. Civilization is defined by a "sense of permanence," notes historian Kenneth Clark. "Civilized man, or so it seems to me, must feel that he belongs somewhere in space and time."[7] Consciously doing all we can to free ourselves from the last boundaries of space and time, we are ultimately trading our cultural and societal anchors for an age of glorious freedom, technological innovation—and darkness. As our attentional skills are squandered, we are plunging into a culture of mistrust, skimming, and a dehumanizing merging between man and machine. As we cultivate lives of distraction, we are losing our capacity to create and preserve wisdom and slipping toward a time of ignorance that is paradoxically born amid an abundance of information and connectivity. Our tools transport us, our inventions are impressive, but our sense of perspective and shared vision shrivels. This is why Umberto Eco has called Western society "neomedieval," comparing our own anxious, postliterate, and highly mobile age with the first post-Roman millennium in Europe. The late Jane Jacobs, who wrote the classic *Death and Life of Great American Cities* a generation ago, warned of an impending time of darkness brought on by fatal cracks in various pillars of American society, such as ethics and science. Critic Harold Bloom calls this era a "Dark Age of the Screens."[8]

Although a time of decline may take generations or even centuries to unfold, the first evidence of its shadowy embrace may be seen all around us, if we can rise above the muddle of our days and see clearly. With this in mind, I want to lure you, the reader, into pausing and reflecting on our daily lives and our era. I do not propose to, nor could I, write *The Decline and Fall of the American Empire,* nor could I tackle the enormous political or economic implications of such changes. Nor is this a how-to, although hopefully this book will have a positive impact on a reader's life. Rather, my scope is *how we live and what that means* for our individual and collective futures.

Consider the issue of attention deficit disorder. This is not a book about whether millions of distractible children and adults belong on Ritalin and other stimulants. Yet alongside the voracious debates about the disorder festers a discomfiting realization: this condition, or at least some portion of it, may be exacerbated by the way we are living. With a mixture of self-mockery, perverse pride in our busyness, and real uneasiness, we accept that ADD has spilled far past the confines of the medical world. Educators fret about "vaccinating" children against ADD through better teaching and parenting. A growing roster of defenders venerates the upsides of being attention-deficient. Students pop Adderall and other "wakefulness" pills to focus better on tests. "How do you know you have ADD or a severe case of modern life?" asks Edward Hallowell, a psychiatrist who warns of an epidemic of attention deficit trait. "Everyone these days is super-busy and multitasking and keeping track of more data points than ever. The actual condition is just that—taken to a more extreme level."[9] ADD and ADT are both causes of worry and badges of honor, but above all, they signal disturbing slippages in an asset that we cannot afford to lose.

Not long ago, an old school friend called me. We hadn't talked in years. After hearing about my book, he wanted to get together. E-mails sallied back and forth, like bumper cars bouncing off one another, with no solid hits. After repeated cancellations and postponements, we set a date for lunch. Arriving at his office, I waited while he wound up a meeting, took a phone call, dashed around. (Luckily, I had brought a book.) It was long past noon when we hurried to a coffee shop, where he mentioned that he'd eaten already. I gulped a sandwich, he half-heartedly sipped a soda, then raced back to work. It was all very friendly, yet I stood on the street corner for a few minutes, feeling unsettled. In school, I was studious and he was goofy. But he was never this, well, *diluted.* I thought we were going to catch up. Instead, I got the face-to-face equivalent of an MTV montage. Several times, he uneasily joked about his inability to focus.

We all share the joke. Nearly a third of workers feel they often do not have time to reflect on or process the work they do. More than half typically have to juggle too many tasks simultaneously and/or are so often interrupted that they find it difficult to get work done.[10] One yearlong study found that workers not only switch tasks every three minutes during their workday but that nearly half the time they interrupt themselves.[11] People are so dazed that they have almost no time to reflect on the world around them, much less their futures. Not too long ago, I stood on a New York street corner, watching a businessman who was so busy shouting into a cell phone and hailing a taxi that for some minutes he didn't notice that his colleague already had found a cab and was ready to roll. Speaking at a lunch for forty lawyers in Philadelphia, I talked about our mobile lives, technology's impact on the home, flexible work—and the erosion of focus. They pounced. That was the lightning rod issue: divided, diluted attention. Two hours passed, without a BlackBerry in sight. Finally, the leader of the group tentatively asked, "Is it just me, or is it true that we don't seem to go deeply into anything anymore?" Around the table, heads nodded. "Is all of this really progress?" she wondered.

Is all this progress? We have reason to worry. Kids are the inveterate multitaskers, the technologically fluent new breed that is better suited for the lightning-paced, many-threaded digital world, right? After all, they are bathed in an average of nearly six hours a day of nonprint media content, and a quarter of that time they are using more than one screen, dial, or channel. Nearly a third of fourteen- to twenty-one-year-olds juggle five to eight media while doing homework.[12] Yet for all their tech fluency, kids show less patience, skepticism, tenacity, and skill than adults in navigating the Web, all while overestimating their prowess, studies show.[13] Meanwhile, US fifteen-year-olds rank twenty-fourth out of twenty-nine developed countries on an Organization for Economic Cooperation and Development (OECD) test of problem-solving skills related to analytic reasoning—the sort of skills demanded in today's workforce. Nearly 60 percent of fifteen-year-olds in our country score at or below the most *basic* level of problem solving, which involves using single sources of well-defined information to solve challenges such as plotting a route on a map.[14] Government and other studies show that many US high school students can't synthesize or assess information, express complex thoughts, or analyze arguments. In other words, they often lack the critical thinking skills that are the bedrock of an informed citizenry and the foundation of scientific and other advancements.[15] Is it just a coincidence that they lack the skills nurtured by the brain's executive attention network, the seat of our highest-level powers of focus?

While undoubtedly the reasons for this state of affairs are myriad, what's certain is that we can't be a nation of reflective, analytic problem solvers while cultivating a culture of distraction. I am not alone in wondering how often our children will experience the hard-fought pleasures of plunging deeply into a thought, a conversation, a state of being. Will focusing become a lost art, quaintly exhibited alongside blacksmithing at the historic village? ("Look, honey, that man in twentieth-century costume is doing just one thing!") An executive at a top accounting firm, who was researching the future workforce, confided to me his deep concerns that young workers are less and less able to concentrate, think deeply, or mine a vein of inquiry. Knowledge work can't be done in sound bites, he warned.

And yet again, perhaps it is silly to worry. What if we're all slowly, and with lots of stumbles, learning to adapt to a new world, where multitasking, split-second decision making, information surfing, bullet pointing, and virtual romancing is the new norm? What if our technologies are ushering us into an even more glorious future? Just hang on for the ride! Perhaps the smart folks are creating a new definition of smarts. Those clinging to the power of the word, the mysterious miracles of the human mind and spirit, and a reverence for the sensuality of physical togetherness will be soon left behind!

It's true that our tools are shaping us and teaching us, as they have since man first picked up a stick, sword, or pen. And today's technologies are making us smarter ... in some ways. We don't yet know whether video games teach us problem-solving, pattern recognition, or how to construct order from chaos, as Steven Johnson and others argue.[16] Early evidence shows that many computer games teach the kind of iconic and spatial skills useful for playing more computer games, and not much more. While some carefully crafted computer-based exercises can and are being powerfully used to educate, many games on the market are simply "training wheels" for improving *computer* literacy, some researchers conclude. Video games also can boost your ability to pay attention to multiple stimuli in your field of vision, a skill useful for driving but not analytical thinking.[17] Limited doses of educational television produce some language, math, and reading gains in young children, but there's no evidence that, as Johnson argues, the growing numbers of sitcom characters or "complexity" of plot lines in adult fare offer us anything more than a diet of loose threads.[18] If crafted well and used wisely, our high-tech tools have the potential to make us smarter, but too often so far they seem to be doing so in narrow ways.

"It's like, instead of writing the whole book, you're just writing the back cover," explained Brendan, age ten.[19] One sultry June day in library class, Brendan was giving me a primer on the difference between a written report—"writing, research, more research, more writing"—and his PowerPoint presentation on piranha fish—"a brief summary." Although Brendan was hardly a boy of few words in person, his slides took bullet points to new heights of brevity. "Habitat. Amazon River. Warm Water. Murky Water. Always Have Food. Lots of Predators," one read. He ticked off the benefits of PowerPoint. It's shorter, animated, fun, and easier, even though you don't learn as much from it. His classmates and other students at a suburban elementary school outside Hartford, Connecticut, agreed with him. They liked PowerPoint's short sentences, bouncing words, the fact that their parents are amazed by the results, and above all, its bright colors. No one wants to read long sentences or too much information, they assured me. Not surprisingly, the information in their presentations was mostly cut and pasted from Web sites. The results? "You get a smattering of information," said the school librarian, whose job is to teach tech skills, not content. "You get a snippet of this and that." When I asked several children about specific words in their slides or why they included a particular and sometimes nonsensical piece of information, most shrugged. "I don't know," they said.

Channeling our thoughts and ideas into outlines and bullet points—is this a new definition of smart? With four hundred million copies in circulation, PowerPoint is the world's most popular presentation tool. Some books get taken off class lists if they don't give good PowerPoint.[20] Many corporate employees, bureaucrats, and military officers hardly dare to make a presentation without it. Proponents, including Microsoft (naturally), argue that in a world of information overload, we need brevity and distillation. PowerPoint's shortcomings stem from people's inexperience with this new tool, they say. But opponents, led by information theorist Edward Tufte, are blistering in their criticism. They say the software shapes thoughts and data into alluringly professional yet narrow and simplistic formats, fostering uninformative and often misleading presentations that discourage creativity or argument. Partly as a result of Tufte's work, NASA blamed its reliance on PowerPoint for a pattern of obfuscation and miscommunication that helped doom the *Challenger* space shuttle.[21] "When presentation becomes its own powerful idea, we diminish our appreciation of complexity," concluded MIT professor Sherry Turkle after studying PowerPoint's use in classrooms.[22] PowerPoint "tells you how to think," quips rock musician David Byrne in "Envisioning Emotional Epistemological Information," a satirical PowerPoint artwork set to his own compositions. "This can be an enjoyable experience."[23]

PowerPoint doesn't make us dumb, and a judicious use of such slide-ware likely can help us navigate a world of information overload. I'm not angling for a return to some sort of pastoral, unmechanized Eden in order to halt the erosion of attention. We cannot blame technology for society's ills. Nor can we fall into the opposite and increasingly commonplace trap of blindly trusting that our new tools will automatically usher us into a glorious new age. The tools we are wholeheartedly embracing today are inherently powerful, and we ignore that truth at our peril. You can use a stick for digging potatoes or stabbing your neighbor, so how you use a stick is important, but equally important is the fact that a stick is not a wheel. It's crucial that we better understand how our new high-tech tools, from video games to PowerPoint, may be affecting us. Moreover, our tools reflect the values of our time, so it's no coincidence that PowerPoint is a tool of choice in a world of snippets and sound bites. This is the messy soup that makes up our relation to technology, and explains why technology plays a starring but ultimately subordinate role in this book. Technology is a key to understanding our world, but it is not the full story. Instead, we must ask: how do we want to define progress? We are adapting to a new world, but in doing so are we redefining "smart" to mostly mean twitch speed, multitasking, and bullet points? Are we similarly redefining intimacy and trust? Are we so enamored of our alluring surface gains that we are failing to stem or even notice the deeper, human costs of these "advances"? We may be getting expert at pushing buttons and wiring our thoughts with bells and whistles and tracking two virtual enemies across a screen but losing the skills needed to thrive in an increasingly complex world: deep learning, reasoning, and problem solving. We may be getting better at juggling three people simultaneously over a screen or wire but forgetting that what we need more than ever in a time of growing mistrust and seemingly expendable relations is honesty, unhurried presence, and care.

I think we're beginning to see a time of darkness when, amid a plethora of high-tech connectivity, one-quarter of Americans say they have no close confidante, more than double the number twenty years ago. It's a darkening time when we think togetherness means keeping one eye, hand, or ear on our gadgets, ever ready to tune into another channel of life, when we begin to turn to robots to tend to the sick and the old, when doctors listen to patients on average for just eighteen seconds before interrupting, and when two-thirds of children under six live in homes that keep the television on half or more of the time, an environment linked to attention deficiencies. We should worry when we have the world at our fingertips but half of Americans age eighteen to twenty-four can't find New York state on a map and more than 60 percent can't similarly locate Iraq.[24] We should be concerned when we sense that short-term thinking in the workplace eclipses intellectual pattern making, and when we're staking our cultural memory largely on digital data that is disappearing at astounding rates. We should worry when attention slips through our fingers.

For nothing is more central to creating a flourishing society built upon learning, contentment, caring, morality, reflection, and spirit than attention. As humans, we are formed to pay attention. Without it, we simply would not survive. Just as our respiration [and] circula- tory systems are made up of multiple parts, so attention encompasses three "networks" related to different aspects of awareness, focus, and planning.[25] In a nutshell, "alerting" makes us sensitive to incoming stimuli, while the "orienting" network helps us select information from among the millions of sensations we receive from the world, vol- untarily or in reaction to our surroundings. A baby's first job is to hone these skills, which are akin to "awareness" and "focus," respectively. In a class of its own, however, is the executive network, the system of attention responsible for complex cognitive and emotional operations and especially for resolving conflicts between different areas of the brain. (We fire up four separate areas of the brain just to solve a simple word recognition problem, such as coming up with a use for the word *hammer*.)[26] All three networks are crucial and often work together, and without strong skills of attention, we are buffeted by the world and hindered in our capacity to grow and even to enjoy life. People who focus well report feeling less fear, frustration, and sadness day to day, partly because they can literally deploy their attention away from negatives in life. In contrast, attentional problems are one of the main impediments to attaining "flow," the deep sense of contentment that people find when they are stretching themselves to meet a challenge.[27] For example, schizophrenics tend to suffer from *anhedonia*, or liter- ally "lack of pleasure," because they usually are unable to sift stimuli. "Things are coming in too fast," said one patient. "I am attending to everything at once and as a result I do not really attend to anything."[28] Without a symphonic conductor, the music of the brain disintegrates into cacophonic noise.

Attention also tames our inner beast. Primates that receive training in attention become less aggressive.[29] One of attention's highest forms is "effortful control," which involves the ability to shift focus deliberately, engage in planning, and regulate one's impulses. Six- and seven-year- olds who score high in tests of this skill are more empathetic, better able to feel guilt and shame, and less aggressive. Moreover, effortful control is integral to developing a conscience, researchers are discovering.[30] In order to put back the stolen cookie, you must attend to your uneasy feelings, the action itself, and the abstract moral principles—then make the right response. All in all, attention is key to both our free will as individuals and our ability to subordinate ourselves to a greater good. The *Oxford English Dictionary* defines attention as "the act, fact or state of attending or giving heed; earnest direction of the mind," and secondarily as "practical consideration, observant care, notice." The word is rooted in the Latin words *ad* and *tendere*, meaning to "stretch toward," implying effort and intention.[31] Even the phrase "attention span" literally means a kind of bridge, a reaching across in order to widen one's horizons. Attention is not always effortful, but it carries us toward our highest goals, however we define them. A culture that settles for numb distraction cannot shape its future.

This morning, I sat in the library trying to harness my thoughts, but like runaway horses, they would not be reined in. We missed the first birthday of a baby whose parents are two of our closest friends, and I stewed about that for a while. Someone I interviewed for my newspaper column was peeved that an editor hadn't confirmed this evening's photo shoot, and a flurry of e-mails ensued. A man outside my study room made a long, illicit phone call and gestured threateningly when I asked him to stop. The old water pipes hissed in a new, odd way. I have never thought of myself as easily distracted, although I always have had an Olympic capacity for daydreaming, failing to complete my sentences, and slips of the tongue. (Go put on your pajamas, I'll tell my daughter at noon, when I really mean bathing suit.) A friend generously diagnoses me as having "too many words" in my head. But perhaps the ultimate weak spot in my own capacity for focus is that I'm observant and "sensitive"—a label I grew to hate as a child. I notice much of the ceaseless swirl of social intonations, bodily signals, and facial expressions around me. Even in the relative quiet of the library, the world tends to come rushing in, jumbling and splashing about inside me, a restless sea.

Yet isn't that essentially the starting point of attention? Attention is a process of taking in, sorting and shaping, planning, and decision making—a mental and emotional forming and kneading of the bread of life, or, if you prefer, an inner mountain climb. The first two forms of attention—alertness and orienting—allow us to sense and respond to our environment, while the third and highest network of executive attention is needed to make ultimate sense of our world. Our ability to attend is partly genetic, yet also dependent upon a nurturing environment and how willing we are to reach for the highest levels of this skill, just as a naturally gifted athlete who lacks the opportunity, encouragement, and sheer will to practice can never master a sport. Today, our virtual, split-screen, and nomadic era is eroding opportunities for deep focus, awareness, and reflection. As a result, we face a real risk of societal decline. But there is much room for hope, for attention can be trained, taught, and shaped, a discovery that offers the key to living fully in a tech-saturated world. We need not waste our potential for reaching the heights of attention. We don't have to settle for lives mired in detachment, fragmentation, diffusion. A *renaissance of attention* is within our grasp.

I didn't set out to write about attention. I was curious why so many Americans are deeply dissatisfied with life, feeling stressed, and often powerless to shape their futures in a country of such abundant resources. At first, I sought clues in the past, assuming that lessons from the first high-tech era—the heyday of the telegraph, cinema, and railway—could teach us how to better manage our own shifting experiences of space and time. Instead, I discovered that our gadgets are bringing to a climax the changes seeded in these first revolutions. Is this a historical turning point, a "hinge of history," in Thomas Cahill's words? In researching this next question, I discovered stunning similarities between past dark ages and our own era. At the same time, I began studying the astonishing discoveries made just in our own generation about the nature and workings of attention. As I explored these seemingly unrelated threads, I realized that they formed a tapestry: the story of what happens when we allow our powers of attention to slip through our fingers. Realizing this loss is intriguing. Considering the consequences is alarming.

When a civilization wearies, notes Cahill, a confidence based on order and balance is lost, and without such anchors, people begin to return to an era of shadows and fear.[32] Godlike amid our five hundred television channels and three hundred choices of cereal, are we failing to note the creeping arrival of a time of impermanence and uncertainty? Mesmerized by streams of media-borne eye candy and numbed by our faith in technology to cure all ills, are we blind to the realization that our society's progress, in important ways, is a shimmering mirage? Consumed by the vast time and energy simply required to survive the ever-increasing complexity of our systems of living, are we missing the slow extinction of our capacity to think and feel and bond deeply? We just might be too busy, wired, split-focused, and *distracted* to notice a return to an era of shadows and fear.

On the August day in 410 when the Goths brutally sacked Rome, the emperor was at his country house on the Adriatic, attending to his beloved flock of prize poultry.[33] Informed by a servant that Rome had perished, the emperor, Honorius, was stunned. "Rome perished?" he said. "It is not an hour since she was feeding out of my hand." The chamberlain clarified himself. He'd been talking about the city, not the imperial bird of that name. Apocryphal as this story may be, the point is apt. For in the years leading into a dark age, societies often exhibit an inability to perceive or act upon a looming threat, such as a declining resource. Twilight cultures begin to show a preference for veneer and form, not depth and content; a stubborn blindness to the consequences of actions, from the leadership on down. In other words, an epidemic erosion of attention is a sure sign of an impending dark age.

Welcome to the land of distraction.

Endnotes

1. Daniel Ho, *"1 + 1 = 0."* Also Richard Dresser, "Greetings from the Home Office," and Malcolm Messersmith, "Chip" (presented at the State University of New York, Albany, November 2003).
2. Jay Palmer, "High-Wired Act," *Barron's*, April 17, 2007, p. 27. Also *Books in Print 2007–8* (New Providence, NJ: Bowker, 2007), 1:vii.
3. William James, *The Principles of Psychology*, ed. Frederick Burkhardt (Cambridge, MA: Harvard University Press, 1981; originally published, 1890), 1:381–2.
4. Barbara Tuchman, *A Distant Mirror: The Calamitous Fourteenth Century* (New York: Knopf, 1978), p. 55. Also Chiara Frugoni, *Books, Bank, Buttons and Other Inventions of the Middle Ages*, trans. William McCuaig (New York: Columbia University Press, 2001, 2003), pp. ix–x.
5. Thomas Cahill, *How the Irish Saved Civilization: The Untold Story of Ireland's Heroic Role from the Fall of Rome to the Rise of Medieval Europe* (New York: Nan A. Talese, Doubleday, 1995), p. 181.
6. Dan Stanislawski, "Dark Age Contributions to the Mediterranean Way of Life," *Annals of the Association of American Geographers* 63, no. 4 (1973): 397–410, here, p. 398. Also Anthony Snodgrass, *The Dark Age of Greece: An Archeological Survey of the Eleventh to the Eighth Centuries BC* (Edinburgh: University of Edinburgh Press, 1971), pp. 2, 21, 363, 367, 381, 399–402.
7. Kenneth Clark, *Civilization: A Personal View* (London: British Broadcasting Corp. and John Murray, 1969), pp. 14, 17.
8. Umberto Eco, *Travels in Hyper Reality: Essays*, trans. William Weaver (San Diego: Harcourt Brace Jovanovich, 1986), p. 73. Jane Jacobs, *Dark Age Ahead* (New York: Random House, 2004), p. 3. Harold Bloom, "Great Dane," *Wall Street Journal*, April 20, 2005, p. A16.
9. Hallowell quoted in Kris Maher, "The Jungle: Focus on Recruitment, Pay and Getting Ahead," *Wall Street Journal*, March 2, 2004, p. B8.
10. Ellen Galinsky et al., *Overwork in America: When the Way We Work Becomes Too Much* (New York: Families and Work Institute, 2005), pp. 2–4.
11. Gloria Mark, Victor Gonzalez, and Justin Harris, "No Task Left Behind? Examining the Nature of Fragmented Work," *Proceedings of the Conference on Human Factors in Computer Systems* (2005): 321–30. Also Victor Gonzalez and Gloria Mark, "Constant, Constant Multi-tasking Craziness: Managing Multiple Working Spheres," *Proceedings of Conference on Human Factors in Computing Systems* (2004): 113–20.
12. Victoria Rideout and Donald Roberts, *Generation M: Media in the Lives of Eight to 18-Year-Olds* (Menlo Park, CA: Henry J. Kaiser Family Foundation, March 2005), pp. 6, 23.
13. Deborah Fallows, *Search Engine Users* (Washington, DC: Pew Internet and American Life Project), January 23, 2005, pp. iii–iv, 27, Also Patti Caravello et al., *Information Competence at UCLA: Report of a Survey Project* (Los Angeles: UCLA Library Instructional Services Advisory Committee, Spring 2001), pp. 1–3. Hoa Loranger and Jakob Nielsen, *Teenagers on*

the Web: Usability Guidelines for Creating Compelling Websites for Teens* (Fremont, CA: Nielsen Norman Group, 2005), pp. 5–6, 12–13, 17–18.

14. *Problem Solving for Tomorrow's World* (Paris: Organization of Economic Co-operation and Development, 2004), pp. 40–42, 47, 144.

15. H. Persky, M. Daane, and Y. Jin, *The Nation's Report Card: Writing 2002* (Washington, DC: US Department of Education, Institute of Educational Sciences, 2003), pp. 11, 19, 21. Also Steven Ingels et al., *A Profile of the American High School Sophomore in 2002: Initial Results from the Base Year of the Education Longitudinal Study of 2002* (Washington, DC: US Department of Education, National Center for Education Statistics, 2005), pp. 25–26. Also *Crisis at the Core: Preparing All Students for College and Work* (Iowa City: ACT, 2005), pp. 3, 24.

16. Steven Johnson, *Everything Bad Is Good for You: How Today's Popular Culture Is Actually Making Us Smarter* (New York: Riverhead Books, 2005), pp. 41–46, 61–62.

17. Kaveri Subrahmanyam et al., "The Impact of Home Computer Use on Children's Activities and Development," *Future of Children* 10, no. 2 (2000): 123–44, here, p. 129. Also Sandra Calvert, "Cognitive Effects of Videogames," in *Handbook of Computer Game Studies*, ed. J. Raessens and J. Gudstein (Cambridge, MA: MIT Press, 2005), pp. 125–31. Also June Lee and Aletha Huston, "Educational Televisual Media Effects," in *Faces of Televisual Media*, ed. Edward Palmer and Brian Young (Mahwah, NJ: L. Erlbaum Associates, 2003), pp. 83–105. Also C. Shawn Green and Daphne Bavelier, "Action Video Game Modifies Visual Selective Attention," *Nature* 423, no. 29 (2003): 534–37.

18. Johnson also argues that nonverbal IQ scores are rising globally because more than ever we live in a world dominated by images, although others attribute the gains to better nutrition or even simply to the increasing complexity of society. See Ulric Neisser, *The Rising Curve: Long-Term Gains in IQ and Related Measures* (Washington, DC: American Psychological Association, 1998).

19. Interviews with Brendan, his classmates, and the librarian, June 2005.

20. Ian Parker, "Absolute PowerPoint: Can a Software Package Edit Our Thoughts?" *New Yorker*, May 28, 2001, pp. 76–87.

21. Edward Tufte, *The Cognitive Style of PowerPoint* (Cheshire, CT: Graphics Press, 2003). Clive Thompson, "PowerPoint Makes You Dumb," *New York Times*, December 14, 2003, p. 88.

22. Sherry Turkle, "From Powerful Ideas to Powerpoint," *Convergence* 9, no. 2 (2003): 24.

23. David Byrne, *Envisioning Emotional Epistemological Information* (Gottingen, Germany: Steidel Verlag, 2003).

24. Miller McPherson, Matthew Brashears, and Lynn Smith-Lovin, "Social Isolation in America: Changes in Core Discussion Networks over Two Decades," *American Sociological Review* 71 (2006): 353–75. Jerome Groopman, *How Doctors Think* (New York: Houghton Mifflin, 2007), p. 17. Victoria Rideout, Elizabeth Vandewater, and Ellen Wartella, *Zero to Six: Electronic Media in the Lives of Infants, Toddlers and Preschoolers* (Menlo Park, CA: Henry J. Kaiser Family Foundation, 2003), p. 4. Dimitri Christakis, Frederick Zimmerman, David DiGiuseppe, and Carolyn McCarty, "Early Television Exposure and Subsequent Attentional Problems in Children," *Pediatrics* 113, no. 4 (2004): 708–13. *Final Report: National Geographic-Roper Public Affairs 2006 Geographic*

Literacy Study (Washington, DC: National Geographic Education Foundation, May 2006), pp. 6, 28.

25. Michael Posner and Jin Fan, "Attention as an Organ System," in *Topics in Integrative Neuroscience: From Cells to Cognition*, ed. James Pomerantz (New York: Cambridge University Press, 2007).

26. Michael Posner and Mary K. Rothbart, "Attention, Self-Regulation and Consciousness," *Philosophical Transactions: Biological Sciences* 353, no. 1377 (1998): 1916.

27. Mihaly Csikzsentmihalyi, *Flow: The Psychology of Optimal Experience* (New York: Harper Perennial, 1991), pp. 84–85.

28. Ibid.

29. Duane Rumbaugh and David Washburn, "Attention and Memory in Relation to Learning," in *Attention, Memory and Executive Function* (Baltimore, MD: Paul H. Brookes Publishing, 1995), pp. 199–219. Also e-mail communications with Washburn, September 2007.

30. Mary K. Rothbart and M. Rosario Rueda, "The Development of Effortful Control," in *Developing Individuality in the Human Brain: A Tribute to Michael I. Posner*, ed. Ulrich Mayr, Edward Awh, and Steven Keele (Washington, DC: American Psychological Association), p. 170.

31. *Oxford English Dictionary*, vol. 1 (Oxford: Clarendon Press, 1989), p. 765.

32. Cahill, *Irish Saved Civilization*, p. 59.

33. Lewis Lapham, *Waiting for the Barbarians* (London: Verso, 1997), p. 210.

Critical Reading Questions

Summarizing the Text

1. Jackson's argument in this piece (which is necessarily general, given that it is an introduction to a much longer work) posits a cause and an effect. What is the cause? What is the effect? And how, precisely, does the cause create the effect?

2. Jackson also works by analogy, arguing that our present time period is similar to another. In fact, she uses the term *dark age* for both. What earlier dark age is she referring to? And how does she define a dark age—what are its characteristics that we are in danger of recreating?

Establishing the Context

3. It is a commonplace idea that we are overwhelmed by information, and the popular metaphor of web "surfing" suggests that we can only skim over the top of a very deep ocean of information. Do you agree with Jackson's argument, though, that this information overload has caused Americans to be melancholy and detached from one another?

4. Because this piece is just the introduction to a longer book, Jackson cannot sufficiently support her very broad claims with evidence here—it would be tough to prove that we are facing a coming dark age in twenty pages and

several anecdotes. How persuasive is this introduction? Does it lead you to believe that she can marshal convincing evidence in support of her points, or can you discern large holes in her argument or flaws in her logic?

Responding to the Text

5. A popular application for Macintosh computers is a widget that blocks all Internet access—Web, email, Facebook—for a set period of time. It is meant for people who cannot pull themselves away from interconnection in order to concentrate. Do you think you might need this? Do you have difficulty focusing because of all the technological distractions (your phone, email, social-network accounts, and the like)?

6. One definition of an "addict" is "someone who cannot stop engaging in a particular activity, even when the results of that activity have caused him or her great harm." Do you think we are "addicted" to our devices and to being online and available at all times? What harm can you see in this, apart from what Jackson identifies? Do the benefits outweigh the damage?

iPhone Advertisement

The image below is a still from a television commercial for Apple Computer's iPhone.

1. What is the argument of the iPhone ad?
2. How does the image use space to convey its message?
3. How does this image response to Jackson?
4. Find other Web or television advertisements for Apple products. What kinds of design elements does Apple rely on? How does the company attempt to make an argument about its products through the design of its ads?

Why I Blog

Andrew Sullivan

A British-born, gay, HIV-positive conservative, Andrew Sullivan edited the venerable New Republic *magazine while still in his twenties. In 2000, Sullivan became one of the first mainstream journalists to experiment with the new form of writing called "blogging," and he currently edits one of the most read and most influential blogs out there, "The Daily Dish." This article appeared, ironically, in the print magazine* The Atlantic.

The word *blog* is a conflation of two words: *Web* and *log*. It contains in its four letters a concise and accurate self-description: it is a log of thoughts and writing posted publicly on the World Wide Web. In the monosyllabic vernacular of the Internet, *Web log* soon became the word *blog*.

This form of instant and global self-publishing, made possible by technology widely available only for the past decade or so, allows for no retroactive editing (apart from fixing minor typos or small glitches) and removes from the act of writing any considered or lengthy review. It is the spontaneous expression of instant thought—impermanent beyond even the ephemera of daily journalism. It is accountable in immediate and unavoidable ways to readers and other bloggers, and linked via hypertext to continuously multiplying references and sources. Unlike any single piece of print journalism, its borders are extremely porous and its truth inherently transitory. The consequences of this for the act of writing are still sinking in.

A ship's log owes its name to a small wooden board, often weighted with lead, that was for centuries attached to a line and thrown over the stern. The weight of the log would keep it in the same place in the water, like a provisional anchor, while the ship moved away. By measuring the length of line used up in a set period of time, mariners could calculate the speed of their journey (the rope itself was marked by equidistant "knots" for easy measurement). As a ship's voyage progressed, the course came to be marked down in a book that was called a log.

In journeys at sea that took place before radio or radar or satellites or sonar, these logs were an indispensable source for recording what actually happened. They helped navigators surmise where they were and how far they had traveled and how much longer they had to stay at sea. They provided accountability to a ship's owners and traders. They were designed to be as immune to faking as possible. Away from land, there was usually no reliable corroboration of events apart from the crew's own account in the middle of an expanse of blue and gray and green; and in long journeys, memories always blur and facts disperse. A log provided as accurate an account as could be gleaned in real time.

As you read a log, you have the curious sense of moving backward in time as you move forward in pages—the opposite of a book. As you piece together a narrative that was never intended as one, it seems— and is—more truthful. Logs, in this sense, were a form of human self-correction. They amended for hindsight, for the ways in which human beings order and tidy and construct the story of their lives as they look back on them. Logs require a letting-go of narrative because they do not allow for a knowledge of the ending. So they have plot as well as dramatic irony—the reader will know the ending before the writer did.

Anyone who has blogged his thoughts for an extended time will recognize this world. We bloggers have scant opportunity to collect our thoughts, to wait until events have settled and a clear pattern emerges. We blog now—as news reaches us, as facts emerge. This is partly true for all journalism, which is, as its etymology suggests, daily writing, always subject to subsequent revision. And a good columnist will adjust position and judgment and even political loyalty over time, depending on events. But a blog is not so much daily writing as hourly writing. And with that level of timeliness, the provisionality of every word is even more pressing—and the risk of error or the thrill of pre-science that much greater.

No columnist or reporter or novelist will have his minute shifts or constant small contradictions exposed as mercilessly as a blogger's are. A columnist can ignore or duck a subject less noticeably than a blogger committing thoughts to pixels several times a day. A reporter can wait—must wait—until every source has confirmed. A novelist can spend months or years before committing words to the world. For bloggers, the deadline is always now. Blogging is therefore to writing what extreme sports are to athletics: more free-form, more accident-prone, less formal, more alive. It is, in many ways, writing out loud.

You end up writing about yourself, since you are a relatively fixed point in this constant interaction with the ideas and facts of the exterior world. And in this sense, the historic form closest to blogs is the diary. But with this difference: a diary is almost always a private matter. Its raw honesty, its dedication to marking life as it happens and remembering life as it was, makes it a terrestrial log. A few diaries are meant to be read by others, of course, just as correspondence could be—but usually posthumously, or as a way to compile facts for a more considered autobiographical rendering. But a blog, unlike a diary, is instantly public. It transforms this most personal and retrospective of forms into a painfully public and immediate one. It combines the confessional genre with the log form and exposes the author in a manner no author has ever been exposed before.

I remember first grappling with what to put on my blog. It was the spring of 2000 and, like many a freelance writer at the time, I had some vague notion that I needed to have a presence "online." I had no clear idea of what to do, but a friend who ran a Web-design company offered to create a site for me, and, since I was technologically clueless, he also agreed to post various essays and columns as I wrote them. Before too long, this became a chore for him, and he called me one day to say he'd found an online platform that was so simple I could henceforth post all my writing myself. The platform was called Blogger.

As I used it to post columns or links to books or old essays, it occurred to me that I could also post new writing—writing that could even be exclusive to the blog. But what? Like any new form, blogging did not start from nothing. It evolved from various journalistic traditions. In my case, I drew on my mainstream-media experience to navigate the virgin sea. I had a few early inspirations: the old Notebook section of *The New Republic*, a magazine that, under the editorial guidance of Michael Kinsley, had introduced a more English style of crisp, short commentary into what had been a more high-minded genre of American opinion writing. *The New Republic* had also pioneered a Diarist feature on the last page, which was designed to be a more personal, essayistic, first-person form of journalism. Mixing the two genres, I did what I had been trained to do—and improvised.

I'd previously written online as well, contributing to a listserv for gay writers and helping Kinsley initiate a more discursive form of online writing for Slate, the first magazine published exclusively on the Web. As soon as I began writing this way, I realized that the online form rewarded a colloquial, unfinished tone. In one of my early Kinsley-guided experiments, he urged me not to think too hard before writing. So I wrote as I'd write an e-mail—with only a mite more circumspection. This is hazardous, of course, as anyone who has ever clicked Send in a fit of anger or hurt will testify. But blogging requires an embrace of such hazards, a willingness to fall off the trapeze rather than fail to make the leap.

From the first few days of using the form, I was hooked. The simple experience of being able to directly broadcast my own words to readers was an exhilarating literary liberation. Unlike the current generation of writers, who have only ever blogged, I knew firsthand what the alternative meant. I'd edited a weekly print magazine, *The New Republic*, for five years, and written countless columns and essays for a variety of traditional outlets. And in all this, I'd often chafed, as most writers do, at the endless delays, revisions, office politics, editorial fights, and last-minute cuts for space that dead-tree publishing entails. Blogging—even to an audience of a few hundred in the early days—was intoxicatingly free in comparison. Like taking a narcotic.

It was obvious from the start that it was revolutionary. Every writer since the printing press has longed for a means to publish himself and reach—instantly—any reader on Earth. Every professional writer has paid some dues waiting for an editor's nod, or enduring a publisher's incompetence, or being ground to literary dust by a legion of fact-checkers and copy editors. If you added up the time a writer once had to spend finding an outlet, impressing editors, sucking up to proprietors, and proofreading edits, you'd find another lifetime buried in the interstices. But with one click of the Publish Now button, all these troubles evaporated.

Alas, as I soon discovered, this sudden freedom from above was immediately replaced by insurrection from below. Within minutes of my posting something, even in the earliest days, readers responded. E-mail seemed to unleash their inner beast. They were more brutal than any editor, more persnickety than any copy editor, and more emotionally unstable than any colleague.

Again, it's hard to overrate how different this is. Writers can be sensitive, vain souls, requiring gentle nurturing from editors, and oddly susceptible to the blows delivered by reviewers. They survive, for the most part, but the thinness of their skins is legendary. Moreover, before the blogosphere, reporters and columnists were largely shielded from this kind of direct hazing. Yes, letters to the editor would arrive in due course and subscriptions would be canceled. But reporters and columnists tended to operate in a relative sanctuary, answerable mainly to their editors, not readers. For a long time, columns were essentially monologues published to applause, muffled murmurs, silence, or a distant heckle. I'd gotten blowback from pieces before—but in an amorphous, time-delayed, distant way. Now the feedback was instant, personal, and brutal.

And so blogging found its own answer to the defensive counterblast from the journalistic establishment. To the charges of inaccuracy and unprofessionalism, bloggers could point to the fierce, immediate scrutiny of their readers. Unlike newspapers, which would eventually publish corrections in a box of printed spinach far from the original error, bloggers had to walk the walk of self-correction in the same space and in the same format as the original screwup. The form was more accountable, not less, because there is nothing more conducive to professionalism than being publicly humiliated for sloppiness. Of course, a blogger could ignore an error or simply refuse to acknowledge mistakes. But if he persisted, he would be razzed by competitors and assailed by commenters and abandoned by readers. In an era when the traditional media found itself beset by scandals as disparate as Stephen Glass, Jayson Blair, and Dan Rather, bloggers survived the first assault on their worth. In time, in fact, the high standards expected of well-trafficked bloggers spilled over into greater accountability, transparency, and punctiliousness among the media powers that were. Even *New York Times* columnists were forced to admit when they had been wrong.

The blog remained a *superficial* medium, of course. By superficial, I mean simply that blogging rewards brevity and immediacy. No one wants to read a 9,000-word treatise online. On the Web, one-sentence links are as legitimate as thousand-word diatribes—in fact, they are often valued more. And, as Matt Drudge told me when I sought advice from the master in 2001, the key to understanding a blog is to realize that it's a broadcast, not a publication. If it stops moving, it dies. If it stops paddling, it sinks.

But the superficiality masked considerable depth—greater depth, from one perspective, than the traditional media could offer. The reason was a single technological innovation: the hyperlink. An old-school columnist can write 800 brilliant words analyzing or commenting on, say, a new think-tank report or scientific survey. But in reading it on paper, you have to take the columnist's presentation of the material on faith, or be convinced by a brief quotation (which can always be misleading out of context). Online, a hyperlink to the original source transforms the experience. Yes, a few sentences of bloggy spin may not be as satisfying as a full column, but the ability to read the primary material instantly—in as careful or shallow a fashion as you choose— can add much greater context than anything on paper. Even a blogger's chosen pull quote, unlike a columnist's, can be effortlessly checked against the original. Now this innovation, pre-dating blogs but popularized by them, is increasingly central to mainstream journalism.

A blog, therefore, bobs on the surface of the ocean but has its anchorage in waters deeper than those print media is technologically able to exploit. It disempowers the writer to that extent, of course. The blogger can get away with less and afford fewer pretensions of authority. He is—more than any writer of the past—a node among other nodes, connected but unfinished without the links and the comments and the track-backs that make the blogosphere, at its best, a conversation, rather than a production.

A writer fully aware of and at ease with the provisionality of his own work is nothing new. For centuries, writers have experimented with forms that suggest the imperfection of human thought, the inconstancy of human affairs, and the humbling, chastening passage of time. If you compare the meandering, questioning, unresolved dialogues of Plato with the definitive, logical treatises of Aristotle, you see the difference between a skeptic's spirit translated into writing and a spirit that seeks to bring some finality to the argument. Perhaps the greatest single piece of Christian apologetics, Pascal's *Pensées*, is a series of meandering, short, and incomplete stabs at arguments, observations, insights. Their lack of finish is what makes them so compelling—arguably more compelling than a polished treatise by Aquinas.

Or take the brilliant polemics of Karl Kraus, the publisher of and main writer for *Die Fackel*, who delighted in constantly twitting authority with slashing aphorisms and rapid-fire bursts of invective. Kraus had something rare in his day: the financial wherewithal to self-publish. It gave him a fearlessness that is now available to anyone who can afford a computer and an Internet connection.

But perhaps the quintessential blogger *avant la lettre* was Montaigne. His essays were published in three major editions, each one longer and more complex than the previous. A passionate skeptic, Montaigne amended, added to, and amplified the essays for each edition, making them three-dimensional through time. In the best modern translations, each essay is annotated, sentence by sentence, paragraph by paragraph, by small letters (A, B, and C) for each major edition, helping the reader see how each rewrite added to or subverted, emphasized or ironized, the version before. Montaigne was living his skepticism, daring to show how a writer evolves, changes his mind, learns new things, shifts perspectives, grows older—and that this, far from being something that needs to be hidden behind a veneer of unchanging authority, can become a virtue, a new way of looking at the pretensions of authorship and text and truth. Montaigne, for good measure, also peppered his essays with myriads of what bloggers would call external links. His own thoughts are strewn with and complicated by the aphorisms and anecdotes of others. Scholars of the sources note that many of these "money quotes" were deliberately taken out of context, adding layers of irony to writing that was already saturated in empirical doubt.

To blog is therefore to let go of your writing in a way, to hold it at arm's length, open it to scrutiny, allow it to float in the ether for a while, and to let others, as Montaigne did, pivot you toward relative truth. A blogger will notice this almost immediately upon starting. Some e-mailers, unsurprisingly, know more about a subject than the blogger does. They will send links, stories, and facts, challenging the blogger's view of the world, sometimes outright refuting it, but more frequently adding context and nuance and complexity to an idea. The role of a blogger is not to defend against this but to embrace it. He is similar in this way to the host of a dinner party. He can provoke discussion or take a position, even passionately, but he also must create an atmosphere in which others want to participate.

That atmosphere will inevitably be formed by the blogger's personality. The blogosphere may, in fact, be the least veiled of any forum in which a writer dares to express himself. Even the most careful and self-aware blogger will reveal more about himself than he wants to in a few unguarded sentences and publish them before he has the sense to hit Delete. The wise panic that can paralyze a writer—the fear that he will be exposed, undone, humiliated—is not available to a blogger. You can't have blogger's block. You have to express yourself now, while your emotions roil, while your temper flares, while your humor lasts. You can try to hide yourself from real scrutiny, and the exposure it demands, but it's hard. And that's what makes blogging as a form stand out: it is rich in personality. The faux intimacy of the Web experience, the closeness of the e-mail and the instant message, seeps through. You feel as if you know bloggers as they go through their lives, experience the same things you are experiencing, and share the moment. When readers of my blog bump into me in person, they invariably address me as Andrew. Print readers don't do that. It's Mr. Sullivan to them.

On my blog, my readers and I experienced 9/11 together, in real time. I can look back and see not just how I responded to the event, but how I responded to it at 3:47 that afternoon. And at 9:46 that night. There is a vividness to this immediacy that cannot be rivaled by print. The same goes for the 2000 recount, the Iraq War, the revelations of Abu Ghraib, the death of John Paul II, or any of the other history-making events of the past decade. There is simply no way to write about them in real time without revealing a huge amount about yourself. And the intimate bond this creates with readers is unlike the bond that *The Times*, say, develops with its readers through the same events. Alone in front of a computer, at any moment, are two people: a blogger and a reader. The proximity is palpable, the moment human—whatever authority a blogger has is derived not from the institution he works for but from the humanness he conveys. This is writing with emotion not just under but always breaking through the surface. It renders a writer and a reader not just connected but linked in a visceral, personal way. The only term that really describes this is *friendship*. And it is a relatively new thing to write for thousands and thousands of friends.

These friends, moreover, are an integral part of the blog itself—sources of solace, company, provocation, hurt, and correction. If I were to do an inventory of the material that appears on my blog, I'd estimate that a good third of it is reader-generated, and a good third of my time is spent absorbing readers' views, comments, and tips. Readers tell me of breaking stories, new perspectives, and counterarguments to prevailing assumptions. And this is what blogging, in turn, does to reporting. The traditional method involves a journalist searching for key sources, nurturing them, and sequestering them from his rivals.

A blogger splashes gamely into a subject and dares the sources to come to him.

Some of this material—e-mails from soldiers on the front lines, from scientists explaining new research, from dissident Washington writers too scared to say what they think in their own partisan redoubts—might never have seen the light of day before the blogosphere. And some of it, of course, is dubious stuff. Bloggers can be spun and misled as easily as traditional writers—and the rigorous source assessment that good reporters do can't be done by e-mail. But you'd be surprised by what comes unsolicited into the in-box, and how helpful it often is.

Not all of it is mere information. Much of it is also opinion and scholarship, a knowledge base that exceeds the research department of any newspaper. A good blog is your own private Wikipedia. Indeed, the most pleasant surprise of blogging has been the number of people working in law or government or academia or rearing kids at home who have real literary talent and real knowledge, and who had no outlet—until now. There is a distinction here, of course, between the edited use of e-mailed sources by a careful blogger and the often mercurial cacophony on an unmediated comments section. But the truth is out there—and the miracle of e-mail allows it to come to you.

Fellow bloggers are always expanding this knowledge base. Eight years ago, the blogosphere felt like a handful of individual cranks fighting with one another. Today, it feels like a universe of cranks, with vast, pulsating readerships, fighting with one another. To the neophyte reader, or blogger, it can seem overwhelming. But there is a connection between the intimacy of the early years and the industry it has become today. And the connection is human individuality.

The pioneers of online journalism—Slate and Salon—are still very popular, and successful. But the more memorable stars of the Internet—even within those two sites—are all personally branded. Daily Kos, for example, is written by hundreds of bloggers, and amended by thousands of commenters. But it is named after Markos Moulitsas, who started it, and his own prose still provides a backbone to the front-page blog. The biggest news-aggregator site in the world, the Drudge Report, is named after its founder, Matt Drudge, who somehow conveys a unified sensibility through his selection of links, images, and stories. The vast, expanding universe of The Huffington Post still finds some semblance of coherence in the Cambridge-Greek twang of Arianna; the entire world of online celebrity gossip circles the drain of Perez Hilton; and the investigative journalism, reviewing, and commentary of Talking Points Memo is still tied together by the tone of Josh Marshall. Even Slate is unimaginable without Mickey Kaus's voice.

What endures is a human brand. Readers have encountered this phenomenon before—*I.F. Stone's Weekly* comes to mind—but not to this extent. It stems, I think, from the conversational style that blogging rewards. What you want in a conversationalist is as much character as authority. And if you think of blogging as more like talk radio or cable news than opinion magazines or daily newspapers, then this personalized emphasis is less surprising. People have a voice for radio and a face for television. For blogging, they have a sensibility.

But writing in this new form is a collective enterprise as much as it is an individual one—and the connections between bloggers are as important as the content on the blogs. The links not only drive conversation, they drive readers. The more you link, the more others will link to you, and the more traffic and readers you will get. The zero-sum game of old media—in which *Time* benefits from *Newsweek*'s decline and vice versa—becomes win-win. It's great for *Time* to be linked to by *Newsweek* and the other way round. One of the most prized statistics in the blogosphere is therefore not the total number of readers or page views, but the "authority" you get by being linked to by other blogs. It's an indication of how central you are to the online conversation of humankind.

The reason this open-source market of thinking and writing has such potential is that the always adjusting and evolving collective mind can rapidly filter out bad arguments and bad ideas. The flip side, of course, is that bloggers are also human beings. Reason is not the only fuel in the tank. In a world where no distinction is made between good traffic and bad traffic, and where emotion often rules, some will always raise their voice to dominate the conversation; others will pander shamelessly to their readers' prejudices; others will start online brawls for the fun of it. Sensationalism, dirt, and the ease of formulaic talking points always beckon. You can disappear into the partisan blogosphere and never stumble onto a site you disagree with.

But linkage mitigates this. A Democratic blog will, for example, be forced to link to Republican ones, if only to attack and mock. And it's in the interests of both camps to generate shared traffic. This encourages polarized slugfests. But online, at least you see both sides. Reading *The Nation* or *National Review* before the Internet existed allowed for more cocooning than the wide-open online sluice gates do now. If there's more incivility, there's also more fluidity. Rudeness, in any case, isn't the worst thing that can happen to a blogger. Being ignored is. Perhaps the nastiest thing one can do to a fellow blogger is to rip him apart and fail to provide a link.

A successful blog therefore has to balance itself between a writer's own take on the world and others. Some bloggers collect, or "aggregate," other bloggers' posts with dozens of quick links and minimalist opinion topspin: Glenn Reynolds at Instapundit does this for the right-of-center; Duncan Black at Eschaton does it for the left. Others are more eclectic, or aggregate links in a particular niche, or cater to a settled and knowledgeable reader base. A "blogroll" is an indicator of whom you respect enough to keep in your galaxy. For many years, I kept my reading and linking habits to a relatively small coterie of fellow political bloggers. In today's blogosphere, to do this is to embrace marginality. I've since added links to religious blogs and literary ones and scientific ones and just plain weird ones. As the blogosphere has expanded beyond anyone's capacity to absorb it, I've needed an assistant and interns to scour the Web for links and stories and photographs to respond to and think about. It's a difficult balance, between your own interests and obsessions, and the knowledge, insight, and wit of others—but an immensely rich one. There are times, in fact, when a blogger feels less like a writer than an online disc jockey, mixing samples of tunes and generating new melodies through mashups while also making his own music. He is both artist and producer—and the beat always goes on.

If all this sounds postmodern, that's because it is. And blogging suffers from the same flaws as postmodernism: a failure to provide stable truth or a permanent perspective. A traditional writer is valued by readers precisely because they trust him to have thought long and hard about a subject, given it time to evolve in his head, and composed a piece of writing that is worth their time to read at length and to ponder. Bloggers don't do this and cannot do this—and that limits them far more than it does traditional long-form writing.

A blogger will air a variety of thoughts or facts on any subject in no particular order other than that dictated by the passing of time. A writer will instead use time, synthesizing these thoughts, ordering them, weighing which points count more than others, seeing how his views evolved in the writing process itself, and responding to an editor's perusal of a draft or two. The result is almost always more measured, more satisfying, and more enduring than a blizzard of posts. The triumphalist notion that blogging should somehow replace traditional writing is as foolish as it is pernicious. In some ways, blogging's gifts to our discourse make the skills of a good traditional writer much more valuable, not less. The torrent of blogospheric insights, ideas, and arguments places a greater premium on the person who can finally make sense of it all, turning it into something more solid, and lasting, and rewarding.

The points of this essay, for example, have appeared in shards and fragments on my blog for years. But being forced to order them in my head and think about them for a longer stretch has helped me understand them better, and perhaps express them more clearly. Each week, after a few hundred posts, I also write an actual newspaper column. It invariably turns out to be more considered, balanced, and evenhanded than the blog. But the blog will always inform and enrich the column, and often serve as a kind of free-form, free-associative research. And an essay like this will spawn discussion best handled on a blog. The conversation, in other words, is the point, and the different idioms used by the conversationalists all contribute something of value to it. And so, if the defenders of the old media once viscerally regarded blogging as some kind of threat, they are starting to see it more as a portal, and a spur.

There is, after all, something simply irreplaceable about reading a piece of writing at length on paper, in a chair or on a couch or in bed. To use an obvious analogy, jazz entered our civilization much later than composed, formal music. But it hasn't replaced it; and no jazz musician would ever claim that it could. Jazz merely demands a different way of playing and listening, just as blogging requires a different mode of writing and reading. Jazz and blogging are intimate, improvisational, and individual—but also inherently collective. And the audience talks over both.

The reason they talk while listening, and comment or link while reading, is that they understand that this is a kind of music that needs to be engaged rather than merely absorbed. To listen to jazz as one would listen to an aria is to miss the point. Reading at a monitor, at a desk, or on an iPhone provokes a querulous, impatient, distracted attitude, a demand for instant, usable information, that is simply not conducive to opening a novel or a favorite magazine on the couch. Reading on paper evokes a more relaxed and meditative response. The message dictates the medium. And each medium has its place—as long as one is not mistaken for the other.

In fact, for all the intense gloom surrounding the newspaper and magazine business, this is actually a golden era for journalism. The blogosphere has added a whole new idiom to the act of writing and has introduced an entirely new generation to nonfiction. It has enabled writers to write out loud in ways never seen or understood before. And yet it has exposed a hunger and need for traditional writing that, in the age of television's dominance, had seemed on the wane.

Words, of all sorts, have never seemed so now.

This article available online at: http://www.theatlantic.com/magazine/archive/2008/11/why-i-blog/7060/

Critical Reading Questions

Summarizing the Text

1. What is Sullivan's argument? What is his definition of a *blog*? What are the crucial elements of a blog, and how does it differ from other forms of journalism and/or personal writing?

2. "Aggregating content" is, Sullivan argues, a key virtue of a blog. What does it mean to aggregate content?

Establishing the Context

3. Sullivan celebrates the "superficial" nature of blogging and online writing in general. How can something superficial be of value, especially when it deals (as Sullivan's blog does) with such weighty issues?

4. Apply Jackson's argument to Sullivan's explanation of the value of blogging. Where Jackson appears to fear superficiality, Sullivan celebrates it. Where, however, might these two be in agreement?

5. Describing a blog by writing in a more traditional medium (the long-form magazine feature) might be considered ironic. How does Sullivan use this form to underscore the strengths of a blog? When might long-form magazine journalism be superior to or more useful than a blog?

Responding to the Text

6. Do you agree that this is a "golden era for journalism"? Why does Sullivan believe this? What purpose does journalism serve in our society?

7. What kinds of things might you write about in a blog? What might you save for a more formal medium?

8. Wikipedia and blogs both undermine the "authority of the writer," Sullivan argues. How?

Confessions of a 30-Year-Old Gamer

Ta-Nehisi Coates

Coates, a Baltimore native brought up in an unconventional home (documented in his 2008 memoir The Beautiful Struggle: A Father, Two Sons, and an Unlikely Road to Manhood), *has written for publications such as the* Village Voice *and* Time, *where this essay appeared. In this essay, he reminisces about his former — and ongoing — obsession with MMOGs (Massive Multiplayer Online Games) and how it has affected his domestic life.*

Last spring I took the measure of my life, and decided that my favorite video game, World of Warcraft, had to go.

I was 30, and by most objective standards, was doing pretty well. I lived in an old building in majestic Harlem, with a lovely son and partner, and made a show of wearing a suit and fedora to a job that merely requested jeans and a collar. I had a joint bank account and dental insurance. Yet, on any given day, if you'd asked me about my greatest accomplishment, it invariably began with my second life — the one in which I was a seven-foot blue elf whose hobbies included firing crossbows, trapping wild boars and reenacting the video for Michael

Jackson's "Billie Jean." In May I quit because I didn't want any illusions about which of my two lives [was] more important.

Like most of my generation, I was raised on video games. Like most of my generation, I assumed that this obsession would pass at the proper time—say when I turned 30. But like most of my generation, I was wrong. Our assumptions were based on the idea that video games would never grow up. But no genre has worked harder to disprove that maxim than MMOGs—Massively Multiplayer Online Games. Unlike with normal video games, where you interact with just a computer, MMOGs allow millions of people to play with each other in sprawling online virtual worlds. Most MMOGs target people like me who, as kids, took 20-sided dice and J.R.R. Tolkien a little too seriously, and none do it better than World of Warcraft. At last count there were 8 million people journeying through its fantasy world known as Azeroth.

All those trips to Azeroth add up to a lot of money. WoW subsists on a monthly subscription fee of $14.95, which means Blizzard rakes in hundreds of millions of dollars monthly. Their clientele are mostly young men like myself—the same young men who've been giving studio executives headaches as we abandon the box office and TV.

It doesn't take much to see why. This summer I could have paid 10 bucks to watch *Superman Returns* for three hours. Or I could have paid 15 bucks to be Superman whenever I wanted. It isn't just the thrill of playing dress-up either; *Superman Returns* is static, always saddled with the same ending. But WoW, like the real world, changes with every choice I make. Fighting with two swords instead of one gives me a better shot at beating down an opposing mage, while spending hours wending through a haunted manse might win me a coveted staff. Also, unlike with old media, my choices affect people around me. I can form guilds, essentially virtual clubhouses, band together to quest for rare breastplate, recite the assorted lore of Vin Diesel or Chuck Norris, or simply hang out in front of the local inn doing the electric slide.

WoW wasn't the first MMOG I'd ever played, but it is the best. The interface is clean and easy to master. The world feels mammoth and its geography runs the gamut from painted deserts and sprawling savannahs to snow-covered mountains and swamps teeming with gators and fish men. Despite its size, players easily navigate the world via roads, ships, zeppelins, giant bats and mythological creatures like hippogriffs. Players in Azeroth choose to be members of races like humans, orcs, trolls or night elves, and then pledge allegiance to one of two factions. But unlike in other fantasy games, neither side is wholly good or evil, and both factions are under siege from a plague that turns its victims into mindless undead.

Its biggest draw, without a doubt, is its human factor, and WoW's fans have quickly shaped Azeroth into a second Earth. Players hunt for gold, and epic items, then put them up for sale on eBay, thus turning a hobby into a livelihood. They have cyber-sex, date, and get married. They hang out with old friends who may live hundreds of miles away.

I'd started playing MMOGs six years ago, shortly after my son was born. The kid was great from the moment he popped out. My lady and I were not. She was hospitalized with pregnancy-related heart problems. I was fired by a small alternative weekly newspaper in Philadelphia. In those days, we lived in a small one-bedroom apartment in Delaware. Paychecks floated into our mailbox randomly. We ate take-out more then we cooked. Our rent was habitually late. We spent many hours home together with a new son, and when we weren't looking, the walls closed in on us.

It was at that point that I retreated to my old haven of video games and purchased Everquest, the forerunner to WoW. The dude at the counter rang me up and laughed as he said "Picking up Evercrack, I see." I didn't fully get the joke until two years later. By then I was playing the game 16 hours a day. I'd gained 30 pounds. I didn't have a job. The end came one weekend when I played a marathon session, which I only interrupted for trips to Dunkin' Donuts. I quit, lost the weight, and put my life back in order. But when WoW premiered in 2004, it promised to be the MMOG that allowed you to have a life. The game even gives bonuses to players who don't log in for periods of time. Its loading screen features quotes like, "Moderation in all things, even World of Warcraft."

I played two characters—a hunter named Longaxe, and a shadow priest named Salaam. When I brought Longaxe, from his meager starting zone in the quiet forest of Tendrassil to the capital city of Stormwind, I felt like I had actually gone from Wisconsin to New York. The people were of all races, from gnomes to dwarves to regular old humans. Vendors sold cheeses, meats, cloaks and hats. Monks would train you in the art of swords. Giant griffins ferried you to smaller far-flung towns. WoW's art style is cartoonish, and each of its many worlds more fantastical than the last, so it always amazed me that, on an emotional level, I believed it.

But there was something else about it, something I really didn't want to admit. I asked Paul Sams, the Blizzard COO, why people played WoW and his answer was simple, if a bit depressing: "How often in your everyday world do you get to feel heroic?" he said. "How often do you get to step into a world and do something big and meaningful? People need an escape from ordinary life. It's just something people need."

What's implicit in that, however, is a sense of defeat, an admission that for the denizens of Azeroth, our normal lives just aren't good enough. This is why most adults who play WoW are ashamed, and, on a scale of morals, rate their hobby only slightly above porn. We ourselves razz those who are ultra-accomplished in WoW, asserting that they are either kids with no responsibilities, or more likely, dudes who can't get laid. This unspoken envy only conceals a potentially darker truth—that we've all come to accept that WoW is fundamentally better than our real lives.

That conclusion, of course, can have unfortunate consequences for people in our real lives. Shelly Quintana, a 30-year-old New Jersey housewife and mother of three, is one such person, but she isn't taking it lying down. A native of New Zealand, Quintana has been married for 10 years, but she says her husband has spent much of their marriage cruising through games like WoW. "He's excellent with the kids, but our relationship is nonexistent," says Quintana. "I'm completely torn—he provides for us, and he works really long hours. But at the same time I believe he owes me some companionship."

Quintana enlisted the Internet, of all things, to strike back. She started the website gamingsucks.com, which features a blog that chronicles the travails of "gamer widows," women whose husbands are more interested in building up their character in-game than building relationships with their wives. Quintana's site simmers with sexual tension; a comic strip that she draws tells married gamers to cut off the PC and "push some real buttons."

Most of the attacks on MMOGs sounded familiar to me—in the '80s when I played Dungeons & Dragons, it was taken as practically gospel that the game was the devil's work. But while I knew, even as a kid, that those claims were stupid, I wasn't so sure about WoW. I believed that there was something wrong about how easy excitement came in WoW.

And indeed, the summer after I abandoned WoW, I learned much more subtle pleasures. I took a basic Spanish class. I purchased a book on drawing. I woke up at 5 a.m. and ran through Central Park. But still, I felt like I had left something behind, something old and essential, that went back long before I started playing WoW.

I was born into a big family with four brothers, and it is no stretch to say many of my great memories are virtual. We were all very different, some of us bookish, some of us athletic. When I was seven, my father brought home a used Commodore 64, and it almost immediately became a bonding point for my brothers and me. Our contests were no longer as simple as who had the best natural jump-shot, or an innate feel for chess; video games featured all sorts of contests, and thus became a lingua franca for us all.

But while some of my fondest memories are based around video games, it's the people involved that I remember the most. Even with WoW, my best times were spent playing with my younger brother. We lived five hours apart, and saw each other only a few times a year.

But when we were online, it was almost as if we were sitting in the same bar, presiding over the same pitcher.

What I came to understand was that WoW was not necessarily an escape, but a surrogate for a community that is harder and harder to find in the real world. I lived further from my parents and siblings than my parents had. I wasn't raised in the church. In my 20s, I built a shocking amount of community around illicit substances and bars. But with age and a child, that was no longer as attractive or even possible. Into that void, I brought WoW, which instantly connected me with the world—not just mine, but others I could never have imagined or found on my own.

It may not shock you to learn that by September of last year, I had returned to WoW. I missed the ores, the swords and the small hamlets of make-believe. But more than that, I missed my guild, Gnomeland Security, a loose cross-section of military guys, history majors, high school students, writers and singers. They were the place where every-one knew my name—even if they didn't.

Of course, even as I write this, I'm not completely convinced. The anonymity of the Internet and digital worlds allows for amazing inci-vility. And in mid-November I watched one of the most devious acts I've ever seen in a MMOG. A guild decided to hold an online memorial service for a player who'd died in real life. In a macabre but heart-felt gesture, the player's character was accessed and brought out to a lake in an area known as Winterspring. A rival guild caught word of the event and ambushed the other players, killing the deceased person's character first and then killing everyone else in the guild. The rival guild then posted a video of the entire event online.

I suppose these are just the same kind of problems we deal with in the so-called real world—certainly I see my share of the same walking down any street in New York.

But even getting past that, I still have one problem of my own, one that I still haven't solved. My son is six now, and no longer willing to accept my proclamations unquestioningly. On Saturday evening, he is liable to wander into the room, stare at the screen for a few seconds and then ask questions—Who is that? Where are you going? Did you win?—that I am too afraid to answer. I still can't shake the old taboos, and part of me wants desperately to impute them on my son. I am clear on what's being recreated on this second earth. But in [an] age of climate change and war, I afraid I might be teaching him to abandon the first.

Find this article at http://www.time.com/time/arts/article/0,8599,1577502.00.html

Critical Reading Questions

Summarizing the Text

1. Is Coates making an argument here? Or is this just a personal reminiscence?
2. What larger point is he trying to make about the online "memorial service" and its ambush by rival players?

Establishing the Context

3. In many ways, Coates's article is interesting for what it leaves out. As he details in his memoir, he was brought up by a father who kept multiple households and who was a political radical, a former Black Panther. Coates also grew up in the tough streets of West Baltimore, Maryland. Yet in this article, he mentions none of this and instead writes of himself as just a "gamer," a type often associated with middle-class, socially inept white males. How does this self-portrayal affect the piece's message?
4. What role have MMOGs played in his life? How, he suggests, will this change now that his son is old enough to question what he's doing?

Responding to the Text

5. Role-playing games, from Dungeons & Dragons to The Sims to Second Life to World of Warcraft, provide their players with an alternate persona. Why do we seek out alternate personae? For those who do not play online games, what other ways can they access and inhabit an alternate persona?
6. This piece is an odd inclusion in a chapter that is largely about *information* on the Internet. How can an online game be seen as part of the "universe of information" on the Internet? How might Katherine Mangu-Ward analyze MMOGs and the actions (such as the ambush of the memorial service) players have their characters commit?

Questions for Short Projects or Group Presentations

1. How reliant are you on technology? Is Vaidhyanathan right that you are not as dependent upon, or conversant with, electronic information as many people think you are? Or is Jackson right that we have become so addicted to our devices that it is harming our quality of life in ways we can't yet even see?

2. Contribute to a Wikipedia site. Add valuable material to a preexisting site, and track the changes that are made to your contributions (use the "History" tab for this). Add false information to a popular Wikipedia page and see whether, and how quickly, it is corrected or taken down. What does this tell you about the ultimate reliability of the information on Wikipedia?

3. The "distraction" that Jackson speaks about and the overconfidence in their own digital skills that Vaidhyanathan attributes to young people might contribute to the phenomenon that Manjoo sees. After all, we are more likely to swallow a story if we don't have the patience and concentration to really think about and investigate it. Discuss an instance of this that you see going on in the world today.

4. With your group, empty your pockets and purses and backpacks. Among you, how many devices do you have that can access information wirelessly—your phone, your music player, your pager, your PDA, your laptop? What information do you get from each? How long could you go without all of these devices?

Questions for Formal Essays

1. Is there such a thing as "Person 2.0," as Zadie Smith suggests? Synthesize several of the readings—Carr, Manjoo, Vaidhyanathan— with Smith. Do they add up to a coherent (if pessimistic) portrait of a new kind of person?
2. Jackson and Carr both argue that deep processes in our brains are being altered and even atrophied as a result of our dependence on technology. How are Jackson's and Carr's arguments different, though, in terms of how these alterations will manifest themselves? How might they respond to Andrew Sullivan's embrace of precisely the kind of hit-and-run writing and thinking that characterizes blogs, and digital writing in general?
3. Wikipedia and the net in general encourage people to think, as many early Internet enthusiasts argued, that "content wants to be free" (in all senses of the word). However, in the academic environment, many ideas are owned and are, in fact, sources of income. How might universities adapt to students' changing views of the ownership of ideas? How might plagiarism policies reflect the new reality?

What's an Education For? 5

CHAPTER INTRODUCTION

The "American Dream," a founding myth of our nation and one that continues to draw immigrants to the United States, says that in America anyone, no matter what circumstances they were born into, can be a success. Taking advantage of America's public education and higher education systems has always been a part of that dream. In the United States, elementary schools became free and mandatory in the late nineteenth century; by the time of World War I, free public high schools were almost universal, as well, and according to the *Statistical Abstract of the United States*, the percentage of 25-year-olds with a high school diploma rose from 7 percent in 1900 to 25 percent in 1940 to 85 percent today.

Elementary and secondary schools weren't just a way for individuals to improve their lives. At the turn of the twentieth century, public education became the primary means for a nation that was becoming much more culturally diverse to create a common experience and body of knowledge for all of its citizens. Public schools were the places where children were taught what it meant to be an American citizen. As many historians have noted, the American public education system in a very real sense created the modern American nation.

This is not as much the case anymore. Although public school enrollments remain strong, a significant minority of students attend private schools that have much more curricular freedom. More students are homeschooled today than ever before, and those numbers continue to grow (although they still account for only about 1 percent of primary-school-aged children).

Public schools themselves are no longer monolithic. Income disparities between rich and poor school districts create unequal public schools (as schools are largely funded by local taxes), and a powerful "school-choice" movement seeks to give parents "vouchers" to take their children out of failing neighborhood schools and use the money for private school tuition. Within the public school system, "charter school" organizers seek to create public schools with specialized missions and curricula. If we were to sum up these trends, we'd have to say that a dominant and largely standardized public school system and curriculum that dominated through the 1960s or 1970s is fading away, and today the schools, while still a powerful means by which society conveys its values, are no longer as effective or influential in "creating America" as they used to be.

Higher education has experienced even more dramatic changes from the late 1800s to today. At the end of the nineteenth century, only about 3 percent of the population earned a bachelor's degree. In 1950, the number was approximately 14 percent. In 2000, almost 25 percent of Americans had a bachelor's degree or higher, and in 2009 the Census Bureau reported that 55 percent had attended at least some college.

If a quarter of the population graduates from college, why are they going? Why do people invest, at times, more than $100,000 in their education? What do they get out of it? And how is a college education changing as the population of students is growing, and growing much more diverse? These are the questions that interest the authors included in this chapter.

A basic question about higher education has always been whether one should be educated *for* something, or whether being "educated" was a benefit in itself. Those who argue the latter tend to support what's called the "liberal arts" curriculum—a broad set of classes in a wide variety of subjects. The liberal arts curriculum familiarizes students with the timeless questions and ideas that advocates of such a curriculum believe all educated people should know. If you have distribution requirements or a core curriculum at your college or university, you are receiving at least a little bit of a liberal arts education—you learn about the arts and about how science works, you learn to do higher math, you learn some history, you read some literature, and so forth. The idea behind the liberal education is twofold: first, that as members of the same culture, we should all know some basic things in common; second, that engaging with these different "ways of knowing" represented by the arts, humanities, social sciences, and sciences trains you to be a better thinker and, thus, gives you a wide variety of basic problem-solving and communications skills that you can use in any profession.

Several arguments counter the liberal arts model. People have always objected that a liberal arts education doesn't really train you for anything in particular, except graduate school—we've all heard the jokes about how an English or philosophy or art history degree should also train students to say, "Do you want fries with that?" But as college tuitions have skyrocketed in the past twenty years, this is a more serious concern than ever. Many private liberal arts schools charge more than $40,000 a year just for tuition, but what is even more remarkable is the precipitous rise in tuition at public universities, where state funding has been cut by 70 or 80 percent over the past decades. (Some of your parents might recall paying their semester's tuition bill with a $100 bill, and getting change in return.) If you are going to invest that kind of money in an education, shouldn't you be able to start earning that money back right away? Shouldn't colleges prepare you for a job that you can step into right away? Perhaps a tacit response to this rhetorical question is the fact that business administration is the most popular major among American college students.

Other voices question the way that college is delivered. The American higher educational system as we know it today is actually a hybrid, blending the student-centered liberal arts training of pre-twentieth-century colleges with the research-intensive demands of doctoral-granting universities. But, many ask, why is this necessary? Why should those who teach also be required to do research? Why do we need ivy-covered buildings, idyllic campus quads, sports teams, and campus clubs? Entrepreneurs such as John Sperling of the University of Phoenix have said, "We don't—we can run a university like a business, turn a profit, and provide our students with precisely what they want and need from an education." Shedding themselves of almost all of the traditional trappings of college life, online and for-profit universities are growing rapidly.

The essays included here fall into two broad clusters. The first collects several "takes" on the meaning or purpose of a college education, particularly a liberal arts education. The second cluster looks not at theoretical questions about the purpose of a college education but at practical issues about how education is delivered and funded. As you read these essays, ask yourself: Why are you here? Why are you in college? What do you want out of college? An April 2010 survey conducted by WiseChoice, a college guidance firm, found that the top three answers to the question "Why are you going to college?" were (1) to have better job opportunities, (2) to reach goals in life, and (3) to earn more money. Well down the list was "to broaden my mind and learn more." Where do you fall on this?

CLUSTER ONE: WHAT'S SO SPECIAL ABOUT A LIBERAL ARTS EDUCATION?

What's a Liberal Arts Education Good For?

Michael Roth

Michael Roth is the president of Wesleyan College in Connecticut, one of the leading liberal arts colleges in the nation. In his role as president of Wesleyan, Roth has sought to reach out beyond his office and contribute to the larger societal debate about the cost of higher education and the value of a liberal education. This article appeared as a blog post on the "aggregator" site The Huffington Post, and Roth even keeps his own blog at http://roth.blogs.wesleyan.edu/.

Over the next few months, in homes across America, seventeen and eighteen-year-olds will be conferring with one another and with their parents about a life changing decision: What college to go to! After months of research, visits, and advice from "experts," these young men and women must now decide: Where will I be happy? Where will I make friends? Where will I get an education I can afford now, and an education that will remain valuable for years after graduation?

In this same time period, our government officials will be deciding where an investment in America's economic infrastructure will do the most good. Commentators from different political perspectives have often noted that one of the great advantages of America is its peerless higher education system. Although other sectors have diminished international roles, higher education in this country continues to inspire admiration around the globe. When politicians talk about this, they often emphasize the research output of large universities, but the focus should also be on American undergraduate liberal arts education. Liberal arts in the USA provide not only a pipeline of talented and prepared students to the great graduate schools, but also a model for life-long learning that other countries are beginning to emulate.

But in these challenging times, what's an education in the liberal arts good for?

Rather than pursuing business, technical or vocational training, some students (and their families) opt for a well-rounded learning experience. Liberal learning introduces them to books and the music, the science and the philosophy that form disciplined yet creative habits of mind that are not *reducible* to the material circumstances of one's life (though they may depend on those circumstances). There is a promise of freedom in the liberal arts education offered by America's most distinctive, selective, and demanding institutions; and it is no surprise that their graduates can be found disproportionately in leadership positions in politics, culture and the economy. A quick look at several members of President-elect Obama's leadership team can stand as an example of how those with a liberal arts education are shaping the future of our society.

What does liberal learning have to do with the harsh realities that our graduates are going to face after college? The development of the capacities for critical inquiry associated with liberal learning can be enormously practical because they become resources on which to draw for continual learning, for making decisions in one's life, and for making a difference in the world. Given the pace of technological and social change, it no longer makes sense to devote four years of higher education entirely to specific skills. Being ready on DAY ONE may have sounded nice on the campaign trail, but being able to draw on one's education over a lifetime is much more practical (and precious). Post secondary education should help students to discover what they love to do, to get better at it, and to develop the ability to continue learning so that they become agents of change—not victims of it.

A successful liberal arts education develops the capacity for innovation and for judgment. Those who can image how best to reconfigure existing resources and project future results will be the shapers of our economy and culture. We seldom get to have all the information we would like, but still we must act. The habits of mind developed in a liberal arts context often result in combinations of focus and flexibility that make for intelligent, and sometimes courageous risk taking for critical assessment of those risks.

The possibilities for free study, experimentation and risk taking need protection and cultivation. Looking around the world, we find no shortage of thugs who desecrate or murder those who seek to produce a more meaningful culture. And here at home we can easily see how mindless indifference to the contemporary arts and sciences facilitates the destruction of cultural memory and creative potential.

America's great universities and colleges must continue to offer a rigorous and innovative liberal arts education. A liberal education remains a resource years after graduation because it helps us to address problems and potential in our lives with passion, commitment and a sense of possibility. A liberal education teaches freedom by example, through the experience of free research, thinking and expression; and ideally, it inspires us to carry this example, this experience of meaningful freedom, from campus to community.

The American model of liberal arts education emphasizes freedom and experimentation as tools for students to develop meaningful ways of working after graduation. Many liberal arts students become innovators and productive risk takers, translating liberal arts ideals into effective, productive work in the world. That is what a liberal education is good for.

We were surprised last week to hear reports from several liberal arts colleges and universities that they had seen significant increases in 'early decision' applications. At Wesleyan, we were up almost 40%, an increase none of us on the staff would have predicted. Early decision applicants have already decided that if they are accepted at the one school to which they apply in the fall, they will attend that school the following year. Many of the highly selective schools like Wesleyan have robust financial aid programs, accepting students regardless of their ability to pay.

In these turbulent economic times, it appears that students want to know as quickly as possible if they are going to be able to attend their first choice school. Many of our talented high school seniors are doubtless deciding that the significant investment of time and money in a liberal arts education will give them the capacity for a sustainable and creative future. Perhaps they have something to teach us!

Critical Reading Questions

Summarizing the Text

1. How does Roth define "liberal education," and from what does he differentiate the term?

2. According to Roth, what is most valuable or important about a liberal education?

Establishing the Context

3. Roth wrote this column in December 2008, when the American economy was in its worst crisis since the Great Depression. How might this economic climate have affected people's feelings about going to, and paying for, college?

4. How does Roth anticipate and respond to the counterargument that people need specialized training from "DAY ONE" of leaving school?

Responding to the Message

5. Roth's argument is largely abstract, using terms such as *rigorous and innovative, free study, experimentation and risk taking,* and *critical inquiry.* He does not provide many specific examples of how these skills can be helpful in real terms. Does this weaken his argument? Or can you think of examples that support Roth's argument?

6. Why did you choose the school you are attending? Why did you choose a liberal education (if you did) or professional training? Think back to when you were selecting a school, and imagine that Roth is writing this to you, attempting to get you to attend Wesleyan. How might you respond to his argument?

College Degree an Overrated Product

Marty Nemko

*Marty Nemko, who bills himself as "One of the Nation's Top Career Coaches,"
holds a Ph.D. in education from the University of California at Berkeley.
He hosts shows on education and career issues on radio stations in the San
Francisco Bay Area and appears frequently on television to talk about these
topics. This article appeared on the opinion page of the* Atlanta Journal-
Constitution *newspaper.*

Among my saddest moments as a career counselor is when I hear a
story like this: "I wasn't a good student in high school, but I wanted to
prove that I can get a college diploma. I'd be the first one in my family
to do it. But it's been five years and $80,000, and I still have 45 credits
to go."

I have a hard time telling such people a killer statistic: Among
high school students who graduated in the bottom 40 percent of their
classes, and whose first institutions were four-year colleges, two-thirds
had not earned diplomas 8 1/2 years later.

Yet four-year colleges admit and take money from hundreds of
thousands of such students each year.

Most college dropouts leave campus having learned little of value,
and with a mountain of debt and devastated self-esteem. Perhaps
worst of all, even those who do manage to graduate too rarely end up
in careers that require a college education. So when you hop in a cab or
walk into a restaurant, you're likely to meet workers who spent years
and their family's life savings on college, only to end up with a job they
could have done as a high school dropout.

Many students are grossly unprepared for college, and even those
who are fully qualified are increasingly unlikely to derive enough
benefit to justify the often six-figure cost and four to six years (or more)
it takes to graduate.

Colleges trumpet the statistic that, over their lifetimes, college
graduates earn more than nongraduates, but that's misleading.
College-bound individuals tend to start out brighter and more
motivated and with better family connections.

Also, their advantage in the job market is eroding as employers
send more professional jobs offshore and hire part-time workers.
Many college graduates are forced to take some very nonprofessional
positions like driving a truck or tending bar.

Colleges are quick to argue that an education is more about enlightenment than employment. That may be the biggest deception of all.
Colleges and universities are businesses, and students are a cost item,
while research is a profit center. As a result, many institutions tend

to educate students in the cheapest way possible: large lecture classes, with necessary small classes staffed by rock-bottom-cost graduate students.

That's not to say that professor-taught classes are so worthwhile. The more prestigious the institution, the more likely that faculty members are hired and promoted more for their research than for their teaching.

So, no surprise, in the latest annual national survey of freshmen conducted by the Higher Education Research Institute at the University of California at Los Angeles, 44.6 percent said they were not satisfied with the quality of instruction they received. Imagine if that many people were dissatisfied with a brand of car: It would quickly go off the market.

Meanwhile, 43.5 percent of freshmen reported "frequently" feeling bored in class, the survey found.

Despite that, do they learn? A 2006 study supported by the Pew Charitable Trusts found that 50 percent of college seniors scored below "proficient" levels on a test that required them to understand the arguments of newspaper editorials or compare credit card offers. The Spellings Report, released in 2006 by a federal commission that examined the future of higher education, said: "Over the past decade, literacy among college graduates has actually declined. . . Employers report repeatedly that many new graduates they hire are not prepared to work, lacking the critical thinking, writing and problem-solving skills needed in today's workplaces."

What must be done to improve undergraduate education?

Colleges should be held at least as accountable as tire companies are.

To be government-approved, all tires must have—prominently molded into the sidewall—ratings of tread life, temperature resistance and traction compared with national benchmarks. Colleges should be required to prominently report the following on their Web sites and in recruitment materials:

- Results of a "value added" test. Just as the No Child Left Behind Act mandates strict accountability of elementary and second-ary schools, all colleges should be required to administer a test to entering freshmen and to students about to graduate. The test should measure skills important for responsible citizenship and career success, such as the ability to draft a persuasive memo, analyze a financial report or use online research tools to develop content for a report.

- The average cash, loan and work-study financial aid for varying levels of family income and assets, broken out by race and gender. And because some colleges use the drug-dealer scam—give the first dose cheap, and then jack up the price—they should be required to provide the average not just for the first year, but also for each year.

- Retention data. Institutions should reveal the percentage of students returning for a second year, broken out by SAT score, race and gender.

- The four-, five- and six-year graduation rates, broken out by SAT score, race and gender.

- Employment data. They should list the percentage of graduates who, within six months of graduation, are in graduate school, unemployed or employed in a job requiring college-level skills, along with salary data.

- Results of recent student-satisfaction surveys.

Meanwhile, what should parents and guardians of prospective students do?

If your child's high school grades and test scores are in the bottom half for his class, resist the attempts of four-year colleges to woo him. Colleges make money whether or not a student learns or graduates or finds good employment. Consider an associate-degree program at a community college, or such nondegree options as apprenticeship programs (examples can be found at www.khake.com), shorter career-preparation programs at community colleges, the military or on-the-job training, especially at the elbow of a successful small-business owner. If your student is in the top half of his high school class and motivated to attend college for reasons other than going to parties and being able to say he went to college, have him apply to perhaps a dozen colleges. It's often wise to choose the college that requires you to pay the least cash and take out the smallest loan.

If your child is one of the rare breed who knows what he wants to do and isn't unduly attracted to academics or to the "Animal House" environment that characterizes many college living arrangements, then take solace in the fact that countless other people have success-fully taken the noncollege road. Some examples: Maya Angelou, David Ben-Gurion, Richard Branson, Coco Chanel, Walter Cronkite, Michael Dell, Walt Disney, Thomas Edison, Henry Ford, Bill Gates, Alex Haley, Ernest Hemingway, Wolfgang Puck, John D. Rockefeller Sr., Ted Turner, Frank Lloyd Wright and nine U.S. presidents, from Washington to Truman.

College is a wise choice for far fewer people than are encouraged to consider it. It's crucial that they evenhandedly weigh the pros and cons of college versus the alternatives. The quality of their lives may depend on that choice.

Critical Reading Questions

Summarizing the Text

1. The article is a rebuttal of the claim that "A college education will benefit anyone who has it." No, Nemko says. Why?

2. What is the unspoken assumption Nemko brings to this article about *why* an education is valuable?

Establishing the Context

3. Engaging in critical analysis of statistics, Nemko grants that college graduates will earn more than nongraduates, but dismisses this conclusion as irrelevant (he says college graduates are on the whole more motivated and privileged anyway, and thus are more likely to succeed). How might you respond similarly to some of the statistics that Nemko uses?

4. Nemko seems to be arguing for a kind of "consumer-information" guide to colleges—something similar to the "Nutritional Information" panel you can find on all packaged food. Certainly, many places (from the Princeton Review to *US News and World Report* to CollegeProwler.com) offer this kind of information now, but Nemko wants the universities themselves to make it available. Do you think that a college education can be quantified and analyzed like any other consumer product?

Responding to the Message

5. Nemko largely refutes the claim that a college education will inevitably be of *economic* benefit to those who obtain it, but Michael Roth and others argue that the benefits of an education cannot be quantified in financial terms. What do you think about this? Are there benefits to college that cannot be quantified?

6. One of Nemko's proposals is that colleges should have what he calls a "value-added" test—an exam administered at the start and end of college that would measure what students had learned. What kinds of questions might be on that exam? How could you write such an exam so that it would apply to everyone, from philosophy majors to pre-meds to engineers?

Mallard Fillmore

Bruce Tinsley

Bruce Tinsley's comic strip "Mallard Fillmore" chronicles the adventures of a politically conservative duck who works at a fictional television station. The strip appears in more than 400 newspapers and online.

Critical Reading Questions

Summarizing the Text

1. What is the joke here?

Establishing the Context

2. Students and parents often lament that a liberal arts degree doesn't prepare students for immediate entry into a job. The comic, though, seems to suggest that a liberal arts education will *never* provide a fulfilling career. Do you agree with this?

Responding to the Message

3. The duck's jab at psychology majors could easily be aimed at English majors, or philosophy majors, or art history majors. How might you rewrite this joke to aim it at those who pursue a preprofessional field of study?

Plan B: Skip College

Jacques Steinberg

Jacques Steinberg covers the higher education beat for the New York Time *and also keeps a* Times *blog, "The Choice," that focuses on college admissions and financial aid. He is the author of* The Gatekeepers: Inside the Admissions Process of an Elite College *(2002). In this article, which appeared on the op-ed page of the* New York Times, *Steinberg questions the assumption that all high school graduates should attend college.*

What's the key to success in the United States?

Short of becoming a reality TV star, the answer is rote and, some would argue, rather knee-jerk: Earn a college degree.

The idea that four years of higher education will translate into a better job, higher earnings and a happier life—a refrain sure to be repeated this month at graduation ceremonies across the country—has been pounded into the heads of schoolchildren, parents and educators. But there's an underside to that conventional wisdom. Perhaps no more than half of those who began a four-year bachelor's degree program in the fall of 2006 will get that degree within six years, according to the latest projections from the Department of Education. (The figures don't include transfer students, who aren't tracked.)

For college students who ranked among the bottom quarter of their high school classes, the numbers are even more stark: 80 percent will probably never get a bachelor's degree or even a two-year associate's degree.

That can be a lot of tuition to pay, without a degree to show for it.

A small but influential group of economists and educators is pushing another pathway: for some students, no college at all. It's time, they say, to develop credible alternatives for students unlikely to be successful pursuing a higher degree, or who may not be ready to do so.

Whether everyone in college needs to be there is not a new question; the subject has been hashed out in books and dissertations for years. But the economic crisis has sharpened that focus, as financially struggling states cut aid to higher education.

Among those calling for such alternatives are the economists Richard K. Vedder of Ohio University and Robert I. Lerman of American University, the political scientist Charles Murray, and James E. Rosenbaum, an education professor at Northwestern. They would steer some students toward intensive, short-term vocational and career training, through expanded high school programs and corporate apprenticeships.

"It is true that we need more nanosurgeons than we did 10 to 15 years ago," said Professor Vedder, founder of the Center for College Affordability and Productivity, a research nonprofit in Washington. "But the numbers are still relatively small compared to the numbers of nurses' aides we're going to need. We will need hundreds of thousands of them over the next decade."

And much of their training, he added, might be feasible outside the college setting.

College degrees are simply not necessary for many jobs. Of the 30 jobs projected to grow at the fastest rate over the next decade in the United States, only seven typically require a bachelor's degree, according to the Bureau of Labor Statistics.

Among the top 10 growing job categories, two require college degrees: accounting (a bachelor's) and postsecondary teachers (a doctorate). But this growth is expected to be dwarfed by the need for registered nurses, home health aides, customer service representatives and store clerks. None of those jobs require a bachelor's degree.

Professor Vedder likes to ask why 15 percent of mail carriers have bachelor's degrees, according to a 1999 federal study.

"Some of them could have bought a house for what they spent on their education," he said.

Professor Lerman, the American University economist, said some high school graduates would be better served by being taught how to behave and communicate in the workplace.

Such skills are ranked among the most desired—even ahead of educational attainment—in many surveys of employers. In one 2008 survey of more than 2,000 businesses in Washington State, employers said entry-level workers appeared to be most deficient in being able to "solve problems and make decisions," "resolve conflict and negotiate," "cooperate with others" and "listen actively."

Yet despite the need, vocational programs, which might teach such skills, have been one casualty in the push for national education standards, which has been focused on preparing students for college.

While some educators propose a radical renovation of the community college system to teach work readiness, Professor Lerman advocates a significant national investment by government and employers in on-the-job apprenticeship training. He spoke with admiration, for example, about a program in the CVS pharmacy chain in which aspiring pharmacists' assistants work as apprentices in hundreds of stores, with many going on to study to become full-fledged pharmacists themselves.

"The health field is an obvious case where the manpower situation is less than ideal," he said. "I would try to work with some of the major employers to develop these kinds of programs to yield mastery in jobs that do demand high expertise."

While no country has a perfect model for such programs, Professor Lerman pointed to a modest study of a German effort done last summer by an intern from that country. She found that of those who passed the Abitur, the exam that allows some Germans to attend college for almost no tuition, 40 percent chose to go into apprenticeships in trades, accounting, sales management, and computers.

"Some of the people coming out of those apprenticeships are in more demand than college graduates," he said, "because they've actually managed things in the workplace."

Still, by urging that some students be directed away from four-year colleges, academics like Professor Lerman are touching a third rail of the education system. At the very least, they could be accused of lowering expectations for some students. Some critics go further, suggesting that the approach amounts to educational redlining, since many of the students who drop out of college are black or non-white Hispanics.

Peggy Williams, a counselor at a high school in suburban New York City with a student body that is mostly black or Hispanic, understands the argument for erring on the side of pushing more students toward college.

"If we're telling kids, 'You can't cut the mustard, you shouldn't go to college or university,' then we're shortchanging them from experiencing an environment in which they might grow," she said.

But Ms. Williams said she would be more willing to counsel some students away from the precollege track if her school, Mount Vernon High School, had a better vocational education alternative. Over the last decade, she said, courses in culinary arts, nursing, dentistry and heating and ventilation system repair were eliminated. Perhaps 1 percent of this year's graduates will complete a concentration in vocational courses, she said, compared with 40 percent a decade ago.

There is another rejoinder to the case against college: People with college and graduate degrees generally earn more than those without them, and face lower risks of unemployment, according to figures from the Bureau of Labor Statistics.

Even those who experience a few years of college earn more money, on average, with less risk of unemployment, than those who merely graduate from high school, said Morton Schapiro, an economist who is the president of Northwestern University.

"You get some return even if you don't get the sheepskin," Mr. Shapiro said.

He warned against overlooking the intangible benefits of a college experience—even an incomplete experience—for those who might not apply what they learned directly to their chosen work.

"It's not just about the economic return," he said. "Some college, whether you complete it or not, contributes to aesthetic appreciation, better health and better voting behavior."

Nonetheless, Professor Rosenbaum said, high school counselors and teachers are not doing enough to alert students unlikely to earn a college degree to the perilous road ahead.

"I'm not saying don't get the B.A," he said. "I'm saying, let's get them some intervening credentials, some intervening milestones. Then, if they want to go further in their education, they can."

Critical Reading Questions

Summarizing the Text

1. What is Steinberg's thesis?
2. How does Steinberg anticipate and defuse some of the objections to his thesis?

Establishing the Context

3. Marty Nemko's article and this one make extremely similar claims, but they differ in the reason behind their claims and in the type of evidence offered to support the reason. What support or evidence does Steinberg offer to back up his reasoning? What authorities does he cite?
4. Encouraging some students not to go to college, Steinberg admits, might be taken as discriminating against ethnic minorities or the poor (who currently graduate from college at lower rates than do the white and affluent). Do you think this is true? How would Steinberg's proposal affect the fact that that African-American and Latino students attend college at lower rates than white students?

Responding to the Message

5. In his first line, Steinberg asks, "What is the key to success in the United States?" For Steinberg, "success" is directly equivalent to "greater earning power"—all of his evidence is about people who do *not* go to college and yet earn a good living. But how else might "success" be defined?

2005 Commencement Address to Kenyon College

David Foster Wallace

David Foster Wallace was one of America's leading fiction writers and an accomplished journalist. Wallace was also a dedicated teacher and spent many years as a creative writing professor at Illinois State University and then at Pomona College. Wallace also suffered from crippling depression that led to his suicide in 2008 at the age of 46. In this speech to Kenyon College's graduating class of 2005, Wallace both embraces and subverts the conventions of the commencement address, and at the same time he provides a powerful endorsement of the value of a liberal education.

Greetings and congratulations to Kenyon's graduating class of 2005. There are these two young fish swimming along and they happen to meet an older fish swimming the other way, who nods at them and says "Morning, boys. How's the water?" And the two young fish swim on for a bit, and then eventually one of them looks over at the other and goes "What the hell is water?"

This is a standard requirement of US commencement speeches, the deployment of didactic little parable-ish stories. The story turns out to be one of the better, less bullshitty conventions of the genre, but if you're worried that I plan to present myself here as the wise, older fish explaining what water is to you younger fish, please don't be. I am not the wise old fish. The point of the fish story is merely that the most obvious, important realities are often the ones that are hardest to see and talk about. Stated as an English sentence, of course, this is just a banal platitude, but the fact is that in the day to day trenches of adult existence, banal platitudes can have a life or death importance, or so I wish to suggest to you on this dry and lovely morning.

Of course the main requirement of speeches like this is that I'm supposed to talk about your liberal arts education's meaning, to try to explain why the degree you are about to receive has actual human value instead of just a material payoff. So let's talk about the single most pervasive cliché in the commencement speech genre, which is that a liberal arts education is not so much about filling you up with knowledge as it is about "teaching you how to think." If you're like me as a student, you've never liked hearing this, and you tend to feel a bit insulted by the claim that you needed anybody to teach you how to think, since the fact that you even got admitted to a college this good seems like proof that you already know how to think. But I'm going to posit to you that the liberal arts cliché turns out not to be insulting at all, because the really significant education in thinking that we're supposed to get in a place like this isn't really about the capacity to think, but rather about the choice of what to think about. If your total freedom of choice regarding what to think about seems too obvious to waste time discussing, I'd ask you to think about fish and water, and to bracket for just a few minutes your scepticism about the value of the totally obvious.

Here's another didactic little story. There are these two guys sitting together in a bar in the remote Alaskan wilderness. One of the guys is religious, the other is an atheist, and the two are arguing about the existence of God with that special intensity that comes after about the fourth beer. And the atheist says: "Look, it's not like I don't have actual reasons for not believing in God. It's not like I haven't ever experimented with the whole God and prayer thing. Just last month I got caught away from the camp in that terrible blizzard, and I was totally lost and I couldn't see a thing, and it was 50 below, and so I tried it: I fell to my knees in the snow and cried out 'Oh, God, if there is a God, I'm lost in this blizzard, and I'm gonna die if you don't help me.'" And now, in the bar, the religious guy looks at the atheist all puzzled. "Well then you must believe now," he says, "After all, here you are, alive." The atheist just rolls his eyes. "No, man, all that was was a couple Eskimos happened to come wandering by and showed me the way back to camp."

It's easy to run this story through kind of a standard liberal arts analysis: the exact same experience can mean two totally different things to two different people, given those people's two different belief templates and two different ways of constructing meaning from experience. Because we prize tolerance and diversity of belief, nowhere in our liberal arts analysis do we want to claim that one guy's interpretation is true and the other guy's is false or bad. Which is fine, except we also never end up talking about just where these individual templates and beliefs come from. Meaning, where they come from INSIDE the two guys. As if a person's most basic orientation toward the world, and the meaning of his experience were somehow just hard-wired, like height or shoe-size; or automatically absorbed from the culture, like language. As if how we construct meaning were not actually a matter of personal, intentional choice. Plus, there's the whole matter of arrogance. The nonreligious guy is so totally certain in his dismissal of the possibility that the passing Eskimos had anything to do with his prayer for help. True, there are plenty of religious people who seem arrogant and certain of their own interpretations, too. They're probably even more repulsive than atheists, at least to most of us. But religious dogmatists' problem is exactly the same as the story's unbeliever: blind certainty, a close-mindedness that amounts to an imprisonment so total that the prisoner doesn't even know he's locked up.

The point here is that I think this is one part of what teaching me how to think is really supposed to mean. To be just a little less arrogant. To have just a little critical awareness about myself and my certainties. Because a huge percentage of the stuff that I tend to be automatically certain of is, it turns out, totally wrong and deluded. I have learned this the hard way, as I predict you graduates will, too.

Here is just one example of the total wrongness of something I tend to be automatically sure of: everything in my own immediate experience supports my deep belief that I am the absolute centre of the universe; the realest, most vivid and important person in existence. We rarely think about this sort of natural, basic self-centredness because it's so socially repulsive. But it's pretty much the same for all of us. It is our default setting, hard-wired into our boards at birth. Think about it: there is no experience you have had that you are not the absolute centre of. The world as you experience it is there in front of YOU or behind YOU, to the left or right of YOU, on YOUR TV or YOUR monitor. And so on. Other people's thoughts and feelings have to be communicated to you somehow, but your own are so immediate, urgent, real.

Please don't worry that I'm getting ready to lecture you about compassion or other-directedness or all the so-called virtues. This is not a matter of virtue. It's a matter of my choosing to do the work of somehow altering or getting free of my natural, hard-wired default setting which is to be deeply and literally self-centred and to see and interpret everything through this lens of self. People who can adjust their natural default setting this way are often described as being "well-adjusted," which I suggest to you is not an accidental term.

Given the triumphant academic setting here, an obvious question is how much of this work of adjusting our default setting involves actual knowledge or intellect. This question gets very tricky. Probably the most dangerous thing about an academic education—least in my own case—is that it enables my tendency to over-intellectualise stuff, to get lost in abstract argument inside my head, instead of simply paying attention to what is going on right in front of me, paying attention to what is going on inside me.

As I'm sure you guys know by now, it is extremely difficult to stay alert and attentive, instead of getting hypnotised by the constant monologue inside your own head (may be happening right now). Twenty years after my own graduation, I have come gradually to understand that the liberal arts cliché about teaching you how to think is actually shorthand for a much deeper, more serious idea: learning how to think really means learning how to exercise some control over how and what you think. It means being conscious and aware enough to choose what you pay attention to and to choose how you construct meaning from experience.

Because if you cannot exercise this kind of choice in adult life, you will be totally hosed. Think of the old cliché about "the mind being an excellent servant but a terrible master."

This, like many clichés, so lame and unexciting on the surface, actually expresses a great and terrible truth. It is not the least bit coincidental that adults who commit suicide with firearms almost always shoot themselves in: the head. They shoot the terrible master. And the truth is that most of these suicides are actually dead long before they pull the trigger.

And I submit that this is what the real, no bullshit value of your liberal arts education is supposed to be about: how to keep from going through your comfortable, prosperous, respectable adult life dead, unconscious, a slave to your head and to your natural default setting of being uniquely, completely, imperially alone day in and day out. That may sound like hyperbole, or abstract nonsense. Let's get concrete. The plain fact is that you graduating seniors do not yet have any clue what "day in day out" really means. There happen to be whole, large parts of adult American life that nobody talks about in commencement speeches. One such part involves boredom, routine and petty frustration. The parents and older folks here will know all too well what I'm talking about.

By way of example, let's say it's an average adult day, and you get up in the morning, go to your challenging, white-collar, college-graduate job, and you work hard for eight or ten hours, and at the end of the day you're tired and somewhat stressed and all you want is to go home and have a good supper and maybe unwind for an hour, and then hit the sack early because, of course, you have to get up the next day and do it all again. But then you remember there's no food at home. You haven't had time to shop this week because of your challenging job, and so now after work you have to get in your car and drive to the supermarket. It's the end of the work day and the traffic is apt to be very bad. So getting to the store takes way longer than it should, and when you finally get there, the supermarket is very crowded, because of course it's the time of day when all the other people with jobs also try to squeeze in some grocery shopping. And the store is hideously lit and infused with soul-killing muzak or corporate pop and it's pretty much the last place you want to be but you can't just get in and quickly out; you have to wander all over the huge, over-lit store's confusing aisles to find the stuff you want and you have to manoeuvre your junky cart through all these other tired, hurried people with carts (et cetera, et cetera, cutting stuff out because this is a long ceremony) and eventually you get all your supper supplies, except now it turns out there aren't enough check-out lanes open even though it's the end-of-the-day rush. So the checkout line is incredibly long, which is stupid and infuriating. But you can't take your frustration out on the frantic lady working the register, who is overworked at a job whose daily tedium and meaninglessness surpasses the imagination of any of us here at a prestigious college.

But anyway, you finally get to the checkout line's front, and you pay for your food, and you get told to "Have a nice day" in a voice that is the absolute voice of death. Then you have to take your creepy, flimsy, plastic bags of groceries in your cart with the one crazy wheel that pulls maddeningly to the left, all the way out through the crowded, bumpy, littery parking lot, and then you have to drive all the way home through slow, heavy, SUV-intensive, rush-hour traffic, et cetera et cetera.

Everyone here has done this, of course. But it hasn't yet been part of you graduates' actual life routine, day after week after month after year.

But it will be. And many more dreary, annoying, seemingly meaningless routines besides. But that is not the point. The point is that petty, frustrating crap like this is exactly where the work of choosing is gonna come in. Because the traffic jams and crowded aisles and long checkout lines give me time to think, and if I don't make a conscious decision about how to think and what to pay attention to, I'm gonna be pissed and miserable every time I have to shop. Because my natural default setting is the certainty that situations like this are really all about me. About MY hungriness and MY fatigue and MY desire to just get home, and it's going to seem for all the world like everybody else is just in my way. And who are all these people in my way? And look at how repulsive most of them are, and how stupid and cow-like and dead-eyed and nonhuman they seem in the checkout line, or at how annoying and rude it is that people are talking loudly on cell phones in the middle of the line. And look at how deeply and personally unfair this is.

Or, of course, if I'm in a more socially conscious liberal arts form of my default setting, I can spend time in the end-of-the-day traffic being disgusted about all the huge, stupid, lane-blocking SUV's and Hummers and V-12 pickup trucks, burning their wasteful, selfish, 40-gallon tanks of gas, and I can dwell on the fact that the patriotic or religious bumper-stickers always seem to be on the biggest, most disgustingly selfish vehicles, driven by the ugliest (this is an example of how NOT to think, though) most disgustingly selfish vehicles, driven by the ugliest, most inconsiderate and aggressive drivers. And I can think about how our children's children will despise us for wasting all the future's fuel, and probably screwing up the climate, and how spoiled and stupid and selfish and disgusting we all are, and how modern consumer society just sucks, and so forth and so on.

You get the idea.

If I choose to think this way in a store and on the freeway, fine. Lots of us do. Except thinking this way tends to be so easy and automatic that it doesn't have to be a choice. It is my natural default setting. It's the automatic way that I experience the boring, frustrating, crowded parts of adult life when I'm operating on the automatic, unconscious belief that I am the centre of the world, and that my immediate needs and feelings are what should determine the world's priorities.

The thing is that, of course, there are totally different ways to think about these kinds of situations. In this traffic, all these vehicles stopped and idling in my way, it's not impossible that some of these people in SUVs have been in horrible auto accidents in the past, and now find driving so terrifying that their therapist has all but ordered them to get a huge, heavy SUV so they can feel safe enough to drive. Or that the Hummer that just cut me off is maybe being driven by a father whose little child is hurt or sick in the seat next to him, and he's trying to get this kid to the hospital, and he's in a bigger, more legitimate hurry than I am: it is actually I who am in HIS way.

Or I can choose to force myself to consider the likelihood that everyone else in the supermarket's checkout line is just as bored and frustrated as I am, and that some of these people probably have harder, more tedious and painful lives than I do.

Again, please don't think that I'm giving you moral advice, or that I'm saying you are supposed to think this way, or that anyone expects you to just automatically do it. Because it's hard. It takes will and effort, and if you are like me, some days you won't be able to do it, or you just flat out won't want to.

But most days, if you're aware enough to give yourself a choice, you can choose to look differently at this fat, dead-eyed, over-made-up lady who just screamed at her kid in the checkout line. Maybe she's not usually like this. Maybe she's been up three straight nights holding the hand of a husband who is dying of bone cancer. Or maybe this very lady is the low-wage clerk at the motor vehicle department, who just yesterday helped your spouse resolve a horrific, infuriating, red-tape problem through some small act of bureaucratic kindness. Of course, none of this is likely, but it's also not impossible. It just depends what you want to consider. If you're automatically sure that you know what reality is, and you are operating on your default setting, then you, like me, probably won't consider possibilities that aren't annoying and miserable. But if you really learn how to pay attention, then you will know there are other options. It will actually be within your power to experience a crowded, hot, slow, consumer-hell type situation as not only meaningful, but sacred, on fire with the same force that made the stars: love, fellowship, the mystical oneness of all things deep down.

Not that that mystical stuff is necessarily true. The only thing that's capital-T True is that you get to decide how you're gonna try to see it.

This, I submit, is the freedom of a real education, of learning how to be well-adjusted. You get to consciously decide what has meaning and what doesn't. You get to decide what to worship.

Because here's something else that's weird but true: in the day-to-day trenches of adult life, there is actually no such thing as atheism. There is no such thing as not worshipping. Everybody worships. The only choice we get is what to worship. And the compelling reason for maybe choosing some sort of god or spiritual-type thing to worship—be it JC or Allah, be it YHWH or the Wiccan Mother Goddess, or the Four Noble Truths, or some inviolable set of ethical principles—is that pretty much anything else you worship will eat you alive. If you worship money and things, if they are where you tap real meaning in life, then you will never have enough, never feel you have enough. It's the truth. Worship your body and beauty and sexual allure and you will always feel ugly. And when time and age start showing, you will die a million deaths before they finally grieve you. On one level, we all know this stuff already. It's been codified as myths, proverbs, clichés, epigrams, parables; the skeleton of every great story. The whole trick is keeping the truth up front in daily consciousness.

Worship power, you will end up feeling weak and afraid, and you will need ever more power over others to numb you to your own fear. Worship your intellect, being seen as smart, you will end up feeling stupid, a fraud, always on the verge of being found out. But the insidious thing about these forms of worship is not that they're evil or sinful, it's that they're unconscious. They are default settings.

They're the kind of worship you just gradually slip into, day after day, getting more and more selective about what you see and how you measure value without ever being fully aware that that's what you're doing.

And the so-called real world will not discourage you from operating on your default settings, because the so-called real world of men and money and power hums merrily along in a pool of fear and anger and frustration and craving and worship of self. Our own present culture has harnessed these forces in ways that have yielded extraordinary wealth and comfort and personal freedom. The freedom all to be lords of our tiny skull-sized kingdoms, alone at the centre of all creation. This kind of freedom has much to recommend it. But of course there are all different kinds of freedom, and the kind that is most precious you will not hear much talk about in the great outside world of wanting and achieving. ... The really important kind of freedom involves attention and awareness and discipline, and being able truly to care about other people and to sacrifice for them over and over in myriad petty, unsexy ways every day.

That is real freedom. That is being educated, and understanding how to think. The alternative is unconsciousness, the default setting, the rat race, the constant gnawing sense of having had, and lost, some infinite thing.

I know that this stuff probably doesn't sound fun and breezy or grandly inspirational the way a commencement speech is supposed to sound. What it is, as far as I can see, is the capital-T Truth, with a whole lot of rhetorical niceties stripped away. You are, of course, free to think of it whatever you wish. But please don't just dismiss it as just some finger-wagging Dr. Laura sermon. None of this stuff is really about morality or religion or dogma or big fancy questions of life after death.

The capital-T Truth is about life BEFORE death.

It is about the real value of a real education, which has almost nothing to do with knowledge, and everything to do with simple awareness; awareness of what is so real and essential, so hidden in plain sight all around us, all the time, that we have to keep reminding ourselves over and over:

"This is water."

"This is water."

It is unimaginably hard to do this, to stay conscious and alive in the adult world day in and day out. Which means yet another grand cliché turns out to be true: your education really IS the job of a lifetime. And it commences: now.

I wish you way more than luck.

Critical Reading Questions

Summarizing the Text

1. Wallace draws a distinction between what he calls our natural tendency to live inside of our own heads and the ability, fostered by a liberal education, to "remind ourselves over and over: 'This is water.'" What does he mean by this?

2. What does he mean when he says that a liberal education allows you to choose "what to worship"?

Establishing the Context

3. The commencement address is a formalized type of speech, with iron-clad conventions. (In fact, talking about how conventionalized the commencement address form is has become one of the conventions of the commencement address!) How does Wallace use this form, and how does he try to break through its conventionality to reach these students?

4. Ordinarily, in a commencement address, the speaker doesn't talk extensively about him- or herself, but instead focuses on helping the graduates understand where they now stand in the world. Wallace, on the other hand, makes himself the central character of this speech. How does this use of *ethos* affect the speech? How would you respond to this, if Wallace had been your commencement speaker?

Responding to the Message

5. Wallace accepts the clichéd proposal that a liberal education teaches one "how to think," but he expands that to say that this means that "thinking" prevents us from being "uniquely, completely, imperially alone day in and day out." What does he mean by that? Has your education up to this point given you any insight on this?

6. Few people during Wallace's life were aware of the depth of his emotional problems, but in reading this it is difficult *not* to see prefigurations of Wallace's suicide. Where do you think that his concerns are universal, and where do they seem particular to one who is fighting depression?

CLUSTER TWO: HOW IS EDUCATION DELIVERED?

The Hard Life and Restless Mind of America's Education Billionaire

Bill Breen

Bill Breen is a senior editor for Fast Company, *a business magazine that focuses on new technologies and digital media, business leadership, and business ethics. Breen is also the author of* The Future of Management *and* The Responsibility Revolution: How the Next Generation of Business Will Win. *This article is what is known as a "feature" or a "profile"—an article that takes more liberties with storytelling and perspective than a standard news story—and appeared in* Fast Company.

At first glance, he doesn't look like a street fighter. John Sperling, an 82-year-old former history professor, is an elf-sized fellow with gold-rimmed aviator glasses and a halo of gray hair. Twice divorced, he lives alone in an Italian-style estate near the sere hills of north Phoenix, where he is surrounded by citrus and pecan trees and paintings by Andy Warhol. As we meet in his poolside office on a sun-splashed winter day, he is retiring, almost shy.

But make no mistake: John Sperling, the man who put the profit into for-profit higher education, hasn't amassed a billion-dollar fortune by letting himself get pushed around. The longer we talk, the more his hard-charging attitude emerges. He drives a Jaguar. He favors a black leather biker jacket and a Greek sailor cap. He is direct, profane. And he enjoys nothing more than sticking it to the powers that be—whether it's smug academic princes in the ivory tower or zealous antidrug warriors in the Bush administration.

Sperling is chairman of the Apollo Group Inc., a Nasdaq-traded holding company with a market cap of $7.5 billion, and founder of the University of Phoenix, the least by-the-book university imaginable. The Apollo Group owns the university, which makes it a school that you can attend and invest in at the same time. Comprised entirely of working adults (the minimum age is 23), the University of Phoenix is the largest private university system in the United States, with more than 140,000 students attending classes at 41 campuses. Factor in its distance-learning operation, and the University of Phoenix's reach extends across the world.

Sperling's Apollo Group is a rare success story in this down economy. Since going public in 1994, Apollo has racked up an annual growth rate of roughly 25%. Last year, it had $1 billion in revenue—a 31% increase over 2001. Its distance-learning division claims nearly 60,000 students and an enrollment that's increasing at a rate of about 60% a year. Its stock has split twice and nearly tripled in price since its IPO in 2000, making it one of the few Internet companies to have prospered.

For those reasons and more, Sperling is beloved on Wall Street. For those reasons and more, he is loathed in many academic quarters. His critics accuse him of commodifying education, turning a social good into a market product. They dismiss the University of Phoenix as a "McUniversity" that delivers mass-produced fare at bland locations.

"John Sperling's vision of education is entirely mercenary. It is merely one more opportunity to turn a buck," says Scott Rice, a San Jose State University English professor who is writing a book on the effort to monetize higher education. "When education becomes one more product, we obey the unspoken rule of business: to give consumers as little as they will accept in exchange for as much as they will pay. Sperling is a terrible influence on American education." Sperling is used to such biting commentary. In fact, he seems to welcome it. "Why do people say such things about us?" he asks. "Fear! Fear! Fear! They're scared to death of us."

Even Sperling's harshest critics must concede that he is a visionary. He foresaw a growing demand for adult learning—which now accounts for more than half of all college students—and built a fortune by getting there first. Then, years before Marc Andreessen unveiled the Mosaic browser and supercharged the Web, Sperling saw that he could reach tens of thousands of additional students by putting the University of Phoenix's curriculum online.

By his own description, Sperling is an "unintentional" entrepreneur, an ex–trade unionist who is now on the *Forbes* 400 list of America's wealthiest people. He is also a provocateur: He enraged animal-rights activists when he underwrote a successful attempt to clone a cat named CC, the first-ever genetically engineered pet. He still unnerves conservatives by helping bankroll 17 drug-reform ballot initiatives—and winning every one. "Popular causes find money everywhere. What's the point of backing them?" he grouses.

Sperling is a battler—a man who views the business world as a "nasty, brutish" place and likes nothing more than to wage a good fight—against complacency, against convention, and against those who would crush him. "When you're in the middle of a brawl, your animal instincts are at their peak," he exclaims. "When you face death—that is, the death of your company—that's when you're most effective. You're most in focus. You're most alive."

Rough Start: The Makings of an Accidental CEO

Sperling's rags-to-riches life is the stuff of an American fable. He was born in the Missouri Ozarks in a cabin that already housed a family of six. His mother was overbearing. His father habitually beat him. In his autobiography, *Rebel With a Cause* (Wiley, 2000), he recalls that when his father died, "I could hardly contain my joy." Sperling got pneumonia at the age of seven, and doctors used just a local anesthetic when they sawed out a piece of a rib and drained pus from an infected lung. He spent the next six months in bed. The experience left him with a lifelong aversion to boredom. "I learned nothing from my childhood," he muses. "Except that it's a mean world out there, and you've got to bite and scratch to get by."

Years later, Sperling discovered that he was dyslexic. He prints everything—except for his signature, which he inks in a wobbly cursive script. When he graduated from high school, he could barely read. His real education began when he joined the merchant marine and took a job in a freighter's engine room. Once at sea, he met several older, well-educated crewmen who shared their personal libraries. Sailing between Japan and Shanghai, Panama and New York, he devoured such classics as *Notes from Underground* and *The Great Gatsby*. Many of the ship's crew members were socialists—some were Trotskyites and Stalinists—and they introduced him to a leftist ideological culture. He remains an unabashed liberal who delights in challenging the status quo.

After two years at sea, he left the merchant marine and paid his tuition at Portland, Oregon's Reed College by working the swing shift in a Columbia River shipyard. Lacking family connections or any notion of how to make his way in the business world, he fell into academe. "It was the path of least resistance," he says. He earned a PhD from Cambridge University and became a tenured humanities professor at San Jose State University. Professor Scott Rice describes Sperling's time at the school in less-than-charitable terms. "Teaching was all right, but I'm an activist," Sperling concedes. The passive life just didn't appeal to me."

It was at San Jose State that he discovered his first true calling: union organizing. He joined the local chapter of the American Federation of Teachers (AFT) and rose to state and national positions of leadership during the next 10 years. But then he overplayed his hand. In 1968, he persuaded the leaders of the AFT at San Jose State to mount a sympathy strike with professors at San Francisco State University. After 31 days of picketing, 100 professors narrowly averted a mass firing, and the strike unraveled. As for Sperling, he lost his credibility as a leader and became the most reviled man on campus. Still, the humiliating defeat delivered an invaluable lesson.

"The strike was one of the most liberating experiences of my life," he says. He found that "it didn't make a goddamn bit of difference what people thought of me. Without that psychological immunity, it would have been impossible to create and protect the University of Phoenix from hostility, legal assaults, and attempts to legislate us out of existence." He does not recommend this behavior to others. ("You don't get anywhere in an organization if you're utterly indifferent to how people feel about you," he says.) But for him, it worked. The experience steeled him for the life of an entrepreneur.

No Retreat: Defiling the Ivory Tower

Sperling dislikes the goal-oriented mind-set that drives many businesspeople. "If you have a goal, you're constrained by that goal," he says. "You should never delude yourself into thinking that you know exactly where you're going." By the early 1970s, Sperling's academic career was going nowhere. But while he didn't know it at the time, he was about to embark on a life-changing journey into the world of business.

In 1972, he was chosen to run a series of workshops at San Jose State that would prepare police officers and teachers to work with juvenile delinquents. He built the program around some of the same pedagogical tools that he would later employ at the University of Phoenix: He brought in teachers who were experts in their fields, divided the class into small groups, and challenged each group to complete a project. He was surprised when the enthusiastic students lobbied him to create degree programs. Which is exactly what he did.

Sperling sketched out a curriculum for working adults and pitched it to the academic vice president at San Jose State, who promptly slapped it down. "My university said they didn't need no more stinkin' students, that they had all they could handle," Sperling acidly recalls. "They told me to go back and behave—be a professor." Naturally, he ignored that advice. Even though he held business in contempt—as would any right-thinking, left-leaning humanities professor—the marketplace intrigued him. And he sensed an enormous market for degree-based programs targeted at working adults who were anxious to take the road to higher education.

Gambling that he could take the adult-education curriculum that San Jose State had rejected and make it succeed elsewhere, Sperling set about putting his ideas to work. He sought out the vice president of development at Stanford University, a man named Frank Newman, who threw a dash of reality onto his ambitions. Newman warned that educational bureaucracies innovate only out of fiscal desperation. In a letter, he advised Sperling to "find a school in financial trouble and convince the people running it that your program will generate a profit." Sperling found the University of San Francisco, a cash-strapped, Jesuit-run institution that became his first client.

Newman's advice was appealing. For starters, Sperling was itching to test his vision in the marketplace. "Either we'd grow or we'd die," he says. "The market is a jungle, and I love it." But there was an equally compelling motivator for making his enterprise a for-profit effort. After losing control of the United Professors of California, the union that he had built almost single-handedly, he vowed that he would never again lead a nonprofit, "which some board could yank away from me." By launching a corporation—the forerunner of his Apollo Group—he would control his own destiny. At age 53, Sperling became the thing that he had cursed for so many years: a businessman.

His program at USF proved to be an "immediate financial success." His biggest challenge was handling the growth. But soon, a larger problem loomed. As he signed up other schools, word spread among California's regulators that Sperling had committed the ultimate blasphemy: He had dragged the profit motive into the ivory tower. His assault on academic orthodoxy, recalls Sperling, "was met with hostility bordering on rage. If they could have killed me, they would have."

Smart Money: The Un-University Arrives

Sperling had sparked a culture war that pitted his notion of a radically different learning system against California's higher-education establishment. In many academic circles, his vision of a stripped down, utilitarian curriculum that provided working adults with real-world tools and information was viewed as a naked attempt to dethrone the professorate.

Although he was a tenured professor at San Jose State, Sperling forbade tenure in his own programs. (Even now, the faculty consists primarily of 8,000 professionals who teach at night what they do for work by day.) He banned lectures and developed standardized courses. The University of Phoenix's curriculum is built around peer-based learning groups where the instructor isn't exactly viewed as a fount of knowledge. "The faculty member is an equal in the classroom," says Sperling. "His job isn't to expound wisdom, it's to serve a learning group."

Bureaucrats and politicians branded Sperling's operation a diploma mill, and after a futile five-year battle to win accreditation, he abandoned California and decamped to Phoenix, where he thought regulators would be more receptive. But his struggles in Arizona proved to be just as vicious as they were in California. It wasn't until 1979—after an all-out campaign waged in the media, the Arizona state legislature, and the conference rooms of higher-education regulators— that Sperling's newly named University of Phoenix was finally accredited. Still, the fights continue. Today, the Apollo Group retains an army of 30 political lobbyists to help Sperling further his dream of building a for-profit, global university.

The University of Phoenix's main campus sits on a side road just off of Interstate 10. Three red-brick buildings, which house classrooms and administrative offices, cluster around a courtyard that's ringed with conifers. And that's it. There's no student center, no fine-arts buildings, no athletic center. In a school that offers undergraduate and graduate-degree programs in business, information technology, accounting, management, marketing, and the like, ivy-covered quads are deemed superfluous. At least, that's one explanation. But in a larger sense, this spartan campus is simply the physical manifestation of Sperling's assault on the traditional college experience. It is the embodiment of his notion of how a university for working adults should look, feel, and function.

In mid-afternoon, when many colleges are bustling with students, the university's courtyard is deserted. All of that changes as night falls and students begin to arrive from their day jobs. As the classrooms fill with thirtysomething and fortysomething professionals dressed for work, the place takes on its true character: that of a corporate campus. The average student is 34 years old and earns between $50,000 and $60,000 a year. About 60% of students receive some tuition reimbursement from their employers, which include such blue-chip behemoths as AT&T, Boeing, IBM, Intel, Lockheed Martin, and Motorola—not to mention the U.S. military.

Sperling's critics, of course, question whether the Intels and Motorolas of the world are getting their money's worth from the University of Phoenix. "Many CEOs and hiring partners report that these newly minted business majors aren't as literate and as broadly educated as they need to be," says Carole Fungaroli Sargent, an English professor at Georgetown University and author of *Traditional Degrees for Nontraditional Students: How to Earn a Top Diploma From America's Great Colleges at Any Age* (Farrar, Straus, and Giroux, 2000). "When places like the University of Phoenix strip the arts and humanities out of a degree because those studies are deemed unnecessary, they don't serve the business world, and they certainly don't serve the student."

Sperling dismisses such talk, countering that if the school were failing to educate, it wouldn't be attracting students by the tens of thousands. Then he scribbles two numbers onto a piece of paper: "160,000" and "30%." I ask what he means. "We have a student enrollment of 160,000, which is growing at 30% per annum. At that rate, in five years we will have nearly 600,000 students. That would make us the largest higher-education system in the world."

Still the First Mover

Sperling is a restless soul. He likes to say that his whole life has been a flight from boredom. Twice he nearly bankrupted the Apollo Group when he pushed the company into new markets before it was ready. But when the Internet arrived in the mid-1990s and dotcoms rushed to launch virtual universities, they soon found that Sperling had gotten there first.

In 1989, he purchased a defunct distance-learning company and assigned a team of techies a task that no one had ever accomplished: Create a viable and profitable electronic education system. It took five years to translate a classroom education experience into bits and bytes. But in 2000, just as the Internet wave was cresting, the university's online enrollment jumped 81%. Phoenix Online now generates $327 million in revenue. Analysts at William Blair & Co. call it one of the best-performing tracking stocks of all time.

These days, Sperling can barely contain his excitement over a new high-tech experiment that could turn out to be as revolutionary as the university's distance-learning effort. Eighteen months ago, at a dinner party for San Francisco venture capitalists, Sperling saw his first demo of an electronic textbook: "I was fascinated by it, although I didn't know what the hell to do with it." He brought the e-book idea to Adam Honea, the university's dean of information systems and technology, and used it to issue a challenge: Brainstorm a way to eliminate all of the system's textbooks and replace them with customized learning materials that exist entirely in digital form.

"At first, it doesn't seem that revolutionary. But think about it: We become publishing's version of a general contractor," says Honea. "We contract authors and experts to create course materials exactly to our specs. That lets us bypass textbook publishers. It eliminates the fixed costs of moving 140,000 books every five to six weeks. John Sperling reinvented the traditional model of the student, the instructor, and the classroom. And now he's reinventing the textbook."

Even if he fails in this latest adventure, you can't help but marvel at the man's audacity—and energy. Sperling may be an octogenarian, but he still gets up at 5:30 every morning to work out, he still puts in a 12-hour day, and he still lives by that 1999 mantra: Change or die. "We'll put the textbook publishers out of business if they don't adapt," he exclaims. Then his eyebrows rise in mock wonder: "Isn't this what you guys call a 'disruptive technology'?"

Critical Reading Questions

Summarizing the Text

1. How is Sperling's approach to designing a university structure and curriculum different from that of a traditional university?

2. Breen centers his portrait of Sperling on the notion of "risk taking." What are some of the risks that Sperling has taken in his life, and how did they turn out? How did the University of Phoenix represent a risk to him?

Establishing the Context

3. What does it mean to accuse a school of being a "McUniversity"? What negative results do Sperling's critics fear that the profit motive will bring to education?

4. Breen argues in this piece that the values of the business world and the values of the traditional world of higher education are fundamentally in conflict. How?

Responding to the Message

5. Research one of the University of Phoenix's degree programs through its website. What are the requirements for the degree? How do these requirements differ from the requirements for a similar degree at your institution?

6. How might Sperling respond to the arguments in favor of liberal education (and the traditional college) made by Michael Roth or David Foster Wallace?

University of Phoenix Building and Low Library of Columbia University

Compare these two photographs. The one on the left is of the Tucson, Arizona, campus of the University of Phoenix; the one on the right is of the Low Library at Columbia University in New York City. The University of Phoenix is one of the fastest growing schools in the nation and offers online and in-person classes to a student body that is largely composed of employed adults who are seeking to earn

a degree while they work. Whether it is intentional or not, the University of Phoenix often situates its campuses in office buildings located in suburban locations.

Columbia University's Low Library, on the other hand, was always meant to be an academic building. Built in 1895 by the famous architects McKim, Mead, and White, the building uses the neoclassical style popular at the time and is modeled in part on the ancient Pantheon in Rome.

Critical Reading Questions

Summarizing the Text

1. Describe the features of each building. What sorts of adornments does the Phoenix building have? Where have you seen these kinds of buildings? What about the Columbia library is notable—the steps leading up, the dome, the columns, the architrave (the part on top of the columns)?

Establishing the Context

2. A university's main buildings—its administration building, its library, and for a religious school its chapel or temple—are key elements of a school's public image. They tell outsiders what the institution values, and they reinforce the identity and personality of the school to the university community. What does each building say about what goes on inside? How does each building express the personality and values of the institution, and what roles its graduates will fill in society?

Responding to the Message

3. Go outside the building in which your class takes place and look at the building from its front entrance. How does this building express the values of your institution?

Why I Changed My Mind on Charter Schools

Diane Ravitch

Diane Ravitch is one of America's leading historians of education, and a distinguished writer and teacher, but she also served as assistant secretary of education under President George H. W. Bush. Initially a strong advocate of President George W. Bush's "No Child Left Behind" law, which mandated increased use of standardized tests in public schools, Ravitch changed her mind about this law, and about the prevalence of testing in general, by the end of the Bush administration. This article appeared in the Wall Street Journal.

I have been a historian of American education since 1975, when I received my doctorate from Columbia. I have written histories, and I've also written extensively about the need to improve students' knowledge of history, literature, geography, science, civics and foreign languages. So in 1991, when Lamar Alexander and David Kearns invited me to become assistant secretary of education in the administration of George H.W. Bush, I jumped at the chance with the hope that I might promote voluntary state and national standards in these subjects.

By the time I left government service in January 1993, I was an advocate not only for standards but for school choice. I had come to believe that standards and choice could co-exist as they do in the private sector. With my friends Chester Finn Jr. and Joseph Viteritti, I wrote and edited books and articles making the case for charter schools and accountability.

I became a founding board member of the Thomas B. Fordham Foundation and a founding member of the Koret Task Force at the Hoover Institution, both of which are fervent proponents of choice and accountability. The Koret group includes some of the nation's best-known conservative scholars of choice, including John Chubb, Terry Moe, Caroline Hoxby and Paul Peterson.

As No Child Left Behind's (NCLB) accountability regime took over the nation's schools under President George W. Bush and more and more charter schools were launched, I supported these initiatives. But over time, I became disillusioned with the strategies that once seemed so promising. I no longer believe that either approach will produce the quantum improvement in American education that we all hope for.

NCLB received overwhelming bipartisan support when it was signed into law by President Bush in 2002. The law requires that schools test all students every year in grades three through eight, and report their scores separately by race, ethnicity, low-income status, disability status and limited-English proficiency. NCLB mandated that 100% of students would reach proficiency in reading and math by 2014, as measured by tests given in each state.

Although this target was generally recognized as utopian, schools faced draconian penalties—eventually including closure or privatization—if every group in the school did not make adequate yearly progress. By 2008, 35% of the nation's public schools were labeled "failing schools," and that number seems sure to grow each year as the deadline nears.

Since the law permitted every state to define "proficiency" as it chose, many states announced impressive gains. But the states' claims of startling improvement were contradicted by the federally sponsored National Assessment of Educational Progress (NAEP). Eighth grade students improved not at all on the federal test of reading even though they had been tested annually by their states in 2003, 2004, 2005, 2006 and 2007.

Meanwhile the states responded to NCLB by dumbing down their standards so that they could claim to be making progress. Some states declared that between 80%–90% of their students were proficient, but on the federal test only a third or less were. Because the law demanded progress only in reading and math, schools were incentivized to show gains only on those subjects. Hundreds of millions of dollars were invested in test-preparation materials. Meanwhile, there was no incentive to teach the arts, science, history, literature, geography, civics, foreign languages or physical education.

In short, accountability turned into a nightmare for American schools, producing graduates who were drilled regularly on the basic skills but were often ignorant about almost everything else. Colleges continued to complain about the poor preparation of entering students, who not only had meager knowledge of the world but still required remediation in basic skills. This was not my vision of good education.

When charter schools started in the early 1990s, their supporters promised that they would unleash a new era of innovation and effectiveness. Now there are some 5,000 charter schools, which serve about 3% of the nation's students, and the Obama administration is pushing for many more.

But the promise has not been fulfilled. Most studies of charter schools acknowledge that they vary widely in quality. The only major national evaluation of charter schools was carried out by Stanford economist Margaret Raymond and funded by pro-charter foundations. Her group found that compared to regular public schools, 17% of charters got higher test scores, 46% had gains that were no different than their public counterparts, and 37% were significantly worse.

Charter evaluations frequently note that as compared to neighboring public schools, charters enroll smaller proportions of students whose English is limited and students with disabilities. The students who are hardest to educate are left to regular public schools, which makes comparisons between the two sectors unfair. The higher graduation rate posted by charters often reflects the fact that they are able to "counsel out" the lowest performing students; many charters have very high attrition rates (in some, 50%–60% of those who start fall away). Those who survive do well, but this is not a model for public education, which must educate all children.

NAEP compared charter schools and regular public schools in 2003, 2005, 2007 and 2009. Sometimes one sector or the other had a small advantage. But on the whole, there is very little performance difference between them.

Given the weight of studies, evaluations and federal test data, I concluded that deregulation and privately managed charter schools were not the answer to the deep-seated problems of American education. If anything, they represent tinkering around the edges of the system. They affect the lives of tiny numbers of students but do nothing to improve the system that enrolls the other 97%.

The current emphasis on accountability has created a punitive atmosphere in the schools. The Obama administration seems to think that schools will improve if we fire teachers and close schools. They do not recognize that schools are often the anchor of their communities, representing values, traditions and ideals that have persevered across decades. They also fail to recognize that the best predictor of low academic performance is poverty—not bad teachers.

What we need is not a marketplace, but a coherent curriculum that prepares all students. And our government should commit to providing a good school in every neighborhood in the nation, just as we strive to provide a good fire company in every community.

On our present course, we are disrupting communities, dumbing down our schools, giving students false reports of their progress, and creating a private sector that will undermine public education without improving it. Most significantly, we are not producing a generation of students who are more knowledgeable, and better prepared for the responsibilities of citizenship. That is why I changed my mind about the current direction of school reform.

Critical Reading Questions

Summarizing the Text

1. Is Ravitch arguing against reforming the public school system? What is her thesis?
2. Why did Ravitch change her mind about "school choice"?

Establishing the Context

3. How does Ravitch establish her credibility with the audience that reads the (conservative) *Wall Street Journal* opinion page?
4. Ravitch points to a problem in the way school success was measured: differing definitions of "proficiency." How might this invalidate the data?

Responding to the Message

5. What exactly is a "charter school"? What relationship do charter schools have to the public school system? How are they different from private schools? What has been their promise, and what does Ravitch argue is the reality?
6. How is educational achievement measured? What are some of the sources of data that Ravitch uses? What are some competing sources of data that charter school and school choice advocates use to bolster their arguments?

Come Study La Raza
Grievance and Distortion 101
Liam Julian

Liam Julian is the managing editor of Policy Review, *the journal of the conservative Hoover Institution, and a leading voice on the right on education policy issues. This article drew early nationwide attention to the Tucson (AZ) Unified School District's so-called "Raza Studies" curriculum, a set of classes and programs aimed at Mexican American students. Julian writes for many publications, and this article appeared in the* National Review, *the most important journal of conservative opinion in the United States.*

The name of the nation's most visible, self-defined Latino civil-rights organization, the National Council of La Raza, translates as the National Council of The Race. The official website denies it, of course, but we have dictionaries. That controversial term—*La Raza*—is gaining currency: Some K–12 public schools now teach something called "Raza Studies."

Like those in Tucson, for example. The Tucson Unified School District (TUSD) has, in fact, welcomed Raza Studies in its classrooms for about a decade, but it's been mighty secretive about the association.

What, exactly, is Raza Studies? Arizona Superintendent of Public Instruction Tom Horne asked that question in November 2007 when he inquired if it wouldn't be too much trouble for TUSD to send to him the Raza curricula it was teaching and the textbooks from which it taught them. Actually, TUSD replied to Horne, meeting his request would be a *heckuva* lot of trouble.

Then the local papers piled on Arizona's superintendent. The first sentence of a November 26th editorial in the *Tucson Citizen* read, "Memo to Tom Horne: Butt out." Another editorial, titled "Horne meddling in TUSD's ethnic studies efforts," this one in Tucson's *Arizona Daily Star*, noted that "Students enroll in these classes because they cover information that is not offered in other classes. While U.S. history classes and textbooks do a better job than those of the past of including more about our shared history, much is left out."

What is left out of traditional syllabi, of course, is the grievance and distortion. When Horne finally acquired the program materials he requested, they included texts with titles such as *Occupied America* and *The Pedagogy of Oppression*. And according to John Ward, a Tucson teacher who saw his U.S. history course coopted by the Raza Studies department, the Raza curriculum's focus is "that Mexican-Americans were and continue to be victims of a racist American society driven by the interests of middle and upper-class whites."

When Ward raised concerns about Raza Studies (which is part of TUSD's larger Ethnic Studies department) he was, despite being Hispanic himself, called a racist and eventually reassigned to another course. Ward told a reporter from the *Arizona Republic* that by the time he left the Raza Studies class, he had observed a definite change in the students: "An angry tone. They taught them not to trust their teachers, not to trust the system. They taught them the system wasn't worth trusting."

A persuasive case can and should be made that teaching students history and literature (not to mention science and math) through some concocted ethnic perspective that the pupils supposedly possess is balderdash. It does Hispanic youngsters a profound disservice to predicate their educations on ethnic identity, to have them skip the great works of literature and read only tracts by, say, Mexican authors, and to teach them only the history that involves Latin America(ns).

But when an ethnically based education, which is bad enough, transmogrifies into an ethnically based education of grievance and oppression that vilifies the United States and anyone with white skin—well, this is simply untenable. And yet this product is exactly that which goes by the name Raza Studies and that Tucson blithely pushes.

Moreover, the city is intransigent about the whole thing. To valid concerns about its Raza Studies department, the school board responded last month, according to the *Arizona Republic*, "by announcing plans to hugely expand the [entire Ethnic Studies] program, making it a required course of studies for freshmen. And, eventually, expanding it into elementary schools." Within a year, it seems, all of Tucson's children will be taught based on their ethnicities distinctive curricula that will share no common denominator as strong as the condemnation of whites and of the United States.

The school district is also sponsoring in two weeks, in partnership with the University of Arizona School of Education, the 10th Annual Institute for Transformative Education seminar, at which "Classroom teachers will have the opportunity to learn . . . the areas of Latino critical race theory, critical race theory, critical multicultural education, Chicana/o studies, ethnic studies, cultural studies, critical pedagogy, and critical race pedagogy." Ugh.

To defend and then expand an educational program that reveres Che Guevara, that paints American history as a series of lamentable and dishonorable events, that divides students by their ethnicities and then attempts to instill in them a defiant stance toward authority and country is a form of noxious educational malpractice. But beyond that, it's a direct challenge to the values that millions of Americans hold dear and will this Friday, on the Fourth of July, celebrate. One hopes that the citizens of Tucson have had their fill of this nonsense in their schools, and that they'll stand up and say so.

Critical Reading Questions

Summarizing the Text

1. What is wrong with Tucson's Ethnic Studies program, according to Julian?

2. Julian is arguing to a conservative audience here, as his article appeared in a conservative publication. What unspoken assumptions does he make about his audience, and how do these assumptions inform his text?

Establishing the Context

3. Public education has traditionally been the most important institution in American life that defined what it means to be an American. Julian fears that these "ethnic studies" classes undermine this role for public education. Do you agree? Why or why not?

Responding to the Message

4. Julian predicates this article on the idea that there is a unified "American" identity (typified by the celebration of the Fourth of July), and that this "ethnic studies" curriculum teaches students to hold an angry or defiant attitude toward that American identity. What do you think? To what degree do you identify as "American," and to what degree are other elements of your ethnic

or linguistic or religious identity central to who you are? And how should a public school system deal with this?

5. HB 2281, the Arizona state law that penalized Tucson USD for this ethnic studies program, came soon after the controversial and sweeping SB 1070, which established a much more punitive and aggressive police approach to illegal immigration. Research SB 1070 and HB 2281—how did public opinion about one influence the other?

New Arizona Law Could Be Detrimental to Students

Angela Yeager

Angela Yeager is a newspaper reporter and wrote this story while pursuing a master's degree in English at Oregon State University. The article is a "news release" for the university—a form of public relations through which colleges and universities publicize the discoveries and accomplishments of their professors and students.

A new Arizona law targeting ethnic studies classes could negatively affect students' academic achievement and reverse academic gains made over the last several years, according to two Oregon State University researchers.

Susan Meyers, assistant professor and director of writing in the English department at OSU, and Rick Orozco, an assistant professor in the College of Education at OSU, both earned their Ph.D.s at the University of Arizona in Tucson, Ariz. and are intimately familiar with the program that spurred the new law in Arizona.

The bill, HB 2281, prevents " ... courses or classes that either: 1) are designed primarily for pupils of a particular ethnic group, or 2) advocate ethnic solidarity instead of the treatment of pupils as individuals."

The types of courses that this bill targets are known as ethnic studies courses, a field of study that is commonly offered on many university campuses, including OSU, as well as on increasing numbers of high school campuses.

Meyers and Orozco said this specific bill started as a reaction to the Mexican-American Studies Department, also known informally as Raza Studies, in the Tucson Unified School District.

Arizona School Superintendent Tom Horne advocated against the program saying it promotes "ethnic chauvinism." After failed attempts to oust school board members who supported the program, he took his appeal to state political leaders. They drafted HB 2281, which went into law May 11. Proponents of the bill argue that programs like Raza Studies pose a threat to political and social stability, while program advocates say it is an important means of supporting minority students.

Some educators argue that programs aimed at empowering students and increasing literacy are particularly important in a state like Arizona, which ranks among the lowest states in the nation in terms of dollars invested in public education—and is one of the highest in student homelessness and teen pregnancy (ranking second).

Meyers and Orozco are concerned about the proposed elimination of programs that have been documented to help student learning and success. The researchers said that Raza Studies students graduate at rates that are higher than their white peers, and enroll in college at a rate that approaches 70 percent. Raza Studies students also outperform their peers in Arizona's standardized testing.

"Ample scholarship in a variety of disciplines now conclude[s] that rates of student success—particularly among minority students—is positively correlated with culturally relevant and community-minded curriculum," Orozco said.

Before coming to OSU, Orozco spent 15 years as a teacher at a predominately Mexican-American school in Tucson. His research there focused on analyzing mission statements of schools and school districts that served predominantly white versus predominantly Mexican ethnic populations to see if expectations and attitudes differed. Orozco found that there were lower expectations and more negative attitudes toward the Mexican ethnic students.

"For minority students—whether ethnic minorities, first-generation college students, disabled students, etc.—ethnic studies program can provide meaningful connective experiences that aid both their understanding of academic content and increase their motivation to pursue formal education," he said.

Orozco said he had many students who pursued post-secondary education in Tucson and credits Mexican-American studies curricula with providing the impetus they needed.

Meyers has been involved for the past two years in a qualitative research project that investigates the educational experiences of students whose families immigrate to the United States from Mexico. In particular, she concentrates on the ways in which these students adapt to education in the United States and she has focused specifically on these students' relative success and motivation—and their decision as to whether to pursue further levels of education.

Her findings indicate that when students encounter curriculum that does not include cultural references or awareness of their backgrounds, they feel alienated by the education process, and they are less likely to complete high school and/or go on for professional or academic training.

In contrast, Meyers said, curriculum that encourages students to think critically about a variety of topics—from cultural differences to gender equity to transnational relationships—is a more effective means of engaging students and preparing them for higher levels of education.

In addition to this research project, Meyers also worked with a college readiness program in Tucson called GEAR UP, which serves the Tucson school district and a neighboring district, Sunnyside Unified School District. GEAR UP is a federal grant that aligns school districts and local universities in order to help prepare students from low-income schools for college programs. Many of these students become the first members of their families to attend college; in Tucson, many of these students are Latino.

Through her work with GEAR UP, Meyers said she witnessed some of the kinds of culturally integrated programming that HB 2281 will eliminate.

"GEAR UP programming itself seeks to create culturally relative programming that invites students to critically engage with their educational experiences so that they better understand the education system and are better prepared for college," she said. "I saw how important programs that recognize a student's culture and heritage are, not only to their educational attainment, but also to their sense of self-worth and confidence."

Critical Reading Questions

Summarizing the Text

1. While the article from the *National Review* was a strong statement of opinion, this is a "news" article—it just reports the facts. What are the facts, according to Yeager?

2. Does this article make an argument in favor of or against HB 2281?

Establishing the Context

3. What evidence do Orozco and Myers use to make their argument that HB 2281 is "detrimental"? How does Yeager establish their authority?

Responding to the Message

4. Yeager does not allude to the fiery controversy about whether or not these ethnic studies programs undermine students' identity as Americans or their feelings about American culture and society as a whole. However, this is the central question behind this bill. Why does she not do so?

Questions for Short Projects or Group Presentations

1. Look at the advertising and publicity materials for your university (you might take a class field trip to the admissions office). Perform a rhetorical analysis on the brochures and handouts you find there. How does your school describe the education offered there? Does the school use the rhetoric of the liberal arts or of the practical use of the degrees its students earn? How do the photographs and images interact with the language the school uses to describe itself?

2. Why are you in college? In a small group, debate the issue of what your college education is for. How can or should your university change its requirements to better match what you want out of your education?

3. How do universities, school districts, or the government measure educational achievement? Is testing a sufficient means of assessing how well a school is performing? Should universities institute exit examinations specific to each major? Research and present to the class your group's ideas on these topics.

Questions for Formal Essays

1. Are college students "consumers" in the same way that someone who buys an iPod or goes to a movie is a consumer? If so, what is the product the consumer is buying—an education or a degree? How does the relationship between the consumer and the provider of the service or product differ in these cases? What about doctors or lawyers— are their clients consumers? If college students are consumers, what rights do they have versus the rights of the company (the university or college) that is selling them the product (the education)?

2. Public school boards are some of the most intensely local of governmental bodies—we have a deeply personal relationship with our public schools, and the schools not only reflect, but often do much to create a sense of community. However, public schools are also responsible for educating students to standards that a state sets out, and for helping students learn the values of the nation itself. Compare the controversies surrounding the No Child Left Behind act and the ethnic studies program at Tucson Unified School District in Arizona. What does each controversy say about what happens when local, state, and national laws, values, and priorities conflict?

3. Using the school board's website, the local newspaper, and local blogs, research a current controversy in your town's public schools. What is at issue? What are the primary points of view on it? What do you think about it and how does it compare with your own experience with primary and secondary education?

4. In small groups, take photographs of the primary buildings on your campus (and on other campuses in your city, if there are any). What do these buildings say about the values of your school? Is there a difference between the library and more student-centered buildings such as the dormitories?

How Do We Work Today, and How Will We Work Tomorrow?

CHAPTER INTRODUCTION

Except for a few, the rest of us have to work to earn a living. And although we have to do it, people tend not to be (at least openly) very enthusiastic about it. Perhaps the most common connotation of "work" is that it is something best avoided or finished quickly; it is something that, given a choice, we wouldn't do. Such synonyms as "drudgery," "labor," "toil," or "chore" express this sense that we would rather be doing almost anything else besides working.

But for many people—in fact, probably for most—work isn't necessarily a bad thing, or something to be avoided. One doesn't need to be a cheerleader for the so-called "Protestant work ethic" to feel that, in some ways, human beings need to work, to contribute, to create value, to be productive. To those in the Judeo-Christian tradition, the book of Genesis tells that God created Adam in part to "till the soil" of the Garden of Eden, and generations of theologians have interpreted that to mean that labor is one of the central purposes of human life. Almost every major cultural tradition places a great deal of positive value upon work. For many, if not most, of us, work gives meaning to our lives.

A seemingly superficial but probably telling indicator of the centrality of work to American culture is the fact that the "workplace" situation comedy has been a staple of television almost since it began. As Thomas Schatz details in this chapter, early workplace situation comedies such as the *Dick Van Dyke Show* helped establish a template that would continue through *The Mary Tyler Moore Show*, *The Bob Newhart Show*, *M*A*S*H*, *Taxi*, *Cheers*, and *The Office* or *30 Rock* today. In his overview of the history of the workplace program, Schatz points out that television has been a repository of the stories Americans like to tell themselves about their culture, and it has also provided an outlet for our anxieties about just how much time and energy and attention we expend on our jobs.

You "work" in college, of course; studying and writing papers and interning and conducting lab experiments are certainly work. And most students (more than half, according to recent statistics) hold at least a part-time job while they are enrolled in college. But for Americans, college—particularly the traditional full-time, four-year experience one enters upon completing high school—is understood to be different from "work" in the sense of a full-time occupation.

Popular culture reinforces the idea that there's college, and then there's the "real world." Staying in college to avoid responsibility, or returning to the seeming freedom of college, is the theme of dozens of well-known movies, from *Animal House* to *Van Wilder* to *Old School*. (It's funny that in these films male college students tend to be the ones who fear entering the real world, whereas females are the responsible ones.)

Increasingly, though, students have a foot in both worlds—college and the "real" one. More than 10 percent of full-time students also work full-time jobs, and many of those are so-called "nontraditional" students or older students returning to school. College itself is changing to better reflect the realities of the working world, too, responding to demands from parents, students, and employers. And the fastest growing sector of higher education is the "for-profit" school, such as Strayer University or the University of Phoenix, that cater specifically to students who are working full-time while pursuing their degrees.

Even given all this, the transition from college to the working world can still be a shock. The readings in this chapter touch upon many of the issues faced by recent college graduates as they leave their studies for a paycheck. Or hoping for a paycheck: the unemployment rate for recent college graduates has, in recent years, been at historic highs because of the "Great Recession" of 2008–10. In 2010, only 24 percent of college graduates had a job waiting for them upon graduation, according to a study by the National Association of Colleges and Employers.

The nature of skilled work and of the workplace itself is also changing. As it has fundamentally transformed almost every area of our lives, information technology and electronic communications are radically changing what jobs are available, what working conditions are like, and the nature of the relationship between employer and employee.

Taking an entirely different stance on the issue of "skilled" work is Matthew Crawford, a political science Ph.D. who has chosen to work in a motorcycle repair shop. In his essay "Shop Class as Soulcraft," Crawford argues that "skilled" or "professional" work as it is increasingly understood—doing things with computers or through computers—alienates us from the product of our labor, with ominous consequences.

Speaking of computers, both Rebecca Traister and Wei Du focus on other ways in which our connected lives can negatively affect our professional lives. Wei discusses how employers are increasingly looking at applicants' online presences (such as a Facebook page) to learn more about a potential employee. Traister complains about the negative effects of our desire and need to be constantly connected, pointing out that we lose an important space in our life that is *away* from work. As we live increasingly online, and as our online presence and information are increasingly available to the world at large, how will the way we work change?

Nicholas Kristof and the activist group China Labor Watch examine two sides of the kind of work that few American college graduates experience—factory work that takes place in so-called "sweatshops." A holdover term from the late nineteenth century, *sweatshop* refers to a factory—originally, a small unventilated shop that produced clothing—in which employees work long hours in unpleasant, crowded conditions doing tedious, repetitive work for low wages. As much manufacturing has moved out of the United States to cheaper labor markets in Asia, sweatshops have also moved there—and flourished. China Labor Watch has studied one manufacturer in particular (the Chinese company Foxconn that assembles high-technology products for Chinese, American, and European brands) and accuses Foxconn of running sweatshops with inhumane conditions. Included in this chapter is a personal narrative of a Foxconn employee, describing the conditions in which he works and lives.

But, Kristof says, although most of *us* wouldn't want to do it, it's hard to argue against the benefits that sweatshops bring to their employees, many of whom would live lives of dire poverty without their sweatshop jobs. A generally liberal commentator for the *New York Times*, Kristof here takes a contrarian view, arguing that judging working conditions in China by American standards is foolish—and adding that the Chinese factory economy is the envy of many much poorer nations, whose citizens cannot aspire even to the modest living standards of a Chinese sweatshop worker.

CLUSTER ONE: WHAT IS THE WORKPLACE, AND HOW IS IT CHANGING?

The "Trophy Kids" Go to Work

Ron Alsop

Ron Alsop is a news editor and senior writer at the Wall Street Journal, *the preeminent American daily newspaper covering the worlds of business and finance. Alsop edits the annual* Wall Street Journal Guide to the Top Business Schools *and is the author of* The 18 Immutable Laws of Corporate Reputation. *This essay, which originally appeared in the* Journal, *is adapted from Alsop's 2008 book* The Trophy Kids Grow Up: How the Millennial Generation Is Shaking Up the Workplace.

When Gretchen Neels, a Boston-based consultant, was coaching a group of college students for job interviews, she asked them how they believe employers view them. She gave them a clue, telling them that the word she was looking for begins with the letter "e." One young man shouted out, "excellent." Other students chimed in with "enthusiastic" and "energetic." Not even close. The correct answer, she said, is "entitled." "Huh?" the students responded, surprised and even hurt to think that managers are offended by their highfalutin opinions of themselves.

If there is one overriding perception of the millennial generation, it's that these young people have great—and sometimes outlandish— expectations. Employers realize the millennials are their future work force, but they are concerned about this generation's desire to shape their jobs to fit their lives rather than adapt their lives to the workplace.

Although members of other generations were considered somewhat spoiled in their youth, millennials feel an unusually strong sense of entitlement. Older adults criticize the high-maintenance rookies for demanding too much too soon. "They want to be CEO tomorrow," is a common refrain from corporate recruiters.

More than 85% of hiring managers and human-resource executives said they feel that millennials have a stronger sense of entitlement than older workers, according to a survey by CareerBuilder.com. The generation's greatest expectations: higher pay (74% of respondents); flexible work schedules (61%); a promotion within a year (56%); and more vacation or personal time (50%).

"They really do seem to want everything, and I can't decide if it's an inability or an unwillingness to make trade-offs," says Derrick Bolton, assistant dean and M.B.A. admissions director at Stanford University's Graduate School of Business. "They want to be CEO, for example, but they say they don't want to give up time with their families."

Millennials, of course, will have to temper their expectations as they seek employment during this deep economic slump. But their sense of entitlement is an ingrained trait that will likely resurface in a stronger job market. Some research studies indicate that the millennial generation's great expectations stem from feelings of superiority. Michigan State University's Collegiate Employment Research Institute and MonsterTrak, an online careers site, conducted a research study of 18- to 28-year-olds and found that nearly half had moderate to high superiority beliefs about themselves. The superiority factor was measured by responses to such statements as "I deserve favors from others" and "I know that I have more natural talents than most."

For their part, millennials believe they can afford to be picky, with talent shortages looming as baby boomers retire. "They are finding that they have to adjust work around our lives instead of us adjusting our lives around work," a teenage blogger named Olivia writes on the Web site Xanga.com. "What other option do they have? We are hard working and utilize tools to get the job done. But we don't want to work more than 40 hours a week, and we want to wear clothes that are comfortable. We want to be able to spice up the dull workday by listening to our iPods. If corporate America doesn't like that, too bad."

Where do such feelings come from? Blame it on doting parents, teachers and coaches. Millennials are truly "trophy kids," the pride and joy of their parents. The millennials were lavishly praised and often received trophies when they excelled, and sometimes when they didn't, to avoid damaging their self-esteem. They and their parents have placed a high premium on success, filling resumes with not only academic accolades but also sports and other extracurricular activities.

Now what happens when these trophy kids arrive in the workplace with greater expectations than any generation before them? "Their attitude is always 'What are you going to give me,'" says Natalie Griffith, manager of human-resource programs at Eaton Corp. "It's not necessarily arrogance; it's simply their mindset."

Millennials want loads of attention and guidance from employers. An annual or even semiannual evaluation isn't enough. They want to know how they're doing weekly, even daily. "The millennials were raised with so much affirmation and positive reinforcement that they come into the workplace needy for more," says Subha Barry, managing director and head of global diversity and inclusion at Merrill Lynch & Co.

But managers must tread lightly when making a critique. This generation was treated so delicately that many schoolteachers stopped grading papers and tests in harsh-looking red ink. Some managers have seen millennials break down in tears after a negative performance review and even quit their jobs. "They like the constant positive reinforcement, but don't always take suggestions for improvement well," says Steve Canale, recruiting manager at General Electric Co. In performance evaluations, "it's still important to give the good, the bad and the ugly, but with a more positive emphasis."

Millennials also want things spelled out clearly. Many flounder without precise guidelines but thrive in structured situations that provide clearly defined rules and the order that they crave. Managers will need to give step-by-step directions for handling everything from projects to voice-mail messages to client meetings. It may seem obvious that employees should show up on time, limit lunchtime to an hour and turn off cellphones during meetings. But those basics aren't necessarily apparent to many millennials.

Gail McDaniel, a corporate consultant and career coach for college students, spoke to managers at a health-care company who were frustrated by some of their millennial employees. It seems that one young man missed an important deadline, and when his manager asked him to explain, he said, "Oh, you forgot to remind me." Parents and teachers aren't doing millennials any favors by constantly adapting to their needs, Ms. McDaniel says. "Going into the workplace, they have an expectation that companies will adapt for them, too."

Millennials also expect a flexible work routine that allows them time for their family and personal interests. "For this generation, work is not a place you go; work is a thing you do," says Kaye Foster-Cheek, vice president for human resources at Johnson & Johnson.

Although millennials have high expectations about what their employers should provide them, companies shouldn't expect much loyalty in return. If a job doesn't prove fulfilling, millennials will forsake it in a flash. Indeed, many employers say it's retention that worries them most.

In the Michigan State/MonsterTrak study, about two-thirds of the millennials said they would likely "surf" from one job to the next. In addition, about 44% showed their lack of loyalty by stating that they would renege on a job-acceptance commitment if a better offer came along.

These workplace nomads don't see any stigma in listing three jobs in a single year on their resumes. They are quite confident about landing yet another job, even if it will take longer in this dismal economy. In the meantime, they needn't worry about their next paycheck because they have their parents to cushion them. They're comfortable in the knowledge that they can move back home while they seek another job. The weak job market may make millennials think twice about moving on, but once jobs are more plentiful, they will likely resume their job-hopping ways.

Justin Pfister, the founder of Open Yard, an online retailer of sports equipment, believes he and his fellow millennials will resist having their expectations deflated. If employers fail to provide the opportunities and rewards millennials seek, he says, they're likely to drop out of the corporate world as he did and become entrepreneurs. "We get stifled when we're offered single-dimensional jobs," he says. "We are multi-dimensional people living and working in a multi-dimensional world."

These outspoken young people tend to be highly opinionated and fearlessly challenge recruiters and bosses. Status and hierarchy don't impress them much. They want to be treated like colleagues rather than subordinates and expect ready access to senior executives, even the CEO, to share their brilliant ideas. Recruiters at such companies as investment-banking firm Goldman Sachs Group Inc. and Amazon.com describe "student stalkers" who brashly fire off emails to everyone from the CEO on down, trying to get an inside track to a job.

Companies have a vested interest in trying to slow the millennial mobility rate. They not only will need millennials to fill positions left vacant by retiring baby boomers but also will benefit from this generation's best and brightest, who possess significant strengths in teamwork, technology skills, social networking and multitasking. Millennials were bred for achievement, and most will work hard if the task is engaging and promises a tangible payoff.

Clearly, companies that want to compete for top talent must bend a bit and adapt to the millennial generation. Employers need to show new hires how their work makes a difference and why it's of value to the company. Smart managers will listen to their young employees' opinions, and give them some say in decisions. Employers also can detail the career opportunities available to millennials if they'll just stick around awhile. Indeed, it's the wealth of opportunities that will prove to be the most effective retention tool.

In the final analysis, the generational tension is a bit ironic. After all, the grumbling baby-boomer managers are the same indulgent parents who produced the millennial generation. Ms. Barry of Merrill Lynch sees the irony. She is teaching her teenage daughter to value her own opinions and to challenge things. Now she sees many of those challenging millennials at her company and wonders how she and other managers can expect the kids they raised to suddenly behave differently at work. "It doesn't mean we can be as indulgent as managers as we are as parents," she says. "But as parents of young people just like them, we can treat them with respect."

Critical Reading Questions

Summarizing the Text

1. What is the "millennial generation"? How is it defined demographically? What characteristics are its members commonly seen to share?
2. According to the article, what are some of the adjustments that employers should make for "millennial" employees?

Establishing the Context

3. Many of the characteristics of the "millennial generation" that Alsop identifies might be questionable or might apply to any group of people. What are some of the unsupported generalizations that Alsop makes? How does he use ethos to support them? How might you refute these generalizations?
4. Alsop, in his conclusion, acknowledges the "irony" of this "generational tension." What does he mean by this? Who are the "baby boomers" and what are *their* generational characteristics?

Responding to the Message

5. Are you a member of the "millennial generation"? If so, do you believe that Alsop's portrayal is accurate? Why or why not?
6. What sort of job do you envision yourself having? When you think about adjectives describing your dream job, what are they? Does this match with Alsop's anecdotal report on the desires of the "millennials"?

Shop Class as Soulcraft
Matthew Crawford

Matthew Crawford holds a Ph.D. in political science from the University of Chicago and is a fellow at the Institute for Advanced Studies in Culture at the University of Virginia. He also fixes motorcycles for a living. This seeming split is at the heart of Crawford's essay "Shop Class as Soulcraft" (later turned into a book), which appeared in the New Atlantis, *a magazine that seeks "to clarify the nation's moral and political understanding of all areas of technology." In this essay, Crawford examines the nature of two kinds of work: manual labor and "knowledge work," which college students are training to do. Because we have moved too far into the world of "knowledge work," Crawford argues, we are becoming "more passive and more dependent."*

Anyone in the market for a good used machine tool should talk to Noel Dempsey, a dealer in Richmond, Virginia. Noel's bustling warehouse is full of metal lathes, milling machines, and table saws, and it turns out that most of it is from schools. EBay is awash in such equipment, also from schools. It appears shop class is becoming a thing of the past, as educators prepare students to become "knowledge workers."

At the same time, an engineering culture has developed in recent years in which the object is to "hide the works," rendering the artifacts we use unintelligible to direct inspection. Lift the hood on some cars now (especially German ones), and the engine appears a bit like the shimmering, featureless obelisk that so enthralled the cavemen in the opening scene of the movie *2001: A Space Odyssey*. Essentially, there is another hood under the hood. This creeping concealedness takes various forms. The fasteners holding small appliances together now often require esoteric screwdrivers not commonly available, apparently to prevent the curious or the angry from interrogating the innards. By way of contrast, older readers will recall that until recent decades, Sears catalogues included blown-up parts diagrams and conceptual schematics for all appliances and many other mechanical goods. It was simply taken for granted that such information would be demanded by the consumer.

A decline in tool use would seem to betoken a shift in our mode of inhabiting the world: more passive and more dependent. And indeed, there are fewer occasions for the kind of spiritedness that is called forth when we take things in hand for ourselves, whether to fix them or to make them. What ordinary people once made, they buy; and what they once fixed for themselves, they replace entirely or hire an expert to repair, whose expert fix often involves installing a pre-made replacement part.

So perhaps the time is ripe for reconsideration of an ideal that has fallen out of favor: manual competence, and the stance it entails toward the built, material world. Neither as workers nor as consumers are we much called upon to exercise such competence, most of us anyway, and merely to recommend its cultivation is to risk the scorn of those who take themselves to be the most hard-headed: the hard-headed economist will point out the opportunity costs of making what can be bought, and the hard-headed educator will say that it is irresponsible to educate the young for the trades, which are somehow identified as the jobs of the past. But we might pause to consider just how hard-headed these presumptions are, and whether they don't, on the contrary, issue from a peculiar sort of idealism, one that insistently steers young people toward the most ghostly kinds of work.

Judging from my admittedly cursory survey, articles began to appear in vocational education journals around 1985 with titles such as "The Soaring Technology Revolution" and "Preparing Kids for High-Tech and the Global Future." Of course, there is nothing new about American future-ism. What is new is the wedding of future-ism to what might be called "virtualism": a vision of the future in which we somehow take leave of material reality and glide about in a pure information economy. New and yet not so new—for fifty years now we've been assured that we are headed for a "post-industrial economy." While manufacturing jobs have certainly left our shores to a disturbing degree, the manual trades have not. If you need a deck built, or your car fixed, the Chinese are of no help. Because they are in China. And in fact there are reported labor shortages in both construction and auto repair. Yet the trades and manufacturing are lumped together in the mind of the pundit class as "blue collar," and their requiem is intoned. Even so, the *Wall Street Journal* recently wondered whether "skilled [manual] labor is becoming one of the few sure paths to a good living." This possibility was brought to light for many by the bestseller *The Millionaire Next Door,* which revealed that the typical millionaire is the guy driving a pickup, with his own business in the trades. My real concern here is not with the economics of skilled manual work, but rather with its intrinsic satisfactions. I mention these economic rumors only to raise a suspicion against the widespread prejudice that such work is somehow not viable as a livelihood.

The Psychic Appeal of Manual Work

I began working as an electrician's helper at age fourteen, and started a small electrical contracting business after college, in Santa Barbara. In those years I never ceased to take pleasure in the moment, at the end of a job, when I would flip the switch. "And there was light." It was an experience of agency and competence. The effects of my work were visible for all to see, so my competence was real for others as well; it had a social currency. The well-founded pride of the tradesman is far from the gratuitous "self-esteem" that educators would impart to students, as though by magic.

I was sometimes quieted at the sight of a gang of conduit entering a large panel in a commercial setting, bent into nestled, flowing curves, with varying offsets, that somehow all terminated in the same plane. This was a skill so far beyond my abilities that I felt I was in the presence of some genius, and the man who bent that conduit surely imagined this moment of recognition as he worked. As a residential electrician, most of my work got covered up inside walls. Yet even so, there is pride in meeting the aesthetic demands of a workmanlike installation. Maybe another electrician will see it someday. Even if not, one feels responsible to one's better self. Or rather, to the thing itself—craftsmanship might be defined simply as the desire to do something well, for its own sake. If the primary satisfaction is intrinsic and private in this way, there is nonetheless a sort of self-disclosing that takes place. As Alexandre Kojève writes:

> The man who works recognizes his own product in the World that has actually been transformed by his work: he recognizes himself in it, he sees in it his own human reality, in it he discovers and reveals to others the objective reality of his humanity, of the originally abstract and purely subjective idea he has of himself.

The satisfactions of manifesting oneself concretely in the world through manual competence have been known to make a man quiet and easy. They seem to relieve him of the felt need to offer chattering *interpretations* of himself to vindicate his worth. He can simply point: the building stands, the car now runs, the lights are on. Boasting is what a boy does, who has no real effect in the world. But craftsmanship must reckon with the infallible judgment of reality, where one's failures or shortcomings cannot be interpreted away.

Hobbyists will tell you that making one's own furniture is hard to justify economically. And yet they persist. Shared memories attach to the material souvenirs of our lives, and producing them is a kind of communion, with others and with the future. Finding myself at loose ends one summer in Berkeley, I built a mahogany coffee table on which I spared no expense or effort. At that time I had no immediate prospect of becoming a father, yet I imagined a child who would form indelible impressions of this table and know that it was his father's work. I imagined the table fading into the background of a future life, the defects in its execution as well as inevitable stains and scars becoming a surface textured enough that memory and sentiment might cling to it, in unnoticed accretions. More fundamentally, the durable objects of use produced by men "give rise to the familiarity of the world, its customs and habits of intercourse between men and things as well as between men and men," as Hannah Arendt says. "The reality and reliability of the human world rest primarily on the fact that we are surrounded by things more permanent than the activity by which they were produced, and potentially even more permanent than the lives of their authors."

Because craftsmanship refers to objective standards that do not issue from the self and its desires, it poses a challenge to the ethic of consumerism, as the sociologist Richard Sennett has recently argued. The craftsman is proud of what he has made, and cherishes it, while the consumer discards things that are perfectly serviceable in his restless pursuit of the new. The craftsman is then more possessive, more tied to what is present, the dead incarnation of past labor; the consumer is more free, more imaginative, and so more valorous according to those who would sell us things. Being able to think materially about material goods, hence critically, gives one some independence from the manipulations of marketing, which typically divert attention from *what a thing is* to a back-story intimated through associations, the point of which is to exaggerate minor differences between brands. Knowing the production narrative, or at least being able to plausibly imagine it, renders the social narrative of the advertisement less potent. The tradesman has an impoverished fantasy life compared to the ideal consumer; he is more utilitarian and less given to soaring hopes. But he is also more autonomous.

This would seem to be significant for any political typology. Political theorists from Aristotle to Thomas Jefferson have questioned the republican virtue of the mechanic, finding him too narrow in his concerns to be moved by the public good. Yet this assessment was made before the full flowering of mass communication and mass conformity, which pose a different set of problems for the republican character: enervation of judgment and erosion of the independent spirit. Since the standards of craftsmanship issue from the logic of things rather than the art of persuasion, practiced submission to them perhaps gives the craftsman some psychic ground to stand on against fantastic hopes aroused by demagogues, whether commercial or political. The crafts-man's habitual deference is not toward the New, but toward the distinction between the Right Way and the Wrong Way. However narrow in its application, this is a rare appearance in contemporary life—a disinterested, articulable, and publicly affirmable idea of the good. Such a strong ontology is somewhat at odds with the cutting-edge institutions of the new capitalism, and with the educational regime that aims to supply those institutions with suitable workers—pliable generalists unfettered by any single set of skills.

Today, in our schools, the manual trades are given little honor. The egalitarian worry that has always attended tracking students into "college prep" and "vocational ed" is overlaid with another: the fear that acquiring a specific skill set means that one's life is *determined.* In college, by contrast, many students don't learn anything of particular application; college is the ticket to an *open* future. Craftsmanship entails learning to do one thing really well, while the ideal of the new economy is to be able to learn new things, celebrating potential rather than achievement. Somehow, every worker in the cutting-edge workplace is now supposed to act like an "intrapreneur," that is, to be actively involved in the continuous redefinition of his own job. Shop class presents an image of stasis that runs directly counter to what Richard Sennett identifies as "a key element in the new economy's idealized self: the capacity to surrender, to give up possession of an established reality." This stance toward "established reality," which can only be called psychedelic, is best not indulged around a table saw. It is dissatisfied with what Arendt calls the "reality and reliability" of the world. It is a strange sort of ideal, attractive only to a peculiar sort of self—gratuitous ontological insecurity is no fun for most people.

As Sennett argues, most people take pride in being good at something specific, which happens through the accumulation of experience. Yet the flitting disposition is pressed upon workers from above by the current generation of management revolutionaries, for whom the ethic of craftsmanship is actually something to be rooted out from the workforce. Craftsmanship means dwelling on a task for a long time and going deeply into it, because one wants to get it right. In management-speak, this is called being "ingrown." The preferred role model is the management consultant, who swoops in and out, and whose very pride lies in his lack of particular expertise. Like the ideal consumer, the management consultant presents an image of soaring freedom, in light of which the manual trades appear cramped and paltry.

The Cognitive Demands of Manual Work

In *The Mind at Work*, Mike Rose provides "cognitive biographies" of several trades, and depicts the learning process in a wood shop class. He writes that "our testaments to physical work are so often focused on the values such work exhibits rather than on the thought it requires. It is a subtle but pervasive omission....It is as though in our cultural iconography we are given the muscled arm, sleeve rolled tight against biceps, but no thought bright behind the eye, no image that links hand and brain."

Skilled manual labor entails a systematic encounter with the material world, precisely the kind of encounter that gives rise to natural science. From its earliest practice, craft knowledge has entailed knowledge of the "ways" of one's materials—that is, knowledge of their nature, acquired through disciplined perception and a systematic approach to problems. And in fact, in areas of well-developed craft, technological developments typically preceded and gave rise to advances in scientific understanding, not vice versa. The steam engine is a good example. It was developed by mechanics who observed the relations between volume, pressure, and temperature. This at a time when theoretical scientists were tied to the caloric theory of heat, which later turned out to be a conceptual dead end. The success of the steam engine contributed to the development of what we now call classical thermodynamics. This history provides a nice illustration of a point made by Aristotle:

> Lack of experience diminishes our power of taking a comprehensive view of the admitted facts. Hence those who dwell in intimate association with nature and its phenomena are more able to lay down principles such as to admit of a wide and coherent development; while those whom devotion to abstract discussions has rendered unobservant of facts are too ready to dogmatize on the basis of a few observations.

Another example is the Vernier scale used on machinists' calipers and micrometers. Invented in 1631, it is a sort of mechanical calculus that renders continuous measurement in discrete digital approximation to four decimal places. Such inventions capture a reflective moment in which some skilled worker has made explicit the assumptions that are implicit in his manual skill.

In what has to be the best article ever published in an education journal, the cognitive scientists Mike Eisenberg and Ann Nishioka Eisenberg give real pedagogical force to this reflective moment, and draw out its theoretical implications ("Shop Class for the Next Millennium: Education Through Computer-Enriched Handicrafts," in the *Journal of Interactive Media in Education*). They offer a computer program to facilitate making origami, or rather Archimedean solids, by unfolding these solids into two dimensions. But they then have their students actually make the solids, out of paper cut according to the computer's instructions. "Computational tools for crafting are entities poised somewhere between the abstract, untouchable world of software objects and the homey constraints of human dexterity; they are therefore creative exercises in making conscious those aspects of craft work ... that are often more easily represented 'in the hand' than in language." It is worth pausing to consider their efforts, as they have implications well beyond mathematics instruction.

> In our early work with HyperGami, we often ran into situations in which the program provided us with a folding net that was mathematically correct—i.e., a technically correct unfolding of the desired solid—but otherwise disastrous. Figure 7 shows an example. Here, we are trying to create an approximation to a cone—a pyramid on a regular octagonal base. HyperGami provides us with a folding net that will, indeed, produce a pyramid; but typically, no paper crafter would come up with a net of this sort, since it is fiendishly hard to join together those eight tall triangles into a single vertex. In fact, this is an illustrative example of a more general idea—the difficulty of formalizing, in purely mathematical terms, what it means to produce a 'realistic' (and not merely technically correct) solution to an algorithmic problem derived from human practice.

I take their point to be that the crafting problem is in fact not reducible to an algorithmic problem. More precisely, any algorithmic solution to the crafting problem cannot itself be generated algorithmically, as it must include ad hoc constraints known only through practice, that is, through embodied manipulations. Those constraints cannot be arrived at deductively, starting from mathematical entities. It is worth noting in passing that this has implications for the theory of mind favored by artificial intelligence researchers, as it speaks to the "computability" of pragmatic cognition. It would be a task for cognitive science to determine if these considerations place a theoretical limit on the automation of work, but I can speak firsthand to how one area of work is resistant to algorithmic thinking.

Following graduate school in Chicago, I took a job in a Washington, D.C. think tank. I hated it, so I left and opened a motorcycle repair shop in Richmond. When I would come home from work, my wife would sniff at me and say "carbs" or "brakes," corresponding to the various solvents used. Leaving a sensible trace, my day was at least imaginable to her. But while the filth and odors were apparent, the amount of head-scratching I'd done since breakfast was not. Mike Rose writes that in the practice of surgery, "dichotomies such as concrete versus abstract and technique versus reflection break down in practice. The surgeon's judgment is simultaneously technical and deliberative, and that mix is the source of its power." This could be said of any manual skill that is diagnostic, including motorcycle repair. You come up with an imagined train of causes for manifest symptoms and judge their likelihood before tearing anything down. This imagining relies on a stock mental library, not of natural kinds or structures, like that of the surgeon, but rather the functional kinds of an internal combustion engine, their various interpretations by different manufacturers, and their proclivities for failure. You also develop a library of sounds and smells and feels. For example, the backfire of a too-lean fuel mixture is subtly different from an ignition backfire. If the motorcycle is thirty years old, from an obscure maker that went out of business twenty years ago, its proclivities are known mostly through lore. It would probably be impossible to do such work in isolation, without access to a collective historical memory; you have to be embedded in a community of mechanic-antiquarians. These relationships are maintained by telephone, in a network of reciprocal favors that spans the country. My most reliable source, Fred Cousins in Chicago, had such an encyclopedic knowledge of obscure European motorcycles that all I could offer him in exchange was regular shipments of obscure European beer.

There is always a risk of introducing new complications when working on decrepit machines, and this enters the diagnostic logic. Measured in likelihood of screw-ups, the cost is not identical for all avenues of inquiry when deciding which hypothesis to pursue. For example, the fasteners holding the engine covers on 1970s-era Hondas are Phillips-head, and they are *always* stripped and corroded. Do you *really* want to check the condition of the starter clutch, if each of ten screws will need to be drilled out and extracted, risking damage to the engine case? Such impediments can cloud one's thinking. Put more neutrally, the attractiveness of any hypothesis is determined in part by physical circumstances that have no logical connection to the diagnostic problem at hand, but a strong pragmatic bearing on it (kind of like origami). The factory service manuals tell you to be systematic in eliminating variables, but they never take such factors into account. So you have to develop your own decision tree for the particular circumstances. The problem is that at each node of this new tree, your own, unquantifiable risk aversion introduces ambiguity. There comes a point where you have to step back and get a larger gestalt. Have a cigarette and walk around the lift. Any mechanic will tell you that it is invaluable to have other mechanics around to test your reasoning against, especially if they have a different intellectual disposition.

My shop-mate Tommy Van Auken was an accomplished visual artist, and I was repeatedly struck by his ability to literally *see* things that escaped me. I had the conceit of being an empiricist, but seeing things is not a simple matter. Even on the relatively primitive vintage bikes that were our specialty, some diagnostic situations contain so many variables, and symptoms can be so under-determining of causes, that explicit analytical reasoning comes up short. What is required then is the kind of judgment that arises only from experience; hunches rather than rules. There was more thinking going on in the bike shop than in the think tank.

Socially, being the proprietor of a bike shop in a small city gave me a feeling I never had before. I felt I had a place in society. Whereas "think tank" is an answer that, at best, buys you a few seconds when someone asks what you do, while you try to figure out what it is that you in fact do, with "motorcycle mechanic" I got immediate recognition. I bartered services with machinists and metal fabricators, which has a very different feel than transactions with money, and further increased my sense of social embeddedness. There were three restaurants with cooks whose bikes I had restored, where unless I deceive myself I was treated as a sage benefactor. I felt pride before my wife when we would go out to dinner and be given preferential treatment, or simply a hearty greeting. There were group rides, and bike night every Tuesday at a certain bar. Sometimes one or two people would be wearing my shop's T-shirt. It felt good.

Given the intrinsic richness of manual work, cognitively, socially, and in its broader psychic appeal, the question becomes why it has suffered such a devaluation in recent years as a component of education. The economic rationale so often offered, namely that manual work is somehow going to disappear, is questionable if not preposterous, so it is in the murky realm of culture that we must look to understand these things. To this end, perhaps we need to consider the origins of shop class, so that we can better understand its demise.

ARTS, CRAFTS, AND THE ASSEMBLY LINE

At a time when Teddy Roosevelt preached the strenuous life and elites worried about their state of "over-civilized" spiritual decay, the project of getting back in touch with "real life" took various forms. One was romantic fantasy about the pre-modern craftsman. This was understandable given changes in the world of work at the turn of the century, a time when the bureaucratization of economic life was rapidly increasing the number of paper shufflers. The tangible elements of craft were appealing as an antidote to vague feelings of unreality, diminished autonomy, and a fragmented sense of self that were especially acute among the professional classes.

The Arts and Crafts movement thus fit easily with the new therapeutic ethic of self-regeneration. Depleted from his workweek in the corporate world, the office worker repaired to his basement workshop to putter about and tinker, refreshing himself for the following week. As T. J. Jackson Lears writes in his history of the Progressive era, *No Place of Grace*, "toward the end of the nineteenth century, many beneficiaries of modern culture began to feel they were its secret victims." Various forms of antimodernism gained wide currency in the middle and upper classes, including the ethic of craftsmanship. Some Arts and Crafts enthusiasts conceived their task to be evangelizing good taste as embodied in the works of craft, as against machine-age vulgarity. Cultivating an appreciation for *objets d'art* was thus a form of protest against modernity, with a view to providing a livelihood to dissident craftsmen. But it dovetailed with, and gave a higher urgency to, the nascent culture of luxury consumption. As Lears tells the story, the great irony is that antimodernist sentiments of aesthetic revolt against the machine paved the way for certain unattractive features of late-modern culture: therapeutic self-absorption and the hankering after "authenticity," precisely those psychic hooks now relied upon by advertisers. Such spiritualized, symbolic modes of craft practice and craft consumption represented a kind of compensation for, and therefore an accommodation to, new modes of routinized, bureaucratic work.

But not everyone worked in an office. Indeed, there was class conflict brewing, with unassimilated immigrants accumulating in America's Eastern cities and serious labor violence in Chicago and elsewhere. To the upper classes of those same cities, enamored of the craft ideal, the possibility presented itself that the laboring classes might remain satisfied with their material lot if they found joy in their labor. Shop class could serve to put the proper spin on manual work. Any work, it was posited, could be "artful" if done in the proper spirit; somehow a movement that had started with reverence for the craftsman now offered an apologetic for factory work. As Lears writes, "By shifting their attention from the conditions of labor to the laborer's frame of mind, craft ideologues could acclaim the value of any work, however monotonous."

The Smith-Hughes Act of 1917 gave federal funding for manual training in two forms: as part of general education and as a separate vocational program. The invention of modern shop class thus serviced both cultural reflexes of the Arts and Crafts movement at once. The children of the managerial class could take shop as enrichment to the college-prep curriculum, making a bird-feeder to hang outside mom's kitchen window, while the children of laborers would be socialized into the work ethic appropriate to their station through what was now called "industrial arts" education. The need for such socialization was not simply a matter of assimilating immigrants from Southern and Eastern Europe who lacked a Protestant work ethic. It was recognized as a necessity for the broader working-class population, precisely because the institutions that had previously served this socializing function, apprenticeship and guild traditions, had been destroyed by new modes of labor. Writing in 1918, one Robert Hoxie worried thus:

> It is evident...that the native efficiency of the working class must suffer from the neglect of apprenticeship, if no other means of industrial education is forthcoming. Scientific managers, themselves, have complained bitterly of the poor and lawless material from which they must recruit their workers, compared with the efficient and self-respecting craftsmen who applied for employment twenty years ago.

Needless to say, "scientific managers" were concerned more with the "efficient" part of this formula than with the "self-respecting" part, yet the two are not independent. The quandary was how to make workers efficient and attentive, when their actual labor had been degraded by automation. The motivation previously supplied by the intrinsic satisfactions of manual work was to be replaced with ideology; industrial arts education now concerned itself with moral formation. Lears writes that "American craft publicists, by treating craftsmanship ... as an agent of socialization, abandoned [the] effort to revive pleasurable labor. Manual training meant specialized assembly line preparation for the lower classes and educational or recreational experiences for the bourgeoisie."

Of the Smith-Hughes Act's two rationales for shop class, vocational and general ed, only the latter emphasized the learning of aesthetic, mathematical, and physical principles through the manipulation of material things (Dewey's "learning by doing"). It is not surprising, then, that the act came four years after Henry Ford's innovation of the assembly line. The act's dual educational scheme mirrored the assembly line's severing of the cognitive aspects of manual work from its physical execution. Such a partition of thinking from doing has bequeathed us the dichotomy of "white collar" versus "blue collar," corresponding to mental versus manual. These seem to be the categories that inform the educational landscape even now, and this entails two big errors. First, it assumes that all blue collar work is as mindless as assembly line work, and second, that white collar work is still recognizably mental in character. Yet there is evidence to suggest that the new frontier of capitalism lies in doing to office work what was previously done to factory work: draining it of its cognitive elements. Paradoxically, educators who would steer students toward cognitively rich work options might do this best by rehabilitating the manual trades, based on a firmer grasp of what such work is really like. And would this not be in keeping with their democratic mission? Let them publicly honor those who gain real craft knowledge, the sort we all depend on every day.

The Degradation of Blue Collar Work

The degradation of work in the last century is often tied to the evils of technology in one way or another. And it is certainly true that "technical progress has multiplied the number of simplified jobs," as one French sociologist wrote in the 1950s. This writer pointed out a resemblance between the Soviet bloc and the Western bloc with regard to work; both rival civilizations were developing "that separation between planning and execution which seems to be in our day a common denominator linking all industrial societies together." Yet while technology plays a role in facilitating this separation of planning and execution, the basic logic that drives the separation rests not on technological progress, but rather on a certain mode of economic relations, as Harry Braverman has shown in his masterpiece of economic reflection, *Labor and Monopoly Capital: The Degradation of Work in the Twentieth Century.* Braverman was an avowed Marxist, writing in 1974. With the Cold War now safely decided, we may consider anew, without defensive ire, the Marxian account of alienated labor. Braverman gives a richly descriptive account of the degradation of many different kinds of work. In doing so, he offers nothing less than an explanation of why we are getting more stupid with every passing year—which is to say, the degradation of work is ultimately a cognitive matter.

The central culprit in Braverman's account is "scientific management," which "enters the workplace not as the representative of science, but as the representative of management masquerading in the trappings of science." The tenets of scientific management were given their first and frankest articulation by Frederick Winslow Taylor, an unembarrassed evangelist of efficiency whose *Principles of Scientific Management* was hugely influential in the early decades of the twentieth century. Stalin was a big fan, as were the founders of the first MBA program, at Harvard, where Taylor was invited to lecture annually. Taylor writes, "The managers assume...the burden of gathering together all of the traditional knowledge which in the past has been possessed by the workmen and then of classifying, tabulating, and reducing this knowledge to rules, laws, and formulae." Scattered craft knowledge is concentrated in the hands of the employer, then doled out again to workers in the form of minute instructions needed to perform some *part* of what is now a work *process*. This process replaces what was previously an integral activity, rooted in craft tradition and experience, animated by the worker's own mental image of, and intention toward, the finished product. Thus, according to

Taylor, "All possible brain work should be removed from the shop and centered in the planning or lay-out department." It is a mistake to suppose that the primary purpose of this partition is to render the work process more efficient. It may or may not result in extracting more value from a given unit of labor *time*. The concern is rather with labor *cost*. Once the cognitive aspects of the job are located in a separate management class, or better yet in a process that, once designed, requires no ongoing judgment or deliberation, skilled workers can be replaced with unskilled workers at a lower rate of pay. Taylor writes that the "full possibilities" of his system "will not have been realized until almost all of the machines in the shop are run by men who are of smaller caliber and attainments, and who are therefore cheaper than those required under the old system."

What becomes of the skilled workers? They go elsewhere, of course. But the competitive labor-cost advantage now held by the more modern firm, which has aggressively separated planning from execution, compels the whole industry to follow the same route, and entire skilled trades disappear. Thus craft knowledge dies out, or rather gets instantiated in a different form, as process engineering knowledge. The conception of the work is remote from the worker who does it.

Scientific management introduced the use of "time and motion analysis" to describe the physiological capabilities of the human body in machine terms. As Braverman writes, "the more labor is governed by classified motions which extend across the boundaries of trades and occupations, the more it dissolves its concrete forms into the general types of work motions. This mechanical exercise of human faculties according to motion types which are studied independently of the particular kind of work being done, brings to life the Marxist conception of 'abstract labor.'" The clearest example of abstract labor is thus the assembly line. The *activity* (in the Aristotelian sense) of self-directed labor, conducted by the worker, is dissolved into abstract parts and then reconstituted as a *process* controlled by management.

At the turn of the last century, the manufacture of automobiles was done by craftsmen recruited from bicycle and carriage shops: all-around mechanics who knew what they were doing. In *The Wheelwright's Shop*, George Sturt relates his experience in taking over his family business of making wheels for carriages, in 1884, shortly before the advent of the automobile. He had been a school teacher with literary ambitions, but now finds himself almost overwhelmed by the cognitive demands of his new trade. In Sturt's shop, working exclusively with hand tools, the skills required to build a wheel regress all the way to the selection of trees to fell for timber, the proper time for felling them, how to season them, and so forth. To select but one minor task out of the countless he describes, here is Sturt's account of fabricating a part of a wheel's rim called a felloe:

> Yet it is in vain to go into details at this point; for when the simple apparatus had all been gotten together for one simple-looking process, a never-ending series of variations was introduced by the material. What though two felloes might seem much alike when finished? It was the wheelwright himself who had to make them so. He it was who hewed out that resemblance from quite dissimilar blocks, for no two felloe-blocks were ever alike. Knots here, shakes there, rind-galls, waney edges (edges with more or less bark in them), thicknesses, thinnesses, were for ever affording new chances or forbidding previous solutions, whereby a fresh problem confronted the workman's ingenuity every few minutes. He had no band-saw (as now [1923]) to drive, with ruthless unintelligence, through every resistance. The timber was far from being prey, a helpless victim, to a machine. Rather it would lend its own special virtues to the man who knew how to humour it.

Given their likely acquaintance with such a cognitively rich world of work, it is hardly surprising that when Henry Ford introduced the assembly line in 1913, workers simply walked out. One of Ford's biographers wrote, "So great was labor's distaste for the new machine system that toward the close of 1913 every time the company wanted to add 100 men to its factory personnel, it was necessary to hire 963."

This would seem to be a crucial moment in the history of political economy. Evidently, the new system provoked natural revulsion. Yet, at some point, workers became habituated to it. How did this happen? One might be tempted to inquire in a typological mode: What sort of men were these first, the 100 out of 963 who stuck it out on the new assembly line? Perhaps it was the men who felt less revulsion because they had less pride in their own powers, and were therefore more tractable. Less republican, we might say. But if there was initially such a self-selection process, it quickly gave way to something less deliberate, more systemic.

In a temporary suspension of the Taylorist logic, Ford was forced to double the daily wage of his workers to keep the line staffed. As Braverman writes, this "opened up new possibilities for the intensification of labor within the plants, where workers were now anxious to keep their jobs." These anxious workers were more productive. Indeed, Ford himself later recognized his wage increase as "one of the finest cost-cutting moves we ever made," as he was able to double, and then triple, the rate at which cars were assembled by simply speeding up the conveyors. By doing so he destroyed his competitors, and thereby destroyed the possibility of an alternative way of working. (It also removed the wage pressure that comes from the existence of more enjoyable jobs.) At the Columbian World Expo held in Chicago in 1893, no fewer than seven large-scale carriage builders from Cincinnati alone presented their wares. Adopting Ford's methods, the industry would soon be reduced to the Big Three. So workers eventually became habituated to the abstraction of the assembly line. Evidently, it inspires revulsion only if one is acquainted with more satisfying modes of work.

Here the concept of wages as *compensation* achieves its fullest meaning, and its central place in modern economy. Changing attitudes toward consumption seemed to play a role. A man whose needs are limited will find the least noxious livelihood and work in a subsistence mode, and indeed the experience of early (eighteenth-century) capitalism, when many producers worked at home on a piece-rate basis, was that only so much labor could be extracted from them. Contradicting the assumptions of "rational behavior" of classical economics, it was found that when employers would increase the piece rate in order to boost production, it actually had the opposite effect: workers would produce less, as now they could meet their fixed needs with less work. Eventually it was learned that the only way to get them to work harder was to play upon the imagination, stimulating new needs and wants. The habituation of workers to the assembly line was thus perhaps made easier by another innovation of the early twentieth century: consumer debt. As Jackson Lears has shown in a recent article, through the installment plan, previously unthinkable acquisitions became thinkable, and more than thinkable: it became normal to carry debt. The display of a new car bought on installment became a sign that one was trustworthy. In a wholesale transformation of the old Puritan moralism, expressed by Benjamin Franklin (admittedly no Puritan) with the motto "Be frugal and free," the early twentieth century saw the moral legitimation of spending. Indeed, 1907 saw the publication of a book with the immodest title *The New Basis of Civilization*, by Simon Nelson Patten, in which the moral valence of debt and spending is reversed, and the multiplication of wants becomes not a sign of dangerous corruption but part of the civilizing process. That is, part of the disciplinary process. As Lears writes, "Indebtedness could discipline workers, keeping them at routinized jobs in factories and offices, graying but in harness, meeting payments regularly."

The Degradation of White Collar Work

Much of the "jobs of the future" rhetoric surrounding the eagerness to end shop class and get every warm body into college, thence into a cubicle, implicitly assumes that we are heading to a "post-industrial" economy in which everyone will deal only in abstractions. Yet trafficking in abstractions is not the same as thinking. White collar professions, too, are subject to routinization and degradation, proceeding by the same process as befell manual fabrication a hundred years ago: the cognitive elements of the job are appropriated from professionals, instantiated in a system or process, and then handed back to a new class of workers—clerks—who replace the professionals. If genuine knowledge work is not growing but actually shrinking, because it is coming to be concentrated in an ever-smaller elite, this has implications for the vocational advice that students ought to receive.

"Expert systems," a term coined by artificial intelligence researchers, were initially developed by the military for battle command, then used to replicate industrial expertise in such fields as oil-well drilling and telephone-line maintenance. Then they found their way into medical diagnosis, and eventually the cognitively murky, highly lucrative, regions of financial and legal advice. In *The Electronic Sweatshop: How Computers Are Transforming the Office of the Future into the Factory of the Past*, Barbara Garson details how "Extraordinary human ingenuity has been used to eliminate the need for human ingenuity." She finds that, like Taylor's rationalization of the shop floor, the intention of expert systems is "to transfer knowledge, skill, and decision making from employee to employer." While Taylor's time and motion studies broke every concrete work motion into minute parts,

> The modern knowledge engineer performs similar detailed studies, only he anatomizes decision making rather than bricklaying. So the time-and-motion study has become a time-and-thought study. . . .To build an expert system, a living expert is debriefed and then cloned by a knowledge engineer. That is to say, an expert is interviewed, typically for weeks or months. The knowledge engineer watches the expert work on sample problems and asks exactly what factors the expert considered in making his apparently intuitive decisions. Eventually hundreds or thousands of rules of thumb are fed into the computer. The result is a program that can 'make decisions' or 'draw conclusions' heuristically instead of merely calculating with equations. Like a real expert, a sophisticated expert system should be able to draw inferences from 'iffy' or incomplete data that seems to suggest or tends to rule out. In other words it uses (or replaces) judgment.

The human expert who is cloned achieves a vast dominion and immortality, in a sense. It is *other* experts, and future experts, who are displaced as expertise is centralized. "This means that more people in the advice or human service business will be employed as the disseminators, rather than the originators, of this advice," Garson writes. In his 2006 book *The Culture of the New Capitalism*, Richard Sennett describes just such a process, "especially in the cutting-edge realms of high finance, advanced technology, and sophisticated services": genuine knowledge work comes to be concentrated in an ever-smaller elite. It seems we must take a cold-eyed view of "knowledge work," and reject the image of a rising sea of pure mentation that lifts all boats. More likely is a rising sea of clerkdom. To expect otherwise is to hope for a reversal in the basic logic of the modern economy—that is, cognitive stratification. It is not clear to me what this hope could be based on, though if history is any guide we have to wonder whether the excitation of such a hope has become an instrument by which young people are prepared for clerkdom, in the same perverse way that the craft ideology prepared workers for the assembly line. Both provide a lens that makes the work look appealing from afar, but only by presenting an image that is upside down.

THE CRAFTSMAN AS STOIC

We are recalled to the basic antagonism of economic life: work is toilsome and necessarily serves someone else's interests. That's why you get paid. Thus chastened, we may ask the proper question: what is it that we really want for a young person when we give them vocational advice? The only creditable answer, it seems to me, is one that avoids utopianism while keeping an eye on the human good: work that engages the human capacities as fully as possible. What I have tried to show is that this humane and commonsensical answer goes against the central imperative of capitalism, which assiduously partitions thinking from doing. What is to be done? I offer no program, only an observation that might be of interest to anyone called upon to give guidance to the young.

Since manual work has been subject to routinization for over a century, the nonroutinized manual work that remains, outside the confines of the factory, would seem to be resistant to much further routinization. There still appear developments around the margins; for example, in the last twenty years pre-fabricated roof trusses have eliminated some of the more challenging elements from the jobs of framers who work for large tract developers, and pre-hung doors have done the same for finish carpenters generally. But still, the physical circumstances of the jobs performed by carpenters, plumbers, and auto mechanics vary too much for them to be executed by idiots; they require circumspection and adaptability. One feels like a man, not a cog in a machine. The trades are then a natural home for anyone who would live by his own powers, free not only of deadening abstraction, but also of the insidious hopes and rising insecurities that seem to be endemic in our current economic life. This is the stoic ideal.

So what advice should one give to a young person? By all means, go to college. In fact, approach college in the spirit of craftsmanship, going deep into liberal arts and sciences. In the summers, learn a manual trade. You're likely to be less damaged, and quite possibly better paid, as an independent tradesman than as a cubicle-dwelling tender of information systems. To heed such advice would require a certain contrarian streak, as it entails rejecting a life course mapped out by others as obligatory and inevitable.

Critical Reading Questions

Summarizing the Text

1. The text rests on a distinction between *knowledge work* and *skilled manual labor*. How does Crawford define each term? What are the essential qualities of each?

2. What do the terms *white collar* and *blue collar* mean? What is his argument about how white collar work is being "degraded"?

Establishing the Context

3. Although his piece is primarily about work, Crawford's argument has strong ramifications for how we are *trained* for jobs. What does he have to say about education in this essay? How does he rebut common ideas about the value of a college education?

4. Crawford writes like an academic—he brings in concepts and terms from other writers and thinkers and makes them tools in his argument. Make a list of all of the writers he alludes to, and what he takes from them. What does this tell you about how he constructs his *ethos* and his argument?

Responding to the Message

5. This is a "counterintuitive" argument—a highly educated person arguing in a journal aimed at intellectuals that the "knowledge economy" is a dead end. What do you think about this? What are the benefits of knowledge work that he *doesn't* mention? What are some of the drawbacks of working in a skilled trade that he fails to bring up?

6. Crawford argues that one should attend college but should "approach college in the spirit of craftsmanship." What does this mean? How might you approach your studies in such a spirit? How might one design a program of study that would promote such an approach?

A Foxconn Worker's Story

China Labor Watch

China Labor Watch is a nonprofit organization, founded by the Chinese labor activist Li Qiang in 2000, that seeks to "protect the rights of workers in China." The group conducts investigations of some of the larger manufacturing plants in China (many of which are producing goods for American and European markets), issues reports on their findings, and urges companies that do business with these Chinese firms to press for better working conditions in those factories. This personal narrative comes from an anonymous worker at a Foxconn factory in the city of Shenzhen that makes computer drives for companies such as Lenovo, Nintendo, Sony, and Philips.

I was raised in a farmer's family with five family members: my grand-father, parents, older brother and I. We own about eight acres of land, but since my grandfather is elderly, he cannot help my parents grow crops. My older brother is in college, and as for me, I am currently 19 years old, and just last month I was recruited by Foxconn through the arrangement [at] my school. Besides the earnings from growing crops, there is no additional income for my family. In the past, we had owed some money to relatives because my parents had to support my brother[s] and my education. Since I just graduated from a technical school, I was able to leave home to work and send some money home to pay for my brother's education and other debts.

After graduation, I was told by my school that it could arrange for my classmates and me to work at Shenzhen Foxconn. The school then gave us an introduction to Foxconn. At that time, I knew Foxconn's campus in Shenzhen is huge, but had no idea just how big it was until I got there. There were about 200 of us, guided by school teachers heading to Shenzhen. It took us about 30 hours by train and then by bus to reach Shenzhen Foxconn.

I was placed in a dormitory that has ten three-level bunk beds, thus accommodating 30 people. While many people refused to stay there at that time, the management said that it is much better than the other dormitories on site that are shared by hundreds of workers. Although I still had some negative feelings towards the dorm room, at the same time, I felt lucky for not having to live in a dorm room shared by hun-dreds, Just the second day living in the dorm, however, I found my safe box open, and my Walkman gone. There was nothing I could do but to try to tell myself that I was lucky because it was not that expensive.

The training begins immediately on the second day upon our arrival. At first I thought we would be informed of some professional operative skills and knowledge, but instead, we were taught the fac-tory's regulations, culture, and acknowledgment of Foxconn's business concept. By now, I think it is safe to say that the training is a part of Foxconn's brainwashing process. A supervisor told us that working at Foxconn requires total obedience; you do not need to be intelligent or highly skilled. After a week of training, we concluded that at Foxconn, we shouldn't treat ourselves as human beings, we are just machines. During the week, we also had a health examination, a very simple blood test, a blood pressure test and a vision test. We did not receive any results afterwards.

After the one week of in-class training, we begin our on-site train-ing, which is a modest way of telling us that we have to work as long as regular workers, with minimal compensation. Since we are still under training, Foxconn did not give us a contract to sign.

I consider myself lucky because one week after the on-site training I was selected by a CCPBG recruiter, which means I am officially a regular worker. When the selection takes place, it seems like a slave market where slave owners get to pick suitable slaves. There were about a couple hundred of us going through on-site training, and when the recruiters from other companies on Foxconn campus come, all of us have to stand straight in lines, putting our hands behind our backs, and wait for these recruiters to pick. After the selection ends, those who did not get picked go back to their work post. They cannot become regular workers until being picked so I was very lucky to be selected the first week. Many of my classmates are still doing on-site training waiting to be picked.

Twenty people including myself were selected and brought to the workshop where I will finally begin as a regular worker. First, the supervisor and assistant manager explain to us the rules of the workshop: no talking at work, no leaving work post at will, and etc. Then, the section supervisor gave us a lecture, emphasizing that we are no longer in school and that we have to work hard. Afterwards, I was assigned to my post, and few days later, I was offered a contract to sign. Since I was very inexperienced at that time, I did not even look at the contract details, and I still have yet to take a look at what exactly is on my contract.

My work post at that time was connecting computer wires. Later, I was assigned to another production line that produces CD-ROMs. I believe the whole workshop is producing for Sony.

Everyday I wake up at 7 AM, head to the workshop at 7:30 AM, place all personal items that contain metal, such as mobile phones, keys, pens and etc., into the shoe shelf, change into my uniform, and begin working at 8 AM. Although CCPBG states that work begins at 8 AM, it actually requires workers to be present at the workshop by 7:30 AM, and those 30 minutes are unpaid.

My current position is at the end of the production belt, installing four screws onto each CD-ROM case. At first I was not very skilled, and many times, either I was not able to install screws fast enough, decelerating the production or the screws were too loose. Thus the first week, I was often insulted by my supervisor. It was at that time when many workers decided to quit, not having been paid the adequate wages that we deserved. Like those workers, I was on the verge of quitting, but after I thought about my brother's education, and my family's limited income, I stayed. I am much better at my job now, though the speed of the production line moves so quickly that I have to continue to install screws on the CD-ROMs nonstop until lunch time, which is at noon. Before exiting the workshop, we have to go through a metal detector test, and if the alarm goes off, security will need to conduct a search to find the cause. If the cause is not work-related, we are allowed to pass.

We have a one hour lunch break. During break, the whole campus is filled with people, and we have to be very careful not to run into anyone. The situation in the canteen is even worse, and I generally have to wait more than ten minutes to get the meal. The lunch meal consists of two meat dishes and one vegetable dish, and rice is self-service, though I don't recommend taking too much rice since left over rice results in a fine. Since I always finish what I have on the plate, I am not too certain of the details of the fine.

At 1 PM, we return to our work and continue what was left off earlier this morning.

The afternoon is the most difficult part of the day, and since there is no time for nap after lunch, I often feel drowsy. We get off work at 5 PM, have dinner, rest for a while, and then at 6 PM overtime begins. We usually get off work at 8 PM, having completed two hours of overtime. However, if we were unable to complete the production quota in the allotted time, we would be insulted by supervisors and asked to work until the quota is reached. Moreover, those additional hours are unpaid. I was told by other experienced workers that each month there are about ten overtime hours uncounted, excluding the extra 30 minutes of unpaid work each morning.

Since I have been standing at the same spot working for more than ten hours, when I return to the dorm at night, I feel so exhausted and don't want to move. The dormitory is very inconvenient. I have to walk to the other side of the dormitory to take a shower, drink water, or use the bathroom. Since there's only one shower room on each floor, I often have to wait for a long time before I can take a shower and go to sleep.

Although the dormitory is free, my classmate and I decided to move out for safety reasons. Now, I live in a one bedroom apartment about 25 minutes' drive from Foxconn. The rent is 300 RMB [approx. $48] and we split the cost. Including the bus fare, which is 4 RMB roundtrip, about 120 RMB a month, I spend about a total of 270 RMB a month. Although I have to wake up much earlier to go to work, I feel much safer.

I was told by other workers that it is difficult to distinguish between peak and slow season at Foxconn. When it is busy, we have to work more than ten hours a day and most likely get one off day a month. When work is slow, we still have to work over ten hours a day, though we have three to four off days a month. This month I have only two off days, and since the crime rate at where I live is high, and I have often heard cases of robberies nearby, I usually stay home when I don't have to work. When my classmate and I miss our homes, we cook some of our local dishes as a remedy to our homesickness.

There is too much pressure during the day. I never have time to think, and only at night would I think about my parents at home. I want to call them, but there's no time to call during the day, and at night, I feel guilty calling because my parents are probably exhausted from working in the field all day. The only chance I have to call them is on my off days. Perhaps in the future, when the company switches me to night shifts I would have more opportunities to call home.

As for the future, I have not thought about it yet. Currently I earn about 1,500 RMB a month, which includes the minimum wage of 750 RMB and all the overtime hours I have worked. I will continue to work at Foxconn until my brother graduates and all the debts in the family paid off. Life is too difficult here. I feel like I have no self-esteem.

Critical Reading Questions

Summarizing the Text

1. This story, on its own, appears largely informational, but the activist group China Labor Watch included it in its report on what it considers poor working conditions at this factory. Where does the speaker directly express his opinions on the factory? What other details about the factory might China Labor Watch use to support its arguments?

2. What surprises you about the working and living conditions at Foxconn? How do these conditions differ from what you might expect in a factory?

Establishing the Context

3. Do you think Foxconn's Shenzhen factory, as described by this worker, qualifies as a sweatshop? What does that term mean? Is it a loaded term? If so, what are its connotations?

4. Much of this worker's narrative centers on the fact that as first he lives in a Foxconn dormitory and eats at a Foxconn "canteen" or dining hall. How does this affect a worker's relationship to his or her employer? His or her ability to stand up for his or her interests? Why would an employer provide these services to its employees?

Responding to the Message

5. Many of the workers who actually produce our expensive high-technology devices—computers, smart phones, e-readers—are low-skilled, low-paid employees of large Chinese factories. This is even more so when it comes to other, less expensive products that we use every day, from our clothing to our cookware. Should we be willing to pay more for our goods in order to ensure that the Chinese workers who actually produce these goods earn a living wage? Do consumers have any responsibility toward the workers who produce the products they consume?

6. Increasingly popular on campuses is the "sweatshop-free" movement—the idea that university-branded and licensed products (such as t-shirts or binders or backpacks) sold on campuses should not be produced in sweatshops. Activists on many campuses have received assurances from bookstore

managers and even university presidents that they will contract with sweat-shop-free vendors to provide those products. What do you think? Where are your bookstore's sweatshirts and polo shirts made? Is there a sweatshop-free movement on your campus? Should this be a priority at your school?

Where Sweatshops Are a Dream
Nicholas Kristof

As a columnist for the opinion page of the New York Times, *Nicholas Kristof has one of the most influential positions a persuasive writer can have. And although he writes on many subjects (generally from a center-left perspective), Kristof has become known over the past decade for his advocacy for the poor of the developing world: China, Darfur, India, and other places. Here, Kristof writes that although sweatshops are not an end, they are a means to bettering the material conditions of millions—even billions—of people, Kristof insists.*

PHNOM PENH, Cambodia

Before Barack Obama and his team act on their talk about "labor standards," I'd like to offer them a tour of the vast garbage dump here in Phnom Penh.

This is a Dante-like vision of hell. It's a mountain of festering refuse, a half-hour hike across, emitting clouds of smoke from subterranean fires.

The miasma of toxic stink leaves you gasping, breezes batter you with filth, and even the rats look forlorn. Then the smoke parts and you come across a child ambling barefoot, searching for old plastic cups that recyclers will buy for five cents a pound. Many families actually live in shacks on this smoking garbage.

Mr. Obama and the Democrats who favor labor standards in trade agreements mean well, for they intend to fight back at oppressive sweatshops abroad. But while it shocks Americans to hear it, the central challenge in the poorest countries is not that sweatshops exploit too many people, but that they don't exploit enough.

Talk to these families in the dump, and a job in a sweatshop is a cherished dream, an escalator out of poverty, the kind of gauzy if probably unrealistic ambition that parents everywhere often have for their children.

"I'd love to get a job in a factory," said Pirn Srey Rath, a 19-year-old woman scavenging for plastic. "At least that work is in the shade. Here is where it's hot."

Another woman, Vath Sam Oeun, hopes her 10-year-old boy, scavenging beside her, grows up to get a factory job, partly because she has seen other children run over by garbage trucks. Her boy has never been to a doctor or a dentist, and last bathed when he was 2, so a sweatshop job by comparison would be far more pleasant and less dangerous.

I'm glad that many Americans are repulsed by the idea of importing products made by barely paid, barely legal workers in dangerous factories. Yet sweatshops are only a symptom of poverty, not a cause, and banning them closes off one route out of poverty. At a time of tremendous economic distress and protectionist pressures, there's a special danger that tighter labor standards will be used as an excuse to curb trade.

When I defend sweatshops, people always ask me: But would you want to work in a sweatshop? No, of course not. But I would want even less to pull a rickshaw. In the hierarchy of jobs in poor countries, sweltering at a sewing machine isn't the bottom.

My views on sweatshops are shaped by years living in East Asia, watching as living standards soared—including those in my wife's ancestral village in southern China—because of sweatshop jobs.

Manufacturing is one sector that can provide millions of jobs. Yet sweatshops usually go not to the poorest nations but to better-off countries with more reliable electricity and ports.

I often hear the argument: Labor standards can improve wages and working conditions, without greatly affecting the eventual retail cost of goods. That's true. But labor standards and "living wages" have a larger impact on production costs that companies are always trying to pare. The result is to push companies to operate more capital-intensive factories in better-off nations like Malaysia, rather than labor-intensive factories in poorer countries like Ghana or Cambodia.

Cambodia has, in fact, pursued an interesting experiment by working with factories to establish decent labor standards and wages. It's a worthwhile idea, but one result of paying above-market wages is that those in charge of hiring often demand bribes—sometimes a month's salary—in exchange for a job. In addition, these standards add to production costs, so some factories have closed because of the global economic crisis and the difficulty of competing internationally.

The best way to help people in the poorest countries isn't to campaign against sweatshops but to promote manufacturing there. One of the best things America could do for Africa would be to strengthen our program to encourage African imports, called AGOA, and nudge Europe to match it.

Among people who work in development, many strongly believe (but few dare say very loudly) that one of the best hopes for the poorest countries would be to build their manufacturing industries. But global campaigns against sweatshops make that less likely.

Look, I know that Americans have a hard time accepting that sweatshops can help people. But take it from 13-year-old Neuo Chanthou, who earns a bit less than $1 a day scavenging in the dump. She's wearing a "Playboy" shirt and hat that she found amid the filth, and she worries about her sister, who lost part of her hand when a garbage truck ran over her.

"It's dirty, hot and smelly here," she said wistfully. "A factory is better."

Critical Reading Questions

Summarizing the Text

1. What is Kristof's argument here? Are sweatshops a good thing? If so, are they a universal good (for everyone at all times) or a conditional good (good depending on the context)?

2. What does Kristof mean by the terms *labor-intensive* and *capital-intensive*? How do these terms contribute to his argument?

Establishing the Context

3. Kristof says that sweatshops are *not* a feature of the poorest and least developed nations. Why? Why does he think that more nations, and the world in general, should support and fund the growth of sweatshops in poor nations?

4. "I'm glad that many Americans are repulsed by the idea of importing products made by barely paid, barely legal workers in dangerous factories," Kristof says. "Yet sweatshops are only a symptom of poverty, not a cause, and banning them closes off one route out of poverty." How does he use these two sentences to establish his ethos with his audience?

Responding to the Message

5. Kristof is writing here about sweatshops in the poorest nations (such as Cambodia), but anti-sweatshop activists have pointed out that we still have these establishments in the United States. Is this true? Research sweatshops in the United States: what kinds of industries use them?

6. Kristof mentions the idea of a *living wage*. What does this term mean? How is it used? Several cities have passed living wage ordinances in the past twenty years—what do those laws do? Does your city have a living wage ordinance? Do you think it should?

Workplace Programs
Thomas Schatz

Thomas Schatz is a professor of communications at the University of Texas at Austin and the author of four books on the Hollywood film industry. He writes for academic publications as well as general-interest outlets such as the New York Times and Premiere. In this short, informational article, Schatz traces the history of "workplace programs"—television programs, dramatic or comedic, that take place largely in the workplace (as opposed to "domestic" programs, whose action is centered in the home). The article appears on the website of the Museum of Broadcast Communications, a museum and educational institution located in downtown Chicago.

U.S. television, from its earliest years, has developed prime-time programs which focus on the workplace. This trend is understandable enough, given TV's essential investment in the "American work ethic" and in consumer culture, although it also evinces TV's basic domestic impulse. By the 1970s and 1980s, in fact, TV's most successful workplace programs effectively merged the medium's work-related and domestic imperatives in sitcoms like *The Mary Tyler Moore Show*, *M*A*S*H*, *Taxi*, and *Cheers*, and in hour-long dramas like *Hill Street Blues*, *St. Elsewhere*, and *LA Law*. While conveying the working conditions and the professional ethos of the workplace, these programs also depicted co-workers as a loosely knit but crucially interdependent quasi-family within a "domesticated" workplace. This strategy was further refined in 1990s sitcoms like *Murphy Brown* and *Frasier*, and even more notably in hour-long dramas like *ER*, *NYPD Blue*, *Picket Fences*, *Chicago Hope*, and *Homicide: Life in the Streets*. These latter series not only marked the unexpected resurgence of hour-long drama in prime time, but in the view of many critics evinced a new "golden age" of American television.

This integration of home and work was scarcely evident in 1950s TV, when the domestic arena and the workplace remained fairly distinct. The majority of workplace programs were male-dominant law-and-order series which generally focused less on the workplace itself than on the professional heroics of the cops, detectives, town marshals, bounty hunters, who dictated and dominated the action. *Dragnet*, TV's prototype cop show, did portray the workaday world of the L.A. police, albeit in uncomplicated and superficial terms. The rise of the hour-long series in the late 1950s brought a more sophisticated treatment of the workplace in courtroom dramas like *Perry Mason*, detective shows like *77 Sunset Strip*, and cop shows like *Naked City* (which ran as a half-hour show in 1957–58 and then returned as an hour-long drama in 1960). More than simply a "home base" for the protagonists, the workplace in these programs was a familiar site of personal and professional interaction.

The year 1961 saw three new important hour-long workplace dramas: *Ben Casey, Dr. Kildare,* and *The Defenders.* The latter was a legal drama whose principals spent far less time in the court-room and more time in the office than did Perry Mason. And while Mason's cases invariably were murder mysteries, with Mason functioning as both lawyer and detective, *The Defenders* treated the workaday legal profession in more direct and realistic terms. Both *Ben Casey* and *Dr. Kildare,* meanwhile, were medical dramas set in hospitals, and they too brought a new degree of realism to the depiction of the workplace setting—and to the lives and labors of its occupants. As *Time* magazine noted in reviewing *Ben Casey,* the series "accurately captures the feeling of sleepless intensity of a metropolitan hospital."

Another important and highly influential series to debut in 1961 was a half-hour comedy, *The Dick Van Dyke Show,* which effectively merged the two dominant sitcom strains—the workplace comedy with its ensemble of disparate characters, and the domestic comedy center-ing on the typical (white, middle-class) American home and family. At the time, most workplace comedies fell into three basic categories: school-based sitcoms like *Mr. Peepers* and *Our Miss Brooks;* working-girl sitcoms like *Private Secretary* and *Oh Suzanna;* and military sitcoms like *The Phil Silvers Show* and *McHale's Navy.* The vast majority of half-hour comedies were domestic sitcoms extolling (or affectionately lam-pooning) the virtues of home and family. These occasionally raised work-related issues–via working-stiffs like Chester Riley (*The Life of Riley*) lamenting an American Dream just out of reach, for instance, or on an "unruly" housewife like Lucy Ricardo (*I Love Lucy*) comically resisting her domestic plight. And some series like *Hazel* centered on "domestic help" (maids, nannies, etc.), thus depicting the home itself as a workplace.

The Dick Van Dyke Show created a hybrid of sorts by casting Van Dyke as Rob Petrie, an affable suburban patriarch and head writer on the fictional Alan Brady Show. Setting the trend for workplace com-edies of the next three decades, *The Dick Van Dyke Show* featured a protagonist who moved continually between home and work, thus creating a format amenable to both the domestic sitcom and the workplace comedy. The series' domestic dimension was quite conven-tional, but its treatment of the workplace was innovative and influ-ential. The work itself involved television production (as would later workplace sitcoms like *The Mary Tyler Moore Show, Buffalo Bill,* and *Murphy Brown),* and thus the program carried a strong self-reflexive dimension. More importantly, *The Dick Van Dyke Show* developed the prototype for the domesticated workplace and the work-family ensemble—Rob and his staff writers Buddy (Morey Amsterdam) and Sally (Rose Marie); oddball autocrat Alan Brady (Carl Reiner, the creator and executive producer of *The Dick Van Dyke Show*); and Alan's producer and brother-in-law, the ever-flustered and vaguely maternal Mel (Richard Deacon). Significantly, Rob was the only member of the workplace ensemble with a stable and secure "home life," and thus he served as the stabilizing, nurturing, mediating force in the comic-chaotic and potentially dehumanizing workplace.

The influence of *The Dick Van Dyke Show* on TVs workplace programs was most obvious and direct in the sitcoms produced by MTM Enterprises in the early 1970s, particularly *The Mary Tyler Moore Show* and *The Bob Newhart Show*. While these and other MTM sitcoms featured a central character moving between home and work, *The Mary Tyler Moore Show* was the most successful in developing the workplace (the newsroom of a Minneapolis TV station, WJM) as a site not only of conflict and comedic chaos but of community and kinship as well. And although Moore, who had played Rob's wife on *The Dick Van Dyke Show*, was cast here as an independent single woman, her nurturing instincts remained as acute as ever in the WJM newsroom.

While the MTM series maintained the dual focus on home and work, another crucial workplace comedy from the early 1970s, *M*A*S*H*, focused exclusively on the workplace—in this case a military surgical unit in war-torn Korea of the early 1950s (with obvious pertinence to the then-current Vietnam War). Alan Alda's Hawkeye Pierce was in many ways the series' central character and governing sensibility, especially in his caustic disregard for military protocol and his fierce commitment to medicine. Yet *M*A*S*H* was remarkably "democratic" in its treatment of the eight principal characters, developing each member of the ensemble as well as the collective itself into a functioning work-family. While ostensibly a sitcom, the series often veered into heavy drama in its treatment of both the medical profession and the war; in fact, the laugh track was never used during the scenes set in the operating room. And more than any previous workplace program, whether comedy or drama, *M*A*S*H* was focused closely on the professional "code" of its ensemble, on the shared sense of duty and commitment which both defined their medical work and created a nagging sense of moral ambiguity about the military function of the unit—that is, patching up the wounded so that they might return to battle.

A domestic sitcom hit from the early 1970s, *All in the Family*, also is pertinent here for several reasons. First, in Archie Bunker (Carroll O'Connor) the series created the most endearing and comic-pathetic working stiff since Chester Riley. Second, parenting on the series involved two grown "children," with the generation-gap squabbling between Archie and son-in-law Mike (Rob Reiner) frequently raising issues of social class and work. Moreover, their comic antagonism was recast in other generation-gap sitcoms set in the workplace, notably *Sanford and Son* and *Chico and the Man*. And third, *All in the Family* itself evolved by the late 1970s into a workplace sitcom, *Archie Bunker's Place*, with the traditional family replaced by a work-family ensemble.

The trend toward workplace comedies in the early 1970s was related to several factors both inside and outside the industry. One factor, of course, was the sheer popularity of the early-1970s workplace comedies, and their obvious flexibility in terms of plot and character development. These series also signaled TV's increasing concern with demographics and its pursuit of "quality numbers"—i.e., the upscale urban viewers coveted by sponsors. Because these series often dealt with topical and significant social issues, they were widely praised by critics, thus creating an equation of sorts between quality demographics and "quality programming." And in a larger social context, this programming trend signaled the massive changes in American lifestyles which accompanied a declining economy and runaway inflation, the sexual revolution and women's movement, the growing ranks of working wives and mothers, rising divorce rates, the aging of the baby-boom generation, and so on.

Thus the domestic sitcom with its emphasis on traditional home and family all but disappeared from network schedules in the late 1970s and early 1980s, replaced by workplace comedies like *Alice, Welcome Back Kotter, WKRP in Cincinnati, Taxi, Cheers, Newhart,* and *Night Court.* The domestic sitcom did rebound in the mid-1980s with *The Cosby Show* and *Family Ties,* and by the 1990s the domestic and workplace sitcoms had formed a comfortable alliance—with series like *Murphy Brown, Coach,* and *Frasier* sustaining the MTM tradition of a central, pivotal character moving between home and the workplace.

TV's hour-long workplace dramas underwent a transformation as well in the 1970s, which was a direct outgrowth, in fact, of MTM's workplace sitcoms. In 1977, MTM Enterprises retired *The Mary Tyler Moore Show* and created a third and final spin-off of that series, *Lou Grant,* which followed Mary's irascible boss (Ed Asner) from WJM-TV in Minneapolis to the *Los Angeles Tribune,* where he took a job as editor. Lou Grant was created by two of MTM's top comedy writer-producers, James Brooks and Allan Burns, along with Gene Reynolds, the executive producer of *M*A*S*H.* It marked a crucial new direction for MTM not only as an hour-long drama, but also because of its primary focus on the workplace (a la *M*A*S*H*) and its aggressive treatment of "serious" social and work-related issues. In that era of Vietnam, Watergate, and *All the President's Men, Lou Grant* courted controversy week after week, with Lou and his work-family of investigative journalists not only pursuing the "Truth" but agonizing over their personal lives and professional responsibilities as well.

MTM's hour-long workplace dramas hit their stride in the 1980s with *Hill Street Blues* and *St. Elsewhere*, which effectively revitalized two of television's oldest genres, cop show and doc show. Each shifted the dramatic focus from the all-too-familiar heroics of a series star to an ensemble of co-workers and to the workplace itself—and not simply as a backdrop but as a social-service institution located in an urban-industrial war zone with its own distinctive ethos and sense of place. Each also utilized serial story structure and documentary-style realism, drawing viewers into the heavily populated and densely plotted programs through a heady, seemingly paradoxical blend of soap opera and cinema verite. Documentary techniques—location shooting, hand-held camera, long takes and reframing instead of cutting, composition in depth, and multiple-track sound recording—gave these series (and the workplace itself) a "look" and "feel" that was utterly unique among police and medical dramas.

Hill Street Blues and *St. Elsewhere* also emerged alongside prime-time soap operas like *Dallas* and *Falcon Crest*, and shared with those series a penchant for "continuing drama." While this serial dimension enhanced both the Hill Street precinct and St. Eligius hospital as a "domesticated workplace," the genre requirements of each series (solving crimes, healing the sick) demanded action, pathos, jeopardy, and a dramatic payoff within individual episodes. Thus a crucial component of MTM's workplace dramas was their merging of episodic and serial forms. The episodic dimension usually focused on short-term, work-related conflicts (crime, illness), while the serial dimension involved the more "domestic" aspects of the characters' lives—and not only their personal lives, since most of the principals were "married to their work," but also the ongoing interpersonal relationships among the co-workers.

Hill Street co-creator Steven Bochco left MTM in the mid-1980s and developed *LA Law*, which took the ensemble workplace drama "upscale" into a successful big-city legal firm. While a solid success, this focus on upscale professionals marked a significant departure from *Hill Street* and *St. Elsewhere*—and from most workplace dramas in the 1990s as well. Indeed, prime-time network TV saw a remarkable run of MTM-style ensemble dramas in the 1990s, notably *ER, Homicide, Law and Order, Chicago Hope*, and another Bochco series, *NYPD Blue*. Most of these were set, like *Hill Street* and *St. Elsewhere*, in decaying inner cities, and they centered on co-workers whose commitment to their profession and to one another was far more important than social status or income. Indeed, a central paradox in these programs is that their principal characters, all intelligent, well-educated professionals, eschew material rewards to work in under-funded social institutions where commitment outweighs income, where the work is never finished nor the conflicts satisfactorily resolved, and where the work itself, finally, is its own reward.

Despite these similarities to *Hill Street* and *St. Elsewhere*, the 1990s workplace dramas differed in their emphasis on workaday cops and docs. Those earlier MTM series carried a strong male-management focus, privileging the veritable "patriarch" of the work-family—Capt. Frank Furillo and Dr. Paul Westphall, respectively—whose role (like Lou Grant before them) was to uphold the professional code and the familial bond of their charges. The 1990s dramas, conversely, concentrated mainly on the workers in the trenches, whose shared commitment to one another and to their work defines the ethos of the workplace and the sense of kinship it engendered.

More conventional hour-long workplace programs have been developed alongside these MTM-style dramas, of course, from 1970s series like *Medical Center, Ironside,* and *Baretta* to more recent cop, doc, and lawyer shows like *Matlock, T.J. Hooker,* and *Quincy.* In the tradition of *Dragnet* and *Marcus Welby*, the lead characters in these series are little more than heroic plot functions, with the plots themselves satisfying the generic requirements in formulaic doses and the workplace setting as mere backdrop. Two recent hour-long dramas more closely akin to the MTM-style workplace programs are *Northern Exposure* and *Picket Fences*. Both are successful ensemble dramas created by MTM alumni who took the workplace form into more upbeat and off-beat directions—the former a duck-out-of-water doc show set in small-town Alaska which veered into magical realism, the latter a hybrid cop-doc-legal-domestic drama set in small-town Wisconsin. But while both are effective ensemble dramas with an acute "sense of place," they are crucially at odds with urban-based medical dramas like *ER* and *Chicago Hope*, and police dramas like *Homicide* and *NYPD Blue*, whose dramatic focus is crucially wed to the single-minded professional commitment of the ensemble and is deeply rooted in the workplace itself.

Indeed, *ER* and *Homicide* and the other MTM-style ensemble dramas posit the workplace as home and work itself as the basis for any real sense of kinship we are likely to find in the contemporary urban-industrial world. As Charles McGrath writes in the *New York Times Magazine*, "The Triumph of the Prime-Time Novel," such shows appeal to viewers because "they've remembered that for a lot of us work is where we live more of the time; that, like it or not, our job relationships are often as intimate as our family relationships, and that work is often where we invest most of our emotional energy." McGrath is one of several critics who view these workplace dramas as ushering in a renaissance of network TV programming, due to their Dickensian density of plot and complexity of character, their social realism and moral ambiguity, their portrayal of workers whose heroics are simply a function of their everyday lives and labors.

The workplace in these series ultimately emerges as a character unto itself, and one which is both harrowing and oddly inspiring to those who work there. For the characters in *ER* and *NYPD Blue* and the other ensemble workplace dramas, soul-searching comes with the territory, and they know the territory all too well. They are acutely aware not only of their own limitations and failings but of the inadequacies of their own professions to cure the ills of the modern world. Still they maintain their commitment to one another and to a professional code which is the very life-blood of the workplace they share.

Critical Reading Questions

Summarizing the Text

1. Is this simply an informational article or is it persuasive? If it is persuasive, what is its thesis?

2. In Schatz's mind, how does the role of the workplace change for the characters of these shows from the early *Dick Van Dyke Show* to the later *ER* or *NYPD Blue*?

Establishing the Context

3. How have television programs depicted the workplace? Some theorists argue that workplace television serves to make the tedium of office work seem tolerable, and others say that workplace television attempts to reinforce the fundamentally capitalist argument that we must work and contribute and refrain from questioning the system as a whole. Given the workplace shows that you might know, what do you think?

4. Compare your favorite workplace show with your favorite domestic show. How do the two dramatize the proper roles of women and men? Of bosses versus workers? Of children versus parents?

Responding to the Message

5. Schatz's article is a little out of date—the last programs it examines flourished in the late 1990s. What workplace programs are the most popular and influential today? What do they tell us about our attitude toward work that is different from that in *ER* or *Cheers* or other earlier workplace programs?

6. Schatz writes at a time when broadcast network television (ABC, NBC, CBS, and Fox) dominated televised entertainment. Today, many of the most interesting and some of the more popular original programs air on cable

networks: AMC's *Mad Men*, Showtime's *Weeds*, HBO's *Entourage* or *The Sopranos*, USA's *NCIS*, or Disney's *Hannah Montana*, for example. But in a larger sense, fewer and fewer viewers are watching scripted television programs on the networks than ever before. How might these changes affect the kinds of workplace stories that we watch?

Workplace Program Publicity Stills

*These four photographs are examples of "publicity stills"—images used to advertise a television show or film or any kind of video. In this instance, the stills are from television programs that are set primarily in the workplace. The first two are from extremely popular hour-long dramas—*ER, *a medical show set in a Chicago public hospital's emergency room, and* CSI Miami, *a police procedural drama centering on the investigations performed by the Miami Police Department's crime-scene investigation unit. The other two stills are from half-hour workplace comedies:* 30 Rock *(behind the scenes at a sketch comedy show) and* NewsRadio *(about a New York City 24-hour news radio station).*

Critical Reading Questions

1. "Read" the photos. What does each tell you about the program? If you knew nothing about the program, what would you learn from the photo? If you are familiar with the program, what aspects of the program does the image reinforce?

2. How are the stills for the dramas and the stills for the comedies different in their composition and emotion? What different messages do they give you about what the shows are like?

CLUSTER TWO: HOW IS TECHNOLOGY GOING TO CHANGE THE WORKPLACE FOR THE MILLENNIAL GENERATION?

Job Candidates Get Tripped Up by Facebook
Wei Du

Wei Du is a business reporter for CNBC and Bloomberg News. She holds a journalism degree from Renmin University in Beijing, China. In this article (which originally appeared on MSNBC's website), Wei outlines some of the difficulties young job seekers have encountered with potential employers when those employers access their online profiles (including Facebook or MySpace pages), and she talks to employers about how they use the information they find about applicants online.

Many students learn the hard way that online image can limit opportunity.

Van Allen runs a company that recruits job candidates for hospitals and clinics across the country. With physicians in short supply, he was happy to come across the resume of a well-qualified young female psychiatrist.

As part of his due diligence check, Allen looked her up in Facebook, a popular social networking Web site, and found things that made him think twice.

"Pictures of her taking off her shirt at parties," he said. "Not just on one occasion, but on another occasion, then another occasion."

Concerned about those pictures, he called the candidate and asked for an explanation. She didn't get the job.

"Hospitals want doctors with great skills to provide great services to communities," Allen said. "They also don't want patients to say to each other, 'Heard about Dr. Jones? You've got to see those pictures.'"

Job candidates who maintain personal sites on Facebook or MySpace are learning—sometimes the hard way—that the image they present to their friends on the Internet may not be best suited for landing the position they're seeking.

Although many employers are too old to qualify as members of the Facebook Generation, they're becoming increasingly savvy about using social networking sites in their hiring due diligence. That has both job candidates and human resources professionals debating the ethics and effectiveness of snooping on the Web for the kind of information that may not come up in a job interview.

According to a March survey by Ponemon Institute, a privacy think tank, 35 percent of hiring managers use Google to do online background checks on job candidates, and 23 percent look people up on social networking sites. About one-third of those Web searches lead to rejections, according to the survey.

Social networking sites have gained popularity among hiring managers because of their convenience and a growing anxiety about hiring the right people, researchers say.

Big corporations long have retained professional investigators to check job applicants' academic degrees, criminal records and credit reports. But until now the cost has deterred the ability of smaller firms to do the same level of checking, said Sue Murphy, a director of National Human Resources Association.

One problem is that there is little to prevent hiring managers from discriminating on the basis of personal information discovered through social Web sites.

"There's just not much legislation on that yet," Murphy said.

New college graduates, the most active social networkers, are most likely to be the target of Web research.

"For people new to a field, companies just don't have a lot to look back on," Murphy said. "They can't call up your former boss. They look you up on Facebook."

Financial services firms and health care providers are among the biggest users of social networking sites, said Larry Ponemon, founder of the Ponemon Institute.

"These industries are stewards of people's property and health, and companies really look for a high level of integrity," he said.

Professional services like law and consulting firms are also big users, because companies care about how employees present themselves to clients and look for clues in how applicants present themselves online.

Risqué pictures are not the only way a job applicant can be tripped up. Pictures of illegal behavior like drug use or heavy alcohol use could disqualify a candidate too. Some also suggest poor writing and bad grammar in Facebook profiles and in blog entries can raise a red flag about communication skills. Derogatory comments or complaints or radical political positions also can draw the scrutiny of a prospective ·employer.

One job applicant indicated in his Facebook profile that he was a leading hacker, and he was applying to be a computer security analyst, said Ponemon. He too didn't get the job.

"It's amazing how many things people just put out there," said Murphy of the human resources association.

Facebook users often don't expect their personal information to be monitored by potential employers, and many consider their online profile information to be private.

A study by Adecco, a work force consulting firm, showed that 66 percent of Generation Y respondents, those in their late teens and 20s, were not aware that the information they put online can be factored into hiring decisions. Fifty-six percent said they think the practice is unfair.

Originally Facebook was seen as a safe "closed circuit" site, in which profiles would only be visible to people in a limited group. The site originally required users to register with a valid college e-mail address. But it loosened the restriction last summer to allow registration with any e-mail account. Facebook networks, which had been relatively small, expanded to include companies and even large geographic areas.

The new policies of Facebook drew public attention this year when Miss New Jersey Amy Polumbo nearly lost her crown after being blackmailed over pictures of her that were taken off her Facebook profile. Ultimately the judges decided not to take away her title, but her crown was tarnished.

"This was meant to be private," Polumbo told *Today Show* host Matt Lauer, referring to photos that showed her fully clothed but posing provocatively and drinking at clubs.

"People have a common misconception about how big their networks really are," said Michael Fertik, CEO of Reputationdefender. com, a year-old startup offering services to minimize the damage of Web background checks. "Nothing on the Internet is private. Period."

Reputationdefender.com offers to monitor one's Web reputation for $10 a month plus a onetime fee of $30 to remove from the Web an unwanted item that may have slipped out of the user's control.

In one high-profile case last spring, a group of law school students found that pictures were taken off their Facebook accounts and reposted onto an online discussion board without their permission. Whoever posted the pictures then invited suggestive comments.

The law students tried to have their pictures removed from the discussion board, complaining that they had been shunned in job interviews.

"People also have to understand the standard you will be judged against in hiring," said Fertik. "Employers don't have to believe what they see—they only have to decide not to take a chance on you."

Critical Reading Questions

Summarizing the Text

1. How are employers using applicants' online profiles in the hiring process?
2. Why do employers think that what happens in a potential employee's private life is fair game for them to discover? What kinds of employers are particularly interested in this information? Why?

Establishing the Context

3. If *ethos* has to do with how you present yourself to an audience, your self-presentation in a job interview is very much a question of *ethos*. How might the information about you that is freely available online affect your *ethos* to a potential employer?

4. How does Wei balance anecdotal evidence with evidence that indicates the actual pervasiveness of these practices? How well do her anecdotes illustrate the "harder" factual evidence she has to offer? Research this issue yourself—what other statistics or facts can you find on this phenomenon?

Responding to the Message

5. Should the information that you post online about yourself "belong" to you? What does this mean?

6. Do you believe that a potential employer researching you on the Web is a violation of privacy? Why or why not?

No More Vacation: How Technology Is Stealing Our Lives

Rebecca Traister

Rebecca Traister writes on women's issues for Salon.com, an online magazine. She is also the author of Big Girls Don't Cry, *a study of the 2008 presidential election. In this article, she turns her focus to how our gadgets and the pressure to be constantly available for texts, emails, IMing, and the like are sapping our attentions and energies. This article originally appeared in Salon.com in July 2010.*

Friday before the 4th of July, my friend Sara and I walked to the local pool, talking about work stress, anxiety, difficulty relaxing. We were both struck by how lately, after 15 years of full-time work, we were so unreasonably tired. Why now, we wondered, when we have more experience and self-assurance, when we are amply compensated for our labor at comparatively cushy white-collar jobs, do we feel more spent than when we were strapped entry-level drones, running our tails off to please insatiable bosses? Why has our recent exhaustion felt so bone-deep and dire? Childless, we marveled at how our mothers managed kids and jobs, while we were so wrecked. As we entered the locker room, we were briskly reminded of the strict New York City public pool rules: no street clothes on the pool deck, no food or drink, no cellphones. Stowing our stuff in the cubbie above us, both of our hands paused in midair as I checked my phone and Sara eyed her BlackBerry nervously. As we headed out to the concrete and chlorine oasis, Sara said with an unconvincingly nonchalant laugh, "I hope nobody's looking for me." It was late afternoon before a holiday weekend, I assured her. But I quietly worried that an associate I'd been playing phone tag with might leave a message. If I didn't return it till later that night, would she surmise that I wasn't working?

This, I realized after one lap in the bracing blue water, is why we are so tired.

There's been a lot written about how the beeping and flashing gadgets with which we now surround ourselves keep us from sleeping, keep us from concentrating, keep us, ironically, from working. The thing that I have noticed of late is how often they seem to keep us from *living*.

Perhaps I'm feeling a loss of leisure so keenly these days because of my romanticized (but real) memories of summer days from not so long ago. Not just the ones in which I was a kid on a three-month vacation, but in which I was the daughter of parents who came home from their jobs at night and were *at home,* who cooked dinner, or maybe drove us to a movie or watched television or read a book without so much as a glance at a Palm Pilot or an e-mail in box. It's not that my academic parents didn't work overtime: They often read, graded papers and caught up on administrative work late into the night. But that extra work was done on what was once generously regarded as "their time." They found ways to fit it in around hours or days during which their colleagues or superiors had no idea where they were, in which they were unreachable and there was no notion that they should be otherwise.

Those rusty memories are decades old, but even as recently as 12 summers ago, while I tried to keep my head above water at my first job, my legendary and demanding boss would, at some magic moment on a Friday afternoon, disappear to her country house, where she could be reached primarily by an unreliable fax machine. She was gone for the weekend.

Now, it often seems, there is no "gone for the weekend." There is certainly no "gone for the night." Sometimes there's not even a gone on vacation.

Earlier this month, on my honeymoon in California, I found myself checking my computer compulsively for days, not for fun, but because I was afraid of being professionally remiss. It was simultaneously an irrational and a perfectly sane concern: Every day *did* bring some new professional demand or question that supposedly could not wait, though I also answered the ones that obviously could.

Halfway through the trip, my brain began to ease into vacation mode and my typing fingers stopped twitching. As soon as I recovered myself a bit, I also recovered some perspective on the vortex into which I'd been pulled. I'd catch sight of my innocent white Mac sitting on a hotel room desk, suddenly less a seraphic emissary of important information than a sinister conveyor of work stress. *What will you want from me today?* I'd wonder as I stared it down. *What anxieties lie waiting within you?*

We have created a monster that is consuming us. And I don't mean that "the Internet is bad" in that hypocritical and falsely ascetic way. I mean that we, along with the phones that travel with us, the texts we type in movie theaters, the instant messages we receive now even on some planes, the social media many of us are expected to participate in on behalf of our jobs, and the complexes and work ethics we have all inherited from our diverse array of guilt-generating forebears, have bubbled together into a frenzy of ceaseless professional engagement that is boiling us dry.

It's certainly a first-world problem, a privileged concern. In so many ways, the Internet has been a democratizing force, has made our lives so much easier. In most of the world, cellphone technology doesn't weigh people down; it gives them an opportunity to make a living.

But those disparities of experience don't change the fact that in certain sectors, not just the one I inhabit, technology is allowing our work to eat our lives. In Canada, labor leaders have pushed to make employers pay for the hours workers spend on their BlackBerrys out of the office, and in the United States, lawsuits to recoup overtime pay for time spent on hand-held devices are piling up. Perhaps making bosses pay for out-of-office texting time will be just the thing to get them to discourage it, but I fear that irreversible shifts in attitude and metabolism make this an unlikely hope. Professional rhythms have quickened to match technological possibility in ways that make resistance futile.

I don't own an iPhone or a BlackBerry because I do not want to receive e-mail all day every day. Increasingly I understand this preference to be naive, impractical and really rather twee. On several occasions in the past year, days when I've run between appointments and not brought my laptop, I've had to call my boyfriend to ask him to log into my e-mail and tell me whether I've missed anything urgent. I should get a smart phone because I live in the real world. And in the real world, where I used to receive a few dozen e-mails a day, I now receive hundreds.

During a recent visit from a cousin, we ran out to do errands and get lunch, realizing only once we'd gone too far to turn around that she had accidentally left both of her BlackBerrys in my apartment. After a brief panic and a strong Bloody Mary, she confessed that the 120 minutes she'd just spent without her PDAs was the longest period of technological unavailability she'd experienced in years. As soon as we walked back in the door, she rushed to catch up on the scores of work exchanges she'd left unfinished. My cousin is a primary school principal. This was a Saturday in July.

I don't think the notion that we have to be constantly plugged in is just in our heads: I think it's also in the heads of our superiors, our colleagues, our future employers and our prospective employees. There will be judgment, or at least a note made, perhaps by a boss who's tried to reach you unsuccessfully, or an employee who has an urgent question that goes briefly unanswered.

To not be reachable if called upon at any time, except perhaps the dead of night, feels sinful; unavailability betrays disconnectedness, and disconnectedness has come to stand for idleness and indolence. How many people have sent needless e-mails at 7 a.m. or perhaps 11 p.m., with the thought, if not the conscious intention, of communicating an intensity of professional commitment, demonstrating defensively or passive-aggressively or in the hopes of beating the next round of layoffs that they were beavering away at every odd hour of the day and night.

America's excesses are never far from sight: Our endless enthusiasms for boundless capitalism, materialism and hedonism persist. But these three have always had a complicated but close relationship with their uptight buddy, Puritanism, and I can't help feeling these days like Cotton Mather and Jonathan Edwards have insinuated themselves into everyone's friends and family network, preaching the gospel of a work world without end.

Without retreating to some heretical call to smash the machines, I wonder if it wouldn't do us all some good to stuff them all in a locker for an hour and go for a swim.

Critical Reading Questions

Summarizing the Text

1. What is Traister's thesis—how is technology "stealing our lives"?
2. How does Traister "temper" or qualify her argument? What effect does this have on her *logos* and her *ethos*?

Establishing the Context

3. What does Traister mean by her allusion to Cotton Mather and Jonathan Edwards? Who are these people, what is Puritanism, and what does it have to do with work?
4. Much of Traister's argument relies solely on her own experience of her life today, and comparing that with her memories of her childhood and the way her parents lived their lives. Does this undermine the validity of her claims? Why? When is anecdotal evidence not enough?

Responding to the Message

5. Traister writes as a professional woman in her 30s with a job that is based largely on writing and communicating; in a sense, it's not surprising that she is particularly susceptible to the exhaustion of being constantly "reachable." Does her portrait of tech exhaustion apply as well to younger people—college students, for instance? Do you find yourself similarly drained? And do you think that her "exhaustion" is in any way a function of her generation—one that did not grow up with cellphones, IMing, and the Internet?

6. The ease of electronic communications has profoundly changed the nature of work—particularly white-collar work—in America. Electronic communications allow us to "telecommute," to outsource expensive jobs (customer-service call centers, for instance) to cheaper contractors overseas. But as Traister argues, it also makes employees always *available* to their employers. The lines between work time and free time blur. How do you feel about this? Do you look forward to being able to be always at work if you choose? Or would you prefer a job that you leave at work?

Digital "Natives" Invade the Workplace

Lee Rainie

Lee Rainie is the director of the Pew Internet & American Life Project, which describes itself as "a non-profit, non-partisan 'think tank' that studies the social impact of the internet." Before coming to the Pew Center, Rainie worked as the managing editor for the weekly magazine U.S. News & World Report. *He is the coauthor, with Barry Wellman, of the forthcoming book* Networked: The New Social Operating System. *In this article, Rainie examines—using anecdotal, polling, and research data—the changes that "digital natives" are bringing to the American workplace.*

Young people may be newcomers to the world of work, but it's their bosses who are immigrants into the digital world.

As consultant Marc Prensky calculates it, the life arc of a typical 21-year-old entering the workforce today has, on average, included 5,000 hours of video game playing, exchange of 250,000 emails, instant messages, and phone text messages, 10,000 hours of cell phone use. To that you can add 3,500 hours of time online.

Our work at the Pew Internet Project shows that an American teen is more likely than her parents to own a digital music player like an iPod, to have posted writing, pictures, or video on the internet, to have created a blog or profile on a social networking web site like MySpace, to have downloaded digital content such as songs, games, movies, or software, to have shared a remix or "mashup" creation with friends, and to have snapped a photo or video with a cell phone.

"Today's younger workers are not 'little us-es,':" argues Prensky, an educator, gaming expert, author of *Don't Bother Me, Mom—I'm Learning.* "Their preference is for sharing, staying connected, instantaneity, multi-tasking, assembling random information into patterns, and using technology in new ways. Their challenge to the established way of doing things in the business world has already started."

Those challenges often flow from young workers' embrace of technologies that have grown up with them. Today's 21-year-old was born in 1985—10 years after the first consumer computers went on sale and the same year that the breakthrough "third generation" video game, Nintendo's "Super Mario Brothers," first went to market. When this young worker was a toddler, the basic format of instant messaging was developed. And at the time this young worker entered kindergarten in 1990, Tim Berners-Lee wrote a computer program called the World Wide Web. Upon entering middle school, our worker might have organized his schedule with a gadget called a Palm Pilot (first shipped in 1996). And at the dawn of high school for our worker in 1999, Sean Fanning created the Napster file-sharing service. When the worker graduated from high school four years later, his gifts might have included an iPod (patented in 2002) and a camera phone (first shipped in early 2003).

Our worker's college career saw the rise of blogs (already two years old in 2000), RSS feeds (coded in 2000), Wikipedia (2001), social network sites (Friendster was launched in 2002), tagging (Del.icio.us was created in 2003), free online phone calling (Skype software was made available in 2003), podcasts (term coined in 2004), and the video explosion that has occurred as broadband internet connections become the norm in households (YouTube went live in 2005).

Now, we have a reversal of the normal situation, where young people migrate into a workplace manned by seasoned natives. Instead, in this digitalized age, this 21-year-old and his peers are showing up in human resources offices as digital natives in a workplace world dominated by digital immigrants—that is, elders who often feel less at ease with new technologies.

How different are they? Several years ago when she was interviewing a 17-year-old girl named LaShonda for a project about the future of work, Rebecca Ryan, founder of a hip consulting firm named Next Generation Consulting, noted the difference between digital natives and their digital immigrant elders. In an email, she explains:

"We were at a food court in a mall outside Seattle. While I was interviewing her, she was IM'ing, had her PDA on, her cell phone, the whole thing. . . . I was so put off. I thought, 'She's not paying attention!' And so I asked her, 'LaShonda, what do you think will be the impact of technology on the future of work?' She looked me in the eye and asked, 'What do you mean by technology?' I looked at all of her gadgets on the table and said, 'Like this stuff!' She said, 'This is only technology for people who weren't raised with it.' Whoa. The point that came home to rest for me is that for LaShonda, IM'ing and texting are like breathing. Fish don't know they're in water. LaShonda didn't consider her gadgets technology."

This generational difference will inevitably pose challenges and create opportunities for the firms that hire them because natives have experiences and values that are different from digital immigrants. Herewith, five new realities of the digital natives' lives that should be understood by their new employers:

Reality 1—They are video gamers and that gives them different expectations about how to learn, work, and pursue careers.

A host of experts have affirmed that today's young workers have internalized the new realities of work. "In contrast to a generation ago, job entrants now do not expect lifetime employment from a single employer; they do not expect a full menu of paid corporate benefits; they do not relish jobs in hierarchical bureaucracies," argues Edward Lawler, Director of the Center for Effective Organizations at the University of Southern California, and co-author of the forthcoming book, *The New American Workplace.* "To them, the word 'career' is plural."

These attitudes clearly reflect the larger realities of the changing nature of work. Yet there is also some evidence that the ethos of video gaming plays a role. Studies at the Pew Internet & American Life Project show that virtually all college students play video, computer, or internet games and 73% of teens do so. John Beck and Mitchell Wade argue in their book, *Got Game: How the Gamer Generation Is Reshaping Business Forever*, that games are the "training program" for young workers that helps form their attitudes about the way the work-world operates—a world full of data-streams, where analysis and decisions come at twitch speed, where failure at first is the norm, where the game player is the hero, and where learning takes place informally.

For companies, this puts a premium on designing engaging work that allows workers to make a clear contribution and be rewarded for same. If "organization man" has become "gaming man," then the importance of worker morale is elevated—as is the value of basing work on completed tasks, rather than other measures of work effort such as hours on the job. "Give them projects to complete and then stand out of the way," argues James Ware, who helps run *Future of Work*, an organization for facilities, information technology, and human resources professionals based in Prescott, Arizona. "These kids quit when they are frustrated trying to finish an effort that will 'get them to the next level.'"

Reality 2—They are technologically literate, but that does not necessarily make them media literate.

Our research has found consistently that the dominant metaphor for the internet in users' minds is a vast encyclopedia—more than it is a playground, a commercial mall, a civic commons, a kaffee klatch, or a peep show. This is especially true for younger users, who have grown up relying on it to complete school assignments, perhaps too often clipping and pasting material from websites into term papers.

Sandra Gisin, who oversees knowledge and information management at reinsurance giant Swiss Re, says her colleagues marvel at the speed with which younger workers communicate and gather information. Still, she has had enough bad experiences with credulous younger workers accepting information from the top link on a Google search result that she says the firm will begin new training programs next year to teach workers how to evaluate information and to stress that "not all the best information is free."

Dow Jones news organizations have similar worries. They have created programs for journalism educators and reporters-in-training to drive home the point that journalists should not rely on Web sources without checking their origins and confirming them in other ways. "We drive home the point that it's not good enough to say, 'I read it on the internet,' without taking other steps to verify it," notes Clare Hart, Executive Vice President of Dow Jones and President of the Enterprise Media Group.

At the same time, younger workers' comfort with online tools can be a boon to marketing departments. Hart, 45, says younger workers on the staff "convinced us Baby Boomers" to put more information from Dow Jones conference presentations online and to create podcasts of the best of them. Since then, email offering podcasts gets opened about 20% more frequently than traditional marketing email.

Reality 3—They are content creators and that shapes their notions about privacy and property.

More than half of American teenagers have created a blog, posted an artistic or written creation online, helped build a website, created an online profile, or uploaded photos and videos to a website. They think of the internet as a place where they can express their passions, play out their identities, and gather up the raw material they use for their creations.

So, why shouldn't young employees think it clever and fun to post on their blogs pictures of Apple computers being delivered to the loading bay at Microsoft headquarters? That is what Michael

Hanscom, a temp employee for a Microsoft vendor, did and was quickly fired for violating the company's non-disclosure rules. An even more benign episode ended the same way when Bill Poon, a database marketing manager for Collectors Universe, a sports memorabilia authenticating company in Los Angeles, posted a photo of his department's president on his MySpace profile. Poon also filed a few comments poking fun at the firm's dress code and cubicle culture and was axed based on the company's concerns about "identity theft."

In the many-to-many broadcast environment of the internet, the prospects for data hemorrhage from companies have grown exponentially. The rise of consumer-creations online also means that outsiders have all manner of ways to record and report on the behavior of employees—as AOL discovered recently when a customer recorded and posted a frustrating telephone encounter with a customer service representative who refused his request to change his service plan and persistently pressed him with other options.

Clearly, firms need to create policies about how internal bloggers should treat company information, what kinds of intellectual property need to be protected, and basic norms of behavior that should guide people who want to create online material.

Reality 4—They are product and people rankers and that informs their notions of propriety.

This is the wisdom-of-crowds generation that grew up rating peers' physical attributes (amihotornot.com), pop culture creations (metacritic.com reviews), teachers' style and grading practices (ratemyprofessors.com), products and services (epinions.com), and even weddings (bridezilla.com). No surprise, then, that there are websites drawing decent traffic for people to rate their bosses, their clients, and their customers. The tone of online commentary is often flame-oriented, racy, and retaliatory. This, too, is the generation that has given rise to cyber-bullying.

So, organizations might ponder adding a new clause or two to the policy manual about online etiquette inside and outside the workplace. "Most companies have policies in place against harassment based on things like sex, race, and ethnicity," says Lynn Karoly, an economist at the RAND Corporation who has studied the 21st-century workplace. "But we should probably create new categories of policies to handle unacceptable online behaviors where liability might emerge."

Reality 5—They are multi-taskers often living in a state of "continuous partial attention" and that means the boundary between work and leisure is quite permeable.

The ubiquity of gadgets and media allows younger workers to toggle back and forth quickly between tasks for work and chatter with their friends, research for projects and diversions on their screens. Many marvel at their capacity to juggle multiple tasks at once. An even sharper insight comes from Linda Stone, a technology consultant, who has noted that many technophiles function in a condition she calls "continuous partial attention," where they are scanning all available data sources for the optimum inputs.

Those who operate in such a state are not as productive as those who stay on task. They also do not make distinctions between the zones of work and leisure, consumer and producer, education and entertainment. "Their worlds bleed together," argues Charles Grantham, another principal at Future of Work. "It is pretty useless to try to draw borders around different spheres of life for them. It's better to let them shift among them at their own choosing as long as the work gets done."

Rebecca Ryan of Next Generation Consulting says she has recently gained a new appreciation for young workers' capacity to multi-task even when it seems rude and inattentive. In an email, she explained:

"We currently have an intern who's working on several critical projects. She's brilliant and a great fit for our team. At meetings, she's online the whole time. At first, I was totally put off by this—Why isn't she looking me in the eye? But then I realized that our 'to do' lists were a LOT shorter after these meetings because she would locate the information we needed in real time, which eliminated the need for a lot of follow-up work. So, something that I initially perceived as 'poor manners' on her part actually ended up being a great efficiency in our team meetings."

Again, companies would be wise to spell out their tolerance levels for the amount of personal activity workers are allowed on the clock and their expectations about the availability of workers outside the office and after hours.

Many firms see no option but to embrace the world of digital natives. Agilent Technologies, a top global measurement company, began early this year to distribute iPod Nanos to new employees hired from U.S. college campuses. The Nanos were preloaded with podcasts describing each of the benefits offered by the company, such as the 401(k) retirement plan and options for health insurance. "The college kids loved getting the benefit overviews preloaded on the iPod, while our older workers often preferred to read about these things on our web site," notes human resources manager Cathy Taylor. "There are different generational learning styles."

Still, the ethic of podcasting information has now begun to spread through the company and some of those older workers have caught the bug, too. For a recent retirement party, staffers from Agilent's far-flung offices collaborated on a podcast for the retiree. "You Raise Me Up" by Andrea Bocelli was dubbed over the voiced well wishes and the podcast was played over a WebEx teleconference. "It was a first for a virtual retirement party," enthuses Taylor. "We'll be doing it again."

Critical Reading Questions

Summarizing the Text

1. Rainie uses the anecdote of a 17-year-old named LaShonda to illustrate his key point about "digital natives'" relationship to technology. What point is he making with her story?
2. What is Rainie's thesis here? Who is his audience?

Establishing the Context

3. What is the difference between "technologically literate" and "media literate"? How does this affect the preparation of young workers?
4. Rainie's article appeared on the website of the nonprofit, nonpartisan Pew Center. How does this affect its *ethos*?

Responding to the Message

5. What are some other ways in which the millennial generation's comfort with technology might affect—negatively or positively—their attitude toward work? Their abilities? Their strengths and weaknesses as employees?
6. Rainie, like Maggie Jackson in Chapter 4, argues that being a digital native means that a young person is in a "state of continual partial attention." What does this mean? What are the ramifications of *this*?

LittleBrother Is Watching You

Miriam Shulman

Miriam Schulman is the director of communications and administration at Santa Clara University's Markkula Center for Applied Ethics. She has written on ethics for publications ranging from the San Jose Mercury-News *to her the 2000 collection* Cyberethics. *Here, Schulman looks at what was in 1998, when she wrote the article, a brand-new phenomenon: workers spending time surfing the Internet rather than working, and employers being able to monitor, down to the click and keystroke, what their employees were doing. This article appeared in* Issues in Ethics, *an academic publication aimed at philosophers, ethicists, and others who think about and design policies regarding ethics in daily life.*

Last year, a software package came on the market that allows employers to monitor their workers' Internet use. It employs a database of 45,000 Web sites that are categorized as "productive," "unproductive," or "neutral," and rates employees based on their browsing. It identifies the most frequent users and the most popular sites. It's called LittleBrother.

Though the title is tongue-in-cheek, LittleBrother does represent the tremendous capabilities technology has provided for employers to keep track of what their work force is up to. There are also programs to search e-mails and programs to block objectionable Web sites. Beyond installing monitoring software, your boss can simply go into your hard drive, check your cache to see where you've been on the Net, and read your e-mail.

Did you delete that message you sent about his incompetence? Not good enough. The e-mail trash bin probably still exists on the server, and there are plenty of computer consultants who can retrieve the incriminating message.

All told, such monitoring is a widespread-and-growing-phenomenon. Looking just at e-mail, a 1996 survey by the Society for Human Resource Management found that 36 percent of responding companies searched employee messages regularly and 70 percent said employers should reserve the right to do so.

The Law

Legally, employees have little recourse. The most relevant federal law, the 1986 Electronic Communications Privacy Act, prohibits unauthorized interception of various electronic communications, including e-mail. However, the law exempts service providers from its provisions, which is commonly interpreted to include employers who provide e-mail and Net access, according to David Sobel, legal counsel for the Electronic Privacy Information Center in Washington, D.C. A federal bill that would have required employers at least to notify workers that they were being monitored failed to come to a vote from 1993 to 1995.

The situation in the courts is similar. "There aren't many cases, and they tend to go against the employee," according to Santa Clara University Professor of Law Dorothy Glancy. "Often, court opinions take the point of view that when the employees are using employers' property—the employers' computers and networks—the employees' expectation of privacy is minimal." When courts take this view, Glancy continues, "if employees want to have private communications, they can enjoy them on their own time and equipment."

In a presentation on employee monitoring, Mark S. Dichter and Michael S. Burkhardt of the law firm Morgan, Lewis & Bockius explain that courts have tried to balance "an employee's reasonable expectation of privacy against the employer's business justification for monitoring."

For example, in *Smyth* v. *Pillsbury Co.*, Michael Smyth argued that his privacy was violated and he was wrongfully discharged from his job after his employers read several e-mails he had exchanged with his supervisor. In the electronic messages, among other offensive noteces, he threatened to "kill the backstabbing bastards" in sales management.

The court ruled that Smyth had "no reasonable expectation of privacy" on his employer's system, despite the fact that Pillsbury had repeatedly assured employees that their e-mail was confidential. In addition, the court held that the company's interest in preventing "inappropriate and unprofessional" conduct outweighed Smyth's privacy rights.

Privacy as a Moral Matter

But the fact that employee monitoring is legal does not automatically make it right. From an ethical point of view, an employee surely does not give up all of his or her privacy when entering the workplace. To determine how far employee and employer moral rights should extend, it's useful to start with a brief exploration of how privacy becomes a moral matter.

Michael J. Meyer, SCU professor of philosophy, explains it this way: "Employees are autonomous moral agents. Among other things, that means they have independent moral status defined by some set of rights, not the least of which is the right not to be used by others only as a means to increase overall welfare or profits."

Applying this to the workplace, Meyer says, "As thinking actors, human beings are more than cogs in an organization—things to be pushed around so as to maximize profits. They are entitled to respect, which requires some attention to privacy. If a boss were to monitor every conversation or move, most of us would think of such an environment as more like a prison than a humane workplace." But, like all rights, privacy is not absolute. Sometimes, as in the case of law enforcement, invasions of privacy may be warranted. In "Privacy, Morality, and the Law," William Parent, also a philosophy professor at SCU, sets out six criteria for determining whether an invasion of privacy is justifiable:

1. For what purpose is the undocumented personal knowledge sought?
2. Is this purpose a legitimate and important one?
3. Is the knowledge sought through invasion of privacy relevant to its justifying purpose?

4. Is invasion of privacy the only or the least offensive means of obtaining the knowledge?
5. What restrictions or procedural restraints have been placed on the privacy-invading techniques?
6. How will the personal knowledge be protected once it has been acquired?

These questions can offer guidance as we consider both sides of the controversy.

The Case for Workplace Monitoring

If an employer uses a software package that sweeps through office computers and eliminates games workers have installed, few people will feel such an action is an invasion of privacy. Our comfort with this kind of intrusion suggests that most of us don't fault an employer who insists that the equipment he or she provides be used for work, at least during working hours.

Why, then, should we balk when an employer tries to ensure that his equipment is not being used to surf non-job-related Web sites? Hours spent online browsing the recipe files of Epicurious are no less a breach of the work contract than games playing.

"The underlying principle is value for money," says Joseph R. Garber, a columnist for *Forbes* magazine. "If you don't deliver value for money, in some sense, you're lying."

Garber gives this illustration: If we hired someone to paint our house, and they didn't do the northern wall, we would feel moral outrage. Similarly, if we pay workers to give a good day's work and they are, instead, surfing X-rated Web sites, we are also morally outraged.

Such "cyberlollygagging" is no small problem. A study by Nielsen Media Research found that employees at major corporations such as IBM, Apple, and AT&T logged onto the online edition of *Penthouse* thousands of times a month.

Beyond worry about lost productivity, employers have legitimate concerns about the use of e-mail in thefts of proprietary information, which, according to the "Handbook on White Collar Crime," account for more than $2 billion in losses a year. The transfer of such information can be monitored by programs that search employee e-mails for suspect word strings or by employers simply going into the employee's hard drive and reading the messages.

In a case last year, a former employee of Cadence Systems was charged with stealing proprietary information and intending to bring it to the rival software maker Avant! According to prosecutors, before leaving Cadence, he e-mailed a file containing 5 million bytes to a personal e-mail account. Such large messages suggested that he might be sending source code for the company's products and prompted Cadence to contact the police.

Electronic communications can pose other dangers for employers besides breached security and lost productivity. More and more, employers are being held legally liable for the atmosphere in the workplace. Although the case was ultimately dismissed, employers worry about litigation like the $70 million suit brought by Morgan Stanley employees, who claimed that racist jokes on the company's electronic mail system created a hostile work environment.

Sexual harassment cases also often hinge on allegations of a hostile work environment, which might be evidenced by employees downloading or displaying pornographic material from the Web or sending off-color e-mails. "The days of guys putting naked bunnies up on their computer screens are gone because that's actionable stuff," Garber comments.

To prevent such abuses, Garber argues, employers need to be allowed to monitor: "We can't make corporations responsible for stopping unacceptable forms of behavior and then deny them the tools needed to keep an eye out for that behavior."

The Case Against Workplace Monitoring

Consider this scenario: It's lunch hour. An employee writes a note to her boyfriend. She puts it in an envelope, affixes her own stamp, and drops it in the basket where outgoing mail is collected. Does the fact that the pencil and paper she used belong to her employer give her boss the right to open and read this letter?

Although most people would answer no, that's just the argument employers are making to defend monitoring e-mail, according to the Electronic Privacy Information Center's Sobel: Employers claim that because they own the computer, they have the right to read the e-mail it produces. The situation is complicated by the fact that work and personal life are not as clearly delineated as they once were, due, in part, to the very technologies that are being monitored. Employees may telecommute, doing much of their business through e-mail and the Net. Often, they work a good deal more than 40 hours a week. If they take a moment to send a message to Aunt Margaret in Saskatoon, do they not have a right to expect their e-mail will be confidential?

"Most people don't work 8 to 5," says Anthony Pozos, senior vice president for human resources and corporate services at Amdahl Corp. "We pay people to do a job; we don't really pay by time increment. Employees probably do use our e-mail or Web access for personal matters; it's analogous to using the telephone. People do sometimes need to do personal things on the job, but as long as it doesn't interfere with work, that should be okay."

Another ethical consideration in the debate is fairness. Usually, it's not corporate higher-ups who are subject to monitoring, but line workers. That's particularly true when it comes to key-stroke monitoring, a form of electronic surveillance that measures the speed of data entry. According to an article in Public Personnel Management, "The majority of employees being electronically monitored are women in low-paying clerical positions."

Then there's Parent's question about whether the invasion of privacy (represented by monitoring) is the only or the least offensive means of obtaining the information employers seek. In a survey conducted by *PC World*, slightly more than half of the executives interviewed were opposed to monitoring employees' Internet use. Scott Paddock, manager of PC Brokers, told the magazine, "First, I trust my employees; that's why they work for me. If there were to be any problems with an employee, those problems would present themselves without the need for me to get involved in cloak-and-dagger shenanigans. And second, if I spent time monitoring their Web usage, I would be just as guilty of wasting time as my behavior implies they are."

Trust is often mentioned by opponents of monitoring as a major ethical issue. As Rita C. Manning writes in the *Journal of Business Ethics*, "When we look at the workplaces in which surveillance is common, we see communities in trouble. What is missing in these communities is trust."

If, Manning continues, employers create trust, employee behavior "will conform to certain norms, not as a result of being watched, but as a result of the care and respect which are part of the communal fabric."

Some Possibilities for Common Ground

It is possible to moot many of these ethical issues by arguing that monitoring all comes down to a question of contract. That is the view of David Friedman, an economist and professor at SCU's School of Law.

"There isn't an agreement that is morally right for everybody. The important thing is what the parties agree to," he says. "If the employer gives a promise of privacy, then that should be respected." If, on the other hand, the employer reserves the right to read e-mail or monitor Web browsing, the worker can either accept those terms or look else-where for employment, Friedman continues.

Friedman's argument doesn't address the problems of lower-income workers who may not have a choice about whether to accept a job or, if they do, may be choosing between entry-level positions where monitoring is a feature of the work environment.

But he does point to an area where some common ground may exist between opponents and proponents of monitoring. Most parties to the debate agree that companies should have clear policies on electronic surveillance and that these should be effectively communicated to employees.

A recent study by International Data Corp. suggests that such clarity does not currently prevail. A survey of employees at 110 businesses showed that 45 percent thought their company had no policy on e-mail at all. Most of those who did know the company policy had either learned it by word of mouth or were directly involved in writing it.

Spelling out company policy "is our bottom line," says Sobel. "We would like to see an outright prohibition on e-mail monitoring in the workplace, but, at the very least, there needs to be notice to employees if that's the policy."

Pozos believes that involving employees in the creation of a monitoring policy is also a way to find common ground. By bringing employees and managers together to develop principles and guide-lines for electronic mail, Amdahl was able to create a policy that was acceptable to both sides, Pozos says.

In any case, employers who reserve the right to monitor should attend to the considerations Parent proposes, ensuring at least that the monitoring serves a legitimate purpose and follows clear procedures to protect a worker's personal life from unnecessary prying, either by LittleBrother or by Big Brother.

Critical Reading Questions

Summarizing the Text

1. What is Schulman's thesis here? Where does she side, if anywhere, on the question of whether employers should be able to monitor their employees' Internet use?

2. What are the unspoken assumptions behind the two main arguments here (that employers should or should not be able to monitor their employees' Internet use)?

Establishing the Context

3. Schulman's article appeared in 1998, just at the beginning of the "Internet age." Certainly, the actual conditions of how permeated our work and per-sonal lives are by digital technology has radically changed since then. How?

4. With his six-point framework, for determining whether an invasion of privacy is justifiable, William Parent's goal is to provide a system by which we can judge the legitimacy of any—not just employee-Internet-use-monitoring—snooping. Do you agree with this framework? Why or why not? Does the greater permeation of technology today make it necessary to revise this?

Responding to the Message

5. When you are "on the clock," what does that mean? Has your employer paid for all of your time and all of your energy and all of your attention during that time? What space should you still have for yourself, if any?

6. Is there a difference between an employer monitoring your keystrokes and an employer looking through your purse or pockets or locker? Why or why not?

Internet Usage Software

WorkExaminer.com

WorkExaminer sells software that tracks a company's employees' use of the Internet—who is visiting what pages, what they are doing there, how long they are staying. This Web page describes how the software monitors "Internet usage"; other pages detail how the company's products can monitor all of an employee's activities or filter the Internet. Among WorkExaminer's products is WorkExaminer Academic, specifically designed to "monitor students' activities in real time . . . examine whether a student has been using chat/web [and] block all inappropriate applications and websites during an examination."

According to the latest research by Salary.com, the average worker spends 1.7 hours doing nothing during a typical 8-hour working day. Mainly this time is spent on personal web surfing (34.7 %), talking with friends and colleagues (20.3 %), or on a hobby (17.0 %).

EfficientLab has developed a software product—Work Examiner—that can solve problems with Internet usage in your company.

Work Examiner analyzes not only what your employees are engaged in, but also what they spend time on. Moreover, you can analyze time spent on surfing, blogs and chats both by individual employees or company departments.

Work Examiner allows supervisors to see which applications and web sites employees and groups are using. It simplifies the introduction of Internet usage tracking into your workplace. At the same time, we understand that each company might define "personal time" differently and might allow employees varying levels of freedom, so Work Examiner users can adjust settings at their discretion.

Work Examiner software also can form detailed internet usage reports.

The report can be exported in 10 popular formats, including PDF, HTML, MS Word, MS Excel. It can create reports automatically through its Report Jobs function. All you need to do is set the parameters of the job and every manager in the company will receive a detailed weekly Internet usage report on every employee.

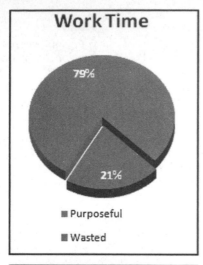

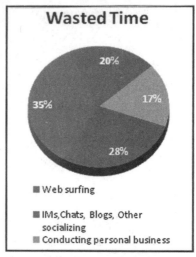

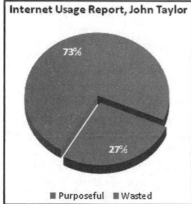

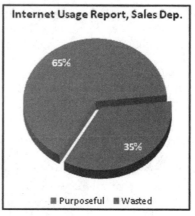

In addition to monitoring, Work Examiner can also restrict internet usage. The "Internet Filter" feature can block access to sites or groups of sites based on varying criteria: time of day, hours, particular users, particular computers.

Critical Reading Questions

1. Judging from the points made on this page, what anxieties do employers have about their employees' use of the Internet?

2. Is this product sinister? Is it justified? How would you feel about working at a place where your Internet usage was monitored?

Questions for Short Projects or Group Presentations

1. According to the writers in this chapter, the Internet and other electronic communications technologies are fundamentally changing the nature of the workplace. Compare and evaluate their claims. What do you think will be the long-term effect of this change on your career?

2. Many of the essays and articles in this chapter were written during the depths of the "Great Recession" that began in 2008—a crisis that included the crash of the real-estate market, the failure of several large investment and consumer banks, unemployment rates above 10 percent, and massive government bailout and stimulus spending. For a group project, research how economic conditions have changed since then, and how this might affect the job prospects of this year's graduates.

Questions for Formal Essays

1. Several of the essays in this chapter (Sandler's, Chen's, and others) translate primary-source scientific research for a more general, non-specialist audience. Compare how each author uses his or her sources by consulting those original sources. Do the authors accurately represent the research they are presenting to their audiences?

2. Rainie's and Alsop's arguments are quite similar on the surface—how the digital-native millennial generation is changing the workplace—but their conclusions and evidence are quite different. Compare the two: where do they agree on the characteristics of the generation in question, on the causes of these characteristics, and on the effects they will have? Where do they disagree? Compare these ideas to Maggie Jackson's in Chapter 4.

3. How does television represent the workplace today? Analyze the depictions of the workplace in five or six current popular television programs. What do the characters get out of their time at work? What is their attitude toward work? How does the program "teach" its viewers to understand the proper balance of work and life?

4. As the United States moves away from being a manufacturing economy toward being a service economy, the nations of Asia, in particular, have taken up the mantle of "manufacturer for the world." But as the Foxconn worker's story indicates, the conditions under which factory laborers toil can be trying, and their wages would be unacceptable to most Americans. What can or should we do about this? Should the United States give up on manufacturing, given that our labor costs will always exceed those of poorer nations? If not, how can we revive our manufacturing sector?

What Makes a Family?

CHAPTER INTRODUCTION

We all know what the traditional American family is: a mom who stays at home, a dad who works, two kids (probably boy and girl), and maybe a dog. And a house in the suburbs. With a picket fence. And a station wagon, or perhaps (to update our image) a hybrid SUV. The images that the term *traditional American family* evokes are so deeply ingrained in all of us that we have stopped questioning them, assuming that they reflect an ideal or natural state, even though today most families don't match up with this "traditional" profile.

So where did this traditional image come from? In part, it came from facts. First of all, in 1950 (in that mythical decade that the traditional American family supposedly dominated) almost 90 percent of households—groups of people living together—were families. Of those families, the overwhelming majority were two-parent families. But in 2000, only 68 percent of households were families, and of those only two-thirds were two-parent families. So, it's true that the United States used to have more two-parent families, and that more households consisted of families.

Facts, as you have been learning throughout this book, can be bolstered by arguments and images, as well. And for many of us, we learn as much about "real" families from media sources as we do from our own family or from our friends' families. The 1950s television comedy *Leave It to Beaver* is arguably more influential as a model of family life than as a pioneering sitcom; in fact, many who have never seen the program use "Leave It to Beaver" as a sarcastic phrase for a kind of idyllic suburban family life (it is a common trope in hip-hop lyrics). Other television programs of the 1950s—*Ozzie and Harriet, The Donna Reed Show, The Dick Van Dyke Show*—reinforced this notion that "real" American families looked like these TV families. And this image lives on, in television, in films, and even on political commercials where candidates pose in their living rooms with their spouses, children, and pets to offer us objective evidence that they are "just like us"—or, at least, just like what we think we should be.

As families in America changed, television reflected those changes. In the 1960s, television began to depict single-parent families in programs such as *My Three Sons* or *Here's Lucy*; blended families were immortalized in *The Brady Bunch*; divorced women lived together in *Kate & Allie*; and *Full House* depicted the very uncommon, if comedically fertile, arrangement of three men and a woman jointly raising two children.

Although many of these television programs played such domestic situations for laughs, the reality was that the American family was actually changing in profound ways. The divorce rate shot up in the 1960s and 1970s as state laws changed and the feminist movement empowered many women to leave unsatisfactory marriages. Because of this, more children grew up shuttling between parents, or with only one parent in their lives.

What do American families look like today? Well, those traditional families of beloved television memory still survive, albeit in much smaller numbers. The biggest change is in work status: today, two-thirds of two-parent families are also *two-earner* families—that is, in two-thirds of families with two parents, both parents work. In 1950, in only a small minority of two-parent families did both parents work. Households in general are growing smaller today (as a greater percentage of households consists of unmarried, unrelated people), but even family households are shrinking, from 3.8 people per family household in 1950 to 3.14 in 2000. Americans are getting married later, and having fewer children.

Even as both households and families are getting smaller, another demographic trend is working in the opposite direction. In the past twenty years, the proportion of "multigenerational" families (defined by the Census Bureau as "three or more generations of parents and their families") has risen—just from 1990 to 2000 that number rose 60 percent, to 3.9 million households. The reasons are partly demographic (grandparents and even great-grandparents are living longer); partly economic; and partly cultural, particularly due to rising numbers of Hispanic and Asian families whose cultures encourage all of the generations to live together.

These demographic changes are significant, but much *louder* and more controversial are other changes to the nature of the American family. In 2003, Massachusetts became the first American state to allow same-sex couples to marry. Soon afterward, several other states—Connecticut, Vermont, Iowa, and New Hampshire—joined, as did New York in 2011. As a result, since 2003 same-sex marriage has been one of the hottest, most emotional, and most charged issues in the United States. Fought simultaneously in state courts, federal courts, state legislatures, Congress, and election campaigns, the battle over whether same-sex couples should be allowed to marry is certain to continue for years, if not decades. Included in this chapter is a powerful argument by the lawyer Ted Olsen, who is suing to invalidate an anti-gay-marriage amendment to the California state constitution.

What's undeniable is that general public acceptance of same-sex relationships is growing. Polls conducted by the Gallup organization in 2010 found that a majority (52 percent) of Americans found homosexual relationships "morally acceptable," and 44 percent supported legal recognition of same-sex marriage—still a minority, but up from 27 percent in 1996. A 2010 CNN poll found that young people in particular (18- to 29-year-olds) support gay marriage at the highest rate—52 percent—of any age group. The first cluster of readings in this chapter examines this question of same-sex marriage from several different perspectives.

Heather Has Two Mommies, a picture book introducing young children to families with same-sex parents, was used for many years as an emotional symbol of how the "homosexual agenda" was seeping into schools with the intent of making children think that it was "normal" to be gay. Now more children than ever are growing up with same-sex parents—for many children, it's no longer unusual or remarkable that Heather, or Brynne, or Jameer has two mommies or two daddies.

The second section of this chapter looks at other changes affecting the American family. Writers in this section use the tools of "demography"—the study of populations—to draw a picture of what American families look like today, and what trends we are seeing in terms of changes to the family. Heavy immigration from Hispanic nations has brought cultural changes to the traditional American family, Rosa Villareal points out, but she argues that such changes are being misrepresented by those who want to attack immigration. Other writers in this section write about those who choose *not* to have children, or those who choose so-called "plural marriage"—polygamy. As you read these articles, think for yourself about what a family is, what a family can be, and what a family should be.

CLUSTER ONE: SAME-SEX MARRIAGE AND "REAL" AMERICAN VALUES

The Conservative Case for Gay Marriage
Why same-sex marriage is an American value

Ted Olsen

After representing George W. Bush in the 2000 case Bush v. Gore, *which ended a Florida vote recount and, in effect, made Bush president, Theodore Olsen served as the U.S. Solicitor General (the lawyer who represents the United States in cases argued before the Supreme Court) from 2001 to 2004. So it was surprising to many when the reliably conservative Olsen teamed up with his* Bush v. Gore *adversary, David Boies, to challenge a California state constitutional amendment barring same-sex marriage. In this column for* Newsweek *magazine, Olsen lays out what he believes to be the "conservative" argument for same-sex marriage.*

Together with my good friend and occasional courtroom adversary David Boies, I am attempting to persuade a federal court to invalidate California's Proposition 8—the voter-approved measure that overturned California's constitutional right to marry a person of the same sex.

My involvement in this case has generated a certain degree of consternation among conservatives. How could a politically active, life-long Republican, a veteran of the Ronald Reagan and George W. Bush administrations, challenge the "traditional" definition of marriage and press for an "activist" interpretation of the Constitution to create another "new" constitutional right?

My answer to this seeming conundrum rests on a lifetime of exposure to persons of different backgrounds, histories, viewpoints, and intrinsic characteristics, and on my rejection of what I see as superficially appealing but ultimately false perceptions about our Constitution and its protection of equality and fundamental rights.

Many of my fellow conservatives have an almost knee-jerk hostility toward gay marriage. This does not make sense, because same-sex unions promote the values conservatives prize. Marriage is one of the basic building blocks of our neighborhoods and our nation. At its best, it is a stable bond between two individuals who work to create a loving household and a social and economic partnership. We encourage couples to marry because the commitments they make to one another provide benefits not only to themselves but also to their families and communities. Marriage requires thinking beyond one's own needs. It transforms two individuals into a union based on shared aspirations, and in doing so establishes a formal investment in the well-being of society.

The fact that individuals who happen to be gay want to share in this vital social institution is evidence that conservative ideals enjoy widespread acceptance. Conservatives should celebrate this, rather than lament it.

Legalizing same-sex marriage would also be a recognition of basic American principles, and would represent the culmination of our nation's commitment to equal rights. It is, some have said, the last major civil-rights milestone yet to be surpassed in our two-century struggle to attain the goals we set for this nation at its formation.

This bedrock American principle of equality is central to the political and legal convictions of Republicans, Democrats, liberals, and conservatives alike. The dream that became America began with the revolutionary concept expressed in the Declaration of Independence in words that are among the most noble and elegant ever written: "We hold these truths to be self-evident, that all men are created equal, that they are endowed by their Creator with certain unalienable Rights, that among these are Life, Liberty and the pursuit of Happiness."

Sadly, our nation has taken a long time to live up to the promise of equality. In 1857, the Supreme Court held that an African American could not be a citizen. During the ensuing Civil War, Abraham Lincoln eloquently reminded the nation of its founding principle: "our fathers brought forth on this continent, a new nation, conceived in liberty and dedicated to the proposition that all men are created equal."

At the end of the Civil War, to make the elusive promise of equality a reality, the 14th Amendment to the Constitution added the command that "no State shall deprive any person of life, liberty or property, without due process of law; nor deny to any person the equal protection of the laws."

Subsequent laws and court decisions have made clear that equality under the law extends to persons of all races, religions, and places of origin. What better way to make this national aspiration complete than to apply the same protection to men and women who differ from others only on the basis of their sexual orientation? I cannot think of a single reason—and have not heard one since I undertook this venture—for continued discrimination against decent, hardworking members of our society on that basis.

Various federal and state laws have accorded certain rights and privileges to gay and lesbian couples, but these protections vary dramatically at the state level, and nearly universally deny true equality to gays and lesbians who wish to marry. The very idea of marriage is basic to recognition as equals in our society; any status short of that is inferior, unjust, and unconstitutional.

The United States Supreme Court has repeatedly held that marriage is one of the most fundamental rights that we have as Americans under our Constitution. It is an expression of our desire to create a social partnership, to live and share life's joys and burdens with the person we love, and to form a lasting bond and a social identity. The Supreme

Court has said that marriage is a part of the Constitution's protections of liberty, privacy, freedom of association, and spiritual identification. In short, the right to marry helps us to define ourselves and our place in a community. Without it, there can be no true equality under the law.

It is true that marriage in this nation traditionally has been regarded as a relationship exclusively between a man and a woman, and many of our nation's multiple religions define marriage in precisely those terms. But while the Supreme Court has always previously considered marriage in that context, the underlying rights and liberties that marriage embodies are not in any way confined to heterosexuals.

Marriage is a civil bond in this country as well as, in some (but hardly all) cases, a religious sacrament. It is a relationship recognized by governments as providing a privileged and respected status, entitled to the state's support and benefits. The California Supreme Court described marriage as a "union unreservedly approved and favored by the community." Where the state has accorded official sanction to a relationship and provided special benefits to those who enter into that relationship, our courts have insisted that withholding that status requires powerful justifications and may not be arbitrarily denied.

What, then, are the justifications for California's decision in Proposition 8 to withdraw access to the institution of marriage for some of its citizens on the basis of their sexual orientation? The reasons I have heard are not very persuasive.

The explanation mentioned most often is tradition. But simply because something has always been done a certain way does not mean that it must always remain that way. Otherwise we would still have segregated schools and debtors' prisons. Gays and lesbians have always been among us, forming a part of our society, and they have lived as couples in our neighborhoods and communities. For a long time, they have experienced discrimination and even persecution; but we, as a society, are starting to become more tolerant, accepting, and understanding. California and many other states have allowed gays and lesbians to form domestic partnerships (or civil unions) with most of the rights of married heterosexuals. Thus, gay and lesbian individuals are now permitted to live together in state-sanctioned relationships. It therefore seems anomalous to cite "tradition" as a justification for withholding the status of marriage and thus to continue to label those relationships as less worthy, less sanctioned, or less legitimate.

The second argument I often hear is that traditional marriage furthers the state's interest in procreation—and that opening marriage to same-sex couples would dilute, diminish, and devalue this goal. But that is plainly not the case. Preventing lesbians and gays from marrying does not cause more heterosexuals to marry and conceive more children. Likewise, allowing gays and lesbians to marry someone of the same sex will not discourage heterosexuals from marrying a person of the opposite sex. How, then, would allowing same-sex marriages reduce the number of children that heterosexual couples conceive?

This procreation argument cannot be taken seriously. We do not inquire whether heterosexual couples intend to bear children, or have the capacity to have children, before we allow them to marry. We permit marriage by the elderly, by prison inmates, and by persons who have no intention of having children. What's more, it is pernicious to think marriage should be limited to heterosexuals because of the state's desire to promote procreation. We would surely not accept as constitutional a ban on marriage if a state were to decide, as China has done, to discourage procreation.

Another argument, vaguer and even less persuasive, is that gay marriage somehow does harm to heterosexual marriage. I have yet to meet anyone who can explain to me what this means. In what way would allowing same-sex partners to marry diminish the marriages of heterosexual couples? Tellingly, when the judge in our case asked our opponent to identify the ways in which same-sex marriage would harm heterosexual marriage, to his credit he answered honestly: he could not think of any.

The simple fact is that there is no good reason why we should deny marriage to same-sex partners. On the other hand, there are many reasons why we should formally recognize these relationships and embrace the rights of gays and lesbians to marry and become full and equal members of our society.

No matter what you think of homosexuality, it is a fact that gays and lesbians are members of our families, clubs, and workplaces. They are our doctors, our teachers, our soldiers (whether we admit it or not), and our friends. They yearn for acceptance, stable relationships, and success in their lives, just like the rest of us.

Conservatives and liberals alike need to come together on principles that surely unite us. Certainly, we can agree on the value of strong families, lasting domestic relationships, and communities populated by persons with recognized and sanctioned bonds to one another. Confining some of our neighbors and friends who share these same values to an outlaw or second-class status undermines their sense of belonging and weakens their ties with the rest of us and what should be our common aspirations. Even those whose religious convictions preclude endorsement of what they may perceive as an unacceptable "lifestyle" should recognize that disapproval should not warrant stigmatization and unequal treatment.

When we refuse to accord this status to gays and lesbians, we discourage them from forming the same relationships we encourage for others. And we are also telling them, those who love them, and society as a whole that their relationships are less worthy, less legitimate, less permanent, and less valued. We demean their relationships and we demean them as individuals. I cannot imagine how we benefit as a society by doing so.

I understand, but reject, certain religious teachings that denounce homosexuality as morally wrong, illegitimate, or unnatural; and I take strong exception to those who argue that same-sex relationships should be discouraged by society and law. Science has taught us, even if history has not, that gays and lesbians do not choose to be homosexual any more than the rest of us choose to be heterosexual. To a very large extent, these characteristics are immutable, like being left-handed. And, while our Constitution guarantees the freedom to exercise our individual religious convictions, it equally prohibits us from forcing our beliefs on others. I do not believe that our society can ever live up to the promise of equality, and the fundamental rights to life, liberty, and the pursuit of happiness, until we stop invidious discrimination on the basis of sexual orientation.

If we are born heterosexual, it is not unusual for us to perceive those who are born homosexual as aberrational and threatening. Many religions and much of our social culture have reinforced those impulses. Too often, that has led to prejudice, hostility, and discrimination. The antidote is understanding, and reason. We once tolerated laws throughout this nation that prohibited marriage between persons of different races. California's Supreme Court was the first to find that discrimination unconstitutional. The U.S. Supreme Court unanimously agreed 20 years later, in 1967, in a case called *Loving v. Virginia*. It seems inconceivable today that only 40 years ago there were places in this country where a black woman could not legally marry a white man. And it was only 50 years ago that 17 states mandated segregated public education—until the Supreme Court unanimously struck down that practice in *Brown v. Board of Education.* Most Americans are proud of these decisions and the fact that the discriminatory state laws that spawned them have been discredited. I am convinced that Americans will be equally proud when we no longer discriminate against gays and lesbians and welcome them into our society.

Reactions to our lawsuit have reinforced for me these essential truths. I have certainly heard anger, resentment, and hostility, and words like "betrayal" and other pointedly graphic criticism. But mostly I have been overwhelmed by expressions of gratitude and good will from persons in all walks of life, including, I might add, from many conservatives and libertarians whose names might surprise. I have been particularly moved by many personal renditions of how lonely and personally destructive it is to be treated as an outcast and how meaningful it will be to be respected by our laws and civil institutions as an American, entitled to equality and dignity. I have no doubt that we are on the right side of this battle, the right side of the law, and the right side of history.

Some have suggested that we have brought this case too soon, and that neither the country nor the courts are "ready" to tackle this issue and remove this stigma. We disagree. We represent real clients—two wonderful couples in California who have longtime relationships. Our lesbian clients are raising four fine children who could not ask for better parents. Our clients wish to be married. They believe that they have that constitutional right. They wish to be represented in court to seek vindication of that right by mounting a challenge under the United States Constitution to the validity of Proposition 8 under the equal-protection and due-process clauses of the 14th Amendment. In fact, the California attorney general has conceded the unconstitutionality of Proposition 8, and the city of San Francisco has joined our case to defend the rights of gays and lesbians to be married. We do not tell persons who have a legitimate claim to wait until the time is "right" and the populace is "ready" to recognize their equality and equal dignity under the law.

Citizens who have been denied equality are invariably told to "wait their turn" and to "be patient." Yet veterans of past civil-rights battles found that it was the act of insisting on equal rights that ultimately sped acceptance of those rights. As to whether the courts are "ready" for this case, just a few years ago, in *Romer v. Evans,* the United States Supreme Court struck down a popularly adopted Colorado constitutional amendment that withdrew the rights of gays and lesbians in that state to the protection of anti-discrimination laws. And seven years ago, in *Lawrence v. Texas,* the Supreme Court struck down, as lacking any rational basis, Texas laws prohibiting private, intimate sexual practices between persons of the same sex, overruling a contrary decision just 20 years earlier.

These decisions have generated controversy, of course, but they are decisions of the nation's highest court on which our clients are entitled to rely. If all citizens have a constitutional right to marry, if state laws that withdraw legal protections of gays and lesbians as a class are unconstitutional, and if private, intimate sexual conduct between persons of the same sex is protected by the Constitution, there is very little left on which opponents of same-sex marriage can rely. As Justice Antonin Scalia, who dissented in the *Lawrence* case, pointed out, "[W]hat [remaining] justification could there possibly be for denying the benefits of marriage to homosexual couples exercising '[t]he liberty protected by the Constitution'?"

He is right, of course. One might agree or not with these decisions, but even Justice Scalia has acknowledged that they lead in only one direction.

California's Proposition 8 is particularly vulnerable to constitutional challenge, because that state has now enacted a crazy-quilt of marriage regulation that makes no sense to anyone. California recognizes marriage between men and women, including persons on death row, child abusers, and wife beaters. At the same time, California prohibits marriage by loving, caring, stable partners of the same sex, but tries to make up for it by giving them the alternative of "domestic partnerships" with virtually all of the rights of married persons except the official, state-approved status of marriage. Finally, California recognizes 18,000 same-sex marriages that took place in the months between the state Supreme Court's ruling that upheld gay-marriage rights and the decision of California's citizens to withdraw those rights by enacting Proposition 8.

So there are now three classes of Californians: heterosexual couples who can get married, divorced, and remarried, if they wish; same-sex couples who cannot get married but can live together in domestic partnerships; and same-sex couples who are now married but who, if they divorce, cannot remarry. This is an irrational system, it is discriminatory, and it cannot stand.

Americans who believe in the words of the Declaration of Independence, in Lincoln's Gettysburg Address, in the 14th Amendment, and in the Constitution's guarantees of equal protection and equal dignity before the law cannot sit by while this wrong continues. This is not a conservative or liberal issue; it is an American one, and it is time that we, as Americans, embraced it.

Critical Reading Questions

Summarizing the Text

1. What is the fundamental nature and purpose of marriage, for Olsen?
2. Why, according to Olsen, should marriage be a "fundamental right" of all Americans, protected by the Constitution?

Establishing the Context

3. In essence, Olsen is arguing that the *legal principle* underlying marriage is more fundamental than the *traditional definition* of the word. How does he separate the two?
4. Sometimes the most powerful argument on a controversial issue is one made by a surprising rhetor. Olsen's *ethos* is a key element of this argument. Describe Olsen's *ethos* appeal, both explicit (what he says) and implicit (what readers know about him and about the larger context of conservative views of marriage).

Responding to the Message

5. How do Olsen's assumptions about the purpose of marriage inform his argument? Do you agree with his assumptions? Does this make you agree with him? Why or why not?

6. Although many radical gay activists have argued for decades that marriage is something that gays should be happy to avoid—as it is an oppressive or bourgeois institution in itself—in recent years a strong strain of "conservative" gay thought, embodied in writers such as Jonathan Rauch and Andrew Sullivan, has made the case that gays should want to live their lives in traditional models. Research this controversy—what are the objections to gay marriage raised by homosexual activists and theorists?

Photograph: 2008 Anti-Proposition 8 Demonstration in California

In 2008, California voters approved Proposition 8, an amendment to the California state constitution that stipulated that "only marriage between a man and a woman is valid and recognized in California." The proposition was in response to a state supreme court ruling that same-sex couples have a constitutional right to marry. In the vote on the proposition, 52.24 percent of voters voted "yes," while 47.76 percent voted "no." The proposition was fiercely opposed by gay activists and their sympathizers (such as those depicted in the photo) and strongly supported by conservative groups and churches, in particular the Church of Jesus Christ of Latter-Day Saints (the Mormons), who experienced a backlash for their pro–Prop 8 support.

Critical Reading Question

1. How do the protesters understand the nature of marriage (judging from their signs—do not ascribe motives to them without evidence)?

Gay Wedding Bells Ring; So Do Cash Registers

Steve Roth

Stephen A. Roth is the founder and principal partner of OutThink Partners, a Los Angeles–based communications and marketing consulting firm that specializes in outreach to the lesbian and gay communities. He also blogs for Advertising Age, *the major trade publication for the advertising industry. This article appeared in* Advertising Age *in 2008.*

It's midnight in Los Angeles, and I'm sitting in front of my computer typing away. Two important things happened in my day today and I want to share them with you. One is that I attended my first bona fide gay wedding reception. The second is that Hallmark just unveiled its first line of same-sex wedding cards.

My two friends John and John (yes, that happens more often than you'd think with same-sex couples) were legally married in the afternoon. Their wedding reception started at 8 p.m. with cocktails at The Abbey, L.A.'s biggest and most famous gay bar, which was featured in a reality show recently.

Mind you, it was a Thursday night, and most of us had to work today. But the two mothers of the grooms—one in her 70s and the other in her 80s—were keeping up with the best of them, so I had to go along.

This was not the kind of wedding reception I grew up with in semi-rural Missouri, the kind that took place at the Knights of Columbus Hall with a lame DJ and bad catered food. Nope. Instead, after the cocktails, we boarded one of those red, faux-London double-decker tour buses and proceeded to drive around Los Angeles as we drank Champagne out of Red Bull-sized cans.

We cruised through West Hollywood and stopped at Hollywood and Highland, home of the Kodak Theatre and lots of confused straight tourists. We ended up at the home of an art dealer in the Hollywood Hills and listened to an opera diva sing wedding-themed showtunes as we ate cupcakes and drank more Champagne. I love being gay.

Continuing to the second important thing that happened in my day yesterday, Hallmark Cards rolled out its first gay wedding cards. Yes, that Hallmark. The one based in Kansas City that has been a bastion of middle-American "values" and sentiments for almost 100 years.

Ken Wheaton beat me to this news, but I still want to reiterate its significance. In June, I blogged about the potential economic impact of legal gay marriage in California, and the marketing opportunities that are destined to accompany it. Since then, we've seen major mainstream companies like Macy's take out full-page, gay-oriented wedding registry ads in major daily newspapers like the San Francisco Chronicle and the Los Angeles Times.

We've also seen the major gay publications, like *Frontiers* and *IN* magazine in Los Angeles, introduce regular, multipage ad spreads dedicated to wedding-related companies from caterers to bagpipers. Robbins Brothers Jewelers took out a full-page ad in the most recent issue of IN.

Gay couples are marrying at record rates in California, and now out-of-state gays can marry in Massachusetts, too. Companies clearly see the commercial opportunities and are acting accordingly.

But it's Hallmark's decision—perhaps more than any other—that signifies a sea change in cultural attitudes in this country and bodes well for the future of gay rights and acceptance in America. After all, this is the company that sells Precious Moments figurines and that can be found in most shopping malls across the country.

Granted, Hallmark has said that its stores can choose whether to add the latest offerings. But as far as I'm concerned, the cat is out of the bag. By 5 p.m. yesterday, I had seen news of Hallmark's new card line on AdAge.com, AP, the *Los Angeles Times* and even CNN. If nothing else, this has been a huge PR coup for the company. Granted, protests may come, but I haven't heard of any yet.

My point in all this is to celebrate the fact that smart companies as mainstream as Hallmark are recognizing and responding to the consumer demand they see in the gay market. Just as they have rolled out their Spanish-language and Mahogany lines in the last few decades, they are now courting the gay market. Not to make a political statement but because it makes sound business sense.

And for my part, I'll take the double-decker tour bus over the Knights of Columbus wedding reception anytime.

Critical Reading Questions

Summarizing the Text

1. What is Roth's thesis? What is the significance of Hallmark's decision to roll out a line of same-sex wedding cards?

2. Does Roth make his own sexual preference an issue in this piece? If so, how does it affect the argument? How does it change the argument's *pathos*?

Establishing the Context

3. What was the legal status of gay marriage in the state of California in August 2008? What has happened since then? Does this affect the validity of Roth's thesis?

4. Underlying Roth's argument is the factual claim that general public acceptance of same-sex marriage is increasing. Is this true? What evidence can you use to support your point?

Responding to the Message

5. Roth compares the introduction of same-sex themed wedding cards to Hallmark's "Spanish-language and Mahogany lines." What are these? What is Roth's implicit argument in equating these three things? Do you agree? Why or why not?

6. In some areas, popular culture is ahead of the law, and in others the law is ahead of popular culture. Roth here is arguing that popular culture—particularly business—is ahead of the law in this area. Do you agree that American culture has grown more accepting of homosexuality, and of gay marriage in particular, because popular culture and business have normalized them by trying to make money from them? Is this a positive or negative development? Explain your answer.

The Kids Aren't All Right

Judith "Jack" Halberstam

Judith "Jack" Halberstam is a professor of English and director of the Center for Feminist Research at the University of Southern California. In this 2010 post from the "Bully Bloggers" site, Halberstam discusses what she sees as the shortcomings of the 2010 film The Kids Are All Right, *which depicted a lesbian family thrown into turmoil when the sperm donor who fathered the couple's son appears in their lives. In this article, Halberstam takes on what she sees as Hollywood's natural tendency to try to fit lesbian relationships (and families) into models more appropriate for heterosexual pairings—even when the filmmaker herself is a lesbian.*

In the pre-punk, post-mod anthem "The Kids Are Alright" by The Who, Roger Daltrey sings about leaving domesticity behind and moving on: "Sometimes, I feel I gotta get away/Bells chime, I know I gotta get away/And I know if I don't, I'll go out of my mind/Better leave her behind with the kids, they're alright/The kids are alright."

This song has been brilliantly covered by The Queers and The Ramones among others and has become part of the powerful legacy of The Who, a rock band that created the violent and dynamic foundations for punk, emo, for The Strokes, The White Stripes and a whole host of other genre-bending bands. Given the raucous power of the song and the anti-domestic sentiment it expresses, it sets expectations high for Lisa Cholodenko's new film by the same name, and promises to deliver us from suffocating domesticity into some other arrangement of bodies, biology and desire. No such luck!

The Kids Are All Right is a soul-crushing depiction of long-term relationships, lesbian parenting and mid-life crisis. Nic (Annette Bening) and Jules (Julianne Moore) are mushed into one category by their kids Laser (Josh Hutcherson) and Joni (Mia Wasikowska) who call them "moms" or "the moms." The moms have merged into one maternal entity and although they have distinct personalities, their parenting function is depicted as one amorphous smothering gesture after another. The kids suffer through the over-parenting but crisis ensues when Laser decides to track down his sperm donor dad, Paul, played by Mark Ruffalo. Once Paul rides onto the scene on his classic black BMW motorcycle, bearing organic veggies and good wine, the cracks in the façade of lesbian domesticity appear and a rather predictable cycle of betrayal, infidelity and domestic upheaval begins.

Obviously the *mise-en-scene* for *The Kids are All Right* is rife with narrative and dramatic possibilities and the film is being hailed as a universal depiction of the travails of long-term relationships. The acting is fine and nuanced throughout and yet the film is depressing and sadly trades in stale stereotypes about lesbians in particular. While Cholodenko's first film played against stereotype by setting its lesbian drama in a drugged out world of high-art, this film loads sexual inertia, domestic dowdiness and bourgeois complacency onto the lesbian couple and leaves the sperm donor dad in the enviable position of being free, cool and casually sexual. Early on in the film, Jules and Nic watch gay porn while making a grand effort to have sex—in this cringe-worthy scene, Jules goes under the covers to go down on Nic who keeps watching the bad porn with no particular desire. Eventually we hear the whirr of a vibrator but still there is no money shot (either in the bed or on the TV screen), no real desire between the two women and we don't even see flesh! Cut to Paul making love to a gorgeous AfricanAmerican woman, one of his employees no less, with much gusto, much nakedness and free abandon. Ok, we get the picture, long-term relationships struggle with desire, short-term involvements struggle with commitment. The long-term couple may not have great sex but they do have the family and togetherness, the single guy has great sex and lots of it but no one to go home to.

While the film's moral outcome is supposed to favor the women and leave Paul out in the cold, it actually delivers, whether the film means to or not, a scathing critique of gay marriage. If the message here is "see gay marriages are just like straight ones—we all face the same problems," then surely the outcome of the film would be the end of marriage, the desire to find other kinds of arrangements that work. But no, this film, like many a heterosexual drama that turns the family inside out only to return to it at the film's end, shows that marriage is sexless, families turn rotten with familiarity, lesbians over parent and then it asks us to invest hope into this very arrangement.

The Kids Are All Right is beautifully acted and has moments where it gets everything right—the awkwardness between Paul and Joni and Laser, for example, at their first meeting; the anger sparked by Paul trying to step in and offer parenting advice to Nic—she responds: "I need your advice like I need a dick up my butt!" possibly the best line in the film—the irritation between Nic and Jules as they try to absorb the daddy-come-lately into their family unit. But all the acting in the world cannot save a conservative script from its own conclusions. And so, even though the film is quite good at showing how superfluous and redundant the father role has become in an era of the supermom, by refusing to distinguish between the "moms" and by not making much of a gender distinction between Nic (vaguely butch) and Jules (vaguely femme), we are left with too much mothering and a sense that fatherhood is necessary to intervene in the cloying attentions of maternal love.

In one stinging exchange, Laser is leaving for the evening and both moms reach out their arms to him asking for hugs. Laser says to Nic—"hug her," meaning Jules, "that's what she's there for!" It is a laugh line for sure but it somehow seals the moms in asexual pathos and interferes with our ability to really identify with them. As Laser leaves, we want to leave with him: as they songs says, "I know I gotta get away, and I know if I don't, I'll go out of my mind."

There are parts of the movie that fuel the disdain that the audience might begin to feel for the moms—we are not given enough info about the basis for their original love and attraction—a quick story about how they met refers to flirtatious attraction between the two but this is a sexual energy that we are told about rather than shown. At the same time, Paul's effect on women is shown but not told—he does not charm or romance women, with no action on his part, women simply throw themselves at him. This naturalization of his sexual power and the naturalization of the lack of charisma of the moms again stabilize a grid of desire that always tips in favor of male heterosexuality and leaves lesbians stranded. With the scales tipped this way, it becomes inevitable that Jules will sleep with Paul, that she will become dick-obsessed, that Nic will be cast as the sad, slightly butch partner who loses out to the dynamic, phallic dad. Again, this could have been played differently—Nic could have been a butch; she would have been much more likely in fact to ride the BMW motorbike than Paul (classic beemers are a popular queer choice of motorcycle in fact); she could have been phallic with a dildo instead of flaccid with a vibrator. I am not saying that the lesbian relationship should have been positive and male heterosexuality should have been slammed—but I am saying that Cholodenko is working the well-worn grooves of the cinematic depiction of lesbian desire as a flickering flame always on the verge of extinction and of lesbian-male rivalry as always a mismatch.

Finally, if *The Kids Are All Right* wanted to weigh in on the gay marriage debate by saying that marriage sucks anyway and here's a realistic depiction of what long-term relationships look like, I could live with that. If the film wanted to take a hard look at lesbian parenting and refute the idea that too many moms spoil the broth, I would have embraced that. If it wanted to offer a critique of fatherhood as always too little too late, I would have applauded that. But to give us cloying lesbian moms, charismatic fathers, inert long-term relationships and then to tell us to accept it, get used to it and like it or lump it ... well, why? Also, why does Julianne Moore have to be dowdy—she is a luminescent actress in most of her films; even when she is playing frigid housewives, as she does for Todd Haynes, Moore is gorgeous. But suddenly, when she is a femme lesbian, she loses her looks! Annette Bening is great as always, and except for a slightly embarrassing scene involving a Joni Mitchell song, her acting carries the film a long way.

A couple of moments of casual racism in the film (the depiction of the Latino gardener as a half-wit and the AfricanAmerican restaurant hostess as voracious) remind us that this is a deeply conservative film. Perhaps the right anthem for this film is not "The Kids Are Alright" given that the kids seem not to be all right but "My Generation"—in this song the "kids" tell the parent culture to fade away, not to try to understand them but to leave them to their "strange" teenage activities. The key line, of course, is a kind of anti-oedipal refusal of a futurity in which the kids become the adults: "things they do look awful cold/hope I die before I get old." The protest here is not against old people but against a form of aging that involves giving up on life, lust, change and that means settling in for the long haul. If I learned anything from Cholodenko's film, it is that trading in sex for comfort, change for stability, and improvised relationships for marriage are all bad deals and if we don't change the social structures we inherit, we are doomed to repeat them.

Critical Reading Questions

Summarizing the Text

1. What is Halberstam's objection to the depiction of the married couple in the film?

2. Halberstam argues that the film is both homophobic and racist. What is her evidence for this?

Establishing the Context

3. *The Kids Are All Right* was praised for depicting a lesbian family without sensationalizing the family arrangement or making the lesbianism itself the subject of the movie—in the film, the characters played by Annette Bening and Julianne Moore are just like any other long-married couple. How does this film contribute to the societal debate about legalizing gay marriage? What is the current state of this issue?

4. Why and how does Halberstam use lyrics of songs by The Who to frame her argument?

Responding to the Message

5. Research reviews of this film through review-aggregator sites such as RottenTomatoes.com. How do other reviewers respond to the depiction of the lesbian family?

6. Think of other recent films about families. What are the different models of the married relationship that tend to dominate? What kinds of portrayals of the relationship between parents and older children are most common? What does this tell us about the American family?

CLUSTER TWO: HOW IS THE AMERICAN FAMILY CHANGING DUE TO ECONOMICS, IMMIGRATION, AND SOCIAL FACTORS?

Farewell, June Cleaver: "Non-Traditional Families" and Economic Opportunity

Michelle Chen

Michelle Chen writes for many progressive publications (including AirAmerica, Extra!, and Alternet.com) and has freelanced for other nonpolitical publications, such as the South China Morning Post. *She is a member of the board of editors of* In These Times, *a left-wing magazine and website, and this article appeared in* In These Times *in May 2010.*

As the traditional nuclear family fades into history, we've entered the era of the "non-traditional" family: single parents, pairs of moms and dads, blended families, multi-generational households, grand-parent caregivers. With a growing share of babies today born outside marriage, American society seems to be finally leaving behind the *Leave It to Beaver* model.

A new study by Pew Economic Mobility Project asks how family structure—a divorced or single-parent household versus a conventional married one—affects a child's economic opportunities later in life. Society's attitude toward divorce and single parenthood has become more open over the past few generations, but has our economy?

It's easy to assume that divorce or single-parenthood would lead to some hardships, and Pew did find a link between marital status and socioeconomic advancement across generations. But the outcomes are also heavily influenced by race and class factors, which persist among poor households whether children grow up with one parent or two.

For children who start at the bottom third of the economic ladder, Pew found, "only 26 percent with divorced parents move up to the middle or top third as adults, compared to 42 percent of children born to unmarried mothers and 50 percent of children with continuously married parents."

In terms of "absolute mobility," or the potential to rise relative to their parents' income level, divorce does not have a clear impact on children's mobility:

> Among children who start in the bottom third, 74 percent with divorced parents exceed their parents' family income when they reach adulthood, compared to 90 percent of children with continuously married parents.

Still, the study concluded:

> Perhaps surprisingly, there is no evidence that being born to an unmarried mother reduces upward absolute mobility from the bottom third of the income distribution—the rates for those children and for children with continuously married parents are statistically indistinguishable.

When you slice the data by race, a different picture emerges. Divorce appears to make a bigger difference for black children's future prospects.

> Among African-American children who start in the bottom third of the income distribution, 87 percent with continuously married parents exceed their parents' income in adulthood, while just 53 percent of those with divorced parents do.
>
> Among white children who start in the bottom third, about the same proportion of adult children exceed their parents' income regardless of whether their parents were continuously married (91 percent exceeding) or divorced (92 percent exceeding).

Pointing out that "family structure can explain only some of the differences in economic mobility rates between African Americans and whites," the study raises intriguing questions about how social policy interacts with parents' life choices.

The sweeping welfare reforms of the Clinton era continue to reveal the ramifications of using welfare to impose certain social norms at the expense of those who don't fit the mold. As Kate Boo explained in her trenchant 2003 *New Yorker* article "The Marriage Cure," the supposed correlation between marriage and economic well-being became perverted into the rationale that promoting marriage could reduce systemic poverty.

The "reforms" targeted urban black single mothers who were stereotyped as antithetical to the "traditional" family: degenerate, shiftless women who couldn't stop having babies. The result was a national crusade to push impoverished single mothers simultaneously into the labor market and the marriage market, for better or worse.

To antipoverty and racial justice activists, the pro-marriage credo has simply repackaged the old blame-the-poor canard in the rhetoric of "family values." In fact, poor single mothers have been systematically locked out of the social privileges that their middle-class married counterparts typically take for granted. Welfare rights activists since the 1960s have shown that policies intended to relieve poverty end up punishing women for not being June Cleaver.

In addition to the patriarchal conservatism inherent in pro-marriage ideology, women face practical barriers to getting hitched: Black women especially may have trouble finding long-term male partners in communities devastated by mass incarceration. Not to mention, some old-fashioned types see marriage as a matter of conjugal love rather than social engineering. Go figure.

Despite the talk of "personal responsibility" in welfare policy, the real barriers poor single mothers face are rooted in poverty itself. According to a 2002 policy paper by Stephanie Coontz and Nancy Folbre:

- Non-marriage is often a result of poverty and economic insecurity rather than the other way around.

- The quality and stability of marriages matters. Prodding couples into matrimony without helping them solve problems that make relationships precarious could leave them worse off.

- Two-parent families are not immune from the economic stresses that put children at risk. More than one third of all impoverished young children in the U.S. today live with two parents.

Pew doesn't directly critique welfare reform's legacy, but the research does point to policy changes that could help break the cycle of intergenerational poverty. The Earned Income Tax Credit, for instance, has helped lift millions of children out of poverty through targeted income supports. Paid family leave time, subsidized child care, and career training and unemployment insurance programs that recognize challenges unique to working single parents, would help move non-married families toward long-awaited equity.

Regardless of what you think about the institution of marriage, there's no justification for forcing children to pay an economic penalty for their parents' decision to divorce or remain unmarried. And a parent's decision not to tie the knot shouldn't be an economic shackle on the next generation.

While our concept of the family has grown and diversified since the days of Mrs. Cleaver, for households striving toward advancement, our labor market and social policy remain stuck in the past.

Critical Reading Questions

Summarizing the Text

1. What are the basic conclusions of the Pew Economic Mobility Project study that Chen's article summarizes?

2. According to the study, what is more important in terms of children's economic future: their race or the marital status of their parents?

Establishing the Context

3. Who is "June Cleaver"? What is Chen trying to convey by the phrase "Farewell, June Cleaver"?

4. Chen's article is an example of a common type of article in the mainstream media that translates for a general public the results of a research study that was originally aimed at academic specialists. Use the Web to find the original study—what does Chen leave out, if anything? How might you summarize the study differently? What do the study's authors find to be the study's most significant findings, as opposed to what Chen finds most important?

Responding to the Message

5. Chen alludes to a popular and influential argument that marriage reduces poverty. This argument had real-world policy ramifications (including government promotion of marriage and disincentives for single parents) and provided backing to a general American feeling that it was "normal" or ideal for parents to be married. Is it true that children are better off *economically* when their parents are married? Should government policy encourage parents to stay married?

6. Chen is clearly a left-wing writer. Where does she use loaded language? What does she use it for? What effect does this have on her *ethos* and

pathos? Does her left-wing stance color the way she interprets the Pew study for her audience? What conservative arguments does she ignore or misrepresent?

The Changing American Family
Herbert S. Klein

Herbert S. Klein is a research fellow at the Hoover Institution, a conservative think tank, as well as a professor of history at Stanford University. He has written extensively on Latin America in books such as African Slavery in Latin America and the Caribbean *(1986) and* A Concise History of Bolivia *(2003). Among his many honors are a Guggenheim Fellowship, a Woodrow Wilson Fellowship, and several appointments as a Fulbright Lecturer. This short article, which appeared in the Hoover Institution's journal* Hoover Digest, *is adapted from his 2004 book* A Population History of the United States.

For all the changes in fertility and mortality that Americans have experienced from the colonial period until today, there has been surprisingly little change in the structure of the family until the past quarter century. Until that point, the age of marriage changed from time to time, but only a minority of women never married and births outside marriage were traditionally less than 10 percent of all births.

But this fundamental social institution has changed profoundly since 1980. In fact, if one were to define the most original demographic feature in the post-1980 period in the United States, it would be the changes that were occurring in both families and households for all sections of the national population. The traditional American family has been undergoing profound transformations for all ages, all races, and all ethnic groups. Every aspect of the American family is experiencing change. These include the number of adults who marry, the number of households that are formed by married people, the number of children that are conceived, the economic role of mothers, the number of non-family households, and even the importance of marriage in accounting for total births.

The proportion of persons over 15 years of age who had never married reached historic levels in 2000 when a third of the men and a quarter of the women were listed as never having married. The decline in marriage among whites is occurring at a slower pace than among blacks, but both are experiencing rising trends in unmarried adults. By 2000, 22 percent of adult white women and 42 percent of adult black women had never married. This rise in the ratio of persons never married is also reflected in historical changes in the relation between families and households. Non-family households had always existed as a small share of the total households in the United States, usually made up of elderly persons with no families left. But now they are formed by young adults, many of whom never married, or by older persons who no longer reside with children. Also, the proportion of two-parent households, even in family households with children, is on the decline, as single-parent-plus-children households are on the rise. As late as 1960, at the height of the Baby Boom, married families made up almost three-quarters of all households; but by the census of 2000 they accounted for just 53 percent of them, a decline that seems to have continued in the past few years. Non-family households now account for 31 percent of households, and families headed by a single parent with children account for the rest, making up to 27 percent of all such families with children. Black families experienced the fastest decline of dual-parent households; by the end of the century married couples with children accounted for only 4 out of 10 of all black family households with children. But no group was immune to this rising trend of single-parent households.

More older people than ever before are also living alone or without other generations present. Declining mortality and morbidity, the development of Social Security and other retirement benefits, all meant that older persons could financially live alone and were generally healthier and lived longer than in earlier periods. A change in cultural values during the second half of the twentieth century seems to have increased the value of privacy among older adults. In 1910, for example, most widows over 65 years of age lived with their children; only 12 percent lived alone. By 1990, almost 70 percent of such widows were living alone. There was also a major rise in "empty nest" households, with elderly couples no longer having resident children of any age. Extended family arrangements were progressively disappearing for the majority of the population. There were also more couples surviving into old age than ever before, so that by 2000 more than half of the adults over 65 who resided in independent households lived with their spouses. With better health and more income, more elderly persons have the ability and the desire to "buy" their privacy as never before.

Not only have family households been on the decline, as a consequence of the rise of single-person and childless-couple households, but even women giving birth are now having far fewer children, are spacing them further apart, and are ending their fertility at earlier ages than ever before, which has brought fertility levels in the United States to their lowest level in history. In the colonial period the average woman produced more than seven children during the course of her lifetime. Since the 1970s the rate has been under two children for the majority non-Hispanic white population. The national fertility total currently barely reaches its replacement level; fluctuated between 2.0 and 2.1 children per woman over the past quarter century; by 2000 non-Hispanic white women were averaging just 1.8 children. Among all groups it was only the Hispanic women—who are at a total fertility rate of 2.5 children—who are above the replacement level. Even among Hispanic women, it is primarily Mexican-American women, the largest single group, which maintained very high fertility rates. Cuban-American women were close to the non-Hispanic whites, and the Puerto Rican women were closer to the fertility patterns of non-Hispanic black women.

Although the U.S. fertility rate declined to the lowest level in history, single women now make up an increased percentage of those having children. The rapid and very recent rise in births outside marriage means that married women no longer are the exclusive arbiters of fertility. Whereas at mid-century such extramarital births were an insignificant phenomenon, accounting for only 4 percent of all births, by 2000 they accounted for a third of births, and that proportion is rising. Although all groups experienced this change, non-Hispanic whites experienced a slower rise than all other groups. Although some have thought this to be a temporary aberration in historic patterns, the increasing illegitimacy rates in Europe suggest that North America is following modern advanced Western European trends.

In the 1970s, when the issue began to be perceived by the public as one of major concern, it was the teenagers who had the highest rates of births outside marriage, and those births seemed to be rising at the time. But by the end of the century older women's rates of illegitimacy were highest and rising; those for teenage girls were falling in both relative and absolute numbers. That this increase of births outside marriage was not due to poverty per se can be seen in the fact that the United States was not unique in this new pattern of births and the declining importance of traditional marriage. Other wealthy countries, such as Sweden, have also experienced this trend. Although Sweden in 1950 had fertility patterns comparable to those of the United States, by the end of the century its rate of non-marital births was more than half of all births. Even such Catholic countries as Spain and Portugal had arrived at 16 percent and 22 percent illegitimacy rates, respectively, and France was up to 38 percent by 1996. Thus the belief that this was a temporary or uniquely North American development does not appear to be the case. The factors influencing these trends everywhere in the modern industrial world seem to be the same—late marriages, women increasing their participation in the workforce and thus having higher incomes, and changing beliefs in the importance and necessity of marriage. These changes seem to be affecting all Europe and North America at approximately the same time.

This trend is also reflected in the changing economic role of women even in dual-parent households with children. The traditional family with a single male breadwinner working alone to sustain the family is no longer the norm. By the end of the century, only one in five married couples had just a single male breadwinner working outside the home. Among married couples with children under six years of age, only 36 percent had the mother staying at home with the children and not working, and in families where women had given birth to a child during the previous year, the majority of these mothers at the end of the year were working outside the home—more than half of them in 2000 compared to just under one third in 1967. Not only were more women in the workforce—a ratio that was constantly on the rise through the second half of the century—but the vast majority of married mothers with young children were working outside the home by 2000.

All of these changes are having an impact on U.S. fertility rates. Not only is formal marriage no longer the exclusive arbiter of fertility, but more and more women are reducing the number of children they have. This is not due to women forgoing children. In fact, there has been little change in the number of women going childless, which has remained quite steady for the past 40 years. This decline in fertility is due to the fact that women are deliberately deciding to have fewer children. They are marrying later, thus reducing their marital fertility, they are beginning childbearing at ever later ages, they are spacing their children farther apart, and they are terminating their fertility at earlier ages. Not only did the average age of mothers having their first children rise by 2.7 years from 1960 to 1999, but it rose significantly for every subsequent child being born as well, while the spacing between children also increased. Although the average age of mothers at first birth for the entire population was now 24.9 years, for non-Hispanic white women it was 25.9 years.

Clearly the American family, like all families in the Western industrial countries, is now profoundly different from what it had been in the recorded past. It typically is a household with few children, with both parents working, and with mothers producing their children at ever older ages. At the same time, more adults than ever before are living alone or with unmarried companions and more women than ever before are giving birth out of wedlock. These trends have profoundly changed the American family and are unlikely to be reversed any time soon.

Critical Reading Questions

Summarizing the Text

1. What are the most important changes in the nature of the American family over the past two decades, according to Klein?

2. What does Klein mean by "illegitimacy"? Do you think this is the appropriate word for this idea? Why or why not?

Establishing the Context

3. The "traditional" family—a married mother and father, the father employed outside of the house and the mother not in the workforce, and at least two children—has been held forth as an ideal for many decades, and families

that differed from this model were often ostracized. What do the statistics that Klein highlights indicate will happen to the "traditional" family?

4. All American politicians, but particularly conservative ones, argue that the family is the basic unit of American culture, and it is generally assumed that "family" means mother, father, and children. How might the rhetorical use of "family" change over the next few decades as a result of these demographic changes?

Responding to the Message

5. Many affluent European nations and Japan are, like the United States, seeing their birthrates decline, and they look forward with fear to a significant decline in population. However, the American population continues to rise. Why? What might be the long-term significance of this difference between the United States and other developed nations?

6. American women are having fewer children, Klein points out. What do you think the long-term ramifications of this will be on American society in terms of economics, demographics, and culture?

The Only Child: Debunking the Myths
Lauren Sandler

Lauren Sandler is an independent journalist who has written for national publications such as The Atlantic Monthly, *the* New York Times, *the* Nation, *and* Time *(where this article originally appeared in 2010). She is the author of the 2006 book* Righteous: Dispatches from the Evangelical Youth Movement. *In this feature story for* Time, *Sandler attempts to refute what she considers to be common "myths" about only children.*

It's a conversation I have most weeks—if not most days. This time, it happens when my 2-year-old daughter and I are buying milk at the supermarket. The cashiers fawn over her pink cheeks and applaud when she twirls for them, and then I endure the usual dialogue.

"Your first?"

"Yup."

"Another one coming soon?"

"Nope—it might be just this one."

"You'll have more. You'll see."

"At the moment, I'm not planning on it."

"You wouldn't do that to your child. You'll see."

I offer no retort, but if I did, I'd start by asking these young minimum-wage earners to consider the following: the U.S. Department of Agriculture reports that the average child in the U.S. costs his or her parents about $286,050—before college. Those costs have actually risen during the recession. The milk I'm buying adds up to $50 a month, and we're pushing toilet training just to drop the cost of diapers—about $100 a month—from our monthly budget. It's a marvel to me these days that anyone can manage a second kid—forget about a third.

And since I celebrated my 35th birthday, I have to ask myself not when but if. My parents asked themselves that question when I was my daughter's age and decided the answer was no. They wanted the experience of parenting but also their careers, the freedom to travel and the lower cost and urbane excitement of making a home in an apartment rather than a suburban house. Back then, their choice was rare, but if we too choose to stop at one child, my daughter will likely feel far less alone in her only status than I did.

"The recession has dramatically reshaped women's childbearing desires," says Larry Finer, the director of domestic policy at the Guttmacher Institute, a leading reproductive-health research organization. The institute found that 64% of women polled said that with the economy the way it is, they couldn't afford to have a baby now. Forty-four percent said they plan to reduce or delay their childbearing—again, because of the economy. This happens during financial meltdowns: the Great Depression saw single-child families spike at 23% of all families, and that was back when onlies were still an anomaly. Since the early '60s, according to the National Center for Health Statistics, single-child families have almost doubled in number, to about 1 in 5—and that's from before the markets crashed. Birth control has quickly become one of the recession's few growth industries.

Meanwhile, friends and relatives—not to mention supermarket cashiers, pastors and, I've found, strangers on the subway—continue to urge parents of only children to have another baby. There are certain time-honored reasons for having that baby: in many countries and communities, the mandate to be fruitful and multiply is a powerful religious directive. And family size can be dictated by biology as much as by psychology. But the entrenched aversion to stopping at one mainly amounts to a century-old public-relations issue. Single children are perceived as spoiled, selfish, solitary misfits. No parents want that for their kid. Since the 1970s, however, studies devoted to understanding the personality characteristics of only children have debunked that idea. I, for one, was happy without siblings. A few ex-boyfriends aside, people seem to think I turned out just fine. So why, at a time when so many parents worry about being able to support more than one, do we still worry that there's something wrong with just one? And what will it mean for future generations if more parents than ever before decide that one is enough?

A Stereotype Is Born

The image of the lonely only—or at least the legitimizing of that idea—was the work of one man, Granville Stanley Hall. About 120 years ago, Hall established one of the first American psychology-research labs and was a leader of the child-study movement. A national network of study groups called Hall Clubs existed to spread his teachings. But what he is most known for today is supervising the 1896 study "Of Peculiar and Exceptional Children," which described a series of only-child oddballs as permanent misfits. Hall—and every other fledgling psychologist—knew close to nothing about credible research practices. Yet for decades, academics and advice columnists alike disseminated his conclusion that an only child could not be expected to go through life with the same capacity for adjustment that children with siblings possessed. "Being an only child is a disease in itself," he claimed.

Later generations of scholars tried to correct the record, but their findings never filtered into popular parenting discourse. Meanwhile, the "peculiar" only children—"overprivileged, asocial, royally autonomous...self-centered, aloof and overly intellectual," as sociologist Judith Blake describes them in her 1989 book *Family Size and Achievement*— permeated pop culture, from the demon children in horror films (*The Omen, The Bad Seed*) to the oddball sidekicks in '80s sitcoms (*Growing Pains, Family Ties*). Even on the new show *Modern Family*, the tween singleton is a cringingly precocious loner with a coddling mother. Such vehicles have evangelized Hall's teachings more than his clubs did. Of course we ask when someone is going to have "kids," not "a kid." Of course we think that one is the loneliest number. No one has done more to disprove Hall's stereotype than Toni Falbo, a professor of educational psychology and sociology at the University of Texas at Austin. An only child herself and the mother of one, Falbo began investigating the only-child experience in the 1970s, both in the U.S. and in China (where the government's one-child policy, the world's biggest experiment in population control, went into effect in 1979), drawing on the experience of tens of thousands of subjects. Twenty-five years ago, she and colleague Denise Polit conducted a meta-analysis of 115 studies of only children from 1925 onward that considered developmental outcomes of adjustment, character, sociability, achievement and intelligence. The studies, mainly from the U.S., cut across class and race.

Generally, those studies showed that singletons aren't measurably different from other kids—except that they, along with firstborns and people who have only one sibling, score higher in measures of intelligence and achievement. No one, Falbo says, has published research that can demonstrate any truth behind the stereotype of the only child as lonely, selfish and maladjusted. (She has spoken those three words so many times in the past 35 years that they run together as one: lonely-selfishmaladjusted.) Falbo and Polit later completed a second quantitative review of more than 200 personality studies. By and large, they found that the personalities of only children were indistinguishable from their peers with siblings.

"For most people, this still hasn't sunk in," she tells me after a meeting of her graduate seminar in social psychology. She's just spent a couple of hours pacing a linoleum classroom floor in platform heels, presenting data to her students—all of whom have siblings, except for an exchange student from China (who is a product of the one-child policy)—but they still don't seem to have internalized the lesson. After class, a student from West Texas chats with a student from India. He had astute things to say during class regarding how cultures adapt over time, offering sharp observations about the psychology of collectivism. But now he refers to how there's "no only-child problem" in his big family. "I'm not saying only children are socially retarded or anything, but, you know ..." he laughs.

Undiluted Resources

At California State University at Dominguez Hills, Adriean Mancillas— an only child and the mother of triplets—has studied the prevalence of only-child stereotypes. They can be found cross-culturally from Estonia to Brazil, she says, dating to "when people needed bigger families to farm the land." And they stick. "You can tell people all the research in the world that contradicts it," she says, but the same cognitive psychology that maintains any sort of prejudice, large or small, applies. Of course, part of the reason we assume only children are spoiled is that whatever parents have to give, the only child gets it all. The argument Blake makes in *Family Size and Achievement* as to why onlies are higher achievers across socioeconomic lines can be stated simply: there's no "dilution of resources," as she terms it, between siblings. No matter their income or occupation, parents of only children have more time, energy and money to invest in their kid, who gets all the dance classes, piano lessons and prep courses, as well as all their parents' attention when it comes to helping work out an algebra problem. That attention, researchers have noticed, leads to not just higher SAT scores but also higher self-esteem.

And as Falbo tells her students, the cocktail of aptitude and confidence yields results: only children tend to do better in school and get more education—college, medical or law degrees—than other kids. Not that having siblings will necessarily thwart you; Einstein had a sister and did just fine. But for every Venus and Serena Williams you can find a luminary singleton: Cary Grant, Elvis Presley, John Updike, Lance Armstrong or Frank Sinatra.

But if only children do get it all, doesn't that mean there's truth to the stereotype that they're overindulged? In Austin, I seek out the counseling practice of psychologist Carl Pickhardt, who meets with patients in his office on the ground floor of a Victorian house. The low lamplight—and Kleenex box on his coffee table—renders an inversion of Falbo's fluorescent-lit classroom. Pickhardt, author of *The Future of Your Only Child*, is neither cheerleading nor hectoring, as participants in the stratified conversation about only children tend to be. His soft-voiced presence is a reminder that clinical sampling can take us only so far, that human behavior cannot be entirely reduced to numbers on a questionnaire.

"There's no question that only children are highly indulged and highly protected," he tells me. But that doesn't mean the stereotype is true, he says, at least not based on his four decades of seeing singletons—both kids and adults—unburden themselves in his office. "You've been given more attention and nurturing to develop yourself. But that's not the same thing as being selfish. On balance, that level of parental involvement is a good thing. All that attention is the energy for your self-esteem and achievement." But, he adds, "everything is double-edged. And everything is formative."

In a suburb outside Austin, Zoe and Don Mullican live with their 9-year-old daughter Sophia in a rented house with a red pickup parked outside. The beige sectional couch in the family room was a free Craigslist find; folding mesh chairs make up the outdoor furniture in the yard. On the tailgate of their truck is a purple sticker that bears the name of the private Austin Waldorf School, which Sophia attends. Zoe recently lost her job as an executive assistant in a law firm, and the new gig she found is only part time, resulting in a significant cut in their family income. (Don works as a civil engineer.) They've scaled back on "everything from gas to groceries to clothing," Zoe says, but Sophia's attendance at her school is nonnegotiable. As is her status as an only child. "We have such limited resources financially, and we want to give one person the best we could give," Zoe tells me over Don's home-brewed beer at a backyard barbecue.

Researchers have crunched the numbers from years of standardized tests like the National Merit Scholarship exam to measure verbal and mathematical abilities. In each category, only children performed better than children from larger families. Furthermore, they're expected to. Falbo tells her class that parents have significantly higher expectations of academic achievement and attainment when they have just one kid. But Pickhardt notes that parental expectations are merely part of the pressure only children can feel. Much of it is self-imposed, he says, because of their notions of themselves as performing at a peer level with their parents. It's the other edge of all that adulticizing: pressure and responsibility usually accompany success, and neither feels much like childhood.

But Zoe doesn't sound that worried about it as we talk over the sound of Sophia belting out *High School Musical* karaoke upstairs in her room with two other singleton friends. Zoe was an only child herself until she was a teenager; so was her oldest friend, whose only child's voice joins the chorus of Vanessa Hudgens impersonators. When Sophia and her friends come downstairs for grilled turkey burgers, Sophia expresses dismay that I haven't heard of the band Ghostland Observatory, which she saw perform at Austin City Limits with her parents last year. "Mom, you gotta play it for her!" she says. "They're one of our favorite bands," the 9-year-old tells me. Zoe puts on the album, sits down next to Sophia and gives her a hug. "Isn't this great?" they say together. To my only-child eyes, their dynamic looks ideal, but I can hear the nay-saying voices in my head wondering if this is the fullest form of childhood.

Will It Make Us Happier?

As parents, we tend to ask ourselves two questions when we talk with our partners about having more children. First, will it make our kid happier? And then, will it make us happier?

When University of Pennsylvania demography professor Samuel Preston was conducting research to help him predict the future of fertility, he told me the discovery that surprised him most was that parents felt so madly in love with their first child, they wanted a second. That's an unusual finding. Talk to parents and you'll often hear that they opt to have another because they think it will be better for the child they already have. Not many say they do it for themselves, no matter how much they may love the experience of parenting.

But I bring it up because of how deeply I feel all that love for my kid. I am not someone who spent my first three decades imagining a glowing pregnancy followed by maternal bliss. In fact, I used to suspect that mothers who talked about their children with such unbridled wonder didn't have much else going on in their lives. Then I had my daughter—and now I gush like the rest of them. When I was interviewing the parents of only children, several paraphrased the words of one mother I spoke with: "If I knew I could have him all over again, I'd do it in a heartbeat. But being a mother, and loving being a mother, means being his mother—at least that's how I experience it." I can relate, which is why it amazes me when people seem to think that parents who choose to have one kid don't love their child as much as parents who have more—that somehow they are doing their kid harm.

Parents who intend to have only one say they can manage the drudgery with an eye on the light at the end of the tunnel. Beth Nixon, a Pennsylvania artist and mother of a 1-year-old, says she finds reassurance every day in the fact that "it's not going to be an endless chain of need which is going to be fulfilled for years and years." When her daughter Ida wakes up every hour and a half, screaming with the pain of teething, Nixon feels like it's no big deal. "I can be fully present for this and do my best at trying to appreciate it, because it's like, this is the only time I am going to do this."

Rochelle Rosen works full time running her own educational-consulting firm in Massachusetts while a nanny stays with her young daughter. "People judge me for working full time and for saying I don't want another kid, like these things mean I don't love my daughter. They tell me I'd be happier if I didn't work as much, if I had another kid," she says. "If I have another child, in five years or 10 years will I be happy that I did it? Maybe. But I try to imagine the first couple of years and try to imagine the impact on my daughter. I am so torn in different directions already."

A 2007 survey found that at a rate of 3 to 1, people believe the main purpose of marriage is the "mutual happiness and fulfillment" of adults rather than the "bearing and raising of children." There must be some balance between the joy our kids give us and the sacrifices we make to care for them. Social scientists have surmised since the 1970s that singletons offer the rich experience of parenting without the consuming efforts that multiple children add: all the wonder and giggles and shampoo mohawks but with leftover energy for sex, conversation, reading and so on. The research of Hans-Peter Kohler, a population sociologist at the University of Pennsylvania, gives weight to that idea. In his analysis of a survey of 35,000 Danish twins, women with one child said they were more satisfied with their lives than women with none or more than one. As Kohler told me, "At face value, you should say that you'll stop at one child to maximize your subjective well being."

"Most people are saying, I can't divide myself anymore," says social psychologist Susan Newman. Before technology made the office a 24-hour presence, we actually spent less time actively parenting, she explains. "We no longer send a child out to play for three hours and have those three hours to ourselves," she says. "Now you take them to the next practice, the next class. We've been consumed by our children. But we're moving back slowly to parents wanting to have a life too. And people are realizing that's simply easier with one."

The New Traditional Family

While singleton households may become "the new traditional family," as Newman puts it, in Leslie and Jarrod Moore's church community in Amarillo, Texas, tradition means something quite different. The couple decided to become parents when Leslie was 25, but pregnancy didn't come easily. It was years before Leslie finally conceived, and by the time Bryar—now 9—arrived healthy, the Moores decided their hard-won baby boy was "the one God meant for us to have and the only one we want." Jarrod, who has his own home-design company, is one of six and says he knows how hard it is to share resources with siblings. Bryar plays four sports, and "it's already expensive," says Leslie.

"Forget college, insurance and a car. Imagine if we were running around to twice as many sporting events, buying twice as many uniforms and tennis shoes," she says. "People around here think we're crazy. But to tell you the truth, if by some weird twist I got pregnant accidentally, we would be devastated."

If you comb the World Values Survey, you'll find religiosity and fertility go hand in hand, whether in more secular Europe or in more pious America. As much as family size is a deeply personal issue, for many people it is also a spiritual one. And as Samuel Preston writes in his 2008 paper "The Future of American Fertility," high fertility can beget high fertility: children who inherit their parents' religious beliefs inherit at least one of the reasons to have many children themselves. No wonder churches nationwide vied to book Jon and Kate Gosselin (predivorce) for guest spots in their pulpits. Evangelicals—the biggest share of their viewership—saw the Gosselins' brood as proof of pure piety.

Back when the mandate to be fruitful and multiply was first chiseled in stone, there was a true impetus behind the idea. It was pretty elementary evolutionary psychology: the more you bred, the more likely your line was to survive. Large families were social networks and insurance policies. More kids meant more helping hands, more productivity, more comfort. In much of the world, that is still the case.

Most American families aren't of biblical proportions any longer, but a plurality of adults (46%) say two children is the ideal number, according to a 2010 Pew survey on American motherhood. Only 3% said one child was ideal—the same number that said zero. But Kohler says his happiness study contributes to a consensus that a metamorphosis is afoot. "If people feel they have to give in to these social expectations to have more children, then they might have another child for reasons other than their own happiness," he told me. "But as the acceptability of one-child families increases over time, there's an absence of these pressures to have more children—and so people don't."

Falbo has observed that in some urban areas in China where the one-child policy has been relaxed and permission has been given to have more than one child, families still choose to have only one—largely because of economic uncertainty. And that's not just an Asian phenomenon. A paper by Joshua Goldstein, a director of the Max Planck Institute for Demographic Research in Germany, made a stir at population conferences: he presented research on how the next generation of German and Austrian parents will be the first in Europe to see only children as more common.

Ascent of the Onlies?

Goldstein's paper is just one of many exacerbating angst about the current low-fertility "crisis" that has European economists and policy wonks in a panic. In the early 1960s, Europe represented 20% of the world's population. About a century later, those numbers are projected to drop to about 7.5%, despite the rise in minority and immigrant birthrates. Between now and 2030, demographers forecast the E.U. will have lost 13 million—or almost 4%—of people ages 15 to 64. Meanwhile, the number of people over 65 will increase by more than 40%. On a continent where the fertility rate is well below 2, these questions arise: Who will make up the workforce? Who will care for the disproportionate number of elderly citizens?

The latter is a question felt even more acutely on a personal level—particularly in the microcosm of the single-child family. A 2001 study found that one of the most consistent self-perceived challenges for only children was concern about being the sole caretaker for aging parents (including feelings of anxiety about being the sole survivor in the family once their parents died). My parents address my unspoken anxiety with monthly payments into a long-term health care insurance plan. But there are limits to what can be managed by logistics, even for families with the resources to plan ahead. Like many only children, I've lined up emotional and practical support—in my case, my spouse. My husband is like a son to my parents. He will be the first to spoon pureed food into my mother's mouth, like he did for my grandmother, or help my father in the bathroom, like he did for my grandfather. And yet I know my parents are not his. I know it's not the same.

Of course, having siblings is no guarantee that the burden of elder care will be shared equally or even shared at all. But imagining this emotionally fraught inevitability impels many people I know to have more kids, especially if they can afford them. (As one Park Avenue obstetrician told me, in her practice "three is the new black.")

It may be tough to trace the overall impact of single-child families in the U.S., if, as some experts predict, they trend upward alongside an increase in larger families—not of the 9 by Design ilk but three- and four-child families. While demographers expect to see a slip in population because of the recession, the champion breeders among us will likely offset the continuing ascent of onlies. Preston, the University of Pennsylvania demographer, projects that in the U.S. both the number of larger families and the number of only children will keep growing. But our national picture will probably look a little different: the recent Pew study on American motherhood shows a major uptick in the share of births to Hispanic women, who now give birth to 1 in 4 babies, while white motherhood has declined by 12 percentage points since 1990. (The share of births to Asian mothers has also increased, though not nearly as dramatically, while African-American families have stayed stable.)

Even with those population segments in mind, Andrew Oswald, a professor at the University of Warwick who studies the relationship between economics and happiness, predicts many families will continue to shrink, assuming the nation doesn't slide far deeper into economic crisis. Ironically, it seems that if economic pressures can bring about lower fertility, so can economic prosperity. "I love my own daughters to bits. But skiing and sports cars without baby seats can be fun too," he says. "That's why only children are the secular trend of a rich society we've been moving toward for the past 100 years."

That trend is what is known as the second demographic transition, a concept Ron Lesthaeghe at the University of Michigan advanced 25 years ago. It refers to the fertility shift that occurred when the industrial world moved from high birth and death rates to low ones. Now postponement of parenthood—or refusal of it—in favor of greater focus on education and career, longer periods of searching for the ideal mate and a more flexible and pleasure-seeking life has given us the second demographic transition. Because of these "rich society" tendencies, Oswald guesses that 50-odd years from now, the U.S. will be worrying about declining population, just like Europe and Japan are today.

What shape might that worry take? Nicholas Eberstadt of the American Enterprise Institute has furrowed his brow a great deal over what he calls "the depopulation bomb" in Russia and China, but he says even if it were to go off in the U.S., we wouldn't face the same kinds of collective problems. "It's not like we don't have the social capital, the rule of law, the sorts of institutional infrastructure that we in the West take for granted," he told me. He says he's not even that worried about Europe. "That's a whole lot less consequential than in China, where there is no national public pension system, where people have relied on relatives for economic backup since time immemorial." He's not just talking about siblings: in China, as generations of only children follow each other, the cousin disappears from the family tree.

On the other hand, no one in the U.S. is taking Social Security for granted these days. If they needed it, I wouldn't be able to financially support my parents in their decline without their long-term-care plan—especially with another year or two of day care still to go. If it were easier to be a parent in this country and if the current economic situation weren't so dire, I might feel more inclined to have a second child myself.

As I enter what my obstetrician calls advanced maternal age, it's a choice my husband and I need to make soon. In doing so, we talk about the idea that to be good parents, we have to be happy people.

How we determine our happiness and our daughter's will be based on the love we feel for her and the realities—both joyful and trying—of what a larger family would mean. What we won't consider is whether being an only child will screw her up; we'll do that fine in other ways.

If we end up having no other children, we'll have to be mindful to raise her to be part of something bigger than just us three. But must we share DNA to do that? Stepparents and stepsiblings have become firmly normative in American culture. Single, unmarried and gay parents have headed in that direction too. As Susan Newman tells me, "What really changes, the fewer siblings we have, is how we define family." I've been part of this redefinition all my life. Like most only children, I've cast cousins and friends as ersatz siblings since I was a child, knowing it's not the same as having a brother or a sister but not necessarily missing what I don't have. For now, my kid is happy enough to dance down supermarket aisles by herself or with her friends and cousins. And with her, sometimes, I do too.

Critical Reading Questions

Summarizing the Text

1. What are some of the powerful pressures on women in particular to have more than one child? Where do these pressures come from?
2. What stereotypes do people have about only children? Do those stereotypes differ between nations or cultures?

Establishing the Context

3. Sandler brings up the work of the nineteenth-century psychologist Granville Hall to help ground her argument. Who is Hall? How does Sandler use him to establish her *ethos* and *logos*? Research Hall and his work—do you think she is fair to him?
4. Sandler makes a conscious decision to bring herself into this argument—she, a woman who is making decisions about how many children to have, is the lens through which she examines this issue. How do you think this rhetorical choice affects the impact and validity of her argument?

Responding to the Message

5. What do you believe are the drawbacks, if any, to having a single child—to the child, to the family, and to society in general?
6. Family size, Sandler points out, can be a deeply religious issue. How does religion affect these decisions? How do you feel about only children—are you one? If you have a child, do you want only one, or multiple? What influences in your life have led you to this preference?

One Man, Many Wives, Big Problems

Jonathan Rauch

Jonathan Rauch, a journalist and writer, is one of the leading pro-gay-marriage voices in mainstream American culture, but (like Andrew Sullivan, whose essay "Why I Blog" appears in Chapter 4) he is also known as a gay conservative—to many Americans' minds, an oxymoron. Rauch, whose conservatism is manifested in skepticism about the value and efficacy of governmental programs to achieve social ends, initially gained fame by speaking out against hate-crime laws and, in the 1990s, began writing frequently about the benefits to society of allowing same-sex couples to marry. In this article from Reason (a libertarian magazine), he takes a different perspective on the issue of marriage, arguing that it is right to limit the institution to paired partners.

"And now, polygamy," sighs Charles Krauthammer, in a recent *Washington Post* column. It's true. As if they didn't already have enough on their minds, Americans are going to have to debate polygamy. And not a moment too soon.

For generations, taboo kept polygamy out of sight and out of mind in America. But the taboo is crumbling. An HBO television series called "Big Love," which benignly portrays a one-husband, three-wife family in Utah, set off the latest round of polygamy talk. Even so, a federal lawsuit (now on appeal), the American Civil Liberties Union's stand for polygamy rights, and the rising voices of pro-polygamy groups such as TruthBearer.org (an evangelical Christian group) and Principle Voices (which *Newsweek* describes as "a Utah-based group run by wives from polygamous marriages") were already making the subject hard to duck.

So far, libertarians and lifestyle liberals approach polygamy as an individual-choice issue, while cultural conservatives use it as a bloody shirt to wave in the gay-marriage debate. The broad public opposes polygamy but is unsure why. What hardly anyone is doing is thinking about polygamy as social policy.

If the coming debate changes that, it will have done everyone a favor. For reasons that have everything to do with its own social dynamics and nothing to do with gay marriage, polygamy is a profoundly hazardous policy.

To understand why, begin with two crucial words. The first is "marriage." Group love (sometimes called polyamory) is already legal, and some people freely practice it. Polygamy asserts not a right to love several others but a right to marry them all. Because a marriage license is a state grant, polygamy is a matter of public policy, not just of personal preference.

The second crucial word is "polygyny." Unlike gay marriage, polygamy has been a common form of marriage since at least biblical times, and probably long before. In his 1994 book *The Moral Animal: The New Science of Evolutionary Psychology,* Robert Wright notes that a "huge majority" of the human societies for which anthropologists have data have been polygamous.

Virtually all of those have been polygynous: that is, one husband, multiple wives. Polyandry (one wife, many husbands) is vanishingly rare. The real-world practice of polygamy seems to flow from men's desire to marry all the women they can have children with.

Moreover, in America today the main constituents for polyga-mous marriage are Mormons[*] and, as *Newsweek* reports, "a growing number of evangelical Christian and Muslim polygamists." These religious groups practice polygyny, not polyandry. Thus, in light of current American politics as well as copious anthropological experi-ence, any responsible planner must assume that if polygamy were legalized, polygynous marriages would outnumber polyandrous ones—probably vastly.

Here is something else to consider: As far as I've been able to determine, no polygamous society has ever been a true liberal democ-racy, in anything like the modern sense. As societies move away from hierarchy and toward equal opportunity, they leave polygamy behind. They monogamize as they modernize. That may be a coincidence, but it seems more likely to be a logical outgrowth of the arithmetic of polygamy.

Other things being equal (and, to a good first approximation, they are), when one man marries two women, some other man marries no woman. When one man marries three women, two other men don't marry. When one man marries four women, three other men don't marry. Monogamy gives everyone a shot at marriage. Polygyny, by contrast, is a zero-sum game that skews the marriage market so that some men marry at the expense of others.

For the individuals affected, losing the opportunity to marry is a grave, even devastating, deprivation. (Just ask a gay American.) But the effects are still worse at the social level. Sexual imbalance in the marriage market has no good social consequences and many grim ones.

Two political scientists, Valerie M. Hudson and Andrea M. den Boer, ponder those consequences in their 2004 book *Bare Branches: Security Implications of Asia's Surplus Male Population.* Summarizing their findings in a *Washington Post* article, they write: "Scarcity of women leads to a situation in which men with advantages—money, skills, education—will marry, but men without such advantages—poor, unskilled, illiterate—will not. A permanent subclass of bare branches [unmarriageable men] from the lowest socioeconomic classes is cre-ated. In China and India, for example, by the year 2020 bare branches will make up 12 to 15 percent of the young adult male population."

The problem in China and India is sex-selective abortion (and sometimes infanticide), not polygamy; where the marriage market is concerned, however, the two are functional equivalents. In their book, Hudson and den Boer note that "bare branches are more likely than other males to turn to vice and violence." To get ahead, they "may turn

---

[*]Author's note: My wording left some readers under the impression that the modern Mormon church may endorse or practice polygamy. It does not. I should have made clearer that I was referring to certain people who claim to be Mormons, not to the church or mainstream practice.

to appropriation of resources, using force if necessary." Such men are ripe for recruitment by gangs, and in groups they "exhibit even more exaggerated risky and violent behavior." The result is "a significant increase in societal, and possibly intersocietal, violence."

Crime rates, according to the authors, tend to be higher in polygynous societies. Worse, "high-sex-ratio societies are governable only by authoritarian regimes capable of suppressing violence at home and exporting it abroad through colonization or war." In medieval Portugal, "the regime would send bare branches on foreign adventures of conquest and colonization." (An equivalent today may be jihad.) In 19th-century China, where as many as 25 percent of men were unable to marry, "these young men became natural recruits for bandit gangs and local militia," which nearly toppled the government. In what is now Taiwan, unattached males fomented regular revolts and became "entrepreneurs of violence."

Hudson and den Boer suggest that societies become inherently unstable when sex ratios reach something like 120 males to 100 females: in other words, when one-sixth of men are surplus goods on the marriage market. The United States as a whole would reach that ratio if, for example, 5 percent of men took two wives, 3 percent took three wives, and 2 percent took four wives—numbers that are quite imaginable, if polygamy were legal for a while. In particular communities—inner cities, for example—polygamy could take a toll much more quickly. Even a handful of "Solomons" (high-status men taking multiple wives) could create brigades of new recruits for street gangs and drug lords, the last thing those communities need.

Such problems are not merely theoretical. In northern Arizona, a polygamous Mormon sect has managed its surplus males by dumping them on the street—literally. The sect, reports *The Arizona Republic*, "has orphaned more than 400 teenagers ... in order to leave young women for marriage to the older men." The paper goes on to say that the boys "are dropped off in neighboring towns, facing hunger, homelessness, and homesickness, and most cripplingly, a belief in a future of suffering and darkness."

True, in modern America some polygynous marriages would probably be offset by group marriages or chain marriages involving multiple husbands, but there is no way to know how large such an offset might be. And remember: *Every* unbalanced polygynous marriage, other things being equal, leaves some man bereft of the opportunity to marry, which is no small cost to that man.

The social dynamics of zero-sum marriage are ugly. In a polygamous world, boys could no longer grow up taking marriage for granted. Many would instead see marriage as a trophy in a sometimes brutal competition for wives. Losers would understandably burn with resentment, and most young men, even those who eventually won, would *fear* losing. Although much has been said about polygamy's inegalitarian implications for women who share a husband, the greater victims of inequality would be men who never become husbands.

By this point it should be obvious that polygamy is, structurally and socially, the opposite of same-sex marriage, not its equivalent. Same-sex marriage stabilizes individuals, couples, communities, and society by extending marriage to many who now lack it. Polygamy destabilizes individuals, couples, communities, and society by withdrawing marriage from many who now have it.

As the public focuses on a subject it has not confronted for generations, the hazards of polygamy are likely to sink in. In time, debating polygamy will remind us why our ancestors were right to abolish it. The question is whether the debate will reach its stride soon enough to prevent polygamy from winning a lazy acquiescence that it in no way deserves.

Critical Reading Questions

Summarizing the Text

1. What is the difference between polygamy, polygyny, and polyandry? What is the significance of this difference for Rauch's argument?

2. What is the most immediate negative societal effect of polygyny, according to Rauch?

Establishing the Context

3. Why is polygamy "the opposite of same-sex marriage, not its equivalent"?

4. A common argument against gay marriage is that opening the door of marriage to same-sex couples will leave no logical way to deny the benefits of marriage to other unconventional combinations: several women and a man (polygamy), several same-sex partners, even a human and an animal. Rauch clearly disagrees with this slippery-slope argument. What is his underlying assumption about what is unique and valuable about marriage? Why does it only allow two partners?

Responding to the Message

5. Americans have become more familiar with polygamists recently because of events in the news (the arrest and trial of polygamist leader Warren Jeffs) and products of popular culture (the HBO series *Big Love* and TLC's "reality" TV show *Sister Wives*). Do you think that polygamy is becoming "normalized" because of this—that is, as we see it in the media it begins to seem more normal to us and thus more acceptable? Do you think the presence of polygamy in pop culture results from our search for ever-stranger things to watch? Or is there another reason?

6. What is your definition of marriage? In terms of government policy and law (not religion), what should the purpose of marriage be, and what kinds of partnerships should be allowed to marry and receive the legal benefits of marriage? What are those benefits?

Illegitimate Mexican Family Values?

Rosa Martha Villareal

Martha Rosa Villareal is a Northern California–based writer and professor of writing at Los Rios Community College, near Sacramento. She is the author of several works of fiction, including 2008's The Stillness of Love and Exile, *winner of the Josephine Miles Literary Award. She also contributes to the website Mexidata.info, where this article originally appeared. In the article, Villareal responds to and refutes claims that Latino families—particularly families of illegal Mexican immigrants in the United States—have significantly higher rates of illegitimacy than other populations.*

In the public debate over illegal immigrants, advocates on both sides of the issue have included Hispanic family values into their arguments. Interlocutors such as President George W. Bush have praised the family values of Hispanic immigrants and argued that, in an era of moral relativism, they would strengthen the national character. Not to be outdone, the opposing camp has published a plethora of articles suggesting that Hispanic family values are, in actuality, the very antithesis of American values.

Leading the charge are Heather MacDonald of *City Journal*, and Steven Camarota of the Center for Immigration Studies. Citing statistics on "illegitimate births," Mr. Camarota's recent article, "Illegitimate Nation," paints not only a grim picture, but proposes that there is an endemic pathology in Hispanic culture with regards to illegitimate births. The arguments therein are, without a doubt, compelling, but flawed and untruthful in their conclusion because, as I remind my students, an argument may be "nothing but the truth" but not the "whole truth." A partial truth, thus, while creating a technically "valid" syllogism may still be fallacious.

First of all, let us concede that the numbers don't lie. Being that most of the populations of Latin America—including those who migrate illegally into the United States—are poor, the fact that an astonishing number of births occur outside of wedlock is not entirely surprising. However, one must ask if this phenomenon is more of a result of the *culture of poverty.* As Mr. Camarota points out, the rate of illegitimacy is even higher in Haiti, a Francophone, ethnic African, and even *poorer* country.

It doesn't take a lot of imagination to see the same dilemma in poor white and black America as anyone who's watched the despairing spectacle of *The Jerry Springer Show* can attest. Moreover, no one has yet chronicled how many European peasant immigrants in previous migrations left behind spouses and children and started anew once in America and, thus, technically produced their own "illegitimate nation."

But legitimacy of birth is beside the point. As Jean Jacques Rousseau noted, the family is a *natural,* not a civil, institution. In our evolutionary history, what made a family was a cohesive unit based on kinship. The natural values of the family were and are based on the biological parents living together and caring for and feeding their offspring and older members of their kin group. Just because the legal form of marriage did not exist prior to the rise of organized societies does not mean that families and the values of responsibility did not exist.

In today's class of the immigrant poor, many parents may not have legitimized their union but nonetheless live, work, and raise their children together *and* send remittances back home to support elderly parents and even younger siblings. It is not as though the lack of a marriage certificate precludes people from being responsible. And it is not as though the vast majority of these "illegitimate" children are being raised in single households.

What is most troubling about Mr. Camarota's assertion is that he ascribes the disregard for legal marriage as endemic not to the cultures of the poor, regardless of their ethnicity, but to Hispanic culture, proving at the very least the superficiality of the argument and the ignorance of the writer. Legal marriage and the legitimate birth of children are actually *highly* valued in the Hispanic middle and upper classes, just as they are in other European-based cultures.

In researching my own genealogy on the American continent—which by the way is descendent of legitimate births all the way back to my Spanish ancestors in the 1500's—I found that, unlike U.S. birth certificates, Spanish certificates list a birth as either "legitimate" or "natural." Additionally, the social distinction *"somos de buenas familias"* not only signifies respect for the legal institution of marriage but for honor and integrity as well.

There are many sincere arguments against illegal immigration and equally as many against amnesty, but disparaging the entire Hispanic culture is not one of them. This smear campaign—known as the Black Legend in the 16th century—equates anything from the Spanish culture as inherently inferior to that of Northern Europe.

With that said, if one criticism of Hispanic culture needs to be pointed out it is that it is too traditional, perpetuating the absurd Biblical assertion that man is in the image of God and woman in the image of man. Paradoxically, many of the commentators who argue so passionately against illegal immigration are equally passionate about denying women in this country their reproductive rights and advocate for a return to traditional (and lesser) roles for women.

Perhaps the reason we don't have as many illegitimate births in our country is because women have more rights in the first place.

Critical Reading Questions

Summarizing the Text

1. What does Villareal do with her introductory paragraph? What points does it set up? Does she reveal her thesis here?

2. One of Villareal's counterclaims is that high rates of illegitimacy among Hispanic families are proof not of a flaw in "Hispanic family values" but of the effects of "the culture of poverty." What does she mean by this? What evidence does she offer in support of this claim?

Establishing the Context

3. Villareal responds to critics of so-called "Hispanic family values" with a rhetorical analysis: she claims that although their arguments are truthful, this does not mean that their arguments are actually *valid*. Why not?

4. How does Villareal refer to historical evidence to support her claim that "Hispanic family values" are, contrary to some critics' claims, highly pro-legitimacy?

Responding to the Message

5. Villareal ends her argument with a strongly feminist claim: that the flaw in Hispanic culture is that it is too patriarchal, and that the old-fashioned roles for women prescribed by patriarchal culture, ironically, encourage illegitimacy. Do you agree with this? Do you find that this concluding point strengthens or weakens her overall argument? How?

6. Villareal's conclusion is an excellent example of a writer using a conclusion not simply to restate an earlier point but to expand on the points she has just made, and to show how her argument has larger ramifications. Look at your most recent paper—what did you do with your conclusion? How might you more effectively use the conclusion?

Questions for Short Projects or Group Presentations

1. Using 2010 U.S. census data, look at the state of the American family today. What percentage of families is headed by married couples? How many states allow gay marriage or civil unions? Is the divorce rate climbing or sinking? How big is the average American family?

2. Highly developed nations are experiencing declining birthrates; poorer nations tend to have high birthrates and populations where the average age is low—15 years old or so. What are the reasons for this? What are the effects of this? How might this change as some of the poorer nations—India or Brazil, for instance—grow wealthier? And how has China managed its population?

Questions for Formal Essays

1. Several of the essays in this chapter (Sandler's, Chen's, and others) translate primary-source scientific research for a more general, non-specialist audience. Compare how each author uses his or her sources by consulting those sources. Do the authors accurately represent the research they are presenting to their audiences?

2. Conservative activists tend to argue that the responsibilities and mutual support we develop in a traditional family are essential to the health of our larger society. Others, however, argue that the traditional family isn't at all a natural formation—that there are any number of valid and healthy ways to organize domestic life, from communes to polygamy to happy singlehood. What is the value and importance of a family, in your opinion—not for the individuals themselves, but for society as a whole?

3. What are "family values"? Where does this term come from? Who uses it, and for what ends? What kinds of values are not considered family values? What power comes from control of this term?

4. Should the United States loosen its definition of marriage to include same-sex couples or even polygamous arrangements? Or should it codify marriage as being "one man, one woman"? Why? Answer this by referring to the arguments made in this chapter.

What Spaces Do You Inhabit?

CHAPTER INTRODUCTION

Where are you? Where have you been? Where are you going? What's it like there? These questions all refer to location, of course—in these questions, someone is asking about a physical location.

At least, that's true most of the time. Space can also be metaphorical. If a classmate asks you "Where are you in the reading?" you probably understand that she is asking how *far* into the reading you've gotten. But let's change the preposition in that sentence from "in" to "on": "Where are you on the reading?" That question probably isn't inquiring about physical space, but rather asks about your *opinion* of the stance taken on the reading. One might ask, similarly, "where are you on what we should be doing about global warming?" Location here means where one is on a spectrum of opinion.

Space can be mental as well. If you stare off into the ether while your mind wanders, your roommate might ask "where are you?" She knows that you are *physically* next to her, but your brain and attention are elsewhere—worrying about a class or watching a video on your computer.

Writers have always been interested in space—physical space as well as metaphorical space—and the first cluster of this chapter provides several different perspectives on the physical spaces we use and inhabit. Who controls the space where you find yourself right now? What limitations are there on its use? How does the space attempt to make an argument to you about it, and about what you should be doing or thinking or feeling?

The design of spaces can effectively link emotions and ideas. The apparel retailer Abercrombie & Fitch intensively uses its space—the interior of the store—to associate, in the customer's "lizard brain" (a humorous term for one's most primitive mental space), the store's brand with a particular kind of sexed-up Californian beach culture that many young—and older—people find appealing. Using the décor, the music, the colors of the walls and doors, and even the appearance and bearing of the sales staff, the stores put you in a particular place, even if you are actually in a drab shopping mall in the middle of winter. Creating this association in visitors' minds is, for the A&F staff, perhaps even more important than having them buy something there and then (for they can always "visit" the A&F website).

The first two essays in this cluster examine spaces similar to an A&F store in their intentional design—Starbucks Coffee restaurants and a shopping mall in central Los Angeles called "The Grove." The authors argue that each space is intended to create or re-create a kind of experience that consumers find pleasurable. Both authors, as well, insist that the emotional associations each place creates—feelings of community, democracy, urban life—are actually in conflict with the values that the Grove and Starbucks actually enforce in their spaces and promote through their businesses.

Moving from commercial spaces to public spaces, the rest of the essays in this cluster offer different perspectives on whether and how much the government should control public space. "Sprawl," or uncontrolled suburban development, is anathema to many people, who argue that it is ugly, environmentally toxic, and unhealthy. Others disagree and see sprawl (or "low-density development," a less loaded term) as merely the manifestation of people's freedom to pursue happiness as they see fit, even if that is simply through owning a large house in a safe neighborhood with easy access to a wide variety of stores.

Finally, the last essay in the section applies the idea of the "ownership society" (the notion, popularized most recently by President George W. Bush, that if people own things, they tend to take better care of them than if the government owned them and made decisions about their care) to America's national parks. Should these parks remain the property of the government—of all of the people, essentially—when government ownership is costly and government management inefficient? Or should the private sector have a greater role in our parks and conservation system?

Space isn't just physical, of course. Increasingly, we use metaphors of physical space and motion to describe our interactions with computers and the Internet. The Web has "sites," and you "surf" or "jump" from one site to another. Programmers seek to create an appealing "environment" on their websites that will encourage users to "visit" and "stay."

Early Web surfers excitedly described the experience of staying up all night clicking on sites that were located in Eastern Europe, Africa, East Asia, and everywhere else; breathlessly, they told us that they could visit the entire physical world without ever leaving their desk chairs. Today, the Internet has become such a mundane part of our lives that we don't even think about the physical locations that we are virtually visiting—the server farms in Moldova or Seoul or Arlington, Virginia, with which our computers talk. The Internet is no longer "like" physical space—it is a completely immersive space with its own physical geography.

And people are spending a lot of time there. A 2009 Kaiser Family Foundation study found that children ages 8–18 spend an average of 7.5 hours a day with media technologies (the Internet via computers and phones, as well as television and other media), and since most of us "multitask," or do several things at once, it's probably more accurate to say that young people experience almost 11 hours of media a day.

While some of that time is spent in the passive activity of watching television or listening to music, more is spent with so-called "interactive" technologies such as the Internet, video games, or cell phones. These activities dominate our attention as we watch, listen, and respond to text messages, games, or Web content. They become the "virtual spaces" we inhabit.

What, then, are these spaces like? Who makes the rules for them? What can we do while there—and what can be done with us there? The second cluster in this chapter looks at the site that has become the most important space in the virtual world (and the most popular website in the United States): Facebook.

Facebook is a profit-driven business that depends primarily on advertising for its revenue. Like Google and many other popular sites, Facebook uses computer algorithms and "bots" to harvest information about its users and then sells that information to advertisers, who can thus better target their advertising. For example, if your status updates and photo tags and inbox messages mention the Boston Red Sox with great frequency, you will soon see Red Sox- and Boston-related advertising appearing on your home page.

The problem is that many of us use Facebook like a private social space. We don't like it when others eavesdrop on our private conversations and make a profit on the information they glean from that. Since its founding, Facebook (and its founder, Mark Zuckerberg) has been consistently pushing for users to make more information more public, and users have been pushing back. Included here are several takes on changes that Zuckerberg instituted in early 2010.

Finally, the Internet can serve as the world's biggest enabler of over-sharing—it's a space in which we can say anything, even if it should probably remain unsaid. In her controversial 2008 article "Exposed," blogger and former Gawker.com writer Emily Gould chronicles how her blog, and eventually her job, created an almost unstoppable momentum behind her own natural tendency to make far too much of her personal information public. In this article, she argues that she learned that the Internet was a much more public space—with all of the dangers that go along with public life—than even she originally understood.

As you read these pieces, think about "space"—how do these writers use the idea of space as a controlling idea or metaphor? Who should set the rules for the spaces we inhabit? How careful should we be in public space? Who protects us from the dangers of public space? And what are the dangers of private (in both senses—personal and commercial) space?

CLUSTER ONE: PRIVATE RIGHTS AND THE PUBLIC GOOD IN THE SPACES WE INHABIT

It Looks Like a Third Place

Bryant Simon

Bryant Simon is a professor of history and director of the American Studies program at Temple University in Philadelphia, Pennsylvania. In his book Everything But The Coffee: Learning About America from Starbucks, *Simon examines the role that the coffee chain Starbucks has taken on in American culture, and he places Starbucks within the long history of coffeehouses and democracy. In this excerpt, he questions whether and how Starbucks functions as a "third place," a location separate from home or work where people gather to socialize and create community. In terms of its audience, Simon's book on Starbucks is aimed at both academics and a more general public interested in the critical examination of culture.*

Like a lot of people, *Boston Globe* columnist and seasoned Starbucks watcher Alex Beam thought Howard Schultz coined the term *third place.* He didn't—retired University of South Florida sociology professor Ray Oldenburg came up with the term to describe sites where people gather other than work or home. Still, it is easy to see why Beam would make this mistake. Every chance he gets, Schultz uses this expression to describe his company's often busy and bustling stores. When he does so, he makes yet another implicit promise from the brand. He links its outlets to the coffeehouse traditions of connections, conversation, debate, and, ultimately, the ongoing and elusive desire for community and belonging in the modern world.

Lots of brands these days sell the idea that a shared sense of buying—or taste—adds up to community. Schultz, however, grasped
that his consumers wanted something more than just a nod of the
head between buyers of pricey, specialty coffee; that is, he understood
how brand communities work. Customers wanted a throwback to the
past—a sense of touch, the sound of voices, and the noise and intimacy
of laughter and conversation. So that's what he promised latte drinkers. Yet his stores offer less belonging and fewer real connections than
they do a quick cup of coffee and a predictable and safe meeting place,
a retreat from the world and from other people.

Nonetheless, Schultz repeats his third place community-building
promises all the time. His stores, he tells talk-show hosts, journalists,
and stockholders, are places between work and home where people
can meet, unwind, establish connections, and deepen their sense of
community. Asked once how Starbucks differed from McDonald's and
Burger King, the two-time company CEO and majority stockholder
said, "We're not in the commodity business. We've created a third
place." In his memoir, he boasts, "Almost everywhere we open a store
we add value to the community. Our stores become an instant gathering space, a Third Place, that draws people together."

Starbucks didn't start out creating third places or even getaways.
This was a case where the customers, not the company, drove the
changes. At first, Starbucks sold bulk coffee, and then it sold espresso-
based drinks, but it turns out people didn't just pick up some beans or
grab a cup of coffee and go. Sometimes, they lingered. Employees here
and there put in a few stools, and then a few tables, and more people
stayed. Starbucks' more deliberate building of third places was really
something of an accident of real estate.

When Starbucks tried to break into the New York area, it shifted
its growth model. In the late 1980s and early 1990s in Chicago and
Washington, DC, the company established itself downtown with the
high-earning grab-and-go crowd first and then moved outward like
the spokes on a wheel to the suburbs. In New York, however, the company couldn't get into the downtown market right away, so it opened
initially in the suburbs. Store managers, and then executives, noticed
that profits at these stores were high in part because customers stayed
longer. Soon an employee got the idea of putting a couch in the corner,
and people sat there—and the people in line liked the look of things and
the promise of comfort, connections, and conversation. So Starbucks
had a new template: it was not just a repository of coffee knowledge or
a dispenser of authenticity or a producer of predictability; now it was
also a maker of socially vital third places.

Once again Howard Schultz had a sense for what people wanted.
He gave them a taste, a somewhat contradictory taste, of community. "If
you look at the landscape of America," he observed in 1992, "we have

an opportunity to change the way people live." Twenty-five years later, Schultz proclaimed, "I think we have managed to, with a simple cup of coffee and a very unique experience, enhance the lives of millions of people by recreating a sense of community, by bringing people together and recognizing the importance of *place* in people's lives." ...

Weak Ties

I spent a lot of time eavesdropping at Starbucks. When there is talk at Starbucks, it is largely between workers and customers. The ties that are made there, then, are generally weak ties, not really what Ray Oldenburg had in mind when he talked about third places. Still, that is not to say that Oldenburg and others won't recognize the social and psychological usefulness of these kinds of weaker connections. "To be known," Oldenburg says, "is important. It gives you a sense of belonging."

In many ways, Starbucks deliberately manufactures these weak ties and this casual sense of belonging. Company manuals and managers encourage workers to perform all kinds of what sociologist Arlie Hochschild so aptly called "emotion work." Like the flight attendants she studied, Starbucks calls on its clerks not only to deliver coffee but also to create, through their tone, faces, and moods, "a particular emotional state in others." The Green Apron book, a shorter, handier version of the company manual, reminds "partners" to be "welcoming, genuine, considerate, knowledgeable." "It is a little forced," one veteran worker admitted: "We are judged if we say hello. You have to smile and make eye contact." If you want to go "above and beyond to deliver legendary service, you have to start customer conversations." "You have to pretend you care," she continued, "about their vacations plans and car troubles, what they drank yesterday and what they will eat today." One time her shift manager scolded her for not smiling enough with her eyes. However, she recognized, as others do, that these conversations and facial expressions create relationships and a sense of belonging. That's why they have value.

In 1943, psychologist Abraham Maslow laid out his famous pyramid of needs. Once the basic needs of air, food, sleep, water, and sex are met, human beings, he argued, seek to satisfy higher longings. He laid these out in ascending order. After safety and security (things Starbucks surely pays attention to), he listed love and belonging as the next-highest needs. People, Maslow observed, seek a sense of belonging and acceptance from larger groups—families, neighbors, church members, business associates, peers, and the guys at the barbershop and the women at the beauty salon. Without these kinds of connections, we are susceptible to loneliness and social anxiety. No doubt familiar with Maslow's ideas, Starbucks designers engineered a sense of belonging knowing that customers will pay extra for recognition, especially as community ties get weaker and nods and hellos are harder to find. That is surely one of the benefits of the corporate-created language. Only people in the know—the people who belong—can talk there. That is also why shift managers remind employees to smile with their eyes and remember everyone's name in line.

When I tell some people about how Starbucks manufactures a sense of belonging, they sometimes cringe. Others look disappointed, like their friendly barista wasn't really their friend after all. But most see the conversations at the Starbucks counter for what they are and value the weak ties that they get from the company, with their simultaneous closeness and distance, inclusiveness and exclusiveness. "I like that they recognize me," my former dean explained to me, "but also I like that I don't have to talk when I don't want to." Maybe we can call this customer-controlled belonging. "I don't work for Starbucks," one regular wrote on the online discussion board starbucksgossip.com, "but every time I'm in there ... the baristas greet me cheerfully and always without fail, compliment something about me: my hair, my outfit, my jewelry, my purse." With a touch of modesty, she continued, "there's nothing exceptional about me, but they seem to go out of their way to make me feel good. I always leave a little happier than when I arrived. Maybe it's part of the 'sell,'" she acknowledged, "but I don't care. A kind word goes a long way." These pleasantries—corporate-generated recognition and banter—kept her coming back to Starbucks, singing the company's praises, and paying the premium. Weak ties, even manufactured ones, have value, and people will pay for them.

Still, neither weak ties nor the coffee shop turned into an office or private meeting place was what Oldenburg had in mind when he talked about third places. For him, third places had their own sort of weak tie to Jürgen Habermas's weightier ideas about public spaces. The influential German philosopher defined the public sphere as a place where individuals who won't meet in other situations come together at a site, like a club, tavern, or coffeehouse, outside the influence of the state and away from the private realm. But they need to be doing more than just sharing space. Gathered as carpenters or artists or coffee drinkers, they must start to talk, then connect, and then meld together into a public. After this happens—and for Habermas this was the real payoff—they become capable of debating politics and talking about the larger civic good. Democracy, Habermas argued, can't function without vibrant public spaces, spaces that do not serve primarily as sites of buying and selling, but as places for thinking and talking. Oldenburg would basically agree, although he is more interested in smaller-scale community than the more grandiose project of democracy. But, he would concede, the process of bringing people together is similar. In third places that work, people who wouldn't otherwise meet get to know and eventually trust each other. For this to happen, there has to be conversation; there has to be talk.

Sociologist Elijah Anderson shared similar concerns and hopes. In a tight and perceptive essay, he developed a model that is perhaps closest to how a Starbucks might work as a public space or third place. He called such a location the "cosmopolitan canopy." These were sites where different kinds of people gather and feel safe enough to let down their guard and open themselves up to new music, new food, new experiences, new ideas, and even new people. This takes some repetition. Usually the same people come over and over again to these kinds of places, and the people working there are also the same each time. This familiarity creates a sense of security and gives these places great potential for meaningful talk. Sharing a table and then a conversation with, say, an AfricanAmerican man can encourage a white man—to imagine one example suggested by Anderson—to rethink his thoughts about race. Maybe through this interaction he revises his belief system to feel that not all young black men are criminals; then the next time that he approaches a young black man on his way to work, he doesn't automatically cross the street. But this change of heart and newfound tolerance requires not just observing the other, but talking and exchanging stories, news reports, gossip, rumors, and, maybe most important, theories for why things happen the way they happen. Unregulated talk, then, is absolutely essential for Anderson, as it is for Oldenburg, Habermas, and anyone else interested in cosmopolitan canopies and third places.

For about nine months, while I was doing research for this book, I spent, on average, ten to fifteen hours a week at Starbucks. On only a dozen or so occasions did I speak to someone I didn't already know. However, on any number of occasions, I have seen teenagers, sometimes from the same school and sometimes from different schools, gather there and take advantage of being away from their parents to try on slightly new personalities and talk to each other, exchanging ideas, secrets, gossip, and phone numbers. Moreover, I have heard stories from others about meaningful talk among adults at Starbucks, about people over twenty making connections there beyond their usual social circles.

My friend Sarah Igo told me, for instance, about a New Haven Starbucks on the edge of Yale's campus, where students and locals, professors and the unemployed gather around a chessboard to play, talk strategy, and swap stories. Wright Massey, the 1990s Starbucks store designer, told a similar story. These days he stops by a Starbucks store near his home in suburban, strip-malled Orlando every morning. When he walks in the door, he sees the same people, sitting in the same places. They are his coffeehouse friends. He talks with them about politics, the weather, business, whatever. His mornings at

Starbucks provide him with a connection—a hard thing to find in Orlando, a large, fast-growing, and spread-out place with seemingly more tourists than full-time residents and few walkable neighborhoods anchored by corner bars and diners.

Thirty-seven-year-old Kathleen Dalaney lived in a place like Orlando—the suburbs of Charlotte, North Carolina, the placeless sort of place where Starbucks seems more likely than in the cities to become a central meeting spot. In 2005, she had just had a baby. Her husband worked long hours, turning her into a stay-at-home mom who couldn't get an Elmo song out of her head. "It can be so isolating sometimes," Dalaney admitted. Looking for connections, she logged onto meetup.com, "a web site where people with similar interests can find likeminded people close by." Pretty soon, she discovered other area stay-at-home moms. They started to meet at a Starbucks. Now, she says, she has someone to talk to about the daily pressures in her life. The women are even planning a cruise someday—without their kids or their husbands.

Yet Igo's, Massey's, and Dalaney's stories seem to me to represent the exception rather than the rule. I have been to plenty of Starbucks without much talk. Most times when I have talked with people I didn't know at Starbucks, my kids were involved. I have seen this with others as well. With a four-year-old by your side, you are marked as safe. Twice outside the United States, I talked with people I didn't know— other Americans. Another time, I was sitting in the tiny Starbucks in Margate, New Jersey, a shore town a couple of miles south of Atlantic City. A man started talking about his plans to develop condos in Atlantic City. But he blurted out he would have to sell them to New York Jews, not Philadelphia Jews, because Philly Jews, he bellowed, knew all about Atlantic City, a city I understood him to say with an AfricanAmerican majority. Then he asked everyone in the coffee shop if they agreed. Two did, and one wasn't sure. I didn't vote. I didn't know what to say or how to raise questions about the proposition on the table with people I didn't know. Most of my Starbucks interactions, then, were one-off deals, even at outlets where I often went and sat for a long time. The conversations never lasted long, or involved a lot of back-and-forth, or got renewed the next day or the day after that—a key for Oldenburg and Anderson.

Judi Schmitt of Northern Virginia went searching for a third place at Starbucks and didn't find it, either. For three years, she said over e-mail, she and a friend played weekly, two-hour long Scrabble games at a local Starbucks. "We kind of hoped to start something," she noted with regret, but "we have not ... started a trend." Not a single person ever asked to join them, though a few customers looked up from their "babies, laptops, [and] school books" and shared "fond memories of playing Scrabble." But that's it.

In search of that elusive third place, I went back to the busy wedge-shaped Starbucks on Dupont Circle I had visited in DC before I talked with Philadelphia reporter Alfred Lubrano and declared Starbucks "a perfect third place." This time it was a crisp but comfortable January night. Again, a diverse crowd of people came and went and kept the store packed. Students sat behind laptops and stacks of papers. Friends talked to friends. Businessmen barked instructions into cell phones about delayed orders and discounts. Lovers whispered to each other. A few customers exchanged hellos and the occasional "How are you?" with the employees. But no one talked with anyone they didn't seem to already know or hadn't come there to meet. None of the talk was addressed to anyone else. For my part, I couldn't find a way to enter a dialogue with anyone.

I left and came back the next day. Again the place was crowded and thick with chatter. I looked around, but I didn't recognize anyone from my other visits. Still, this time I was determined to talk to someone. I sat on one of the comfy chairs in the back of the room. My knees just about touched the knees of the guy next to me. I made eye contact with him. But not a word—a nod, but not a word. I suppose I should have said hello, made a comment about the Tony Hillerman mystery he was reading, but I didn't know how to start the conversation. Or maybe I knew—and he knew—not to talk at Starbucks. We had been trained into silence, into recognizing the coffee shop as a place with boundaries. If you are there by yourself, you are off limits. I went back to the Dupont Circle Starbucks again later that day and the next day. Never did I find a conversation that I could easily—for me—join in. Again, maybe I should have tried harder.

Not long after my very unscientific and unsuccessful Washington-based third place experiment, I went to a Philadelphia Starbucks and pulled out my copy of Ray Oldenburg's *The Great Good Place: Cafes, Coffee Shops, Bookstores, Bars, Hair Salons, and Other Hangouts at the Heart of a Community*, the book where he first introduced the term *third place*. Reading it again and thinking about my own Starbucks experiences, I realized that Howard Schultz had cited and put into practice only part of the third place idea. Third places certainly function, Oldenburg says, as spaces to hang out between work and home, something Schultz and other Starbucks officials point out all the time, but they remain, the sociologist insists, so much more. For starters, they are idiosyncratic, one-of-a-kind hangouts. Each has its own feel and decor. Uniqueness gives them value to customers and gives them the chance to become agents of cohesion and community. But, again, it is the talk that happens in these quirky third places that matters. Oldenburg is not simply romantic for a lost urban past of mom-and-pop corner stores and manly neighborhood taverns, although he can come off this way at times. To him, third places serve not just as refuges or hideouts from the world or as steady producers of weak ties, things that Starbucks does quite well. They are not about the individual; they are about the collective. They are not about passive participation; they are about active engagement. This is key for Oldenburg, just as it is for Anderson. Like cosmopolitan canopies, third places perform a vital public service: they bring people together who would not come into contact with one another in any other setting. They do this not just for commerce but also for the larger social good.

Not long after I reread his book, I went to talk with Oldenburg. Thin and graying, with a bad back that made him move slower than he might have for his age, the retired professor blended into the early-morning crowd at a Pensacola pancake house. Starbucks, he told me, had once asked him to work for the company. He turned down the offer only to have an executive lecture him in the back of a limo about the true nature of third places.

While Oldenburg admitted that Starbucks has done some "good things," he scoffed at the notion of Starbucks as a third place. "It is an imitation," he said as he took a bite of his ham and eggs, adding, "It's all about safety for them." Fully realized and functioning third places, he insisted, must have wide-open doors, a whiff of danger, and a hint of uncertainty. They must value easy access for everyone over predictability. In Oldenburg's mind, owners play a key part in creating the unique, transformative character of a third place. Standing behind the bar or the counter day and night, they are a constant presence, not a shift worker like a Starbucks barista, fit into a complex and ever-changing schedule. More important, the owners set the tone for the place through their jokes, political commentary, wall hangings, jukebox choices, and gruff or gentle gestures. They welcome strangers and bring them into the community by introducing them to the regulars. And they don't do this for money alone; they do it for themselves, out of a desire for social connections and in service to their town or neighborhood. "Would Starbucks," Oldenburg asked me, "give a guy who is down on his luck a job?"

Essentially, Oldenburg continued, third places are conversational zones, places to talk freely and openly, sound off and entertain, experiment with ideas and arguments. With its "overriding concern for safety," predictability, and reassurance, Starbucks "can't achieve the kinds of connections I had in mind," Oldenburg concluded.

Coffeehouse Quotes

The music of Miles Davis and Dave Brubeck has always had a kind of countercultural cool. This was the sophisticated urban sound of intellectuals, hipsters, painters, and novelists—the imagined coffeehouse crowd. That's why Starbucks pumped this music into its stores, especially in the early days before it turned itself into an alternative to Tower Records.

More quotes appeared on the walls. Artists, essayists, and writers made a home for themselves in the penny university coffeehouses. They gave these places a sense of romance, intrigue, and intensity. Starbucks makes gestures in this direction as well. Art hangs on the walls of all its stores. Yet this is never edgy, raucous, or iconoclastic art. Rarely is it locally produced art, either. It is instead Starbucks-made and -generated art created at some centralized studio factory. From Portland, Oregon, to Portland, Maine, Starbucks stores display inflated abstract expressionist and pop art–infused homages to coffee. As tall as a basketball hoop and as wide as a garage door, these mixed-medium, earth-toned montages show steaming mugs of coffee, a few lines of poetry or prose about coffee and community, photographs of coffee plants covered by squiggly lines, and preprogrammed random-looking drops of paint. But as experience architect Greg Beck told me, the art still works. It tells people, he explained, that Starbucks cares about art, and so do its customers, then, by going to Starbucks.

In another quote from the past, Starbucks promised community. So did the Someday Café in Somerville, Massachusetts. Opened in 1993, this was a Beat-era throwback. The owners of the coffeehouse decorated it with mismatched furniture and photographs from local artists. They play a blistering soundtrack of alternative music. On the back walls, they let customers plaster fliers in a rainbow of colors announcing shows of punk bands at cramped bars and alt-country acts at reconverted theaters. Handwritten notes dot the community board, making it look like a paper patchwork quilt. Bands seek new guitar players. Someone is looking for a "sunny room in home with vegan/macro kitchen." ACT UP announces an emergency meeting, anarchists call for a protest against the death penalty, and the local Pagans invite anyone interested to a Wednesday night potluck.

Tucked back in the corner of most Starbucks stores are the company's own version of community boards with phrases like "What's Happening" or "Starbucks Happenings" running along the top. Like everything at Starbucks, the company has a policy on the community boards. Over coffee at a store in Austin, Texas, a former employee let me peek at the "Dos/Don'ts of Community Boards" from the late 1990s. The list went like this:

Do—showcase Starbucks' participation and involvement in the local community.

Do—post community events that Starbucks is involved in or sponsored.

Do—post photos of Starbucks partners' involvement in community events.

> Do—post positive news articles about your store's community involvement.

> Do—post "thank you" letters and awards or certificates pertaining to our support within the community.

The rules instructed store managers not to post anything about politics or religion. Groups involved in recycling and conservation could use the boards, but not environmental activists. Classified ads or calls for roommates are also not allowed. Generally, the company reminds employees, "Do not post any information on any event not sponsored by Starbucks."

The manager of a Washington, DC, Starbucks clearly followed the rules. When I stopped for a coffee in 2006, three items hung on the "Our Neighborhood" board. There was an advertisement for subscriptions to the official Starbucks paper, the *New York Times*. "Coffee," the ad said, "Makes News More Interesting and Vice Versa." Below this was a flier about Ethos Water, Starbucks' bottled water product and the clean-water projects it funded in the developing world. Also tacked up was a copy of the company's social responsibility brochure.

When I asked Leslie Celeste, the manager of a busy Starbucks in Austin, Texas, about the community board in her store, she chuckled. But she quickly got back to company policy, saying that she won't let religious or political groups put fliers there. Occasionally, she told me, she pinned up calls for auditions at local theaters and notices about art openings at nearby galleries. When we went to look at the store's community board, it was empty. That's the way it usually was, she laughed.

With its third place quotes, jazz soundtrack, abstract expressionist-looking art, and heavily edited community boards, Starbucks tries again and again to link itself to coffeehouse culture. The search for a connection to the past extends even to talk, that central feature of the penny university. "In the tradition of coffee houses everywhere," the company's Web page proclaims, "Starbucks has always supported a good, healthy discussion." With a statement like this, the company shows that it recognizes the desire for something beyond just a better cup of coffee than the diner serves. However vague, it does seem that creative class types like the possibility of contact, connections, free-wheeling art forms, and vigorous, spirited, and contentious debate. Or they like the sophistication and urbanity that others associate with these kinds of exchanges. Over the years, therefore, Starbucks' branders have tried to connect the company to the impulse to talk about big ideas.

In 1999, Starbucks teamed up with Time Custom Publishing to launch the magazine *Joe*. According to the venture's managing editor, the glossy aimed to "replicate the ideas, conversations, and encounters in a coffeehouse." "Life is interesting. Discuss." That's what *Joe*'s subtitle declared. The magazine didn't make it past a few issues. Starbucks, however, didn't give up on creating the appearance of coffeehouse conversations.

On a second try at getting the discussion going, Starbucks officials plastered quotes—now more than three hundred of them—on the company's take-away cups. "Our goal with The Way I See It is to promote free and open exchange of ideas," explained Starbucks spokesperson Tricia Moriarty. "We think this tradition of dialogue and discussion is an important facet of the coffeehouse experience." On one cup, Dan Rapp, a Starbucks customer from Cincinnati, intones, "I think every professional athlete should have to attend at least five kids' games every year, just so they remember what the sport is really about." That is quote number 73. (I tripped over this one in a parking lot.) I picked number 278 off a subway floor. On it Ben Kweller, who is described on the cup as a "rock musician" whose "songs can be heard on Starbucks XM Café Channel 45," asserted, "In the end we're all the same." Number 59 (found on the sidewalk in front of my house) featured Andy Roddick, the tennis star and the youngest American ever to climb to the top of the world rankings. He said, "Having two older brothers is a healthy reminder that you're always closer to the bottom than the top." In case anyone disagreed with Rapp, Kweller, Roddick, or any of the other coffee cup philosophers, the company denied responsibility for the content. "This is the author's opinion," it says at the bottom of every cup, "not necessarily that of Starbucks." Even as it distances itself from the cup quotes, Starbucks, nodding in the direction of coffeehouse tradition, invites customers to join online exchanges about the views expressed on its containers, although it is hard to imagine who could quarrel with most of the lines. Who isn't in favor of recognizing our commonality or adults watching kids play baseball or demonstrating humility? But, of course, when you are as ubiquitous as Starbucks, someone is going to be opposed to something.

"My only regret about being gay is that I repressed it for so long," novelist Armistead Maupin laments on a Starbucks cup. "I surrendered my youth to the people I feared when I could have been out there loving someone. Don't make that mistake yourself. Life's too damn short." For one Baylor University faculty member, this quote was too long and too gay. In response to the professor's protest, the Starbucks store on the campus of the Waco, Texas, Baptist school stopped serving coffee in the Maupin cups. Linda Ricks, a university official, reported that the dining services agreed to ditch the offending containers out of what she called respect for "Baylor culture." "There are different viewpoints on ... campus," Ricks elaborated. "We pulled the cup to be sensitive." She told the press that Starbucks had supported the removal. "They aren't intending to generate conflict at all," Ricks said about the cup quotes. "Starbucks fully supported our decision because they understand our environment."

Starbucks, then, doesn't reproduce the English coffeehouse or any other sort of genuine public space. What it does, rather, is simulate the coffeehouse. French cultural theorist Jean Baudrillard first developed the idea of simulacrums. Based on an idealized version, kind of like Weston's version of the penny university, the simulacrum is a reproduction. Over time, the reproduction becomes less and less like the imagined original, so even though it looks like the first cut of something, it doesn't function in the same way, for the same purposes.

Under Starbucks' reign, the coffeehouse has become something to consume more than an actual public gathering place. You rent out space for work or a meeting or pay for a chair for twenty minutes of relaxation, or maybe you use it as a place to show off your good taste. In all these scenarios where something beyond the functional is involved, you drink up form rather than substance. Thinking about these same issues, though in a different way, a business blogger asked, "Why is Starbucks the giant they are? Sure, they have good coffee, but that's not the whole picture. It's the brand. It's the barista experience. It's being surrounded by jazz music and modern art and people wearing turtleneck sweaters." In other words, it is the appearance of the coffeehouse that matters. Go to this place with art on the walls and jazz flowing out of the speakers, and you turn yourself into a witty, handsome, and urbane character from the TV show *Friends*. Or maybe you become a sophisticated, arty, and cosmopolitan individual. "You feel creative there," adds a midwestern journalist, like you've "got metro style down, ... like [you're] writing an indie film script, starting a start up or composing a term paper." But this isn't necessarily who you are; this is an image you pay a premium to display. You spend money to say something about yourself. At the classic coffeehouse or at a real third place, you participate by talking and listening; you don't just sit there, and it isn't just about you. At Starbucks, the coffeehouse quotes are there to sell Starbucks and to lend out, for a price, a sophisticated, cool image, but not really to promote free exchange, artistic engagement, or lasting community connections.

Starbucks simulates the coffeehouse in another way. ABC Radio reporter Aaron Katersky lived alone in a small Upper West Side apartment. He went to Starbucks because he liked to spread out every now and then and, even more, because he liked to be around other people. But he didn't necessarily want to talk to them. He picked Starbucks because the tables were set far apart and "protect[ed] his privacy." Increasingly, for Katersky and others, the ideas behind the original coffeehouses have vanished. Starbucks was all that they knew of the coffeehouse tradition and how to act in these places. Now, Katersky expected to get his better-than-decent cup of coffee, find a seat, and be left alone. Actually, if someone did try to talk with him about the fall in New York real estate prices or the Iraq war, he might think, like I did with that conversation about race and Atlantic City's development, that they had breached the boundaries of his individual coffeehouse space.

"Maybe," *New York Times* reporter Anemona Hartocollis speculated after visiting a Starbucks, "we only wish to drown our sorrows in a strong cup of coffee in cushy chairs surrounded by strangers who will grant us the illusion of community yet respect our privacy." Alfred Polgar, an Austrian writer and Viennese coffeehouse regular, noted in a similar vein that Starbucks was "a place for people who want to be alone, but need company for it."

Hartocollis and Polgar captured how Starbucks worked as a simulacrum, how it stamped out the real essence of the original ideal of the coffeehouse and, through proliferation and endless insistence, became itself the real thing for many bobo and creative class types. Just as Baudrillard suggested, this covering up takes place in the service of profit. At Starbucks, the coffeehouse quotes are there to sell the aura of Starbucks, to tell customers they can get what they want and be who they want, there and only there. Heated exchanges and avant-garde art might invigorate democracy, but they also run the risk of alienating potential customers. So Starbucks, as a business aimed at the upper edges of the mass market, understandably shies away from the contentious and divisive. The problem is that once the fake proliferates—without admitting that it is a fake—it can overwhelm the original. We forget that an older ideal dedicated to meaningful talk ahead of the market ever existed. We never learn how to push past our anxieties and talk with people we don't know, so we never hear their thoughts and opinions. Now many coffee drinkers think that solo-friendly, closely regulated, tightly scripted Starbucks, with its extra milky faux cappuccinos, is what a coffeehouse is and should be. As this happened, another chance for dialogue, the foundation of democracy and a potential counterforce against the privatization of everyday life and politics, slipped away as Starbucks consumed more space and more ideas.

Critical Reading Questions

Summarizing the Text

1. What does Starbucks *claim* to do and be, and how does it in reality not do this, according to Simon?

2. Simon divides his chapter into smaller sections, each with its own sub-argument. Two are included here: "Weak Ties" and "Coffeehouse Quotes." What is the thesis of each section, and how does it support the argument of the chapter as a whole?

Establishing the Context

3. Simon brings in many theorists—Baudrillard, Habermas, Ray Oldenburg, and others—and uses their ideas in his analysis of Starbucks. Discuss how he briefly summarizes four of them and how he employs their ideas. How do the writers he chooses to cite help construct his *ethos* as a writer?

4. Simon is largely critical of the "idea" or "brand" of Starbucks, but he pays little attention to what the retailer actually sells: coffee drinks, food, and coffee- and tea-related items. Is this fair? Is Starbucks more about the "experience" he believes it sells, or is it more about its actual products?

Responding to the Message

5. Do you frequent a Starbucks or other similar coffee chain? Do you patronize an independent store? Do you go just to get take-out drinks, or do you stay? How has that coffee shop obtained your loyalty? Apply some of Simon's theoretical ideas to your response.

6. Visit a local business. What does its interior design tell you about the values of the place and its relationship to its customers? How does the business send out signals about the kinds of customers it expects, or wants?

The Once and Future Mall
Alan A. Loomis

Alan Loomis is an architect and the principal urban designer of the city of Glendale, California (a suburb of Los Angeles). His website, DeliriousLA. net, collects "research and essays on landscape, urbanism, and architecture" in Southern California. In this essay, Loomis looks at The Grove mall in Los Angeles, an enclosed shopping center in the middle of the city. "The Once and Future Mall" appeared in the 2004 annual review of the Los Angeles Forum for Architecture and Urban Design *(a publication intended largely for architects, designers, and planners) as well as on the L.A. Forum's website.*

Near the end of 2001 no fewer than three urban malls opened their doors to the shoppers of greater Los Angeles. These malls— and at least another three are in the final stages of construction or planning—represent a prodigious production of retail space, over 4 million square feet of shopping. Moreover, their scale, density, and architectural typology are also stunning, and unprecedented since the opening of the notorious Beverly Center in 1982.[1] As perceived by the popular press and consumers, these malls represent a reinvestment in the city as a social and economic site—Hollywood & Highland

Aerial view of The Grove

Los Angeles Farmers Market in the 1940's

is the keystone for the LA Community Redevelopment Agency's revitalization of Hollywood Boulevard, and a civic center plan commissioned by the City of Pasadena dictated the urban configuration of Paseo Colorado. For others, these malls signal the final capitulation of the city to suburban cultural and economic norms. These critics attack the homogenous mixture of national and global retail chains typical of any high-rent, centralized management structure. Yet beyond the proliferation of Baby Gap and Banana Republic, the creeping suburbanization of urban malls indicates a shift of a more systemic nature—one that significantly diminishes the palette of urban design tools and, more disturbingly, reduces our understanding of urban life.

Of the three malls, The Grove most clearly illustrates these issues, particularly because its adjacency to the venerable Farmers Market at Third and Fairfax amplifies the history and future of the urban shopping mall. A visit to both the Market and The Grove reveals strikingly different spatial experiences. The former is a semienclosed, claustrophobic labyrinth of small shops, housed in anonymous agricultural shacks and set on an asphalt parking lot. The newer mall is more like Main Street Disneyland or the Forum Shops at Caesar's Place in Las Vegas, albeit without an artificial sky or animatronic fantasy figures. The Grove's medium and big box stores and multiplex cinema face a central open-air walk and are housed in vigorous reproductions

Olvera Street market, mid–20th century

of historic commercial architecture, detailed throughout in materials luxurious for a shopping mall. Only a set of mid-sized buildings by the Market's architectural stewards of twenty years, Koning Eizenberg, mediates between its one-story casualness and the three-story deliberations of The Grove and its massive, computer-monitored parking garage.[2]

Yet the gap between the two is bridged with a straight line—for the Market is essentially the prototype for the suburban shopping mall and The Grove is its most current incarnation. Although its relaxed attitude suggests the Market was an outgrowth of ad-hoc gatherings, its rural aesthetic was a calculated marketing strategy not so different from the Mexican stylism of its contemporary at Olvera Street. The unique environment of the Market was designed to encourage leisure shopping. "With little outlay, a bazaar-like atmosphere was cultivated to enhance the experience so that shopping for food would seem more akin to a leisure than a routine pursuit. Fueled by an aggressive advertising campaign, the Farmers Market began to attract an affluent trade of movie stars and others who sought the unusual goods sold there and took pleasure in the novel ambience."[3] The historicist imagery of The Grove engages in the same manipulative choreography, albeit updated by seventy years of market research and with architect Jon Jerde as mediator. Less skillfully executed than a Jerde Partnership "experience," such as San Diego's Horton Plaza or Universal CityWalk, The Grove's narrative architecture and programming clearly [owe] much to their innovations.[4]

Yet the fundamental innovation of the Farmers Market is that unlike the shopping courts of its day it has no retail street frontage, but is an internalized court located in the middle of a parking lot. This typology, of course, would become the dominant model of late twentieth century shopping malls. In Los Angeles, Lakewood Center was the first mall to conform to this now-classic model, firmly established by earlier structures such as Seattle's Northgate and Boston's Shoppers World.[5] The juggernaut of this type is now the 4.2 million square foot Mall of America outside of Minneapolis, although the title of world's largest mall once belonged to 3+ million square foot Del Amo Fashion Center in Torrance. In the transition from the Farmers Market to the Mall of America stands late modern architect Victor Gruen, the father of the modern shopping mall. Gruen organized the parking strategy and pedestrian-only environment of the Market with economic proformas of department stores and the technical innovations of modern architecture and transportation planning into a codified formula for producing suburban shopping malls.[6] Over the next twenty-five years, the regional mall quickly became one of the most recognizable architectural and marketing typologies in America suburbia.[7] Inevitably, as retailers rediscovered the city, the suburban mall was imported to the city. Although surface parking generally does not surround urban malls—cars are located under the mall as at Century City or next door in gigantic parking garages as at The Grove—the spatial organization remains decidedly suburban. Even if the roof has been removed, opening the mall interior to the sky, shops and pedestrian passages remain focused inward towards privately controlled "public" space, disconnected from the street life of sidewalks.

But as the penultimate evolution of the mall, The Grove is neither innovative nor particularly imaginative. For architects, the dilemma of The Grove is not its postmodern pastiche of architectural styles, but its failure to expand the mall's range of typological or urban performance. More troubling, The Grove's popular success also reinforces entertainment retail (retailtainment) as the only legitimate activity for creating urban places. The dominance of shopping—exacerbated in California's sales tax addicted cities—establishes retail centers as the only tool of urban design, to the exclusion of production (the workplace) and living (housing), and at the expense of a sustainable urban economy founded in a physical form that balances land uses with transit needs.

For a divorce between consumption (represented by shopping/entertainment) and the productive, domestic, or civic / political life has occurred during the evolution of the Farmers Market to The Grove. At The Grove, shopping has no connection to the surrounding Fairfax neighborhood, or even to greater Los Angeles. Whereas the Farmers Market married rural agricultural production with urban life at the local scale, the corporate enclave of The Grove, like most malls, is occupied by branch stores of national retail / entertainment corporations, with little relationship to the industry of the city. Shopping at The Grove does not prime the economic engine of Los Angeles manufacturers or retail companies.[8]

Although the Market's connection with local production was quickly lost as its architectural typology was applied to regional shopping malls, malls briefly retained elements of local civic culture. Gruen viewed the shopping mall as the suburbs' social center, and the inclusion of local cultural and political establishments was integral to his early mall formulas. Yet for the most part, even storefront post offices are absent from major shopping centers. In its place, The Grove features two European-feeling pedestrian streetscapes that converge on centralized park, with a small pond and actual grass. Although it is essentially an outdoor version of the atrium typical of suburban malls, including its set-to-music water fountain created by WET Design of Bellagio Vegas fame, this park nonetheless is immensely popular. Yet this very popularity makes The Grove that much more problematic. In one corner of the park is a collection of bronze sculptures, representing a gaggle of (white) children in 50's attire selling lemonade. At Christmas, the park features a gigantic fir tree—which signage proudly explains is taller than the Rockefeller Center tree. The references to the Rockefeller Center and mid-century Americana symbolically equate The Grove with the archetypal public green of New England villages and the democratic, urban civic culture such archetypes carry. But The Grove is entirely private space, created, owned and governed by Caruso Affiliated Holdings. Its primary and only purpose is shopping and entertainment: public facilities and institutions associated with democratic government are absent; offices and workshops of middle-class and working-class labor are not to be found; and the products of regional businesses are not sold here. The congested popularity of The Grove and its architectural and decorative symbolism gives it the appearance of a vibrant, rich urban place—yet it is ultimately a place where urban life is rendered in one-dimension, reduced to consumption only. The simulated city is just a marketing tool to amplify sales-per-square-foot numbers. This concentration of hyper-consumerism is not a problem per se—after all, commerce constitutes a certain kind of "publicness" and is one of the city's primary functional reasons to exist. Rather, the problem is that within popular perception The Grove's success quietly and insidiously eliminates other possible definitions of urban

life, leaving architects and developers only one option for activating
the city—shopping.

Meanwhile, The Grove is hidden from Pan Pacific Park by its massive parking garage and presents a blank wall to the real public face
of Third Street. The architectural cinema of The Grove's interior is not
directed towards the sidewalk and none of its storefronts open on the
street. The urban design of The Grove does nothing to positively contribute to the pedestrian life of Fairfax's streets—it merely increases
traffic. One suspects Byzantine conventions and the machinations of
retail real estate played a greater role in shaping the disposition of The
Grove than LA City planners, who should have rejected its "Berlin
Wall" as a matter of course.

The Grove's defiant rejection of Los Angeles' streets is all the more
distressing because of the latent transformative effect LA's commercial corridors could have in solving the region's planning challenges.
Beginning with Doug Suisman's 1989 *Los Angeles Boulevard* pamphlet,
the under-performing commercial mileage of Los Angeles boulevards
has been viewed in the context of a cataclysmic housing shortage,
no-growth single-family neighborhoods, and the prospect of transportation gridlock. Suisman and others have argued that LA's boulevards
are the optimum site for mixed-use corridors combining high-density
housing, sidewalk pedestrian-oriented retail, and, critically, either
bus-way or fixed-rail transit lines.[9] From this ideological perspective,
it is sadly ironic that The Grove's "streets" feature a double-decker,
state-of-the-art electric-powered trolley to transport shoppers from
the parking garage to the Farmers Market. Meanwhile, a mid-density
residential development, similar to many others appearing across the
city, is nearing completion across Third Street, yet the relationship
between housing and retail seems to have been given no thought by
either the designers of The Grove, of the housing development, or the
planners charged with imagining the City's future.[10]

Yet there are alternatives to The Grove—commercial projects by
mainstream developers that incorporate ground level, street-facing retail
with upper-level condos or apartments—Paseo Colorado in Pasadena,
Hollywood/Western in Hollywood, and CityPlace in Long Beach. Of
course, none of these three projects represent an ideal model. Half of
CityPlace's sidewalk frontage is service yards and parking garages,
including that facing the adjacent Blue Line light rail stop; the clunky
brown and orange stucco detailing of Hollywood/Western is simply
ugly and garish, even by Hollywood standards; and Paseo Colorado
retains internalized shopping courts while its architecture is deadly
flat and uniform, as if it were a full-scale enlargement of a cardboard model.[11] Nonetheless, each of these three malls has partially
turned the conventional typology of the mall inside-out and upside-
down: storefronts face the sidewalk and the airspace above the stores

is occupied by housing. As architectural prototypes, they inject new imagination into the standards of large-scale urban shopping centers. As urban design, they are part of broader strategies to increase the residential density of traditional office/commercial cores with an aim towards creating the proverbial 24/7 city.[12] As financial propositions, they also seem to be meeting early success: Paseo Colorado was recently sold at a considerable profit to its original developer.[13] Certainly the mythical days of shop owners living above their wares are over, but neither do these recent projects promote that myth. Rather they suggest that, although just opened, The Grove is already an obsolete model for the mall. For The Grove is nothing more than Fairfax's version of CityWalk, incorporating its spatial choreography, but also its isolation as a destination. When exhausted as an entertainment destination (for assuredly something "newer" will come along), its single-purpose architecture will be obsolete, like its "dead mall" predecessors on the suburban fringe. Although the Pasadena, Hollywood and Long Beach projects share many of The Grove's stores and therefore engage in the same consumerist fantasies, they are constructed in an architectural form that responds to the city's present social dilemmas, yet is adaptable to incremental change, where storefront tenants will reflect the evolving nature of the city's street life. As such, they represent a more sustainable investment of city's resources and its long-term future. With their mix of residential and commercial uses oriented towards the city's sidewalks and suggestion of transit corridors on boulevards, these projects are the first gestures towards the future of the mall in Southern California.

Notes

1. The three malls are, of course, Hollywood & Highland at 640,000 sq ft, The Grove at 575,000 sq ft, and Pasadena's Paseo Colorado at 565,000 sq ft. Also open or in development at the beginning of 2003 is West Hollywood Gateway at 245,000 sq ft, Long Beach's Pike at Rainbow Harbor at 369,000 sq ft, The Promenade at Howard Hughes Center at 250,000 sq ft, Sunset Millennium in Hollywood at 200,000 sq ft, Pasadena's The Shops on South Lake Avenue at 150,000 sq ft, and the reconstruction of Long Beach CityPlace at 450,000 sq ft, Sherman Oaks Galleria at 300,000 sq ft, and Santa Monica Place at 278,000 sq ft. The Beverly Center is a whopping 876,000 sq ft.
2. Carolyn Ramsay, "A Market Fresh Look," *Los Angeles Times*, 03 Jan 2002, and Koning Eizenberg Architects.
3. Roger Dahlhjelm established The Farmers Market in 1934. Olvera Street (formerly Olivera Street) opened in 1930, thanks to the efforts of Christine Sterling. (Richard Longstreth, *City Center to Regional Mall*, MIT Press, 1997, pp 279–283.)
4. The rooftops and HVAC equipment of The Grove can be seen from the upper levels of its parking garage, a lapse in the coherency of the design/

fantasy narrative that one would not expect of the Jerde Partnership. For more on Jerde, see Frances Anderton, editor, *You Are Here: The Jerde Partnership International*, Phaidon Press, 1999 or www.jerde.com. For more on the narrative design of The Grove, see Morris Newman, "The Grove's Groove" in *Grid*, May 2002.

5. Lakewood Center opened in 1952, Shopper's World in 1951 and Northgate in 1950. (Richard Longstreth, *City Center to Regional Mall*, MIT Press, 1997, pp 332–333.)

6. Victor Gruen and Larry Smith, *Shopping Towns USA: The Planning of Shopping Centers*, Reinhold Publishing Corporation, 1960.

7. Peter Rowe, *Making a Middle Landscape*, MIT Press, 1991, pp 109–147.

8. The Farmers Market was established to sell local produce. (Richard Longstreth, *City Center to Regional Mall*, MIT Press, 1997, p 282.) Some might argue that the cinemas at The Grove are outposts of the local film industry. Considering that marketing and finances of cinema makes little variation for local circumstance, I do not find this convincing.

9. Doug Suisman, *Los Angeles Boulevard: Eight X-Rays of the Body Public*, Los Angeles Forum for Architecture and Urban Design, 1989. Also see John Kaliski, "The Form of Los Angeles's Quotidian Millennium" in *The Edge of the Millennium: An International Critique of Architecture, Urban Planning, Product and Communication Design* edited by Susan Yelavich (Washington, D.C.: Smithsonian Institute, 1993), pp 106–119. Research by the Planning Center in Orange County studied the viability of converting commercial corridors into housing sites from a design perspective, and a 14 June 2002 Solimar Research Group brief authored by William Fulton confirms that this conversion is in fact taking place, The City of LA's General Plan Framework, adopted in 1996/2001, promotes mixed-use corridors, but it is only recently that zoning codes have caught up with policy. See Ordinance No. 174999 Residential/Accessory Services Zone, reported by Jocelyn Stewart. "The Sky's the Limit with New Zoning," *Los Angeles Times*, 29 Nov 2002 and Howard Fine, "City to Ease Way for Residences in Business Districts," *Los Angeles Business Journal*, 2 Sept 2002.

10. The proliferation of housing without street-facing retail is an equal failure of urban imagination, but that is the topic of yet another essay.

11. For a more extended critique of CityPlace, see Michael Bohn, "The Good, the Bad, and the Monotony" in this edition of the LA Forum newsletter. For Paseo Colorado, see Nicolai Ouroussoff, "Pasadena's Paseo Colorado: Shopping for Reality, in Vain," *Los Angeles Times*, 9 Nov 2001. For a general critique of new pedestrian malls, see Nicolai Ouroussoff, "No Sale in a Faux Town," *Los Angeles Times*, 27 Jan 2002.

12. Jesus Sanchez, "An Upscale Urban Village Emerges in Genteel Pasadena," *Los Angeles Times*, 30 Nov 2002 and Marshall Allen, "Living Large in Pasadena," Pasadena *Star News*, 16 Sept 2002. Both articles note the significant dollar premium paid for such "urbane" living and the affordable housing gap this presents. Recent plans for Santa Monica Place also propose to "invert" the mall and top it with housing: see Carolanne Sudderth, "One Little Shopping Mall and How it Grew and Grew and Grew," Ocean Park *Gazette*, 5 June 2002.

13. Danny King "Trizec Said Near Sale of Successful Pasadena Project," *Los Angeles Business Journal*, 2 Sept 2002 and "Developers Diversified Realty Announces Acquisition of Paseo Colorado Shopping Center," 16 Jan 2003. DDR, curiously, is also the developer/owner of CityPlace and The Pike in Long Beach. The housing component of Paseo Colorado is owned by Post Properties and was not part of the sale. TrizecHahn developed both Paseo Colorado and Hollywood&Highland—the latter project, with an exclusive focus on tourist-oriented entertainment/retail, has been a financial loss.

Critical Reading Questions

Summarizing the Text

1. In the opening paragraph, Loomis argues that a mall such as The Grove "reduces our understanding of urban life." How does he develop this argument in the rest of the essay?

2. Although he is very harsh about The Grove and shopping malls in general, later in the essay Loomis argues that some of these "large-scale urban shopping centers" are more imaginative and less one-dimensional. What counterexamples does he offer, and what makes them different?

Establishing the Context

3. Shopping malls have been criticized as being soulless almost since they came into existence after World War II. How is The Grove different from a typical suburban mall, in Loomis's mind?

4. Loomis alludes to the growing popularity of urban living today, a trend that has been accelerating since the 1990s. (From the 1950s through the 1980s, cities were often seen, in the American popular imagination, as dangerous, dirty places.) Using Loomis's description, The Grove's website, or photos on the Web, describe how The Grove imports the positive aspects of urban life into a traditional mall setting. Why does it do this? How does this appeal to shoppers?

Responding to the Message

5. Loomis argues that in The Grove, "urban life is rendered in one dimension, reduced to consumption only.... The Grove's success quietly and insidiously eliminates other possible definitions of urban life, leaving architects and developers only one option for activating the city: shopping." What does he mean by this? Is this a fair criticism to make of what is, after all, a shopping mall? Defend your answer.

6. Simon's and Loomis's articles are what's called "cultural criticism"—writing that applies theoretical ideas to analyze everyday objects or businesses or experiences on a deeper level. Using Simon and Loomis as a model, perform "cultural criticism" on a business or building or experience that is a central part of your everyday life.

Population Growth and Suburban Sprawl: A Complex Relationship *and* Global Warming: Sprawling Across the Nation

The Sierra Club

The Sierra Club is the nation's oldest and largest environmental and conservation organization. It promotes outdoor activities such as hiking and camping, but more importantly it also advocates for environmental protection through lobbying, contributions to candidates, and publications such as the ones included here. Here, the Sierra Club attempts to show how "suburban sprawl" (unchecked commercial and residential development of rural lands, often outside cities, that turns forests and farmlands into highways, residential subdivisions, and strip malls) is an environmental issue, not just an aesthetic one. These two position papers were intended either to be read on the Web or to be printed and distributed.

Population Growth and Suburban Sprawl

A Complex Relationship

A recent survey by the Pew Center for Civic Journalism found that suburban sprawl ties with crime as a top local concern for most Americans. It's not hard to figure out why: Americans are fed up with losing parks to pavement, breathing polluted air and spending an average of 55 workdays in traffic every year. We can do better to rein in out-of-control sprawl and slow population growth with simple solutions such as good land use planning, greater transportation choices, and increased support for family planning.

So why do we keep sprawling and overdeveloping? Sprawl has more than one source. As Sierra Club's two most recent national sprawl reports have shown, a complex mix of billions of dollars in government subsidies and poor federal, state and local planning policies fuels haphazard growth. Beyond that, in many but not all regions, rapid population growth further fuels sprawl.

Nationwide, land consumed for building far outpaces population growth. Urban areas expand at about twice the rate the population is growing.[1] A regional breakdown of the data shows some significant variations. In some regions of the United States, sprawl is largely a consequence of residents moving from urban centers to suburbs, but in others, population growth plays a larger role.

Population growth is clearly a bigger sprawl factor in the South and the West than the Midwest and Northeast, particularly along the Atlantic coast.[2]

In fact, according to a recent study of 277 metropolitan areas, from 1960 to 1990 our western cities nearly doubled in population, southern cities increased 70 percent, and population in cities in the Midwest and the Northeast grew by a more modest 25 percent and 12.5 percent respectively.[3]

Sprawl in many parts of the Midwest and Northeast is largely a product of poor land-use planning, irresponsible development and the migration of people to sprawl areas. In these communities, poor planning and lack of regional cooperation play larger roles than population growth.

Some notable examples of this phenomenon include Detroit, Pittsburgh and Chicago. From 1970 to 1990, Detroit's population shrank by 7 percent but its urbanized area increased by 28 percent. Pittsburgh's population shrank 9 percent in the same period and its area increased by 30 percent. Chicago's population did increase between 1970 and 1990 by one percent. Meanwhile, its urbanized area grew by 24 percent.[4]

As affluent residents flee, the tax base and quality of city schools declines, crime increases, green spaces shrink, and infrastructure is neglected—ultimately leading to more flight.

In the southern and western regions, these same factors combine with population growth to drive sprawl.[5] Nashville, Charlotte, and Phoenix depict how rapidly expanding population contributes to sprawl. Between 1970 and 1990, Nashville's population grew by 28 percent while its urbanized area grew by 41 percent. Charlotte's population grew by a significant 63 percent during this period while its urbanized area grew by a staggering 129 percent.

Sprawl and concurrent population growth in Phoenix provide a frightening glimpse of the repercussions of unchecked growth combined with poor planning: From 1950 to 1970, while its population grew 300 percent, its urbanized area grew by an incredible 630 percent.[6] More recently, its population grew 132 percent from 1970 to 1990; its urbanized area grew by a similarly significant 91 percent.

Solutions

There are effective ways to curb both sprawl and slow population growth. While slowing population growth is one critical step, it alone isn't the only answer. We also need to invest more in cleaner public transportation alternatives like trains, invest more in our existing communities rather than subsidizing fringe sprawl to help us rein in suburban sprawl. Cutting subsidies that feed sprawl, reinvesting in existing communities and smart-growth techniques, such as mixed-use, infill, and transit-oriented development, can channel growth away from open space and sensitive habitat into areas with established infrastructure and existing resources.

But no matter how smart the growth or how good the planning, a rapidly growing population can overwhelm a community's best efforts. Access to affordable family planning offers families a proven way to slow population growth. When families have the freedom to choose how many children to have and when to have them, families tend to be smaller and healthier. Women who have access to reproductive health care and family planning are better equipped to protect their health and the health of their families. Access to quality family planning programs truly is a win-win situation for the environment.

Notes

1. "The State of the Cities 2000," U.S. Department of Housing and Urban Development.
2. Diamdriand Noonan, *Land Use in America*, Island Press 1996, p. 87; Benfield Raimi, and Chen, *Once There Were Greenfields,* Natural Resources Defense Fund, p. 5; Porter, *Managing Growth in America's Communities*, Island Press 1997, p. 4; See also Bartlett, Mageean, O'Connor, "Residential Expansion as a Continental Threat to U.S. Coastal Ecosystems," *Population and Environment*, Volume 21, Number 5, May 2000.
3. Janet Rothenberg Pack, "Metropolitan Areas: Regional Differences," *Brookings Review*, Fall 1998, p. 27.
4. U.S. Census Bureau.
5. Bartlett, Mageean, O'Connor, "Residential Expansion as a Continental Threat to U.S. Coastal Ecosystems," *Population and Environment*, Volume 21, Number 5, May 2000.
6. U.S. Census Bureau.

Global Warming

"Our duty is to use the land well, and sometimes not to use it at all."

—PRESIDENT BUSH

Global Warming Degrades the Environment and Comes With a Huge Price-Tag

Global warming is caused by the build-up of heat-trapping carbon dioxide pollution in the atmosphere. Scientists predict that global warming will damage our coasts and crops, encourage the spread of infectious diseases and lead to the extinction of many plant and animal species.

The burning of ever-increasing quantities of coal, oil and natural gas in our cars and power plants is the source of the carbon dioxide pollution; however, we can take responsible steps to solve this problem.

The Problem at Home

Sprawling development creates homes further from jobs, shopping and other services. This causes two major problems: increased vehicle miles traveled (VMT) and increased infrastructure needs. The infrastructure needs arising from sprawling development cost a household $630 more per year and produce 8 more tons of CO_2 emissions.

These statistics conceal a stark truth: the hidden costs of sprawl require us to pay for the destruction of our environment from our own bank accounts whether we want to or not.

Could Sprawling Development Be Increasing Global Warming? YES!

As development stretches further from urban centers, services and infrastructure are extended, and more land is paved for parking lots and roads. Almost 70% of the recent increases in driving were due to the impacts of sprawl.

Stuck in Our Cars

Sprawl and a lack of transportation options force people to own and drive cars in order to reach most destinations. Sprawling cites have driving related energy consumption rates that can be three times that of better planned, more compact cities that offer transportation choices. Between 1980 and 1997, VMT in cars, trucks, and buses increased an astounding 68%.

The average U.S. household spends about 18% of its budget on transportation, making it the second largest household expense.

Smart Growth Plays a Key Role in Curbing Global Warming

Smart growth is intelligent, well-planned development that channels growth into existing areas, provides transportation choices and preserves farm land and open space. Through better planning, smart growth reduces dependence upon cars and alleviates congestion, thus reducing the sprawl-created burdens to our budgets and our environment.

Smart growth makes it possible to design homes and neighborhoods so that they are closer to jobs, shopping, and transit. In combination with improved transit systems, more pedestrian and bicycle friendly design, it is possible to greatly reduce residents' contributions to global warming.

Benefits of Smart Growth

- Placing new development within already built areas reduces VMT by as much as 61% and CO2 emissions by 50%.

- Planning pedestrian-friendly development along with good transit systems would save the average household over $2000 a year on transportation and save 40 million tons of carbon emissions.

- If 25 million units of new housing built in the U.S. over the next twenty-five years are placed in a more space-efficient way, 3 million acres of land would be preserved, 3,000 fewer new miles of state roads would be needed, and at least $250 billion would be saved.

- In another 50 years, implementing smart growth measures would save 200 million metric tons of carbon emissions per year.

- Design improvements to homes can result in at least 30% greater energy efficiency in heating, cooling, and water heating.

Choices for Easing Congestion

Often, building more roads is the proposed solution to traffic congestion, but as people around our nation are learning, more roads often mean more traffic, not less. Let your neighbors and local governments know about the link between global warming and sprawl. If you are interested in taking further action, the Sierra Club offers many tools to help you promote smart growth and curb global warming.

Solutions

Smart Growth provides a range of solutions to the problem of global warming. These include:

- ***LAND USE PLANNING***——*through land use policies such as mixed use ordinances, traditional neighborhood development standards, growth boundaries, and infill development, transportation options can be increased, reducing both car dependency and infrastructure needs;*

- ***PUBLIC TRANSPORTATION***——*through increased spending on transit, the creation of regional transit authorities, transit oriented development, and transportation control measures, it is possible to increase use of public transportation options and decrease global warming pollution;*

- ***COMMUNITY REVITALIZATION***——*through affordable housing development code provisions, community land trusts, and neighborhood conservation policies, homes can be located closer to jobs and in already developed neighborhoods.*

Critical Reading Questions

Summarizing the Text

1. What are the theses or main claims of these two press releases?
2. What is "sprawl," and why is it a bad thing?

Establishing the Context

3. *Sprawl* is itself a loaded term with strongly negative connotations. What is the term that the Sierra Club uses for the type of development it prefers? How is this choice of words an attempt to persuade an audience?

4. In these two papers, how does the Sierra Club link sprawl to other issues that people may feel more strongly about?

Responding to the Message

5. The "Global Warming" press release uses short paragraphs, numerous images, and short sentences, whereas the "Population Growth" press release uses longer paragraphs and scholarly footnotes. What does this tell you about the audience for each of these? Are there other ways in which these two releases target different audiences?

6. The Sierra Club seems to take for granted that population growth is itself a negative. Is this true? What are the advantages of population growth for particular regions? Is your region growing? How is your city or town managing its growth?

In Defense of Sprawl

Robert Bruegmann

Robert Bruegmann is a historian of architecture and planning and currently teaches in the department of Art History at the University of Illinois at Chicago. His 2005 study Sprawl: A Compact History *made the argument, rare in academia, that sprawl was not the unadulterated blight it was frequently assumed to be. In this article, he provides some historical context for the debate about suburban sprawl and rebuts the argument (made in this volume by the Sierra Club) that slowing sprawl will also help slow global warming. This article appeared in* Forbes *and on Forbes.com, a general-interest publication that covers business and tends to be friendly to business interests.*

If you really want to see urban sprawl, take a look at London.

Yes, it's true that Britain has some of the toughest anti-sprawl measures in the world today. But I mean 19th-century London—the miles and miles of brick row houses in Camberwell and Islington. If sprawl is the outward spread of settlement at constantly lower densities without any overall plan, then London in the 19th century sprawled outward at a rate not surpassed since then by any American city.

London's sprawl was attacked just like sprawl today. Although the middle-class families moving into those row houses were thrilled to have homes of their own, members of the artistic and intellectual elite were nearly unanimous in their condemnation. They castigated the row houses as ugly little boxes put up by greedy speculators willing to ruin the beautiful countryside in order to wrest the last penny out of every square inch of land. They were confident that they would become slums within a generation. The Duke of Wellington spoke for many when he denounced the railroads that made these suburban neighborhoods possible as only encouraging "common people to move around needlessly."

Of course, today these neighborhoods are widely considered to be the very essence of central London, the kind of place that the current elite feels must be protected at all cost from the terrible development going on at the new edge of the city. And so it has gone with every major boom period in urban history, from the ancient Romans until today. As each new group has moved up to newer and better housing by moving out from the central city, there has always been another group of individuals ready to denounce the entire process.

Today, the complaints about sprawl are louder than ever, but as in the past, they are built on an extremely shaky foundation of class-based aesthetic assumptions and misinformation. If history is any guide, some modern anti-sprawl prescriptions will prove as ineffective as the Duke of Wellington's. Others will actually backfire.

Even many of the most basic facts usually heard about sprawl are just wrong. Contrary to much accepted wisdom, sprawl in the U.S. is not accelerating. It is declining in the city and suburbs as average lot sizes are becoming smaller, and relatively few really affluent people are moving to the edge. This is especially true of the lowest-density cities of the American South and West. The Los Angeles urbanized area (the U.S. Census Bureau's functional definition of the city, which includes the city center and surrounding suburban areas) has become more than 25% denser over the last 50 years, making it the densest in the country.

This fact, together with the continued decline in densities in all large European urban areas, coupled with a spectacular rise in car ownership and use there, means that U.S. and European urban areas are in many ways converging toward a new 21st-century urban equilibrium. In short, densities will be high enough to provide urban amenities but low enough to allow widespread automobile ownership and use. The same dynamics are at work in the developing world. Although urban densities there are much higher than anything seen in the affluent West, they are plummeting even faster.

A lack of reliable information underlies many of the complaints against sprawl. Take just one example that is considered by many the gravest charge of all: that sprawl fosters increased automobile use; longer commutes; and more congestion, carbon emissions and, ultimately, global warming.

There is no reason to assume that high-density living is necessarily more sustainable or liable to damage the environment than low-density living. If everyone in the affluent West were to spread out in single-family houses across the countryside at historically low densities (and there is plenty of land to do this, even in the densest European counties), it is quite possible, with wind, solar, biomass and geothermal energy, to imagine a world in which most people could simply decouple themselves from the expensive and polluting utilities that were necessary in the old high-density industrial city. Potentially, they could collect all their own energy on-site and achieve carbon neutrality.

Certainly the remedy usually proposed by the anti-sprawl lobby—increasing densities and encouraging public transit—will not solve the global warming problem. Even if all urban dwellers the world over were brought up to "ideal" urban consumption standards—say, that of a Parisian family living in a small apartment and using only public transportation—it would not reduce energy use and greenhouse emissions, since it would require such large increases in energy use by so many families who today are so poor they can't afford the benefits of carbon-based energy.

Unless we deliberately keep most of the world's urban population in poverty, packing more people into existing cities won't solve anything. The solution is finding better sources of energy and more efficient means of doing everything. As we do this, it is quite possible that the most sustainable cities will be the least dense.

But let's assume for a moment that I'm entirely wrong and that sprawl is terrible. Could we stop it if we wanted to?

The record is not encouraging. The longest-running and best-known experiment was the one undertaken by Britain starting right after World War II. At that time, the British government gave unprecedented powers to planners to remake cities and took the draconian step of nationalizing all development rights to assure that these plans could be implemented. The famous 1944 Greater London plan, for example, envisioned a city bounded by a greenbelt. If there happened to be any excess population that couldn't be accommodated within the greenbelt, it was supposed to be accommodated in small, self-contained garden cities beyond the belt.

Did the plan work? In one sense it did: The greenbelt is still there, and some people consider that an aesthetic triumph. But the plan certainly did not stop sprawl. As usual, the planners were not able to predict the future with any accuracy. The population grew, household size declined and affluence rose faster than predicted. Development jumped right over the greenbelt—and not into discreet garden cities, because this policy was soon abandoned.

The ultimate result was that much of southeastern England has been urbanized. Moreover, because of the greenbelt, many car trips are longer than they would have been otherwise, contributing to the worst traffic congestion in Europe.

Finally, since the 1990s, with a new push to try to prevent greenfield development outside the belt, land and house prices have skyrocketed in London, creating an unprecedented crisis in housing affordability there and in virtually every other place that has tried extensive growth management.

Certainly sprawl has created some problems, just as every settlement pattern has. But the reason it has become the middle-class settlement pattern of choice is that it has given them much of the privacy, mobility and choice once enjoyed only by the wealthiest and most powerful.

Sprawl in itself is not a bad thing. What is bad is the concept of "sprawl" itself, which by lumping together all kinds of issues, some real and important and some trivial or irrelevant, has distracted us from many real and pressing urban issues. It also provides the dangerous illusion that there is a silver bullet solution to many of the discontents created by the fast and chaotic change that has always characterized city life.

Critical Reading Questions

Summarizing the Text

1. How does London's nineteenth-century sprawl compare to ours today? What point is Bruegmann making with this comparison?

2. Why won't making cities more compact and promoting public transportation have an effect on global warming?

Establishing the Context

3. Bruegmann argues that even if sprawl is a bad thing (and he does not admit that it is), it is probably unstoppable. What is his evidence for this? Can you find other examples of cities (Portland, Oregon, for example) that attempted to halt sprawl? What happened?

4. Opposing sprawl is a priority often associated with left-leaning groups and people, whereas conservative or pro-business groups oppose anti-sprawl measures. Why? How do these positions square with the philosophical orientations of those groups?

Responding to the Message

5. The sprawl argument often boils down to whether property owners have the right to do what they want with their land, or whether the government has the authority to determine what a city will look like. Where do you stand on this issue?

6. Bruegmann states that arguments against sprawl "are built on an extremely shaky foundation of class-based aesthetic assumptions and misinformation." What does he mean by this? Do you agree? Why or why not?

Word Cloud Representations of Loomis's and Bruemann's Articles

A "word cloud" is a graphic representation of a text, in which words that appear most frequently are larger. (Word-cloud generators tend to eliminate common words such as "and" or "the.") Displayed as a word cloud, aspects of piece of writing that might not be obvious at first reading or hearing jump out at the viewer. Several websites offer the free service of turning any text into a word cloud; these were generated by Wordle.net.

1. Judging from these word clouds, what words or types of words are most prevalent in each of the articles?

2. Does this word-prevalence depiction match your impression of the articles' emphases after you read them?

3. Are these depictions misleading, or do they accurately—if idiosyncratically—illustrate the articles' arguments?

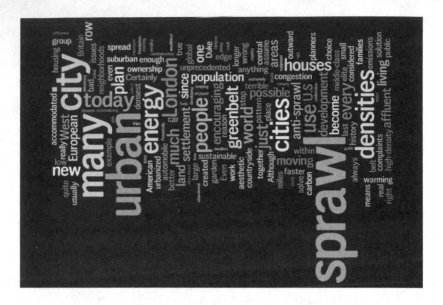

Protecting the Environment Through the Ownership Society

The National Center for Policy Analysis

The National Center for Policy Analysis (NCPA) is a conservative think tank, an orga-
nization that conducts research and produces reports intended to advocate for par-
ticular policies. According to its own materials, the NCPA's goal is to "develop and
promote private alternatives to government regulation and control, solving problems
by relying on the strength of the competitive, entrepreneurial private sector."

Introduction

A bedrock principle upon which the United States was founded is private property ownership as the ultimate guarantor of individual liberty and prosperity. Yet, more than 40 percent of the land is owned by
government. Leaving aside federal office buildings and military bases:

- The federal government owns and controls more than 650 million
  acres, totaling more than 29 percent of the land in the United States.[1]
- These lands include more than 83.6 million acres managed by the
  National Park Service, 193 million acres managed by the Forest Service
  and 258 million acres controlled by the Bureau of Land Management.[2]
- More than 96 million acres are set aside in national wildlife refuges
  supervised by the U.S. Fish and Wildlife Service.[3]

The government owns some of the nation's most magnificent landscapes and treasured resources but it also owns some lands with no particularly striking characteristics or special environmental value. It also manages other natural resources, like ocean fisheries. Unfortunately, the federal government has managed the public's natural resources as poorly as it has managed the federal budget. Unable to balance land use and preservation, government management of public lands has shifted between periods of exploitation or overuse and periods of "protection" or "preservation" bordering on neglect. The result of both has been degradation of the public lands and the wildlife that depends on them. Government efforts to regulate ocean resources have been even more schizophrenic, simultaneously subsidizing the fishing industry while imposing restrictions to halt declining fish populations.

President George W. Bush has promoted the concept of the "Ownership Society" as a solution to a variety of public policy issues including health care, housing and retirement. The idea behind the ownership society is that the welfare of individuals (and thus the nation) is best served by and directly related to the ability of people to control their own lives and pursue their own goals. After more than a hundred years of federal management of natural resources and legislative dominance of environmental law, it is time to re-explore the extent to which ownership can improve the environment.[4]

Garret Hardin provided a modern economic analysis of the idea that public ownership of natural resources leads to poor management and environmental degradation, using the example of herders who share common grazing land.[5] Herders who overgraze commonly-owned land reap all the benefits. Yet all herders share the cost of the resulting land degradation, whether or not they contributed to its cause. Consequently, herders who overgraze bear only part of the cost, while herders who resist the temptation in order to protect the land bear the immediate cost of their forbearance, but realize only a fraction of the benefits. This is because the benefits of their good behavior (long-term preservation) are shared by all herders, not just those who act to preserve the land. Indeed, their selfless actions may have no effect on overgrazing—except to increase the share of the common pasture available to the others. Everyone, therefore, faces perverse incentives to overgraze. To the degree that they act on those incentives, environmental destruction results.

Public lands are also a commons, facing the same problem many other valuable common-pool resources face: overuse. Public commons are controlled through the political process, leading to disparate, sometimes contradictory and shifting goals for their management. As a result, public land managers are often rewarded for making what others perceive as perverse decisions.

This study will show that many of the environmental problems faced by public lands can be solved through a property rights
approach. The environmental management of resources for which
strict private property rights cannot be established due to technological or political reasons can be improved by creating new markets or
economic incentives.

A previous NCPA study, "Protecting the Environment through
the Ownership Society—Part One," applied this concept to agriculture
subsidies, subsidized flood insurance and the Endangered Species
Act.[6] It showed how government programs and policies, some instituted more than a century ago, are causing environmental harm.
In Part Two, the analysis is extended to government ownership and
management of public lands and to ocean fisheries.

National Parks, National Problem

The mission of the National Park Service is to preserve land for the
"benefit and enjoyment of the people." The system now consists of 390
parks, historic sites, scenic rivers and recreation areas totaling nearly
84 million acres.[7]

Problems became apparent almost immediately after the Park
Service was created in 1916, as the goals of "preservation" and providing for the "enjoyment of the people" arguably conflicted. Too many
people using anything will destroy it, and parks—many of which are
ecologically fragile—are no exception. In addition, actions taken to
enhance visitors' short-term enjoyment can have disastrous long-term
consequences.

For example, to encourage the enjoyment of the parks by the
maximum number of people, the Park Service maintained low or no
entrance fees for most of the 20th century. It also suppressed the natural fire cycle in the parks—spending billions of dollars fighting and
preventing forest fires. In addition, predators were actively hunted
and trapped in order to increase populations of animals popular
with park visitors—deer, elk, pronghorn sheep and bison.[8]

The Park Service was successful in both attracting visitors (287 million
people in 1999) and increasing the number of grazing animals—but
success came at a high price.[9]

- High visitor numbers, low fees and limited congressional appro-
  priations have led to a record multibillion-dollar backlog in repairs
  and maintenance.

- The absence of predators to keep their populations in check and
  periodic fires to stimulate plant growth led to an overpopulation
  of grazing animals.[10]

- In Yellowstone, elk have almost entirely driven out deer, bighorn sheep, pronghorn sheep and even beaver populations, or pushed them into poorer habitats with less nourishment, leaving them prey to disease and boom-and-bust population cycles.

Furthermore, in the most popular parks, visitors regularly complain of air pollution from automobiles, cars interfering with scenic views and traffic jams hampering the natural experience.

Changing Park Policies   In recent years, the Park Service has begun to shift its focus away from providing visitor enjoyment toward preservation. It has raised entrance fees substantially for the most popular parks. Management goals for individual parks are also shifting. For example:[11]

- In Yellowstone, elk have been relocated, wolves—once extirpated within the region—have been reintroduced, naturally occurring fires have been allowed to burn unless they threaten human lives or property, and limits have been placed on the number and types of watercraft and snowmobiles in the park.

- In the Everglades National Park, a multibillion-dollar water-flow and wetlands restoration effort has begun.

- In Yosemite, in order to restore a more natural experience, park officials limit the number of cars entering on busy days, closed some camp sites, cabins, roads and trails, and plan to implement a shuttle service for visitors throughout the park (a similar plan is being considered for Yellowstone).

- In the Grand Canyon, limits have been placed on the number of plane and helicopter flyovers.

Changes Spark Controversies   The Park Service's shifting focus toward preservation has not been without controversy. User groups and communities that are economically dependent on park visitors have objected to the increases in entrance fees, camp closures, and restrictions on vehicle access and activities.[12] Many also argue:

- Even if additional revenues from higher fees are used to fix the maintenance backlog, it is a form of double billing since visitors have already paid for park access through taxes; and higher fees can be a barrier to park use by lower-income Americans.

- Concerning the purported damage caused by motorized vehicles, a recent Park Service report found little if any evidence that the number of snowmobiles entering the parks during the winter harms park wildlife.[13]

- Allowing lightning-sparked wildfires to burn is dangerous since they occasionally spread beyond park boundaries and destroy homes and businesses.

Another major controversy has been the reintroduction of wolves in Yellowstone in order to reduce elk overpopulation. Wolves do not stay within park boundaries and pose a threat to livestock on neighboring ranches. In order to lessen opposition, the nonprofit Defenders of Wildlife established a fund to compensate livestock owners for losses to wolf predation.[14]

However, problems in Yellowstone have brought planned wolf reintroduction efforts on other public lands to a virtual standstill. As predicted, wolves have thrived. And as expected, some livestock has been killed. But many ranchers say their claims for compensation have been unjustly denied because of disputes over whether wolves caused the deaths. Some also claim the compensation did not equal the fair market value of their losses. And while the wolves have had the desired impact on the elk population within the park, wolf predation of elk outside the park has begun to raise the ire of sportsmen's groups. They note the decline in elk and fear future restrictions on hunting.

These controversies have prompted members of Congress to propose altering the mission of the Park Service laid out in the 1916 National Park Service Organic Act.[15] At a congressional hearing, Rep. Steve Pearce (R-N.M.), Chairman of the House Resources Subcommittee on National Parks, Recreation and Public Lands, criticized recent park management decisions that appeared to favor preservation over visitor access and enjoyment, stating, "I don't view the Organic Act as Congress' attempt to preserve parks *from* Americans (emphasis added)."[16]

In particular, Pearce targeted what he believed was an attempt to freeze time, rather than allowing the parks to change. "Success should not be determined exclusively by whether the resources look like they did when our ancestors landed on Plymouth Rock," he said.[17]

For now, the national park management is caught between the conflicting goals of preservation and visitor enjoyment. The multibillion-dollar maintenance backlog continues to grow and has become an annual albatross hanging around the neck of multiple Congresses and presidential administrations. In each election cycle, environmental lobbyists cite poor maintenance as evidence that neither Congress nor the administration care about the environment....

Conclusion

President Bush's innovative concept of the ownership society is indebted to Western intellectuals. Great thinkers from Aristotle to Locke to the American founders recognized that secure individual property rights are an effective means of promoting both individual happiness and social welfare, and of maintaining political liberty. However, they did not recognize that property rights could also be used effectively to protect the environment.

People typically use their property to increase their well-being, which, as Adam Smith argued, redounds to the benefit of society. But property use comes with responsibilities. First, property owners bear the costs of the bad decisions they make with their property if their choices result in economic losses or in the destruction of the property itself. Secondly, they have the responsibility to use their property in ways that do not violate the rights of others—and should be penalized when they do.

Government ownership and management of natural resources severs the link between the decisions of those using the resources and the negative consequences of their choices. It leads to a variety of economic ills, but also results in environmental destruction. Applying the concept of the ownership society would reduce incentives to destroy the environment. Indeed, it could create positive incentives for entrepreneurs to provide or expand environmental amenities on privately owned land, including former federally owned land, and to protect and enhance the world's fisheries.[*]

Notes

1. This does not include inland surface water controlled by the U.S. Army Corps of Engineers. See "Federal Land and Building Ownership" Republican Study Committee, U.S. House of Representatives, updated May 19, 2005; available at http://www.house.gov/pence/rsc/doc/Federal_Land_Ownership_05012005.pdf; or see, "Public Land Statistics of the United States 1999: Part I—Land Resources and Information," U.S. Bureau of Land Management, Vol. 184, March 2000, Table 1-3; available at http://www.blm.gov/natacq/pls99/99p11-3.pdf.

2. "The National Park System Acreage," National Park Service, undated; available at http://www.nps.gov/legacy/acreage.html; and "BLM Facts," U.S. Bureau of Land Management, updated November 28, 2006; available at http://www.blm.gov/nhp/facts/index.htm.

3. "America's National Wildlife Refuges," U.S. Fish and Wildlife Service, Fact Sheet, July 2002; available at http://www.fws.gov/refuges/generalInterest/factSheets/FactSheetAmNationalWild.pdf.

4. John Baden, "Destroying the Environment: Government Mismanagement of Our Natural Resources," National Center for Policy Analysis, Policy Report No. 124, 1986.

5. Garrett Hardin, "Tragedy of the Commons," *Science*, Vol. 162, November 11, 1986, pages 1,243-48.

---

[*]NOTE: Nothing written here should be construed as necessarily reflecting the views of the National Center for Policy Analysis or as an attempt to aid or hinder the passage of any bill before Congress.

6. H. Sterling Burnett, "Protecting the Environment through the Ownership Society—Part One," National Center for Policy Analysis, Policy Report No. 282, January 2006.

7. National Park Service, "History," Web page, undated; available at http://www.nps.gov/aboutus/history.htm.

8. John Baden, "Destroying the Environment: Government Mismanagement of Our Natural Resources," National Center for Policy Analysis, Policy Report No. 124, 1986.

9. U.S. National Park Service, "Frequently Asked Questions," undated; available at http://www.nps.gov/faqs.htm.

10. For instance, the population of deer in the Kaibab Plateau region of the Grand Canyon exploded from approximately 15,000 in 1918 to as many as 100,000 by 1923. In 1924, 60 percent of the deer died of starvation. See John Baden, "Destroying the Environment: Government Mismanagement of our Natural Resources," National Center for Policy Analysis, Policy Report No. 124, 1986.

11. National Park Service, "Program Goals, Purpose and Definitions," updated April 17, 2006; available at http://science.nature.nps.gov/im/monitor/ProgramGoals.cfm.

12. See, for instance, Peter Chilson, "The Land Is Still Public, but It's No Longer Free," HighCountryNews.org, October 13, 1997; available at http://www.hcn.org/servlets/hcn.Article?article_id=3693; and Sarah Foster, "Park Wars, Part 1: Debate Roars over Future of Yosemite," WorldNetDaily.com, May 12, 2003; available at http://www.worldnetdaily.com/news/article.asp?ARTICLE_ID=32503.

13. Dan Berman, "NPS Urges Congress to Avoid Changing the Organic Act," Greenwire, December 14, 2005.

14. Defenders of Wildlife, "Wildlife: Wolves," Web page, undated; available at http://www.defenders.org/wildlife/new/wolves.html.

15. Dan Berman, "NPS Urges Congress to Avoid Changing the Organic Act," Greenwire, December 14, 2005.

16. *Ibid.*

17. *Ibid.*

Critical Reading Questions

Summarizing the Text

1. What does the NCPA mean by the "ownership society"? Why is this an important concept in this report?

2. The NCPA does not explicitly argue, in this excerpt, for privatizing or even partially privatizing the management of the national parks. What is the argument of this section? How might this smaller argument contribute to a larger argument about privatization?

Establishing the Context

3. A PBS documentary series called the National Parks system "America's best idea." Implicit in this documentary was the assumption that what was "best" about this idea was that the parks were protected, forever, from the pressures of private development or the profit motive. The NCPA's report, though, asks us to reconsider whether this is such a great idea. How might privatization or partial privatization affect the national parks?

4. Unlike the Sierra Club press releases included in this chapter, this report is not intended for a wide audience but is primarily circulated among politicians, staffers, government administrators, and media organizations. What about the rhetoric of this report demonstrates that it is intended to sway people who have direct influence over these policies, rather than the general public?

Responding to the Message

5. Do you use the national parks? Do you have a favorite park—Yellowstone, Joshua Tree, the Great Smokies, or another? How do you think that the park or the experience of visiting the park would change if private industry were given a greater role in running the park, or if private businesses were allowed to operate within the park?

6. The National Center for Policy Analysis often advocates a "libertarian" approach to public issues. "Libertarianism" seeks to minimize the role of government in people's lives and in society as a whole, and it advocates for much greater freedom for individuals and businesses. Research libertarianism. How do you feel about it? Should the government provide only roads, police, and an army, and let the private sector create innovative solutions to society's other needs and problems (as many libertarians believe)? Or should the government serve to protect citizens from dangers and make decisions about people's lives?

CLUSTER TWO: HOW PRIVATE IS YOUR ONLINE SPACE?

Facebook, MySpace Confront Privacy Loophole

Emily Steel and
Jessica E. Vascellaro

Emily Steel is a reporter and Jessica Vascellaro is the deputy bureau chief of the Media & Marketing Bureau for the Wall Street Journal, *a national newspaper and news website based in New York that covers the worlds of business and finance. In this news article from May 21, 2010, Steel and Vascellaro explain the "privacy loophole" that Facebook and MySpace used to sell user data to advertising companies, contrary to their own assurances that they would keep user data confidential.*

Facebook, MySpace and several other social-networking sites have been sending data to advertising companies that could be used to find consumers' names and other personal details, despite promises they don't share such information without consent.

The practice, which most of the companies defended, sends user names or ID numbers tied to personal profiles being viewed when users click on ads. After questions were raised by *The Wall Street Journal*, Facebook and MySpace moved to make changes. By Thursday morning Facebook had rewritten some of the offending computer code.

Advertising companies are receiving information that could be used to look up individual profiles, which, depending on the site and the information a user has made public, include such things as a person's real name, age, hometown and occupation.

Several large advertising companies identified by the *Journal* as receiving the data, including Google Inc.'s DoubleClick and Yahoo Inc.'s Right Media, said they were unaware of the data being sent to them from the social-networking sites, and said they haven't made use of it.

Across the Web, it's common for advertisers to receive the address of the page from which a user clicked on an ad. Usually, they receive nothing more about the user than an unintelligible string of letters and numbers that can't be traced back to an individual. With social networking sites, however, those addresses typically include user names that could direct advertisers back to a profile page full of personal information. In some cases, user names are people's real names.

Most social networks haven't bothered to obscure user names or ID numbers from their Web addresses, said Craig Wills, a professor of computer science at Worcester Polytechnic Institute, who has studied the issue.

The sites may have been breaching their own privacy policies as well as industry standards, which say sites shouldn't share and advertisers shouldn't collect personally identifiable information without users' permission. Those policies have been put forward by advertising and Internet companies in arguments against the need for government regulation.

The problem comes as social networking sites—and in particular Facebook—face increasing scrutiny over their privacy practices from consumers, privacy advocates and lawmakers.

At the same time, lawmakers are preparing legislation to govern websites' tactics for collecting information about consumers, and the way that information is used to target ads.

In addition to Facebook and MySpace, LiveJournal, Hi5, Xanga and Digg also sent advertising companies the user name or ID number of the page being visited. (MySpace is owned by News Corp., which also owns *The Wall Street Journal*.) Twitter—which doesn't have ads on profile pages—also was found to pass Web addresses including user names of profiles being visited on Twitter.com when users clicked other links on the profiles.

For most social-networking sites, the data identified the profile being viewed but not necessarily the person who clicked on the ad or link. But Facebook went further than other sites, in some cases signaling which user name or ID was clicking on the ad as well as the user name or ID of the page being viewed. By seeing what ads a user clicked on, an advertiser could tell something about a user's interests.

Ben Edelman, an assistant professor at Harvard Business School who studies Internet advertising, reviewed the computer code on the seven sites at the request of the *Journal*.

"If you are looking at your profile page and you click on an ad, you are telling that advertiser who you are," he said of how Facebook operated, if a user had clicked through a specific path, before the fix. Mr. Edelman said he had sent a letter on Thursday to the Federal Trade Commission asking them to investigate Facebook's practices specifically.

The sharing of users' personally identifiable data was first flagged in a paper by researchers at AT&T Labs and Worcester Polytechnic Institute last August. The paper, which drew little attention at the time, evaluated practices at 12 social networking sites including Facebook, Twitter and MySpace and found multiple ways that outside companies could access user data.

The researchers said in an interview they had contacted the sites, which some sites confirmed. But nine months later, the issue still exists.

The issue is particularly significant for Facebook on two fronts: the company has been pushing users to make more of their personal information public and the site requires users to use their actual names when registering on the site.

A Facebook spokesman acknowledged it has been passing data to ad companies that could allow them to tell if a particular user was clicking an ad. After being contacted by the *Journal*, Facebook said it changed its software to eliminate the identifying code tied to the user from being transmitted.

"We were recently made aware of one case where if a user takes a specific route on the site, advertisers may see that they clicked on their own profile and then clicked on an ad," the Facebook spokesman said. "We fixed this case as soon as we heard about it."

Facebook said its practices are now consistent with how advertising works across the Web. The company passes the "user ID of the page but not the person who clicked on the ad," the company spokesman said. "We don't consider this personally identifiable information and our policy does not allow advertisers to collect user information without the user's consent."

The company said it also has been testing changing the formatting for the text it shares with advertisers so that it doesn't pass through any user names or IDs.

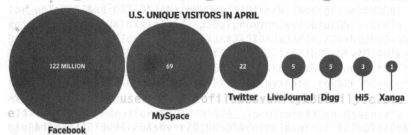

MySpace, Hi5, Digg, Xanga and Live Journal said they don't consider their user names or ID numbers to be personally identifiable, because unlike Facebook, consumers are not required to submit their real names when signing up for an account. They also said since they are passing along the user name of the page the ad is on, not for the person clicking on the ad, there is nothing advertisers can do with the data beyond seeing on what page their ad appeared.

MySpace said in a statement it is only sharing the ID name users create for the site, which permits access only to the information that a user makes publicly available on the site.

Nevertheless, a MySpace spokeswoman said the site is "currently implementing a methodology that will obfuscate the 'FriendID' in any URL that is passed along to advertisers."

A Twitter spokeswoman said passing along the Web address happens when people click a link from any Web page. "This is just how the Internet and browsers work," she said.

Although Digg said it masks a user's name when they click on an ad and scrambles data before sharing with outside advertising companies, the site does pass along user names to ad companies when a user visits a profile page. "It's the information about the page that you are visiting, not you as a visitor," said Chas Edwards, Digg's chief revenue officer.

The advertising companies say they don't control the information a website chooses to send them. "Google doesn't seek in any way to make any use of any user names or IDs that their URLs may contain," a Google spokesman said in a statement.

"We prohibit clients from sending personally identifiably information to us," said Anne Toth, Yahoo's head of privacy. "We have told them. We don't want it. You shouldn't be sending it to us. If it happens to be there, we are not looking for it."

Critical Reading Questions

Summarizing the Text

1. Exactly what kind of information were the advertisers receiving, and how was this information generated?

2. How is this kind of information gathering and sharing different from what these companies usually do?

Establishing the Context

3. Internet companies and websites that track your behavior online generally try to reassure Web surfers by saying that your *personal* information isn't linked only your IP address (the unique identifier of your computer or Internet router). How is this meant to calm users' fears?

4. Read the graph that accompanies this article. What information does this graph provide? How does it comment on the article itself?

Responding to the Message

5. Every time you click on a link when you are online, that information—where you were, what you were looking at, and what you clicked—is recorded and, probably, sold. How do you feel about this?

6. This article is a news story; the writers are not supposed to express any opinion on the subject. Do you think that this is an objective treatment of this issue? If not, where do you see the writers forwarding an opinion?

The Relationship Between Facebook and Privacy: It's Really Complicated

Matthew Ingram

Matthew Ingram is a Toronto-based technology journalist and columnist. In this article for the technology news site Gigaom, he defends—somewhat—Facebook from its fierce and (he believes) underinformed critics. Some of these critics speak back in the comments section, as well.

The tension between Facebook and its users—and governments, and advocacy groups—over privacy is one of the biggest thorns in the company's side right now, as it tries to balance the demands of the network (and of advertisers) with the desires of users, and with the law. And all of this is taking place in an environment where the very meaning of what is "private" and what is "public" is being redefined, by Facebook and other online giants such as Google, and even users themselves sometimes can't decide what information they want to share with the world and what they don't.

Over the past few weeks, the social network has been caught at the center of a privacy maelstrom, with consumer groups attacking it—15 of them filed a formal letter of complaint with the Federal Trade Commission late yesterday—senators sending threatening letters, and growing numbers of users canceling or deactivating their accounts over privacy concerns. The company has been struggling to respond to security holes that expose private data such as chats, and a survey released yesterday by *Consumer Reports* says that more than 50 percent of people engage in what it calls "risky behavior" on the social network. Another survey of Facebook users finds that their use of the network is inherently shallow and largely unfulfilling.

Even as he is being hailed as a billionaire genius akin to Microsoft founder Bill Gates, the empire Mark Zuckerberg has built seems to be taking fire from critics on all sides. But is all of this criticism fair? Probably not. It's true that Facebook's launch of recent changes involving "instant personalization" and the creation of community pages related to users' profile interests has been badly handled. And it doesn't help that many people are confused by how to adjust their privacy settings, how to control what information is displayed, and how to disable applications (we put together a comprehensive guide to the new changes and how to disable them if you want to).

But it's also true that Facebook exists, and has accumulated almost half a billion users worldwide, because it makes it easy for people to connect with their friends and family and to share things with them: photos, thoughts, social games, goofy gifts and yes, even birth dates. Plenty of people clearly want to do this, even after they have been repeatedly warned about the risks, because they believe the trade-off is worth it. And perhaps Facebook doesn't make it as clear as it could what is involved, or how to fine-tune its privacy controls—but at the same time, some of the onus for doing these things has to fall to users.

The complaint filed by the 15 consumer advocacy groups states that:

> Facebook now discloses personal information to the public that Facebook users previously restricted. Facebook now discloses personal information to third parties that Facebook users previously did not make available. These changes violate user expectations, diminish user privacy, and contradict Facebook's own representations. These business practices are Unfair and Deceptive Trade Practices.

The complaint specifically mentions the "instant personalization" feature that allows Microsoft's Doc.com, Yelp, and Pandora to personalize their services when a user is logged in to Facebook, and also refers to the fact that Facebook connects profile details such as hometown, movie and music preferences, etc. to public "community pages."

Those criticisms are all well and good, and the "instant personalization" feature probably wouldn't have drawn as much fire if it wasn't turned on by default, but Facebook does allow people to turn it off, and it tells them that their interests will be connected to community pages and become public, and allows them to opt out. It's not clear from the complaint what the 15 privacy groups would rather the social network do, except not share any of that information at all. But here's the rub: personalization is a useful feature, and community pages might be as well (it's still too early to tell).

The *Consumer Reports* survey, meanwhile, says 52 percent of people post risky information on Facebook. It looked at 2,000 online households in January and found that 9 percent of social network users had been the victim of some form of online abuse in the past year such as malware infections, scams, identity theft or harassment. The report warned about a number of different "risky" activities such as posting your address, when you are home, and so on. But it also mentioned posting photos of family members as a risky behavior (stalking), along with your birth date (potential for identity theft), and other fairly commonplace activities. Isn't posting photos and names and birthdays part of what Facebook is about? It wouldn't be much of a social network without them.

Another survey, done by a Dutch company, interviewed readers of *Fast Company* about Facebook, including asking questions designed to determine whether they were really getting what they wanted out of the social network. The study determined that many users were not really engaging in deep social relationships and therefore weren't getting a lot out of being on the network. "Online social networks make it easy for people to accumulate friends rapidly and to make commitments easily," the study said, concluding that "what define social networks most [is] a lack of depth in relationships."

But even this supposes a false dichotomy, between the connections we make through a social network and "real" relationships, where we phone each other and talk about our personal problems or the death of a loved one. The idea behind social networks, as described by sociologists, is that they help to create an "ambient awareness" of significant people in our lives—friends, family, acquaintances, co-workers—and allow us to stay in touch with them in some small way, not that they replace or mimic real-world relationships. If anything, they should help strengthen them.

And privacy? That's complicated in the real world, too— Facebook didn't invent that, or even pioneer it online. People have been breaching each other's privacy for decades. Just because Facebook is making some mistakes doesn't mean it should become the lightning rod for all of our pent-up dissatisfaction with normal human behavior.

Excerpts from the Comment Thread for this article

- *docthrax* Thursday, May 6 2010

  Facebook is creating a lot o problems it just not that it have privacy problem it has other problems too ...

- *bryan s* Thursday, May 6 2010

  "Just because Facebook is making some mistakes doesn't mean it should become the lightning rod for all of our pent-up dissatisfaction with normal human behavior."

  No, it should be a lightning rod because it is one of the largest publicly accessible database or personal informtation in existence, and constantly makes changes to expose that data and then telling its users. Do you really not get that?

- *Mathew Ingram* Friday, May 7 2010

  I'm not saying it shouldn't be criticized at all, Bryan, or that we shouldn't point out mistakes it is making. Just trying to keep things in perspective.

- *mr-crash* Thursday, May 6 2010

I think the overall theme here from privacy advocates etc is "You changed the rules by default – that's not very nice" and the response by facebook is essentially "but you can turn it off".

The issue here then is not only one of privacy but one of trust. Substantial changes to the direction a platform is going in are understandably of concern to some portion of the users who feel ill at ease perhaps not just for what facebook is doing now, but what it might do in the future.

Facebook does understand this. At f8, all announcements about this were heavily couched in terms to make this as appealing as possible to developers, without sounding scary to the general public.

But I think the response by Facebook is still insufficient. When you see how Google reacted (albeit belatedly) after the fracas over Buzz, It might seem more appropriate for Facebook to at least have offered an option across the network to explicitly turn it on or off – rather than engaging it by default.

On a more technical front, the recent private chat exploit seems not to engender much faith in their ability to keep things together in that respect either.

- *Mathew Ingram* Friday, May 7 2010

I agree that the opt-in nature of some of the new features was a bad move, and that Facebook needs to be careful about losing trust.

- *MacSmiley* Thursday, May 6 2010

Sorry, I'm not giving Facebook a break in this regard.

FB accumulated 400 million users on the premise that "what happened on the Facebook stayed on the Facebook". Now Facebook is changing tack and is FORCING users to publicize sensitive personal information that can be easily abused. Choices are being obliterated.

There's no choice where Pages are concerned. Either you link your profile to public Pages, or you have a blank profile. Only a double bind would be worse.

RE: Instant Personalization. There is no doubt in my mind that Facebook has deliberately made it hard to opt-out. One SINGLE click should do the trick. But it takes clicking 5 different settings to plug the holes (for now, based on only 3 partners), and even that's not a done deal??

And if you want out altogether? Ha! Deactivation versus deletion. That's a joke. If you don't already know the URL for the REAL delete your account page, it takes what? 8 clicks to get there?? It's an obstacle course, and Zuckerberg's no dumb bunny. He knows full well that people give up half-way through the process.

Zuckerberg does not deserve the benefit of the doubt you so generously give him.

Facebook makes a huge deal of how many locks they allow you to have on the front door, and all the while it's shipping your belongings out the windows and the back door.

I don't know why people put up with this nonsense. I won't.

- *ghosh* Thursday, May 6 2010

  Interesting article. In fact Electronic Frontier Foundation came out with time line on the changes over privacy controls over time in FB. Here the link, you might want to check it out Facebook's Eroding Privacy Policy: A Timeline http://eff.org/n/10206

- *Mathew Ingram* Friday, May 7 2010

  Thanks for the link, Ghosh.

- *M. Edward (Ed) Borasky* Thursday, May 6 2010

  Actually, Om, it's really not complicated at all. The first few times Facebook started making more stuff public, there was a lot of noise from the blogosphere, but ordinary people weren't frightened and even the rabid naysayers were still maintaining a presence on Facebook.

  This time it's different. The US Senate is involved. Attorneys are involved. Defects have caused privacy breaches beyond even what was intended by Facebook. And executives of Facebook are saying, "Are we perfect? No." The question they *aren't* asking is "Are we *competent*?" And sadly, I think the answer to that one is "Hell, No!"

  Do I think Facebook will survive? Probably. But they are going to need a serious competence transplant, and *fast!* It's really not complicated at all – they're simply a bunch of incompetent managers who've stumbled onto something that's taken the world by storm and can't manage it.

  And yes, I still have a Facebook account. But I don't think I will for long – it's not giving me any value.

- *vnpshop* Friday, May 7 2010

  Ya, it's complicated, Facebook does understand this. At f8, all announcements about this were heavily couched in terms to make this as appealing as possible to developers, without sounding scary to the general public.

- *mr-crash* Saturday, May 8 2010

  Awesome spam that copies bits from my previous comment. Clever ;)

"all announcements about this were heavily couched in terms to make this as appealing as possible to developers, without sounding scary to the general public"

- *gbp* Friday, May 7 2010

  More than half a billion accounts which includes companies, events ... and such.

- *John Zhu* Friday, May 7 2010

  I agree w/ MacSmiley. I can't give FB a break on this. The general issue of privacy may be complicated, but here's something that isn't: People hate default opt-ins. FB surely knows this (especially considering its prior experience with Beacon), but went ahead and did it anyway with Instant Personalization and didn't tell you how to opt out. We all know that it's more profitable for FB if its users share more personal info. It's also secure in the knowledge that barring some catastrophic breach of privacy, its users aren't likely to defect en masse. So in the absence of a financial motive for the company to really protect its users' private info, you have to rely on the company's ethical standards to protecting privacy. That's why FB's "ask for forgiveness rather than permission" approach is a cause for concern. The eff.org link someone provided below is an excellent analysis of how FB's attitude on privacy has changed over its existence.

- *fjpoblam* Friday, May 7 2010

  Regarding the relationship of Facebook to privacy: may it not, simply, be summed up into one word, "enmity"?

  Facebook's Zuckerberg Says The Age of Privacy is Over http://bit.ly/aYMnrl

- *causerie* Friday, May 7 2010

  As MacSmiley notes, there is no true opt-out for the community pages. Facebook will delete the info on your profile if you choose to "opt out." This is tantamount to extortion, which, I have a theory, is exactly where they're going: they'll offer a pay option to keep your info truly private.

- *Arun Krishnan* Friday, May 7 2010

  Hi Matthew

  Not to get all Confucian on your blog – but it does seem to me that the essence of a social networking site is trust. And Facebook seems to be on the verge of losing that trust by putting very sensitive privacy policies in place—on an opt-out basis.

  Facebook has always been an innovative site. Innovation is important – but it has to happen responsibly. Privacy policies could very well end up being the subprime mortgages of the advertising industry. With the new data sharing policies, we are once incident away from an unfortunate end user and an angry government getting involved in a big mess.

Thanks for the posts and for your point of view. Enjoy the weekend.

Arun Krishnan

blog.pontiflex.com

- Mathew Ing*ram* Friday, May 7 2010

  Thanks for the comment, Arun. You and others are right that trust is the central issue—and with government already circling around the privacy problem, it could definitely turn into a big mess for all concerned.

- *Jtoll* Friday, May 7 2010

  Trust is the central issue BUT all other forms of trust across the web have been destroyed by hackers/crackers/assorted criminals/et al ...

  FB will not get back the trust, they are leaving mistrust in their wake.

  They will have to completely change how they "monetize" the product if they want to maintain their user growth.

- *Chucky* Friday, May 7 2010

  There was a breach in Facebook few days back ... i think it had a crash or something and all personal files locked were open to friends in the groups ... later those people diagnosed the problem and said it will be closed for a few hours ... .was very shocked to hear this!!!!!!

- *ken* Friday, May 7 2010

  Mathew, you end your piece by saying that we have been invading each other's privacy for decades, which may be true, but you must admit that FB takes our personal information and shoves it into the public sphere like no other organization in history. MZ honestly believes that privacy does not exist any more and is willing to build powerful tools that make that believe a self-fulfilling prophecy.

- *Mathew Ingram* Friday, May 7 2010

  I'm not sure whether Zuckerberg believes that privacy doesn't exist any more—much of that talk is based on a single offhand comment from an anonymous FB employee. I think he and Facebook are trying to find a happy medium between the comfort of users and the needs of their business, and they clearly haven't found it yet.

- Sanjay Maharaj Friday, May 7 2010

  Why is it that each time Facebook comes out with new features which deals with privacy they seem to do a very poor job on the PR end of it in terms of not only explaining in detail how it works but they fail to sell it as a benefit to their users.

  They had similar problems with Beacon. They need to do a better job on this.

- *alan p* Friday, May 7 2010

  "Complicated" is not the word I'd use. ... "bloody simple" more like. The financial value of any user in a freeconomic service is the net present value of their future spend, and the more Facebook can expose of it to merchants and advertisers and Joe Public etc, the more of their valuation they can justify.

  It's worth republishing the link ghosh put up below re the steady erosion:

  Facebook's Eroding Privacy Policy: A Timeline http://eff.org/n/10206

  Given that their business model demands continual privacy erosion, and competition is not mitigating this, the only recourse is regulation.

Critical Reading Questions

Summarizing the Text

1. Why are the critics of Facebook wrong, according to Ingram?
2. Ingram differentiates between what people do on social networks and what they do in "real" relationships. How does this point relate to his larger thesis?

Establishing the Context

3. In the comments thread, Ingram responds to some of his critics. How does this feature of online journalism affect the relationship between the publication (website) and its readers?
4. Read all of the comments included below Ingram's article. Comment threads are often dismissed as being a place for misinformed or malicious "trolls" to leave anonymous, irrelevant comments. Do these arguments fall into this category? Do they provide any additional insight on the issue that Ingram doesn't cover in his article?

Responding to the Message

5. Ingram's criticism of Facebook centers not on the company's privacy policies but on how the company *explained* itself—it is a PR problem, he believes. In this, Ingram makes a similar argument to Dylan Martin in the student point-counterpoint editorial later in this chapter. How do Martin's and Ingram's arguments differ? Sketch out their claims, reasons, and implicit assumptions.

Privacy Is Dead on Facebook—Get Over It
Helen Popkin

Helen Popkin writes on popular culture and technology for MSNBC.com and many other forums. Embracing the Internet model of journalism and cultural commentary, Popkin is on Facebook and Twitter and blogs, as well. In this article, she comes down hard on the CEOs of Internet companies who are trying to persuade their customers that privacy isn't important. This article originally appeared in the Technotica section of MSNBC.com, a news website associated with the cable TV network MSNBC—itself a joint venture between a traditional media company (NBC) and the computer-software giant Microsoft.

Once upon a time at Facebook, or so the story from an anonymous Facebook employee goes, there was a general password employees could use to access Facebook accounts. For kicks and giggles, some Facebook employees, including the one recently interviewed on the Rumpus Web site, did just that.

Two Facebook employees got fired, says Anonymous Facebook Employee, for manipulating user profile information. Others, such as Anonymous Facebook Employee, just peeked.

Is this story even true? Regarding the veracity of Anonymous Facebook Employee's claims, a company spokesperson stated via e-mail: "This piece contains the kind of inaccuracies and misrepresentations you would expect from something sourced 'anonymously,' and we'll leave it at that."

Specifics of the alleged inaccuracies above were not addressed, nor was this other thing: You know all those e-mails you send and receive on Facebook, along with those sent and received by more than 350 million users worldwide? They live forever on a Facebook database that doesn't require a tool and a reason to access it; just a search query, says Anonymous Facebook Employee.

Shocked? Whether or not this story is in any way true, you shouldn't be. Facebook founder and CEO Mark Zuckerberg recently went on record speaking the same sentiments blathered by the big money data farmers that came before him; none of the cool kids care about privacy. Neither should you.

"You have zero privacy anyway," Sun Microsystems chief executive Scott McNealy famously said in 1999. "Get over it."

This past December, Google Chief Executive Eric Schmidt glibly stated in a CNBC interview, "If you have something that you don't want anyone to know, maybe you shouldn't be doing it in the first place."

Does that include your address, credit card statements, social security number, medical records, legal and financial documents, competitive business secrets, fan fiction, bad poetry, love letters or any ill-advised photos or videos taken in one's hormone-addled youth? Schmidt didn't say.

Then, last week, during an interview at the 2010 TechCrunch awards, Facebook's Zuckerberg said this:

" ... in the last 5 or 6 years, blogging has taken off in a huge way and all these different services that have people sharing all this information. People have really gotten comfortable not only sharing more information and different kinds, but more openly and with more people. That social norm is just something that's evolved over time."

Zuckerberg was addressing last month's latest privacy evisceration on Facebook; the one that ripped the curtain off user activities, photos, even birthdays, making a whole lot of information previously controlled by users available for anyone on God's green Google (advertisers, identity thieves, stalkers et al.) to see.

What's more, the thick coating of doublespeak made understanding and changing Facebook privacy settings less intuitive than ever.

For some casual Internet users, Zuckerberg's smooth'n savvy sound bites may seem to make sense. It's true, we as a society are less bashful (a lot of us full-on narcissistic) when it comes to sharing the personal minutiae—be it breakfast choice or sexual exploits—previously kept behind closed doors.

But choosing to share your bra color in your Facebook status in an effort to spread breast cancer awareness—or just because —a whole lot different than having your metaphorical shirt ripped off in the middle of the roller rink by a social network that built its empire luring you and assuring that you that it had nothing but respect for your privacy.

Facebook stomped predecessors MySpace and Friendster not (only) because it wasn't lousy with glitter GIFs or hobbled by crippled servers seemingly riddled with the consumption. College students, then their parents and grandparents, flocked to what is now the world's largest social network site because it offered non-tech heads wary of cyberspace a secluded booth at the back of the Internet where they could hang out with chosen circle of family and friends.

Now, as Facebook successfully copies Twitter in order to compete with it, and monetizes even the virtual kitchen sink as it moves toward its initial public stock offering (IPO), your privacy is the first thing to go. While tech and business bloggers call shenanigans, Facebook's general users are lulled into compliance via public relations double-speak meant to make you believe this corporate titan is doing it for you, all for you.

For example, according to Facebook's privacy guide, information that users previously had the power to make private—your photo, city, friends, networks and fan pages—are public and searchable, for your own good:

"Making connections—finding people you know, learning about people, searching for what people are saying about topics that interest you—is at the core of our product. This can only happen when people make their information available and choose to share more openly."

Unmentioned is the fact that by decreasing control over your profile, Facebook can compete with Twitter by bringing in more traffic when your info shows up on Google and other search engines. (Meanwhile, users knew Twitter was open and searchable going in.)

Ripping the privacy carpet out from under its users is the kind of shifty behavior that will no doubt result in lawsuits topping that of Facebook's Beacon debacle back in 2007, when user purchases and other Internet activity popped up in Facebook's "news feed" for all friends to see. But what will most users do? Quit Facebook? Maybe. But probably not.

While there are those privacy advocates who will make a big blogging deal of doing just that, most of us will stay for the many positive aspects Facebook offers: Connection with far-away friends and family, a one-stop shop for free e-mail and FarmVille. Technotica, of course, will stay on Facebook as long as you're still there, as it's my job to screech about the importance of your privacy and blah blah blah.

Because here's the thing: Privacy is important—as important, if not more important, than it ever was. You have a right to access popular technology without worrying that anonymous Facebook employees are rifling photos or e-mails. In the larger picture, it is a company's responsibility to spell out policy changes in clear language free of legalese and public relations doubletalk.

What's more, as we live more of our lives online, this goes beyond Facebook. Privacy isn't just about you, even if you have nothing to hide. Privacy is also about those in power abusing personal information, or those in power having their personal information abused in ways that can eventually affect us, the little people.

It's not impossible that Facebook may fall under the weight of its privacy follies. Remember MySpace? Remember Friendster? Come to think of it, Friendster wasn't all that bad. Maybe it's time to give Friendster another try.

Critical Reading Questions

Summarizing the Text

1. Does Popkin think that we should accept the loss of privacy that comes with online convenience? Why or why not?

2. Popkin differentiates here between information that is "open and searchable" and information that is private. What does "open and searchable" mean? What kinds of information are *not* "open and searchable"?

Establishing the Context

3. Popkin argues that Zuckerberg is using "doublespeak" in order to confuse Facebook users about his real intentions. What is "doublespeak," and exactly how do Zuckerberg's comments qualify as doublespeak, in Popkin's argument?

4. Much of the public response to Facebook's evolving privacy settings has been negative—just do a search for "Facebook privacy"—but among the people who hold the power, such as the directors of Google and Facebook and Yahoo and all of the advertising and data collection companies that remain invisible to you, these objections have little effect. How might citizens have a direct effect on the privacy policies of these companies?

Responding to the Message

5. What is the "Beacon debacle" to which Popkin refers? Research this on the Web—and be sure to find arguments from Facebook itself explaining what Beacon was intended to accomplish.

6. Have you changed your online behavior in response to privacy concerns? How?

Point-Counterpoint: Does Facebook Violate Your Privacy?

Matt Dodge and
Dylan Martin

Matt Dodge and Dylan Martin write for the University of Southern Maine's student newspaper, the Free Press. *In this point-counterpoint argument, they debate the changes that Facebook made to its privacy policies in spring 2010—changes that made it much easier for "corporate partners" to track the activities of Facebook users and provide those users with targeted advertising, and changes that made it the default setting for Facebook users to share their information with the wider public, rather than restricting that information to friends or networks. Although the newspaper industry in general is suffering economically and looking for a new business model, student newspapers such as the USM* Free Press *continue to thrive and to serve as training grounds for young journalists.*

Point: New Facebook privacy practices are deceptive and controlling

By Dylan Martin

While people always bellow and moan over the new interface changes at Facebook.com, that should be the least of their worries. Over the past few years, Facebook has been slowly making efforts to make all user information public so that advertisers can mine the data and make personalized ads. And over that time, the practices have become more deceptive and controlling.

In January, Facebook founder Mark Zuckerberg stated that if he had a chance to start Facebook over, he wouldn't give people an option to privatize their information. Privacy has been a hot-button topic for Facebook in the past few years, but in recent months, Facebook has made some alarming changes that make it harder for users to keep their information private. In fact, Facebook is encouraging users to use new features including "Instant Personalization" and "Community Pages" in trade for personal information, sometimes without them ever knowing.

With every major change to the Facebook interface, there is usually a change in the privacy policy, and this update is no different. The policy has been updated to make it harder for users to hide their information from prospective advertisers. In fact, users are forced into the "Community Pages" feature, which makes every single interest you list in your "About" section a "Community Page."

This might be fine for more innocent interests and activities like "camping," but do you want everyone to know that your favorite activities are "smoking weed" and "having sex"? For some, there should be no shame in doing either activity, but the trouble starts when information you publish on Facebook can be seen by all users on the website. Facebook doesn't make it immediately apparent how you can privatize all of your information, and that's where the problem lies.

Facebook has a way of automatically signing up all users for these features, only giving them an opportunity to "opt-out" if they realize they have the option to. But even then, there are now some pieces of information you have no control over, including your name, profile picture, gender, current city, networks, friend list, and pages. All of that info is made public with no way of hiding it.

Back in 2007, Facebook implemented a service called Beacon which allowed users to post their activity from other websites to their news feeds. The activity information was also used for personalized ads. Like the "Instant Personalization" feature, Beacon was an opt-out only service, misleading some users into sharing too much content with fellow users and advertisers. This led to a class-action lawsuit lead by MoveOn.org, which ultimately caused Facebook to remove the Beacon service in late 2009.

As a corporation, Facebook is entitled to use our information for advertising dollars if we grant it, but if they do it by deceiving us and undermining our freedom to privacy, then something needs to be done. Facebook has proved itself to be the best social networking tool in the world, but at what cost will we continue to use it? Facebook needs to have more transparency in their monetization efforts and tell users the truth about what information is being seen by others. More control on privacy wouldn't hurt, either.

Counterpoint: Mining of personal info is the price of social networking

By Matt Dodge

Facebook's recent efforts to standardize and connect users' profile information are seen by some as an underhanded, deceitful attempt to make more advertising revenue. While the new changes are confusing and perhaps purposefully opaque, it's important to remember that despite how fully integrated into our everyday lives the website has become, it is ultimately just a money-making venture, and a very successful one at that: Microsoft bought a 1.6% stake for $240 million in October 2008, which would suggest that the company is worth around $15 billion.

But every "like," wall post, and FarmVille harvest costs the website something. Server space doesn't come cheap, and while Facebook reported $300 million in revenues in 2008 it also spends tens-of-millions of dollars each year upgrading its server infrastructure, including securing $100 million in 2008 in debt financing to finance leases on more server space, according to *BusinessWeek*.

With a third of all global internet users visiting the social networking mecca, Facebook is now the second-most visited site on the internet, and the world's largest photo hosting site, according to tracking service alexa.com. It is perhaps the internet's best and most comprehensive tool for connecting people, and the most cohesive agent in modern relationships. So how much is all that worth to you?

The generation who relies most on Facebook to track, display, and conduct our interpersonal relationships is known colloquially as "Generation Y," which in this context, could stand for "why should we have to pay for anything?" Coming of age in the era of P2P file-sharing services like Napster, and then torrent search engines like The Pirate Bay, we have lived most of our lives in a happy little bubble where any media we want to consume can be found for free somewhere on the internet with little effort. Given this culture of piracy, it's easy to understand why the Ys would be so hesitant to have their personal info mined for advertising revenue. But such an attitude shows a general ignorance of internet economics.

Facebook's new changes are simply a way of better indexing user demographics and interests in a way that helps the site to better target its advertisements and draw more ad revenue. Facebook integrates a myriad of services—the ability to post photos, run a chat client, post event listings, or challenge a friend to a game—all in one place, fulfilling the role of at least half a dozen websites. Given this all-inclusive functionality, one has to make some concessions for the site's advertising methods.

With its clean, minimalist interface, Facebook only really has a single column along the right side of a browser in which to display ads, whereas other websites are littered with them. Facebook's ads are also fairly unobtrusive, devoid of the distracting flash animations and well-regulated for spam and fraud. You might be freaked out when the ads start alluding to your professed love for Jagermeister or starts advertising sex toys, but the fact is the service is convenient, helpful, and mutually beneficial to the user, the advertiser, and the platform itself.

We need to recognize that the invaluable service offered by Facebook is worth something to us, and that, while it might seem creepy to some, the site's advertising model is the most effective way to make money and keep Facebook running, and is as unobtrusive to the user's experience as possible.

Critical Reading Questions

Summarizing the Text

1. What is Martin's thesis or main claim? What reasons does he offer to support this claim?

2. What is Dodge's thesis or main claim? What reasons does he offer to support this claim?

Establishing the Context

3. Dodge makes the compelling argument that "Generation 'why should we have to pay for anything?'" has become accustomed to getting everything online for free, even when those services and products cost something. Apart from the social networking on Facebook, do you receive other services or products (including information) for free on the Web? Who actually pays to provide that information?

4. Martin says that he has no problem with Facebook "monetizing" (or making money from) users' information; his objection is with what he sees as Facebook's lack of transparency. Does he provide sufficient evidence to support his claim that Facebook is deceptive or misleading? If not, what is missing? What might be more persuasive?

Responding to the Message

5. When you sign up for an account on almost any online site, from Facebook to Hotmail to YouTube, your information—including what you do while you are online—is recorded and sold to advertisers. As we have become more dependent upon the Web, many users have also become much more leery about how much personal information is being used by advertising and are demanding that websites adopt "opt-in" policies. What is the difference between "opt-in" and "opt-out" advertising? Research how some sites that you frequent collect and use your personal information (you can do this by reading the "Terms of Service" agreements you probably ignore).

6. Write a rebuttal to either Dodge or Martin using an entirely different claim and reasons than the ones that appear in these arguments. You might, for example, argue that Facebook should supply *no* user information to advertisers under any circumstances (unlike Martin, who only wants Facebook to be more open about how it does this).

Signs of the Social Networking Times
Nitrozack and Snaggy Cartoon

This cartoon, aimed at professionals in the computer industry Joy Of Tech website, satirizes the phenomenon of people allowing embarrassing photos, videos, or details about themselves to circulate online.

Signs of the social networking times.

Summarizing the Text

1. What is the implicit argument of this cartoon?

Establishing the Context

2. Stories about Human Resources departments looking up Facebook or MySpace pages of potential employees have become clichéd, but these stories are true: employers *do* research the online presences of their potential hires. Are you aware of friends or family members encountering this problem?

Responding to the Message

3. Should employers be able to use information such as a Facebook profile in a hiring decision? Why or why not?

Exposed

Emily Gould

Emily Gould is a writer, blogger, and author of the memoir And The Heart Says Whatever. *An early employee of the popular gossip website Gawker, Gould details in this article how her job for Gawker exacerbated her natural tendency to "overshare," and how this tendency caused great harm to her personal life. This article originally appeared in the* New York Times Magazine, *and the Web version of the article received more comments—the vast majority harsh and insulting—than any other article that had ever appeared on the* Times's *website.*

Back in 2006, when I was 24, my life was cozy and safe. I had just been promoted to associate editor at the publishing house where I'd been working since I graduated from college, and I was living with my boyfriend, Henry, and two cats in a grubby but spacious two-bedroom apartment in Greenpoint, Brooklyn. I spent most of my free time sitting with Henry in our cheery yellow living room on our stained Ikea couch, watching TV. And almost every day I updated my year-old blog, Emily Magazine, to let a few hundred people know what I was reading and watching and thinking about.

Some of my blog's readers were my friends in real life, and even the ones who weren't acted like friends when they posted comments or sent me e-mail. They criticized me sometimes, but kindly, the way you chide someone you know well. Some of them had blogs, too, and I read those and left my own comments. As nerdy and one-dimensional as my relationships with these people were, they were important to me. They made me feel like a part of some kind of community, and that made the giant city I lived in seem smaller and more manageable.

The anecdotes I posted on Emily Magazine occasionally featured Henry, whom my readers knew as a lovably bumbling character, a bassist in a fledgling noise-rock band who said unexpectedly insightful things about the contestants on "Project Runway" and then wondered aloud whether we had any snacks. I didn't write about him often, but when I did, I'd quote his best jokes or tell stories about vacationing with his family.

Henry, seemingly alone among our generation, went out of his way to keep his online presence minimal. Now that we've broken up, I appreciate this about him—it's pretty much impossible to torture myself by Google-stalking him. But back then, what this meant was that he was never particularly thrilled to be written about. Sometimes he was enraged.

Once, I made fun of Henry for referring to "Project Runway" as "Project Gayway." He worried that "people"—the shadowy, semi-imaginary people who read my blog and didn't know Henry well enough to know that he wasn't a homophobe—would be offended. He insisted that I take down the offending post and watched as I sat at my desk in our bedroom, slowly, grudgingly making the keystrokes necessary to delete what I'd written. As I sat there staring into the screen at the reflection of Henry standing behind me, I burst into tears. And then we were pacing, screaming at each other, through every room of our apartment, facing off with wild eyes and clenched jaws.

My blog post was ridiculous and petty and small—and, suddenly, incredibly important. At some point I'd grown accustomed to the idea that there was a public place where I would always be allowed to write, without supervision, about how I felt. Even having to take into account someone else's feelings about being written about felt like being stifled in some essential way.

As Henry and I fought, I kept coming back to the idea that I had a right to say whatever I wanted. I don't think I understood then that I could be right about being free to express myself but wrong about my right to make that self-expression public in a permanent way. I described my feelings in the language of empowerment: I was being creative, and Henry wanted to shut me up. His point of view was just as extreme: I wasn't generously sharing my thoughts; I was compulsively seeking gratification from strangers at the expense of the feelings of someone I actually knew and loved. I told him that writing, especially writing about myself and my surroundings, was a fundamental part of my personality, and that if he wanted to remain in my life, he would need to reconcile himself to being part of the world I described.

After a standoff, he conceded that I should be allowed to put the post back up. As he sulked in the other room, I retyped what I'd written, feeling vindicated but slightly queasy for reasons I didn't quite understand yet.

Oversharing

One of the strangest and most enthralling aspects of personal blogs is just how intensely personal they can be. I'm talking "specific details about someone's S.T.D.'s" personal, "my infertility treatments" personal. There are nongynecological overshares, too: "My dog has cancer" overshares, "my abusive relationship" overshares.

It's easy to draw parallels between what's going on online and what's going on in the rest of our media: the death of scripted TV, the endless parade of ordinary, heavily made-up faces that become vaguely familiar to us as they grin through their 15 minutes of reality-show fame. No wonder we're ready to confess our innermost thoughts to everyone: we're constantly being shown that the surest route to recognition is via humiliation in front of a panel of judges.

But is that really what's making people blog? After all, online, you're not even competing for 10 grand and a Kia. I think most people who maintain blogs are doing it for some of the same reasons I do: they like the idea that there's a place where a record of their existence is kept—a house with an always-open door where people who are looking for you can check on you, compare notes with you and tell you what they think of you. Sometimes that house is messy, sometimes horrifyingly so. In real life, we wouldn't invite any passing stranger into these situations, but the remove of the Internet makes it seem O.K.

Of course, some people have always been more naturally inclined toward oversharing than others. Technology just enables us to overshare on a different scale. Long before I had a blog, I found ways to broadcast my thoughts—to gossip about myself, tell my own secrets, tell myself and others the ongoing story of my life. As soon as I could write notes, I passed them incorrigibly. In high school, I encouraged my friends to circulate a notebook in which we shared our candid thoughts about teachers, and when we got caught, I was the one who wanted to argue about the First Amendment rather than gracefully accept punishment. I walked down the hall of my high school passing out copies of a comic-book zine I drew, featuring a mock superhero called SuperEmily, who battled thinly veiled versions of my grade's reigning mean girls. In college, I sent out an all-student e-mail message revealing that an ex-boyfriend shaved his chest hair. The big difference between these youthful indiscretions and my more recent ones is that you can Google my more recent ones.

Online Life

In the fall of 2006, I got a call from the managing editor of Gawker Media, a network of highly trafficked blogs, asking me to come by the office in SoHo to talk about a job. Since its birth four years earlier, the company's flagship blog, Gawker, had purported to be in the business of reporting "Manhattan media gossip," which it did, sometimes—catty little details about writers and editors and executives, mostly. But it was also a clearinghouse for any random tidbit of information about being young and ambitious in New York. Though Gawker was a must-read for many of the people working at the magazines and newspapers whose editorial decisions the site mocked and dissected, it held an irresistible appeal for desk-bound drones in all fields—tens of thousands of whom visited the site each day.

I had been one of those visitors for as long as I'd had a desk job. Sometimes Gawker felt like a source of essential, exclusive information, tailored to the needs of people just like me. Other times, reading Gawker left me feeling hollow and moody, as if I'd just absentmindedly polished off an entire bag of sickly sweet candy. But when the call came, I brushed this thought aside. For a young blogger in New York in 2006, becoming an editor at Gawker was an achievement so lofty that I had never even imagined it could happen to me. The interview and audition process felt a little surreal, like a dream. But when I got the job, I had the strange and sudden feeling that it had been somehow inevitable. Maybe my whole life—all the trivia I'd collected, the knack for funny meanness I'd been honing since middle school—had been leading up to this moment.

When I started, the site was posting about 40 items per day, and I was responsible for 12 of them. The tone of these posts was smart yet conversational, and often funny in a merciless way. Confronted with endless examples of unfairness, favoritism and just plain stupidity among New York's cultural establishment, the Gawker "voice" was righteously indignant but comically defeated, sighing in unison with an audience that believed nothing was as it seemed and nothing would ever really change. Everyone was fatter or older or worse-skinned than he or she pretended to be. Every man was cheating on his partner; all women were slutty. Writers were plagiarists or talentless hacks or shameless beneficiaries of nepotism. Everyone was a hypocrite. No one was loved. There was no success that couldn't be hollowed out by the revelation of some deep-seated inadequacy.

Shortcuts

At my old job, it would have taken me years to advance to a place where I would no longer have to humor the whims of important people who I thought were idiots or relics or phonies. But at Gawker, it was my *responsibility* to expose the foibles of the undeserving elite. I felt liberated—finally, a job where I could really be myself! Never again would I have to censor my office-inappropriate sentiments or shop the sale racks at Club Monaco for office-appropriate outfits. But at the same time, I wasn't quite convinced that the system of apprenticeship and gradual promotion that I'd left behind when I left book publishing was as flawed as establishment-attacking Gawker made it out to be. I'd been lucky enough, in my publishing job, to have the kind of boss who actually cared about my future. At Gawker, I barely had a boss, and my future was always in jeopardy. In my old job, I'd been able to slowly, steadily learn the ropes, but now I was judged solely on what I produced every day. I had a kind of power, sure, but it was only as much power as my last post made it seem like I deserved.

Sometimes I worried that I'd been chosen not in spite of my inexperience but because of it. Hiring women in their early 20s with little or no background in journalism was a tactic that worked for the site's owner twice before, and I expected to be a victim of the same kind of hazing my predecessors were subjected to as they learned how to do their jobs—and how to navigate New York—in public. I'd once heard someone refer to us as "sacrificial virgins," which didn't seem too far off.

Then again, being a sacrificial virgin has always had its perks. The career arc of Gawker's popular outgoing editor, Jessica Coen, seemed like evidence that talent could and should trump dues-paying. After college, she worked as an assistant in L.A. and maintained a personal blog. When, at age 24, she decided to move to New York, she had two career options: Columbia Journalism School or Gawker. She chose Gawker. Two years later, every magazine editor in town knew her name, and she was hired as the online editor of *Vanity Fair*. Maybe the days were over when young comers were slowly mentored as they prepared to assume their bosses' titles, covering community-board meetings or fetching coffee.

The Feedback Loop

"I tried not to read the comments," Jessica told me when we met for a drink just before I started work at Gawker. "Well, I went back and forth. But, you know, you really shouldn't read the comments." An hour into my first day on the job, I disobeyed her. I needed to know what people were saying about me. Dozens of readers had commented on the post introducing me, some of them dissecting the accompanying photo, some of them talking about how much they already hated me. Every time I wrote a post, the comments would pile up within minutes, disagreeing with or amplifying whatever I just said. Reading the comments created a sense of urgency, which came in handy when trying to hit deadlines 12 times a day.

I relayed some of the choicest bits to Henry, who also thought I shouldn't be reading the comments. But how could I convey to Henry—who sometimes, onstage with his band, played entire shows with his back to the audience—the thrill of delivering a good line to a crowd that would immediately respond, that would fall over themselves to one-up your joke or fill in the blanks with their own suggestions and information?

The commenters at Emily Magazine had been like friends. Now, with Gawker's readers, I was having a different kind of relationship. It wasn't quite friendship. It was almost something deeper. They were co-workers, sort of, giving me ideas for posts, rewriting my punch lines. They were creeps hitting on me at a bar. They were fans, sycophantically praising even my lamer efforts. They were enemies, articulating my worst fears about my limitations. They were the voices in my head. They could be ignored sometimes. Or, if I let them, they could become my whole world.

When Jessica cautioned me against reading the comments, she also told me that the commenters loved it when she revealed personal details. Not only did I find this to be true, I found it to be almost necessary. Injecting a personal aside into a post that wasn't otherwise about me not only kept things interesting for me, it was also a surefire way of evoking a chorus of assenting or dissenting opinions, turning the solitary work of writing posts into something that felt more social, almost like a conversation.

The commenters' compliments were reassuring. And though I was reluctant to admit it, there was even something sort of thrilling about being insulted by strangers. This was brand-new, having so many strangers pay attention to me, and at that point, every kind of attention still felt good. Occasionally, a particularly well-aimed barb would catch me off-guard, and I'd spend a moment worrying that I really was the worst writer ever to work for the site, or unfunny, or ugly, or stupid. But mostly, in the beginning, I was able to believe the compliments and dismiss the insults, even though they were both coming from the same place and sometimes the same people.

Hooked

Like most people, I tend to use the language of addiction casually, as in, "I can't wait for the new season of *America's Next Top Model* to start— I'm totally going through withdrawal." And when talking about how immersed I became in my online life, I'm tempted to use this language because it provides such handy metaphors. It's easy to compare the initial thrill of evoking an immediate response to a blog post to the rush of getting high, and the diminishing thrills to the process of becoming inured to a drug's effects. The metaphor is so exact, in fact, that maybe it isn't a metaphor at all.

When Henry and I fought about my job, we fought on two fronts: whether what I was doing was essentially unethical, and whether I was too consumed by doing it. I would usually end up agreeing with him on the first count—my posts could be petty or cruel—but that only made him more frustrated. It must have been hard for him to understand how someone could keep committing small-scale atrocities with such enthusiasm and single-minded devotion.

My Buddy List

Though Gawker's bloggers often worked from home, I went to the office every day at first. I was used to communicating with most people I knew via instant messenger, but it seemed important to see Alex, my co-editor, in person. I figured that we'd be able to express ourselves more easily by actually turning to each other and speaking words and making facial expressions rather than typing instant messages. But because we were so busy, we continued to I.M. most of the time, even when we were sitting right next to each other. Soon it stopped seeming weird to me when one of us would type a joke and the other one would type "Hahahahaha" in lieu of actually laughing.

Another person I ended up I.M.-ing daily was one of Gawker's most frequent targets, a blogger named Julia Allison, who, within a year, parlayed a magazine dating column into a six-figure TV talking-head job and then into a reality show, all while updating her blog several times a day. Julia wore skimpy, Halloween-style costumes to parties and dated high-profile men in high-profile ways—her tech-millionaire boyfriend collaborated with her on a blog where they took turns chronicling their relationship's ups and downs. I was initially put off by Julia's naked attention-whoring—"Attention is my drug," she often confessed. In thousands of photos on her Flickr feed she posed, caked in makeup, like a celebrity on the red carpet, always thrusting out her breasts and favoring her good side. But in the midst of this artifice she was disarmingly straightforward about how badly she craved the attention that Internet exposure gave her—even though it came at the expense of constant, intensely vitriolic mockery.

I also I.M.-ed constantly with my co-worker Josh, who joined the site as "after hours editor" a few months into my tenure, which meant that he wrote about parties and restaurants. He was cute, and given the number of hours a day we spent trapped at our desks, the flirtation that developed between us seemed unavoidable. And the medium made it seem harmless—sure, maybe our I.M. avatars wanted to hook up, but our flesh-and-blood selves would be careful to make sure things stayed professional.

In Public

It was 11 p.m. on an April night in 2007, and I was in the back seat of a speeding Town Car on my way home from the CNN studios. I was on the phone with Alex, who was at a bar. "I don't think I did a very good job," I told him. I was still full of adrenaline from being on TV, and the noise of the bar in the background as he reassured me made me think it might be fun to join him, but the driver was already headed to Greenpoint, and I was too dazed to give him new directions.

I'd been a guest on an episode of *Larry King Live*, with Jimmy Kimmel as the host in King's absence. I had been told that I would be talking about "celebrities and the media." But Kimmel launched an attack on one of Gawker's regular features, a celebrity "stalker map" that relied on unsourced tipsters, one of whom claimed to have spotted Kimmel looking drunk a few months earlier. It took me a minute to catch on to the fact that Kimmel wasn't acting out some blustery caricature—he was serious about the idea that Gawker had violated his privacy, and he was genuinely, frighteningly angry.

Back at home, after wiping off the TV makeup, I logged into my Gawker e-mail account and found my in-box flooded. I scrolled through the first of what would eventually be hundreds—and then, as the clip of my appearance was dissected on other blogs over the course of the next few days, thousands—of angry e-mail messages. I ended up posting some representative ones on my personal blog:

"You got blown away. You looked like a little girl in awe of your surroundings."

"I just want to tell you how uneducated and STUPID you came off during the appearance on The LKL Show. You truly are a cheap heartless human being, who will one day have to deal with the same kind of SCUM you are."

"You were this giggling, hyper adolescent that did more to hurt your message, your site and your credibility than even coming close to simply neutralizing the debate."

Watching the clip now makes me cringe. Called upon to defend Gawker's publication of anonymous e-mail tips of celebrity sightings, I was dismissive and flip. My untrained, elastic face betrayed the shock and amusement I was feeling about being asked, somewhat aggressively, to justify something that I thought of as not only harmless but also a given: the idea that anyone who makes their living in public was subject to the public's scrutiny at all times.

I expected the miniature scandal to flare and fade quickly, but for a while it seemed as if it would never go away. The clip made its way to Yahoo's front page, and a reporter called my parents for comment. After a week or so, the volume of angry e-mail and blog comments subsided, but they stayed under my skin. I decided to try to develop a steely, defiant numbness. I told myself that the strangers who'd taken the time to e-mail me their rants were wrong and crazy, that there was nothing so bad about what I'd done.

There was a harder truth that I refused to confront, though. After all, by going on TV and having a daily blog presence in front of thousands of people, I had put myself in the category of "people who make their livings in public," and so, by my own declared value system, I was an appropriate target for the kind of flak I was getting. But that didn't mean I could handle it. A week later, I found myself lying on the floor of the bathroom in the Gawker office (where, believe me, no one should ever lie), felled by a panic attack that put me out of commission for the rest of the day.

I started having panic attacks—breathless bouts of terror that left me feeling queasy, drained and hopeless—every day. I didn't leave my apartment unless I absolutely had to, and because I had the option of working from home, I rarely had to. But while my actual participation in life shrank down to a bare minimum, I still responded to hundreds of e-mail messages and kept up a stream of instant-messenger conversations while I wrote. Depending on how you looked at it, I either had no life and I barely talked to anyone, or I spoke to thousands of people constantly.

Famous for 15 People

I started seeing a therapist again, and we talked about my feelings of being inordinately scrutinized. "It's important to remember that you're not a celebrity," she told me. How could I tell her, without coming off as having delusions of grandeur, that, in a way, I was? I obviously wasn't "famous" in the way that a movie star or even a local newscaster or politician is famous—I didn't go to red-carpet parties or ride around in limos, and my parents' friends still had no idea what I was talking about when I described my job—but I had begun to have occasional run-ins with strangers who knew what I did for a living and felt completely comfortable walking up to me on the street and talking about it. The Monday after my disastrous CNN appearance, as I stood in line at Balthazar's coffee bar, a middle-aged man in a suit told me to keep my chin up. "Emily, don't quit Gawker!" a young guy shouted at me from his bicycle as I walked down the street one day. If someone stared at me on the subway, there was no way to tell whether they were admiring my outfit or looking at the stain on my sweater or whether they, you know, Knew Who I Was. The more people e-mailed the Gawker tip line with "sightings" of me—laden with bags from Target and scarfing ice cream while walking down Atlantic Avenue—the more I was inclined to believe it was the latter.

Oversharing on Gawker

I didn't want to go to Fire Island. The trip would take two hours, and it would involve the subway, the Long Island Railroad, a van and a ferry. For a month, I'd been doing my best to avoid any venture more ambitious than the trip to the grocery store a block and a half away, whose clerks were, besides Henry, pretty much the only people I still spoke to aloud on a regular basis. Whenever I left this comfort zone, I would be seized by one of my irrational, heart-pounding meltdowns, which I would studiously conceal from my fellow subway passengers or pedestrians. The panic attacks were about a desire to be invisible, but if I showed any sign that I was having one, everyone would pay attention to me. It was kind of funny when you thought about it, and if you weren't me.

But Choire, my boss, urged me to attend the staff retreat at a house near the beach so that we could all bond as a team. Henry discouraged me from going—he didn't want me to push myself, and we were comfortable, weren't we, in our sad little world together? He was as surprised as I was when, the morning of the retreat, I managed to pry myself out of bed and get myself onto the subway. Walking into Penn Station, I saw Josh and his stylish duffel leaning against a pillar. He looked up at me and smiled in a way that immediately distracted me from thoughts of how miserable I felt. The freakout I was dreading never came, and over the course of the next few days, I forgot to always be anticipating its arrival.

We each wrote our allotment of Gawker posts in the mornings, and in the afternoons we went to the beach. The water was freezing—it was still early in the summer—and we all ran into the waves together screaming. At night Choire cooked us elaborate feasts, and afterward we played Scrabble and watched bad movies. Josh and I sat together on the couch, and I put my head on his shoulder in a completely friendly, professional way. The next day, I let him apply sunscreen to the spot in the middle of my back that I couldn't reach. As a joke, we walked down the wood-plank paths that crisscross the island holding hands. I also remember joking, via I.M. as we worked, about us wanting to cross the hallway that separated our bedrooms and crawl into bed with each other at night when we couldn't sleep. On our last day, I congratulated myself on having made it through the trip without letting these jokes turn into real betrayal. And then, 20 minutes outside the city on the Long Island Railroad on the way home, Josh kissed me.

The next few weeks eliminated every constant from my life except my job. I moved out of the apartment where I'd lived for four years with Henry, and while I looked for a place on my own, I stayed in a tiny room in a loft full of hippies who brewed their own kombucha tea. I quit smoking pot cold turkey. My parents moved out of my childhood home to a different state because my dad had a new job. My best friend, Ruth, lived a hemisphere away in New Zealand, and though we sent each other epic e-mail messages and talked on the phone, I still felt unmoored in the way you can only feel after a breakup, as if you're the last living speaker of some dying language. But even though this sense of disconnection from my old self and my old life was confusing, it felt mostly good. After all, what was so great about my old self and my old life, anyway?

I immersed myself in my job in a way I hadn't even realized was possible—I thought about Gawker, one way or another, 24 hours a day, thrilling to the idea that a review of the restaurant where Josh and I were eating dinner might find its way onto the site the following day; pillow-talking about the site's internal politics and our hopes and dreams about what we would do next. Just a few weeks earlier, I was scared to walk down my own block. Now I felt totally comfortable posting a picture of myself in a bathing suit on the site, inspiring Josh to do the same. I felt blazingly, insanely energized, and the posts came more easily than they ever had before.

I was happy, but I also wasn't a complete idiot—I knew that the euphoria I was feeling was leading to a massive crash. I'd been clinging to Henry for months in spite of our differences because, in addition to the comfort and stability he gave me, he was my sounding board— someone with whom I could share my unfiltered thoughts, without worrying about being entertaining. In his absence, I was becoming more and more open on Gawker.

After the first night Josh and I spent together, I woke up as the sun rose and sat down at my desk to write a post that was nominally about a recent *New York Times* article about the shelf-life of romantic love. My boyfriend and I had just broken up, I revealed, and so I had been wondering whether love really exists. I wrote that I had concluded that it does. We can't expect other people to make us happy, I informed my readers with total sincerity and earnestness, and we should live in the moment and stop obsessing about the future.

I shudder involuntarily when I read this post now. It's like stumbling across a diary I kept as a teenager. It's probably one of the worst things that I've ever written. The commenters loved it.

Gawker had recently added a counter beside each post that displayed how many views it received. Now it was easy to see exactly how many people cared about my feelings. The site's owner didn't like my "I believe in love" post, he told me, but he said he was O.K. with it because, as everyone could see, more than 10,000 people disagreed with him. Readers e-mailed me their own breakup horror stories and posted hundreds of comments, advising me about flavors of ice cream to eat, and I reveled in the attention. I had managed to turn my job into a group therapy session. "Emily, I don't really know you any more than I know the people I see every morning walking the dogs," one of them wrote. "It's more of an imagined familiarity born out of reading your words for a year. But that took guts, all the way around. And I'm in your corner, inasmuch as a somewhat anonymous, faceless, nameless commenter can be."

Would anyone still be in my corner if they knew the truth—that I hadn't in fact been dumped, and that I'd thrown myself headlong into a rebound affair with a co-worker? I wished that I could tell my old Emily Magazine readers everything that was going on in my life and ask them for advice. I wanted to organize my stories into coherence and put them out into the world. But the Internet had changed, and my place in it had changed, too: I no longer had the luxury of writing something and imagining that the only people who might read it would be a handful of funny, supportive friends.

The Fork and the Spoon

My oldest and most responsible friend, Farrin, is a 37-year-old executive editor at a publishing house. Over breakfast, she was complaining to me that she had a problem at work: the head of her department had asked her to add a photo to her profile on the department's Web page, and she wasn't comfortable with having a picture of herself posted online.

The table we were sitting at was wide, maybe four feet across, and made of planks like a picnic table. I positioned my fork all the way on the left side of the table. "So here's the spectrum of Internet self-exposure," I told her. "And here's you. You're the fork." Then I put my spoon at the right end of the table. "And here, at the other end of the spectrum ... Julia Allison."

"So where are you on the spectrum?"

"Well, I used to be here," I said, moving a toast crust a few inches to the left of my plate, the table's midpoint. "And now I'm here." I put the crust halfway between my plate and Julia.

Farrin looked up at me, concerned. "That's not good. I think you should start moving closer to the plate."

Instead, though, I kept moving blithely closer to the spoon.

Heartbreak Soup

About a month after I broke up with Henry, my best friend, Ruth, and I created a new, anonymous blog on which we wrote to each other, as we had been doing via e-mail, about breakups and cooking. We named it Heartbreak Soup. At the beginning, we didn't tell anyone it existed, but then we decided to add a sidebar of links to other sites we liked, and a tiny amount of traffic began to trickle our way.

We used pseudonyms for the people we wrote about, but otherwise our concessions to privacy—other peoples' and our own—were very limited. I knew this wasn't smart in the same way that I knew that dating a co-worker wasn't smart, but my curiosity won out. I wanted to know what would happen if I showed myself as little mercy as I showed everyone else. "I'm bad at describing sex, or maybe everyone is," I wrote at one point, but I didn't let that stop me from trying! I ratted myself out for being a bad daughter: "I love my mom more than I love probably anyone else in the world, really. Also, she is more like me than anyone else in the world. But I often want to kill her. The thing that keeps her alive is how incredibly sad I would be if she died." I described the symptoms and probable causes of a urinary tract infection. And I wrote about how painful it was to pack up my things in my old apartment as Henry—whom I referred to as "William"—stood over me watching. I puzzled over "how comfortable I feel around him, in spite of the fact that at this point I basically feel that he's a crazy person who I sort of hate."

Josh was one of the first people I told about the blog. I wanted him to know everything there was to know about me, after all, and besides, we talked about writing all the time, showing off what we thought were our best turns of phrase. He seemed flattered that some of the posts were about him, but he said he wasn't sure how he felt about how candid I was being—though we'd never discussed it, it seemed like a good idea not to explicitly reveal that we were seeing each other, even though we left the office for makeout coffee breaks and broadcast maudlin love songs on the shared office speakers.

A few weeks later, I arrived home in the early morning hours after abruptly extricating myself from Josh's bed—he had suddenly revealed plans for a European vacation with another girl—and immediately sat down at my computer to write a post about what had happened. On Heartbreak Soup, I wrote a long rant about the day's events, including a recipe for the chicken soup I made the previous afternoon and the sex that I'd been somehow suckered into even after finding out about how serious things were with the other girl. Then I opened another tab in my browser and logged into Gawker to start compiling the morning's gossip. For a few hours, my personal dramas took a backseat—sort of—to news that a Pulitzer-winning author had described his wife's affair with a media mogul in a crazy e-mail message to his graduate students. I used the opportunity of this public figure's indiscretion to pontificate about the idea that all heartbreak is essentially the same, though everyone thinks his feelings are somehow original and special. I was essentially talking to myself.

After Josh and I broke up, I started writing more and more on Heartbreak Soup—about my friendship with Ruth, my family and the weird, sad, terrifying, exciting aspects of being single for the first time in my adult life. Word had spread through my immediate circle of friends about the blog, and it was now getting a few hundred visitors a day—about the same as Emily Magazine before I started at Gawker. I lulled myself into imagining that these Heartbreak Soup readers, like those old Emily Magazine readers, might not even know what Gawker was, that they were reading just because they liked my stories.

One night, after writing a post about my first summer in New York, I put a link to Heartbreak Soup on my Facebook page under "Web sites." By the next morning, this had begun to feel like a very bad idea, and I took the link down. The traffic spike that day seemed ominous.

Not long after, Josh told me he wanted to have a talk with me about how unsecret my "secret" blog had become. I had started working from home again, but I came into the city, and we stood, smiling awkwardly, outside the Gawker office, trying to figure out what to say to each other. I remembered the fight I had with Henry about the "Project Gayway" post. This time, I knew, I wouldn't win—but then I hadn't really won the last time either.

I offered to make the posts that mentioned Josh inaccessible by password-protecting them.

"You should be password-protected," he said, and I laughed. When he went back into the office, I walked to the subway via the alleys where we'd once secretly kissed. At home, I wrote about what had just happened on Heartbreak Soup, and then I password-protected the post, feeling strange and sad.

Losing the Will to Blog

In October, *New York* magazine published a cover article about Gawker's business model and cultural relevance. I took the magazine from my therapist's waiting room into her office and read aloud from the article because, I figured, why waste any of my 45 minutes by struggling to summarize it? The article painted Gawker as a clearinghouse for vitriol and me as a semisympathetic naïf who half-loved and half-loathed what her job was forcing her to become. That week, when I walked around at parties, trying to elicit funny quotes from whatever quasi-famous people were there, all anyone wanted to talk to me about was Gawker. How could I sleep at night? someone wondered. I was getting tired of justifying my job to strangers, trotting out truisms about the public's right to know and the Internet's changing the rules of privacy. And I was getting tired of writing the same handful of posts over and over again. At the end of November, I announced my resignation via a post on Gawker.

For a year, I had been getting up each morning at 7 a.m., my thoughts jostling in my head, eager to escape. I wrote constantly, responding to the events of the day in real time, under perpetual pressure to condense everything I thought and read into something readers could consume. But now I was burned out and directionless, and without an audience, I lost the narrative thread. If no one was going to get on my case for not having read and catalogued every gossip item in the morning papers by 9 a.m., why get out of bed? For months, I thought that I hated the commenters who tormented me. Now, sickeningly, I missed them. I wasn't reading the Sunday the *Times* or *New York* magazine, because what was the point? I wasn't logging into instant messenger. I had terrible writer's block. My grandfather died, and I couldn't even come up with a heartfelt paragraph to read aloud at his funeral.

On Heartbreak Soup, I was reduced to writing about not having anything to write about. I wasn't cooking much, or reading much, or thinking about much of anything besides how miserable and emptied out I felt. When I posted about a week spent wandering around deadeyed in Florida's artificial beauty the week after the funeral, one reader left a comment recommending specific brands of antidepressants. Soon after that, I lost the will to blog altogether.

The will to blog is a complicated thing, somewhere between inspiration and compulsion. It can feel almost like a biological impulse. You see something, or an idea occurs to you, and you have to share it with the Internet as soon as possible. What I didn't realize was that those ideas and that urgency—and the sense of self-importance that made me think anyone would be interested in hearing what went on in my head—could just disappear.

Unprotected

Two months after I quit Gawker, Josh wrote an article in the *New York Post*'s Sunday magazine about how violated he felt when I wrote about him on Heartbreak Soup, quoting extensively from my blog posts to make his points.

On the morning that the article hit the newsstands, I made Ruth—who had moved back to New York and become my roommate—read it first. When she finished, she looked stricken. "Emily, he's so evil," she said, sounding not at all reassuring.

I slumped to the kitchen floor and lay there in the fetal position. I didn't want to exist. I had made my existence so public in such a strange way, and I wanted to take it all back, but in order to do that I'd have to destroy the entire Internet. If only I could! Google, YouTube, Gawker, Facebook, WordPress, all gone. I squeezed my eyes shut and prayed for an electromagnetic storm that would cancel out every mistake I'd ever made.

"I'm taking it down," Ruth called to me from the living room, where my laptop sat on a table, displaying our no-longer-so-secret blog.

I opened my eyes. "Don't delete it," I managed to say. "Just make it all password-protected."

I lay there for a while longer. Eventually I read the article, which was, as personal betrayals go, far worse than I'd thought it could be. But the real power of the article, as Josh must have known when he wrote it, lay in the way that it exposed me to the new Gawker regime, which had already proved itself to be even more vicious than we'd ever been. If the article had been published when I was still working at Gawker, I would have been able to steer the conversation that it provoked. But now I was no longer simultaneously sniper and target—I was just a target, and I felt powerless.

Over the next couple of weeks, I sat on the sidelines and watched as the commenters—on Gawker, on other blogs and even on Emily Magazine—talked about me the same way they once talked about the targets I'd proffered for them to aim at. Many of them explicitly pointed out that this drubbing was my karmic comeuppance—after all, I'd punished other people this way. Now it was my turn. It was only fair.

By revealing my flaws to whoever wanted to look, I thought—incorrectly, as it turned out—that I was inoculating myself against the criticism my Gawker co-workers and I leveled most often. Maybe I was talentless, bad-complected, old-looking and slutty, but no one could call me a hypocrite. I had said that everyone was subject to judgment and scrutiny, and then, by judging and scrutinizing myself relentlessly, I'd invited others to do the same.

But maybe I was a hypocrite after all, because now I was beginning to feel that no one should be subject to that kind of scrutiny. Not Josh, not Jimmy Kimmel and especially not me.

Real Life

If I were going to completely disavow self-scrutiny and unedited opinion-broadcasting, it would mean the end of my life as a blogger. While I couldn't make the Internet disappear, it had always been entirely within my power to shutter Emily Magazine the same way I'd locked up Heartbreak Soup. For about a week after Josh's article came out, I thought about doing so every time I looked at my computer. But then, as panic and sadness faded and anger set in, I started having impulses in the exact opposite direction: I wanted to defend myself and set the record straight! A few months earlier, I probably would have done it too: typed feverishly for hours perfecting the most cutting blog post possible, aired every sad secret at my disposal in a quest for revenge, published the post as soon as I was finished, then checked back compulsively to see whether it had made things better or worse. But I'd finally realized that some defenses always backfire. True, I had the ability to say whatever I wanted and an audience of people who would listen, but the best possible thing for me to do was to ignore them and do nothing. And that is what I did. For two entire weeks.

Late one night, I unlocked Heartbreak Soup and wrote one last post there. In it, I talked about how a single blog post can capture a moment of extreme feeling, but that reading an accumulated series of posts will sometimes reveal another, more complete story. I talked about how taking the once-public blog and making it private, though tempting, felt like trying to revise history.

Knowing that the worst of my online oversharing is still publicly accessible doesn't thrill me, but it doesn't scare me anymore either. I might hate my former self, but I don't want to destroy her, and in a way, I want to respect her decision to show the world her vulnerability. I'm willing to let that blog exist now as a sort of memorial to a time in my life when I thought my discoveries about myself and what I loved were special enough to merit sharing with the world immediately.

I understand that by writing here about how I revealed my intimate life online, I've now revealed even more about what happened during the period when I was most exposed. Well, I'm an oversharer—it's not like I'm entirely reformed. But lately, online, I've found myself doing something unexpected: keeping the personal details of my current life to myself. This doesn't make me feel stifled so much as it makes me feel protected, as if my thoughts might actually be worth honing rather than spewing. But I still have Emily Magazine as a place to spew when I need to. It will never again be the friendly place that it was in 2004—there are plenty of negative comments now, and I don't delete them. I still think about closing the door to my online life and locking them out, but then I think of everything else I'd be locking out, and I leave it open.

Critical Reading Questions

Summarizing the Text

1. This article is an example of a personal memoir—a reflective piece of writing in which a person meditates on an earlier, significant time in his or her life. Does Gould make an argument in this memoir?

2. What is the relationship between Gould's work at Gawker and her relationship with Henry?

Establishing the Context

3. Gawker.com is often very funny, but also often very mean. Its controversial "Gawker Stalker" asks users to alert the site to the location of celebrities; these celebrities, in turn, have accused Gawker of putting them in danger. How does Gawker's sarcastic attitude toward celebrities bleed into Gould's personal life?

4. Describe the voice and *ethos* of this article. How does Gould come across to you? How does this affect her message?

Responding to the Message

5. The immediacy of the Web for bloggers and users of social-networking sites, Gould seems to argue, encourages burgeoning exhibitionists to share much more of their personal life than is probably healthy, for them or for the people in their lives. Have you or people in your life "overshared"? How? What was the effect?

6. Visit the electronic version of this article on the NYTimes.com website and read some of the comments in the comment thread. What do you think of the tone they take? What do you think of the "advice" they offer Gould?

Questions for Short Projects or Group Presentations

1. In a small group, compare how three important sites—Google, Facebook, and Hotmail—collect user data and use it to sell advertising. In a class presentation, describe the differences and similarities among these sites.
2. Using a digital camera or camera phone, take photographs of your campus's most important or photogenic locations—the quad, the old main building, the football stadium, the library. Create a presentation in which you describe the rhetoric of these spaces and explain what they tell the world about your school.

Questions for Formal Essays

1. Land use is a topic that young people rarely pay any attention to, but it often provides the backdrop for the most explosive and bitterly fought battles in a local community. Research a recent land-use controversy in your community (either your home community or the community in which you now live). You might want to consult the local newspaper, a local political or neighborhood association blog, or the websites of your city council or county board of commissioners. What specifically was at issue? What arguments did citizens make? What was the end result?

2. Are we citizens or are we consumers? In the wide world out there, how do these two roles interact or cancel each other out? Implicit in all of the essays in Cluster One are assumptions about what rights and responsibilities and roles we have as *citizens* in public spaces versus what rights and responsibilities and roles we have as *consumers* in a marketplace. Respond to all of the pieces in Cluster One and describe their visions of the citizen versus the consumer, and what this has to do with public versus private spaces.

3. Are you worried about your private information becoming public? How much do you think about the information you provide online—whether on a public blog, on your social-networking site, or when filling out questionnaires or order forms? What precautions do you take, if any?

4. Mark Zuckerberg of Facebook isn't the first new-media titan to argue that privacy is dead: as Popkin points out, as early as 1999 the chief of Sun Microsystems blithely said the same thing. In exchange for making much of our information public or at least available to corporations and advertisers, we get all of the advantages of the Internet age. And as Emily Gould demonstrates, some of us have a natural tendency to overshare, anyway. What do you think? Is privacy a value that is increasingly irrelevant? Should we get accustomed to anyone being able to learn about us? And how are people responding to this by creating alternative Internet avatars of themselves?

How True Is Scientific "Truth"?

CHAPTER INTRODUCTION

Everything's a matter of opinion—except science. The laws of science are inarguable, immutable, and eternal. Except, that is, when they aren't. In this chapter, you will find a number of short, opinionated "takes" or perspectives about one corner where science and public policy intersect, and several longer pieces about the nature of scientific truth, and how scientific truth or fact is used in the public arena.

The first cluster here "When is a drug not a drug?" deals with substances and ingredients that are often called "supplements," and with whether and how such "supplements" should be treated as drugs by the medical establishment and government. Supplements—which run the gamut from vitamin pills, to the ginseng and taurine included in energy drinks, to "miracle cures" sold in alternative medicine shops and on television infomercials—promise to do something beneficial for us. In this, they are like drugs. However, they are *not* like drugs in other ways: most importantly in that they have not been proven by reliable scientific testing to achieve what they promise to achieve.

Manufacturers and marketers of supplements tend to like living in this zone, as they avoid regulation while still being able to claim that their product is "good for you." In the United States, the Federal Trade Commission (FTC) and the Food and Drug Administration (FDA) enforce rules about the kinds of claims that drug or supplement manufacturers can make in advertising, and what sort of evidence they have to have for their claims. Advertising for these supplements and energy drinks can suggest that such products bring health benefits, but the advertisers cannot assert that their products actually *do* anything—make you smarter, stronger, healthier, and so on—without actual and credible testing bolstering that claim. So they often use slippery terms and avoid making concrete statements of fact.

Verifiable or not, these claims have found a receptive audience among consumers, though, many of whom have become skeptical about the medical establishment and the pharmaceutical industry. After a series of embarrassing and costly incidents in which FDA-approved drugs were shown later to be ineffective or even harmful (as with the diet drug Phen-Fen and the analgesic Vioxx), many consumers have come to believe that the FDA works hand-in-glove with a greedy and reckless drug industry. The drug companies are out for a profit even when they know their drugs are harmful, goes the argument, and the government enables them and fails to protect consumers' interests. Such cynicism is often fueled by rumors or stories that circulate on the Internet.

Capitalizing on this cynicism about the medical establishment is the alternative medicine world. Encompassing a vast array of approaches ranging from acupuncture to Rolfing to yoga to homeopathy, alternative medicine asserts that there are other ways of healing the body apart from those that dominate Western medicine. And to consumers wary of what they perceive to be a profit-driven medical establishment, or to patients for whom traditional therapies don't work, alternative medicine is very attractive. But for *New Yorker* writer and science journalist Michael Specter, though, such "alternative medicine" is the problem. Wanting something (such as "this herb will work better than this drug") to be true doesn't *make it* true, he insists, and he coins the term *denialism* to describe the phenomenon of dismissing scientific evidence that points to conclusions we don't want to accept.

Whether or not alternative medicine "works" isn't really an answerable question, in the end. There are so many forms of alternative medicine used for so many different conditions that it is impossible to generalize. What is certain is that many, many people believe that alternative medicine therapies and cures *have* worked for them. Moreover, many alternative medicine approaches call into question what we mean by being "healthy" or "cured." Advocates and providers of these approaches frequently cannot "prove," to Western scientific standards, that they "work"—but is this important when so many people attest that such therapies have worked for them? This issue touches upon deeper questions we have about consumer freedom, irresponsible corporations, the responsibility of the government to "protect" citizens from making bad choices (or to constrain their choices altogether), and the nature of Western scientific knowledge.

The final pair of pieces in this cluster looks at the health effects of so-called "energy drinks," nonalcoholic beverages popular among young people. Such drinks (which include Red Bull, Full Throttle, and Rockstar) include substances such as taurine, ginseng, and guarana, in addition to caffeine. In a controversial paper in the leading medical journal *Pediatrics*, a team of researchers concluded that energy drinks should be more tightly regulated than they are, as they are potentially harmful to young people who consume them frequently. Responding to this article, the American Beverage Association (the trade group for beverage manufacturers) rebuts its claims and tries to call its methods into question. Scientists and nonspecialists will respond differently to these issues, and the American Beverage Industry's response to the study attempts to sow doubt about the science in the audience.

The energy-drinks controversy brings up several key questions about how we and our families use and are affected by science, questions that you might want to take up in a class discussion or a longer paper. How much evidence does science need in order to decide that something is "true"? Can nonscientists understand the scientific research that must underlie governmental decisions to regulate a product? How can an industry defend itself against threats to its business model? Should parents be responsible for whether they allow their children to drink energy drinks? Should the government step in and regulate these products, as it does with tobacco and alcohol? And how reliable is the evidence that the researchers offer? Are they interpreting the evidence of those studies correctly? Might there be other studies that contradict these?

The second cluster of this chapter delves into more philosophical territory. What are the limits of science and what science can know? In his profile of New York City Police Department forensic scientist Lisa Faber, legal writer Jeffrey Toobin counters the "CSI effect"—the idea, promoted by CBS Television's *CSI* franchise, that crime-scene investigators are scientific magicians who can identify killers beyond any reasonable doubt by using forensic science. Underlying Toobin's article is the fact that while much forensic science can point to a *likely* conclusion, it's important to remember that "likely" and "true" may be very far apart indeed.

Barbara Ehrenreich and Natalie Angier, two skeptical intellectuals, use the issue of scientific certainty to point to what they see as the credulousness or gullibility of the American public. In an excerpt from her book on the subject, Ehrenreich takes on the American faith in the beneficial effects of positive thinking. We are so eager (or conditioned) to believe that positive thinking will bring us what we want, she argues, that this faith can overwhelm our willingness to believe even in the most basic properties of the physical world. At the same time, she continues, we will swallow any kind of pseudo-science if it confirms beliefs we already have.

Angier, on the other hand, turns to the scientists and questions them. Why get so worked up about Americans' unwillingness to accept the truth of Darwinism, she says, when other beliefs that are shared by an ever-greater percentage of our population are even more ridiculous, when judged from a scientific perspective? Angier points to Christian beliefs in resurrection and virgin birth as particularly far-fetched, and she cynically concludes that scientists fear rocking the boat of public opinion on these issues because their grant money might be the next thing that devout Christians will question.

Finally, in the last essay in the chapter philosopher William Dembski provides a very technical refutation of the process of deciding on scientific truth. He's particularly interested in how we go from "it's an explanation that can't be ruled out" to "it's very likely that this is the right explanation" to "this is the truth." Here, Dembski wants to prove that even by science's own set of rules, so-called "intelligent design" is the most likely explanation for the world as we know it, but in the abstract his discussion of how a hypothesis becomes truth can be applied to many other science-based controversies: what's causing climate change, whether life may exist on other planets, or whether the MMR vaccine is to blame for the rise in autism rates since 1980.

CLUSTER ONE: WHEN IS A DRUG NOT A DRUG?

The Era of Echinacea

Michael Spector

Michael Specter is a staff writer at the New Yorker *magazine, and he has won numerous awards for his science and medical journalism. His 2009 book* Denialism, *from which this excerpt is taken, purports to expose (in the words of the subtitle) "how irrational thinking hinders scientific progress, harms the planet, and threatens our lives." In the book, he examines several examples of what he dubs "denialism," or "replac[ing] the rigorous and open-minded skepticism of science with the inflexible certainty of ideological commitment."*

Not long ago, for reasons I still don't understand, I began to feel unfocused and lethargic. Work was no more stressful than it had ever been, and neither was the rest of my life. The bulk of my savings had been sucked into the vortex of the newly recognized black hole called the economy. But whose had not? I try to eat properly, exercise regularly, sleep peacefully, and generally adhere to the standard conventions of fitness. It didn't seem to be working. My doctor found nothing wrong and my blood tests were fine. Still, I felt strange, as if I were lacking in energy—or in something. So I did what millions of Americans do every day. I sought salvation in vitamins.

First, though, I had to figure out what variety of salvation to seek. There are many thousands of pills, potions, powders, gels, elixirs, and other packaged promises of improved vitality for sale within just a few blocks of my home. I walked to the closest store, a place called The Health Nuts, and told the proprietor I was feeling sluggish. He nodded gravely and took me straight to the amino acid section. To counteract my deficit of energy, he recommended a supplement of glutamine, which is one of the few amino acids that passes the blood-brain barrier. When people are under stress—physical or psychological—they begin to draw down on their stores of glutamine. "This stuff repairs brain cells and it's good for depression, too," he told me. A leaflet attached to the bottle described the amino acid as a magical aid for mental acuity. ("It is helpful with focus, concentration, memory, intellectual performance, alertness, attentiveness, improving mood, and eliminating brain fog & cloudiness.") I dropped it into my basket.

The store also had a garlic section—not actual garlic, but various pills with names like Kyolic and Garlicin, GarliMax and Gar-lique, all of which claimed to possess the healing properties of garlic, which for centuries has been thought to help ward off the common cold, clear up respiratory infections, and soothe sore throats. Garlic, its advocates claim, is also effective in treating heart problems, lowering cholesterol, and keeping arteries free of blood clots. I grabbed a bottle and moved on to the main supplement section, where multivitamins in every conceivable size, shape, dosage, strength, and formulation were lined up in rows. (There were vitamins for vegans, and for people allergic to gluten, for those who don't need iron and those who do; and there were specific pills for every age group, from the fetus right through to the "well-derly.") Antioxidants were next to them, all seemingly fueled by the "natural" power of prickly pear, goji, and açaí, the intensely popular Brazilian berry that supposedly offers benefits such as rejuvenation, skin toning, and weight loss, not to mention prevention of various illnesses like heart disease. There was also something called "BlueGranate," a combination of blueberries and pomegranates, both of which "possess wondrous health properties," as the bottle put it. "A synergistic blend of powerful and potent phytonutrient antioxidants." Into the basket it went.

Almost everything advertised itself as an antioxidant. Oxidation is a natural result of metabolic processes that can cause harmful chain reactions and significant cellular damage. Those broken cells in turn release unstable molecules called free radicals, which are thought to be the cause of many chronic diseases. Set loose, free radicals can turn into scavengers, ransacking essential proteins and DNA by grabbing their electrons for spare parts. Antioxidants prevent those reactions, but standing there, it was impossible to know how, or if, they worked. The collection of pills was so enormous, the choice so vast, and the information so humbling that while I may not have been depressed when I arrived at The Health Nuts, spending half an hour there did the trick.

I went home and consulted the Internet, which was even more intimidating: there are millions of pages devoted to vitamins and dietary supplements. You could spend your life combing through them and then another life trying them all out. Fortunately, my eye was drawn immediately to the Vitamin Advisor, a free recommendation service created by Dr. Andrew Weil, the ubiquitous healer, whose domed head and bearded countenance are so profoundly soothing that with a mere glance at his picture I felt my blood pressure begin to drop.

Dr. Weil is America's most famous and influential practitioner of complementary medicine—he prefers to call it integrative—which seeks to combine the best elements of conventional treatment with the increasingly popular armamentarium of alternatives, everything from supplements to colonic irrigation, spiritual healing, and homeopathy.

The public's hunger for novel remedies (and alternatives to expensive drugs) has transformed the integrative approach into one of the more potent commercial and social forces in American society. Nearly every major medical school and hospital in the country now has a department of integrative or complementary medicine. (A few years ago the Harvard Medical School even tussled with its affiliate, the Dana Farber Cancer Institute, over which would win the right to house such a program. Harvard prevailed.) While the movement has grown immensely since he opened his Center for Integrative Medicine in Arizona in 1994, Weil remains at its heart. Educated at Harvard University, both as an undergraduate and at its medical school, Weil embraces herbal therapies, New Age mysticism, and "spontaneous healing," which is the title of one of his books. But he also understands science and at times even seems to approve of it.

Weil offers sound advice in his many books—calling refined foods, excess starches, corn sweeteners, and trans fats dangerous, for example, and noting that exercise and a proper diet are far more beneficial even than the vitamins and supplements he recommends. His influence is immense, and in a country embarking on an urgent debate about how to make its health care system more affordable, rational, and responsive, that influence has never been felt more powerfully. Weil is in great demand as a public speaker, testifies before Congress, and has twice appeared on the cover of *Time* magazine. For advocating the many health benefits of mushrooms, Weil is a hero to mycologists the world over. (He is one of the rare Americans to have had a mushroom named after him, *Psilocybe weilii.*)

Andrew Weil seemed like just the man to lead me out of the forest of nutritional darkness into which I had inadvertently wandered. His Vitamin Advisor Web site assured me that, after answering a few brief questions, I would receive "a personalized comprehensive list of supplements based on my lifestyle, diet, medications, and health concerns"—all at no cost, without obligation, and prepared specially to meet my "unique nutritional needs." In addition, if I so chose, I could order the "premium quality, evidence-based" supplements in the proper doses that would "exactly match the recommendations from Dr. Weil." The supplements would be "custom packed in a convenient dispenser box and shipped directly to [me] each month." The only thing Dr. Weil doesn't do for you is swallow the pills.

I filled out the form, answering questions about my health and providing a brief medical history of my family. Two minutes after I pressed "submit," Dr. Weil responded, recommending a large number of dietary supplements to address my "specific health concerns." In all, the Vitamin Advisor recommended a daily roster of twelve pills, including an antioxidant and multivitamin, each of which is "recommended automatically for everyone as the basic foundation for insurance against nutritional gaps in the diet." Since, as he points out on the Web site, finding the proper doses can be a "challenge," Dr. Weil offered to "take out the guesswork" by calculating the size of every pack, which, over the previous ninety seconds, had been customized just for me. That would take care of one challenge; another would be coming up with the $1,836 a year (plus shipping and tax) my new plan would cost. Still, what is worth more than our health? If that was how much it would cost to improve mine, then that was how much I was willing to spend.

Also on my list: milk thistle, "for those who drink regularly or have frequent chemical exposure," neither of which applies to me; ashwagandha, an herb used in ayurvedic medicine to help the body deal with stress and used traditionally as an energy enhancer; cordyceps, a Chinese fungus that for centuries has been "well known" to increase aerobic capacity and alleviate fatigue; and eleuthero, also known as Siberian ginseng, often employed to treat "lethargy, fatigue and low stamina." In addition, there was 1000 milligrams of vitamin C (high doses of which, the information said, *may* provide additional protection against the oxidative stress of air pollution and acute or chronic illness); saw palmetto complex, mixed with stinging nettle root to "support prostate health"; an omega-3 pill (which *may* help reduce the symptoms of a variety of disorders); Saint-John's-wort (to support healthy mood); folic acid (which in addition to offering pregnant women proven protection against neural tube defects, *may* have a role to play in heart health, and *may* also help protect against cancers of the lung and colon, and even *may* slow the memory decline associated with aging); and finally another ayurvedic herb, triphala (a mixture of three fruits that help tone the muscles in the digestive tract).

Dr. Weil, who argues that we need to reject the prevailing impersonal approach to medicine, reached out from cyberspace to recommend each of these pills wholeheartedly and specifically, just for me. Before sending off a check, however, I collected some of the information on nutrition and dietary health offered by the National Institutes of Health, the Harvard School of Public Health, and the Memorial Sloan-Kettering Cancer Center. It turned out that my pills fell essentially into three categories: some, like cordyceps and triphala, seemed to do no harm but have never been shown in any major, placebo-controlled study to do any particular good; others, like Saint-John's-wort, may possibly do some good in some cases for some people, but can also easily interfere with and negate the effects of a large number of prescribed medicines, particularly the protease inhibitors taken by many people with AIDS. Most of the pills, however, including the multivitamin and antioxidant, seemed just plain dangerous.

Despite Dr. Weil's electronic assurances that his selections were "evidence-based," not one of those twelve supplements could be seen to hold anything more than theoretical value for me. At best. One study, completed in 2008, of the omega-3 fatty acids so beneficial when eaten in fish, found that in pill form they had no discernible impact on levels of cholesterol or any other blood lipids. The study was not large enough to be definitive; other trials are needed (and already under way). But it would be hard to argue with Jeffrey L. Saver, vice chairman of the American Heart Association's Stroke Council, professor of neurology at UCLA, and the director of its department of Stroke and Vascular Neurology, who called the findings "disappointing."

Others agreed. "You know, most of that stuff just comes right out at the other end," former surgeon general C. Everett Koop told me. The ninety-four-year-old Koop is congenitally incapable of ignoring facts or pretending they shouldn't matter. "Selling snake oil has always been one of Americas greatest con games. But the more we know about our bodies, the more people seem to buy these pills. That part I never did understand; you would have hoped it would be the other way around. But every day it becomes clearer: we need to eat properly and get exercise. And every day more people seem to ignore the truth."

New data keeps streaming in, and almost all of it confirms that assessment. In 2009, researchers from the Women's Health Initiative, working at dozens of major medical centers under the direction of the National Heart, Lung, and Blood Institute, concluded a fifteen-year study that focused on strategies for preventing heart disease, various cancers, and bone fractures in postmenopausal women. After following 161,808 women for eight years, the team found no evidence of any benefit from multivitamin use in any of ten conditions they examined. There were no differences in the rate of breast or colon cancer, heart attack, stroke, or blood clots. Most important, perhaps, vitamins did nothing to lower the death rate.

Another recent study, this time involving eleven thousand people, produced similar results. In 2008, yet another major trial, of men, had shown that the risk for developing advanced prostate cancer, and of dying from it, was in some cases *actually twice as high* for people who took a daily multivitamin as it was for those who never took them at all. There are hundreds of studies to demonstrate that people who exercise regularly reduce their risk of coronary artery disease by about 40 percent, as well as their risk of stroke, hypertension, and diabetes, also by significant amounts. Studies of vitamin supplements, however, have never produced any similar outcome.

Antioxidants, often described in the press as possessing wondrous powers, and recommended to every American by Dr. Weil, among others, are taken each day by millions. That should stop as soon as possible. While a diet rich in antioxidants has been associated with lower rates of chronic disease, those associations have never been reflected in trials in which people took antioxidants in supplement form. In 2007, for example, the *Journal of the American Medical Association* published the results of the most exhaustive review yet of research on such supplements. After examining sixty-eight trials that had been conducted during the previous seventeen years, researchers found that the 180,000 participants received no benefits whatsoever. In fact, vitamin A and vitamin E, each immensely popular, actually increased the likelihood of death by 5 percent. Vitamin C and selenium had no significant effect on mortality. (Vitamin C has long been controversial. Linus Pauling, the twentieth century's greatest chemist, was convinced it would cure cancer. He was wrong. In fact, too much vitamin C actually seems to help cancer cells withstand some kinds of treatment.)

"The harmful effects of antioxidant supplements are not confined to vitamin A," said the review's coauthor, Christian Gluud, a Danish specialist in gastroenterology and internal medicine and head of the trial unit at the Centre for Clinical Intervention Research at Copenhagen University Hospital. "Our analyses also demonstrate rather convincingly that beta-carotene and vitamin E lead to increased mortality compared to placebo." More than a quarter of all Americans over the age of fifty-five take vitamin E as a dietary supplement, yet among healthy people in the United States it would be hard to cite a single reported case of vitamin E deficiency.

It gets worse: folic acid supplements, while of unquestioned value for pregnant women, have been shown to increase the likelihood that men would develop prostate cancer. "Unfortunately, the more you look at the science the more clearly it tells you to walk away," Kelly Brownell said. Brownell, director of the Rudd Center for Food Policy and Obesity at Yale University, has for years studied the impact of nutrition on human health. "Vitamins in food are essential. And that's the way to get them. In food." With a couple of exceptions like folic acid for pregnant women, and in some cases vitamin D, for the vast majority of Americans dietary supplements are a complete waste of money. Often, in fact, they are worse.

That brings us back to Dr. Weil, who understands the arguments against using vitamin supplements in a country where, with rare exceptions, people have no vitamin deficiencies. He actually makes them pretty well in his book *Healthy Aging: A Lifelong Guide to Your Physical and Spiritual Well-Being*. "Not only is there insufficient evidence that taking [antioxidants] will do you any good, some experts think they might be harmful," he wrote. Excellent analysis, pithy and true. In fact, the evidence of harm keeps growing. In May 2009, researchers from Germany and the United States reported in the *Proceedings of the National Academy of Sciences* that antioxidants like vitamins C and E actually reduce the benefits of exercise. "If you promote health, you shouldn't take large amounts of antioxidants," said Michael Ristow, a nutritionist at the University of Jena, who led the international team of scientists. "Antioxidants in general ... inhibit otherwise positive effects of exercise, dieting and other interventions." Despite news like that, Dr. Weil still thinks you need to take his ("I continue to take a daily antioxidant formula and recommend it to others as well").

Weil doesn't buy into the idea that clinical evidence is more valuable than intuition. Like most practitioners of alternative medicine, he regards the scientific preoccupation with controlled studies, verifiable proof, and comparative analysis as petty and one-dimensional. The idea that accruing data is simply *one way* to think about science has become a governing tenet of the alternative belief system. The case against mainstream medicine is simple, repeated often, and, like most exaggerations, at least partially true: scientists are little more than data collectors in lab coats, people wholly lacking in human qualities. Doctors focus on disease and tissues and parts of the anatomy that seem to have failed, yet they act as if they were repairing air conditioners or replacing carburetors rather than attending to the complex needs of an individual human being. And pharmaceutical companies? They serve no interest but their own. Complementary and alternative medicine, on the other hand, is holistic. It cares. In the world of CAM, evidence matters no more than compassion or belief. Weil spells it all out in *Healthy Aging*:

> To many, faith is simply unfounded belief, belief in the absence of evidence, and that is anathema to the scientific mind. There is a great movement toward "evidence-based medicine" today, an attempt to weed out ideas and practices not supported by the kind of evidence that doctors like best: results of randomized controlled trials. *This way of thinking discounts the evidence of experience.* I maintain that it is possible to look at the world scientifically

and also to be aware of nonmaterial reality, and I consider it important for both doctors and patients to know how to assess spiritual health. [Italics added.]

Evidence of experience? He is referring to personal anecdotes, and allowing anecdotes to compete with, and often supplant, verifiable facts is evidence of its own kind—of the denialism at the core of nearly every alternative approach to medicine. After all, if people like Weil relied on the objective rules of science, or if their methods were known to work, there would be nothing alternative about them. If an approach to healing has a positive physical effect (other than as a placebo), then it leaves the alternative world of sentiment and enters the world of science and fact. The only attribute that alternatives share is that they do not meet the scientific standards of mainstream medicine.

Data is not warm or kind. It is also, however, not cold or cruel. Assessing data and gathering facts are the only useful tools we have to judge whether a treatment succeeds or fails. Weil understands that, and yet he mixes perfectly sensible advice with lunacy. ("I would look elsewhere than conventional medicine for help if I contracted a severe viral disease like hepatitis or polio, or a metabolic disease like diabetes," not to mention "treatment for cancer, except for a few varieties.")

That makes him a uniquely dangerous proponent of magical thinking. It is much easier to dismiss a complete kook—there are thousands to choose from—than a respected physician who, interspersed with disquisitions about life forces and energy fields, occasionally has something useful to say. Still, when Weil writes about a "great movement toward 'evidence-based medicine'" as if that were regrettable or new, one is tempted to wonder what he is smoking. Except that we don't need to wonder. He tells us.

Weil believes in what he calls "stoned thinking" and in intuition as a source of knowledge. This he juxtaposes with "straight" or "ordinary" thinking. You know, the type weighed down by silly rules and conventional thought. Like every alternative healer, Weil believes in the supremacy of faith and compassion. I certainly wouldn't argue against faith (if only because for many people it provides the single form of alternative medicine that seems clearly to work, a placebo effect). And here is my definition of compassion: the desire to alleviate suffering. Nothing in the course of human history meets that definition so fully as the achievements of evidence-based, scientifically verifiable medicine.

The world of CAM is powered by theories that have almost never been tested successfully, and its proponents frequently cite that fact as proof of their unique value, as if they represent a movement that cannot be confined (or defined) by trivialities. It would be terrific if Weil were correct when he says that evidence-based medicine is now in vogue; given its astounding record of success, it certainly ought to be. There is at least one compelling reason that the scientific method has come to shape our notion of progress and of modern life. It works.

But pendulums swing in more than one direction. As Steven Novella, director of general neurology at the Yale University School of Medicine, has written, the biggest victory won by proponents of complementary and alternative medicine was the name itself. "Fifty years ago what passes today as CAM was snake oil, fraud, folk medicine, and quackery," he wrote on Neurologica, his blog, which is devoted heavily to critical thinking. "The promoters of dubious health claims were charlatans, quacks, and con artists. Somehow they managed to pull off the greatest con of all—a culture change in which fraud became a legitimate alternative to scientific medicine, the line between science and pseudoscience was deliberately blurred, regulations designed to protect the public from quackery were weakened or eliminated, and it became politically incorrect to defend scientific standards in medicine."

The integrity of our medical system is certainly subject to doubts and debate. Doctors can be smug and condescending, and they often focus on treating diseases rather than preventing them. But in the alternate universe of CAM treatment nobody has to prove what is safe, what works and what doesn't. And that's dangerous because Americans are desperate for doctors who can treat their overall health, not just specific illnesses. Perhaps that is why this particular universe, populated by millions of people, has been fueled by one of American history's most unlikely coalitions—the marriage of the extreme right with the heirs of the countercultural left.

The political right has never wavered in its support for dietary supplements, and Orrin Hatch, the Utah Republican, has long been the industry's most powerful supporter. Hatch doesn't share a lot of political space with Tom Harkin, the populist liberal from Iowa. They don't agree on abortion rights, gun control, or many other issues. But when it comes to the right of every American to swallow any pill he or she can find in a health food store, the two are welded by a bond of steel. "For many people, this whole thing is about much more than taking their vitamins," Loren D. Israelsen, an architect of the 1994 legislation that deregulated the supplement industry, said. "This is really a belief system, almost a religion. Americans believe they have the right to address their health problems in the way that seems most useful to them. Often, that means supplements. When the public senses that the government is trying to limit its access to this kind of thing, it always reacts with remarkable anger—people are even willing to shoulder a rifle over it. They are ready to *believe anything* if it brings them a little hope."

That kind of fervent belief, rather than facts, feeds disciplines like ayurvedic medicine, which argues for the presence of demonic possession in our daily life, and Reiki, the Japanese practice of laying on the hands, which is based on the notion that an unseen, life-giving source of energy flows through each of our bodies. Then there is iridology (whose practitioners believe they can divine a person's health status by studying the patterns and colors of his iris), Healing—or Therapeutic—Touch, qi gong, magnet therapy. None of it works. Acupuncture, while effective in reducing arthritic pain and the impact of nausea, has never been demonstrated to help people quit smoking or lose weight—two of its most popular applications.

Homeopathy, perhaps the best-known alternative therapy, is also the most clearly absurd, based as it is on the notion that "like cures like." In other words, it presumes that a disease can be treated by ingesting infinitesimally small dilutions of the substance that caused the disease in the first place. No matter what the level of dilution, homeopaths claim, the original remedy leaves some kind of imprint on the water molecules. Thus, however diluted the solution becomes, it is still imbued with the properties of the remedy. No homeopathic treatment has ever been shown to work in a large, randomized, placebo-controlled clinical trial, but nothing seems to diminish its popularity. With logic that is both ridiculous and completely sensible, the federal government has taken a distant approach to regulating homeopathy *precisely because* it contains no substance that can possibly cause harm (or good). "Homeopathic products contain little or no active ingredients," Edward Miracco, a consumer safety officer with the FDA's Center for Drug Evaluation and Research explained. As a result, "from a toxicity, poison-control standpoint" there was no need to worry about the chemical composition of the active ingredient or its strength.

On those rare occasions when data relating to alternative medicine does become available, it is almost invariably frightening: in 2004, for example, a large group of researchers reported in the *Journal of the American Medical Association* that more than 20 percent of the ayurvedic medicines the group purchased on the Internet contained detectable and dangerous levels of lead, mercury, and arsenic. Soon afterward, the FDA warned consumers to exercise caution when purchasing ayurvedic products....

Almost 40 percent of American adults made use of some form of alternative medical therapy in 2007, according to the most recent *National Health Statistics Reports.* They spent $23.7 billion on dietary supplements alone. It has become one of the America's biggest growth industries. (And one that almost uniquely profits during times of economic distress. People are far more likely to turn to herbs and other supplements when they can't afford genuine medical care—and when they have no access to any other health system.) There were approximately 4,000 supplements on the market in 1994, when the industry was deregulated by Congress. Today the exact number is almost impossible to gauge, but most experts say there are at least 75,000 labels and 30,000 products. Those numbers don't include foods with added dietary ingredients like fortified cereals and energy drinks, which seem to fill half the supermarket shelves in the country.

The attraction isn't hard to understand. For all that medicine has accomplished, millions of people still suffer the considerable aches and pains of daily life. Arthritis and chronic pain plague America, and much of that agony is no more amenable to pharmaceutical relief today than it was thirty years ago. The drugs one needs to alleviate chronic pain—aspirin, for instance—can cause their own complications when taken in high enough doses over a long enough period. The pharmaceutical industry is a monolith that often acts as if there is, or soon will be, a pill for everything that ails you. Too much cholesterol? We can melt it away. Depressed? Try one of a dozen new prescriptions. Can't sleep? Blood pressure too high? Obese, sexually dysfunctional, or bald? No problem, the pharmaceutical industry is on the case.

Even our medical triumphs cause new kinds of problems. Reducing deaths from heart disease and cancer, for example, permits us to live longer. And *that* exposes us to a whole new set of conditions, most notably Alzheimer's disease, a debilitating, costly, and humiliating illness for which there is no cure and few treatments of any value.

So what could it hurt to try something new? It is an era of patient empowerment. People have access to more information than ever, their expectations have changed, and they demand greater control over their own health. Supplements and herbal alternatives to conventional drugs, with their "natural" connotations and cultivated image of self-reliance, fit in perfectly. They don't require machines or complex explanations. People can at least try to relate to an herb like echinacea, which has been around for centuries, no matter how useless it is, or a practice like qi gong, which means "cosmic breathing" and suggests that human life forces can be marshaled to flow through our body in a system of "meridians." Homeopathy is nothing more than fraud, as any number of scientists, studies, reports, and institutions have pointed out. Yet, in a complex world simplicity offers an escape from the many moving parts of the medical machine. As with organic food, if science seems allied with corporations and conglomerates—all distant and unfathomable—well, then, nature feels just right.

Under the banner of natural and alternative treatments Americans reflexively accept what they would never tolerate from a drug company (and never should). Vioxx made that clear. Without post-marketing surveys, the unacceptable risks of Vioxx would never have been known. Maybe none of the tens of thousand of herbal supplements for sale in the United States carries any similar risk. But how would we know, since that kind of monitoring has never been required of supplements? Doctors could not have continued to prescribe Vioxx after news of its dangers was made public. Yet compare the way Vioxx was removed from the market—amid the greatest possible publicity and under threat from billions of dollars' worth of lawsuits—to what happened in 2004 with ephedra, which was Americas, most popular dietary supplement.

Ephedra, derived from the Asian herb ma huang, has been used for thousands of years; the herb's active ingredient, ephedrine, boosts adrenaline, stresses the heart, raises blood pressure, and is associated with an increased risk of heart attack, stroke, anxiety, psychosis, and death. None of that was in question. But the FDA's decision to pull it from the market certainly was. Many of the Americans who were outraged that Vioxx had been approved in the first place were just as outraged when ephedra was banned. It took the FDA years of legal battle to get the supplement removed from the shelves of vitamin shops. Ephedrine-containing supplements have caused deaths in many countries, not just in America. But people still want it, and what people want, the Internet provides. "We're growing ma huang (ephedra), which has been used in Traditional Chinese Medicine for 5,000 years but is now banned in America thanks to the criminally-operated FDA," one foreign supplier wrote in 2009. And he will be more than happy to sell it to anyone foolish enough to send money. And why would anyone do that? Because a supplement is not a drug. Its value is taken on faith and no amount of evidence will ever convince true believers to turn away.

Belief outranks effectiveness. Vitamin worship demonstrates that fundamental tenet of denialism with depressing regularity. In 2003, a study that compared the efficacy of echinacea to a placebo in treating colds received considerable attention. Researchers followed more than four hundred children over a four-month period, and found not only that a placebo worked just as well, but that children treated with echinacea were significantly more likely to develop a rash than those who took nothing at all.

Subsequent studies have been even more damning. In 2005, researchers from the Virginia School of Medicine reported in the *New England Journal of Medicine* that echinacea had no clinical impact, whether taken as a prophylactic or after exposure to a virus. Nor did it lessen the duration or intensity of any symptom. In addition, the American College of Pediatricians has urged parents to avoid echinacea mixtures for children who are less than a year old. The response? According to the latest data released by the federal government in 2008, echinacea remains the most heavily used supplement in the childhood arsenal. (It is still wildly popular with adults too, but fish oil is now in greater demand.)

Almost no restrictions were placed on the sale of supplements, vitamins, or other home remedies until 1906, when, reacting to the revelations in Upton Sinclair's book *The Jungle,* Congress passed the Pure Food and Drug Act. The law permitted the Bureau of Chemistry, which preceded the Food and Drug Administration, to ensure that labels contained no false or misleading advertising. Since then, the pendulum has swung regularly between unregulated anarchy and restrictions that outrage many Americans. In 1922, the American Medical Association made an effort to limit the indiscriminate use of vitamins, describing their widespread promotion as "gigantic fraud." It helped for a while. By 1966, the FDA tried to require the manufacturers of all multivitamins to carry this notice: "Vitamins and minerals are supplied in abundant amounts in the foods we eat.... Except for persons with special medical needs, there is no scientific basis for recommending routine use of dietary supplements." The vitamin industry made certain that no such warning was ever issued.

The relationship between food, drugs, and supplements began to blur in the 1970s as connections between diet, food, and medicine became more fully understood. What began as a federal effort to improve nutrition and prevent confusion has ended up as a tacit endorsement of chaos and deceit. First, with a major report issued in 1977 by the Senate Select Committee on Nutrition and Human Needs, and then with studies by the National Academy of Sciences and other research groups, the government started telling Americans to alter their diets if they wanted to have long and healthy lives. That made sense, of course. Advice about ways to reduce the risk of heart disease, diabetes, many cancers, and other chronic illnesses became routine. There were food pyramids and instructions to eat less salt and fat and add fiber as well as whole grains; eat more fruits and vegetables and watch the calories. Still, it was against the law to suggest that there was a relationship between the ingredients in a commercial food and the treatment or prevention of a disease.

Then, in 1984, came the Original Sin. That year, the National Cancer Institute lent its unparalleled credibility to the Kellogg Company when together they launched a campaign in which All-Bran cereal was used to illustrate how a low-fat, high-fiber diet might reduce the risk for certain types of cancer. All-Bran was the first food permitted to carry a statement that was interpreted widely as "Eating this product will help prevent cancer." That led to the era of product labels, and completely changed the way Americans think about not only foods but dietary supplements and ultimately about their health. Food was no longer simply food; it was a way to get healthy. Some of those changes made sense: flour was fortified with folate; juice enriched with calcium; and in 2004, in the name of health, General Mills started making every one of its breakfast cereals from whole grains.

They were exceptions. It would require Dickens's narrative skills and Kafka's insight into bureaucratic absurdity to decipher the meaning of most products for sale in American health food stores today. In the world of alternative medicine, words have become unmoored from their meanings. As long as a company doesn't blatantly lie or claim to cure a specific disease such as cancer, diabetes, or AIDS, it can assert—without providing evidence of any kind—that a product is designed to support a healthy heart, or that it protects cells from damage or improves the function of a compromised immune system.

It's still against the law to claim a product cures a disease—unless it actually does. But there is no injunction against saying that a food or supplement can affect the structure or function of the body. Such claims can appear on any food, no matter how unhealthy. You cannot advertise a product as a supplement that "reduces" cholesterol, but you can certainly mention that it "maintains healthy cholesterol levels." It would be illegal to state that echinacea cures anything, since of course it has been shown to cure nothing. But it's perfectly acceptable to say that echinacea is "an excellent herb for infections of all kinds," although no such thing has been proven to be true.

Even claims that are true are often irrelevant. Vitamin A, for example, is essential for good vision—as supplements for sale in any health food store will tell you. Insufficient consumption of vitamin A causes hundreds of thousands of cases of blindness around the world each year, but not in the United States; here people don't have vision problems arising from a lack of vitamin A. Although statements advertising vitamin A for good vision may, like many others, be legally permissible, they are meaningless. And since too much vitamin A can cause birth defects and osteoporosis, for example, its potential to harm American consumers is far greater than the likelihood that it will do good.

Not long ago, I was given a free bottle of Lifewater at my gym. "It's the perfect energy drink," the woman handing it out said, "because it's an antioxidant and nutritious. And of course, it's water." Except that Lifewater is not really any of those things. Water has no calories. My "Agave Lemonade Vitamin Enhanced Beverage" with natural flavors contained 40 calories per eight-ounce serving. That's five calories per fluid ounce, a little less than half the calorie count of regular Pepsi, the signature product of the corporation that sells Lifewater. Even that number, of course, is misleading. Nobody drinks eight ounces; Lifewater comes in a twenty-ounce bottle, which brings the calorie count to 100.

Okay, 100 calories is not that big a deal. But the main ingredient in the drink is sugar: 32 grams in what many people assume to be vitamin-enriched *water*. And that is not the kind of water we need to be drinking in a country where one-third of adults are obese, 8 percent are diabetics, and both of those numbers are rising rapidly. Lifewater contains no meaningful amount of agave, lemonade, yerba mate, or taurine, all of which are listed invitingly on the bottle.

Lifewater is hardly the only beverage created, named, or designed to dupe people into buying the opposite of what they are looking for; it's probably not even the worst offender. In January 2009, the Center for Science in the Public Interest sued the Coca-Cola Company in federal district court, saying that the company's Glacéau division relied on deceptive advertising and unsubstantiated claims when promoting VitaminWater as a "Nutrient-Enhanced Water Beverage" and by employing the motto "vitamins + water = all you need," for a product that has almost as much sugar in it as a similarly sized can of Coke. "VitaminWater is Coke's attempt to dress up soda in a physician's white coat," the CSPI litigation director Steve Gardner said when he filed the lawsuit. "Underneath, it's still sugar water, albeit sugar water that costs about ten bucks a gallon."

Critical Reading Questions

Summarizing the Text

1. A key term for Specter is "evidence-based" science. What does this term mean? What role does it play in scientific and medical policy today? What might be its opposite?

2. Specter both analyzes and uses loaded language throughout this chapter—he calls attention to the ways the alternative medicine community renamed and rebranded itself to sound more mainstream, but he himself uses freighted words to describe both "his" and "the other" side. List the terms he uses to describe each side—what do they have in common? What is the rhetorical effect of using such language?

Establishing the Context

3. Specter calls out media-friendly alternative medicine figures such as Andrew Weil for their fast-and-loose attitude about evidence-based science in their promotion of alternative medicine. How do such figures win influence? How do they use the media to gain prominence?

4. In the rest of his book, Specter looks at several other examples of what he calls "denialism"—the belief that the measles-mumps-rubella (MMR) vaccine causes autism, the belief that "organic" foods are healthier than conventionally produced foods, and the belief that pharmaceutical companies care only about profits and cannot be trusted to make safe drugs. Research one of these controversies in more detail—does this seem to you an example of "denialism"?

Responding to the Message

5. What is the role of faith and belief in healing? Can you find examples of credible studies in which such intangible factors contributed to better medical outcomes? Do these studies undermine Specter's argument?

Voodoo Priests, Botanicas, Herbs, and Amulets

Jennifer Steinhauer

Jennifer Steinhauer is a longtime reporter for the New York Times, *where she has covered Congress and was the Los Angeles bureau chief. She is also coauthor of* Beverly Hills Adjacent, *a 2009 novel. In this short feature, Steinhauer takes a different angle on the "alternative medicine" question, focusing on how traditional healing methods persist among immigrant communities but are changed by the American imperative to sell. This article appeared in the* New York Times *in August 2000.*

Voodoo Priests, Botanicas, Herbs and Amulets

When in August of 2000 investigators shuttered a large, unlicensed medical clinic in Flushing, New York, that they said offered Chinese and Western remedies, they provided a glance behind a curtain that shrouds an expansive underground health care system serving hundreds of thousands of the city's immigrants.

While the clinic, the New York Beijing Hospital of Traditional Chinese Medicine, may have been more brazen than other centers—it advertised in a local Chinese paper and ran a Web site promising care for a variety of ills—it is only one of perhaps thousands of clinics, herbalists, spiritual centers and makeshift medical offices where many of the city's immigrants go for medical care.

Stymied by a lack of health insurance, fearful of the medical centers' potential connections to immigration authorities and longing for familiar remedies dispensed by someone who speaks their language, many of the city's immigrants have been driven to create their own complex methods of getting health care.

The landscape of their alternative medical sources is as vast and textured as the city's immigrant population, comprising herbal healers used by many people from the Caribbean and South and Central America, voodoo priests frequented by some Haitians, pharmacists who double as internists and doctors, from regions ranging from Russia to India to Poland, who lack an American license but set up shop offering some form of care to those who seek them.

"There is a whole unregulated sector of medicine at work in New York," said Dr. Francesca M. Gany, the executive director of the New York Task Force on Immigrant Health.

About 65 percent of the hundreds of immigrants in Queens who responded to a survey said they used an alternative source of care in addition to or instead of the city's larger health care system, Dr. Gany said. She added that she believed the same held true for the city's broader immigrant population.

And the treatments doled out by these centers vary: herbal remedies used to treat stomachaches and cradle cap; exorcisms for patients with chronic stomach pain; amulets attached to babies to ward off evil spirits; and antibiotics that are dubiously obtained and unwisely administered.

Most often, patients who are new immigrants mingle in two medical worlds, the city's vast array of hospitals and clinics, and a second sphere, where folk remedies are obtained. A few avoid the American medical system entirely, believing they cannot afford it or fearing the doctors, and rely totally on other healers. Others get no health care at all, relying on home remedies until they become terribly ill and end up in a hospital emergency room.

Maria Sambrano, an immigrant from Honduras, said she inhabited both worlds, depending on her needs. "I think some plants work better than medicine," said Ms. Sambrano, who was waiting to meet with a spiritualist at Botanica Santa Barbara in Washington Heights last week.

While many doctors say some folk treatments like herbs are harmless or even beneficial, health care experts are concerned that vast swaths of immigrant groups lack access to conventional health care, and that more centers like the one in Queens may be offering wholly unregulated medicine that they are ill equipped to provide.

And patients may end up paying more for some care than they could be getting at city clinics that charge on a sliding scale based on income. "In the minds of our patients, alternative medicine is the standard of care and what we do is alternative medicine," said Dr. Guillermo Santos the medical director of Betances Health Unit, a community health center on the Lower East Side.

"This poses two problems," Dr. Santos said. "People may have serious: illnesses they may be trying to cure at home. Or they don't tell provider what they are using out of fear." The center's doctors try to stay current or the herbs that patients tend to use, and have worked with neighborhood shamans, showing them how to spot the basic symptoms of diseases like tuberculosis.

Dr. Jackson Kuan, the assistant director of gastroenterology at Flushing Hospital, said he occasionally saw patients who had misused herbs on the advice of alternative healers. He said he recently saw a Korean patient who had been given an herbal concoction that led to fatal liver failure.

And health care workers have been alarmed in recent years by the increased use of mercury among Caribbean residents, especially in the Crown Heights section of Brooklyn.

Illegal centers usually operate far below the radar screen of law enforcement, advertising mostly by word of mouth or through subtle marketing in the language of their intended customers, an increasingly diverse group.

"It is hard just to become aware of the various services that are being provided," said Wayne M. Osten, director of the State Department of Health's Office of Health System Management. Mr. Osten said the department closes twenty to twenty-five unlicensed medical centers a year. "We are looking to hire staff with those skills to better police it, because as you get more and more communities it does become a tougher problem to monitor."

Yet many healers operate legally, if on the fringes. For instance, according to Dr. Gany and other experts, some of the centers serve as entrees to the larger medical world, where new immigrants are directed to clinics and hospitals and assured that immigration officials will not be notified if the immigrants are patients.

Further, understanding how immigrants use alternative centers helps doctors better treat patients who do not share their language and culture. "I don't think these places are necessarily an impediment to care," said Dr. Mary McCord, a pediatrician in Washington Heights who had an intern conduct a study of her patients' herbal use.

"If we can get people to tell us what they are doing, we can negotiate, because people do make choices," Dr. McCord added. "They might say, 'I have asthma but I have heard bad things about those medicines so let me try honey and onions.' So maybe we can get them to use honey and onions and something else. One skill in being a doctor is to accept where people are coming from and to be willing to negotiate according to their beliefs."

The folk healers range greatly from group to group, neighborhood to neighborhood, with much overlap. Hispanics, Russians and people in the Caribbean alike use herbal medicine, although often in different preparations. Russians, according to health care workers, lean more toward vitamins. Shamans have different functions, sometimes performing voodoo ceremonies for Caribbean clients, or doing what they say is healing work with their hands.

The Chinese gravitate toward herbal treatments and acupuncture, as do some Koreans. Southeast Asians often practice yoga and use medicines from their countries.

Each nation offers its own folk remedies, herbs and medical concoctions—rose water for nerves; shark oil for various flu symptoms; cordial de monell, a sedative mixed with oil, for teething; and anise for nausea, to name just a few. These treatments are most often purchased at botanicas, stores that specialize in herbal medicines, oils and religious wares. At Botanica Santa Barbara, one can find fresh rosemary, dozens of ointments, creams and oils to keep away evil spirits, ignite romance or invite prosperity.

Lisa Garcia, a card reader, helps customers with personal problems and says she removes pain with her hands.

"Sometimes people go to the doctor and when it doesn't work, come here," said Antonio Mora, the store's owner.

But while many immigrants prefer many folk or home remedies to conventional medicine, far too many are shut out of the health care system because they lack insurance or are unaware of what is available to them cheaply, experts said. About 40 percent of legal immigrants are uninsured, said David Sandman, a program officer at the Commonwealth Fund, a private philanthropic organization in New York. Among illegal immigrants, the number is far higher, he said.

And then there is the intense distrust many immigrants feel toward the medical establishment. Dr. McCord said that many of her Dominican patients had negative notions about asthma medicine. Dr. Santos said many Jamaican patients shunned hypertension medicine, preferring herbs. And some Asians are afraid to have blood drawn because they think it will only weaken them, said Dinah Surh, the administrator of Sunset Park Family Health Center in Brooklyn.

Her center, with its diverse staff, has gone to great pains to attract many immigrant groups. It set up a mosque for Muslim patients to pray in. It offers acupuncture—now used by patients around the world—as one way of attracting Chinese patients.

The center went for other touches, Ms. Surh said. "We wanted to have a fish tank. Some Chinese groups said we need gold-colored fish for good luck, so we added those. But the tank is right below a skylight, and they told us the good luck would go out of the skylight. So we put a shade there."

Many doctors said that thousands of years of herbal medicine are nothing to sneeze at, and pointed to a highly increased interest among American patients in Eastern techniques like yoga and acupuncture. Indeed many large hospitals have adopted these types of practices in recent years.

And conventional doctors have a few tips to learn from folk and traditional healers, some experts concurred, like advertising in various languages and getting the word out through community groups. But still, many, many immigrants will always rely on a mix of services.

"I use conventional medicine," said Ray Gongora, who immigrated from Cuba in the 1960s and often turns to herbs. "But emotionally I don't get what I need. They give you a blood test and send you on your way, but if you're not prepared mentally, you get depressed."

Critical Reading Questions

Summarizing the Text

1. Does this article have a thesis or an argument? If so, what is it? If not, what is its main point (if it is not an arguable claim)?
2. What are the advantages and problems stemming from these immigrants' reliance on traditional or alternative medicines?

Establishing the Context

3. Steinhauer writes this about New York, a city of immigrants; in 2000, when this article appeared, 36 percent of the city's population was foreign born. How might her article be different if she wrote it about your city or town?

Responding to the Message

4. As the foreign-born population of the United States surges (due to both legal and illegal immigration), immigrant communities will continue to bring their healing and medical traditions here. What sort of regulation do you think that federal, state, and local authorities should impose upon these stores and clinics and practitioners?
5. What are some ways that the U.S. health care system can become more welcoming to immigrants? Should this be a social priority?

Health Effects of Energy Drinks on Children, Adolescents, and Young Adults

Sara M. Seifert,

Judith Schaechter,

Eugene Hershorin, and

Steven E. Lipschulz

At the time this article appeared, Sara M. Seifert was a third-year medical student and Judith Schaechter, Eugene Hershorin, and Steven E. Lipschulz were faculty members at the Leonard M. Miller School of Medicine at the University of Miami. For this article, Seifert and her coauthors conducted a "literature review" of scientific studies related to the ingredients and consumers of energy drinks. Synthesizing all of the relevant studies, Seifert and her collaborators concluded that energy drinks "have no therapeutic benefit" (contrary to some of their advertising claims) and that more research on these drinks should be conducted to see if their sale should be regulated by the government. This article appeared in Pediatrics, the journal of the American Academy of Pediatrics, in February 2011.

OBJECTIVE: To review the effects, adverse consequences, and extent of energy-drink consumption among children, adolescents, and young adults.

METHODS: We searched PubMed and Google using "energy drink," "sports drink," "guarana," "caffeine," "taurine," "ADHD," "diabetes," "children," "adolescents," "insulin," "eating disorders," and "poison control center" to identify articles related to energy drinks. Manufacturer Web sites were reviewed for product information.

RESULTS: According to self-report surveys, energy drinks are consumed by 30% to 50% of adolescents and young adults. Frequently containing high and unregulated amounts of caffeine, these drinks have been reported in association with serious adverse effects, especially in children, adolescents, and young adults with seizures, diabetes, cardiac abnormalities, or mood and behavioral disorders or those who take certain medications. Of the 5448 US caffeine overdoses reported in 2007, 46% occurred in those younger than 19 years. Several countries and states have debated or restricted their sales and advertising.

CONCLUSIONS: Energy drinks have no therapeutic benefit, and many ingredients are understudied and not regulated. The known and unknown pharmacology of agents included in such drinks, combined with reports of toxicity, raises concern for potentially serious adverse effects in association with energy-drink use. In the short-term, pediatricians need to be aware of the possible effects of energy drinks in vulnerable populations and screen for consumption to educate families. Long-term research should aim to understand the effects in at-risk populations. Toxicity surveillance should be improved, and regulations of energy-drink sales and consumption should be based on appropriate research.

"Energy drinks" are beverages that contain caffeine, taurine, vitamins, herbal supplements, and sugar or sweeteners and are marketed to improve energy, weight loss, stamina, athletic performance, and concentration.[1-3] Energy drinks are available in >140 countries and are the fastest growing US beverage market; in 2011, sales are expected to top $9 billion.[4-10] Half of the energy-drink market consists of children (<12 years old), adolescents (12–18 years old), and young adults (19–25 years old).[7-10]

Although healthy people can tolerate caffeine in moderation, heavy caffeine consumption, such as drinking energy drinks, has been associated with even more serious consequences such as seizures, mania, stroke, and sudden death.[6-8,12-14] Numerous reports exist in the popular media, and there are a handful of case reports in the literature that associate such adverse events with energy-drink consumption; it is prudent to investigate the validity of such claims. Children, especially those with cardiovascular, renal, or liver disease, seizures, diabetes, mood and behavioral disorders, or hyperthyroidism or those who take certain medications, may be at higher risk for adverse events from energy-drink consumption.[6-8,14-24] Although the US Food and Drug Administration (FDA) limits caffeine content in soft drinks, which are categorized as food, there is no such regulation of energy drinks, which are classified as dietary supplements.[1-3] Despite the large, unregulated market for energy drinks and reports in the literature and popular media of serious adverse events associated with their consumption, research into their use and effects has been sparse.[25] However, schools, states, and countries increasingly are exploring content and sales regulations of these drinks.[1,8,13,26-35]

Given the rapidly growing market and popularity among youth, we reviewed the literature to (1) determine what energy drinks are, (2) compile consumption data of energy drinks by children, adolescents, and young adults, (3) compile caffeine and energy-drink overdose data, (4) examine the physiologic effects of the ingredients in energy drinks, (5) identify potential problems of energy drinks among children and adolescents, (6) assess the marketing of energy drinks, (7) report current regulation of energy drinks, and (8) propose educational, research, and regulatory recommendations.

Methods

We searched PubMed by using "energy drink," "sports drink," "guarana," "caffeine," 'taurine," "ADHD" (attention-deficit/hyperactivity disorder), "diabetes," "children," "adolescents," "insulin," "eating disorders," and "poison control center" singly or in combination. We limited searches to English-language and foreign-language articles with English-language abstracts and selected articles by relevance to energy-drink use in children and adolescents. We similarly searched Google for print and trade media. We reviewed articles and Internet sources by the above search through June 2010 and updated sections as new information became available through January 2011.

Results

Two-thirds of the 121 references we found on energy drinks were in the scientific literature, although reports by government agencies and interest groups also contained much useful information. Most information came from the United States, but European, Canadian, Australian, New Zealand, and Chinese sources are also represented.

Discussion

What Are Energy Drinks?

Energy drinks may contain caffeine, taurine, sugars and sweeteners, herbal supplements, and other ingredients and are distinct from sports drinks and vitamin waters.[6,8] In 2008, the National Federation of State High School Associations, while recommending water and sports drinks for rehydration, specifically did not recommend energy drinks and cited potential risks, the absence of benefit, and drug interactions.[36,37]

Caffeine is the main active ingredient in energy drinks; many of them contain 70 to 80 mg per 8-oz serving (~3 times the concentration in cola drinks).[8,31] Caffeine content can be nearly 5 times greater than that in 8 oz of cola drinks when packaged as "energy shots" (0.8–3 oz) or as 16-oz drinks.[8,29,38]

Energy drinks often contain additional amounts of caffeine through additives, including guarana, kola nut, yerba mate, and cocoa.[6,7,14,25] Guarana (*Paullinia cupana*) is a plant that contains caffeine, theobromine (a chronotrope), and theophylline (an inotrope).[39] Each gram of guarana can contain 40 to 80 mg of caffeine, and it has a potentially longer half-life because of interactions with other plant compounds.[7,14] Manufacturers are not required to list the caffeine content from these ingredients.[7,14] Thus, the actual caffeine dose in a single serving may exceed that listed.[9,29]

Consumption of Energy Drinks by Children, Adolescents, and Young Adults

In the United States, adolescent caffeine intake averages 60 to 70 mg/day and ranges up to 800 mg/day.[24,40] Most caffeine comes from soda; however, energy drinks are becoming increasingly popular.[7,24,41,42] The following self-report studies have examined energy-drink consumption by children, adolescents, and young adults.[7,24,41,42]

One study found that 28% of 12- to 14-year-olds, 31% of 12- to 17-year olds, and 34% of 18- to 24-year-olds reported regularly consuming energy drinks.[5,43] Shortly after energy drinks were approved in Germany, a study of 1265 adolescents found that 94% were aware of energy drinks, 53% had tried them, 23% drank <1 can per week, and 3% drank 1 to 7 cans per week.[44] Among 10- to 13-year-olds, 31% of girls and 50% of boys had tried energy drinks, and 5% of girls and 23% of boys reported drinking them regularly but at a rate of <1 can per week.[44] Most children in the study consumed energy drinks in moderation, but a small group consumed extreme amounts.[44]

A survey of 496 college students found that 51% of those surveyed regularly consumed >1 energy drink per month; the majority of them habitually drank energy drinks several times per week.[9] Insufficient sleep (67%) and the desire to increase energy (65%) were the most common reasons for use.[9] In this study, 54% of the respondents reported mixing energy drinks with alcohol, and 49% drank ≥3 of them while partying.[9] Another study of 795 college students found that 39% of the respondents had consumed an energy drink in the previous month and that, on average, men drank energy drinks 2.5 days/month, whereas women drank 1.2 days/month.[45]

The estimated caffeine exposure of consuming energy drinks or energy shots was calculated for New Zealand children (5–12 years old), teenagers (13–19 years old), and young men (19–24 years old).[46] After consuming a single retail unit, 70% of the children and 40% of the teenagers who consumed caffeine were estimated to have exceeded the adverse-effect level of 3 mg/kg body weight per day beyond their baseline dietary exposure.[46] An average child, teenager, or young man would all, on average, exceed the adverse-effect level after consuming a single retail unit of energy drink/energy shot above their baseline dietary caffeine exposure.[46]

Caffeine and Energy-Drink Overdoses

US poison centers have not tracked the prevalence of overdoses attributed to energy drinks, because exposures were coded as "caffeine" or "multisubstance exposures" and combined with other caffeine sources (American Association of Poison Control Centers Board of Directors, personal communication, 2010).[47] Energy drinks were recently given unique reporting codes, so their toxicity can now be tracked (American Association of Poison Control Centers Board of Directors, personal communication, 2010).[47]

Germany has tracked energy-drink-related incidents since 2002.[33] Reported outcomes include liver damage, kidney failure, respiratory disorders, agitation, seizures, psychotic conditions, rhabdomyolysis, tachycardia, cardiac dysrhythmias, hypertension, heart failure, and death.[33] Ireland's poison center reported 17 energy-drink adverse events including confusion, tachycardia, and seizures and 2 deaths between 1999 and 2005.[25] New Zealand's poison center reported 20 energy-drink/shot-related adverse events from 2005 to 2009; 12 cases were referred for treatment of vomiting, nausea, abdominal pain, jitteriness, racing heart, and agitation.[46] The minimum and maximum symptomatic caffeine levels were 200 mg (4 mg/kg) in a 13-year-old with jitteriness and 1622 mg (35.5 mg/kg) in a 14-year-old. The maximum volume consumed was fifteen 250-mL cans (11.5 mg/kg caffeine) during 1 hour.[46] One 23-year-old chronic energy-drink consumer had a myocardial infarction.[46]

Physiologic Effects of the Ingredients in Energy Drinks

Caffeine Pharmacology and Physiology   Caffeine, the most commonly used psychoactive drug worldwide, may be the only psychoactive drug legally available over-the-counter to children.[39,48] Caffeine is an adenosine and benzodiazepine receptor antagonist, phosphodiesterase inhibitor, and central nervous system stimulant.[29,38,49] In healthy adults, a caffeine intake of ≤400 mg/day is considered safe; acute clinical toxicity begins at 1 g, and 5 to 10 g can be lethal.[29]

Physiologically, caffeine causes coronary and cerebral vasoconstriction, relaxes smooth muscle, stimulates skeletal muscle, has cardiac chronotropic and inotropic effects, reduces insulin sensitivity, and modulates gene expression in premature neonates.[9,29,50–52] Large amounts of caffeine increase urine flow and sweat excretion and alter blood electrolyte levels.[11,53] Although caffeine is a mild diuretic, consumption of ≤500 mg/day does not cause dehydration or chronic water imbalance.[54,55]

Caffeine is a ventilatory stimulant with anti-inflammatory and bronchoprotective effects.[56] Caffeine has been linked to dyspnea on exertion from central and peripheral chemoreceptor stimulation.[56] In addition, increased breathing work may divert blood flow away from locomotor muscles and negate any ergogenic advantage.[56] Caffeine's cardiovascular effects include decreased heart rate from stimulation of medullary vagal nuclei and increased blood pressure.[24,57–61]

Adults who consume low-to-moderate amounts of caffeine (1–3 mg/kg or 12.5–100 mg/day) have improved exercise endurance, cognition, reaction time, and mood with sleep deprivation.[9,24,56,62] However, these studies typically involve habitual caffeine consumers, and results reflect withdrawal-symptom reversal.[58]

Consuming 4 to 12 mg/kg of caffeine has been associated with undesirable symptoms, including anxiety and jitteriness.[63] Headache and fatigue, common withdrawal symptoms, can occur after short-term, high-dose use.[64] Caffeine intoxication is a clinical syndrome of nervousness, irritability, anxiety, insomnia, tremor, tachycardia, palpitations, and upset stomach.[6,7,9,14,26,65] Additional adverse effects include vomiting and abdominal pain, hypokalemia, hallucinations, increased intracranial pressure, cerebral edema, stroke, paralysis, rhabdomyolysis, altered consciousness, rigidity, seizures, arrhythmias, and death.[1,2,8,29,48]

Caffeine intakes of >300 mg/day have been associated with miscarriage and low birth weight.[38,66,67] Long-term caffeine consumption relates to a lower risk of Parkinson disease and a slower age-related cognitive decline.[58]

Effects of Caffeine in Children and Adolescents   Adolescent and child caffeine consumption should not exceed 100 mg/day and 2.5 mg/

kg per day, respectively.[7,38,63] For example, 8 oz of Red Bull (Fuschl am See, Austria) provides 77 mg of caffeine, or 1.1 mg/kg for a 70-kg male or 2.2 mg/kg for a 35-kg pre-teen.[40] Whether the effects of caffeine in adults can be generalized to children remains unclear.[63] In a study of 26 boys and 26 men, the same dose of caffeine affected blood pressure similarly, but heart rate was significantly lowered in boys, whereas there was no effect on heart rate in men.[68] Boys also exhibited increased motor activity and speech rates and decreased reaction times than did men.[69]

Caffeine can improve attention, but it also increases blood pressure and sleep disturbances in children.[24,63,70,71] After cessation in children who habitually consume caffeine, attention decreases and reaction time increases transiently.[24–39] Similarly, reaction time has been shown to decrease as the dose of caffeine in children increases.[24]

In a study of 9- to 11-year-olds with habitual (mean intake: 109 mg/day) and low (mean intake: 12 mg/day) caffeine consumption given 50 mg of caffeine after overnight abstention, habitual caffeine users reported withdrawal-symptom (headache and dulled cognition) reversal. The children who did not habitually consume caffeine reported no marked changes in cognitive performance, alertness, or headache.[63]

Caffeine may affect future food and beverage preferences by acting on the developing child's brain reward-and-addiction center; this effect may be gender specific.[5] A study of 12- to 17-year-olds revealed that boys found caffeinated soda more reinforcing than did girls regardless of usual caffeine consumption.[72]

Physiologic Effects of Other Ingredients in Energy Drinks and Potential Synergistic Effects

Popular media and case reports have associated adverse events with energy-drink consumption. Yet, few studies have examined the physiologic effects of individual ingredients or potential synergistic effects; furthermore, results of experimental studies have been inconclusive and occasionally contradictory.[24,25,59,73]

Some studies of adults revealed improved mental alertness, reaction times, and concentration with energy drinks;[59,74] others revealed no improvement compared with caffeine or glucose alone.[73] One study of 14 young adults compared a complete energy-drink mixture to the glucose fraction, the caffeine fraction, and the herbal fraction.[9,59] Although individual components did not enhance cognition, the combined ingredients did.[9,59] Caffeine and taurine combined may synergistically decrease heart rate initially; one study found that 70 minutes after consumption, heart rate returned to normal and blood pressure increased.[25,75] Taurine similarly produced a reflex bradycardia when injected into the rat cerebroventricular system.[75] Another study of 15 healthy young adults in a 7-day trial in which they consumed 500 mL of an energy drink each day with 160 mg of caffeine and 2000 mg of taurine, reported an average increase in systolic blood pressure of 9 to 10 mm Hg and an average increased heart rate of 5 to 7 beats per minute 4 hours after consumption.[25,58]

Caffeine- and taurine-containing beverages increased left atrial contractility in 13 athletes, thereby increasing left ventricular end-diastolic volume and stroke volume.[76] The caffeine-only group showed no changes in left ventricular function.[76] Taurine may cause this increase in stroke volume by suppressing sympathetic nervous stimulation and influencing calcium stores in cardiac muscle.[8] Results of human and animal studies have suggested that long-term taurine exposure may cause hypoglycemia[25] but a decreased risk of coronary heart disease.[77] In animal experiments, taurine also has shown anticonvulsive and epileptogenic properties.[25]

Among 50 young adults who drank one sugar-free energy drink, hematologic and vascular effects included increased platelet aggregation and mean arterial pressure and a decrease in endothelial function.[78] Guarana has antiplatelet aggregation properties in vitro, but how it functions physiologically in energy drinks is unknown.[79] A study of 20 healthy subjects revealed that caffeinated espresso had no effects on endothelial function.[80] Caffeine alone did not affect platelet function.[81]

Ginseng, a common ingredient in many energy drinks, may lower blood glucose levels, but its actions in energy drinks are unclear.[82]

Potential Problems of Energy Drinks Among Children and Adolescents

Cardiovascular Effects of Energy Drinks on Children and Adolescents High doses of caffeine may exacerbate cardiac conditions for which stimulants are contraindicated.[17,18,84–86] Of particular concern are ion channelopathies and hypertrophic cardiomyopathy, the most prevalent genetic cardiomyopathy in children and young adults, because of the risk of hypertension, syncope, arrhythmias, and sudden death.[11,86,87]

Effects of Energy Drinks on Children and Adolescents With ADHD ADHD occurs in 8% to 16% of US school-aged children and may be more prevalent in children with heart disease.[88,89] Some 2.5 million US children take stimulants for ADHD, which may increase heart rate and blood pressure.[89–91] Children with ADHD have higher rates of substance abuse, including the abuse of caffeine, which blocks the A2A adenosine receptors and thereby enhances the dopamine effect at the D2 dopamine receptor, similarly to the way guanfacine works for ADHD.[92,95] As with the ADHD stimulants, the combined effects of energy drinks and antidepressants are unknown.[94] For the subpopulation with methylphenidate cardiotoxicity, energy-drink use may increase cardiac events.[95,96]

Energy-Drink Use in Children and Adolescents With Eating Disorders Children and adolescents with eating disorders, especially anorexia nervosa, may regularly consume high amounts of caffeine to counter caloric-restriction-associated fatigue, suppress appetite, and produce looser stools and some diuresis.[71–100] The risk of cardiac dysrhythmias and intracardiac conduction abnormalities from high-caffeine energy drinks in children with eating disorders at higher risk for cardiac-related morbidity/mortality and electrolyte abnormalities is disconcerting.[91–99]

Effects on Caloric Intake and Diabetes Because obesity is epidemic, caloric increases from energy-drink consumption become important. Additional calories may increase blood pressure, blood glucose levels, BMI, calcium deficiency, dental problems, depression, and low self-esteem.[4,101,102] Sugar and caffeine may also synergistically increase postprandial hyperglycemia, which is of concern for children with diabetes.[38,51,52]

Effects on Bone Mineralization Early adolescence is the time of maximal calcium deposition in bone, and caffeine interferes with intestinal calcium absorption.[103,104] It remains controversial whether caffeine itself has the most marked effect on bone acquisition during adolescence or whether replacement of milk intake by caffeinated beverages is the leading contributor.[103,104]

Marketing of Energy Drinks

Youth-targeted marketing strategies date to 1987 when Red Bull was introduced in Austria.[100] When it took 5 years to get permission to export Red Bull to Germany, rumors about its legality and dangerous effects helped fuel its popularity, and it became known as "speed in a can," "liquid cocaine," and a "legal drug."[100]

Energy-drink marketing strategies include sporting event and athlete sponsorships, alcohol-alternative promotion, and product placement in media (including Facebook and video games) oriented to children, adolescents, and young adults.[43,105] Newer alcoholic energy drinks, the cans of which resemble the nonalcoholic counterparts, target risk-taking youth.[43]

Contrasting with brand design is the voluntary fine-print warning label on some products, which state that they may not be safe for children, those who are sensitive to caffeine, or for pregnant or nursing women.[105–107]

Regulation of Energy Drinks

The FDA imposes a limit of 71 mg of caffeine per 12 fl oz of soda.[1,2] Energy-drink manufacturers may circumvent this limit by claiming that their drinks are "natural dietary supplements."[1,2] Thus, safety determinations of energy drinks are made solely by the manufacturers, and there are no requirements for testing, warning labels, or restriction against sales or consumption by minors.[1-3] In contrast, over-the-counter dedicated caffeine stimulants (eg, No-Doz) must list the minimum age for purchase (12 years), adverse effects, cautionary notes, recommended dose, and the total daily recommended dose of caffeine. In November 2009, the FDA asked manufacturers of alcoholic energy drinks to prove their safety.[108] The US Senate is considering a bill that would require supplement manufacturers to register annually with the FDA and allow FDA recalls of supplements suspected of being unsafe. Ingredients may also be restricted to those that have already been approved by the FDA.[109]

Regulatory controversies also extend internationally. When France banned Red Bull, the manufacturers challenged the ban through the European Commission, which determined that the caffeine and taurine concentrations in energy drinks had not been proven to be health risks and ordered France to lift the ban; the European Food Safety Authority has encouraged international data-pooling to better assess risks in children, adolescents, and young adults.[33,110] In 2008, authorities in Germany, Hong Kong, and Taiwan detected 0.13 µg per can of cocaine (average) in Red Bull Cola. Red Bull manufacturers insisted that active cocaine was removed from the coca leaf during processing and that the extract was used for flavoring. However, 11 of 16 German states banned the product.[111]

Conclusions

On the basis of this review, we conclude that (1) energy drinks have no therapeutic benefit, and both the known and unknown pharmacology of various ingredients, combined with reports of toxicity, suggest that these drinks may put some children at risk for serious adverse health effects;[11,16,24,25,38] (2) typically, energy drinks contain high levels of caffeine, taurine, and guarana, which have stimulant properties and cardiac and hematologic activity,[7,8,11] but manufacturers claim that energy drinks are nutritional supplements, which shields them from the caffeine limits imposed on sodas and the safety testing and labeling required of pharmaceuticals;[7,8,11] (3) other ingredients vary, are understudied, and are not regulated; (4) youth-aimed marketing and risk-taking adolescent developmental tendencies combine to increase overdose potential; (5) high consumption is suggested by self-report surveys but is underdocumented in children (deleterious associations with energy-drink consumption have been reported globally in case reports and popular media[7,8,11,25,31,38]); and (6) interactions between compounds, additive and dose-dependent effects, long-term consequences, and dangers associated with risky behavior in children remain to be determined.[5,14,25,38]

Educational, Research, and Regulatory Recommendations

In the short-term, pediatric health care providers need to be aware of energy-drink consumption by children, adolescents, and young adults and the potentially dangerous consequences of inappropriate use.[112] Diet and substance-use histories should include screening for episodic/chronic energy-drink consumption, both alone and with alcohol. Screening is especially important for athletes, children with high-risk behaviors, certain health conditions (eg, seizures, diabetes, hypertension, cardiac abnormalities), and children with behavioral changes, anxiety, poor nutrition, or sleep disturbances.[11]

For most children, adolescents, and young adults, safe levels of consumption have not been established. Yet, heavy use may be harmful or interact with medications and cause untoward adverse effects. Health care providers should educate families and children at risk for the potential adverse effects of energy drinks.

Routine high school athletic physicals do not identify everyone at risk for sudden cardiac death.[11,113] Children with cardiac conditions should be counseled regarding the risks of caffeine-containing products, including irregular heart rhythms, syncope, dysrhythmias, and sudden death.[17,18,85]

Community partners, including schools, athletic groups, and regulatory bodies, also need to promote risk awareness."[3] The fourth edition of the "Preparticipation Physical Evaluation" monograph will feature a revamped health questionnaire focused on cardiac health problems that may be exacerbated by physical activity; thus, adding questions about stimulant use, including energy-drink consumption, becomes important.[113]

Long-term research objectives should aim to better define maximum safe doses, the effects of chronic use, and effects in at-risk populations (eg, those with preexisting medical conditions, those who consume energy drinks during and after exercise, or those who consume them in combination with alcohol), and better documentation and tracking of adverse health effects.[47] Unless research establishes energy-drink safety in children and adolescents, regulation, as with tobacco, alcohol, and prescription medications, is prudent.[11]

This approach is essential for reducing morbidity and mortality, encouraging research, and supporting families of children and young adults at risk for energy-drink overdose, behavioral changes, and acute/chronic health consequences.

References

1. Lee J. Energy drinks vs. sports drinks: know thy difference. Available at: http://speedendurance.com/2009/07/O9/ energy-drinks-vs-sports-drinks-know-thy-difference. Accessed January 17, 2011

2. McCarthy M. Overuse of energy drinks worries health pros. Available at: www.usatoday.com/sports/2009-07-01-Drinks_N.htm. Accessed January 17, 2011

3. US Food and Drug Administration. Overview of dietary supplements. Available at: www.fda.gov/Food/DietarySupplements/ConsumerInform ation/ucm110417.htm. Accessed January 17, 2011

4. Nitzke S, Tanumihardjo S, Salomon J, Coleman G. Energy drinks, sports drinks, and other functional/enhanced beverages are often a waste of money. Available at: www.uwex.edu/ces/wnep/specialist/nfl/ mmpdfs/0810.pdf#page = 1. Accessed January 17, 2011

5. Oddy WH, O'Sullivan TA. Energy drinks for children and adolescents, erring on the side of caution may reduce long term health risks. *BMJ.* 2009;339:b5268

6. Reissig CJ, Strain EC, Griffiths RR. Caffeinated energy drinks: a growing problem. *Drug Alcohol Depend.* 2009;99(1–3):1–10

7. Babu KM, Church RJ, Lewander W. Energy drinks: the new eye-opener for adolescents. *Clin Pediatr Emerg Med.* 2008;9(1):35–42

8. Clauson KA, Shields KM, McQueen CE, Persad N. Safety issues associated with commercially available energy drinks. *J Am Pharm Assoc (Wash DC).* 2008;48(3): e55–e63; quiz e64–e67

9. Malinauskas BM, Aeby VG, Overton RF, Carpenter-Aeby T, Barber-Heidal K. A survey of energy drink consumption patterns among college students. *Nutr J.* 2007;6:35. Available at: www.nutritionj.com/ content/6/1/35. Accessed January 17, 2011

10. Press Office. New report predicts energy drink sales in the U.S. to exceed $9 billion by 2011 [press release]. Available at: www.reportbuyer.com/ press/new-report-predicts-energy-drink-sales-in-the-us-to-exceed-9-billion-by-2011. Accessed January 17, 2011

11. Lipshultz S. High risk: Ban energy drinks from schools. *Miami Herald.* April 20, 2008:4L, L4

12. Broderick P, Benjamin AB. Caffeine and psychiatric symptoms: a review. *J Okla State Med Assoc.* 2004;97(12):538–542

13. Hedges DW, Woon FL, Hoopes SP. Caffeine-induced psychosis. CNS *Spectr.* 2009;14(3):127–129

14. Heneman K, Zidenberg-Cherr S. Some facts about energy drinks. Available at: http://nutrition.ucdavis.edu/content/infosheets/EnergyDrinks.pdf. Accessed January 17, 2011

15. Brecher EJ. Study: caffeine in sodas risky for black kids. *Miami Herald.* May 18, 2004:7E

16. Cohen H. Dangerous jolt: energy drink dangers for children. *Miami Herald.* April 1, 2008:E10,10E

17. Frassica JJ, Orav EJ, Walsh EP, Lipshultz SE. Arrhythmias in children prenatally exposed to cocaine. *Arch Pediatr Adolesc Med.* 1994;148(11): 1163–1169

18. Lipshultz SE, Frassica JJ, Orav EJ. Cardiovascular abnormalities in infants prenatally exposed to cocaine. *J Pediatr.* 1991;118(1):44–51

19. Lipshultz SE. Ventricular dysfunction clinical research in infants, children and adolescents. *Prog Pediatr Cardiol.* 2000;12(1):1–28

20. Lipshultz SE, Wilkinson JD, Messiah SE, Miller TL. Clinical research directions in pediatric cardiology. *Curr Opin Pediatr.* 2009;21(5):585–593

21. Lipshultz SE. Realizing optimal care for children with cardiovascular disease: funding challenges and research approaches. *Prog Pediatr Cardiol.* 2005;20(1)71–90

22. Mone SM, Gillman MW, Miller TL, Herman EH, Lipshultz SE. Effects of environmental exposures on the cardiovascular system: prenatal period through adolescence. *Pediatrics.* 2004;113(4 suppl):1058–1069

23. Chrissos J. Cold medicines taboo for kids under 4: further restricting the use of cold medicines for young children, drug companies now say they shouldn't be used in children younger than 4. *Miami Herald.* October 8, 2008: Living-Health

24. Temple JL. Caffeine use in children: what we know, what we have left to learn, and why we should worry. *Neurosci Biobehav Rev.* 2009; 33(6);793–806

25. Federal Institute for Risk Assessment. New human data on the assessment of energy drinks. Available at: www.bfr.bund.de/cm/245/new_human_data_on_the_ assessment_of_energy_drinks.pdf. Accessed January 17, 2011

26. Health Canada. Energy drinks safety and health effects. Available at: www.enotalone.com/article/10272.html. Accessed January 17, 2011

27. Iyadurai SJ, Chung SS. New-onset seizures in adults: possible association with consumption of popular energy drinks. *Epilepsy Behav.* 2007; 10(3):504–508

28. Berger AJ, Alford K. Cardiac arrest in a young man following excess consumption of caffeinated "energy drinks." *MedJAust.* 2009;190(1):41–43

29. Cannon ME, Cooke CT, McCarthy JS. Caffeine-induced cardiac arrhythmia: an unrecognised danger of healthfood products. *MedJAust.* 2001;174(10): 520–521

30. Bestervelt L. Raising the red flag on some energy drinks. Available at: www.nsf.org/media/enews/documents/energy_drinks.pdf.   Accessed January 17, 2011

31. Nordqvist C. French ban on Red Bull (drink) upheld by European Court. Available at: www.medicalnewstoday.com/articles/5753.php. Accessed January 17, 2011

32. Parikh RK. Red alert on energy drinks. *Los Angeles Times.* September 1, 2008: Health

33. Starling S. Energy drinks safety questioned by German agency. Available at: www.beveragedaily.com/content/view/print/166290. Accessed January 17, 2011

34. High school students warned about energy drink: Smokey Hill student hospitalized after drinking SPIKE. Available at: www.thedenverchannel.com/news/11070908/detail.html. Accessed January 17, 2011

35. Quinones D. Sidelined college football freshman plans medical path. *Miami Herald.* July 30, 2009: Sports

36. National Federation of State High School Associations, Sports Medicine Advisory Committee. Position statement and recommendations for the use of energy drinks by young athletes. Available at: www.nfhs.org/search.aspx?searchtext=Energy%20Drinks. Accessed January 17, 2011

37. National Federation of State High School Associations, Sports Medicine Advisory Committee. Minimize the risk for dehydration and heat illness. Available at: www.nfhs.org/search.aspx?searchtext=Energy%20Drinks. Accessed January 17, 2011

38. Federal Institute for Risk Assessment. Health risks of excessive energy shot intake. December 2, 2009. Available at: www. bfr.bund.de/cm/245/health_risks_of_excessive_energy_shot_intake.pdf. Accessed January 17, 2011

39. O'Connor E. A sip into dangerous territory. *Monit Psychol.* 2001;32(6). Available at: www.apa.org/monitor/jun01/dangersip. aspx.Accessed January 17, 2011

40. Pollak CP, Bright D. Caffeine consumption and weekly sleep patterns in US seventh-, eighth-, and ninth-graders. *Pediatrics.* 2003;111(1):42–46

41. Bernstein GA, Carroll ME, Thuras PD, Cos-grove KP, Roth ME. Caffeine dependence in teenagers. *Drug Alcohol Depend.* 2002; 66(1):1–6

42. Strain EC, Mumford GK, Silverman K, Griffiths RF. Caffeine dependence syndrome: evidence from case histories and experimental evaluations. *JAMA.* 1994;272(13):1043–1048

43. Simon M, Mosher J. Alcohol, energy drinks, and youth: a dangerous mix. Available at: www.marininstitute.org/alcopops/resources/Energy DrinkReport.pdf. Accessed January 17, 2011

44. Viell B, Grabner L, Fruchel G, Boczek P. New caffeinated beverages: a pilot survey of familiarity and consumption by adolescents in north-Rhine West-phalia and Berlin and considerations of consumer protection [in German]. *Z Ernahrungswiss.* 1996;35(4):378–386

45. Miller KE. Wired: energy drinks, jock identity, masculine norms, and risk taking. *J Am Coll Health.* 2008;56(5):481–489

46. Thomson B, Schiess S. Risk profile: caffeine in energy drinks and energy shots. Available at: www.nzfsa.govt.nz/science/risk-profles/fw10002-caffeine-in-beverages-risk-proflle.pdf. Accessed January 17, 2011

47. Bronstein AC, Spyker DA, Cantilena LR Jr, Green JL, Rumack BH, Heard SE; American Association of Poison Control Centers. 2007 Annual Report of the American Association of Poison Control Centers' National Poison Data System (NPDS): 25th Annual Report. *Clin Toxicol (Phila).* 2008;46(10): 927–1057

48. Holmgren P, Norden-Pettersson L, Ahlner J. Caffeine fatalities: four case reports. Fo-rensic SciInt. 2004;139(1):71–73

49. Greenwood MRC, Oria M. Use of dietary supplements by military personnel. Available at: www.nap.edu/catalog/12095.html. Accessed January 17, 2011

50. Connolly S, Kingsbury TJ. Caffeine modulates CREB-dependent gene expression in developing cortical neurons. *Biochem Bio-phys Res Commun.* 2010;397(2):152–156

51. Dworzanski W, Opielak G, Burdan F. Side effects of caffeine in Polish]. *Pol Merkur Lekarski.* 2009;27(161):357–361

52. Koines AJ, Ingvaldsen A, Boiling A, et al. Caffeine and theophylline block insulin-stimulated glucose uptake and PKB phosphorylation in rat skeletal muscles. *Acta Physiol.* 2010;200(1):65–74

53. Del Coso J, Estevez E, Mora-Rodriguez R. Caffeine during exercise in the heat: thermoregulation and fluid-electrolyte balance. *Med Sci Sports Exerc.* 2009;41(1):164–173

54. Armstrong LE. Caffeine, body fluid-electrolyte balance, and exercise performance. *Int J Sport Nutr Exerc Metab.* 2002;12(2):189–206

55. Armstrong LE, Pumerantz AC, Roti MW, et al. Fluid, electrolyte, and renal indices of hydration during 11 days of controlled caffeine consumption. *Int J Sport Nutr Exerc Metob.* 2005;15(3):252–265

56. Chapman RF, Mickleborough TD. The effects of caffeine on ventilation and pulmonary function during exercise: an often-overlooked response. *Phys Sportsmed.* 2009;37(4):97–103

57. Rogers PJ, Dernoncourt C. Regular caffeine consumption: a balance of adverse and beneficial effects for mood and psychomotor performance. *Pharmacol Biochem Behav.* 1998;59(4);1039–1045

58. Rogers PJ. Caffeine, mood and mental performance in everyday life. Br *Nutr Found Nutr Bull.* 2007;32(suppl 1):84–89

59. Scholey AB, Kennedy DO. Cognitive and physiological effects of an "energy drink": an evaluation of the whole drink and of glucose, caffeine and herbal flavouring fractions. *Psychopharmacology (Berl).* 2004;176 (3–4):320–330

60. Lipshultz SE. Vote for children's health. *Miami Herald.* October 25, 2008; Opinion-Other Views-Healthcare

61. Whelton PK, He J, Appel LJ, et al. National High Blood Pressure Education Program Coordinating Committee. Primary prevention of hypertension: clinical and public health advisory from the national high blood pressure education program. *JAMA.* 2002;288 (15):1882–1888

62. Burke LM. Caffeine and sports performance. *Appl Physiol Nutr Metab.* 2008;33(6):1319–1334

63. Heatherley SV, Hancock KM, Rogers PJ. Psychostimulant and other effects of caffeine in 9-to 11-year-old children. *J Child Psychol Psychiatry.* 2006;47(2):135–142

64. Griffiths RR, Woodson PP. Caffeine physical dependence: a review of human and laboratory animal studies. *Psychopharmacology (Berl).* 1988;94(4):437–451

65. Steinke L, Lanfear DE, Dhanapal V, Kalus JS. Effect of "energy drink" consumption on hemodynamic and electrocardiographic parameters in healthy young adults. *Ann Pharmacother.* 2009;43(4):596–602

66. Hinds TS, West WL, Knight EM, Harland BF. The effect of caffeine on pregnancy outcome variables. *Nutr Rev.* 1996;54(7):203–207

67. Dlugosz L, Belanger K, Hellenbrand K, Hol-ford TR, Leaderer B, Bracken MB. Maternal caffeine consumption and spontaneous abortion: a prospective cohort study. *Epidemiology.* 1996;7(3):250–255

68. Turley KR, Desisso T, Gerst JW. Effects of caffeine on physiological responses to exercise: boys versus men. *Pediatr Exerc Sci.* 2007;19(4): 481–492

69. Rapoport JL, Jensvold M, Elkins R, et al. Behavioral and cognitive effects of caffeine in boys and adult males. *JNervMent Dis.* 1981;169(11):726–732

70. Bancalari E. Caffeine for apnea of prematurity. *N Engl J Med.* 2006;354(20):2179–2181

71. Bancalari E. Caffeine reduces the rate of bronchopulmonary dysplasia in very low birth weight infants. *J Pediatr.* 2006;149(5):727–728

72. Temple JL, Bulkley AM, Briatico L, Dewey AM. Sex differences in reinforcing value of caffeinated beverages in adolescents. *Behav Pharmacol.* 2009;20(8):731–741

73. Smit HJ, Cotton JR, Hughes SC, Rogers PJ. Mood and cognitive performance effects of "energy" drink constituents: caffeine, glucose and carbonation. *Nutr Neurosci.* 2004;7(3):127–139

74. Warburton DM, Bersellini E, Sweeney E. An evaluation of a caffeinated taurine drink on mood, memory and information processing in healthy volunteers without caffeine abstinence. *Psychopharmacology (Berl)*. 2001;158(3):322–328

75. Terlizzi R, Rocchi C, Serra M, Solieri L, Cor-telli P. Reversible postural tachycardia syndrome due to inadvertent overuse of red bull. *Clin Auton Res*. 2008;18(4):221–223

76. Baum M, Weiss M. The influence of a taurine containing drink on cardiac parameters before and after exercise measured by echocardiography. *Amino Acids*. 2001;20(1):75–82

77. Wojcik OP, Koenig KL, Zeleniuch-Jacquotte A, Costa M, Chen Y. The potential protective effects of taurine on coronary heart disease. *Atherosclerosis*. 2010;208(1):19–25

78. Worthley Ml, Prabhu A, De Sciscio P, Schultz C, Sanders P, Willoughby SR. Detrimental effects of energy drink consumption on platelet and endothelial function. Am J Wed. 2010;123(2):184–187

79. Subbiah MT, Yunker R. Studies on the nature of anti-platelet aggregatory factors in the seeds of the Amazonian herb guarana *(Paullinia cupana)*. *Int J Vitam Nutr Res*. 2008;78(2):96–101

80. Buscemi S, Verga S, Batsis JA, et al. Acute effects of coffee on endothelial function in healthy subjects. *Eur J Clin Nutr*. 2010;64(5):483–489

81. Natella F, Nardini M, Belelli F, et al. Effect of coffee drinking on platelets: inhibition of aggregation and phenols incorporation. *Br J Nutr*. 2008;100(6):1276–1282

82. Hui H, Tang G, Go VL. Hypoglycemic herbs and their action mechanisms. *Chin Med*. 2009;4:11

83. Dangerous supplements. *Consum Rep*. September 2010;16–20

84. Lipshultz SE, Wong JC, Lipsitz SR, et al. Frequency of clinically unsuspected myocardial injury at a children's hospital. *Am Hearf J* 2006;151(4): 916–922

85. Sokol KC, Armstrong FD, Rosenkranz ER, et al. Ethical issues in children with cardiomyopathy: making sense of ethical challenges in the clinical setting. *ProgPe-diatr Cardiol*. 2007;23(1):81–87

86. Lipshultz SE, Sleeper LA, Towbin JA, et al. The incidence of pediatric cardiomyopathy in two regions of the united states. *N Engl J Med*. 2003;348(17):1647–1655

87. Colan SD, Lipshultz SE, Lowe AM, et al. Epidemiology and cause-specific outcome of hypertrophic cardiomyopathy in children: findings from the pediatric cardiomyopathy registry. *Circulation*. 2007;115(6): 773–781

88. Barbaresi WJ, Katusic SK, Colligan RC, et al. How common is attention-deficit/ hyperactivity disorder? Incidence in a population-based birth cohort in Rochester, Minn. *Arch Pediatr Adolesc Med*. 2002; 156(3):217–224

89. Vetter VL, Elia J, Erickson C, et al. American Heart Association, Council on Cardiovascular Disease in the Young Congenital Cardiac Defects Committee; American Heart Association, Council on Cardiovascular Nursing. Cardiovascular monitoring of children and adolescents with heart disease receiving stimulant drugs: a scientific statement from the American Heart Association Council on Cardiovascular Disease in the Young congenital cardiac defects committee and the council on cardiovascular

nursing [published correction appears in *Circulation*. 2009:120(7):e55-e59]. *Circulation*. 2008:117(18): 2407–2423

90. Wilens TE, Gignac M, Swezey A, Monuteaux MC, Biederman J. Characteristics of adolescents and young adults with ADHD who divert or misuse their prescribed medications. *J Am Acad Child Adolesc Psychiatry*. 2006;45(4):408–414

91. Wilens TE, Prince JB, Spencer TJ, Biederman J. Stimulants and sudden death: what is a physician to do? *Pediatrics*. 2006; 118(3):1215–1219

92. Biederman J, Wilens T, Mick E, Spencer T, Faraone SV. Pharmacotherapy of attention-deficit/hyperactivity disorder reduces risk for substance use disorder. *Pediatrics*. 1999;104(2). Available at: www.pediatrics.org/cgi/content/full/104/2/e20. Accessed January 17, 2011

93. Fredholm BB, Svenningsson P. Striatal adenosine A2A receptors: where are they? What do they do? *Trends Pharmacol Sci*. 1998;19(2):46–48

94. Wilens TE, Biederman J, Baldessarini RJ, et al. Cardiovascular effects of therapeutic doses of tricyclic antidepressants in children and adolescents. *J Am Acad Child Adolesc Psychiatry*. 1996;35(11):1491–1501

95. Dadfarmay S, Dixon J. A case of acute cardiomyopathy and pericarditis associated with methylphenidate. *Cardiovasc Toxicol*. 2009;9(1):49–52

96. Take G, Bahcelioglu M, Oktem H, et al. Dose-dependent immunohistochemical and un-trastructural changes after oral methylphenidate administration in rat heart tissue. *Anat Histol Embryol*. 2008;37(4): 303–308

97. Krahn DD, Hasse S, Ray A, Gosnell B, Drewnowski A. Caffeine consumption in patients with eating disorders. *Hosp Community Psychiatry*. 1991;42(3):313–315

98. Stock SL, Goldberg E, Corbett S, Katzman DK. Substance use in female adolescents with eating disorders. *J Adolesc Health*. 2002;31(2):176–182

99. Striegel-Moore RH, Franko DL, Thompson D, Barton B, Schreiber GB, Daniels SR. Caffeine intake in eating disorders. *Int J Eat Disord*. 2006;39(2):162–165

100. Popkin B. We are what we drink. *In The World Is Fat: The Fads, Trends, Policies, and Products That Are Fattening the Human Race*. New York, NY: Penguin Group; 2002:43–65

101. Moreno MA, Furtner F, Frederick PR. Sugary drinks and childhood obesity. *Arch Pediatr Adolesc Med*. 2009;163(4):400

102. National Center for Chronic Disease Prevention and Health Promotion. Obesity: halting the epidemic by making health easier. Available at: www.cdc.gov/nccdphp/ publications/AAG/pdf/obesity.pdf. Accessed January 17, 2011

103. Heaney RP. Effects of caffeine on bone and the calcium economy. *Food Chem Toxicol*. 2002;40(9):1263–1270

104. Lloyd T, Rollings NJ, Kieselhorst K, Eggli DF, Mauger E. Dietary caffeine intake is not correlated with adolescent bone gain. *J Am Coll Nutr*. 1998;17(5):454–457

105. Hein K. A bull's market: the marketing of Red Bull energy drink. Available at: http://flndarticles.com/p/articles/mi_mOBDW/is_22_42/ai_75286777/?tag=content% 3Bcol1. Accessed January 17, 2011

106. Thomsen SR, Fulton K. Adolescents' attention to responsibility messages in magazine alcohol advertisements: an eye-tracking approach. *J Adolesc Health*. 2007;41(1):27–34

107. Fischer PM, Richards JW Jr, Berman EJ, Krugman DM. Recall and eye tracking study of adolescents viewing tobacco advertisements. *JAMA.* 1989;261(1):84–89

108. Weise E. Petition calls for FDA to regulate energy drinks. *USA Today.* October 22, 2008: News, Health & Behavior

109. Our view on pills and potions: do you really know what's in that dietary supplement? Available at: www.usatoday.com/news/opinion/cditorials/2010-06-07-editorial07_ST_N.htm?loc=interstitialskip. Accessed January 17, 2011

110. European Food Safety Authority. EFSA adopts opinion on two ingredients commonly used in some energy drinks [press release]. Available at: www.efsa.europa.eu/en/press/news/ans090212.htm. Accessed January 17, 2011

111. Red Bull pulled from shelves in Hong Kong. Available at: http://content.usatoday.com/communities/ondeadline/post/2009/06/67549503/1. Accessed October 27, 2009

112. Anderson BL, Juliano LM, Schulkin J. Caffeine's implications for women's health and survey of obstetrician-gynecologists' caffeine knowledge and assessment practices. *J Womens Health (Larchmt).* 2009; 18(9): 1457–1466

113. Pepine CJ. Panel endorses preparticipation sports physicals for every child. *Cardiol Today.* 2010;13(6). Available at: www.cardiologytoday.com/print.aspx?rid=65042. Accessed January 17, 2011

114. Cerimele JM, Stern AP, Jutras-Aswad D. Psychosis following excessive ingestion of energy drinks in a patient with schizophrenia. *Am J Psychiatry.* 2010;167(3):353

115. Convertino VA, Armstrong LE, Coyle EF, et al. American college of sports medicine position stand: exercise and fluid replacement. *MedSci Sports Exerc.* 1996;28(1):i–vii

116. Bruce B. Energy drinks banned over caffeine levels in Australia. Available at: www.foodbev.com/news/energy-drinks-banned-over-caffeine-levels-in-australia. Accessed January 17, 2011

117. Neuman W. "Energy shots" stimulate power drink sales. Available at: www.nytimes.com/2009/07/11/business/11energy.html. Accessed January 17, 2011

118. Derbyshire D. Energy drinks "should have caffeine health warning on cans." Mail-Online. Available at: www.dailymail.co.uk/news/article-1060705/Energy-drinks-caffeine-health-warning-cans.html. Accessed January 17, 2011

119. Energy drinks' caffeine buzz can land the unwary in the ER. *REDORBIT News.* 2005. Available at: www.redorbit.com/news/display/?id=833954. Accessed January 17, 2011

120. Nutra Ingredients.com. Ireland to review safety of energy drinks. Available at: www.nutraingredients.com/Regulation/Ireland-to-review-safety-of-energy-drinks. Accessed January 17, 2011

121. Red Bull banned in Dutch schools. *Dutch Daily News.* Available at: www.dutchdailynews.com/red-bull-banned-in-dutch-schools. Accessed January 17, 2011

Critical Reading Questions

Summarizing the Text

1. A scientific article reporting on research can be daunting for a nonspecialist to read. However, this article is a "literature review"—a survey of other articles. How do Seifert and her coauthors use the other articles?

2. What are the main claims of each subsection of the article (separated by the headers)? How do the claims work together to generate the thesis of the article?

Establishing the Context

3. What are the most difficult sections of this article to understand? Does the vocabulary or the concepts cause the difficulty? What are some strategies to improve one's comprehension of this article?

4. How do studies like this enter the public debate, given that most people don't read *Pediatrics*? Use the Web to research this article, its authors, and the process by which the conclusions of this article were disseminated to the public.

Responding to the Message

5. Why should the government consider regulating these drinks? What might be the counterargument to this? Why shouldn't consumers be responsible for making their own choices?

6. Could the evidence Seifert and her collaborators use to prove that energy drinks are dangerous be used to prove that they are not? Is all of the evidence relevant? What causal claims are being made in this article? Can you find claims in this article for which there is insufficient evidence?

Full Throttle Billboard Advertisement

Full Throttle is an energy drink manufactured by the Coca-Cola Corporation. This billboard promoting the drink appeared on the sides of freeways in 2005.

1. What is the argument of this advertisement?

2. What is the rhetorical effect of the font, the words, the layout of this advertisement? What audiences (gender, age, etc.) might respond to this ad? What audiences might not? Why?

3. Full Throttle's website is http://www.drinkfullthrottle.com/. Visit the website and describe the visuals and the rhetorical appeal of the advertising there. Who is the intended audience? What are the implicit arguments being made about why this audience should purchase this product?

American Beverage Association Statement on *Pediatrics* Article on Energy Drinks

The American Beverage Association is a trade association (a group that represents the interests of companies in a particular industry) for "non-alcoholic refreshment beverage" manufacturers such as PepsiCo, Coca-Cola, and other companies. Trade organizations often sponsor research or public-relations efforts intended to counter negative publicity, as with this press release, which seeks to rebut and undermine the argument of Sara Seifert's Pediatrics *study (included earlier in this chapter).*

In response to "Health Effects of Energy Drinks on Children, Adolescents, and Young Adults," a literature review published in the journal *Pediatrics*, Dr. Maureen Storey, senior vice president of science policy for the American Beverage Association, issued the following statement:

"This literature review does nothing more than perpetuate misinformation about energy drinks, their ingredients and the regulatory process.

Like all foods, beverages and supplements sold in the United States, energy drinks and their ingredients are regulated by the U.S. Food and Drug Administration.

When it comes to caffeine, it's important to put the facts in perspective. Most mainstream energy drinks actually contain about half the caffeine of a similar size cup of coffeehouse coffee. In fact, young adults getting coffee from popular coffeehouses are getting about twice as much caffeine as they would from a similar size energy drink.

Importantly, children and teens are not large consumers of energy drinks. According to government data from the National Health and Nutrition Examination (NHANES) Survey, the caffeine consumed from energy drinks for those under the age of 18 is less than the caffeine derived from all other sources including soft drinks, coffee and teas. And total caffeine consumption from energy drinks among pre-teens is nearly zero. In fact, the data show that caffeine consumption from energy drinks for children and teens, on average, is far less than even one can of an energy drink per day.

Further, the review misinterprets the data from a 2007 study by the American Association of Poison Control Centers, which reported more than 5400 caffeine cases from pharmaceutical exposures, not exposure to caffeine from foods or beverages. (Pharmaceutical exposures refer to over-the-counter caffeine pills and other caffeinated medicines.)

What we do know is that caffeine is one of the most thoroughly tested ingredients in the food supply today. It has been deemed safe by the U.S. Food and Drug Administration, as well as more than 140 countries around the world. Many of our member companies voluntarily list the amount of caffeine on their products' labels and have provided caffeine content information through their websites and consumer hotlines for years.

ABA members encourage all consumers to stay informed about the products they consume. Reading the nutrition facts panel, as well as other information such as caffeine content and heeding voluntary advisory statements may be particularly important to those who are sensitive to caffeine."

Critical Reading Questions

Summarizing the Text

1. What is the thesis of the press release?

2. How does the American Beverage Association construct its ethos? How does it rebut the implicit claim of the *Pediatrics* article that the beverage industry is more concerned about money than consumer health?

Establishing the Context

3. The ABA's statement specifies that the *Pediatrics* article is a "literature review." What is a literature review? How does it differ from a research

study? What might be the rhetorical aim behind the ABA's use of that term?

4. On what grounds does the ABA attempt to refute the *Pediatrics* article?

Responding to the Message

5. Compare the ABA statement, the *Pediatrics* article, and Michael Specter's *Denialism* chapter. The ABA and the *Pediatrics* study clash about what kind of evidence is valid, and how the study's authors use previously published research studies. Is the ABA practicing "denialism"?

6. The American Beverage Association is a "trade association." What is a trade association? What is the purpose of a trade association? Why does it issue press releases?

CLUSTER TWO: HOW DOES SCIENCE BECOME TRUTH?

My God Problem—and Theirs

Natalie Angier

Natalie Angier is one of the leading science writers in the mainstream American media and has written for Discover, Time, *and the* New York Times, *where she won the 1991 Pulitzer Prize for Beat Reporting for her coverage of science. She is the author of* Natural Obsessions *(about cancer research labs) and* Woman: An Intimate Geography. *An outspoken atheist, Angier here questions why the American scientific and educational establishment laments Americans' willingness to accept creationism, when (as she sees it) even greater numbers of Americans accept even more unscientific ideas, such as resurrection. This article appeared in* The American Scholar, *the quarterly magazine of the Phi Beta Kappa Society.*

In the course of reporting a book on the scientific canon, and pestering hundreds of researchers at the nation's great universities about what they see as the essential vitamins and minerals of literacy in their particular disciplines, I have been hammered into a kind of twinkle-eyed cartoon coma by one recurring message. Whether they are biologists, geologists, physicists, chemists, astronomers, or engineers, virtually all my sources topped their list of what they wish people understood about science with a plug for Darwin's dandy idea.

Would you please tell the public, they implored, that evolution is for real? Would you please explain that the evidence for it is overwhelming, and that an appreciation of evolution serves as the bedrock of our understanding of all life on this planet?

In other words, the scientists wanted me to do my bit to help fix the terrible little statistic they keep hearing about, the one indicating that many more Americans believe in angels, devils, and poltergeists than in evolution. According to recent polls, about 82 percent are convinced of the reality of heaven (and 63 percent think they're headed there after death); 51 percent believe in ghosts; but only 28 percent are swayed by the theory of evolution.

Scientists think this is terrible, the public's bizarre underappreciation of one of science's great and unshakeable discoveries—how we and all we see came to be—and they're right.

Yet I can't help feeling tetchy about the limits most of them put on their complaints. You see, they want to augment this particular figure—the number of people who believe in evolution—without bothering to confront a few other salient statistics that pollsters have revealed about America's religious cosmogony. Few scientists, for example, worry about the 77 percent of Americans who insist that Jesus was born to a virgin, an act of parthenogenesis that defies everything we know about mammalian genetics and reproduction. Nor do the researchers wring their hands over the 80 percent who believe in the resurrection of Jesus, the laws of thermodynamics be damned.

No, most scientists are not interested in taking on any of the mighty cornerstones of Christianity. They complain about irrational thinking, they despise creationist "science," they roll their eyes over America's infatuation with astrology, telekinesis, spoon bending, reincarnation, and UFOs, but toward the bulk of the magic acts that have won the imprimatur of inclusion in the Bible, they are tolerant, respectful, big of tent. Indeed, many are quick to point out that the Catholic Church has endorsed the theory of evolution, and that it sees no conflict between a belief in God and the divinity of Jesus and the notion of evolution by natural selection. If the Pope is buying, the reason for most Americans' resistance to evolution must have less to do with religion than with a lousy advertising campaign.

So, on the issue of mainstream monotheistic religions and the irrationality behind many of religion's core tenets, scientists often set aside their skewers, their snark, and their impatient demand for proof, and instead don the calming cardigan of a kiddie-show host on public TV. They reassure the public that religion and science are not at odds with one another, but rather that they represent separate "magisteria," in the words of the formerly alive and even more formerly scrappy Stephen Jay Gould. Nobody is going to ask people to give up their faith, their belief in an everlasting soul accompanied by an immortal memory of every soccer game their kids won, every moment they spent playing fetch with the dog. Nobody is going to mock you for your religious beliefs. Well, we might if you base your life decisions on the advice of a Ouija board; but if you want to believe that someday you'll be seated at a celestial banquet with your long-dead father to your right and Jane Austen to your left— and that she'll want to talk to you for another hundred million years or more—that's your private reliquary, and we're not here to jimmy the lock.

Consider the very different treatments accorded two questions presented to Cornell University's "Ask an Astronomer" Web site. To the query, "Do most astronomers believe in God, based on the available evidence?" the astronomer Dave Rothstein replies that, in his opinion, "modern science leaves plenty of room for the existence of God ... places where people who do believe in God can fit their beliefs in the scientific framework without creating any contradictions." He cites the Big Bang as offering solace to those who want to believe in a Genesis equivalent, and the probabilistic realms of quantum mechanics as raising the possibility of "God intervening every time a measurement occurs," before concluding that, ultimately, science can never prove or disprove the existence of a god, and religious belief doesn't—and shouldn't—"have anything to do with scientific reasoning."

How much less velveteen is the response to the reader asking whether astronomers believe in astrology. "No, astronomers do not believe in astrology," snarls Dave Kornreich. "It is considered to be a ludicrous scam. There is no evidence that it works, and plenty of evidence to the contrary." Dr. Kornreich ends his dismissal with the assertion that in science "one does not need a reason not to believe in something." Skepticism is "the default position" and "one requires proof if one is to be convinced of something's existence."

In other words, for horoscope fans, the burden of proof is entirely on them, the poor gullible gits; while for the multitudes who believe that, in one way or another, a divine intelligence guides the path of every leaping lepton, there is no demand for evidence, no skepticism to surmount, no need to worry. You, the religious believer, may well find subtle support for your faith in recent discoveries—that is, if you're willing to upgrade your metaphors and definitions as the latest data demand, seek out new niches of ignorance or ambiguity to fill with the goose down of faith, and accept that, certain passages of the Old Testament notwithstanding, the world is very old, not everything in nature was made in a week, and (can you turn up the mike here, please?) Evolution Happens.

And if you don't find substantiation for your preferred divinity or your most cherished rendering of the afterlife somewhere in the sprawling emporium of science, that's fine, too. No need to lose faith when you were looking in the wrong place to begin with. Science can't tell you whether God exists or where you go when you die. Science cannot definitively rule out the heaven option, with its helium balloons and Breck hair for all. Science in no way wants to be associated with terrifying thoughts, like the possibility that the peri-century of consciousness granted you by the convoluted, gelatinous, and transient organ in your skull just may be the whole story of you-dom. Science isn't arrogant. Science trades in the observable universe and testable hypotheses. Religion gets the midnight panic fêtes. But you've heard about evolution, right?

So why is it that most scientists avoid criticizing religion even as they decry the supernatural mind-set? For starters, some researchers are themselves traditionally devout, keeping a kosher kitchen or taking communion each Sunday. I admit I'm surprised whenever I encounter a religious scientist. How can a bench-hazed Ph.D., who might of an afternoon deftly puree a colleague's PowerPoint presentation on the nematode genome into so much fish chow, then go home, read a two-thousand-year-old chronicle, riddled with internal contradictions, of a meta-Nobel discovery like "Resurrection from the Dead," and say, gee, that sounds convincing? Doesn't the good doctorate wonder what the control group looked like?

Scientists, however, *are* a far less religious lot than the American population, and the higher you go on the cerebro-magisterium, the greater the proportion of atheists, agnostics, and assorted other paganites. According to a 1998 survey published in *Nature,* only 7 percent of members of the prestigious National Academy of Sciences professed a belief in a "personal God." (Interestingly, a slightly higher number, 7.9 percent, claimed to believe in "personal immortality," which may say as much about the robustness of the scientific ego as about anything else.) In other words, more than 90 percent of our elite scientists are unlikely to pray for divine favoritism no matter how badly they want to beat a competitor to publication. Yet only a flaskful of the faithless have put their nonbelief on record or publicly criticized religion, the notable and voluble exceptions being Richard Dawkins of Oxford University and Daniel Dennett of Temple University. Nor have Dawkins and Dennett earned much good will among their colleagues for their anticlerical views; one astronomer I spoke with said of Dawkins, "He's a really fine parish preacher of the fire-and-brimstone school, isn't he?"

Even a recent D&D-driven campaign to spruce up the image of atheism by coopting the word "bright"—to indicate, as Dawkins put it in a newspaper piece, "a person whose world view is free of supernatural and mystical elements"—has yet to gain much candle-power. Admittedly, the new lingo has problems. To describe oneself at a cocktail party as "a bright," however saucily and sunnily the phrase is delivered, makes one sound like a member of a Rajneeshee-style cult, not exactly the image a heathen wants to project.

But I doubt that semantics is what keeps most scientists quiet about religion. Instead, it's probably something closer to that trusty old limbic reflex called "an instinct for self-preservation." For centuries science has survived quite nicely by cultivating an image of reserve and objectivity, of being above religion, politics, business, table manners. Scientists want to be left alone to do their work, dazzle their peers, and hire grad students to wash the glassware. When it comes to extramural combat, scientists choose their crusades cautiously. Going after Uri Geller or the Raelians is risk-free entertainment, easier than making fun of the sociology department. Battling the creationist camp has been a much harder and nastier fight, but those scientists who have taken it on feel they have a direct stake in the debate and are entitled to wage it, since the creationists, and more recently the promoters of "intelligent design" theory, claim to be as scientific in their methodology as are the scientists.

But when a teenager named Darrell Lambert was chucked out of the Boy Scouts for being an atheist, scientists suddenly remembered all those gels they had to run and dark matter they had to chase, and they kept quiet. Lambert had explained the reason why, despite a childhood spent in Bible classes and church youth groups, he had become an atheist. He took biology in ninth grade, and rather than devoting himself to studying the bra outline of the girl sitting in front of him, he actually learned some biology. And what he learned in biology persuaded him that the Bible was full of ... short stories. Some good, some inspiring, some even racy, but fiction nonetheless. For his incisive, reasoned, scientific look at life, and for refusing to cook the data and simply lie to the Boy Scouts about his thoughts on God—as some advised him to do—Darrell Lambert should have earned a standing ovation from the entire scientific community. Instead, he had to settle for an interview with Connie Chung, right after a report on the Gambino family.

Scientists have ample cause to feel they must avoid being viewed as irreligious, a prionic life-form bent on destroying the most sacred heifer in America. After all, academic researchers graze on taxpayer pastures. If they pay the slightest attention to the news, they've surely noticed the escalating readiness of conservative politicians and an array of highly motivated religious organizations to interfere with the nation's scientific enterprise—altering the consumer information Web site at the National Cancer Institute to make abortion look like a cause of breast cancer, which it is not, or stuffing scientific advisory panels with anti-abortion "faith healers." Recently, an obscure little club called the Traditional Values Coalition began combing through descriptions of projects supported by the National Institutes of Health and complaining to sympathetic congressmen about those they deemed morally "rotten," most of them studies of sexual behavior and AIDS prevention. The congressmen in turn launched a series of hearings, calling in institute officials to inquire who in the Cotton-pickin' name of Mather cares about the perversions of

Native American homosexuals, to which the researchers replied, um, the studies *were* approved by a panel of scientific experts, and, gee, the Native American community has been underserved and it is having a real problem with AIDS these days. Thus far, the projects have escaped being nullified, but the raw display of pious dentition must surely give fright to even the most rakishly freethinking and comfortably tenured professor. It's one thing to monkey with descriptions of Darwinism in a high school textbook ... but to threaten to take away a peer-reviewed grant! That Dan Dennett; he *is* something of a pompous leaf-blower, isn't he?

Yet the result of wincing and capitulating is a fresh round of whacks. Now it's not enough for presidential aspirants to make passing reference to their "faith." Now a reporter from *Newsweek* sees it as his privilege, if not his duty, to demand of Howard Dean, "Do you see Jesus Christ as the son of God and believe in him as the route to salvation and eternal life?" In my personal fairy tale, Dean, who as a doctor fits somewhere in the phylum Scientificus, might have boomed, "Well, with his views on camels and rich people, he sure wouldn't vote Republican!" or maybe, "No, but I hear he has a Mel Gibson complex." Dr. Dean might have talked about patients of his who suffered strokes and lost the very fabric of themselves, and how he has seen the centrality of the brain to the sense of being an individual. He might have expressed doubts that the self survives the brain, but, oh yes, life goes on, life is bigger, stronger, and better endowed than any Bush in a jumpsuit, and we are part of the wild, tumbling river of life, our molecules were the molecules of dinosaurs, and before that of stars, and this is not Bulfinch mythology, this is corroborated reality.

Alas for my phantasm of fact, Howard Dean, M.D., had no choice but to chime, oh yes, he certainly sees Jesus as the son of God, though he at least dodged the eternal life clause with a humble mumble about his salvation not being up to him.

I may be an atheist, and I may be impressed that, through the stepwise rigor of science, its Spockian eyebrow of doubt always cocked, we have learned so much about the universe. Yet I recognize that, from there to here, and here to there, funny things are *everywhere.* Why is there so much dark matter and dark energy in the great Out There, and why couldn't cosmologists have given them different enough names so I could keep them straight? Why is there something rather than nothing, and why is so much of it on my desk? Not to mention the abiding mysteries of e-mail, like why I get exponentially more spam every day, nine-tenths of it invitations to enlarge an appendage 1 don't have.

I recognize that science doesn't have all the answers and doesn't pretend to, and that's one of the things I love about it. But it has a pretty good notion of what's probable or possible, and virgin births and carpenter rebirths just aren't on the list. Is there a divine intelligence, separate from the universe but somehow in charge of the universe, either in its inception or in twiddling its parameters? No evidence. Is the universe itself God? Is the universe aware of itself? We're here. We're aware. Does that make us God? Will my daughter have to attend a Quaker Friends school now?

I don't believe in life after death, but I'd like to believe in life before death. I'd like to think that one of these days we'll leave superstition and delusional thinking and Jerry Falwell behind. Scientists would like that, too. But for now, they like their grants even more.

Critical Reading Questions

Summarizing the Text

1. If scientists object so strongly to Americans' rejection of evolution, according to Angier, why aren't they equally impatient with other tenets of Christianity?
2. Why, in Angier's view, is the scientific explanation of the world more compelling and believable than the religious explanation?

Establishing the Context

3. How would you characterize Angier's tone here? Look particularly at the imagery she uses to describe people's religious beliefs. How does this construct her own voice, and how does it affect the audience that might be reading this article?
4. Angier calls herself a "proud atheist" and has spoken and written a great deal about her rejection of religion or any belief in a God. How does this affect her credibility with the 95 percent of Americans who do believe?

Responding to the Message

5. How did your high schools teach evolution? Did it cover "intelligent design" as a plausible option? Do you think schools should "teach the controversy," as former President George W. Bush urged, or should they stick to one explanation and teach it as fact?
6. Angier argues that belief in virgin birth, resurrection, and divine creation is the same as belief in astrology. Do you agree with this? If not, why—how do they differ?

From *Bright-Sided: How The Relentless Promotion of Positive Thinking Has Undermined America*

Barbara Ehrenreich

Barbara Ehrenreich is a prolific author and commentator on political and cultural issues. Coming from the left of the political spectrum, Ehrenreich combines a sharp perspective with a plainspoken voice and a great deal of on-the-spot reporting. In Bright-Sided, *Ehrenreich turns her attention to the characteristically American insistence on "positive thinking" and "a good attitude." Although not all readers will agree with her conclusion that the emphasis we place on "thinking positively" tends to serve the powerful (after all, Ehrenreich says, if we are ultimately responsible for our own plights, we can't blame an unjust economic system), in this essay Ehrenreich also takes on what she sees as Americans' schizophrenic faith in science.*

The Menace of Negative People

The promise of positivity is that it will improve your life in concrete, material ways. In one simple, practical sense, this is probably true. If you are "nice," people will be more inclined to like you than if you are chronically grumpy, critical, and out of sorts. Much of the behavioral advice offered by the gurus, on their Web sites and in their books, is innocuous. "Smile," advises one success-oriented positive-thinking site. "Greet coworkers." The rewards for exuding a positive manner are all the greater in a culture that expects no less. Where cheerfulness is the norm, crankiness can seem perverse. Who would want to date or hire a "negative" person? What could be wrong with him or her? The trick, if you want to get ahead, is to simulate a positive outlook, no matter how you might actually be feeling.

The first great text on how to *act* in a positive way was Dale Carnegie's *How to Win Friends and Influence People*, originally published in 1936 and still in print. Carnegie—who was born Carnagey but changed his name apparently to match that of the industrialist Andrew Carnegie—did not assume that his readers *felt* happy, only that they could manipulate others by putting on a successful act: "You don't feel like smiling? Then what? Two things. First, force yourself to smile. If you are alone, force yourself to whistle or hum a tune or sing." You could "force" yourself to act in a positive manner, or you could be trained: "Many companies train their telephone operators to greet all callers in a tone of voice that radiates interest and enthusiasm." The operator doesn't have to feel this enthusiasm; she only has to "radiate" it. The peak achievement, in *How to Win*

Friends, is to learn how to fake sincerity: "A show of interest, as with every other principle of human relationships, must be sincere."[1] How do you put on a "show" of sincerity? This is not explained, but it is hard to imagine succeeding at it without developing some degree of skill as an actor. In a famous study in the 1980s, sociologist Arlie Hochschild found that flight attendants became stressed and emotionally depleted by the requirement that they be cheerful to passengers at all times.[2] "They lost touch with their own emotions," Hochschild told me in an interview.

As the twentieth century wore on, the relevance of Carnegie's advice only increased. More and more middle-class people were not farmers or small business owners but employees of large corporations, where the objects of their labor were likely to be not physical objects, like railroad tracks or deposits of ore, but other people. The salesman worked on his customers; the manager worked on his subordinates and coworkers. Writing in 1956, sociologist William H. Whyte viewed this development with grave misgivings, as a step toward the kind of spirit-crushing collectivization that prevailed in the Soviet Union: "Organizational life being what it is, out of sheer necessity, [a man] must spend most of his working hours in one group or another." There were "the people at the conference table, the workshop, the seminar, the skull session, the after-hours discussion group, the project team." In this thickly peopled setting, the "soft skills" of interpersonal relations came to count for more than knowledge and experience in getting the job done. Carnegie had observed that "even in such technical lines as engineering, about 15 percent of one's financial success is due to one's technical knowledge and about 85 percent is due to skill in human engineering."[3]

Today, hardly anyone needs to be reminded of the importance of interpersonal skills. Most of us work with people, on people, and around people. We have become the emotional wallpaper in other people's lives, less individuals with our own quirks and needs than dependable sources of smiles and optimism. "Ninety-nine out of every 100 people report that they want to be around more positive people," asserts the 2004 self-help book *How Full Is Your Bucket? Positive Strategies for Work and Life.*[4] The choice seems obvious— critical and challenging people or smiling yes-sayers? And the more entrenched the cult of cheerfulness becomes, the more advisable it is to conform, because your coworkers will expect nothing less. According to human resources consultant Gary S. Topchik, "the Bureau of Labor Statistics estimates that U.S. companies lose $3 billion a year to the effects of negative attitudes and behaviors at work" through, among other things, lateness, rudeness, errors, and high turnover.[5] Except in clear-cut cases of racial, gender, age, or religious discrimination, Americans can be fired for anything, such as failing to generate positive vibes. A computer technician in

Minneapolis told me he lost one job for uttering a stray remark that was never identified for him but taken as evidence of sarcasm and a "negative attitude." Julie, a reader of my Web site who lives in Austin, Texas, wrote to tell me of her experience working at a call center for Home Depot:

> I worked there for about a month when my boss pulled me into a small room and told me I "obviously wasn't happy enough to be there." Sure, I was sleep deprived from working five other jobs to pay for private health insurance that topped $300 a month and student loans that kicked in at $410 a month, but I can't recall saying anything to anyone outside the lines of "I'm happy to have a job." Plus, I didn't realize anyone had to be happy to work in a call center. My friend who works in one refers to it [having to simulate happiness] as the kind of feeling you might get from getting a hand job when your soul is dying.

What has changed, in the last few years, is that the advice to at least act in a positive way has taken on a harsher edge. The penalty for nonconformity is going up, from the possibility of job loss and failure to social shunning and complete isolation. In his 2005 best seller, *Secrets of the Millionaire Mind*, T. Harv Eker, founder of "Peak Potentials Training," advises that negative people have to go, even, presumably, the ones that you live with: "Identify a situation or a person who is a downer in your life. Remove yourself from that situation or association. If it's family, choose to be around them less."[6] In fact, this advice has become a staple of the self-help literature, of both the secular and Christian varieties. "GET RID OF NEGATIVE PEOPLE IN YOUR LIFE," writes motivational speaker and coach Jeffrey Gitomer. "They waste your time and bring you down. If you can't get rid of them (like a spouse or a boss), reduce your time with them."[7] And if that isn't clear enough, J. P. Maroney, a motivational speaker who styles himself "the Pitbull of Business," announces:

> Negative People SUCK!
> That may sound harsh, but the fact is that negative people do suck. They suck the energy out of positive people like you and me. They suck the energy and life out of a good company, a good team, a good relationship.... Avoid them at all cost. If you have to cut ties with people you've known for a long time because they're actually a negative drain on you, then so be it. Trust me, you're better off without them.[8]

What would it mean in practice to eliminate all the "negative people" from one's life? It might be a good move to separate from a chronically carping spouse, but it is not so easy to abandon the whiny toddler, the colicky infant, or the sullen teenager. And at the workplace, while it's probably advisable to detect and terminate those who show signs of becoming mass killers, there are other annoying people who might actually have something useful to say: the financial officer who keeps worrying about the bank's subprime mortgage exposure or the auto executive who questions the company's overinvestment in SUVs and trucks. Purge everyone who "brings you down," and you risk being very lonely or, what is worse, cut off from reality. The challenge of family life, or group life of any kind, is to keep gauging the moods of others, accommodating to their insights, and offering comfort when needed.

But in the world of positive thinking other people are not there to be nurtured or to provide unwelcome reality checks. They are there only to nourish, praise, and affirm. Harsh as this dictum sounds, many ordinary people adopt it as their creed, displaying wall plaques or bumper stickers showing the word "Whining" with a cancel sign through it. There seems to be a massive empathy deficit, which people respond to by withdrawing their own. No one has the time or patience for anyone else's problems.

In mid-2006, a Kansas City pastor put the growing ban on "negativity" into practice, announcing that his church would now be "complaint free." Also, there would be no criticizing, gossiping, or sarcasm. To reprogram the congregation, the Reverend Will Bowen distributed purple silicone bracelets that were to be worn as reminders. The goal? Twenty-one complaint-free days, after which the complaining habit would presumably be broken. If the wearer broke down and complained about something, then the bracelet was to be transferred to the other wrist. This bold attack on negativity brought Bowen a spread in *People* magazine and a spot on the *Oprah Winfrey Show.* Within a few months, his church had given out 4.5 million purple bracelets to people in over eighty countries. He envisions a complaint-free world and boasts that his bracelets have been distributed within schools, prisons, and homeless shelters. There is no word yet on how successful they have been in the latter two settings.

So the claim that acting in a positive way leads to success becomes self-fulfilling, at least in the negative sense that not doing so can lead to more profound forms of failure, such as rejection by employers or even one's fellow worshipers. When the gurus advise dropping "negative" people, they are also issuing a warning: smile and be agreeable, go with the flow—or prepare to be ostracized.

It is not enough, though, to cull the negative people from one's immediate circle of contacts; information about the larger human world must be carefully censored. All the motivators and gurus of positivity agree that it is a mistake to read newspapers or watch the news. An article from an online dating magazine offers, among various tips for developing a positive attitude: "Step 5: Stop Watching the News. Murder. Rape. Fraud. War. Daily news is often filled with nothing but negative stories and when you make reading such material a part of your daily lifestyle, you begin to be directly affected by that environmental factor."

Jeffrey Gitomer goes further, advising a retreat into one's personal efforts to achieve positive thinking: "All news is negative. Constant exposure to negative news can't possibly have a positive impact on your life. The Internet will give you all the news you need in about a minute and a half. That will free up time that you can devote to yourself and your positive attitude."[9]

Why is all news "negative"? Judy Braley, identified as an author and attorney, attributes the excess of bad news to the inadequate spread of positive thinking among the world's population:

> The great majority of the population of this world does not live life from the space of a positive attitude. In fact, I believe the majority of the population of this world lives from a place of pain, and that people who live from pain only know how to spread more negativity and pain. For me, this explains many of the atrocities of our world and the reason why we are bombarded with negativity all the time.[10]

At the NSA [National Speakers Association] convention, I found myself talking to a tall man whose shaved head, unsmiling face, and stiff bearing suggested a military background. I asked him whether, as a coach, he felt people needed a lot of pumping up because they were chronically depressed. No, was his answer, sometimes they're just lazy. But he went on to admit that he, too, got depressed when he read about the war in Iraq, so he now scrupulously avoids the news. "What about the need to be informed in order to be a responsible citizen?" I asked. He gave me a long look and then suggested, sagely enough, that this is what I should work on motivating people to do.

For those who need more than the ninety-second daily updates permitted by Gitomer, there are at least two Web sites offering nothing but "positive news." One of them, Good News Blog, explains that "with ample media attention going out to the cruel, the horrible, the perverted, the twisted, it is easy to become convinced that human beings are going down the drain. *'Good News'* was going to show site visitors that bad news is news simply because it *is* rare and unique." Among this site's recent top news stories were "Adoptee Reunited with Mother via Webcam Reality Show," "Students Help Nurse Rescued Horses Back to Good Health," and "Parrot Saves Girl's Life with Warning." At happynews.com, there was a surprising abundance of international stories, although not a word about Darfur, Congo, Gaza, Iraq, or Afghanistan. Instead, in a sampling of a day's offerings, I found "Seven-Month-Old from Nepal Receives Life-Saving Surgery," "100th Anniversary of the US-Canada Boundary Waters Treaty," "Many Americans Making Selfless Resolutions," and "Childhood Sweethearts Attempt Romantic Adventure."

This retreat from the real drama and tragedy of human events is suggestive of a deep helplessness at the core of positive thinking.

Why not follow the news? Because, as my informant at the NSA meeting told me, "You can't do anything about it." Braley similarly dismisses reports of disasters: "That's negative news that can cause you emotional sadness, but that you can't do anything about." The possibilities of contributing to relief funds, joining an antiwar movement, or lobbying for more humane government policies are not even considered. But at the very least there seems to be an acknowledgment here that no amount of attitude adjustment can make good news out of headlines beginning with "Civilian casualties mount ... " or "Famine spreads ... "

Of course, if the powers of mind were truly "infinite," one would not have to eliminate negative people from one's life either; one could, for example, simply choose to interpret their behavior in a positive way—maybe he's criticizing me for my own good, maybe she's being sullen because she likes me so much and I haven't been attentive, and so on. The advice that you must change your environment—for example, by eliminating negative people and news—is an admission that there may in fact be a "real world" out there that is utterly unaffected by our wishes. In the face of this terrifying possibility, the only "positive" response is to withdraw into one's own carefully constructed world of constant approval and affirmation, nice news, and smiling people.

The Law of Attraction

If ostracism is the stick threatening the recalcitrant, there is also an infinitely compelling carrot: think positively, and positive things will come to you. You can have anything, anything at all, by focusing your mind on it—limitless wealth and success, loving relationships, a coveted table at the restaurant of your choice. The universe exists to do your bidding, if only you can learn to harness the power of your desires. Visualize what you want and it will be "attracted" to you. "Ask, believe, and receive," or "Name it and claim it."

This astonishingly good news has been available in the United States for over a century, but it hit the international media with renewed force in late 2006, with the runaway success of a book and DVD entitled *The Secret*. Within a few months of publication, 3.8 million copies were in print, with the book hitting the top of both the *USA Today* and *New York Times* best seller lists. It helped that the book was itself a beautiful object, printed on glossy paper and covered in what looked like a medieval manuscript adorned with a red seal, vaguely evoking that other bestseller *The Da Vinci Code*. It helped also that the author, an Australian TV producer named Rhonda Byrne, or her surrogates won admiring interviews on *Oprah,* the *Ellen DeGeneres Show,* and *Larry King Live.* But *The Secret* relied mostly on word-of-mouth, spreading "like the Norwalk virus through Pilates classes, get-rich-quick websites and personal motivation blogs," as the *Ottawa Citizen* reported.[11] I met one fan, a young African-American woman, in the bleak cafeteria of the community college she attends, where she confided that it was now *her* secret.

Despite its generally respectful media reception, *The Secret* attracted—no doubt unintentionally, in this case—both shock and ridicule from Enlightenment circles. The critics barely knew where to begin. In the DVD, a woman admires a necklace in a store window and is next shown wearing it around her neck, simply through her conscious efforts to "attract" it. In the book, Byrne, who struggled with her weight for decades, asserts that food does not make you fat—only the *thought* that food could make you fat actually results in weight gain. She also tells the story of a woman who "attracted" her perfect partner by pretending he was already with her: she left a space for him in her garage and cleared out her closets to make room for his clothes, and, lo, he came into her life.[12] Byrne herself claims to have used "the secret" to improve her eyesight and to no longer need glasses. Overwhelmed by all this magic, *Newsweek* could only marvel at the book's "explicit claim ... that you can manipulate objective physical reality—the numbers in a lottery drawing, the actions of other people who may not even know you exist—through your thoughts and feelings."[13]

But Byrne was not saying anything new or original. In fact, she had merely packaged the insights of twenty-seven inspirational thinkers, most of them still living and many of them—like Jack Canfield, a coauthor of *Chicken Soup for the Soul*—already well known. About half the space in the book is taken up by quotes from these gurus, who are generously acknowledged as "featured co-authors" and listed with brief bios at the end. Among them are a "feng shui master," the president of a company selling "inspirational gifts," a share trader, and two physicists. But the great majority of her "co-authors" are people who style themselves as "coaches" and motivational speakers, including Joe Vitale, whose all-encompassing love I had experienced at the NSA meeting. The "secret" had hardly been kept under wraps; it was the collective wisdom of the coaching profession. My own first exposure to the mind-over-matter philosophy of *The Secret* had come three years before that book's publication, from a less than successful career coach in Atlanta, who taught that one's external conditions, such as failure and unemployment, are projections of one's "inner sense of well-being."

The notion that people other than athletes might need something called "coaching" arose in the 1980s when corporations began to hire actual sports coaches as speakers at corporate gatherings. Many salesmen and managers had played sports in school and were easily roused by speakers invoking crucial moments on the gridiron. In the late 1980s, John Whitmore, a former car racer and sports coach, carried coaching off the playing fields and into the executive offices, where its goal became to enhance "performance" in the abstract, including the kind that can be achieved while sitting at a desk. People who might formerly have called themselves "consultants" began to call themselves "coaches" and to set up shop to instill ordinary people, usually white-collar corporate employees, with a "winning" or positive attitude. One of the things the new coaches brought from the old world of sports coaching was the idea of visualizing victory, or at least a credible performance, before the game, just as Byrne and her confederates urge people to visualize the outcomes they desire.

Sports was only one source of the new wisdom, which had been bubbling up for years from the world of self-help gurus and "spiritual teachers," most of them not referenced by Byrne. For example, there was the 2004 docudrama *What the Bleep Do We Know?*, produced by a New Age sect led by a Tacoma woman named JZ Knight, who channels a 35,000-year-old warrior spirit named Ramtha. In the film, actor Marlee Matlin gives up Xanax for a spiritual appreciation of life's limitless possibilities. At the Ramtha School of Enlightenment, students write down their goals, post them on a wall, and attempt to realize them through strenuous forms of "meditation" involving high-decibel rock music. On the more businesslike side, "success coach" Mike Hernacki published his book *The Ultimate Secret to Getting Absolutely Everything You Want* in 1982; the genre continued with, among others, Michael J. Losier's 2006 book, *Law of Attraction: The Science of Attracting More of What You Want and Less of What You Don't*. T. Harv Eker's *Secrets of the Millionaire Mind* explains that "the universe, which is another way of saying 'higher power,' is akin to a big mail order department," an image also employed by Vitale.[14] If you send in your orders clearly and unambiguously, fulfillment is guaranteed in a timely fashion.

What attracts the coaching profession to these mystical powers? Well, there's not much else for them to impart to their coachees. "Career coaches" may teach their clients how to write resumes and deliver the self-advertisements known as "elevator speeches," but they don't have anything else by way of concrete skills to offer. Neither they nor more generic "success coaches" will help you throw a javelin farther, upgrade your computer skills, or manage the flow of information through a large department. All they can do is work on your attitude and expectations, so it helps to start with the metaphysical premise that success is guaranteed through some kind of attitudinal intervention. And if success does not follow, if you remain strapped for funds or stuck in an unpromising job, it's not the coach's fault, it's yours. You just didn't try hard enough and obviously need more work.

The metaphysics found in the coaching industry and books like *The Secret* bears an unmistakable resemblance to traditional folk forms of magic, in particular "sympathetic magic," which operates on the principle that like attracts like. A fetish or talisman—or, in the case of "black magic," something like a pinpricked voodoo doll—is thought to bring about some desired outcome. In the case of positive thinking, the positive thought, or mental image of the desired outcome, serves as a kind of internal fetish to hold in your mind. As religious historian Catherine Albanese explains, "In material magic, symbolic behavior involves the use of artifacts and stylized accoutrements, in ritual, or ceremonial, magic," while in "mental magic," of the positive-thinking variety, "the field is internalized, and the central ritual becomes some form of meditation or guided visualization."[15]

Sometimes, though, an actual physical fetish may be required. John Assaraf, an entrepreneur and coach featured in *The Secret*, explains the use of "vision boards":

> Many years ago, I looked at another way to represent some of the material-istic things I wanted to achieve in my life, whether it was a car or a house or anything. And so I started cutting out pictures of things that I wanted. And I put those vision boards up. And every day for probably about just two to three minutes, I would sit in [*sic*] my desk and I would look at my board and I'd close my eyes. And I'd see myself having the dream car and the dream home and the money in the bank that I wanted and the money that I wanted to have for charity.[16]

The link to older, seemingly more "primitive" forms of magic is unabashed in one Web site's instructions for creating a kind of vision board:

> Leaving the four corners of the card (posterboard) blank, decorate the rest of the face with glitter, ribbons, magical symbols, herbs, or any other items linked with the attributes of prosperity. Next, take the dollar bill and cut off the four corners. Glue the bill's triangular corners to the four corners of your card. This is sympathetic magic—one must have money to attract money. Then either on the back of the card or on a separate piece of paper, write out these instructions for using the talisman:
> This is a talisman of prosperity. Place it where you will see it every day, preferably in a bedroom.
> At least once a day hold it to your heart and spend several minutes reciting the chant: talisman of prosperity, All good things come to me.
> Notice the magic begin.[17]

Homemade talismans aside, most coaches would be chagrined by any association with magic. What gives positive thinking some purchase on mainstream credibility is its claim to be based firmly on science. Why do positive thoughts attract positive outcomes? Because of the "law of attraction," which operates as reliably as the law of gravity. Bob Doyle, one of the "featured co-authors" of *The Secret* and founder of the "Wealth Beyond Reason" training system, asserts on his Web site: "Contrary to mainstream thinking, the Law of Attraction is NOT a 'new-age' concept. It is a scientific principle that absolutely is at work in your life right now." The claims of a scientific basis undoubtedly help account for positive thinking's huge popularity in the business world, which might be more skittish about an ideology derived entirely from, say, spirit channeling or Rosicrucianism. And science probably helped attract major media attention to *The Secret* and its spokespeople, a panel of whom were introduced by the poker-faced Larry King with these words: "Tonight, unhappy with your love, your job, your life, not enough money? Use your head. You can think yourself into a lot better you. Positive thoughts can transform, can attract the good things you know you want. Sound far-fetched? Think again. It's supported by science."

Coaches and self-help gurus have struggled for years to find a force that could draw the desired results to the person who desires them or a necklace in a store window to an admirer's neck. In his 1982 book, Hernacki settled on the familiar force of gravity, offering the equation linking the mass of two objects to their acceleration. But even those whose science educations stopped at ninth grade might notice some problems with this. One, thoughts are not objects with mass; they are patterns of neuronal firing within the brain. Two, if they were exerting some sort of gravitational force on material objects around them, it would be difficult to take off one's hat.

In an alternative formulation offered by Michael J. Losier, the immaterial nature of thoughts is acknowledged; they become "vibrations." "In the vibrational world," he writes, "there are two kinds of vibrations, positive (+) and negative (−). Every mood or feeling causes you to emit, send-out or offer a vibration, whether positive or negative."[18] But thoughts are not "vibrations," and known vibrations, such as sound waves, are characterized by amplitude and frequency. There is no such thing as a "positive" or "negative" vibration.

Magnetism is another force that has long lured positive thinkers, going back to the 1937—and still briskly selling—*Think and Grow Rich!*, which declared that "thoughts, like magnets, attract to us the forces, the people, the circumstances of life which harmonize with [them]." Hence the need to "magnetize our minds with intense DESIRE for riches."[19] Now, as patterns of neuronal firing that produce electrical activity in the brain, thoughts do indeed generate a magnetic field, but it is a pathetically weak one. As *Scientific American* columnist Michael Shermer observes, "The brain's magnetic field of 10 [to the minus 15th power] tesla quickly dissipates from the skull and is promptly swamped by other magnetic sources, not to mention the earth's magnetic field of 10 [to the minus 5th power] tesla, which overpowers it by 10 orders of magnitude!" Ten orders of magnitude—or a ratio of 10,000,000,000 to one. As everyone knows, ordinary magnets are not attracted or repelled by our heads, nor are our heads attracted to our refrigerators.[20]

There does exist one way for mental activity to affect the physical world, but only with the intervention of a great deal of technology. Using biofeedback techniques, a person can learn, through pure trial and error, to generate brain electrical activity that can move a cursor on a computer screen. The person doing this must be wearing an electrode-studded cap, or electroencephalograph, to detect the electrical signals from inside the head, which are then amplified and sent to an interface with the computer, usually for the purpose of aiding a severely paralyzed person to communicate. No "mind over matter" forces are involved, except metaphorically, if the technology is taken as representing our collective "mind." A technologically unassisted person cannot move a computer cursor by thought alone, much less move money into his or her bank account.

Into this explanatory void came quantum physics, or at least a highly filtered and redacted version thereof. Byrne cites quantum physics in *The Secret,* as does the 2004 film *What the Bleep Do We Know?*, and today no cutting-edge coach neglects it. The great promise of quantum physics, to New Age thinkers and the philosophically opportunistic generally, is that it seems to release humans from the dull tethers of determinism. Anything, they imagine, can happen at the level of subatomic particles, where the familiar laws of Newtonian physics do not prevail, so why not in our own lives? Insofar as I can follow the reasoning, two features of quantum physics seem to offer us limitless freedom. One is the wave/particle duality of matter, which means that waves, like light, are also particles (photons) and that subatomic particles, like electrons, can also be understood as waves—that is, described by a wave equation. In the loony extrapolation favored by positive thinkers, whole humans are also waves or vibrations. "This is what we be," NSA speaker Sue Morter announced, wriggling her fingers to suggest a vibration, "a flickering," and as vibrations we presumably have a lot more freedom of motion than we do as gravity-bound, 150-or-so-pound creatures made of carbon, oxygen, and so forth.

Another, even more commonly abused notion from quantum physics is the uncertainty principle, which simply asserts that we cannot know both the momentum and position of a subatomic particle. In the more familiar formulation, we usually say that the act of measuring something at the quantum level affects what is being measured, since to measure the coordinates of a particle like an electron is to pin it down into a particular quantum state—putting it through a process known as "quantum collapse." In the fanciful interpretation of a New Agey physicist cited by Rhonda Byrne, "the mind is actually shaping the very thing that is being perceived."[21] From there it is apparently a short leap to the idea that we are at all times creating the entire universe

with our minds. As one life coach has written: "We are Creators of
the Universe.... With quantum physics, science is leaving behind the
notion that human beings are powerless victims and moving toward
an understanding that we are fully empowered creators of our lives
and of our world."[22]

In the words of Nobel physicist Murray Gell-Mann, this is so
much "quantum flapdoodle." For one thing, quantum effects come
into play at a level vastly smaller than our bodies, our nerve cells, and
even the molecules involved in the conduction of neuronal impulses.
Responding to *What the Bleep Do We Know?*, which heavily invokes
quantum physics to explain the law of attraction, the estimable Michael
Shermer notes that "for a system to be described quantum-mechan-
ically, its typical mass (m), speed (v) and distance (d) must be on the
order of Planck's constant (h) [6.626×10^{-34} joule-seconds]," which is far
beyond tiny. He cites a physicist's calculations "that the mass of neural
transmitter molecules and their speed across the distance of the syn-
apse are about two orders of magnitude too large for quantum effects
to be influential."[23] In other words, even our thought processes seem
to be stuck in the deterministic prison of classical Newtonian physics.

As for the mind's supposed power to shape the universe: if anything, quantum physics contains a humbling reminder of the *limits* of
the human mind and imagination. The fact that very small things like
electrons and photons can act like both waves and particles does not
mean that they are free to do anything or, of course, that we can morph
into waves ourselves. Sadly, what it means is that we cannot envision
these tiny things, at least not with images derived from the everyday,
nonquantum world. Nor does the uncertainty principle mean that
"the mind is shaping the very thing that is being perceived," only that
there are limits to what we can ever find out about, say, a quantum-level
particle. Where is it "really" and how fast is it going? We cannot know.
When contacted by *Newsweek,* even the mystically oriented physicists
enlisted by Byrne in *The Secret* backed off from the notion of any
physical force through which the mind can fulfill its desires.

But no such qualms dampened the celebration of quantum
physics, or perhaps I should say "quantum physics," at the gathering of the NSA conference in San Diego. Sue Morter fairly bounded
around the stage as she asserted that "your reality is simply determined by whatever frequency [of energy] you choose to dive
into." Unfortunately, she added, "we've been raised in Newtonian
thought," so it can be hard to grasp quantum physics. How much
Morter, a chiropractor by profession, grasped was unclear; quite
apart from the notion that we are vibrations choosing our own frequency, she made small annoying errors such as describing "the
cloud of electrons around an atom." (Electrons are part of the atom,
orbiting around its nucleus.) But the good news is that "science has

shown without a shadow of a doubt" that we create our own reality. Somehow, the fact that particles can act like waves and vice versa means that "whatever you decide is true, is true"— an exceedingly hard proposition to debate.

After Morter's presentation, I went to a workshop entitled "The Final Frontier: Your Unlimited Mind!," led by Rebecca Nagy, a "wedding preacher" from Charlotte, North Carolina, who described herself as a member of the "quantum spiritual world." We started by repeating after her, "I am a co-creator," with the prefix "co" as an apparent nod to some other, more traditional form of creator. Slide after slide went by, showing what appeared to be planets with moons—or electrons?—in orbit around them or announcing that "human beings are both receivers and transmitters of quantum (LIGHT ENERGY) signals." At one point Nagy called for two volunteers to come to the front of the room to help illustrate the unlimited powers of mind. One of them was given two dowsing rods to hold and told to think of someone she loves. But no matter how much Nagy fiddled with the position of the rods, nothing happened, leading her to say, "No judgment here! Can we agree on that? No judgment here!" Finally, after several more minutes of repositioning, she mumbled, "It ain't working," and suggested that this could be "because we're in a hotel."

I began to make it my business to see what other conference goers thought of the inescapable pseudoscientific flapdoodle. They were an outgoing lot, easy to strike up conversations with, and it seemed to me that my doubts about the invocation of quantum physics might get us past the level of "How are you enjoying the conference?" to either some common ground or a grave intellectual rupture. Several modestly admitted that it went right over their heads, but no one displayed the slightest skepticism. In one workshop, I found myself sitting next to a woman who introduced herself as a business professor. When I told her that I worried about all the references to quantum physics, she said, "You're supposed to be shaken up here." No, I said, I was worried about what it had to do with actual physics. "It's what I'm here for," she countered blandly. When I could come up with nothing more than a "Huh?" she explained that quantum physics is "what's going to affect the global economy."

I did find one cynic—a workshop leader who had introduced himself as a "leadership coach" and "quantum physicist," though actually he claimed only a master's degree in nuclear physics. When I cornered him after the workshop, he allowed as how "there is some crap" but insisted that quantum physics and New Age thinking "overlap a lot." When I pushed harder, he told me that it wouldn't do any good to challenge the ongoing abuse of quantum physics, because "thousands of people believe it." But the most startling response I got to my quibbling came from an expensively dressed life coach from Southern California. After I summarized my discomfort with all the fake quantum physics in a couple of sentences, she gave me a kindly therapeutic look and asked, "You mean it doesn't work for you?"

I felt at that moment, and for the first time in this friendly crowd, absolutely alone. If science is something you can accept or reject on the basis of personal tastes, then what kind of reality did she and I share? If it "worked for me" to say that the sun rises in the west, would she be willing to go along with that, accepting it as my particular take on things? Maybe I should have been impressed that these positive thinkers bothered to appeal to science at all, whether to "vibrations" or quantum physics, and in however degraded a form. To base a belief or worldview on science or what passes for science is to reach out to the nonbelievers and the uninitiated, to say that they too can come to the same conclusions if they make the same systematic observations and inferences. The alternative is to base one's worldview on revelation or mystical insight, and these are things that cannot be reliably shared with others. In other words, there's something deeply sociable about science; it rests entirely on observations that can be shared with and repeated by others. But in a world where "everything you decide is true, is true," what kind of connection between people can there be? Science, as well as most ordinary human interaction, depends on the assumption that there are conscious beings other than ourselves and that we share the same physical world, with all its surprises, sharp edges, and dangers.

But it is not clear that there *are* other people in the universe as imagined by the positive thinkers or, if there are, that they matter. What if they want the same things that we do, like that necklace, or what if they hope for entirely different outcomes to, say, an election or a football game? In *The Secret* Byrne tells the story of Colin, a ten-year-old boy who was initially dismayed by the long waits for rides at Disney World. He had seen Byrne's movie, however, and knew it was enough to think the thought "Tomorrow I'd love to go on all the big rides and never have to wait in line." Presto, the next morning his family was chosen to be Disney's "First Family" for the day, putting them first in line and leaving "hundreds of families" behind them.[24] What about all those other children, condemned to wait because Colin was empowered by *The Secret?* Or, in the case of the suitor who was magically drawn to the woman who cleared out her closets and garage to make room for him, was this what he wanted for himself or was he only a pawn in her fantasy?

It was this latter possibility that finally provoked a reaction from Larry King the night he hosted a panel of *The Secret's* "teachers." One of them said, "I've been master planning my life and one of the things that I actually dreamed of doing is sitting here facing you, saying what I'm about to say. So I know that it [the law of attraction] works." That was too much for King, who was suddenly offended by the idea of being an object of "attraction" in someone else's life. "If one of you have a vision board with my picture on it," he snapped, "I'll go to break." This was an odd situation for a famous talk show host—having to insist that he, Larry King, was not just an image on someone else's vision board but an independent being with a will of his own.

It's a glorious universe the positive thinkers have come up with, a vast, shimmering aurora borealis in which desires mingle freely with their realizations. Everything is perfect here, or as perfect as you want to make it. Dreams go out and fulfill themselves; wishes need only to be articulated. It's just a god-awful lonely place.

Notes

1. Dale Carnegie, *How to Win Friends and Influence People* (New York: Pocket Books, 1982), 70, 61, 64.
2. Arlie Russell Hochschild, *The Managed Heart: Commercialization of Human Feeling* (Berkeley: University of California Press, 1983).
3. William H. Whyte, *The Organization Man* (Philadelphia: University of Pennsylvania Press, 2002), 46–47, 14.
4. Tom Rath and Donald O. Clifton, *How Full Is Your Bucket? Positive Strategies for Work and Life* (New York: Gallup Press, 2004), 47.
5. Quoted on the American Management Association's Web site, http://www.amanet.org/books/book.cfm?isbn=9780814405826.
6. T. Harv Eker, *Secrets of the Millionaire Mind: Mastering the Inner Game of Wealth* (New York: HarperBusiness, 2005), 101.
7. Jeffrey Gitomer, *Little Gold Book of YES!* (Upper Saddle River; FT Press, 2007), 138.
8. http://guruknowledge.Org/articles/255/1/The-Power-of-Negative-Thinking/ The-Power-of-Negative-Thinking.html.
9. Gitomer, *Little Gold Book,* 45.
10. Judy Braley, "Creating a Positive Attitude," http://ezinearticles.com/?Creating -a-Positive-Attitude&id=759618.
11. Quoted in http://www.nationmaster.com/encyclopedia/The-Secret-(2006-film).
12. Rhonda Byrne, *The Secret* (New York: Atria Books/Beyond Words, 2006), 116.
13. Jerry Adler, "Decoding 'The Secret,'" *Newsweek,* March 5, 2007.
14. Eker, *Secrets,* 67; Vitale quoted in Byrne, *The Secret,* 48.
15. Catherine L. Albanese, A *Republic of Mind and Spirit: A Cultural History of American Metaphysical Religion* (New Haven: Yale University Press, 2007), 7.
16. *Larry King Live,* CNN, Nov. 2, 2006.
17. http://www.globalpsychics.com/empowering-you/practical-magic/prosperity .shtml.

18. Michael J. Losier, *Law of Attraction: The Science of Attracting More of What You Want and Less of What You Don't* (Victoria: Michael J. Losier Enterprises, 2006), 13.

19. Napoleon Hill, *Think and Grow Rich!* (San Diego: Aventine Press, 2004), 21.

20. Michael Shermer, "The (Other) Secret," *Scientific American*, July 2007, 39.

21. Byrne, *The Secret*, 21.

22. http://ezinearticles.com/?The-Law-of-Attraction-and-Quantum-Physics&id =223148.

23. Michael Shermer, "Quantum Quackery," *Scientific American*, Dec. 20, 2004.

24. Byrne, *The Secret*, 88.

Critical Reading Questions

Summarizing the Text

1. In the story about attending the motivational speakers' conference, Ehrenreich points out how the audience fundamentally misunderstands physics. Why is this important? Does this undermine *their* credibility, or does it seem like Ehrenreich is nitpicking or trying to ridicule people she dislikes?

2. How does the pressure to think and act positively serve the interests of employers, according to Ehrenreich?

Establishing the Context

3. Early in the essay, Ehrenreich goes back to the 1930s and describes the impact and argument of Dale Carnegie's *How To Win Friends and Influence People*. She also describes economic changes in the United States and how they have made "positive thinking" more important in the workplace. What happened to the U.S. economy between now and then? Do you think that the Internet communications revolution will change this? If so, how?

4. Ehrenreich draws an implicit distinction between "science" (such as quantum physics and the laws of magnetism) and "magic" or "metaphysics." How does she create and reinforce this distinction? What authorities does she use to characterize each side—and how does she establish or undermine their credibility?

Responding to the Message

5. What is wrong with adopting a positive attitude, or accepting the "law of attraction," according to Ehrenreich? How might you refute her claims or implicit assumptions in this chapter?

The CSI Effect: The Truth About Forensic Science

Jeffrey Toobin

Jeffrey Toobin is a legal analyst for CNN and a writer for the New Yorker.
*A graduate of Harvard and Harvard Law, Toobin worked for the investigative
team on the 1980s "Iran-Contra" affair (a high-profile political scandal during the
presidency of Ronald Reagan). He is the author of several books on American
law and jurisprudence, most recently* The Nine: Inside the Secret World of the
Supreme Court *(2007). Here, he profiles the forensics department of the largest
city police department in the United States and compares the reality of this gritty
work to the image disseminated by the popular CSI television franchise. This
article appeared in the* New Yorker *magazine in 2007.*

On the evening of March 10, 2003, two New York Police Department
detectives, James V. Nemorin and Rodney J. Andrews, were shot and
killed in an unmarked police car while attempting an undercover
purchase of a Tec-9 assault pistol on Staten Island. The case was significant not just because two officers had died but because the man
who was eventually charged with the murders, Ronell Wilson, faced
the possibility of becoming the first person in more than fifty years to
be executed for a crime in New York State.

The government's theory was that Wilson, who was with an
accomplice in the back seat of the car, shot the detectives during a
robbery attempt. Among the evidence retrieved from the crime scene
were hundreds of hairs and fibres, and prosecutors enlisted Lisa Faber,
a criminalist and the supervisor of the N.Y.P.D. crime lab's hair-and-
fibre unit, to testify at Wilson's trial, last winter. Under questioning in
Brooklyn federal court, Faber said that she had compared samples of
fabric from the detectives' car with fibres found on gloves, jeans, and
a baseball cap that Wilson had allegedly been wearing on the night
of the crime. The prosecutor asked Faber to describe the methods and
equipment she had used to make her analysis. Then she asked Faber
what she had found. "My conclusion is that all of those questioned
fibres could have originated from the interior of the Nissan Maxima,
from the seats, and/or the backrests," Faber said. She added that in her
field "the strongest association you can say is that 'it could have come
from'" the source in question.

Faber's testimony was careful and responsible—and not very significant. She could not say how common the automobile fabric that she
had examined is, or how many models and brands use it. Nor could
she say how likely it was that the fabric from the car would show up on
Wilson's clothes. Faber used no statistics, because there was no way to

establish with any precision the probability that the fibres came from the detectives' car. DNA tests had proved that blood from one of the detectives was on Wilson's clothes, and based on this fact, as well as on testimony from his accomplice and from Faber, Wilson was convicted and sentenced to death. "Given how much evidence they had in the case, I wasn't crucial," Faber told me. "The prosecutors liked the idea of fibre evidence in addition to everything else. Maybe they thought the jury would like it because it was more 'CSI'-esque."

"CSI: Crime Scene Investigation," the CBS television series, and its two spinoffs—"CSI: Miami" and "CSI: New York"—routinely appear near the top of the Nielsen ratings. (A recent international survey, based on ratings from 2005, concluded that "CSI: Miami" was the most popular program in the world.) In large part because of the series' success, Faber's profession has acquired an air of glamour, and its practitioners an aura of infallibility. "I just met with the conference of Louisiana judges, and, when I asked if 'CSI' had influenced their juries, every one of them raised their hands," Carol Henderson, the director of the National Clearinghouse for Science, Technology and the Law, at Stetson University, in Florida, told me. "People are riveted by the idea that science can solve crimes." At the Las Vegas criminalistics bureau where the original version of the show is set, the number of job applications has increased dramatically in the past few years. In the pilot for the series, which was broadcast in 2000, Gil Grissom, the star criminalist, who is played by William Petersen, solved a murder by comparing toenail clippings. "If I can match the nail in the sneaker to the suspect's clipping ... " Grissom mused, then did just that. In the next episode, the Las Vegas investigators solved a crime by comparing striation marks on bullets. "We got a match," one said. Later in the same show, Nick Stokes (George Eads) informs Grissom, his boss, "I just finished the carpet-swatch comparisons. Got a match."

The fictional criminalists speak with a certainty that their real-life counterparts do not. "We never use the word 'match,'" Faber, a thirty-eight-year-old Harvard graduate, told me. "The terminology is very important. On TV, they always like to say words like 'match,' but we say 'similar,' or 'could have come from' or 'is associated with.'"

Virtually all the forensic-science tests depicted on "CSI"—including analyses of bite marks, blood spatter, handwriting, firearm and tool marks, and voices, as well as of hair and fibres—rely on the judgments of individual experts and cannot easily be subjected to statistical verification. Many of the tests were developed by police departments more than a hundred years ago, and for decades they have been admitted as evidence in criminal trials to help bring about convictions. In the mid-nineteen-nineties, nuclear-DNA analysis—which can link suspects to crime-scene evidence with mathematical certainty—became widely available, prompting some legal scholars to argue that older, less reliable tests, such as hair and fibre analysis, should no longer be allowed in court. In 1996, the authors of an exhaustive study of forensic hair comparisons published in the *Columbia Human Rights Law Review* concluded, "If the purveyors of this dubious science cannot do a better job of validating hair analysis than they have done so far, forensic hair comparison analysis should be excluded altogether from criminal trials."

Last week, a commission on forensic science sponsored by the National Academy of Sciences held an open session in Washington at which several participants questioned the validity of hair and fibre evidence. Max Houck, the director of the Forensic Science Initiative at West Virginia University and the co-author of an important study that reviewed hair analyses by the F.B.I., was fiercely criticized by several members of the commission, including one of the co-chairs, Harry T. Edwards, a senior federal-appeals-court judge. "It sounds like there is a lot of impressionistic and subjective examination going on," Edwards said, after Houck described the study. "Follow-up examiners repeated [the analyses] and made the same mistakes," Edwards said. "That's the scariest part."

Sir Robert Peel is credited with creating the first modern police force, the bobbies, in London, in 1829, but the transformation of law enforcement, and especially forensic science, into a professional discipline was a haphazard affair. Scientists occasionally took an interest in police work, and courts sometimes accepted their testimony. Oddly, one prominent early figure in the field developed specialties in both bullets and hair, which have little in common except that both are often found at crime scenes. In 1910, Victor Balthazard, a professor of forensic medicine at the Sorbonne, published the first comprehensive study of hair, "Le Poil de I'Homme et des Animaux," and three years later, in an influential article, he theorized that the grooves inside every gun barrel leave a unique imprint on bullets that pass through it. In the mid-twenties, Calvin Goddard, a New York doctor, began using a comparison microscope, which allows an analyst to examine two slides at the same time, to study bullets. In 1929, he analyzed bullets collected at the site of the St. Valentine's Day massacre, in which gunmen wearing police uniforms shot and killed six members of George (Bugs) Moran's gang and a seventh man. Goddard test-fired all eight machine guns owned by the Chicago police and found no match with the bullets used in the crime. Two years later, he examined two submachine guns retrieved from the home of Fred Burke, a sometime hit man for Al Capone, Moran's great rival. Goddard pronounced Burke's guns the murder weapons, and the feat so impressed local leaders that they established a crime lab, the nation's first, and installed Goddard as its director.

The comparison microscopes in the N.Y.P.D. crime lab are more powerful than Goddard's model was, but many of the techniques the lab uses haven't changed substantially in decades. Situated in a remote part of Queens, in a sprawling office building that formerly belonged to York College of the City University of New York, the crime lab combines municipal decrepitude and state-of-the-art technology. The seating area in the lobby includes an old minivan bench, complete with a dangling seat belt. There are six analysts in Faber's hair-and-fibre unit, and each has a polarized-light microscope, which costs about fifteen thousand dollars. In addition, the unit has two comparison microscopes, which cost fifty thousand dollars, but only one phone line, which doesn't have voicemail. Having worked for the N.Y.P.D. for nearly a decade, Faber has acquired a weary proficiency in the department's eccentricities. "We have some of the best lab equipment in the country, maybe as good as the F.B.I.," she told me recently, when I visited her at the lab. "But for the little stuff we have to scrounge."

Faber's father, a German businessman, was transferred by his company to Manchester, New Hampshire, in 1966, two years before Lisa was born. She was in junior high school when she became interested in trace-evidence analysis, which includes hair and fibre. "It was the time of the Atlanta child murders," she recalled, referring to the killings of more than two dozen children and young men in the city between 1979 and 1981. "I would sit there watching the news and see how they were connecting the murders through fibres at the murder scenes. It just fascinated me that you could have a body floating in a river and still find fibre evidence that would connect it to a car." The trace evidence was critical in the case against Wayne Williams, a twenty-three-year-old aspiring music promoter, who was convicted of two of the murders and sentenced to two life terms. No one has been charged in connection with the other deaths. (In February, following years of unsuccessful appeals by Williams, lawyers for Georgia agreed to allow DNA tests on some of the hair used as evidence in the case. Results of the tests have not yet been reported.)

At Harvard, Faber majored in East Asian Studies. "I still followed murder cases, and the Internet was just getting started not long after I graduated," she recalled. "So I looked around to see what kind of graduate programs in forensic science there might be around the country. There were four." One was at George Washington University, where she enrolled. Her first class, in trace analysis, was taught by a former F.B.I. special agent named Hal Deadman. "He passed around materials on that first day, and they were from the Atlanta murders. He had been an investigator on the case. I thought, I can't believe this. This is perfect for me." Two years later, having completed a master's degree, Faber joined the N.Y.P.D., where she earns about seventy thousand dollars a year. A tall woman, who usually wears her long blond hair in a barrette, Faber has an apartment in Greenwich Village, where few other N.Y.P.D. employees live. "No one ever steals my lunch out of the office refrigerator," she said. "People ask me, 'That's all you're eating—vegetables?'"

When a piece of evidence, usually a garment, arrives in Faber's unit, a junior analyst pats a strip of clear tape on the fabric, to pick up any loose hairs or fibres. The tape strips are then placed face down on a plastic sheet, which is given to a more senior person to study under a relatively low-powered stereo microscope. "I've got to do a screening at this point, just to see what might be useful to examine in greater detail," Faber told me. "As far as hair goes, I'm looking only for head hair and pubic hair, because arm or chest hair doesn't have enough variation to be useful for comparison. If I see a fibre, I'll circle it with my green Sharpie. If I see a hair, I'll circle it in red. A brown circle means I'm not sure what it is. When I'm done, I take my tweezers and remove each hair and fibre and glue them onto slides. Now I'm really ready to begin my analysis."

According to a long-established practice of hair analysis, the examiners study between twenty and thirty characteristics of each hair. (Only hairs whose roots are intact—typically because they have been pulled from someone's head—and are in the growing stage have nuclear DNA, which is unique to each person; the vast majority of hairs found at crime scenes lack roots suitable for testing.) "The first thing we look at is pigment—color," Faber said. "Is there dye or bleach, and how much of it? We like it when there's dye, because it makes a hair distinctive. Then there is the cuticle, which is like the yellow on a pencil—the outside—and we see if it's damaged or serrated." One of the things that make hair analysis so challenging is that a person can have hairs of many different colors on his or her head. Nor can ethnicity be established with certainty on the basis of hair samples alone. "Hair is curly because of diameter variation," Faber explained. "A black person's hair typically has a lot of diameter variation. Asian people have little variation, which is what makes it straight." Faber has hundreds of slides of hair that she has collected from around the world and uses to train junior analysts. "I ask my friends to give me their hair," she said.

For the Wilson case, Faber examined more than a hundred pieces of evidence, including the victims' clothes, the suspects' clothes, and the interior of the car, along with two do-rags and other items seized from the street. From this material, Faber recovered thousands of fibres and hundreds of hairs, each of which had to be assessed under a microscope.

"The examinations involving the car were especially difficult and timeconsuming," she said. For Faber, the key question in the case was whether she could identify fibres on Wilson's clothing which resembled those taken from the car. "There were hundreds of fibres that looked stereoscopically similar at lower power magnifications—that is, up to fifty times—but many of them were in fact different in chemical composition," she said. "I could tell them apart only when I mounted each fibre on a slide and examined it under two hundred to four hundred magnification with a polarized-light microscope. It's only at that level that you can see what you need to know to identify the chemical composition of the fibre, like whether it's polyester, nylon, or acrylic." Once she had eliminated those fibres which could not have come from the car, Faber performed two additional tests on the remaining set: a Fourier Transform Infrared Spectroscopy, to establish and compare chemical composition, and microspectrophotometry, to compare color. Working quickly, Faber said, she could complete perhaps five F.T.I.R. and MSP analyses a day; evaluating all the evidence in the case took her two and a half years.

Several times a year, at the New York Police Academy, Faber lectures about trace analysis in a criminal-investigations course, which generally attracts about a hundred mid-career detectives and other investigators. Earlier this spring, she had the misfortune of appearing late in the three-week course, which meant that the students—about ninety beefy men and six women in an overheated classroom—listened and observed in varied states of consciousness.

"With trace analysis, what we are doing is comparing a 'q' to a 'k,'" Faber told the group. "A 'q' is a questioned sample from a crime scene—a paint chip on someone's clothing from a hit and run, a hair in the hand of a murder victim. The source is unknown. The 'k' is a known sample—a hair from the autopsy, or one that you take from a suspect. What we do in the trace-analysis unit are comparisons with 'q's' and 'k's.' We see if there is a connection."

Faber's brief summary defined the dilemma at the heart of forensic science. "There are really two kinds of forensic science," says Michael J. Saks, a professor of law and psychology at Arizona State University, and a prominent critic of the way such science is used in courtrooms. "The first is very straightforward. It says, 'We have a dead body. Let's see what chemicals are in the blood. Is there alcohol? Cocaine?' That is real science applied to a forensics problem. The other half of forensic science has been invented by and for police departments, and that includes finger-prints, handwriting, tool marks, tire marks, hair and fibre. All of those essentially share one belief, which is that there are no two specimens that are alike except those from the same source." Saks and other experts argue that there is no objective basis for making the link between a "q" and a "k." "There is no scientific evidence, no validation studies, or anything else that scientists usually demand, for that proposition—that, say, two hairs that look alike came from the same person," Saks said. "It's the individualization fallacy, and it's not real science. It's faith-based science."

Virtually all experts agree about the reliability of DNA evidence. "DNA is based on a well-known technology and scientific principles that have a lot of uses outside the lab and a lot of good validation data," D. Michael Risinger, a professor at Seton Hall University School of Law, said. "You will typically know what the error rates are. The tests produce actual probability statements about results. It's real science." Currently, two kinds of DNA are subject to forensic testing: nuclear DNA and mitochondrial DNA (mtDNA), which is passed from mother to child. Unlike nuclear DNA, mtDNA can be extracted even from hairs that lack roots; though mtDNA tests cannot establish a precise match, they can eliminate many potential suspects. In the past two years, New York authorities have begun conducting mtDNA tests on some evidence.

At last week's session on forensic science in Washington, Max Houck explained that he and his co-author, Bruce Budowle, a senior scientist at the F.B.I. Laboratory, had used mtDNA technology to test the validity of hair analysis. The authors reviewed the results of a hundred and seventy microscopic hair examinations, which produced eighty associations between "q" and "k" samples. But subsequent mtDNA tests of the hairs showed that in nine cases—more than ten per cent—the samples could not have come from the same person. The number of errors was concerning, Judge Edwards said. According to his calculations, he added, the study's error rate was actually close to thirty-five per cent. How, he asked Houck, was such a flawed process acceptable?

Houck challenged Judge Edwards's use of the word "error," arguing that mtDNA tests provided a way to refine the more general conclusions of microscopic examinations. To illustrate his point, Houck offered an analogy: "Suppose you have an art expert who is looking at three possible van Goghs. He sees that all three are consistent with his style. But then a chemical test comes along that shows two of them were painted after van Gogh died. They're not van Goghs, but that doesn't mean that the art expert was wrong about them. They may have been consistent with his style. It's the same with hair analysis. The subsequent DNA tests don't mean that the original tests were wrong, just that a more refined test has come along."

"I don't think your analogy holds at all," Edwards said. "Those are real errors, and this is not about art history. My great worry is that there are a lot of people going to jail on bad information."

Margaret A. Berger, a professor at Brooklyn Law School, added, "We know from a lot of DNA exonerations that they come from bad hair evidence. So the real question raised by your study is whether the courts should ever allow microscopic evidence when there is no DNA to back it up? If there is no mtDNA, I think it should be excluded."

"Let me ask you this," Channing R. Robertson, a professor of chemical engineering at Stanford, said to Houck. "Suppose your son or daughter was accused of a crime, and someone came on the stand and gave their qualifications as a hair examiner, and made an association based on microscopic examination, and that led to the conviction of your child. Would you feel that justice had been served?"

After an awkward pause, Houck said, "Not unless there was mtDNA as well."

Houck's critics focussed on the possibility of errors by well-meaning hair-and-fibre analysts, but the field has also been beset by scandals. Incompetent or malevolent trace-evidence examiners in several states, including Texas, West Virginia, and Illinois, have produced scores of tainted verdicts, many of which have been uncovered by the Innocence Project, the legal-advocacy group founded fifteen years ago by the defense attorneys Barry Scheck and Peter Neufeld. In a 1987 case involving the rape of an eight-year-old girl, Arnold Melnikoff, the manager of the Montana state crime lab, testified that there was a "less than one in ten thousand chance" that hairs found at the crime scene did not belong to the defendant, Jimmy Ray Bromgard, who was convicted. In 2002, a DNA test of sperm found on the victim's underwear established Bromgard's innocence, and several more cases in which Melnikoff testified have been overturned or called into question. (John Grisham's recent best-seller, "The Innocent Man," is a nonfiction account of a 1988 murder case in Oklahoma, in which faulty hair analysis, among other things, led to an unjust conviction.) As Faber acknowledges, "There have been horrible cases involving bad hair examiners." (Last month, the N.Y.P.D. released the results of an internal investigation of its crime lab, which revealed that in 2002 two technicians in the controlled-substances division had failed a department proficiency test. This information was not reported to the national accreditation body for forensic labs, as the department is required by law to do. The police commissioner, Raymond W. Kelly, replaced the deputy chief who supervised the lab and ordered the creation of an oversight panel.)

Faber and her colleagues, unlike their fictional counterparts on TV, do not visit crime scenes, leaving evidence collection to specially trained N.Y.P.D. officers. Nevertheless, working in the hair-and-fibre lab has given Faber a macabre expertise in city life. She is often called on to examine the clothing of crime victims and suspects, and she has noticed that patterns recur. "They like big clothes," she told me, referring to the suspects. "We frequently see sizes like 4X."

Faber has recently taken steps to combine traditional hair and fibre analysis with more modern, and accurate, technology. One day last month, Faber's colleague Debbie Hartmann was working over a gray Rocawear sweatshirt with tape and tweezers, trying to find hairs to analyze. The sweatshirt had been left behind during a burglary of a house in Queens, and Hartmann was examining it as part of a new project that Faber has implemented in the crime lab. "The city has had a program in place for a long time where we see if we can do DNA testing in every murder and rape," Faber told me. "But we thought there was no reason not to do burglaries as well. We know that burglars often change their clothes when they're inside a house, so they don't look the same coming out as they did coming in. They leave their tools like screwdrivers behind. They eat food and drink the beer in the fridge. They don't want to leave fingerprints, so they wear rubber gloves and leave them behind. That turns out to be better, because the gloves have DNA from their skin cells, which is better evidence than fingerprints. All of that stuff they leave behind can be tested for DNA, so we decided to do it." (The N.Y.P.D. crime lab, unlike police departments in many other cities, does no DNA testing itself; Faber and her colleagues send evidence for testing to the medical examiner in the Department of Health, or to private contractors.)

The burglary program, which is known as Biotracks and is funded with a grant from the National Institute of Justice, began in 2003, with a pilot program in northern Queens. It was soon expanded to cover the whole city. As of last week, Faber's team—it consists of, in addition to Faber, a police sergeant and another criminalist—had analyzed twenty-three hundred and thirty cases and found DNA profiles in fifteen hundred and forty-one of them. The results of these tests have been placed in the F.B.I.'s Combined DNA Index System (CODIS), a database of more than four million DNA profiles from across the country, and almost three hundred suspects have been identified.

Some of Biotracks' success stories resemble plots of "CSI" episodes. In 2004, Stanley Jenkins, a forty-seven-year-old man who had a criminal record, broke into a residence in Queens and stole jewelry and camera equipment. He used a tissue to wipe away his fingerprints, and no prints were found in the house. But the tissue yielded a DNA sample, and Jenkins was convicted after a trial and sentenced to twenty years to life. The same year, Faber's team found matching DNA on broken windows in a series of smash-and-grab burglaries at several Manhattan stores, including Tourneau, Coach, and Fendi. Police officers picked up a man named David Gibson because he resembled the suspect in the case, and detectives noticed that he had a bandaged wound on his left hand. They offered to change the dressing and submitted the old bandage for DNA testing, which tied Gibson to the crimes.

In 2005, in perhaps the most bizarre case to date, the Biotracks group took a DNA sample from a soda bottle that a burglar had drunk from at a house in the Bronx. The DNA profile identified a pair of identical twins, Kenneth Williams and Andre Fuller, who were both in the CODIS system because they had criminal records. (Only identical twins have the same nuclear DNA.) It turned out that at the time of the burglary Williams was incarcerated, so when Fuller was arrested in an unrelated case he was charged with the burglary. (The case is pending.) "We never did figure out how twins had different last names," Faber said.

Faber regards Biotracks as one way of tethering her field to the rigorous science of DNA. "I know everyone wants to go straight to the DNA lab these days, and I don't blame them," she said. "But they have to come to us first, and for good reason. Ninety per cent of the hair recovered at a crime scene doesn't have roots in the right stage of growth. You need roots for nuclear DNA. You might ask, Why is microscopic trace examination necessary? Why not submit all hairs for DNA analysis immediately? But you cannot go to the medical examiner with two hundred hairs. We have so many crimes and hairs. Hairs are everywhere. We couldn't possibly give every hair to the m.e. We have to screen it first, see if there is a possibility of any kind of DNA test, and then we can send it over."

There is wisdom, but also some poignancy, in Faber's efforts to modernize the N.Y.P.D.'s hair-and-fibre unit. The success of the Biotracks program suggests that the best thing hair analysts can do is turn themselves into initial screeners for the test that really matters—DNA. Soon the demand for the kind of testimony that Faber provided in the Ronell Wilson case may be limited, especially if the commission sponsored by the National Academy of Sciences publishes a report harshly critical of the field's current practices. (In 1992, a similar commission released a blue-ribbon federal report that resulted in the widespread use of DNA evidence in courtrooms.)

Faber is ambivalent about "CSI"—flattered by the attention it has brought to her profession but mindful of the cinematic license taken by the program's creators. She has noticed, for example, a new kind of applicant for jobs at the crime lab. "They're waiting for their interviews, and they look like they're auditioning for a hip profession," she said. "It's not the nerdy-looking people anymore. They don't realize that there is nothing cool or funky about this job."

A few years ago, when CBS was considering launching the "CSI: New York" spinoff, Faber showed Anthony Zuiker, the creator of "CSI," and his colleagues around the crime lab. "They were great, really nice, and we were happy that they decided to do the show," she said. "But in the end they decided to do it in their studio in California."

Critical Reading Questions

Summarizing the Text

1. What is the *"CSI* effect"?
2. What are some of the ways that seemingly ironclad forensic evidence can be shown to be unreliable?
3. Does Toobin have a thesis here—is he making an argument? If so, what is it?

Establishing the Context

4. Toobin briefly touches on some of the history of forensic science. What does this add to his argument?

Responding to the Message

5. The history of criminology, in many ways, has seen a series of seemingly objective, "scientific" methods of determining guilt that have dominated and then been discarded—"phrenology," or the pseudo-science of determining personality by the shape of the cranium, was accepted in courts in the nineteenth century but is now utterly discredited, for example, and more and more today eyewitness testimony has come into question. Toobin here points out how *CSI*-style forensic evidence can never be as conclusive as the television show seems to suggest. Might the same thing happen to DNA evidence? How?

6. Forensics experts such as Faber realize that their discoveries can be unreliable and their conclusions less than unassailable, but juries make the decisions in murder trials. Do you think that the *CSI* franchise has an effect on juries' willingness to accept forensic evidence that experts might find to be shaky? What can our legal system do about this?

Science and Design

William A. Dembski

William Dembski is a professor of philosophy at Southwestern Baptist Theological Seminary in Fort Worth, Texas. The son of a biology professor in Chicago, Dembski has used his training in science, philosophy, and mathematics to argue for "intelligent design"—the idea that random evolution through natural selection cannot account for the complexity of life. The mathematics of probability, Dembski insists, cannot account for how well living organisms are adapted to their environments. Dembski is affiliated with the "Discovery Institute," a leading advocate for intelligent design. This article originally appeared in First Things, *a conservative Catholic magazine.*

When the physics of Galileo and Newton displaced the physics of Aristotle, scientists tried to explain the world by discovering its deterministic natural laws. When the quantum physics of Bohr and Heisenberg in turn displaced the physics of Galileo and Newton, scientists realized they needed to supplement their deterministic natural laws by taking into account chance processes in their explanations of our universe. Chance and necessity, to use a phrase made famous by Jacques Monod, thus set the boundaries of scientific explanation.

Today, however, chance and necessity have proven insufficient to account for all scientific phenomena. Without invoking the rightly discarded teleologies, entelechies, and vitalisms of the past, one can still see that a third mode of explanation is required, namely, intelligent design. Chance, necessity, and design—these three modes of explanation—are needed to explain the full range of scientific phenomena.

Not all scientists see that excluding intelligent design artificially restricts science, however. Richard Dawkins, an arch-Darwinist, begins his book *The Blind Watchmaker* by stating, "Biology is the study of complicated things that give the appearance of having been designed for a purpose." Statements like this echo throughout the biological literature. In *What Mad Pursuit*, Francis Crick, Nobel laureate and co-discoverer of the structure of DNA, writes, "Biologists must constantly keep in mind that what they see was not designed, but rather evolved."

The biological community thinks it has accounted for the apparent design in nature through the Darwinian mechanism of random mutation and natural selection. The point to appreciate, however, is that in accounting for the apparent design in nature, biologists regard themselves as having made a successful scientific argument against actual design. This is important, because for a claim to be scientifically falsifiable, it must have the possibility of being true. Scientific refutation is a double-edged sword. Claims that are refuted scientifically may be wrong, but they are not necessarily wrong—they cannot simply be dismissed out of hand.

To see this, consider what would happen if microscopic examination revealed that every cell was inscribed with the phrase "Made by Yahweh." Of course cells don't have "Made by Yahweh" inscribed on them, but that's not the point. The point is that we wouldn't know this unless we actually looked at cells under the microscope. And if they were so inscribed, one would have to entertain the thought, as a scientist, that they actually were made by Yahweh. So even those who do not believe in it tacitly admit that design always remains a live option in biology. A priori prohibitions against design are philosophically unsophisticated and easily countered. Nonetheless, once we admit that design cannot be excluded from science without argument, a weightier question remains: Why should we want to admit design into science?

To answer this question, let us turn it around and ask instead, Why shouldn't we want to admit design into science? What's wrong with explaining something as designed by an intelligent agent? Certainly there are many everyday occurrences that we explain by appealing to design. Moreover, in our workaday lives it is absolutely crucial to distinguish accident from design. We demand answers to such questions as, Did she fall or was she pushed? Did someone die accidentally or commit suicide?

Was this song conceived independently or was it plagiarized? Did someone just get lucky on the stock market or was there insider trading?

Not only do we demand answers to such questions, but entire industries are devoted to drawing the distinction between accident and design. Here we can include forensic science, intellectual property law, insurance claims investigation, cryptography, and random number generation—to name but a few. Science itself needs to draw this distinction to keep itself honest. Just last January there was a report in *Science* that a Medline web search uncovered a "paper published in *Zentralblatt für Gynäkologie* in 1991 [containing] text that is almost identical to text from a paper published in 1979 in the *Journal of Maxillofacial Surgery*." Plagiarism and data falsification are far more common in science than we would like to admit. What keeps these abuses in check is our ability to detect them.

If design is so readily detectable outside science, and if its detectability is one of the key factors keeping scientists honest, why should design be barred from the content of science? Why do Dawkins and Crick feel compelled to constantly remind us that biology studies things that only appear to be designed, but that in fact are not designed? Why couldn't biology study things that are designed?

The biological community's response to these questions has been to resist design absolutely. The worry is that for natural objects (unlike human artifacts) the distinction between design and non-design cannot be reliably drawn. Consider, for instance, the following remark by Darwin in the concluding chapter of his *Origin of Species*: "Several eminent naturalists have of late published their belief that a multitude of reputed species in each genus are not real species; but that other species are real, that is, have been independently created.... Nevertheless they do not pretend that they can define, or even conjecture, which are the created forms of life, and which are those produced by secondary laws. They admit variation as a vera causa in one case, they arbitrarily reject it in another, without assigning any distinction in the two cases." Biologists worry about attributing something to design (here identified with creation) only to have it overturned later; this widespread and legitimate concern has prevented them from using intelligent design as a valid scientific explanation.

Though perhaps justified in the past, this worry is no longer tenable. There now exists a rigorous criterion—complexity-specification—for distinguishing intelligently caused objects from unintelligently caused ones. Many special sciences already use this criterion, though in a pre-theoretic form (e.g., forensic science, artificial intelligence, cryptography, archeology, and the Search for Extra-Terrestrial Intelligence). The great breakthrough in philosophy of science and probability theory of recent years has been to isolate and make precise this criterion. Michael Behe's criterion of irreducible complexity for establishing the design of biochemical systems is a special case of the complexity-specification criterion for detecting design (cf. Behe's book *Darwin's Black Box*).

What does this criterion look like? Although a detailed explanation and justification is fairly technical (for a full account see my book *The Design Inference*, published by Cambridge University Press), the basic idea is straightforward and easily illustrated. Consider how the radio astronomers in the movie *Contact* detected an extraterrestrial intelligence. This movie, which came out last year and was based on a novel by Carl Sagan, was an enjoyable piece of propaganda for the SETI research program—the Search for Extra-Terrestrial Intelligence. In the movie, the SETI researchers found extraterrestrial intelligence. (The nonfictional researchers have not been so successful.)

How, then, did the SETI researchers in *Contact* find an extraterrestrial intelligence? SETI researchers monitor millions of radio signals from outer space. Many natural objects in space (e.g., pulsars) produce radio waves. Looking for signs of design among all these naturally produced radio signals is like looking for a needle in a haystack. To sift through the haystack, SETI researchers run the signals they monitor through computers programmed with pattern-matchers. As long as a signal doesn't match one of the pre-set patterns, it will pass through the pattern-matching sieve (even if it has an intelligent source). If, on the other hand, it does match one of these patterns, then, depending on the pattern matched, the SETI researchers may have cause for celebration.

The SETI researchers in *Contact* found the following signal:
110111011111011111101111111111101111111111111011111111111111
110111111111111111111101111111111111111111111101111111111111
111111111111101111111111111111111111111111101111111111111111
111111111111111111111101111111111111111111111111111111111111
110111111111111111111111111111111111111111111101111111111111
111111111111111111111111111111101111111111111111111111111111
111111111111111111111101111111111111111111111111111111111111
111111111111111111111101111111111111111111111111111111111111
111111111111111111111111111101111111111111111111111111111111
111111111111111111111111111111111101111111111111111111111111
111111111111111111111111111111111111111111111101111111111111
111111111111111111111111111111111111111111111111111111111111
111111110111111111111111111111111111111111111111111111111111
111111111111111111111111111111101111111111111111111111111111
111111111111111111111111111111111111111111111111111111110111
111111111111111111111111111111111111111111111111111111111111
111111111111111111111111111111101111111111111111111111111111
111111111111111111111111111111111111111111111111111111111111
1111111111

In this sequence of 1126 bits, 1's correspond to beats and 0's to pauses. This sequence represents the prime numbers from 2 to 101,where a given prime number is represented by the corresponding number of beats (i.e., 1's), and the individual prime numbers are separated by pauses (i.e., 0's).

The SETI researchers in *Contact* took this signal as decisive confirmation of an extraterrestrial intelligence. What is it about this signal that decisively indicates design? Whenever we infer design, we must establish two things—complexity and specification. Complexity ensures that the object in question is not so simple that it can readily be explained by chance. Specification ensures that this object exhibits the type of pattern that is the trademark of intelligence.

To see why complexity is crucial for inferring design, consider the following sequence of bits:

110111011111

These are the first twelve bits in the previous sequence representing the prime numbers 2, 3, and 5 respectively. Now it is a sure bet that no SETI researcher, if confronted with this twelve-bit sequence, is going to contact the science editor at the *New York Times,* hold a press conference, and announce that an extraterrestrial intelligence has been discovered. No headline is going to read, "Aliens Master First Three Prime Numbers!"

The problem is that this sequence is much too short (i.e., has too little complexity) to establish that an extraterrestrial intelligence with knowledge of prime numbers produced it. A randomly beating radio source might by chance just happen to put out the sequence "110111011111." A sequence of 1126 bits representing the prime numbers from 2 to 101, however, is a different story. Here the sequence is sufficiently long (i.e., has enough complexity) to confirm that an extraterrestrial intelligence could have produced it.

Even so, complexity by itself isn't enough to eliminate chance and indicate design. If I flip a coin 1,000 times, I'll participate in a highly complex (or what amounts to the same thing, highly improbable) event. Indeed, the sequence I end up flipping will be one in a trillion trillion trillion ... , where the ellipsis needs twenty-two more "trillions." This sequence of coin tosses won't, however, trigger a design inference. Though complex, this sequence won't exhibit a suitable pattern. Contrast this with the sequence representing the prime numbers from 2 to 101. Not only is this sequence complex, it also embodies a suitable pattern. The SETI researcher who in the movie *Contact* discovered this sequence put it this way: "This isn't noise, this has structure."

What is a suitable pattern for inferring design? Not just any pattern will do. Some patterns can legitimately be employed to infer design whereas others cannot. It is easy to see the basic intuition here. Suppose an archer stands fifty meters from a large wall with bow and arrow in hand. The wall, let's say, is sufficiently large that the archer can't help but hit it. Now suppose each time the archer shoots an arrow at the wall, the archer paints a target around the arrow so that the arrow sits squarely in the bull's-eye. What can be concluded from this scenario? Absolutely nothing about the archer's ability as an archer. Yes, a pattern is being matched; but it is a pattern fixed only after the arrow has been shot. The pattern is thus purely ad hoc.

But suppose instead the archer paints a fixed target on the wall and then shoots at it. Suppose the archer shoots a hundred arrows, and each time hits a perfect bull's-eye. What can be concluded from this second scenario? Confronted with this second scenario we are obligated to infer that here is a world-class archer, one whose shots cannot legitimately be explained by luck, but rather must be explained by the archer's skill and mastery. Skill and mastery are of course instances of design.

Like the archer who fixes the target first and then shoots at it, statisticians set what is known as a rejection region prior to an experiment. If the outcome of an experiment falls within a rejection region, the statistician rejects the hypothesis that the outcome is due to chance. The pattern doesn't need to be given prior to an event to imply design. Consider the following cipher text:

nfuijolt ju jt mjlf b xfbtfm

Initially this looks like a random sequence of letters and spaces—initially you lack any pattern for rejecting chance and inferring design.

But suppose next that someone comes along and tells you to treat this sequence as a Caesar cipher, moving each letter one notch down the alphabet. Behold, the sequence now reads,

methinks it is like a weasel

Even though the pattern is now given after the fact, it still is the right sort of pattern for eliminating chance and inferring design. In contrast to statistics, which always tries to identify its patterns before an experiment is performed, cryptanalysis must discover its patterns after the fact. In both instances, however, the patterns are suitable for inferring design.

Patterns divide into two types, those that in the presence of complexity warrant a design inference and those that despite the presence of complexity do not warrant a design inference. The first type of pattern is called a specification, the second a fabrication. Specifications are the non–ad hoc patterns that can legitimately be used to eliminate chance and warrant a design inference. In contrast, fabrications are the ad hoc patterns that cannot legitimately be used to warrant a design inference. This distinction between specifications and fabrications can be made with full statistical rigor (cf. *The Design Inference*).

Why does the complexity-specification criterion reliably detect design? To answer this, we need to understand what it is about intelligent agents that makes them detectable in the first place. The principal characteristic of intelligent agency is choice. Whenever an intelligent agent acts, it chooses from a range of competing possibilities.

This is true not just of humans and extraterrestrial intelligences, but of animals as well. A rat navigating a maze must choose whether to go right or left at various points in the maze. When SETI researchers attempt to discover intelligence in the radio transmissions they are monitoring, they assume an extraterrestrial intelligence could have chosen to transmit any number of possible patterns, and then attempt to match the transmissions they observe with the patterns they seek. Whenever a human being utters meaningful speech, he chooses from a range of utterable sound-combinations. Intelligent agency always entails discrimination—choosing certain things, ruling out others.

Given this characterization of intelligent agency, how do we recognize that an intelligent agent has made a choice? A bottle of ink spills accidentally onto a sheet of paper; someone takes a fountain pen and writes a message on a sheet of paper. In both instances ink is applied to paper. In both instances one among an almost infinite set of possibilities is realized. In both instances one contingency is actualized and others are ruled out. Yet in one instance we ascribe agency, in the other chance.

What is the relevant difference? Not only do we need to observe that a contingency was actualized, but we ourselves need also to be able to specify that contingency. The contingency must conform to an independently given pattern, and we must be able independently to formulate that pattern. A random ink blot is unspecifiable; a message written with ink on paper is specifiable. Wittgenstein in *Culture and Value* made the same point: "We tend to take the speech of a Chinese for inarticulate gurgling. Someone who understands Chinese will recognize language in what he hears."

In hearing a Chinese utterance, someone who understands Chinese not only recognizes that one from a range of all possible utterances was actualized, but he is also able to identify the utterance as coherent Chinese speech. Contrast this with someone who does not understand Chinese. He will also recognize that one from a range of possible utterances was actualized, but this time, because he lacks the ability to understand Chinese, he is unable to tell whether the utterance was coherent speech.

To someone who does not understand Chinese, the utterance will appear gibberish. Gibberish—the utterance of nonsense syllables uninterpretable within any natural language—always actualizes one utterance from the range of possible utterances. Nevertheless, gibberish, by corresponding to nothing we can understand in any language, also cannot be specified. As a result, gibberish is never taken for intelligent communication, but always for what Wittgenstein calls "inarticulate gurgling."

Experimental psychologists who study animal learning and behavior employ a similar method. To learn a task an animal must acquire the ability to actualize behaviors suitable for the task as well as the ability to rule out behaviors unsuitable for the task. Moreover, for a psychologist to recognize that an animal has learned a task, it is necessary not only to observe the animal making the appropriate discrimination, but also to specify this discrimination.

Thus to recognize whether a rat has successfully learned how to traverse a maze, a psychologist must first specify which sequence of right and left turns conducts the rat out of the maze. No doubt, a rat randomly wandering a maze also discriminates a sequence of right and left turns. But by randomly wandering the maze, the rat gives no indication that it can discriminate the appropriate sequence of right and left turns for exiting the maze. Consequently, the psychologist studying the rat will have no reason to think the rat has learned how to traverse the maze. Only if the rat executes the sequence of right and left turns specified by the psychologist will the psychologist recognize that the rat has learned how to traverse the maze.

Note that complexity is implicit here as well. To see this, consider again a rat traversing a maze, but now take a very simple maze in which two right turns conduct the rat out of the maze. How will a psychologist studying the rat determine whether it has learned to exit the maze? Just putting the rat in the maze will not be enough. Because the maze is so simple, the rat could by chance just happen to take two right turns, and thereby exit the maze. The psychologist will therefore be uncertain whether the rat actually learned to exit this maze, or whether the rat just got lucky.

But contrast this now with a complicated maze in which a rat must take just the right sequence of left and right turns to exit the maze. Suppose the rat must take one hundred appropriate right and left turns, and that any mistake will prevent the rat from exiting the maze. A psychologist who sees the rat take no erroneous turns and in short order exit the maze will be convinced that the rat has indeed learned how to exit the maze, and that this was not dumb luck.

This general scheme for recognizing intelligent agency is but a thinly disguised form of the complexity-specification criterion. In general, to recognize intelligent agency we must observe a choice among competing possibilities, note which possibilities were not chosen, and then be able to specify the possibility that was chosen. What's more, the competing possibilities that were ruled out must be live possibilities, and sufficiently numerous (hence complex) so that specifying the possibility that was chosen cannot be attributed to chance.

All the elements in this general scheme for recognizing intelligent agency (i.e., choosing, ruling out, and specifying) find their counterpart in the complexity-specification criterion. It follows that this criterion formalizes what we have been doing right along when we recognize intelligent agency. The complexity-specification criterion pinpoints what we need to be looking for when we detect design.

Perhaps the most compelling evidence for design in biology comes from biochemistry. In a recent issue of *Cell* (February 8, 1998), Bruce Alberts, president of the National Academy of Sciences, remarked, "The entire cell can be viewed as a factory that contains an elaborate network of interlocking assembly lines, each of which is composed of large protein machines.... Why do we call the large protein assemblies that underlie cell function machines? Precisely because, like the machines invented by humans to deal efficiently with the macroscopic world, these protein assemblies contain highly coordinated moving parts."

Even so, Alberts sides with the majority of biologists in regarding the cell's marvelous complexity as only apparently designed. The Lehigh University biochemist Michael Behe disagrees. In *Darwin's Black Box* (1996), Behe presents a powerful argument for actual design in the cell. Central to his argument is his notion of irreducible complexity. A system is irreducibly complex if it consists of several interrelated parts so that removing even one part completely destroys the system's function. As an example of irreducible complexity Behe offers the standard mousetrap. A mousetrap consists of a platform, a hammer, a spring, a catch, and a holding bar. Remove any one of these five components, and it is impossible to construct a functional mousetrap.

Irreducible complexity needs to be contrasted with cumulative complexity. A system is cumulatively complex if the components of the system can be arranged sequentially so that the successive removal of components never leads to the complete loss of function. An example of a cumulatively complex system is a city. It is possible successively to remove people and services from a city until one is down to a tiny village—all without losing the sense of community, the city's "function."

From this characterization of cumulative complexity, it is clear that the Darwinian mechanism of natural selection and random mutation can readily account for cumulative complexity. Darwin's account of how organisms gradually become more complex as favorable adaptations accumulate is the flip side of the city in our example from which people and services are removed. In both cases, the simpler and more complex versions both work, only less or more effectively.

But can the Darwinian mechanism account for irreducible complexity? Certainly, if selection acts with reference to a goal, it can produce irreducible complexity. Take Behe's mousetrap. Given the goal of constructing a mousetrap, one can specify a goal-directed selection process that in turn selects a platform, a hammer, a spring, a catch, and a holding bar, and at the end puts all these components together to form a functional mousetrap. Given a pre-specified goal, selection has no difficulty producing irreducibly complex systems.

But the selection operating in biology is Darwinian natural selection. And by definition this form of selection operates without goals, has neither plan nor purpose, and is wholly undirected. The great appeal of Darwin's selection mechanism was, after all, that it would eliminate teleology from biology. Yet by making selection an undirected process, Darwin drastically reduced the type of complexity biological systems could manifest. Henceforth biological systems could manifest only cumulative complexity, not irreducible complexity.

As Behe explains in *Darwin's Black Box:* "An irreducibly complex system cannot be produced ... by slight, successive modifications of a precursor system, because any precursor to an irreducibly complex system that is missing a part is by definition nonfunctional.... Since natural selection can only choose systems that are already working, then if a biological system cannot be produced gradually it would have to arise as an integrated unit, in one fell swoop, for natural selection to have anything to act on."

For an irreducibly complex system, function is attained only when all components of the system are in place simultaneously. It follows that natural selection, if it is going to produce an irreducibly complex system, has to produce it all at once or not at all. This would not be a problem if the systems in question were simple. But they're not. The irreducibly complex biochemical systems Behe considers are protein machines consisting of numerous distinct proteins, each indispensable for function; together they are beyond what natural selection can muster in a single generation.

One such irreducibly complex biochemical system that Behe considers is the bacterial flagellum. The flagellum is a whip-like rotary motor that enables a bacterium to navigate through its environment. The flagellum includes an acid-powered rotary engine, a stator, O-rings, bushings, and a drive shaft. The intricate machinery of this molecular motor requires approximately fifty proteins. Yet the absence of any one of these proteins results in the complete loss of motor function.

The irreducible complexity of such biochemical systems cannot be explained by the Darwinian mechanism, nor indeed by any naturalistic evolutionary mechanism proposed to date. Moreover, because irreducible complexity occurs at the biochemical level, there is no more fundamental level of biological analysis to which the irreducible complexity of biochemical systems can be referred, and at which a Darwinian analysis in terms of selection and mutation can still hope for success. Undergirding biochemistry is ordinary chemistry and physics, neither of which can account for biological information. Also, whether a biochemical system is irreducibly complex is a fully empirical question: Individually knock out each protein constituting a biochemical system to determine whether function is lost. If so, we are dealing with an irreducibly complex system. Experiments of this sort are routine in biology.

The connection between Behe's notion of irreducible complexity and my complexity-specification criterion is now straightforward. The irreducibly complex systems Behe considers require numerous components specifically adapted to each other and each necessary for function. That means they are complex in the sense required by the complexity-specification criterion.

Specification in biology always makes reference in some way to an organism's function. An organism is a functional system comprising many functional subsystems. The functionality of organisms can be specified in any number of ways. Arno Wouters does so in terms of the viability of whole organisms, Michael Behe in terms of the minimal function of biochemical systems. Even Richard Dawkins will admit that life is specified functionally, for him in terms of the reproduction of genes. Thus in *The Blind Watchmaker* Dawkins writes, "Complicated things have some quality, specifiable in advance, that is highly unlikely to have been acquired by random chance alone. In the case of living things, the quality that is specified in advance is ... the ability to propagate genes in reproduction."

So there exists a reliable criterion for detecting design strictly from observational features of the world. This criterion belongs to probability and complexity theory, not to metaphysics and theology. And although it cannot achieve logical demonstration, it does achieve a statistical justification so compelling as to demand assent. This criterion is relevant to biology. When applied to the complex, information-rich structures of biology, it detects design. In particular, we can say with the weight of science behind us that the complexity-specification criterion shows Michael Behe's irreducibly complex biochemical systems to be designed.

What are we to make of these developments? Many scientists remain unconvinced. Even if we have a reliable criterion for detecting design, and even if that criterion tells us that biological systems are designed, it seems that determining a biological system to be designed is akin to shrugging our shoulders and saying God did it. The fear is that admitting design as an explanation will stifle scientific inquiry, that scientists will stop investigating difficult problems because they have a sufficient explanation already.

But design is not a science stopper. Indeed, design can foster inquiry where traditional evolutionary approaches obstruct it. Consider the term "junk DNA." Implicit in this term is the view that because the genome of an organism has been cobbled together through a long, undirected evolutionary process, the genome is a patchwork of which only limited portions are essential to the organism. Thus on an evolutionary view we expect a lot of useless DNA. If, on the other hand, organisms are designed, we expect DNA, as much as possible, to exhibit function. And indeed, the most recent findings suggest that designating DNA as "junk" merely cloaks our current lack of knowledge about function. For instance, in a recent issue of the *Journal of Theoretical Biology*, John Bodnar describes how "non-coding DNA in eukaryotic genomes encodes a language which programs organismal growth and development." Design encourages scientists to look for function where evolution discourages it.

Or consider vestigial organs that later are found to have a function after all. Evolutionary biology texts often cite the human coccyx as a "vestigial structure" that hearkens back to vertebrate ancestors with tails. Yet if one looks at a recent edition of *Gray's Anatomy*, one finds that the coccyx is a crucial point of contact with muscles that attach to the pelvic floor. The phrase "vestigial structure" often merely cloaks our current lack of knowledge about function. The human appendix, formerly thought to be vestigial, is now known to be a functioning component of the immune system.

Admitting design into science can only enrich the scientific enterprise. All the tried and true tools of science will remain intact. But design adds a new tool to the scientist's explanatory tool chest. Moreover, design raises a whole new set of research questions. Once we know that something is designed, we will want to know how it was produced, to what extent the design is optimal, and what is its purpose. Note that we can detect design without knowing what something was designed for. There is a room at the Smithsonian filled with objects that are obviously designed but whose specific purpose anthropologists do not understand.

Design also implies constraints. An object that is designed functions within certain constraints. Transgress those constraints and the object functions poorly or breaks. Moreover, we can discover those constraints empirically by seeing what does and doesn't work. This simple insight has tremendous implications not just for science but also for ethics. If humans are in fact designed, then we can expect psychosocial constraints to be hardwired into us. Transgress those constraints, and we as well as our society will suffer. There is plenty of empirical evidence to suggest that many of the attitudes and behaviors our society promotes undermine human flourishing. Design promises to reinvigorate that ethical stream running from Aristotle through Aquinas known as natural law.

By admitting design into science, we do much more than simply critique scientific reductionism. Scientific reductionism holds that everything is reducible to scientific categories. Scientific reductionism is self-refuting and easily seen to be self-refuting. The existence of the world, the laws by which the world operates, the intelligibility of the world, and the unreasonable effectiveness of mathematics for comprehending the world are just a few of the questions that science raises, but that science is incapable of answering.

Simply critiquing scientific reductionism, however, is not enough. Critiquing reductionism does nothing to change science. And it is science that must change. By eschewing design, science has for too long operated with an inadequate set of conceptual categories. This has led to a constricted vision of reality, skewing how science understands not just the world, but also human beings.

Martin Heidegger remarked in *Being and Time* that "a science's level of development is determined by the extent to which it is capable of a crisis in its basic concepts." The basic concepts with which science has operated these last several hundred years are no longer adequate, certainly not in an information age, certainly not in an age where design is empirically detectable. Science faces a crisis of basic concepts. The way out of this crisis is to expand science to include design. To admit design into science is to liberate science, freeing it from restrictions that can no longer be justified.

Critical Reading Questions

Summarizing the Text

1. "Claims that are refuted scientifically may be wrong, but they are not necessarily wrong—they cannot be dismissed out of hand." What does this mean?

2. This is a complicated article that uses analogies in a sophisticated way. Read the article carefully: is this a *proof* of intelligent design, or a *refutation* of the idea that design is impossible? And what is the difference?

Establishing the Context

3. How does Dembski use the example of the SETI (Search for Extra-Terrestrial Intelligence) search in the film *Contact*? What does this "complexity" prove, and how?

4. What is the "complexity-specification criterion"? Explain it in your own words, and explain how choice plays into it.

Responding to the Message

5. Part of the mission of the Discovery Institute is to make available scientific and mathematical grounding for beliefs that many people feel are solely religious ideas. Why is this part of the institute's mission?

6. Do you find Dembski's argument plausible? Find some of the refutations of intelligent design—a good place to start would be to research the *Kitzmiller v. Dover Area School District* decision of 2005—and weigh the arguments against each other.

Questions for Short Projects or Group Presentations

1. The questions "What is science? and What kind of evidence, and how much evidence, do we need in order to prove something?" underpin many of the essays in this chapter. Analyze how Specter, Dembski, and Ehrenreich depict and use science.

2. How might Dembski respond to Specter? Does his threshold for scientific proof match Specter's in *Denialism*?

3. The articles on energy drinks and natural cures raise the question of what role government regulators should play in the market. Should natural cures or energy drinks be regulated? What should the rules be? Do people have the right to choose to take whatever drugs they want or to decide which soft drinks their children consume?

Questions for Formal Essays

1. Dembski's description of how a scientific fact is established, and how much "proof" is necessary for a conclusion to become a fact, is complicated and involved. Summarize Dembski's argument about complexity and design in less than a thousand words, and respond to it. Is his explanation good enough? How would Dembski's model handle other scientific revolutions such as heliocentrism (the idea that the earth orbits the sun) or relativity? Can it account for the development, in bacteria, of resistance to antibiotic drugs?

2. Does religion have any place in science? Does science have any place in religion? Using Angier's article as a starting point, examine these questions. Are the two realms just fundamentally different ways of knowing about the world, and are they thus incompatible? Can a scientist be a believer? Should a scientist be a believer?

3. Even more contentious and complicated than the debate about natural supplements versus drugs has been the question of whether and to what extent human activity is causing the planet to warm, and what the ultimate effects of this warming will be. Investigate this question, making sure to identify as many different, credible opinions as you can find. What happens when a scientific question such as this becomes an urgent national priority—and one that directly affects many people and corporations? How do the interest groups use the rhetoric of science when presenting their viewpoints?

4. Provide a summary and overview of a scientific controversy—climate change, evolution, whether vaccines cause autism, or any other scientific controversy that interests you—in visual or multimedia fashion. You might use PowerPoint, a Web page or blog with links, a photograph, or even a short digital-video film. Take a stand on the issue, and take advantage of the visual or audio or interactive nature of your chosen medium as part of your rhetorical approach.

5. Both Farhad Manjoo, in Chapter 4, and Michael Specter in this chapter deal with forms of denialism and of the selective acceptance of scientific truth. Compare their approaches—is there a commonality between them in terms of their explanation of how this denialism has, in their view, become so widespread?

Are We What We Eat?

CHAPTER INTRODUCTION

In a sign of the centrality of food to our current politics, the *New York Times* editorial page announced in January 2010 that Mark Bittman, a food writer and chef, would be contributing a weekly column to the *Times* focused on food and politics. That same month, conservative politician Sarah Palin attacked Michelle Obama's endorsement of organic foods for public schools, accusing the Obamas of wanting to institute a "nanny state" in which the government tells citizens what to eat. Nevertheless, cities across the nation, attempting to combat juvenile diabetes and obesity, are using zoning to eliminate so-called "food desert" neighborhoods where grocery stores selling fresh produce are absent but fast-food outlets thrive. Eating—perhaps the most instinctual of human activities—is as politicized as it's ever been.

Food politics has been with us for more than a century, of course—particularly public outrage at contaminated food and the system (or lack of one) that allows such food to reach consumers. Theodore Roosevelt attested that Upton Sinclair's 1906 novel *The Jungle*, with its nauseating portrayal of unsanitary meatpacking plants, spurred him to propose the Pure Food and Drug Act that year. (Ironically, Sinclair's intent in the novel was to push not for reform of the food industry, but rather for socialism and the labor movement.) Political scandals involving contaminated food sold to the U.S. Army cropped up during World Wars I and II, and the fast-food industry came under attack in the 1990s for serving hamburgers that caused fatal *E. coli* infections. And in the past ten years, Americans have been killed by contaminated scallions, spinach, beef, chicken, and many other foods. The response has been to strengthen inspection of the facilities in which food is produced and processed.

But for an initially small, now significant, contingent of the public, this failed to address the root of the problem. The United States needed to move away from "factory farming," producing food on a massive industrial scale, they argue. To these people, food ideally should be produced "organically"—without chemical fertilizers, antibiotics, or hormones. Rooted in the 1960s counterculture, this organic-foods movement steadily gained adherents through the 1970s, 1980s, and 1990s. In the 2000s, motivated by a desire to diminish the "carbon footprint" of food production, a new idea emerged: "locavorism," or the idea that we should strive, for environmental and epicurean reasons, to consume food produced near us. Such food (often sold at farmers' markets) would embody the character of a region, would promote biodiversity, and would drastically reduce the fossil-fuel consumption associated with shipping food across the world. In addition, consumers would *know* more about food produced locally, making it less likely that such food would be contaminated.

Nonsense, claimed the defenders of the food industry. Although deaths due to contaminated food receive sensational media coverage, the food that Americans eat is significantly safer than it ever has been. The same industrial procedures that make food less expensive also make it safer. At the same time, some organic farms were themselves becoming industrial-scale operations—Horizon Dairy, Stonyfield Farms, Cascadian Farms. This forced some consumers to ask themselves what actually defined an "organic" product—was it the lack of chemicals and hormones, as the Food and Drug Administration defined it, or was it a more nebulous set of feel-good associations with being small, local, and noncorporate? And since leading organic retailer Whole Foods became a major national grocery chain, and Walmart aggressively moved into the local- and organic-foods business, many longtime organic-foods advocates have had to confront their own preconceptions about what it means to be organic.

Food consumption—kind and amount—is closely linked to issues of health, as well. Over the past decade, the federal Centers for Disease Control and Prevention (CDC) has insisted that the United States is suffering from what it calls an "obesity epidemic." In 2009, according to CDC research, only one state (Colorado) could boast that fewer than 20 percent of its citizens were obese (with a body mass index of 30 or greater), and in nine states, more than 30 percent of citizens were obese. Doctors, demographers, and activists point to several major factors contributing to the prevalence of obesity: cheap calories resulting from industrial efficiencies in and government support of food production, a culture that celebrates abundance, effective advertising by the food industry, and ineffective health education.

But is there an "obesity epidemic"? How does the CDC define "obesity"? How does the declaration of an obesity epidemic stigmatize people? And what business is it of the CDC if some people choose to be obese—and not to adhere to conventional standards of what their bodies "should" be? Such questions are raised by many critics of the CDC and of the government's actions in the area of obesity.

The readings that follow are divided into two sections and cover these topics. The first, longer section collects various perspectives on the question of what we should eat, and how our alimentary choices have political ramifications. Beginning with a set of articles touching on locavorism—the desire to buy and consume food that is produced locally—the readings then touch on larger ethical issues regarding the roles of the marketplace and the government in the production and consumption of food. Concluding this section is a long piece by Michael Pollan, the most influential writer on the intersection of food and ethics and politics today, on how our society has moved from being in touch with how our food is produced and prepared to being enthralled only with the act of consuming food. The second section collects shorter pieces from a variety of outlets—from a scientific journal to a blog—on whether the so-called "obesity epidemic" actually exists.

CLUSTER ONE: THE ETHICS OF EATING

Our Language: Locavorism

William Safire

Although he began his career as a public relations executive and, later, became a speechwriter for the Nixon adminstration, the late William Safire also became one of the leading observers of the American vernacular through his weekly column in the New York Times Magazine, *"On Language." "Locavore"—which the* New Oxford American Dictionary *named its "word of the year" in 2007—was coined, as Safire shows, in 2005, and the word has become shorthand for those people who want the way they eat to harm the environment as little as possible.*

Like many of us (a smarmily folksy phrase used by demagogues), at breakfast I breeze through the editorial pages of several newspapers and then focus on the newsworthy information on the packages of cereal, milk and juice.

Headline type on some orange-juice cartons these days smites the consumer with the words "Home Squeezed." That product claim is puzzling; certainly the juice wasn't squeezed in my home. Could it be that instead of being squeezed in some vast, impersonal factory, thousands of miles away, the juice was lovingly squeezed by hand in the nearby individual homes of thousands of orange pickers?

I checked with the product manager at Florida's Natural of Lake Wales, Fla., a division of Citrus World Inc., to pose the question: In whose "home" had my orange juice been squeezed? As a professional alarmist, I had visions of a farmhand, half a fruit in his fist, grinding away at a green glass juicer in a broken-down shack on the edge of alligator-infested Everglades.

"When you squeeze oranges at home," replied Nikki Black, the friendly manager at Florida's Natural fresh and unfrozen headquarters, "you get more pulp. We use 'home squeezed' to differentiate between our pulpy product and our nonpulp juice."

I get it; the meaning of home-squeezed is not "squeezed at home," as a lexicographer might assume from the inexplicably unhyphenated compound adjective; instead, the selling phrase means only "squeezed as if you had squeezed it in your own home." Only the consumer-cognoscenti are expected to know that, as you and I now do.

The reason for beating that juicy subject to a pulp today is to illustrate the hunger of the food industry to get on the "local is best" bandwagon. No longer is the exotic product of a foreign land the object of the gourmand's desire; indeed, arugula—the pungent, purple-veined, edible leaves of the Mediterranean annual herb of the mustard family—has become a symbol of culinary elitism, replacing the brie and Chablis of yesteryear. (When Barack Obama asked an Iowa crowd, "Anybody gone into Whole Foods lately and see what they charge for arugula?" The *Washington Post* compared that with Michael Dukakis's suggestion in his 1988 campaign that Midwest farmers diversify by raising endive; Obama has been munching good ol' local lettuce ever since.)

As the economy began its downturn last year and imports became more expensive, localness challenged cleanliness as being next to god-liness in the food dodge. The lust for the local is even competing with organic—food grown or raised without a chemical assist but often transported around the world—and Wal-Mart, having joined the organic parade two years ago, is now touting its purchases of produce grown in-state near its supercenters.

Naturally, a name was needed to describe the new anti-exoticism. The word locavore was coined in 2005 on the analogy of carnivore, "flesh eater" (which most dictionaries prefer to "meat eater" because the Latin *caro* is translated as "flesh," but nobody eats fattening flesh these days), and herbivore, "plant eater." The suffix -vorous means "eating, devouring" and spawned the adjective "voracious."

The coiner is Jessica Prentice, who had left a job at the Ferry Plaza Farmers Market in San Francisco to write a book about "food and the hunger for connection." While working on that, she decided to urge people in the Bay Area to eat local food for a month; Olivia Wu, a food writer for the *Chronicle*, challenged her to come up with a name for what Prentice had been calling the nearby foodshed, I presume on the analogy of "watershed." She promptly melded the Latin locus, "place," with vorare, "swallow, devour" and (gulp!) there was locavore, the noun that became the *Oxford American Dictionary*'s word of the year for 2007.

"The Rise of the 'Locavore'" was a *Business Week* headline this spring about the spread of farmers' markets: "Consumers increasingly are seeking out the flavors of fresh, vine-ripened foods grown on local farms rather than those trucked to supermarkets from faraway lands." Name of the trend in a recent review in *The New York Sun*, which lamentably set last month: locavorism.

The trend was confirmed in a macabre *New Yorker* cartoon last month by Bruce Eric Kaplan. A man-eating shark, munching on a human arm, says to another shark, "I'm trying to eat more locals."

Critical Reading Questions

Summarizing the Text

1. How was this new word, locavore, coined and popularized?
2. What does the word mean, and in what contexts is it being used?

Establishing the Context

3. Safire's column appeared in 2008, which means that the word *locavore* had been in existence for only three years before this column appeared. What does this tell you about the importance of the issues of "sustainable eating" and "locavorism"?
4. Does Safire take a stand on the use of the word or on the concept itself? One might expect that, as a politically conservative writer, Safire might oppose or ridicule the idea of locavorism, which is often associated with affluent urban liberals. Does his text or tone convey such a stance?

Responding to the Message

5. What assumptions underlie the locavorism movement? Who or what benefits when we eat food produced within a 100-mile radius? What might be the counterarguments to the locavorism stance?
6. New words tend to come out of hotly debated issues or fields in which society or technology is quickly changing. What other neologisms (newly coined or created words) can you identify? Do you use any of them? What areas or issues generate such words today?

No Cranberries in Texas? No Lobster in Colorado? Blame the "Locavores"
Center for Consumer Freedom

The Center for Consumer Freedom (CCF), a nonprofit organization, says that it is "devoted to promoting personal responsibility and protecting consumer choice." Funded by companies in industries such as tobacco, restaurants, processed foods, and alcohol, the group has been a prominent voice against government regulation. Criticized by some on the left as being just a front group for corporations, the center argues instead that it stands up for individual responsibility and choice. In this press release, the center argues that locavorism is undermining consumers' ability to enjoy foods that might come from far-away places.

Researchers at MIT and Columbia University believe the answer to the so-called obesity "epidemic" lies in getting Americans to eat more regional food. So they're outlining different "foodsheds" that we should all be relying on for our needs—especially if we live in a U.S. city. Will it work? Can we afford it? Let's take a look.

The PhysOrg news service spells out the proposal:

> Each metropolitan area, the researchers say, should obtain most of its nutrition from its own "foodshed," a term akin to "watershed" meaning the area that naturally supplies its kitchens ... [T]hese local efforts should form a larger "Integrated Regional Foodshed" system, intended to lower the price and caloric content of food by lowering distances food must travel, from the farm to the dinner table.

Lower the price? We don't know about shopping in New England, but the farmers' markets selling "local" foods in our nation's capital are where people go for $11-per-pound pork chops and $5 pints of raspberries, not discounts. As for lowering the caloric content, it's hard to see how a local carrot might have fewer calories from a carrot that's traveled 500 miles. Unless it's a scrawny organic veggie, of course—which makes the price differential even more appalling.

We suspect that these researchers' real motive is to attack what they see as a food system that's *too efficient* and provides *too many* calories. But with over 1 billion hungry people in the world, efficient food production is hardly a bad thing.

So-called "locavore" advocates usually make environmental arguments for reducing our "food miles," the distance food travels from farm to fork. This, too, is just another trendy foodie myth. In 2006, researchers at New Zealand's Lincoln University compared the emissions and energy performance of their country's domestic agriculture industry. They found that shipping lamb from New Zealand to

England was four times *less* emissions-intensive than serving the Brits lamb produced right in the UK.

Why is this so? Because of economies of scale. It's the same reason fresh flowers grown in Kenya and shipped to England have a smaller environmental impact than blooms grown by Dutch producers closer to home. The production process in Kenya is much more efficient, and emits fewer greenhouse gases per flower. This efficiency more than makes up for the jet (or truck) fuel burned to bring it to market. Food miles, the New Zealand researchers aptly note, is "a very simplistic concept."

But back to today's "foodshed" research: If switching to a regional-food-only diet has any chance of reducing our waistlines, it's likely to be the result of food boredom. Maybe people in Boise will eventually get sick of eating recipes dominated by sugar beets and potatoes. And as for Alaskans and North Dakotans, a long canned-food winter is enough to make anyone eat less. Especially when they see everything Californians would be allowed to eat in a locavore utopia.

Of course, instead of slimming down by ditching our whole food production system, people could simply balance their calorie intake with physical activity. Or would that be too simplistic?

Critical Reading Questions

Summarizing the Text

1. What is the argument here? What is the article's thesis?

2. The article proposes what's called a "causal claim"—an argument that X causes Y. What is X here, and what is Y? And what are the steps between the two?

Establishing the Context

3. How does the Center for Consumer Freedom characterize those against whom it is arguing? How does it question their claims?

4. The CCF is an "interest group" that forwards arguments advocating the position of a certain group but plays down any explicit association with that group. How might this argument benefit the food producers and restaurants that fund CCF? Are those facts addressed here?

Responding to the Text

5. In many ways, this selection attempts to appeal to the kinds of people who would be tempted to become locavores and to come up with reasons that would sway them. Describe the ways in which this article is aimed at an audience of "socially conscious" eaters.

6. Many conservatives argue that the United States is becoming a nanny state in which the government tells citizens what to do and does not allow them to make choices. They point to regulations about seatbelts, smoking, and trans fats. Do you think we are, or are becoming, a nanny state?

Photo Comparison

The first photograph is of a family shopping at a farmers' market, while the second shows part of the organic food section at a Walmart store.

Critical Reading Questions

1. What is the argument of the first photograph? What does it say about the family's relationship to the farmers' market?

2. What implicit argument does the first photograph make about shopping at grocery stores or buying processed foods?

3. What, on the other hand, is the impression that Walmart seeks to elicit by its array of organic produce?

Swallowing the Eco-Hype

Christina Gillham and James McWilliams

James E. McWilliams, a professor of history at Texas State University, is the author of Just Food: Where Locavores Get It Wrong and How We Can Truly Eat Responsibly, *as well as other books about the history of food and eating in the United States. He is also a well-known critic of locavorism. In this interview with Christina Gillham (which appeared in* Newsweek*), he explains his basic argument against locavorism and the trendiness of farmers' markets.*

Among foodies, there are certain green truths that are self-evident: fruits and vegetables grown within 100 miles of your home means you're eating fresher, better-tasting foods that help to enhance the social and physical health of your entire community. And buying locally is good for the environment—or is it?

James E. McWilliams, author of a new book, *Just Food: Where Locavores Get It Wrong and How We Can Truly Eat Responsibly* (Little, Brown), argues that being a locavore is not going to save the planet, much as its proponents seem to believe. In fact, he says, it may even be worse than eating food from miles and miles away: after all, a few crates of apples being trucked in from 50 miles away can expend more energy than a large one trucking in tons of apples from hundreds or thousands of miles away. The diktat to "eat locally" is wrongheaded if you're not considering the bigger environmental picture, he says. It's important to consider a food's life-cycle assessment, or the energy that gets put into its production and distribution—that means not just "food miles," but water and pesticide use, harvesting techniques, packaging, disposal, and many other factors.

McWilliams also makes a strong case against eating only organic foods and for the potential benefits of genetically modified foods. He also explains why grass-fed beef can be bad for the environment. He spoke to *Newsweek* by phone from his office at Texas State University–San Marcos, where he is a professor of history.

You take issue with the locavore movement and its emphasis on food miles, which you say is only a small part of the equation when it comes to having a sustainable food system. Is shopping at the farmers' market pointless, then?

No, it's not pointless. One thing I try to make clear is that I support a lot of the values and the ethics of the locavore movement. But I'm concerned about the movement becoming fundamentalist. Like any movement, it can become the victim of its own success. When I listen to locavores, I'm just not hearing enough about this looming global food crisis I think we're facing. I'm not in any way dismissing them; I'm just realistic about how far [reducing food miles] is going to get us in terms of addressing this bigger question about having to produce a lot more food with fewer resources over the next 50 years. We have to think about what happens to our food once it gets into our kitchen, and what we do to get that food, and most importantly, how that food was produced. Transportation/food miles count for only about 10 percent of overall energy that goes into producing our food.

According to your research, 14 percent of total food purchases are tossed in the trash, and about 27 percent of that is produce. That's a lot of food.

It's a ton of food. Especially for people who have kids. I have two of them, and it's horrifying how much food we waste. I'm sure if someone did a calculation of the energy that went into the food we're throwing out, I'm the problem. But it's not because my food came in on an airplane, it's because I'm throwing it out. But you could also ask questions about the kind of stoves we use. It's common now to just have these enormous gas stoves with these burners that could run a commercial kitchen. It's another way to remind ourselves that when we look at the carbon footprint of our diet, it's so much more immensely complicated than asking where our food came from.

You wrote that an all-organic food industry is simply not possible and can be in fact more dangerous than conventional food farming. Why is that?

Well, first of all, it's a hypothetical: [all-organic farming] is never going to happen. Two percent of the food that's produced in this country is produced organically. So when we get overly obsessed with organic food and say, "I'm only going to buy organic food," I think we're missing a real opportunity to figure out incentives for the other 98 percent to become more efficient without becoming organic. And there are so many ways this can be done that we're not talking about, like getting conventional farmers to judiciously use chemicals. Right now these products are so heavily subsidized that farmers really do not have an incentive to use them judiciously. They're incredibly cheap, so they dump these things indiscriminately.

You mean they're using more than they need to?

Oh, absolutely. It's especially true with fertilizers. There are some high-level fertilizers out there that are expensive but they are much more efficient. The environmental savings would be enormous if we subsidized the use of them. Most conventional farmers I talk to have a profoundly deep respect for the environment. They want to be good environmental stewards, but it's often too expensive for them to do so. And the fact is, there are fungal diseases, there are viruses, there are blights that organic methods cannot control. A lot of farmers want to go as organic as they possibly can, but they don't want to give up access to those weapons in case of an emergency.

How much more organic farming could this country sustain given that, as you say, it requires so much more land than conventional farming?

That's a difficult question to answer. On the whole, conventional has higher yields. We can't ignore that when we think of expanding organic culture. Especially given that with climate change, we are going to confront new fungal diseases, new viruses, and new pests that organic may not be able to control. With the question of yield aside, it's safe to say you would need more land for organic farming. And you would also need many thousands of pounds of manure for a single acre of organic crops, and if we're going to have large organic farms, [then we'll need to] transport that product all over the country. There is also a chemical reliance in organic agriculture; they just happen to be natural chemicals, like nicotine sulfate, which is horribly dangerous. But just because I'm pointing out potential problems with organic farming doesn't mean I'm saying this is a system we shouldn't be pursuing. But we should be pursuing it alongside other solutions.

Perhaps by growing genetically modified (GM) food? You argue that genetic modification allows for food-growing on a larger scale, feeding more people and reducing the needs for pesticides. You also acknowledge that there are unknown health risks in consuming GM foods, but that that shouldn't stop us from growing them. Do you really think it's worth the risk?

There are lots of concerns with GM foods, but we haven't seen any evidence of it. Anyone who eats processed food is eating GM corn or soy. Half our sugar is GM now. Ninety percent of the corn in this country is genetically modified, and it's not just going to animals, it's going to high-fructose corn syrup. There's a movement to start testing these products and finding out if they're GMO [genetically modified organism]-free and labeling it.

There's no regulation for that?

None at all. And the FDA seems really resistant to moving in that direction.

Why is that?

The argument that the seed companies make is that you impugn their product by labeling other products GMO-free. And the fact that there is no evidence to support any negative health consequences is justification for their arguments. I tend to think the consumer deserves to know. There are possible concerns with all kinds of seeds that are conventionally bred as well. When we conventionally breed seeds to acquire certain traits, who's to say that that breeding technique might not have negative health consequences? There's just no predicting. And there's no way you can test for every possible negative consequence of a seed. I've talked to too many plant biologists who said this is a technology that if used properly can serve very real environmental and humanitarian needs, and I'm not willing to ignore them. I'm not terribly fearful of the health consequences.

According to your book, you're not terribly fearful of synthetic pesticides either, even though numerous studies have pointed to their potentially deleterious effects. Why?

I'm much more fearful of a food-borne allergen than I am of the effect of pesticides on my health. I support organic farming because they don't use synthetic pesticides, but I also support a much more rational use by conventional farmers. In the late 19th century they were dumping arsenic and lead on fruits and vegetables, so the pesticides we're using today are nowhere near as dangerous as what we were using in the past. Which is not to say they're not dangerous, but for me there are lots of other concerns that come before the impact of trace pesticides on myself.

By now, many of us are aware that we need to reduce our meat consumption because of its terrible effect on the environment. Factory farming is bad for the air, the water, and the land—not to mention the animals. Consequently, many people have turned to grass-fed beef. But you say that comes with its own set of environmental problems. What do you mean?

Many grass-fed cows are eating grass that's been fertilized or irrigated. As a result, the amount of greenhouse gases that go into its production is a lot higher. You also need eight to 10 acres a cow. If everyone ate grass-fed beef, it would mean giving up a lot of arable land and chopping down rainforests, which is already happening in some places. The bottom line is, animals are inefficient. By the end of the day, I don't care if it's grass-fed or if it's from a conventional system, only 40 percent of it is turned into edible meat.

You became a vegetarian after writing this book.

I did. [After looking] at the research I did into meat production, I couldn't reconcile eating meat with the kind of environmentalist I want to be. I certainly don't preach that others become vegetarian; I advocate becoming as vegetarian as you can.

You say that you wrote your book "somewhat against" your will. What do you mean by that?

I don't like having to write a chapter telling people to eat less meat, because meat tastes good. It's a sacrifice. That's something that's missing in a lot of our discussions about environmentalism and sustainability—the idea of sacrifice. What kind of personal sacrifices are we willing to make? Putting our glass into the right container and dragging it out to the curb is not much of a sacrifice, but I think giving up meat certainly is. I would loved to have been able to say that what we need to do is put all of our eggs in the organic basket, but when I honestly scaled it up I could not ignore these potential problems. I would have preferred to find a silver bullet, but I couldn't.

Critical Reading Questions

Summarizing the Text

1. What is wrong with a strict adherence to locavorism, in McWilliams's view?

2. If paying attention to *where* our food comes from isn't all that important, what does McWilliams see as being more important ethical concerns regarding our eating?

Establishing the Context

3. McWilliams, unlike the Center for Consumer Freedom, is quite concerned with the ethics of eating (the CCF's primary concerns are what it sees as infringements upon our freedoms). How does he appeal to an audience of people who sympathize with locavorism differently than the CCF does?

4. According to McWilliams, what are some ways in which our choices about eating affect the environment?

Responding to the Text

5. McWilliams is what one might call a "contrarian"—someone who shares many fundamental beliefs with a group, but who rejects their proposed solutions to the problems that concern them. What values does he share with the locavorism movement?

6. McWilliams argues that we simply cannot feed a large population solely from small, local producers. Do you agree? Think about where you live. How would your eating habits change if you were able to eat only what was produced within 100 miles of you?

Do We Really Need a Few Billion Locavores?

Stephen J. Dubner

Stephen Dubner—author of the popular books Freakonomics *and* Superfreakonomics—*contributes to the discussion among advocates and detractors of locavorism largely by using qualitative evidence. In this selection, he identifies the assumptions held by those who want people to eat more local food and attempts to debunk the contentions underlying those assumptions.*

We made some ice cream at home last weekend. Someone had given one of the kids an ice cream maker a while ago and we finally got around to using it. We decided to make orange sherbet. It took a pretty long time and it didn't taste very good but the worst part was how expensive it was. We spent about $12 on heavy cream, half-and-half, orange juice, and food coloring—the only ingredient we already had was sugar—to make a quart of ice cream. For the same price, we could have bought at least a gallon (four times the amount) of much better orange sherbet. In the end, we wound up throwing away about three-quarters of what we made. Which means we spent $12, not counting labor or electricity or capital costs (*somebody* bought the machine, even if we didn't) for roughly three scoops of lousy ice cream.

As we've written before, it is a curious fact of modern life that one person's labor is another's leisure. Every day there are millions of people who cook and sew and farm for a living—and there are millions more who cook (probably in nicer kitchens) and sew (or knit or crochet) and farm (or garden) because they love to do so. Is this sensible? If people are satisfying their preferences, who cares if it costs them $20 to produce a single cherry tomato (or $12 for a few scoops of ice cream)?

This is the question that came to mind the other day when we received an e-mail from a reader named Amy Kormendy:

I emailed Michael Pollan recently to ask him this question, and nice guy that he is, he promptly answered "Good question, I don't really know" and suggested I pose it to you good folks:

Wouldn't it be more resource-intensive for us all to raise our own food, than if we paid an expert to raise lots of food that s/he could sell to us? Couldn't it therefore be more sustainable to purchase food from large professional producers?

We're taught that the invention of division of labor gives us a more efficient way to use resources on a societal scale. I love gardening, but it takes me more time and overall investment to get inferior produce to what I could buy from a professional farmer nearby. Similarly, a friend once attempted to sew a skirt for herself. Adding up the time and energy to visit the store, select and buy the fabric & pattern, go home and measure, cut, and stitch, she says the skirt cost her $200, resulted in lots of wasted fabric, and she stitched the hem crooked. "I could have bought a better skirt for $50 at Nordstrom," she said—her experiment in self-sufficiency was a bigger overall resource hog than the conventional supply chain to her local retailer. So, some of Professor Pollan's advice seems to be that we would be better off as a society if we did more for ourselves (especially growing our own food). But I can't help but think that the economies of scale and division of labor inherent in modern industrial agriculture would still render the greatest efficiencies in resource investment. The extra benefit of growing your own food only works out if you count the unquantifiables such as the sense of accomplishment, learning, exercise, suntan, etc.

I very much understand the locavore instinct. To eat locally grown food or, even better, food that you've grown yourself, seems as if it should be 1) more delicious; 2) more nutritious; 3) cheaper; and 4) better for the environment. But is it?

1. "Deliciousness" is subjective. But one obvious point is that no one person can grow or produce all the things she would like to eat. As a kid who grew up on a small farm, I can tell you that after I had my fill of corn and asparagus and raspberries, all I really wanted was a Big Mac.

2. There's a lot to be said for the nutritional value of home-grown food. But again, since one person can grow only so much variety, there are bound to be big nutritional gaps in her diet that will need to be filled in.

3. Is it cheaper to grow your own food? It's not impossible but, as my little ice cream story above illustrates, there are huge inefficiencies at work here. Pretend that instead of just me making ice cream last weekend, it was all 100 people who live in my building. Now we've collectively spent $1,200 to each have a few scoops of ice cream. Let's say you decide to plant a big vegetable garden this year to save money. Now factor in everything you need to buy to

make it happen—the seeds, fertilizer, sprout cups, twine, tools, etc.—along with the transportation costs and the opportunity cost. Are you sure you really saved money by growing your own zucchini and corn? And what if 1,000 of your neighbors did the same? Or here's another, non-food example: building your own home from scratch versus buying a prefab home. With a site-built home, you need to invest in all the tools, material, labor, and transportation costs to make it happen, and the myriad inefficiencies of having dozens of workmen's pickup trucks retrace the same route hundreds of times all for the sake of erecting one family's home— whereas factory-built homes like these create the opportunity for huge efficiencies by bundling labor, materials, transportation, etc.

4. But growing your own food *has* to be good for the environment, right? Well, keeping in mind the transportation inefficiencies mentioned above, consider the "food miles" argument and a recent article in *Environmental Science and Technology* by Christopher L. Weber and H. Scott Matthews of Carnegie Mellon University:

> We find that although food is transported long distances in general (1640 km delivery and 6760 km life-cycle supply chain on average) the GHG emissions associated with food are dominated by the production phase, contributing 83% of the average U.S. household's 8.1 t CO2e/yr footprint for food consumption. Transportation as a whole represents only 11% of lifecycle GHG emissions, and final delivery from producer to retail contributes only 4%. Different food groups exhibit a large range in GHG-intensity; on average, red meat is around 150% more GHG-intensive than chicken or fish. Thus, we suggest that dietary shift can be a more effective means of lowering an average household's food-related climate footprint than "buying local." Shifting less than one day per week's worth of calories from red meat and dairy products to chicken, fish, eggs, or a vegetable-based diet achieves more GHG reduction than buying all locally sourced food.

This is a pretty strong argument against the perceived environmental and economic benefits of locavore behavior—mostly because Weber and Matthews identify the fact that is nearly always overlooked in such arguments: specialization (which Michael Pollan mostly dislikes, and which has been around for a long, long time) is ruthlessly efficient. Which means less transportation, lower prices—and, in most cases, far more *variety*, which in my book means more deliciousness and more nutrition. The same store where I blew $12 on ice cream ingredients will happily sell me ice cream in many flavors, dietetic options, and price points.

Whereas I am now stuck with about 99% of the food coloring I bought, which will probably sit in the cupboard until I die (hopefully not soon).

Critical Reading Questions

Summarizing the Text

1. What are the four ideas underlying locavorism, according to Dubner? How does he refute each point?

2. What does "carbon footprint" mean? What is GHG? Must one understand those terms in order to understand Dubner's argument?

Establishing the Context

3. Although this article appeared in the *New York Times*, it is not the same kind of formal article that appears in the news or features or opinion sections of the paper. Like many other publications, the *Times* is experimenting with offering a "blog" section—casual and offhanded observations on particular issues, often put into conversation with other writers' contributions. Discuss the ways in which this article takes a casual tone.

4. How is Dubner's take on locavorism different from McWilliams's?

Responding to the Text

5. Dubner, McWilliams, and the Center for Consumer Freedom all provide different arguments against strict locavorism. Compare the three—which do you find most persuasive? Can you add other arguments to theirs?

Paying Attention to Food

Stephanie Kaza

Stephanie Kaza, a professor of environmental studies at the University of Vermont, has written extensively on the relationship of Buddhism to environmentalism. Here, she turns her focus to eating, and how eating is an act that must be considered in ethical terms. "Theravada," "Chan," "Zen," and "Tibetan" refer to schools of Buddhist belief and practice. This article appeared in Tikkun, *a monthly magazine with a Jewish spiritual focus.*

Eating, these days, is a political act. Every choice of food carries moral and economic implications, whether we are aware of them or not. Take a simple breakfast for starters. Orange juice from Brazil, grapes from Chile, apples from New Zealand, coffee from Vietnam, bananas from Costa Rica—all of these appear on our plates without us giving them a second thought. And yet the average bite of American food travels 2,000 kilometers from field to fork. The ecological implications of this global food travel are astounding: forests are cleared, soils poisoned, water tables drained, and oil wells drilled to ship the annual load of 650 million tons of food from producer to eater.

As a practicing Buddhist and environmental studies professor, I have long engaged this question of what to eat and why. There are many well-established Western arguments for being a vegetarian, but what does Buddhism have to offer on this politically hot topic? What kind of advice can we find in the Buddhist literature for addressing the complex ethical dilemmas in everyday eating?

At the heart of Buddhist moral guidelines is the central philosophy of nonharming. The first precept is: do not kill. The Buddha's prescription for reducing suffering, the Eightfold Path, defines "right livelihood" as prohibiting Buddhists from being butchers. And yet today's modern agricultural production is far from nonharming to soils, laborers, and ecosystems. Using nonharming as a guideline, one might choose those foods that have been raised in healthy soil free of chemical assaults and foods that have been grown locally and use the least energy for processing and packaging.

The Bodhisattva vow to "save all sentient beings" adds further urgency to this practice of nonharming. If we save all the beings, then who do we eat? Eating becomes an impossible koan we must solve or else starve. The Chinese Buddhist tradition offers up a beautiful metaphor of interdependence that can inform our eating choices. The "Jeweled Net of potatoes and pill bugs" is a vast web of infinitely linked beings, each a shining node of infinite facets. Western environmentally minded Buddhists often refer to this web as the ecological metaphor for our global times. Every item of food prepared for our tables was generated from many sources, through many complex relations and many causal links across the web. Using this Buddhist metaphor we could investigate each food choice for its ecological footprint; we could study the labor practices, the moral questions raised by the markets.

Contemporary Buddhist teachers such as Thich Nhat Hanh work with food to practice mindfulness, bringing the eater's attention to truly experiencing the food that is eaten. This deliberate slowing down and observing of biting, chewing, desiring, enjoying—a tangerine, for instance—helps cultivate a concentrated mind able to consider food choices in more depth. Conscious consumption naturally becomes an ethical practice path. "Socially engaged" or politically active Buddhists take up food choice and preparation as an active practice for liberating all beings.

Based on these ethical approaches, should all Buddhists be vegetarians? Indeed, some have argued that the principle of nonharming requires us not to eat meat. One of my students surveyed Buddhists of different lineages and found that, in fact, only 63 percent of Theravada practitioners were vegetarian, 50 percent of Chan, 44 percent Zen, and 31 percent Tibetan. The rest were meat-eaters to varying degrees. The survey comments showed a wide range of health concerns, prayers, and ethical thought supporting various personal choices. I then surveyed Buddhist retreat centers and found a similar spread of eating practices across the United States. Clearly, the various Buddhist lineages and personal practitioners do not all agree on this politically challenging subject.

Where, then, does this leave the concerned eater? From a Buddhist perspective, it leaves us with no absolute answers. Instead we are called by the teachings to actively cultivate a questioning mind and a compassionate heart. To take up these dilemmas with any seriousness, we must develop our intention and attention. Food, eating, production, farm health, and fair labor offer a virtually infinite practice field with abundant opportunities for Buddhists and non-Buddhists alike to contemplate these complexities. In some of my classes, I ask my students to write personal credos regarding food that lay out their concerns, beliefs, and intentions. It is a good place for them to start on what I hope will be life-long ethical practice. Maybe Buddhist sanghas could take up this work too and make public the struggle to sort these questions out. Though Buddhist teachings provide no absolute guidelines, facing the dilemmas with full heart and mind keeps the practice (and thus us) quite alive.

Critical Reading Questions

Summarizing the Text

1. What is Kaza's argument here? Must we be vegetarians in order to be ethical? Must Buddhists be vegetarians?
2. What are the counterarguments that Kaza brings up? What is her response to them?

Establishing the Context

3. *Tikkun* is a liberal Jewish magazine, yet this article is specifically about a Buddhist understanding of the relationship between food and ethics. What assumptions is Kaza making about her audience?
4. Is Kaza's argument relevant to non-Buddhists? Why or why not?

Responding to the Text

5. What ethical responsibilities do we have as eaters?
6. Many religions—most, in fact—impose on their adherents strictures about eating. Describe several other religions' laws about eating and food preparation. What do you think the purpose of these rules is?

PETA ad

People for the Ethical Treatment of Animals (PETA) is an outspoken animal-rights group known for its ability to generate publicity through using sexual imagery and celebrities in its television, Web, and print advertisements. PETA's outrageous photographs and publicity stunts infuriate even its supporters at times, but it has been a strong voice against animal cruelty, particularly in the meat-production industry. Being so outspoken, though, has made PETA a ripe target for carnivores, the meat industry, and bloggers.

Critical Reading Questions

1. What is the argument of the first photograph? "Read" the image of Barbie Hsu (a Taiwanese actor and singer)—what does it say about vegetarianism?

2. How does the advertisement attempt to appeal to a target audience? What is that audience? What values does that audience hold that are reflected in the ad?

Out of the Kitchen, Onto the Couch
Michael Pollan

In this article, Michael Pollan—the most visible spokesperson for the sustainable-eating movement—argues that the ways contemporary culture has fetishized food has caused us to lose touch with what it means to actually prepare food. Pollan teaches journalism at the University of California at Berkeley, and among his recent books are The Omnivore's Dilemma *and* In Defense of Food: An Eater's Manifesto.

1. Julia's Children

I was only 8 when "The French Chef" first appeared on American television in 1963, but it didn't take long for me to realize that this Julia Child had improved the quality of life around our house. My mother began cooking dishes she'd watched Julia cook on TV: boeuf bourguignon (the subject of the show's first episode), French onion soup gratinée, duck à l'orange, coq au vin, mousse au chocolat. Some of the more ambitious dishes, like the duck or the mousse, were pointed toward weekend company, but my mother would usually test these out on me and my sisters earlier in the week, and a few of the others—including the boeuf bourguignon, which I especially loved—actually made it into heavy weeknight rotation. So whenever people talk about how Julia Child upgraded the culture of food in America, I nod appreciatively. I owe her. Not that I didn't also owe Swanson, because we also ate TV dinners, and those were pretty good, too.

Every so often I would watch "The French Chef" with my mother in the den. On WNET in New York, it came on late in the afternoon, after school, and because we had only one television back then, if Mom wanted to watch her program, you watched it, too. The show felt less like TV than like hanging around the kitchen, which is to say, not terribly exciting to a kid (except when Child dropped something on the floor, which my mother promised would happen if we stuck around long enough) but comforting in its familiarity: the clanking of pots and pans, the squeal of an oven door in need of WD-40, all the kitchen-chemistry-set spectacles of transformation. The show was taped live and broadcast uncut and unedited, so it had a vérité feel completely unlike anything you might see today on the Food Network, with its A.D.H.D. editing and hyperkinetic soundtracks of rock music and clashing knives. While Julia waited for the butter foam to subside in the sauté pan, you waited, too, precisely as long, listening to Julia's impro-vised patter over the hiss of her pan, as she filled the desultory min-utes with kitchen tips and lore. It all felt more like life than TV, though Julia's voice was like nothing I ever heard before or would hear again until Monty Python came to America: vaguely European, breathy and singsongy, and weirdly suggestive of a man doing a falsetto impres-sion of a woman. The BBC supposedly took "The French Chef" off the air because viewers wrote in complaining that Julia Child seemed either drunk or demented.

Meryl Streep, who brings Julia Child vividly back to the screen in Nora Ephron's charming new comedy, "Julie & Julia," has the voice down, and with the help of some clever set design and cinematog-raphy, she manages to evoke too Child's big-girl ungainliness—the woman was 6 foot 2 and had arms like a longshoreman. Streep also captures the deep sensual delight that Julia Child took in food—not just the eating of it (her virgin bite of sole meunière at La Couronne in Rouen recalls Meg Ryan's deli orgasm in "When Harry Met Sally") but the fondling and affectionate slapping of ingredients in their raw state and the magic of their kitchen transformations.

But "Julie & Julia" is more than an exercise in nostalgia. As the title suggests, the film has a second, more contemporary heroine. The Julie character (played by Amy Adams) is based on Julie Powell, a 29-year-old aspiring writer living in Queens who, casting about for a blog conceit in 2002, hit on a cool one: she would cook her way through all 524 recipes in Child's "Mastering the Art of French Cooking" in 365 days and blog about her adventures. The movie shut-tles back and forth between Julie's year of compulsive cooking and blogging in Queens in 2002 and Julia's decade in Paris and Provence a half-century earlier, as recounted in "My Life in France," the memoir published a few years after her death in 2004. Julia Child in 1949 was in some ways in the same boat in which Julie Powell found herself in 2002: happily married to a really nice guy but feeling, acutely, the lack of a life project. Living in Paris, where her husband, Paul Child, was posted in the diplomatic corps, Julia (who like Julie had worked as a secretary) was at a loss as to what to do with her life until she realized that what she liked to do best was eat. So she enrolled in Le Cordon Bleu and learned how to cook. As with Julia, so with Julie: cooking saved her life, giving her a project and, eventually, a path to literary success.

That learning to cook could lead an American woman to success of any kind would have seemed utterly implausible in 1949; that it is so thoroughly plausible 60 years later owes everything to Julia Child's legacy. Julie Powell operates in a world that Julia Child helped to create, one where food is taken seriously, where chefs have been welcomed into the repertory company of American celebrity and where cooking has become a broadly appealing mise-en-scène in which success stories can plausibly be set and played out. How amazing is it that we live today in a culture that has not only something called the Food Network but now a hit show on that network called "The Next Food Network Star," which thousands of 20- and 30-somethings compete eagerly to become? It would seem we have come a long way from Swanson TV dinners.

The Food Network can now be seen in nearly 100 million American homes and on most nights commands more viewers than any of the cable news channels. Millions of Americans, including my 16-year-old son, can tell you months after the finale which contestant emerged victorious in Season 5 of "Top Chef" (Hosea Rosenberg, followed by Stefan Richter, his favorite, and Carla Hall). The popularity of cooking shows—or perhaps I should say food shows— has spread beyond the precincts of public or cable television to the broadcast networks, where Gordon Ramsay terrorizes newbie chefs on "Hell's Kitchen" on Fox and Jamie Oliver is preparing a reality show on ABC in which he takes aim at an American city with an obesity problem and tries to teach the population how to cook. It's no wonder that a Hollywood studio would conclude that American audiences had an appetite for a movie in which the road to personal fulfillment and public success passes through the kitchen and turns, crucially, on a recipe for boeuf bourguignon. (The secret is to pat dry your beef before you brown it.)

But here's what I don't get: How is it that we are so eager to watch other people browning beef cubes on screen but so much less eager to brown them ourselves? For the rise of Julia Child as a figure of cultural consequence—along with Alice Waters and Mario Batali and Martha Stewart and Emeril Lagasse and whoever is crowned the next Food Network star—has, paradoxically, coincided with the rise of fast food, home-meal replacements and the decline and fall of everyday home cooking.

That decline has several causes: women working outside the home; food companies persuading Americans to let them do the cooking; and advances in technology that made it easier for them to do so. Cooking is no longer obligatory, and for many people, women especially, that has been a blessing. But perhaps a mixed blessing, to judge by the culture's continuing, if not deepening, fascination with the subject. It has been easier for us to give up cooking than it has been to give up talking about it—and watching it.

Today the average American spends a mere 27 minutes a day on food preparation (another four minutes cleaning up); that's less than half the time that we spent cooking and cleaning up when Julia arrived on our television screens. It's also less than half the time it takes to watch a single episode of "Top Chef" or "Chopped" or "The Next Food Network Star." What this suggests is that a great many Americans are spending considerably more time watching images of cooking on television than they are cooking themselves—an increasingly archaic activity they will tell you they no longer have the time for.

What is wrong with this picture?

2. The Courage to FLIP

When I asked my mother recently what exactly endeared Julia Child to her, she explained that "for so many of us she took the fear out of cooking" and, to illustrate the point, brought up the famous potato show (or, as Julia pronounced it, "the poh-TAY-toh show!"), one of the episodes that Meryl Streep recreates brilliantly on screen. Millions of Americans of a certain age claim to remember Julia Child dropping a chicken or a goose on the floor, but the memory is apocryphal: what she dropped was a potato pancake, and it didn't quite make it to the floor. Still, this was a classic live-television moment, inconceivable on any modern cooking show: Martha Stewart would sooner commit seppuku than let such an outtake ever see the light of day.

The episode has Julia making a plate-size potato pancake, sautéing a big disc of mashed potato into which she has folded impressive quantities of cream and butter. Then the fateful moment arrives:

"When you flip anything, you just have to have the courage of your convictions," she declares, clearly a tad nervous at the prospect, and then gives the big pancake a flip. On the way down, half of it catches the lip of the pan and splats onto the stovetop. Undaunted, Julia scoops the thing up and roughly patches the pancake back together, explaining: "When I flipped it, I didn't have the courage to do it the way I should have. You can always pick it up." And then, looking right through the camera as if taking us into her confidence, she utters the line that did so much to lift the fear of failure from my mother and her contemporaries: "If you're alone in the kitchen, WHOOOO"—the pronoun is sung—"is going to see?" For a generation of women eager to transcend their mothers' recipe box (and perhaps, too, their mothers' social standing), Julia's little kitchen catastrophe was a liberation and a lesson: "The only way you learn to flip things is just to flip them!"

It was a kind of courage—not only to cook but to cook the world's most glamorous and intimidating cuisine—that Julia Child gave my mother and so many other women like her, and to watch her empower viewers in episode after episode is to appreciate just how much about cooking on television—not to mention cooking itself—has changed in the years since "The French Chef" was on the air.

There are still cooking programs that will teach you how to cook. Public television offers the eminently useful "America's Test Kitchen." The Food Network carries a whole slate of so-called dump-and-stir shows during the day, and the network's research suggests that at least some viewers are following along. But many of these programs—I'm thinking of Rachael Ray, Paula Deen, Sandra Lee—tend to be aimed at stay-at-home moms who are in a hurry and eager to please. ("How good are you going to look when you serve this?" asks Paula Deen, a Southern gal of the old school.) These shows stress quick results, shortcuts and superconvenience but never the sort of pleasure—physical and mental—that Julia Child took in the work of cooking: the tomahawking of a fish skeleton or the chopping of an onion, the Rolfing of butter into the breast of a raw chicken or the vigorous whisking of heavy cream. By the end of the potato show, Julia was out of breath and had broken a sweat, which she mopped from her brow with a paper towel. (Have you ever seen Martha Stewart break a sweat? Pant? If so, you know her a lot better than the rest of us.) Child was less interested in making it fast or easy than making it right, because cooking for her was so much more than a means to a meal. It was a gratifying, even ennobling sort of work, engaging both the mind and the muscles. You didn't do it to please a husband or impress guests; you did it to please yourself. No one cooking on television today gives the impression that they enjoy the actual work quite as much as Julia Child did. In this, she strikes me as a more liberated figure than many of the women who have followed her on television.

Curiously, the year Julia Child went on the air—1963—was the same year Betty Friedan published "The Feminine Mystique," the book that taught millions of American women to regard housework, cooking included, as drudgery, indeed as a form of oppression. You may think of these two figures as antagonists, but that wouldn't be quite right. They actually had a great deal in common, as Child's biographer, Laura Shapiro, points out, and addressed the aspirations of many of the same women. Julia never referred to her viewers as "housewives"—a word she detested—and never condescended to them. She tried to show the sort of women who read "The Feminine Mystique" that, far from oppressing them, the work of cooking approached in the proper spirit offered a kind of fulfillment and deserved an intelligent woman's attention. (A man's too.) Second-wave feminists were often ambivalent on the gender politics of cooking. Simone de Beauvoir wrote in "The Second Sex" that though cooking could be oppressive, it could also be a form of "revelation and creation; and a woman can find special satisfaction in a successful cake or a flaky pastry, for not everyone can do it: one must have the gift." This can be read either as a special Frenchie exemption for the culinary arts (féminisme, c'est bon, but we must not jeopardize those flaky pastries!) or as a bit of wisdom that some American feminists thoughtlessly trampled in their rush to get women out of the kitchen.

3. To The Kitchen Stadium

Whichever, kitchen work itself has changed considerably since 1963, judging from its depiction on today's how-to shows. Take the concept of cooking from scratch. Many of today's cooking programs rely unapologetically on ingredients that themselves contain lots of ingredients: canned soups, jarred mayonnaise, frozen vegetables, powdered sauces, vanilla wafers, limeade concentrate, Marshmallow Fluff. This probably shouldn't surprise us: processed foods have so thoroughly colonized the American kitchen and diet that they have redefined what passes today for cooking, not to mention food. Many of these convenience foods have been sold to women as tools of liberation; the rhetoric of kitchen oppression has been cleverly hijacked by food marketers and the cooking shows they sponsor to sell more stuff. So the shows encourage home cooks to take all manner of shortcuts, each of which involves buying another product, and all of which taken together have succeeded in redefining what is commonly meant by the verb "to cook."

I spent an enlightening if somewhat depressing hour on the phone with a veteran food-marketing researcher, Harry Balzer, who explained that "people call things 'cooking' today that would roll their grandmother in her grave—heating up a can of soup or microwaving a frozen pizza." Balzer has been studying American eating habits since 1978; the NPD Group, the firm he works for, collects data from a pool of 2,000 food diaries to track American eating habits. Years ago Balzer noticed that the definition of cooking held by his respondents had grown so broad as to be meaningless, so the firm tightened up the meaning of "to cook" at least slightly to capture what was really going on in American kitchens. To cook from scratch, they decreed, means to prepare a main dish that requires some degree of "assembly of elements." So microwaving a pizza doesn't count as cooking, though washing a head of lettuce and pouring bottled dressing over it does. Under this dispensation, you're also cooking when you spread mayonnaise on a slice of bread and pile on some cold cuts or a hamburger patty. (Currently the most popular meal in America, at both lunch and dinner, is a sandwich; the No. 1 accompanying beverage is a soda.) At least by Balzer's none-too-exacting standard, Americans are still cooking up a storm—58 percent of our evening meals qualify, though even that figure has been falling steadily since the 1980s.

Like most people who study consumer behavior, Balzer has developed a somewhat cynical view of human nature, which his research suggests is ever driven by the quest to save time or money or, optimally, both. I kept asking him what his research had to say about the prevalence of the activity I referred to as "real scratch cooking," but he wouldn't touch the term. Why? Apparently the activity has become so rarefied as to elude his tools of measurement.

"Here's an analogy," Balzer said. "A hundred years ago, chicken for dinner meant going out and catching, killing, plucking and gutting a chicken. Do you know anybody who still does that? It would be considered crazy! Well, that's exactly how cooking will seem to your grandchildren: something people used to do when they had no other choice. Get over it."

After my discouraging hour on the phone with Balzer, I settled in for a couple more with the Food Network, trying to square his dismal view of our interest in cooking with the hyperexuberant, even fetishized images of cooking that are presented on the screen. The Food Network undergoes a complete change of personality at night, when it trades the cozy precincts of the home kitchen and chirpy softball coaching of Rachael Ray or Sandra Lee for something markedly less feminine and less practical. Erica Gruen, the cable executive often credited with putting the Food Network on the map in the late '90s, recognized early on that, as she told a journalist, "people don't watch television to learn things." So she shifted the network's target audience from people who love to cook to people who love to eat, a considerably larger universe and one that—important for a cable network—happens to contain a great many more men.

In prime time, the Food Network's mise-en-scène shifts to masculine arenas like the Kitchen Stadium on "Iron Chef," where famous restaurant chefs wage gladiatorial combat to see who can, in 60 minutes, concoct the most spectacular meal from a secret ingredient ceremoniously unveiled just as the clock starts: an octopus or a bunch of bananas or a whole school of daurade. Whether in the Kitchen Stadium or on "Chopped" or "The Next Food Network Star" or, over on Bravo, "Top Chef," cooking in prime time is a form of athletic competition, drawing its visual and even aural vocabulary from "Monday Night Football." On "Iron Chef America," one of the Food Network's biggest hits, the cookingcaster Alton Brown delivers a breathless (though always gently tongue-in-cheek) play by play and color commentary, as the iron chefs and their team of iron sous-chefs race the clock to peel, chop, slice, dice, mince, Cuisinart, mandoline, boil, double-boil, pan-sear, sauté, sous vide, deep-fry, pressure-cook, grill, deglaze, reduce and plate—this last a word I'm old enough to remember when it was a mere noun. A particularly dazzling display of chefly "knife skills"—a term bandied as freely on the Food Network as "passing game" or "slugging percentage" is on ESPN—will earn an instant replay: an onion minced in slo-mo. Can we get a camera on this, Alton Brown will ask in a hushed, this-must-be-golf tone of voice. It looks like Chef Flay's going to try for a last-minute garnish grab before the clock runs out! Will he make it? [The buzzer sounds.] Yes!

These shows move so fast, in such a blur of flashing knives, frantic pantry raids and more sheer fire than you would ever want to see in your own kitchen, that I honestly can't tell you whether that "last-minute garnish grab" happened on "Iron Chef America" or "Chopped" or "The Next Food Network Star" or whether it was Chef Flay or Chef Batali who snagged the sprig of foliage at the buzzer. But impressive it surely was, in the same way it's impressive to watch a handful of eager.

Young chefs on "Chopped" figure out how to make a passable appetizer from chicken wings, celery, soba noodles and a package of string cheese in just 20 minutes, said starter to be judged by a panel of professional chefs on the basis of "taste, creativity and presentation." (If you ask me, the key to victory on any of these shows comes down to one factor: bacon. Whichever contestant puts bacon in the dish invariably seems to win.)

But you do have to wonder how easily so specialized a set of skills might translate to the home kitchen—or anywhere else for that matter. For when in real life are even professional chefs required to conceive and execute dishes in 20 minutes from ingredients selected by a third party exhibiting obvious sadistic tendencies? (String cheese?) Never, is when. The skills celebrated on the Food Network in prime time are precisely the skills necessary to succeed on the Food Network in prime time. They will come in handy nowhere else on God's green earth.

We learn things watching these cooking competitions, but they're not things about how to cook. There are no recipes to follow; the contests fly by much too fast for viewers to take in any practical tips; and the kind of cooking practiced in prime time is far more spectacular than anything you would ever try at home. No, for anyone hoping to pick up a few dinnertime tips, the implicit message of today's prime-time cooking shows is, Don't try this at home. If you really want to eat this way, go to a restaurant. Or as a chef friend put it when I asked him if he thought I could learn anything about cooking by watching the Food Network, "How much do you learn about playing basketball by watching the N.B.A.?"

What we mainly learn about on the Food Network in prime time is culinary fashion, which is no small thing: if Julia took the fear out of cooking, these shows take the fear—the social anxiety—out of ordering in restaurants. (Hey, now I know what a shiso leaf is and what "crudo" means!) Then, at the judges' table, we learn how to taste and how to talk about food. For viewers, these shows have become less about the production of high-end food than about its consumption—including its conspicuous consumption. (I think I'll start with the sawfish crudo wrapped in shiso leaves....)

Surely it's no accident that so many Food Network stars have themselves found a way to transcend barriers of social class in the kitchen—beginning with Emeril Lagasse, the working-class guy from Fall River, Mass., who, though he may not be able to sound the 'r' in "garlic," can still cook like a dream. Once upon a time Julia made the same promise in reverse: she showed you how you, too, could cook like someone who could not only prepare but properly pronounce a béarnaise.

So-called fancy food has always served as a form of cultural capital, and cooking programs help you acquire it, now without so much as lifting a spatula. The glamour of food has made it something of a class leveler in America, a fact that many of these shows implicitly celebrate. Television likes nothing better than to serve up elitism to the masses, paradoxical as that might sound. How wonderful is it that something like arugula can at the same time be a mark of sophistication and be found in almost every salad bar in America? Everybody wins!

But the shift from producing food on television to consuming it strikes me as a far-less-salubrious development. Traditionally, the recipe for the typical dump-and-stir program comprises about 80 percent cooking followed by 20 percent eating, but in prime time you now find a raft of shows that flip that ratio on its head, like "The Best Thing I Ever Ate" and "Diners, Drive-Ins and Dives," which are about nothing but eating. Sure, Guy Fieri, the tattooed and spiky-coiffed chowhound who hosts "Diners, Drive-Ins and Dives," ducks into the kitchen whenever he visits one of these roadside joints to do a little speed-bonding with the startled short-order cooks in back, but most of the time he's wrapping his mouth around their supersize creations: a 16-ounce Oh Gawd! burger (with the works); battered and deep-fried anything (clams, pickles, cinnamon buns, stuffed peppers, you name it); or a buttermilk burrito approximately the size of his head, stuffed with bacon, eggs and cheese. What Fieri's critical vocabulary lacks in analytical rigor, it more than makes up for in tailgate enthusiasm: "Man, oh man, now this is what I'm talkin' about!" What can possibly be the appeal of watching Guy Fieri bite, masticate and swallow all this chow?

The historical drift of cooking programs—from a genuine interest in producing food yourself to the spectacle of merely consuming it—surely owes a lot to the decline of cooking in our culture, but it also has something to do with the gravitational field that eventually overtakes anything in television's orbit. It's no accident that Julia Child appeared on public television—or educational television, as it used to be called. On a commercial network, a program that actually inspired viewers to get off the couch and spend an hour cooking a meal would be a commercial disaster, for it would mean they were turning off the television to do something else. The ads on the Food Network, at least in prime time, strongly suggest its viewers do no such thing: the food-related ads hardly ever hawk kitchen appliances or ingredients (unless you count A.1. steak sauce) but rather push the usual supermarket cart of edible foodlike substances, including Manwich sloppy joe in a can, Special K protein shakes and Ore-Ida frozen French fries, along with fast-casual eateries like Olive Garden and Red Lobster.

Buying, not making, is what cooking shows are mostly now about—that and, increasingly, cooking shows themselves: the whole self-perpetuating spectacle of competition, success and celebrity that, with "The Next Food Network Star," appears to have entered its baroque phase. The Food Network has figured out that we care much less about what's cooking than who's cooking. A few years ago, Mario Batali neatly summed up the network's formula to a reporter: "Look, it's TV! Everyone has to fall into a niche. I'm the Italian guy. Emeril's the exuberant New Orleans guy with the big eyebrows who yells a lot. Bobby's the grilling guy. Rachael Ray is the cheerleader-type girl who makes things at home the way a regular person would. Giada's the beautiful girl with the nice rack who does simple Italian food. As silly as the whole Food Network is, it gives us all a soapbox to talk about the things we care about." Not to mention a platform from which to sell all their stuff.

The Food Network has helped to transform cooking from something you do into something you watch—into yet another confection of spectacle and celebrity that keeps us pinned to the couch. The formula is as circular and self-reinforcing as a TV dinner: a simulacrum of home cooking that is sold on TV and designed to be eaten in front of the TV. True, in the case of the Swanson rendition, at least you get something that will fill you up; by comparison, the Food Network leaves you hungry, a condition its advertisers must love. But in neither case is there much risk that you will get off the couch and actually cook a meal. Both kinds of TV dinners plant us exactly where television always wants us: in front of the set, watching.

4. Watching What We Eat

To point out that television has succeeded in turning cooking into a spectator sport raises the question of why anyone would want to watch other people cook in the first place. There are plenty of things we've stopped doing for ourselves that we have no desire to watch other people do on TV: you don't see shows about changing the oil in your car or ironing shirts or reading newspapers. So what is it about cooking, specifically, that makes it such good television just now?

It's worth keeping in mind that watching other people cook is not exactly a new behavior for us humans. Even when "everyone" still cooked, there were plenty of us who mainly watched: men, for the most part, and children. Most of us have happy memories of watching our mothers in the kitchen, performing feats that sometimes looked very much like sorcery and typically resulted in something tasty to eat. Watching my mother transform the raw materials of nature—a handful of plants, an animal's flesh—into a favorite dinner was always a pretty good show, but on the afternoons when she tackled a complex marvel like chicken Kiev, I happily stopped whatever I was doing to watch. (I told you we had it pretty good, thanks partly to Julia.) My mother would hammer the boneless chicken breasts into flat pink slabs, roll them tightly around chunks of ice-cold herbed butter, glue the cylinders shut with egg, then fry the little logs until they turned golden brown, in what qualified as a minor miracle of transubstantiation. When the dish turned out right, knifing through the crust into the snowy white meat within would uncork a fragrant ooze of melted butter that seeped across the plate to merge with the Minute Rice. (If the instant rice sounds all wrong, remember that in the 1960s, Julia Child and modern food science were both tokens of sophistication.)

Yet even the most ordinary dish follows a similar arc of transformation, magically becoming something greater than the sum of its parts. Every dish contains not just culinary ingredients but also the ingredients of narrative: a beginning, a middle and an end. Bring in the element of fire—cooking's deus ex machina—and you've got a tasty little drama right there, the whole thing unfolding in a TV-friendly span of time: 30 minutes (at 350 degrees) will usually do it.

Cooking shows also benefit from the fact that food itself is—by definition—attractive to the humans who eat it, and that attraction can be enhanced by food styling, an art at which the Food Network so excels as to make Julia Child look like a piker. You'll be flipping aimlessly through the cable channels when a slow-motion cascade of glistening red cherries or a tongue of flame lapping at a slab of meat on the grill will catch your eye, and your reptilian brain will paralyze your thumb on the remote, forcing you to stop to see what's cooking. Food shows are the campfires in the deep cable forest, drawing us like hungry wanderers to their flames. (And on the Food Network there are plenty of flames to catch your eye, compensating, no doubt, for the unfortunate absence of aromas.)

No matter how well produced, a televised oil change and lube offers no such satisfactions.

I suspect we're drawn to the textures and rhythms of kitchen work, too, which seem so much more direct and satisfying than the more abstract and formless tasks most of us perform in our jobs nowadays. The chefs on TV get to put their hands on real stuff, not keyboards and screens but fundamental things like plants and animals and fungi; they get to work with fire and ice and perform feats of alchemy. By way of explaining why in the world she wants to cook her way through "Mastering the Art of French Cooking," all Julie Powell has to do in the film is show us her cubicle at the Lower Manhattan Development Corporation, where she spends her days on the phone mollifying callers with problems that she lacks the power to fix.

"You know what I love about cooking?" Julie tells us in a voiceover as we watch her field yet another inconclusive call on her headset. "I love that after a day where nothing is sure—and when I say nothing, I mean nothing—you can come home and absolutely know that if you add egg yolks to chocolate and sugar and milk, it will get thick. It's such a comfort." How many of us still do work that engages us in a dialogue with the material world and ends—assuming the soufflé doesn't collapse—with such a gratifying and tasty sense of closure? Come to think of it, even the collapse of the soufflé is at least definitive, which is more than you can say about most of what you will do at work tomorrow.

5. The End of Cooking

If cooking really offers all these satisfactions, then why don't we do more of it? Well, ask Julie Powell: for most of us it doesn't pay the rent, and very often our work doesn't leave us the time; during the year of Julia, dinner at the Powell apartment seldom arrived at the table before 10 p.m. For many years now, Americans have been putting in longer hours at work and enjoying less time at home. Since 1967, we've added 167 hours—the equivalent of a month's full-time labor—to the total amount of time we spend at work each year, and in households where both parents work, the figure is more like 400 hours. Americans today spend more time working than people in any other industrialized nation—an extra two weeks or more a year. Not surprisingly, in those countries where people still take cooking seriously, they also have more time to devote to it.

It's generally assumed that the entrance of women into the work force is responsible for the collapse of home cooking, but that turns out to be only part of the story. Yes, women with jobs outside the home spend less time cooking—but so do women without jobs. The amount of time spent on food preparation in America has fallen at the same precipitous rate among women who don't work outside the home as it has among women who do: in both cases, a decline of about 40 percent since 1965. (Though for married women who don't have jobs, the amount of time spent cooking remains greater: 58 minutes a day, as compared with 36 for married women who do have jobs.) In general, spending on restaurants or takeout food rises with income. Women with jobs have more money to pay corporations to do their cooking, yet all American women now allow corporations to cook for them when they can.

Those corporations have been trying to persuade Americans to let them do the cooking since long before large numbers of women entered the work force. After World War II, the food industry labored mightily to sell American women on all the processed-food wonders it had invented to feed the troops: canned meals, freeze-dried foods, dehydrated potatoes, powdered orange juice and coffee, instant everything. As Laura Shapiro recounts in "Something From the Oven: Reinventing Dinner in 1950s America," the food industry strived to "persuade millions of Americans to develop a lasting taste for meals that were a lot like field rations." The same process of peacetime conversion that industrialized our farming, giving us synthetic fertilizers made from munitions and new pesticides developed from nerve gas, also industrialized our eating.

Shapiro shows that the shift toward industrial cookery began not in response to a demand from women entering the work force but as a supply-driven phenomenon. In fact, for many years American women, whether they worked or not, resisted processed foods, regarding them as a dereliction of their "moral obligation to cook," something they believed to be a parental responsibility on par with child care. It took years of clever, dedicated marketing to break down this resistance and persuade Americans that opening a can or cooking from a mix really was cooking. Honest. In the 1950s, just-add-water cake mixes languished in the supermarket until the marketers figured out that if you left at least something for the "baker" to do—specifically, crack open an egg—she could take ownership of the cake. Over the years, the food scientists have gotten better and better at simulating real food, keeping it looking attractive and seemingly fresh, and the rapid acceptance of microwave ovens—which went from being in only 8 percent of American households in 1978 to 90 percent today—opened up vast new horizons of home-meal replacement.

Harry Balzer's research suggests that the corporate project of redefining what it means to cook and serve a meal has succeeded beyond the industry's wildest expectations. People think nothing of buying frozen peanut butter-and-jelly sandwiches for their children's lunchboxes. (Now how much of a timesaver can that be?) "We've had a hundred years of packaged foods," Balzer told me, "and now we're going to have a hundred years of packaged meals." Already today, 80 percent of the cost of food eaten in the home goes to someone other than a farmer, which is to say to industrial cooking and packaging and marketing. Balzer is unsentimental about this development: "Do you miss sewing or darning socks? I don't think so."

So what are we doing with the time we save by outsourcing our food preparation to corporations and 16-year-old burger flippers? Working, commuting to work, surfing the Internet and, perhaps most curiously of all, watching other people cook on television.

But this may not be quite the paradox it seems. Maybe the reason we like to watch cooking on TV is that there are things about cooking we miss. We might not feel we have the time or the energy to do it ourselves every day, yet we're not prepared to see it disappear from our lives entirely. Why? Perhaps because cooking—unlike sewing or darning socks—is an activity that strikes a deep emotional chord in us, one that might even go to the heart of our identity as human beings.

What?! You're telling me Bobby Flay strikes deep emotional chords?

Bear with me. Consider for a moment the proposition that as a human activity, cooking is far more important—to our happiness and to our health—than its current role in our lives, not to mention its depiction on TV, might lead you to believe. Let's see what happens when we take cooking seriously.

6. The Cooking Animal

The idea that cooking is a defining human activity is not a new one. In 1773, the Scottish writer James Boswell, noting that "no beast is a cook," called Homo sapiens "the cooking animal," though he might have reconsidered that definition had he been able to gaze upon the frozen-food cases at Wal-Mart. Fifty years later, in "The Physiology of Taste," the French gastronome Jean-Anthelme Brillat-Savarin claimed that cooking made us who we are; by teaching men to use fire, it had "done the most to advance the cause of civilization." More recently, the anthropologist Claude Lévi-Strauss, writing in 1964 in "The Raw and the Cooked," found that many cultures entertained a similar view, regarding cooking as a symbolic way of distinguishing ourselves from the animals.

For Lévi-Strauss, cooking is a metaphor for the human transformation of nature into culture, but in the years since "The Raw and the Cooked," other anthropologists have begun to take quite literally the idea that cooking is the key to our humanity. Earlier this year, Richard Wrangham, a Harvard anthropologist, published a fascinating book called "Catching Fire," in which he argues that it was the discovery of cooking by our early ancestors—not tool-making or language or meat-eating—that made us human. By providing our primate forebears with a more energy-dense and easy-to-digest diet, cooked food altered the course of human evolution, allowing our brains to grow bigger (brains are notorious energy guzzlers) and our guts to shrink. It seems that raw food takes much more time and energy to chew and digest, which is why other primates of our size carry around substantially larger digestive tracts and spend many more of their waking hours chewing: up to six hours a day. (That's nearly as much time as Guy Fieri devotes to the activity.) Also, since cooking detoxifies many foods, it cracked open a treasure trove of nutritious calories unavailable to other animals. Freed from the need to spend our days gathering large quantities of raw food and then chewing (and chewing) it, humans could now devote their time, and their metabolic resources, to other purposes, like creating a culture.

Cooking gave us not just the meal but also the occasion: the practice of eating together at an appointed time and place. This was something new under the sun, for the forager of raw food would likely have fed himself on the go and alone, like the animals. (Or, come to think of it, like the industrial eaters we've become, grazing at gas stations and skipping meals.) But sitting down to common meals, making eye contact, sharing food, all served to civilize us; "around that fire," Wrangham says, "we became tamer."

If cooking is as central to human identity and culture as Wrangham believes, it stands to reason that the decline of cooking in our time would have a profound effect on modern life. At the very least, you would expect that its rapid disappearance from everyday life might leave us feeling nostalgic for the sights and smells and the sociality of the cook-fire. Bobby Flay and Rachael Ray may be pushing precisely that emotional button. Interestingly, the one kind of home cooking that is actually on the rise today (according to Harry Balzer) is outdoor grilling. Chunks of animal flesh seared over an open fire: grilling is cooking at its most fundamental and explicit, the transformation of the raw into the cooked right before our eyes. It makes a certain sense that the grill would be gaining adherents at the very moment when cooking meals and eating them together is fading from the culture. (While men have hardly become equal partners in the kitchen, they are cooking more today than ever before: about 13 percent of all meals, many of them on the grill.)

Yet we don't crank up the barbecue every day; grilling for most people is more ceremony than routine. We seem to be well on our way to turning cooking into a form of weekend recreation, a backyard sport for which we outfit ourselves at Williams-Sonoma, or a televised spectator sport we watch from the couch. Cooking's fate may be to join some of our other weekend exercises in recreational atavism: camping and gardening and hunting and riding on horseback. Something in us apparently likes to be reminded of our distant origins every now and then and to celebrate whatever rough skills for contending with the natural world might survive in us, beneath the thin crust of 21st-century civilization.

To play at farming or foraging for food strikes us as harmless enough, perhaps because the delegating of those activities to other people in real life is something most of us are generally O.K. with. But to relegate the activity of cooking to a form of play, something that happens just on weekends or mostly on television, seems much more consequential. The fact is that not cooking may well be deleterious to our health, and there is reason to believe that the outsourcing of food preparation to corporations and 16-year-olds has already taken a toll on our physical and psychological well-being.

Consider some recent research on the links between cooking and dietary health. A 2003 study by a group of Harvard economists led by David Cutler found that the rise of food preparation outside the home could explain most of the increase in obesity in America. Mass production has driven down the cost of many foods, not only in terms of price but also in the amount of time required to obtain them. The French fry did not become the most popular "vegetable" in America until industry relieved us of the considerable effort needed to prepare French fries ourselves. Similarly, the mass production of cream-filled cakes, fried chicken wings and taquitos, exotically flavored chips or cheesy puffs of refined flour, has transformed all these hard-to-make-at-home foods into the sort of everyday fare you can pick up at the gas station on a whim and for less than a dollar. The fact that we no longer have to plan or even wait to enjoy these items, as we would if we were making them ourselves, makes us that much more likely to indulge impulsively.

Cutler and his colleagues demonstrate that as the "time cost" of food preparation has fallen, calorie consumption has gone up, particularly consumption of the sort of snack and convenience foods that are typically cooked outside the home. They found that when we don't have to cook meals, we eat more of them: as the amount of time Americans spend cooking has dropped by about half, the number of meals Americans eat in a day has climbed; since 1977, we've added approximately half a meal to our daily intake.

Cutler and his colleagues also surveyed cooking patterns across several cultures and found that obesity rates are inversely correlated with the amount of time spent on food preparation. The more time a nation devotes to food preparation at home, the lower its rate of obesity. In fact, the amount of time spent cooking predicts obesity rates more reliably than female participation in the labor force or income. Other research supports the idea that cooking is a better predictor of a healthful diet than social class: a 1992 study in *The Journal of the American Dietetic Association* found that poor women who routinely cooked were more likely to eat a more healthful diet than well-to-do women who did not.

So cooking matters—a lot. Which when you think about it, should come as no surprise. When we let corporations do the cooking, they're bound to go heavy on sugar, fat and salt; these are three tastes we're hard-wired to like, which happen to be dirt cheap to add and do a good job masking the shortcomings of processed food. And if you make special-occasion foods cheap and easy enough to eat every day, we will eat them every day. The time and work involved in cooking, as well as the delay in gratification built into the process, served as an important check on our appetite. Now that check is gone, and we're struggling to deal with the consequences.

The question is, Can we ever put the genie back into the bottle? Once it has been destroyed, can a culture of everyday cooking be rebuilt? One in which men share equally in the work? One in which the cooking shows on television once again teach people how to cook from scratch and, as Julia Child once did, actually empower them to do it?

Let us hope so. Because it's hard to imagine ever reforming the American way of eating or, for that matter, the American food system unless millions of Americans—women and men—are willing to make cooking a part of daily life. The path to a diet of fresher, unprocessed food, not to mention to a revitalized local-food economy, passes straight through the home kitchen.

But if this is a dream you find appealing, you might not want to call Harry Balzer right away to discuss it.

"Not going to happen," he told me. "Why? Because we're basically cheap and lazy. And besides, the skills are already lost. Who is going to teach the next generation to cook? I don't see it.

"We're all looking for someone else to cook for us. The next American cook is going to be the supermarket. Takeout from the supermarket, that's the future. All we need now is the drive-through supermarket."

Crusty as a fresh baguette, Harry Balzer insists on dealing with the world, and human nature, as it really is, or at least as he finds it in the survey data he has spent the past three decades poring over. But for a brief moment, I was able to engage him in the project of imagining a slightly different reality. This took a little doing. Many of his clients—which include many of the big chain restaurants and food manufacturers—profit handsomely from the decline and fall of cooking in America; indeed, their marketing has contributed to it. Yet Balzer himself made it clear that he recognizes all that the decline of everyday cooking has cost us. So I asked him how, in an ideal world, Americans might begin to undo the damage that the modern diet of industrially prepared food has done to our health.

"Easy. You want Americans to eat less? I have the diet for you. It's short, and it's simple. Here's my diet plan: Cook it yourself. That's it. Eat anything you want—just as long as you're willing to cook it yourself."

Critical Reading Questions

Summarizing the Text

1. Pollan sets up his article with a basic question: why are we so eager to watch people cook, and so reluctant to actually cook? What answer does he offer to this question?

2. Pollan proposes a kind of "genealogy" of cooking shows, beginning with Julia Child and ending with today's Food Network. What is the nature of the evolution that he identifies?

3. What does "cook" mean in this article? How does Pollan use Harry Balzer to offer a definition of this seemingly obvious word?

Establishing the Context

4. Pollan states that "so-called fancy food has always served as a form of cultural capital, and cooking programs helped you acquire it, now without so much as lifting a spatula." What is "cultural capital"? Can you define that term from context?

5. Having created and moderated much of the cultural discussion about locavorism and sustainability, Pollan here attempts to expand this discussion to include feminism, consumer culture, and even the influence of television. Is his argument strengthened or weakened by its broad scope? How so?

Responding to the Text

6. Do you watch Food Network shows? Do others whom you know? Do those shows make you want to cook, eat, or both?

7. Food here is just a metaphor for the larger culture, it seems. Do you agree with Pollan's argument that we are becoming a nation that is much more concerned with consuming than with producing? What other examples of this can you offer?

CLUSTER TWO: IS THERE AN OBESITY EPIDEMIC?

Halting the Obesity Epidemic: A Public Health Policy Approach

Marion Nestle and
Michael F. Jacobson

Marion Nestle is one of the leading researchers on food and public policy. Currently she is the Paulette Goddard Professor of Nutrition, Food Studies, and Public Health at New York University. Author of such books as Food Politics *and* Safe Food, *she has been an outspoken opponent of the food industry, blaming it for putting profits above public health. In this article, written with Center for Science in the Public Interest director Michael Jacobson, Nestle argues that only public policy—laws and education—can combat the "obesity epidemic" raging in the United States. This article appeared in the peer-reviewed journal* Public Health Reports.

Synopsis

Traditional ways of preventing and treating overweight and obesity have almost invariably focused on changing the behavior of individuals, an approach that has proven woefully inadequate, as indicated by the rising rates of both conditions. Considering the many aspects of American culture that promote obesity, from the proliferation of fast-food outlets to almost universal reliance on automobiles, reversing current trends will require a multifaceted public health policy approach as well as considerable funding. National leadership is needed to ensure the participation of health officials and researchers, educators and legislators, transportation experts and urban planners, and businesses and nonprofit groups in formulating a public health campaign with a better chance of success. The authors outline a broad range of policy recommendations and suggest that an obesity prevention campaign might be funded, in part, with revenues from small taxes on selected products that provide "empty" calories—such as soft drinks—or that reduce physical activity—such as automobiles.

In 1974, an editorial in *The Lancet* identified obesity as "the most important nutritional disease in the affluent countries of the world,"[1] yet a quarter century later, its prevalence has increased sharply among American adults, adolescents, and children.[2-4] The deleterious effects of obesity on chronic disease risk, morbidity, and mortality[5,6]; its high medical, psychological, and social costs[7,8]; its multiplicity of causes[9]; its persistence from childhood into adulthood[10]; the paucity of successful treatment options[11]; the hazards of pharmacologic treatments[12]; and the complexities of treatment guidelines[13] all argue for increased attention to the prevention of excessive weight gain starting as early in life as possible. Prevention, however, requires changes in individual behavioral patterns as well as eliminating environmental barriers to healthy food choices and active lifestyles—both exceedingly difficult to achieve.

Because obesity results from chronic consumption of energy (calories) in excess of that used by the body, prevention requires people to balance the energy they consume from food and drinks with the energy expended through metabolic and muscular activity. Although the precise relationship between the diet and activity components of this "equation" is still under investigation,[14,15] it is intuitively obvious that successful prevention strategies—individual and societal—must address both elements.[16]

Guidelines Focus on Individuals

Concern about obesity is not new. By 1952, the American Heart Association had already identified obesity as a cardiac risk factor modifiable through diet and exercise.[17] Subsequently, a number of federal agencies and private organizations devoted to general health promotion or to prevention of chronic conditions for which obesity is a risk factor—coronary heart disease, cancer, stroke, and diabetes—issued guidelines advising Americans to reduce energy intake, raise energy expenditure, or do both to maintain healthy weight. Typically, these guidelines focused on individuals and tended to state the obvious. For example, the otherwise landmark 1977 Senate report on diet and chronic disease prevention, *Dietary Goals for the United States*, omitted any mention of obesity. (The second edition was amended to advise: "To avoid overweight, consume only as much energy [calories] as is expended; if overweight, decrease energy intake and increase energy expenditure."[18]) Overall, the nearly half-century history of such banal recommendations is notable for addressing both physical activity and dietary patterns, but also for lack of creativity, a focus on individual behavior change, and ineffectiveness.

Only rarely did such guidelines deal with factors in society and the environment that might contribute to obesity. Participants in the 1969 White House Conference on Food, Nutrition, and Health recommended a major national effort to reverse the trend toward inactivity in the population through a mass-media campaign focused on milder forms of exercise such as walking or stair-climbing; school physical education programs; and federal funding for community recreation facilities.[19] The 1977 *Dietary Goals* report described certain societal influences on dietary intake, such as television advertising, but made no recommendations for government action beyond education, research, and food labeling.[19]

The most notable exception was the report of a 1977 conference organized by the National Institutes of Health (NIH) to review research and develop recommendations for obesity prevention and management. In one paper, A.J. Stunkard thoroughly reviewed social and environmental influences on obesity.[20] As a result, the conference report included an extraordinarily broad list of proposals for federal, community, and private actions to foster dietary improvements and more active lifestyles. These ranged from coordinated health education and model school programs to changes in regulations for grades of meat, advertising, taxes, and insurance premiums.[21] Some of the proposals cut right to the core of the matter: "Propose that any national health insurance program ... recognize obesity as a disease and include within its benefits coverage for the treatment of it." "Make nutrition counseling reimbursable under Medicare." and "Fund demonstration projects at the worksite."[22] Perhaps because the recommendations took 23 pages to list, conveyed no sense of priority, would be expensive to implement, but specified no means of funding, they were largely ignored and soon forgotten. Subsequent reports on obesity prevention continued to emphasize individual approaches to decreasing energy intake and increasing energy expenditure without much consideration of the factors in society that act as barriers to such approaches.

National Objectives

Prevention of obesity by individuals and population groups has been an explicit goal of national public health policy since 1980. In developing its successive 10-year plans to reduce behavioral risks for disease through specific and measurable health objectives, the US Public Health Service (PHS) said that the government should "lead, catalyze, and provide strategic support" for implementation through collaboration with professional and industry groups.[23] In developing the specific *Promoting Health/Preventing Disease* objectives for obesity prevention and the methods to implement them, PHS suggested that government agencies do such things as work with public and private agencies to distribute copies of the *Dietary Guidelines for Americans*[24] and other educational materials; encourage development of nutrition education and fitness programs through grants to states; and support research on methods to prevent and control obesity among adults and children. Although these obesity objectives were assigned to the Department of Health and Human Services (DHHS), the implementation activities were distributed among multiple agencies within the Department, with no one agency taking lead responsibility. Thus, the Centers for Disease Control and Prevention (CDC) were to encourage adoption of model school curricula, the Food and Drug Administration (FDA) was to develop a mass-media campaign to educate the public about food labels, and NIH was to sponsor workshops and research on obesity. Implementation steps to achieve the physical activity objectives were distributed among at least nine federal agencies.[25] The words used to describe the implementation steps reflected—and continue to reflect—political and funding realities. Government agencies can encourage, publicize, and cooperate with—but usually cannot implement—programs to achieve national obesity objectives.

Nevertheless, evidence of rising rates of obesity in the late 1980s and 1990s[2,13] has focused increasing attention on the need for prevention strategies. In PHS's second 10-year plan, *Healthy People 2000*, the section on physical activity and fitness appears first among the 22 priority areas for behavior change, and the nutrition objectives appear second, emphasizing PHS's view of obesity as a priority public health problem. Among the objectives in these areas, reducing rates of overweight among adults and adolescents appeared second in order only to prevention of cardiovascular disease. *Healthy People 2000* listed specific objectives for promotion of nutrition and physical education in schools, work sites, and communities—public health approaches that would surely create a more favorable environment for prevention of obesity.[26]

Despite these efforts, the activity levels of Americans appear to have changed little, if at all, from the 1970s to the 1990s.[5,27] Discerning such trends is exceedingly difficult due to the lack of reliable methods for measuring energy expenditure in the population. Moreover, the average caloric intake reported by Americans rose from 1826 kilocalories per day (kcal/d) in 1977–1978 and 1774 kcal/d in 1989–1991[28] to 2002 kcal/d in 1994–1996.[29] No matter how imprecise the data, these trends suggest why average body weights are increasing so significantly. According to data from the 1976–1980 and 1988–1994 National Health and Nutrition Examination Surveys, the prevalence of overweight (defined as at or above the 85th percentile of body mass index [BMI] in 1976–1980) rose from 25.4% to 34.9% among American adults, from 24.1% to 33.3% among men and from 26.5% to 36.4% among women; nearly doubled among children ages 6–11 years from 7.6% to 13.7%; and rose from 5.7% to 11.5% among adolescents.[2,4] (The BMI is defined as body weight in kilograms divided by height in meters squared [kg/m^2].) According to the results of telephone surveys conducted by the CDC, the prevalence of obesity (defined as a BMI ≥30), increased from 12% to nearly 18% in just the few years from 1991 to 1998.[2] Trends in prevention and treatment of obesity are also moving in precisely the wrong direction. The proportions of schools offering physical education, overweight people who report dieting and exercising to lose weight, and primary-care physicians who counsel patients about behavioral risk factors for obesity and other conditions have all declined.[7]

In response to these alarming developments, the third PHS 10-year plan, *Healthy People 2010*, continues to emphasize goals related to regular exercise, noting that people with risk factors for coronary heart disease, such as obesity and hypertension, may particularly benefit from physical activity.[30] The first *three* objectives in the nutrition section now focus on increasing the prevalence of healthy weight (BMI 19–25), reducing the prevalence of obesity, and reducing overweight among children and adolescents. But the plan offers little guidance as to how the objectives are expected to be achieved beyond calling for "a concerted public effort" in that direction.[30]

Barriers to Obesity Prevention

Although the impact of obesity on health has been recognized for nearly a half century and its increasing prevalence among adults and children shows no sign of reversal, national action plans consist mostly of wishful thinking and admonitions to individuals rather than public health strategies that could promote more healthful lifestyles (such as those presented by Stunkard in 1977 and later).[20,21] Public health officials need to recognize that when it comes to obesity, our society's environment is "toxic."[31] Unintended consequences of our post-industrial society are deeply rooted cultural, social, and economic factors that actively encourage overeating and sedentary behavior and discourage alterations in these patterns, a situation that calls for more active and comprehensive intervention strategies.

Energy intake   The data indicate that Americans are consuming more calories but are not compensating for them with increased physical activity. If recommendations to consume fewer calories have so little effect, it may be in part because such advice runs counter to the economic imperatives of our food system.[32] While not the sole reason for high caloric intake, massive efforts by food manufactures and restaurant chains to encourage people to buy their brands must undoubtedly play a role. Promotions, pricing, packaging, and availability all encourage Americans to eat *more* food, not less.

The food industry spends about $11 billion annually on advertising and another $22 billion or so on trade shows, supermarket "slotting fees," incentives, and other consumer promotions.[33] In 1998, promotion costs for popular candy bars were $10 million to $50 million, for soft drinks up to $115.5 million, and for the McDonald's restaurant chain just over a *billion* dollars.[34] Such figures dwarf the National Cancer Institute's $1 million annual investment in the educational component of its 5-A-Day campaign to increase consumption of fruit and vegetables[35] or the $1.5 million budget of the National Heart, Lung, and Blood Institute's National Cholesterol Education Campaign.[36] American children are bombarded daily with dozens of television commercials promoting fast foods, snack foods, and soft drinks.[37] Advertisements for such products are even commonplace in schools, thanks to Channel One, a private venture that provides free video equipment and a daily television "news" program in exchange for mandatory viewing of commercials by students,[38] and school district contracts for exclusive marketing of one or another soft drink in vending machines and sports facilities.[39] Advertising directly affects the food choices of children,[40] who now have far more disposable income than they had several decades ago and far greater influence on their parents' buying habits.[41]

Americans spend about half of their food budget and consume about one-third their daily energy[42] on meals and drinks consumed outside the home, where it is exceedingly difficult to estimate the energy content of the food. About 170,000 fast-food restaurants[43] and three million soft drink vending machines[44] help ensure that Americans are not more than a few steps from immediate sources of relatively non-nutritious foods. As a Coca-Cola Company executive proclaimed, "[T]o build pervasiveness of our products, we're putting ice-cold Coca-Cola classic and our other brands within reach, wherever you look: at the supermarket, the video store, the soccer field, the gas station—everywhere."[45]

Food eaten outside the home, on average, is higher in fat and lower in micronutrients than food prepared at home.[42] Many popular table-service restaurant meals—lunch or dinner—provide 1000 to 2000 kcal each,[46] amounts equivalent to 35% to 100% of a full day's energy requirement for most adults.[47] Restaurants and movie theaters charge just a few cents more for larger-size orders of soft drinks, popcorn, and French fries, and the standard serving sizes of these and other foods have increased greatly in the past decade.[48] For example, in the 1950s, Coca-Cola was packaged only in 6.5-oz bottles; single-serving containers expanded first to 12-oz cans and, more recently, to 20-oz bottles. A 12-oz soft drink provides about 150 kcal, all from sugars, but contains no other nutrients of significance.[49]

Taken together, such changes in the food environment help explain why it requires more and more will power for Americans to maintain an appropriate intake of energy.

Energy expenditure Influencing Americans to increase energy expenditure is as daunting a task as encouraging reductions in energy intake. Twentieth-century labor-saving devices, from automobiles to e-mail, are ubiquitous and have reduced energy needs, as has the shift of a large proportion of the workforce from manual labor to white-collar jobs that require nothing more active than pressing keys on a computer.[50] Wonders of modern civilization such as central heating lessen the energy cost of maintaining body temperature, and air conditioning makes it much more comfortable on hot summer days to stay inside and watch television or play computer games than to engage in outdoor activities. Dangerous neighborhoods—or the perception of danger—discourage people from walking dogs, pushing strollers, playing ball, jogging, or permitting children to play outdoors.[51] Many suburban neighborhoods are structured for the convenience of automobile drivers; they may not have sidewalks and may lack stores, entertainment, or other destinations within walking distance. Meanwhile, the decline in tax support for many public school systems and the need to fulfill competing academic priorities have forced them to relegate physical education to the category of "frill." Many school districts have had to eliminate physical education classes entirely, and fewer and fewer schools offer any opportunity for students to be physically active during the school day.[6] Such barriers make it clear why an attempt to "detoxify" the present environment and create one that fosters healthful activity patterns deserves far more attention than it has received since the 1977 recommendations in *Obesity in America*.[20,22]

Public Health Approaches

In an environment so antagonistic to healthful lifestyles, no quick and easy solution to the problem of obesity should be expected. Meaningful efforts must include the development of government policies and programs that address both the "energy in" and "energy out" components of weight maintenance. Although privately funded campaigns to educate the public and mobilize physicians to combat obesity, such as Shape Up America,[52] are useful adjuncts, they cannot be expected to achieve significant population wide behavior change. What is needed is *substantial* involvement of and investment by government at all levels. Governmental policies and programs affect many of the environmental determinants of poor diets and sedentary lifestyles. Communities, workplaces, schools, medical centers, and many other venues are subject to federal and other governmental regulations that could be modified to make the environment more conducive to healthful diet and activity patterns. Just as the environmental crisis spurred the public to make a huge financial investment in seeking solutions, so should the obesity epidemic.

In Figure 1, we provide recommendations for a variety of such modifications along with suggestions for new policies targeted to

Figure 1 Reducing the prevalence of obesity: policy recommendations
Education

- Provide federal funding to state public health departments for mass media health promotion campaigns that emphasize healthful eating and physical activity patterns.
- Require instruction in nutrition and weight management as part of the school curriculum for future health-education teachers.
- Make a plant-based diet the focus of dietary guidance.
- Ban required watching of commercials for foods high in calories, fat, or sugar on school television programs (for example, Channel One).
- Declare and organize an annual National "No-TV" Week.
- Require and fund daily physical education and sports programs in primary and secondary schools, extending the school day if necessary.
- Develop culturally relevant obesity prevention campaigns for high-risk and low-income Americans.
- Promote healthy eating in government cafeterias, Veterans Administration medical centers, military installations, prisons, and other venues.
- Institute campaigns to promote healthy eating and activity patterns among federal and state employees in all departments.

Food labeling and advertising

- Require chain restaurants to provide information about calorie content on menus or menu boards and nutrition labeling on wrappers.
- Require that containers for soft drinks and snacks sold in movie theaters, convenience stores, and other venues bear information about calorie, fat, or sugar content.
- Require nutrition labeling on fresh meat and poultry products.
- Restrict advertising of high-calorie, low-nutrient foods on television shows commonly watched by children or require broadcasters to provide equal time for messages promoting healthy eating and physical activity.
- Require print advertisements to disclose the caloric content of the foods being marketed.

Food assistance programs

- Protect school food programs by eliminating the sale of soft drinks, candy bars, and foods high in calories, fat, or sugar in school buildings.
- Require that any foods that compete with school meals be consistent with federal recommendations for fat, saturated fat, cholesterol, sugar, and sodium content.

- Develop an incentive system to encourage Food Stamp recipients to purchase fruits, vegetables, whole grains, and other healthful foods, such as by earmarking increases in Food Stamp benefits for the purchase of those foods.

Health care and training

- Require medical, nursing, and other health professions curricula to teach the principles and benefits of healthful diet and exercise patterns.
- Require health care providers to learn about behavioral risks for obesity and how to counsel patients about health-promoting behavior change.
- Develop and fund a research agenda focused on behavioral as well as metabolic determinants of weight gain and maintenance, and on the most cost-effective methods for promoting healthful diet and activity patterns.
- Revise Medicaid and Medicare regulations to provide incentives to health care providers for nutrition and obesity counseling and other interventions that meet specified standards of cost and effectiveness.

Transportation and urban development

- Provide funding and other incentives for bicycle paths, recreation centers, swimming pools, parks, and sidewalks.
- Develop and provide guides for cities, zoning authorities, and urban planners on ways to modify zoning requirements, designate downtown areas as pedestrian malls and automobile-free zones, and modify residential neighborhoods, workplaces, and shopping centers to promote physical activity.

Taxes

- Levy city, state, or federal taxes on soft drinks and other foods high in calories, fat, or sugar to fund campaigns to promote good nutrition and physical activity.
- Subsidize the costs of low-calorie nutritious foods, perhaps by raising the costs of selected high-calorie, low-nutrient foods.
- Remove sales taxes on, or provide other incentives for, purchase of exercise equipment.
- Provide tax incentives to encourage employers to provide weight management programs.

Policy development

- Use the National Nutrition Summit to develop a national campaign to prevent obesity.
- Produce a Surgeon General's Report on Obesity Prevention.
- Expand the scope of the President's Council on Physical Fitness and Sports to include nutrition and to emphasize obesity prevention.
- Develop a coordinated federal implementation plan for the Healthy People 2010 nutrition and physical activity objectives.

obesity prevention. These recommendations, reflecting the disparate influences on diet and activity, address education, food regulation and advertising, food assistance, health care and the training of health professionals, transportation and urban development, taxation, and the development of federal policy. We offer the suggestions, some of which have been proposed by others,[20,22,53,54] to stimulate discussion of a much wider range of approaches than is typically considered. In doing so, we suggest changes in existing policies and practices[55] that affect health behaviors. We believe these proposals are politically and economically feasible and, collectively, capable of producing a significant effect in helping people to maintain healthy weight. Each of the suggestions could benefit from further discussion and analysis. Here, we comment on just a few of them.

Using media campaigns   Media advertising should be a vital part of any campaign to reduce obesity through promotion of positive changes in behavior, such as eating more fruits, vegetables, and whole grains; switching to lower-fat meat or dairy products; eating fewer hamburgers and steaks; and drinking water instead of soda. Campaigns of this kind can be remarkably effective. For example, the Center for Science in the Public Interest's "1% Or Less" program doubled the market share of low-fat and fat-free milk in several communities through intensive, seven-week paid advertising and public relations campaigns that cost as little as 22 cents per person.[56–58] Those efforts illustrate that advertising can be an affordable, effective method for promoting dietary change—even in the context of media advertising for less nutritious foods. Similar mass-media motivational campaigns could be developed to encourage people to walk, jog, bicycle, and engage in other enjoyable activities that expend energy.

Discouraging TV watching and junk-food advertising   Anti-obesity measures need to address television watching, a major sedentary activity as well as one that exposes viewers to countless commercials for high-calorie foods. The average American child between the ages of 8 and 18 spends more than three hours daily watching television and another three or four hours with other media.[59] Television is an increasingly well-established risk factor for obesity and its health consequences in both adults and children.[60,61] At least one study now shows that reducing the number of hours spent watching television or playing video games is a promising approach to preventing obesity in children.[62] Government and private organizations could sponsor an annual "No TV Week" to remind people that life is possible, *even better*, with little or no television and that watching television could well be replaced by physical and social activities that expend more energy. The Department of Education and DHHS could sponsor a national campaign, building on previous work by the nonprofit TV-Free America.[63]

Advertisements for candy, snacks, fast foods, and soft drinks should not be allowed on television shows commonly watched by children younger than age 10. Researchers have shown that younger children do not understand the *concept* of advertising—that it differs from program content and is designed to sell, not inform—and that children of all ages are highly influenced by television commercials to buy or demand the products that they see advertised.[64] It makes no sense for a society to allow private interests to misshape the eating habits of the next generation, and it is time for Congress to repeal the law that blocks the Federal Trade Commission from promulgating industry-wide rules to control advertising during children's television programs.[65]

Promoting physical activity Federal and state government agencies could do more to make physical activity more attractive and convenient. They could provide incentives to communities to develop safe bicycle paths and jogging trails; to build more public swimming pools, tennis courts, and ball fields; to pass zoning rules favoring side walks in residential and commercial areas, traffic-free areas, and traffic patterns that encourage people to walk to school, work, and shopping; and safety protection for streets, parks, and playgrounds. Government could also provide incentives to use mass transit, and disincentives to drive private cars, thereby encouraging people to walk to bus stops and train stations.

Reaching children through the schools State boards of education and local school boards have an obligation to promote healthful lifestyles. Physical education should again be required, preferably on a daily basis, to encourage students to expend energy and to help them develop lifelong enjoyment of jogging, ball games, swimming, and other low-cost activities. School boards should be encouraged to resist efforts of marketers to sell soda and high-calorie, low-nutrient snack foods in hallways and cafeterias. Congress could support more healthful school meals by insisting that the US Department of Agriculture (USDA) set stricter limits on sales of foods high in energy (calories), fat, and sugar that compete with the sale of balanced breakfasts and lunches.

Adjusting food prices. Price is a factor in food purchases. Lowering by half the prices of fruits and vegetables in vending machines and school cafeterias can result in doubling their sales.[66] The government could adopt policies to decrease the prices of more healthful foods and increase the prices of foods high in energy.[67] Local governments and the media might offer free publicity, awards, or other incentives to restaurants to offer free salads with meals, to charge more for less nutritious foods, and to reduce the prices of more nutritious foods.

Financing Obesity Prevention

The principal barrier to meaningful health-promotion programs is almost always lack of funds, and the educational campaigns and certain other measures we propose would not be inexpensive. But to put such costs in perspective, it is important to understand that the annual costs of direct health care and lost productivity resulting from obesity and its consequences have been estimated at 5.7% of total US health care expenditures, or $52 billion in 1995 dollars.[68] More conservative estimates still suggest that obesity accounts for 1% to 4% of total health care costs.[7] Notwithstanding these enormous costs, Congress and state legislatures provide virtually no funding specifically targeted to anti-obesity measures other than basic research. The $5 million recently granted to the CDC for nutrition and obesity programs represents a small but important step in the right direction.

To compensate for state and federal legislatures' failure to apply general revenues to anti-obesity measures, other commentators have suggested that revenues from taxes on "junk foods" be used to subsidize the costs of more healthful foods.[31] While onerous taxes on commonly purchased products would be highly unpopular and politically unrealistic, small taxes are feasible. Such taxes would likely have little effect on overall sales but could generate sufficient revenues to fund some of the measures that we are suggesting. Legislatures have long levied taxes on products deemed to be unhealthful. Thus, the federal government and states impose taxes on alcoholic beverages and cigarettes; these taxes are supported by large public majorities, especially when the revenues are earmarked for health purposes.[69] Several states currently tax soft drinks and snack foods. In California, for example, soft drinks are the only foods subject to the 7.25% sales tax; we calculate on the basis of population[43] and consumption[70] statistics that this tax alone raises about $200 million per year. A two-cent-per-can tax on soft drinks in Arkansas raises $40 million per year (Personal communication, Tamra Huff, Arkansas Department of Finance and Administration, September 1998). In these and several other states, the tax revenues go into the general treasury. West Virginia, however, uses the revenues from its soft drink tax to support its state medical, dental, and nursing schools, and Tennessee earmarks 21% of the revenues from its tax for cleaning up highway litter.

To fund the television advertisements, physical education teachers, bicycle paths, swimming pools, and other measures that we propose, we suggest that small taxes be levied on several widely used products that are likely to contribute to obesity. We estimate that each of the following hypothetical taxes would generate revenues of about $1 billion per year:

- A 2/3-cent tax per 12 oz on soft drinks.[70]

- A 5% tax on new televisions and video equipment.[43]

- A $65 tax on each new motor vehicle (about 0.3% on a $20,000 car), or an extra penny tax per gallon of gasoline.[43]

A national survey found that 45% of adults would support a one-cent tax on a can of soft drink, pound of potato chips, or pound of butter if the revenues funded a national health education program.[71] Such taxes are too small to raise serious concerns about their regressive nature.

Toward National Action

The USDA and DHHS have announced plans for a National Nutrition Summit, scheduled for May 30–31, 2000. This Summit could catalyze an unprecedented effort to reverse the obesity epidemic. Its focus will be on behavioral factors—especially those that could help prevent overweight and obesity.[72] The Summit provides an ideal opportunity for public and private institutions to initiate the kinds of policies and programs that we are advocating. We believe that the Summit should emphasize ways to improve both government policies and corporate practices that affect individual behavior change.

Government officials could use the Summit to announce actions, including proposed legislation, that their departments will seek to implement (see Figure 3). For example, USDA could announce incentives to encourage Food Stamp recipients to buy more produce, whole grains, and reduced-fat animal products. The Surgeon General could announce a campaign to reduce television watching. Justice Department officials could announce initiatives for reducing inner-city crime to make playing outside safer for children, while the Department of Housing and Urban Development could announce grants for inner-city recreational facilities. The Department of Transportation could announce increased funding to enable states to expand mass transit and provide more bicycle paths. Finally, the futility of current efforts demonstrates the urgent need for research on which to base more effective public health policies. Ending the obesity epidemic will require much greater knowledge of effective diet and activity strategies than is currently available. The research focus must extend beyond genetic, metabolic, and drug development studies to encompass—and emphasize—population-based behavioral interventions, policy development, and program evaluation.

Thus, we propose that the measures outlined in Figure 3 be implemented on a trial basis and evaluated for their effectiveness. We do not pretend that these suggestions alone will eliminate obesity from American society, but they will be valuable if they help to produce even small reductions in the rate of obesity, as even modest weight loss confers substantial health and economic benefits.[73] Without such a national commitment and effective new approaches to making the environment more favorable to maintaining healthy weight, we doubt that the current trends can be reversed.

References

1. Infant and adult obesity [editorial]. Lancet 1974;i:17–18.
2. Mokdad AH, Serdula MK, Dietz WH, Bowman BA, Marks JS, Koplan JP. The spread of the obesity epidemic in the United States, 1991–1998. JAMA 1999;282:1519–22.
3. Troiano RP, Flegal KM, Kuczmarski RJ, Campbell SM, Johnson CL. Overweight prevalence and trends for children and adolescents. Arch Pediatr Adolesc Med 1995;149:1085–91.
4. Update: prevalence of overweight among children, adolescents, and adults—United States, 1988–1994. MMWR Morb Mortal W kly Rep 1997;46:199–202.
5. Must A, Spadano J, Coakley EH, Field AE, Colditz G, Dietz WH. The disease burden associated with overweight and obesity. JAMA 1999;282:1523–9.
6. Allison DB, Fontaine KR, Manson JE, Stevens J, Vanltallie TB. Annual deaths attributable to obesity in the United States. JAMA 1999;282:1530–8.
7. Allison DB, Zannolli R, Narayan KMV. The direct health care costs of obesity in the United States. Am J Public Health 1999;89:1194–9.
8. Rippe JM, Aronne LJ, Gilligan VF, Kumanyika S, Miller S, Owens GM, et al. Public policy statement on obesity and health from the Interdisciplinary Council on Lifestyle and Obesity Management. Nutr Clin Care 1998;1:34–7.
9. Grundy SM. Multifactorial causation of obesity: implications for prevention. Am J Clin Nutr 1998;67(3 Suppl):536S–72S.
10. Whitaker RC, Wright JA, Pepe MS, Seidel KD, Dietz WH. Predicting obesity in young adulthood from childhood and parental obesity. N Engl J Med 1997;337:869–73.
11. Methods for voluntary weight loss and control: Technology Assessment Conference statement. Bethesda (MD): National Institutes of Health (US); 1992.
12. Williamson DF. Pharmacotherapy for obesity. JAMA 1999;281:278–80.
13. Expert Panel on the Identification, Evaluation, and Treatment of Overweight in Adults. Clinical guidelines on the identification, evaluation, and treatment of overweight in adults. Bethesda (MD): National Institutes of Health (US); 1998.
14. US Preventive Services Task Force. Guide to clinical preventive services. 2nd ed. Alexandria (VA): International Medical Publishing; 1996.
15. Dalton S. Overweight and weight management. Gaithersburg (MD): Aspen; 1997.
16. Koplan JP, Dietz WH. Caloric imbalance and public health policy. JAMA 1999;282:1579–80.

17. Harvard School of Public Health, Department of Nutrition. Food for your heart: a manual for patient and physician. New York: American Heart Association; 1952.
18. Senate Select Committee on Nutrition and Human Needs (US). Dietary goals for the United States. 2nd ed. Washington: Government Printing Office; 1977.
19. White House Conference on Food, Nutrition, and Health: final report. Washington: Government Printing Office; 1970.
20. Stunkard AJ. Obesity and the social environment: current status, future prospects. In: Bray GA, editor. Obesity in America. Washington: Department of Health, Education, and Welfare (US); 1979. NIH Pub. No.:79–359.
21. Stunkard A. The social environment and the control of obesity. In: Stunkard AJ, editor. Obesity. Philadelphia (PA): WB Saunders; 1980. p. 438–62.
22. Fullarton JE. Matrix for action: nutrition and dietary practices [appendix]. In: Bray GA, editor. Obesity in America. Washington: Department of Health, Education, and Welfare (US); 1979. p. 241–64. NIH Pub. No.: 79-359.
23. Department of Health and Human Services (US). Promoting health/ preventing disease: objectives for the nation. Washington: Government Printing Office; 1980.
24. Department of Agriculture (US) and Department and Health and Human Services (US). Nutrition and your health: dietary guidelines for Americans. Washington: Government Printing Office; 1980.
25. Department of Health and Human Services (US). Promoting health/preventing disease: Public Health Service implementation plans for attaining the objectives for the nation. Public Health Rep 1983;Sept–Oct Suppl.
26. Department of Health and Human Services (US). Healthy People: national health promotion and disease prevention objectives. Washington: Government Printing Office; 1990.
27. Department of Health and Human Services (US). The 1990 Health Objectives for the Nation: a midcourse review. Washington: Office of Disease Prevention and Health Promotion (US); 1986.
28. Life Sciences Research Office, Federation of American Societies for Experimental Biology. Third report on nutrition monitoring in the United States. Vol 2. Prepared for Interagency Board for Nutrition Monitoring and Related Research, US Department of Health and Human Services, US Department of Agriculture. Washington: Government Printing Office; 1995.
29. Department of Agriculture (US). Data Tables: Results from USDA's 1994–96 Continuing Survey of Food Intakes by Individuals and 1994–96 Diet and Health Knowledge Survey, December 1997 [cited 1999 Feb 23]. Available from: URL: http://www.barc.usda.gov/bhnrc/foodsurvey/home.htm
30. Department of Health and Human Services (US). Healthy People 2010: understanding and improving health. Conference edition. Washington: Government Printing Office; 2000.
31. Battle EK, Brownell KD. Confronting a rising tide of eating disorders and obesity: treatment vs. prevention and policy. Addict Behav 1996;21:755–65.
32. Department of Agriculture, Economic Research Service (US). U.S. Food Expenditures [cited 1999 Dec 11]. Available from: URL: http://www.econ.ag.gov

33. Gallo AE. The food marketing system in 1996. Agricultural Information Bulletin No. 743. Washington: Department of Agriculture (US); 1998.
34. 44th annual: 100 leading national advertisers. Advertising Age 1999 Sept 27;S1–S46.
35. Gov't & industry launch fruit and vegetable push; but NCI takes back seat. Nutr Week 1992;22(26):1–2.
36. Cleeman Jl, Lenfant C. The National Cholesterol Education Program: progress and prospects. JAMA 1998;280:2099–104.
37. Kotz K, Story M. Food advertisements during children's Saturday morning television programming: are they consistent with dietary recommendations? J Am Diet Assoc 1994;94:1296–1300.
38. Hays CL. Channel One's mixed grades in schools. New York Times 1999 Dec 5;Sect. C:1,14–15.
39. Hays CL. Be true to your cola, rah! rahl: battle for soft-drink loyalties moves to public schools. New York Times 1998 Mar 8;Sect. D:1,4.
40. Sylvester GP, Achterberg C, Williams J. Children's television and nutrition: friends or foes. Nutr Today 1995;30(1):6–15.
41. McNeal JU. The kids market: myths and realities. Ithaca (NY): Paramount Market Publishing; 1999.
42. Lin B-H, Frazão E, Guthrie J. Away-from-home foods increasingly important to quality of American diet. Agricultural Information Bulletin No. 749. Washington: Department of Agriculture (US); 1999.
43. Bureau of the Census (US). Statistical abstract of the United States: the national data book: 1997. 117th ed. Washington: Government Printing Office; 1997.
44. Vended bottled drinks. Vending Times 1998;38(9):15,21–2.
45. Annual Report. Atlanta: Coca-Cola Co.; 1997. Available from Coca-Cola Co., One Coca-Cola Plaza, Atlanta GA 30313.
46. Burros M. Losing count of calories as plates fill up. New York Times 1997 Apr 2;Sect. C:1,4.
47. National Research Council. Recommended dietary allowances. 9th rev. ed. Washington: National Academy Press; 1989.
48. Young LR, Nestle M. Portion sizes in dietary assessment: issues and policy implications. Nutr Rev 1995;53:149–58.
49. Jacobson MF. Liquid candy: how soft drinks are harming Americans' health. Washington: Center for Science in the Public Interest; 1998.
50. President's Council on Physical Fitness and Sports (US). Physical activity and health: a report of the Surgeon General. Washington: Department of Health and Human Services (US); 1996.
51. Neighborhood safety and the prevalence of physical inactivity—selected states, 1996. MMWR Morb Mortal Wkly Rep 1999;48:143–6.
52. Welcome to Shape Up America! [cited 1999 Dec 4]. Available from: URL: http://www.shapeup.org
53. Jeffery RW. Public health approaches to the management of obesity. In: Brownell KD, Fairburn CG, editors. Eating disorders and obesity: a comprehensive handbook. New York: Guilford Press; 1995. p. 558–63.
54. Hirsch J. Obesity prevention initiative. Obes Res 1994;2:569–84.
55. Zepezauer M, Naiman A. Take the rich off welfare. Tucson (AZ): Odonian Press; 1996.

56. Reger B, Wootan MG, Booth-Butterfield S. Using mass media to promote healthy eating: a community-based demonstration project. Prev Med 1999;29:414–21.

57. Reger B, Wootan MG, Booth-Butterfield S, Smith H. 1% or less: a community-based nutrition campaign. Public Health Rep 1998;113:410–19.

58. Nestle M. Toward more healthful dietary patterns—a matter of policy. Public Health Rep 1998;113;420–3.

59. McClain DL. Where is today's child? probably watching TV. New York Times 1999 Dec 6;Sect. C:18.

60. Anderson RE, Crespo CJ, Bartlett SJ, Cheskin LJ, Pratt M. Relationship of physical activity and television watching with body weight and level of fatness among children: results from the Third National Health and Nutrition Examination Survey. JAMA 1998;279:938–42.

61. Jeffery RW, French SA. Epidemic obesity in the United States: are fast foods and television viewing contributing? Am J Public Health 1998;88:277–80.

62. Robinson TN. Reducing children's television viewing to prevent obesity: a randomized controlled trial. JAMA 1999;282:1561–7.

63. Ryan M. Are you ready for TV-Turnoff Week? Parade 1998 Apr 12;18–19.

64. Fox RF. Harvesting minds: how TV commercials control kids. Westport (CN): Praeger; 1996.

65. Federal Trade Commission Improvements Act of 1980, Pub. L. No. 96–252, 94 Stat. 374 (1980).

66. French SA, Story M, Jeffery RW, Snyder P, Eisenberg M, Sidebottom A, Murray D. Pricing strategy to promote fruit and vegetable purchase in high school cafeterias. J Am Diet Assoc 1997;97:1008–10.

67. French SA, Jeffery RW, Story M, Hannan P, Snyder M. A pricing strategy to promote low-fat snack choices through vending machines. Am J Public Health 1997;87:849–51.

68. Wolf AM, Colditz GA. Current estimates of the economic cost of obesity in the United States. Obes Res 1998;6:97–106.

69. Conference Research Center. Special consumer survey report: to tax or not to tax. New York: Conference Board; 1993 Jun.

70. Putnam JJ, Allshouse JE. Food consumption, prices, and expenditures, 1970–97. Statistical Bulletin No. 965. Washington: Department of Agriculture (US); 1999.

71. Bruskin-Goldring Research. Potato chip labels/health programs, January 30–31, 1999. Edison (NJ): Center for Science in the Public Interest; 1999.

72. Department of Agriculture (US) and Department of Health and Human Services (US). National Nutrition Summit: notice of a public meeting to solicit input in the planning of a National Nutrition Summit. Fed Reg 1999;64(Nov 26):66451.

73. Oster G, Thompson D, Edelsberg J, Bird AP, Colditz GA. Lifetime health and economic benefits of weight loss among obese persons. Am J Public Health 1999;89:1536–42.

Critical Reading Questions

Summarizing the Text

1. What is the thesis of this article—what is the problem that Nestle and Jacobson identify, and what is their solution?
2. What specific recommendations does this article propose for combating the obesity epidemic?

Establishing the Context

3. Why does the article detail the history of this obesity epidemic?
4. What are some of the other ways in which this article is clearly aimed at an audience of specialists?
5. Implicit in this selection are responses to the counterargument—made most forcefully by groups such as the Center for Consumer Freedom—that obesity prevention should be strictly an individual, not a governmental, matter. How do Nestle and Jacobson make their case that obesity is a public concern and should be addressed with laws and wide-scale education campaigns?

Responding to the Text

6. Nestle and Jacobson's work—and similar research and policy proposals by many other scientists—have come under harsh attack by food industry groups. On what grounds do they rebut the proposals of these public-health researchers? You might want to consult the websites of groups such as the Center for Consumer Freedom.
7. The Center for Consumer Freedom isn't the only advocacy group involved in this debate. Although this article appeared in a peer-reviewed journal, Jacobson's Center for Science in the Public Interest—a nonprofit that supports the kinds of governmental actions that Nestle and Jacobson propose—endorses this kind of research and even makes it available on its website. What are some other groups that call for greater governmental intervention to slow this obesity epidemic?

CDC State-by-State Obesity Maps, 1999 and 2009

The maps, taken from a PowerPoint presentation on the CDC's website, show state-by-state obesity rates in 1999 and 2009.

1. What conclusions can you draw from these two maps? What has happened to American obesity rates in the ten years represented by the maps?
2. What important data about American health and obesity do these maps leave out?

1999

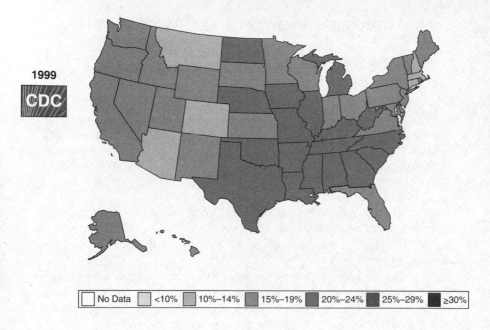

☐ No Data   ☐ <10%   ☐ 10%–14%   ☐ 15%–19%   ☐ 20%–24%   ☐ 25%–29%   ☐ ≥30%

2009

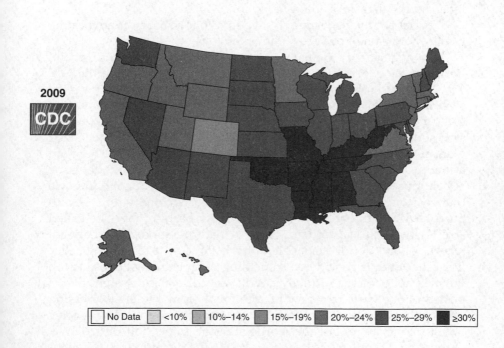

☐ No Data   ☐ <10%   ☐ 10%–14%   ☐ 15%–19%   ☐ 20%–24%   ☐ 25%–29%   ☐ ≥30%

America's War on the Overweight

Kate Dailey and
Abby Ellin

Disentangling the ways in which the campaign against obesity as a public-health issue has morphed into a public campaign to demonize overweight people, Newsweek lifestyle editor Kate Dailey and journalist Abby Ellin here survey the controversy about "fat" in the United States and how it has been affected by the supposed obesity epidemic.

Practically the minute President Obama announced Regina M. Benjamin, a zaftig doctor who also has an M.B.A. and is the recipient of a MacArthur "genius grant," as a nominee for the post of Surgeon General, the criticism started.

The attacks were vicious—Michael Karolchyk, owner of a Denver "anti-gym," told Fox News' Neil Cavuto, "Obesity is the No. 1 issue facing our country in terms of the health and wellness, and she has shown not that she was born this way, not that she woke up one day and was obese. She has shown through being lazy, and making poor food choices, that she's obese."

"This is totally disgusting to have some one so big to be advocating health," wrote one YouTube commenter.

The anger about Benjamin wasn't the only example of vitriol hurled at the overweight. Cintra Wilson, style columnist for the *New York Times*, recently wrote a column so disdainful of JCPenney's plus-size mannequins that the *Times'* ombsbudman later wrote that he could read "a virtual sneer" coming through her prose. A *Newsweek* post about *Glamour's* recent plus-size model (in fact, a normal-sized woman with a bit of a belly roll) had several commenters lashing out at the positive reaction the model was receiving. "This model issue is being used as a smoke screen to justify self-destructive lifestyle that cost me more money in health care costs," one wrote. Health guru MeMe Roth has made a career out of bashing fat—she called size 12 *American Idol* Jordan Sparks a "bad role model" on national television, and derided size 2 Jennifer Love Hewitt for having cellulite. (That Roth is considered something of an extremist doesn't stop the media attention.) Virtually any news article about weight that is posted online garners a slew of comments from readers expressing disgust that people let their weight get so out of control. The specific target may change, but the words stay the same: Self-destructive. Disgusting. Disgraceful. Shameful. While the debate rages on about obesity and the best ways to deal with it, the attitudes Americans have toward those with extra pounds are only getting nastier. Just why do Americans hate fat people so much?

Fat bias is nothing new. "Public outrage at other people's obesity has a lot to do with America from the turn of the 20th century to about World War I," says Deborah Levine, assistant professor of health policy and management at Providence College. The rise of fat hatred is often seen as connected to the changing American workplace; in the early 20th century, companies began to offer snacks to employees, white-collar jobs became more prominent, and fewer people exercised. As thinness became rarer, says Peter N. Stearns, author of *Fat History: Bodies and Beauty in the Modern West* and professor of history at George Mason University, it was more prized, and conversely, fatness was more maligned.

At the same time, people also paid a lot of attention to President Taft's girth; while Taft was large, he wasn't all that much heavier than earlier presidents. Newspapers questioned how his weight would affect diplomacy and solicited the funniest "fat Taft" joke. "This [period] is also when you get ready-to-wear clothing," says Levine. "For the first time, [people were] buying clothes in a certain size, and that encourages a comparison amongst other people." Actuarial tables began to connect weight and shorter lifespan, and cookbooks published around World War I targeted the overweight. "There was that idea that people who were overweight were hoarding resources needed for the war effort," Levine says. She adds that early concerns were that overweight American men would not be able to compete globally, participate in international business, or win wars.

Fatness has always been seen as a slight on the American character. Ours is a nation that values hard work and discipline, and it's hard for us to accept that weight could be not just a struggle of will, even when the bulk of the research—and often our own personal experience—shows that the factors leading to weight gain are much more than just simple gluttony. "There's this general perception that weight can be controlled if you have enough willpower, that it's just about calories in and calories out," says Dr. Glen Gaesser, professor of exercise and wellness at Arizona State University and author of *Big Fat Lies: The Truth About Your Weight and Your Health*, and that perception leads the nonfat to believe that the overweight are not just unhealthy, but weak and lazy. Even though research suggests that there is a genetic propensity for obesity, and even though some obese people are technically healthier than their skinnier counterparts, the perception remains "[that] it's a failure to control ourselves. It violates everything we have learned about self control from a very young age," says Gaesser.

In a country that still prides itself on its Puritanical ideals, the fat self is the "bad self," the epitome of greed, gluttony, and sloth. "There's a widespread belief that fat is controllable," says Linda Bacon, author of *Health at Every Size: The Surprising Truth About Your Weight.* "So then it's unlike a disability where you can have compassion; now you can blame the individual and attribute all kinds of mean qualities to them. Then consider the thinner people that are always watching what they eat carefully—fat people are symbols of what they can become if they weren't so virtuous."

But considering that the U.S. has already become a size XL nation—66 percent of adults over 20 are considered overweight or obese, according to the Centers for Disease Control—why does the stigma, and the anger, remain?

Call it a case of self-loathing. "A lot of people struggle themselves with their weight, and the same people that tend to get very angry at themselves for not being able to manage their weight are more likely to be biased against the obese," says Marlene Schwartz, director of the Rudd Center for Food Policy and Obesity at Yale University. "I think that some of this is that anger is confusion between the anger that we have at ourselves and projecting that out onto other people." Her research indicates that younger women, who are under the most pressure to be thin and who are also the most likely to be self-critical, are the most likely to feel negatively toward fat people.

As many women's magazines' cover lines note, losing the last five pounds can be a challenge. So why don't we have more compassion for people struggling to lose the first 50, 60, or 100? Some of it has to do with the psychological phenomenon known as the fundamental attribution error, a basic belief that whatever problems befall us personally are the result of difficult circumstances, while the same problems in other people are the result of their bad choices. Miss a goal at work? It's because the vendor was unreliable, and because your manager isn't giving you enough support, and because the power outage last week cut into premium sales time. That jerk next to you? He blew his quota because he's a bad planner, and because he spent too much time taking personal calls.

The same can be true of weight: "From working with so many people struggling with their weight, I've seen it many times," says Andrew Geier, a postdoctoral fellow in the psychology department at Yale University. "They believe they're overweight due to a myriad of circumstances: as soon as my son goes to college, I'll have time to cook healthier meals; when my husband's shifts change at work, I can get to the gym sooner...." But other people? They're overweight because they don't have the discipline to do the hard work and take off the weight, and that lack of discipline is an affront to our own hard work. (Never mind that weight loss is incredibly difficult to attain: Geier notes that even the most rigorous behavioral programs result in at most about a 12.5 percent decrease in weight, which would take a 350-pound man to a slimmer, but not svelte, 306 pounds).

But why do the rest of us care so much? What is it about fat people that makes us so mad? As it turns out, we kind of like it. "People actually enjoy feeling angry," says Ryan Martin, associate professor of psychology at the University of Wisconsin, Green Bay, who cites studies done on people's emotions. "It makes them feel powerful, it makes them feel greater control, and they appreciate it for that reason." And with fat people designated as acceptable targets of rage—and with the prevalence of fat people in our lives, both in the malls and on the news—it's easy to find a target for some soul-clearing, ego-boosting ranting.

And it may be, that like those World War I–era cookbook writers, we feel that obese people are robbing us of resources, whether it's space in a row of airline seats or our hard-earned tax dollars. Think of health care: when president Obama made reforming health care a priority, it led to an increased focus on obesity as a contributor to health-care costs. A recent article in *Health Affairs,* a public-policy journal, reported that obesity costs $147 billion a year, mainly in insurance premiums and taxes. At the same time, obesity-related diseases such as type 2 diabetes have spiked, and, while diabetes can be treated, treatment is expensive. So the overweight, some people argue, are costing all of us money while refusing to alter the behavior that has put them in their predicament in the first place (i.e., overeating and not exercising).

The reality is much more complicated. It's a fallacy to conflate the unhealthy action—overeating and not exercising—with the unhealthy appearance, says Schwartz: some overweight people run marathons; eat only organic, vegetarian fare; and have clean bills of health. Even so, yelling at the overweight to put down the doughnut is far from productive. "People are less likely to seek out healthy behaviors when they're criticized by friends, family, doctors, and others," says Schwartz. "If people tell you that you're disgusting or a slob enough times, you soon start to believe it." In fact, fat outrage might actually make health-care costs higher. In a study published in the 2005 issue of the *Journal of Health Politics, Policy and Law,* Abigail Saguy and Brian Riley found that many overweight people decide not to get help for medical conditions that are more treatable and more risky than obesity because they don't want to deal with their doctor's harassment about their weight. (For instance, a study from the University of North Carolina found that obese women are less likely to receive cervical exams than their thinner counterparts, in part because they worry about being embarrassed or belittled by the doctor because of their weight.)

The bubbling rage against fat people in America has put researchers like Levine in a difficult position. On the one hand, she says, she wants to ensure that obesity is taken seriously as a medical problem, and pointing out the costs associated with obesity-related illnesses helps illustrate the severity of the situation. On the other hand, she says, doing so could increase the animosity people have toward the overweight, many of whom may already live healthy lives or may be working hard to make healthier choices.

"The idea is to fight obesity and not obese people," she says, and then pauses. "But it's very hard for many people to disentangle the two."

Critical Reading Questions

Summarizing the Text

1. What evidence do Dailey and Ellin have to support their claim that our culture has become "vitriolic" about fat people who are in the public eye?

2. Do Dailey and Ellin propose a solution to a problem (stereotyping and attacking the overweight)? Are they proposing a potential cause for this problem? Or are they just identifying and describing the problem?

Establishing the Context

3. This article is what's called a "Web exclusive"—it did not appear in the print version of the magazine and appeared only online. How does the audience of the article differ from the audience of an article in the printed edition of *Newsweek*?

4. We have become accustomed to "commenting" on everything we read or see on the Web: YouTube videos, blog posts, even products sold on Amazon.com. How do Dailey and Ellin use such comments as evidence in their argument? What are the drawbacks of using Web comments to represent a general opinion about an issue?

Responding to the Text

5. For decades, feminists have argued that our culture demands that women, especially, be unrealistically thin. How has the obesity epidemic changed this?

6. Do you agree that there is an unrealistic expectation for Americans, and women in particular, to be thin? Leaving out the obvious example of the fashion industry, where do you see this? What has been the most surprising place in which you have seen women pressured (explicitly or subtly) to lose weight?

Fat vs. Fiction

Kate Harding

Jezebel contributor Kate Harding attempts to debunk the obesity epidemic argument. The website Jezebel.com employs a team of bloggers to write short, punchy posts about women's issues.

Newsweek, currently hosting a series called "The Fat Wars," is featuring dueling op-eds today, one arguing that fatties need to put down the forks, the other that obesity is genetic. Neither one gets it quite right.

If you've ever read a word I've written, you've already guessed that I come down on the side of the second argument. Which is basically this, words of Jeffrey Friedman, who wrote the op-ed:

The heritability of obesity—a measure of how much obesity is due to genes versus other factors—is about the same as the heritability of height. It's even greater than that for many conditions that people accept as having a genetic basis, including heart disease, breast cancer, and schizophrenia. As nutrition has improved over the past 200 years, Americans have gotten much taller on average, but it is still the genes that determine who is tall or short today. The same is true for weight. Although our high-calorie, sedentary lifestyle contributes to the approximately 10-pound average weight gain of Americans compared to the recent past, some people are more severely affected by this lifestyle than others. That's because they have inherited genes that increase their predisposition for accumulating body fat. Our modern lifestyle is thus a necessary, but not a sufficient, condition for the high prevalence of obesity in our population.

But Friedman had already pissed me off before he even got to that. In an apparent effort to prove that he's a Serious Person and not just some delusional fatass with an axe to grind (hi!), he acknowledges that obesity is a risk factor for a bunch of diseases, claiming it has "consequences that include diabetes, heart disease, and cancer, and that cause nearly 300,000 deaths in the United States each year."

Y'all, the 300,000 deaths thing was debunked in 2005. By the CDC, not delusional fatties with axes to grind. Same folks who came up with the original stat, in fact. They just f**ked up the first time:

According to the [second] study, obesity and extreme obesity cause about 112,000 deaths per year, but being overweight was found to prevent about 86,000 deaths annually. **Based on those figures, the net U.S. death toll from excess weight is 26,000 per year.** By contrast, researchers found that being underweight results in 34,000 deaths per year.
Emphasis added.

Seeing that error—*four years* after that crucial revision came out—automatically makes me think I can't take the person talking seriously. Which sucks, because in this particular debate, Friedman is, generally speaking, the one dealing in reality.

Ken Thorpe and Christine Ferguson, on the other hand, get it wrong from the headline: "We Have the Power to Change Our Weight" (And no, they probably didn't write the headline, but they wrote the op-ed that made that a logical summary.) Sure, most of us have the power to change our weight, *temporarily.* I was a champion dieter for a while there, losing 65 lbs. the first time I got serious about it, and 45 the second time. Haters will go to their graves believing that's because I gave up, both times, and started mainlining powdered sugar delivered to me via an elaborate pulley system constructed so I'd never to leave the couch, but those who have even a passing interest in facts might consider looking at the research on long-term weight loss. Such as the 2007 UCLA study, in which researchers reviewed 31 earlier studies and concluded that on the whole:

> [D]ieters were not able to maintain their weight losses in the long term, and there was not consistent evidence that the diets resulted in significant improvements in their health. In the few cases in which health benefits were shown, it could not be demonstrated that they resulted from dieting, rather than exercise, medication use, or other lifestyle changes. It appears that dieters who manage to sustain a weight loss are the rare exception, rather than the rule. Dieters who gain back more weight than they lost may very well be the norm, rather than an unlucky minority.

The part about not being able to identify which variables actually produced the (few demonstrated) health benefits is crucial. Thorpe and Ferguson write, "We know that as little as a 5 to 10 percent weight loss can significantly reduce risk factors for chronic disease, including lower blood-glucose levels, lower blood pressure, and reduced cholesterol levels," but they don't question how those studies proved it was the weight loss itself, as opposed to the lifestyle interventions that elicited eating, exercise and (wonder of wonders self-acceptance, all without regard to weight loss—delivers *better* health outcomes than dieting. No one disputes that a steady diet of junk food and a sedentary lifestyle are bad for your health. But A) many fat people can and do eat balanced diets and exercise just as much as thin people without losing weight—that's where the whole genetic thing comes in—and B) plenty of thin people suffer from health issues related to lifestyle choices, but the default assumption is that they're "taking care of themselves" because they don't happen to have fat genes. Eating a balanced diet and exercising can be beneficial for all of us, but they will not cause permanent weight loss in most of us—and there's no real proof that we'd be markedly better off if they did. (Even if being thinner is theoretically advantageous—and again, "overweight" people win the longevity game—we must keep in mind that a fat person who's lost weight is not the same thing as a person who's always been thin.)

Friedman gets this mostly right:

> There is no evidence that obese individuals need to "normalize" their weight to reap health benefits. In fact, it is not even clear whether there are enduring health benefits to weight loss among obese individuals who do not suffer from diabetes, heart disease, hypertension, or liver disease.

---

*I've said many times that I weigh around 200 lbs., though I haven't weighed myself since I jumped on a dog scale at the vet's office to prove a point 2 years ago. I weighed 185 then, after which I gained size, which probably represents 10–15 lbs. But as it happens, I have recently dropped a pants size, so am probably somewhere around 190. Yes, the Queen of the Fat-o-Sphere has lost weight! And because I love you, I will share the secret of how I did it: I went off the pill.

But then, once again, he blows it, basically reiterating Thorpe and Ferguson's point about losing 5-10% of your weight:

> What is known is that the obese who do suffer from these conditions receive a disproportionately large benefit from even modest weight loss, which together with exercise and a heart-healthy diet can go a long way toward improving health.

Apart from what I've already said about the variables involved in weight loss and the fact that permanent weight loss is a pipe dream for all but a few statistical outliers, here's the obvious question about "just lose 5-10%" thing: What happens when I do that and am still fat? Losing 10% of my weight (+/–19 lbs.*) would leave me squarely in the obese category, not improving their statistics one little bit—even if my health improved, would anyone actually quit bitching about the "obesity crisis"? Oh, but wait—enough people are on the cusp of BMI categories that if we all lost 5-10% of our weight, we'd see a dramatic drop in "obesity" and "overweight" population-wide, at which point we could all congratulate ourselves on no longer being a nation of embarrassing fatties who are going to die younger than our parents, even though individual losses would generally be quite small. The important thing is, on paper, that would look fantastic. At least until *everyone gained it back.*

Thorpe and Ferguson argue for many of the public health interventions I addressed in an inexplicably controversial post last week, and as always, I'm in favor of several of them, e.g., "lowering copays on preventive care ... reinstating physical education and requiring school lunches to meet nutritional standards ... ensuring that all Americans have access to a place to be physically active and purchase healthy foods." What I'm not in favor of are undefined "programs to help overweight Americans" (unless they mean programs to help us overcome the ill effects of relentless fat-hatred, see above about diets not working) and "tax credits to employers that offer wellness benefits and encourage health inside and outside of the workplace"—which sound fairly unobjectionable until you consider that this is what leads to demeaning "Biggest Loser" competitions at the office, employers badgering their workers to join specific commercial weight loss programs, and hysteria about a plate of cupcakes in the break room. If we're talking about tax credits for offering employees free or discounted gym memberships—and then leaving them the hell alone to work out as they please, or not—then great, have at it. But that's never all we're talking about. We're talking about diet culture invading the workplace even more than it already has, and a whole new layer of shame for fat people who aren't interested in joining Weight Watchers—probably because they've already been on it multiple times, and gained back everything they lost.

"[T]o win the fight against obesity," Thorpe and Ferguson write, "all of us need to be individually committed." Really? All of us? What role do people who aren't fat play in this, exactly? If you mean they need to be constantly reminding fat people that we're disgusting, unlovable, smelly, lazy, undisciplined, and above all, unhealtheeeeeee, then as a whole, they're doing a bang-up job already. (This does not, of course, apply to all thin people. Some of my best friends are thin!) So I'm pretty sure what you mean is "Fat people need to be individually committed" to fighting their own bodies. To which I'd point out: *Most already are.* Who the f**k do you think is keeping the $50 billion dollar weight loss industry afloat? Magic sprites?

Oh, and about that. You know that population-wide weight gain that happened in the last 30 years? (Friedman says the average is about 10 lbs.; I've heard anywhere from 7 to 20). Check out that last sentence from the UCLA researchers I quoted above: "Dieters who gain back more weight than they lost may very well be the norm, rather than an unlucky minority." Not only does dieting not work, but a lot of times it *makes you fatter.* And the weight loss industry has been growing right along with our asses all that time. Is that the only reason for the gain over that period? I have no idea, probably not. But it's something obesity alarmists never, ever factor in, even though common sense suggests somebody really ought to explore that correlation.

If you're a regular reader of mine and you feel like you've heard everything in this post a million, billion times, you have my apologies. I am so sick of making these arguments, I cannot even tell you. Unfortunately, people can't even get it through their heads that diets don't work—despite both a mountain of scientific evidence to that effect *and* a friggin' "results not typical" disclaimer on every ad—let alone that it is possible to be fat and healthy, that it is equally possible to be thin and unhealthy, that correlation does not equal causation, that there is strong evidence that obesity is highly heritable, that calories in/calories out is a ludicrously simplistic equation unless you think human beings are Bunsen burners, and that, above all, *fat people are human beings.* Which means *we can hear you.* And our continued fatness is not a personal attack on you or our country or our healthcare system, but the result of complex factors science is only beginning to understand, and in very many cases, something *we have already tried our damnedest to change.*

Or, as Friedman puts it:

> While research into the biologic system that controls weight is moving toward the development of effective therapies for obesity, we are not there yet. In the meantime we must change our attitudes toward the obese and focus less on appearance and more on health. In their efforts to lose weight they are fighting against their biology. But they also are fighting against a society that wrongly believes that obesity is a personal failing.

I've stopped fighting against my biology, but I am still fighting against that society every goddamned day. And I don't just mean the trolls who swing by to tell me things like,

My fear that a woman with the legal power to take half of my possessions might some day become so fat and sexually unappealing that I'd sooner cut my own penis off than have sex with the manatee that used to be my wife is unfortunately all too common and blogs like this one that dangerously suggest to naive future fatties that it's ok are only leading your victims down the primrose path to a battle they can't win."

Or:

I personally dislike most fat people for their lack of will power or mental strength. If fat people would just have a strong mental will power, then they would either be able to deal with the jokes, or become skinny by actually sticking to their dieting and exercise plan without giving up.

Or:

FATTIES ARE GROSS FATTIES ARE GROSS FATTIES ARE GROSS FATTIES ARE GROSS FATTIES ARE GROSS FATTIES ARE GROSS FATTIES ARE GROSS
FATTIES ARE GROSS FATTIES ARE GROSS FATTIES ARE GROSS FATTIES ARE GROSS FATTIES ARE GROSS FATTIES ARE GROSS FATTIES ARE GROSS
FATTIES ARE GROSS FATTIES ARE GROSS FATTIES ARE GROSS FATTIES ARE GROSS FATTIES ARE GROSS FATTIES ARE GROSS FATTIES ARE GROSS
FATTIES ARE GROSS FATTIES ARE GROSS FATTIES ARE GROSS FATTIES ARE GROSS FATTIES ARE GROSS FATTIES ARE GROSS FATTIES ARE GROSS
FATTIES ARE GROSS FATTIES ARE GROSS FATTIES ARE GROSS FATTIES ARE GROSS FATTIES ARE GROSS FATTIES ARE GROSS FATTIES ARE GROSS
FATTIES ARE GROSS FATTIES ARE GROSS FATTIES ARE GROSS FATTIES ARE GROSS FATTIES ARE GROSS FATTIES ARE GROSS FATTIES ARE GROSS
FATTIES ARE GROSS FATTIES ARE GROSS FATTIES ARE GROSS FATTIES ARE GROSS

(I truncated that one. By a lot.)

It's not just those s***heads, who are incredibly easy to dismiss. I'm talking about the people who swear they are really only *concerned for my health,* without ever having heard of Health at Every Size. The people who write screeds on how much obesity (theoretically) costs our healthcare system, and exhort individuals to fix that problem, without acknowledging that pile of research showing permanent weight loss is virtually impossible. I'm talking about the people who try to sell good ideas for improving public health as cures for childhood obesity, making fat kids feel like enemies of their entire communities, and yet not making them noticeably thinner. I'm talking even about people like Friedman, who are starting to get the message about the basic intractability of fat—and kudos to him for spreading it—but still repeat debunked, alarmist statistics in an effort to boost their own *credibility* before daring to suggest that fat people might not be a bunch of lazy slobs. I'm talking about everyone who's ever said, "I don't thing we should treat fat people badly, but ..."

Because that right there? Is treating fat people badly. It's still treating us as a problem to be solved, not as human beings.

To win the fight against fat hatred and discrimination, we all must be individually committed.

Critical Reading Questions

Summarizing the Text

1. What is Harding's argument about the obesity epidemic? Does she believe it exists?

2. What sources does she use to support her argument?

Establishing the Context

3. Blogs are a much more "intertextual" medium than almost any other type of writing that has come before; we assume that a blog will link to many other sites and will quote lengthy pieces of other people's writing. What is the rhetorical effect, here, of the quotes that Harding uses—from peer-reviewed medical studies to comment threads?

4. Blogs, as Andrew Sullivan explains in "Why I Blog" (Chapter 4), also offer a contingent kind of writing, including facts and contentions that might have to be quickly revised. Bloggers expect that their readers will return multiple times in a day. How does this post make its argument in a particularly "bloggy" way? What holes can you find?

Responding to the Text

5. Compare this argument to Dailey and Ellin's. How is their logic different? How is their rhetoric different?

6. Harding argues with several other writers about the *cause* of obesity and its persistence in certain people. Is she oversimplifying the debate? What other factors can you think of that might contribute?

Questions for Short Essays/Group Projects

1. What are some of the key terms in this chapter whose definitions are called into question? How do the writers go about defining the terms? How do they take their audience's values into consideration when creating their definitions?
2. In Chapter 1, you read about the conflict between "centralism" and "federalism"; basically, this indicates the struggle between those who think that rules on issues of social importance should be imposed from the top level of government (the "central authority") and those who think that local communities should make rules that suit their particular circumstances ("federalism"). How does this debate play into these issues about food and obesity?
3. Using PowerPoint or another multimedia application, create a presentation of images (still and moving) to illustrate the contentions or arguments of several of these readings.

Essay Prompts

1. Pollan's article touches on many issues: localism, feminism, consumer culture, and media literacy. Do you agree with his underlying idea that our addiction to the "media" (here you might reread Maggie Jackson's article from Chapter 1) encourages us to disengage with the processes of our life, and to instead prefer to watch those things happen? Are there other examples you can provide?

2. Put the CCF in conversation with Pollan. Do they share any assumptions about individual freedom and choice? If the CCF opposes governmental intervention in our lives, what might Pollan think about a heavier government presence in our eating lives?

3. Research the obesity epidemic and how it has changed since the early 2000s. Is mortality due to obesity declining? Have new studies undermined the conclusions of the study included here?

4. Create a blog or a website that aggregates various arguments—including the ones we have here—on one of these topics: locavorism or the obesity epidemic. Use links to allow your readers to go directly to your sources, but put them " in conversation" with one another. Are there other poles of opinion not included here?

Credits

Page 2: Alex Wong/Getty Images. Page 11: Venice Wow. Pages 11–13: Ice Kobe: A Guest Post by Scott Andrews, Weekly Rader Blog, May 10, 2010. Used by permission of Scott Andrews. Pages 14–16: Used by permission of the author, Kevin Chong. Pages 20–22: Steve Chapman, "Terrorists in the Heartland? Chill," Chicago Tribune, Dec 17, 2009. Used by permission of Chicago Tribune via PARS, Intl. Page 28: Wikipedia. Page 32: Harm Reduction Coalition. Pages 37–41: William Martin, "Guest Column: The Conservative Case for Needle Exchange," The Texas Tribune, Feb 23, 2011. Used by permission of The Texas Tribune, www.texastribune.org. http://www.texastribune.org/texas-legislature/texas-legislature/why-texas-should-allow-needle-exchange-for-addicts. Page 63: Barry Sweet/Landov. Page 67: Kevin Lamarque/Reuters/Landov. Pages 72–77: Used by permission of the author, Michael B Wong. Page 79: http://www.flickr.com/photos/will-lion/2595497078/. Pages 81–90: Nicholas Carr, "Is Google Making Us Stupid?" The Atlantic, July/August 2008. Used by permission of the author. Pages 107–112: Matthew S. Willen, "Reflections on the Cultural Climate of Plagiarism," Liberal Education, Fall 2004. Reprinted with permission of the Association of American Colleges and Universities 2011. Pages 121–133: Zadie Smith, "Generation Why," The New York Review of Books, November 25, 2010. Used by permission of A.P. Watt, Ltd. Page 134: ph: Merrick Morton/© Columbia Pictures/Courtesy Everett Collection. Pages 135–149: Katherine Mangu-Ward is a senior editor for Reason magazine and Reason.com, where this column first appeared in the June 2007 issue. Used by permission of Reason Magazine and Reason.com. Pages 150–162: From Maggie Jackson, Distracted: The Erosion of Attention and the Coming Dark Age (Amherst, NY: Prometheus Books, 2009). Copyright (c) 2008 by Maggie Jackson. Reprinted with permission of the publisher; www.prometheusbooks.com. Page 165: Adrian Lyon/Alamy. Pages 166–176: "Why I Blog" by Andrew Sullivan, originally published by The Atlantic. Copyright © 2008 by Andrew Sullivan, used by permission of The Wylie Agency LLC. Pages 188–190: Michael Roth, "What's a Liberal Arts Education good For?", Huffington Post, Dec 1, 2008. Used by permission. Pages 191–194: Marty Nemko, America's Most Overrated Product: the Bachelor's Degree, Chronicle of Higher Education,

Index